On Dragonwings

On Dragonwings

DRAGONSDAWN
DRAGONSEYE
MORETA

Anne McCaffrey

BALLANTINE BOOKS • NEW YORK

THE DRAGONRIDERS OF PERN
is a trademark of Anne McCaffrey. Reg. U.S. Pat & Tm. Off.

A Del Rey® Book
Published by The Random House Publishing Group

www.delreydigital.com

ISBN 0-345-46565-2

Library of Congress Control Number
is available upon request from the publisher.

Book design by Julie Schroeder
Maps by Bob Porter

Manufactured in the United States of America

First Edition: October 2003

1 3 5 7 9 10 8 6 4 2

PROFOUND ACKNOWLEDGMENTS

This book could not have been written without the advice, assistance, and aid of Dr. Jack Cohen, D.Sc., lately Senior Lecturer of Reproductive Biology at Birmingham University, England, whose expertise and enthusiasm helped me create the dragons of Pern, and attendant botany/biology/ecology. Jack made fact out of myth, and science out of legend. I am not the only writer of his acquaintance who owes him a tremendous debt of gratitude.

I am also indebted to Harry Alm, Naval Engineer of New Orleans, Louisiana, for his configuration of the Thread Fall Patterns, based on only casual remarks in various of my books. To his wife, Marilyn, I owe the patient and correct transmission by Compuserve of this incredible technical data.

CONTENTS

Dragonsdawn
· 1 ·

Dragonseye
· 329 ·

Moreta: Dragonlady of Pern
· 589 ·

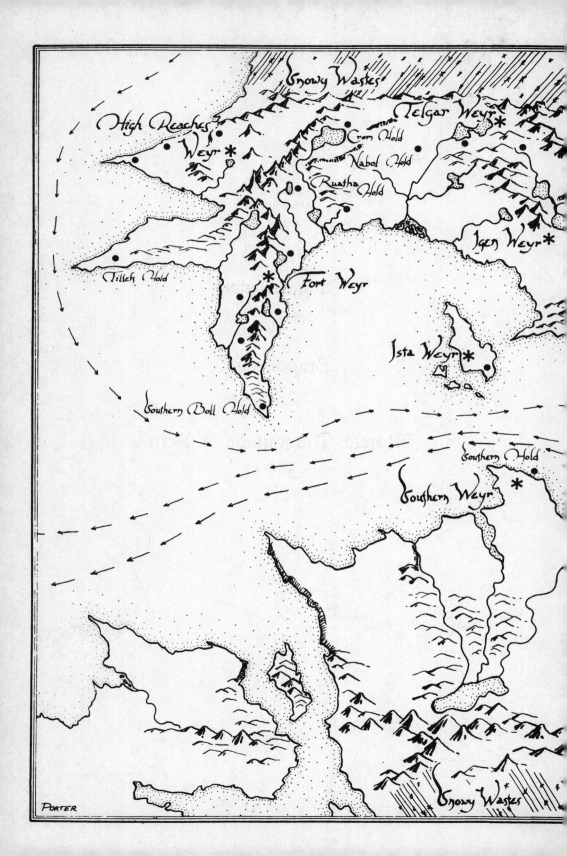

Benden Weyr
Bitra Hold
Keroon Hold
Nerat Hold
N
W
E
S
Southern Current
Cove
Pern

Pern

at the time of Landing

On
Dragonwings

Dragonsdawn

This book was always for
Judy-Lynn Benjamin del Rey

Part One

✣

LANDING

"Probe reports coming through, sir," Sallah Telgar announced without taking her eyes from the flickering lights on her terminal.

"On the screen, please, Mister Telgar," Admiral Paul Benden replied. Beside him, leaning against his command chair, Emily Boll kept her eyes steadily on the sunlit planet, scarcely aware of the activity around her.

The Pern Colonial Expedition had reached the most exciting moment of its fifteen-year voyage: the three colony ships, the *Yokohama*, the *Bahrain*, and the *Buenos Aires* were finally approaching their destination. In offices below the bridge deck, specialists eagerly awaited updates on the reports of the long-dead Exploration and Evaluation team that, 200 years earlier, had recommended Rukbat's third planet for colonization.

The long journey to the Sagittarian Sector had gone without a hitch, the only excitement being the surprise when the Oort cloud encircling the Rukbat system had been sighted. That phenomenon had continued to engross some of the space and scientific personnel, but Paul Benden had lost interest when Ezra Keroon, captain of the *Bahrain* and the expedition's astronomer, had assured him that the nebulous mass of deep-frozen meteorites was no more than an astronomical curiosity. They would keep an eye on it, Ezra had said, but although some comets might form and spin from its depths, he doubted that they would pose a serious threat to either the three colony ships or the planet the ships were fast approaching. After all, the Exploration and Evaluation team had not mentioned any unusual incidence of meteor strikes on the surface of Pern.

"Screening probe reports, sir," Sallah confirmed, "on two and five." Out of the corner of her eye, she saw Admiral Benden smile slightly.

"This is sort of anticlimactic, isn't it?" Paul murmured to Emily Boll as the latest reports flashed onto the screens.

Arms folded across her chest, she hadn't moved since the probes had been launched, except for an occasional twiddling of fingers along her upper arms. She lifted her right eyebrow in a cynical twitch and kept her eyes on the screen.

"Oh, I don't know. It's one more procedure which gets us nearer to the surface. Of course," she added dryly, "we're sort of stuck with whatever's reported, but I expect we can cope."

"We'll have to, won't we?" Paul Benden replied a trifle grimly.

The trip was one-way—it had to be, considering the cost of getting over six thousand colonists and supplies to such an out-of-the-way sector of the galaxy. Once they reached Pern the fuel left in the great transport ships would be enough only to achieve and maintain a synchronous orbit above their destination while people and cargo were shuttled down to the surface. To be sure, they had homing capsules that would reach the headquarters of the Federated Sentient Planets in a mere five years, but to a retired naval tactician like Paul Benden, a fragile homing capsule did not offer much in the way of an effective backup. The Pern expedition was composed of committed and resourceful people who had chosen to eschew the high-tech societies of the Federated Sentient Planets. They expected to manage on their own. And though their destination in the Rukbat system was rich enough in ores and minerals to support an agriculturally based society, it was poor enough and far enough from the center of the galaxy that it should escape the greed of the technocrats.

"Only a little while longer, Paul," Emily murmured, her voice reaching his ears alone, "and we'll both be able to lay down the weary load."

He grinned up at her, knowing that it had been as difficult for her as it had been for him to escape the blandishments of technocrats who had not wished to lose two such charismatic war heroes: the admiral who had prevailed in the Cygni Space Battle, and the governor-heroine of First Centauri. But no one could deny that the two were the ideal leaders for the Pern expedition.

"Speaking of loads," she went on more loudly, "I'd better be there to referee my team now the reports are coming in. I suppose specialists *have* to consider their own disciplines the most important ones, but such contentiousness!" She stifled a groan, then grinned, her blue eyes twinkling in her rather homely face. "Just a few more days of talking, and it'll be action stations, Admiral."

She knew him well. He hated the interminable debate over minor points that seemed to obsess those in charge of the landing operation. He preferred to make quick decisions and implement them immediately, instead of talking them to death.

"You're more patient with your teams than I am," the admiral said quietly. The last two months, as the three ships had decelerated into the Rukbat system, had been made tedious with meetings and discussions which seemed to Paul to be nit-picking over procedures that had been thoroughly thrashed out seventeen years before in the planning stages of the venture.

Most of the twenty-nine hundred colonists on the *Yokohama* had passed the entire journey in deep sleep. Personnel essential to the operation and maintenance of the three great ships had stood five-year watches. Paul Benden had elected to stand the first and last five-year periods. Emily Boll had been revived shortly before the rest of the environmental specialists, who had spent their time railing at the superficiality of the Exploration and Evaluation Corps report. She saw no point in reminding them of their enthusiasm for the same words when they had signed up for the Pern expedition.

Paul continued to absorb the display information, eyes flicking from one screen to another, absently rubbing the thumb of his left hand across three fingers. Though not the sort of man Emily was attracted to, Paul Benden was undeniably handsome, and Emily much preferred him with his hair grown out of the spaceman's crop that had been his trademark. She thought that the thick blond mass softened the strong features: the blunt nose, the forceful jaw, and the wide thin-lipped mouth, just then pulled slightly to the left in a little smile.

The trip had done him good: he looked fit and well able to face the rigors of their next few months. Emily remembered how terribly thin he had been at the official ceremony commemorating his brilliant victory at Cygnus, where he and the Purple Sector Fleet had turned the tide of war against the Nathis. Legend said that he had remained awake and on duty for the entire seventy hours of the crucial battle. Emily believed it. She had done something of the sort herself during the height of the Nathis attack on her planet. There were many things a person could do if pushed, she knew from experience. She expected that one paid for such physical abuses later on in life, but Benden, well into his sixth decade, looked vigorously healthy. And she certainly felt no diminution of her own energies. Fourteen years of deep sleep seemed to have cured the terrible fatigue that had been the inevitable result of her defense of First Centauri.

And what a world they were now approaching! Emily sighed, still unable to look away from the main screen for more than a second. She knew that all those on duty on the bridge, along with those of the previous watch who had not left, were totally bemused by the magnificent sight of their destination.

Who had named it Pern, she did not recall—quite probably the single letters blazoned across the published report had stood for something else entirely—but it was Pern officially, and it was theirs. They were on an equatorial heading; as she watched, the planet's lazy rotation hid the northern continent and the spine of mountains up its coast, while the western desert of the southern landmass was revealed. The dominant topographical feature was the wide expanse of ocean, slightly greener than that of old Earth, with a ring of islands splattered across it. The atmosphere was currently decorated with the swirling cloud curl of a low-pressure area moving rapidly northeast. What a beautiful, beautiful world! She sighed again and caught Paul's quick glance. She smiled back at him without really taking her eyes from the screen.

A beautiful world! And theirs! By all the Holies, this time we won't botch it! she assured herself fervently. With all that magnificent, productive land, the old imperatives don't apply. No, she added in private cynicism, people are already discovering new ones. She thought of the friction she had sensed between the charterers, who had raised the staggering credits needed to finance the Pern expedition, and the contractors, the specialists hired to round out the basic skills required for the undertaking. Each could end up with a largeous amount of land or mineral rights on this new world, but the fact that the charterers would get first choice was a bone of contention.

Differences! Why did there always have to be distinctions, arrogantly displayed as superiorities, or derided as inferiorities? Everyone would have the same opportunity, no matter how many stake acres they could claim as charterer or had been granted as contractor. On Pern, it would truly be up to the individual to succeed, to prove his claim and to manage as much land as he and his cared for. That would be the catholic distinction. Once we've landed, everyone will be too bloody busy to fret over "differences," she consoled herself, and watched in fascination as a second low-pressure area began to spin down from the hidden north across the sea. If the two weather systems melded, there would be a tremendous storm over the eastern curve of the oceanic islands.

"Looking good," Commander Ongola murmured in his deep, sad bass voice. Emily had not seen him smile once in the six months she had been awake. Paul had told her that Ongola's wife, children, and entire family had been vaporized when the Nathis had attacked their service colony; Paul had specifically requested him to join the expedition. Stationed at the science desk, Ongola was monitoring the meteorology and atmospherics displays. "Atmospheric content as expected. Southern continent temperatures appear to be normal for this late winter season. Northern continent enjoying considerable precipitation due to low-pressure air masses. Analyses and temperatures consistent with EEC report."

The first probe was doing a high-altitude circumnavigation in a pattern that would allow it to photograph the entire planet. The second, taking a low-level course, could reexamine any portion required. The third probe was programmed for topographical features.

"Probes four and six have landed, sir. Five is on hold," Sallah went on, as she interpreted the new lights that had begun to flash. "Scuttlebugs deployed."

"Show them on the screens, Mister Telgar," the admiral said. She transferred the displays to screens three, four, and six.

Pern's image continued to dominate the main screen as the planet rotated slowly to the east, from night to day. The southern continent's coastline was day-lit; the spinal range of mountains and the tracks of several rivers were visible. The thermal scan was showing the effect of daylight on the late winter season of the southern continent.

Probe scuttlebugs had been landed at three not-yet-visible specific points in the southern hemisphere and were relaying updates on current conditions and terrain. The southern continent had always been favored as the landing site: the survey-team report mentioned the more clement weather patterns on the high plateaus; a wider variety of plant life, some of it edible by humans; eminently suitable farmland; and good harbors for the tough siliplex fishing vessels that existed as numbered pieces in the holds of the *Buenos Aires* and the *Bahrain*. The seas of Pern teemed with aquatic life, and at least a few of the species could be safely consumed by humans. The marine biologists had high hopes of populating the bays and estuaries with Terran piscine types without harming the present ecological balance. The deep-freeze tanks of the *Bahrain* contained twenty-five dolphins who had volunteered to come along. Pern's seas were eminently suitable for the support of the intelligent mammals, who enjoyed sea-shepherding as well as the opportunity to see new worlds.

Soil analyses had indicated that Terran cereals and legumes, which had already adapted well to Centauran soil, should flourish on Pern, a necessity as the native grasses were unsuitable for Terran animals. One of the first tasks facing the agronomists would be to plant fodder crops to sustain the variety of herbivores and ruminants that had been brought as fertilized ova from the Animal Reproduction Banks of Terra.

In order that the colonists could ensure the adaptability of Terran animals to Pern, permission to use certain of the advanced biogenetic techniques of the Eridanis—mainly mentasynth, gene paring, and chromosome enhancements—had been grudgingly granted. Even though Pern was in an isolated area of the galaxy, the Federated Sentient Planets wanted no further disasters like the bio-alts, which had aroused the strong Pure Human Life Group.

Emily Boll repressed a shudder. Those memories belonged to the past. Displayed on the screen in front of her was the future—and she had best get down and help the specialists organize it. "I've dallied long enough," she murmured to Paul Benden, touching his shoulder in farewell.

Paul pulled his gaze from the screen and smiled at her, giving her hand a friendly pat. "Eat first!" He waggled a stern finger at her. "You keep forgetting we're not rationed on board the *Yoko*." She gave him a startled look. "I will. I promise."

"The next few weeks are going to be rough."

"Hmm, but so stimulating!" Her blue eyes twinkled. Then her stomach audibly rumbled. "Gotcha, Admiral." She winked again and left.

He watched her as she walked to the nearest exit off the bridge, a lean, almost bony woman, with gray and naturally wavy hair which she wore shoulder length. What Paul liked most about her was her wiry strength, both moral and physical, which was combined with a ruthlessness that sometimes startled him. She had tremendous personal vitality—just being in her presence gave one's spirits a lift. Together they would make something of their new world.

He looked back to the main screen and the enthralling vista of Pern.

❖ ❖ ❖

The large lounge had been set up as an office for the heads of the various teams of exobiology, agronomy, botany, and ecology, along with six representatives of the professional farmers, who were still a bit groggy from their term in deep sleep. The room was ringed by multiple screens displaying a constantly altering range of microbiology reports, statistics, comparisons, and analyses. There was much debate going on. Those hunched over desk monitors, busily collating reports, tried to ignore the tension emanating from the departmental heads who occupied the very center of the room in a tight knot, each one with an eye out for the screens displaying reports on his or her specialty.

Mar Dook, head agronomist, was a small man whose Earth Asiatic ancestry was evident in features, skin tone, and physiology: he was wiry, lean, and slightly bowed in the shoulders, but his black eyes gleamed with eager intelligence and the excitement of the challenge.

"The schedule has long been decided, my dear colleagues. We're in the first wave down. The probes do not contradict any of the information we already have. The dirt and vegetation samples match. There's the same sort of red and green algae reported along the shoreline. Marine life has been sighted by the sea probe. One of the low probes has caught a comforting variety of insects, which the EEC also found. The aerial fax that came up with that flyer reported—what did the team call them?—wherries."

"Why 'wherries'?" Phas Radamanth asked. He scrolled through the report searching for that particular annotation. "Ah," he said when he found it. "Because they resemble airborne barges—squat, fat, and full." He allowed himself a little smile for the whimsy of that long-dead team.

"Yeah, but I don't see mention of any other predators," Kwan Marceau said, his rather high forehead creased, as usual, with a frown.

"There's sure to be something that eats them," Phas replied confidently.

"Or they eat each other," Mar Dook suggested. He received a stern frown from Kwan. Suddenly Mar Dook pointed excitedly to a new fax coming up on one screen. "Ah, look! The scuttlebug got a reptiloid. Rather a large specimen, ten centimeters thick and seven meters long. There's your wherry eater, Kwan."

"Another scuttle has just run through a puddle of excretal matter, semiliquid, which contains intestinal parasites and bacteria," Pol Nietro said, hurriedly tagging the report for later reference. "There do seem to be plenty of wormlike soil dwellers, too. Rather a significant variety, if you ask me. Worms like nematodes, insectoids, mites that really wouldn't be out of place in a Terran compost heap. Ted, here's something for you: plants like our mycorrhizas—tree fungi. Speaking of that, I wonder where the EEC team found that luminous mycelium."

Ted Tubberman, one of the colony botanists, gave a contemptuous snort. He was a big man, not carrying any extra flesh after nearly fifteen years in deep sleep, who tended to be overbearing. "Luminous organisms are usually found in deep caves, Nietro, as they use their light to attract their victims, generally insects. The mycelium reported by that team was in a cave system on that large island south of the northern continent. This planet seems to have a considerable number of cave systems. Why weren't any scuttles scheduled for subterranean investigations?" he asked in an aggrieved tone.

"There were only so many available, Ted," Mar Dook said placatingly.

"Ah, look! Now, this is what I've been waiting for," Kwan said, his usually solemn face lighting up as he bent until his nose almost touched the small screen before him. "There are reef systems. And yes, a balanced if fragile marine ecology along the ring islands. I'm much encouraged. Possibly those polka dots they saw are from a meteorite storm."

Ted dismissed that instantly. "No. No impact, and the formation of new growth does not parallel that sort of phenomenon. I intend looking into that problem the first moment I can."

"What we have to do first," Mar Dook said, his tone gently reproving, "is select the appropriate sites, plow, test, and, where necessary, introduce the symbiotic bacteria and fungi, even beetles, needed for pastureland."

"But we still don't know *which* landing site will be chosen." Ted's face was flushed with irritation.

"The three that are now being surveyed are much of a muchness," Mar Dook replied with a tolerant smile. He found Tubberman's petulant restlessness tedious. "All three give us ample scope for experimental and control fields. Our basic tasks will be the same no matter where we land. The essential point is not to miss this first vital growing season."

"The brood animals must be revived as soon as possible," Pol Nietro said. The head zoologist was as eager as everyone else to plunge into the practical work ahead. "And reliance on the alfalfa trays for fodder is not going to adjust their digestions to a new environment. We must begin as we mean to go on, and let Pern supply our needs."

There was a murmur of assent to his statement.

"The only new factor in these reports," Phas Radamanth, the xenobiologist, said encouragingly, without turning his eyes from his screens, "is the density of vegetation. We may have to clear more than we thought in the forty-five south eleven site. See here—" He gestured to the disparate images. "Where the EEC pic showed sparse ground cover, we now have heavy vegetation, some of it of respectable size."

"There should be at least that, after two-hundred-odd years," Ted Tubberman said irritably. "I never was happy about the barrenness. Smacked of a depauperate ecology. Hey, most of those circular features are overgrown. Felicia, run up the EEC pics that correspond." He bent his big frame to peer over her shoulder at the double screen below the probe broadcast. "See, those circles are barely discernible now. The team was right about botanical succession. And that isn't a grassoid. If that's mutant vegetation . . ." He trailed off, shaking his head and jutting his chin out. He had loudly and frequently insisted that the success of Pern as a colony would depend on botanical health.

"I, too, am happier to see succession, but according to the EEC reports, it's—" Mar Dook began.

"Shove the EEC reports. They didn't tell us the half of what we really need to know," Ted exclaimed. "Survey, they called it. Quick dip at the trot. No depth to it at all. The most superficial survey I've ever read."

"I quite agree," said the calm voice of Emily Boll, who had entered while the botanist was ranting. "The initial EEC report does seem to have been less than complete now that we can compare it to our new home. But the most crucial, salient points were covered for us. We know what we needed to know, and the FSP was quite happy to turn the planet over to us because it certainly doesn't have anything to interest them. And it's not a planet that the syndicates would fight over. Which is why *we* were allowed to have it. I think we have to be grateful to that team, not critical." Her smile swept everyone in the crowded room. "The important elements—atmosphere, water, arable soil, ores, minerals, bacteria, insects, marine life—are all present, and Pern is eminently suitable for human habitation. The gaps, the in-depth investigations that report did not contain, are what we shall spend a lifetime filling in. A challenge for each and every one of us, and our children!" Her low-pitched voice rang in the crowded room. "Let's not worry at this very late date about what we weren't told. We'll find the answers soon enough. Let's concentrate now on the great work we have to begin in just two days' time. We're ready for any surprises Pern might have for us. Now, Mar Dook, have you seen anything in the updates to suggest we must alter the schedule?"

"Nothing," Mar Dook replied, warily glancing at Ted Tubberman, who was frowning at Emily Boll. "But those soil and vegetable matter samples would occupy us usefully."

"I'm sure they would." Emily grinned broadly at him. "We'll be busy enough—ah, here's the information you need. And what a bumper crop to digest."

"We still don't know *where* we're landing," Ted complained.

"The admiral is discussing that right now, Ted," Emily replied equably. "We'll be among the first to know."

Agronomists were to be in the first shuttleloads to reach the surface, for it was vital to the colony's future to break land for crops as soon as possible. Even while the engineers were setting up the landing grids, agronomists would be plowing fields, and Ted Tubberman and his group would be setting up sheds and seeding the precious soil brought from Earth. Pat Hempenstall would set up a control shed using indigenous dirt, to see if Earth or colonial variants would thrive unassisted in an alien soil. Sufficient packaged organisms had also been brought to introduce symbiotic bacteria.

"I will be very glad," Pol Nietro murmured, "if the reports confirm those insectoids, winged and subterranean, reported by the EEC team. If they should prove sufficient to do the work of dung beetles and flies on our Terran-style detritus, agronomy will be off to a good start. We've got to get nutrients back into the soil and introduce the rumen bacteria, protozoans, and yeasts for our cows, sheep, goats, and horses so they'll thrive."

"If not, Pol," Emily replied, "we can ask Kitti to work a bit of her micro-magic and rearrange innards that can deal with what Pern has to offer." She smiled with great deference at the tiny lady seated in the center of the little cluster.

"Soil samples coming up," Ju Adjai said into the pause. "And here's vegetable mash for you, Ted. Get your teeth in that."

Tubberman launched himself to the position next to Felicia, his big fingers nimble and accurate over the keyboard.

In moments the rattling of keys, punctuated by assorted mutters and other monosyllables of concentration, filled the room. Emily and Kit Ping exchanged glances tinged with amused condescension for the vagaries of their younger colleagues. Kit Ping then turned her eyes back to the main screen and continued her contemplation of the world they were rapidly approaching.

As Emily sat down at her workspace, she wondered how under the suns the expedition had lucked out enough to include the most eminent geneticist in the Federated Sentient Planets—the only human who had ever been trained by the Eridanis. Emily had only seen pics of the altered humans who had made the first abortive mission to Eridani. She suppressed a shudder. Pern wouldn't ever require that kind of abominable tinkering. Maybe that's why Kit Ping was willing to come to the edge of the galaxy—to end what had already been a long and incredible life in a quiet backwater where she, too, could practice selective amnesia. There were many on the colony's roll who had come to forget what they had seen and done.

"The grassoid on that eastern landing site is going to be hell to cut through," Ted Tubberman said, scowling. "High boron content. It'll dull cutting edges and foul gear."

"It'd cushion the landing," Pat Hempenstall said with a chuckle.

"Our landing craft have landed safely on far more inhospitable terrain than that," Emily reminded the others.

"Felicia, run a comparison on the botanical succession around those crazy polka dots," Ted Tubberman went on, staring at his own screens. "There's something about that configuration that still bothers me. The phenomenon is all over the planet. And I'd be happier if we could get an opinion from that geologist whiz, Tarzan—" He paused.

"Tarvi Andiyar," Felicia supplied, accustomed to Ted's memory lapses.

"Well, memo him to meet me when he's revived. Damn it, Mar, how can we function with only half the specialists awake?"

"We're doing fine, Ted. Pern is coming up roses for us. Not a joggle off the report data."

"That's almost worrying," Pol Nietro said blandly.

Tubberman snorted, Mar Dook shrugged, and Kitti Ping smiled.

◆ ◆ ◆

Admiral Benden's chrono tingled against his wrist, reminding him that it was time for his own meeting.

"Commander Ongola, take the conn." Reluctantly, his eyes focusing on the main screen until the access panel of the exit closed, Paul left the bridge.

The corridors of the great colony ship were becoming more crowded by the hour, Paul noticed as he made his way to the wardroom. Newly revived people, clutching the handrails, were jerkily exercising stiff limbs and trying to focus body and mind on the suddenly hazardous task of remaining upright. The old *Yoko* would be packed tighter than reserve rations while colonists awaited their turns to reach the surface. But with the promise of the freedom of a whole new world as the reward of patience, the crowding could be endured.

Having paid close attention to the various probe reports, Paul had already decided which of the three recommended landing sites he would choose. Naturally he would accord his staff and the other two captains the courtesy of a hearing, but the obvious choice was the vast plateau below a group of strato volcanoes. The current weather there was clement, and the nearly level expanse was adequate to accommodate all six shuttles. The updates had only confirmed a tentative preference made seventeen years ago when he had first studied the EEC reports. He had never anticipated much difficulty with landing; it was a smooth and accident-free debarkation that caused him anxiety. There was no rescue backup hovering solicitously in the skies of Pern, nor disaster teams on its surface.

In organizing the debarkation, Paul had chosen as flight officer Fulmar Stone, a man who had served with him throughout the Cygnus campaign. For the past two weeks, Fulmar's crews had been all over the *Yoko*'s three shuttle vehicles and the admiral's gig, ensuring that there would be no malfunction after fifteen years in the cold storage of the flight deck. The *Yoko*'s twelve pilots, under Kenjo Fusaiyuki, had gone through rigorous simulator drills well spiced with the most bizarre landing emergencies. Most of the pilots had been combat fighters, and were fit and fully experienced at extricating themselves from tricky situations, but none had quite the record of Kenjo Fusaiyuki. Some of the less experienced shuttle pilots had complained about Kenjo's methods; Paul Benden had courteously listened to the complaints—and ignored them.

Paul had been surprised and flattered when Kenjo had signed up with the expedition. Somehow, he had thought the man would have signed on to an exploratory unit where he could continue to fly as long as his reflexes lasted. Then Paul remembered that Kenjo was a cyborg, with a prosthetic left leg. After the war, the Exploration and Evaluation Corps had had their choice of experienced, whole personnel, and cyborgs had been shunted into administrative positions. Automatically, Paul made his left hand into a fist, his thumb rubbing against the knuckles of the three replacement fingers which had always worked as well as his natural ones. But there was still no feeling in the pseudoflesh. Consciously, he relaxed the hand, certain once again that he could hear a subtle plastic squeak in the joints and the wrist.

He turned his mind to real problems, like the debarkation ahead, knowing that unforeseeable delays or foul-ups could stall the entire operation as cargo and passengers began to flow from the orbiting ships. He had appointed good men as super-cargoes: Joel Lilienkamp as surface coordinator, and Desi Arthied on the *Yoko*. Ezra and Jim, of *Bahrain* and *Buenos Aires*, were equally confident in their own debarkation personnel, but one minor hitch could cause endless rescheduling. The trick would be to keep everything moving.

The admiral turned starboard off the main corridor and reached the wardroom. Once again, he hoped that the meeting would not drag on. As he raised his hand to brush the access panel, he could see that he had arrived with two minutes to spare before the other two captains screened in. First there would be the brief formality of Ezra Keroon, as fleet astrogator, confirming the exact ETA at their parking orbit, and then the landing site would be chosen.

"The betting's eleven to four now, Lili," Paul heard Drake Bonneau saying to Joel as the access panel to his wardroom *whoosh*ed open.

"For or against?" Paul asked, grinning as he entered. Those present, led by Kenjo's example, shot to their feet, despite Paul's dismissing gesture. He took in the two blank screens which in precisely ninety-five seconds would reveal the faces of Ezra Keroon and Jim Tillek, and to the center one where Pern swam tranquilly in the black ocean of space.

"There're some civilians don't think Desi and me can make the deadline, Paul," Joel answered with a smug wink at Arthied, who nodded solemnly. Not a tall man, Lilienkamp was chunkily built; he had an engaging monkey face, framed with graying dark hair that curled tightly against his skull. His personality was ebullient, volatile, and could be caustic. His quick wits included an eidetic memory that allowed him to keep track of not only any bet he made, for how much and with whom and what odds, but every parcel, package, crate, and canister in his keeping. Desi Arthied, his second-in-command, often found his superior's levity a trial, but he respected Lilienkamp's abilities. It would be Desi's job to shift the cargo that Joel designated to the loading decks and on board the shuttles.

"Civilians? Who don't know you very well, do they?" Paul asked dryly, taking his seat and smiling noncommittally at Avril Bitra, who had been in charge of the simulation exercises. Ambition had hardened her. He wished that he had not spent so much of his waking time during the voyage involved with the sultry brunette, but she *was* stunning. Soon they would all be too busy for personal relationships. More and more attractive young women were appearing in the corridors. He wanted one of them to want to marry Paul Benden, not "the admiral." Just then, the two screens lit up, the right-hand one displaying Ezra Keroon's saturnine countenance, with his distinctive fringe of gray hair, and the left showing Jim Tillek, his square face wearing his usual cheerful expression.

"G'day, Paul," he said, just ahead of Ezra's more formal salute.

"Admiral," Ezra said solemnly. "I beg to report that we have maintained our programmed course to the minute. Estimated arrival to parking orbit is now forty-six hours, thirty-three minutes, and twenty seconds. No deviations anticipated at this point in time."

"Very good, Captain," Paul said, returning the salute. "Any problems?"

Both captains reported that their revival programs were continuing without incident and that their shuttles were ready for launch once orbit had been achieved.

"Now that we know when, the matter of where is open for discussion," Paul said, leaning back in his chair to signal that comment was invited.

"So, tell us, Paul," Joel Lilienkamp said with his usual disregard for protocol, "where're we landing?" All through the Nathi War, Joel's impertinence had amused Paul Benden at a time when amusement was scarce, and he had consistently proved himself a near miraculous scavenger. His impudence caused Ezra Keroon to frown, but Jim Tillek chuckled.

"What are the odds, Lili?" he asked, his expression sly.

"Let us discuss the matter without prejudice," Paul suggested wryly. "The three sites recommended by the EEC team have now all been probed. If you will refer to the chart, the sites are at thirty south by thirteen point thirty, forty-five south by eleven, and forty-seven south by four point seven five."

"There's really only one, Admiral, from my point of view," Drake Bonneau interrupted excitedly, jabbing his finger at Paul's own choice, the strato site. "Scuttlebug scans say it's almost as level as if it had been graded for us, and broad enough to accommodate all six shuttles. The site at forty-five south eleven is waterlogged right now, and the western one is too far from the ocean. Temperature readings are near freezing."

Paul saw Kenjo's nod of agreement. He glanced at the two screens. Ezra's growing bald spot was evident as he bent to consult his notes; unconsciously, Paul smoothed back his own thick hair.

"That thirty south is nearer sea for me," Jim Tillek remarked amiably.

"Good harbor about fifty klicks away. River's navigable, too." Tillek's interest in sailing vessels was exceeded only by his love of dolphins. Accessibility to open water would be a high factor in his choice.

"Good heights for observatory and met stations all right," Ezra replied, "though we've no real criterion from those reports about climatology. Don't fancy settling that close to volcanoes myself."

"A point, Ezra, but—" Paul paused to screen the relevant data for a quick scan. "No seismic readings were recorded, so I don't see volcanic activity as an immediate problem. We can have Patrice de Broglie do a survey. Ah, yes, no seismic readings from the EEC, so even the one that has erupted has been dormant for well over two hundred years. And the weather and general conditions on the other two sites do mitigate against them."

"Hmm, so they do. Doesn't look from a met point of view as if the conditions at either will improve in two days," Ezra conceded.

"Hell, we don't have to *stay* where we land," Drake exclaimed.

"Unless there's some freak weather brewing up," Jim Tillek said, "which I'm sure the met boys will be able to spot, let's settle on the thirty-south site. That's the one the EEC team favored, anyhow. Besides, the scuttlebugs say it's got a thick ground cover. That should cushion the shock when you bounce, Drake."

"Bounce?" Drake's gray eyes widened at the mild jibe. "Captain Tillek, I haven't bounced a landing since my first solo."

"Very well, then, gentlemen, have we settled on our landing site?" Paul asked. Ezra and Jim nodded. "Relevant updates and detailed charts will be in your hands by 2200 hours."

"Well, Joel," Jim Tillek said, his sly grin broadening, "didja win?"

"Me, Captain?" Joel's expression was that of injured innocence. "I never bet on a sure thing."

"Any other problems to raise at this point, Captains?" Paul paused courteously, looking from one screen to the other.

"All ahead go, Paul, now I know I'll land this bucket in her parking space on time," Jim said, "and where to send my shuttle." He waved a casual salute toward Ezra and then his screen blacked out.

"Good evening, Admiral," Ezra said more formally. His image faded.

"Is that all now, Paul?" Joel asked.

"We've got the time and the place," Paul replied, "but that's a tough timetable you've set, Joel. Can you keep it?"

"There's a lot of money says he will, Admiral," Drake Bonneau quipped.

"Why do you think it took me so long to load the *Yoko*, Admiral?" Joel Lilienkamp replied with a wide grin. "I knew I'd have to unload it all fifteen years later. You'll see." He winked at Desi, whose expression showed the faintest hint of skepticism.

"Then, gentlemen," the admiral said, standing up, "I'll be in my cabin if any problems do arise."

As he swung out of the wardroom, Paul heard Joel asking for bets on how soon knowledge of the landing site would circulate the *Yoko*.

Avril's throaty voice replied. "Those odds, Lili." Then the door panel *whoosh*ed shut.

Morale was high. Paul hoped that Emily's meeting had been as satisfactory. Seventeen years of planning and organization were about to be put to the test.

◆ ◆ ◆

On the deep-sleep decks of all three colony ships, the medics were working double shifts to arouse the fifty-five hundred or so colonists. Technicians and specialists were being revived in order of their usefulness to the landing operation, but Admiral Benden and Governor Boll had been insistent that everyone be awake by the time the three ships achieved their temporarily programmed parking position in a stable Lagrangian orbit, sixty degrees ahead of the larger moon, in the L–5 spot. Once the three great ships had been cleared of passengers and cargo, there would be no more chance to view Pern from outer space.

Sallah Telgar, coming off duty from her watch on the bridge, decided that she had had quite enough space travel for one lifetime. As the only surviving dependent of serving officers, she had spent her childhood being shunted from one service post to another. When she had lost both parents, she had been eligible to sign on as a charter member of the colony. War compensations had permitted her to acquire a substantial number of stake acres on Pern, which she could claim once the colony had become solidly established. Above all other considerations, Sallah yearned to set herself down in one place and stay there for the rest of her natural life. She was quite content that that place be Pern.

As she exited bridge territory for the main corridors, she was surprised to see so many people about. For nearly five years she had had a cabin to herself. The cabin was not spacious even for single-occupancy, and with three sharing, it offered no privacy at all. Not eager to return, Sallah made for the off-duty lounge, where she could get something to eat and continue planet-gazing, courtesy of the lounge's large screen.

At the lounge entrance, Sallah hauled up sharp, surprised at how few seats were available. In the brief moments it took her to collect food from the dispensers, her options were narrowed down to one: a wall-counter seat well to the port side of the big room, with a slightly distorted view of Pern.

Sallah shrugged diffidently. Like an addict, she would take any view she could get of Pern. However, as she slipped into the seat, she realized that her nearest neighbors were also the people she least liked on board the *Yokohama*: Avril Bitra, Bart Lemos, and Nabhi Nabol. They were seated with three men she did not know, whose collar tabs identified them as mason, mechanical engineer, and miner. The six were also about the only people in the room not avidly watching the screen. The three specialists were listening to Avril and Bart, their faces carefully expressionless, though the oldest man, the engineer, occasionally glanced around to check on the attention of those nearby. Avril had her elbows on the table, her handsome face marred by the arrogant, supercilious sneer she affected, her black eyes glinting as she leaned forward toward homely Bart Lemos, who was enthusiastically punching his right fist into his left palm to emphasize his quick low words. Nabhi was wearing his perpetual expression of hauteur, an expression not far removed from Avril's sneer, as he watched the geologist.

Their attitudes were enough to spoil anyone's appetite, Sallah thought. She craned her neck to see Pern.

Gossip had it that Avril had spent a good deal of the last five years in Admiral Paul Benden's bed. Candidly, Sallah could see why a virile man like the admiral would be sexually attracted by the astrogator's dark and flashing beauty. A mixture of ethnic ancestors had given her the best of all possible features. She was tall, neither willowy nor overripe, with luxuriant black hair that she often wore loose in silky ripples. Her slightly sallow complexion was flawless and her movements gracefully studied, but her eyes, snapping with black fire, indicated a highly intelligent and volatile personality. Avril was not a woman to cross, and Sallah had carefully maintained her distance from Paul Benden, or anyone else seen more than three times in Avril's company. If the unkind pointed out Paul Benden's recent marked absence from Avril's side, the charitable said that he was needed for long conferences with his staff, and the time for dalliance was over. Those who had been victims of Avril's sharp tongue said that she had lost her bid to be the admiral's lady.

However, Sallah had other matters on her mind than Avril Bitra's ploys. She was waiting to hear which site had been chosen for landing. She knew that a decision had been made, and that it was to be kept secret until the admiral's formal announcement. But she knew, too, that the news was bound to leak. Bets had been surreptitiously made about how soon the rest of the ship would know. The news should percolate through the lounge real soon now, Sallah thought.

"This is where," a man suddenly exclaimed. He strode to the screen, jabbing his forefinger at a point that had just become visible. He wore the agronomy plow tab on his collar. "Right—" He paused as the screen image moved fractionally. "Here!" He planted his forefinger at the base of a volcano, discernible only as a pinpoint but nevertheless recognizable as a landmark.

"How much did Lili win on that one?" someone demanded.

"Don't care about him," the agronomist shouted. "I've just won an acre off Hempenstall!"

There was a ripple of applause and good-natured joking, infectious enough to make Sallah grin, until her gaze happened to spot the contemptuous smile of superiority on Avril's face. Seeing the astrogator's expression, Sallah knew that Avril had known the secret and withheld the information from her table companions. Bart Lemos and Nabhi Nabol leaned closer to exchange terse sentences.

Avril shrugged. "The landing site is immaterial." Her sultry voice, though low, carried to Sallah's ears. "The gig's equipped to do the job, believe me." She glanced away and caught Sallah's eyes. Instantly her body tensed and her eyes narrowed. With a conscious effort she relaxed and leaned indolently back in her chair, maintaining eye contact with an insolence that Sallah found aggravating.

Sallah looked away, feeling slightly soiled. She drank the last gulp of coffee, grimacing at the bitter aftertaste. The ship's coffee was lousy, but she would miss even that facsimile when the supply was exhausted. Coffee had failed on all the colony planets so far, for reasons no one had yet discerned. The survey team had discovered and recommended a Pernese shrub bark as a coffee substitute, but Sallah did not have much faith in that.

After the identification of the landing site, the noise level in the lounge had risen to an almost intolerable pitch. With a sigh, Sallah ditched her rubbish in the disposer, passed her tray under the cleanser, and stacked it neatly with others. She permitted herself one last long look at Pern. We won't spoil this planet, she thought. I personally won't let anyone spoil it.

As she turned to leave, her glance fell on Avril's dark head. Now there's an odd one to be a colonist, Sallah thought, not for the first time. Avril was listed as a contractor, with a handsome stake as a professional fee, but she scarcely seemed the sort who would be comfortable in a rural environment. She had all the sophisticated manners of the citified. The Pern expedition had attracted some first-rate talents, but most of those to whom Sallah had talked had been motivated to leave behind the syndicate-ridden technocracy and its ever-spiraling need for resources.

Sallah liked the notion of joining a self-reliant society so far from Earth and her other colonies. From the moment she had read the Pern prospectus she had been eager to be part of the venture. At sixteen, with service compulsory at that point in the bitterly fought Nathi War, she had chosen pilot training, with additional studies in probe and surveillance techniques. She had completed her training just as the war ended and then used her skills to map devastated areas on one planet and two moons. When the Pern expedition was put together, she had not only been eligible to be a charterer, but had the experience and skills that would make her a valuable addition to the professional complement.

She left the off-duty lounge to return to her quarters, but she was not sure she would be able to sleep. In two days, they would reach their long-awaited goal. Then life would get interesting!

Just as Sallah turned into the main corridor, a little girl with burnished deep red hair lurched into her, tried to regain her balance, and fell heavily at Sallah's feet. Bursting into loud sobs, more from frustration than from hurt, the child clung to Sallah's leg in a grip astonishingly strong for one so young.

"There now, not to cry. You'll get your balance back, pet," Sallah said soothingly, reaching down to stroke the child's silky hair and then to loosen her frantic grip.

"Sorka! Sorka!" An equally redheaded man holding a little boy by one hand, and a very pretty brunette woman by the other, moved unsteadily toward Sallah. The woman had all the signs of someone only just awake: her eyes didn't quite focus, and while she was trying to respond to the situation, she was unable to concentrate.

The man's eyes flicked to Sallah's collar emblem. "I do apologize, Pilot," the redheaded man said, grinning apologetically. "We're really not awake yet."

He was trying to disencumber one hand to come to Sallah's assistance, but the woman refused to relinquish her grasp, and plainly he could not let go of the tottering boy.

"You need help," Sallah said pleasantly, wondering which medic had let the totally unstable quartet out on their own.

"Our quarters are only a few steps along." He nodded toward the splinter aisle behind Sallah. "Or so I was told. But I never appreciated how far a few steps could be."

"What's the number? I'm off duty."

"B–8851."

Sallah looked at the plates on the corridor corners and nodded. "It *is* just the next aisle. Here, I'll help. There now, Sorka—is that your name? Here, I'll just—"

"Excuse me," the man interrupted as Sallah moved to lift the child into her arms. "They kept telling us we'd be better off walking. Trying to walk, that is."

"I can't walk," Sorka cried. "I'm lopsided." She clung more fiercely to Sallah's legs.

"Sorka! Behave yourself!" The redhead frowned at his daughter.

"Got an idea!" Sallah said in a brisk friendly tone. "You take both my hands—" She peeled Sorka's fingers from her leg and grasped each little hand firmly in her own. "—and walk in front of me. I'll keep you on an even keel."

Even with Sallah's help, the family made slow progress, impeded by the more agile walkers rushing by on private errands, and by the uncertainty of their own steps.

"I'm Red Hanrahan," the man said when their progress improved.

"Sallah Telgar."

"Never thought I'd need help from a pilot before we reached Pern," he said with a wide grin. "This is my wife, Mairi, my son, Brian, and you've got Sorka."

"Here we are," Sallah said, reaching their compartment and throwing open the door. She grimaced at the size of the accommodation and then reminded herself that their occupancy would only be for a short time. Even though the bunks were strapped up against the walls in their daytime position, the remaining floor space allowed for little movement.

"Not much larger than the quarters we just vacated," Red remarked equably.

"How are we supposed to exercise in here?" his wife demanded, a rather shrill note in her voice as she rolled her body around the doorjamb and got a good look at the size of their cabin.

"One by one, I guess," Red said. "It's only for a few days, pet, and then we'll have a whole planet to range. In you go, Brian, Sorka. We've kept Pilot Telgar long enough. You really saved us, Telgar. Thanks."

Sorka, who had propped herself against the inside wall of their cabin as her father encouraged the rest of his family to enter, slid to a sitting position on the floor, her little knees against her chest. Then she cocked her head to peer up at Sallah. "Thanks from me, too," she said, sounding more self-possessed. "It's really silly not knowing up from down, and side from side."

"I agree, but the effect will disappear very quickly. We all had to go through it when we woke up."

"You did?" Sorka's incredulous expression turned into the most radiant smile Sallah had ever seen, and she found herself grinning, too.

"We did. Even Admiral Benden," she said mendaciously. She ruffled the child's silky, magnificently titian hair. "I'll see you around. Okay?"

"While you're in that position, Sorka, do those exercises we were shown.

Then it'll be Brian's turn," Red Hanrahan was saying as Sallah closed the door behind her.

She reached her own quarters without further incident, though the corridors were filled with recent sleepers lurching about, their expressions ranging from intense concentration to horrified dismay. The moment Sallah opened her door, she was aware of the occupants asleep inside. She grimaced. Very carefully she slid the panel back and leaned against it, wondering what to do. She was too keyed up to sleep yet; she had to wind down somehow. She decided to go to the pilots' ready room for some stimulating simulator practice. The moment of truth for her abilities as a shuttle pilot was rapidly approaching.

Her route was impeded by another recently awakened colonist whose coordination suffered from prolonged disuse. He was so rake-thin that Sallah feared he would break a bone as he lurched from side to side.

"Tarvi Andiyar, geologist," he said, courteously introducing himself as soon as she had supported him to a vertical stance. "Are we really orbiting Pern?" His eyes crossed as he looked at her, and Sallah managed to suppress the grin that his comical expression evoked. She told him their position. "And you have seen with your own bright and pretty eyes this marvelous planet?"

"I have and it's every bit as lovely as forecast," Sallah assured him warmly. He smiled broadly in relief, showing her very white and even teeth. Then he gave a shake of his head, which seemed to correct the aberrant focus of his eyes. He had one of the most beautiful faces she had ever seen on a man—not Benden's rugged, warrior features, but a sophisticated and subtle arrangement, almost sculpted, like some of the ancient Indic and Cambodian princes on ruined stone murals. She flushed as she remembered what those princes had been doing in the murals.

"Would you know if there are any updated probe reports? I am exceedingly eager to get to work."

Sallah laughed, amusement easing the sensual jolt his face had given her. "You can't even walk and you want to get to work?"

"Isn't fifteen years' holiday long enough for anyone?" His expression was mildly chiding. "Is that not cabin C–8411?"

"It is indeed," she said, guiding him across the corridor.

"You are as beautiful as you are kind," he said, one hand on the panel for support as he tried to make a very courtly bow. She had to grab at his shoulders as he overbalanced. "And quick." With a more judicious inclination of his head, and with considerable dignity under the circumstances, he opened his door.

"Sallah!" Drake Bonneau exclaimed, striding down the corridor toward her. "Anybody told you where we're landing?" He had the eager expression of someone about to confer a favor on a friend.

"It took no more than nine minutes for the scuttlebutt to circulate," she said coolly.

"That long?" He pretended disdain and then produced one of the smiles that he assumed would charm anyone. "Let's drink to it. Not much longer to enjoy our leisure, eh? Just you and me, huh?"

She suppressed her distrust of his flattery. He was probably not even conscious of the triteness of his glib phrases. She had heard him trot out the same smooth lines for any reasonably attractive female, and at the moment, his casual insincerity irritated her. Yet he was not a bad sort, and certainly he had had courage enough to spare during the war. Then she realized that her uncharacteristic annoyance was a reaction to the sudden bustle, noise, and proximity of so many people after the last few years of quiet. Relax, she told herself sternly, it's only for a few days and then you'll be too busy flying to worry about crowds and noise.

"Thanks, Drake, but Kenjo has me down for simulator practice in—" She glanced at her wrist. "—five minutes. Getcha another time."

To avoid the crowded corridors, she took the emergency tube down to the flight deck, then made her way past the variety of cargo secured there to the admiral's gig, the *Mariposa*. It was a compact little craft, with its delta wing and its perky, pointed nacelle, but it would be full of quiet and unoccupied space. Sallah punched the hatch release.

Sallah shared her next watch, the dogwatch, with Kenjo Fusaiyuki. There was little for either of them to do, barring reacting if a glitch halted the programs. Sallah was hacking around, trying to find something interesting enough to keep her awake, when she noticed that Kenjo had activated one of the smaller screens on his position.

"What have you got there?" she asked before she remembered Kenjo was not generally outgoing and might resent her interruption.

"I was decoding the gen on that eccentric wanderer," he replied, without looking up from the screen.

"Oh, the one that had the astronomers all excited?" Sallah asked. She grinned, remembering the unusual spectacle of the rather staid, pedantic astronomer, Xi Chi Yuen, flushed with excitement and dancing about the bridge.

"Quite likely," Kenjo said. "It does seem to have an enormously eccentric orbit, more cometary than planetary, though its mass indicates its planetary size. Look." He tapped out a sequence that brought up the satellites of Pern's star system in relation to their primary and to one another. "It computes to come in farther than the usual fourth planet position and actually intrudes on the Oort cloud at aphelion. This is supposed to be an old system, or so the EEC report leads one to believe, and that planet ought to have a more conventional orbit."

"There was talk that it could be a stray that the Rukbat sun attracted."

Kenjo shook his head. "That has been ruled out." He typed out another sequence and the diagram on the screen shifted to another projection. In a few seconds, equations overlaid the system diagram. "Look at the odds against that." He pointed to the blinking nine-figure probability. "It would have to be a cometary-type orbit, right into the system. But it's not." His long, bony fingers reset the screen. "I can't find a harmonic with the other planets. Ah, Captain Keroon registers the opinion that it might have been captured by Rukbat about ten of its cycles ago."

"No, I think Xi Chi Yuen ruled that out. He computed it to be just after aphelion right now," Sallah said. "What did he say? Ah . . ." She tried to remember.

Kenjo was already accessing that file. "His report actually says that the eccentric planetoid had just exited the Oort cloud, pulling some of the cloud matter with it."

"He also said, and I remember that distinctly, that in about eight years' time, we'll have a rather spectacular meteorite show as our new world goes through the wisps of Oort material."

Kenjo snorted. "I'd rather we didn't. I don't have much faith in that EEC report now that it's being compared with what's there. Those polka dots may be meteor damage after all."

"I'm not going to lose any sleep over it."

"Nor I." Kenjo crossed his arms over his chest as the report continued to scroll up the screen. "Yuen apparently believes that with such an eccentric, almost parabolic orbit, this Pluto body may exit the star system again, or fall into the sun."

"Which wouldn't much notice, would it?"

Kenjo shook his head, his eyes still scanning the report. "Frozen solid. Much too far from Rukbat to get any warmth during most of its orbit. There's a possibility of a cometary tail visible when it's close in." He exited that program and tapped out a new sequence. "Pern's two moons are much more interesting."

"Why? We're not colonizing *them*. Anyway, fuel consumption allows for only the one trip to the moons, to set up the relay disks."

Kenjo shrugged. "You *always* leave yourself an escape route."

"To a moon?" Sallah was openly skeptical. "C'mon, Kenjo, we're not at war with anyone or anything this far from the Hub. Give over." She spoke kindly, knowing that Kenjo had had several very narrow escapes in the Nathi War.

"Old habits die hard," he murmured in such a low voice that she almost missed it.

"Yeah, they do. But we're all going to be able to start fresh."

Kenjo merely grunted, signaling an end to his talkative mood.

◆ ◆ ◆

As the colony ships slowed, they were filled with constant activity as sleepers continued to be awakened, and the immense cargo pods were opened and their contents transferred to decks, spilling into access corridors. When the shuttles had been secured for the long voyage, they had already been loaded with the grid components and other necessities to build a safe landing field for the mass of matériel and people to be discharged from the colony ships. The urgency was to have the next shipment—agricultural tools and supplies— ready to be hustled on board as soon as the shuttles returned. The agronomists had promised to break ground before the next shuttle flight could reach the planet.

There were six shuttles between the three ships: three in the *Yoko*, two in the *Buenos Aires*, and one in the *Bahrain*, the latter equipped with special fittings for transporting livestock. Once the vessels had achieved their Lagrangian orbit, debarkation would commence.

Twelve hours before that event, all the sleepers had been revived. There was a fair amount of grumbling about the crowding. Many felt that the unessential people, especially young children, should have slept on until planetside accommodations were completed. But despite the inconvenience, Sallah agreed with the governor's announcement that no one should be denied the chance to witness the end of the long journey and the incredible vision of their new world spinning in black space. Sallah could not keep her eyes off Pern and watched on whatever screen was available, even the tiny one in her quarters. She had also managed to get on the duty roster for the most important watch of the entire trip.

Afterward, Sallah always stoutly averred that she had known the instant the *Yokohama* reached its orbital position. The great ship had been slowing for days; the slight puff of the retros as they reduced the forward motion to a match with the planet below was infinitesimal. Suddenly they were turning with the planet, in position over a real point on Pern, seeming to come to a halt in relation to the geography below them. Somehow Sallah sensed that moment. She actually looked up from her console just as the helmsman, with suppressed excitement, turned to salute the commander.

"We have arrived, sir," the helmsman announced.

At the same instant, a similar report came in from the *Bahrain* and the *Buenos Aires*, and those on the bridge erupted into cheers and undisciplined expressions of relief and exultation. Commander Ongola immediately informed the admiral of the completion of the maneuver and received formal thanks. Then he ordered all screens to focus on the planet spread out below them, curving away into night on the one side, and into brilliant day on the other.

Sallah joined in the hullabaloo until she noticed a break in the chatter from the probe and checked the monitor. The probe was merely switching its site as programmed. As she looked up, she caught a very sad, oddly pensive expression on Commander Ongola's face. Aware of her scrutiny, he arched one eyebrow in query.

Sallah smiled back in sympathy. The end of his last voyage, she thought. Who wouldn't be sad?

Both of Ongola's heavy eyebrows went up, and with great dignity he turned his head away, giving the order for the shuttle-bay doors to be opened. The crew and the initial landing party were already strapped into their seats aboard the shuttles, awaiting the history-making order. Under her breath, Sallah murmured a good luck to Kenjo, Drake, and Nabol, who were piloting the *Yoko*'s three shuttles.

Klaxons announced the imminent departure, and immediately the main screen turned its eye to the landing site. The watch officers sat alert at their stations. Smaller screens showed the opened shuttle-bay doors from several angles, so that the bridge personnel could watch the shuttles begin to drift from their mother ship, dropping quickly on puffs of their jets before the main engines were ignited. They would spiral down across the planet, entering Pern's atmosphere on the western edge of the northern continent, and braking as they continued on down and around the globe until they reached their landing site on the eastern end of the southern continent. Exterior cameras picked up the other three shuttles, which took their positions in the flotilla. Gracefully, all six arrowed down and then out of sight over the curve of the planet.

Sallah's watch ended before the estimated time of arrival on Pern, but she made herself small against the side wall, along with everyone else from her watch, in order to have the best view possible. She knew that every screen on the ship was broadcasting the same information, and that the visual of the actual landing would flash simultaneously on all three colony vessels—but somehow it seemed more official to see it all from the bridge. So she stayed, reminding herself to breathe from time to time and shifting from one tired swollen leg to another. She would be relieved when the spin went down in order to facilitate the moving of cargo—but soon she would be planet-side, with no convenient spin to turn off to reduce the effects of gravity.

◆　◆　◆

"Got rid of your mates?" Stev Kimmer asked, stepping quickly into Avril's room after a quick glance over his shoulder. He closed the door behind him.

Avril turned to face him, arms extended; she flicked her fingers to indicate unoccupied space, and smiled in smug satisfaction. "Rank has privileges. I used mine. Lock it. Occasionally that oaf Lensdale tries to foist someone off on me, but I added three names below mine, and he may have given up."

Kimmer, due shortly at the loading bay to take his place in one of the *Yoko*'s shuttles, got straight to the point. "So where is this incontrovertible proof of yours?"

Still smiling, Avril opened a drawer and took out a dark wood box with no apparent seam. She handed it to him, and he shook his head.

"I told you I've no time for puzzles. If this is a ploy to get a man into your bed, Avril, your timing's way off."

She grimaced, annoyed by his phrasing as well as the fact that changed circumstances forced her to seek assistance from others. But her first plan had run aground on the reef of Paul Benden's sudden and totally unexpected indifference to her. Smiling away her distaste, she repositioned the box on her left palm, made a pass at the side facing her, then effortlessly lifted the top. As she had predicted, Stev Kimmer inhaled in surprise, the sparkle in his eyes fleetingly reflecting the rich glow of the ruby that sat nestled in the box. His hands made a movement toward it, and she tilted the box ever so slightly, causing the gem to twinkle wickedly in the light.

"Magnificent, isn't it?" Avril's voice was soft with affectionate possession as she turned her hand, letting him see the brilliance in the heart of the rose-cut gem. Abruptly, she took the jewel from its bed and handed it to him. "Feel it. Look at it through the light. Flawless."

"How did you get it?" He shot her an accusing glance, his features set with a combination of envy, greed, and admiration. The latter was all for the magnificent jewel as he held it up to the lighting strip and examined its perfection.

"Believe it or not, I inherited it." At his suspicious expression, she leaned gracefully against the small table, arms folded across her well-formed breasts, and grinned. "My grandmother at seven removes was a member of the EEC team that explored this mudball. Shavva bint Faroud, to give her her maiden name."

"Fardles!" Stev Kimmer was genuinely astounded.

"Furthermore," Avril went on, enjoying his reaction, "I have her original notes."

"How did your family manage to keep this all those years? Why, it's priceless."

Avril raised her lovely arched eyebrows. "Great-grandmother was no fool. That bauble was not the only thing she brought back from here, or the other planets she explored."

"But to bring this with you?" It was all Kimmer could do not to clench his fingers around the beautiful gem.

"I'm the last of my line."

"You mean, you can claim part of this planet as a direct descendant of the EEC team?" Stev was beginning to warm to such possibilities.

She shook her head angrily at his misconstruction. "The EEC takes bloody good care that doesn't happen. Shavva knew that. She also knew that sooner or later the planet would be opened for colonization. The ruby and her notes—" Avril paused dramatically. "—were handed down to me. And I—and her notes—are now in orbit around Pern."

Stev Kimmer regarded her for a long moment. Then she reached over and took the ruby from him, negligently tossing it in one hand while Kimmer nervously watched.

"Now, do you want in on my scheme?" she asked. "Like my beloved and far-seeing predecessor, I have no wish to remain at the end of the galaxy on a seventh-rate world."

Stev Kimmer narrowed his eyes and shrugged. "Have the others seen the ruby?"

"Not yet." She smiled slowly with sly malice. "If you'll help me, they may never need to."

By the time Stev Kimmer made a hurried departure to the loading dock, Avril was sure of his participation. She glanced at the chrono and was pleased to see that her timing was perfect. She smoothed her hair, dabbed on a bit more of the heavy musk scent she preferred, and burnished her nails for a few moments before she heard a discreet knock on the door.

Nabhi Nabol entered. "Are your roommates out?"

◆ ◆ ◆

Kenjo Fusaiyuko tensed at the first shudder as the shuttle hit atmosphere. The admiral, seated between Kenjo and Jiro Akamoto, the copilot, leaned forward eagerly, straining at his safety harness and smiling in anticipation. Kenjo permitted himself to smile, too. Then he carefully blanked his expression. Things were going far too well. There had been no problems with the countdown checklist. For all its fifteen years of inactivity, the shuttle *Eujisan* handled perfectly. They had achieved an excellent angle of entry and should make a perfect landing on a site that, according to probe report, was as level as a natural area could be.

Kenjo had always worried about possible contingencies, a habit that had made him one of the best transport pilots in Cygnus Sector Fleet in spite of the fact that the few emergencies he had faced had never been ones that he could have foreseen. He had survived because, in planning for foul-ups, he had been ready for anything.

But the Pern landing was different. No one, apart from the long-dead Exploration and Evaluation team, had set foot on Pern. And, in Kenjo's estimation, the EEC team had not spent enough time on the planet to have made a proper assessment.

Beside him, Jiro murmured reassuring readings from his instrumentation, and then both pilots felt the resistance as the shuttle dug deeper into the atmospheric layer. Kenjo tightened his fingers around the control yoke, setting his feet and his seat deep for steadiness. He wished the admiral would lean back—it was unnerving to have someone breathing down his neck at a time like this. How had the man managed to find so much slack in his safety harness?

The exterior of the shuttle was heating up, but the internal temperature remained steady. Kenjo shot a glance at the small screen. The passengers were riding well, too, and none of the cargo had shifted under its straps. His eyes flicked from one dial to the next, noting the performance and health of his vehicle. The vibration grew more violent, but that was to be expected. Had he not pierced the protective gases of a hundred worlds in just the same way, slipping like a penknife under the flap of an envelope, like a man into the body of his beloved?

They were on the nightside now, one moon casting a brilliant full light on the dark landmass. They were racing toward day over the immense sea of Pern. He checked the shuttle's altitude. They were right on target. The first landing on Pern simply could not be perfect. Something would have to go amiss, or his faith in probability would be shattered. Kenjo searched his control panel for any telltale red, of any blinking yellow malfunction light. Yet the shuttle continued its slanting plunge as the sweat of apprehension ran down Kenjo's spine, and moisture beaded his brow under his helmet.

Beside Kenjo, Jiro looked outwardly calm, but then he bit nervously at the corner of his lower lip. Seeing that, Kenjo turned his head away, careful not to let his expression betray the satisfaction he felt at the revelation that his copilot, too, was experiencing tension. Between them Admiral Benden's breath was becoming more rapid.

Would the old man expire in joy beside him? Kenjo felt a sudden stab of alarm. Yes, that could be it. The shuttle would land safely, but Admiral Benden would die on the point of arrival at his promised land. Yes, that would be the flaw in the trip. A human error, not a mechanical failure.

As Kenjo's mind played with the ramifications of that disaster, resistance on the skin of the shuttle decreased as it dropped below the speed of sound.

Skin heat was okay, the shuttle was responding smoothly to the helm, and they were at the correct altitude, dropping as programmed.

Remember, Kenjo, use as little fuel in retro as possible. The more fuel saved, the more trips can be made. And then—Kenjo cut off that line of thinking. There would still be the atmosphere planes to drive for many years to come. Power packs lasted for decades if carefully recharged. And if he could scrounge the right parts . . . His spirit would not be grounded for a long time yet.

He took quick altitude readings, checked his compass, trimmed the flaps, did a quick calculation on his speed, and squinted ahead toward the shoreline, which was coming up in plain sight ahead of him. His screens told him that the other shuttles were following at the prescribed safe intervals. The shuttle *Eujisan*, with Kenjo at the helm and both Admiral Benden and Governor Boll aboard, would be the first to touch down on Pern.

The shuttle was hurtling over the eastern ocean, its shadow preceding it on the water as it overpassed the lumps of islets and larger masses in the archipelago that extended northeastward from their landing site. As he spotted a perfect strato volcano rising above the water, Kenjo nearly lost his concentration: its resemblance to the famed Mount Fuji was incredible. Surely that volcano was a good sign.

Kenjo could see surf boiling at the base of the rocky promontory that signaled their approach to the chosen landing site.

"Retro-rockets, two-second blast," he said, pleased to hear his voice steady and calm, almost bored. Jiro acknowledged, and the shuttle tugged back slightly but evenly as the retros broke its forward speed. Kenjo lifted the nose, slightly bleeding airspeed. "Landing gear down."

Jiro nodded. As Kenjo watched, hand hovering over the retros in case the landing gear failed to emerge, the green lights came on unwinkingly, and then he felt the pull of air against the great wheels as they locked into position. The shuttle's speed was a shade too high for landing. The vast field was coming up under them, a field that undulated like the sea. Kenjo fought down the panic. He checked drag, windspeed, and, wincing at the necessity, fired the retros again briefly and pulled the nose up as he persuaded the shuttle to settle to the surface of Pern.

Once the big wheels touched, the shuttle bounced a bit over the uneven ground. Braking judiciously and making full use of his flaps, Kenjo swung the shuttle in a wide circle so that it faced the way it had just come and rolled to a complete stop.

Kenjo permitted himself a small smile of satisfaction, then returned his attention to the control panel to begin the landing checklist. Noting the fuel expended, he gave a grunt of pleasure at his economy. Liters under the allowance.

"Fine landing, Kenjo! Jiro! My compliments," the admiral exclaimed. Kenjo decided that he would forgive him that enthusiastic clout on the shoulder. Then suddenly he and Jiro were startled by unexpected sounds: the snapping of metal clasps, and the sudden noise of air rapidly evacuating.

Alarmed, Kenjo turned just in time to see the admiral and the governor disappearing down the cabin's escape hatch. Kenjo glanced frantically at his console, certain that the expedition's leaders must be reacting to an emergency of some sort, but only the red brake light was on. Smells of burning grass and oil and rocket fuel wafted up to the two pilots through the open hatch. Simultaneously they were aware of the shouts from the passenger cabin—shouts of joy, not cries of panic. A glance in the screens proved to Kenjo that their passengers were releasing their safety harnesses. A few had risen and were tentatively stretching legs and arms, talking excitedly in anticipation of stepping out on the surface of their new home. But why had the admiral and the governor left the shuttle so precipitously—and through the escape hatch instead of the main exit?

Jiro eyed him questioningly. All Kenjo could think to do was shrug. Then, as the cheering subsided into a silence punctuated by nervous whispers, Kenjo realized that, as pilot, it fell to him to take charge. He activated the cargo-hold release mechanism, then switched the sensors to exterior, setting the cameras to record the historic moment. Above all, he must pretend that everything was in order, despite the strange behavior of the admiral and the governor.

Kenjo unstrapped himself, motioning for Jiro to do the same. He stooped, briefly, to activate the hatch closure. Then he took the three steps to the panel between the two cabins and palmed it open.

Cheers greeted him and, modestly, he dropped his head and eyes. The cheers subsided expectantly as he reached the rear of the payload cabin and undogged the passenger hatch. With an unnecessary but satisfying force, he pushed open the door. As the aperture widened and the ramp extended, the fresh air of the new world poured in. He was not the only one to take a deep breath of the oxygen-rich, aromatic air. Kenjo was debating with himself the protocol of such an occasion, since the logical candidates had already evacuated the vehicle, but Jiro, beside him, began to point excitedly. Kenjo peered around the slowly opening hatch and blinked in astonishment.

There, visible not only to him but to the other five shuttles which had landed in due order behind him, were two brilliant banners. One was the gold and blue of the Federated Sentient Planets. The other was the brand-new standard for the planet Pern: blue, white, and yellow, with the design of sickle and plow in the upper left-hand corner, signifying the pastoral nature of the colony. Occasionally hidden by the flapping of the banners in the steady breeze over the meadow were the triumphant figures of Admiral Benden and Governor Boll. The pair of them were grinning like idiots, Kenjo saw, as they enthusiastically beckoned the passengers to emerge.

"Let us welcome you, my friends, to the planet Pern," the admiral cried in a stentorian voice.

"Welcome to Pern!" the governor shouted. "Welcome! Welcome!"

They looked at each other and then began the formal words in an obviously well rehearsed unison.

"By the power vested in us by the Federated Sentient Planets, we hereby claim this planet and name it Pern!"

CHAPTER

III

The engineers, the power-resource group, the jacks-of-all-trades, and every able-bodied man and woman who knew which end of a hammer to grip were set to work putting down the landing-strip grids. A second work force erected the prefabricated sections of the landing control and meteorology tower, in which Ongola and the other meteorologists would be based.

The tower was three stories high, two square sections supported by a wider and longer rectangular base. Initially the ground level would serve as headquarters for the admiral, the governor, and the informal council. When the proper administrative square had been built later on, the entire installation would be turned over to meteorology and communications.

The third and smallest group—all eight of Mar Dook's agronomists, plus a dozen able-bodieds, Pol Nietro from zoology, Phas Radamanth and A. C. Sopers of xenobiology, and Ted Tubberman and his crew—had the task of choosing the site for the experimental farm. Others were detailed to scout for varieties of vegetation that might be efficiently converted into various plastics which the colony would need for building. On the one minisled brought along, Emily Boll flew between the agronomy survey and the control tower, correlating data. Once the emergency infirmary was set up, medics were kept busy patching bruises and scrapes, and peremptorily ordering rest periods for the older workers who were overextending themselves in their enthusiasm.

By midday, those in orbit had a nonstop show of the disciplined but constant activities on the surface.

"It keeps people home," Sallah remarked to Barr Hamil, her copilot, as they traversed nearly empty corridors on their way back from the main hangar where they had been checking cargo manifests for their first trip down.

"It's fascinating, Sal. And *we'll* be there tomorrow!" Barr's eyes were shining, and she wore a silly grin. "I really can't believe we're here, and will be there!" She pointed downward. "It's like a dream. I keep being afraid I'll wake up suddenly."

They had reached their own quarters and both had eyes only for the vid screen in the corner.

"Good," Barr said with a relieved sigh. "They've got the donks assembled."

Sallah chuckled. "Our job is to get the shuttle down in one piece, Barr. Unloading is someone else's problem." But she, too, was relieved to see the sturdy load handlers lined up at the end of the almost completed landing strip. The donks would greatly facilitate unloading, and speed up the shuttles' return to their mother ships for the next run. Already there were informal competitions between the various units to bring their projects in faster and more efficiently than programmed time allowed.

Sallah and Barr watched, as everyone did, until the dark tropical moonless night rendered the broadcasts impossible to interpret. Broadcasts from the surface would be primitive until Drake Bonneau and Xi Chi Yuen, in the admiral's gig, had a chance to install the commsats on the two moons. Nonetheless, the last scene raised a nostalgic lump in Sallah's throat, reminding her of the hunting trips that she and her parents had enjoyed in the hills around First on Centauri.

The screen showed tired men and women seated around an immense campfire, eating an evening meal that had been prepared in a huge kettle from freeze-dried Terran vegetables and meats. In the failing light, the white strips of the runway grids and the wind sock having convulsions in the brisk breeze, were just barely visible. The planetary flag, so proudly displayed that morning, had wrapped itself around the pole above the control tower. Someone began to play softly on a harmonica, an old, old tune so familiar that Sallah couldn't name it. Someone else joined in with a recorder. Softly and hesitantly at first, then with more confidence, the tired colonists began to sing or hum along. Other voices added harmony, and Sallah remembered that the song was called "Home on the Range." There certainly had been no "discouraging words" that day. And the evening serenade did make the landing site seem a bit more like a home.

The next morning Sallah and Barr had been up long before the klaxon sounded, assembling their passengers and making last-minute weight calculations. The pilots had been given a very serious briefing from Lieutenant Commander Ongola on the necessity of conserving fuel.

"We have just enough liquid fuel to get every man, woman, and child, beast, parcel, package, and reusable section of the ships down to the surface. Waste not, want not. Fools waste fuel! We have none to waste. Nor," he added, with his sad wistful smile, "fools among us."

Watching on the loading-bay screens, Sallah and Barr could follow the six shuttles lifting from the planet's surface. Then the scene shifted to a panoramic view of the main landing site.

"It's breathtaking, Sal, breathtaking," Barr said. "I've never seen so much unoccupied, unused land at one time in my life."

"Get used to it," Sallah replied with a grin.

With the activities of the landing party to watch, it seemed like no time at all before the shuttles were locking on. The loading detail were trundling the first crates into the hold before Kenjo and Jiro could exit. Sallah was a little annoyed with Kenjo for his brusque dismissal of Barr's excited questions. Even Jiro looked abashed by his senior's truculence as Kenjo succinctly briefed Sallah on landing procedures, advice on handling the shuttle's idiosyncrasies, and the frequency for the tower meteorological control. He wished her a safe drop, saluted, and, turning on his heel, left the bay.

"Well, hail and farewell," Barr said, recovering from the snub.

"Let's do the preflight even if Fussy Fusi has made such a big deal of turnover," Sallah said, sliding into the lock of the *Eujisan* an inch ahead of the next big crate being loaded. They had finished their check by the time loading was complete. Barr did passenger inspection, making very certain that General Cherry Duff, the oldest charterer and the pro tem colony magistrate, was comfortable, and then they were cleared for the drop.

◆ ◆ ◆

"We were barely there," Barr complained as Sallah taxied the *Eujisan* into takeoff position at the end of the runway eight hours later. "And now we're away again."

"Efficiency is our guide. Waste not, want not," Sallah told her, eyes on the instrumentation as she opened the throttle on the *Eujisan* for lift-off thrust. She grimaced, eyes flicking between fuel gauge and rev counter, not wanting to use a cc more of fuel than necessary. "Kenjo and the next eager set of colonists will be chewing hunks out of the cargo hatch. We must up, up, and away!"

"Kenjo never made an error in his life?" Barr asked of Sallah sometime later after the famous pilot had made a disparaging remark about the shuttle's consumption of fuel during the trips made by the two women.

"That's why he's alive today," Sallah replied. But his comment rankled. Though she knew that she had expended no more fuel than was absolutely necessary, she began keeping a private record of consumption on each of her trips. She noticed that Kenjo generally oversaw the *Eujisan*'s refueling and supervised its fifty-hour checks. She knew that she was a better than average pilot, in space or atmospheric craft, but she did not want to make waves with a hero pilot who had far more experience than she did—not unless she absolutely had to, and not without the ammunition of accurate records.

Patterns were quickly established. Those on the ground began each morning by erecting the housing and work areas for those due to arrive during the day. The agronomy teams handily cleared the designated fields. The infirmary had already dealt with its first clients; fortunately, all the accidents so far had been minor. And despite all the hard work, senses of humor prevailed. Some wit had put up street signs with estimated distances in light-years for Earth, First Centauri, and the homeworlds of the other members of the Federated Sentient Planets.

◆ ◆ ◆

Like everyone else waiting to drop, Sorka Hanrahan spent a lot of time watching the progress of the settlement, which had been informally dubbed "Landing." To Sorka, watching was only a way to pass the time. She was not really interested, especially after her mother kept remarking that they were seeing history made. History was something one read about in books. Sorka had always been an active child, so the enforced idleness and the constriction of shipboard life quickly became frustrating. It was small comfort to know how important her father's profession of veterinary surgeon was going to be on Pern when all the kids she had met in the mess halls and corridors were getting down to Pern faster than she and her brother were.

Brian, however, was in no hurry. He had made friends with the Jepson twins, two aisles away. They had an older brother Sorka's age, but she did not like him. Her mother kept telling her that there would be girls her age on Pern whom she would meet once she got to school.

"I need a friend now," Sorka murmured to herself as she wandered through the corridors of the ship. Such freedom was a rare privilege for a girl who had always had to be on guard against strangers. Even home on the farm in Clonmel, she had not been allowed out of sight of an adult, even with old Chip's protective canine presence. On the *Yokohama*, not only did she not have to watch out, but the whole ship was open to her, provided she kept out of engineering or bridge territory and didn't interfere with crew. But at that moment she did not feel like exploring; she wanted comfort. So she headed for her favorite place, the garden.

On her first long excursion, she had discovered the section of the ship where great broad-leafed plants arched over the ceiling, their branches intertwining to make green caves below. She loved the marvelous aroma of moist earth and green things, and felt no inhibition about taking deep lungfuls of air that left a clean, fresh taste at the back of her mouth. Beneath the giant bushes were all sorts of herbs and smaller plants with tags on them, soon to be transported to the new world. She did not recognize most of the names, but she knew some of the herbs by their common names. Back at home her mother had kept an herb garden. Sorka knew which ones would leave their fragrances on her fingers and she daringly fingered the marjoram, then the tiny thyme leaves. Her eyes drank in the blues and pale yellows and pinks of the flowers that were in bloom, and she gazed curiously at the hundreds of racks of shoots in little tubes of water—nutrient fluids, her dad had told her—sprouted only a few months back, to be ready for planting once they reached Pern.

She had just bent to gently feel the surface of an unfamiliar hairy sort of silver-green leaf—she thought it had a nice smell—when she saw a pair of very blue eyes that no plant had ever sprouted. She swallowed, reminding herself that there were no strangers on the ship; she was safe. The eyes could belong only to another passenger who, like herself, was investigating the peaceful garden.

"Hello," she said in a tone between surprise and cordiality.

The blue eyes blinked. "Go 'way. You don't belong here," a young male voice growled at her.

"Why not? This is open to anyone, so long as you don't damage the plants. And you really shouldn't be crouched down in there like that."

"Go 'way." A grubby hand emphasized the order.

"I don't have to. Who're you?"

Her eyes, adjusted to the shadows, clearly read the boy's resentful expression. She hunkered down, looking in at him. "What's your name?" she asked.

"I doan gotta tell nobody my name." He spoke with a familiar accent.

"Well, excuse me, I'm sure," she said in an affected tone. Then she realized that she recognized his accent. "Hey, you're Irish. Like me."

"I'm *not* like you."

"Well, deny you're Irish." When he didn't—because he couldn't, and they both knew it—she cocked her head at him, smiling agreeably. "I can see why you'd hide in here. It's quiet and it smells so fresh. Almost like home. I don't like the ship either; I feel—" Sorka hugged herself. "—sort of cramped and squashed all the time." She lengthened the words to make them express her feelings. "I come from Clonmel. Ever been there?"

"Sure." The boy's tone was scornful, but he brushed a strand of long orange hair from his eyes and shifted his position so that he could keep his eyes on her.

"I'm Sorka Hanrahan." She looked inquiringly at him.

"Sean Connell," he admitted truculently after considerable delay.

"My dad's a vet. The best in Clonmel."

Sean's expression cleared with approval. "He works with horses?"

She nodded. "With any sick animal. Did you have horses?"

"While we was still in Ballinasloe." His expression clouded with resentful grief. "We had good horses," he added with defensive pride.

"Did you have your own pony?"

The boy's eyes blinked, and he dropped his head.

"I miss my pony, too," Sorka said compassionately. "But I'm to get one on Pern, and my dad said that they'd put special ones in the banks for you." She wasn't at all sure of that, but it seemed the proper thing to say.

"We'd better. We was promised. We can't get anywhere 'thout horses 'cause this place isn't to have hovervans er nothing."

"And no more gardai." Sorka grinned mischievously at him. She had just figured out that he must be one of the traveling folk. Her father had mentioned that there were some among the colonists. "And no more farmers chasing you out of their fields, and no more move-on-in-twenty-four-hours, or lousy halts, and no roads but the ones you make yourself, and—oh, just lots of things you really want, and none of the bad things."

"Can't be all that good," Sean remarked cynically.

Suddenly the comm unit in the garden erupted into sound. "The boarding call has been issued for the morning drop. Passengers will assemble immediately in the loading bay on Deck Five."

Like a turtle, Sean drew back into the shadows.

"Hey, does he mean you?" Sorka tried to make out Sean's face in the darkness. She thought she saw a faint nod. "Boy, are you lucky, going so soon. Third day! What's the matter? Don't you *want* to go?" She got down on her hands and knees to peer in at him. Then slowly she drew back. She had seen real fear often enough to recognize it in Sean. "Gee, I'd trade places with you. I can't wait to get down. I mean, it's not that long a trip. And it'll be no different from getting to the *Yoko* from Earth," she went on, thinking to reassure him. "That wasn't so bad, was it?" She had been so excited, even knowing that she would be put in deep sleep almost as soon as they got on board, that she had been unaware of anything but the first pressure of take-off.

"We was shipped up asleep." His words were no more than a terrified mutter.

"Gee, you missed the best part. Of course, half the adults," she added condescendingly, "were weeping about their last view of old Terra. I pretended that I was Spacer Yvonne Yves, and my brother, Brian, he's much younger than we are, but he made like he was Spacer Tracey Train."

"Who're they?"

"C'mon, Sean. I know you all had vidscreens in your caravans. Didn't you ever see *Space Venturers*?"

He was openly scornful. "That's kid stuff."

"Well, you're a Space Venturer right now, and if it's only kid stuff, there's nothing to be afraid of, is there?"

"Who said I was afraid?"

"Well, aren't you? Hiding away in the garden."

"I just needed a decent breath of fresh air." Suddenly he pushed himself out.

"When you've a planet full of fresh air below you, only hours away?" Sorka grinned at him. "Just pretend you're a space hero."

The comm unit came alive, and she could hear the edge to the embarkation officer's voice. Desi Arthied had not had to remind any other load of passengers to assemble. "The shuttles drop in precisely twenty minutes. Passengers scheduled for this drop who default go to the end of the list."

"He's angry," Sorka told Sean. She gave him a little push toward the door. "You'd better git. Your parents'll skin you alive if you keep them from making their drop."

"That's all you know," he said savagely. He stomped out of the garden room.

"Scaredy-cat," she said softly, then sighed exaggeratedly. "Well, he can't help it."

Then she turned back to examine the fragrant plant.

◆　◆　◆

By the sixth day all essential personnel were on the surface. Seating was removed from all but one of the shuttles and set about the bonfire square until needed again. Mountains of supplies were dropped, distributed, and stored. Delicate instruments packed in shockproof cocoons followed, along with sperm and the precious fertilized ova from Earth and First—Sallah was certain that Barr did not take a deep breath throughout those drops. Immediately fertilized eggs were implanted in those cows, goats, and sheep that had fully recovered from their deep sleep. Small sturdy types had been brought, not themselves the best genotypes available on Earth but suitable as surrogate dams; the embryos were different again, specially adapted for hardiness and resistance. The resultant progeny would, it was hoped, be able to digest Pern-grown fodder, which would have much more boron in it than the usual Terran produce, and a good variety of native weeds. If there were problems, Kitti Ping and her granddaughter, Wind Blossom, would use the Eridani techniques to alter the next generation appropriately. The plan was for at least some of the animals to be tailored to make the required enzymes in their own glands, instead of using symbiotic bacteria as their ancestors had on Earth.

Admiral Benden proudly remarked that by the time the ships were completely evacuated, the first chicken eggs were likely to hatch on Pern. He went on to announce that there was evidence that the planet harbored its own egg-layers, too, for broken shells had been found above the high-tide line on the beach where the harbor and the fish hatchery were being constructed. Zoologists were trying to figure out what sort of creature had laid the chickenlike eggs; they hoped it was the rather beautiful and unusual avaians mentioned by the EEC team, but so far, the reptiloid creatures mentioned in the survey report had not been observed. As the analysis of the shells showed a high level of boron, the team put egg and its inhabitant on the dubious list of indigenous inedibles.

The shuttles made only two trips a day for the next four, since the loading and unloading of all that matériel was time-consuming.

"I prefer a few passengers," Barr remarked as the off-duty pilots were enjoying dinner in the mess hall, "as a leaven to crates and crates, big, little, medium. Or all those absolutely irreplaceable herbs and bushes. There's still plenty of people to go down." The mess hall, not nearly so crowded anymore, was still full of diners.

Looking about, Sallah noticed the redheaded family seated at the far left. She waved, smiling brightly because the youngsters looked so glum.

"Gorgeous red hair, isn't it?" Sallah said wistfully.

"Too unusual," Avril Bitra said derisively.

"I dunno," Drake remarked, staring at the party. "Makes a nice change."

"She's too young for you, Bonneau," Avril said.

"I'm a patient man," Drake countered, grinning because it was not often that he got a rise out of the sultry beauty. "I'll know where to find her when she grows up." He appeared to consider the prospect. "Of course, the boy is much too young for you, Avril. A full generation away."

Avril gave him a long, disgusted look and, grabbing the wine carafe, stalked to the dispensers. Sallah exchanged glances with Barr. Avril was scheduled first the next morning, and the wind factors provided sufficient danger even without alcohol-blurred reactions. They both looked toward Nabol, her copilot, but he shrugged indifferently. Sallah hadn't hoped for much support from the man. No one had much influence on Avril.

"Hey, Avril, hold off on the sauce," Drake began, rising to intercept her. "You did promise me a rematch in gravity ball. The court'll be empty now." His smile was challenging, and from where she sat, Sallah could see his hand slide caressingly up Avril's arm. The astrogator's mouth assumed a less discontented line. "We'd best use it while we may," he added, his smile deepening. Moving his arm up to her shoulders, he took the carafe from her hand and placed it on the nearest table as he guided her out of the mess hall without a backward look.

"Wow! Charm has its uses," Barr said.

"Shall we see if it's ball they're playing in the grav court?" Nabol suggested, an unsettling glitter in his eyes.

"There's ball games and ball games," Sallah said with a diffident shrug. "I've seen 'em all. Excuse me." She stood up and strode over to the Hanrahans' table. She knew she had left her friend stranded, but Barr could leave, too, if Nabol made her uncomfortable. "Hi, there. When do you drop?" she asked, as she reached the Hanrahans.

"Tomorrow," Red said with a welcoming grin. He pulled a chair over from the next table. "Join us? I think we're on your ship."

"We are." Sorka beamed at Sallah.

"You've had a long wait," Sallah remarked, sitting down.

"I'm vet, and Mairi's childcare," Red replied. "We aren't exactly essential personnel."

"Perhaps not now," Sallah replied with a wide grin that acknowledged the future importance of their specialties.

"Is it really as nice down there as it looks?" Sorka asked.

"I can't say I've had much time to find out," Sallah said with a rueful expression. "We drop, unload, and lift. But the air is like wine." She flared her nostrils in deprecation of the recycled atmosphere of the ship. "And a breeze, too." She laughed. "Sometimes a bit stiff." She pantomimed fighting with the control yoke of the shuttle. Mairi looked wistful, while her husband looked eager. Sallah turned to the kids. "And school's great. Outdoors! Teaching you all we know about our new home." The two children had groaned at her first phrase, but began to brighten as she went on. "Sometimes the teachers are just a skip ahead of the students."

"They didn't have bonfires last night," Brian said, disappointed.

"That's because they got light pylons up, but watch tonight. You aren't the only one who missed 'em. I heard they decided to have a bonfire square, and every night someone new gets a chance to light it, if they've worked very hard and earned the privilege."

"Wow!" Brian was elated. "Whaddya have to do to get to light it?"

"You'll think of something, Brian," his father assured him.

"See you all bright and early?" Sallah rose, giving Sorka's hair a ruffle.

"Be there before you," Red replied with a grin.

To Sallah's surprise, they were, for Mairi had insisted on reassuring herself that their precious personal baggage was safely stowed in the cargo hold. Mairi had worried and worried about her precious family heirlooms, especially the rosewood dower chest which had been in her family for generations. It had been carefully unglued and took up most of the weight allowed them, but Mairi had insisted that it accompany them to Pern. Indeed Sorka could not recall her parents' bedroom without the dower chest under the window. Sorka had been forced to reduce her treasured collection of toy horses to three of the smallest, and her book tapes to ten. Brian's ship models had been dismantled, and he, too, fretted about finding the proper glue.

That was his urgent question when Sallah and Barr greeted them.

"Glue?" Sallah repeated in surprise. "They've dropped everything else; why on earth would they leave glue out?" She winked at Red, who grinned. "Otherwise our local experts are sure to be able to whomp something up. Pern seems to be well supplied. On board with you now, Clan Hanrahan. We're only a skip ahead of today's horde."

As the first arrivals, the Hanrahans got their choice of seats, and Sorka suggested that they take the last row so they would be the first out. It was almost agonizing to have to wait until everyone else was strapped in and the drop begun. Excitement almost strangled Sorka. She was disappointed that the forward screen was malfunctioning, because then she did not know exactly when the shuttle left its bay. And a display would have given her something to distract her from the shuttle's vibrations. She looked anxiously at her parents, but they had their eyes closed. Brian looked as bug-eyed as she felt, but she would not give him the satisfaction of appearing scared. Then, suddenly, she remembered Sean Connell, hiding in the garden, and forced herself to imagine Spacer Yvonne Yves leading an exciting mission to a mysterious planet.

And then they were there. The retros pushed her back into her padded seat, nearly depriving her of breath, and the shuttle bumped lightly as its landing gear made contact.

"We've landed! We made it!" she cried.

"Don't sound so surprised, lovey!" her father said with a laugh, and reached over to give her knee a pat.

"Can we eat when we get out?" Brian asked petulantly. Someone up front chuckled.

Sorka heard the *whoosh* as the passenger hatch was cracked. Then the two pilots appeared at the top of the aisle and gave the order to disembark. A blast of sunlight and fresh air streamed into the spacecraft, and Sorka felt her heart give an extra thump of gladness.

Laughing, her father flipped open her safety belt and urged her to move. But a moment of nervousness held her back.

"Go on, you little goose," Red said, grinning to let her know that he understood her hesitation.

"Hey, Sorka, you can leave now," Sallah called.

Sorka's legs were a bit wobbly as she stood. "I'm heavy again," she exclaimed. Full weight was a new sensation after the half gravity of the *Yoko*. At the exit, she stopped, awed by her first glimpse of Pern, a vast panorama of the grassy plateau, with its knobs of funny bluish bushes and the green-blue sky.

"Don't block the exit, dear," said a woman who was standing outside by the ramp.

Sorka hastily obeyed, though how she got down the ramp with so much looking around to do, she never knew. The ground cover was subtly different from grass on the farm. The bushes were more blue than green, and had funny-shaped leaves, like the put-together geometric shapes of a toy she had played with as a toddler.

"Look, Daddy, clouds! Just like home!" she cried, excitedly pointing to the sky.

Her father laughed and, with an arm about her shoulders, moved her forward with him.

"Maybe they followed us, Sorka," he said kindly, smiling broadly. Sorka knew that he was just as excited as she was to be landing on Pern at last.

Sorka threw her head back to the fresh breeze which rippled across the plateau. It smelled of marvelous things, new and exciting. She wanted to dance, free once more under a sky, without ceiling or walls to constrict her.

"Are you Hanrahan or Jepson?" the woman asked, a recorder in her hand.

"Hanrahan," Red replied. "Mairi, Peter, Sorka, and Brian."

"Welcome to Pern," she said, smiling graciously before she made a tick on her sheet. "You're House Fourteen on Asian Square. Here's your map. All the important facilities are clearly marked. Now, if you'll just lend a hand to unload and clear the shuttle . . ." She handed him a sheet, gestured toward the float that was backing up to the open cargo hatch, then moved on to the Jepsons, who had just emerged.

"We made it, Mairi love," Red said, embracing his wife. Sorka was surprised to see tears in her parents' eyes.

There was more to be unloaded than just the personal luggage of the passengers. Cartons of stores still had to be checked off the supercargo's lists.

"Tell the dispatcher that more furnishings are required," Sallah was told once the shuttle's hold had been emptied. "Or some people won't have beds tonight."

"That's efficiency for you," Sallah remarked to Barr. She waved to the Hanrahans as she closed the hatch to prepare for the return flight. "Soon there won't be anyone above and precious little left of the ships but the hulls."

"I know," Barr replied. "I half expect to find our bunks already gone."

The two began their take-off check and Sallah grinned as she made her notations. She had the glide down to perfection, which meant that she was saving nearly twenty liters every journey. The wind was veering to stern, and she warned Barr to speed up her checklist.

"Want to take advantage of that tail wind. Saves fuel."

"Good God, Sal, you're as bad as Fussy Fusi." But Barr completed her list with a flourish. "What I want to know is why are we busting ass saving fuel? We can't go anyplace useful with what we'd be saving. And once the ships are gutted, there isn't any use for space shuttles, now is there?"

Sallah gave her a searching stare and then chuckled drolly. "A very good point, my friend. A very good point. I think," she added after a moment's thought, "I'll check the tanks while Fussy's dropping."

But when she had done that, she was not that much wiser. If they were saving so much fuel, then the level in the tanks should have been higher. Barr, who was enjoying a flirtation with one of the resource engineers, forgot her idle observation. But Sallah did not. During one of Kenjo's drops, she did a bit of checking in the mainframe's banks.

Fuel consumption was at acceptable levels in both of *Yoko*'s remaining tanks. Sallah computed in her average fuel consumption per trip, plus an estimate of Kenjo's, and came up with a total that should have left them with an extra two thousand liters of available fuel. She knocked off a percentage, based on consumption during her heavier trips, when drift and wind factors had required a higher expenditure of fuel. Once again she came up with a deficit figure, slightly lower than before but still higher than the amount available.

What good would it do anyone to hoard fuel? Avril? But Avril and Kenjo were not at all friendly. In fact, Avril had made snide remarks about Kenjo on several occasions, unacceptable ethnic-based slander.

"Of course, if you wanted to put someone off the track . . ." Sallah murmured to herself.

Checking the distance to the nearest system, which had been interdicted a century before by the EEC team, and the distance to the nearest habitable system, and computing in the cruising range and speed of the captain's gig, Sallah came up with the answer that the *Mariposa* could, even with the most careful management, make it only to the uninhabitable system. But what good would that do anyone? Disgusted by the waste of the afternoon, Sallah went in search of Barr. They had the evening run to make, and that meant that they would get to sleep planetside.

To Sorka's utter delight, school on Pern concentrated on adapting the students to their new home. Everyone was given safety instruction about common tools, and those over fourteen were taught how to operate some of the less dangerous equipment. They were shown specimens of the plants to be avoided and lectured on the botany so far catalogued: the varieties of fruit, leafy vegetables, and tubers that were innocuous and could be eaten in moderation. One of the jobs for the young colonists, they were told, would be to gather any edible plants they found to supplement the transported foodstuffs. They were also shown slides of native insectoids and herpetoids. Finally those under twelve gathered in the main classroom, while the older ones assembled outside to be assigned work with adult team leaders.

"During this settling-in period," Rudi Shwartz, the official headmaster, told the older children, "you will have a chance to work with a variety of specialists, learning what craft or profession you'd like to pursue within the context of the work force on Pern. We're going to revive an apprentice system here. It worked pretty well on old Earth, has been successful on First Centauri, and is particularly suitable to our pastoral colony. All of us will have to work hard to establish ourselves on Pern, but diligence will be rewarded."

"What with?" asked a boy at the back of the class. He sounded slightly contemptuous.

"A sense of achievement and," Mr. Shwartz added, raising his voice and grinning at the skeptic, "grants of land or material when you reach your maturity and want to strike out for yourself. All of us have the same opportunities here on Pern."

"My dad says the charterers will still end up with all the good land," a young male voice said from the anonymity of the group.

Surveying the children through slightly narrowed eyes, Rudolph Shwartz waited to answer until his audience began to move restlessly.

"The charter permits them first choice, it is true. This is a large planet with millions of acres of arable land. Even charterers have to prove the land they claim. There will be some left for your father, and for you. Now . . . how many of you already know how to manage the basic sled controls?"

Sorka had been sizing up her fellow students, and reluctantly concluded that there were no girls her age. The clutch of teenaged girls had already formed a group excluding her, and the other girls were all much younger than she was. Resigned, Sorka then looked in vain for Sean Connell. Wasn't it just like a tinker to skip school as soon as possible?

That initial morning session was concluded with instructions on how to apply to the commissary for their needs, from the carefully rationed candy and treats of Earth, to field boots or fresh clothing. Everyone, their headmaster insisted, had the right to certain luxury items. If an item was available, it would be issued. After a short lecture on moderation, the students were dismissed to enjoy a lunch served from the communal kitchens set up near Bonfire Square and told to report back to the school at 1300 hours for their afternoon duties.

After nearly two weeks of inactivity on the ship, Sorka welcomed the fetch-and-carry tasks. She was almost alone in her preference. The older girls in particular were appalled to be put to rough labor. Farmbred Sorka felt rather superior to those city lilies, and worked so diligently in helping to clear stones from the fields that her agronomist team leader cautioned her to take it easy.

"Not that we don't appreciate your vigor, Sorka," the woman said with a wry grin, "but don't forget you were inactive for fifteen years. Work those muscles in gently."

"Well, at least I've got some," Sorka replied with a scornful glance at a team of girls who scowled sullenly as they held plastic poles in place for fencing.

"They'll get used to Pern. They're here to stay." The team leader gave a sort of snort. "We all are."

Sorka sighed with such contentment that the older woman reached out to ruffle her hair. "Ever consider a career as an agronomist?"

"Naw, I'm going to be a vet like my dad," Sorka replied cheerfully.

The agronomist team leader was the first of many adults who would have liked to have Sorka Hanrahan as an apprentice. She was only a few days on the rock-picking detail before she and five others were sent down to the harbor and the hatchery.

"You've proved you can work without supervision, Sorka," Headmaster Shwartz told her approvingly. "Just the attitude we need to get Pern going."

After a morning learning to recognize those marine specimens that had already been catalogued, she and the other five youngsters were split into two groups and sent in opposite directions along the immense sweep of the natural harbor to gather any unidentified types of seaweeds and grasses, or anything new that might have been trapped in tidal pools after the previous night's storm. Delighted, Sorka went off happily with Jacob Chernoff, who, as the oldest, was appointed leader and given a beeper for emergencies.

"This sand ought to be different, not just the same," the third member of the group complained as they set off.

"Chung, oceans grind stones on Pern the same way they do it on Earth and the result just has to be the same: sand," Jacob said amiably. "Where were you from?"

"Kansas," Chung replied. "Betcha don't know where that is." His mocking glance fell on Sorka.

"Bounded by the old states of Missouri on the east, Oklahoma on the south, Colorado in the west, and Nebraska on the north," Sorka replied with studied diffidence. "And you don't have sand out there. You got dirt!"

"Say, you know your geography," Jacob said to Sorka with a smile of admiration. "Where are you from?"

"Colorado?" Chung demanded sarcastically.

"Ireland."

"Oh, one of those European islands," Chung said dismissively.

Sorka pointed to a large purplish branch of weed just ahead of them. "Hey, do they have this one yet?"

"Don't touch," Jacob warned as they reached it. With tongs, he lifted the weed for a closer examination. It had thick leaves that branched irregularly from a central stem.

"Looks like it grew from the sea bottom," Sorka remarked, pointing to a clump of tendrils at the base that looked like roots.

"They didn't show us anything that big," Chung said. So they wrapped it in a specimen bag to bring back for study.

That was almost their only find that afternoon, though they sifted through many piles of already identified sea vegetation. Then they rounded an outcropping of the rough gray stone that punctuated the long crescent beach, and came upon a sizable pool in which were trapped a variety of marine life, things that scurried on multiple legs, a couple of purple bladderlike objects that Sorka was certain would be poisonous, and some finger-long transparent creatures that seemed almost like fish.

"How can they be almost fish?" Chung demanded when Sorka voiced her opinion. "They're in the water, aren't they? That makes them fish."

"Not necessarily," Jacob replied. "And they don't really look like fish. They look like . . . well, I don't know what they look like," he admitted. The life-form seemed to have layers of fins along its side, some of which were in constant motion. "Hairy, they look."

"All I know is we didn't see anything like 'em in the tanks at the hatchery," Chung said. Taking out a specimen bottle, he lowered himself to the edge of the pool to catch one.

Though Jacob was able to get one of the bladders into a jar, and three samples of the many-legged species almost leaped into captivity, the finger fish eluded both boys.

When Sorka's suggestions for capture were dismissed, she wandered farther down the beach. Around a second pile of boulders, she found a massive outcropping that resembled a man's heavy-featured head, complete with brow ridges, nose, lips, and chin, though part of the chin was buried in the sand and lashed by the waves. Delighted and awed, Sorka stood in rapt admiration. It was wonderful, and *she* had found it. One of the girls in her own Asian Square had fallen down a hole that turned out to be one of the many entrances to a series of caves to the south and west of Landing. They had been officially named the Catherine Caves after their inadvertent discoverer.

Sorka's Head? She murmured the title under her breath. No, people might think it was her head, and she didn't look like that at all. As she pondered the question she glanced above the splendidly imposing cliff. It was then that she saw the creature, seemingly suspended in the air. She gasped in wonder, for in that moment the sun caught and dazzled the creature into a golden statue. Abruptly it dove and swooped out of sight, behind the pate of the stone head.

No one had shown her anything that resembled that marvelous creature, and Sorka was filled with excitement. She would have something stupendous to report when she got back to the hatchery. She ran toward the vast head, which was beginning to lose its illusory resemblance. That no longer mattered to Sorka. She had discovered something far more important: a creature of Pern.

She had to scramble up a series of boulders to reach the summit. She paused just before she reached the top and peered over, hoping to catch a closer glimpse of the winged life-form. But she stood up in disappointment. There was nothing visible but naked rock, pitted here and there by faults and holes. She drew back hastily when the surf, beating against the cliff face, became a fountaining plume through one of the holes, showering her with cold seawater.

Disconsolate, she completed her climb onto the pate, keeping well away from the spume holes. The height gave her a splendid view of the crescent harbor. She could see Jacob and Chung sprawled by the tidal pool and even distinguish some activity at the hatchery and the first of the fishing ships riding at anchor. She looked to the west and saw a magnificent vista of small beaches bounded by more outcroppings of the same type of rock she stood on. Ahead of her was nothing but ocean, though she knew that the northern continent was somewhere over the curve of the planet.

She turned about, looking at the thick vegetation growing up to the edge of the cliff. She was thirsty suddenly. Seeing what she thought was a red fruit tree, she decided to pick one. She could cut a few to bring to the boys, too. They were probably ready for a break.

Two things happened at once: she nearly stepped into a large hollow that was occupied by a number of pale, mottled eggs, and something dove at her, its claws just missing her head.

Sorka dropped to the stone surface, peering anxiously about to see what had attacked her. It zoomed in on her again, talons extended, and she waited, as she had done once with an angry bull, to roll away at the last moment. A wave of anger and outrage swept over her, so intense that Sorka inadvertently called out.

Confused by the unexpected emotions but fully aware of her immediate danger, Sorka scrambled to her feet and ran, half-crouched, to the cliff edge. Screams of rage and frustration split the air and lent speed to Sorka's descent. She heard a *whoosh* of air and ducked instinctively to evade another attack, then edged under a rocky overhang. Flattening herself against the rock face, she had an all too vivid look at her assailant, something dominated by eyes that rippled with red and orange fire. The creature's body was gold; its almost translucent wings were a paler shade against the green-blue sky, their dark frames clearly outlined.

The creature screamed in confusion and surprise, and soared up, out of sight. Sorka wondered if it could not see her in the shadow under the ledge. She heard it calling again, the sound muted by, she hoped, distance and the noise of the waves.

Abruptly a wave broke over the rocks about her, soaking her thoroughly. Anxiously she realized that the slight Pernese tide was bringing waves higher on the shoreline, and she would be well advised to move. Soon.

Cautiously she looked about her, listening, but the creature's cries were still distant. A second wave added a certain urgency, and Sorka began to edge down and toward the bluff. Her feet slipped on the wet rocks, and the last meter was an uncontrollable fall. Arms thrashing for balance, she landed on the beach. Still young enough to cry when she was hurt, Sorka let out an anguished wail, as hands, chin, and knees were scraped in the bruising fall.

From overhead came such a replica of her sounds that she forgot her pain and stared above her to where the flying creature hovered.

"Are you making fun of me?" Sorka suddenly felt as irritated as if one of her peer group had taunted her. "Well, are you?" she demanded of the golden creature. Abruptly it disappeared.

"Wow!" Sorka blinked, then scanned the sky for the creature, amazed by the speed with which it had disappeared from sight. "Wow! Faster than light."

Rising slowly to her feet, Sorka turned a complete circle, certain that the flyer had to be visible somewhere. Then another wave crashed at her feet, and she hastily stepped back, though she was thoroughly soaked already. But her hands and knees were stinging from the salty water, and she had a long walk back to the hatchery ahead of her with really nothing to show for her scrapes. She had subconsciously decided not to mention the flyer to anyone yet.

She jumped in surpise when the bushes on the bluff above her parted and a blond head poked through.

"You fecking gobshite, you iggerant townie. You skeered her away!"

Sean Connell came slithering down the slope, his skin no longer white but red with sunburn, his blue eyes flashing. "I've been lying doggo since dawn, hoping she'd walk into my snare, and you, you blow it all on me. Fecking useless you are!"

"You'd snare her? That lovely creature? And keep her from her eggs?" Appalled, Sorka flung herself on Sean, her hands automatically flattening, her fingers tight as she sliced at the boy in hard blows. "Don't you dare! Don't you dare harm her!"

Sean ducked and managed to evade the full force of her blows.

"Not to harm! To tame!" he yelled, dodging with his hands up to deflect her jabs. "We don't kill nuthing. I want her. For me!"

In an unexpected lunge, Sean tackled Sorka, sending her sprawling onto the sand where he fell on top of her. His longer and slightly heavier frame effectively pinned her. Recovering her breath, she squirmed, trying to angle her legs to kick at him.

"Don't be so stupid, girl. I wouldn't harm her. I've been watching her for two days. An' I haven't told a soul about her."

Finally understanding what he was saying, Sorka lay quiescent, eyeing him suspiciously. "You mean that?"

"Yup."

"It'd still be wrong." Sorka heaved against him experimentally, but he pressed her harder into the sand. Stones were bruising her back. "Taking her from her eggs."

"I was gonna keep watch on 'em."

"But you don't know if her hatchlings need her or not. You can't take her."

Sean regarded Sorka with equally angry suspicion. "An' what were *you* going to do? There's a reward for such as her. An' we need the money a lot more than you do."

"There isn't any money on Pern! Who needs it?" Sorka regarded him with surprise and then sympathy for the dismay in his face. "You can get anything you need at Stores. Didn't they explain that to you when you went to school?" Sean regarded her warily. "Oh, you didn't even stay in school long enough to learn that, did you?" She gave a disgusted snort. "Let me up. I've got stones digging holes in my back. You really are the absolute end." She got to her feet and swatted at the worst of the sand on her clothes. She faced Sean again. "Did you at least wait to find out what was poisonous?" When he gave her a slow nod, she exhaled in relief. "School isn't all bad. At least, not here."

"No money?" Sean seemed unable to grasp that astonishing idea.

"Not unless someone brought some old coins for keepsake. I doubt it: coins'd be heavy. Look," she said quickly, catching his arm when he started to twist away. "You go to the Stores building at Landing. It's the biggest one. Tell them what you want, sign your name on a chit, and if they have it, they give it to you. That's called requisitioning, and every one of us, kids included, are entitled to requisition things from Stores. Well, reasonable things." She grinned, hoping to lighten his scowl. "What are you doing way out here?" She felt a twinge of annoyance as she realized that if he and his family were in that area, then she had not been the first person to see the headland, and she could not ask to have it named after her.

"Like you told me on the spaceship—" He grinned suddenly, a smile full of charm and mischief. "Once we got here, we could go where we please. Only we can't go really far yet until we get some horses."

"Don't tell me you brought your wagons with you?" Sorka was appalled at the weight those would take up in a cargo hold.

"Wagons were brought for us," he told her. "Only we've nothing to pull 'em with." He waved toward the thick underbrush. "But we are free again, and camping where we want until we get our animals."

"That's going to take a couple of years, you know," she said earnestly. Once again he nodded solemnly. "But we've started. My dad's a vet and he said they'd woken up some horse and donkey mares, cows, goats, and sheep and made 'em pregnant with our kinds of animals."

"Woken up?" Sean's eyes protruded.

"Sure, who could muck livestock out for fifteen years? But it'll still take eleven months for the horses to be born, if that's what you're waiting for."

"Horses, always. We were promised horses." Sean sounded wistful as well as emphatic, and she experienced a moment of kindliness toward him.

"You'll get them, too. My father said so," she added mendaciously. "He said that the ti—the traveling folk were first on the list."

"We'd better be." Sean glowered darkly. "Or there'll be trouble."

"You see me before you make any trouble here. My da always got on well with your people in Clonmel. Believe me, you'll get your horses." She could see that he was skeptical. "Now, mind, I hear that you've harmed our creature and I'll see you don't, Sean Connell!" She held up a warning hand, the flat edge in an offensive position. "Not that you could catch her. She's smart, that one. She understands what you're thinking."

Sean eyed her, more scornful than skeptical. "You know so much about her?"

"I'm good with animals." She paused, then grinned. "Just like you are. See you 'round. And remember about requisitioning!"

She turned and started back down the beach to catch up with Jacob and Chung—just in time to help carry the samples back to the hatchery.

◆ ◆ ◆

When Sallah Telgar heard the call for volunteers to make up a skeleton crew so that those who had not yet been down to the surface would have a weekend break on Pern, she hesitated until she saw the names of the first three volunteers: Avril, Bart, and Nabhi. That trio did nothing that did not further themselves. Why would *they* volunteer? Suspicious, she scrawled her name down immediately. Also, she was still curious about what Kenjo had been up to with his fuel economies. The *Eujisan* had drawn its quota regularly, yet her private calculations indicated a growing balance that had neither been burned up by the *Eujisan* nor was in the *Yoko*'s fuel tanks. Very strange. Soon there would be no place on the old *Yoko* to hide a thimbleful of fuel, much less the volume of the shortfall she had calculated. But Kenjo was not among the volunteers.

All six shuttles went up to relieve the ships' crews and to bring down more bits and pieces. Sallah flew the *Eujisan* up with the skeleton crew for the *Yoko*. Avril had a smile on her face, smug enough to satisfy Sallah that the woman had personal plans for her weekend. Bart Lemos looked apprehensive and fidgeted while Nabhi continued to look supercilious. They were up to something, Sallah was sure. But what it might be she couldn't imagine.

When Sallah sprang the hatch on the *Yoko*'s landing deck, she was nearly bowled over by the jubilant men and women waiting to board the *Eujisan* for their first trip to the surface of their new home. Sallah had never seen a faster loading. Shortly all that would remain of the *Yoko* would be bare hull and the corridors leading to the bridge, where the mainframe computer banks would remain intact. Most of the computer's vast memory had been duplicated for use on the surface, but not all—the bulk of the naval and military programs were protected and, in any case, irrelevant. Once passengers and crew left the three spaceships in their orbit, there would be no need to know how to fight space battles.

The volunteers were given their orders by the crew members they were replacing and then the shore-leave party merrily departed.

"Gawd, this place is eerie," Boris Pahlevi whispered as he and Sallah made their way to the bridge through the echoing corridors, which had been stripped of siding and were down to the central plank of flooring.

"Will the last man off roll the plank up behind him?" Sallah asked facetiously. She shuddered when she noticed that the safety hatches between sections had been removed. Lighting had been reduced to three units per corridor. She watched where she put her feet.

"It's rape, though," Boris remarked in a lugubrious tone, as he gazed around, "gutting the old girl this way."

"Ivan the Terrible," Sallah said. That was the pilots' nickname for the ship's quartermaster in charge of the removal process. "He's Alaskan, you know, and a real scrounger scrooge."

"Tut-tut," Boris said with a mock stern expression. "We're all Pernese now, Sal. But what's Alaskan?"

"Fardles, you is the most iggerant bastard, Boris, even for a second-generation Centauran. Alaska was a territory on Earth, not far from its arctic circle, and cold. Alaskans had a reputation for never throwing anything away. My father never did. Must have been a genetic trait because he was reared on First, although my grandparents were Alaskan." Sallah sighed with nostalgia. "Dad never threw anything away. I had to chuck the whole nine yards before we shipped out. Eighteen years of accumulated—well, it wasn't junk, because I got good prices on practically everything in the mountain, but it was some chore. Hercules and the Augean stables were clean in comparison."

"Hercules?"

"Never mind," Sallah said, wondering if Boris was teasing her by pretending ignorance of old Earth legends and peoples. Some people had wanted to throw everything out, literature, legend, language, all the things that had made people so interestingly different from each other. But wiser, more tolerant heads had prevailed. General Cherry Duff, the colony's official historian and librarian, had insisted that records of all ethnic written and visual cultures be taken to Pern. Those who had craved a completely fresh start consoled themselves with the fact that anything not valid in the new context would eventually fall into disuse as new traditions were established.

"You never know," Cherry Duff frequently admonished, "when old information becomes new, viable, and valuable. We keep the whole schmear!" The valiant lady defender of Cygnus III, a healthy woman in her eleventh decade with great-grandchildren making the trip with her on the *Buenos Aires*, affected idiomatic speech in order to make her points memorable. "Takes up no space at all on the chips we've got."

Sallah and Boris found the bridge territory reassuringly intact. Even the danger doors were still in place. Boris took the command chair and asked Sallah to confirm the stability of their orbit. He was an engineer who dabbled in computer programming, and as weekend duty officer, he would probably spend all his time on the mainframe. He was certainly competent to detect and deal with any untoward deviation from orbit. He had welcomed the respite from outdoor work, as he had forgotten to protect a fair skin against sunburn while he was helping to erect temporary power pylons for the hydroelectric unit. He was annoyed with himself for ignoring a simple precaution just because everyone around him had been shucking shirts to get planet-brown.

"Program's been left up," Sallah told him, sliding into the chair at the navigator's position. "The *Yoko*'s smack dab on orbit."

"The duty officer really should have remained here until I officially took over," Boris muttered. Then he exhaled. "But I suppose she was afraid that they'd leave without her. No harm done, at any rate."

Boris began calling in the other manned stations, confirming the duty personnel from the roster he had been given. Avril Bitra and Bart Lemos were assigned to Life Support, and Nabhi Nabol was in Supply. While Boris was involved in roll call, Sallah began some discreet checking of her own from the big terminal. She initiated a program to discover who else had been accessing the mainframe. That sort of internal check was a function of the bridge terminal and not available on any of the others, except the one that had once been in the admiral's suite. By the time Sallah left the *Yoko*, she would know who had asked for what, if not why.

"D'you know if they've got all the library tapes down below yet?" Boris asked, relaxing in the command chair once the call had been completed and logged in.

"I think General Duff said they are, but why not get your own copies while there's tape left?"

"Well, I'll just do a few for private consumption. After all, my hide has been flayed to produce power to run 'em."

Sallah laughed, but she could not help but feel compassion. Poor Boris's face was raw with sunburn, and he wore the loosest possible clothing. She regarded him casually until he became absorbed in a perusal of the library; then she turned back to the computer.

Avril was asking for figures on the remaining fuel in the tanks of all three colony ships. Nabol was inquiring about machine parts and replacement units that had already been landed. He was accessing their exact locations in Stores. So he won't have to ask to get them, Sallah thought. More worrisome were Avril's programs, for she was the only fully qualified and experienced astrogator. If anyone could make use of available fuel, it was Avril. And where were the liters and liters that Kenjo had scrounged?

Avril requested the coordinates for the nearest planet capable of sustaining humanoids. Two had EEC reports that indicated developing sentient life. They were distant, but within the range of the admiral's gig. Just. Sallah could not quite see why Avril would be at all interested in those planets, even if they were within reach of the *Mariposa*. Granted Avril could calculate her way there, but it would be a long, harrowing trip even at the maximum speed the gig could achieve. Then Sallah remembered that the gig had two deep-sleep tanks: a last resort and not one she herself would undertake. If she were in deep sleep, she would prefer to have someone awake and checking the dials. The method was not as foolproof as all that. But there were two tanks. So who was the lucky one to go with Avril? If escape from Pern was what she planned. But why would anyone escape from Pern when she had just got there, Sallah wondered, mystified. A whole new sparkling world, and Avril was not going to wait until she had given it a chance? Or was she?

Sallah continued her surveillance throughout the three-day stint and took hard copy before she erased the file. By the time she boarded the shuttle to return planetside, she understood why the crews had needed shore leave. The poor old nearly gutted *Yoko* was a depressing place. The two smaller ships, *Buenos Aires* and *Bahrain*, would be claustrophobic. But the stripping was nearly complete, and soon the three colony ships would be abandoned to their lonely orbit, visible at dawn and dusk only as three points of light reflecting Rukbat's rays.

Despite her parents' tacit disapproval of Sean Connell as a friend for their daughter, Sorka found many reasons to continue seeing him, once he had relaxed his natural suspicions of her. Curiously enough, Sorka also noticed that his family was no keener on his friendship with her than her own was. That added a certain fillip.

They were bound together by their fascination with their creature and her clutch of eggs. Sorka was watching the nest with Sean, as much to be sure that he did not succeed in his efforts to snare her as to be present when the eggs hatched.

That morning—a rest day—Sorka had come prepared for a long vigil with sandwiches in her pack. She had brought enough to share with Sean. The two children had hidden, bellies down, in the underbrush that bordered the headland rock, in a spot where they could keep the nest in sight. The little gold animal sunned herself on the seaside; they could see her eyes glittering as she maintained her watch over her eggs.

"Just like a lizard," Sean murmured, his breath tickling Sorka's ear.

"Not at all," Sorka protested, recalling illustrations in a book of fairy tales. "More like a little dragon. A dragonet," she said almost aggressively. She did not think that "lizard" was at all appropriate for such a gorgeous being.

She carefully waved away another one of the many-legged bugs that was urgently trundling its three-sectioned body through the underbrush. Felicia Grant, the children's botany teacher, had called them a form of millipede and was happy to see them. She had explained their reproductive cycle to the class: the adult produced young, which remained attached to the parent until it reached the same size, whereupon it was dropped off. Two maturing off-spring were often in tow.

Sean was idly building a dam of leaves to turn the bug away from him. "Snakes eat a lot of these, and wherries eat snakes."

"Wherries also eat wherries," Sorka said in a disgusted tone of voice, re-calling the scavengers at work.

A subtle crooning alerted them as they sprawled, half-drowsing in the midday heat. The little golden dragonet spread her wings.

"Protecting them," Sorka said.

"Nope. Welcoming them."

Sean had a habit of taking exactly the opposite line in any discussions they had. Sorka had grown used to it, even expected it.

"It could be both," she suggested tolerantly.

Sean only snorted. "I'll bet that trundle-bug was running from snakes."

Sorka suppressed a shudder. She would not let Sean see how much she detested the slithery things. "You're right. She's welcoming them." Sorka's eyes widened. "She's singing!"

Sean smiled at the sound that was growing more lyrical. The little crea-ture tilted her head so that they could see her throat vibrating.

Suddenly the air about the rock was busy with dragonets. Sean grasped Sorka's arm, as much in surprise as to command her to silence. Open-mouthed in astonishment, Sorka could not have uttered a sound; she was too delighted with the assembly to do more than stare. Blue, brown, and bronze dragonets hovered in the air, blending their voices with that of the little gold.

"There must be hundreds of the dragonets, Sean." The way they were wheeling and darting about, the air seemed over-laden with them.

"Only twelve lizards," Sean replied, impervious. "No, sixteen."

"Dragonets," Sorka said firmly.

Sean ignored her interruption. "I wonder why."

"Look!" She pointed to a new flight of dragonets that appeared suddenly, trailing large branches of dripping seaweeds. More arrived, each with some-thing wiggling in its mouth, the burden deposited on the seaweeds that made an uneven circle about the nest. "Like a dam," Sorka murmured won-deringly. More avians, or perhaps the same ones on a return trip, brought trundle-bugs and sandworms, which flopped or burrowed in the weeds.

Then, as they saw the first of the eggs crack and a little wet head poke through, Sorka and Sean clung to each other in order to contain their excite-ment. Pausing in their harvesting, the airborne creatures warbled an intricate pattern of sound.

"See, it is welcome!" Sean knew that he had been right all along.

"No! Protection!" Sorka pointed to the blunt snouts of two huge mottled snakes at the far side of the underbrush.

The intruders were spotted by the flyers, and half a dozen dove at the protruding heads. Four of the dragonets sustained the attack right into the vegetation, and there was considerable agitation of branches until the attackers emerged, chittering loudly. In that brief interval, four more eggs had cracked open. The adult avians were a living chain of supply as the first arrival shed its shell and staggered about, keening woefully. Its dam herded it, with wing motion and encouraging chirps, toward a nearby dragonet that was holding a flopping fishling for the hatchling to devour.

A bolder snake, emerging from the sand where it had hidden itself, attempted a rush up the rock face toward another hatchling. It braced its middle limbs as it raised its head, its turtlelike mouth agape, to grab its prey. Instantly the snake was attacked by the airborne dragonets. With a good sense of preservation, the hatchling lurched over the damlike ramparts of seaweed, toward the bush under which Sorka and Sean hid.

"Go away," Sean muttered between clenched teeth. He waved his hand at the keening juvenile, shooing it away from them. He had no wish to be attacked by its adult kin.

"It's starving, Sean," Sorka said, fumbling for the packet of sandwiches. "Can't you *feel* the hunger in it?"

"Don't you dare mother it!" he muttered, though he, too, sensed the little thing's craving. But he had seen the flyers rend fish with their sharp talons. He would prefer not to be their next victim.

Before he could stop her, Sorka tossed a corner of her sandwich out onto the rock. It landed right in front of the weaving, crying hatchling, who pounced and seemed to inhale the bit. Its cry became urgently demanding, and it hobbled more purposefully toward the source. Two more of the little creatures raised their heads and turned in that direction, despite their dam's efforts to shoo them to the adults holding out succulent marine life.

Sean groaned, "Now you've done it."

"But it's hungry." Sorka broke off more bits and lobbed them at the three hatchlings.

The other two scurried to secure a share of the bounty. To Sean's dismay, Sorka had crawled out of their hiding place and was offering the foremost hatchling a piece directly from her fingers. Sean made a grab for her but missed, bruising his chin on the rock.

Sorka's creature took the offered piece and then climbed into her hand, snuffling piteously.

"Oh, Sean, it's a perfect darling. And it can't be a lizard. It's warm and feels soft. Oh, do take a sandwich and feed the others. They're starving of the hunger."

Sean spared a glance at the dam and realized with intense relief that she was far more concerned with getting the others fed than with coming after the three renegades. His fascination with the creatures overcame caution. He grabbed a sandwich and, kneeling beside Sorka, coaxed the nearer brown dragonet to him. The second brown, hearing the change in its sibling's cries, spread its wet wings and, with a screech, joined it in a frantic dive. Sean found that Sorka was right: the critters had pliant skins and were warm to the touch. They did not feel at all lizardlike.

In short order, the sandwiches had been reduced to bulges in lizard bellies, and Sorka and Sean had unwittingly made lifelong friends. They had been so preoccupied with their three that they had failed to note the disappearance of the others. Only the empty shards of discarded eggs in a hollow of the rock bore witness to the recent event.

"We can't just leave them here. Their mother's gone," Sorka said, surprised by the abandonment of dragonet kin.

"I wasn't going to leave mine any road," Sean said, slightly derisive of her quandary. "I'm keeping 'em. I'll keep yours, too, if you don't want to bring it back to Landing. Your mother won't let you have a wild thing."

"This one's not wild," Sorka replied, taking offense. With her forefinger, she stroked the back of the tiny bronze lizard curled in the crook of her arm. It stirred and snuggled closer, exhaling on something remarkably like a purr. "My mother's great with babies. She used to save lambs that even my father thought might die."

Sean was pacified. He had put the browns in his shirt, one on either side, and tightened the leather belt he had dared requisition. The ease with which he had accomplished that at the Stores building had encouraged him to trust Sorka. It had also proved to his father that the "others" were fairly distributing the wealth of matériel carried to Pern in the spaceships. Two days after getting his belt, Sean began to see proper new pots replacing discarded tins over the campfire, and his mother and three sisters were wearing new shirts and shoes.

The brown dragonets felt warm against his skin and a bit prickly where their tiny spikes pressed, but he was more than pleased with his success. They only had three toes, the front one folded against the back two. Everyone in his father's camp had been hunting for lizard—well, dragonet—nests and snake holes along the coast. They looked for signs of the legendary lizards for fun, and hunted the snakes for safety. The scavenging reptiles were dangerous to people who camped in rough shelters of woven branches and broadleaf fronds. Reptiles had eaten their way into the shelters and had bitten sleeping children in their blankets. Nothing was safe from their predatory habits. And they were not good eating.

Sean's father had caught, skinned, and grilled several snakes. He had sampled a tiny bite of each variety and instantly had to wash his mouth out, as the snake flesh stung and caused his mouth to swell. So the order had gone to everyone in the camp: snare and kill the vermin. Of course, as soon as they had terriers or ferrets to go down the holes, they could make short work of the menace. Porrig Connell had been upset because the other members of the expedition seemed not to understand how urgent it was for his people to have dogs. The animals were not pets—they were necessary adjuncts of his folk's lifestyle. It was proving the same on Pern as on Earth: the Connells were the last to get anything useful and the first to be given the back of the hand. But he had had each of his five families put in for a dog.

"Your dad'll be pleased," Sorka said, expansive in her own pleasure. "Won't he, Sean? Bet they'll be better even than dogs at going after snakes. Look at the way they attacked the mottleds."

Sean snorted. "Only because the hatchlings were being attacked."

"I doubt it was just that. I could almost feel the way they hated the snakes." She wanted to believe that the flying lizards were unusual, just as she had always believed that their marmalade tom, Duke, was the best hunter in the valley, and old Chip the best cattle dog in Tipperary. Doubt suddenly assailed her. "But maybe we should leave them here for their dam."

Sean frowned. "She was shooing the others off to the sea fast enough."

Of one mind, they rose and, walking carefully so as not to disturb their sleeping burdens, headed for the summit of the headland.

"Oh, look!" Sorka cried, pointing wildly just as something pulled the tattered body of a hatchling under the water. "Oh, oh, oh." Sean watched impassively. Sorka turned away, clenching her fists. "She's not a very good mother after all."

"Only the best survive," Sean said. "Our three are safe. They were smart enough to come to us!" Then he turned, cocking his head and peering at her through narrowed eyes. "Will yours be *safe* at Landing? They've been after us to bring 'em specimens, you know. 'Cause my dad's special at trapping and snaring."

Sorka hugged her sleeping charge closer to her body. "My father wouldn't let anything happen to this lad. I know he wouldn't."

Sean was cynical. "Yeah, but he's not head of his group, is he? He has to obey orders, doesn't he?"

"They just want to *look* at life-forms. They don't want to cut 'em up or anything."

Sean was unconvinced, but he followed Sorka as she moved away from the sea and made her way through the undergrowth to the edge of the plateau.

"See ya tomorra?" Sean asked, suddenly loath to give up their meetings now that their mutual vigil had come to an end.

"Well, tomorrow's a workday, but I'll see you in the evening?" Sorka didn't even pause a moment to think about her reply. She was no longer hampered by the stern tenets of Earth restrictions on her comings and goings. She was beginning to accept her safety on Pern as easily as she accepted her responsibility to work for her future there. Sean was also part of that sense of personal safety, despite his innate distrust of all but his own people. Even if Sean was unaware of it, a special link had been forged between Sean and her after their momentous experience on the rock head.

◆ ◆ ◆

"Are you sure these creatures will hunt the snake?" Porrig Connell asked as he examined one of Sean's sleeping acquisitions. It remained motionless when he extended one of the limp wings.

"If they're hungry," Sean replied, holding his breath lest his father inadvertently hurt his little lizard.

Porrig snorted. "We'll see. At least it's a creature of this place. Anything's better than being eaten alive. One of the blue mottled ones took a huge chunk out of Sinead's babee last night."

"Sorka says the snakes can't get in *their* house. Plastic keeps 'em out."

Porrig gave another of his skeptical grunts, then nodded toward the sleeping hatchling. "Watch 'em now. They're your problem."

At Residence Fourteen in Asian Square, there was considerably more enthusiasm about Sorka's creature. Mairi dispatched Brian to bring his father from the veterinary shed. Then she made a little nest in one of the baskets she had been weaving from the tough Pernese reeds, lining it with dried plant fiber. Tenderly she transferred the creature from Sorka's arm to its new bed, where it immediately curled itself into a ball and, with a tremendous sigh that inflated its torso to the size of its engorged belly, fell deeper into sleep.

"It's not really a lizard, is it?" she said, softly stroking the warm skin. "It feels like good suede. Lizards are dry and hard to the touch. And it's smiling. See?"

Obediently Sorka peered down and smiled in response. "You should have seen it wolf down the sandwiches."

"You mean, you've had no lunch?" Aghast, Mairi immediately bustled about to remedy that situation.

Though the communal kitchens catered for most of the six thousand

regular inhabitants of Landing, more and more of the family units were beginning to cook for themselves for all but the evening meal. The Hanrahans'
home was a typical accommodation for a family: one medium-sized bedroom, two small, a larger room for general purposes, and a sanitary unit; all
the furnishings but the treasured rosewood dower chest were salvaged from the
colony ships or made by Red in his infrequent spare time. At one end of
the largest room was a food-preparation unit, compact but adequate. Mairi
prided herself on her culinary skills and was enjoying a chance to experiment
with new foods.

Sorka was halfway through her third sandwich when Red Hanrahan arrived with zoologist Pol Nietro and microbiologist Bay Harkenon.

"Don't wake the little thing," Mairi instantly cautioned them.

Almost reverently the three peered at the sleeping lizard. Red Hanrahan
let the specialists monopolize it while he gave his daughter a hug and a kiss,
ruffling her hair with affectionate pride. "Who's the clever girl!" he exclaimed.

He sat down at the table, stretching his long legs underneath, and slid
his hands into his pockets as he watched the two tut-tutting over a genuine
Pernese native.

"A most amazing specimen," Pol remarked to Bay as they straightened.

"So like a lizard," she replied, smiling with wonder at Sorka. "Will you
please tell us exactly how you enticed the creature to you?"

Sorka hesitated only briefly, then, at her father's reassuring nod, she told
them all she knew about the lizards, from her first sight of the little gold beast
guarding her eggs, to the point where she had coaxed the bronze one to eat from
her hand. She did not, however, mention Sean Connell, though she knew from
the glances her parents exchanged that they surmised that he had been with her.

"Were you the only lucky one?" her father asked her in a low voice while
the two biologists were engrossed in photographing the sleeping creature.

"Sean took two brown ones home. They have an awful time with snakes
in their camp."

"There're homes waiting for them on Canadian Square," her father reminded her. "And they'd have the place to themselves."

All the ethnic nomads in the colony's complement had been duly allotted living quarters, thoughtfully set to the edge of Landing, where they
might not feel so enclosed. But after a few nights, they had all gone, melting
into the unexplored lands beyond the settlement. Sorka shrugged.

Then Pol and Bay began a second round of questions, to clarify her
account.

"Now, Sorka, we'd like to borrow your new acquisition for a few hours."
Bay emphasized the word "borrow." "I assure you we won't harm a—well, a

patch of its hide. There's a lot we can determine about it simply from obser-vation and a judicious bit of hands-on examination."

Sorka looked anxiously at her parents.

"Why don't we let it get used to Sorka first?" Red said easily, one hand resting lightly on his daughter's clenched fists. "Sorka's very good with ani-mals; they seem to trust her. And I think it's far more important right now to reassure this bitty fellow than find out what makes it tick." Sorka remem-bered to breathe and let her body relax. She knew she could count on her fa-ther. "We wouldn't want to scare it away. It only hatched this morning."

"Zeal motivates me," Bay Harkenon said with a rueful smile. "But I know you're right, Red. We'll just have to leave it in Sorka's capable care." The woman gathered herself to rise when her associate cleared his throat.

"But if Sorka would keep track of how much it eats, how often, what it prefers—" Pol began.

"Besides bread and sandwich spread," Mairi said with a laugh.

"That would improve our understanding." Pol had a charming grin that made him appear less gray and frowzy. "And you say that all you had to do was entice it with food?"

Sorka had a sudden mental image of the rather stooped and unathletic Pol Nietro lurking in bushes with a basket of goodies, luring lizards to him.

"I think it had something to do with its being so dreadfully hungry after it hatched," she replied thoughtfully. "I mean, I've had sandwiches in my pockets every morning this week on the beach, and the dam never came near me for food."

"Hmmm. A good point. The newly hatched are voracious." Pol contin-ued to mumble to himself, mentally correlating the information.

"And the adults actually held food for the hatchlings?" Bay murmured. "Fish and insects? Hmm. Sort of an imprinting ritual, perhaps? The juveniles could fly as soon as the wings dried? Hmmm. Yes. Fascinating. The sea would be the nearest source of food." She gathered up her notes and thanked Sorka and her parents. Then the two specialists left the house.

"I'd best go back myself, loves," Red said. "Good work, Sorka. Just shows what old Irish know-how can achieve."

"Peter Oliver Plunkett Hanrahan," his wife immediately chided him. "Start thinking Pernese. Pernese. Pernese." With each repetition she raised her voice in mock emphasis.

"Pernese, not Irish. We're Pernese," Red obediently chanted. Grinning unrepentantly, he did a dance step out of the house to the tempo of "Pernese, Pernese."

That night, to Sorka's intense and embarrassed surprise, and to the total disgust of her envious brother, she was called upon to light the evening bonfire. When Pol Nietro announced why, there were cheers and vigorous applause. Sorka was astonished to see that Admiral Benden and Governor Boll, who had made a point of attending that little evening ceremony, were shouting and clapping like everyone else.

"It wasn't just me," Sorka said in a loud clear voice as she was formally presented with the torch by the acting mayor of Landing. "Sean Connell got two brown lizards, only he isn't here tonight. But you should know that he found the nest first, and both of us watched it."

She knew that Sean Connell would not care if he was given due credit or not, but she did. With that thought, she plunged the burning brand into the heart of the bonfire. She jumped back quickly as the dry material caught and flared brightly.

"Well done, Sorka," her father said, lightly resting his hands on her shoulders. "Well done."

◆ ◆ ◆

Sorka and Sean remained the only proud owners of the pretty lizards for nearly a full week, even though there was an evening rush to the beaches and headlands. But bit by bit, nests were staked and vigilantly guarded. Guided by the routine that Sorka had accurately reported, several more of the little creatures were finally acquired. And her name for the creatures—"dragonets"—was adopted popularly.

The acquisition, as Sorka soon discovered, had two sides. Her little dragonet, whom she nostalgically named Duke after her old marmalade tomcat, was voracious. It ate anything at three-hour intervals, the first night disturbing the entire square with its hungry keening. Between feedings, it slept. When Sorka noticed that its skin was cracking, her father prescribed a salve, prudently concocted of local fish oils, with the help of a pediatrician and a biologist. The pediatrician was so pleased with the result that she had the pharmacist make up more as an ointment for dry skin in general.

"Duke is growing, and his skin is stretching," was Red's diagnosis.

The male designation was arbitrary, since no one had been able to examine the creature closely enough to discover its sex, or even if it had any. The golden dragonets had demonstrated a generally more feminine role in egg-laying, though one of the biologists qualified that by reminding people that the males of some species on Earth were the egg-tenders. The dead skin flakes were assiduously collected for analysis. The eager zoologists had not been able to X-ray Duke, for he seemed to know the moment someone had designs on him. On the second day of his advent, the zoologists had attempted to place him under the scope, while Sorka waited nervously in the next room.

"My word!"

"What?"

Sorka heard the startled exclamations from Pol and Bay at the same moment that Duke reappeared above her head, considerably agitated. Dropping to her shoulder with cries of relief and anger, he wrapped his tail firmly about her neck and hooked his talons into her hair, scolding furiously, his many-faceted eyes rippling with angry reds and oranges.

The door behind Sorka opened suddenly, and Pol and Bay burst into the room, their eyes wide with amazement.

"He just appeared," the girl told the two scientists.

Recovering their composure, the two exchanged glances. Pol's broad face became wreathed in a smile, and Bay looked remarkably pleased.

"So the Amigs do *not* have a monopoly on telekinetic abilities," Bay said with a smug smile. "I always maintained, Pol, that they could not be unique in the galaxy."

"How did he do that?" Sorka asked, not quite certain as she remembered other instances of perplexingly rapid departures.

"Duke must have been frightened by the scope. He is rather small, and it does look menacing," Bay said. "So he teleported himself away. Fortunately back to you, whom he considers his protector. The Amigs use teleportation when threatened. A very useful capability."

"I wonder if we can discover how the little creatures *do* it?" Pol mused.

"We could try the Eridani equations," Bay suggested.

Pol looked at Duke. The lizard's eyes were still red with anger, and he continued to cling tenaciously to Sorka, but he had folded his wings to his back.

"To try them, we need to know more about this chap and his species. Perhaps if you held him, Sorka?" Pol suggested.

Even with Sorka's gentle reassurance, Duke would not permit himself to be placed under the scope. After a half hour, Pol and Bay reluctantly allowed their unwilling subject to be taken away. Reassuring him every step, Sorka carried her still-outraged lizard to his birthplace. Sean was there, stretched out in the shade cast by the bushes, his two browns curled up against his neck. They heard Sorka coming and peered up at her, their eyes whirling a mild blue-green. Duke chirped a greeting to which they replied in kind.

"I was just getting some sleep," Sean muttered petulantly, not bothering to open his eyes to see who had arrived. "M'da made me bunk in with the babees to see if these fellers would scare off the snakes."

"Well, did they?" Sorka asked when he seemed to be falling asleep again.

"Yup." Sean yawned hugely and swatted idly at an insect. One of the browns immediately snapped it out of the air and swallowed it.

"They do eat anything." Sorka's tone was admiring. "Omnivorous, Dr.

Marceau called them." She sat down on the rock beside Sean. "And they can go between places when they're scared. Dr. Nietro tried to scope Duke and made me leave the room. The next thing I knew Duke was clinging to me like he'd never let go. They said he can teleport. He uses telekinesis." She was proud that she had gotten the words out without stumbling over them.

Sean opened one eye and cocked his head to stare up at her. "What does that mean?"

"He can project himself out of danger instantly."

Sean gave a huge yawn. "Yeah? We've both seen them do their disappearing act. And they don't do it always because of danger." He yawned again. "You were smart to take only one. If one isn't eating, the other is. What with that and guarding the babees, I'm fair knackered." He closed his eye again, settled his hands across his chest, and went back to sleep.

"I shall play gold then and guard you, lest a big nasty mottled blunt-nose comes and takes a bite out of you!"

She did not rouse him even when she saw a flight of the lizards in the sky, looping and diving in an aerial display that left her breathless. Duke watched with her, crooning softly to himself, but despite her initial consternation that he might choose to join them, he did not even ease his tailhold about her neck. Before she returned home, Sorka left Sean a jar of the ointment that had been made for Duke's skin.

◆ ◆ ◆

Sorka was not the only person on Pern watching aerial acrobatics that day. Half a continent to the south and west, Sallah Telgar's heart was in her mouth as she watched Drake Bonneau pull the little air sled out of a thermal elevator above the vast inland lake that he was campaigning to call Drake's Lake. No member of their small mining expedition would deny him that privilege, but Drake had a tendency to beat a subject to death. Similarly, he would not stop showing off; he seemed bent on stunning everyone with his professional skill. His antics were a foolish waste of power, Sallah thought, and certainly not the way to her heart and esteem. He had taken to hanging around her quarters, but so far he had met with no great success.

Ozzie Munson and Cobber Alhinwa emerged from the shelter where they had just stored their gear and paused to see what Sallah was staring at.

"Oh, my word, he's at it again," Ozzie said, grinning maliciously at Sallah.

"He'll crash hisself," Cobber added, shaking his head, "and that bleeding lake's so deep we'd never find 'im. Or the sled. And we need that."

Seeing Svenda Olubushtu coming to join them, Sallah hastily turned and headed for the main shelter of the small prospecting camp. She did not care to listen to Svenda's snide, jealous remarks. It was not as if Sallah encouraged

Drake Bonneau. On the contrary, she had emphatically, publicly, and frequently made her disinterest plain enough.

Maybe I'm going about discouraging him the wrong way, she thought. Maybe if I'd run after him, hang on his every word, and ambush him every chance I get, the way Svenda's doing, he'd leave me alone, too.

In the main shelter, she found Tarvi Andiyar already marking the day's findings on the big screen, muttering to himself as he did so, his spidery fingers flicking at the terminal keys so fast that even the word processor had trouble keeping up with him. No one understood him when he talked to himself like that; he was speaking in his first language, an obscure Indic dialect. When asked about his eccentricity, he would respond with one of his heart-melting smiles.

"For other ears to hear this beautiful liquid language, so it will be spoken even here on Pern, so that there will be one person alive who still speaks it fluently, even after all these centuries," he always told those who asked. "Is it not a lovely language, lilting, melodic, a joy to the ear?"

An intuitive, highly trained mining engineer, Tarvi had a reputation of being able to trace elusive veins through many subterranean shifts and faults. He had joined the Pern expedition because all the glorious hidden "blood and tears of Mother Earth," as he chose to describe the products of mining, had been pried from her bosom. He had prospected on First, too, but the alien metals had eluded his perceptions and so he had traveled across a galaxy to ply his trade in what he called his "declining years."

As Tarvi Andiyar had only reached his sixth decade, that remark generally brought the reassurances he required from the kindly, or hoots of derision from those who knew his ploys. Sallah liked him for his wry and subtle wit, which he generally turned on his own shortcomings, and would never think to use to offend anyone else.

Since Sallah had first encountered him after coldsleep, he had not put even so much as an ounce more on his long, almost emaciated frame. "My family has had generations of gurus and mahatmas, all intent on fasting for the purification of their souls and bowels, until it has become a genetic imperative for all Andiyars to be of the thinness of a lathe. But I am strong. I do not need bulk and thews and bulging muscles. I am every bit as strong as the strongest sumo wrestler." Everyone who had seen him work all day without respite beside Ozzie and Cobber knew that his claim was no idle boast.

Sallah found herself more attracted to the lanky engineer than to any of the other men in the colony. But if she could not impress on Drake Bonneau how little she cared for him, she was equally unable to get closer to Tarvi.

"What's the tally, Tarvi?" she asked, nodding to Valli Lieb, who was already relaxing with a quikal drink.

One of the first things human settlers seemed to do on any new world was to make an immediate and intensive search for fermentables, and to devise an alcoholic beverage in the quickest possible time. Every lab at Landing, no matter what its basic function, had experimented with distilling or fermenting local fruits into potable beverages. The quikal still had been the first piece of equipment assembled when the mining expedition had set up its base camp, and no one had objected when Cobber and Ozzie had spent the first day producing imbibables from the fermented juices they had brought along. Svenda had berated them fiercely, while Tarvi and Sallah had merely carried on with the surveying. That first evening in the camp the drink had been more than a tradition: it was an achievement.

As Svenda entered the shelter, Sallah poured herself a glass of quikal. Valli moved over on the bench to make room for her. Valli looked freshly washed and in far better shape than when she had emerged from the brush that afternoon, covered with slime but bearing some very interesting samples for assay.

At that moment they heard the sound of the sled landing outside the shelter. Svenda craned her neck to watch Drake's progress up from the pad; she barely moved as Ozzie and Cobber brushed past her to enter the room.

"What was the assay, Valli?" Sallah asked.

"Promising, promising," the geologist said, her face glowing with achievement. "Bauxite has so many uses! This strike alone makes this expedition profitable."

"However, your find—" Cobber bowed formally to Valli. "—will be far easier to work in an open pit."

"Ha! We have enough to mine both," Ozzie said. "High-grade ore's always needed."

"And," Tarvi put in, joining them at the table though he refused the drink Svenda always offered him, "there is copper and tin enough within reasonable distance so that a mining town could profitably be established by this beautiful lake, with hydroelectric from the falls to power refineries, and a good waterway to transport the finished products to the coast, and thence to Landing."

"So," Svenda asked, "this site is viable?" She looked about her with an air of possession that struck Sallah as slightly premature. Charterers had first choice, before contract specialists.

"I shall certainly recommend it," Tarvi said, smiling in the avuncular way he had that always annoyed Sallah. He was not old. He was very attractive, but if he kept thinking of himself as everyone's uncle, how could she get him to really look at her? "I *have* recommended it," he went on. "Especially as that slime into which you fell today, Valli, is high-yield mineral oil."

When the cheers had subsided, he shook his head. "Metals, yes. Petroleum, no. You all know that. To establish this as an effective colony, we must learn how to function efficiently at a lower technological level. That's where the skill comes in, and how skills are remembered."

"Not everyone agrees with our leaders on that score," Svenda said, scowling.

"We signed the charter and we all agreed to honor it," Valli said, quickly glancing at the others to see if anyone else concurred with Svenda.

"Fools," was the blond girl's derisive rejoinder. Slopping more quikal into her beaker, Svenda left the shelter.

Tarvi looked after her, his mobile face anxious.

"She's all wind and piss," Sallah said softly to him.

He raised his eyebrows, his dark eyes regarding her expressionlessly for a moment. Then his usual smile reappeared, and he patted her shoulder— unfortunately just as one would pat an obedient child. "Ah, and here is Drake with our supplies and news of our comrades."

"Hey, where is everyone?" Drake demanded the moment he entered, well laden with bundles. "There's more in the sled, too."

Sallah dropped her head to hide her expression. "We're celebrating, Drake," Valli said, taking him a glass of quikal. "Two new finds, both of them rich and easily worked. We're in business."

"So, the Drake's Lake Mining and Refinery is in business?"

Everyone laughed and, when he raised his glass in a toast, no one refuted the title.

"And I've news for you," he said after he drank. "We're all to go back to Landing three days from now."

His announcement was met with great consternation. Grinning with anticipated pleasure, Drake raised his free hand for silence. "For a Thanksgiving."

"For this? How'd they know?" Valli asked.

"That should be in the fall, after harvest," Sallah said.

"Why?" was Tarvi's simple response.

"For this auspicious start to our new life. The last load from the starships has reached Landing. We are officially landed."

"Why make a fuss over that?" Sallah asked.

"Not everyone is a workaholic like you, my lovely Sallah," Drake said, pinching her chin affectionately. Seeing that he meant to kiss her, Sallah ducked away, grinning to take away the sting of her rejection. He pouted. "Our gracious leaders have so decided, and it is to be the occasion of many marvelous announcements. All the exploratory teams are being called back, and a grand time will be had by all."

Sallah was almost resentful. "We only got here last week!"

As an escape from several unpalatable but unprovable conclusions, she had taken on the assignment of flying the geologists and miners to the immense inland lake where the EEC survey had reported ore concentrations. She had hoped that distance might provide some objective answers to the events she had witnessed.

A week before, returning one evening to the *Mariposa* to look for a tape she had left on board during one of her early stints as Admiral Benden's pilot, she had seen Kenjo emerging from the small rear service hatch, a brace of sacks in each hand. Curious, she had followed him as he hurried off into the shadows. Then he had seemed to disappear. She hid behind a bush and waited until he had reemerged empty-handed. Then she retraced his steps, and tried to find out where he had put his burden.

After some scrambling about, a couple of bruised shins, and a scraped hand, she had stumbled into a cave—and she was appalled to see the amount of fuel he had purloined. Tons of it, she judged, checking a tag for the quantity, all stashed in easily handled plasacks. The rock fissure was well hidden at the extreme end of the landing grid behind a clump of the tough thorny bushes that the farmers were clearing from the arable acres.

Two nights later, she had overheard a disturbing conversation between Avril and Stev Kimmer, the mining engineer whom Sallah had seen her with the day the landing site had been announced.

"Look, this island is stuffed with gemstones," Avril was saying, and Sallah, dropping into the shadow of the delta wing of the shuttle, could hear the sound of plasfilm being unrolled. "Here's the copy of the original survey report, and I don't need to be a mining specialist to figure out what these cryptic symbols mean." The plasfilm rippled as Avril jabbed her finger at various points. "A fortune for the taking!" There was a ring of triumph in her wheedling voice. "And I intend to take it."

"Well, I grant you that copper, gold, and platinum are useful on any civilized world," Stev began.

"I'm not talking industrial, Kimmer," Avril said sharply. "And I don't mean little stones. That ruby was a small sample. Here, read Shavva's notes."

Kimmer snorted in dismissal. "Exaggerations to improve her bonus!"

"Well, I have forty-five carats of exaggeration, man, and you saw it. If you're not in this with me, I'll find someone who can take a challenge."

Avril certainly knew how to play her hook, Sallah thought grimly.

"That island's not on the schedule for years," Stev pointed out.

Avril gave a low laugh. "I can navigate more than spaceships, Stev. I'm checked out on a sled and I'm as free as everyone else on this mudball to look for the measly amount of stake acres I'm entitled to as a contractor.

But you're charter, and if we pool our allotments, we could own the entire island."

Sallah heard Kimmer's intake of breath. "I thought the fishers wanted the island for that harbor."

"They only want a harbor, not an island. They're fishermen, dolphineers. The land's no use to them."

He muttered, shifting his feet uneasily.

"Who'd know anyhow?" Avril demanded silkily. "We could go in, on the weekends, begin on the most accessible stuff, stash it in a cave. There're so many that you could search for years and never find the right one. And we wouldn't have to draw attention to our activities by staking it officially, unless we're forced to."

"But you said there was stuff in the Great Western Range."

"And so there is," Avril agreed with a little chuckle. "I also know where. A short hop from the island."

"You've got it all worked out, haven't you?" Kimmer's voice had an edge of sarcasm.

"Of course," Avril agreed easily. "I'm not going to live out the rest of my life in this backwater, not when I've discovered the means to live the style of life I very much prefer." Again there was that rippling laugh and then a long silence, broken by the sound of moist lips parting. "But while I'm here, and you're here, Kimmer, let's make the most of it. Here and now, under the stars."

Sallah had slipped away, both embarrassed and disgusted by Avril's blatant sexuality. Small wonder Paul Benden had not kept the woman in his bed. He was a sensual man, Sallah thought, but unlikely to appreciate Avril's crude abandon for long. Ju Adjai, elegant and serene, was far more suitable, even if neither appeared to be rushing a noticeable alliance.

But Avril's voice had dripped with an insatiable greed. Had Stev Kimmer heard what Sallah had? Or had her enticement clouded his thinking? Sallah had always been aware of Pern's gemstone wealth. The Shavva Ruby had been as much part of the legend of Pern as the Liu Nugget. Pern's distance from the Federated Sentient Planets outweighed any major temptation its gem deposits might have held for the greedy. But if a person did manage to return to Earth with a shipload of gems, he or she would undoubtedly be able to retire to a sybaritic life-style.

Avril's plot would hardly deplete Pern's resources. What worried Sallah was *how* Avril would contrive the fuel for such a journey. Sallah knew that there was fuel left in the Admiral's gig, the *Mariposa*. That was not common knowledge, but as a pilot, Avril would have access to that information. Judging by the computations Avril had made during her time on the *Yokohama*,

Sallah knew that the woman could actually make it to an uninhabited system. But then what?

Sallah had liked surveying with Ozzie, Cobber, and the others, and she had been kept too tired to think of her dilemma. But with return to Landing imminent, her questions came flooding back. While she had no compunction about reporting Avril, she realized that she would also have to mention Kenjo's activities. She wished she knew why Kenjo had held back fuel. Did he have some crazy notion about exploring the two moons? Or the wayward planet which was expected to cross Pern's orbit in roughly eight years?

It was impossible to imagine Kenjo being involved with someone like Avril Bitra. Sallah was certain that the obvious animosity between the two was not feigned. She suspected that to Kenjo flying was both a religion and an incurable disease. But he did have all of Pern to fly over, and the packs that powered the colony's air sleds would, if used circumspectly, allow for several decades of such flight.

What worried Sallah most was the possibility, however remote, of Avril's discovering Kenjo's cache. She had thought of confiding in one of the other pilots, but Barr Hamil could not handle such a problem, Drake would not take it seriously, and Jiro, Kenjo's copilot, would never betray his superior. She did not know the others well enough to judge their reactions to such a disclosure. Go to the top, she told herself. This sort of thing is safest there. She was sure that Ongola would listen to her. And he would know whether or not to burden Paul and Emily with her suspicions.

Damn! Sallah's fists clenched at her sides. Pern was supposed to be above petty schemes and intrigues. We're all working to a common goal, she thought. A secure, bountiful future, without prejudice. Why must someone like Avril touch that beautiful vision with her sour egocentricity?

Then Ozzie touched her arm, bringing her out of her depressing thoughts.

"You'll gimme a dance, Sallah?" he asked in his slightly nasal twang, his eyes twinkling with a challenge.

Sallah grinned and accepted. As soon as she returned to Landing, she would find Ongola and tell him. Then she would be able to trip the light fantastic with an easy conscience.

"And then," Ozzie went on irrepressibly, "Tarvi can dance with you and give me time to rest my sore toes."

Tarvi gave her a look of rueful assent, not having much choice, Sallah realized, with so many witnesses and without a chance to prepare an excuse. But she was grateful to sly old Ozzie.

◆ ◆ ◆

By the time the mining party returned to Landing, the fire was well started in Bonfire Square and the party was gathering momentum. From her high vantage point as she swung the sled to the perimeter and down to the strip, Sallah almost did not recognize the utilitarian settlement. Lights were on in almost every window, and every lamp standard glowed. A dais had been erected across one side of Bonfire Square, and colored spotlights strung on a frame above it. Drake had said that there was a call out for anyone who could play an instrument to take a turn that evening. The white cubes of old plastic packers dotted the dais to serve as stools for the musicians.

Tables and chairs had been brought from residences and set up in a freshly mowed space beyond the square. Firepits had been dug to roast huge wherries; on smaller spits the last of the frozen meats brought from Earth browned along with several other carcasses. The aroma of roasting meat and grilling fish was mouth-watering. The colonists were all dressed in their best clothes. Everyone was bustling around, helping, toting, arranging, and fixing the last of the delicacies brought from the old worlds and saved for one last gorge on the new.

Sallah parked her sled crosswise on the landing grid, thinking that if more were set down at random along the straightaway, the *Mariposa* parked at the other end of the field would not have sufficient space for takeoff. But how long would there be that many sleds at Landing?

"Hey, hurry up, Sallah," Ozzie called as he and Cobber jumped out of the sled.

"Gotta check in at the tower," she said, waving cheerfully at them to go on.

"Oh, leave it the once," Cobber suggested, but she waved them on again.

Ongola was just leaving the meteorology tower as she reached it. He gave her a resigned nod and opened the door again, noticing as he did so the position of her sled. "Wise to leave it like that, Sallah?"

"Yes. A precautionary measure, Commander," she said in a tone intended to warn him that she had come on a serious errand.

He did not seat himself until she was halfway through her suspicions, and then he lowered himself into the chair with such weariness that she hated herself for speaking out.

"Forewarned is forearmed, sir," she said in conclusion.

"It is, indeed, Mister Telgar." His deep sigh stressed the return of doubt. He motioned her to be seated. "How much fuel?"

When she reluctantly gave him the precise figures, he was surprised and concerned.

"Could Avril know of Kenjo's hoard?" Ongola sat up so quickly that she realized he found her suspicions of the astrogator far more worrying than Kenjo's theft. "No, no," he corrected himself with a quick wave of his hand. "Their dislike of each other is genuine. I will inform the admiral and the governor."

"Not tonight, sir," Sallah said, inadvertently raising her hand to protest. "It's only because this was the first chance I've had to approach you . . ."

"Forewarned is forearmed, Sallah. Have you mentioned these suspicions to anyone else?"

She shook her head vigorously. "No, sir! It's bad enough suspecting there are maggots in the meat without offering anyone else a bite."

"True! Eden is once again corrupted by human greed."

"Only one human," Sallah felt obliged to remind him.

He held up two fingers significantly. "Two, Kimmer. And who else was she speaking to on board?"

"Kimmer, Bart Lemos, and Nabhi Nabol, and two other men I've never met."

Ongola did not seem surprised. He took a deep breath and sighed before he put both hands on his thighs and rose to his full height. "I am grateful, and I know that the admiral and the governor will also be grateful."

"Grateful?" Sallah stood, feeling none of the relief she had hoped to gain from telling her superior.

"We had actually anticipated some problems as people began to realize that they are *here*," Ongola said, stabbing one long finger downward, "and cannot go anywhere else. The euphoria of the crossing is over; tonight's celebration is planned to defuse a rebound as that realization sinks in. Well-fed, well-oiled people who have tired themselves with dancing are unlikely to plot sedition."

Ongola opened the door, gesturing courteously for her to precede him. No one locked doors on Pern, even doors to official administrative offices. Sallah had been proud of that fact, but now she was worried.

"We're not that stupid, Sallah," Ongola said, as if he had read her mind. He tapped his forehead. "This is still the best memory bank ever invented."

She gave a sigh of relief and managed a more cheerful expression.

"We still have a great deal to be thankful for on Pern, you know," he reminded her.

"Indeed I do!" she replied, thinking of her dance with Tarvi.

By the time she had washed, changed into her own finery, and reached Bonfire Square, the party was in full swing and the impromptu orchestra was playing a polka. Halting in the darkness beyond all that light and sound, Sallah was astonished at the number of unexpected musicians who were stomping time as they waited their turns.

The music changed constantly as new musicians replaced those who had already played. To Sallah's utter amazement, even Tarvi Andiyar produced pan pipes and played an eerie little melody, quite haunting and a quiet change after the more raucous sets.

The informal group went from dance tunes to solos, calling on the audience to sing old favorites. Emily Boll took a turn on the keyboard, and Ezra Keroon enthusiastically fiddled a medley of hornpipes that had everyone foot-tapping while several couples did hilarious imitations of the traditional seamen's dance.

Sallah had enjoyed not one dance with Tarvi, but two. In the middle of the second, as they swayed to an ancient tune in three-quarter time, there came a heart-stopping moment when it seemed as if Pern, too, had decided to dance to the new tunes it heard. Every dish on the trestle tables rattled, dancers were thrown off balance, and those seated felt their chairs rock.

The quake lasted less than the time between two heartbeats and was followed by complete and utter silence.

"So Pern wants to dance, does it?" Paul Benden's amused voice rang out. He jumped to the musicians' platform, arms outspread as if he considered the quake an oblique sign of welcome. His comment caused whispers and murmurs, but it eased the tension. Even as Paul signaled the musicians to resume their music, he was scanning the audience, looking for certain faces.

Beside Sallah, Tarvi gave an almost imperceptible nod of his head and dropped his arms away from her. "Come, we must go check the rhythm of this dance."

Sallah tried to hide her intense disappointment at having her dance with Tarvi cut short. The quake had to be given precedence. She had never felt an earth tremor before, but that had not prevented her from instantly understanding what had just occurred. Even as she and Tarvi made their way from the dancing square, she moved warily, as if to forestall the surprise of another shock.

Jim Tillek gathered his mariners to see that the boats were moored well within the newly reinforced breakwater, and hoped that if there were a tsunami, it would dissipate its force against the intervening islands. The dolphineers, with the exception of Gus, who was coerced into remaining behind to play his accordion, went to the harbor to speak to the marine mammals. They could signal the arrival of the tsunami and estimate its destructiveness.

Patrice de Broglie took a group to go set seismic cores, but in his professional opinion the shock had been a very gentle one, originating from a far-distant epicenter.

Sallah got to finish her dance with Tarvi, but only because he was told that the absence of too many specialists might cause alarm.

By morning, the epicenter had been located, east by northeast, far out in the ocean, where volcanism had been mentioned by the EEC team. As there were no further shocks penetrating to the mainland, the geologists were able to dispel the ripple of uncertainty that had marred the Thanksgiving festivities.

When Tarvi wanted to join Patrice to investigate the epicenter, Sallah volunteered to pilot the big sled. She did not even mind that the sled was crowded with curious geologists and packed with equipment. She saw to it that Tarvi occupied the right hand driving seat.

CHAPTER

VI

After the Thanksgiving celebration, the colonists settled down to more routine work. The dolphins had a high old time tracking the tsunami wave; it had, as Tarvi had predicted, raced across the Northern Sea, spending the worst of its violence on the eastern extrusion and the western tip of the northern continent and the big island. Jim Tillek's harbor was safe, although combers brought a ridge of bright red seawrack well up the beaches. The deep-sea plant was unlike anything so far discovered, and samples were rushed to the lab for analysis. An edible seaweed would be valuable.

The dolphins were excited by the earthquake, for they had sensed its imminence from the reactions of the larger marine forms that scurried for safety, and they were pleased to learn of such awareness in the life of their new oceans. As Teresa had told Efram in indignant clicks and hisses, they had rung and rung the seabell installed at the end of the jetty, but no one had come. The marine rangers had had their work cut out to soothe and placate the blues and bottlenoses.

"What was the sense," Teresa, the biggest blue, had demanded, "of going through all that mentasynth infection if you humans don't come to hear what we have to tell you?"

Meanwhile, high-quality copper, tin, and vanadium ores were assayed in the north at the foot of a great range, fortuitously near a navigable river by which one could be carried down to the great estuary. Tarvi, who was now head of mine engineering on Pern, had inspected the site with that mining team's leader, and they had proposed to the council that a secondary settlement there would be feasible. Ore could be processed in situ and shipped downriver, saving a lot of time, effort, and trouble. The power resources committee agreed that the nearby cataracts would provide ample hydroelectric power. The council proposed to bring the matter up at the next monthly congregation. In the meantime, the geology teams were to continue their explorations of both continents.

Other progress was being made on land and sea. Wheat and barley were thriving; most of the tubers were doing well; and though several species of squash were having trouble, those crops were being sprayed with nutrients. Unfortunately, the roots of cucumbers and all but two of the gourds seemed to be susceptible to a Pernian fungus-worm, and unless the agronomists could combat it with a little cross-parasitism, they might lose the entire family Cucurbitacae. Technology was looking into the problem.

The orchard stock, bar a few samples of each variety, had bloomed and was leafing well. Transplants of two varieties of Pern fruit plants appeared to thrive near Earth types, and technology was hoping for some symbiosis. Two Pernian food plants showed evidence of being attacked by a human-brought virus, but it was too early to tell if it would prove symbiotic or harmful. Land suitable for rice cultivation still had not been found, but the colony cartographer, busy translating probe pictures to survey maps, thought that the southern marshlands might work out.

Joel Lilienkamp, the stores manager, reported no problems and thanked everyone, especially the children, for doing such a grand job of bringing in edible stuffs. The mariners, too, got special thanks for their catches. Some of the indigenous fishlike creatures were very tasty despite their appearance. He once again warned people to be careful of the fins on what they had dubbed "packtails," for they would infect any cuts or scratches. He would gladly supply gloves now that plastics was able to produce a tough, thin film for handwear.

On the zoological front, Pol Nietro and Chuck Havers delivered a cautious report on the success of gestations. Some of each big species were progressing well, but the initial turkey eggs had not survived. Three bitches were expecting imminently, and there were seventeen kittens from four tabbies, though one mother cat had given birth to only one. Six more bitches and the other two female cats would be in heat soon and would shortly be inseminated or receive embryos. It had regretfully been decided not to use the Eridani techniques, especially mentasynth, on the dogs, due to the considerable trouble with such adaptations on Earth. Some of the stock, and indeed many of the human beings, had ancestors who had been so "enhanced," and their descendants still showed signs of extreme empathy, something that dogs apparently could not adapt to.

Geese, ducks, and chickens had no problems, and were laying regularly. They were kept in outdoor runs, too valuable yet to be allowed to range free, and the runs were much visited by both adults and children. It took nearly six weeks for the omnivorous wherries, as the EEC team had named the awkward fliers, to discover that new source of food and for hunger to overcome their cautious, though some termed it cowardly, nature. But when they finally attacked, they attacked with a vengeance.

Fortunately, by that time there were thirty of the little dragonets in Landing. Although smaller than their adversaries, the dragonets were more agile aerial fighters and seemed able somehow to communicate with one another so that as soon as one wherry had been driven off, one dragonet, usually a big bronze, would keep pace with it to be sure it left the area, while the other dragonets would go to assist their fellows in fending off the next attacker.

Watching from the crowd of onlookers, Sorka noticed something very odd in the dragonets' staunch defense: her Duke had appeared to attack one very aggressive wherry with what looked suspiciously like a little flame. Certainly there was smoke puffing up above the combatants, and the wherry broke off its attack and fled. It happened so fast that she was not sure what she had seen, so she did not mention the phenomenon to anyone.

There was always a cloud of smell accompanying wherries, like the sulfurous odor of the river estuary and the mud flats. If the fliers were anywhere upwind their presence was obvious. The dragonets smelled cleanly of sea and salt and sometimes, Sorka noticed when Duke lay curled on her pillow, a little like cinnamon and nutmeg, spices that would soon be memories unless there was more success in the greenhouses.

There was no question in the colonists' minds that the dragonets had preserved the poultry from danger.

"By all that's holy! What warriors they make," Admiral Benden declared respectfully. He and Emily Boll had seen the attack from their vantage point in the met tower and hurried to help conduct the defense.

Though startled and unprepared, the settlers had rushed to the poultry run, grabbing up brooms, rakes, sticks—whatever was near to hand. The firemen, who were well drilled and had already had to control small fires, arrived with firehoses, which held off the few wherries that evaded the little defenders. Adults and kids herded the squawking, frightened poultry back into their hutches. One of the funnier sights, Sorka told Sean afterward, was watching the very dignified scientists trying to catch chicks. Although some people bore scratches from the raking talons of the wherries, there would have been more—and probably serious—casualties if the dragonets had not intervened.

"Too bad they're not bigger," the admiral remarked, "they'd make good

watch animals. Maybe our biogeneticists can create a few flying dogs for us."
He inclined his head respectfully toward Kitti and Wind Blossom Ping. Kitti
Ping gave him a frosty nod. "Not only did those dragonets use their own initiative, but, by all that's holy, I swear they were communicating with each
other. Did you see how they set up a perimeter watch? And how they combined their attacks? Superb tactics. Couldn't have improved on it myself."

Pol Nietro, himself impressed by the incident, was momentarily between
phases of his scheduled projects and not the sort of personality to put leisure
time to leisure use. So, when order had been restored and reliable young
colonists set as sentinels against a repeat of the incursion, he and Boy paid a
visit to Asian Square.

Mairi Hanrahan smiled at his request. "You're in luck, Pol, for she happens to be home. Duke's getting an extra-special meal for his defense of the
poultry yard."

"Ah, he was there, then."

"Sorka would have it that he led the fair of dragonets," Mairi said in a
low voice, her eyes twinkling with maternal pride and tolerance. She ushered
him into their living room, which had been transformed from utilitarian to
homey, with bright curtains at the windows, and pots of flowering plants,
some native and some obviously from Terran seed. Several etchings made the
walls seem less bare, and brightly colored pillows improved the comfort of
the plastic chairs.

"Fair of dragonets? Like a pride of lions? Or a gaggle of geese? Yes, a very
'fair' description," Pol Nietro said, his eyes twinkling at mother and daughter. "Not that you're apt to have that kind of cooperation in the ordinary
'fair.' "

"Pol Nietro, if you're casting aspersions on Donnybrook Fairs . . ." Mairi
began with a grin.

"Cast aspersions, Mairi? Not my way at all." Pol winked at her. "But that
fair of dragonets proved very useful. They did, indeed, seem to work well together to a common goal. Paul Benden noticed this particularly and wants
Kitti and myself to—"

Mairi caught his arm, her expression altered. "You wouldn't—"

"Of course not, my dear." He patted her hand reassuringly. "But I think
Sorka can help us, and Duke, if they're willing. We have already amassed
quite a good deal of information about our small friends. Their potential has
just taken a quantum leap. And our understanding of them! We brought no
creatures with us to ward off such vicious aerial scavengers as the wherries."

Sorka was feeding a nearly sated Duke, who sat upright, tail extended on
the top of the table, the tip twitching with a more decisive movement each

time he daintily secured the morsel Sorka offered him. There was about him an odd, not completely pleasant odor which, out of deference to his heroism, she was trying to ignore.

"Ah, the servant is worthy of his hire," Pol said.

Sorka gave him a long look. "I don't mean to be cheeky, sir, but I don't think of Duke as a servant of any kind. And he certainly proved he was a friend to us!" She waved her hand to indicate the entire settlement.

"He and his . . . cohorts," Pol said tactfully, "most certainly proved their friendship today." He said down beside Sorka, watching the little creature pinch the next piece of food in its claws. Duke regarded the morsel from all sides, sniffed, licked, and finally took a small bite. Pol watched admiringly.

Sorka giggled. "He's stuffed, but he never turns down food." Then she added, "Actually, he's not eating as much as he used to. He's down to one meal a day, so he may be reaching maturity. I've kept notes on his growth, and really, sir, he does seem to be as big as the wild ones."

"Interesting. Do please give me your records, and I shall add them to the file." Pol shifted his body a bit. "Really, you know, this is a fascinating evolution. Especially if those plankton eaters the dolphins report could represent a common ancestor for the tunnel snakes and dragonets."

Mairi was surprised. "Tunnel snakes *and* dragonets?"

"Hmm, yes, for life evolved from the seas here on Pern just as it did on Earth. With variations, of course." Pol settled happily into his lecturing mode with an attentive if incredulous audience. "Yes, an aquatic eellike ancestor, in fact. With six limbs. The first pair—" He pointed at the dragonet still clutching his morsel in his front pincers. "—originally were nets for catching. See the action of the front claw against the stationary back pair. The dragonets dropped the net in favor of three digits. They opted for wings instead of stabilizing middle fins, while the hind pair are for propulsion. The dry-land adaptation, our tunnel snake, was to make the front pair diggers, the middle set remained balancers, especially when they have food in the front pair, and the rear limbs are for steering or holding on. Yes, I'm sure we'll find that the plankton eaters are like the common ancestors of our good friends here." Pol beamed warmly down at Duke, who was deliberating taking a fresh morsel from Sorka. "However . . ." He paused.

Sorka waited politely, knowing that the zoologist had some purpose in his visit.

"Would you happen to know of any undisturbed nests?" he asked finally.

"Yes, sir, but it's not a big clutch, and the eggs are rather smaller than others I've seen."

"Ah, yes, perhaps the eggs of the smaller green female," Pol said, placatingly. "Well, since the green is not as protective of her nest as the gold, she will suffer no great pangs if we borrow a few. But I did want to ask you one other, greater favor. I particularly remember your mentioning seeing the body of a hatchling in the water. Is this a frequent hazard?"

Sorka considered that and replied in the same objective tone of voice. "I think so. Some of the hatchlings just don't make it. Either they can't feed themselves enough to make up for the hatching trauma," she began to explain. She didn't see the slight grin tugging at Pol Nietro's mouth. "Or they are struck down by wherries. You see, just before hatching, the older dragonets bring seaweed to form a ring about the clutch, and offer fish and crawlies and anything else they can find to the hatchlings."

"Hmm, definitely imprinting, then," Pol murmured.

"By the time they've filled their stomachs, their wings have dried, and they can fly off with the rest of the fair. The older dragonets do a first-rate job of keeping off snakes and wherries, to give the babies a chance. One day, though, Sean spotted some eellike thing attacking from the sea during a high tide. The hatchling didn't have a chance."

"Sean is your elusive but oft-mentioned ally?"

"Yes, sir. He and I discovered the first nest together and kept watch on it."

"Would he assist us in finding nests, and . . . the hatchlings?"

Sorka regarded the zoologist for a long moment. He had always kept his word to her, and he had been very good about Duke that first day. She decided that she could trust him, but she was also aware of his high rank in Landing, and what he might be able to do for Sean.

"If you promise, *promise*—and I'd vouch for you, too—that his family gets one of the first horses, he'll do just about anything for you."

"Sorka!" Mairi was embarrassed by her daughter's proposal. The girl spent entirely too much time with that boy and was learning some bad habits from him. But to her amazement, Pol smiled cheerfully and patted Sorka's arm.

"Now, now, Mairi, your daughter has good instincts. Barter is already practiced as an exchange system on Pern, you know." He regarded Sorka with proper solemnity. "He's one of the Connells, is he not?" When she nodded solemnly, he went on briskly. "In point of fact, that is the first name on the list to receive equines. Or oxen, if they prefer."

"Horses. Horses are what they've always had," Sorka eagerly affirmed.

"And when can I have a few words with this young man?"

"Anytime you want, sir. Would this evening do? I know where Sean is likely to be." Out of lifelong habit, she glanced at her mother for consent. Mairi nodded.

◆　◆　◆

On consultation, Sean agreed that there were only green eggs nearby, but suggested that they would do well to look on the beaches a good distance from Landing's well-trampled strands. Sorka had found him on the Head, his two dragonets fishing in the shallows for the finger fish often trapped between tides.

"May we request your services in this venture, Sean Connell?" Pol Nietro asked formally.

Casually, Sean cocked his head and gave the zoologist a long and appraising look. "What's in it for me to go off hunting lizards?"

"Dragonets," Sorka said firmly.

Sean ignored her. "There ain't no money here, and me da needs me in the camp."

Sorka moved restlessly beside Pol, unsure if the scientist would rise to the occasion. But Pol had not been head of a prestigious zoology department in the huge university on First without learning how to deal with touchy, opinionated fellows. The young rascal who eyed him with ancient, inherited skepticism merely presented a slightly different aspect of a well-known problem. To any other young person, the zoologist might have offered the chance to light the evening bonfire, which had become a much-sought-after privilege, but he knew that Sean would not care about that.

"Did you have your own pony on Earth?" Pol asked, settling himself against a rock and folding his short arms across his chest.

Sean nodded, his attention caught by such an unexpected question.

"Tell me about him."

"What's to tell? He's long gone to meat, and even them what ate him is probably worms, too."

"Was he special in some way? Apart from being special to you?"

Sean gave him a long sideways look, then glanced briefly at Sorka, who kept her face expressionless. She was not going to get involved further; she was feeling the slightest twinge of guilt for having given Pol a hint about Sean's deepest desire.

"He was part Welsh mountain, part Connemara. Not many like him left."

"How big?"

"Fourteen hands high," Sean said almost sullenly.

"Color?"

"Steel gray." Sean frowned, growing more suspicious. "Why d'ya wanna know?"

"D'you know what I do on this planet?"

"Cut things up."

"That, too, of course, but I also combine things, among them, traits, color, gender. That is what I and my colleagues generally do. By a judicious manipulation of gene patterns, we can produce what the client—" Pol waved one hand toward Sean. "—wants."

Sean stared at him, not quite understanding the terms used and not daring to hope what Pol Nietro seemed to be suggesting.

"You could have Cricket again, here on Pern," Sorka said softly, her eyes shining. "He can do it, too. Give you a pony just like Cricket."

Sean caught his breath, darting glances from her to the old zoologist who regarded him with great equanimity. Then he jerked his thumb at Sorka. "Is she right?"

"In that I could produce a gray horse—if I may venture to suggest that you're too tall now for a pony—with all the physical characteristics of your Cricket, yes, she's correct. We brought with us sperm as well as fertilized eggs from a wide variety of the Terran equine types. I know we have both Connemara and Welsh genotypes. They're both hardy, versatile breeds. It's a simple matter."

"Just to find lizard eggs?" Sean's suspicious nature overcame his awe.

"Dragonet eggs," Sorka doggedly corrected him. He scowled at her.

"We're trading eggs for eggs, young man. A fair exchange, with a riding horse from your egg in the bargain, altered to your specifications as a gratuity for your time and effort in the search."

Sean glanced once more at Sorka, who nodded reassurance. Then, spitting into the palm of his right hand, he extended it to Pol Nietro. Without hesitation, the zoologist sealed the bargain.

The speed with which Pol Nietro organized an expedition left many of his colleagues as well as the administration staff gasping for breath. By morning, Jim Tillek had agreed that they could use the *Southern Cross* if he captained the crew. He was asked to provision it for a coastal trip of up to a week's length; the Hanrahans and Porrig Connell had given their permission for Sorka and Sean to go; and Pol had persuaded Bay Harkenon to bring along her portable microscope and a quantity of specimen cases, slides, and similar paraphernalia. To Sorka's surprise and Sean's amusement, Admiral Benden was at the jetty to wish them good luck with the venture, and helped the crew cast off the stern lines. With that official blessing, the *Southern Cross* glided out of the bay on a fine brisk breeze.

Landbred Sean was not all that happy about his first sea voyage, but he managed to suppress both fear and nausea, determined to earn his horse and not to show weakness in front of Sorka, who showed every evidence of enjoying the adventure. He spent most of the voyage sitting with his back against the mast, facing forward and stroking his brown dragonets, who liked to sleep stretched out on the sunny deck. Sorka's Duke remained perched on her shoulder, one pincer holding delicately to her ear to balance himself while his tail was lightly but firmly wrapped about her neck. From time to time, she would nuzzle him reassuringly or he would croon some comment in her ear just as if he was certain of her understanding.

The forty-foot sloop, *Southern Cross,* could be sailed with a crew of three, slept eight, and had been designed to serve as an exploratory ship as well as a fast courier. Jim Tillek had already sailed as far west as the river they had christened the "Jordan," and, along with a crew to measure volcanism, as far east as the island volcano whose eruption had interrupted the Thanksgiving feast. He was hoping to get permission to make the longer crossing to the large island off the northern continent, and to explore the delta of the river proposed to carry the ore or finished metals from the projected mining site. He had, he told the enthralled Sorka, sailed all the seas and oceans of Earth during his leaves from captaining a merchantman on the Belt runs, and up as many rivers as were navigable: Nile, Thames, Amazon, Mississippi, St. Lawrence, Columbia, Rhine, Volga, Yangtze, and less well known streams.

"Course, I wasn't doing that as a professional man, and there wasn't much call on a sailor on First yet, so this expedition was my chance to ply my hobby as trade, as 'twere," he confided. "Damned glad I came!" He inhaled deeply. "The air here's fabulous. What we used to have back on Earth. Used to think it was the ozone! Take a deep breath!"

Sorka inhaled happily. Just then Bay Harkenon emerged from the cabin, looking much better than she had when she had hastily descended to be nauseated in private.

"Ah, the pill worked?" Jim Tillek inquired solicitously.

"I cannot thank you enough," the microbiologist said with a tremulous but grateful smile. "I'd no idea I was susceptible to motion sickness."

"Had you ever sailed?"

Bay shook her head, the clusters of gray curls bobbing on her shoulders.

"Then how would you know?" he asked affably. He squinted into the distance, where the peninsula and the mouth of the Jordan River were already visible. Portside, the towering Mount Garben—named after the senator who had done so much to smooth the expedition's way through the intricacies of the Federated Sentient Planets' bureaucracy—dominated the landscape, its cone suitably framed against the bright morning sky. There had been some lobbying to name its three small companions after Shavva, Liu, and Turnien, the original EEC landing party, but no decision had yet been made at the monthly naming sessions held around the evening campfire after the more formal official sittings of the council.

Captain Tillek dropped his gaze to the charts and, using his dividers, measured the distance from the jetty to the river mouth, and again to the land beyond.

"Why do the colors stop here?" Sorka asked, noticing that the bulk of the chart was uncolored.

Grinning in approval, he tapped the chart. "Fremlich did this for me from the probe pics, and they've been accurate to the last centimeter so far, but as we ourselves walk across the land and sail the coast, I color it in appropriately. A good way of knowing where we've been and where we've yet to go. I've also added notations that a sailor might need, about prevalent winds and current speeds."

It was only then that Sorka noticed those additional marks. "It's one thing to see, and another to know, isn't it?"

He tweaked one of her titian braids. "Indeed, it is being there that matters."

"And we'll really be the first people—here?" She laid the tip of her forefinger on the peninsula.

"Indeed we shall," Tillek said with heartfelt satisfaction.

Jim Tillek had never been so contented and happy before in a life that had already spanned six decades. A misfit in a high-tech society because of his love of seas and ships, bored by the monotonous Belt runs to which his lack of tact or incorruptible honesty restricted him, Tillek found Pern perfect, and now he had the added fillip of being one of the first to sail its seas and discover their eccentricities. A strongly built man of medium height, with pale blue, far-seeing eyes, he looked his part, complete with visored cap pulled down about his ears and an old guernsey wool sweater against the slight coolness of the fresh morning breeze. Though the *Southern Cross* could have been sailed electronically from the cockpit with the touch of buttons, he preferred to steer by the rudder and use his instinct for the wind to trim the sheets. His crew were forward, making all lines fair on the plasiplex decks and going about the routine of the little ship.

"We'll put in at dusk, probably about here, where the chart tells me there's a deep harbor in a cove. More color to be added. We might even find what we're looking for there, too." He winked at Sorka and Bay Harkenon.

When the *Southern Cross* was anchored in six fathoms, Jim took the shore party to the beach in the little motorboat. Sean, who had had quite enough company for a while, told Sorka to search for dragonet nests to the east while he went west along the beach. His two browns circled above his head, calling happily as they flew. Galled at the way Sean ordered the girl about, Jim Tillek was about to take the lad to task, but Pol Nietro sent him a warning look and the captain subsided. Sean was already ducking into the thick vegetation bordering the strand.

"We'll have a hot meal for you when you return," Pol called after the two youngsters. Sorka paused to wave acknowledgment.

When they returned at dusk for the promised food, both children reported success.

"I think the first three I found are only greens," Sorka said with quiet authority. "They're much too close to the water for a gold. Duke thinks so, too. He doesn't seem to like greens. But the one we found farthest away is well above high-tide marks, and the eggs are bigger. I think they're hard enough to hatch soon."

"Two green clutches and two I'm positive are gold," Sean said briskly, and began to eat, pausing only to offer his two browns their share of his meal. "There's a lot of 'em about, too. Are you going to take back all you can find?"

"Heavens, no!" Pol exclaimed, throwing both hands up in dismay. His white hair, wiry and thick, stood out about his head like a nimbus, giving him a benign appearance that matched his personality. "We won't make *that* mistake on Pern."

"Oh, no, never," Bay Harkenon said, leaning toward Sean as if to touch him in reassurance. "Our investigative techniques no longer require endless specimens to confirm conclusions, you know."

"Specimens?" Sean frowned, and Sorka looked apprehensive.

"Representative would perhaps be the better word."

"And we'd use the eggs . . . of the green, of course," Pol added quickly, "since the female greens do not appear to be as maternally inclined as the gold."

Sean was confused. "You don't want a gold's eggs at all?"

"Not all of them," Bay repeated earnestly. "And only a dead hatchling of the other colors if one can be obtained. We've had more than enough green casualties."

"Dead is the only way you'd get one," Sean muttered.

"You're likely correct," Bay said with a little sigh. She was a portly woman in her late fifth decade but fit and agile enough not to hinder the expedition. "I've never been able to establish a rapport with animals." She looked wistfully at Sorka's bronze lying in the total relaxation of sleep around the girl's neck, legs dangling down her chest, the limp tail extending almost to her waist.

"A dragonet's so hungry when it's born, it'll take food anywhere it can," Sean said with marked tactlessness.

"Oh, I don't think I could deprive someone of—"

"We're all supposed to be equal here, aren't we?" Sean demanded. "You got the same rights as anyone else, y'know."

"Well said, young nipper," Jim Tillek said. "Well said!"

"If the dragonets were only a little bigger," Pol murmured, as much to himself as to the others, and then he sighed.

"If dragonets were only a little bigger what?" Tillek asked.

"Then they'd be an equal match for the wherries."

"They already are!" Sean said loyally, stroking one of his browns. If he had named them, he kept their names to himself. He had trained them to answer his various whistled commands. Sorka felt too shy to ask him how he had done it. Not that Duke ever disobeyed her—once he figured out what she wanted.

"Perhaps you're right," Pol said, giving his head a little shake.

"Tinkering isn't something lightly undertaken. You know how many efforts abort or distort." Bay smiled to ease her gentle chiding.

"Tinker?" Sean came alert.

"They didn't mean you, silly," Sorka assured him in a low voice.

"Why would you want to . . . ahem . . . manipulate," Jim Tillek asked, "critters that have been doing quite well in protecting themselves for centuries? And us."

"Out of the stew of creation so few survive, and often not the obvious, more perfectly designed or environmentally suited species," Pol said with a long patient sigh. "It is always amazing to me what does win the evolutionary race to become the common ancestors of a great new group. I'd never have expected anything as close to our vertebrates as wherries and dragonets on another planet. The really strange coincidence is that our storytellers so often invested a four-legged, two-winged creature in fantasy, although none ever existed on Earth. Here they are, hundreds of light-years away from the people who only imagined them." He indicated the sleeping Duke. "Remarkable. And not as badly designed as the ancient Chinese dragons."

"Badly designed?" the seaman asked, amused.

"Well, look at him. It's redundant to have both forelimbs and wings. Earth avian species opted for wings instead of forelimbs, though some have vestigial claws of what had once been the forefinger before the limb became a wing. I'll grant you that a curved rear limb is useful for springing off the ground—and the dragonet's are powerful, with muscles into the back to provide assistance—but that long back is vulnerable. I wonder how they arrange their mechanics so that they can sit up for so long without moving." Pol peered at the sleeping Duke and touched the limp tail. "There is one slight improvement: the excretory hole in the fork of the tail instead of under it. And there are dorsal nostrils and lungs, which are a distinct improvement. Humans are very poorly designed, you know," he went on, happy to be able to exercise his favorite complaint to a rapt audience.

"I mean, surely you can see how ridiculous it is to have an air pipe—" He touched his nose. "—that crosses the food pipe." He touched his rather prominent Adam's apple. "People are always choking themselves to death. And a vulnerable cranium: one good crack, and the concussion can cause impairment if not fatality. Those Vegans have their brains well protected in tough internal sacs. You'd never concuss a Vegan."

"I'd rather have bellyaches in my middle than headaches," Tillek said in a droll tone. "Though, from what I saw once, some of the other Vegan operating mechanisms are exceedingly unhandy, particularly the sexual and reproductive arrangements."

Pol snorted. "So you think having the playground between the sewers makes more sense?"

"Didn't say that, Pol," Jim Tillek answered hurriedly with a glance at the two children, though neither were paying the adults much heed. "It's a bit handier for us, though."

"And more vulnerable. Oh my, oh my, there I go again, falling into the lecture attitude. But there are endless ways in which we humans could be profitably improved . . ."

"We are doing that, though, aren't we, Pol, dear?" Bay said kindly.

"Oh, yes, cybernetically we do, and *in vitro* we can correct certain gross genetic mistakes. It's true that we are allowed to use the Eridani mentasynth, though personally I don't know whether our response to it is a boon or not. It makes people too empathic with their experimental animals. But we can't do much yet, of course, with the laws that the Pure Humans forced through to prohibit drastic changes."

"Who'd want to?" Tillek asked with a frown.

"Not us," Bay assured him hastily. "We don't have that kind of need on this world. But I sometimes feel that the Pure Human Life Group was wrong to oppose alterations that would permit humans to use those water worlds in Ceti IV. Lungs exchanged for gills and webbing on hands and feet is not that great or blasphemous an adaptation. The fetus still goes through a similar stage *in utero*, and there's good evidence for a more aquatic past for adults. Think how many planets would be open to humans if we weren't so limited to land areas that met our gravitational and atmospheric requirements! Even if we could provide special enzymes for some of the dangerous gases. Cyanides have kept us out of so many places. Why . . ." She threw up her hands as words failed her.

Sean was peering at the two specialists with some suspicion.

"Campfire talk," Sorka told him sagely. "They don't mean it."

Sean snorted and, carefully positioning his two brown dragonets, rose to

his feet. "I plan to be up tomorrow before dawn. Best time to catch the dragonets feeding and know who's minding the nests."

"Me, too," Sorka said, standing.

Tillek had rigged shelters well above the high-tide marks, protection
against the sudden squalls that seemed characteristic of the early summer season. Thermal blankets had been stitched into sleeping bags, and Sorka gratefully crawled into one. Duke, without apparently waking, accommodated
himself to her new position. She had a little trouble falling asleep because,
for a while, the beach seemed to heave beneath her, mimicking the motions
of the waves.

A little warning chirp from Duke roused her. Snores drifted over from
the adults, but as her eyes grew accustomed to the predawn darkness, she saw
Sean rising. She could just see him turn his head toward her and then westward. With an economy of movement he crept to the ashes of the previous
night's fire and rummaged quietly in the supply sacks, taking several items
which he stuffed into his shirt.

Sorka waited until he was out of sight and then she rose. Then, after taking a pack of rations and one of the red fruits they had gathered before dinner, she left a note telling the adults that she and Sean had gone to check
nests and would be back soon after dawn to report.

As she trotted along the beach, she ate the red fruit, discarding the blem-
ished side where a mold had gotten at it, just as she had once eaten windfall
apples and thrown away the brown bits back on Earth. At a little distance from
each of the nests, she had piled small cairns of white, ocean-smoothed stones
so that she could find each clutch without stepping into it. She found the first
two with no problem and hurried toward the third, the one she thought might
be a gold's nest. There was a faint trace of brightness in the eastern sky, and she
wanted to be hidden in the bushes before day actually broke.

It was wonderful to be alone, and safe, in a part of a world that had never
felt the tread of feet. Sorka had studied the EEC survey reports and maps
often enough to know that those intrepid people had not been on that particular beach. She exulted in the special magic of being first and sighed at being so privileged. Her earlier desire to be able to tag a special place with *her*
name had altered to a dream of finding the most beautiful spot on the new
world, a really unique place for which she, too, could be remembered. Better
still would be for the colonists to wish to name a mountain or a river or a valley after Sorka Hanrahan because of something special that she had done.

She was so lost in that dream that she nearly stumbled over the cairn and
into the half-buried clutch. Duke saved her from the error with a warning
cheep.

She stroked his little head in gratitude. If she could alter one thing about Duke, it would be to give him speech. She had learned to interpret his various noises accurately and was able to understand what other dragonets said to their owners, but she wished she could communicate with Duke in a common language. But someone had said that forked tongues could not manage speech, and she certainly did not want any drastic changes in Duke—especially not in his size. Any bigger and he would not fit on her shoulder so comfortably.

Maybe she should have a chat with the marine rangers who worked with the dolphins. They communicated with one another about complex matters. It was just as likely that the dragonets did, too, judging by the way they had routed the wherries. Even Admiral Benden had commented on it.

Thinking of the hero of Cygnus, she decided that she, too, must use careful strategy and hide her tracks. The gold dragonets were a lot smarter than the stupid green ones. She found a thickly fronded branch from the underbrush and covered her footprints in the dry sand, retreating into the brush before making her way back to a good vantage point close to but obscured from the beach and the nest.

Dawn coincided with a cheerful morning chorus as a fair of dragonets swooped down to the foreshore. Only the gold approached the nest; the others, brown and bronze and blue, remained a discreet distance from it. Watching their bodies outlined against the white sands, Sorka could appreciate the difference in their sizes. The golden female was the largest, taller in the shoulder by the span of two fingers than the bronzes, who seemed to be the next in size, though one or two of the browns were nearly as big. The blues were definitely smaller, moving with quick nervous steps, examining seaweeds, discarding some and hauling others toward the nest with many smug chirps. The bronzes and browns seemed to be discussing something, murmuring and cheeping to themselves while the blues were clearly interested only in what might be edible. Or were they? The nest was being surrounded by a circle of weed. When it was completed, the browns and bronzes got busy, depositing the scuttling sea things she had seen at Duke's hatching.

With an almost peremptory screech, the gold female rose from the nest, swooping down over the heads of the bronzes and browns and dipping wings at the blues as she raced toward the sea. The others followed, not as gracefully, Sorka thought, but swiftly. She saw them climb over the gently lapping surf and then suddenly dive at the waves, chirping triumphantly as they fished. Then, abruptly, they all disappeared. One moment they were there, suspended above the ocean; the next moment the sky was completely clear of flashing dragonet bodies. Sorka blinked in astonishment.

Then she had an idea: If the eggs were that close to hatching, and if she could get one back to Bay Harkenon in time for her to feed it, Bay would finally have a creature of her own. The scientist was a nice, kind lady, not the least bit stuffy like some of the section heads were, and a dragonet would be a companion to her.

Sorka didn't think about it any further; she acted. Darting out of her hiding place, she streaked to the nest, made a grab for the nearest egg on the top of the pile, and scurried as fast as she could back to the underbrush.

She was only just in time, the branches still swaying from her swift passage, when the dragonets were back again, in what seemed to be greater numbers than before. The little golden one landed right by the eggs while bronzes, browns, and blues were depositing helplessly flapping fish within the seaweed circle. Suddenly the welcoming chorus began, and Sorka was torn between the desire to watch the magical moment of hatching and the need to get her purloined egg to Bay in time. Then she felt the egg, which she had tucked under her pullover for warmth and protection, move against her skin.

"Don't you dare make a sound, Duke!" she whispered harshly when she heard Duke's chest begin to rumble. She caught his little jaw between her fingers and glared straight into his faceted eyes, which had begun to whirl with happy colors. "She'll kill me!"

He clearly understood her warning and hunched closer to her, clinging with sharp nails to her hair and hiding his face against her braid. Then she crawled backward from the beach edge until she was screened sufficiently to risk standing up. Dead fronds and branches tangled her feet as she ran, and she encountered a disheartening variety of thorny bushes and needly plants. But she plunged on.

When she could no longer hear the cries of the dragonets, she turned west and crashed back out to the beach. She pelted down the sands as fast as she could, ignoring the stitch in her side in deference to the antics of the egg beating at her ribs. Duke circled about her head, keening with obediently muted anxiety.

Surely she must be almost back at the camp. Was that the first cairn she had passed, or the second? She stumbled, and Duke cried out in terrible alarm, a shrill strident shriek like the cries of the peacocks that had inhabited her father's farm, a ghastly sound like someone in extreme agony. He swooped, tugging valiantly at her shoulder, as if he himself could support her.

His shriek had been sufficient to rouse the sleepers. Jim Tillek was the first one to struggle to his feet, which got tangled in the bag for the first few steps. Pol and Bay were more laggard until they recognized Sorka.

Sorka, ignoring both Tillek's urgent queries and helping hands, staggered to the plump microbiologist, dropping heavily to her knees and fumbling to get the egg into Bay's hands for she could feel a crack beginning to run along the shell.

"Here! Here, this is yours, Bay!" she gasped, grabbing the astonished woman's hands and closing them about the egg.

Bay's reaction was to thrust it back to Sorka, but the girl had thrown herself toward the supply packs, rummaging for something edible, fumbling to open a packet of protein bars and break one into tiny pieces.

"It's cracking, Sorka. Pol! What do I do with it? It's cracking all over!" Bay exclaimed uncertainly.

"It's yours, Bay, an animal that will love only you," Sorka said in gasps, floundering back with full hands. "It's hatching. It'll be yours. Here, feed it these. Pol, Captain, see what you can find under the seaweed for it to eat. You be bronzes. See, watch what Duke's going after."

Duke, chirping with exultation, was dragging a huge branch of seaweed up from the high-tide line.

"Just bundle the seaweed up, Pol," Tillek said moments later as he demonstrated.

"It's cracked!" Bay cried, half-afraid, half-delighted. "There's a head! Sorka! What do I do now?"

Twenty minutes later the risen sun shone on a weary but excited quartet as Bay, with the most beatific and incredulous expression on her face, cradled a lovely golden dragonet on her forearm. Its head was an ornament on the back of her hand, its forearms loosely encircled her wrist. Its distended belly had support from Bay's well-fleshed limb, its hind legs dangled by her elbow, and its tail was lightly twined around her upper arm. A slight noise, similar to a snore, could be discerned. Bay stroked the sleeping creature from time to time, amazed by the texture of its skin, by the strong but delicate claws, the translucent wings, and the strength of the newborn's tail about her arm. She constantly extolled its perfections.

Jim Tillek regenerated the fire and served a hot drink to counteract the chilly breeze from the sea.

"I think we should go back to the nest, Pol," Sorka said, "to see if . . . if . . ."

"Some didn't make it?" Jim finished for her. "You need to eat."

"But then it'll be too late."

"It's probably too late already, young lady," Tillek said firmly. "And you've acquitted yourself superbly anyhow, delivering the gold. That's the highest status of the species, isn't it?"

Pol nodded, peering detachedly at Bay's sleeping charge. "I don't think any other biologist actually has one yet. Ironic that."

"Always the last to know, huh?" Jim asked, screwing his eyebrows sardonically but grinning. "Ah, what have we here?" He pointed his long cooking fork at the figure plodding from the west. "He's got something. Can you make it out better, Sorka, with your young eyes?"

"Maybe he's got more eggs and you'll have one, too, Pol and Jim."

"I tend to doubt Sean's altruism, Sorka," Pol remarked dryly. She flushed. "Now, now, child. I'm not being critical. It's a difference of temperament and attitude."

"He's carrying something, and it's larger than an egg, and his two dragonets are very excited. No," Sorka amended. "They're upset!"

On her shoulder, Duke raised up on to his hind legs, uttering one shrill query. She could feel him sag as he received an answer, and he gave a little moan, almost a sob, she thought. She reached up to stroke him. He nuzzled her hand as if he appreciated her sympathy. She could feel the tension in his small frame, and in the way his feet gripped her pullover. Once again she was glad that her mother had reinforced the fabric to prevent his claws from puncturing through to her skin. She turned her head, rubbing his side with her cheek.

Everyone watched as Sean made his way toward the camp. Soon his bundle could be distinguished as layers of wide leaves, closely wrapped and bound with green climber vine. He was aware of their scrutiny and he looked tired. Sorka thought he also looked unhappy. He came right up to the two scientists and carefully deposited his bundle by Pol.

"There you are. Two of 'em. One barely touched. And some of the green eggs. Had to search both nests to find some that snakes hadn't sucked dry."

Pol laid one hand on Sean's offering. "Thank you, Sean. Thank you very much. Are the two . . . from a gold's clutch or a green's?"

"Gold's, of course," Sean said with a disgusted snort. "Greens rarely hatch. They're snake-eaten. I got there just in time." He looked almost challengingly at Sorka.

She did not know what to say.

"So did Sorka," Jim Tillek replied proudly, nodding to Bay.

Only then did Sean see the sleeping dragonet. A fleeting look of surprise, admiration, and annoyance crossed his face, and he sat down with a thump.

Sorka did not quite meet his eyes. "I didn't do as well," she heard herself saying. "I didn't get what we were sent after. You did."

Sean grunted, his face expressionless. Above his head, his browns exchanged news with her bronze in a rapid fire of cheeps, chirps, and murmurs. Then each gave a flip to its wings to close them back and settled in the sun to catch the warming rays.

"Chow's up," Jim Tillek said. He began filling plates with fried fish and rings of one of the fruit nuts that was improved by cooking.

CHAPTER
VII

"Go, Ongola, what have you to report?" Paul Benden asked.

Emily Boll poured a measure of Benden's precious brandy into three glasses and passed them around before taking her own seat. Ongola used the interval to organize his thoughts. The three had gathered, as they often did, in the meteorology tower beside the landing grid now used by the sleds and the one shuttle that had been altered for sparing use as a cargo carrier.

Both admiral and governor, naturally pale of skin, had become almost as brown as the swarthy Ongola. All three had worked hard in the fields, in the mountains, and on the sea, actively participating in every aspect of the colony's endeavors.

Once the colonists took up their stake acres and Landing's purpose had been accomplished, the ostensible leaders would turn consultants, with no more authority than other stakeholders. The council would convene regularly to discuss broad topics and redress problems that affected the entire colony. A yearly democratic meeting would vote on any issues that required the consent of all. Magistrate Cherry Duff administered justice at Landing and would have a circuit for grievances and any litigation. By the terms of the Pern Charter, charterers and contractors alike would be autonomous on their stake acres. The plan was idealistic, perhaps, but as Benden repeatedly insisted, there was more than enough land and resources to allow everyone plenty of latitude.

There had been no more than a few grumbles so far about Joel Lilienkamp's disposition of supplies and matériel from their stores. Everyone knew that once the imported supplies were exhausted, all would have to learn to make do with what they had, to replace with their own industry, or to barter with the appropriate crafters. Many people prided themselves on being able to improvise, and everyone took good care of irreplaceable tools and equipment.

Between the weekly informal gatherings and the monthly mass meeting where most administrative matters were put to a democratic vote, the colony was running smoothly. An arbitration board had been voted on at one of the first mass meetings, comprising three ex-judges, two former governors, and four nonlegal people who would hold their offices for two years. The board would look into grievances and settle such disputes as might occur about staking acres or contractual misunderstandings. The colony had four trained legists and two attorneys, but it was hoped that the need for such representations would be minimal.

"There is no dispute so bitter that it cannot be arbitrated by an impartial board or by a jury of peers," Emily Boll had stated fervently and persuasively at one of the earliest mass meetings attended by everyone, including sleeping babies in their cradles. "Most of you know war firsthand." She had paused dramatically. "Wars of attrition over land and water, wars of terrible annihilation in space itself. Pern is now far, far from those former battlefields. You are here because you wished to avoid the contagion of territorial imperatives that has plagued humans since time began. Where there is a whole planet, with diverse and magnificent lands and wealth and prospects, there is no longer a need to covet a neighbor's possessions. Stake your own acres, build your homes, live in peace with the rest of us, and help us all build a world truly a paradise."

The power of her ringing voice and the sincerity of her fervent phrases had, on that glorious evening, motivated everyone to fulfill that dream. Also a realist, Emily Boll knew very well that there were dissident factors among those who had listened so politely before giving her a cheering ovation. Avril, Lemos, Nabol, Kimmer, and a handful of others had already been tagged as possible troublemakers. But Emily devoutly hoped that the dissidents would become so involved in their new lives on Pern that they would have little time, energy, or occasion to indulge in intrigue.

The charter and the contracts had incorporated the right to discipline the signatories for "acts against the common good." Such acts had as yet to be defined.

Emily and Paul had argued about the necessity for any sort of penal code. Paul Benden favored the "punishment fitting the crime" as an object lesson for miscreants and frequent breakers of the "peace and tranquility of the settlement." He also preferred to mete out community discipline on the spot, shaming offenders in public and requiring them to do some of the more disagreeable tasks necessary to the running of the colony. So far that rough justice had been sufficient.

Meanwhile, the discreet surveillance continued on a number of folk, and Paul and Emily met with Ongola from time to time to discuss the general morale of the community and those problems that were best kept discreet. Paul and Emily also made sure to be constantly accessible to all the colonists, hoping to solve small discontents before they could grow into serious problems. They kept official "office hours" six days of the established seven-day week.

"We may not be religious in the archaic meaning of the word, but it makes good sense to give worker and beast one day's rest," Emily stated in the second of the mass meetings. "The old Judean Bible used by some of the old religious sects on Earth contained a great many commonsensible suggestions for an agricultural society, and some moral and ethical traditions which are worthy of retention"—she held up a hand, smiling benignly—"but without any hint of fanatic adherence! We left *that* back on Earth along with war!"

While the two leaders knew that even that loose form of democratic government might be untenable once the settlers had spread out from Landing to their own acres, they did hope that the habits acquired would suffice. Early American pioneers on that western push had exhibited a keen sense of independence and mutual assistance. The later Australian and New Zealand communities had risen above tyrannical governors and isolation to build people of character, resource, and incredible adaptability. The first international Moonbase had refined the art of independence, cooperation, and resourcefulness. The original settlers on First had been largely the progeny of indigenous Moon and asteroid-belt miner parents, and the Pern colony included many descendants of those original pioneering groups.

Paul and Emily proposed to institute yearly congregations of as many people from the isolated settlements as possible to reaffirm the basic tenets of the colony, acknowledge progress, and apply the minds of many to address any general problems. Such a gathering would also be the occasion for trading and social festivities. Cabot Francis Carter, one of the legists, had proposed setting aside a certain area, midway on the continent, that would be the center for these annual assemblies.

"That would be the best of all possible worlds," Cabot had said in a mellifluous bass voice that had often stirred Supreme Courts on Earth and First. Emily had once told Paul that Cabot was the most unlikely of their charter members, but it was his legal guild that had produced the actual charter and rammed it through the bureaucracy to be ratified by the FSP council. "We may not achieve it on Pern. But we can damn sure try!"

Alone with Emily and Ongola, Paul recalled that stirring challenge as he ticked off names on his long callused fingers. "Which is why I think we should continue to keep tabs on people like Bitra, Tashkovich, Nabol, Lemos, Olubushtu, Kung, Usuai, and Kimmer. The list is, mercifully, short, considering our numbers. I'm not adding Kenjo, because he's shown absolutely no connection with any of the others."

"I still don't like it. Secret surveillance smacks too much of the subterfuges used by other governments in more parlous times," Emily said grimly. "It feels demeaning to myself and to my office to use such tactics."

"There's nothing demeaning in knowing who's agin you," Paul argued. "An intelligence section has always proved invaluable."

"In revolutions, wars, power struggles, yes, but not here on Pern."

"Here as well as everywhere else in the galaxy, Em," Paul replied forcefully. "Mankind, not to mention Nathi, and even the Eridanites to some degree, prove in many ways that greed is universal. I don't see the bounty of Pern changing that trait."

"Forgo that futile old argument, my friends," Ongola said with one of his wise, sad smiles. "The necessary steps have already been taken to defunction the gig. I have, as you recommended—" He inclined his head to Paul. "—stripped the gig of several minor but essential parts in the ignition system, the effect of which would be obvious early on, and substituted two dud chips in the guidance module, something that would not be so obvious." He gestured out the window. "Sleds are allowed to park any which way, effectively but surreptitiously blocking the gig from taking off. But I don't really know why she would."

Paul Benden winced, and the other two looked away from him, knowing that he had allowed himself to be too intimate with her for an injudicious length of that outward voyage.

"Well, I'd be more worried if Avril knew about that cache of Kenjo's," Paul said. "Telgar's figures indicate that there's half a tank's worth for the *Mariposa*." He grimaced. He had found it hard enough to believe that Kenjo Fusaiyuko had scrounged so much fuel. Paul had a grudging admiration for the sheer scope of the theft, even if he could not understand the motive, and especially for the risks that Kenjo had gotten away with during all those fuel-saving shuttle trips.

"Avril favors us so seldom with her company that I don't worry that she'd discover the hoard," Emily said with a wry smile. "I've also managed to have Lemos, Kimmer, and Nabol assigned to different sections, with few occasions to return here. 'Divide and conquer,' the man said."

"Inappropriate, Emily," Paul replied, grinning.

"If, and I do stress that improbability, Avril should discover and use

Kenjo's purloined fuel," Ongola began, holding up a finger for each point, "manage to find the missing pieces, and fly the gig out of here undetected, she would have a half-full tank. She would not then drain the ships' reserves to a danger point. Frankly, we would be well rid of her and whoever she deigns to take with her. I think we dwell too much on the matter. Those seismic reports from the eastern archipelago are far more worrying. Young Mountain is smoking again and twitching its feet."

"I agree," Paul said, quite willing to turn to the more immediate problem.

"Yes, but for what purpose did Kenjo take so much fuel?" Emily asked. "You haven't answered that question. Why would he risk the safety of passengers and cargo? And he is a genuinely eager colonist! He's already chosen his stake acreage."

"A pilot of Kenjo's ability risked nothing," Paul replied smoothly. "His shuttle flights were without incident. I do know that flying is his life."

Ongola regarded the admiral in mild surprise. "Hasn't he done enough flying for one lifetime?"

Paul smiled with understanding. "Not Kenjo. What I do completely appreciate is that flying a mere power sled is a come-down, a loss of prestige, face, considering the kind of craft he's flown and where he's been. You say that he's chosen his acres, Emily? Where?"

"Down beyond what people are beginning to call the Sea of Azov, as far away from Landing as he can get but on rather a pleasant plateau, to judge by the probe report," Emily replied. She hoped that the meeting would conclude soon. Pierre had promised her a special meal, and she found that she was enjoying those quiet dinners far more than she had thought she would.

"How in hell is Kenjo going to get those tons of fuel there?" Benden asked.

"I suspect we'll have to wait and see," Ongola replied with the trace of a smile on his lips. "He's got the same right as everyone else to use power sleds to transport his goods, and he's done some close trading with work units at the commissary. Shall I have a word with Joel about Kenjo's requisitions?"

Emily glanced quickly at Paul, who was adamant in his defense of Kenjo. "Well, I don't like unsolved riddles. I'd prefer some sort of explanation, and I think you would, too, Paul." When Benden nodded reluctantly, Emily said that she would speak to Joel Lilienkamp.

"Which brings us back to that third tremor," Paul Benden said. "How's work progressing on buttressing the stores warehouses and the one with all the medical supplies? We can't afford to lose such irreplaceable items."

Ongola consulted his notes. He wrote with a bold angular script that looked, from Emily's angle, like ancient manuscript ornamentations. All three of them, as well as most section heads, had made a point of reverting to less sophisticated methods of note-taking than speech processors. The power packs, whose rechargeability was good but not infinite, were to be reserved for essential uses, so everyone was rediscovering the art of calligraphy.

"The work will be completed by next week. The seismic net has been extended as far as the active volcano in the eastern archipelago and to Drake's Lake."

Paul grimaced. "Are we going to let him get away with that?"

"Why not?" Emily asked, grinning. "No one's contesting it. Drake was the first to see it. A community settling there would have ample space to grow, and plenty of industry to support it."

"Is it scheduled for a vote?" Paul asked after an appreciative sip of his brandy.

"No," Ongola said with another hint of a grin. "Drake is still campaigning. He doesn't want any opposition, and whatever there might have been is now worn down."

Paul snorted, and Emily cast her eyes upward in amused exasperation with the flamboyant pilot. Then Paul pensively regarded the remainder of the brandy in his glass. As Emily went on to the next point on their informal agenda, he took another sip, rolling the liquor around in his mouth, savoring the soon-to-be-exhausted beverage. He could and did drink the quikal but found it harsh to a palate trained to subtleties.

"We are proceeding well in general terms," Emily was saying briskly. "You heard that one of the dolphins died, but Olga's death was accepted by her community with considerable equanimity. According to Ann Gabri and Efram, they had expected more fatalities. Olga was, apparently," she added with a grin, "older than she said she was and hadn't wished to let her last calf go into the unknown without her."

All three chuckled and followed Paul's lead as he raised a toast to maternal love.

"Even our . . . nomads . . . have settled in," Emily went on, after checking her notepad. "Or, rather, spread out." She tapped it with her pencil, still unused to handwriting notes but struggling to get accustomed to archaic memory assists. The only voice-activated device still operable was the surface interface with the main computer banks on the *Yokohama*, but it was rarely used anymore. "The nomads've made rather a lot of inroads on clothing fabrics, but when those are depleted, that's the end of it and they'll have to make their own or trade, the same as the rest of us. We have located all the campsites. Even on foot, the Tuareg contingent can travel astonishing distances, but they camp for a while, in two separate sections."

"Well, they've a whole planet to lose themselves in," Paul said expansively. "Have they posed any other problems, Ongola?"

The dark man shook his heavy head, lowering the lids of his deep-set eyes. He was agreeably surprised by the nomads' smooth transition to life on Pern. Every week each tribe sent a representative to the veterinary sheds. The forty-two mares brought in coldsleep by the colony were all in foal, and the nomads' leaders had accepted the fact that a mare's gestation period was eleven months on Pern as it had been on Earth.

"As long as the vets keep their sense of humor. But Red Hanrahan seems to understand their ways and deals with them."

"Hanrahan? Didn't his daughter find the dragonets?"

"She and a boy, one of the travelers," Ongola replied. "They also provided the corpses which the bios have been clucking over."

"Could be useful creatures," Benden said.

"They already are," Emily added stoutly.

Ongola smiled. One day, Ongola thought, he would find a nest at the critical hatching point and he would have one of those charming, friendly, nearly intelligent creatures as a pet. He had once learned Dolphin, but he had never been able to overcome his fear of being constricted underwater to share their world properly. He needed space about him. Once, when Paul was sharing one of the long watches with him on the journey to Pern, the admiral had argued most eloquently that the dangers of outer space were even more inimical to human life than those of inner sea.

"Water is airless," Paul had said, "although it contains oxygen, but when and if the Pure Lives' hold on human adaptations is broken, humans will be able to swim without artificial help. Space has no oxygen at all."

"But you are weightless in space. Water presses down on you. You feel it."

"You'd better not feel space," Paul had replied with a laugh, but he had not argued the point further.

"Now, to more pleasant matters," Paul said. "How many contract marriages are to be registered tomorrow, Emily?"

Emily smiled, riffling pages of her notepad to come to the next seventh-day sheet, since that had become the usual time for such celebrations. In order to widen the gene pool in the next generation, the charter permitted unions of varying lengths, first insuring the support of a gravid woman and the early years of the resultant child. Prospective partners could choose which conditions suited their requirements, but there were severe penalties, up to the loss of all stake acres, for failing to fulfill whatever contract had been agreed and signed before the requisite number of witnesses.

"Three!"

"The numbers are falling off," Paul remarked.

"I've done my bit," Ongola said, slyly glancing at the two staunchly single leaders.

Ongola had courted Sabra Stein so adroitly that neither of his close friends had realized he had become attached until the couple's names had appeared on the marital schedule six weeks earlier. In fact, Sabra was already pregnant, which had led Paul to remark that the big gun was not firing blanks. He had let his bawdy humor disguise his relief, for he knew that Ongola still grieved for the wife and family of his youth. Ongola's hatred of the Nathi and his implacable desire for revenge had sustained the man throughout the war. For a long while, Paul had worried that his favorite aide and valued commander might be unable to alter that overpowering hatred even in a more peaceful clime.

"Emily, has Pierre consented yet?" Ongola asked, a knowing grin lighting a somber face that even his present felicitous state did not completely brighten.

Emily was astonished. She had thought that she and Pierre had been discreet. But she had recently noticed in herself a tendency to smile more easily and to lose the thread of conversations for no apparent reason.

She and Pierre were an unlikely combination of personalities, but that was half the pleasure of it. Their relationship had begun quite unexpectedly about the fifth week after Landing, when Pierre had asked her opinion of a casserole composed entirely of indigenous ingredients. He administered the mass catering of Landing, and very well, she thought, considering the wide range of tastes and dietary requirements. He had started to serve her special dishes when she ate at the big mess hall. Then, when she would often have to work through the lunch hour, Pierre de Courci would bring over the tray she ordered.

"If I were the possessive type, I would keep his cooking to myself," she replied. "Kindly remember that I am past childbearing, an advantage you men have over me. How about it, Paul? Will you do your bit?" Emily knew that her tone had a snap to it, born of envy. None of her children, all adults, had wished to accompany her on a one-way journey.

Unperturbed, Paul Benden merely smiled enigmatically and sipped at his brandy.

◆ ◆ ◆

"Caves!" Sallah cried, nudging Tarvi's arm and pointing to the rock barrier in front of them. Sunlight outlined openings in its sheer face.

He reacted instantly and enthusiastically, with the kind of almost innocent joy of discovery that Sallah found so appealing in him. The continually unfolding beauties of Pern had not palled on Tarvi Andiyar. Each new wonder was greeted with as much interest as the last one he had extolled for its magnificence, its wealth, or its potential. She had wangled ruthlessly to get herself assigned as his expedition pilot. They were making their third trip together—and their first solo excursion.

Sallah was playing it cautiously, concentrating on making herself so professionally indispensible to Tarvi that an opportunity to project her femininity would not force him to retreat into his usual utterly courteous, utterly impersonal shell. She had seen other women who made a determined play for the handsome, charming geologist rebuffed by his demeanor; they were surprised, puzzled, and sometimes hurt by the way he eluded their ploys. For a while, Sallah wondered if Tarvi liked women at all, but he had shown no preference for the acknowledged male lovers in Landing. He treated everyone, man, woman, and child, with the same charming affability and understanding. And whatever his sexual preference, he was nonetheless expected to add to the next generation. Sallah was already determined to be the medium and would find the moment.

Perhaps she had found it. Tarvi had a special fondness for caves; he had at various times called them orifices of the Mother Earth, entrances to the mysteries of her creation and construction, and windows into her magic and bounty. Even though this was Pern, he worshipped the same mystery that had dominated his life so far.

Their current trip was to make an aerial reconnaissance of the location of several mineral deposits noted by the metallurgy probes. Iron, vanadium, manganese, and even germanium were to be found in the mountainous spine that Sallah was aiming at as they followed the course of a river to its source. She was also operating under the general directive that unusual sites should be recorded and photographed to offer the widest possible choice. Only a third of those with stake acreage had made their selection. There was a subtle pressure to keep everyone in the southern continent—at least in the first few generations—but there was no such directive in the charter. The broad, long river valley that lay to their right as they approached the precipice was, to Sallah's mind, the most beautiful they had seen so far.

Rene Mallibeau, the colony's most determined vintner, was still looking for the proper type of slope and soil for his vineyards, though to get his project started he had actually released some of his hoard of special soils from their sealed tanks for his experiments in viniculture. Quikal was not a universally accepted substitute for the traditional spirits. Despite being poured through a variety of filters with or without additives, nothing could completely reduce the raw aftertaste. Rene had been promised the use of ceramic-lined metal fuel tanks which, once thoroughly cleansed, would provide him with wine vats of superior quality. Of course, once the proper oak forests had reached adequate size for use as staves, his descendants could move back to the traditional wooden barrel.

"Rather spectacular, that precipice, isn't it, Tarvi?" Sallah said, grinning rather foolishly, as if the view were a surprise that she herself had prepared for him.

"Indeed it is. 'In Xanadu did Kubla Khan,' " he murmured in his rich deep voice.

" 'Caverns measureless to man'?" Sallah capped it, careful not to sound smug that she recognized his source. Tarvi often quoted obscure Sanskrit and Pushtu texts, leaving her groping for a suitable retort.

"Precisely, O moon of my delight."

Sallah suppressed a grimace. Sometimes Tarvi's phrases were ambiguous, and she knew that he did not mean what his phrase suggested. He would not be so obvious. Or would he? Had she penetrated that bland exterior after all? She forced herself to contemplate the immense stone bulwark. Its natural fluted columns appeared carved by an inexperienced or inattentive sculptor, yet the imperfection contributed to the overall beauty of the precipice.

"This valley is six or seven klicks long," she said quietly, awed by the truly impressive natural site.

From the steep, right-angled fall of a spectacular *diedre*, the palisade led in a somewhat straight line for about three klicks before falling back into a less perfectly defined face that sloped down in the distance to meet the floor of the valley. She angled the sled to starboard, facing upriver, and they were nearly blinded by the brilliant sunlight reflecting from the surface of the lake that had been charted by the probe.

"No, land here," Tarvi said quickly, actually catching her arm to stress his urgency. He was not much given to personal contact, and Sallah tried not to misinterpret excitement for anything else. "I must see the caves."

He released the safety harness and swiveled his seat around. Then he walked to the back of the sled, rummaging among the supplies.

"Lights, we'll need lights, ropes, food, water, recording devices, specimen kit," he muttered as his deft movements filled two backpacks. "Boots? Have you on proper boots . . . ah, those will do, indeed they will. Sallah, you are always well prepared." He compounded his inadvertent injury to her feelings by one of his more ingratiating smiles.

Once again, Sallah shook her head over her whimsical fancy, which had managed to settle on one of the most elusive males of her acquaintance. Of course, she consoled herself, anything easily had is rarely worth having. She landed the sled at the base of the towering precipice, as near to the long narrow mouth of the cave as she could.

"Pitons, grappling hook—that first slab looks about five meters above the scree. Here you are, Sallah!"

He handed her pack over, waiting only long enough to see her grab a strap before he released the canopy, jumped down, and was striding toward the towering buttress. With a resigned shrug, Sallah flipped on beacon, comm unit, and recorder for incoming messages, fastened her jacket, settled the rather hefty pack on her back, and followed him, closing the canopy behind her.

He scrambled up the scree and stood with one palm flat against the slab, looking up its imposing and awesome spread, his face rapt with wonder. Gently, as if in a caress, he stroked the stone before he began to look right and left, assessing how best to climb to the cave. He flashed her an ingenuous smile, acknowledging her presence and assuming her willingness.

"Straight up. Not much of a climb with pitons."

The climb proved strenuous. Sallah could have used a breather as she crawled onto the ledge, but there was the cave opening, and nothing was going to deter Tarvi from immediate entrance and a leisurely inspection. Ah, well, it was just 1300 hours. They had time in hand. She rolled to her feet, unlatching the handlight from her belt just a few seconds after he had done the same, and was at his side as he peered into the opening.

"Lords, gods, and minor deities!"

His invocation was a mere whisper, solemn and awed, a susurrous echo. The vast initial cavern was larger than the cargo hold of the *Yokohama*. Sallah made that instant comparison, remembering how eerie that immense barren space had seemed on her last trip, and in the next second, she wondered what the cavern would look like occupied. It would make a spectacular great hall, in the tradition of medieval times on Earth—only even more magnificent.

Tarvi held his breath, hesitantly extending his still-dark handlight, as if reluctant to illuminate the majesty of the cavern. She heard his intake of breath, in the manner of one steeling himself to commit sacrilege, and then the light came on.

Wings whirred as shadows made silent sinuous departures to the darker recesses. They both ducked as the winged denizens departed in flight lines just clearing their heads, though the cave entrance was at least four meters high. Ignoring the exodus, Tarvi moved reverently into the vast space.

"Amazing," he murmured as he shined the light up and judged that the shell of the outer wall above them was barely two meters thick. "A very thin face."

"Some bubble," Sallah said, feeling impious and wanting to regain her equilibrium after her initial awe. "Look, you could carve a staircase in that," she said, her light picking out a slanting foot of rock that rose to a ledge where a large darkness indicated yet another cave.

She spoke to inattentive ears, for Tarvi was already prowling about, determining the width of the entrance and the dimensions of the cave. She hurried after him.

The first chamber of the cave complex measured an awesome fifty-seven meters deep at its widest, tapering at either end to forty-six meters on the left and forty-two meters on the right. Along the back wall, there were innumerable irregular openings at random levels; some were on the ground level leading into apparent tunnel complexes, most of which were high enough to admit Tarvi's tall frame with considerable head space; others, like great dead eyes, peered down from higher up the inside wall. Entranced as Tarvi was by their discovery, he was a trained scientific observer. With Sallah's aid, he began to draft an accurate plan of the main chamber, the openings of secondary ones, and the tunnel complexes leading inward. He penetrated each to a depth of a hundred meters, roped to a nervous Sallah who kept glancing back at the cave's opening for the reassuring sight of the waning day.

His rough notes were refined by the light of the gas fire on which Sallah cooked their evening meal. Tarvi had elected to camp far enough into the cave to be protected from the stiff breeze that blew down the valley, and far enough to the left so as not to interfere with the habits of the cave's natural residents. Later, a low flame from the protected gas fire would discourage most of Pern's wildlife from investigating the intruders.

Somehow, in the cave Sallah did feel like an intruder, though she had not previously been bothered by that notion. The place was truly awe-inspiring.

Tarvi had gone down to the sled to bring up more drafting tools and the folding table over which he had hunched almost immediately. With no comment, he had eaten the stew she had carefully prepared, absently handing back his plate for a second helping.

Sallah was of two minds about Tarvi's concentration. On the one hand, she was a good cook and liked to have her skill acknowledged. On the other hand, she was as glad that Tarvi was distracted. One of the pharmacists had given her a pinch of what she swore was a potent indigenous aphrodisiac; Sallah had used it to season Tarvi's share. She did not need it herself, not with her mind and body vibrating to his presence and their solitude. But she was beginning to wonder if the aphrodisiac was strong enough to overcome Tarvi's enchantment with the cave. Just her luck to get him to herself for a night or two and then have him be totally enthralled by Dear Old Mother Earth in Pernese costume. But she had not bided her time to waste a sterling opportunity. She could wait. All night. And tomorrow. She had enough of the joy dust to use the next night, too. Maybe it just took a while to act.

"It is truly magnificent in its proportions, Sallah. Here, look!" He straightened his torso, arching his back against his cramped muscles, and

Sallah came up behind him, knelt, and considerately began to knead his taut shoulder muscles as she peered over his shoulder.

The two-dimensional sketch had been deftly drawn with bold lines: he had added back, front, and side elevations, truthfully ending them where his measurements ended. But that only made the cavern more imposing and mysterious.

"What a fort it would have been in the olden days!" He looked toward the black interior, his wide liquid eyes shining, his face alight as imagination altered the chamber before him. "Why, it would have housed whole tribes. Kept them secure for years from invasion. There's fresh water, you understand, down the third left-hand tunnel. Of course, the valley itself would be defensible and this the protected inner hold, with that daunting slab to defeat climbers. There are no less than eighteen different exits from the main chamber."

She had worked her hands up the column of his neck, then across the trapezius muscles, and down to the deltoids, massaging firmly but letting her fingers linger in a movement that she had found immensely effective on other occasions when she had wished to relax a man.

"Ah, how kind you are, Sallah, to know where the muscles bind." He twisted slightly, not to evade her seeking, kneading fingers but to guide them to the sorest points. He pushed the low table to one side so that his arms could fall naturally to his lap as he rotated his head. "There's a point, eleventh vertebrae . . ." he suggested, and she dutifully found the knot of muscle and smoothed it expertly. He sighed like a lithe dark feline being stroked.

She said nothing, but moved ever so slightly forward so that her body touched his. As she walked her fingers back to his neck, she dared to press against him so that her breasts lightly touched his shoulder blades. She could feel her nipples harden at the contact, and her respiration quickened. Her fingers ceased to knead and began to caress, moving down over his chest in long slow motions. He caught her hands then, and she could feel the stillness of him, a stillness of mind and breath, as his body began to tremble slightly.

"Perhaps this is the time," he mused as if alone. "There will never be a better. And it must be done."

With the suppleness that was as much a trademark of Tarvi Andiyar as his ineffable charm, he gathered her in his arms, pulling her across his lap. His expression, oddly detached as if examining her for the first time, was not yet quite the tender, loving expression she had so wished to evoke. His expressive and large brown eyes were almost sad, though his perfectly shaped lips curved in an infinintely gentle smile—as if, the thought intruded on Sallah's delight in her progress, he did not wish to frighten her.

"So, Sallah," he said in his rich low and sensual voice, "it is you."

She knew she should interpret that cryptic remark, but then he began to kiss her, his hands suddenly displaying an exceedingly erotic mind of their own, and she no longer wished to interpret anything.

CHAPTER

VIII

Four mares, three dolphins, and twelve cows produced their young at precisely the same moment, or so the records for that dawn hour stood. Sean had even agreed to allow Sorka to observe the birth of the foal designated for him by Pol and Bay. He had maintained a pose of skepticism over the color and sex of the creature although, three days previously, he had already witnessed that the first of the draft animals produced for his father's group was exactly as requested, a sturdy bay mare with white socks and a face blaze who had weighed over seventy kilos at birth and would be the image of the long-dead Shire stallion whose sperm had begot her.

Some wit had quipped that Landing's records were turning into the biblical begottens of Pern's chronicle. In two years, the new generation was well begun and increasing daily. Human births were less minutely reported than the successes of animalkind, but at least as well celebrated.

Sheep and the Nubian strain of goats that had somehow adapted where other tough breeds had failed grazed Landing's meadows and would soon go to farm-stake acres in the temperate belts of the southern continent. The growing herds and flocks were patrolled by such a proliferation of dragonets that the ecologists were becoming concerned that the animals would lose their natural abilities to fend for themselves. The tame dragonets were proving to be extraordinarily faithful to the humans who had impressed them at hatching, even after their voracious appetites abated with maturity and they were well able to forage on their own.

The biology department was learning more about the little creatures every day. Bay Harkenon and Pol Nietro had discovered of a particularly surprising phenomenon. When Bay's little queen mated with a bronze that Pol had impressed, the sensuality of their pets surprised them with its intensity. They found themselves responding to the exciting stimulus in a human fashion. After the initial shock, they came to a mutual conclusion and took a larger residence together. Awed by the empathic potential of the dragonets, Bay and Pol asked for, and got, Kitti Ping's permission to try mentasynth enhancement on the fourteen eggs that Bay's Mariah had conceived in her mating flight. They fussed considerably more over the little golden Mariah than was necessary, but neither the dragonet nor her clutch suffered. When Mariah produced her enhanced eggs in a specially constructed facsimile of a beach, Bay and Pol were smugly pleased.

Incorporation of mentasyth, which had originally been developed by the Beltrae, a reclusive Eridani hive culture, sparked latent empathic abilities. Dragonets had already demonstrated such an ability, amounting to an almost telepathic communication with a few people. The dragonets were clearly a remarkable evolutionary attempt which, like dolphins, had produced an animal that understood its environment—and controlled it. So, inspired by the success of the dolphins' mentasynth enhancement, Bay and Pol hoped that the dragonets would come to an even closer empathy with people.

Initially, humans from Beltrae who had been "touched" were regarded with great suspicion, of course, but as soon as their remarkable empathic powers with animals and other people were realized, the technique became widespread. Many groups eventually had valued healers whose abilities had been amplified that way. Luckily, that all happened well before the Pure Human group became powerful.

From their studies of the tunnel snakes and wherries, Bay and Pol had come to an appreciation of the potential of the charming and useful dragonets. It had taken many experiments with dragonet tissues, and with several generations of the little tunnel snakes, to incorporate the mentasynth system successfully, but longtime experience with such species as dolphins—and, of course, man—paid off.

Everyone in Landing had come to have a working knowledge of the habits of the dragonets, biological as well as psychological, for there was good cause to be grateful to the creatures and to tolerate their few natural excesses. Theoretically, Bay had known that some of the owners seemed to feel the "primitive urges" of the creatures: hunger, fear, anger, and an intense mating imperative. She had simply never thought that she would be as vulnerable as her younger colleagues. It had been an exceedingly delightful surprise.

Red and Mairi Hanrahan were thankful that Sorka and Sean had impressed—the word, meaning the act of imprinting a dragonet, had somehow crept into the language—dragonets that would not want to mate with each other. They still did not approve of Sorka's close attachment to the boy and felt that she was too young to be subject to irresistible sensual urges.

On that morning, nearly twelve months after Landing, the mare Sean had chosen to produce his promised foal was laboring to give birth, there was no doubt that Sorka, who had turned thirteen, and Sean, two years older, were in rapport with their eagerly anticipating dragonets. The two browns and the bronze had perched on the top rail of the stable partition, their eyes whirling with growing excitement as they crooned their birth song. The little chestnut mare dropped to the straw to deliver the forelegs and head of her foal. Above, the rafters of the barn seemed to ripple with its temporary adornment of the dragonet population of Landing, crooning and chirping continual encouragement.

Dragonets were sentimental about births and missed none in Landing, bugling in high-pitched tenor voices at each new arrival. Fortunately, they discreetly remained outside human habitations. The colony's obstetricians had lately been working nonstop and had drafted the nurses and taken on apprentices. An array of dragonets on a roof became an irrefutable sign of impending birth: the dragonets were never wrong. The obstetricians could gauge the labor's progress by the growing intensity of the dragonets' welcoming song. The chorus might deprive neighbors of sleep, but most of the community took it in good humor. Even the most jaundiced had seen the dragonets protecting the flocks and herds, and had to appreciate their value.

The chestnut mare heaved again, extruding the foal farther. Since its legs, head, and forequarters were wet with birth fluids, Sean could not distinguish the animal's color. Then the rest of the body emerged, followed, with a final push, by the hindquarters. There was no doubt that he was not only darkly dappled but male. With a crow of incredulous joy, Sean dropped to the little fellow's head to mop it dry, even before the mare could form her bond. Tears streaming down her dusty face, Sorka hugged herself in joy. Dimly she heard the excited comments of the other animal midwives sharing the large barn.

"He's the only colt," her father said, returning to Sean and Sorka. "As ordered." Though the colony actually needed as many female animals as it could breed, Sean's preference for a colt had been duly considered. And one local stallion would be a safeguard, though there were more than enough varied sperms in reserve. "Grand fellow, though," Red remarked, nodding his head approvingly. "Make a good sixteen hands, if I'm any judge. A sturdy nine stone, I'd say. Fine good fellow, and she bore him like a trooper." He stroked the neck of the little mare, who was licking the colt as he suckled her with vigor. "Come now, Sorka," he went on, seeing her tear-streaked face. "I'll keep my promise that you'll have a horse, too." He gave her a reassuring hug.

ment. That the charterers had more than any contractor, including herself, the astrogator, who had delivered them safely to the wretched place, was a fact that had never set well with her.

Damn Munson and Alhinwa. They could have told her where they had unearthed the turquoise. Pern was a virgin world, with metal and mineral aplenty, untouched as yet by careless prospectors and greedy merchants. There was plenty for everyone. Back on sophisticated worlds, any large, well-colored hunks of that sky-blue stone would be snatched up by ardent collectors—the higher the asking price the more collectible!

And why had she not heard from Nabhi? She suspected that he might be trying to run a program of his own, instead of the one she had set. She would have to watch that one: he was a devious sort. Much as she was. In the long run, she had the upper hand, since she was the astrogator, and Nabhi did not have the skills required to get home by himself. He had to have her, but she did not have to have him—unless it suited her. Nabol was not as good over-all for her purposes as Kimmer was, but he would do in a pinch.

She had almost bridged the distance between continent and island and could see waves lashing the granite rock. She veered to port, looking for the mouth of the natural harbor where the long-dead survey team had made camp. She had told Kimmer to meet her there. She felt better about being someplace that had already been occupied. She could not stand listening to the idiot colonists going on and on about being "first" to see that or "first" to step there, or the naming arguments that continually dominated conversation night after night around the bonfire. Shit in Drake's Lake! Fatuous ass! Lousy gravity-ball player!

She corrected her course as she spotted the two natural spurs of rock that formed a breakwater to the roughly oval natural harbor. Kimmer would have hid the sled anyhow just in case . . . She caught herself and snorted in sour amusement. As if anyone on this goody-good world is checking up on any-one else! "We are all equal here." Our brave and noble leaders have so or-dained it. With equal rights to share in Pern's wealth. You just bet. Only I'll get my equal share before anyone else and shake this planet's dirt off my boots!

Just as she passed over the breakwater, she saw the glint of metal under the lush foliage to starboard on a ledge above the sandy shoreline. Nearby was the smoke of Kimmer's small fire. She landed her sled neatly beside his.

"You were right about this place, baby," he greeted her, a closed fist up-raised and shaken in victory. "I got here yesterday afternoon, good tail wind all the way, so I did a decco. And see what I found first thing!"

"Let me see," she said, displaying a bright breathless eagerness, though she did not at all like his presumptive solo explorations.

He smiled broadly as he slowly opened his fingers and let his hand drop so that she could see the large gray rock he held. Her eagerness drained with discouragement until he turned the stone just slightly and she caught the unmistakable glint of green, half buried in one end.

"Fardles!" She snatched the stone from his hand and whirled to the sun, which had risen over the ocean by then. She wet her finger and rubbed at the green glint.

"I also found this," Kimmer said.

Looking up, she saw him holding a squarish green stone the size of a spoon bowl, rough-edged where it had been prized from a limestone cavity.

She almost threw away the rock with its still-hidden treasure in her eagerness to take the rough emerald from him. She held it to the sun, saw the flaw, but had no complaint about the clear deep green. She weighed it in her hand. Why, it had to be thirty or forty carats. With a clever lapidary to cut beyond the flaw, there would be fifteen carats of gemstone. And if that stone was just a sample . . . The idea of apprenticing as a gemstone cutter and using that magnificent jewel to learn on amused her.

"Where?" she demanded, her breath constricted with urgency.

"Over there." He half turned, pointing up into the thick vegetation. "There's a whole cave of them embedded in the rock."

"You just walked in and it winked at you?" She forced herself to speak lightly, amusedly, smiling up approvingly at his beaming face. He looked so bloody pleased with himself. She continued to smile but ground her teeth.

"I've *klah* for you," he said, gesturing to the fire where he had rigged a spit and a protecting rock for his kettle.

"That abominable stuff," she exclaimed. She had a fleet-incurred preference for strong coffee, and the last had been served at that pathetic Thanksgiving shindig—and spilled when the tremor had shaken the urns from their stands. The last coffee from Earth had seeped, undrunk, into the dirt of Pern.

"Oh, if you use enough sweetening, it's not all that bad." He poured her a cup even though she had not said that she wanted one. "They say it's got as much caffeine in it as coffee or tea. The secret's in drying the bark thoroughly before grinding and steeping it."

He had lashed sweetener into the cup and handed it to her, expecting her to be grateful for his thoughtfulness. She could not afford to alienate Kimmer even if he sounded revoltingly like a good little colonist, approving of good colonial substitutes.

"Sorry, Stev," she said, smiling apologetically at him as she took the cup. "Early morning nerves. I really do miss coffee."

He gave a shrug. "We won't for long, now, will we?"

She kept her smile in place, wondering if he knew how inane he sounded. Then, she cautioned herself severely, if she had only been more careful with Paul, she might have been first lady on Pern. What *had* she done wrong? She could have sworn she would be able to maintain his interest in her. All had gone perfectly right up until they entered the Rukbat system. Then it had been as if she no longer existed. And I got them here!

"Avril?"

She came back to the present at the impatience in Stev Kimmer's voice. "Sorry!" she said.

"I *said* that I've already got food for the day, so as soon as you finish that we can go."

She tipped her cup, watching the dark liquid momentarily stain the white sand. She jiggled the cup to scatter the last drops, put it upside down by the fire like a good little colonist, and rose to her feet, smiling brightly at Kimmer. "Well, let's go!"

Part Two

THREAD

CHAPTER

IX

4.5.08 Pern

Perhaps it was because people were so accustomed to dragonets after nearly eight years of close association that they no longer paid much attention to the creatures' behavior. Those who noticed their unusual antics thought that the dragonets were merely playing some sort of a new game, for they were inventively amusing. Later people would remember that the dragonets attempted to herd the flocks and herds back to the barns. Later marine rangers would remember that the bottlenoses Bessie, Lottie, and Maximilian had urgently tried to explain to their human friends why the indigenous marine life was rushing eastward to a food source.

At her home in Europe Square, Sabra Ongola-Stein actually thought that Fancy, the family dragonet, was attacking her three-year-old son at play in the yard. The little gold was grabbing at Shuvin's shirt, attempting to haul him from his sandpile and his favorite toy truck. As soon as Sabra had rescued the boy, batting at Fancy, the dragonet had hovered over her, cheeping with relief. It was puzzling behavior to be sure, but, though the fabric of the shirt was torn, Sabra could see no marks on Shuvin's flesh from the dragonet talons. Nor was Shuvin crying. He merely wanted to go back to his truck while Sabra wanted to change his shirt.

To her utter surprise, Fancy tried to duck into the house with them, but Sabra got the door closed in time. As she leaned against it, catching her breath, she noticed through the rear window that other dragonets were acting in the most peculiar fashion. She was somewhat reassured by the fact that there had never been reports of dragonets *hurting* people, even in the ardor of mating, but that did not seem to be what was agitating them, because greens were wheeling as frantically as the other colors. Greens always got out of the way when a gold was mating. And it was certainly the wrong time for Fancy to be in season.

As Sabra changed Shuvin's shirt, deftly handling the little boy's squirms, she realized that the cries that penetrated the thick plastic walls of the house sounded frightened. Sabra knew the usual dragonets sounds as well as anyone in Landing. What could they be frightened of?

The large flying creature—perhaps a very big wherry—that had been occasionally spotted soaring near the Western Barrier Range would be unlikely to range so far east. What other danger could there be on a fine early spring morning? That smudge of gray cloud far off on the horizon suggested rain later on in the day, but that would be good for the crops already sprouting in the grain fields. Maybe she should get the clothes in off the line. Sometimes she missed the push-button conveniences that back on old Earth had eliminated the drudgery of monotonous household tasks. Too bad that the council never considered requiring miscreants to do domestic duties as punishment for disorderly conduct. She pulled Shuvin's shirt down over his trousers, and he gave her a moist, loving kiss.

"Truck, Mommie, truck? Now?"

His wistful question made her aware, suddenly, of the silence, of the absence of the usual cheerful cacophony of dragonet choruses which was the background to daily life in Landing and in nearly every settlement across the southern continent. Such a complete silence was frightening. Startled, restraining Shuvin, who wanted urgently to get back out and play in the sand, Sabra peered out the back window, then through the plasglas behind her. She saw not a dragonet in sight. Not even on Betty Musgrave-Blake's house where there had been the usual natal congregation. Betty was expecting her second child; and Sabra had seen Basil, the obstetrician, arriving with Greta, his very capable apprentice midwife.

Where were the dragonets? They never missed a birth.

As well established as Landing was, one was still supposed to report anything unusual on Pern. She tried Ongola's number on the comm unit, but it was engaged. While she was using the handset, Shuvin reached his grubby hand up to the door pull and slid it open, with a mischievous grin over his shoulder at his mother as he performed that new skill. She smiled her acquiescence as she tapped out Bay's number. The zoologist might know what was amiss with her favorite critters.

◆ ◆ ◆

Well east and slightly south of Landing, Sean and Sorka were hunting wherry for Restday meals. As the human settlements spread, foragers were having to go farther afield for game.

"They're not even trying to hunt, Sorka," Sean said, scowling. "They've spent half the morning arguing. Fardling fools." He lifted one muscular brown arm in an angry gesture to his eight dragonets. "Shape up, you winged wimps. We're here to hunt!"

He was ignored as his veteran browns seemed to be arguing with the mentasynths, most aggressively with Sean's queen, Blazer. That was extraordinary behavior: Blazer, who had been genetically improved by Bay Harkenon's tinkering, was usually accorded the obedience that any of the lesser colors granted the fertile gold females.

"Mine, too," Sorka said, nodding as her own five joined Sean's. "Oh, jays, they're coming for *us*!" Slackening her reins, she began to tighten her legs around her bay mare but stopped when she saw Sean, wheeling Cricket to face the oncoming dragonets, hold up an imperious hand. She was even more startled to see the dragonets assume an attack formation, their cries clamors of unspeakable fright and danger.

"Danger? Where?" Sean spun Cricket around on his haunches, a trick that Sorka had never been able to teach Doove despite Sean's assistance and her own endless patience. He searched the skies and stayed Cricket as the dragonets solidly turned their heads to the east.

Blazer landed on his shoulder, swirling her tail about his neck and left bicep, and shrieked to the others. Sean was amazed at the interaction he sensed. A queen taking orders from browns? But he was distracted as her thoughts became vividly apprehensive.

"Landing in danger?" he asked. "Shelter?"

Once Sean had spoken, Sorka understood what her bronzes were trying to convey to her. Sean was always quicker to read the mental images of his enhanced dragonets, especially those of Blazer, who was the most coherent. Sorka had often wished for a golden female, but she loved her bronzes and brown too much to voice a complaint.

"That's what they all give me, too," Sorka said, as her five began to tug various parts of her clothing. Though Sean could hunt bare to the waist, she bobbled too much to ride topless comfortably; her sleeveless leather vest provided support, as well as protection from the claw holds of the dragonets. Bronze Emmett settled on Doove's poll long enough to secure a grip on one ear and the forelock, trying to pull the mare's head around.

"Something big, something dangerous, and shelter!" Sean said, shaking his head. "It's only a thunderstorm, fellas. Look, just a cloud!"

Sorka frowned as she looked eastward. They were high enough on the plateau to have just a glimpse of the sea.

"That's a funny-looking cloud formation, Sean. I've never seen anything like it. More like the snowclouds we'd have now and again in Ireland."

Sean scowled and tightened his legs. Cricket, picking up on the dragonets' urgent fears, pranced tensely in place in the piaffe he had been taught, but it was clear that he would break into a mad gallop the minute Sean gave him his head. The stallion's eyes were rolling white in distress as he snorted. Doove, too, was fretting, spurred by Emmett's peculiar urgency.

"Doesn't snow here, Sorka, but you're right about the color and shape. By jays, whatever it's raining, it's damned near visible. Rain here doesn't fall like that."

Duke and Sean's original two browns saw it and shrieked in utter frustration and terror. Blazer trumpeted a fierce command. The next thing Sean and Sorka knew, both horses had been spurred by well-placed dragonet stabs across their rumps into a headlong stampede which the massed fair of dragonets aimed north and west. Rein, leg, seat, or voice had no effect on the two pain-crazed horses, for whenever they tried to obey their riders, they got another slash from the vigilant dragonets.

"Whatinell's got into them?" Sean cried, hauling on the hackamore that he used in place of a bit in Cricket's soft mouth. "I'll break his bloody nose for him, I will."

"No, Sean," Sorka cried, leaning into her mare's forward plunge. "Duke's terrified of that cloud. All of mine are. They'd never hurt the horses! We'd be fools to ignore them."

"As if we could!"

The horses were diving headlong down a ravine. Sean needed all his skill to stay on Cricket, but his mind sensed Blazer's relief that she had succeeded in moving them toward safety.

"Safety from what?" he muttered in a savage growl, hating the feeling of impotence on an animal that had never disobeyed him in its seven years, an animal that he had thought he understood better than any human on the whole planet.

The headlong pace did not falter, even when Sean felt the gray stallion, fit as he was, begin to tire. The dragonets drove both horses onward, straight toward one of the small lakes that dotted that part of the continent.

"Why water, Sean?" Sorka cried, sitting back and hauling on Doove's mouth. When the mare willingly slowed, Duke and the other two bronzes screamed a protest and once again gouged her bleeding rump.

Neighing and white-eyed with fear, the mare leapt into the water, nearly unseating her rider. The stallion plunged beside her, galled by the spurred talons of Sean's dragonets.

The lake, a deep basin collecting the runoff from the nearby hills, had little beach and the horses were soon swimming, determinedly herded by the dragonets toward the rocky overhang on the far side. Sean and Sorka had often sunbathed on that ledge; they enjoyed diving from their high perch into the deep water below.

"The ledge? They want us *under* the ledge? The water's fardling deep there."

"Why?" Sorka still asked. "It's only rain coming." She was swimming beside Doove, one hand on the pommel of her saddle, the other holding the reins, letting the mare's efforts drag her forward. "Where'd they all go?"

Sean, swimming alongside Cricket, turned on his side to look back the way they had come. His eyes widened. "That's not *rain*. Swim for it, Sorka! Swim for the ledge!"

She cast a glance over her shoulder and saw what had startled the usually imperturbable young man. Terror lent strength to her arm; tugging on the reins, she urged Doove to greater efforts. They were nearly to the ledge, nearly to what little safety that offered from the hissing silver fall that splatted so ominously across the woods they had only just left.

"Where are the dragonets?" Sorka wailed as she crossed into the shadow of the ledge. She tugged at Doove, trying to drag the mare in behind her.

"Safer where they are, no doubt!" Sean sounded bitterly angry as he forced Cricket under the ledge. There was just room enough for the horses' heads to remain above the level of the water, but there was no purchase for their flailing legs.

Suddenly both horses ceased resisting their riders and began to press Sean and Sorka against the inner wall, whinnying in abject terror.

"Jack your legs up, Sorka! Balance against the inside wall!" Sean shouted, demonstrating.

Then they heard the hiss on the water. Peering around the frightened horses' heads, they could actually see the long, thin threads plunging into the water. The lake was suddenly roiling and cut every which way with the fins of the minnows that had been seeded in the streams.

"Jays! Look at that!" Sean pointed excitedly to a small jet of flame just above the lake's surface that charred a large tangle of the stuff before it landed in the water.

"Over there, too!" Sorka said, and then they heard the agitated but exultant chatter of dragonets. Crowded back under the ledge, they caught only fleeting glimpses of dragonets and the unexpected flames.

All at once Sorka remembered that long-ago day when she had first witnessed the dragonets defending the poultry flocks. She had been certain then that Duke had flamed at a wherry. "That happened before, Sean," Sorka said, her fingers slipping on his wet shoulder as she grabbed at it to get his attention. "Somehow they breathe fire. Maybe that's what the second stomach is for."

"Well, I'm glad they weren't cowards," Sean muttered, cautiously propelling himself to the opening. "No," he said in a relieved voice, expelling a big sigh. "They're by no means cowards. C'mere, Sorka."

Glancing anxiously at Doove, Sorka joined Sean and cried out with surprised elation. Their fair of dragonets had been augmented by a mass of others. The little warriors seemed to take turns diving at the evil rainfall, their spouts of flame reducing the terror to char, which fell as ashes to the surface of the lake, where quick fish mouths gobbled it up.

"See, Sorka, the dragonets are protecting this ledge."

Sorka could see the menacing rain falling unimpeded to the lake on either side of the dragonet fire zone.

"Jays, Sean, look what it does to the bushes!" She pointed to the shoreline. The thick clumps of tough bushes they had ridden through only moments before were no longer visible, covered by a writhing mass of "things" that seemed to enlarge as they watched. Sorka felt sick to her stomach, and only intense concentration prevented her from heaving her breakfast up. Sean had gone white about the mouth. His hands, moving rhythmically to keep him in position in the water, clenched into fists.

"No bleeding wonder the dragonets were scared." He smashed impotent fists into the water, sending ripples out. Sorka's Duke appeared instantly, hovering just outside and peering in. He waited just long enough to squeak a reassurance, and then literally disappeared. "Well, now," Sean said. "If I were Pol Nietro, I'd call that instantaneous flit of theirs the best defense mechanism a species could develop." A long thread slithered from the ledge and hung a moment in front of their horrified eyes before a flame charred it.

Revolted, Sean splashed water on the remains, whisking the floating motes away from Sorka and himself. Behind them the horses' breathing showed signs of real distress.

"How long?" Sean said, gliding over to Cricket's head and soothing the horse with his hands. "How long?"

◆ ◆ ◆

"It is *not* mating activity," Bay told Sabra when she called, "and it is a totally irrational pattern of behavior." Her mind riffling through all she knew and had observed about the dragonets, Bay continued to peer out her window. As she watched, a sled lifted from a parking spot near the met tower, and it headed at full speed toward the storm. "Let me check my behavioral files and have a word with Pol. I'll call you back. It really is most unusual."

Pol was working on the vegetable patch behind their home. He saw her coming and waved cheerfully, tipping back his visored cap and mopping his brow. The garden soil had been carefully enriched and enhanced by a variety of Terran beetles and worms that were as happy to aerate the soil of Pern as of Earth and augmented the local, lazier kinds. Bay saw Pol stop, his hand in midwipe, and stare about him; she guessed he had only then noticed the absence of the dragonets.

"Where've they all gone?" He glanced toward other residential squares and Betty's empty roof. "That was sudden, wasn't it?"

"Sabra's just been on to me. She said their Fancy appeared to attack little Shuvin. For no reason, although her claws did not pierce the skin. Fancy then attempted to enter the house with them. Sabra said she sounded frightened."

Pol raised his eyebrows in surprise and continued to wipe his brow and then the hat band before recovering his head. Leaning on his hoe, he glanced all around. It was then that he saw the gray clouds.

"Don't like the look of that, m'luv," he said. "I'll take a bit of a break until it blows over." He smiled at her. "While we access your notes on the menta-breed. Fancy's a menta, not a native."

Suddenly the air was full of shrieking, screaming, bugling, and very frightened dragonets.

"Where have they been, the little pests?" Pol demanded, snatching off his cap to wave it furiously in front of his face. "Faugh! They stink!"

Bay pinched her nostrils, hurrying toward the refuge of the house. "They do, indeed. Positively sulfurous."

Six dragonets detached themselves from the swirling hundreds and dove for Bay and Pol, battering at their backs and screeching to hurry them forward.

"I do believe they're driving us into the house, Pol," Bay said. When she stopped to study the eccentric behavior, her queen grabbed a lock of her hair, and the two bronzes secured holds on the front of her tunic, pulling her forward. Their cries grew more frantic.

"I believe you're correct. And they're doing it to others, too."

"I've never seen so many dragonets. We don't normally have such a concentration here," Bay went on, cooperating to the point of a lumbering jog trot. "Most of them are wilds! Look how much smaller some queens are. A preponderance of greens as well. Fascinating."

"Extremely," Pol remarked, mildly amused that the dragonets who were their particular friends had entered the house and were cooperating in a joint effort to close the door behind the humans. "Most remarkable."

Bay was already sitting down at the terminal. "Patently, it's something harmful to them as well as to us."

"I'd prefer them to settle," Pol said. Their dragonets were flitting about the lounge and into the bedroom, the bathroom, and even the addition to the house that had been made into a small but well-equipped home laboratory for the two scientists. "This is a bit much. Bay, tell your queen to settle, and the others will follow suit."

"Tell her yourself, Pol, while I access the behavioral program. She'll obey you as well as me."

Pol attempted to coax Mariah to land on his arm. But the moment she touched down she was off again, and the others after her. A tidbit of her favorite fish was ignored. Pol was no longer amused. He looked out the window to see if others were experiencing the same mass hysteria and noticed that the squares had been cleared of people. He could see clouds of dust over by the veterinary barns, and the dark dashes of dragonets attempting to herd the animals. He could also hear the distant discord of frightened beasts.

"There had better be an explanation for this," he murmured, pausing behind Bay to read the screen. "My word, look at Betty's house!" He pointed over the screen and out the window toward a structure fully clothed in dragonets. "My God, should I call them to see if they need help?"

When he put his hand out to reach for the door pull, Mariah, screaming with anger, dove at his hand and pushed it away, scratching him.

"Don't go, Pol. Don't go out, Pol! Look!"

Bay had half risen from her chair and remained frozen in the semi-crouch, a look of utter horror on her face. As Pol threw a protective arm about her shoulders, they both heard the hiss of the terrible rain that fell on Landing. They could see the individual elongated "raindrops" strike the surface, sometimes meeting only dust, other times writhing about the shrubs and grasses, which disappeared, leaving behind engorged sluglike forms that rapidly attacked anything green in their way. Pol's nicely sprouting garden became a waste of squirming grayish "things," bloating larger within seconds on each new feast.

Mariah let out a raucous call and disappeared from the house. The other five dragonets followed instantly.

"I don't believe what I saw," Pol said in an amazed whisper. "They're teleporting in droves, almost formations. So the telekinesis was developed as a survival technique first. Hmm."

The hideous rain had advanced, spreading its mindless burden behind and inexorably falling across Pol's neatly patterned stonework patio toward the house.

"They can't devour stone," Pol remarked with clinical detachment. "I trust our silicon plastic roof provides a similar deterrent."

"The dragonets have more than one unexplored skill, Pol, my dear," Bay said proudly and pointed.

Outside, their dragonets were swooping and soaring, breathing flame to incinerate the attacking life-form before it could reach the house.

"I would be happier if I knew the things could not penetrate plastic," Pol repeated with a slight tremor in his voice, looking up at the opaque roof. He winced and hunched in self-protection as he heard a slithering impact, then another, then saw the flame spurt briefly in gouts across the dark roof material.

"Well, that's a relief," he said, straightening his shoulders.

"They did strike the roof, however, until the dragonets, bless their little hearts, set them ablaze." Bay peered out the window facing Betty Musgrave-Blake's house. "My word! Look at that!"

The house seemed to be ringed by fiery whirls and gouts as an umbrella of dragonets frantically made certain that not a single piece of the grotesque rain reached the home of a woman in labor.

Pol had the presence of mind to collect his binoculars from the clutter on a shelf. He turned them on the fields and the veterinary sheds. "I wonder if they'll protect our livestock. There're too many animals to get all safely under shelter. But dragonets do seem to be massing in that area."

Keenly interested in the safety of the herds and flocks they had helped to create, Pol and Bay took turns watching. Bay suddenly dropped the glasses, shuddering as she passed them wordlessly to Pol. She had been shocked by the sight of a full-grown cow reduced in a few moments to a seared corpse covered by masses of writhing strings. Pol altered the focus and then groaned in helpless dismay, dropping the binoculars.

"Deadly, they are. Voracious, insatiable. It would appear they consume anything organic," he murmured. Taking a deep, resolute breath, he raised the binoculars again. "And, unfortunately, to judge by the marks on the roofs of some of those shelters we put up first, carbon-based plastics, too."

"Oh, dear. That could be terrible. Could this be a regional phenomenon?" Bay asked, her voice still trembling. "There were those odd circles on the vegetated areas, the ones in the original survey fax . . ." Turning away from the disaster, she sat down at the keyboard and, clearing the screen, began to call up files.

"I hope no one is foolish enough to go out after those last few cows and sheep," Pol said, an edge to his voice. "I hope they got all the horses in safely. The new equine strain is too promising to lose, even to a ravening disaster."

Almost as an afterthought the alarm klaxon on the meteorology tower began to bleat.

"Now that's a bit after the fact, old fellow," Pol said, turning to focus the binoculars on the tower. He could see Ongola in the tower, holding a rag against his cheek. The sled that had gone out to investigate the storm was parked so close to the tower entrance that Pol guessed that Ongola had probably dived directly from sled to the tower door.

"No, the sound carries and sets off the relays," Bay said absently as her fingers flew over the keys.

"Ah, yes, I'd forgot that. Quite a few people went out on hunting parties this morning, you know."

Bay's quick fingers stilled, and she turned slowly in the swivel chair to stare at Pol, her face ashen.

"There now, old dear, so many people have dragonets now, and at least one of the smarter mentas you developed." He crossed to her and gave her a reassuring pat on the head. "They've done a first-class job of warning and protecting us. Ah! Listen!"

There was no mistaking the exultant warble of the dragonets that always heralded a birth. Despite the bizarre disaster occurring on Pern at that moment, a new life had entered it. The welcome did not, however, interfere with the protective net of flame about the house.

"The poor baby! To be born now!" Bay mourned. Her plump cheeks were drawn, her eyes sunken in her face.

◆ ◆ ◆

Heedless of the stinging pain on the left side of his face, Ongola kept one finger on the klaxon even as he began calling out to the other stations on the network.

"Mayday! Mayday! Mayday at Landing! Take shelter! Get livestock under cover! Extreme danger. Shelter all living things." He shuddered, recalling the horrific sight of two wayward sheep consumed in an eye-blink by the descending vileness. "Shelter under rock, metal, in water! An unnatural rain heading westward in uneven fall. Deadly! Deadly! Shelter. Mayday from Landing. Mayday from Landing. Mayday from Landing!" Drops of blood from his head and neck dripped in punctuation to his terse phrases. "Cloud unnatural. Rainfall deadly. Mayday from Landing! Take shelter! Mayday. Mayday."

His own home was barely visible through the sheeting fall, but he did see the gouts of flame above those houses in Landing still occupied. He accepted the amazing reality of the thousands of dragonets massing to assist their human friends, of the living, flaming shield over Betty Musgrave-Blake's home, of the multitude swirling above the veterinary sheds and the pastures, and he remembered that Fancy had tried to fly into the window where he had been sitting out his watch. When he had suddenly realized that none of the meteorological devices were registering the cloud mass approaching steadily from the east, he had phoned Emily at her home.

"Go have a look, Ongola. Looks like just a good stiff equinoctial squall, but if the water-vapor instruments are not registering, you'd better check the wind speed and see if there's hail or sleet in the clouds. There're hunters and fishers out today, as well as farmers."

Ongola had gotten close enough to the cloud to register its unusual composition—and to see the damage it did. He tried to raise Emily on the sled's comm unit. When that did not work, he tried to reach Jim Tillek at Harbor Control. But he had taken the nearest sled, a small, fast one that did not have the sophisticated equipment the bigger ones did. He tried every number he could think of and only reached Kitti, who generally stayed in her home, frail in her tenth decade despite prostheses that gave her some mobility.

"Thank you for the warning, Ongola. A prudent person is well advised. I will contact the veterinary sheds for them to get the livestock under cover. A hungry rain?"

Ongola had thrown the little sled to its maximum speed, hoping that there was enough power in the packs to withstand such a drain. The sled responded, but he only just made it back to the tower, the engine dying just as he touched ground.

The stuff pelted down on the sled canopy. He had not managed to outrun the leading edge. He grabbed the flight-plan board, an inadequate shield from the deadly rain but better than nothing. Taking a deep breath, he punched auto-close, then ducked out. He took three long strides, more jump than run, and made it to the tower door just as a tangle descended. The tilted edge of the board deflected the stuff right onto the unprotected left side of his head. Screaming with pain, Ongola batted the stuff from his ear just as a dragonet came flaming up to his assistance. Ongola shouted a "Thanks" for the dragonet's aid as he threw himself inside and slammed the door. Automatically, he threw the bolt, snorting at useless instinct, and took the steps to the tower in twos and threes.

The stinging pain continued, and he felt something oozing down his neck. Blood! He blotted at the injury with his handkerchief, noticing that the blood was mixed with black fragments, and he became aware of the stench of burned wool. The dragonet's breath had scorched his sweater.

The warning delivered, he was flipping on the recording when a second stinging pain on his left shoulder made him glance down. He saw the front end of a waving strand that did not look at all like wool. The pain seemed to accompany the strand. He had never undressed as fast as he did then. And he was just fast enough: the strand had become thicker and was moving with more rapidity and purpose. Even as he watched in horror at his close escape, the wool was ingested, and the grotesque, quivering segment left in its place filled him with revulsion.

Water! He reached for both the water pitcher and the klah thermos and emptied them over the . . . the thing. Writhing and bubbling, it slowly subsided into a soggy inert mass. He stamped on it with as much satisfaction as he had felt destroying Nathi surface positions.

Then he looked at his shoulder and saw the thin bloodied line scored in his flesh by his close encounter with that deadly piece of thread. A convulsive shudder took hold of his body, and he had to grab a chair to keep from falling to his knees.

The comm unit began to bleat at him. Taking several deep breaths, he got to his feet and back on duty.

◆ ◆ ◆

"Thanks for the klaxon, Ongola. We had just time enough to batten down the hatches. Knew the critters were telling us something but howinell could we guess *that*?" Jim Tillek reported from the bridge of the *Southern Star*. "Thank the powers that be, our ships are all siliplex."

Monaco Bay harbor office reported overturned small craft and was instigating rescues.

The infirmary reported that human casualties in and about Landing had been minimal: mainly dragonet scratches. They had the dragonets to thank for saving lives.

Red Hanrahan at Vet said that they had lost fifty to sixty assorted livestock of the breeding herds pastured about Landing, thanking the good fortune of having just shipped out three hundred calves, lambs, kids, and piglets to new homes the previous month. There were, however, large numbers at nearby stakes that did not have stabling facilities and were in the path of the abominable rain. Red added that all of the animals left loose to graze could be considered lost.

Two of the larger fishing vessels reported severe burn injuries for those who had not made it under cover in time. One of the Hegelman boys had jumped overboard and drowned when the things landed in a clump on his face. Maximilian, escorting the *Perseus*, had been unable to save him. The dolphin had added that native marine life was swarming to the surface, fighting over the drowning wrigglers. He himself did not much like the things: no substance.

Messages were rapidly stacking up on Ongola's board; he rang Emily to send him some assistance.

The captain of *Maid of the Sea*, fishing to the north, wanted to know what was happening. The skies about him were clear to the southern horizon. Patrice de Broglie, stationed out at Young Mountain with the seismic team, asked if he should send his crew back. There had been only a few rumbles in the past weeks, though there were some interesting changes in the gravity meter graphs. Ongola told him to send back as many as he could, not wanting to think what might have happened to homesteads in the path of that malevolent Threadfall.

Bonneau phoned in from Drake's Lake, where it was still night and very clear. He offered to send a contingent.

Sallah Telgar-Andiyar got through from Karachi Camp and said that assistance was already on its way. How widespread was the rain? she wanted to know.

Ongola shunted all those calls when the first of the nearby settlements reported.

"If it hadn't been for those dragonets," said Aisling Hempenstahl of Bordeaux, "we'd all be—have been eaten alive." Her swallow was audible. "Not a green thing to be seen, and all the livestock gone. Except the cow the dragonets drove into the river, and she's a mess."

"Any casualties?"

"None I can't take care of myself, but we've little fresh food. Oh, and Kwan wants to know do you need him at Landing?"

"I'd say yes, indeed we do," Ongola replied fervently. Then he tried again to raise the Du Vieux, the Radelins, the Grant van Toorns, the Ciottis, and the Holstroms. "Keep trying these, Jacob." He passed the list over to Jacob Chernoff, who had brought three young apprentices to help. "Kurt, Heinrich, try the River numbers, Calusa, Cambridge, and Vienna." Ongola called Lilienkamp at Stores. "Joel, how many checked out for hunting today?"

"Too many, Ongola, too many." The tough Joel was weeping.

"Including your boys?"

Joel's response was the barest whisper. "Yes."

"I am sorry to hear that, Joel. We've organized searches. And the boys have dragonets."

"Sure, but look how many it took the protect Landing!" His voice rose shrilly.

"Sir." Kurt tugged urgently at Ongola's bare elbow. "One of the sleds—"

"I'll get back to you, Joel." Ongola took the call from the sled. "Yes?"

"Whaddya do to kill this stuff, Ongola?" Ziv Marchane's anguished cry sent a stab of pure terror and fury to Ongola's guts.

"Cautery, Ziv. Who is it?"

"What's left of young Joel Lilienkamp."

"Bad?"

"Very."

Ongola paused and closed his eyes tightly for a moment, remembering the two sheep. "Then give him mercy!"

Ziv broke the connection, and Ongola stared at the console, paralyzed. He had given mercy several times, too many times, during the Nathi War when his men had been blown apart after Nathi hits on his destroyer. The practice was standard procedure in surface engagements. One never left one's wounded to Nathi mercy. Mercy, yes, it was mercy to do so. Ongola had never thought that necessity would ever arise again.

Paul Benden's vibrant voice broke through his pained trance. "What in hell's happening, Ongola?"

"Wish the hell I knew, Admiral." Ongola shook his head and then gave him a precise report and a list of casualties, known or suspected.

"I'm coming in." Paul had staked his claim on the heights above the delta on the Boca River. It would soon be dawn there. "I'll check other stakes on the way in."

"Pol and Kitti want samples if they can be safely got—of the stuff in the air. It scores holes through thin materials, so be sure to use heavy-gauge metal or siliplex. We've got enough of what ate our fields bare. I've sent all our big sleds out to track the frigging Fall. Kenjo's flying in from Honshu in that augmented speeder of his. The stuff just came out of nowhere, Paul, nowhere!"

"Didn't register on anything? No? Well, we'll check it all out."

The absolute confidence in Paul Benden's voice was a tonic for Ongola. He had heard that same note all through the Cygnus Battle and he took heart.

He needed it. Before Paul Benden arrived late that afternoon, the casualties had mounted to a frightening total. Only three of the twenty who had gone hunting that morning had returned: Sorka Hanrahan, Sean Connell, and David Catarel, who had watched, helpless, from the water as his companion, Lucy Tubberman, dissolved under the rain on the riverbank despite the frantic efforts of their dragonets. He had deep scores on his scalp, left cheek, arms, and shoulders, and he was suffering from shock and grief.

Two babies, obviously thrust at the last moment into a small metal cabinet, were the only survivors of the main Tuareg camp on the plains west of the big bend in the Paradise River. Sean and Sorka had gone to find the Connells, who had last been reported on the eastern spur of Kahrain Province. No one answered from the northern stakes on the Jordan River. It looked bad.

Porrig Connell had, for once, listened to the warnings of the dragonets and had taken shelter in a cave. It had not been large enough to accommodate all his horses, and four of the mares had died. When they screamed outside, the stallion had gone berserk in the confines of the cave, and Porrig had had to cut his throat. There was no fodder for the remaining mares, so Sean and Sorka returned with hay and food rations. Then they went off to search for other survivors.

The Du Vieux and Holstroms at Amsterdam Stake, the Radelins and Duquesnes at Bavaria, and the Ciottis at Milan Stake were dead; no trace remained of them or their livestock. The metals and heavy-gauge, silicon-based plastic roofing, though it was heavily pocked, remained as the only evidence of their once thriving settlement. They had used the newly pressed vegetable-fiber slabs for their homes. No one on Pern ever would use such building material again.

From the air, the swath of destruction cut by the falling threadlike rain was obvious, the fringes seething with bloated wormlike excrescences which squadrons of dragonets attacked with flaming breath. The path ended seventy-five klicks beyond the narrow Paradise River, where it had annihilated the Tuareg camps.

That evening, the exhausted settlers fed their dragonets first, and left out mounds of cooked grain for the wild ones that would not approach near enough to be hand-fed.

"Nothing was said about this sort of thing in the EEC report," Mar Dook muttered in a bitter tone.

"Those wretched polka dots no one ever explained," Aisling Hempenstahl said, her voice just loud enough to be heard.

"We've been investigating that possibility," Pol Nietro said, nodding to a weary Bay, who was resting her head against his shoulder.

"Nevertheless, I think we should arrive at some preliminary conclusions before tomorrow," Kitti said. "People will need facts to be reassured."

"Bill and I looked up the reports we did on the polka dots—" Carol Duff-Vassaloe smiled grimly. "—during Landing Year. We didn't investigate every site, but the ones we examined where tree development could be measured suggests a time lapse of at least a hundred and sixty or seventy years. I think it's rather obvious that it was this terrible life-form which caused the patterning, turning all organic material it meets into more of itself. Thank heavens most of our building plastics are silicon-based. If they were carbon-based, we'd all have been killed, without a doubt. This infestation—"

"Infestation?" Chuck Havers's voice broke in incredulous anger.

"What else to call it?" Phas Radamanth remarked in his dogmatic fashion. "What we need to know is how often it occurs? Every hundred and fifty years? That patterning was planet-wide, wasn't it, Carol?" She nodded. "And how long does it last once it occurs?"

"Last?" Chuck demanded, appalled.

"We'll get the answers," Paul Benden said firmly.

CHAPTER

X

The colony's two psychologists flew in late that evening when the infirmary was still crowded with the injured and shocked, and set to work immediately to help reduce traumas. Cherry Duff had suffered a stroke at the news, but was recovering splendidly. Joel and his wife were both prostrated by the loss of their sons. Bernard Hegelman had submerged his own grief to comfort his shattered wife and the other families bereft by loss.

Sean and Sorka had tirelessly sledded in the wounded they located. Even those uninjured were dazed, some weeping uncontrollably until sedated, others pathetically quiet. Porrig Connell had sent his eldest daughter and his wife to help cope with the survivors, while he stayed with his extended family in the cave.

"The first time Porrig Connell ever did anything for anyone else," his son remarked under his breath to Sorka, who berated him for such cynicism. "He wants to use Cricket to service the rest of his mares when they foal. He expects me to give up *my* stallion because he hadn't trained his!"

Sorka wisely said nothing.

With one exception, the distant holdings had contacted Landing, offering either assistance or sympathy. The one exception was the Big Island mining camp, comprised of Avril Bitra, Stev Kimmer, Nabhi Nabol, and a few others. Ongola, running over the log, noticed the absence.

Kenjo, appearing like magic from his distant Honshu plateau, headed the aerial survey. By nightfall, he and his team produced accurate maps and pics of the extent of the terrible "Threadfall," as it soon came to be called. The original complement of biologists reconvened at Landing to ascertain the nature of the beast. Kitti Ping and Wind Blossom lent their special skills to analyze the life-forms as soon as samples were brought in.

Unfortunately too many, acquired at considerable danger to the volunteers, were found apparently moribund in the metal or heavy plastic containers in which they had been contained. Seemingly, after about twenty minutes, all the frenetic activity, the replications of the original strand several thousand times into big wriggling "sausages," ceased. The form unraveled, blackened, and turned into an utterly lifeless, sticky, tarry mess, within a tougher shell.

The captain of the *Mayflower*, which had been trawling at the ragged northern edge of the Fall, inadvertently discovered a segment of Thread in a pail of fish bait, slapped on a tight lid, and reported the find to Landing. He was told to keep it alive, if possible, by judicious feeding until it could be flown to Landing.

By then, the Thread had to be housed in the biggest heavy-gauge plastic barrel on board the *Mayflower*. Ongola transported the tightly sealed barrel, using a long steel cable attached to the big engineering sled. Only when the crew saw the sled disappearing in the distance would they come on deck. The captain was later astonished to learn that his act was considered one of extreme bravery.

By the time the pulsing life-form reached Landing, it coiled, a gross meter long and perhaps ten centimeters in circumference, resembling a heavy hawser. Double-thick slabs of transparent silicon-based building plastic, tightly banded with metal strips, were rigged into a cage, its base quikplased to the floor. Several thin slits with locking flaps were created. A hole the size of the barrel opening was incised in the top, the barrel lid readied, and with the help of grimly anxious volunteers the terrible creature was transferred from barrel to cage. The top opening was sealed as soon as the life-form was dropped into the plastic cube.

One of the men scrambled for a corner to be sick in. Others averted their faces. Only Tarvi and Mar Dook seemed unmoved by the creature's writhing as it engulfed the food that had been placed in the cube.

In its urgency to ingest, the thing rippled in waves of gray, greasy colors: sickly greens, dull pink tones, and an occasional streak of yellow flowed across its surface, the image sickeningly distorted by the thick clear plastic. The outer covering of the beast seemed to thicken. The thick shell probably formed at its demise, the observers guessed, for such remains had been found in rocky places where the organism had starved. The interior of the beast evidently deteriorated as rapidly as it had initially expanded. Was it really alive? Or was it some malevolent chemical entity feeding on life? Certainly its appetite was voracious, although the very act of eating seemed to interfere with whatever physical organization the beast had, as if what it consumed hastened its destruction.

"Its rate of growth is remarkable," Bay said in a very calm voice, for which Pol later praised her, saying that it had provided an example to the others, all stunned by the sight of that gross menace. "One expects such expansion under the microscope but not in the macrocosm. Where can it have come from? Outer space?"

Blank silence met her astonishing query, and those in the room exchanged glances, partly of surprise, partly of embarrassment at Bay's suggestion.

"Do we have any data on the periodicity of comets in this system?" Mar Dook asked hopefully. "That eccentric body? Something brought in from our Oort cloud? Then there's the Hoyle-Wickramansingh theory, which has never been totally discredited, citing the possibility of viruses."

"That's one helluva virus, Mar," Bill Duff said skeptically. "And didn't someone on Ceti III confound that old theory?"

"Considering it drops from the skies," Jim Tillek said, "why couldn't it have a space origin? I'm not the only one who's noticed that red morning star in the east getting brighter these past weeks. A bit of coincidence, isn't it, that the planet with the crazy orbit is coming right into the inner planets, right at the same time this stuff hits us? Could that be the source? Is there any data in the library on that planet? On this sort of thing?"

"I'll ask Cherry. No," Bill Duff corrected himself before anyone could remind him that the redoubtable magistrate was indisposed. "I'll access the information myself and bring back hardcopy to study." He hurried from the room as if glad to have a valid excuse to leave.

"I'll get a sample from that section pressing against the lower slot," Kwan Marceau said, gathering up the necessary implements in the rush of someone who dared not consider overlong what he was about to do.

"A record's being kept of the . . . intake?" Bay asked. She could not quite say "food," remembering what the creatures had already consumed since they had fallen on Pern.

"Now, to judge the frequency of . . . intake"—Pol seized gratefully on that euphemism—"sufficient to keep the . . . organism alive."

"And to see how it dies," Kitti added in a voice so bland that it rang with satisfaction.

"And why all its ilk died in this first infestation," Phas Radamanth added, pulling the EEC pics out of the welter of hardcopy in front of him.

"*Did* all die?" Kitti asked.

By morning, with no report from scientists who had worked through the night, the muttering began: a still-shocked whisper over morning *klah*; a rumor that began to seep into every office and the hastily reopened living quarters on the abandoned residential squares. A huge blaze had been started the previous evening and continued to burn at Bonfire Square. Torches, pitched and ready to be lit, had been piled at each corner, and more were added to the piles throughout the day.

Many of the lighter sleds that had been on the ground at Landing needed new canopies. Sweeping out the detritus of putrid Thread shells was undertaken with masks and heavy work gloves.

There was a new and respectful title for the winged friends: fire-dragons. Even those who had previously scorned the creatures carried tidbits for them in their pockets. Landing was dotted with fat-bellied dragonets sleeping in the sun.

By lunchtime, a meal was served from the old communal kitchens, and rumor was rife. By midafternoon, Ted Tubberman and a fellow malcontent, their faces streaked and drawn by grief, led bereaved relatives to the door of the containment unit.

Paul and Emily came out with Phas Radamanth and Mar Dook.

"Well? Have you discovered what that thing is?" Ted demanded.

"It is a complex but understandable network of filaments, analogous to a Terran mycorrhiza," Mar Dook began, resenting Tubberman's manner but respecting his grief.

"That explains very little, Mar," Ted replied, belligerently sticking out his chin. "In all my years as a botanist, I never saw a plant symbiont danger-ous to humans. What do we get next? A death moss?"

Emily reached out to touch Tubberman's arm in sympathy, but he jerked away.

"We have little to go on," Phas said in a sharp tone. He was tired, and working all night near the monstrosity had been a terrible strain. "Nothing like this has ever been recorded on any of the planets humans have explored. The nearest that has been even imagined were some of the fictional inven-tions during the Age of Religions. We're still refining our understanding of it."

"It's still alive? You're *keeping* it alive!" Ted was livid with irrational out-rage. Beside him, his companions nodded agreement as fresh tears streamed down their faces. Murmuring angrily among themselves, the delegation crowded closer to the entrance, every one of them seeking an outlet for frus-tration and impotent grief.

"Of course, we have to study it, man," Mar Dook said, keeping his voice steady. "And find out exactly what it is. To do that, it must be fed to . . . con-tinue. We've got to ascertain if this is only the beginning of its life cycle."

"Only the beginning!" Tubberman cried. Paul and Phas leapt forward to restrain the grief-mad botanist. Lucy had been his apprentice as well as his daughter, and the two had shared a deep and affectionate bond. "By all that's holy, I'll end it now!"

"Ted, be rational. You're a scientist!"

"I'm a father first, and my daughter was . . . devoured by one of those creatures! So was Joe Milan, and Patsy Swann, Eric Hegelman, Bob Jorgensen, and . . ." Tubberman's face was livid. His fists clenched at his sides, his whole body strained with rage and frustration. He glared accusingly at Emily and Paul. "We trusted you two. How could you bring us to a place that devours our children and all we've achieved the past eight years!" The murmurs of the delegation supported his accusation. "We"—his wide gesture took in the packed numbers behind him—"want that thing dead. You've had long enough to study it. C'mon, people. We know what we have to do!" With a final bitter, searing look at the biologists, he turned, roughly pushing aside those in his path. "Fire kills it!"

He stomped off, raging. His followers left with him.

"It won't matter what they do, Paul," Mar Dook said, restraining Paul Benden from going after Ted. "The beast is moribund now. Give them the corpse to vent their feelings on. We've about finished what examinations we can make anyhow." He shrugged wearily. "For all the good it does us."

"And that is?" Paul inquired encouragingly. Mar Dook and Phas gestured to him and Emily to reenter the containment unit where Pol, Bay, and the two geneticists were still writing up their notes.

Wearily, Mar Dook scrubbed at his face, his sallow skin nearly gray as he slumped onto a table that was littered with tapes and slide containers. "We now know that it is carbon based, has complex, very large proteins which flick from state to state and produce movement, and others which attack and digest an incredible range of organic substances. It is almost as if the creature was designed specifically to be inimical to our kind of life."

"I'm glad you kept that to yourself," Emily said wryly, looking over her shoulder at the door swinging shut on a view of the angry group heading away.

"Mar Dook, you can't mean what you just said," Paul began, resting both hands on the shoulders of the weary biologist. "It may be dangerous, yes—but designed to kill *us*?"

"That *is* just a thought," Mar Dook replied, looking a bit sheepish. "Phas here has a more bizarre suggestion."

Phas cleared his throat nervously. "Well, it's come out of the blue so unexpectedly, I wondered if it could possibly be a weapon, preparing the ground for an invasion?" Dumbfounded, Paul and Emily stared at him, aware of Bay's sniff of disagreement and the amused expression on Kitti Ping's face. "That is not an illogical interpretation, you know. I like it better than Bay's suggestion, that this might be only the beginning of a life cycle. I dread what could follow."

Paul and Emily glanced around them, stunned by such a dreadful possibility. But Pol Nietro rose from his chair and cleared his throat, a tolerant expression on his round face.

"That is also a suggestion from the fiction of the Age of Religions, Mar," Pol said with a wry smile. He glanced apologetically at his wife and then noticed Kitti Ping's reassuring smile. He felt heartened. "And, in my opinion, highly improbable. If the life cycle produced inimical forms, where are the descendants of subsequent metamorphoses? The EEC team may have erred in considering the polka dots nondangerous, but they also discovered no other incongruous life-forms.

"As for an invasion from outer space, every other planet in this sector of space was found to be inimical to carbon-based life-forms." Pol began to warm to his own theory and saw Emily recovering from the shock of the other revelations. "And we have determined that *that*—" He jerked his thumb at the discolored cube. "—is carbon based. So that would seem to more or less limit it to this system. And we will find out how." Pol's burst of explanation seemed to have drained the last of his energy, and he leaned wearily against the high laboratory stand. "I believe I'm right, though. Airing the worst possible interpretations of the data we have gleaned has cleared the air, so to speak." He gave a little, almost apologetic shrug and smiled hopefully at Phas and Bay.

"I still feel we have missed something in our investigations," Phas said, shaking his head. "Something obvious, and important."

"No one thinks straight after forty hours on the trot," Paul said, clasping Phas by the shoulder to give him a reassuring shake. "Let's look at your notes again when you've had some rest and something to eat, away from the stench in here. Jim, Emily, and I will wait and deal with Ted's delegation. They're overreacting." He sighed. "Not that I blame them. Sudden grief is always a shock. However, I personally would rather plan for the worst that can happen. As you've suggested several dire options, we won't be surprised by anything that happens. And we should plan to reduce its effects on the settlements."

Paul had a quiet word with one of the psychologists, whose opinion was that the thwarted tensions of the bereaved might be eased by what he termed "a ritual incineration." So they stepped aside when Ted Tubberman and his adherents demanded the cube and destroyed it in a blazing fire. The resultant stench gagged many, which helped to speed the dispersal of the onlookers. Only Ted and a few others remained to watch the embers cool.

The psychologist shook his head slowly. "I think I'll keep an eye on Ted

Tubberman for a while," he told Paul and Emily. "That was apparently not enough to assuage his grief."

Telescopes were trained on the eccentric planet early the next morning. Its reddish appearance was due, Ezra Keroon suggested, to the aggregated dust swirls it had brought in from the edge of the system. Despite the lack of any proof, the feeling among the observers was that the planet was somehow responsible for the disaster.

During the day, Kenjo's group discovered traces of an earlier fall on Ierne Island, which a witness remembered as more of a rainstorm littered with black motes than a fall of Thread. A scout sent to the northern continent reported traces of recent destruction across the eastern peninsula there. That discovery dispersed the vain hope that the Fall was unique or confined to a specific area. A review of the probe pics from the EEC did nothing to alleviate tension, for the fax incontrovertibly showed the Fall two hundred years before to have been widespread. They figured that the event must have happened just prior to the team's arrival. The demand to know the extent and frequency of the falls increased ominously.

To assuage mounting fears and tension, Betty Musgrave-Blake and Bill Duff undertook to review the survey's original botanical data. Ted Tubberman was the only trained botanist who had survived, but he spent his days tracking down every Thread shell and his evenings burning the piles. The psychologists continued to monitor his aberrant behavior.

Based on the original data, Betty and Bill deduced a two-hundred-year gap between incursions, allowing a span of ten to fifteen years for the vegetation to regenerate on the damaged circles after taking into account the age of some of the largest trees in and near the previous occurrence. Betty delivered their conclusion as a positive statement, meant to engender optimism, but she could provide no answer to the vital question of how long the deadly rain would continue to fall.

In an attempt to disprove Mar's theory of purposeful design or Phas's equally disturbing suggestion of invasion, Ezra Keroon spent that day on the link with the *Yokohama*'s mainframe. His calculations confirmed beyond question that the eccentric planet had an orbit of 250 years. But it only stayed in the inner system for a little while, the way Halley's comet periodically visited Sol. It was too much to suppose there was no connection, and, after consulting Paul and Emily, Ezra programmed one of the *Yokohama*'s few remaining probes to circumnavigate the planet and discover its composition and, especially, the components of its apparently gaseous envelope.

Though all reports were honestly and fully presented to the community as soon they came in, by evening speculation had produced alarming interpretations. Grimly the more responsible members tried to calm those who gave way to panic.

Then a perplexed Kenjo sought Betty out with a disturbing observation. She immediately informed Paul and Emily, and a quiet meeting was arranged with those who were able to discuss the situation with some detachment.

"You all know that I've overflown to map the damage," Kenjo began. "I didn't know what I'd seen until I'd seen it often enough to realize what was *not* there." He paused, as if steeling himself for rebuke or disbelief. "I don't think all thread starved to death. And crazy Tubberman hasn't gotten as far as I have. In most places, there are shells! But in nine circles that I have seen—and I landed to be sure I make no mistake—there were no shells." He made a cutting gesture with both hands. "None. And these circles were by themselves, not in a group, and the area—demolished—was not as big as usual." He glanced at each of the serious faces about him. "I see. I observe. I have pics, too."

"Well," Pol said, heaving a weary sigh and absently patting the folded hands of his wife beside him at the table. "It is biologically consistent that to perpetuate a species many are sent and few are chosen. Perhaps the journey through space vitiates most of the organisms. I'm almost relieved that a few can survive and flourish. It makes more sense. I prefer your theory to some of the others that have been bruited about."

"Yes, but what do they become in the next metamorphosis?" Bay wondered, her face reflecting depression. Sometimes being right was another sort of failure.

"We'd better find out," Paul said, glancing around for support. "Is there one nearby, Kenjo?" When the pilot pointed to its position on the map, Paul nodded. "Good, then. Phas, Pol, Bill, Ezra, Bay and Emily, just slip out of Landing in small sleds. Let's see if we can prevent a new batch of wild notions. Report back here as soon as you can."

Paul sent Betty back to her home and her new baby, telling her to rest. Boris Pahlevi and Dieter Clissman were summoned and set to work designing a comprehensive computer program to analyze the data as it continued to come in. Then Paul and Ongola settled back to wait tensely for the other specialists to return.

Pol, Bay, and Phas were the first back, and they brought little good news.

"All the insects, slug-forms, and grubs we found on those sites," Phas reported, "appear harmless enough. Some of them have already been catalogued, but," he added with a shrug, "we've barely begun to identify creatures and their roles in the ecology of this planet. Kenjo was right to alert us. Clearly some of the Thread survives to propagate itself, so Bay's theory is the most viable to date." Phas seemed relieved. "But I won't rest easy until we have discovered the entire cycle."

Late in the afternoon of the third day after that first Fall, an almost hysterical call came in from Wade Lorenzo of Sadrid in Macedonia Province. Jacob Chernoff, who took the call, immediately contacted Ongola and Paul at the administration building. "He says it's coming straight across the sea, right at him, sir. His stake is due west on the twenty-degree line. I'm holding him on channel thirty-seven."

Even as Paul picked up the handset and punched for the channel, he located the coastal stake of Sadrid on the big map of the continent.

"Get everyone in under silicon plastic," he ordered. "Use fire to ignite the stuff where it hits the surface. Use torches if necessary. D'you have any dragonets?"

The stakeholder's deep breath was audible as he fought for self-control. "We have some dragonets, sir, and we've two flamethrowers—used 'em to cut down bush. We thought it was just a very bad rain squall until we saw the fish eating. Can't you come?"

"We'll get there as soon as possible!"

Paul told Jacob to tell no one of the new Fall.

"I don't want to cause more panic than there already is, sir," Jacob agreed.

Paul smiled briefly at the boy's fervor, then dialed Jim Tillek at the Monaco Bay harbormaster's office. He inquired if there were any trawlers southwest near Sadrid.

"Not today. Any trouble?"

So much for trying to sound casual, Paul thought. "Can you get here to admin without appearing to rush?"

Ongola was looking grimly at the map, his eyes flicking from Macedonia to Delta. "Your Boca River Stake is not that far from Sadrid," he told the admiral.

"I noticed." Paul dialed the channel link to his stake and in terse sentences told his wife the grim news and instructed her on what precautions to take. "Ju, it may not reach us but . . ."

"It's best to be on the safe side with something like this, isn't it?"

Paul was proud of her calm response. "I'll give you an update as soon as we've got one. With any luck, you've got at least an hour's leeway if it's just now at Sadrid. I'll be there as soon as I can. Quite possibly, Boca's far enough north. This stuff seems to fall in a southwesterly drift."

"Ask her if her dragonets are acting normally," Ongola suggested.

"Sunning themselves, as always at this time of day," Ju replied. "I'll watch them. They really do anticipate this stuff?"

"Ongola thinks so. I'll check with you later, Ju."

"I've just got through to the Logorides at Thessaly," Ongola said. "They might be in the path. Had we better warn Caesar at Roma Stake? He's got all that livestock."

"He was also smart enough to put up stone buildings, but call him and then find out if Boris and Dieter have run their new program. I wish the hell we knew when it started, how far it'll travel," Paul muttered anxiously. "I'll organize transport." He dialed the main engineering shed and asked for Kenjo.

"There's more Thread? How far away?" Kenjo asked. "Sadrid? On the twentieth? I've got something that could make it in just over an hour." There was a ripple of excitement in Kenjo's usually even tone. "Fulmar worked out jet-assist units on one of the medium sleds. Fulmer thinks we could get seven hundred kph out of it, at least, even fully loaded. More if we run light."

"We're going to have to pack as many of the flamethrowers as possible plus emergency supplies. We'll use HNO_3 cylinders—they'll be like using fire *and* water at once on the Thread. Pol and Bay don't weigh much, and they'll be invaluable as observers. We need at least one medic, a couple of joats, Tarvi, Jim, and me. Eight. All right, then, we'll be with you directly." Paul turned to Ongola. "Any luck?"

"Since we can't tell them when it started, they want to know when it ends," Ongola said. "The more data we can give them, the more accurate they will be . . . next time. Am I among the eight?"

Paul shook his head with regret. "I need you here to deal with any panic. Blast it, but we've got to get organized for this."

Ongola snorted to himself. Paul Benden was already a legend in organizing and operating at high efficiency in emergency situations. Observers, crew, and supplies boarded the augmented sled within twenty minutes of the initial call, and it was airborne and out of sight before Ongola heard the muted roar of its improved drive.

Kenjo drove the sled at its maximum speed, passengers and supplies securely strapped in safety harnesses. They sped across the verdant tip of the untouched peninsula past the Jordan River, and then out to sea where the turbulence of sporadic but heavy squalls added more discomfort to an already rough ride in a vehicle not designed for such velocities.

"No sign of the leading edge of Fall. Half of that cloud to the south of us is more squalls," Paul said, looking up from the scope and rubbing his eyes. "Maybe, just maybe," he added softly, "those squalls also saved Sadrid."

Despite the excessive speed, the journey, mainly over water, seemed to continue endlessly. Suddenly, Kenjo reduced speed. The sea became less of a blur to starboard, and on the port side, the vast, approaching land was just visible through the mist of squall. Sunlight broke through cloud to shine impartially on tossing vegetation and denuded alleys.

"It's an ill wind," Jim Tillek remarked, pointing to the sea, which was disturbed more by underwater activity than by wind. "By the way, before I left Monaco Bay, I sent our finny friends to see what they could find out."

"Good heavens!" Bay exclaimed, pressing her face against the thick plastic canopy. "They can't have made it here so fast."

"Not likely," Jim replied, chuckling, "but the locals are feeding very well indeed."

"Stay seated!" Kenjo cried, fighting the yoke of the sled.

"If the dolphins can find out where it started . . . Data, that's what Dieter and Boris need." Paul resumed manning the forward scope. "Sadrid wasn't entirely lucky," he added, frowning. "Just as if someone had shaved the vegetation off the ground with a hot knife," he muttered under his breath, and turned away. "Get us down as fast as possible, Kenjo!"

"It was the wind," Wade Lorenzo told the rescue team. "The wind saved us, and the squall. Came down in sheets, but it was water, not Thread. No, we're mostly okay," he assured them, pointing to the dragonets, grooming themselves on the rooftrees. "They saved us, just like I heard they did at Landing." The younger children were just being shepherded out of one of the larger buildings, wide-eyed with apprehension as they looked about them. "But we don't know if Jiva and Bahka are all right. They were trawling." He gestured hopelessly to the west.

"If they went west and north, they'd've had a good chance," Jim told him.

"But we are ruined," Athpathis added. The agronomist's face was a picture of defeat as he indicated the ravaged fields and orchards.

"There're still plenty of seedlings at Landing," Pol Nietro assured him, patting his back with clumsy sympathy. "And one can grow several crops a year in this climate."

"We'll be back to you later," Paul said, helping to unload flamethrowers. "Jim, will you organize the mop-up here? You know what to do. We've got to track the main Fall to its end. There you are, Wade. Go char the bastards!"

"But Admiral—" Athpathis began, the whites of his large fearful eyes accentuated in his sun-darkened face.

"There's two other stakes in the way of this menace," Paul said, climbing back into the sled and fastening the hatch.

"Straight to your place, Paul?" Kenjo asked, lifting the sled.

"No, I want you to go north first. See if we can find Jiva and Bahka. And until we find the edge of the Fall."

As soon as Kenjo had hoisted the sled, he slapped on the jet assist, slamming his passengers back into their seats. But almost immediately he eased back on the power. "Sir, I think it's missed your place."

Instantly Paul pressed his eyes to the scope and, with incredible relief, saw the vegetation along the beach tossing in the wake of squall winds. Reassured, he could concentrate on the job at hand without divided priorities.

"Why, it just cuts off," Bay said, surprised.

"Rain, I think," Pol remarked as he, too, craned his neck to see out the siliplex canopy. "And look, isn't that an orange sail?"

Paul looked up from the scope with a weary smile. "Indeed it is, and intact. Mark your position, Mister Fusaiyuki, and let's get to Caesar's with all available speed." He took a more comfortable position in his seat and gripped the arm rests.

"Aye, aye, sir."

The six passengers once again endured the effects of speed and, once again, Kenjo's abrupt braking. That time he added such a turn to port that the sled seemed to spin on its tail.

"I've marked my position, Admiral. Your orders, sir?"

Paul Benden's spine gave an involuntary shudder, which he hoped was due more to the unexpected maneuver than to Kenjo's naval address.

"Let's follow the path and see how wide a corridor it punches. I'll contact the other stakes to stand down from the alert."

He permitted himself to contact his wife first and gave her a brief report, as much to lock the details in his own mind as to relieve hers.

"Shall I send a crew to help?" she asked. "Landing's report says the stuff often has to be burnt to be killed."

"Send Johnny Greene and Greg Keating in the faster sled. We've spare flamethrowers with us."

Others volunteered to send their sons, and Paul accepted those offers. Caesar Galliani, making the same offer, added that he wanted his sons back in time to milk the big Roma herd.

"I was right, wasn't I," the vet said with a chuckle, "to spend so much energy on stone buildings?"

"You were indeed, Caesar."

"There's nothing like stone walls to make you feel secure. The boys'll be on their way as soon as you give me a position. You'll keep us posted, won't you, Admiral?"

Paul winced at that second unconscious use of his former rank. After seven happy years as a civilian agronomist, he had no wish to resume the responsibilities of command. Then his eyes were caught by the circles of destruction, so hideously apparent from the air, interspersed with untouched swaths where squally rain had drowned Thread before it could reach the surface. Rain and dragonets! Fragile allies against such devastation. If he had his way . . . Paul halted that train of thought. He was not in command; he did not wish to be obliged to take command. There were younger men to assume such burdens.

"I make the corridor fifty klicks wide, Admiral," Kenjo announced. Paul realized that the others had been quietly conferring on details.

"You can watch vegetation disintegrating by the yard," Bay said anxiously. She caught Paul's eyes. "Rain isn't enough."

"It helped," Tarvi answered her, but he, too, looked at Paul.

"We've got reinforcements coming from Thessaly and Roma. We'll scorch where we have to on our way back to Sadrid. Set down where you can, Kenjo. Landing will need to know the details we've gotten today. Data they want, data they'll have."

By the time all the available HNO_3 cylinders were exhausted, so were the crews. Pol and Bay had followed diligently after the flamethrower teams, taking notes on the pattern of the stuff, grateful that squall activity had somewhat limited the destruction. When Paul had thanked the men from Thessaly and Roma, he told Kenjo to make reasonable speed to Sadrid to collect Jim Tillek.

"And so we must arm ourselves with tongues of flame against this menace to our kind and generous planet," Tarvi said softly to Paul as they finally headed eastward toward a fast-approaching night. "Will Sadrid be safe now?"

"On the premise that lightning doesn't strike twice in the same place?" Paul's tone was droll. "No promises can be made on that score, Tarvi. I am hoping, however, that Boris and Dieter will soon come up with a few answers." Then, his expression anxious, he turned to Pol. "This couldn't fall at random, could it?"

"You prefer the theory that it's planned? No, Paul, we've established that we're dealing with an unreasoning, voraciously hungry organism. There isn't a discernible intelligence," Pol replied, clenching and releasing his fist, surprised at his own vehemence, "much less a trace of sentience. I continue to favor Bay's theory of a two- or three-stage life cycle. Even so, it is only remotely possible that intelligence develops at a later stage."

"The wherries?" Tarvi asked facetiously.

"No, no, don't be ridiculous. We've traced them back to a sea eel, a common ancestor for both them and the dragonets."

"The dragonets were more of a help than I expected," Tarvi admitted. "Sallah insists they've a high level of intelligence."

"Pol, have you or Bay attempted to measure that intelligence when you used mentasynth enhancement?" Paul Benden asked.

"No, not really," Pol replied. "There's been no need to, once we demonstrated that an enhanced empathy made them more biddable. There have been other priorities."

"The main priority as of now is establishing the parameters of this menace," Paul muttered. "We'd all better get some rest."

Once the rescue team had returned to Landing, it was impossible to deny the fact of the new incursion. Despite a comm silence on their trip, rumors were inevitable.

"The only good thing about it," Paul told Emily as he consumed a hastily prepared meal, "was that it was sufficiently far away from here."

"We still don't have enough data to establish either frequency or probable corridors of the stuff," Dieter Clissmann announced. "The dolphins apparently could not find out where or when it started. Marine life doesn't keep time. Boris is adding in random factors of temperature variations, high- and low-pressure areas, frequency of rain, and wind velocity to the data." He gave a long sigh, combing thick hair back from his forehead. "Drowns in the rain, huh? Fire and water kill it! That's some consolation."

◆ ◆ ◆

Few were as easily consoled. There were even some at Landing who were relieved that other sections of the continent had suffered the same disaster. The positive benefit of fear and horror was that emergency measures were no longer resisted. Some had felt that precautions emanating from Landing violated their charter autonomy. The more outspoken revised their objections when pictures of the devastation on the Sadrid corridor—as Pol termed it— were distributed. After that, Ongola and his communications team were kept busy briefing distant stakeholders.

Tarvi drafted a crew to work round the clock, adapting empty cylinders into flamethrowers and filling them with HNO_3. The easily made oxidant had not only proved to be very effective at destroying Thread but could be synthesized cheaply from air and water, using only hydroelectricity, and was not a pollutant. Most importantly, dragonet hide and human skin were usually not severely damaged from spillage. A wet cloth, applied within about twenty seconds, prevented a bad burn. Kenjo led a group in rigging holders for flamethrowers on the heavier sleds. He was adamant that the best defense was not only offense but aerial. He had many willing supporters among those at Landing who had lived through the First Fall.

Fire was the top choice for weapon. As one wit said, since no one had ever figured out how to make rain on demand, fire was the only reliable defense. Even the most ardent supporters of the dragonets did not wish to rely totally on their continued assistance.

There were not hands enough to do all the jobs required. Twice Paul and Emily were called in to arbitrate labor-pirating. The agronomists and veterinarians hastily reinforced livestock shelters. Caves were explored as possible alternate accommodations. Empty warehouses at Landing were made into shelters for any stakeholders who wished to house stock for safety's sake. Joel Lilienkamp insisted that due to the worker shortage the holders themselves would have to reinforce any buildings they preempted. Many stakeholders felt that that was Landing's job; some were unwilling to leave their stakes unless, and until, assured of safe quarters. In eight years, the population of the settlers had increased far beyond the point where the original site could house even half the current numbers.

Porrig Connell remained in his cave, having discovered that there were sufficient interlinking chambers to accommodate his entire extended family and their livestock. In addition to stabling for his mares and foals, he had also constructed a stallion box in which Cricket had been made very comfortable. Magnanimously, he allowed the survivors of some other families to remain in his cavesite until they found their own.

Because they had been the colony's leaders, Paul Benden and Emily Boll—as well as Jim Tillek, Ezra Keroon, and Ongola—found that many decisions were being referred to them, despite the fact that they had stepped down from their previous administrative duties.

"I'd far rather they came to me than to Ted Tubberman." Paul remarked wearily to Ongola when the former communications officer brought him the latest urgent queries from outlying stakes. He turned to the psychologist Tom Patrick, who had come to report on the latest round of gripes and rumors. "Tom?"

"I don't think you can stall a showdown much longer," he said, "or you and Emily will lose all credibility. That would be a big error. You two may not want to take command, but someone will have to. Tubberman's constantly undermining community effort and spirit. He's so totally negative that you ought to be thankful that most of the time he's out trying singlehandedly to clear the continent of rotting Threadshell. Grief has totally distorted his perceptions and judgment."

"Surely no one believes his ranting?" Emily asked.

"There're just enough long-buried gripes and resentments, and good honest gut-fear, right now that some people do listen to him. Especially in the absence of authorized versions," Tom replied. "Tubberman's complaints have a certain factual basis. Warped, to be sure." The psychologist shrugged, raising both hands, palms up. "In time, he'll work against himself—I hope. Meanwhile he's roused a substantial undercurrent of resentment which had better be countered soon. Preferably by you gentlemen and Emily and the other captains. They still trust you, you know, in spite of Tubberman's accusations."

"So the Rubicon must be crossed again," Paul said whimsically, and exhaled. He caught himself rubbing his left thumb against the insensitive skin of his replacement fingers and stopped. Leaning wearily back in his chair, he put both hands behind his head as if supporting an extra weight.

◆ ◆ ◆

"I can lead a meeting, Paul," Cabot said when Paul contacted him on a secured comm channel, "but they subconsciously consider you and Emily their leaders. Force of habit."

"Any decision to reinstate us must be spontaneous," Paul replied after a long and thoughtful pause. Slowly Emily nodded. The last days had aged both admiral and governor. "The matter must be handled strictly on the charter protocol, though by all that's holy, I never anticipated having to invoke those contingency clauses."

"Thank all the powers that be that they're there," Cabot said fervently. "It'll take an hour or two to organize things here. Oh, by the way, we also had a few messages across the river early yesterday morning. Didn't notice until about noon today. Hit the southern edge of Bordeaux. We gave Pat and his crew a hand. All's safe here." With that, he rang off, leaving Paul dumbfounded.

"After our little brush with the stuff," Cabot said when he arrived in person, "I'm beginning to appreciate the gravity of the colony's situation." A hopeful smile, not echoed by the expression in his keen gray eyes, curved his strong mouth. "Is it as bad as rumor has it?"

"Probably. Depends on the source of the rumor," Paul answered with an honest grimace.

"Depends on whether you're an optimist or pessimist," Jim Tillek added. "I've been in worse fixes on the asteroid runs and come out with life and lung. I prefer to have a planet to maneuver in, on, over. And the seas."

Cabot's smile faded as he regarded the five people gathered discreetly in the met tower.

"Most of what we *know*," Paul said, "is negative. But—" He began to refute the prevalent rumors by ticking them off on his strong, work-stained fingers. "The Threads are unlikely to be the forerunner of an alien invasion. It was not unique to this area. It did strike the planet in much the same way, to judge by the EEC records, almost exactly two hundred years ago. It may or may not emanate from the eccentric planet, which has a two-hundred-and-fifty-year orbit. And although we do not know what its life cycle is, or even if it does have one—that is the most viable theory—Thread is not the initial stage of tunnel snakes, for example, who have a much more respectable lineage, nor of any of the other kinds of life we've had a look at so far."

"I see." Cabot slowly nodded his handsome leonine head as he fingered his lips in thought. "No reassuring forecast available?"

"Not yet. As Tom here recommends, we need a forum in which to air grievances and correct misconceptions," Paul went on. "It didn't miss Boca Stake because Paul Benden owns it, or drop on Sadrid because they're the newest, or stop short of Thessaly because Gyorgy was one of the first charterers to claim his stake. We can, and will, survive this hazard, but we cannot have the indiscriminate conscriptions of technicians and able-bodied workers. It is apparent to anyone pausing to think that we also cannot survive if everyone hares off in opposite directions. Or if some of the wilder notions, including Tubberman's, are not dismissed and morale restored."

"In short, what you want is a suspension of autonomy?"

"Not what I want," Paul replied clearly and with emphasis, "but a centralized administration"—Cabot grinned at the admiral's choice of words—"will be able to efficiently organize available workers, distribute matériel and supplies, and make sure that the majority survive. Joel Lilienkamp locked up Stores today, claiming inventory, to prevent panic requisitions. People must realize that this *is* a survival situation."

"Together we stand, divided we fall?" Cabot used the old saying with respect.

"That's it."

"The trick will be in getting all our independent spirits to see the wisdom," Tom Patrick said, and Cabot nodded agreement.

"I must emphasize," Paul went on, looking quickly at Emily, who nodded approval, "that it doesn't matter who administers during the emergency so long as some authority is recognized, and obeyed, that will ensure survival."

After a pause, Cabot added thoughtfully, "We're years from help. Did we burn all our bridges?"

◆ ◆ ◆

Considerable surprise and relief permeated Landing the next morning when Cabot Francis Carter, the colony's senior legist, broadcast the announcement that a mass meeting was scheduled for the following evening. Representatives of every major stake, charter, or contract, would be expected to attend.

By the night of the meeting, the electricians had managed to restore power to one end of Bonfire Square by means of underground conduits. Where lamps were still dark, torches had been secured to the standards. The lighted area was filled with benches and chairs. The platform, originally constructed for musicians for the nightly bonfires, contained a long table, set with six chairs along one side. There was light enough to see those who took places there.

When neither Paul Benden nor Emily Boll appeared, a murmur of surprise rippled around those assembled. Cabot Francis Carter led Mar Dook, Pol and Bay Harkenon-Nietro, Ezra Keroon, and Jim Tillek onto the stage.

"We have had time to mourn our losses," Cabot began, his sonorous voice easily reaching to the very last bench. Even the children listened in silence. "And they have been heavy. They could have been worse, and there can't be one among us who doesn't give thanks to our small fire-breathing, dragonlike allies.

"I don't have all bad news for you tonight. I wish I had better. We can give a name to the stuff that killed some of our loved ones and wiped out five stakes: it's a very primitive mycorrhizoid life-form. Mar Dook here tells me that on other planets, including our own Earth, very simple fungi can be generally found in a symbiotic association with trees, the mycelium of the fungus with the roots of a seed plant. We've all seen it attack vegetation—"

"And just about anything else," Ted Tubberman shouted from the left-hand side of the audience.

"Yes, that is tragically true." Cabot did not look at the man or attempt to lighten the tone of the meeting, but he intended to control it. He raised his voice slightly. "What we are only just beginning to realize is that the phenomenon is planetwide and the last occurrence was approximately two hundred years ago." He paused to allow the listeners to absorb that fact, then stolidly held up his hands to silence the murmurs. "Soon we will be able to predict exactly when and where this Threadfall is likely to strike again, because, unfortunately, it will. But this is *our* planet," he stated with an expression of fierce determination, "and no damned mindless Thread is going to make us leave."

"You stupid bastard, we *can't* leave!" Ted Tubberman jumped to his feet, wildly waving clenched fists in the air. "You fixed it so we'll rot here, sucked up by those effing things. We can't leave! We'll all die here."

His outburst started a sullen, murmurous roll in the audience. Sean, sitting with Sorka to the edge of the crowd, was indignant.

"Damnfool loud mouth charterer," Sean murmured to Sorka. "He knew this was a one-way trip, only now everything's not running smooth enough for him, it has to be *someone's* fault." Sean snorted his contempt.

Sorka shushed him to hear Cabot's rebuttal.

"I don't look at our situation as hopeless, Tubberman," Cabot began, his trained voice drowning the murmurs in a firm, confident, and determined tone. "Far from it! I prefer to think positively. I see this as a challenge to our ingenuity, to our adaptability. Mankind has survived more dangerous environments than Pern. We've got a problem and we must cope with it. We must solve it to survive. And survive we will!" When Cabot saw the big botanist gathering breath, he raised his voice. "When we signed the charter, we all knew there'd be no turning back. Even if we could, I, for one, wouldn't consider running home." His voice became rich with contempt for the faint of heart, the coward, and the quitter. "For there's more on this planet for me than First or Earth ever held! I'm not going to let this phenomenon do me out of the home I've built, the stock I plan to raise, the quality of life I enjoy!" With a contemptuous sweep of his hand, he dismissed the menace as a minor inconvenience. "I'll fight it every time it strikes my stake or my neighbors', with every ounce of strength and every resource I possess.

"Now," he went on in a less fervent tone, "this meeting has been called, in the democratic manner outlined by our charter, to make plans on how best to sustain our colony during this emergency. We are, in effect, under siege by this mycorrhizoid. So we must initiate measures and develop the necessary strategy by which to minimize its effect on our lives and property."

"Are you suggesting martial law, Cabot?" Rudi Shwartz demanded, rising to his feet, his expression carefully guarded.

Cabot gave a wry chuckle. "As there is no army on Pern, Rudi, martial law is impossible. However, circumstances force us to consider suspending our present autonomy in order to reduce the damage which this Thread apparently can—and will—do to both the ecology of the planet and the economy of this colony. I'm suggesting that a reversion to the centralized government of our first year on Pern be considered at this point in time." His next words rose to a near bellow to drown out the protests. "*And* whatever measures are required to ensure the survival of the colony, unpalatable though they may be to us as individuals who have enjoyed our autonomy."

"And these measures have already been decided?" someone asked.

"By no means," Cabot assured the woman. "We don't even yet know that much about our—adversary—but plans must be made now, for every possible contingency. We know that Thread falls on a worldwide scale, so sooner or later it will affect every stake. We have to minimize that danger. That will mean centralization of existing food supplies and matériel, and a return to hydroponics. It definitely means that some of you technicians will be asked to return to Landing, since your particular skills can be best exercised here. It means we're all going to have to work together again instead of going our separate ways."

"What option do we have?" another woman asked in the slight pause that followed. She sounded resigned.

"Some of you have fairly large common stakes," Cabot answered in the most reasonable of tones. "You could probably do quite well on your own. Any central organization here at Landing would have to consider the needs of its population first, but it wouldn't be the case of 'Never Darken Our Doorstep Again.' " He gave a brief reassuring smile in her general direction. "That's why we meet here tonight. To discuss all the options as thoroughly as the charter's conditions and the colony's prospects were initially discussed."

"Wait just a minute!" Ted Tubberman cried, jumping to his feet again, spreading out his arms and looking around, his chin jutting forward aggressively. "We've got a surefire option, a realistic one. We can send a homing capsule to Earth and ask for assistance. This is a state of emergency. We need help!"

"I told ya," Sean murmured to Sorka, "squealing like a stuck pig. Earth lands here, girl, and we make for the Barrier Range and stay lost!"

"I wouldn't bet on Earth sending any," Joel Lilienkamp said from the front of the audience, his words drowned by the cries of colonists agreeing with Ted.

"We don't need Earth mucking about Pern," Sean cried, jumping to his feet and flourishing his arm. "This is *our* planet!"

Cabot called for order, but very little of the commotion subsided. Ezra Keroon got to his feet, trying to help. Finally, making a megaphone of his hands, he bellowed his message. "Hold it down, now, friends. I have to remind you all—*listen to me!*—it'd be over ten years before we got a reply. Of any kind."

"Well, I for one don't want old Terra," Jim Tillek said over the loud reaction to that, "or even First, poking their noses in *our* business. That is, if they'd bother to respond. For sure, if they condescended to help, they'd mortgage all of us to the hilt for aid. And end up owning all the mineral rights and most of the arable land. Or have you all forgotten Ceti III? I also don't see why a central administration during this emergency is such a big deal. Makes sense to me. Share and share alike!"

A low murmur of agreement could be clearly heard, although many faces wore discouraged or sullen expressions.

"He's right, Sorka," Sean said in a voice loud enough for others around him to hear.

"Dad and Mother think so, too," Sorka added, pointing to her parents, who were sitting several rows ahead.

"We've got to send a message," Ted Tubberman shouted, shaking off the attempts of his immediate neighbors to make him sit down. "We've got to tell them we're in trouble. We've a right to help! What's wrong in sending a message?"

"What's wrong?" Wade Lorenzo shouted from the back of the audience. "We need help right now, Tubberman, not ten to thirty years from now.

Why, by then, we'd probably have the thing licked. A Fall's not all that bad," he added with the confidence of experience. He sat down amid hoots and shouts of dissent, mainly from those who had been at Landing during the tragedy.

"And don't forget that it took half a century before Earth went to Ceti III's assistance," Betty Musgrave-Blake said, jumping to her feet.

Other comments were voiced.

"Yeah, Captain Tillek's right. We've got to solve our own problems. We can't wait for Earth."

"Forget it, Tubberman."

"Sit down and shut up, Tubberman."

"Cabot, call him to order. Let's get on with this meeting."

Similar sentiments rose from all sides.

His neighbors forced the botanist down and, dismayed by the lack of support, Ted shook off the compelling hands and crossed his arms defiantly on his chest. Tarvi Andiyar and Fulmar Stone moved to stand nearby. Sallah watched apprehensively, although she knew full well the strength belied by Tarvi's lean frame.

Sean nudged Sorka. "They'll shut him up, and then we can get to the meat of all this talking," he said. "I hate meetings like this—people sounding off just to make a noise and act big when they don't know what they're talking about."

Raising a hand to be recognized, Rudi Shwartz again got to his feet. "If, as you've suggested, Cabot, the larger stakes could remain self-governing, how would a central government be organized? Would the large stakes be at all responsible to it?"

"It's more a matter of the fair allocation of food, materials, and shelter, Rudi," Joel Lilienkamp said, rising, "rather than—"

"You mean, we don't have enough food?" an anxious voice broke in.

"For now, we do, but if this Threadstuff is planetwide . . . we all see what it did to Landing's fields," Joel went on, motioning to the dark, ravaged area, "and if it keeps coming back, well—" A woman made a protest of dismay that was clearly audible. "Well," he went on, hitching up his trousers, "everyone deserves a fair share of what we've got. I see nothing wrong with going back to hydroponics for a while. We did just fine for fifteen years on shipboard, didn't we? I'll take any odds we can do it again."

His jovial challenge met with mixed reactions, some cheering, others clearly apprehensive.

"Remember, too, folks, that Thread doesn't affect the sea," Jim Tillek said, his cheerfulness unforced. "We can live, and live well, from the sea alone."

"Most early civilizations lived almost entirely from the sea," Mairi Hanrahan cried in a ringing, challenging tone. "Joel's right—we can use alternate methods of growing. And, as long as we can harvest the sea for fresh protein, we'll be just fine. I think we all ought to buck up, instead of collapsing under the first little snag." She stared significantly at Ted Tubberman.

"Little snag?" he roared. He would have shoved through the crowd to get to Mairi if he had not been restrained. Tarvi and Fulmar moved in closer to him.

"Hardly a *little* snag," Mar Dook said quickly, raising his voice over the ripple of mixed remonstrance and support. "And certainly tragic for many of us. But let's not fight among ourselves. It's equally useless for us to bitch that the EEC team did not do a thorough inspection of this planet and grossly misled us. But this world has already proved that it can survive such an incursion and regenerate. Are we humans any less resilient with the resources we have at hand?" He tapped his forehead significantly.

"I don't want just to survive, hand to mouth," Ted Tubberman shouted, his chin jerking out belligerently, "cooped up in a building, wondering if those things are going to eat their way through to me!"

"Ted, that's the biggest bunch of bilgewash I've ever heard from a grown man," Jim Tillek said. "We got a bit of a problem with our new world that I sure as hell am going to help solve. So quit your bitching, and let's figure out just how to cope. We're here, man, and we're going to survive!"

"I want us to send home for help," someone else said, calm but firm. "I feel that we're going to need the defenses a sophisticated society can supply, especially as we brought so little technology with us. And most especially if this stuff returns so often."

"Once we've sent for help, we have to take what is sent," Cabot said quickly.

"Lili, what odds are you taking that Earth would send us help?" Jim Tillek asked.

Ted Tubberman jumped to his feet again. "Don't bet on it. Vote on it! If this meeting's really democratic, that is, let's vote to send a mayday to Federated Sentient Planets."

"I second the motion," one of the medics said, along with several others.

"Rudi," Cabot said, "appoint two other stewards and let's take a hand vote."

"Not everyone's here tonight," Wade Lorenzo pointed out.

"If they don't wish to attend a scheduled meeting, they will have to abide by the decision of those who did," Cabot replied sternly. He was met with shouts of agreement. "Let the vote be taken on the motion before us. Those in favor of sending a homing capsule to the Federated Sentient Planets for assistance, raise their hands."

Hands were duly raised and counted by the stewards, Rudi Shwartz taking note of the count. When Cabot called for those opposed to sending for help, the majority was marked. As soon as Cabot announced the results, Ted Tubberman was vituperative.

"You're damned fools. We can't lick this stuff by ourselves. There's no place safe from it on this planet. Don't you remember the EEC reports? The entire planet was eaten up. It took more than two hundred years to recover. What chance have we?"

"That is enough, Tubberman," Cabot roared at him. "You asked for a vote. It was taken in sight of all, and the *majority* has decided against sending for help. Even if the decision had been in favor, our situation is serious enough so that certain measures must be initiated immediately.

"One priority is the manufacture of metal sheeting to protect existing buildings, no matter where they are. The second is to manufacture HNO_3 cylinders and flamethrower components. A third is to conserve all materials and supplies. Another problem is keeping a good eastern watch at every stake until a pattern can be established for Threadfall.

"I'm asking that we temporarily reinstate Emily Boll and Paul Benden as leaders. Governor Boll kept her planet fed and free despite a five-year-long Nathi space embargo, and Admiral Benden is by far the best man to organize an effective defense strategy.

"I'm calling for a show of hands now, and we'll make it a proper referendum when we know exactly how long the state of emergency will last." A ripple of assent greeted his crisp, decisive statements. "Rudi, prepare for another count." He waited a moment as the crowd shifted restlessly. "Let's have a show of hands on implementing those priorities tonight, with Admiral Benden and Governor Boll in charge."

Many hands were immediately thrust in the air, while others came up more slowly as the undecided took heart from their neighbors' resolution. Even before Rudi gave him the count, Cabot could see that the vote was heavily in favor of the emergency measures.

"Governor Boll, Admiral Benden, will you accept this mandate?" he asked formally.

"It was rigged!" Ted Tubberman shouted. "I tell you, rigged. They just want to get back into power again." His accusations broke off suddenly as Tarvi and Fulmar pushed him firmly back down on the bench.

"Governor? Admiral?" Cabot ignored the interruption. "You two still have the best qualifications for the jobs to be done, but if you decline, I will accept nominations from the floor." He waited expectantly, giving no hint of his personal preference in the matter and paying no attention to the restless audience and the rising murmur of anxious whispers.

Slowly Emily Boll rose to her feet. "I accept."

"As I do," Paul Benden said, standing beside the governor. "But only for the duration of this emergency."

"You believe that?" Tubberman roared, breaking loose from his restrainers.

"That is quite enough, Tubberman," Cabot shouted, appearing to lose his professional detachment. "The majority supports this temporary measure even if you won't." Slowly the audience quieted. Cabot waited until there was complete silence. "Now, I've saved the worst news until I was certain we were all resolved to work together. Thanks to Kenjo and his survey teams, Boris and Dieter believe that there is a pattern emerging. If they're right, we have to expect this Thread to fall again tomorrow afternoon at Malay River and proceed across Cathay Province to Mexico on Maori Lake."

"On Malay?" Chuck Kimmage jumped to his feet, his wife clutching his arm, both of them horrified. Phas had managed to find and warn all the other stakers at Malay and Mexico, but Chuck and Chaila had arrived just before the meeting, too late to be privately informed.

"And all of us will help preserve your stakes," Emily Boll said in a loud firm voice.

Paul jumped up on the platform, raising his hands and glancing at Cabot for permission to speak. "I'm asking for volunteers to man sleds and flamethrowers. Kenjo and Fulmar have worked out a way of mounting them. Some are already in place on what sleds they could commandeer. Those of you with medium and large sleds just volunteered them. The best way to get the Thread is while it's still airborne, before it has a chance to land. We will also need people on the ground, mopping up what does slip through."

"What about the fire-lizards, or whatever you call 'em? Won't they help?" someone asked.

"They helped us that day at Landing," a woman added, a note of fearful apprehension making her voice break.

"They helped at Sadrid Stake two days ago," Wade said.

"The rain helped a lot, too," Kenjo added, not at all convinced of assistance from a nonmechanical quarter.

"Any of you with dragonets would be very welcome in ground crews," Paul went on, willing to entertain any possible reinforcements. But he, too, was skeptical; he had been too busy to attach a dragonet, though his wife and older son had two each. "I particularly need those of you who've had any combat or flight experience. Our enemy isn't the Nathi this time, but it's our world that is being invaded. Let's stop it, tomorrow and whenever it's necessary!"

A spontaneous cheer went up in response to his rousing words and was repeated, growing in volume as people got to their feet, waving clenched fists. Those on the platform watched the demonstration, relieved and reassured. Perhaps only Ongola took note of those who remained seated or silent.

XI

If Dieter and Boris were correct, the oncoming Fall would give the Kahrain peninsula a near miss, beginning at approximately 1630 hours, roughly 120 klicks northwest of the mouth of the Paradise River, 25 degrees south. Dieter and Boris were not sure if the fall would extend as far southwestward as Mexico on Lake Maori, but precautions were being taken there as well.

Acting Commander Kenjo Fusaiyuki assembled his squadrons at the required point. Though Thread drowned in the sea, his teams would at least have some practice throwing flame at the "real thing."

"Practice" was not the appropriate term for the chaos that resulted. Kenjo was reduced to snarling peremptory orders over the comm unit as the inept but eager sled pilots plummeted through the skies after Thread, frequently favoring one another with a glancing touch of thrown HNO_3.

Fighting Thread required entirely different techniques from hunting wherry or scoring a hit on a large flying machine driven by a reasonably intelligent enemy. Thread was mindless. It just fell—in a slanting southwesterly direction, occasionally buffeted into tangles by gusting winds. It was the inexorability of that insensate fall that infuriated, defeated, depressed, and frustrated. No matter how much was seared to ash in the sky, more followed relentlessly. Nervous pilots swooped, veered, and dove. Unskilled gunners fired at anything that moved into range, which more often than not was another sled chasing down a tangle of Thread. Nine domesticated dragonets fell victim to such inexpertise, and there was suddenly a marked decrease in the number of wild ones who had joined the fray.

In the first half hour of the fall, seven sleds were involved in midair collisions, three badly damaged and two with cracked siliplex canopies which made them unairworthy. Even Kenjo's sled bore scorch marks. Four broken arms, six broken or sprained hands, three cracked collarbones, and a broken leg put fourteen gunners out of action; many others struggled on with lacerations and bruises. No one had thought about rigging any safety harnesses for the flame-gunners.

A hasty conference between the squadron leaders was called on a secured channel at the beginning of the second hour while the Fall was still over water. The squadron leaders—Kenjo, Sabra Stein-Ongola, Theo Force, and Drake Bonneau—and Paul Benden, as leader of the ground-support crews, decided to assign each squadron their own altitude level at hundred-meter intervals. The squadron would fly in a stacked wedge formation back and forth across the fifty-klick width of the Thread corridor. The important factor was for each wedge of seven sleds to stick to its designated altitude.

Once the sleds began to maintain their distances, midair collisions and scorchings were immediately reduced. Kenjo led the most capable fliers at ground level to catch as much missed Thread as possible and to inform the surface crews where tangles got through. Paul Benden coordinated the movements of the fast ground-skimmers, which carried teams with small portable flamers. Channels were kept open to air, ground, and Landing. Joel Lilienkamp organized replacement of empty HNO_3 cylinders and power packs. A medical team remained on standby.

By mid-Fall, Paul knew that his ground-support teams were too thinly spread to be truly effective, even though there were, fortunately, substantial stretches where Thread landed on stony or poor soil and shriveled and died quickly. Toward the end, when weary pilots were running low on energy and the sled power packs were nearly depleted, more Thread got through. It seemed to be part of the growing bad luck that it fell over thick vegetation and the home farm of the Mexico Stake.

The abrupt end of the Fall, on the verge of Maori Lake and the main buildings of Mexico, came as a distinct shock to those who had been concentrating so hard on destroying Thread. Squadron leaders ordered their fighters to land on the lakeside while they had a chance to confer with the ground-crew marshals. Those at Mexico who had not been in ground defense provided hot soup and *klah*, fresh bread, and fruit, and had prepared an infirmary in one of the houses. Tarvi and the Karachi team had managed to complete metal roofing just before the Fall reached the area. Then Joel Lilienkamp's supply barge arrived with fresh power packs and HNO_3 cylinders.

The day was not over yet. Pilots cruised slowly back over the Fall corridor, checking for any "live" Thread. Paul drove himself and his sweat-smeared, soot-covered, weary teams back toward Malay Stake and the coast to try to spot signs of a secondary infestation where no shell or dissolving matter was visible. Only two such points were discovered and, on Paul's order, the ground was saturated with sustained blasts of HNO_3.

One of the ground crew on that detail told the admiral that he thought that was a waste of fuel. "The dragonets weren't at all concerned, Admiral. They are when there's Thread."

"We take no chances at this stage," Paul replied, a slight smile removing any hint of rebuke. He did not look upon the fiery bath as an overkill. The dragonets were palpably alerted by Thread, but were obviously unaware of the presence of the second, and possibly more fearful, stage of its life cycle.

However, Paul Benden's respect for the dragonets was increased by their diligent searching out of newly fallen Thread. Several times during the Fall, he spotted the fair of dragonets fighting alongside Sean Connell and the red-headed Hanrahan girl. The creatures seemed to be obeying orders. Their movements had a discipline, while other groups flitted about in a kind of chaotic frenzy.

On almost too many occasions, Paul saw the little creatures suddenly disappearing just when one seemed certain to be seared by the fiery breath of another. He found himself wishing that sleds had that sort of ability, or even more agility. Sleds were not the most efficient fighter craft. He recalled his admiration of the dragonets during the wherry attack. From accounts of their now legendary "umbrella" defense of Landing from the First Fall, he knew that hundreds of wild ones had assisted their domesticated kin. They could be splendid reinforcements. Paul wondered what the chances were to mobilize *all* the dragonets to be trained by Connell and Hanrahan.

The present Fall had left denuded patches on the surface, but despite all initial bungling and the inexperience of sled and ground crews, the devastation was not as widespread as in the first horrific Fall.

Most of the exhausted fighters chose to remain the night at Malay Stake. Pierre de Courci took it upon himself to act as chef, and his team had prepared baked fish and tubers in great pits on the beach. Weary men, women, and youngsters sat around the reassuring bonfires, too spent to talk, glad enough just to have survived the rigors of the day.

Sean and Sorka opened an emergency clinic on the Malay beach to tend the wounded fire-dragonets, slathering numb-weed on Threadscored wings and seared hide.

"D'you think that once Sira stops crying, my bronze and brown will come back?" Tarrie Chernoff asked. She was dirty with black grease and vegetation-green stains, her wher-hide jerkin showing numerous char spots, new and old, but like all devoted fire-dragonet owners, she was caring for her creature before seeing to her own relief.

Sean shrugged noncommittally, but Sorka laid a reassuring hand on Tarrie's arm. "They usually do. They get pretty upset when one of their own fair's hurt, especially a queen. You get a good night's sleep and see what the morning brings."

"Why'd you give her false comfort like that, Sorka?" Sean asked in a low voice when Tarrie had trudged back to the bonfires, her comforted queen cradled in the crook of her arm. "You know bloody well by now that if it's hurt badly enough, a fire-lizard doesn't come back." Sean was grim. He and Sorka had been lucky with their fair so far, but then, he had seen to it that their dragonets had the discipline to survive.

"She needs a good night's sleep without worrying herself sick. And a lot do come back."

Sorka gave a weary sigh as she closed the medicine case. She arched her back against tired back muscles. "Give me a rub, would you, Sean? My right shoulder." She turned her back to him and sighed in relief as his strong fingers kneaded the strain away.

Sean's hands felt marvelous on her back; he knew just how to ease away the tension. Then his hands moved caressingly up the nape of her neck and lovingly into her hair. Tired as she was, she responded to the silent question. She stepped away from him, smiling as she looked quickly about to see where their fair had taken themselves.

"They've all found quiet nests to curl up in." Sean's low voice was suggestive.

"Then let's find us one of our own." She caught his hand and led him off the beach and into a thick grove of arrow-leaf plants that they had helped save from Threadscore.

◆ ◆ ◆

Revived by the hot meal and a generous beaker of a very smooth quikal fermented by Chaila Xavior-Kimmage from local fruits, Paul and Emily quietly organized a discreet council, which they held in one of the unscathed Malay outbuildings. Besides the admiral and the governor, Ongola, Drake, Kenjo, Jim Tillek, Ezra Keroon, and Joel Lilienkamp attended.

"We'll do better next time, Admiral," Drake Bonneau assured Paul with a cocky salute. Kenjo, entering behind him, regarded the tall war ace with amused condescension. "Today taught us that this Thread requires entirely different flight and strike techniques. We'll refine that wedge maneuver so nothing gets through. Sled pilots must drill to maintain altitude patterns. Gunners must learn to control their blasts. It's more than just holding the button down. We had some mighty close encounters. We lost some of the little dragonets, too. We can't risk so many lives, much less the sleds."

"We can repair the sleds, Drake," Joel Lilienkamp remarked dryly before Paul spoke, "but power packs won't last forever. We can't afford to expend them uselessly on drills. Despite our resupply system, which I bet I can improve, nine pilots had to glide-land at Maori. That's clumsy management. That wedge formation, by the way, Drake, is economical on the packs. But it still takes days to recharge exhausted ones. How long will this stuff keep falling, Paul?" Joel looked up from his calculating pad.

"We haven't established that yet," Paul said, his left thumb rubbing his knuckles. "Boris and Dieter are collating information from the pilot debriefing."

"Hellfire, that's not going to tell us what we need to know, Paul," Drake said, his weary tone a complaint. "Where does this stuff come *from*?"

"Probe's gone off," Ezra Keroon said. "It'll be a couple a more days before any reports come back."

Drake continued almost as if he had not heard. "I want to find out if the stuff mightn't be more vulnerable in the stratosphere. Even if we only have ten pressurized sleds, would a high-altitude strike be more effective? Does this junk hit the atmosphere in clumps and then disperse? Can we develop a defense less clumsy than flamethrowers? We need to know more about this enemy."

"It doesn't fight back," Ongola remarked, rubbing his temples to ease the pounding sort of headache that battle had always given him.

"True," Paul replied with a grim smile as he turned to Kenjo. "I wonder if we would gain any useful data from an orbital reconnaissance flight? How much fuel in the *Mariposa*'s tanks?"

"If I pilot it, enough for three, maybe four flights," Kenjo replied, deliberately avoiding Drake's eyes, "depending on how much maneuvering is required and how many orbits."

"You're the man for it, Kenjo," Drake said with a flourish of his hand and a rueful expression. "You can land on a breath of fuel." Kenjo, smiling slightly, gave a short, quick bow from the waist. "Do we know when, or where, the stuff hits us again?"

"We do," Paul assured them in a flat tone. "If the data is correct, and it was today, stakeholders are lucky. It strikes in two places: 1930 hours across Araby to the Sea of Azov"—his expression reflected his continued regret at the loss of Araby's original stakeowners—"and 0330 from the sea across the tip of Delta. Both those areas are unoccupied."

"We can't let that stuff go unchecked anywhere, Paul," Ezra said in alarm.

"I know, but if we're going to have to mount crews every three days, we'll all soon be exhausted."

"Not everything needs to be protected," Drake said, unfolding his flight map. "Lots of marsh, scrub land."

"The Fall will still be attended," Paul said in an inarguable tone of voice. "Look on it as a chance to refine maneuvers and train teams, Drake. It is undeniably best to get the stuff while it's airborne. Thread didn't eat through as much land today, but we can't to afford to lose wide corridors every time it hits us."

"Draft some more of those dragonets," Joel suggested facetiously. "They're as good on the ground as in the air."

Emily regarded him sadly as the others grinned. "Unfortunately they just aren't big enough."

Paul turned around in his chair to give the governor a searching look. "That's the best idea today, Emily."

Drake and Kenjo looked at each other, puzzled, but Ongola, Joel, and Ezra Keroon sat up, their expressions expectant. Jim Tillek grinned.

◆ ◆ ◆

There were five main islands off the southern coast of Big Island and several small prominences, the remains of volcanoes poking above the brilliant green-blue sea. The one Avril and Stev were eagerly approaching was no more than the crater of a sunken volcano. Its sides sloped into the sea, providing a narrow shore, except to the south where the lip of the crater was lowest. Avril was bouncing with impatience as Stev nosed the prow of the little boat up onto the north shore.

"That Nielsen twit couldn't possibly be right," she muttered, hopping on to the pebbly beach before he had shut off the power. "How could we have missed a whole beach full of diamonds?"

"We had more promising sites. Remember, Avril?"

Steve watched her scoop up a handful of the black stones and sift them through her fingers. She kept only the largest, which she thrust at him.

"Here! Scan it!" As he inserted the palm-sized stone into the portable scanner, she looked about in angry agitation. "It makes no sense. They can't all be black diamonds. Can they?"

"This one is!"

She took back the stone and held it up to the sun for a moment. "And this one?" She grabbed up a fist-sized rock and pushed it at him, but he was quick enough to see her slip the first stone into her pouch. "It's lucky that Nielsen kid's only our apprentice. All this is—ours—too!"

"We'll"—Stev had not missed Avril's quick alteration—"have to be careful not to glut the market." He put the big stone into the scanner with eager and not quite steady fingers. "It is indeed black diamond. Around four hundred carats and relatively unflawed. Congratulations, my dear, you've struck it rich."

She grimaced at his mocking tone and snatched the diamond from him, clasping it against her almost protectively. "It can't all be black diamond," she muttered. "Can it?"

"Why not? There's nothing to keep diamonds from being hatched from a volcano, if you have the right ingredients and sufficient pressure at some point in time. I grant you, this might be the only beach composed of black diamond, or any diamond, in the universe, but that's what"—Stev's grin was pure malice—"*you* have here."

She glanced at him, her eyes weary, and managed an easy smile. "What *we* have, Stev." She leaned into him, her skin warm against his. "This is the most exciting moment of my life." She wound her free hand about his neck and kissed him passionately, her body pressing against him until he felt the diamond gouging his ribs.

"Not even diamonds must come between us, my love," he murmured, taking it from her resisting fingers and dropping it behind him into the open sled.

Stev was not unduly surprised the next morning when he found that both Avril and the fastest sled were gone from their Big Island mining camp. He made a second check in the rock hollow where he knew Avril secreted the more spectacular gemstones that had been found. It was empty.

Stev grinned maliciously. She might have ignored the mayday from Landing, but he had not. He had followed what was happening on the southern continent, and kept an eye to the east whenever a cloud appeared. He had made contingency plans. He doubted that Avril had. He would have liked to see her expression when she found out that Landing was swarming with industrious people, the takeoff grid crammed with sleds and technicians. So he roared with amusement when one of their apprentices anxiously reported that she could not find Avril anywhere.

Nabhi Nabol was not at all pleased.

◆　◆　◆

Kenjo achieved orbit with a minimum of fuel expenditure. He kept his mind on the task at hand, feeling the upward thrust of the versatile craft, and the glorious elation of release from gravity. He could wish that all his cares would fall away as easily. But he had not lost his touch with spacecraft. He slid appreciative fingers down the edge of the console.

The last three days had been frantic, servicing the *Mariposa*'s dormant systems, checking any possible fatigue or perishing of essential parts. He had even allowed Theo Force to command his squadron when Thread fell over the mountains southeast of Karachi and brushed Longwood, on Ierne Island.

It was more important for him to recommission the *Mariposa*. Ongola had spared some time to tune the comm unit circuits and help with the terminal checks. The little ship had been designed for inactivity in the vacuum of space, and although the more important circuits had been stored in vacuum containers, there was always the fear that some minor but critical connection had *not* been properly scrutinized. But finally all systems had proved go-green, and a trial blast of her engines had been reassuringly loud and steady—and Kenjo had objected when forced to rest the last twelve hours before takeoff.

"You may be a bloody good jockey, Kenjo, but there are better mechanics on Pern than you," Paul Benden had told him in no uncertain terms. "You need rest *now*, to keep you alert in space where we can't help you."

A flight plan had been calculated to allow Kenjo to be in the position where Boris and Dieter had predicted the next batch of Thread would enter Pern's atmosphere. Their program indicated that Thread fell in approximately seventy-two-hour bursts, give or take an hour or two. Kenjo's mission was to measure the accuracy of their program, to determine the composition of Thread prior to entry, and, if possible, to trace its trajectory backward. Also, last but scarcely least, he was to destroy it before it entered the atmosphere. The next Fall was due to hit Kahrain Province, just above the deserted Oslo Landing, continue on to fall over Paradise River Stake, and end in the Araby Plains.

Kenjo was a hundred miles below the empty spaceships, but that was too far away for them to register on his scope. Nevertheless he strained to see them, magnifying the viewscope to its limit. Then he shrugged. The ships were past history. He was going to make a new contribution, an unparalleled one. Kenjo Fusaiyuko would discover the source of Thread, eradicate it once and for all, and be a planetary hero. Then no one would condemn him for "conserving" so much fuel for his private use. He could relieve his sense of honor and his scouring bouts of conscience.

Building his extra-light aircraft had been most rewarding. He had found the design on tape in the *Yokohama*'s library, in the history-of-airflight section. It was not the most fuel efficient, even when he had redesigned the engine, but what he had saved from each shuttle drop had made that saucy plane possible. Flying it over his isolated Honshu Stake in the Western Barrier Range had given him satisfaction far beyond his imagining, even if it had given rise to rumors of a large, and hitherto unknown, flying creature. His wife, patient and calm, had ventured no opinion on his avocation, aiding him in its construction. A mechanical engineer, she managed the small hydroelectric plant that served their plateau home and three small stakes in the next valley. She had given him four children, three of them sons, was a good mother, and even managed to help him cultivate the fruit trees that he raised as a credit crop.

She was safe from Thread, for they had cut their home right into the mountain, using wood only on the interior. She had been quite willing to help him carve a hangar for his aircraft with the stone-cutters he had borrowed from Drake Bonneau. But she did not know that he had a second, well-concealed cave in which to store his hoard of liquid fuel. He had not yet managed to transfer all of it to Honshu from the cave at Landing.

Yes, no one would object to what Kenjo had done when he brought them the information they sought. And he would see to it that it took three or four missions to do so. He had missed the tranquility and the challenge of deep space. How pitiful his little atmospheric craft was in comparison to the beautiful, powerful *Mariposa*. How clumsy the sled he had flown as a squadron leader. He had finally returned to his true medium—space!

The ship's alarms went off, and moments later the pinging began. He was in the midst of a shower of small ovoids. With a cry once uttered by long-dead Japanese warriors, Kenjo fired his starboard repulsors and grinned when the screen blossomed with tiny stars of destruction.

◆ ◆ ◆

Avril Bitra was livid. She could not believe the change in Landing, especially as she had counted on it being nearly deserted. When Stev had talked her into taking apprentices so that no one would question exactly what it was they were doing on Big Island, Landing's population had been down to a mere two hundred.

But the Landing she found was crawling with people. There were lights everywhere, and people bustling about despite the late hour. Worst of all, the landing strip was crowded with sleds, large, small, and medium, and technicians swarmed about—and the *Mariposa* was not there! What under the suns had happened?

She had settled her sled to one edge of the strip, near where she had last seen the little space gig. She fumed impotently again over that disappointment. She had a fortune with which to depart this wretched mudball. She had even managed to shake off any companions. She had no qualms about leaving Stev Kimmer. He had been useful, as well as amusing—until just lately, until he had assessed those black diamonds. Yes, she had been right to leave immediately, before he thought to dismantle the sleds or do something drastic so that she would be forced to take him with her. Where in all the hells of seventeen worlds was the *Mariposa*? Who was using up the fuel she needed to get her to the colony ships? She struggled to control her rage. She had to think!

Belatedly she remembered the mayday. She wished now that she had listened in. Well, it could not have been that serious, not with Landing a hive of industry. Still, that could work in her favor. With so many people around, no one would notice another worker poking about.

She shivered, suddenly aware of the chill in the night air of the plateau. She was accustomed to the tropical climate of Big Island. Cursing inventively under her breath, she rooted through the sled's storage compartments and found a reasonably clean coverall. She also girded on the mechanic's belt she found beneath the coverall. It was probably Stev's—he was always well equipped. She smirked. Not always prepared, however.

Before she left to hunt for the *Mariposa*, she would have to hide the sled. In the darkness, she tried to locate at least one of the dense shrubs that grew at the edge of the strip, but she could not find any. Instead she stumbled into a small hole that proved large enough to conceal her sacks of treasure. She retrieved them from the sled, dropped them into the hole, piled loose stone and dirt over them, and then shone her handbeam over the spot to see if they were well hidden. After a few minor adjustments, she was satisfied.

With brazen strides she walked down the grid to the lights and activity.

◆ ◆ ◆

Glancing out of the ground-floor window of the met tower where Drake Bonneau was conducting a training session, Sallah Telgar-Andiyar thought she had to be mistaken: the woman only *looked* like Avril Bitra. She was wearing a tool belt and strode purposefully toward a stripped-down sled. Yet no one else Sallah knew had that same arrogant walk, that provocative swing of the hip. Then the woman stopped and began to work on the sled. Sallah shook her head. Avril was at Big Island; she had not even responded to the mayday, or to the more recent recall to Landing for pilot duty. No one had seen her, or really cared to, but Stev Kimmer's genius with circuits would have been invaluable. Ongola was trying to get Paul Benden to *order* the return of Big Island miners.

"Don't keep your fingers on the release button." Drake's voice penetrated her moment of inattention.

Poor fellow, Sallah thought. He was trying to teach all the eager youngsters how to fight Thread. If half of what Tarvi had told her about the deadly menace was true, it was devilish to combat.

"Always sweep from bow to stern. Thread falls in a sou'westerly direction, so if you come in under the leading edge, you char a larger portion." Drake was running out of space on the operational board, which he had covered with his diagrams and flight patterns. Sallah had yet to fight the stuff, so she had paid attention—until the moment when she had thought she recognized Avril.

The day had had the quality of a reunion for the shuttle pilots. All the old crowd, with the exception of Nabhi Nabol and Kenjo, had answered the summons. Sallah knew where Kenjo was; she was a trifle envious of him, and was glad of Nabol's absence. He would certainly have sneered to be in the company of all the young ones who had earned their flying tickets since Landing. Why, she had known some of them as adolescents.

Settling in at Karachi had eaten more time than she realized. And it had brought so many changes, such as the dragonets perched on young shoulders or curled up on hide-trousered legs. Her own three—a gold and two bronzes—had, just like her older children, picked up some basic manners. They were perched on the top shelves of the big ready room. Two were mentas, and she wondered if they understood what was going on before their watchful rainbow eyes.

Drake's imperative warning interrupted her musing. "*Don't* deviate from your assigned altitude. We're trying to rig cruising devices that will warn your hair-trigger pilots when you're out of line. We've got to maintain flight levels to avoid collisions. We've got more people to fly than sleds to fly in. *You,*" he said, jabbing his finger at his audience, "can be replaced. The sled cannot, and we're going to need every one we can keep in the air.

"Now, a sweep from bow to stern in a one-second blast chars as much Thread as possible for the range of these throwers. Catch the end of the stuff and fire runs back up most of it. Don't waste the HNO_3." His rapid-fire use of the chemical designation made it sound more like "agenothree," Sallah thought, losing concentration once again. Damn, she must pay attention, but she was so used to listening for sounds, not words. And silences. The silence all children made when they were being naughty or trying out forbidden things. And hers were inventive. She felt her lips widen in a proudly maternal smile, then disciplined her expression as Drake's eyes fastened on her face.

She already missed her three older children dreadfully. Ram Da, Sallah's sturdy, reliable seven-year-old son, had promised to look out for Dena and Ben. Sallah had brought three-month-old Cara with her—the baby was safely installed with Mairi Hanrahan's lot—so she was not totally deprived. But Tarvi was back at Karachi, extruding metal sheets on a round-the-clock basis, slaving as hard as the people he drove to their limits.

". . . and make each cylinder last as long as possible," Drake was saying. "Conserve agenothree and power, and you'll last longer in the flight line. Which is where you're needed. Now, most of you have had experience with turbulence. *Don't* shuck your safety harness until you're on the ground. The lighter sleds can be flipped on landing if the wind suddenly gusts, because they're nose-heavy with the flame-thrower mounts."

With Tarvi on such a schedule, it was just as well that she had work of

her own to do, Sallah thought. He had little enough time for her, and she would not even have the comfort of sleeping beside him—or be able to rouse him to a dawn lusting when he was too drowsy to resist her caresses.

What was wrong with her? she wondered for the millionth time. She had not trapped Tarvi. The mutual need and passion that day in the cave could not have been faked. When the chance union had resulted in pregnancy, he had immediately offered to make a formal arrangement. She had not insisted, but she had been much relieved that the initiative had been his. He had been considerate, tender, and solicitous throughout the gestation, and sincerely overjoyed when his firstborn was a strong, healthy boy. He adored all his children, rejoicing at their births and in their development. It was his wife he avoided, dismissed, ignored.

Sallah sighed, and her old friend Barr shot her a quizzical glance. Sallah smiled and gave a shrug, intimating that Drake had caused her reaction. What would her life have been like with Drake Bonneau, happily ensconced on his lake? Svenda looked complacent, boasting about limiting her child-bearing to two. Drake might act the confident flyboy in public, but the previous night he had been noticeably dancing attendance on his imperious wife. Sallah had always thought that Drake was more "show" than "do." Yet for all Tarvi's eccentricities, Sallah preferred the geologist and treasured those ever more rare occasions when she could rouse him to passion. Perhaps that was the problem: Tarvi should be allowed the initiative. No, she had tried that tack, and had gone through a miserable year before she thought of her "dawn attacks."

She had learned some Pushtu phrases from Jivan and artlessly she had inquired about feminine names. Whomever Tarvi called for at the height of passion, it was not another woman. Or another man, from all she could discover.

"So," Drake said, "here is the roster for the next Fall. Remember, it's a double hit, at Jordan and at Dorado. We're going to send you Dorado squadrons on ahead so you can be well rested by the time you have to fight." Again Drake's eagle gaze swept his adoring students. "Now, back to your sleds to lend the technicians what assistance you can. House lights'll go out at midnight. We all need our rest," he concluded cheerfully as he waved their dismissal.

Svenda quickly moved to his side, her scowl a deterrent to those who approached Drake with private questions.

"When did you get in, Sallah?" Barr asked, turning with her usual friendly grin. "I only arrived in from our stake around noon. No one of the old group knew when you'd make it. I didn't realize this thing was so serious until I saw what it had done on my way up."

Sallah laughed. Barr's bubbling personality had not changed a micro, though her figure had rounded. "How many kids do you have now, Barr?" Sallah asked. "We've sort of lost track of each other with you on the other side of the continent."

"Five!" Barr managed a girlish giggle, glancing slyly at Sallah. "The last was a set of twins, which I'd never have expected. Then Jess told me that he was a twin, and twin births were common in his family. I could have strangled him."

"You didn't, though."

"Naw! He's a good man, a loving father, and a hard worker." Barr gave a sharp nod of her head at each virtue, grinning at Sallah again. Then her mobile face changed to one of concern. "Are you all right, Sallah?"

"Me, certainly. I've four kids. Brought Cara with me. She's only three months old."

"Is she at Mairi's or Chris MacArdle-Cooney's?"

"At Mairi's. We'd better check that roster and see when we're on duty. Where's Sorka these days?" Sallah had also lost track of the redheaded Hanrahan girl. "I saw all the others."

"Oh, she's living with another vet. Over on Irish Square."

"How appropriate!" Suddenly Sallah felt a surge of resentment, something to do with the freedom young people had and her frustration with Tarvi's diffidence, along with the sudden realization that she had relatively few responsibilities at that moment and that her professional skills were once again in demand. "C'mon, let's go find a drink and catch up on our lives!"

◆ ◆ ◆

Sorka and Sean arrived at their quarters from different directions, Sean from an unexpected meeting with Admiral Benden, Sorka from the barn. She knew by his jarring stride that Sean was barely containing a fine fit of rage. He held it back until they were inside the house.

"Damn fool, hell'n'damned fool," he said, slamming the door behind him. "That pompous, pig-headed, butt-stupid git."

"Admiral Benden?" she inquired, surprised. Sean had never had reason to criticize the admiral, and he had been proud to be called to a special interview.

"That stupid admiral wants a cavalry unit!"

"Cavalry?" Sorka paused as she picked their evening meal out of the freezer compartment.

"To charge about the countryside with flamethrowers, no less!"

"Doesn't he realize horses hate fire?"

"He does now." Sean went past her to the small cabinet, hauled out a bottle of quickal, and held it up suggestively.

"Yes, please. If I don't unwind, too, my food won't do me any good at all." She curtailed her anxiety. The need for a drink indicated how tense he was, for Sean was not a drinking man.

"We don't have to eat up above, do we?" he asked, jerking his head over his shoulder in the direction of the reestablished community kitchen.

"No, I raided Mother's freezer." She set the container in the warming unit and dialed the appropriate time.

Sean handed over her glass and raised his in a toast. "To idiot admirals who are very good in space and real dumb wash-out stupid about animals. As if we had enough horses to waste in such an asinine caper. He also envisions me training squadrons of fire-lizards"—Sean had persisted in using his own name for them—"swooping down on Thread at command. He even feels that he should have one, too. He doesn't effing know they won't be hatching till summer! That is, if those flyboys don't flame 'em all down."

Sorka had never seen Sean so infuriated. He paced about, his face flushed, throwing his left arm out in extravagant gestures, sipping at his drink between phrases as he vented his anger. He flicked his head to flip the sun-lightened hair out of his eyes. A grimace made him appear inscrutable, almost frightening in his anger. On one level she listened to his words, agreeing with his anxieties and opinions; on another, she reveled in the fact that beneath the contained, almost coldly detached impression he gave most people, there was such a passionate, intelligent, critical, rational, and dedicated personality.

Sorka did not quite know when she had realized that she loved him—it seemed that she always had—but she remembered the day she realized that he loved her: the first time he had exploded in her presence over a minor incident. Sean would never have permitted himself that luxury if he had not felt totally secure in her presence, if he had not unconsciously needed her soothing affection and reassurance. Watching him work off his aggravation, Sorka permitted herself a small smile which she tactfully hid behind her glass.

"Now, Sean, the admiral paid you a compliment, too," she remarked. She caught his surprised glance and smiled. "By consulting *you*. I noticed, even if you didn't, that he watched us out there on the Malay corridor, saw how well our fair behaved. And I'm sure that he knows that you're more likely than anyone else to discover where the queens are hiding their eggs."

"Humph. Yes, I guess that's true enough." Somewhat mollified, Sean continued to pace, but with less agitation.

Sorka loved Sean in every mood, but his infrequent explosions fascinated her. His anger had never been directed at her; he rarely criticized, and then only in a crisp impersonal tone. Some of her girlfriends had wondered how she could stand his taciturn, almost sullen moodiness, but Sorka had never found him sullen in her company. Generally he was thoughtful, unwilling to offend even in a complete disagreement, and certainly a man who kept his own counsel—unless horses were at risk. His lithe figure was graceful even as he thudded back and forth, his heels pounding and leaving dents in the thick wool carpet she had woven for their home. She let his tirade continue, amused by the language in which he described the probable antecedents of the admiral, whom he usually respected, and the idiocy of the entire biological team who tampered with creatures whose natures they had not the wit to understand.

"Well, did you offer to find the admiral a dragonet egg when the time's right?" she asked when he paused for breath after another elaboration of the stupidity of brass asses.

"Ha! I will if I can." He spun on his heel and sprawled beside her on the couch, his face suddenly still, rage and frustration dissipated, his eyes on the amber liquid in his glass. From his expression, she knew that something else was worrying him deeply. She waited for him to continue. "You know as well as I do that we haven't caught a glimmer of any of the wild ones around here. They've made themselves scarce since the Sadrid Fall. Jays, if there were anywhere safe on this planet, they'd find it!"

"There were a lot helping us at the Malay corridor."

"Up until some ijiits started flaming them, too!" Sean finished the last of his drink to drown his disgust. "We won't get the wild ones to help at all if that gets about." He poured himself another drink. "Say, where're yours?" he asked suddenly noticing that the usual perches were vacant.

"Same place yours are, out and about," she answered in a mild tone.

Then Sean began to laugh, as much at himself as at the fact that he had only just realized that his fire-lizards had made themselves scarce the moment he left the admin building.

"Not surprising, is it?" she teased, grinning back at him. He shoved one arm behind her shoulders and pulled her, unresisting, closer to him. "When Emmett told me Blazer was in a tizzy over your righteous wrath, I told mine they'd have to find their own food tonight. They don't like cheesy things anyway."

"It's not often we get a night alone," Sean said softly, his voice a seductive whisper in her ear. "Finish your drink, redheaded gal." He ruffled her fringe, then his hand traveled in a caress down her cheek to her chin. "And turn off the cooker," he added just before he kissed her.

Sorka did as she was told, well pleased. It was awkward having to invent excuses to send the dragonets off on specious errands. But even when they were not in season, the creatures delighted in strong emotions, and with thir-

teen in a chorus of encouragement, the entire neighborhood would know
what was happening in the Hanrahan-Connell quarters.

Later that night, when the sounds of Landing's industry were muted,
Sorka wondered if she had conceived. Sean slept neatly and quietly beside
her, his fingers lightly encircling her upper arm. She had never mentioned a
formal arrangement to Sean, or ever pointed out the common assumption of
Landing's population that they were a tempered team. She and Sean were of
one mind in nearly everything they did, utilizing their veterinary apprenticeship to breed strong horses, finding the very best among the genetic stock
available from either the banks or the live stallions. They were soon to sit
their final exams in veterinary medicine and they had located the perfect spot
for a home—a valley halfway down the Eastern Barrier Range. Sean had
taken Red to see the proposed Killarney Stake, and her father had approved
emphatically of their choice. Sorka took that as a tacit approval of their still
informal union.

Although Sorka's parents had acquiesced, Porrig Connell still treated her
formally as a guest he wished to see less often. His wife had never ceased in
her efforts to bring her son back to his proper hearth. She had chosen another daughter-in-law for Sean and sometimes embarrassed all concerned by
pushing the girl at Sean on every opportunity.

"I won't breed so close, Mam," Sean had informed her when she had
nagged him once too often. "It's bad for the blood. Lally Moorhouse's father
was your first cousin. We need to spread the gene pool, not enclose it."

Sorka had overheard, but she knew Sean well enough by then not to be
hurt that he had said no more about choosing. Perhaps he had not known
then that he loved fifteen-year-old Sorka Hanrahan, who was already certain
where her heart had been given.

She had been seventeen before he had touched her with any kind of passion, and that had been a night to remember. Their roles had become reversed: she, the wanton; he, the hesitant, tender lover. Her ardent response to
his gentle overtures had surprised and pleased them both, but they had not
moved to separate quarters until she had passed her eighteenth birthday. It
had become a custom in their generation to have a trial period prior to a formal declaration before the magistrate.

Sorka wanted Sean's child badly. Ever since that hideous half hour, tread-
ing water under a stone ledge, she had been aware of their mortality. She
wanted something of Sean—just in case. Not that he was wild or incautious,
but the Lilienkamp boys had not been reckless, and certainly poor Lucy Tubberman had not. So many people had been wiped out in that First Fall.

Sorka did not want to be left with nothing of Sean. She had not tried before to conceive, because pregnancy would have interfered with their plans

for Killarney Stake: they needed the work credits for every acre they could purchase. She worried that there was something wrong with her that she had not gotten pregnant before, with all the incautious fooling around that she and Sean had enjoyed. But she was no longer fooling. That night she had meant business.

◆ ◆ ◆

Wind Blossom opened the door to Paul Benden, Emily Boll, Ongola, and Pol and Bay Harkenon-Nietro. Gracefully inclining her head in welcome, she held the door wide for them to enter.

Kitti Ping was seated on a padded chair that, Paul decided, must be raised off the ground under its cover, giving it the semblance of an archaic throne. She looked imposing, a feat for someone half his height. A beautiful soft woven rug had been tucked about a frail body, and a long-sleeved tunic with elaborate embroideries also increased her general look of substance and authority. She raised one delicate hand, no larger than his oldest daughter's, and indicated that they were to be seated on the stools set in an irregular circle in front of her.

As Paul doubled his long legs to sit, he realized that she had achieved a subtle advantage over her visitors. Amused by the tactic, he smiled up at her and thought he could detect the merest hint of an acknowledgment.

Only a few strong ethnic traditions had survived the Age of Religions, but the Chinese, Japanese, Maori, and Amazon-Kapayan were four that had retained some of their ancient ways. In Kitti's Pernese house, which was exquisitely furnished with heirlooms from her family, Paul knew better than to disrupt a hospitality ritual. Wind Blossom served the visitors fragrant tea in delicate porcelain cups. The little plantation of tea bushes, grown to sustain the lovely ceremony, had been a casualty in the First Fall. Paul was poignantly aware that the cup of tea he sipped might be the last he would ever taste.

"Has Mar Dook had a chance to inform you, Kitti Ping, that he had several tea bushes in reserve in the conservatory?" Paul asked when everyone had had time to savor the beverage.

Kitti Ping inclined her head in a deep bow of gratitude and smiled. "It is a great reassurance."

Such a bland reply gave him no opening wedge. Paul moved restlessly, trying to find a comfortable position on the stool, and he knew that Pol and Bay were bursting to discuss the reason for the interview.

"All of us would be more reassured, Kit Ping Yung"—abruptly he modulated his voice, which sounded so much louder after her delicate response— "If we had . . . some form of reliable assistance in combating this menace."

"Ah?" Her pencil-thin eyebrows rose, and then her tiny hands made a vague gesture about the armrests.

"Yes." Paul cleared his throat, annoyed at himself for being so gauche, and more annoyed that he could be so disconcerted by a trivial seating arrangement. She must know why he had arranged the private conference. "The truth is we are very badly positioned to defend ourselves against Thread. Bluntly, we will run out of resources in five years. We do not have the equipment to manufacture either sleds or power packs when what we brought are worn out. Kenjo's attempt to destroy Thread in space was only partially successful, and there isn't much fuel left for the *Mariposa*.

"As you know, none of the colony ships carried any defensive or destructive weaponry. Even if we could construct laser sweep beams, there isn't fuel enough to move even one ship into an effective position to annihilate the pods. Nevertheless the best way to protect the surface is to destroy this menace in the air.

"Boris and Dieter have confirmed our worst fears: Thread will sweep across Pern in a pattern that will denude the planet unless we can stop it. We cannot entertain much hope that Ezra Keroon's probe will bring us any useful information." Paul spread his hands with the hopelessness that threatened to overwhelm him.

Kitti raised her delicate eyebrows in unfeigned surprise. "The morning star is the source?"

Paul sighed heavily. "That is the current theory. We'll know more when the probe returns its survey."

Kitti Ping nodded thoughtfully, her willow-slender fingers tightening on the armrests.

"We are, Kit Ping Yung," Emily said, sitting even more erect on her stool, "in a desperate situation."

Paul Benden was heartened in an obscure way to see the governor as much like a nervous schoolchild as himself. Pol and Bay nodded encouragement. Kitti Ping and Wind Blossom, who stood slightly behind her grandmother's left side, waited patiently.

"If the dragonets were only larger, Kitti," Bay broke in, her manner unusually brusque, "intelligent enough to obey commands, they'd be an immense help to us. I was able to use mentasynth to enhance their own latent empathies, but that's a relatively simple matter. To breed large enough dragonets— dragons—we need them *big*—" Bay stretched her arms full length and flicked her fingers to indicate room size. "—intelligent, obedient, strong enough to do the job needed: flame Thread out of the sky." She ran out of words then, knowing very well how Kitti Ping Yung felt about bioengineering beyond simple adjustments to adapt creatures to new ecological parameters.

Kitti Ping nodded again while her granddaughter regarded her with surprise. "Yes, size, strength, and considerable intelligence would be required," she said in her softly audible voice. Hiding her hands in the cuffs of her long sleeves and folding them across her stomach, she bent her head and was silent for so long that her audience wondered if she had nodded off in the easy sleep of the aged. Then she spoke again. "And dedication, which is easy to instill in some creatures, impossible in others. The dragonets already possess the traits you wish to enhance and magnify." She smiled, a gentle, faintly apologetic smile of great sadness and compassion. "I was the merest student, though a very willing and eager one, in the Great Beltrae Halls of Eridani. I was taught what would happen if I did this or that, enlarged or reduced, severed that synapse or modified this gene pattern. Most of the time what I was taught to do worked, but, alas," she added, raising one hand warningly, "I never knew why sometimes the modification failed and the organism died. Or should have. The Beltrae would teach us the how but never the why."

Paul sighed deeply, despair threatening to overwhelm him.

"But I can try," she said. "And I will. For though my years are nearly accomplished, there are others to be considered." She turned to smile gently upon Wind Blossom, who ducked her head with humility.

Paul shook his head, not quite believing what she had just said.

"You will?" Bay exclaimed, jumping to her feet. She stopped just short of rushing to Kitti's raised chair.

"Of course I will *try*!" Kitti raised one tiny hand in warning. "But I must caution you that success cannot be assumed. What we undertake is dangerous to the species, could be dangerous for us, and cannot be guaranteed. It is good fortune of the highest degree that the little dragonets already possess so many of the qualities required in the genetically altered animal that suits the urgent need. Even so, we may not be able to achieve the exact creature, or even be sure of a genetic progression. We have no sophisticated laboratory equipment, or methods of analysis which could lighten our burden. We must let repetition, the work of many hands and eyes, replace precision and delicacy. The task is appropriate, but the means are barbaric."

"But we have to try!" Paul Benden said, rising to his feet with clenched fists.

XII

All medical staff not on duty in the infirmary or on ground crew duty, the veterinarians, and the apprentices, Sean and Sorka included, worked shifts as Kitti Ping's project was given top priority. Anyone with training in biology, chemistry, or laboratory procedures of any kind—sometimes even those with nimble fingers who could be put to work preparing slides, or those convalescing from Threadfall injuries who could watch monitors—were drafted into service. Kitti, Wind Blossom, Bay, and Pol extracted a genetic code from the chromosomes of the fire-dragonets. Although the creatures were not of Earth, their biology proved not too dissimilar to work with.

"We succeeded with the chiropteroids on Centauri," Pol said, "and they had chains of silicons as their genetic material."

A great deal of schedule-juggling was required in order to muster enough people to fight Fall over populated areas. The detailed sequence of Threadfall, established by the exhausted team of Boris Pahlevi and Dieter Clissmann, gave a structure to which even Kitti's project had to bow. The resultant four-shift roster attempted to provide everyone with some time for themselves—both to relax and to care for their own stakes—though some of the specialists ignored such considerations and had to be ordered to sleep.

Everyone over the age of twelve was brought in when Thread fell. The hope that Kenjo, in the *Mariposa*, could deflect Thread pods in the upper reaches of the atmosphere turned out to be ineffective. The predicted double Fall—over Cardiff in mid-Jordan and Bordeaux in Kahrain, and over Seminole and Ierne Island—was patchy, but the gaps perversely did not include occupied sites.

More double Falls could be anticipated: on the thirty-first day after First

Fall, Thread would sweep across Karachi camp and the tip of the Kahrain peninsula; three days later a single land corridor would range from Kahrain across Paradise River Stake, while a second Fall would pass harmlessly at sea well above the tip of Cibola Province. After another three days, a dangerous double would hit Boca Stake and the thick forests of lower Kahrain and Araby, stocks of the one real wood vitally needed to shore up mine pits at busy Karachi Camp and Drake's Lake.

Ezra spent hours in the booth that housed the link with the *Yokohama's* mainframe, scanning the naval and military histories to find some means of combating the menace. He also sought, with much less optimism, obscure equations or devices that might be able to alter the orbit of the planet. Then the next Fall could, perhaps, be avoided. Meanwhile, however, the present pass had seeded Pern's orbit with spirals of the encapsulated Thread, a danger that the colonists would have to face no matter what. He also did comparisons with data from Kitti's program, delving into science files, using his security ID to access secret or "need to know" information. He was waiting, too, for the probe's findings to be relayed back to him. And because everyone knew where to find Ezra, he often intercepted complaints and minor problems that would have added unnecessary burdens to the admiral and the governor.

Kenjo was sent on three more missions, each time trying to find a more efficient way of destroying enough Thread in space to justify the expenditure of precious fuel. The gauges on the *Mariposa* dropped only slightly with each trip, and Kenjo was commended on his economy. Drake was openly envious of the space pilot's skill.

"Jays, man," Drake would say. "You're driving it on the fumes!"

Kenjo would nod modestly and say nothing. He was, however, rather relieved that he had not managed to transfer all the fuel sacks to their hiding place at Honshu. All too soon, he would have to broach that supply to ensure continued trips into space. Only there did he feel totally aware and alive in every sense and nerve of his body.

But each time he brought back useful information. Thread, it turned out, traveled in a pod that burned away when it hit the atmosphere of Pern, leaving an inner capsule. About 15,000 feet above the surface, the inner capsule opened into ribbons, some of which were not thick enough to survive in the upper reaches. But, as everyone at Landing well knew, plenty fell to the surface.

Most of the sleds were unpressurized, so they had an effective ceiling of 10,000 feet. There was still only one way to clear the Thread from the skies: by flamethrowers.

With Thread due to fall on the Big Island Stake on Day 40, Paul Benden ordered Avril Bitra and Stev Kimmer to return to Landing. When Stev asked what Landing needed in the way of the ores mined at Big Island, Joel Lilienkamp was more than happy to supply a list. So when they arrived at Landing with four sleds crammed canopy-high with metal ingots, no one mentioned their long delinquency.

"I don't see Avril," Ongola commented as the sleds were being unloaded at the metals supply sheds.

Stev looked at him, slightly surprised. "She flew back weeks ago." He peered back at the landing grid and saw the sun glint off the *Mariposa*'s hull. "Hasn't she reported in?" Ongola shook his head slowly. "Well, now, fancy that!" Stev's gaze lingered thoughtfully on the *Mariposa* just long enough for Ongola to notice. "Maybe Thread got her!"

"Maybe her, but not the sled," Ongola replied, knowing that Avril Bitra was too adept at preserving her skin to be scored. "We'll keep an eye out for her."

Threadfall charts were displayed everywhere and constantly updated; previous Falls were deleted and future ones limited to the next three, so that people could plan a week ahead. Avril could not have stopped ten minutes in Landing without learning of the dangers of Thread. Ongola reminded himself that he must remove that guidance chip from the *Mariposa* as soon as Kenjo landed. He knew exactly how the space pilot had extended the fuel; he did not want anyone else, especially Avril Bitra, to discover how. Admiral Benden had been right about Kenjo. Ongola did not want to be right about Bitra!

"Where do you want me to work now I'm back, Ongola?" Stev asked with a wry grin.

"Find out where Fulmar Stone needs you most, Kimmer. Glad to see you in one piece."

◆　◆　◆

Avril had stayed around Landing that night just long enough to know that she did not wish to be conscripted into any of the several teams who could use her special skills. The only skill she preferred to employ—space navigation—was thwarted. So, before dawn broke on Landing and before anyone noticed the existence of a spare sled, she lifted it again, loaded with useful supplies, both food and matériel.

She touched down on the rocky height above the ravaged Milan Stake, where she had a clear view of Landing and, more importantly, a good view of the busy, illuminated grid where the *Mariposa* would touch down. She spent the early morning hours using the metal sheets she had filched to arrange an umbrella over the sled's siliplex canopy. She preferred to take every precaution against the deadly airborne stuff. By mid-morning she had camouflaged her eyrie and tuned the sled's scope on her objective. She was rewarded by a provocative view of Kenjo's return.

By listening carefully to all the channels available on the sled's comm unit, she managed to discover the facts of his mission and its limited success.

Over the next several days, she began to feel secure in her hideout. Because of the old volcanoes, most air traffic took corridors well to either side of her. During the morning the shadow of the biggest peak lurked over the retreat, like a broad digit pointing directly at her. It was enough to make her flesh creep. She had no real appreciation of views, although the fact that she could look up the Jordan to the bay, or down toward Bordeaux meant that she was unlikely to be surprised. She began to relax and wait. Considering the reward, she had trouble practicing patience.

◆ ◆ ◆

"Have you *any* progress to report, Kitti?" Paul Benden asked the tiny geneticist.

He had never found that close surveillance improved performance, but he needed some morsel of encouragement to lighten the depression of his people. The psychologists reported a lowering of morale as the second month of Threadfall ground on. The initial enthusiasm and resolution was being eroded by fierce work schedules and few distractions. Landing's facilities, once generous, were crowded with technicians drafted into the laboratories and stakeholders' families returned to the dubious safety of the first settlement.

No one was idle. Mairi Hanrahan had made it a game for the five- and six-year-olds with good motor control to assemble control panels by the colors of the chips. Even the most awkward ones could help gather fruits and vegetables from the undamaged lands, or compete with one another in collecting the unusual-colored seaweeds from the beaches after high tides or storms. The seven- and eight-year-olds were permitted to help fish with handlines under the watchful eyes of experienced fishermen. But even the youngest toddlers were beginning to react to mounting tensions.

There was considerable talk about allowing more holders to return to their stakes and fly out from their homes to meet Thread. But that would mean splitting up the supply depots and disarranging the work schedules of the more valuable technicians. Paul and Emily finally had to remain adamant on the centralization.

That night Kitti regarded Paul and Emily with a wise and compassionate smile. As she sat erect on the stool by the massive microbiological unit, its minute laser units pushed back from the manipulation chamber, she did not appear fatigued; only her bloodshot eyes showed the strain of her labors. A program was running with whispering clicks, flashing incomprehensible displays on its several monitors. Kitti paused briefly to regard a graph on one screen and a set of equations on another before she returned her gaze to the anxious men.

"There is no way, Admiral, to accelerate gestation, not if you wish a healthy, viable specimen. Not even the Beltrae managed to hasten that process. As I mentioned in my last reports, we pinpointed the cause of our original failures and made the necessary corrections. Time-consuming, I realize, but well worth the effort. The twenty-two bioengineered prototypes we now have are proceeding well into the first semester. We all"—her delicate hand made a graceful sweeping gesture that included all the technicians working in the huge laboratory block—"are immensely cheered by such a high rate of success." She turned her head slightly to watch the flicker of a reading. "We constantly monitor the specimens. They show the same responses as the little tunnel snakes whose development we understand well. Let us earnestly hope that all proceeds without incident. We have been infinitely fortunate so far. Patience is required of you now."

"Patience," Paul echoed ruefully. "Patience is in very short supply."

Kitti raised her hands in a gesture of impotence. "Day by day, the embryos grow. Wind Blossom and Bay continue to refine the program. In two days we shall start a second group. We shall continue to refine the manipulations. Always seeking to improve. We do not stand still. We move forward.

"Our task is great and full of responsibility. One does not irresponsibly change the nature and purpose of any creature. As it was said, the person of intellect is careful in the differentiation of things, so that each finds its place. Before completion, deliberation and caution are the prerequisites of success."

Kitti then smiled a courtly dismissal of the two leaders and turned her complete attention to the rapidly shifting monitors. Paul and Emily executed equally courteous bows to her slender back and left the room.

"Well," Paul began, shrugging off his frustration, "that's that."

"What city wasn't built in a day, Paul?" Emily asked whimsically.

"Rome." Paul grinned at Emily's astonishment at his prompt reply. "Old Earth, first century, I think. Good land fighters and road builders."

"Militarists."

"Yes," Paul said. "Hmm . . . They also had a way of keeping people content. They called it circus. I wonder . . ."

◆ ◆ ◆

On the forty-second day after First Fall, with Thread crossing uninhabited parts of Araby and Cathay and falling harmlessly in the Northern Sea above Delta, missing Dorado's western prong, Admiral Benden and Governor Boll decreed a day of rest and leisure for all. Governor Boll asked department heads to schedule work loads to allow everyone to participate in the afternoon feast and evening dancing. Even the most distant stakeholders were invited to come for whatever time they could spare. Admiral Boll asked for two squadrons of volunteers to fly Thread at 0930 over the eastern corridor, and another two to be ready in the early evening to check the western one.

The platform on Bonfire Square was gay with multicolored bunting, and a new planetary flag was hoisted on the pole to flap in the breeze. Tables, benches, and chairs were placed around the square, leaving its center clear for dancers. Vats of quickal were to be broached, and Hegelman would produce ale—no one wished to think that it might be the last made for a long while. Joel Lilienkamp released generous supplies without grudge. "Thank the kids that gathered them! Child labor can be efficient," he said with a grin. The Monaco Bay fishermen brought in shining loads of fish and the more succulent seaweeds to be baked in the big, long-unused pits; twenty farm stakes donated as many steers to turn on spits; Pierre de Courci had worked all the previous night, baking cakes and making extravagant sweets. "Better to fatten humans than Thread!" He was always happiest when overseeing a large effort.

"It's good to hear music and singing and laughter," Paul murmured to Ongola as they wandered from one group to another.

"I think it would be a good custom to establish," Ongola replied. "Something to look forward to. Reunites old friends, improves bonds, gives everyone a chance to air and compare." He nodded to the group that included his wife, Sabra, Sallah Telgar-Andiyar, and Barr Hamil-Jessup, chatting and laughing together, each with a sleepy child on her lap. "We need to gather more often."

Paul nodded, then glanced at his wrist chrono and, swearing softly under his breath, went off to lead the volunteers against the western Fall.

◆　◆　◆

Ongola was not feeling exactly top of the mark the next morning when he arrived for his watch at the met tower. In fact, he had called in first at the infirmary, where the pharmacist had given him a hangover tablet and assured him that he was one of many. But her comment about disturbing casualties during that Threadfall had only made his headache worse.

The report that awaited him at the met tower was a shock and a surprise. One sled had been totaled and its crew of three killed; a second sled had been badly crumpled, the starboard gunner killed, and pilot and port gunner badly injured in the midair head-on collision. Someone had not been obeying the altitude restrictions. Ongola groaned involuntarily as he read the casualty list: Becky Nielson, mining apprentice just back from Big Island—she had been safer after all with Avril; Bart Nilwan, a very promising young mechanic; and Ben Jepson. Ongola rubbed his eyes to clear the blur. Bob Jepson was the other dead pilot. Two in the same family. Those twins! Farting around in break-ass fashion instead of following orders! Stinkin' air! What could he say to their parents? A minor Fall with a party to come back to, and they died!

Ongola put his hand on the comm unit, about to dial administration. Then he heard someone tapping hesitantly at the door.

"Come!" he called.

Catherine Radelin-Doyle stood there, her eyes round, her face pale.

"Yes, Cathy?"

"Sir, Mr. Ongola . . ."

"Either will do." He mustered an encouraging smile. Considering the amount of trouble Cathy could get into, from stumbling into caves at an early age, to marrying the most feckless joat on the planet, he wondered at her shy demeanor. She was, poor child, just one of those people to whom events tended to occur with no connivance from themselves at all.

"Sir, I've found a cave."

"Yes?" he encouraged when she hesitated. She was constantly finding caves.

"It wasn't empty."

Ongola sat up straight. "It had a lot of fuel sacks in it?" he asked. If Catherine had found it, would Avril? No, Avril did not have the same sort of luck Catherine had.

"However did you know, Mr. Ongola?" She looked faint with relief.

"Possibly because I know they're there."

"You do? They are? I mean, they weren't put there by 'them'?"

"No, by us." He wanted to make as little fuss about Kenjo's hoard as possible. He had been counting the dwindling numbers and wondering why Kenjo seemed so complacent after each trip. Ongola flicked a glance at the corner of the shadowed shelving where the guidance chips were hidden in their dark-foam case.

Catherine suddenly sank to the nearest chair. "Oh, sir, you don't know what a fright it gave me. Thinking that someone else was here, because everyone *knows* there's so little fuel left. And then to see . . ."

"But you saw nothing, Catherine," Ongola told her crisply. "Nothing whatever. There's no cave worth noticing down that particular crevasse and you won't say a thing about it to anyone else. I will personally tell the admiral. But you will tell no one."

"Oh no, sir."

"This information cannot—I repeat, can*not*—be divulged to any other person."

"That's right, Mr. Ongola." She nodded solemnly several times. Then she smiled winsomely. "Shall I keep on looking?"

"Yes, I think you'd better. And find something!"

"Oh, but I have, Mr. Ongola, and Joel Lilienkamp says they're going to be excellent storage space." Her face clouded briefly. "But he didn't say for what."

"Go, Cathy, and find something . . . else."

She left, and Ongola had barely returned to brooding over the first serious losses to their defense when Tarvi came storming up the stairs.

"It's been staring us in the face, Zi," he said, swinging his arms in one of his expansive gestures. His face was alight with enthusiasm, although his skin looked a bit gray from the excesses of the night before.

"What?" Ongola was in no mood for puzzles.

"Them! There!" Tarvi gestured extravagantly out the northern windows. "All the time."

It was probably the headache, Ongola thought, but he had no idea what Tarvi was talking about.

"What do you mean?"

"All this time we have been slavering away at mining ore, refining, molding it, adding weeks to our labors, when all the time we've had what we need in front of us."

"No puzzles, Tarvi."

Tarvi's expressive eyes widened in surprise and consternation. "I give you no puzzles, Zi, my friend, but the source of much valuable metals and materials. The shuttles, Zi, the shuttles can be dismantled and their components used for our specific purposes here and now. Theirs is done. Why let them slowly decay on the meadow?" Tarvi emphasized each new sentence with a flick of long fingers out the window and then, exasperated with Ongola's incomprehension, he hauled the man to his feet and pointed a very long, slightly dirty forefinger directly at the tail fins of the old shuttles. "There. We'll use them. Hundreds of relays, miles of the proper flex and tubing, six small mountains of recyclable material. Have you any idea of how much is in them?" In an instant, all the exuberance drained from the volatile geologist. He put both hands on Ongola's shoulders. "We can replace the sled we lost today even if we cannot replace those marvelous young lives or comfort their stricken families. The parts make a new whole."

◆ ◆ ◆

Work dulled the edge of the sorrow that hung over Landing at the loss of four young people. The two survivors reluctantly admitted that the Jepson twins, toward the end of that Fall, had indulged in some fatal foolery. Ben's sled had been scheduled for servicing after the Fall because its previous pilot had reported a sluggish reaction on port side turns. The sled had been considered safe enough for what should have been a monitoring flight.

Rather than prevent other such collisions, the next few Falls saw a rash of them even as Tarvi's crew began to strip the first shuttle and Fulmar's teams began to service and replace from the bonanza of salvage.

The longest hours were still put in at Kitti Ping's laboratory, monitoring the development of the specimens for any signs of aberration from the program.

"Patience," was Kitti's response to all queries. "All proceeds vigorously."

Three days after the midair collision, Wind Blossom discovered her grandmother still at the electronic microscope, apparently peering at yet another slide. But when Wind Blossom touched Kitti's arm, the movement produced an unexpected result. The dainty fingers slipped from their relaxed position on the keyboard, and the body slumped forward, only kept upright by the brace that held her to the stool for her long sessions at the microscope. Wind Blossom let out a moan and dropped to her knees, holding one tiny cold hand to her forehead.

Bay heard her disconsolate weeping and came to see what had happened. Instantly she called to Pol and Kwan, then phoned for a doctor. Once Wind Blossom had followed the gurney carrying her grandmother's body out of the room, Bay straightened her plump shoulders and stood at the console. She asked the computer if it had finished its program.

PROGRAM COMPLETED flashed on the screen—almost indignantly, Bay thought in the portion of her mind that was not sorrowing. She tapped out an information query. The screen displayed a dazzling series of computations and ended with REMOVE UNIT! DANGER IF UNIT IS NOT IMMEDIATELY REMOVED!

Astonished, Bay recognized the paraphernalia on the workspace beside the electronic microscope. Kitti Ping had been manipulating gene patterns again, a complicated process that Bay found as daunting as Wind Blossom did, despite Kitti Ping's encouragements. So Kitti had made those infinitesimal alterations in the chromosomes. Bay felt the chill of a terrible apprehension sweep through her plump body. She pressed her lips together. That moment was not the time to panic. They must not lose what Kitti Ping had been making of the raw material of Pern.

With hands that were not quite steady, she unlocked the microcylinder, removed the tiny gel-encapsulated unit, and placed it in the culture dish that Kitti had readied. An agony as severe as a knife stab almost doubled Bay up, but she fought the grief and the knowledge that Kit Ping Yung had died to produce that altered egg cell. The label was even prepared: *Trial 2684/16/M: nucleus #22A, mentasynth Generation B2, boron/silicon system 4, size 2H; 16.204.8.*

Walking as fast as her shaky legs would permit and gradually recovering her composure, Bay took the final legacy of the brilliant technician to the gestation chamber and put it carefully beside the forty-one similar units that held the hopes of Pern.

◆ ◆ ◆

"*That* was the second probe to malfunction," Ezra told Paul and Emily, his quiet voice ragged with disappointment. "When the first one blew up, or whatever, I thought it a mischance. Even vacuum isn't perfect insulation against decay. Probe motors could misfire, their recording device clog somehow or other. So I refined the program for the second one. It got exactly as far as the first one, and then every light went red. Either that atmosphere is so corrosive even our probe enamels melt, or the garage on the *Yokohama* has somehow been damaged, and the probes, too. I dunno, guys."

Ezra was not much given to agitated gestures but he paced up and down Paul's office, strutting and waving his arms about him like a scarecrow in a high wind. The last few days had wearied and aged him. Paul and Emily exchanged concerned glances. Kitti Ping's death had been such a shock, following so closely on the sled collision disaster. The geneticist had seemed so indestructible, despite the fact that everyone knew of her physical frailty. She had exuded a quality of immortality, however false that had proved.

"Whose theory was it that we were being bombarded from outer space to reduce us to submission?" Ezra asked, stopping suddenly in his tracks and staring at the two leaders.

"Ah, c'mon now, Ezra!" Paul was bluntly derisive. "Think a minute, man. We're all under a strain, but not one that makes us lose our wits. We all know that there are atmospheres that can and have melted probes. Furthermore—" He halted, not certain what would suffice to reassure Ezra, and himself.

"Furthermore, the organism attacking us," Emily went on with superb composure, "is hydrocarbon based, and if it comes from that planet, its atmosphere is not corrosive. I favor malfunction."

"My opinion, too," Paul said, nodding his head vigorously. "Fardles, Ezra, let's not talk ourselves into more problems than we've got."

"We've *got*"—Ezra brought both fists down on the desk—"to probe that planet, or we won't know enough to combat the stuff. Half the settlers want to know the source and destroy it so we can get back to our lives. Rake up the debris and forget all this."

"What aren't you telling us, Ezra?" Emily asked, cocking her head slightly and regarding the captain with an unflinching gaze.

Ezra stared back at her for a very long moment, then straightened from his half crouch over the desk and began to smile wryly.

"You've been sitting in the interface booth long hours, Ezra, and you weren't playing tiddlywinks while the programs were running," Emily went on.

"My calculations are frightening," he said in a low voice, glancing over each shoulder. "If the program is in any way accurate, and I've run it five times now from start to finish, we have to put up with Thread for long after that red planet crosses out of the inner system."

"How long will that be?" Paul felt his fingers gripping the arm rests and made a conscious effort to relax them while he tried to recall some reassuring facet of planetary orbits.

"I get between forty and fifty years!"

Emily grimaced, her mouth forming an O of surprise before she slowly exhaled. "Forty or fifty years, you say."

"If," Ezra added grimly, "the menace originated from that planet."

Paul caught his eyes and saw the ineffably weary and discouraged look in them. "If? There is another alternative?"

"I have discerned a haze about the planet, irrespective of its atmospheric envelope. A haze that spreads backward in this system and swirls along the eccentric's path. I cannot refine that telescope enough to tell more. It could be space debris, a nebulosity, the remnants of a cometary tail, a whole bunch of things that are harmless."

"But if it should be harmful?" Emily asked.

"That tail would take nearly fifty years to diffuse out of Pern's orbit, some into Rukbat—the rest, who knows?"

There was a long moment of silence.

"Any suggestions?" Paul asked finally.

"Yes," Ezra said, straightening his shoulders with a wrench. He held up two fingers. "Take a trip to the *Yokohama*, find out what's bugging the probes, and send two of 'em down to the planet to gather as much information as we can. Send the other two along the line of that cometary dust and use the *Yoko*'s more powerful space scope with no planetary interference to see if we can identify its source and components." Ezra then locked his fingers together and cracked his knuckles, a habit that always made Emily shudder. "Sorry, Em."

"At least you can recommend some positive action," Paul went on.

"The big question is, Paul, is there enough fuel to get someone to the *Yoko* and back? Kenjo's already made more trips than I thought possible."

"Good pilot," Paul said discreetly. "There's enough for what we need now. Kenjo will pilot, and did you wish to go with him?"

Ezra shook his head slowly. "Avril Bitra has the training for the job."

"Avril?" Paul gave a harsh bark and then shook his head, grinning sourly. "Avril's the last person I'd put on the *Mariposa* for any reason. Even if we knew where she is."

"Really?" Ezra looked at Emily for an explanation, but she shrugged. "Well, then, Kenjo can double. No," he corrected himself. "If something's wrong with the probes, we'd need a good technician. Stev Kimmer. He's back, isn't he?"

"Who else?" Paul jotted down names rather than worry Ezra with more suspicions.

"Kenjo is a very capable technician," Emily insisted.

"There should be two on the mission, for safety's sake," Ezra said, furrowing his brow. "This mission has got to give us the results we need."

"Zi Ongola," Paul suggested.

"Yes, the very one," Ezra agreed. "If he runs into any trouble, I can have Stev at the interface for expert advice."

"Forty years, huh?" Emily said, watching Paul underline the two final choices on the pad. "Rather longer than we'd bargained for, my friend. Let's start training replacements."

Inevitably their thoughts went to Wind Blossom, so obviously a frail vessel to continue the work her grandmother had begun.

◆ ◆ ◆

Avril's suspicious nature was aroused not by anything she heard, although what she did not hear was as significant, but by what she saw in the weary hours she manned the sled's scope. It was usually trained on the *Mariposa*, sitting at the far end of the landing grid. The night before every one of Kenjo's jaunts he had done exterior and internal checks of the craft. Fussy Fusi! Her use of the nickname was not quite derisive, because she simply could not figure out how he had managed to stretch the small reserve of fuel on the *Mariposa* as far as he already had. She had seen some activity about it last night but no sign of Kenjo. In fact, with neither moon out, she had just barely seen the shifting of shadow that indicated activity about the craft. She had been quite agitated. The only thing that reassured her was that several figures were involved. But no one entered the gig. That perplexed her.

At first light, so early that no one was yet working the donks at the skeleton of the shuttle that had been the center of considerable activity all week, she was surprised to see Fulmar Stone and Zi Ongola approaching the vessel. Her apprehension, honed by weeks of waiting, spurred her to remove the protective cover from her sled in preparation for a quick departure. At full speed, she could reach the landing grid in less than fifteen minutes. Early morning traffic into Landing would be sufficient to give her cover.

She had a moment's anxiety thinking that perhaps the *Mariposa* had developed a problem and they were scavenging replacement parts from the shuttle. Kenjo had flown a mission three days before with his usual economical takeoff and landing. She had to hand it to him—he was gliding in smoothly with no power at all. Only where was he getting the fuel to lift?

The three men, moving with almost stealthy speed, slipped inside the little spaceship and closed the airlock. Well, the access to the engines was through exterior panels, so she began to relax. They remained inside the ship for three hours, long enough for a full interior systems check. But that did not presage a usual flight. Maybe the *Mariposa* was bollixed. Scorch Kenjo for ineptitude. The *Mariposa* had to be spaceworthy. Avril swore.

Or had something happened to Kenjo so that Ongola was taking the ship up? But how? There could not be much fuel left. So why were they checking internal systems? Why were they making yet another jaunt? Displeased, Avril finished her preparations to fly.

◆ ◆ ◆

Sallah Telgar-Andiyar was feeding her daughter her breakfast in the shady covered porch of Mairi Hanrahan's Asian Square house when she caught sight of a familiar figure striding down the path. It was covered by loose overalls, and a peaked cap was pulled well down over the face, but the walk was undeniably Avril's, especially from the rear. Never mind the greasy hands, the exhaust pipe carried so ostentatiously in one hand, the clipboard in the other. That was Avril, who only sullied her hands for a good cause. No one had seen her since she had left Big Island. Sallah continued to watch until Avril mingled in with the crowd at the main depot, where technicians jostled one another for parts and matériel.

Ever since Sallah had overheard Avril's conversation with Kimmer, she had known the woman would attempt to leave Pern. Did Avril know of Kenjo's fuel dump? Irritably Sallah shook her head. Cara blinked her huge brown eyes and stared apprehensively at her mother.

"Sorry, love, your mother's mind is klicks away." Sallah gathered more puree on the spoon and deposited it into Cara's obediently open mouth. No, Sallah told herself fiercely, because she wanted to believe it so badly, Avril could not have discovered that fuel: she had been too busy mining gemstones on Big Island. At least, up until three weeks before. And where has

Avril been since then? Sallah asked herself. Watching while Kenjo flew the *Mariposa*? That would certainly set Avril Bitra to thinking hard.

Well, Sallah was due on her shift soon anyway, and as luck would have it, the sled she was servicing was on the grid. She would have a clear view of the *Mariposa* and those who approached it. If Avril came anywhere near, Sallah would set up an alarm.

There had been no talk of Kenjo making another attempt to clear Thread in the atmosphere. Then, too, Kenjo's flights were usually plotted for the dawn window, and Sallah's shift began well past that time.

It all happened rather quickly. Sallah was walking toward the sled she was servicing as Ongola and Kenjo, suited for space travel, left the tower with Ezra Keroon, Dieter Clissmann, and two other overalled figures whom Sallah was astonished to recognize by their postures as Paul and Emily. Ongola and Kenjo had the appearance of men listening to last-minute instructions. Then they continued on, almost at a stroll, toward the *Mariposa*, while the others turned back into the met tower. Suddenly another suited figure began to walk across the grid on a path that would intercept Ongola and Kenjo. Even in the baggy space gear the figure walked as only Avril did!

Sallah grabbed the nearest big spanner and started at a jog-trot across the grid. Ongola and Kenjo disappeared behind the pile of discarded sled parts at the edge of the field. Avril had begun to run, and Sallah increased her own pace. She lost sight of Ongola and Kenjo. Then she saw Arvil pick up a short strut from the pile and disappear out of sight.

Rounding the pile, Sallah saw both Kenjo and Ongola flat on the ground. Blood covered the back of Kenjo's head and Ongola's shoulder and neck. Sallah ran flat out, ducking down to keep scrap heaps between her and the *Mariposa*. As it was, she just made it as the airlock was closing. She threw herself inside and felt something scrape her left foot; there was an immense hissing, and then she blacked out.

XIII

Mairi Hanrahan thought it odd that Sallah had not rung at lunchtime to tell her she was delayed. With so many small ones to feed, every mother tried to be there at mealtimes. Mairi got one of her older children to feed Cara instead, thinking that something very important must have demanded Sallah's attention.

None of the people at the met tower or admin building expected any contact from Ongola or Kenjo while the shuttle was moving through the ionized atmosphere. Ezra, seated at the desk of the voice-activated interface, could follow its course via the activated monitor screens on board the *Yokohama*. The *Mariposa* was closing fast and soon reached the docking port. "Safely there," Ezra announced when he rang through to both tower and administration.

Half an hour later, children playing at the edge of the grid came screaming back to their teacher about the dead men. Actually, Ongola was still barely alive. Paul met the medic team at the infirmary.

"He'll live, but he's lost more blood than I like," the doctor told the admiral. "What 'n hell happened to him and Kenjo?"

"How was Kenjo killed?" Paul asked.

"The old blunt instrument. The paras found a bloodied strut nearby. Probably that. Kenjo never knew what hit him."

Paul was not sure he did either, for his legs suddenly would not support him. The doctor beckoned fiercely for one of the paras to help the admiral to a seat and poured a glass of quikal.

Paul tried to dismiss the eager hands. The implications of the two deaths greatly disturbed him. There was no antidote for Kenjo's loss, though the wretched quikal eased the intense shock that had rocked him. In the back of his mind, as he knocked back the drink, he wondered where Kenjo had cached the rest of the fuel. Why, Paul seethed at himself, had he not asked the man before? He could have done so any time before or after the last few flights Kenjo had taken in the *Mariposa*. As admiral, he knew exactly how much fuel had been left in the gig on its last drop. Now it was too late! Unless Ongola knew. He had mentioned to Paul that there was not much left at the original site, but that Kenjo had been supplying the *Mariposa*. The figures Sallah had initially reported to Ongola indicated a lot more fuel than Paul had seen in that cave the other night. Well, the misappropriation—yes, that was the right term—had had a final appropriate usage. Maybe Kenjo's wife knew where he had stored the remainder.

Paul consoled himself with that thought. Kenjo's wife would certainly know if there were more fuel sacks at the Honshu stake. He forced himself to deal with present issues: a man had been murdered and another lay close to death on a planet that had, until that moment, witnessed no capital crime.

"Ongola will survive," the doctor was saying, pouring Paul a second shot. "He's got a splendid constitution, and we'll work any miracle required. We could probably have saved Kenjo if we'd got there earlier. Brain-dead. Drink this—your color's lousy."

Paul finished the quikal and put the glass down with a decisive movement. He took a deep breath and rose to his feet. "I'm fine, thanks. Get on with saving Ongola. We'll need to know what happened when he recovers consciousness. Keep the rumors down, people!" he added, addressing the others in the room.

He strode out of the emergency facility and turned immediately for the building that housed the interface chamber and Ezra. As he walked, he reviewed the puzzle that rattled his orderly mind. He had seen the *Mariposa* take off. Who had flown her? He stopped off to collect Emily from her office, briefing her on the calamity. Ezra was surprised by the arrival of both admiral and governor; the *Mariposa's* current flight was being treated as routine.

"Kenjo's dead and Ongola seriously injured, Ezra," Paul said as soon as he had closed and locked the door behind them. "So, who's flying the *Mariposa*?"

"Gods in the heavens!" Ezra leapt to his feet and pointed to the monitor, which clearly showed the safely docked *Mariposa*. "The flight was precalculated to hit the right window, but the docking process was left to the pilot. It was very smoothly done. Not everyone can do that."

"I'll run a check on the whereabouts of pilots, Paul," Emily said, picking up a handset.

Paul glared at the monitor. "I don't think we need to do that. Call—" Paul had started to say "Ongola" and rubbed his hand across his face. "Who's at the met tower?"

"Jake Chernoff and Dieter Clissmann," Emily reported.

"Then ask Jake if there's any unmodified sleds on the grid. Find out exactly where Stev Kimmer, Nabol Nahbi, and Bart Lemos are. And—" Paul held up a warning hand. "—if anyone's seen Avril Bitra anywhere."

"Avril?" Ezra echoed, and then clamped his mouth firmly shut.

Suddenly Paul swore in a torrent of abusive language that made even Ezra regard him with amazement, and slammed out of the room. Emily concentrated on finding the pilots and had completed her check before Paul returned. He leaned back against the closed door, catching his breath.

"Stev, Nabhi, and Lemos are accounted for. Where did you go?" Emily asked.

"To check Ongola's space suit. Doc says he'll recover from his injuries. The strut just missed severing the shoulder muscle and leaving him a cripple. But—" Paul held up a crystal packet between forefinger and thumb. "No one is going to get very far in the *Mariposa*." He nodded grimly as Ezra realized what the admiral was holding. "One of the more essential parts of the guidance system! Ongola had not yet put it in place."

"Then how did—Avril?" Emily asked, pausing for confirmation. Paul nodded slowly. "Yes, it has to be Avril, doesn't it? But why would she want to get to the *Yoko*?"

"First step to leaving the system, Emily. We've been stupidly lax. Yes, I know we have this," he acknowledged when Emily pointed to the chip panel. "But we shouldn't have allowed her to get that far in the first place. And we all knew what she was like. Sallah warned us, and the years . . ."

"And recent unusual events," Ezra put in, mildly hinting that Paul need not excoriate himself.

"We should have guarded the *Mariposa* as long as she'd an ounce of fuel in her."

"We also ought to have had the sense to ask Kenjo where he was getting all the fuel," Ezra added.

"We knew that," Emily said with a wry grin.

"You did?" Ezra was amazed.

"At least Ongola took no chances," Paul went on, wincing as he remembered the sight of the man's battered shoulder and neck. "This—" He put the guidance chip very carefully down on the shelf above the worktop. "—was Ongola's special precaution, done with Kenjo's complete concurrence."

Emily sat down heavily in the nearest chair. "So where does that leave us now?"

"The next move would appear to be Avril's." Ezra shook his head sadly. "She's got more than enough fuel to get back down."

"That is not her intention," Paul said.

"Unfortunately," Emily said, "she has a hostage, whether she knows it or not. Sallah Telgar-Andiyar is also missing."

◆ ◆ ◆

Sallah returned to consciousness aware of severe discomfort and a throbbing pain in her left foot. She was bound tightly and efficiently in an uncomfortable position, her hands behind her back and secured to her tied feet. She was floating with her side just brushing the floor of the spacecraft; the lack of gravity told her that she was no longer on Pern. There was a rhythmic but unpleasant background noise, along with the sounds of things clattering and slipping about.

Then she recognized the monotonous and vicious sounds to be the curses of Avril Bitra.

"What in hell did you *do* to the guidance systems, Telgar?" she asked, kicking at the bound woman's ribs.

The kick lifted Sallah off the floor, and she found herself floating within inches of the face of an enraged Avril Bitra. Probably the only reason Sallah was still breathing was because the cabin of the *Mariposa* had its own oxygen supply. Kenjo would have charged the tanks up to full, wouldn't he? Sallah asked herself in a moment of panic as she continued to float beyond Avril. The other woman was suited; the helmet sat on the rack above the pilot's seat, ready for use.

Avril reached up and grabbed Sallah's arm. "What do you know about this? Tell me and be quick about it, or I'll evacuate you and save the air for me to breathe!"

Sallah had no doubt that the woman was capable of doing just that. "I know nothing about anything, Avril. I saw you stalking Ongola and Kenjo and knew you were up to something. So I followed you and got in the airlock just as you took off."

"You followed me?" Avril lashed out with a fist. The impact caused both women to bounce apart. Avril steadied herself on a handhold. "How dare you?"

"Well, as I hadn't seen you in months and longed to know how you were faring, it seemed a good idea at the time." Hang for the fleece, hang for the sheep, Sallah thought. She could not shrug her shoulders. What had she done to her foot? It was an aching mess.

"Bloody hell. You've flown this frigging crate. How do I override the preflight instructions? You must know that."

"I might if you'd let me see the console." She saw hope, and then manic doubt, in Avril's eyes. Sallah was not lying. "How could I possibly tell from over here? I don't know where we are. I've been just another Thread sledder." Even to a woman slightly paranoid, the truth would be obvious. Sallah warned herself to be very careful. "Just let me look."

She did not ask to be untied although that was what she desperately wanted—needed. Her right shoulder must have been bruised by her fall into the cabin, and all the muscles were spasming.

"Don't think I'll untie you," Avril warned, and contemptuously she pushed Sallah across the cabin. Grabbing a handhold, she corrected Sallah's spin to a painful halt against the command console. "Look!"

Sallah did, though hanging slightly upside down was not the best position for the job. She had to think carefully, for Avril had piloted shuttles and knew something of their systems. But the *Mariposa*, though small, was designed to traverse interplanetary distances, dock with a variety of stations or other craft, and had the sophisticated controls to perform a considerable variety of maneuvers in space and on a planetary surface. Sallah dared to hope that much of its instrumentation would be unfamiliar to Avril.

"To find out what this ship just did," she instructed, "hit the return button on the bottom tier of the greens. No, the port side."

Avril jerked at Sallah, tweaking strained arm and back muscles and jamming Sallah's head against the viewscope. Sallah's long hair was freed completely from its pins and flowed over her face.

"Don't get cute!" Avril snapped, her finger hovering on the appropriate button. "This one?"

Sallah nodded, floating away again. Avril punched the button with one hand and hauled her back into position with the other. Then she caught the handhold to keep herself in place.

Every action has a reaction, Sallah thought, trying to clear her head of pain and confusion.

The monitor came up with a preflight instruction plan.

"The *Mariposa* was programmed to dock here on the *Yoko*." It was nice to know where she was, Sallah reflected. "Once you hit the power, you couldn't alter its course."

"Well," Avril said, her tone altering considerably. "I wanted to come here first anyhow. I just wanted to come on my own." Sallah, hair falling over her face, felt a lessening of the tension that emanated from the woman. Some of the beauty returned to a face no longer contorted with frustration. "I don't need you hanging about, then." Avril reached up and gave Sallah's body a calculated shove that sent her to the opposite end of the cabin, to bump harmlessly against the other wall and then hover there. "Well, I'll just get to work."

How long Sallah was suspended in that fashion she did not know. She managed to tilt her head and get her hair to float away from her eyes, but she did not dare to move much—action produced reaction, and she did not wish to draw attention to herself. She ached all over, but the pain in her foot was almost unbearable.

A tirade of malevolent and resentful oaths spun from Avril's lips. "None of the programs run, of all the frigging luck. Nothing runs!"

Sallah had just enough time to duck her head to avoid Avril's projectile arrival against her. As it was, she went head over heels in a spin that Avril, laughing gleefully, assisted until the rotation made Sallah retch.

"You bitch woman!" Avril stopped Sallah before she could expel more vomit into the air. "Okay! If that's the way of it, you know what I need to know. And you're going to tell me, or I'll kill you by inches." A spaceman's knife, with its many handle-packed implements, sliced across the top of Sallah's nose.

Then she felt the blade none too gently cutting the bindings on her hands and feet. Blood rushed through starved arteries, and her strained muscles reacted painfully. If she had not been in free-fall, she would have collapsed. As it was, the agony of release made her sob and shake.

"Clean up your spew first," Avril said, shoving a slop jar at her.

Sallah did as she was told, grateful for the lack of gravity, grateful for the release, and wondering what she could do to gain an upper hand. But she had little opportunity to enjoy her freedom, for Avril had other ways of securing her prisoner's cooperation.

Before Sallah realized what was happening, Avril had secured a tether to the injured foot and tweaked the line. Pain, piercing like a shard of glass, shot through Sallah's leg and up to her groin. There was too little left in her stomach to throw up. Avril jerked Sallah over to the console, pushed her into the pilot's chair, and tied her down, twiching her improvised lead line to remind Sallah of her helplessness.

"Now, check the fuel on board, check the quantity in the *Yoko's* tanks— I've done that, I know the answers, so don't try anything clever." A jerk against Sallah's injured foot reinforced the threat. "Then enter a program that gets me out of this wretched asshole of a midden system."

Sallah did as she was told, though her head ached and her eyes blurred repeatedly. She could not suppress her surprise at the amount of fuel in the *Mariposa's* tanks.

"Yes, someone was holding back on it. You?" There was a jerk on the line.

"Kenjo, I suspect," Sallah replied coolly, managing to suppress a cry. She was determined not to give Avril any satisfaction.

"Fussy Fusi? Yes, that computes. I thought he'd given up all too tamely! Where did he hide it?" The line tightened. Sallah had to bite hard on her lip against a sob.

"Probably at his stake. It's back of beyond. No one goes there. He could hide anything there."

Avril snorted and remained silent. Sallah made herself breathe deeply, forcing more adrenaline into her system to combat pain, fatigue, and fear.

"All right, compute me a course to . . ." Avril consulted a notebook. "Here."

Only because Sallah already knew the coordinates did she recognize the numbers. Avril wished to go to the system nearest them, a system that, though uninhabited, was closer to the populated sectors of space. The course would stretch the *Mariposa* to the end of available fuel, even if Avril also drained the *Yoko*'s tanks. It gave Sallah no consolation to think that the little ship might drift for centuries with Avril safe and composed in deep sleep. Unless, just maybe, Ongola had tampered with the sleep tanks, too. She liked that idea. But she knew Ongola too well to presume that kind of foresight.

Unfortunately, the Avrils of the galaxy could make themselves at home in any time and culture. So if Avril went into deep sleep, eventually someone, or something, would rescue her and the *Mariposa*. Sallah did not need to see them to know that Avril had several fortunes' worth of gemstones and precious metals aboard the *Mariposa*. There had never been any doubt in anyone's mind why Avril had chosen Big Island as her stake, but no one had cared. But then, no one would have imagined that she would be mad enough to attempt to leave Pern, even with Threadfall threatening the planet.

Wondering why Avril, who was an astrogator, after all, had not been able to complete laying in such a simple course, Sallah did as she was ordered. She had more experience than Avril did with the *Mariposa*'s drive board. But the program was not accepted. ERROR 259 AT LINE 57465534511 was the message.

Avril jerked hard on the line, and Sallah hissed against the burning, crippling pain in her foot.

"Try again. There's more than one way of entering a course."

Sallah obeyed. "I'll have to go around the existing parameters."

"Reset the entire effing thing but plot that course," Avril told her.

As Sallah began the more laborious deviation into the command center of the gig's course computer, she was aware that Avril had picked up a long narrow cylinder from the rack by her helmet. She fiddled with it, humming tunelessly under her breath, seemingly thoroughly delighted with herself.

When Sallah finally tapped the "return" tab, she became aware of Avril's intense interest in the flickering console. She chanced a look at what the woman had been fondling. It was a homemade capsule. Not a homer—they were thicker and longer—but something more like the standard beacon. Suddenly she clearly saw Avril's plan.

Avril would take the *Mariposa* as far away from the Rukbat system as possible and then direct the distress beacon toward shipping lanes. Every planetary system involved with the Federated Sentient Planets, and some life-forms who were not, traced distress beacons to origin. The devices, automatically released when a ship was destroyed, were often traced by those who wished to turn whatever profit they could on the flotsam.

Avril's plan was not as insane as it seemed. Sallah felt certain that Stev Kimmer had intended to take the trip with her, to be rescued by the distress beacon he had made for her.

Words flashed on the screen. NO ACCESS WITHOUT STANDARD FCP/120/GM.

"Fuck it! That's all I could get out of it. Try again, Telgar." Avril pressed Sallah's foot against the base of the console module, increasing the pain to the point where Sallah felt herself losing consciousness. Avril viciously pinched her left breast. "You don't pass out on me, Telgar!"

"Look," Sallah said, her voice rather more shaken than she liked, "I've tried twice, you've tried. I've tried the fail-safe I was taught. Someone anticipated you, Bitra. Open up this panel and I'll tell you if we've been wasting effort." She was trembling not only with pain but with the effort not to relieve her bladder. But she did not dare to ask even that favor.

Swearing, her face livid with frustration and rage, Avril deftly removed the panel, kicking the console in her frenzy. Sallah leaned as far away as her bonds permitted, hoping to escape any stray blows.

"How did they do it? What did they take, Telgar, or I'll start carving you up." Avril flattened Sallah's left hand over the exposed chips, and her knife blade cut through the little finger to the bone. Pain and shock lanced through Sallah's body. "You don't need this one at all!"

"Blood hangs in the air just like vomit and urine, Bitra. And if you don't stop, you'll have both in free-fall!"

They locked eyes in a contest of wills.

"What . . . did . . . they . . . remove?" With each word Avril sawed against the little finger. Sallah screamed. It felt good to scream, and she knew that it would complete the picture of her in Avril's mind: soft Sallah had never felt harder in her life.

"Guidance. They removed the guidance chip. You can't go anywhere."

The blade left her finger, and Sallah stared in fascination at the drops of blood that formed and floated. The contemplation took her mind off Avril's ranting until the woman snagged her shoulder.

"Are all the spare parts on the planet? Did they strip everything from the *Yoko*?"

Sallah forced her attention away from the blood and the pain, clamping down on all but the important consideration: how to thwart Avril without seeming to. "I'd say that there would be guidance chips left in the main board that could be substituted."

"There'd better be." Avril slipped the knife through the cord that bound Sallah to the pilot's seat. "Okay. We suit up and head for the bridge."

"Not before I go to the head, Avril," Sallah replied. She nodded at her hand. "And attend to this. You don't want blood on the chips, you know." She let herself scream with the pain of the jerk to her foot. She felt she had handled her submission well. Avril would have suspected a more immediate capitulation. "And another boot."

Finally Sallah could spare a dispassionate look at her foot. Half her heel was missing, and a puddle of blood rocked slowly back and forth, moved by the agitation of Avril's kicks.

"Wait!" Avril had also noticed the blood. She spun away to the lockers by the hatch and came back with a space suit and a dirty cloth. "There! Strip!"

Sallah tied up her finger with the least soiled strip of cloth and used the rest to bind her foot. It hurt badly, and she could feel that fragments of her work boot had been jammed into the flesh. She was allowed the use of the head, while Avril watched and made snide cracks about maternal changes in a woman's body. Sallah pretended to be more humiliated than she actually felt. It made Avril feel so superior. The higher the summit, the harder the fall, Sallah thought grimly. She struggled into the space suit.

✦ ✦ ✦

"She's left the gig, Admiral," Ezra said suddenly into the tense silence in the crowded interface chamber. Tarvi had been called in. Silent tears streamed down his face. "She's passed the sensors at the docking area. No," he corrected himself, "two bodies have passed the sensors." Tarvi let out a ragged sob but said nothing.

Bit by bit, the pieces had been put together to solve the puzzle of Sallah's disappearance and Avril Bitra's reappearance.

A technician, working on a remount job on the sled nearest Sallah's, remembered seeing her leave her task and wander toward the scrap pile at the edge of the grid. He had also noticed Kenjo and Ongola walking to the *Mariposa*. He had not seen anyone else in that vicinity. Shortly afterward he had seen the *Mariposa* lift off.

Once someone thought to look for it, the sled Avril had used was easily spotted. It carried none of the modifications that all other Pernese sleds bore; it had been left at the edge of the grid, among others that had been called in for servicing. Stev Kimmer was called in to identify it. She had removed every trace of her occupancy, although Stev pointed to scrape marks that were new to him. He also kept his personal comments about his erstwhile partner to himself, though his expression had been sufficiently grim for Paul and Emily to suspect that he had been double-crossed. For one moment he had hesitated. Then, with a shrug, he had answered every question they asked him.

"She won't get anywhere," Emily said, firmly, striving for optimism.

"No, she won't." Paul looked at the guidance cartridge, not daring to glance in Tarvi's direction.

"Couldn't she replace it from similar chips on the bridge?" Tarvi asked, his face an odd shade, his lips dry, and his liquid eyes tormented.

"Not the right size," Ezra said, his expression infinitely sad. "The Mariposa was more modern, used smaller, more sophisticated crystals."

"Besides," Paul added heavily, "the chip she really needs is the one Ongola replaced with a blank. Oh, she can probably set a course and it will appear to be accepted. The ship will reverse out of the dock, but the moment she touches the firing pin, it'll just go straight ahead."

"But Sallah!" Tarvi demanded in an anguished voice. "What will happen to my wife?"

◆ ◆ ◆

Sallah waited until Avril had reversed the Mariposa from the dock, let it drift away from the Yokohama's bulk, and ignited the Mariposa's tailflame before she operated the comm unit. Avril had done as much damage to the circuitry in the bridge console as she could, but she had forgotten the override at the admiral's position. As soon as she left the bridge, Sallah accessed it.

"Yokohama to Landing. Come in, Ezra. You must be there!"

"Keroon here, Telgar! What's your position?"

"Sitting," Sallah said.

"Goddamn it, Telgar, don't be facetious at a time like this," Ezra cried.

"Sorry, sir," Sallah said. "I don't have visuals." That was a lie, but she did not wish anyone to see her condition. "I'm accessing the probe garage. There is no damage report for that area. You've three probes left. How shall I program them?"

"Hellfire, girl, don't talk about probes now! How're we going to get you down?"

"I don't think you are, sir," she said cheerfully. "Tarvi?"

"Sal-lah!" The two syllables were said in a tone that brought her heart to her mouth and tears to her eyes. Why had he never spoken her name that way before? Did it mean the long-awaited avowal of his love? The anguish in his voice evoked a spirit tortured and distressed.

"Tarvi, my love." She kept her voice level though her throat kept closing. "Tarvi, who's with you there?"

"Paul, Emily, Ezra," he replied in broken tones. "Sallah! You must return!"

"On the wings of a prayer? No. Go to Cara! Get out of the room. I've got some business to do, Pern business. Paul, make him leave. I can't think if I know he's listening."

"Sallah!" Her name echoed and reechoed in her ears.

"Okay, Ezra, tell me where you want them."

There was a choking, throat-clearing noise. "I want one to go to the body of the cometary, the second to circumnavigate." Ezra cleared his throat again. "I want the other to follow the spiral curve of that nebulosity. If the big scope is operable, I'd like bridge readings all along that damned thing. We can't track it with the telescope we have here—not powerful enough for the definition we need. Never thought we'd need the big one, so we didn't dismantle it." He was maundering, Sallah thought affectionately, to get himself under control. Did she hear someone crying through that conversation? Surely Governor Boll or the admiral would have been kind enough to get Tarvi out of the room.

Then she needed to concentrate on the information Ezra was giving her to encode the duties and destinations of the individual probes.

"Probes away, sir," she said, remembering the last time she had given that response. She saw Pern on the big screen; she had never thought that she would again see from space the world she had come to know as her home. "Now I'm sending some data for Dieter to decipher. Avril said she'd killed both Ongola and Kenjo. Has she?"

"Kenjo, yes. Ongola will pull through."

"Old soldiers don't die easy. Look, Ezra, what I'm sending for Dieter are some notations I made on available fuel. Ongola will know what I mean. And I've sent down Avril's course. She went off in the right direction, but I saw a very odd-looking crystal in that guidance system, one I never saw on the *Mariposa* when I was driving her. Am I right? She won't go anywhere?"

"Once Bitra hits the engine button, she goes in a straight line."

"Very good," Sallah said with a feeling of immense satisfaction. "The straight and narrow for our dear departed friend. Now, I'm activating the big scope. I'll program it to report through the interface to you. All right?"

"Give me the readings yourself, Mister Telgar," Ezra ordered gruffly.

"I don't think so, Captain," she said, glad to rely on the impersonal address. She visualized Ezra Keroon's thin frame hunched over the interface. "I don't have that much time. Only the oxygen in my tanks. They were full when Avril let me put them on, but she told me she was switching off the bridge's independent system. I have no reason to doubt her. That's another reason why I'm switching the scope's readings to you. Space gloves are good, but they don't allow for fine tunings. I just about managed some repairs to the mess Avril made of the console. Jury rig at least, so . . . when someone gets a chance to get up here, most everything will work."

"How much time do you have, Sallah?"

"I don't know." She could feel the blood reaching to her calf in the big boot, and her left glove was full. How much blood did a person have? She felt weak, too, and she was aware that it was getting harder to breathe. It was all of a piece. She would miss knowing Cara better.

"Sallah?" Ezra's voice was very kind. "Sallah, talk to Tarvi. We can't keep him out of here. He's like a madman. He just wants to talk to you."

"Oh, sure, fine. I want to talk to him," she said, her voice sounding funny even to herself.

"Sallah!" Tarvi had managed to get his voice under control. "Get out of here, all of you! She's mine now. Sallah, jewel in my night, my golden girl, my emerald-eyed ranee, why did I never tell you before how much you mean to me? I was too proud. I was too vain. But you taught me to love, taught me by your sacrifice when I was too engrossed in my other love—my worklove—to see the inestimable gift of your affection and kindness. How could I have been so stupid? How could I have failed to see that you were more than just a body to receive my seed, more than an ear to hear my ambitions, more than hands to—Sallah? Sallah! Answer me, Sallah!"

"You—loved—me?"

"I do love you, Sallah. I do! Sallah? Sallah! *Sallllaaaaah!*"

◆ ◆ ◆

"What do you think, Dieter?" Paul asked the programmer as he consulted the figures Ezra had given them.

"Well, this first lot of figures gives us over two thousand liters of fuel. The second is a guesstimate of how much Kenjo used on the four missions he flew and what was used by the *Mariposa* today. There's a substantial quantity unused somewhere down here on the surface. The third set is evidently what was left in the *Yoko*'s tanks and is now in the *Mariposa*'s. But, I do point out, as Sallah does, that there's enough in the *Yoko*'s sumptank for centuries of minor orbital corrections."

Paul nodded brusquely. "Go on."

"Now this section is the course Bitra tried to set. The first course correction should have been initiated about now." Dieter frowned at the equations on his monitor. "In fact, she should be plunging straight toward our eccentric planet. Maybe we'll find out sooner than we knew what the surface is like."

"Not that Avril is likely to stand by and give us any useful information as—as Sallah did." Dieter looked up at the savage tone of the admiral's voice. "Sorry. C'mon. You've the right. And if something goes wrong . . ." Paul left the sentence dangling as he led Dieter down the corridor to the interface room.

Emily had gone with Tarvi to give him what comfort she could, so Ezra was manning the room alone. He looked as old as Paul felt after the wringing emotions of the day.

"Any word?"

"None of it for polite company," Ezra said with a snort. "She's just discovered that the first course correction hasn't occurred." He turned the dial so that the low snarl of vindictive curses was plainly audible.

Paul grinned maliciously at Dieter. "So you said." He turned on the speakers.

"Avril, can you hear me?"

"Benden! What the hell did that bitch of yours do? How did she do it? The override is locked. I can't even maneuver. I knew I should have sawn her *foot* off."

Ezra blanched and Dieter looked ill, but Paul's smile was vindictive. So Avril had underestimated Sallah. He took a deep breath of pride in the valiant woman.

"You're going to explore the plutonic planet, Avril darling. Why don't you be a decent thing and give us a running account?"

"Shove it, Benden. You know where! You'll get nothing out of me. Oh, shit! Oh, shit! It's not the—oh, shiiiitt."

The sound of her final expletive was drowned by a sizzling roar that made Ezra grab for the volume dial.

"Shit!" Paul echoed very softly. " 'It's not the . . .'—the what? Damn you, Avril, to eternity! It's not the *what?*"

❖ ❖ ❖

Emily and Pierre, along with Chio-Chio Yoritomo, who had been Kenjo's wife's cabinmate on the *Buenos Aires* and her housemate on Irish Square, took the fast sled to Kenjo's Honshu Stake. While most of Landing knew about Kenjo's death and Ongola's serious illness, there had been no public announcement. Rumor had been busy discussing the "unknown" assailant.

When Emily returned that night, she brought a sealed message to the admiral.

"She told us," Emily said dryly, "that she would prefer to stay on at Honshu to work the stake herself for her four children. She has few needs and would not trouble us."

"She is very traditional," Chio-Chio told the admiral breathlessly. "She would not show grief, for that belittles the dead." She shrugged, eyes down, her hands clenching and unclenching. Then she looked up, almost defiant in her anger. "She was like that. Kenjo married her because she would not question what he did. He asked me first, but I had more sense, even if he *was* a war ace. Oh!" She brought her arm up to hide her face. "But to die like that! Struck from behind. An ignominious death for one who had cheated it so often!" Then she turned and fled from the room, her sobbing audible as she ran out into the night.

Emily gestured for Paul to open the small note, which was well sealed by wax and stamped with some kind of marking. He broke it open and unfolded the thick, beautiful, handmade paper. Then, mystified, he handed it to Emily and Pierre.

" 'There were two caves cut, to judge by the amount of fuel used and rubble spilled. One cave housed the plane. I do not know where the other was,' " Emily read. "So he did manage to remove some of the fuel? How much?"

"We'll see if Ezra can figure it out—or Ongola, when he recovers. Pierre?" Paul asked the chef for a pledge of silence.

"Of course. Discretion was bred in my family for generations, Admiral."

"Paul," the admiral corrected him.

"For something like this, old friend, you are the admiral!" Pierre clicked his heels together and inclined his body slightly from the waist, smiling with a brief reassurance. "Emily, you are tired. You should rest now. Paul, tell her!"

Paul laid one hand on Pierre de Courci's shoulder and took Emily's arm with the other. "There is one more duty for the day, Pierre, and you'd best be with us."

"The bonfire!" Emily pulled back against Paul's arm. "I'm not sure I—"

"Who can?" Paul broke in when she faltered. "Tarvi has asked it."

All three walked with reluctant steps, joining the trickle of others going in the same direction, down to the dark Bonfire Square. Each house had left one light burning. The thinly scattered stars were brilliant, and the first moon, Timor, was barely a crescent on the eastern skyline.

By the pyramid of thicket and fern, Tarvi stood, his head down, a man as gaunt as some of the branches that had been cast into the pile. Suddenly, as if he knew that all were there who would come, he lit the brand. It flared up to light a face haggard with grief, with hair that straggled across tear-wet cheeks.

Tarvi raised the brand high, turning slowly as if to place firmly in his memory the faces of all those in attendence.

"From now on," he shouted harshly, "I am not Tarvi, nor Andiyar. I am Telgar, so that her name is spoken every day, so that her name is remembered by everyone for giving *us* her life today. Our children will now bear that name, too. Ram Telgar, Ben Telgar, Dena Telgar, and Cara Telgar, who will never know her mother." He took a deep breath, filling his chest. *What is my name?*"

"Telgar!" Paul replied as loud as he could.

"Telgar!" cried Emily beside him, Pierre's baritone repeating it a breath behind her. *"Telgar!"*

"Telgar! Telgar! Telgar! *Telgar! Telgar!*" Nearly three thousand voices took up the shout in a chant, pumping their arms until Telgar thrust the burning torch into the bonfire. As the flame roared up through the dry wood and fern, the name crescendoed. *"Telgar! Telgar! Telgar!"*

The shock of Sallah Telgar's death reverberated across the continent. She had been well known, both as shuttle pilot during debarkation and as an able manager of the Karachi camp. Her courage, however, gave an unexpected boost to morale, almost as if, because Sallah had been willing to devote the last moments of her life to benefit the colony, everyone had to strive harder to vindicate her sacrifice. Or so it seemed for the next eight days until some disturbing rumors began to circulate.

"Look, Paul," Joel Lilienkamp began even before he had closed the door behind him. "Everyone's got a right to access Stores. But that Ted Tubberman's been taking out some unusual stuff for a botanist."

"Not Tubberman again," Paul said, leaning back in his chair with a deep sigh of disgust. Tarv—Telgar, Paul corrected himself, had phoned the previous day, asking if Tubberman had been authorized to scrounge in the shuttle they were dismantling.

"Yes," Joel said. "If you ask me, he's only accessing half his chips. You've got enough on your plate, Paul, but you gotta know what that fool's doing. I'll bet my last bottle of brandy he's up to something."

"At Wind Blossom's request, Pol has denied him further access to the biology labs," Paul said wearily. "Seems he was acting as if *he* was in charge of bioengineering. Bay doesn't like him much, either."

"She's not alone," Joel replied, lowering himself to a chair and scrubbing at his face. "I want your permission to shut the shop door in his face, too. I caught him in Building G, which houses the technically sensitive stuff. I don't want anyone in there without my authorization. And there he was, bald-faced and swaggering like he had every right, he and Bart Lemos."

"Bart Lemos!" Paul sat up again.

"Yeah. He, Bart, and Stev Kimmer're doing a good-old-buddy bit these days. And I don't like the rumors my sources tell me they're spreading."

"Stev Kimmer's in on it?" Paul was surprised.

Joel shrugged. "He's mighty thick with 'em."

Paul rubbed his knuckles thoughtfully. Bart Lemos was a gullible non-entity, but Stev Kimmer was a highly skilled technician. Paul had put a discreet monitor on the man's activities after Avril's departure. Stev had gone on a three-day bender and been found asleep in the dismantled shuttle. Once he had recovered from the effects of quikal, he had gone back to work. Fulmar said that other mechanics did not like pairing with him because he was taciturn, if not downright surly. The thought of Tubberman having access to Kimmer's expertise made Paul uneasy. "What exactly have you heard, Lili?" he asked.

"A load of crap," the little storesman said, folding his fingers across his chest. "I don't think anyone with any sense buys the notion that Avril and Kenjo were in league. Or that Ongola killed Kenjo to keep them from taking the *Mariposa* to go for help. But I'll warn you, Paul, if Kitti's bioengineering program doesn't show positive results, we could be down the tubes. I'll lay odds you and Emily are going to be asked to reconsider sending off that homing capsule."

The previous evening, Paul had discussed that expedient with Emily, Ezra, and Jim. Keroon had been the fiercest opponent of a homing-capsule mayday, which he termed an exercise in futility. As Paul remarked, such technological help was, at the earliest, ten years away. And the chance that the FSP would move with any speed to assist them was depressingly slim. To send for help seemed not only a rejection of Sallah's sacrifice but a cowardly admission of failure when they had not exhausted the ingenuity and resourcefulness of their community.

"What sort of material has Ted been requisitioning, Lili?" Paul asked.

Joel extracted a wad of paper from his thigh pocket and made a show of unfolding and reading from it. "Grab bag from hydroponics to insulation materials, steel mesh and posts, and some computer chips that Dieter says he couldn't possibly need, use, or understand."

"Did you happen to ask Tubberman what he needed them for?"

"I happened to just do that very thing. A bit arrogant he was, too. Said they were needed for his experiments"—Joel was clearly dubious about their value—"to develop a more effective defense against the Thread until help comes."

Paul grimaced. He had heard the botanist's wild claims that *he*, not the biologists and their jumped-up mutated lizards, would protect Pern. "I don't like that 'till help comes' bit," Paul murmured, gritting his teeth.

"So, tell me to lock him out, Paul. He may be a charterer, but he's over-spent his credit and then some." He waved the sheet. "I got records to prove that."

Paul nodded. "Yes, but next time he presents a list, get him to tell you what he wants, then shut the door. I want to know what he's up to."

"Restrict him to his stake," Joel said, rising to his feet, an expression of genuine concern on his round face, "and you'll save all of us a lot of aggro. He's a wild card, and you can't be sure where he'll bounce up next."

Paul grinned at the storesman. "I'd be glad to, Lili, but the mandate doesn't permit that kind of action."

Joel snorted derisively, hesitated a moment longer, and then, shrugging in his inimitable fashion, left the office.

Paul did not forget the conversation, but the morning brought more pressing concerns. Despite the best efforts of Fulmar and his engineering crews, three more sleds had failed airworthiness tests. That meant using more ground crews, the last line of defense and the most enervating for people already worked to the point of exhaustion. Neither Paul nor Emily recognized the significance of three separate reports: one from the veterinary lab, saying that their supply rooms had been rifled overnight; another from Pol Nietro, reporting that Ted Tubberman had been seen in bioengineering; and the third from Fulmar, saying that someone had made off with one of the exhaust cylinders from the dismantled shuttle.

When Joel Lilienkamp's angry call came through, Paul had little trouble arriving at a conclusion.

"May his orifices congeal and his extremities fall off," Joel cried at the top of his voice. "He's got the homing capsule!"

Shock jolted Paul out of his chair, while Emily and Ezra regarded him in astonishment. "Are you sure?"

"Of course I'm sure, Paul. I hid the carton in among stove pipes and heating units. It hasn't been misplaced, but who the hell could *know* that carton #45/879 was a homing capsule?"

"Tubberman took it?"

"I'll bet my last bottle of brandy he did." Joel spoke so fast that his words slurred. "The fucker! The crap-eater, the slime-producing maggot!"

"When did you discover it gone?"

"Now! I'm calling from Building G. I check it out at least once a day."

"Could Tubberman have followed you?"

"What sort of a twat do you think I am?" Joel was as apoplectic at such a suggestion as he was about the theft. "I check every building every day and I can tell you exactly what was requisitioned yesterday and the day before, so I fucking well know when something's missing!"

"I don't doubt you for a moment, Joel." Paul rubbed his hand hard over his mouth, thinking rapidly. Then he saw the anxious expressions of Emily and Ezra. "Hold on," he said into the handset, and reported what Joel had said.

"Well," Ezra replied, a look of intense relief passing over his gaunt features. "Tubberman couldn't launch a kite. He can barely maneuver a sled. I wouldn't worry about him."

"Not him. But I worry a lot about Stev Kimmer and Bart Lemos being seen in Tubberman's company lately," Paul said quietly. Ezra seemed to deflate, burying his head in his hands.

"Ted Tubberman has had it," Emily said, placing the folder she had been studying onto the table in a precise manner and rising to her feet. "I don't give a spent chip for his position as a charterer or the privacy of his stake. We're searching Calusa." She gave Ezra a poke in the shoulder. "C'mon, you'll know what components he'd need."

They all heard the sound of running feet, then the door burst in and Jake Chernoff erupted into the office.

"Sir, sorry, sir," the young man cried, his face flushed, his chest heaving from exertion. "Your phone—" He pointed excitedly at the receiver in the admiral's hand. "Too important. Scanners at met—something blasted off from Oslo Landing, three minutes ago—and it wasn't a sled. Too small."

As one, Paul, Emily, and Ezra made for the door and ran to the interface chamber. Ezra fumbled at the terminal in his haste to implement the program. An exhaust trail was plainly visible, on a northwestern heading. Cursing under his breath, Ezra switched to the *Yoko*'s monitor, which was tracking the blip. For a long moment they watched, rigid with fury and frustration. Then Ezra straightened his long frame, his hands hanging limply.

"Well, what's done's done."

"Not completely," Emily said, her voice harsh as she separated each syllable in a curious lilt. She turned to Paul, her eyes very bright, her lips pursed, and her expression implacable. "Oslo Landing, hmmm? That capsule was just launched. Let's go get the buggers."

Leaving Ezra to monitor the capsule's ascent, Paul and Emily left at a run. The first three big men they encountered on their way to the grid were commandeered to assist. Paul spotted Fulmar and told him to pilot Kenjo's augmented sled.

"Don't ask questions, Fulmar," Paul said, peremptorily seconding two more burly technicians. "Just head us toward Jordan, and everyone keep their eyes open for sled traffic." He reached for the comm unit as he shrugged into his harness. "Who's in the tower? Tarrie? I want to know who's in the air above the river, where they're going, and where they've been."

Fulmar took off in such a steep climb that for a moment the noise blanketed any answer Tarrie Chernoff gave.

"Only one sled above the Jordan, sir, apart from that—other flight." She choked on her words and then recovered the impersonal reserve of a comm officer. "The sled does not acknowledge."

"They will," Paul assured her grimly. "Continue to monitor all traffic in that area."

Tubberman was just stupid enough to be obvious, but somehow Paul did not think that such stupidity was a trait of Stev Kimmer or whomever else Ted had talked into such an arrant abrogation of the democratic decision of the colony.

Tubberman was alone in the sled when Fulmar forced him to land in the riverside desolation of the ill-fated Bavaria Stake. He was unrepentant as he faced them, folding his arms across his chest and jutting his chin out defiantly.

"I've done what should have been done," he stated in pompous righteousness. "The first step in saving this colony from annihilation."

Paul clenched his fists tightly to his sides. Beside him, Emily was vibrating with a fury as intense as his own.

"I want the names of your accomplices, Tubberman," Paul said through his teeth, "and I want them now!"

Tubberman inhaled, bracing himself. "Do your worst, Admiral. I am man enough to take it."

The mock heroic attitude was so absurd to his auditors that one of the men behind Paul let out a short bark of incredulous laughter, which he quickly cut off. But the one burst of derision altered Paul's mood.

"Tubberman, I wouldn't let anyone touch a hair of your head," Paul said, grinning in a release of tension. "There are quite suitable ways to deal with you, plainly set out in the charter—nothing quite as crude or barbaric as physical abuse." Then he turned. "You men take him back to Landing in his sled. Put him in my office and call Joel Lilienkamp. He'll take charge of the prisoner." Paul had the satisfaction of seeing the martyred look fade from Tubberman's eyes, to be replaced by a mixture of anxiety and surprise. Turning on his heel, Paul gestured Emily, Fulmar, and the others back into their sled.

Tarrie reported no other vehicles in the area and apologized that traffic records were no longer kept. "Except for that . . . rocket thing, the pattern was normal, sir. Oh, and Jake's back. Did you want to speak to him?"

"Yes," Paul answered, wishing that Ongola were back in charge. "Jake, I want to know where Bart Lemos and Stev Kimmer are. And Nabhi Nabol." Beside him, Emily nodded approval.

By then, Fulmar had covered the short air distance between Bavaria and Oslo Landing. The remains of the launch platform were still smoking. While Paul went with the others to search the area for sled skids, Fulmar carefully prodded through the overheated circle beneath it, sniffing as he went.

"Shuttle fuel by the smell of it, Paul," he reported. "A homing capsule wouldn't take much."

"It would take know-how," Paul said grimly. "And expertise, and you and I know just how many people are capable of handling that sort of technology." He looked Fulmar square in the eye, and the man's shoulders sagged. "Not your fault, Fulmar. I had your report. I had others. I just didn't put the pieces together."

"Who'd have thought Ted'd pull such a crazy stunt? No one believes half of what he says!" Fulmar protested.

Emily and the others came back then from an inconclusive search. "There're a lot of skid marks, Paul," she reported. "And rubbish." She indicated a collapsed fuel sack and a handful of connectors and wires. Fulmar's look of desolation deepened.

"We're wasting time here," Paul said, curbing his irritation.

"Let's have Cherry and Cabot waiting in my office," Emily murmured as they climbed into the sled.

◆ ◆ ◆

"He's *proud* of what he did," Joel stormed when Paul and Emily called him into Emily's office on their return. "Says it was his *duty* to save the colony. Says we'll be surprised at how many people agree with him."

"He's the one who'll be surprised," Emily replied. Her jaw was set in a resolute line, and her lips curved in a curious smile, which her tired eyes did not echo.

"Yeah, Em, but what *can* we do to him?" Joel demanded in impotent indignation.

Emily poured herself a fresh cup of *klah* and took a sip before she answered. "He will be shunned."

"Who will be shunned?" Cherry Duff demanded in her hoarse voice, entering the room at that instant. Cabot Carter was right behind her, having escorted the magistrate from her office in reply to the summons.

"Shunned?" Carter's handsome face was enlivened by a smile that grew broader as he looked expectantly from Paul to Emily, then faded slightly as he saw the dour storesman.

Paul grinned back. "Shunned!"

"Shunned?" Joel exclaimed in a disgusted tone.

Emily gestured Cherry into the comfortable chair and motioned for the others to be seated. Then, at a nod from Paul, she gave a terse report that culminated in Tubberman's illicit use of the homing capsule.

"So we're to order Tubberman shunned, huh?" Cherry looked around at Carter.

"It's legal all right, Cherry," the legist replied, "since it is not a corporal punishment, per se, which is illegal under the terms of the charter."

"Refresh me on such a process," Cherry said, her tone doubly droll.

"Shunning was a mechanism," Emily began, "whereby passive groups could discipline an erring member. Religious communities resorted to it when someone of their sect disobeyed their peculiar tenets. Quite effective really. The rest of the sect pretended the offending member didn't exist. No one spoke to him, no one acknowledged his presence, no one would assist the shunned in any way or indicate that he—or she—existed. It doesn't seem cruel, but in fact that deprivation is psychologically destructive."

"It'll do," Cherry said, nodding in satisfaction. "An admirable punishment for someone like Tubberman. Admirable!"

"And completely legal!" Cabot concurred. "Shall I draft the announcement, Emily, or do you prefer to do it, Cherry?"

Cherry flicked her hand at him. "You do it, Cabot. I'm sure you learned all the right phrases. But do explain exactly what shunning entails. Not that most of us aren't so fed up with the man's rantings and rumors that they won't be delighted to have an official excuse to . . . ah . . . shun him! Shun him!" She tipped back her head and gave a hoot of outrageous laughter. "By all that's holy—and legal—I like that, Emily. I like that a lot!" In an abrupt switch of mood with no leavening of humor, she added, "It'll cool a lot of hotheads." She swept Paul and Emily with a shrewd look. "Tubberman didn't do it by himself. Who helped?"

"We've no proof," Paul began in the same minute that Joel said, "Stev Kimmer, Bart Lemos, and maybe Nabhi Nabol."

"Let's shun them, too," Cherry cried, banging the arm of her chair with her thin old hands. "Damn it, we don't need dissension. We need support, cooperation, hard work. Or we won't survive. Oh, flaming hells!" She raised both hands up high. "What'll we do if that capsule brings those blood-sucking FSP salvagers down on us?"

"I wouldn't bet on that," Joel answered her, rolling his eyes.

Cherry gave him a hard stare. "I'm relieved to know there is something you won't make book on, Lilienkamp. All right, so what *do* we do about Tubberman's accomplices?"

Cabot leaned over to touch her arm lightly. "First we have to prove that they were, Cherry." He looked expectantly at Paul and Emily. "The charter says that a person is judged innocent until proved guilty."

"We watch 'em," Paul said. "We watch 'em. Carter, compose that notice and see that it's posted throughout Landing, and that every stakeholder is apprised of the fact. Cherry, will you impose the sentence on Tubberman?" He held out his arm to assist her to her feet.

"With the greatest of satisfaction. What a superb way to get rid of a bore," she added under her breath as she marched forward. The unholy joy on her face brightened Joel Lilienkamp's mood as he followed them, rubbing his hands together.

✦ ✦ ✦

The messenger was quite happy to bring a copy of the official notice to Bay and Wind Blossom, on duty in the large incubator chamber. The room was separated from the main laboratory and insulated against temperature changes and noise. The incubator itself stood on heavy shock absorbers, so that in the precarious early stages the embryos in their sacs could not be jarred by equipment moved around the main laboratory.

Although eggs within a natural womb, or even in a proper shell, could handle a great deal of trauma, the initial *ex utero* fertilization and alteration had been too delicate to risk the most minute jolt. Development was not yet canalized, nor was the new genetic structure balanced, and any variation in the embryos' environment would doubtless cause damage. Later, when the eggs were at the stage when naturally they would have been laid in a clutch, they would be transferred to the building where a warmed sand flooring and artificial sun lamps imitated the natural conditions in which dragonet eggs hatched. That point was several weeks ahead.

Special low-light viewing panels had been created, so no light filtered into the womblike darkness while observers had a clear view of the incubator's precious contents. A portable magnifier had been devised which could be set at any position on the incubator's four glass sides for very coarse and routine inspections. In the laboratories of First and Earth, each developing embryo would have been remotely monitored and recorded. But, in Pern's relatively primitive conditions, about which Wind Blossom constantly complained, the necessity for the avoidance of any toxic substances at all meant that no sensors could be allowed close to the embryos in the culture chambers.

Bay was jotting down Wind Blossom's assessment when the messenger delivered the notice. The lad was quite willing to explain any part of the shunning, but Bay shooed him off on his rounds.

"How extraordinary," Bay said when she had finished reading it aloud to Blossom. "Really, Ted has been quite a nuisance lately. Did you hear those rumors he was spreading, Blossom? As if that wretched Bitra had anything but her own plans in mind when she stole the *Mariposa*. Going for help, indeed!" She squinted loyally into the incubator at its forty-two hopes for their future. "But to send off a homing capsule when we most specifically voted against such an action."

"I am relieved," Wind Blossom said, sighing gently.

"Yes, he was beginning to upset you," Bay remarked kindly. She tried to tell herself that the woman was still grieving for her grandmother. There were moments recently, though, when Bay wanted to remind Blossom that it was not just the Yung family who had suffered a grievous loss. She had not, because Blossom had been rather volatile lately and might interpret such a comment as an aspersion on her ability to proceed with her grandmother's brilliant genetic-engineering program. As her mother's primary assistant, she was technically in charge of the program on file in the biology Mark 42 computer. Bay, too, had scanned it to familiarize herself with the procedure. Kitti Ping had left copious notes on how to proceed, anticipating those possible minor alignments, balancing, or other compensations that might be needed. She had apparently anticipated everything but her own death.

"You misunderstand me," Blossom replied, inclining her head in a gesture reminiscent of her grandmother correcting an erring apprentice. "I am relieved that the homing capsule has been sent. Now there is no blame to us."

Bay was not certain that she had heard correctly. "What under the suns do you mean, Blossom?"

Blossom gave Bay a long look, smiling faintly. "All our eggs are in one basket," she said with an inscrutable smile and moved the inspection lens to a new position.

When Pol and Phas Radamanth came to relieve them, Bay lingered. She and Pol did not have much time together anymore, and she did not look forward to another dull supper at the communal kitchen.

"You got a copy, I see," Pol said, indicating the shunning notice.

"Extraordinary, that."

"More than time," Phas said, glancing up from Blossom's notations. "Let's hope he wasn't as incompetent a launcher as he was a botantist."

Bay stared in astonishment at the xenobiologist and Phas had the grace to look embarrassed.

"No one approves of Tubberman's actions, my dear," Pol assured her.

"Yes, but if they come . . ." Bay's gesture took in the incubator and the laboratory, and all that the colonists had managed to do with their new world.

"If it's any consolation," Phas said, "Joel Lilienkamp has not opened a book on an ETA."

"Oh!" Then she asked, "And what's happened to Ted Tubberman?"

"He was escorted back to his stake and told to remain there."

Pol could look quite fierce, she thought, when he wanted to. "What about Mary? And his young children?" she asked.

Pol shrugged. "She can stay or come. She's not shunned. Ned Tubberman was looking pretty upset, but he never was very close to his father, and Fulmar Stone thinks he's a very promising mechanic." He shrugged again and then gave his wife an encouraging smile.

Bay had no sooner turned to go than the ground under them shook. She instinctively lunged toward the incubator, and found Phas and Pol beside her. Even without the magnifier they could see that the amniotic fluid in the sacs was not rippling in response to the earthquake. The shock absorbers had proved adequate.

"That's all we need!" Pol cried, outraged. He stomped to the comm unit and dialed the met tower, slamming down the handset. "Engaged! Bay, reassure them." He gestured toward the first bunch of technicians heading anxiously to the door of the chamber. He dialed again and got through just as Kwan Marceau pushed his way into the room. "Are there going to be more shocks, Jake?" Pol asked. "Why weren't we warned?"

"It was a small one," Jake Chernoff replied soothingly. "Patrice de Broglie called it in but I am obliged to warn infirmary first in case surgery is in progress, and then your line was busy." That explanation placated Pol. "Patrice says there's a bit of tectonic plate action to the east, and there may be more jolts in the next few weeks. The incubator's on shocks anyway, isn't it? You don't have anything to worry about."

"Nothing to worry about?" Pol demanded. He jammed the handset back onto its stand.

◆ ◆ ◆

There was a discreet knock on the door to the admiral's office, and when Paul answered with a noncommittal "Come in," Jim Tillek opened it. Emily smiled with relief. The master of Monaco Bay was always welcome. Paul leaned back in his swivel chair, ready for a break from the depressing inventory of air-worthy sleds and serviceable flamethrowers.

"Hi, there," Jim said. "Just up to get my skimmer serviced."

"Since when have you needed assistance in that job?" Paul asked.

"Since all my spare parts at Monaco got reabsorbed by Joel Lilienkamp." Jim's drawl was cheerful.

"And pigs fly," Paul retorted.

"Oh, is that the next project?" Jim asked with a comic grin. He dropped into the nearest seat and laced his fingers together. "By the way, Maximilian and Teresa reported on the dolphin search Patrice requested. There are significant lava flows from the Illyrian volcano. It's only a small one, so don't be surprised if our easterlies bring in some black dust. It's *not* dead Thread. Just honest-to-Vulcan volcanic dust. I wanted you to know before another rumor started."

"Thanks," Paul said dryly.

"Logical explanations are always welcome," Emily added.

"I also dropped in to see our favorite patient." Jim pushed himself deeper into the chair and met Paul's eyes squarely. "He's raring to go and threatens to move into the second story of the met tower and run communications from there. Sabra threatens to divorce him if he does anything before he gets medical clearance. Myself, I told him he doesn't need to worry, as young Jake Chernoff's been doing a proper job of it. The boy won't even hazard a guess about the weather until he's run the satellite report twice and looked out the window."

Paul and Emily both smiled at his jocular account.

"Ongola *needs* to be back at work," Emily agreed.

"He's sure he'll never use his arm again. He'd do better being so busy he doesn't think such negative thoughts." Jim cocked his head at Paul.

"According to the doctors," Emily said with a grateful smile, "Ongola *will* use that arm—even if he refuses to believe it—but the amount of mobility is still in question."

"He'll get it back," Jim said blandly. "Hey, is there any truth to the rumor that Stev Kimmer was involved with Tubberman?"

Paul pulled a face, and Emily shot him a glance. "I told you that was doing the rounds," she said.

Jim leaned forward, his expression eager. "Any truth to the one that he skitted out with one of the big pressurized sleds which has been seen near the Great Western Barrier where Kenjo staked his claim? Kimmer's a lot more dangerous than Ted Tubberman ever was."

Paul ran his thumb over his artificial fingers and stopped when he saw that Jim Tillek had noticed the nervous habit. "He is indeed. As the comm unit on that stolen sled was in working order when he lifted it, he will also know that he is wanted back here for questioning."

Jim nodded in solemn approval. "Has Ezra made any sense out of the reports of those probes Sallah . . ." He blinked, his eyes suspiciously wet.

"No," Paul said, clearing his throat. "He's still trying to translate them. The printout is unclear."

"Well, now," Jim said, "I've got a few hours to spare while my sled's serviced. I looked at hundreds of EEC survey team reports before I found a planet I liked the look of. Can I help?"

"A fresh eye might be useful," Paul said. "Ezra's been at it nonstop."

"Did I hear correctly," Jim asked gently, "that the *Mariposa* plunged directly into the eccentric?"

Paul nodded. "She made no informative comment." Avril's cryptic penultimate phrase, "It's not the . . ." still rang with some message that Paul felt he must unravel. "Look, Jim, do stop in and see if you can help Ezra. We need some good news. Morale is still low after the murders, and having to shun Ted Tubberman and explain how he got his hands on that homing capsule have not improved the administration's image."

"Clever trick, though," Jim said, chuckling as he rose. "Keeps you from having to breach stake autonomy, and keeps that fool where he can't do more damage. I'll just amble over to Ezra's pod." He left the room with a backhanded wave at Emily and Paul.

Immeasurably cheered by his visit, they went back to the onerous tasks of scheduling crews for the upcoming Threadfalls and mustering teams to collect edible greenery for silage from places as yet untouched by the ravening organism.

"*L*ook, Jim, I just can't find any other logical explanation for the destruction of the probes and *these*." Ezra Keroon waved a handful of probe pics, so blurred that no detail could be seen. "One, maybe two probes could malfunction. But I've sent off seven! And Sallah—" Ezra paused a moment, his face expressing the sorrow he still felt at her loss. "Sallah told us that there had been no damage report for the probe garage. Then we have the *Mariposa*. It did not hit the surface. Something hit it just about the same time one of the probes went bang!"

"So you prefer to believe that something down on the surface prevents inspection?" Jim Tillek asked wryly. He leaned back in his seat, easing shoulder muscles taut from hours of bending and peering through magnifiers. "I can't credit that explanation, Ez. C'mon, man. How can anything on that planet be functioning? The surface has been frozen. It can't have thawed appreciably in the time it's been swinging in to Rukbat."

"One does not have such regular formations on any unpopulated surface. I don't say they can't be natural. They just don't look natural. And I certainly won't make any guesses about what sort of creature made them. Then look at the thermal level here, here, and here." Ezra jabbed a finger at the pics he had been studying. "It's higher than I'd anticipate on a near-frozen surface. That much we got from the one probe that sent data back."

"Volcanic action under the crust could account for that."

"But regular *convex*, not concave, formations along the equator?"

Jim was incredulous. "You *want* to believe that plutonic planet could be the *source* of this attack?"

"I like that better than substantiating the Hoyle-Wickramansingh theory, I really do, Jim."

"If Arvil hadn't taken the gig, we could find out what that nebulosity is. Then we'd know for sure! Hoyle-Wickramansingh or little frozen blue critters." Jim's tone was facetious.

"We've the shuttles," Ezra said tentatively, tapping his pencil.

"No fuel, and there isn't a pilot among those left that I'd be willing to trust to do such a difficult retrieval. You'd have to match its orbital speed. I saw the dents on the *Mariposa*'s hull myself where the defense shields failed. Also, we didn't bring down any heavy worksuits that would protect a man out in a meteor storm. And if your theory's correct, he'll get shot down."

"Only if he gets too close to the planet," Ezra went on cautiously. "But he wouldn't have to, to get a sample of the trail. If the trail is nothing but ice, dirt, and rock, the usual cometary junk, we'd know then that the real menace is the planet, not the trail. Right?"

Jim eyed him thoughtfully. "It'd be dangerous either way. And there's no fuel to do it anyhow!" Jim opened his arms in a gesture of exasperation.

"There *is* fuel."

"There is?" Jim sat bolt upright, eyes wide with surprise.

Ezra gave him a wry smile. "Known only to a chosen few."

"Well!" Jim made his eyebrows twitch, but he grinned to show that he took no offense at having been excluded. "How much?"

"With a thrifty pilot, enough for our purpose. Or maybe, if we can find Kenjo's main cache, more."

"More?" Jim gawked. "Kenjo's cache? He scrounged fuel?"

"Always was a clever driver. Saved it from his drops, Ongola said."

Jim continued to stare at Ezra, amazed at Kenjo's sheer impudence. "So that's why Kimmer's nosing about the Western Barrier Range. He's out trying to find Kenjo's cache. For his own purposes or ours?"

"Not enough to get anyone's hopes up, mind you," Ezra continued, holding up a warning hand. "Maybe it's not too bad a thing that Tubberman sent off the homer. Because if it *is* the planet, we need help, and I'm not too proud to ask for it." Ezra grimaced. "Not that Kimmer said anything to anyone when he made off with the big sled and enough concentrated food and power packs to stay lost for years. Joel Lilienkamp was livid that anyone would *steal* from his Stores. We don't even know how Stev found out about Kenjo's hoard. Except that he knew how much fuel the *Mariposa* had in her tanks eight years ago. So he must have figured out someone had saved fuel back when Kenjo made those reconnaissance flights." Then, as Jim opened his mouth, he added, "Don't worry about Kimmer taking off even if he finds fuel. Ongola and Kenjo disabled the shuttles some time back. Kimmer doesn't know where we stash the fuel sacks here. Neither do I."

"I'm honored—by your confidence and the cares you have so carefully laid on my bowed shoulders."

"You walked in here three days ago and volunteered your services," Ezra reminded him.

"Three days? Feels like three years. I wonder if my skimmer's been serviced." He rose and stretched again until the bones in his spine and joints readjusted with audible clicks. "So, shall we take this mess—" He gestured to the mass of photos and flimsies neatly arranged on the work surface. "—to the guys who have to figure out what we do with it?"

◆　◆　◆

Paul and Emily listened, saying nothing, until both men had finished expressing their conflicting viewpoints.

"But when the planet is past us in the next eight or nine years, Threadfall will stop," Paul said, jumping to a conclusion.

"Depends on whose theory you favor," Jim said, grinning with good-natured malice. "Or how advanced Ezra's aliens are. Right now, if you buy his theory, they're keeping us at arm's length while the Thread softens us up."

Paul Benden brushed away that notion. "I don't credit that, Ezra. Thread was ineffective on the previous try. But the Pluto planet could be defending itself. I could live with that much of your theory based on the evidence."

Emily looked squarely at Jim. "How long will this gunge fall if it's from your cometary tail?"

"Twenty, thirty years. If I knew the length of that tail, I could give a closer estimate."

"I wonder if that's what Avril meant," Paul said slowly, "by 'it's not the . . .' Did she mean that it wasn't the planet we had to fear, but the tail it brought from the Oort cloud?"

"If she hadn't taken the *Mariposa*, we'd have a chance of knowing." Emily's voice had a sharp edge.

"We still do," Ezra said. "There's enough fuel to send a shuttle up. Not as economical a vehicle as the *Mariposa* but adequate."

"Are you sure?" Paul's expression was taut as he reached for a calc pad on which he worked several equations. He leaned back, his face pensive, then passed the pad over to Emily and Jim. "It might just be possible." He caught and held Emily's gaze. "We have to know. We have to know the worst we can expect before we can plan ahead."

Ezra raised a warning hand, his expression wary. "Mind you, they can't get close to the planet! We've lost seven probes. Could be mines, could be missiles—but they blow up."

"Whoever goes will know exactly what and how big the risks are," Paul said.

"There's risk enough in just going up," Ezra said gloomily.

"I hate to sound fatuous, but surely there's one pilot who'd take the challenge to save this world," Paul added.

Drake Bonneau was approached first. He thought the scheme was feasible, but he worried about the risk of a shuttle that had certainly deteriorated from eight years' disuse. He then pointed out that he was married with responsibilities, and that there were other pilots equally as qualified. Paul and Emily did not argue with him.

"Marriage and dependent children will be the excuse of practically everyone," Paul told their private counselors, Ezra, Jim, and Zi Ongola, who had been permitted four hours of work a day by his reluctant medical advisers. "The only one still unattached is Nabhi Nabol."

"He's a clever enough pilot," Ongola said thoughtfully, "though not exactly the type of man on whom the future of an entire planet should ride. However, exactly the type if the reward could be made attractive enough for him to take the risk."

"How?" Emily asked skeptically.

Nabhi had already been reprimanded a dozen times and served Cherry Duff's sentences for social misdemeanors such as being caught "drunk and disorderly," several work delinquencies, and one "lewd advance." Lately he had somewhat redeemed himself by being a good squadron leader, and was much admired by the young men he led.

"He's a contractor," Ongola said. "If he should be offered, say, a charterer's stake rights, I think he might well go for it. He's griped about the disparity in land holdings often enough. That could sweeten him. He also fancies himself a crack pilot."

"We've got some very good young pilots," Jim began.

"Who have had no experience in space with a shuttle." Ongola dismissed that notion. "Though it might be a good idea to choose one to go as copilot and give them the feel. But I'd rather trust Nahbi than a complete space novice."

"If we suggest that he was also our second choice, rather than our last one . . ." Emily remarked.

"We'd better get on with it, whatever we do," Ezra said. "I can't keep stalling questions. We need data and we need a sample of the stuff in that trail. Then we'll know for certain what our future is."

✦ ✦ ✦

Bargaining with Nabhi began that afternoon. He sneered at the flattery and the appeal to his competence and demanded to know just how much the trip was worth in terms of a holding and other rights. When he demanded the entire province of Cibola, Paul and Emily settled down to their task. When Nabhi insisted on being granted charterer status, they agreed with sufficient reluctance to satisfy the man that he was ahead in the bargaining.

Then Emily nonchalantly mentioned that Big Island was now untenanted. She and Paul managed to suppress their relief when he immediately seized on the notion of occupying Avril's former property.

Nabhi said that he wanted the shuttle he had used during the ferrying operation and he specified the personnel who were, under his supervision, to handle the *Moth*'s recommissioning. He waved aside the fact that all the people he named were already heavily involved in crucial projects. He would only make the trip if he was satisfied that the long-disused shuttle checked out technically. But the other inducements were his immediately.

He then demanded Bart Lemos as his copilot, with the condition that Bart, too, would be given charterer status. Paul and Emily found that particularly unpalatable, but agreed reluctantly.

Nabol's attitude toward both admiral and governor immediately altered, becoming so arrogant and pompous that Emily had to struggle to contain her dislike of the man. His smile of triumph was only one degree less than a full sneer as he left their office with the signed charterer's warrant. Then he commandeered one of the speed shuttles, although it was needed for an imminent Threadfall, and went to inspect his new acquisition.

The admiral and the governor formally announced the venture, its aims, and its personnel. The news managed to outweigh every other topic of interest with one exception: the transfer of the twenty-seven mature eggs to their artificial hatching ground.

The full veterinary contingent assisted the biologists in that maneuver. Sorka Hanrahan and Sean Connell, in their capacities as advanced veterinary apprentices, had also done some of the early analysis and tedious documentation for the project, working under Kitti Ping's close supervision. It didn't take long to accomplish the transfer, but Sorka noticed that the amount of dithering was aggravating her lover. But the project meant more to him than his exasperation with worried biologists, and he suppressed his irritation. Finally the eggs were placed to the complete satisfaction of Wind Blossom, Pol, and Bay: in a double circle, seventeen on the inner ring, twenty on the outer, with the warm sand banked high around them to imitate the natural environment of dragonets.

"The whole thing could have been done in a third of the time," Sean muttered darkly to Sorka. "So much fuss is bad for the eggs." He scowled at the precise circles.

"They're much bigger than I thought they'd be," Sorka said after a moment's silence.

"Much bigger than *they* thought they'd be," Sean said in a scoffing tone. "I suppose we're lucky that so many survived to this stage—a credit to Kit Ping, considering all that had to be done to create them."

Sorka knew that it meant as much to Sean to be a part of the project as it did to her. They had, after all, been the first to discover one of the wild nests. Eager but tired, she was balancing on one of the edging timbers, keeping her feet off the uncomfortably warm sands of the artificial hatching ground.

Although the transfer was complete, the helpers had not yet dispersed. Wind Blossom, Pol, and Bay were deep in discussions with Phas, the admiral, and the governor, who had taken an official part in the removal. Sorka thought that Emily Boll particularly looked drawn and exhausted, but her smile remained warm and genuine. They, too, seemed reluctant to leave.

Most of the Landing population of dragonets had been in and out of the Hatching Ground, darting up to the rafters and vying to find roosting room. They seemed content to watch; none of them had been bold enough to examine the eggs closely. Sorka interpreted their little chirps as reverent, awed.

"Would they know what these are?" she asked Sean softly.

"Do we?" Sean retorted with an amused snort. He had both arms folded across his chest; he unlaced one to point to the nearest egg. "That's the biggest. I wonder if it's one of the golds. I've lost track of which was put where in that dance we just did. There were more males than females among the ones lost, and Lili's opened book on which of us get what."

Sorka gave the egg a long speculative look. She thought about whether or not it was a gold, and then decided, somewhat arbitrarily in her own mind, that no, it was not. It was a bronze. She did not tell Sean her conclusion. Sean tended to debate such issues, and that moment, surveying the first clutch of "dragons," was not a moment to spoil. She sighed.

Dragonets had become as important to her as horses. She readily admitted that Sean could make his fair behave better than she could hers. He could and did discipline his for effective use during Threadfall. But she knew that she *understood* any of them—hers, his, or those impressed by anyone else on Pern—better than he did, especially when they were injured fighting Thread. Or maybe her sensitivity, developed over the last couple of months along with her pregnancy, tended toward maternal caring. The doctor had said she was in excellent health and had found nothing in her physical profile to suggest problems. She could continue riding as long as she felt comfortable in the saddle.

"You'll know when you can't ride anymore," he had told her with a grin. "And you'll have to curtail ground crew at five months. That's no time for you to be swinging the weight of a flamethrower about for hours on end."

Sorka had not yet found the proper moment to inform Sean of his impending fatherhood. She fretted about his reaction. They had saved enough work credits to make the Killarney holding a substantial one, but not with Thread falling. Sean had not even mentioned Killarney since the third Fall, but that did not mean he did not think about it. She saw the faraway look in his eyes from time to time.

She had thought he would mention Killarney when his father returned Cricket from his stud duties. But he had not. With everyone working double jobs just to keep essential services going, very few people had time to consider private concerns. Sean and Sorka spent what leisure moments they had keeping their horses fit, riding them out beyond the swath of destruction for an hour's grazing.

The main door opened to admit one of the security engineers, and there was an instant reaction from the gallery of winged watchers. Sean chuckled softly. "They don't need a security system in here," he murmured to Sorka. "C'mon, love, we've got surgery in five minutes."

With backward glances at the circles of mottled eggs, the two apprentices reluctantly went back to work. As they crossed one of the alleys, they had a clear view of the donks slowly moving the shuttle *Moth* into takeoff position.

"D'you think they'll make it?" Sorka asked Sean.

"They've been busy enough," he replied sourly. Neither Nabhi Nabol nor Bart Lemos had made himself popular since the sudden rise to charterer rank. "Still, I wouldn't be in their shoes for anything!"

She giggled. "Spacer Yvonne. You've never told me, Sean, did that help you on the drop?"

He gave her face a long and searching look, a slight smile tugging his lips. Then he put his arm about her and hauled her into his side. "All I could think about was proving to you I wasn't scared. But, by jays, I was!" Then his expression changed and he halted, turning her roughly to him, both hands feeling across her stomach and pulling the bulky shipsuit taut across her body. He glared accusingly at her. "Why didn't you tell me you're pregnant?"

"Well, it's only just been confirmed," she said defiantly.

"Does everyone else know but me?" He was furious with her; for the first time in their years together, he was mad *at* her. His eyes were flashing and his hands rested hard across her thickening waistline.

"No one knows except the doctor, and he doesn't have to ground me for another three months." She pulled defensively at one hand to make him release her. "But there's Killarney and I know you think about it . . ."

"Your mother knows?"

"When do I have a chance to see her? She's minding half of Landing's babies, as well as my latest brother. You're the only other one who knows."

"Sometimes you baffle me, Sorka," Sean said, his anger abating. He shook his head. "Why wait to tell me? Killarney's a long way off in our future now. We're committed here. I thought you understood that." He put both hands on her shoulders and gave her a stern shake. "I've wanted to be the father of your children. I want you to have only mine. I want it to be now, too, Sorka love, but I didn't think I had the right to ask you to bring a child into the world the way it is." His voice fell into the special tender tone he always used when they were making love.

"No, it's the best time to have a child. Something for both of us to have," she said. She did not add "in case," but he knew what she was thinking and tightened his grip on her. His eyes compelled hers to look at him. The fury had been replaced by resolution.

"Immediately after surgery, we're going before Cherry Duff. This is going to be a two-parent child, or my name's not Sean Connell!"

Sorka burst out laughing and did not stop until they reached the surgery shed.

◆ ◆ ◆

Ongola had ended up as arbiter on the reconditioning of the space shuttle *Moth*. Nabhi Nabol had been driving the refit crew demented, interrupting them at critical moments of repair, demanding to know if that circuit or this segment of hull had been checked. Despite the fact that he had a good working knowledge of the complexities of a shuttle, he delayed more than he assisted. The shuttle *Mayfly*, lying next to the *Moth*, had been sectioned off into offices for Ongola, Fulmar, and Nabhi, with a half-dozen comm lines so that Ongola could handle other commitments while on hand at the shuttle. His office was festooned with probe pics and survey maps, as well as with the various launch windows open to Nabhi. Nabhi would often come in and stand broodingly staring at the orbits, picking at his lower lip. Ongola ignored him.

The basic condition of the *Moth* had been surprisingly good: there had been practically no perishing of interior circuits or lines. But everything had to be double-checked. In that Ongola agreed with Nabhi. It put quite a burden on Fulmar's engineering team, but that was not where he disagreed with the autocratic Nabhi.

"I wouldn't care what he asked me to do," Fulmar told Ongola, "if he'd only ask politely. You'd think he was doing *me* a favor. Are you sure he's as good a driver as he thinks he is?"

"He is good," Ongola reluctantly admitted.

"I'd've preferred the mission in Bonneau's hands," Fulmar replied, shaking his head sadly. "But with that big stake, kids and all, I can't fault his refusal. It's just that—" He broke off, raising his big, work-stained hands in a helpless gesture.

"The mission has got to succeed, Fulmar," Ongola said, giving the man an encouraging clout on the shoulder. "And you're the best man to see that it does."

◆ ◆ ◆

In the thirteenth week after Threadfall, the pattern suddenly shifted. As the squadrons reached the projected site, which was mainly over unoccupied lands, only the top of the squadron saw the leading edge. It was well north of their position: the gray shimmering stain on the horizon was all too easily identified.

"Hell and damnation!" Theo Force cried, ramming a call through to Ongola at Landing. "The damned stuff's shifted north, Zi. We'll need reinforcements."

"Give me the coordinates," Ongola said, issuing crisp orders and gesturing to Jake to get in touch with Dieter or Boris. "Go for it. We'll scramble another squadron or two to help. I'll alert Drake."

Boris was found, and made some quick calculations. "It's going to hit Calusa and Bordeaux. It seems to have shifted north by five degrees. That doesn't make sense. Why on earth would it shift so suddenly?"

There was no answer to his question. Ongola rang off. "Have you the week's roster there, Jake? Check where Kwan is today. I'll call Chuck Havers at Calusa."

Sue Havers answered the phone. After her initial shock at the news, she rallied. "We've several hours then, don't we? And it could just miss us? I hope so. I don't know where Chuck is working today. Thank you, Zi. And," she added, her voice less assured, "are you calling Mary Tubberman, or should I warn her?"

"We'll send Ned along." Ongola disconnected.

Shunning was very hard on the relatives. Ned was entitled to assist his mother and his younger brothers and sister in fighting Thread. If he chose also to assist his father in the emergency, there would be only family to witness it. Tubberman had been quick to clad his buildings with metal, so his stake was as safe as those precautions could make it. He would get no other help.

Ongola then contacted Drake and ordered him to avoid the Tubbermans' stake. Drake at first protested that they couldn't leave any Thread on any ground, shunned or not.

"Ned can protect that much with his mother's help, Drake, but we cannot assist Ted Tubberman."

"But it's Thread, man."

"That's an order, man," Ongola replied in a steely tone.

"Gotcha!"

Ongola then informed Paul Benden and Emily Boll of the pattern's alteration.

"Ezra will say that proves intelligence directs Fall," Paul remarked to Emily as they conferred.

"It's heads we lose, tails we lose, as far as I can see," Emily replied, heaving a sigh.

"It's as well we don't have to wait long to find out." Paul nodded toward the grid where the *Moth* was undergoing the final countdown. None of the technicians had been allowed to scramble for additional support squadrons. Their assignments on the shuttle had just become all-important.

◆ ◆ ◆

Following the courtesy now well established, Drake Bonneau checked in at the Havers' stakehold on his way back from end of Fall, which had just tipped Bordeaux across the Jordan River. He landed within sight of the Tubbermans' larger home.

"Ned and Mary were out with flamethrowers," Chuck told the squadron leader, "and then, for some insane reason, Ted drove them back into the house. There couldn't have been much damage, or we'd have seen results."

"Well, you're all right here," Drake said heartily.

"The ground crew arrived well in advance. But does anyone know why the pattern's shifted?" Sue asked. Weary with fighting, she needed some spark of reassurance.

"No," Drake replied cheerfully, "but we'll probably be told!"

He accepted a cup of the refreshing fruit drink that the oldest Havers girl brought him and his crew, then said good-bye. Drake had obeyed Ongola's order to bypass the Tubberman stake during Fall, but after what the Havers had said about Ted, he was curious. In his opinion, all Thread had to be destroyed, even if it fell on a shunned homesite. Thread did not care about human conflicts: it ate. Drake did not want to see a little burrow get started because of man-made restrictions.

Therefore, as he took off, he made a leisurely turn right over the Tubberman property. He saw Ned standing on the green patch surrounding the house. Ned waved and gesticulated rather wildly, at which point Drake felt obliged to follow orders and turn northwest towards Landing.

He was having a quick bite to eat in the dining hall when Ned Tubberman found him.

"You saw it, Drake, I know you did. You have to have seen it," Ned said, excitedly pulling at Drake's sleeve to pull him to his feet. "C'mon, you have to tell them what you saw."

Drake pulled his arm free. "Tell who what?" He forked up another mouthful of the hot food. Thread-fighting gave him an incredible appetite.

"Tell Kwan and Paul and Emily what you saw."

"I didn't *see* anything!" Then suddenly Drake had a flash of pure recall: Ned standing on a green square, a green square that was surrounded by scorched earth. "I don't believe what I saw!" He wiped his mouth, chewing absently as he absorbed that memory. "But Thread had just been across your place, and Chuck and Sue saw your father stop you flaming!"

"Exactly!" Ned grinned hugely and again pulled at Drake. The squadron leader rose and followed Ned out of the room. "I want you to tell them what you saw, to corroborate my statement. I don't *know* what Dad's done." The grin faded and some of the buoyancy drained from Ned Tubberman. "He says shunning works two ways. Mother told me that he locks himself away in his laboratory and won't let anyone near it. My brothers and sister go over to Sue's all the time, but Mother won't leave Dad, even if he isn't in the house much. She keeps the place ticking over."

"Your father's been experimenting with something?" Drake was confused.

"Well, he's got botanical training. He did say that until help came, the only defense was the planet itself." Ned slowed his pace. "And that patch of grass must have defended itself—somehow—against today's Fall, because it's still there!"

Drake did tell Kwan, Paul, Emily, and the hastily summoned Pol and Bay. Ned insisted that he had seen Thread fall on the ground-cover plants, had not seen them wither or be ingested, and that by the time Drake had overflown the stake, there was no evidence that Thread had ever fallen on that twelve-by-twenty-meter rectangle.

"I couldn't hazard a guess as to how he's done it," Pol finally said, looking to Bay for agreement. "Maybe he has been able to adapt Kitti Ping's basic program for use on a less complex life-form. Professionally I have to doubt it."

"But I saw it," Ned insisted. "Drake saw it, too."

There was a long silence, which Emily finally broke. "Ned, we do not doubt *you*, or Drake's verification, but as your father said, shunning works both ways."

"Are you too proud to ask him what he's done?" Ned demanded, his skin blanched under his tan, and his nostrils flaring with indignation.

"Pride is not involved," Emily said gently. "Safety is. He was shunned because he defied the will of the colony. If you can honestly say that he has changed his attitude, then we can discuss reinstatement."

Ned flushed, his eyes dropping away from Emily's tolerant gaze. He sighed deeply. "He doesn't want anything to do with Landing or anyone on it." Then he gripped the edge of the table and leaned across it toward the governor. "But he's done something incredible. Drake saw it."

"I did indeed see ground cover where there shouldn't've been any," Drake conceded.

"Could your mother present evidence on his behalf?" Paul asked, seeking an honorable way out for Ned's sake.

"She says he only talks to Petey, and Petey says he's sworn to secrecy, so she hasn't pushed him." Ned's face twisted with anguish for a long moment, then it cleared. "I'll ask her. I'll ask Petey, too. I can try!"

"This has not been easy for you either, Ned," Emily said. "All of us would like to see the matter happily resolved." She touched his hand where he still gripped the table edge. "We need everyone right now."

Ned looked her steadily in the eyes and gave a slow nod. "I believe you, Governor."

◆　◆　◆

"Sometimes the duties to which rank entitles me are more than it's worth," Emily murmured to Paul as the hatch of the shuttle finally closed on Nabhi Nabol and Bart Lemos. She spoke quietly, because every young man in Nabhi's squadron had come to wish their leader good luck. She turned and smiled at them, leading the way off the grid to the safer sidelines, and waited dutifully with the technicians for the takeoff.

They waited and waited, until both admiral and governor were giving the meteorology tower anxious scrutiny. Just when both had decided that Nabhi was going to renege, as they had half suspected he would, they heard the roar of ignition and saw the yellow-white flame pouring out of the tubes.

"Firing well," Paul bellowed over the noise. Emily contented herself with a nod as she plugged her ears with her fingers.

She did not know much about the mechanics of shuttles, but the young men were grinning and waving their arms triumphantly. The look of relief on Fulmar's face was almost comical. Majestically the shuttle began its run up the grid, its speed increasing at a sensational rate. It became airborne, the engines thrusting it in an abrupt but graceful swoop up. The flame became lost in the blue of the sky as the observers shaded their eyes against the rising sun. Then the puffy contrail blossomed, billowing out as a tracer for the shuttle's path. The technicians who had made it possible cheered, and clapped one another on the back.

"Gawssakes, but it's good to get a bird up again," one of the men shouted. "Hey, what's wrong with them?" he added, pointing to several fairs of dragonets zipping at low level across the grid out of nowhere, crooning oddly.

"Who's having a baby?" Fulmar demanded.

Emily and Paul exchanged glances. "We are," she said, sliding quickly into the skimmer. "See? They're going straight to the Hatching Ground."

Looking up toward Landing, there was no doubt that fairs of dragonets were streaming in that direction. No one lingered on the grid. The roof of the Hatching Ground was covered with the crooning and chittering creatures. The cacophony was exciting rather than irritating. When the admiral and governor arrived, they had to make their way through the crowd to the open double doors.

"Welcome in nine-hundred-part harmony," Emily muttered to Paul as they made it to the edge of the warm sands. Their they halted, awed by the sense of occasion within.

Kitti Ping had left explicit instructions on who was to attend the birth day. Sixty young people between the ages of eighteen and thirty, who had already shown a sympathy for the dragonets, had the privilege of standing around the circle of eggs. Wind Blossom, Pol, Bay, and Kwan stood to one side on a wooden platform, their faces flushed and expectant.

The dragonets' song outside remaining softly jubilant while the crooning of those who had found roosting space inside sounded like subdued encouragement, almost reverent.

"They can't know what we expect for today, can they, Paul?"

"Young Sean Connell"—Paul pointed to where the young man stood beside his wife around the eggs—"would have you believe that they do. But then, they've always been attracted by birthing! After all, they protect their own young against attack."

A hush swept around the arena as a distinct crack was heard. One of the eggs rocked slightly, the motion drawing excited whispers.

Emily crossed her fingers, hiding them in the folds of her trousers. She noticed, with a slight grin, that others were doing the same. So much hung on the events of that day, on the first hatching and on what Nabhi Nabol was irrevocably committed to doing.

Another egg cracked and a third wobbled. The chorus became beguilingly insistent, striking an excited chord in everyone watching.

Then all of a sudden, one of the eggs cracked open and a creature emerged, damp from birth; it shook stubby wings and stumbled over its shell, squawking in alarm. The dragonets answered soothingly. The young people in the circle stood their ground, and Emily marveled at their courage, for that awkward creature was not the graceful being she had been expecting, a beast remembered from old legends and illustrations held in library treasuries. She caught herself holding her breath, and exhaled quickly.

The creature extended its wings; they were wider and thinner than she had expected. It was so spindly, so ungainly, and its very oddly constructed eyes were flashing with red and yellow. Emily felt a flush of alarm. The creature gave a desperate cry, and was answered reassuringly by the multivoiced choir above. It lurched forward, its voice pleading, and then the cry altered to one of joy, held on a high sweet note. It staggered another step and fell at the feet of David Catarel, who bent to help it.

He looked up with eyes wide with wonder. "He wants me!"

"Then accept him!" Pol bellowed, gesturing for one of the stewards to come forward with a bowl of food. "Feed him! No, don't anyone else help you. The bond should be made now!"

Kneeling by his new charge, David offered the little dragon a hunk of meat. It bolted that and urgently cried for more, pushing at David's leg with an imperious head.

"He says he's very hungry," David cried. "He's talking to me. In my head! It's incredible. How did she do it?"

"The mentasynth works, then!" Emily murmured to Paul, who nodded with the air of someone not at all surprised.

"Ye gods, but it's ugly," Paul said in a very low voice.

"You probably weren't much to look at at birth either," Emily surprised herself by saying. She grinned at his quick glance of astonishment.

David coaxed his new friend out of the circle of people and toward the edge of the Hatching Ground, calling for more food. "Polenth says he's starving."

Bay had ordered plenty of red meat to be available, butchered from animals that had adapted well to the improved Pernese grasses. The young dragonets would require plenty of boron for growth in their first months, and would best absorb it from the flesh of cattle.

Another egg cracked, and a second bronze male made a straight-line dash to Peter Semling. A voluntary shrill came from Peter's fair of dragonets. There was a long wait before any more activity. A worried hum developed among the watchers. Then four more eggs abruptly shattered, two with unexpectedly dainty creatures, one golden and one bronze, who partnered themselves with Tarrie Chernoff and Shih Lao; the other two were stolid-looking browns who took to Otto Hegelman and Paul Logorides.

"Do they expect them all to hatch today?" Emily asked Paul.

"Let's go around to Pol and Bay," Paul said. They inched their way to the right, pausing to admire David Catarel's bronze, who was bolting down hunks of meat so fast that he seemed to be inhaling them. David looked ecstatic.

"Well, they could," Pol replied when they reached him. He was masking anxiety well. Wind Blossom was not, and barely acknowledged the quiet greetings of admiral and governor. "They were engineered within a thirty-six-hour period. The six that have hatched were from the first and second groups. We might have to wait. In our observations of wild dragonets, we know that laying the eggs can take several hours. I suspect the greens and golds may be like one of the Earth vipers, which can keep eggs within her body until she finds an appropriate place, or time, to lay them. We know that naturally clutched eggs do hatch more or less simultaneously. This," he said, pointing to the Hatching Ground, "is a concession to Kitti Ping's reverence for the ancestral species' habitat. Ah, another one's cracking." He consulted the flimsy in his hand. "One of the third group!"

"Six males, but only one female," Bay said quietly. "To be frank, I'd rather have more females. What do you think, Blossom?"

"One perfect male and one perfect female are all we need," Wind Blossom said in a tight, controlled voice. She had her hands hidden in her loose sleeves, but there were deep tension lines in her face and her eyes were clouded.

"Peter Semling's bronze looks sturdy," Emily said encouragingly. Wind Blossom did not respond, her gaze was fixed on the eggs. "Are they as you anticipated?" she asked, looking at Pol and Bay.

"No," Bay admitted, "but then it was Kitti who had the requisite image in her mind. If only . . ." She faltered. "Ah, another gold female. I believe that Kitti Ping made the choices gender imperative. For Nyassa Clissmann. And such charming creatures!"

Emily failed to see charm in the hatchlings, but she was glad to see so many live ones. But what had Kitti Ping had in her mind when she altered the dragonet ova? Those were not dragons of any kind Emily knew. And yet she had an unexpected vision of a sky full of the creatures, soaring and diving, breathing flame. Had Kitti Ping had such a vision?

"The shuttle!" Pol said suddenly. "Did I hear it take off?"

"Yes, he made it," Paul replied. "Ongola will keep us informed. We don't have enough fuel for a direct flight. The shuttle'll have to coast a week before it reaches the trail."

"Oh, I see." Then Pol refocused his attention on the eggs.

The crowd shifted as some people had to return to complete unfinished tasks and others moved in to take their places. Food was brought to the biologists and the leaders on their dais, and wooden benches to sit on. Wind Blossom remained standing. Food was also taken to the circle of hopeful dragon riders. The dragonets' encouragement did not abate. Emily wondered how they could keep it up.

It was dark before there was any further movement, and then all at once a brown and two golds cracked their eggs. Marco Galliani got the brown, and Kathy Duff and Nora Sejby the two golds. There was a good deal of cheering.

The crowd at the opening thinned, while the dragonets kept their posts and continued their encouraging song. Emily was becoming weary and she could see fatigue catching up with the others. She was half-asleep when Catherine Radelin-Doyle impressed her gold.

"Do they always go female to female?" Emily asked Pol. "And male to male?"

"Since the males are expected to be fighters and the females egg-carriers, Kitti made it logical."

"Logical to her," Emily said, a trifle bemused. "There aren't any blues or greens among them," she suddenly realized.

"Kitti programmed the heavier males, but I believe they're to carry sperm for the entire range. The greens will be the smallest, the fighters; the blues sturdier, with more staying power; the browns sort of anchor fighters with even more endurance. They'll have to fight four to six hours, remember! The bronzes are leaders and the golds . . ."

"Waiting at home to be egg-carriers."

Pol gave Emily a long look, his tired face reflecting astonishment at her sarcasm.

"In the wild, greens don't have good maternal instincts. The golds do," Bay put in, giving the governor an odd glance. "Kitti Ping kept as much natural instinct as possible. Or so her program reads."

◆ ◆ ◆

"There!" Nabhi said, leaning back from the console, his swarthy face intense with an inner satisfaction. "Kenjo wasn't the only one who could save fuel."

Bart stared at him, surprised and confused. "Save it for what, Nabhi?" He spoke more sharply than he meant to, but he had been wound up with tension that would not ease. It was not that he did not trust Nabhi as a pilot—Nabhi was a good driver, or Bart would not have been talked into participating in the insane venture, not for the choicest land on Pern.

"To maneuver," Nabhi said. His mocking grin did nothing to ease Bart's disquiet.

"Where? You're not . . . you wouldn't be mad enough to try to land on the farking planet?" Bart clawed at the release straps, but Nabhi's indolent gesture of negation aborted the effort.

"No way. I came to get the pods or whatever." His smile then broadened, and Bart was amazed at the humor in it. "Our course is basically the same one Avril took." He turned his head and looked directly at his copilot.

"So?"

"They said the gig blew up." Nabhi's smile was pure malice. "Turn on the screens. There might be some interesting flotsam. Diamonds and gold nuggets and whatever else Avril took with her. No one needs to know what else we scooped up out of space. And it sure beats mining the stuff ourselves."

◆ ◆ ◆

By midnight Pol and Bay decided to examine the remaining eggs and slowly did the rounds. Wooden platforms had been brought out for the candidates to rest on, since the heat in the sand was enervating. None of the chosen was willing to forgo the chance at impressing a hatchling by leaving the Ground.

When the two biologists returned, Pol was shaking his head and Bay looked drawn. She went immediately to Wind Blossom and touched her arm.

"The rest of the first group show no signs of life. But already the outcome is better than projected. We detected viable signs in the others. We can but wait. They were not all conceived at the same time."

Wind Blossom remained an unmoving statue.

◆ ◆ ◆

Sean nudged Sorka in the ribs to wake her up. She had fallen asleep leaning against him, her cheek against his upper arm. She was instantly alert and aware of her surroundings. Sean pointed to the biggest of the eggs, which sat almost directly in front of them. He had taken that position at the outset, and finally, after his long vigil, the egg was rocking slightly.

"What time is it?" she asked.

"Nearly dawn. There's been no other movement. But listen to the dragonets. Listen to Blaze. She'll have no throat left!"

They had noted their own dragonets early during that long day, and Sorka had taken heart from their constant choral encouragements.

"That egg over there has been moving spasmodically for the last two hours," he said in a quiet tone. "The one beyond it rocked for a while, but it's stopped completely."

Sorka tried to contain a yawn, then gave in to the compulsion and felt better for it. She wanted to stretch, but another candidate was draped over her legs, fast asleep. Beyond, the other candidates began to wake.

At some point while Sorka had been dozing, the admiral and the governor had left. Pol and Bay were leaning into each other, and Kwan's head was on his chest, arms limp in his lap. Wind Blossom had apparently not moved since she had taken up her watch.

"She's uncanny," Sorka said, turning away from the geneticist.

A single great crack startled everyone, and the egg before them parted into two ragged halves. The bronze hatchling walked out imperiously, lifted his head, and made a sound like a stuttering trumpet. Everyone came to attention. Sean was on his feet, and Sorka pushed at his legs to urge him on. She need not have worried. As he locked eyes with the hatchling, Sean gave a low incredulous groan and moved forward to meet the beast halfway. Their fair was bugling with triumph.

"Meat, quickly," Sorka called, beckoning to a sleepy steward. Hoping that the heat in the building had not soured the meat, she ran to meet the man, grabbed the bowl, and returned to thrust it into Sean's hands. She had never seen that utterly rapt look in his eyes before.

"He says his name is Carenath, Sorka. He knows his own name!" Sean transferred food from the bowl into Carenath's mouth as fast as he could shovel it. "More meat. Hurry, I need more meat."

Everyone in the Hatching Ground was wakened by his vibrant voice. Then the other egg broke open, and a golden female sauntered forth, chittering and looking about urgently. Sorka was too busy passing bowls of meat to Sean to notice until Betsy tugged at her arm.

"She's looking for you, Sorka. Look at her!"

Sorka turned her head and suddenly she, too, felt the indescribable impact of a mind on hers, a mind that rejoiced in finding its equal, its lifelong partner. Sorka was filled with an exultation that was almost painful.

My name is Faranth, Sorka!

"We have actually learned a great deal from eggs that didn't hatch," Pol told Emily and Paul when he, Wind Blossom, and Bay made their report two evenings later.

"So far, so good?" Paul asked hopefully.

"Oh, very good," Bay said enthusiastically, grinning and nodding her head vigorously. Wind Blossom managed a prim, set smile. The air of impenetrable gloom that had surrounded her on the Hatching Day had been exchanged for an aloof superiority.

"Then you do believe that the eighteen hatchings will all become viable adults?" Paul asked Wind Blossom.

She inclined her head. "We must await their maturity with patience."

"But they *will* be able to produce flame from phosphine-bearing rocks and go *between* as the dragonets do?" Paul asked her.

"I am, myself, much encouraged," Pol said, when Wind Blossom said nothing. "Bay is, too, by the way in which mentasynth has provided a strong empathic bond and telepathic communication."

"A genuine mind-to-mind contact," Bay added with a smile of satisfaction. "Especially strong for Sorka and Sean."

"The dragons were *designed*," Wind Blossom added pompously, "to make Impression with other than their own ancestral species. In that much, the program has succeeded." She held up her hand. "We must contain impatience and strive to achieve the perfect specimen."

"The stabilization of Impression to another species was the most important aspect," Pol said, his brows creasing slightly. "After all, the dragonets have teleported as naturally as they breathe."

"The *dragonets* have," Wind Blossom said coolly. "We have yet to see if the dragons can."

"Kitti Ping did not alter those capabilities, you know. They will, of course, have to be refined and controlled," Pol went on. He did not like Wind Blossom's attitude, her refusal to concede the triumphs already achieved. "I must say, I am very glad that the young Connells both Impressed. With their veterinary training and their general competence, not to mention their proven ability to discipline their dragonet fairs, we couldn't ask for better mates."

Wind Blossom made a slight noise, which the listeners took as disapproval.

"They're qualified," Bay said with unexpected heat. "Someone must make the beginning."

"Their progress must be strictly monitored," Wind Blossom said, "so that we will know what mistakes must be avoided the next time."

"Next time?" Emily blinked in surprise and noticed that Bay and Pol were reacting similarly.

"I do not yet know if these creatures will perform on the other design levels, either natural or imposed." Her sepulchral tone indicated that she had grave doubts.

"How can you not be encouraged—" Pol began with some heat.

A decisive gesture of dismissal cut him off, and he stared at Wind Blossom.

"I will begin anew," Wind Blossom informed them in a tone that almost implied martyrdom. Pol and Bay regarded her in astonishment. "With what we learned from the post mortem examinations, I cannot be sure that any of the living will be fertile or reproduce. More importantly—reproduce themselves! I must try again, and again, until success is assured. This experiment is only begun."

"But, Wind Blossom—" Pol began, astounded.

"Come, you shall assist me." With an imperious gesture, she swept from the room.

◆ ◆ ◆

Neither the veterinarians nor the xenobiologists had any criteria by which to judge the health of eighteen representatives of a new species. But the dragons' hearty appetites, the vibrant color of their suedelike hides, and the ease of their physical exertions—which consisted mainly of eating and exercising their wings—were taken as measures of well-being. In the first week of life, each had grown at least a handspan taller and had filled out; they looked considerably more substantial. And as the toughness of their transparent wings became more and more evident, those who had worried about their fragility were relieved.

Fascinated, the official medical support group watched as the two Connells bathed and oiled their ten-day-old dragons. Large shallow bathing pools of siliplas had been erected near the homes of all the dragonmates. Faranth was coyly aware of the admiring glances.

"She's preening, Dad," Sorka said, amused, as she poured oil on a scaly patch between the dorsal ridges. "Is that the itchy spot, Farrie?"

My name is Faranth and that is that *itchy spot,* Faranth said in tones that went from reproof to relief. *Another is starting on my hind leg.*

"She doesn't like to be called by a nickname," Sorka said tolerantly, grinning at her father. "But jays, she takes scrubbing." A bristle brush had been made for the purpose, firm enough to rub in oil but not harsh enough to mar the tender, smooth hide.

Suddenly everyone was drenched as Carenath, sweeping his glistening wings forward in the low bath, showered them with water.

"Carenath, behave yourself!" Sorka and Sean spoke in the same sharp tone.

I am already clean, you polka-dotted idiot, Faranth said in an excellent mimicry of one of Sorka's favorite admonitions. *I was nearly dry, and now my oiling has to be done again.*

Sean and Sorka laughed and then hurriedly explained to the drenched men that they were amused by what Faranth had said, not by Carenath's playfulness. Sean gestured to the dragonets that perched on the rooftree, obviously watching everything below them. Almost instantly, the soaked observers had towels dropped about them.

"Handy critters, Sean," Red Hanrahan said, drying his face and hands and mopping his clothing.

"Very useful with young dragons, too, Red," Sean replied. "They fish constantly for these walking appetites."

Am I that much trouble to you? Carenath sounded aggrieved.

"Not at all, pet," Sean quickly assured him, lovingly caressing the head that was tilted wistfully. "Don't be silly. You're young, you have a good appetite, and it's our job to keep you fed."

Red was beginning to get accustomed to the sudden non sequiturs from his daughter and son-in-law, but the others were startled. Faranth butted at Sorka for reassurance and when she received it, her eyes settled to the blue of contentment.

"Can't they be ridden yet? And hunt for themselves?" Phas Radamanth asked.

"You don't attempt to ride a foal, even a good big one," Sean replied, brushing oil on the rough patch on Carenath's broad back. "Kitti Ping's program suggests waiting a full year before we attempt it."

"Can we wait long enough for them to mature?" Threadfall and the need to fight it was never far from anyone's mind.

"I've never rushed a horse," Sean said, "and I'm not about to start with my dragon. However, at the rate they're growing, and if we can be sure that their skeletal structure—it's boronsilicate, you know, which is tougher than our calcareous material—is developing properly, I think they'll be capable of manned flight as scheduled." Sean grinned. "Jays, what times we'll have then, old fella, won't we?"

The tenderness, the concern, and the deep affection in Sean's voice were almost embarrassing to hear. Red looked at his son-in-law in surprise. So Impression had affected young Connell, as it had changed all the dragonmates. Even Sorka, who had always been caring and capable, seemed somehow strengthened and exuded a radiance that could not all be attributed to her pregnancy.

Young David Catarel had altered in the most spectacular way. Badly scarred mentally as well as physically by that First Fall and Lucy Tubberman's tragic death, the young man had retreated into a wallow of self-disgust and needless guilt. Not even intensive therapy had broken through the stubborn facade. David fought Thread with a vindictive intensity that was frightening to watch. Only when he had seen how useful dragonets were in ground-crewing had he tolerated their wistful affection.

The renaissance of his personality had begun the moment Polenth nudged his knee. An openly smiling, ecstatic David Catarel had left the hatching sands, solicitously and deftly assisting the staggering little dragon. The changes in the other youths had been felicitous as well, though Catherine Radelin-Doyle's tendency to giggle at some unheard comment from her golden mate could be disconcerting. Shih Lao, who had Impressed bronze Firth, also went about with smiles on his once pensive face, Tarrie Chernoff had stopped apologizing for any minor accident or inconsistency, and Otto Hegelman's stutter had completely disappeared.

"They're credits to you both," Caesar Galliani said to Sean and Sorka. "Though Marco's Duluth, if I say so myself, looks equally as good."

Sean grinned at the Roma stakeholder. "He does, indeed. As long as they're eating, sleeping—"

"Being bathed, cosseted, oiled, and scratched, they have *nothing* to complain of," Sorka finished, giving Faranth's nose a final swipe. "There now, love, why don't you curl up and go to sleep?"

Carenath's not finished, Faranth complained even as she was moving to the sun-warmed plascrete she preferred as her couch. *I like him to lean against. I'm a little hungry.*

Sorka put her fingers between her front teeth and gave a piercing whistle. The dragonets instantly disappeared.

All clean, Carenath cried, hopping out of the bath. Warned by Sean, he did not shake himself all over his audience. Carefully he extended his wet glistening wings, holding them aloft in the slight breeze while Sean, with Sorka's help, mopped his underparts dry.

"D'you need anything, Sean, while we're here?" Red asked.

"Nope," Sean grunted as he bent to dry the claw sheaths. The claw design was one of the few physical modifications that Kitti Ping had made from dragonet to dragon. The fingerlike claws would be more useful, she had thought, for grabbing running animals than the dragonets' pincer-type arrangement. "As soon as they've had their snack, we'll have one, too."

"Amazing couple," Phas Radamanth said, smiling up at Red. "Now if that bronze is fertile, and the gold willing, we'll have our next generation."

"Let's not rush too far ahead in our hopes," Caesar said, looking back over his shoulder at the scene. "Wind Blossom strongly advocates caution about this first batch."

"Her *grandmother* bioengineered them." Phas spoke firmly, stopping in his tracks.

"Well, she also produced imperfect ones that didn't hatch."

"Eighteen was a very good result, and we learned a great deal from dissecting the aborts," Phas said.

They were just turning away when the air filled with dragonets, each carrying a fair-sized packtail in its claws. The dragons lifted their heads, opened their mouths, and took the offerings as rightful homage. The men grinned and continued their morning round.

Once Faranth and Carenath had their snack, they were quite willing to curl up together, Carenath with his triangular head neatly placed on his outstretched forelegs. Faranth draped her head and neck over his forequarters, her tail twitching occasionally just in front of his muzzle, her wings sagging slightly from their folded position on her back. Both freshly oiled hides gleamed in the sun.

"I will be glad when they *can* hunt for themselves," Sean murmured to Sorka as they wearily settled on the ground in the shade of the east wall of their home.

"Meanwhile," Sorka said, reaching for a water jar, "we couldn't manage it without the fair." She sent strong feelings of gratitude to Duke, Emmett, Blazer, and the others. Their response, muted in deference to the somnolent dragons, was clearly "You're welcome."

"The requirements of dragons were never considered by Landing's architects," Sean remarked as he took the water jar in turn. Washing dragons was thirsty business. "When they get bigger, something will have to be done. There aren't enough places to house people in Landing anymore, much less dragons."

"D'you think they'd be comfortable in some of Catherine's caves? She mentioned it again yesterday."

"Yes, so she did. Then she giggled."

The two Connells exchanged amused and tolerant grins. The human dragonmates had abruptly found themselves a group set apart, by occupation and dedication, as well as by the subtler changes within them. Though they had the unqualified support and help of every member of the medical, veterinary, and biological teams, they found that talking minor problems over among themselves brought better results. One had to *be* a dragonmate to appreciate the problems—and the joys!

Sorka noted with quiet pride that it was Sean's opinion that seemed to be sought most frequently by the others. And she agreed. He had always been sensible about animals. But, she realized, she could not really call the dragons "animals." They were too . . . human. Even their voices: Carenath's voice sounded just like Sean's light baritone being spoken through a long tunnel. And Sorka suspected that Faranth's voice was a version of her own.

From the moment they had brought the two hatchlings to Irish Square, Sorka had realized that she heard both Faranth and Carenath, while Sean heard only Carenath. That Sorka could hear both did not seem to distress either dragon. They were amenable to everything in life as long as they had full bellies and oiled hides. Then, as Sean's bond with the bronze developed, Sorka heard fewer private exchanges. She, too, had learned, as she suspected each dragonmate had, to communicate telepathically on a private band.

"I'd say they'll be ready to hunt in another week or two—if we can use a small corral to pen the beasts." Sean found her hand and squeezed it, then laid his hand over her belly. "All this won't harm our child, will it?"

Sorka felt guilty. Lately, she had not had time to think about her condition: there was always something to be done for Faranth, or for one of the other young dragons. And she and Sean were still on duty at the dragonet clinic, treating those injured fighting Thread.

"The doctor said I was healthy and could ride . . ." Sorka groaned. "Will *we* be able to teach them to fly *between*, Sean?" Her voice was low, and she clutched his hand apprehensively.

"Now, dear heart, we'll be able for what we have to do." The unknown clearly did not faze Sean anymore.

"But, Sean . . ."

"If *we* know where we're going, *they* will. They'll see it in our minds. They see everything else. What makes you think directions will be difficult?"

"But we don't even know how the dragonets do it!"

Sean shrugged, grinning down at her. "No, we don't. But if the fire-lizards are capable of the teleportation, the dragons will be, too. Kitti Ping did not tamper with that. Let's not fret ourselves. We won't fret them."

She eyed him sourly, then shook her finger at him. "Then *you* stop worrying about it!"

Laughing, his blue eyes sparkling at her shrewd hit, he took her hand and pulled her into his embrace. She nestled there, taking strength from him and returning it. Although Sorka had never before felt so in charge of herself, so dynamic, there were moments when she was assailed with the fear that she might fail Faranth in some small but essential way. She expressed that to Sean.

"No, you won't," he said, smoothing her sweat-damp hair back from her face. "No more will I Carenath. They're ours, and we belong to them." He turned her face up to look at him, his eyes so intense with love and assurance that her breath caught. Sean embraced her again tightly. "Ever since we dropped to this planet, Sorka, this has been our destiny. Or why else were we the first to find the fire-lizards? Out of all the people exploring the world, why did the fire-lizards come to us? Why did the last of Kitti Ping's creation search *us* out of the crowd? No, believe in yourself, in us and our dragons." He held her a moment longer and then released her. "I think we have to give Cricket and Doove to your father. Brian gets along with Cricket very well."

Sorka had known that some decisions had to be made about their horses, both of whom had from the start been terrified of the wobbling dragons. Red and Brian had taken the horses up to the main veterinary barn. Sorka thought briefly of all the grand moments she had experienced on the bay mare's back, most of them shared with Sean and Cricket. But their dragons had become all-important.

"Yes," she heard herself saying with no further twinge of regret. "I never thought there'd come a day when I wouldn't have time for horses." She looked lovingly at the sleeping figure of Faranth and grinned at the bulge in the golden belly, which would all too quickly disappear. "I'll fix us something to eat."

Sean kissed her on the forehead. His new willingness to display affection was one of the fringe benefits from Carenath, and Sorka loved him more than ever. She leaned against him, inhaling his manly smell mixed with the herbal dragon oil.

"Make sandwiches, love," Sean advised. "Here comes Dave Catarel at the trot. If Polenth's asleep, the others will be along, too."

◆ ◆ ◆

"They've got it," Ongola informed Paul when the admiral answered the comm unit in Emily's quarters, where he was anticipating one of Pierre's excellent dinners. Emily had taken pity on him as Ju had gone back to check on their Boca holding the previous day. "Nabhi just called in. Bart Lemos got a scoopful. Although . . ."

"Although what?" Paul asked, exchanging glances with Emily.

"Although it took them a long time," Ongola finished on a troubled sigh. "They should have been well up in the trail before now." Ongola sounded puzzled. "They have what we need, that's the important thing: the pods. The fax are being relayed to the interface right now. Ezra and Jim should have an analysis sometime tomorrow."

"Are you still at the *Moth*?" Paul asked, frowning. Ongola was not completely recovered from his injuries, and Paul was proprietary in his concern for him. Ongola would be a key man in the coming struggle for autonomy and survival.

"Yes, but Sabra's brought me dinner." Ongola was indulging in one of his rare chuckles as he signed off.

"They've got what we need," Paul told Emily as he reseated himself. "Now I can enjoy this dinner."

◆　◆　◆

The first rumblings occurred the next morning, early enough to rattle many people in their beds. Only the young dragons were unperturbed, sleeping through the commotion made by the excited, frightened humans.

"Will this planet never let up on us?" Ongola demanded as he untangled himself from his bedsack and fumbled for the comm unit set.

"Was that an earthquake?" Sabra asked sleepily. She had left the children with a friend so that she and Ongola could have a few hours together. Sabra felt she needed that comfort almost as much as Ongola must. And she had signed on a charter promising order and tranquillity!

"Go back to sleep," Ongola told her as he dialed. "What does Patrice say, Jake?" he asked his efficient assistant.

"He says the gravity meters have all been registering a disturbance in lava chambers along the island ring. He doesn't know what's going to blow, but the display suggests that something has to. He's trying to guess the most likely escape point."

Ongola's next call was to Paul, at home.

"No rest for the weary, huh?" Paul asked in a resigned tone.

"Volcanic disturbance all along the chain."

"Chain, my foot! That rumble was right under my ear, Ongola, and we do have three volcanoes looming over us."

Ongola was so accustomed to the great peaks that he had forgotten that they, also, could pose a threat; though the experts had all agreed that the last eruption of Mount Garben had occurred a millennium ago.

By midmorning Patrice relieved the worst fears by his announcement that a new volcano was erupting out of the sea beyond the eastern tip of Jordan Province. Young Mountain, which had been monitored for the past eight years, was throwing up a cloud of smoke, gas, and some ash, but magma pressure did not seem to be building there.

A second underground churning startled people midafternoon. When Patrice arrived, parking his sled in Administration Square and going in to consult with Paul and Emily, an anxious crowd quickly gathered to await the result of that meeting. Finally the colony's two leaders appeared on the porch with Patrice, who was smiling and waving fax in both hands.

"A new volcano to be named. Like Aphrodite rising from the sea, but I don't necessarily insist on that name," he shouted.

"Where?"

"Beyond the easternmost tip of Jordan, safely away from us, my friends." He held up the largest photo so that the roiling seas and the protruding tip of the smoking peak could be seen by all.

"Yeah, but that's still the same little tectonic plate we're on, isn't it?" one man shouted. He pointed back over his shoulder at the lofty peak of Mount Garben. "That one could go again. Couldn't it?"

"Of course it could," Patrice answered easily, shrugging his shoulders. "But it is very unlikely in my opinion. It shot its head off thousands of years ago. There has been no evidence of activity here. It's an old one, that volcano. The young ones have more to say, and are saying it. Do not panic. We are safe at Landing." He sounded so certain that the anxious murmurings abated and the crowd dispersed.

All through the day there were sporadic growlings, as Telgar called them. Wandering at random through Landing, he had made himself available to anyone who wished to be reassured. It was the first time since Sallah's death that Telgar had circulated socially. That night, a large proportion of Landing's population gathered in Bonfire Square, and the blaze was built up to an unusual, almost defiant size.

"Our beautiful Pern has popped a pimple on her face," Telgar said with a hint of his former joviality, talking to a group of young people. "She's not so old that her digestion is perfect. And we have been disturbing her with our borings and diggings."

When he moved off, one of the apprentice geologists followed him. "Look, Tar-Telgar," the young man began earnestly. "We're not on basement rock here in Landing."

"That is very true," Telgar replied with a slight smile. "Which is why we are rocking a little. But I am not concerned."

The apprentice flushed. "Well, there's a wide, long strip of basement rock in the northern continent, along the western mountain range."

"Ah, how well you have studied your lessons," Telgar commented. He nodded equably to Cobber Alhinwa and Ozzie Munson, who had just joined them. "Ah, have a glass with us."

Embarrassed by having stated the obvious, the young man hastily excused himself.

"So people are talking of basement rock," Cobber said, and beside him Ozzie smirked.

"I know, you know, and he knows, but we have had enough of insecurity today. The basement rock will not shift. As you know, I have given my opinion to Paul, Emily, and Patrice." Telgar looked beyond the big miner to a distant view that only his eyes saw. Cobber and Ozzie exchanged meaningful glances. The set, pained look on Telgar's face meant that he was remembering something about Sallah.

Cobber nudged Ozzie and leaned conspiratorially toward Telgar. "Are we all to go look at some basement rock now, Telgar?"

◆ ◆ ◆

The next morning a rumble of a different kind finally roused Paul as Ju reached across him for the handset.

"For you," she mumbled sleepily, dropping it on the bedsack and rolling over again.

Paul fumbled for it and cleared his throat. "Benden."

"Admiral," Ongola said urgently, "they've begun reentry, and Nabhi's on a bad course."

Paul pulled loose the fasteners of the bedsack and sat bolt upright. "How could he be?"

"*He* says he's green, Admiral."

"I'm coming." Paul had an irrational desire to slam the handset down and go back to sleep beside his wife. Instead he dialed Emily, who said she would join him at the met tower. Then he alerted Ezra Keroon and Jim Tillek.

"Paul?" Ju asked sleepily.

"Sleep on, honey. Nothing to worry you."

He had tried to keep his voice low and was sorry to have disturbed her. In the second semester of a new pregnancy, Ju needed more sleep. They had stayed up late talking, regretfully aware that they must set the example and close down their stake. The constant drain of Threadfall was having a devastating effect on supplies and resources. Joel particularly fretted over the dwindling efficiency of the power packs. According to Tom Patrick, the psychological profile of Landing's population was, in the main, encouraging, although therapy and medication were increasingly required to keep distressed people functioning. Somehow Paul could not bring himself to hope that Nabhi Nabol and Bart Lemos had brought back something as vital as encouragement.

Yesterday Ezra and Jim had produced the latest analysis of the eccentric's orbit. It was as wayward, in Jim Tillek's phrasing, as a drunken whore on a Saturday night at a space facility in the Asteroid Belt. What had looked to be a reasonable, predictable elliptical orbit through Rukbat's system proved to be even more bizarre, at an angle to the ecliptic. The planet would wobble into the vicinity of Pern every two hundred and fifty years, though Ezra had made extrapolations that provided some variations of its course, due to the effect of other planets in the system. During some of its orbits, it looked as if the eccentric and its cloud of junk would miss Pern.

"The most singular planet I've ever tried to track," Ezra had said apologetically, scratching his head as he summed up his report.

"Natural orbit?" Jim had asked, with a sly grin at the astronomer.

Ezra had given him a long scornful look. "There's nothing natural about that planet."

Although Thread had shifted five degrees to the north in the current—third—round of Falls, the admiral no longer held much hope for Ezra's theory that the Falls were deliberate, a softening-up procedure by some sentient agency. If that had been the case, he argued, the Falls ought to have accelerated in frequency and density after the wild planet swung to its nearest spatial point to Pern. But Thread had continued to drop in mindless patterns, each consistent with the northern shift. Mathematical calculations, checked and double-checked by Boris Pahlevi and Dieter Clissmann, concurred with Ezra's depressing conclusion. The eccentric would swing away from Pern and the inner system, only to swing back again in two hundred and fifty years.

The fax Bart had flashed back to Pern had shown the trail of debris to be endless.

"All the way to the edge of the system," Ezra declared in total capitulation. "The planet pierces the Oort cloud and drags the stuff down with it. Hoyle and Wickramansingh's theory has been vindicated in the Rukbat system."

"Aren't we lucky?" Jim added. "The junk could still be just ice and rock. We won't know for sure until we see what Bart Lemos scooped up out there." Jim was not at all happy that his theory was right. He would almost prefer a sentient intelligence somehow surviving on the eccentric planet. You could usually deal with intelligence. His theory made it tough on Pern.

In the cold light of a new morning, Paul dressed quickly, toeing his feet into his boots and closing the front of his shipsuit. He combed his hair neatly back and then stumbled into the predawn light. He used the skimmer—it would be quieter than him puffing and jogging down to the tower. He tried to practice what he preached in matters of conservation, but that morning he did not wish to be heard passing by.

The last few days, with the *Moth* overdue, had been hard on him. Waiting had never been his forte: decision and implementation were where he shone. Emily had proved once again the staunch, unswerving, resolute governor of herself and her subordinates. She was the best sort of complement to his strengths and flaws.

He saw lights over in Irish Square and, through the lines of dwellings, he caught a glimpse of fluttering wings as the young Connells gave their dragons the early morning meal. In the next square, Dave Catarel was up, too, feeding his young bronze.

At the thought of those young people committed to survival on Pern, Paul felt a sudden surge of confidence that he and Emily would bring everyone through. By all that was holy, they would! Had he not gone through bleaker days before the Battle at Purple Sector? And Emily had been blockaded for five years, emerging with a healthy functioning population despite a shortage of raw materials.

The tower was still dark as Paul parked his skimmer behind it. The windows were shuttered, but the main door was ajar. He went up the stairs as quietly as he could. Lately, with the dormitories so crowded, off-duty communications personnel slept on the ground floor. All of Landing was crowded—with refugees, Paul made himself add. People had even begun to make homes out of some of the Catherine Caves. That may have originated from some atavistic urge, but caves *were* Threadproof, and some of them were downright spacious. Caves might be a good place to lodge the fast-growing dragons, too.

As he reached the top floor, his eyes went immediately to the big screen, which showed the *Moth*'s position above Pern, relayed from the moon installation.

"He has not corrected his course once," Ongola said, swinging his chair toward Paul. He motioned for Jake to vacate the second console chair. The young man's eyes were black holes of fatigue, but Paul knew better than to suggest that Jake stand down until the shuttle was safely landed. "He ought to have fired ten minutes ago. *He* says he doesn't need to."

Paul dropped to the chair and toggled in the comm unit. "Tower to *Moth*, do you read me? Benden here. *Moth*, respond."

"Good morning, Admiral Benden," Nabhi replied promptly and insolently. "We are on course and reentering at a good angle."

"Your instrumentation is giving you false readings. Repeat, you are getting false readings, Nabol. Course correction essential."

"I disagree, Admiral," Nabhi replied, his tone jaunty. "No need to waste fuel! Our descent is on the green."

"Correction, *Moth*! Your descent is red and orange across our board and on our screen. You have sustained instrument malfunction. I will give you the readings." Paul read the numbers off from the calculator pad that Ongola handed to him. He was sure he heard a startled gasp in the background.

But Nabhi seemed undisturbed by Paul's information, and he did indeed report readings consonant with a good reentry.

"I don't believe this," Ongola said. "He's coming in from the wrong quadrant, at too steep an angle, and he's going to crash smack in the center of the Island Ring Sea. Soon."

"Repeat, *Moth*, your angle is wrong. Abort reentry. Nabol, take another orbit. Sort yourself out. Your instruments are malfunctioning." Fardles, if Nabol could not feel the wrongness of that entry, he was nowhere near the driver he thought himself.

"I'm captain of this ship, Admiral," Nabol snapped back. "It's your screen that's malfunctioning . . . Whadidya say, Bart? I don't believe it. You've got to be wrong. Give it a bang! *Kick it!*"

"Yank your nose up and fire a three-second blast, Nabol!" Paul cried, his eyes on the screen and the speed of the incoming shuttle.

"I'm trying. Can't fire. No fuel!" Sudden fear made Nabol's voice shrill.

Paul heard Bart's cries in the background. "I told you it felt wrong. I told you! We shouldn't've . . . I'll jettison. They'll have that much!" Bart shouted. "If the farking relay'll work."

"Use the manual jettison lever, Bart," Ongola yelled over Paul's shoulder.

"I'm trying, I'm trying . . . She's heating up too fast, Nabhi. She's heatin—"

Horrified, Paul, Ongola, and Jake watched the dissolution of the shuttle. One stubby wing sheared off and the shuttle began to spin. The tail section broke off and spun away on a different route, burning up in the atmosphere. The second wing followed suit.

"It'll hit the sea?" Paul asked in a bare whisper, trying to calculate the impact of that projectile on land. Ongola nodded imperceptibly.

Like an obituary, the relay screen lit up with a glorious sunlit spread of many bits and one larger object, disappearing into many faint pricks of glitter.

◆ ◆ ◆

A team of dolphins were sent out to the Ring Sea to find the wreck. Maxmilian and Teresa reported back a week later, tired and not too happy to tell humans that they had seen the twisted hulk wedged into a reef in waters too deep for them to examine closely. All the dolphins were still searching the Ring Sea for the jettisoned scoop.

"Tell them not to bother," Jim Tillek muttered dourly. "There's unlikely to be anything left to analyze. We know that the junk goes back in a years' long tail. We're stuck with it. Hail Hoyle and Wickramansingh!"

"Ezra?" Emily asked the solemn astronomer.

Keroon's butterscotch-colored skin seemed tinged with gray, and he looked bowed by his responsibilities. He heaved a heavy, weary sigh and scratched at the back of his head. "I have to concede that Jim's theory is correct. The contents of the pod would have been the final proof, but I, too, doubt the scoop survived. Even if it did, it could take years to find it in such a vast area. Years also apply to that trail, I fear. We won't be able to judge until the end of that tail comes in sight."

"And where does that leave us?" Paul asked rhetorically.

"Coping, Admiral, coping!" Jim Tillek replied proudly. With a twitch of his sturdy shoulders, he had thrown off his doomsday expression and instead challenged them all. "And we've Thread falling in two hours, so we'd better stop worrying about the future and attend to the present. Right?"

Emily looked at Paul and managed a tentative smile, which she also turned on Zi Ongola, who was watching them impassively.

"Right! We'll cope." She spoke in a firm, resolute voice. Surely we can hold out for ten years, she thought to herself, if we're very careful. She wondered why no one mentioned the homing capsule. Perhaps because no one had much faith in Ted Tubberman. "We've got to."

"Until those dragons start earning their keep," Paul said. "But this settlement must be restructured." Emily and he had been discussing redispositions for days. They had been waiting for the right moment to broach the subject to the others of the informal Landing council.

"No," Ongola said, surprising everyone. "We must resettle completely. Landing is no longer viable. It used to be sort of a link with our origins, with the ships that brought us here. We no longer require that sense of continuity."

"And most especially," Jim picked up the thoughts, "not with volcanoes popping up and spouting off in this vicinity." Jim shifted in his chair, settling in to discuss basics. "I've been listening to what people are saying. So has Ezra. Telgar's notion about moving to that cave system on basement rock in the north is gaining strength. The cave complex is big enough to house

Landing's population—plus dragons! We're not out of raw materials to make plastic and metal for housing. But making it takes time away from the essential task of fighting Thread and keeping us alive. Why not use a natural structure? Use our technology to make the cave system comfortable, tenable, and totally safe from Thread?"

Emily did not even pause to take a breath. "Just what Paul and I have been discussing. There's enough fuel, I believe, to transport some of the heavier equipment by shuttle. Then we can use the metal in situ. Jim, the Pern Navy is about to be commissioned."

Paul grinned at Emily. It was much easier when people made up their own minds to do what their leaders had decided was best for them.

Part Three

CROSSING

11.18.08 Pern

"ℌoliest of holies," Telgar murmured respectfully as he held his torch high and still could not illuminate the ceiling. His voice started echoes in the vast chamber, repeating and repeating down side corridors until finally the noise was absorbed by the sheer distance from its source.

"Oh, I say, mate, this is one big bonzo cave," Ozzie Munson said, keeping his voice to a whisper. His eyes were white and wide in his tanned, wind-seared face.

Cobber Alhinwa, who was rarely impressed by anything, was equally awed. "A bleeding beaut!" His whisper matched Ozzie's.

"There are hundreds of ready-made chambers in this complex alone," Telgar said. He was unfolding the plassheet on which he and his beloved Sallah had recorded their investigations of eight years earlier. "There are at least four openings to the cliff top which could be used for air circulation. Channel down to water level and install pumps and pipe—I came across big reservoirs of artesian water. Core down to the thermal layer and, big as it is, this whole complex could be warmed in the winter months." He turned back to the opening. "Block that up with native stone and this would be an impregnable fort. No safer place on this world during Threadfall. Further along the valley, there are surface-level caves near that pasture land. Of course, it would have to be seeded, but we still have the alfalfa grass propagators that were brought for the first year.

"At the time there was no need to investigate thoroughly, but the facilities exist. As I recall when we overflew the range above us, we discovered a medium-size caldera, well pocked with small cliffs, about a half-hour's flight from here. We didn't think to mark whether it was accessible at ground level. It might be ideal for dragon quarters, so accessibility isn't a problem, provided they do fly as well as dragonets."

"We seen a couple old craters like that," Ozzie said, consulting the battered notebook that habitually lived in his top pocket. "One on the east coast, and one in the mountains above the three drop lakes, when we was prospecting for metal ores."

"So," Cobber began, having recovered from his awe, "the first thing is cut steps to this here level." He walked to the edge of the cave and looked down critically at the stone face. "Maybe a ramp, like, to move stuff up here easy like. That incline over there's nearly a staircase already." He pointed to the left-hand side. "Steps neat as you please up to the next level."

Ozzie dismissed those notions. "Naw, those Landingers will want their smart-ass engineers and arki-tects to fancify it for them with the proper mod cons."

Cobber settled a helmet on his head and switched on its light. "Yeah, else some poor buggers get all closet-phobic."

"Claustrophic, you iggerant digger," Ozzie corrected him.

"Whatever. Inside's safest with that farking stuff dropping on ya alla time. C'mon, Oz, let's go walkabout. The admiral and the governor are counting on our expertise, y'know." He gave an involuntary grunt as he settled the heavy cutter on his shoulder and strode purposefully toward the first tunnel.

Ozzie put on his own helmet and picked up a coil of rope, pitons, and a rock hammer. Thermal and ultraviolet recorders, comm unit, and other mining hand-units were attached to hooks on his belts. Lastly, he slung one of the smaller rock cutters over his shoulder. "Let's go test some claustrophia. We'll start left, right? I'll give ya a holler in a bit, Telgar."

Cobber had already disappeared in the first of the left-hand openings as Ozzie followed him. Alone, Telgar stood for a long moment, eyes closed, head back, arms slightly away from his body, his palms turned outward in supplication. He could hear the slight noises of disturbed creatures and the distorted murmur of low conversations from Ozzie and Cobber as they made their way past the first bend in the tunnel.

There was nothing of Sallah in that cave. Even the place where they had built a tiny campfire had been swept bare to the fire-darkened stone. Yet there she had offered herself to him, and he had not *known* what a gift he had received that night!

The sudden high-pitched keening of the stone cutter shattered all thought and sent Telgar about the urgent business of making the natural fort into a human habitation.

• • •

The hum roused Sorka and she tried to find a more comfortable position for her cumbersome body. Fardles, but she would be grateful when she could finally sleep on her stomach again. The humming persisted, a subliminal sound that made a return to sleep impossible. She resented the noise, because she had not been sleeping at all well during the past few weeks and she needed all the rest she could get. Irritably she stretched out and twitched aside the curtain. It could not be day already. Then, startled, she clutched the edge of the curtain because there *was* light outside her house—the light of many dragon eyes, sparkling in the predawn gloom.

Her exclamation disturbed Sean, who stirred beside her, one hand reaching for her. She shook his shoulder urgently.

"Wake up, Sean. Look!" Whichever way she turned, she felt a sudden stab of pain in her groin so unexpected that she hissed.

Sean sat bolt upright beside her, his arms around her. "What is it, love? The baby?"

"It can't be anything else," she said, laughter bubbling out of her as she pointed out the window. "I've been warned!" She could not stop giggling. "Go look, Sean. Tell me if the fire-dragonets are roosting! I wouldn't want them to miss this, any of them."

Grinding sleep out of his eyes, Sean struggled to alertness. He half glared at her for her ill-timed levity, but annoyance was replaced by concern when her laughter turned abruptly into another hissing intake of breath as a second painful spasm rippled across her distended belly.

"It's time?" He ran one hand caressingly across her stomach, his fingers instinctively settling on the band of contracting muscle. "Yes, it is. What's so funny?" he added. She could not quite see his face in the dim light, but he sounded solemn, almost indignant.

"The welcoming committee, of course! All of them. Faranth, love, are all present and accounted for?"

We are here, Faranth said, *where we should be. You are amused.*

"I am very amused," Sorka said, but then another contraction caught her, and she clutched at Sean. "But that was not at all amusing. You'd better call Greta."

"Jays, we don't need her. I'm as good a midwife as she is," he muttered, shoving feet into the shoes under their bed.

"For horses, cows, and nanny goats, yes, Sean, but it is expected for humans to assist humans . . . oooooh, Sean, these are very close together."

He rose to his feet, pausing to throw the top blanket across his bare shoulders against the early morning's chill, when there was a discreet knock at the door. He cursed.

"Who is it?" he roared, not at all pleased at the idea that someone might have come to summon him for a veterinary emergency right then.

"Greta!"

Sorka started to laugh again, but that became very difficult to do all of a sudden, and she switched to the breathing she had been taught, clutching at her great belly.

"How under the suns did you know, Greta?" she heard Sean ask, his voice reflecting his astonishment.

"I was called," Greta said with great dignity, gently pushing him to one side.

"By whom? Sorka only just woke up," Sean replied, following Greta back to their room. "She's the one who's having the baby."

"Not always the first to know when labor commences," Greta said in a very calm, almost detached manner. "Not in Landing. And certainly not with a queen dragon listening in on your mind." She flicked on the lights as she entered the room and deposited her midwifery bag on the dresser. She had been a gangly girl who had turned into a rangy woman with hair and skin the same coffee color and a dusting of freckles across the bridge of her nose. Her eyes, very brown in her kindly face, missed few details.

"Faranth told you?" Sorka was astonished. A dragon speaking to someone outside of their group was unheard of.

"Not exactly," Greta replied with a chuckle. "A fair of fire-dragonets flew in my window and made it remarkably plain that I was needed. Once I got outside, it wasn't hard to figure out whose baby was coming. Now, let me see what's going on here."

I told them to get her, Faranth told Sorka in a smugly complacent tone of voice. *You like her.*

As Sorka lay back for Greta's examination, she tried to figure that out. She liked her doctor, too, and had no qualms about him attending her delivery. How had Faranth sensed that she really had wanted Greta in attendance? Could Faranth possibly have sensed that she had always been friendly with Greta? Or was it some connection the golden dragon had made because Sorka had assisted Greta in the birth of Mairi Hanrahan's latest, Sorka's newest baby brother? But for Faranth to recognize an unconscious preference . . .

Sean slid cautiously onto the other side of the bed and reached for her hand. Sorka gave him a squeeze, laughter still bubbling up in her. She had so hated the last few weeks when her body had not seemed to be her own, when all its controls seemed to have been assumed by the bouncing, kicking, impertinent, restless fetus that gave her no rest at all. Her laughter was sheer elation that all of *that* was nearly over.

"Now, let me have a look . . . another contraction?"

Sorka concentrated on her breathing, but the spasm was far more painful than she had anticipated. Then it was gone, pain and all. She felt sweat on her forehead. Sean blotted it gently.

You are hurting? Faranth's voice became shrill.

"No, no, Faranth. I'm fine. Don't worry!" Sorka cried.

"Faranth's upset?" Keeping her hand tight in his, Sean crouched to see out the window to the dragons waiting there. "Yes, she is! Her eyes are gaining speed and orange."

"I was afraid of that!" Mutely Sorka appealed to Sean. Expressions flitted across his face. If she read them correctly, he was annoyed with Faranth, indecisive—for once—about what to do, and anxious for her. Then tender concern dominated his face as he looked down at her, and she felt that she had never loved him more than at that moment.

"A pity we can't have your dragon heat a kettle of water to keep her out of mischief," Greta remarked, her strong capable hands finishing the examination. She gave Sorka's distended belly a gentle pat. "We'll take care of her fussing you right now. Can you turn on one side? Sean, help her."

"I feel like an immense flounder," Sorka complained as she struggled to turn. Then Sean, deftly and with hands gentler than she had ever known, helped her complete the maneuver. She had just reached the new position when another mighty spasm caught her, and she exhaled in astonishment. Outside Faranth trumpeted a challenge. "Don't you dare wake everyone up, Faranth. I'm only having a baby!"

You hurt! You are in distress! Faranth was indignant.

Sorka felt a slight push against the base of her spine, the coolness of the air gun, and then a blessed numbness that spread rapidly over her nether region.

"Oh, blessed Greta, how marvelous!"

You don't hurt. That is better. Faranth's alarm subsided back into that curious thrumming of dragons, and Sorka could identify her voice in the hum as clearly as she heard the noise intensify. Oddly enough, the humming was soothing—or was it simply that she no longer had to anticipate that painful clutching of uterine muscles?

"Now, let's get you to your feet for a little walking, Sorka," Greta said. "You're already fairly well dilated. I don't think you're going to be any time delivering this baby, even if you are a primipara."

"I'm numb," Sorka said by way of apology as Greta got her to her feet. Then Sean was on her other side.

He had gotten dressed, but Sorka, trying to watch where her nerveless feet were going, noticed that he did not have his socks on. She thought that endearing of him. Odd the difference between his hands and Greta's—both caring, both gentle, but Sean's loving and worried.

"That's a girl," Greta said encouragingly. "You're doing just fine, three fingers dilated already. No wonder the fairs were alerted. And you're not the only one exciting them tonight." Greta chuckled as they began to retrace their steps across the lounge, up the short hall, and into the bedroom. "It's the walking that's important . . . ah, another contraction. Very good. Your breathing's fine."

"Who else is delivering?" Sorka asked because it helped to concentrate on things other than what her muscles were doing to her.

"Fortunately, Elizabeth Jepson, a new baby will help her get over the loss of the twins."

Sorka felt a pang of grief. She remembered the two boys as mischievous youngsters on the *Yoko*, and recalled how she had envied her brother, Brian, for having friends his own age.

"It's funny that, isn't it?" Sorka said, speaking quickly. "People having two complete families, almost two separate generations. I mean, this baby will have an uncle only six months older. And be part of an entirely different generation . . . really."

"One reason why we have to keep very careful birth records," Greta said.

Sean grunted. "We're all Pernese, that's what matters!"

Sorka's water burst then, and outside the humming went up a few notes and deepened in intensity.

"I think I'd better check you, Sorka," Greta said.

Sean stared at her. "Do you deliver to dragonsong?"

Greta gave a low chuckle. "They've an instinct for birth, Sean, and I know you vets have been aware of it, too. Let's get her back to the bed."

Sorka, involved in the second phase of childbirth, found the dragonsong both comforting and soothing; it was like a blanket of sound shimmering about her, enfolding and uplifting and comforting. The sound suddenly increased in tempo, rising to a climax. Sean's hands grasped hers, giving her his strength and encouragement. Every time she felt the contractions, painless because of the drug, he helped her push down. The spasms were becoming more rapid, almost constant, as if matters had been taken entirely out of her control. She let the instinctive movements take over, relaxing when she could, assisting because she had no other option.

Then she felt her body writhe in a massive effort, and when it had been expended, she felt a tremendous relief of all pressures and pullings. For one moment, there was complete silence outside, then she heard a new sound.

Sean's cry of triumph was lost in the trumpeting of eighteen dragons and who knew how many fire-dragonets! Oh dear, she thought distractedly. They'll wake up the whole of Landing!

"You have a fine son, my dears," Greta said, her voice ringing with satisfaction. "With a crop of thick red hair."

"A son?" Sean asked, sounding immensely surprised.

"Now, don't tell me, after all my hard work, Sean Connell, that you wanted a daughter?" Sorka demanded.

Sean just hugged her ecstatically.

◆　◆　◆

"Sometimes I feel as if everyone's forgotten all about us," Dave Catarel said to Sean as they watched their two bronzes hunting. Sean, his eyes on Carenath, did not reply.

Although all the dragons were well able to fly short distances and had proved capable of hunting down wild wherries, their human partners grew anxious if they flew out of sight. Nor was it always possible to use a sled or a skimmer to accompany them. As a compromise, Sean had talked Red into giving them the culls or injured animals from the main herds. He and the others had rigged a Threadfall shelter for the mixed herd in one of the caves, and each took turns on the succession trays that supplied their fodder.

The young dragons were strong and flew well. But, erring on the side of caution, the veterinary experts had decided that riding should not be attempted until the full year had passed. Sean had railed privately to Sorka about such timidity, but she had talked him out of defiance, reminding him how much they stood to lose in forcing the young dragons. Fortunately the decision had been reached without consultation with Wind Blossom, which made it easier for Sean to accept what he called "sheer procrastination." He did not like her proprietary attitude toward the dragons. She continued to exercise Kitti Ping's program, though without the same success. Her first four batches had not produced any viable eggs, but seven new sacs in the incubator looked promising.

The odds in Joel Lilienkamp's book favored the success of the first Hatching, but only marginally. Sean was privately determined to upset such odds, but he also would not risk official censure or jeopardize the young dragons.

"I really cannot repose the same confidence in Wind Blossom as I did in Kitti Ping," Paul had told Sean and Sorka in a private conference, "but we would all breathe more easily if we could see some progress. Your dragons eat, grow, even fly to hunt. Will they also chew rock?" Paul began to tick off the points on his left hand. "Carry a rider? And preserve their valuable hides during Threadfall? The power pack situation is getting tight, Sean, very tight indeed."

"I know, Admiral," Sean had replied, feeling grim and defensive. "And eighteen fully functional dragons are not going to make fighting Thread all that much easier."

"But self-reproducing, self-sustaining Thread fighters will make one helluva lot of difference in the long run. And it's the long run, frankly, Sean, Sorka, that worries me."

Sean kept his opinion about Wind Blossom to himself. Part of it was loyalty to Carenath, Faranth, and the others of the first Hatching; a good deal stemmed from his lack of confidence in Wind Blossom, where he had had every faith in her grandmother. After all, Kit Ping had been trained at the source, with the Eridani.

As he watched the grace of Carenath, swooping to snatch a fat wether from the stampeding flock, his faith in these amazing creatures was reinforced.

"He really got some altitude there," David said with ungrudging praise. "Look, Polenth's dropped his wings now. He's going for that one!"

"Got it, too," Sean replied in a return of compliment.

Maybe they were all being too cautious, afraid of pushing down the throttle and seeing the result. Carenath flew strongly and well. The bronze was nearly the same height in the shoulder as Cricket, though the conformation was entirely different, Carenath being much longer in the body, deeper in the barrel, and stronger in the hindquarters. In fact, the dragons already were much stronger than similar equines, their basic structure much more durable, utilizing carborundums for strength and resilience. Pol and Bay had gone on about the design features of dragons as if they had been new sleds, which indeed, Sean thought wryly, was what they were intended to replace. According to the program, dragons would gradually increase in size over many generations until they reached the optimum. But in Sean's eyes, Carenath was just right.

"At least they eat neatly," Dave said, averting his eyes from the two dragons who were rending flesh from the carcasses of their kills. "Though I wish they didn't look like they enjoyed it so much."

Sean laughed. "City-bred, were you?"

Dave nodded and smiled weakly. "Not that I wouldn't do anything for Polenth. It's just that it's one thing on three-D, another to watch it live and *know* that your best friend prefers to hunt living animals. What did you say, Polenth?" Dave's eyes took on that curious unfocused look that people had when being addressed by their dragons. Then he gave a rueful laugh.

"Well?" Sean prompted him.

"He says anything's better than fish. He's meant to fly, not swim."

"Good thing he has two bellies," Sean remarked, seeing Polenth devouring the sheep, horns, hooves, fleece, and all. "The way he's squaffing down the wool, he could start a premature blaze when he starts chewing firestone."

"He will, won't he, Sean?" Dave's earnest plea for reassurance worried Sean. The dragonmates could not doubt their beasts for a moment, not on any score.

"Of course he will," Sean said, standing up. "That's enough, Carenath. Two fills your belly. Don't get greedy. There are more to be fed here today."

The bronze had been about to launch himself into the air again, aiming toward the rise into the next valley where the terrified flock had stampeded.

I would really like another one. So tasty. So much better than fish. I like to hunt. Carenath sounded a trifle petulant.

"The queens hunt next, Carenath."

With a peevish swing of his head, Carenath began to amble back down to Sean, spreading his wings to balance himself. Dragons looked odd when they walked, since they had to crouch to their shorter forelegs; some of them fell more easily into a hop-skip gait, dropping to the forequarters every few steps or using their wings to provide frontal lift. Sean disliked seeing the dragons appear so ungainly and unbalanced.

"See you later," he said to David as he and Carenath turned to walk back to the cave they inhabited.

The dragons had quickly outgrown the backyard shelters and, in many cases, the patience of neighbors, some of whom worked night shifts and slept during daylight hours. Dragons were a vocal lot for a species that could not speak aloud, so dragons and partners had explored the Catherine Caves for less public accommodations. Sorka had at first worried about living underground with their baby son, Michael, but the cavesite Sean had chosen was spacious, with several large chambers—their new home actually had far more space than did the house in Irish Square. Faranth and Carenath were delighted. There was even a shelf of bare earth above the cave entrance where dragons could sunbathe, the leisure activity they enjoyed even above swimming.

"We are all much better suited here," Sorka had exclaimed in capitulation, and had set about making their living quarters bright with lamps, her handwoven rugs, fabrics, and pictures that she had cadged from Joel.

But the new quarters had proved to be more than just a physical separation, Sean realized as he and Carenath trudged along. Dave Catarel had put his finger on it in his wistful comment about being forgotten.

This walk is long. I would rather fly on ahead, Carenath said, doing his little hop-skip beside Sean. Once again Sean thought that his brave and lovely Carenath looked like a bad cross between a rabbit and kangaroo.

"You were designed to fly. I'll be happy when we both fly."

Why do you not fly on me, then? I would be easier to ride than that scared creature. Carenath did not think much of Cricket as a mount for his partner.

Scared creature, Sean thought with a chuckle. Poor Cricket. How easy it would be to swing up to Carenath's back and just take off! The notion made the breath catch in his throat. To fly *on* Carenath, instead of shuffling along on the dusty track. The adolescent year for the dragons was nearly over. Sean looked about in deep speculation. Let Carenath drop off the highest point, and he would have enough space to make that first, all-important downsweep of his wings . . .

Sean had spent as much time watching how fire-lizards and dragons handled themselves in the air as he once had patiently observed horses. Yes, a drop off a height would be the trick.

"C'mon, Carenath. I'm glad I didn't let you fill your belly. C'mon, right up to the top."

The top? The ridge? Sean heard comprehension color the dragon's mind, and Carenath scrambled to the height in a burst of speed that left Sean coughing in the dust. *Quickly! The wind is right.*

Rubbing dust particles out of his eyes, Sean laughed aloud, feeling elation and the racing pulse of apprehension. This is the sort of thing you do *now*, at the right time, in the right place, he thought. And the moment was right for him to ride Carenath!

There was no saddle to vault to, no stirrup to assist Sean to the high shoulder. Carenath dipped politely, and Sean, lightly stepping on the proferred forearm, caught the two neck ridges firmly and swung over, fitting his body between them.

"Jays, you were designed for me," he said with a triumphant laugh, and slapped Carenath's neck in affection. Then he grabbed at the ridge in front of him.

Carenath was perched on the very edge of the ridge, and Sean had an awesome view of the bottom of the rockstrewn gorge. He swallowed hastily. Flying Carenath was not at all the same thing as riding Cricket. He took a deep breath. It was also not the time for second thoughts. He took a compulsive hold with legs made strong from years of riding and shoved his buttocks as deeply into the natural saddle as he could.

"Let's fly, Carenath. Let's do it now!"

We will fly, Carenath said with ineffable calm. He tilted forward off the ridge.

Despite years of staying astride bucking horses, sliding horses, and jumping horses, the sensation that Sean Connell experienced in that seemingly endless moment was totally different and completely new. A brief memory of a girl's voice urging him to think of Spacer Yves flitted through his mind. He was falling through space again. A very short space. What sort of a nerd-brain was he to have attempted this?

Faranth wants to know what we are doing, Carenath said calmly.

Before Sean's staggered mind registered the query, Carenath's wings had finished their downstroke and they were rising. Sean felt the sudden return of gravity, felt Carenath's neck under him, felt the weight and a return of the confidence that had been totally in abeyance during that endless-seeming initial drop. The power in those wing sweeps drove his seat deeper between the neck ridges as Carenath continued to beat upward. They were level with the next ridge, the floor of the gorge no longer an imminent crash site.

"Tell Faranth that we're flying, of course," Sean replied. He would never admit it to Sorka—he could barely admit it to himself—but for one moment he had been totally and utterly terrified.

I will not let you fall, Carenath's tone chided him.

"I never thought you would." Sean forced his body to relax, forced his long legs down and around Carenath's smooth neck, but he took a firmer grip on the neck ridge. "I just didn't think I'd stay aboard you for a minute there."

Carenath's wings swept up and down, just behind Sean's peripheral vision. He felt their strong and steady beat even if he did not see them. He could feel the air pressure against his face and his chest. There was nothing around him but air, open, empty, and absolutely marvelous.

Yes, once he got the hang of it, flying his dragon was the most marvelous sensation he had ever had.

I like it, too. I like flying you. You fit on me. This goes well. Where shall we go? The sky is ours.

"Look, we better not do much of this right now, Carenath. You just ate, and we're going to have to think this thing through. It's not enough to fall off a ridge. Oooooooh—" he cried inadvertently as Carenath banked and he saw the wide-open, dusty, Thread-barren ground far, far beneath him. "Straighten up!"

I wouldn't let you fall! Carenath sounded nearly indignant, and Sean freed one hand to give him a reassuring slap. But he quickly replaced his hand on the ridge. Jays, a rider can't fly Thread hanging on for dear life!

"You wouldn't let me fall, my friend, but I might let me!"

Trying to quell his rising sense of panic, Sean hazarded a glance at the ground. They were nearly to the rank of caves that had become their home.

Sean could see Faranth on the height where she must have been sunning herself. She was sitting on her haunches, her wings half-spread. In a few sweeps of Carenath's powerful wings, they had covered a distance that ordinarily took a half hour of up-hill-down-dale slogging.

Faranth says that Sorka says that we had better come down right away. Right away! Carenath's tone was defiant, begging Sean to contradict the golden dragon and anything that shortened their new experience. *We are flying together. It is the right thing to do for dragons and riders.*

"It's a fantastic thing to do, Carenath, but as we are now home, can you land us, say, by Faranth? Then you can tell her just how we did it!"

Sean did not care if Sorka had hysterics over his spontaneous and totally unplanned flight. He had done it, they had succeeded, and all was well that ended well. The dragons of Pern finally had riders! That would change the odds in Joel's book!

◆ ◆ ◆

The other seventeen riders, including Sorka, once Faranth had reassured her about Carenath's prowess, were delighted at their tremendous advance. Dave wanted to know why Sean had been so precipitous.

"Couldn't you have waited for me? Polenth and I were just behind you. You scared the living wits out of me for a moment, you know."

Sean clasped Dave's arm in tacit apology. "It was what you'd said about being forgotten, Dave. I just had to try, but I didn't want to endanger anyone else in case I was wrong." Sean caught Sorka frowning at him and pretended to flinch. "I was all right, love. You *know* that! But—" He glared warningly at the others seated on the rugs around him. "We've got to go about this in a logical and sensible way, folks. Flying a dragon's not like riding a horse."

His glance held Nora Sejby's. She certainly was not the sort of person he would have said would Impress a dragon, but Tenneth had chosen her, and they would have to make the best of it. Nora was accident-prone, and Tenneth had already hauled her partner out of the lake and prevented her from falling into the crevices and holes that pitted the hills around the Catherine Caves. On the other hand, Nora had been sailing across Monaco Bay since she was strong enough to manage a tiller and she had checked out on both sleds and skimmers.

"For one thing, there's all this open air around you. Falling is down onto a hard and injurious surface," Sean made appropriate gestures, smacking one hand into the palm of the other and startling Nora with the noise.

"So?" Peter Semling said. "We use a saddle."

"A dragon's back is full of wings," Sorka replied dryly.

"You ride forward, sitting your butt in the hollow between the last two ridges," Sean went on, grabbing for a sheet of opaque film and a marker. He made a quick sketch of a dragon's neck and shoulders, and the disposition of two straps. "The rider wears a stout belt, wide like a tool belt. You strap yourself in on either side, and the safety harness goes over your thigh for added security. And we're going to need special flying gear and protective glasses—the wind made my eyes water, and I wasn't even aloft all that long."

"What did it really feel like, Sean?" Catherine Radelin asked, her eyes shining in anticipation.

Sean smiled. "The most incredible sensation I've ever had. Beats flying a mechanical all hollow. I mean . . ." He raised his fists, tensing his arms into his chest and giving his hands an upward thrusting turn of indescribable experience. "It's . . . it's between you and your dragon and . . ." He swung his arms out. "And the whole damned wide world."

He made a less dramatic presentation at the impromptu meeting where he was asked to account for such risk-taking. He would rather have reported privately, to maybe Admiral Benden or Pol or Red, but he found himself facing the entire council.

"Look, sir, the risk was justified," he said, looking quickly from the admiral to Red Hanrahan. His father-in-law had been both furious and hurt by what he considered a betrayal. Sean had not anticipated that. "We were almost to the ridge when I suddenly knew I had to prove that dragons could fly us. Sir, all the planning in the world sometimes doesn't get you to the right point at the right time."

Admiral Benden nodded wisely, but the startled expression on Jim Tillek's blunt face and Ongola's sudden attention told Sean that he had said something wrong.

"I could risk my own neck, sir, but no one else's," he went on, "so we've got to take our time getting some of the other riders ready to fly. I've done a lot of riding and sled-driving, but flying a dragon's not the same thing, and I'm not about to go out again until Carenath's got some safety harness on him. And me."

Joel Lilienkamp leaned forward across the table. "And what will that require, Connell?"

Sean grinned, more out of relief than amusement. "Don't worry, Lili, what I need is what Pern's got plenty of—hide. I found a use for all that tanned wher skin you've got in Stores. It's plenty tough enough and it'll be easier on dragons' necks than that synthetic webbing used in sled harnesses. I've made some sketches." He unfolded the diagrams, much improved on by his discussions with the other dragonmates. "These show the arrangement of straps and the belts we'll need, the flying suits, and we can use some of those work goggles plastics turns out."

"Flying suits and plastic goggles," Joel repeated, reaching for the drawings. He examined them with a gradually less jaundiced attitude.

"As soon as I can rig the flying harness for Carenath, Admiral, Governor, sirs," Sean said, politely including all assembled and adding a tentative grin at Cherry Duff's deep scowl, "you can see just how well my dragon flies me."

"You were informed, weren't you," Paul Benden said, and Sean saw him rubbing the knuckles of his left hand, "that there're new eggs on the Hatching Sands?"

Sean nodded. "Like I told you, Admiral, eighteen are not enough to take up much slack. And it'll be generations before there're enough."

"Generations?" Cherry Duff exclaimed in her raspy voice, swinging in accusation on the veterinary team. "Why weren't we told it'd take generations?"

"Dragon generations," Pol answered, smiling slightly at her misinterpretation. "Not human."

"Well, how long's a dragon generation?" she demanded, still affronted. She shot a disgusted scowl at Sean.

"The females should produce their first independent clutches at three. Sean has proved that a male dragon can fly at just under a year—"

Cherry brought both hands down on the table, making a sharp, loud noise. "Give me facts, damn it, Pol."

"Then, four to five years?"

Cherry pursed her lips in annoyance, a habit that made her look even more like a dried prune, Sean thought idly.

"Humph, then I'm not likely to see squadrons of dragons in the sky, am I? Four to five years. And when will they start flaming Thread? That was their design function, wasn't it? When will they start being useful?"

Sean was fed up. "Sooner than you think, Cherry Duff. Open a book on it, Joel." With that he strode from the office. It galled him to the bone to have to take a skimmer back to Sorka and the others who waited to hear what had happened.

Ten days later, when Joel Lilienkamp himself brought them the requisitioned belts, straps, flying kit, and goggles, flight training on the dragons of Pern began in earnest.

◆ ◆ ◆

Landing had grown accustomed over the past year and a half to the grumblings and rumblings underfoot. On the morning of the second day of the fourth month of their ninth spring on Pern, early risers sleepily noted the curl of smoke, and the significance did not register.

Sean and Sorka, emerging from their cave with Carenath and Faranth, also noticed it.

Why does the mountain smoke? Faranth wanted to know.

"The mountain *what?*" Sorka demanded, waking up enough to absorb her dragon's words. "Jays, Sean, look!"

Sean gave a long hard look. "It's not Garben. It's Picchu Peak. Patrice de Broglie was wrong! Or was he?"

"What on earth do you mean, Sean?" Sorka stared at him in amazement.

"I mean, there's been all this talk of basement rock, and shifting Landing to a more practical base, with a special accommodation for dragons and us . . ." Sean kept his eyes on the plume curling languidly up from the peak, dwarfed beside the mightier Garben but certainly as ominous. He shrugged. "Not even Paul Benden can make a volcano erupt on cue. Come, we can get breakfast at your mother's. Let's stuff Mick in his flying suit and go. Maybe your dad will have received some official word." He scowled. "We're always the last ones to get news. I've got to convince Joel to release at least one comm unit for the caves."

Sorka got their wriggling son into his fleece-lined carrying sack before she shrugged into her jacket and crammed helmet and goggles onto her head. Sean carried Mick out to Faranth. With an ease grown of practice, Sorka ran the two steps to her dragon's politely positioned foreleg and vaulted astride. Sean handed her a protesting bundle to sling over her back and then turned to mount the obliging Carenath.

The dragons leapt upward from the ledge before the cave, giving themselves enough airway to take the first full sweep. Over the last few weeks, dragon backs had strengthened and muscled up. They had managed flights of several hours' duration. Riders, even Nora Sejby—Sean had contrived a special harness that made her feel securely fastened to Tenneth—were improving. Long discussions with Drake Bonneau and some of the other pilots who had both fighter experience in the old Nathi War and plenty fighting Thread had improved the dragonriders' basic understanding of the skills needed. And practice had encouraged them.

Three weeks before, Wind Blossom's latest attempt had hatched. The four creatures who had survived had not been Impressed by the candidates awaiting them, although the creatures ate the food presented. Indeed, the poor beasts turned out to be photophobic, but Blossom, much to the disgust of Pol and Bay and against their advice, had insisted on special darkened quarters for the beasts, for the purpose of continued examination of that variant.

Even the fire-lizards were more useful, Sean thought, as the two fairs erupted into the air about them, bugling a morning welcome in their high, sweet voices. Now, if the dragons could only prove capable of *that*, Sean thought enviously. But how do you teach a dragon to do something you do not yourself understand? The dragons got smarter every day and they were fast learners, but it was impossible to explain telekinesis to them or ask them to teleport the way the fire-lizards did. Kitti Ping had called it an instinctive action. Nowhere in the genetics program that Sean had memorized did he find any words of wisdom on how to instruct a dragon to use his innate instinct.

And it was not the sort of exercise one did on a spontaneous basis. First, they would try to chew firestone and make flame. They knew where the fire-lizards got the phosphine-bearing rock; Sean had even watched the browns and Sorka's Duke selecting the pieces to chew and the careful way they concentrated while they chewed. The fire-lizards had learned to produce flame on demand, so Sean felt easy about teaching the dragons that. But going *between* one place and another . . . that was scary.

◆　◆　◆

Flame of a different kind obsessed Landing's counselors three days later.

"What people want to know, Paul, Emily," Cherry Duff said, turning her penetrating stare from admiral to governor, "is how much warning you had of Picchu's activity."

"None," Paul said firmly. Emily nodded. "Patrice de Broglie's reports have not been altered. There's been a lot of volcanic activity all along the ring, as well as that new volcano. You've felt the same shakes I have. Landing and all stakeholders have been apprised of every technical detail. This is as much of an unpleasant surprise to us as it is to you!" Then Paul's stern expression altered. "By all that's holy, Cherry, all that black ash gave me as much a fright yesterday as it did everyone else."

"So?" Cherry demanded, her attitude unsoftened.

"Picchu is officially an active volcano!" Paul spread his hands, looking past Cherry to Cabot Francis Carter and Rudi Shwartz. "And officially, it's likely to continue to spout smoke and ash. Patrice and his crew are up at the crater now. He'll give a full public report this evening at Bonfire Square."

Cherry gave him a long hard stare, her black eyes piercing, her face expressionless. Then she snorted. "I believe him, but that doesn't mean I like it—or the obvious prognosis. Landing moves, doesn't it?"

Emily Boll nodded solemnly.

"And your next statement," Cherry went on in her hard voice, "is that you have prepared a place for us!"

Paul burst into guffaws, though Emily muffled her laughter when she saw how such levity affronted Rudi Shwartz.

"You had no right," Paul said, controlling his laughter, "to steal that line from Emily, Cherry Duff! Damn it, we were working on the official announcement when you barged in. And you fardling well know we've been rushing to complete the northern fort. Landing couldn't continue much longer as a viable settlement even if Picchu hadn't started showering us with ash. That doesn't, of course, mean," he put in quickly, holding up his hand to forestall Cabot's explosion, "that stakeholders will be asked to leave their lands. But the administration of this planet will have to be in the most protected situation we can contrive. Plainly Landing has outlived its usefulness. It was never intended as a permanent installation."

Emily took up the discussion then, passing to each of the delegation copies of the directive she and Paul had been drafting. "The transfer is being organized much as our space journey here. We have the technicians and the equipment to make a northern crossing as easy as possible. We have enough fuel to power two of the shuttles to transport equipment too bulky to fit on any of Jim's ships. It'll be a one-way trip for the shuttles: they'll be dismantled for parts. When there's time, we can send a crew back to scavenge the other three. Joel Lilienkamp has been working on priority shipments for the big sleds, taking as few as possible from the fighting strength."

"Speaking of fighting strength, has that young upstart taught them any new tricks?" Cherry demanded imperiously, looking down her long nose at Paul. "Speaking of eruptions, as we were, how are those beasts of Kitti Ping's progressing? I see them flitting around all the time. Mighty pretty they look in formation, but are they any good in battle?"

"So far," Paul began cautiously, "they've matured well beyond the projections. The young Connells have proved splendid leaders."

"They were the best ground-crew leaders I had," Cabot Carter said, disgruntled.

"They'll be superior as aerial fighters," Paul went on, overriding the legist's unspoken criticism. "Self-perpetuating, too, unlike sleds and skimmers."

"D'you know that for sure?" Cherry demanded in her raspy voice. "Blossom's experiments aren't all that successful."

"Her grandmother's are," Paul replied with a firm confidence he hoped would reassure Cherry. "According to Pol and Bay, the males are producing their equivalent to sperm. Genetic analysis has started but will take months. We might have direct proof of dragon fertility by then, as the gold females mature later." Paul tried not to sound defensive, but he wanted to counter the very bad publicity surrounding Wind Blossom's brutes. Especially when the young dragonriders were trying so very hard to perfect themselves for combat against Thread. Though it was not public knowledge, Sean and his group had already served as messengers and had transported light loads efficiently.

Paul had a report on his desk from Telgar and his group. They had done a survey of the old crater above the fort hold, with its myriad bubble caves and twisting passages, and had pronounced it a suitable accommodation for the dragons and their riders. Telgar had a team working to make the place habitable, while they still had power in the heavy equipment. A stream was being damned up for a dragon-sized bathing lake, water piped into the largest of the ground-level caverns for kitchen use, and a chimney hole had been bored for a large hearth complex.

Obviously, that would be the pattern for future human habitation on Pern, and for some, accustomed to sprawling living space, it would take some getting used to. But it was the best way to survive!

"Pol?"

It took a moment for the biologist to identify the anxious voice. "Mary?" His response was equally tentative, but he pulled at Bay's sleeve to attract her attention away from the monitor she was frowning at. "Mary Tubberman?"

"Please don't turn an old friend away unheard."

"Mary," Pol said kindly, "*you* weren't shunned." He shared the earpiece with Bay, who nodded in vigorous approval.

"I might as well have been." The woman's tone was bitter, then her voice broke on a tremulous note and both Bay and Pol could hear her weeping. "Look, Pol, something's happened to Ted. Those creatures of his are *loose*. I've pulled down the Thread shutters, but they're still prowling about and making awful noises."

"Creatures? What creatures?" Pol locked glances with Bay. Beyond them, their dragonets roused from a doze and chirped in empathic anxiety.

"The beasts he's been rearing." Mary sounded as if she thought Pol knew what she was talking about and was being deliberately obtuse. "He—he stole some frozen in-vitros from veterinary and he used Kitti's program on them to make them obey him, but they're still . . . things. His masterpiece does nothing to stop *them*." Again her bitterness was trenchant.

"What makes you think something has happened to Ted?" Pol asked, picking up on the words Bay mouthed to him as she gestured urgently.

"He would never let those animals *loose*, Pol! They might harm Petey!"

"Now, Mary, calm down. Stay in the house. We'll come."

"Ned's not in Landing!" Her tone became accusatory. "I tried his number. He'd believe me!"

"It's not a question of belief, Mary." Bay pulled the mouthpiece around to speak directly into it. "And anyone can come assist *you*."

"Sue and Chuck won't answer."

"Sue and Chuck moved north, Mary, after that first bad rock shower from Picchu." Bay was patient with her. The woman had a right to sound paranoid, living in seclusion as she had for so long, with an unbalanced husband and so many earthshocks and volcanic rumblings.

"Pol and I are coming down, Mary," Bay said firmly. "And we'll bring help." She replaced the handset.

"Who?" Pol demanded.

"Sean and Sorka. Dragons have an inhibiting effect on animals. And that way we don't have to go through official channels."

Pol looked at his wife with mild surprise. She had never criticized either Emily or Paul, obliquely or bluntly.

"I always felt someone should have investigated the report Drake and Ned Tubberman made. So did they. Sometimes priorities get lost in the shuffle around here." She wrote a hasty note which she then attached to her gold dragonet's right foot. "Find the redhead," she said firmly, holding the triangular head to get Mariah's full attention. "Find the redhead." Bay walked with her to the window and opened it, pointing firmly in Sorka's direction. She filled her mind with an image of Sorka, leaning against Faranth. Mariah chirped happily. "Now, off with you!" Then, as the dragonet obediently flew off, Bay ran a finger over the black grime that was once again settling on the windowsill she had swept earlier. "I'll be glad to move north. I'm so eternally tired of black dust everywhere. Come on, Pol, we'd better get dressed warmly."

"You volunteered to help Mary because it gives you a chance to ride a dragon again," Pol said, chuckling.

"Pol Nietro, I have long been concerned about Mary Tubberman!"

Fifteen minutes later, two dragons came swooping over the rise to settle on the road in front of their house.

"They are so graceful," Bay said, making certain her headscarf was tied, as much against the prevailing dust outside as in hopes of riding. As she left the house, Mariah circled down and settled to the plump shoulder with a chirrup of smug satisfaction. "You're marvelous, Mariah, simply marvelous," Bay murmured to her little queen as she marched right up between Faranth and Carenath. However, it was Sorka she addressed. "Thank you for coming, my dear. Mary Tubberman just contacted us. There's trouble at Calusa. Creatures are loose, and Mary thinks something has happened to Ted. Will you take us there?"

"Officially, or unofficially?" Sean asked as Sorka glanced over at her mate.

"It's all right to help Mary," Bay said, looking for support from Pol, who had just come up to the dragons, his glance as admiring as ever. "And with who knows what sort of beast . . ."

"Dragons are useful," Sorka replied with a grin, arriving at her own decision. She beckoned to Bay. "Give the lady your leg, Faranth. Here's my hand."

With Faranth's assist, Bay was agile enough to settle herself quietly behind Sorka. She would never admit that she was pinched fore and aft between the ridge. Mariah gave her usual squeak of protest.

"Now, Mariah, Faranth's perfectly safe," Bay said, and looked over to see that Pol was settling behind Sean. The young dragonrider's grin was very broad as he winked at Bay. Well, this time it really is an emergency, she told herself. A woman trapped in her home with small children and unidentifiable menaces prowling outside.

"Hang on tight now," Sean said as always. He pumped his arm in the signal to launch.

Bay suppressed an exclamation as Faranth's upward surge pushed her painfully against the stiff dorsal ridge. Her discomfort lasted only a moment, as the golden dragon leveled off and veered leisurely to her right. Bay caught her breath. She would never get accustomed to this; she didn't want to. Riding a dragon was the most exciting thing that had happened to her since . . . since Mariah had first risen to mate.

Calusa was not a long trip by air, but the flight was tremendously exhilarating. The dragons hit one of the many air currents that were the result of Picchu's activity, and Bay clutched at Sorka's belt, stuffing her fingers to the knuckle in the belt loops. Flying on a dragon was so much more immediate an activity than going in the closed sled or skimmer. Really much more exhilarating. Bay turned her head so that Sorka's tall, strong body shielded her from the worst of the airstream and the dust from Picchu that seemed to clog the air even at that altitude.

The journey gave Bay time to ponder what Mary had said about "beasts." Red Hanrahan had reported a late-night entry into the veterinary laboratory. A portable bio-scan had been missing without being logged out, but as the bio lab was always borrowing vet equipment, the absence was dismissed. Later someone had noticed that the order in which the frozen ova of a variety of Earth-type animals were stored had been disarranged. It *could* have happened during the earthquakes.

Ted Tubberman had been very busy in his discontent, Bay thought grimly. One of the strictest dictums of her profession as a microbiologist was a strict limitation of genetic manipulation. She had actually been surprised, if relieved, that Kitti Ping Yung, as the senior scientist on the Pern expedition, had permitted the bioengineering of the fire-dragonets. Had Kitti Ping any idea of what a marvelous gift she had bestowed on the people of Pern?

But for Ted Tubberman, disgruntled *botanist*, to tinker with ova—and he *had not* at all understood the techniques or the process—to make independent alterations was intolerable to her, both professionally and personally. Bay knew herself to be a tolerant person, friendly and considerate, but if Ted Tubberman was dead, she would be tremendously relieved. And she would not be the only one. Just thinking about the man produced symptoms of agitation and pure fury which made Bay lose her professional detachment, and that annoyed her even more. There she was on dragonback, a marvelous opportunity for peaceful reflection, with only the noise of the wind in her ears, with all Jordan spread below her, and she was wasting contemplative time on Ted Tubberman. Bay sighed. One had so few moments of total relaxation and privacy. How she envied young Sorka, Sean, and the others.

She was astonished to see Calusa in the next valley. It was a sturdy complex, built by the Tubbermans as headquarters for their stake acres. The galvanized roofs of the main buildings had grown to a dull dark gray from the repeated showers of volcanic ash that Picchu Peak deposited wherever the wind blew. But Bay had scarcely had time to notice that when Sorka's cry of astonishment blew back to her.

"Jays, that building's a shambles!" Sorka pointed to her right, and Faranth abruptly turned in response to an unspoken request. The dorsal ridge bit into the soft flesh of Bay's crotch, and she gripped Sorka's belt more tightly.

"Look!" Sorka was directing her gaze downward.

Seventy-five meters from the main house, there was a roofed compound with separate enclosures along an L passageway, forming two sides of a fenced-in area. One of the outside walls and several of the interior partitions were smashed, and a corner of the roofing had burst outward. Bay could not recall if there had been any more earthshocks reported in that area to cause such structural damage. No other building was damaged.

As the dragon once more changed direction, Bay grabbed at Sorka, felt the girl's reassuring fingers on hers, and then they were down.

"I do like riding Faranth. She's so very graceful and strong," Bay said, tentatively patting the warm hide of the dragon's neck.

"No, don't dismount," Sorka said. "Faranth says there's something prowling in there. The dragonets will have a look. Whoops!"

The air was suddenly full of the chitterings and chatterings of angry dragonets. Bay's Mariah shrieked in her ear.

"Now, now, it's all right. Faranth won't let anyone harm you." Bay held up her arm for her gold, but Mariah joined the investigating fairs. Bay was astounded to realize that the dragon was growling, a sensation she could also feel through her body contacts. Faranth turned her impressive head toward the compound, the many facets of her eyes gleaming with edges of red and orange.

A piercing yowl was clearly audible and then there was silence. The excited fairs swirled back over the two dragonriders' heads, chittering and clattering with their news. Faranth looked up, her eyes wheeling as she absorbed the dragonets' images.

"There's some kind of very large spotted beast out there," Sorka told Sean. "And something else that is even larger but silent."

"We'll need trank guns, then," he said. "Sorka, have Faranth call up some reinforcements. Marco and Duluth, if possible; Dave, Kathy—we may need a medic. Peter's Gilgath is sturdy, Nyassa won't panic, and ask for Paul or Jerry. I think we should evacuate Mary and the two children until the beasts can be captured."

Her ordeal ended, Mary Tubberman wept copiously on Bay's shoulder. Her son, Peter, usually a cheerful seven-year-old, watched poker-faced and taut with anxiety. His two little sisters clung together on a lounger and would not respond to Pol's efforts to comfort them, though he was generally very deft with children. Mary did not resist the suggestion that she move to a safer location.

"Dad's dead, isn't he?" Petey asked, stepping right up to Sean.

"He could be out trying to recapture the beasts," kindhearted Bay suggested. The boy gave her a scornful look and went off down the corridor to his room.

The dragon reinforcements arrived with the trank guns. Sean was pleased to see them landing in the order they had been drilled in. Sean gave Paul, Jerry, and Nyassa the trankers and sent them off on their dragons to see if they could find and disable the escaped animals.

Leaving Sorka to help the Tubbermans assemble their gear, Sean and the others, armed with the pistols, cautiously approached the wrecked compound. Inside the building, the reek of animal was heavy and mounds of recent dung littered the place. They found Ted Tubberman's mauled and gnawed body pitifully sprawled outside his small laboratory.

"Fardles, nothing we have kills like that!" David Catarel exclaimed, backing out of the corridor.

Kathy knelt by the corpse, her face expressionless. "Whatever it was had fangs and sharp claws," she remarked, slowly getting to her feet. "His back was broken."

Marco grabbed up an old lab coat and some toweling from a rail and covered the corpse. Then he picked up the remains of a chair, made of one of the local pressed vegetable fibers that were used for interior furnishings. "This'll burn. Let's see if we can find enough to cremate him here. Save a lot of awkwardness." He waved in the direction of the main house. Then he shuddered, clearly unwilling to move the mangled body.

"The man was insane," Sean said, poking a rod into the dung pats in one enclosure. "Developing big predators. We've enough trouble with wherries and snakes!"

"I'll go tell Mary," Kathy murmured.

Sean caught her arm as she went by. "Tell her he died quickly." She nodded and left.

"Hey!" Peter Semling picked up a covered clipboard from the littered floor of the laboratory. "Looks like notes," he exclaimed, examining the thin sheets of film covered with notations in a cramped hand. "This is botanical stuff." He shrugged, held it out to Kathy, and picked up another. "This is . . . biological? Humph."

"Let's collect any notes," Sean said. "Anything that would tell us what kind of creature killed him."

"Hey!" Peter said again. He flipped the cover back on a portable bio-scan, complete with monitor and keyboard. "This looks like the one that went missing from the vet lab a while back, along with some AI samples."

Meticulously they gathered up every scrap of material, even taking an engraved plate with the cryptic message *Eureka, Mycorrhiza!* which had been nailed to the splashboard of the sink unit. Dave carried out several sacks to be brought back to Landing. Then Sean and Peter collected enough flammable materials to make a pyre that could be lit once Mary and the children had gone.

"Sean!" David Catarel called. He was hunkered down by a wide green swath that was the only living thing in the raddled and ash-littered plot, though its color was dimmed by the pervasive black ash. "How many Falls has this area had?" he asked, glancing about. He ran his hand over the grass, a tough hybrid that agro had developed for residence landscaping before Thread had fallen.

"Enough to clear this!" Sean knelt beside him and pulled up a hefty tuft. The dirt around the roots contained a variety of soil denizens, including several furry-looking grubs.

"Never seen that sort before," David remarked, catching three deftly as they dropped. He felt in his jacket pocket, extracted a wad of fabric, and carefully wrapped the grubs. "Ned Tubberman was yakking about a new kind of grass surviving Fall down here. I'll just take these back to the agro lab."

Just then Sorka, Pol, Bay, and Peter, each loaded with bundles, came out of the main house. Sean and Dave began to load the eight dragons.

"We can make another run for you, Mary," Sorka suggested tactfully when the woman joined them with two stuffed bedsacks.

"I don't have much besides clothes," Mary said, her glance flicking to the compound. "Kathy said it was quick?" Her anxious eyes begged confirmation.

"Kathy's the medic," Sean assured her smoothly. "Up you go now. David and Polenth will take you. Mount up. You kids ever ridden a dragon before?"

Sean made a game of it for them and passed quickly over the awkwardness of the moment. He saw them all off before he and Pol ignited the funeral pyre. Then they took off in yet another shower of the volcanic dust which would eventually bury Landing.

◆ ◆ ◆

"I can't break Ted's personal code!" Pol exclaimed in exasperation, throwing the stylus down to a worktop littered with clipboards and piles of flimsies. "Wretched, foolish man!"

"Ezra loves codes, Pol," Bay suggested.

"Judging by the DNA/RNA, he was experimenting with felines, but I cannot imagine why. There're already enough running wild here at Landing. Unless—" Pol broke off and pinched his lower lip nervously, grimacing as his thoughts followed uneasy paths. "We *know*—" He paused to bang the table in emphasis. "—that felines do not take mentasynth well. *He* knew that, too. *Why* would he repeat mistakes?"

"What about that other batch of notes?" Bay asked, gesturing to the clipboard lying precariously on the edge.

"Unfortunately, all I can read of them are quotations from Kitti's dragon program."

"Oh!" Bay cocked her jaw sideways for a moment. "He had to play creator as well as anarchist?"

"Why else would he refer to the Eridani genetic equations?" Pol slapped the worktop with his hand, frustrated and anxious, his expression rebellious. "And what did he hope to achieve?"

"I think we can be grateful that he hadn't tried to manipulate the fire-dragonets, though I suspect he was practicing on the ova he appropriated from the vet frozen storage."

Pol rubbed the heels of his hands into his tired eyes. "We can be grateful for small mercies there. Especially when you consider what Blossom has done. I shouldn't have said that, my dear. Forget it."

Bay permitted herself a scornful sniff. "At least Blossom has the good sense to keep those wretched photophobes of hers chained. I cannot think why she persists with them. She's the only one they like." Bay gave a shudder of revulsion. "They positively fawn on her."

Pol snorted. "That's why," he said absently, riffling through the notes on the undecipherable clipboard. "What I don't understand is why he chose the large felines?"

"Well, why don't we ask Petey? He helped his father in the compound, didn't he?"

"You are the essence of rationality, my dear," Pol said. Pushing himself out of the chair, he went over and laid an affectionate kiss on her cheek, ruffling her hair. She was admonishing him when he punched the commcode for Mary Tubberman's quarters. Both he and Bay had been visiting her daily to help her settle back into the community. "Mary, is Peter available?"

When Peter answered, his tone was not particularly encouraging. "Yeah?"

"Those large cats your father was breeding? Did they have spots or stripes?" Pol asked in a conversational tone.

"Spots." Peter was surprised by the unexpected question.

"Ah, the cheetah. Is that what he called them?"

"Yeah, cheetahs."

"Why cheetahs, Peter? I know they're fast, but they wouldn't be any good hunting wherries."

"They were great going after the big tunnel snakes." Peter's voice became animated. "And they'd come to heel and do everything Dad told them—" he broke off.

"I expect they did, Petey. Several ancient cultures on Earth bred them to hunt all manner of game. Speediest things on four legs!"

"Did they turn on him?" Peter asked after a moment's silence.

"I don't know, Petey. Are you coming to the bonfire tonight?" Pol asked brightly, feeling that he could not leave the conversation on such a sour note. "You promised me a rematch. Can't have you winning every chess game." He received a promise for that evening and disconnected. "From what Petey said, it would appear that Ted used mentasynth on cheetahs to enhance their obedience. He used them to hunt tunnel snakes."

"They turned on him?"

"That seems likely. Only why? I wish we knew how many ova he took from vet. I wish we could decipher these notes and discover if he only used mentasynth or if he implemented any part of Kitti's program. Be that as it may—" Pol exhaled in frustration. "We have an unknown number of predatory animals loose in Calusa. Loose in Calusa!" Pol let out a derisory snort for his inadvertent rhyming. "I wonder if Phas Radamanth has had any luck deciphering the notes on those grubs. *They* could be useful."

♦ ♦ ♦

Patrice de Broglie burst into Emily's office. "Garben's getting set to blow. We've got to evacuate. Now!"

"*What!*" Emily rose to her feet, the flimsies she was studying slipping out of her hands to scatter on the floor.

"I've just been to the peaks. There's a change in the sulfur-to-chlorine ratio. It's Garben that's going to blow." He slapped his hand to his forehead in a self-accusatory blow. "Right before my eyes, and I didn't see it."

Alerted by Emily's cry, Paul came through from the adjoining office. "Garben?"

"You've got to evacuate immediately," Patrice cried, his expression contorted. "There've even been significant increases in mercury and radon from the damned crater. And we thought it was leaking from Picchu."

"But it's Picchu that's smoking!" Stunned, Paul struggled to keep his cool. He reached for the comm unit just as Emily did. She grabbed it first, and he jerked his fingers back and let her contact Ongola.

"That Garben is as sly a mountain as the man we named it for. Volcanology still isn't a precise science," Patrice said, rolling his eyes in frustration as he paced up and down the small office. "I've sent a skimmer up with the correlation spectrometer to check on the content of the fumarole emissions that just started in the Garben crater," Patrice went on. "I brought down samples of the latest ash. But that rising sulfur-to-chlorine ratio means the magma is rising."

"Ongola," Emily said. "Sound the klaxon. Volcano alert. Recall all sleds and skimmers immediately. Yes, I know there's Threadfall today, but we've got to evacuate Landing *now*, not later. How long do we have, Patrice?"

He shrugged in exasperation. "I cannot give you the precise moment of catastrophe, my friends, nor which way it will spew, but the wind is a strong nor'easterly. Already the ash increases. Had you not noticed?"

Startled, governor and admiral glanced out the window and saw that the sky was gray with ash that obscured the sunlight, and that Picchu's smoking yellow plume was broader than usual. A similar halo was beginning to grow about Garben's peak.

"One can even become accustomed to living beneath a volcano," Paul remarked with dry humor.

Patrice shrugged again and managed a grin. "But let's not, my friends. Even if the pyroclastic flow is minimal, Landing will soon be covered with ash at the rate it's now falling. As soon as we've decided possible lava flow paths, I'll inform you, so you can clear the most vulnerable areas first."

"How fortunate we already have an evacuation plan," Emily remarked, selecting a file and bringing it up on the terminal. "There!" She ran the sequence to all printers, on emergency priority. "That's going to all department heads. Evacuation is officially under way, gentlemen. What a nuisance to have to do it at speed. Something is bound to be forgotten no matter how carefully you plan ahead."

Trained by repeated drills, the population of Landing reacted promptly to the klaxon alert by going to their department heads for orders. A brief flurry of panic was suppressed, and the exercise went into high gear.

The sky continued to darken as thick black clouds of ash rolled up, covering the peaks of the now active volcanoes that had once appeared so benign. White plumes rose from Garben's awakened fumaroles and from crevasses down its eastern side. Morning became twilight as the air pollution spread. Handlamps and breathing masks were issued.

In charge of the actual evacuation, Joel Lilienkamp supervised from one of the fast sleds, keeping the canopy open so that he could bawl orders and encouragement to the various details and make on-the-spot decisions. The laboratories and warehouses nearest the simmering volcano were being cleared first, along with the infirmary, with the exception of emergency first aid and burn control. The donks trundled everywhere, depositing their burdens at the grid or carrying them on down to temporary shelter in the Catherine Caves.

Patrice's group had already calculated areas of high and low pyroclastic hazard. Warnings had been sent as far east as Cardiff, west to Bordeaux, and south to Cambridge. Already favored with a heavy fall of ash, Monaco was also in range of moderate pyroclastic missile danger. Every boat, ship, and barge was mobilized in the bay, to be loaded and sent off to stand beyond the first Kahrain peninsula.

The last sacks of fuel were emptied into the tanks of the two remaining shuttles. Most of the dragonriders were put to herding the livestock toward the harbor. For the first time, no one assembled to fight Thread at Maori Lake—a more deadly fall threatened.

No one had time to cheer as Drake Bonneau lifted the old *Swallow*, with its cargo of children and equipment, just as daylight receded from the plateau. The technicians moved immediately to the *Parakeet*. Ongola and Jake, monitoring in the tower, took advantage of the respite to eat the hot food that had been sent up to them. The communications equipment had been placed on trolleys and could be quickly shifted if the tower was threatened.

"*Swallow* looks good," Ezra called in from the interface chamber where he was monitoring the flight. He had spent much of that day erecting a shield of heatproof material around the chamber, not quite ready to accept Patrice's hurried assurance that the room's location did not intersect any channels of previous lava flows. Unfortunately the interface with the orbiting *Yokohama* could not be disconnected, relying as it did on a fixed beacon to the receiver on the *Yoko*. Since the setting on the *Yoko* could no longer be altered to a new direction, there was no point in taking the interface and reassembling it.

That night, the air was choking with sulfur fumes and full of gritty particles, and Patrice warned that the buildup was reaching the critical point. White plumes from both Picchu and Garben, ominously rooted in a muted glow from peak and crater, were visible even against the dark sky, casting an eerie light over the settlement.

Drake Bonneau reported that he was safely down after a difficult flight. "Damn crate nearly shook apart, but nothing was damaged. None of the kids so much as bruised, but I don't think any of them will develop a yen for flying. Hard landing, too, plowed a furrow when we overshot the mark. We'll need the rest of the day to clear the site for the *Parakeet*. Tell Fulmar to check the gyros and the stabilizing monitors. I'll swear we had tunnel snakes in the *Swallow*'s."

There was a constant stream of vehicles down to the harbor, as the bigger ships and barges were loaded with protesting animals prodded into stalls erected on deck. Crates of chickens, ducks, and geese were strapped wherever they could be attached, to be off-loaded at the Kahrain cove, safely out of the danger zone. With any luck, most of the livestock would be evacuated. Skimming over the harbor, Jim Tillek managed to be everywhere, encouraging and berating his crews.

By nightfall, Sean called a halt for dragonriders ferrying people and packages to the Kahrain cove. "I'm not risking tired dragons and riders," he told Lilienkamp with some heat. "Too risky, and the dragons are just too young to be under this sort of stress."

"Time, man, we don't have time for niceties!" Joel replied angrily.

"You handle the exodus, Joel, I'll handle my dragons. The riders will work until they drop, but it's bloody stupid to push young dragons! Not while I can prevent it."

Joel gave him an angry, frustrated glare. The dragons had been immensely useful, but he also knew better than to put them at risk. He gunned the sled away, perched behind the console like a small, ash-covered statue.

Sean and the other riders did work until they dropped. Each dragon then curled protectively about his rider as they slept. No one had time to notice that there were few dragonets about.

Then, all too soon, Joel was there again, exhorting them from the air, and they rejoined the Herculean efforts of the people around them.

Suddenly, the klaxon sounded a piercing triple blast. All activity ceased for the message that followed.

"She's going to blow!" Patrice's almost triumphant shout echoed throughout Landing.

Every head turned toward Garben, its peak outlined by the eerie luminosity from its crater.

"Launch the *Parakeet*!" Ongola's stentorian voice broke the awed, stunned silence.

The engines of the shuttle were drowned by the rumbling earth and an ear-splitting roar of tremendous power as the volcano erupted. The attentive stance of observers broke as people scrambled to complete tasks at hand, shouting to one another above the noise. Later, those who watched the peak fracture and the red-hot molten lava begin to ooze from the break said that everything appeared to happen in slow motion. They saw the fissures in the crater outlined by orange-red, saw the pieces blowing out of the lip, even saw some of the projectiles lifting out of the volcano and could track their dizzying trajectory. Others averred that it all happened too fast to be sure of details.

Bright red tongues of lava rolled ominously up and over the blasted lip of Garben, one flow traveling at an astonishing rate directly toward the westernmost buildings of Landing.

In that dawn hour, the wind had dropped, saving much of the eastern section of Landing from the worst of the shower of smaller rocks and hot ash. The larger, devastating projectiles that Patrice had feared did not appear. But the lava was sufficiently frightening a menace.

The *Parakeet*, laden with irreplaceable equipment, pierced the western gloom, her engine blasts visible, if not audible, as she drove northwest and out of danger.

At the sound of the klaxon, the dolphins began to tow heavily laden small boats out of Monaco Bay, a flotilla of vessels not ordinarily suitable for any prolonged sea travel. The dolphins had assured humans that they would get their charges safely to the sheltered harbor beyond the first Kahrain peninsula. *Maid* and *Mayflower*, which were not fully loaded, left the harbor to wait outside the estimated fallout zone until they could return for the last of their cargoes. Jim, on board the *Southern Cross*, shepherded barges and luggers along the coast on their long journey to Seminole, from where they would make the final run north.

Sleds and skimmers streamed between Landing and Paradise River Hold as the nearest safe assembly point. Traffic there was chaotic, as vital supplies were kept available and loads were shunted to designated areas of the beach. Landing was being cleared of all that could be reused in the new northern hold.

Thick sulfur-smelling ash began to cover Landing's buildings. Some of the lighter roofs collapsed under the load, and observers could hear the plastic groaning and shifting. The air was almost unbreathable with traces of chlorine. Everyone used the breathing masks without complaint.

By midafternoon, a haggard Joel Lilienkamp dropped his battered sled on the lee side of the tower beside Ongola's. He waited a moment to gather enough strength to thumb open the comm unit.

"We've cleared all we can," he said in gasps, his voice raspy from the acrid airborne fumes. "The donks are parked in the Catherine Caves until we can strip 'em down for shipment. You can leave now, too."

"We're coming," Ongola replied.

Moments later he appeared, slowly angling a heavy comm package on a grav unit past the door. Jake came next, similarly encumbered. Paul followed, guiding two more components.

"Need a hand?" Joel asked automatically, though the way he slumped at the console made it hard to believe that he had any more energy to spare.

"One more trip," Ongola said when they had positioned the equipment in his sled. "Is your power pack up to a load?" he asked Joel.

"Yup. My last fresh unit."

As Ongola and Jake went back into the tower, Paul went to the flagstaff and, with a bleak expression on his face, solemnly lowered the singed tatters of the colony's flag. He made a ball of it, which he stuffed underneath the seat he took on the sled. He gave the supply master one long look. "Want me to drive, Joel?"

"I got you here, I'll take you out!"

Paul dared not look back at the ruins of Landing, but as Joel veered east and then north in a wide sweep, the admiral saw that he was not the only one with tears coursing down his cheeks.

◆　◆　◆

A stiff nor'easterly wind kept the Kahrain cove clear of ash and the acrid taint of Garben's eruption. The gray pall spread over the eastern horizon as the volcano continued to spew lava and quantities of ash. Patrice and a skeleton team remained to monitor the event after Landing was abandoned.

"We hunt this morning," Sean said to the other riders.

They had found a quiet cove up the beach from the main evacuation camp. None of the dragons sprawled in the warm sun had a very good color, and privately Sean worried that their maturing strengths had been overtaxed.

He decided stoutly that there was nothing wrong that a good meal would not restore. He looked around for fire-lizards and swore under his breath. "Damn them! We *need* all we've got. Four queens and ten bronzes can't possibly catch enough packtail to feed eighteen dragons! Surely they've seen volcanoes erupt before."

"Not on top of them," Alianne Zulueta replied. "I couldn't reassure mine. They just left!"

"Red meat would be better than fish—more iron," David Catarel suggested, his eyes on his pale bronze Polenth. "There's sheep here."

"Hold it," Marco Galliani said firmly, raising both hands in restraint. "My father's shipping them on to Roma as soon as sleds are free. Prime breeding stock."

"So are dragons." Sean rose, an odd grin on his face. "Peter, Dave, Jerry, come with me. Sorka, you run interference—if there is any."

"Hey, wait a minute, Sean," Marco began, dual loyalties in conflict.

Sean grinned slyly, laying a finger along his nose. "What the eye doesn't see, Marco, the heart won't grieve."

"It's for your dragon, man," Dave muttered as he passed him.

An hour later, several dragons disappeared in a westerly direction, skimming the treetops. The other riders were so conspicuous in their efforts to help the crew struggling to organize the chaos on the beach that no one would have noticed that the riders were not all present at any one time. By noon, seventeen brightly hued, sated dragons lolled on the strand. One sat patiently on the headland while fire-dragonets dove into the sea, fishing for packtail.

Caesar and Stefano Galliani, taking a poll count as their sheep were loaded, discovered that the tally was short by some thirty-six animals, including one of the best rams. Caesar called on the dragonriders to search the area and herd the missing sheep back to the shore.

"Useless things, always wandering off," Sean agreed, nodding sympathetically at the frustrated and puzzled Gallianis. "We'll give a look."

When Sean reported back an hour later, he suggested to Caesar that the sheep must have dropped into some of the many potholes in the area. Reluctantly the Gallianis took off with the depleted flock. The big transport sleds had schedules to keep, and shipment could not be postponed.

As the last of the sleds departed, Emily came over to Sean. "Are your dragons fit for duty?"

"Anything you say!" Sean agreed so amiably that Emily shot him a long look. "The fire-lizards worked hard all morning to feed the dragons." He gestured toward the cove where Duluth was accepting a packtail from a bronze.

"Fire-lizards?" Emily was momentarily baffled by "lizards," then remembered that Sean tended to use his own name for the little creatures. "Oh, yes, then your fairs have returned?"

"Not all of them," Sean said ruefully, and then added quickly, "but enough of the queens and bronzes to be useful."

"The eruption scared them all, didn't it?"

Sean gave a snort. "The eruption scared all of us!"

"Not out of our wits, it would seem," Emily said with a crooked smile. "At least nobody acted as foolish as sheep, did they?" Sean pretended neither innocence nor understanding; he returned her look until she broke eye contact. "If your dragons have lost the taste for fish, hunt wherries. That eruption whittled down our herds quite enough, thank you." Sean inclined his head, still noncommittal. "There's so much to be done, and done quickly." Consulting the thick sheets on her clipboard, she paused to rub her forehead. "If only your dragons were fully functional . . ." Then she shot him a penitent smile. "Sorry, Sean, that's an egregious comment."

"I, too, wish we were, Governor," Sean replied without prejudice. "But we're not sure *how* it's done. Not even what to tell them to do." He blotted the sweat from his forehead and neck, a sweat not entirely provoked by the hot sun.

"A point well made and a matter we must look into, but not here and now. Look, Sean, Joel Lilienkamp's worried about the supplies still at Landing. We're shifting loads out of here as fast as we can." She swept her arm over the mounds of color-coded crates and foam-covered pallets. "The orange stuff has to be protected from Threadfall, so it has to go north as fast as possible to be sorted in the Fort Hold. We still have to try to save what's left at Landing before the ash covers it."

"That ash burns, Governor. Burns as easily through dragon wings as—" Sean broke off, staring fixedly toward the western beach, one hand coming up in a futile gesture of warning. Emily twisted around to see what had prompted his concern.

The dragon's trumpet of alarm was faint and thin on the hot air. The driver of the sled on collision course with the creature seemed unaware that he was descending onto another flyer. Then, just before the sled would have hit, dragon and rider disappeared.

"Instinct is marvelous!" Emily exclaimed, her face lit with both relief at the last-minute evasion and joy that a dragon had displayed that innate ability. She looked back to Sean and her expression changed. "What's the matter, Sean?" She glanced quickly up at the sky, a sky empty of both dragon-pair and the sled, which was lost in the many coming and going on the Kahrain cove. "Oh no!" Her hand went to her throat, which seemed to close as she felt the wrenching of fear in her guts. "No. Oh no! Shouldn't they be visible again now? Shouldn't they, Sean? Isn't it supposed to be an instantaneous displacement?"

Distressed, she reached out to clasp his arm, giving him a little shake to attract his attention. He looked down at her, and the anguished expression in his eyes gave her an answer that altered fear to grief. She turned her head slowly from side to side, trying to deny the truth to herself.

Just as one of the cargo supervisors came striding up to her, a sheaf of plasfilm in his hand and an urgent expression on his face, the most appalling keen rose into the air. The dissonant noise was so piercing that half the people on the beach stopped to cover their ears. In the same moment as the unbearable sound mounted steadily, the air was full of fire-dragonets, each adding its own shrill voice to swell the sound of lament.

The other dragons rose, riderless, to fly past the point where one of their number and his human partner had lost their lives. In a complex pattern that would have thrilled watchers on any other occasion, the fire-dragonets flew around their larger cousins, emitting their weird counterpoint to the deeper, throbbing, mournful cry of the dragons.

"I'll find out how that could have happened. The driver of that sled—" Emily stopped as she saw the terrible expression on Sean's face.

"That won't bring back Marco Galliani and Duluth, will it?" He whipped his hand sideways in a sharp, dismissive cut. "Tomorrow we will fly wherever you need us for whatever we can save for you."

For a long long moment Emily stood looking after him until the image of the sorrowing young man was indelibly imprinted in her mind. In the sky, as if escorting him back to the dragonriders' camp, the graceful beasts wheeled, dipped, and glided westward to their beach.

Whatever pain Emily felt, it could be nothing, she realized, to the sense of loss that would be experienced by the dragonriders. She scrubbed at her face, at a chin that trembled, determinedly swallowed the lump in her throat, and irritably gestured for the cargo supervisor to approach her.

"Find out who drove that sled and bring him or her to my tent at noon. Now, what's on your mind?"

◆ ◆ ◆

"Marco and Duluth disappeared, just the way the fire-lizards do," Sean said, his voice oddly gentle.

"But they *didn't* come back," Nora cried out in protest. She started to weep afresh, burying her face in Peter Semling's shoulder.

The shock of the unexpected deaths had been traumatic. The dragons' lament had subsided over the afternoon. By evening, their partners had coaxed them to curl up in the sand and sleep. The dragons seen to, the young people hunched about a small fire, dispirited and apathetic.

"We have to find out what went wrong," Sean was saying, "so that it can never happen again."

"Sean, we don't know even know what Marco and Duluth were doing!" Dave Catarel cried.

"Duluth was exhibiting an instinctive reaction to danger," a new voice said. Pol Nietro, Bay beside him, paused in the light thrown by the fire. "An instinct he was bred to exercise. May we offer condolences from all those connected with the dragon program. We—Bay and I—why, all of you are like family to us." Pol awkwardly dabbed at his eyes and sniffed.

"Please join us," Sorka said with quiet dignity. She rose and drew Bay and Pol into the firelight. Two more packing crates were hauled into the circle.

"We have tried to figure out what went wrong," Pol continued after he and Bay had settled down wearily.

"Neither looked where he was going," Sean said with a heavy sigh. "I was watching. Marco and Duluth took off from the beach and were rising just as the sled driver made an approach turn. He wouldn't have seen Marco and Duluth coming up under him. Dragons aren't fitted with proximity warning devices." Sean raised both hands in a gesture of helplessness. "I have it from very good authority that the sled driver had turned his alarm off because the constant noise in so much traffic was getting on his nerves."

Pol leaned toward him. "Then it is more important than ever that you riders teach your dragons discipline." A ripple of angry denial made him hold up his hands. "That is not meant to sound censorious, my dear friends. Truly I mean to be constructive. But obviously now is the moment to take the next step in training the dragons—training them to make proper use of the instinct that ought to have saved both Marco and Duluth today."

The comment raised murmurs, some angry, some alarmed. Sean held up his hand for silence, his tired face lit by the jumping tongues of flame. Next to him, Sorka was keenly aware of the muscles tightening along his jawline and the stricken look in his eyes.

"I believe we've been thinking along the same lines, Pol," he said in a taut voice that told the biologist just how much strain the young dragonrider was under. "I think that Marco and Duluth panicked. If only they'd just come back to the place they'd left, the farking sled was gone!" His anguish was palpable. He took a deep breath and continued in a level, almost emotionless tone. "All of us have fire-lizards. That's one of the reasons Kit Ping chose us as candidates. We've all sent them with messages, telling them where to go, what to do, or who to look for. We should be able to instruct the dragons to do the same thing. We know now, the hard way, that they can teleport, just as the fire-lizards do. We have to guide that instinct. We have to discipline it, as Pol suggested, so panic doesn't get us the way it got Marco."

"Why did Marco panic?" Tarrie Chernoff asked plaintively.

"I'd give anything to know," Sean said, the edge of anguish returning to his voice. "One thing I do know. From now on, no rider takes off without checking what's in his immediate airspace. We must fly defensively, trying to spot possible dangers. *Caution*," he said, stabbing his index finger into his temple, "should be engraved on our eyeballs." He spoke rapidly, his tone crisp. "We know that the fire-lizards do go wherever it is they go, *between* one place and another, so let's stop taking that talent of theirs for granted and *watch* exactly what they do. Let's scrutinize their comings and goings. Let's send them to specific places, places they haven't been before, to see if they can follow our mental directions. Our dragons hear us telepathically. They understand exactly what we're saying—not like the fire-lizards—so if we get used to giving precise messages to the fire-lizards, the dragons ought to be able to operate on the same sort of mental directions. When we understand as much of fire-lizard behavior as we can, *then* we will attempt to direct our dragons."

The other riders murmured among themselves, Sean watching them with narrowed darting glances.

"Wouldn't that risk our dragonets?" Tarrie asked, stroking the little gold that had nestled in the crook of her arm.

"Better the dragonets than the dragons!" Peter Semling said firmly.

Sean gave a derisive snort. "The fire-lizards're very good at taking care of themselves. Don't misunderstand me—" He held up a hand against Tarrie's immediate protest. "I appreciate them. They've been great little fighters. Jays, we'd never have fed the hatchlings without their help, but—" He paused to look around the circle. "—they have got a well-developed survival mechanism or they wouldn't have lasted through the first pass of that Oort cloud. Whenever that was. As Peter said, it's a lot safer to experiment with the fire-lizards than another dragonpair."

"You've made some very good points there, Sean," Pol said, beginning to take heart himself, "though I trust you mean to use the gold and bronze fire-dragonets. They have always seemed more reliable to Bay and myself."

"I had. Especially since the blues and greens all scarpered off after the eruption."

"I'm game to try," Dave Catarel said, throwing his shoulders back and straightening up, sending a challenging look at the others. "We've got to try something. Cautiously!" He shot Sean a quick glance.

A slow smile broke across Sean's face as he reached across the fire to grasp Dave's hand.

"I'm willing, too," Peter Semling said. Nora tentatively agreed.

"It sounds eminently sensible to me," Otto said, nodding vigorously and looking about him. "It is, after all, what the dragons were bred to do, escape from the danger of Threadfall as the mechanical sleds cannot."

"Thanks, Otto," Sean said. "We all need to think positively."

"And cautiously," Otto amended, raising one finger in warning.

Stirred from their apathy, the riders began murmuring to one another.

"Do you remember, Sorka," Bay said, leaning toward her urgently, "when I sent Mariah to you the day we were called to Calusa?"

"She brought me your message."

"She did indeed, but all I told her was to find the redhead by the caves." Bay paused significantly. "Of course, Mariah has known you all her life and there aren't *that* many redheads in Landing, or on the planet." Bay knew she was babbling, which was something she rarely did, but then she rarely broke down in tears, either, and when she had heard the dreadful news, she had cried for nearly an hour, despite Pol's comforting. As Pol had said, it had been like losing family. Without a terminal to consult for possible solutions, they had spent two frantic hours searching for the crate in which they had packed all their written notes of the dragon program, wanting to have some positive suggestion with which to comfort the young people. "But Mariah did find you with no trouble that day, and you were at our house in minutes. So it can't have taken her very long to do it."

"No, it didn't," Sorka said thoughtfully. She looked around the circle of fire-lit faces. "Think of how many times we told the dragonets to get us fish for the hatchlings."

"Fish are fish," Peter Semling remarked, absently prodding the sand with a branch.

"Yes, but the dragonets knew which ones the dragons like best," Kathy Duff said. "And it takes them no time at all from the moment we issue the command. They just wink out and a couple of breaths later they're back with a packtail."

"A couple of breaths," Sean repeated, looking out to the darkness, his stare fixed. "It took more than a couple of breaths for any of our dragons to realize that . . . Marco and Duluth were not coming back. Can we infer from that that it also only takes a couple of breaths for dragons to teleport?"

"Cautiously . . ." Otto held up his finger again.

"Right," Sean went on briskly, "this is what we do tomorrow morning at first light." He reached over and took Peter's stick, and drew a ragged coastline in the sand. "The governor wants us to ferry stuff out of Landing. Dave,

Kathy, Tarrie, you've all got gold fire-lizards. You make the first run. When you get to the tower, send your fire-lizards back here to me and Sorka. Bay, do you and Pol have to be anywhere else tomorrow?"

Bay gave a derisory sniff. "The pair of us are useless until we get our systems going again at Fort Hold. And we have to wait for transport. We'd be delighted to help you, any way we can!"

"We'll time the fire-lizards. Only, we've got to have handsets to do it on the mark."

"Let me scrounge those," Pol offered.

Sean grinned with real humor. "I was hoping you'd volunteer. Lilienkamp wouldn't deny you, would he?"

Pol shook his head emphatically, feeling much better than he had all afternoon, vainly searching for mislaid documentation during the nadir of his grieving.

"Well then, Bay and I will leave you now," Pol said, rising and giving her a helpful hand to her feet. "To scrounge handsets. How many? Ten? We'll meet you here at dawn, then, with handsets." He made a bow to the others, noting that only Bay understood his whimsy. "Yes, at dawn, we'll begin our scientific observations."

"Let's all get some sleep, riders," Sean said. He began to scoop sand over the dying flames.

◆ ◆ ◆

With a handset to his ear, Pol dropped his finger as Bay, Sean, and Sorka set the mark on their wrist timers. Keeping index fingers hovering over the stop pin, they all looked up toward the eastern sky, Bay squinting against the sunglare from the smooth sea.

"Now!" four voices spoke and four fingers moved as a fire-dragonet erupted into the air over their heads, chirping ecstatically.

"Eight seconds again," Pol exclaimed happily.

"Come, Kundi," Sorka said, holding up her arm as a landing spot. Dave Catarel's bronze cheeped, cocking his head as if considering her invitation, but he veered away as Duke, Sorka's bronze, warned him off. "Don't be ugly, Duke."

"Eight seconds," Sean said, admiringly. "That's all it takes them to travel fifty-odd klicks."

"I wonder," Pol mused, tapping his stylus on the clipboard with its encouraging column of figures. "The figure doesn't vary no matter who we send which direction. How long would it take them to go to say, Seminole or the Fort Hold in the north?" He looked with bright inquiry at the others.

Sean began to shake his head dubiously, but Sorka was more enthusiastic.

"My brother, Brian, is working at the fort. Duke knows him as well as he knows me. And I've seen plenty of fax of the place. He'd go to Brian." As if understanding that he was being discussed, Duke circled in to land on Sorka's shoulder. She laughed. "See, he's game!"

"He may come when he's called," Sean said, "but will he go where he's sent? Landing's one thing—they all know it well."

"We can only try and see," Pol remarked firmly. "And this is a good hour to reach Brian at the Ford Hold." He punched the comm unit. "What a boon that the tower's functional. Ah, yes, Pol Nietro speaking. I need an urgent word with Brian Hanrahan . . . I said urgent! This is Pol Nietro. Get him for me! Idiots," he murmured in an aside. " 'Is this call important?' "

Brian was found and was surprised to hear from his sister. "Look, what's this all about? You don't just scream priority around here. I can assure you that Mother's taking good care of Mick. She dotes on him."

His slightly aggrieved voice was clear to the others, and Sorka was taken aback by his uncooperative response. Sean took the handset from her.

"Brian, Sean here. Marco Galliani and his dragon Duluth died yesterday in an unfortunate accident. We're trying to prevent a recurrence. We're only asking for a few minutes of your time. And this is a priority."

"Marco and Duluth?" Brian's tone was chastened. "Jays, we hadn't heard anything. I'm sorry. What can I do?"

"Are you outside? Someplace where you can be easily spotted from the air?"

"Yes, I am. Why?"

"Then tell Sorka exactly where you are. I'm handing you over to her."

"Hell and damnation, Sorka, I'm sorry I dumped on you. So I'm outside. Have you seen the recent fax? Well, I'm approximately twenty meters from the new ramp. At the vet caves. They finally carved us some more headroom, and there's a huge pile of rock about a meter from me and nearly as high. What do I do now?"

"Just stand there. I'm sending Duke to you. When I say 'mark,' set your timer."

"Come on, now, sis," he began in patent disbelief, "you're in Kahrain Cove, aren't you?"

"Brian! For once in your life, don't argue with me."

"All right. I'm ready to mark the time." He still sounded aggrieved.

Sorka held her arm high, ready to pitch Duke into the air. "Go to Brian, Duke. He's at the new place! Here!" She screwed her eyes shut and concentrated on an image of Brian standing on the site he had described. "Go, Duke."

With a startled squawk, Duke launched himself into the air and vanished.

Mark! Sorka cried.

"Hey, I can hear you loud and clear, sister. You don't need to roar. I don't know what good this is going to do. You can't imagine for one minute that a fire-dragonet could possibly—jays!" Brian's voice in her ear faded into astonishment. "I don't bloody believe it. Shit. I forgot to mark time."

"That's all right," Sorka said, nodding her head with delight, "we used your 'jays' to mark!"

Pol was jumping up and down, holding his wrist chrono and shouting, "Eight seconds! *Eight seconds!*"

He grabbed Bay by the waist and danced around her. Sean lifted Sorka from her feet and kissed her soundly while Mariah and Blazer led an augmented fair of fluting fire-dragonets in a dizzy aerial display.

"Eight seconds to the fort, only eight seconds," Pol gasped, reeling to a standstill, Bay clinging to him.

"That doesn't make much sense, does it?" Bay said, panting, one hand on her heaving chest. "The same time to go fifty klicks or nearly three thousand."

"Hey, Sorka," came Brian's plaintive voice. She put the handset to her ear again, mopping the sweat off her forehead against her sleeve. "I really gotta go, only what am I supposed to do with Duke now you've got him here?"

"Tell him to come back to me. And give us the mark when he disappears."

"Sure, right. On the mark, now . . . Duke, find Sorka! Sorka! Find—he's gone. Shit! Mark!"

On the beach at Kahrain Cove, four fingers pressed sweep hands, four pairs of eyes turned westward to the hot afternoon skies, and four voices counted the seconds.

"Six . . . seven . . . eight . . . He did it!"

Their elation had new confidence as Duke, cheeping happily, settled back to Sorka's shoulder and rubbed a cold muzzle against her cheek.

"Well, this has been most satisfying and productive," Bay said, beaming broadly.

"Report it to Emily, will you, Bay?" Sean asked, tucking his hand under Sorka's elbows. "We'd better go do our share of the donk work today."

◆ ◆ ◆

"So the Galliani boy's death proved to be a catalyst?" Paul Benden asked Emily as they conferred that evening by comm unit.

"Pol and Bay are much encouraged," Emily replied, still unaccountably saddened by the tragedy. She was tired, she knew, and while she spoke to Paul, hoping for the consolation of any sort of good news from the northern continent, half her mind was still on things that *had* to be organized.

"Telgar's group has made a tremendous effort, Em. The quarters are magnificent. You wouldn't know you were twenty or thirty feet in solid rock. Cobber and Ozzie have penetrated several hundred feet down on seven tunnels. There's even an eyrie for Ongola's communications equipment, cut high up in the cliff face. This place is big enough to house the entire population of Landing."

"Not everyone wants to live in a hole in the ground, Paul." Emily spoke for herself.

"There are quite a few ground-level caverns, immediate access," he replied soothingly. "You wait. You'll see. And when are you coming over? I've got to put in an appearance at the next Fall or they'll fire me."

"Don't you wish it!"

"Emily." Paul's flippant tone turned serious. "Let Ezra take over for you. He and Jim can liaise on shipments. Others can handle transportation and sled and skimmer maintenance. Pierre should be here to supervise the catering arrangements. He's got the biggest kitchen unit on Pern."

"That would be a welcome change from the largest single barbecue pit! It's the dragons that I worry about, Paul."

"I think they have to sort it out themselves, Emily. From what you reported, I believe they will."

"Thank you, Paul," she replied fervently, heartened by the absolute confidence in his voice. "I'll reserve a seat on the evening sled tomorrow."

◆ ◆ ◆

After the excitement of sending Duke north, directing fire-dragonets back and forth between Kahrain and Landing was anticlimactic, but it helped to pass the tedium of the long journey. On the way back, Sean had the dragonriders practice flying in both close and loose formations and, more importantly, learning how to identify and benefit from the helpful airstreams.

Their campfire that night was bigger, and Pol and Bay slipped into its light to discuss observations about the fire-dragonets and how to apply them to the dragons. There had been no real need for Sean to promote caution as a byword: Marco and Duluth were still very much in everyone's mind. To counter any morbidity, Sean suggested that they get more formation practice the next day, practice that would stand them in good stead during Threadfall.

"If you know where you are in relation to other wing riders, you'll always know where to come back to," he said, stressing the last word.

"Your dragons are so young," Pol went on, seeing the favorable reaction, "in terms of their species. The fire-dragonets do not appear to suffer from degeneration. In other words, they don't age as we do physiologically."

"You mean, they could go on living after we die?" Tarrie asked, amazed. She glanced around toward Porth, a darker bulk against the shadowy vegetation.

"From what we've discerned, yes, Tarrie," Pol replied.

"Our major organs degenerate," Bay went on, "although modern technology can effect either repair or replacement, permitting us long, and useful, life spans."

"So they're not likely to get sick or to ail?" Tarrie brightened at the prospect.

"That's what we *think*," Pol answered, but he held up a warning finger. "But then we haven't *seen* any elderly dragonets."

Sean gave a snort, which Sorka softened with a laugh. "We've really only *our* generation to judge by," she said. "At that, we only get to treat our own, who trust us, and that's usually for scoring or scorching, or an occasional hide lesion. I find it comforting to know that dragons should be as long-lived."

"So long as *we* don't make mistakes," Otto Hegelman said gloomily.

"So, we *don't* make mistakes!" Sean's tone was decisive. "And so that we don't make mistakes, tomorrow let's split up into three sections. Six, six . . . and five. We need three leaders."

Although Sean had left the choice open, he was nominated at once. Dave and Sorka were selected after a minimum of discussion.

Later, when Sean and Sorka had made themselves comfortable on the sand between Faranth and Carenath, she gave him a long hug and kissed his cheek.

"What's that for?"

"Giving up all hope. But Sean, I'm worried."

"Oh?" Sean stroked her hair away from his mouth and inched his left shoulder into a new hollow.

"I think we oughtn't to wait too long before we try to teleport."

"My thoughts entirely, and I'm grateful to Pol and Bay for their comments on dragon longevity. Cheered me up, too."

"So, as long as *we* keep our wits, we'll keep our dragons." She snuggled against him.

"I wish you'd kept your hair long, Sorka," he muttered, pushing another curl out of his mouth. "I didn't eat so much of it then."

"Short hair's easier under a riding helmet," she replied in a sleepy sort of mumble. Then they both slept.

◆   ◆   ◆

Although they could see the diminution of the parcels and plastic-cocooned equipment at Landing, cargo did not move out of Kahrain Cove as quickly.

That second evening, when Sean was helping his wing riders unload, he caught sight of one of the cargo supervisors seated at a makeshift desk peering at the small screen of a portable unit.

"We'll finish off transferring from Landing by tomorrow, Desi," Sean assured the man.

"That's great, Sean, great," Desi said curtly, with a dismissive wave.

"What the hell's the matter, Desi?" Sean asked.

The edge in his voice caused Desi to look up in surprise. "What's the matter? I've got a beachful of stuff to shift and no transport." Desi's face was so contorted with anxiety that Sean's rancor dissolved.

"I thought the big sleds were coming back."

"Only when they're recharged and serviced. I wish they'd mentioned that earlier." Desi's voice rose in a quiver of frustration. "All my schedules . . . gone. What'm I to do, Sean? We'll be under Threadfall again here soon and all that stuff—" He flourished a sweat-grimed rag at the bulk of orange cartons. "—is irreplaceable. If only—" He broke off, but Sean had a good idea what the man had almost said. "You've done great, Sean, great. I really appreciate it. How much did you say is still to be shipped forward?"

"We'll have cleared it tomorrow."

"Look, then, the day after . . ." Desi rubbed at his face again, trying to hide his flush of embarrassment. "Well, I heard from Paul. He wants you riders to start making your way to Seminole, and cross to the north from there. And . . ." Desi screwed up his face again.

"You'd like us to take some of the orange out of danger?" Sean felt resentment welling up again. "Well, I suppose that's better than being good for nothing at all." He strode off before his temper got the better of him.

Faranth and Sorka come, Carenath said in a subdued tone. Sean altered his course to their point of arrival. He could not fool Sorka, but he could work off some of his fury during the unloading.

"All right, what happened?" Sorka said, pulling him to the seaward side of her golden queen, where they were shielded from the other riders, who were still sorting packages into the color-coded areas.

Sean set his fist violently into the palm of his other hand several times before he could put words to the humiliation.

"We're considered nothing but bloody pack animals, donks with wings!" he said finally. He did remember to keep his voice down, though he was seething.

Faranth turned her head around her shoulder, regarding the two riders, hints of red beginning to gleam through the blue of her eyes. Carenath shoved his head over her back. Beyond them, Sean heard the other dragons muttering. The next thing he knew, he and Sorka were surrounded by dragons, and their riders were weaving into the central point.

"Now, see what you've done," Sorka said with a sigh.

"What's the matter, Sean?" Dave asked, squeezing past Polenth.

Sean took a deep breath, burying anger and resentment. If he could not control himself, he could not control others. There were flares of the yellow of alarm in the dragons who looked down at him. He had to quiet them, himself, and the other riders. Sorka was right. He had done something he had better quickly undo.

"We seem to be the only available aerial transportation unit," he said, managing a sort of a smile. "Desi says all the big sleds are grounded until they've been serviced."

"Hey, Sean," Peter Semling protested, jerking his thumb over his shoulder at the masses of material on the beach. "We can't shift all that!"

"No way." Sean made a decisive cut with his hands. "That's not been laid on us. When we've cleared Landing, Paul wants us to fly across to Seminole and make the final crossing north from there. That's okay." He gave a genuinely rueful smile. "But Desi would like us to take some of the irreplaceable stuff with us."

"So long as everyone understands we're not in the freight business," Peter said in an aggrieved tone that echoed Sean's sentiments.

"That's not at issue, Pete," Sean said firmly. "We're coming along as dragonriders, coming along fine. But Desi's caught between a rock and a hard place and he needs us."

"I just wish we were needed for what we're supposed to do," Tarrie remarked.

"Once we've fulfilled our commitment here," Sean said, "we concentrate on that, and that alone. I mean to see us all teleporting by the time we reach Seminole."

"To places we've never seen?" asked the practical Otto.

"No, to the places we've just been. Look on our flight to Seminole as a chance to see the most important stakes in the south," Sean replied in a bracing tone. He was surprised to find himself believing it. "We'll need such reference points to teleport when we're fighting Thread." Sorka's face was glowing with pride as he managed not only to turn around his own anger but to restate the dignity of their future. Above their heads, the yellow was fading from dragon eyes. "I can smell food. I'm hungry. Let's go eat. We've earned it."

"We're going to have to hunt the dragons before we go skiting across the continent," Peter said, jerking his chin toward the animal enclosures.

Sean shook his head, smiling as he remembered Emily's oblique warning. "Can't go to that well twice, Pete. Tomorrow, we'll hunt the critters that got through the roundup in the Landing area." He began to push through the ring of dragons. "Food tomorrow, Carenath," he said, affectionately clouting the bronze as he passed him.

Fish? Carenath queried in a tone that carried dismay.

"Meat. Red meat," Sean said. He laughed when some of the dragons bugled gratefully. "But this time we won't kidnap it for you." Then he put an arm around Sorka and started up the beach to the cooking fires.

◆ ◆ ◆

The next day, as the three wings of dragonriders crossed the Jordan River, they spread out in three different directions, bypassing the ash-covered settlement and heading south and east at low levels.

Faranth says that she has found running meat, Carenath reported to his rider. *Have we?*

Sean had his binoculars trained on a little valley. They were north of the path of the two Threadfalls that had dropped on that area, so there was vegetation to attract grazers.

"Tell her we've hit pay dirt, too."

Not meat? Carenath asked wistfully.

Sean grinned, and slapped his dragon's shoulder. "Yes, meat, by another name. And all you can eat this time," he added as the small mixed herd of sheep and cattle stampeded to escape the danger above them. He signaled to the rest of his wing in the exaggerated arm gestures that they had been rehearsing. Since the dragons could communicate with one another, the riders had chosen not to use handsets. But Sean had retained those Pol had scrounged. Although too valuable to risk dropping from a height, the handsets were too useful to be surrendered. "Land me on that ridge, Carenath. There's enough room there for the others."

Porth says they've enough for all of us, Carenath reported as he touched down gracefully and dipped his shoulder for Sean to dismount.

"Tell Porth we're grateful, but you'd better hurry to catch that lot," Sean advised. The herd was making all possible speed down the valley. He had to shield his face from the gravel and omnipresent ash thrown up by Carenath's abrupt departure. Bright streaks followed the bronze. "Welcome back," Sean said derisively as he distinguished blues and greens among the small colorful fire-lizard bodies following Blazer as she led the way.

The rest of his wing soon joined him. Even Nora Sejby managed a creditable landing on Tenneth; she was improving all the time. He worried more about Catherine Radelin-Doyle: she had not giggled with Singlath since the tragedy. Nyassa, Otto, and Jerry Mercer completed his wing. Once their dragons followed the hunt, Sean turned his glasses on Carenath in time to see the bronze swoop and grab a steer neatly without slowing his forward motion.

"Nice catch, Carenath!" Sean passed the binoculars to Nyassa to check on Milath.

"Seemed to me there were quite a lot of cattle in that bunch," Jerry said, pulling off his helmet and ruffling his sweat-damp hair. "What'll happen to them?"

Sean shrugged. "The best stock went north. These'll survive, or they won't."

"Sean, look who's come to dinner!" Nyassa pointed northward at the unmistakable outline of five wherries. "Go to it!" she added as she caught a glimpse of fire-dragonets launching an attack on the intruders. "Wait your turn!"

"I brought some lunch," Catherine said, twisting out of her backpack. "We might as well take a meal break, too."

Sean called a halt to the hunt when each dragon had consumed two animals. Carenath complained that he had eaten only one big one, so he needed two of the smaller kind. Sean replied that Carenath's belly would be so full that he would be unable to fly, and they still had work to do. The dragons grumbled, Carenath ingenuously remarking that Faranth wanted another meal, too, but Sean was adamant, and the dragons obeyed.

Sean re-formed the wing once they were aloft.

"All right, Carenath," he said, thinking ahead with relief to the last loads at Landing. "Let's get back to the tower as fast as we can and get this over with!"

He raised his arm and dropped it.

The next instant he and Carenath were enveloped in a blackness that was so absolute that Sean was certain his heart had stopped.

I will not panic! he thought fiercely, pushing the memory of Marco and Duluth to the back of his mind. His heart raced, and he was aware of the stunning cold of the black nothingness.

I am here!

Where are we, Carenath? But Sean already knew. They were *between*. He focused intense thoughts on their destination, remembering the curious ash-filtered light around Landing, the shape of the meterology tower, the flatness of the grid beyond it, and the bundles awaiting them there.

We are at the tower, Carenath said, somewhat surprised. And in that instant, they were. Sean cried aloud with relief.

The he went wide-eyed with sudden terror. "Jays! What have I done?" he shrieked. "Where are the others, Carenath? Speak to them!"

They're coming, Carenath replied with the utmost calm and confidence, hovering above the tower.

Before Sean's unbelieving eyes, his wing suddenly materialized behind him, still in formation.

"Land, Carenath, please, before I fall off you," Sean said in a whisper made weak by the unutterable relief he felt.

As the others circled in to land, Sean remained seated on Carenath, reviewing everything, half in wonder, half in remembered terror at the unthinkable risk that had just been unaccountably survived.

"Keeeeyoooo!" Nyassa's yodel of triumph brought him up short. She was swinging her riding helmet above her head as Milath landed beside Carenath. Catherine and Singlath came in on the other side, Jerry Mercer and Manooth beyond them, and Otto and Shoth beside Tenneth and Nora.

"Hip, hip, hooray!" Jerry led the cheer while Sean stared at them, not knowing what to say.

It was easy, you know. You thought me where to go, and I went. You did tell me to go as fast as possible. Carenath's tone was mildly reproving.

"If that is all there is to it, what took us so long?" Otto asked.

"Anyone got a spare pair of pants?" Nora ask plaintively. "I was so scared I wet myself. But we did it!"

Catherine giggled. The sound brought Sean to his senses, and he allowed himself to smile.

"We were ready to try!" he said, shrugging nonchalantly as he unbuckled his riding straps. Then he realized that he, too, would need to find a clean pair of pants.

CHAPTER

XIX

"I said, we'll maintain silence about Emily's condition," Paul said sternly, glaring at Ongola, Ezra Keroon, and the scowling Joel Lilienkamp. He did *not* want Lilienkamp taking book on whether or not Emily Boll would recover from her multiple fractures. He moderated his expression as his eyes rested on the bent head of Fulmar Stone, who kept pulling with agitated fingers at a wad of grease-stained rag. "As far as Fort Hold is concerned, she's resting comfortably. That is the truth, according to the doctor and all the support systems monitoring her condition. For outside inquiries, she's busy—shunt the call to Ezra."

Abruptly Paul pushed himself to his feet and began to pace his new office, the first apartment on the level above the Great Hall. Its windows gave an unimpeded view of the ordered rows of cargo and supplies that filled that end of the valley. Eventually all those goods would be stored in the vast subterranean caverns of Fort. So much had to be done, and he sorely missed Emily's supportive presence.

He caught himself fingering the prosthetic fingers and jammed both hands into his pockets. His position had required him to contain his distress in order to avoid alarming people already under considerable tension. But before his close and trusted friends, he could give vent to the anxieties that they all shared.

The disastrous failure of the big sled's gyros and its subsequent crash had been visible to the inhabitants of Fort Hold, but few had known that the governor had been a passenger that night. They could be honest about the severity of the pilot's injuries, for he would recover easily from two broken arms and numerous lacerations. None of the other passengers had been severely hurt, and those who rescued the injured had not recognized Emily, her face bloodied by the head wound. At least until she was convalescing, Paul would not allow the facts to be common knowledge. Following so closely after the exodus from Landing, that crash, with the loss of some irreplaceable medical supplies as well as the sled itself, had to be minimized to sustain morale.

"Pierre agrees," Paul went on. He could feel the resistance from the others, the unspoken opinion that suppression would undermine his credibility. "Even insists on it. It's what Emily would want." In his pacing, Paul inadvertently glanced out the deep-set window and averted his eyes from the view of the scar that the sled had gouged two days ago. "Ezra, get someone to smooth that over, will you? I see it every time I look out the window."

Ezra murmured a response and made a note.

"How long can we expect Emily's state to be kept a secret?" Ongola asked, his face craven with new worry lines.

"As long as we have to, dammit, Ongola! We can at least spare people one more worry, especially when we haven't got a positive prognosis." Paul drew in a deep breath. "The head wound wasn't serious—no skull fracture— but it was a while before she was removed from the sled. The trauma wasn't treated quickly enough, and we don't have the sophisticated equipment to relieve the shock of multiple fracture. She must be given time and rest. Fulmar—" Paul swung to the engineer. "There will be a transport sled ready to go south today, won't there? I can't keep stalling Desi."

"All that orange-coded stuff is irreplaceable," Joel added, rearranging himself in the chair. "Not that we've got half the stuff moved inside here yet, but it'd be a sight more protectable in our front yard then on some frigging beach half a world away. Otherwise, you're going to have to send Keroon back for it. And I'll figure out a new schedule of priorities. You couldn't make that two sleds to go, could you, Fulmar?"

Fulmar looked up at him with eyes so reddened by strain and grief that even the doughty storesman recoiled in dismay. He knew that Stone's crews had been working impossible hours to service the big transport sleds. Joel would admit only to himself that more of the blame of that crash could be attributed to Stores than to maintenance. But what could he do with one emergency after another dumping on him?

"Whenever you can, Fulmar," Joel said in a gentler tone. "Whenever they're ready." He walked out of the room without a backward glance.

"We're doing our best, Admiral," Fulmar said wearily, struggling to his feet. He looked at the rag in his hands, perplexed to see it in tatters, and then jammed it into his hip pocket.

"I know, man, I know." Placing his arm across Fulmar's hunched shoulders, Paul guided the man to the door, giving him a final appreciative squeeze. "In all that spare time you have, Fulmar, run up a list of servicing dates on the smaller craft. I've got to know how many I'll have for this Fall.

"The accident was no one's fault," Paul said, returning to his desk and slumping down into his chair. "There's Fulmar, blaming himself for not insisting on servicing earlier. For that matter, I shouldn't have urged Emily to come north. The cargo was inadequately secured in the cabin. However, gentlemen, it is folly to read more into such an accident than bad timing and a lousy concatenation of circumstances. We evacuated Landing in reasonable order. A place had been prepared for us, and we've got to mobilize enough personnel and machines to fight Thread." He no longer hoped for support from either dragonets or dragons.

◆　◆　◆

"You did *what*?" Sorka cried, her skin blanching then flushing brightly in fury. Faranth, her eyes whirling orange in sympathy with her rider, lowered her head. Carenath bugled alarm.

Sean grabbed Sorka by the arms, obscurely irritated by her reaction. He had managed to get the others to wait until Sorka's wing had landed before broadcasting their feat.

"Look, it wasn't something I planned, Sorka! Jays, it was the last thing in my head. I just told Carenath to get back to Landing as fast as possible. He did!"

It was really very simple, Carenath said modestly. *I've told Faranth. She believes me.* He swiveled his head to cast a reproachful look on Sorka.

"How . . . how . . . did the others know?" Fear returned to shadow her eyes. She ignored the general carry-on about her as Sean's wing cavorted with her riders, babbling the good news and going into specific detail at the top of their lungs.

He told them, Faranth replied, an edge to her tone.

"We've spent two hours figuring that out." Sean smiled, hoping to coax a smile from Sorka. Putting his arm about her shoulders, he drew her back to the others. "I think," he said, choosing his words carefully, "we were all scared shitless by Marco and Duluth dying like that. Now we know, firsthand, why Marco panicked. Sorka, it's like nothing you've ever seen, and you can't feel anything, even your dragon between your legs. Otto called it total sensory deprivation."

It is between, Carenath said in an almost didactic tone. He and Faranth followed their riders back to the mass of netted bundles which would be their final load. The dragons of Sean's wing were sitting on their haunches in a loose circle, occasionally shaking themselves to dislodge windblown ash.

Faranth made a noise low in her throat, which made Sean grin. The golden queen was as skeptical as her rider.

"Can Faranth tell me how far away Dave's wing is?" he asked Sorka.

They are in sight now, Carenath said just as Sorka replied, "Faranth says they're in sight now." She pointed northeast. "Polenth says that they hunted well. Meat!" Sorka gave a brief smile, and Sean decided that she was halfway to forgiving him.

There was of course renewed astonishment and rueful congratulations when Dave and his wing riders heard the news.

"Okay then," Sean said, mounting a carton to address them all. "This is what we do, riders. We teleport to Kahrain Cove. We know its aerial aspect as well as we know Landing's. So it's the perfect test. Carenath insists that he told the other dragons where they were going, but I'd prefer that you riders tell your own dragons where to go. I think that has to be as much part of our preflight drill as strapping on and checking the immediate airspace." He grinned at them.

"What're we going to tell *them*?" Dave asked, jerking a thumb in a northerly direction.

"Emily's gone to join the admiral. Pol and Bay were supposed to get the first sled back." Sean paused, looking around again, and then gave Sorka a long look. She nodded slowly in approval. "I think we keep this to ourselves for the time being. We'll spring the finished product on them, fighting-ready dragons! It's one thing to send a fire-lizard north on the strength of fax, but I sure wouldn't want to risk Carenath going someplace *I've* never been." Sean took another deep breath, having gauged the favorable reaction. "Desi said we're to make our way along the coast to Seminole. That'll give us time to practice teleporting between where we are and where we've been. That way we'll know exactly how to get back to any of the major stakes when we need to fight Thread over them."

"Yeah, but the dragons don't flame yet," Peter Semling pointed out.

"There's phosphine-bearing rock all along the coast. We've all watched the fire-lizards chew rock. That's the easiest part of this whole thing," Sean replied dismissively.

"It's one thing to go from one place to another," Jerry began slowly. "We've *done* it now. We go from here—" He stabbed his left index finger. "—to there." He held up his right finger. "And the dragons do the work. But dodging Thread, or a sled—" He broke off.

"Duluth caught Marco off-balance. He panicked." Sean spoke quickly and confidently. "Frankly, Jerry, that place *between* scared me, and I'll lay book the rest of you were scared. But now we know, we adapt. We'll plan emergency evasive tactics." Sean pulled the knife out of his boot cuff and hunkered down. "Most of us have flown sleds or skimmers in Threadfall, so we've seen *how* the junk drops . . . most of the time." He drew a series of long diagonal stripes in the ash. "A rider sees he's on a collision course with Thread . . . here—" He dug his point in. "—and *thinks* a beat forward." He jumped the point ahead. "We'll have to practice skipping like that. It's going to take quick reflexes. We see fire-lizards using such tactics all the time—wink in, wink out—when they're fighting Thread with ground crews. If they can, dragons can!"

The dragons bugled in answer to the challenge, and Sean grinned broadly.

"Right?" Sean's question dared the riders.

"Right!" They all replied enthusiastically, and fists were brandished to show staunch determination.

"Well, then." Sean stood up, bringing his hands together with an audible smack. Ash shifted off his shoulders. "Let's load up and teleport ourselves back to Kahrain."

"What if someone sees us, Sean?" Tarrie asked anxiously.

"What? The flying donks doing what they were designed to do?" he asked sarcastically.

* * *

"Obviously," Paul told the worried pilots, "we're not going to be able to protect as much land with such a depleted aerial coverage."

"Damn it, Admiral," Drake Bonneau said, twisting his face into a frown. "We were supposed to have enough power packs to last fifty years!"

"We did." Joel Lilienkamp jumped to his feet once again. "Under normal usage. They have *not* had what anyone could possibly term normal usage, or even normal maintenance. And don't blame Fulmar Stone and his crew. I don't think they've had a full night's sleep in months. The best mechanics in the world can't make sleds operate on half-charged or badly charged packs." Glaring belligerently around him, he sat down hard, and the chair rocked on the stone floor.

"So it really is a case of taking the greatest care of the sleds and skimmers we have left, or have no aerial vehicles at all in a year?" Drake asked plaintively.

No one answered him immediately.

"That's it, Drake," Paul finally replied. "Burn a swath around your homes and what vegetable crops you've managed to save, keep the home stake clear . . . and thank whatever agency you will that hydroponics are available."

"Where're those dragons? There were eighteen of them," Chaila said.

"Seventeen," Ongola corrected her. "Marco Galliani died at Kahrain, with the brown, Duluth."

"Sorry, forgot that," Chaila murmured. "But where are the others? I thought they were to take up when vehicles failed."

"They're en route from Kahrain," Paul replied.

"Well?" Chaila prompted pointedly.

"The dragons are not yet a year old," Paul said. "According to Wind Blossom"—he noted the subtly disapproving reaction to her name—"Pol, and Bay, the dragons will not be mature enough to be fully . . . . operational . . . for another two or three months."

"In two or three months," someone called out bitterly, "there'll have been between eighteen and twenty more uncontained Falls!"

Fulmar rose, turning to the back of the chamber. "We will have three completely reconditioned sleds back on line in three weeks."

"I heard there were more creatures hatched," Drake said. "Is that true, Admiral?"

"Yes, that's true."

"Are *they* any good?"

"Six more dragons," Paul said, more heartily than he felt.

"Removing six more young people from our defensive strength!"

"Giving us six more potential self-maintaining, self-propagating fighters!" Paul rose to his feet. "Consider the project in the right perspective. We have got to have an aerial defense against Threads. We have bioengineered an indigenous life-form to supply that critical need. They will!" He laced his voice with conviction. "In a few generations—"

"Generations?" The cry elicited angry murmurs from an audience already unnerved by an unpalatable briefing.

"Dragon generations," Paul said, raising his voice over the reactions. "The fertile females are mature enough to reproduce when they're two and a half or three years. A dragon generation is three years. The queens will lay between ten to twenty eggs. We've ten golds from the first Hatching, three from this second one. In five, ten years, we'll have an invincible aerial defense system to combat the intruder."

"Yeah, Admiral, and in a hundred years there won't be any space for humans left on the planet!" The suggestion was met with a ripple of nervous laughter, and Paul smiled, grateful to the anonymous wit.

"It won't come to that," he said, "but we will have a unique defense system, bioengineered to our needs. And useful in other ways. Desi tells me the dragonriders have been delivering supplies to the stakes as they make their way here to Fort. Meanwhile, you have your orders."

Paul Benden rose and left quickly, Ongola right behind him.

"Damn it, Ongola, where the hell are they?" Paul exclaimed when they were alone.

"They check in every morning. Their progress is good. We can't ask more of an immature species. I heard Bay tell you that she and Pol both worried that the dragons had been dangerously extended during the evacuation."

Paul sighed. "Not that there is any other way for them to get here, with the transport situation." He started down the winding iron stairs that went from the executive level to the underground laboratory complex. "Wind Blossom's staff has to be reassigned. We don't have time, personnel, or resources for further experimentation no matter what she says."

"She's going to want to appeal to Emily!" Ongola replied.

"Let's devoutly hope that she can! Any news from Jim this morning?" Paul had reached the state of mind at which he was so saturated with bad news that he did not feel additional blows so keenly. The previous day's news, that Jim Keroon's convoy, sailing past Boca, had been caught in a sudden tropical storm that capsized nine craft, had seemed almost inconsequential.

"He reports no loss of life," Ongola said reassuringly, "and all but two of the boats have been refloated and can be repaired. The dolphins are recovering cargo. There is some heavy stuff, though, that divers will have to locate. Fortunately, they were in shallow water, and the storm didn't last long." Ongola hesitated.

"Well, let me have it," Paul said, pausing on a landing.

"There were no manifests, so there's no way of checking that they've recovered everything."

Paul regarded Ongola stolidly. "Does he have any idea how long that's going to hold him up?" Ongola shook his head. "All the more reason, then, to reassign Wind Blossom's personnel," Paul said then. "When that's done, I'll have a word with Jim. It's incredible that he's got such an ill-assorted flotilla as far as he has! Through fog, Fall, and storm!"

Ongola agreed fervently.

◆ ◆ ◆

While Carenath concentrated very carefully on chewing, Sean stood slightly to one side trying not to be anxious. Fire-dragonets flitted around the dragons, chirping what was obviously encouragement. Duke and some of the other bronzes had found pebbles that they masticated in demonstration.

The dragons and their riders had located the necessary phosphine-bearing rock on an upland plateau halfway between the Malay River and Sadrid. Over the past few days, the confidence of the riders had improved as time and again they were able to teleport to and from given landmarks. Otto Hegelman had suggested that each rider keep a log, noting down reference points for later identifications. The notion had been enthusiastically adopted, although it was immediately necessary for them to request writing materials at the Malay River Stake. They had been surprised to find only children there, with Phas Radamanth's sixteen-year-old daughter in charge.

"Everyone's out fighting Thread, you know," she said, cocking her head at them in what Tarrie later said was pure insolence.

"Desi gave us supplies for you," Sean replied, stifling his resentment of her implied criticism and the current menial status of dragonriders. He gestured for Jerry and Otto to bring the cargo net into the house. "Would you have any notebooks we could have?"

"What for?"

"We're doing a coastline survey," Otto said pompously.

The girl looked surprised, then her face relaxed into a less antagonistic expression. "I guess so. There's all that sort of stuff in the schoolroom over there. Who has time for lessons these days?"

"You're most kind," Jerry said, giving her a quick bow and a broad grin as they withdrew.

The incident had reinforced the riders' determination to accomplish their purpose during their westward journey.

"It isn't as if you can chew for him, Sean," Sorka said, holding out another piece to Faranth. "How much do they need to eat?"

"Who knows how much stoking it takes to start a dragon's fires?" Tarrie sang out cheerfully. "I'd say this—" She hefted the stone in her hand. "—is comparable to the pebble-size I used to feed my gold dragonet. Isn't it, Porth?"

The queen obediently lowered her head and took the offering.

"The dragonets chew at least a handful before they can flame," Dave Catarel said, but he was watching Polenth dubiously as the bronze worked his jaws with the same solemn contemplative look the others had. "Look, Sorka, your fair's setting the example!"

Duke let go a fine long plume of fire, while Blazer took to the air, scolding him.

Just then Porth let out a squawk, her mouth opened, and a green-stained rock fell to the ground, just missing Tarrie's foot. Porth snapped her mouth shut and moaned.

"What did she do?" Dave asked.

"She says she bit her tongue," Tarrie replied. She patted Porth's shoulder sympathetically. "She did, too. Look!" The green ichor on the rock glistened in the sunlight. "Should I look, Sorka? She might have done herself damage."

"What does Porth say?" Sorka asked with professional detachment. She could not recall ever having had to deal with self-inflicted dragonet bites.

"It hurts, and she'll wait until it doesn't before she chews any more rock." Tarrie retrieved the offending piece and put it back in the pile they had gathered.

There was another draconic exclamation of pain, and Nora's Tenneth followed Porth's bad example. Sean and Sorka exchanged worried glances and continued to offer the firestone to their dragons.

Suddenly Polenth burped, and a tiny flame leapt beyond his nose. The startled bronze jumped backward.

"Hey, he did it!" Dave cried proudly. "Phew!" he added, waving the air from his face. "Stand upwind, folks. That stinks."

"Watch it!" Sean leapt sideways as Carenath belched, surprising everyone with a respectable tongue of flame that just missed searing his rider. Overhead the fire-lizards flew in congratulatory circles, alternately chirping or expelling flame, their eyes whirling bright blue with approval.

"Upwind and to one side, riders!" Sean amended. "Try it again, Carenath!" Sean offered a larger chunk.

"Jays, that's awful!" Tarrie said as the wind blew the overpowering stench of the fire-making stone straight into her face. Choking, she ducked around Porth to escape it.

"Where there's fire, there's smell," Jerry quipped. "No, Manooth, turn your head that way!"

Just as the brown dragon obeyed, a blast of flame erupted from his mouth and seared into charcoal one of the scrawny bushes that dotted the plateau.

Jerry pounded his dragon's shoulder in exultation. "You did it! Manooth! Master blaster!"

The others returned to stoking their dragons with renewed enthusiasm. An hour later, all the males had produced flame, but none of the females had; though the golds had chewed and chewed, one after the other they had regurgitated an awful gray pastelike substance.

"As I recall the program," Sean said as the gold riders stood disconsolately about, "the queens aren't mature until they're nearly three. The males are . . . well . . ." Sean cast about for a diplomatic phrase.

"Functional now," Tarrie finished for him, none too pleased.

"Even seven recruits are going to be well received at Fort," Otto said, for once not trying to sound pompous.

Sorka was frowning, though, an expression unusual enough to her that Tarrie inquired as to its cause.

"I was just thinking. Kit Ping was such a traditionalist . . ." Sorka regarded her husband for a long moment, until he ducked his head, unable to maintain the eye contact. "All right, Sean, you know every symbol in that program. Did Kit Ping introduce a gender discrimination?"

"A what?" Tarrie asked. The other queen riders gathered close, while the young men took discreet backward steps.

"A gender inhibition . . . meaning the queens lay eggs, and the other colors fight!" Sorka was disgusted.

"It may just be that the queens aren't mature enough yet," Sean said, temporizing. "I haven't been able to figure out some of Kit Ping's equations. Maybe the flame production is a mature ability. I don't know why the queens all barfed. We'll have to ask Pol and Bay when we get to Fort. But I tell you what, there's no reason you girls can't use flamethrowers. With wands a bit longer, you wouldn't singe your dragon by mistake."

His suggestion did much to mollify the queen riders for the time being, but Sean hoped fervently that Pol and Bay could give a more acceptable verdict. Seventeen dragons made a more impressive display than seven. And he was determined to impress when the dragonriders flew into Fort Hold. The only burdens dragons should ever carry again were their riders and firestone!

• • •

"Actually, Paul," Telgar said, glancing at Ozzie and Cobber, "those photophobes of Wind Blossom's have proved to be extremely useful in subterranean explorations. Their instinct for hidden dangers—pitfalls, in fact, and blind tunnels—is infallible." The geologist gave one of his humorless smiles. "I'd like to keep them now that Wind Blossom has abandoned them, so to speak." Telgar turned to Pol and Bay.

"It's a relief to know they've some use," Pol said, sighing heavily. Both he and his wife had tried to reason with the indignant Wind Blossom when she had been requested to suspend the dragon program. Though she maintained that the emergency transfer from Landing to Fort had damaged many of the eggs in the clutch she had manipulated, Pol and Bay had seen the autopsy reports and knew that claim to be spurious. They had been lucky to hatch six live creatures.

"Once they get to trust you, they're quite harmless," Telgar went on. "Cara adores the latest hatchling, and it won't let her out of its sight unless she leaves the Hold." Again he displayed his mirthless smile. "Keeps watch at her door by night."

"We can't have uncontrolled breeding of those creatures," Paul said quickly.

"We'll see to that, Admiral," Ozzie said solemnly, "but they're right useful little buggers."

"Strong, too. Carry more'n they weigh themselves out of the mines," Cobber added.

"All right, all right. Just limit the breeding."

"Eat anything," Ozzie added for good measure. "Anything. So they keep a place clean."

Paul continued to nod agreement. "I just want any further propagation cleared with Pol and Bay for the biology department."

"We're delighted, I assure you," Bay said. "I didn't approve of them, but I also cannot approve summary termination of any living creature which can be useful."

Telgar rose abruptly, and Bay, wondering if her words had reminded him of Sallah's death, mentally chastised herself for not thinking before she spoke. Ozzie and Cobber sprang to their feet, as well.

"Now that you've finally finished mapping the Fort Hold complex," Paul said, deftly filling the awkward moment, "what are your plans, Telgar?"

A flash of enthusiasm briefly lightened the geologist's face. "The probe reports indicated ore deposits in the Western Range that should be assayed as an alternative to power-costly haulage from Karachi Camp. Best to have resources close to hand." Telgar inclined his head in an abrupt farewell and then strode from the room, Ozzie and Cobber mumbling something suitable as they followed him.

"How that man has changed!" Bay said softly, her round face sad.

Paul observed a respectful silence. "I think we all have, Bay. Now, is anything to be done about Wind Blossom's intransigence?"

"Nothing until she has an interview with Emily herself," Pol said, his expression neutral. Of necessity, the two scientists had been informed of the governor's true condition, which, twelve days after the accident, remained virtually unchanged.

"I don't know why she won't accept your decision, Paul," Bay said, showing some agitation.

"Tom Patrick says Wind Blossom chooses to distrust the male half of this leadership." Paul grinned. Actually he did find the situation ludicrous, but since Wind Blossom had immured herself in her quarters until she "had a fair hearing," he had grasped the opportunity to transfer personnel to more productive employment. Most of them had been grateful. "You will, of course, continue to monitor the new dragon hatchlings."

"Of course. What's the latest word from Sean and the others?" Pol asked, a trifle anxious. He and Bay had discussed their continued absence, beginning to wonder if it was deliberate. They both knew that Sean resented the dragonriders' messenger status. But what else could he expect? Everyone had to do what he could. Pol and Bay themselves were not exactly inspired by Kwan Marceau's project to monitor the grubs from the grass plot at Calusa, but that was where they could perform a useful service.

"They should be here soon." Paul's voice and expression were neutral. "When does Kwan anticipate a northern trial on those worms of his?"

"More grub than worm," Pol said didactically. "Sufficient have been propagated for a ground test."

"That's good news indeed," Paul said heartily, rising to his feet. "Remember, tomorrow won't be a good day for any kind of test!"

Pol and Bay exchanged looks. "Is it true, Admiral," Pol asked, "that you're not going to fly the full Fall across the mountains?"

"That's right, Pol. We have neither the personnel, the power, nor the sleds to do more than protect the immediate area. So, if those grubs are of any assistance, we will all be grateful to you."

When they had left, Paul sank back down in his chair, swiveling to look out the window at the starlit night. The northern climate was colder than that of the south, but the crisp air made the now-familiar star patterns crystal clear. Sometimes he could almost imagine that he was back in space again. He sighed heavily and picked up the terminal. He had to find some vestige of hope in that depressing inventory Joel had submitted.

If they were extremely careful to use sleds and skimmers on only the most critical errands, they might just last out Pern's current pass through the Oort cloud matter. But when it came around again, what would they do? Paul winced as he remembered the arrogance of Ted Tubberman in preempting the dispatch of the homing device. Had the man known how to activate it properly? Ironic, that! Would it be received? Acted upon? With the help of the technological society they had foresworn, his descendants could survive. Did he want them to? Had they any other choice? With adequate technology, the problem of Thread could possibly be solved. So far, ingenuity and natural resources had failed miserably.

Fire-breathing dragons, indeed! A ridiculous concept, straight out of folk tales. And yet . . .

Resolutely Paul began to scroll out the stark facts and figures of the colony's dwindling supplies.

◆ ◆ ◆

"Tarrie!" Peter Chernoff came rushing to greet his sister from the cavernous barn set on the east edge of the Seminole Stake headquarters. A tall young man, he was able to look down at the riders who were surrounding him. "Say, you guys, where have you all been?"

"We've been reporting in to Fort every day," Sean said, surprised.

"I made yesterday's report and even spoke to brother Jake," Tarrie added, her expression anxious. "What's the matter, Petey?"

Reluctant to explain, Peter stamped his feet as he hedged and hawed. "Things are getting tougher. We're not to fly anything anywhere that isn't a priority number one top emergency."

"So that's why we saw so much Thread damage," Otto said, shocked.

Peter nodded solemnly. "And there's Fall at Fort Hold today, and they'll have to sit it out."

"Without any attempt . . ." Dave Catarel was appalled.

"Transporting Landing to the north put too big a strain on sled and power packs." Peter peered down at them, judging their reaction. "And the governor was injured, you know. No one's seen her in weeks."

"Oh, no," Sorka said, leaning into Sean for comfort. Nora Sejby began to weep softly.

Peter gave another of his solemn nods. "It's pretty bad. Pretty bad."

Suddenly everyone was demanding news of his or her own kin, and Peter did his best to answer when he could. "Look, guys, I don't sit on the comm unit all the time. The word is out to sit tight and keep the home stake as clear as possible with ground crews. There's plenty of HNO_3, and it's easy to maintain tanks and wands."

"But not the land," Sean said, raising his voice authoritatively. The babble died abruptly, and his riders looked to him. "There's Thread at Fort today, you said. When?"

"Right now!" Peter replied. "Well, it starts out over the bay—"

"And you have throwers here? Ten of 'em that we could use?" Sean asked eagerly.

"Use? Well, you'd have to ask Cos, and he's not here right now. And what do you need ten throwers for?"

Grinning, Sean turned with a flourish of his hand to indicate the gold riders. "The girls need them to fight Thread! And we've got to work fast to be ready!"

"Whaddya mean?" Peter was dumbfounded. "The Fall's started. You wouldn't even make it out across the sea before it's over. And you're supposed to get in touch with Fort the moment you get here!"

"Peter, be a good lad, don't argue. Show the girls where the throwers are kept and let me see the latest fax of Fort Hold. Or better, the Fort harbor I heard they built. Dragons are a lot faster than that fleet Jim Keroon's shepherding. They haven't passed the Delta West Head yet."

Sean gave Peter no time to think or protest. He sent Otto to run off copies of the installation at the mouth of the Fort Hold River. Tarrie chivvied

her brother into showing them where the flamethrowers were kept and helping the girls check out the tanks. In a flurry of golden wings, the queens
landed at that storehouse and permitted Sean, Dave, and Shih to secure additional tanks to their backs. Sean shouted directions to Jerry and Peter Semling to check the cargo nets of firestone on the browns and bronzes. Peter
Chernoff went from one rider to another, pleading with them to stop. What
was he to do? How was he to explain all this? When would they bring all this
equipment back? They could not leave Seminole defenseless.

Then all the frenzied preparations were completed, and the bronze and
brown dragons had chewed as much firestone as they could swallow.

"Check straps!" Sean roared. He was developing quite a powerful bellow.
Of course, he did not need to shout, as all the dragons were listening to
Carenath, but it served to release adrenaline into his system, and it helped to
encourage those who would soon follow him into danger.

"Checked!" was the prompt response.

"Do we know where we're going?" Setting the example himself, he spread
out the fluttering fax for one last long look at the seafront installation with
its wharf and the metal unloading crane that looked like an awkward alien
species hunched high over the metal beams that had once been part of a
space ship.

"We know!"

"Check your airspace?" He turned his head to the left and the right of
Carenath, who was vibrating in his eagerness to jump off.

"Checked!"

"Remember to skip! Let's go!"

Rising up from Carenath's neck as far as the riding straps would permit,
Sean raised his arm high, rotated his hand, and then dropped it: the signal to
spring.

Seventeen dragons launched themselves skyward, arrowing upward in
the bright tropical sky in two V formations. Then, as a bewildered and incredulous Peter Chernoff watched, the Vs disappeared.

Mouth open, Peter stared for one more long moment. Then he turned
on his heel, raced to the office, and launched himself at the comm unit.
"Fort, this is Seminole. Fort, do you copy? Only you won't."

"Peter, is that you?" his brother Jake asked.

"Tarrie was here, but she left, with a flamethrower."

"Get a hold of yourself, Pete. You're not making any sense."

"They all came. They took our flamethrowers and half the tanks and
left. All of them. All at once."

"Peter, calm down and make sense."

"How can I make sense when I don't believe what I saw anyhow!"

"Who was there? Tarrie and who else?"

"Them. The ones who ride dragons. They've gone to Fort. To fight Thread!"

◆   ◆   ◆

Paul picked up the comm unit. Any occupation was preferable to sitting like a barnacle on a hull in a shuttered room while a voracious organism rained down outside.

"Admiral?" Excitement tingled through Ongola's single word. "We've had word that the dragonriders are on their way here."

"Sean and his group?" Paul wondered why that would excite Ongola. "When did they start?"

"Whenever they started, sir, they're already here." Paul wondered if disappointment had got the better of his imperturbable second-in-command, for he could swear the man was laughing. "The seaport asks should they join the aerial defense of the harbor? And, Admiral, sir, I've got it on visuals! Our dragons are fighting Thread! I'll patch it in to your screen."

Paul watched as the picture cleared and the focus lengthened to show him the unbelievable vision of tiny flying creatures, undeniably spouting flame from their mouths at the silver rain that fell in a dreadful curtain over the harbor. He had that one view before the picture was interrupted by a sheet of Thread. He waited no longer.

Afterward Paul wondered that he had not broken his neck, going down stone steps three at a time. He ran full pelt across the Great Hall and down the metal stairway leading to the garage where the sleds and skimmers were stored. Fulmar and one mechanic were bent over a gyro, and stared in surprise at him.

"You there, get the doors open. Fulmar, you'd better come with me. They may need help." He all but fell into the nearest sled, fumbling with the comm unit. "Ongola, tell Emily and Pol and Bay that their protégés have made it. Record this, by all that's holy, get as much of this on film as you can."

Paul had the sled motor turning over before Fulmar had shut the canopy. He slipped the sled under the door before it was fully open, a maneuver he would have reamed anyone else for attempting, and then, turning on the power, he made an arrow ascent straight up out of the valley. Emerging from the shelter of the cliffs of Fort, he could see the ominous line of Thread.

"Admiral, have you gone mad?" Fulmar asked.

"Use the screen, high magnification. Hell, you don't need it, Fulmar, you can see it with your bare eyeballs!" Paul pointed wildly. "See. Flame. See the bursts. I count fourteen, fifteen emissions. The dragons are fighting Thread!"

◆ ◆ ◆

It was frightening, Sean thought. It was wonderful! It was the finest moment in his life, and he was scared stiff. They had all emerged right on target, just above the harbor, dragon-lengths ahead of the Fall.

Carenath started flaming instantly, and then skipped as they were about to plow through a second tangle of the stuff.

Are the others all right? Sean anxiously asked Carenath as they slipped back into real space.

Flaming well and skipping properly, Carenath assured him with calm dignity, veering slightly to flame again, turning his head from side to side, searing his way through Thread.

Sean glanced around and saw the rest of his wing following in the step formation they had adopted from Kenjo's sled tactics. That gave them the widest possible range of destruction. Even as Sean looked, he saw Jerry and Manooth wink out and back in again, neatly escaping. Then he and Carenath skipped.

A thousand feet below them, he caught a glimpse of Sorka's wing of five and, following that formation, Tarrie leading the remaining queens.

More! Carenath said imperiously, arrowing upward in a trough between Thread. He turned his head backward, mouth wide open. Sean fumbled for a lump of firestone. This will have to be practiced, he thought. Carenath skipped them out.

Shoth has a wing-score, Carenath announced. *He will continue to fly!*

He'll learn to fly the better for it! Sean retorted.

Then the straps strained at the belt as Carenath seemed to stand on his tail to avoid a stream of Thread which he then followed with flame.

Back in formation! Sean ordered. The last thing they needed was to sear one another. He saw that the others had held their positions as Carenath resumed his.

After that first exhilarating cross of the Threadfall, they all got down to business until flame and evasion became instinctive. Carenath went *between* several times to lose Thread that had wrapped about his wings. Sean locked his jaw against his dragon's pain each time Carenath was scored. By then all the bronzes and browns had received minor injuries. Still they had fought on. The queens constantly encouraged them. Then Faranth reported the arrival of a sled; reported again that ground crews were out in the harbor area, destroying the shells that had made it to the surface. The queen riders had used up the tanks they had taken from Seminole. Sorka was going to get more from the harbor hold.

Faranth asks how long will we fight? Carenath asked.

As long as we have firestone to fight with! Sean replied grimly. He had just taken a faceful of char, and his cheeks stung. In the back of his mind he noted that full face masks would be useful.

Manooth says they have no more firestone! Carenath announced suddenly after a nearly mindless length of fighting time. *Shall they see if there is more at Fort Hold?*

Sean had not realized how far inland their battle had taken them. They were indeed over the imposing ramparts of Fort Hold. He stared in a moment of bewilderment, suddenly very much aware of how he ached from cold and strain. His body felt bruised from the riding straps, his face smarted, and his fingers, toes, and knees were numb.

Tell them to land at Fort! he said. *Thread has moved up into the mountains. We can do no more today!*

Good! Carenath replied with such enthusiasm that Sean forgot his sore cheeks and grinned. He slapped affectionately at his dragon's shoulder as the formation executed a right turn, spiraling down to land.

◆ ◆ ◆

"Emily!" Pierre burst into his wife's room. "Emily, you'll never believe it!"

"Believe what?" she said in the tired voice that seemed all she could muster since the accident. She turned her head on the cushioned back of the support chair and smiled wanly at him.

"They've come! I heard, but I had to see it to believe it myself. The dragons and their riders have all reached Fort. They reached it in triumph! They've actually fought Thread, just as you dreamed they would, as Kit Ping designed them to do!" He caught the hand she lifted, the one part of her that had not been broken in the crash. "All seventeen brave fine young people. And they cut a real swath in the Fall, Paul says." He found himself smiling broadly, tears in his eyes as he saw color flushing across her cheeks, the lift of her chest, and the flash of interest in her eyes. She raised her head, and he rattled on. "Paul watched them flame Thread from the skies. They didn't stay for the entire Fall, of course, part of it was over the sea anyhow, and the rest will fall in the mountains where it can't do much harm.

"Paul said it was the most magnificent thing he's ever seen. Better than the relief at Cygnus. They have a record of it, too, so you can see it later." Pierre bent to kiss her hand. He had tears in his eyes for Emily, and for the valiant young people who had ridden against so terrible a menace in the skies of their wondrous and frightening new world. "Paul's gone down to greet them. A triumphant arrival. My word, but it puts heart in all of us. Everyone is yelling and cheering, and Pol and Bay were weeping, which is something quite unscientific for that pair. I suppose they feel that the dragonriders are their creations. I suppose they're right, don't you agree?"

Emily struggled in the support chair, her fingers clutching at him. "Help me to the window, Pierre? I must see them. I must see them for myself!"

◆ ◆ ◆

Most of the inhabitants of Fort Hold turned out to greet them, waving impromptu banners of bright cloth and shouting tumultuously as the dragons backwinged to land on the open field, where here and there ground crews had gotten rid of what Thread had escaped the dragons' fire. The crowd surged forward, mobbing the individual riders, everyone eager to touch a dragon, ignoring at first the riders' strident appeals for something to ease Thread-pierced wings and scored hide.

Gratefully Sean saw a skimmer hovering, and heard the loud-spoken orders to give the dragons room, and let the medics in.

The hubbub subsided a decibel or two. The crowds parted, allowing the medical teams access, giving the dragonriders space to dismount, and whispering sympathetically when the cheering had died down enough so that the dragons could be heard whimpering in pain. Some of those gathered around Carenath eagerly helped Sean doctor him.

Is everyone here to see us? Carenath asked shyly. The bronze turned his left wing so that Sean could reach a particularly wide score and sighed in audible relief as anesthetic cream was slathered on.

"I don't know how we got so lucky," Sean muttered to himself when he was certain that all Carenath's injuries had been attended to. He looked around him, checking to see that all the other dragons had been treated. Sorka gave him a thumbs-up signal and grinned at him, her face smeared with blood and soot. He returned her sign with both fists. "Sheer fluke we got out of that with just sears and scores. We didn't even know what we were doing. Blind luck!" His mind roiled with ways to avoid any sort of scoring and ideas for drills to improve how much Thread a single breath could char. Their fight had been, after all, only the first, brief skirmish in a long, long war.

"Hey, Sean, you need some, too," one of the medics said, pulling off his helmet to anoint his cheeks. "Got to get you looking spruce. The admiral's waiting!"

As if her words were a cue, a murmurous silence fell over the plain. The riders converged together and moved forward to the foot of the ramp where Paul Benden, in the full uniform of a fleet admiral, with Ongola and Ezra Keroon similarly attired flanking him, awaited the seventeen young heroes.

In step, the dragonriders walked forward, past people grinning foolishly in their pride. Sean recognized many faces: Pol and Bay looking about to burst with pride; Telgar, tears streaming down his cheeks, Ozzie and Cobber on either side of him; Cherry Duff upheld by two sons, her black eyes gleaming with joy. He caught sight of the Hanrahans, Mairi holding up his small son to see the pageantry. There was no sign of Governor Emily Boll, and Sean felt his heart contract. What Peter Chernoff had said was true, then. This moment would not be the same without her.

They reached the ramp, and somehow the queen riders had dropped a step behind the others and Sean stood in the center. When they halted, he took a step forward and saluted. It seemed the correct thing to do. Admiral Benden, tears in his eyes, proudly returned the salute.

"Admiral Benden, sir," said Sean, rider of bronze Carenath, "may I present the Dragonriders of Pern?"

Dragonseye

This book is most respectfully
dedicated to
Dieter Clissmann,
who sorts out my various computers
and never fails to answer my pleas for *HELP!*

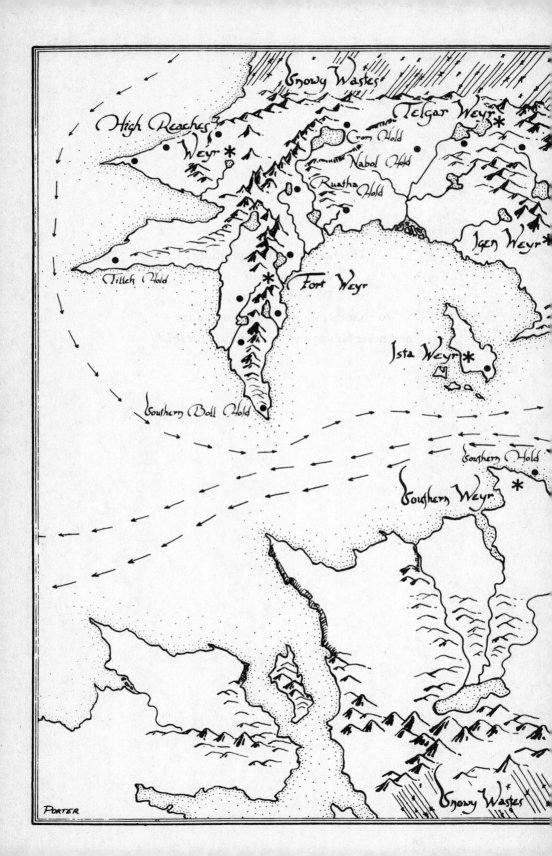

Snowy Wastes

High Reaches
Weyr *

Telgar Weyr *

Crom Hold

Nabol Hold

Ruatha Hold

Igen Weyr *

Tillek Hold

Fort Weyr *

Ista Weyr *

Southern Boll Hold

Southern Hold

Southern Weyr *

Snowy Wastes

PORTER

Benden Weyr

Bitra
Hold

Keroon Hold

Nerat Hold

N
W   E
S

Southern   Current

Cove Hold

Pern

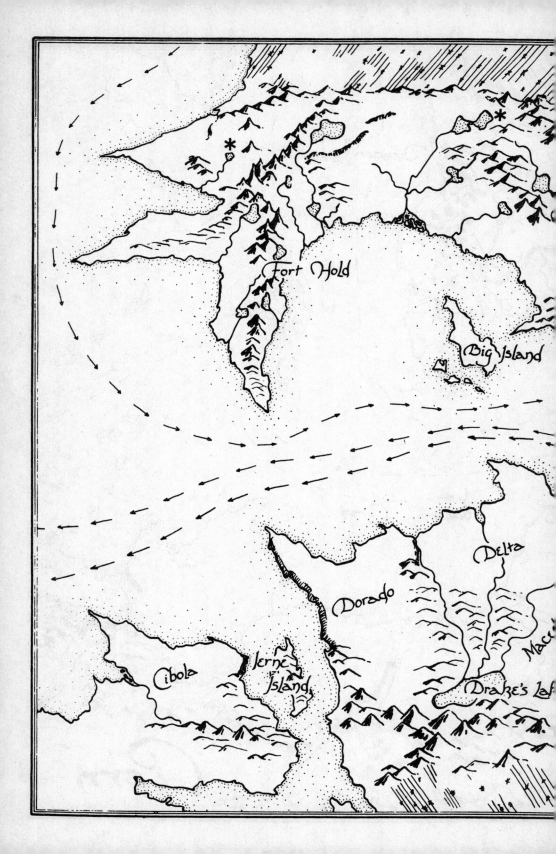

THREADFALLS—TERRITORY COVERED

FIRST *dangerous* FALL: 4

Starts over Jordan Province

Hits	*Monaco Bay*	TZ14–TZ11
	Landing	22S–48S
	Oslo Landing	
	Amsterdam	
	Bavaria	
	Milan	
	Tuareg Camp Site	

SECOND FALL:

Double Hit 5	TZ11–TZ8
Macedonia	2N–30S

Oversea until end

Hits *Sadrid*

(*Thessaly & Roma* warned)

Second wave falls over unoccupied

Bordeaux—unexpectedly

THIRD FALL:

Cathay Province: 6	TZ11–TZ8
	19A–49S

Clips edge of *Malay River*

Mexico on *Maori Lake—stops mid-lake*

FOURTH FALL:

Double Fall: 7	TZ42–TZ8

Araby to Barrier Range: observed

Sea at Equator TZ8–TZ5: observed

FIFTH FALL:

A Baddie: 8	TZ8–5
	20S–485

Macedonia—Dorado

Drake's Lake

Yukon

Narrowly misses *Suweto*

Smack on *Karachi* Camp

SIXTH FALL: Double Hit: 9. Ends just on edge
of Kahrain
TZ13 at sea—observed
Hits Cathay, *Maori Lake* again   TZ8-d.o.

SEVENTH FALL: Double Hit: 10
Jordan—hits TZ14–13.30S-river
Hits *Cardiff,* southern edge of Landing
Calusa & Bordeaux   TZ5–2, 20S–485
Dorado—hits *Seminole* & just misses *Ierne*

EIGHTH FALL: Double hit—11, just tip of Kah-
rain unoccupied end of *Karachi*
Camp—mountains
Longwood area of *Ierne*

NINTH FALL: Kahrain-Cathay—12   TZ13–10/
                                           15S–44S
Paradise River right in the centre

TENTH FALL: Double Hit—13   TZ13–11.50
                                       TZ10–7

Kahrain & Delta
    Killarney (unoccupied)
    Boca River

ELEVENTH FALL: 14—Sea and *Cathay*   TZ10–7
Just misses *Malay River*
Tips southeast edge of *Thessaly*

TWELFTH FALL: 15—Double   TZ10–7
Araby/Cathay
Just misses *Maori Lake*
Clips into *Seminole* East

The Finger points
To an Eye blood-red.
Alert the Weyrs
To sear the Thread.

◆

from
Dragonflight

$\mathcal{R}$ukbat, in the Sagittarian sector, was a golden G-type star. It had five planets, two asteroid belts, and a stray planet it had attracted and held in recent millennia. When men first settled on Rukbat's third planet and called it Pern, they had taken little notice of the stranger planet, swinging around its adopted primary in a wildly erratic orbit—until the desperate path of the wanderer brought it close to its stepsister at perihelion.

When such aspects were harmonious, and not distorted by conjunctions with other planets in the system, the wanderer brought in a life form that sought to bridge the space gap to the more temperate and hospitable planet.

The initial losses the colonists suffered from the voracious mycorrhizoid organism that fell on them were staggering. They had divorced themselves from their home planet, Earth, and had already cannibalized the colony ships, the *Yokohama*, the *Bahrain*, and the *Buenos Aires*, so they would have to improvise with what they had. Their first need was an aerial defense against the Thread, as they named this menace. Using highly sophisticated bioengineering techniques, they developed a specialized variant of a Pernese life form which had two unusual, and useful, characteristics: the so-called fire-lizards could digest a phosphine-bearing rock in one of their two stomachs and, belching forth the resultant gas, create a fiery breath which reduced Thread to harmless char; and they were able both to teleport and to share an empathy that allowed limited understanding with humans. The bioengineered "dragons"—so called because they resembled the Earth's mythical creatures—were paired at hatching with an empathic human, forming a symbiotic relationship of unusual depth and mutual respect.

The colonists moved to the Northern Continent to seek shelter from the insidious Thread in the cave systems, new homes that they called "Holds." The dragons and their riders came, too, housing themselves in old volcanic craters: Weyrs.

The First Pass of Thread lasted nearly fifty years, and what scientific information the colonists were able to gather indicated that Thread would be a cyclic problem, occurring every 250 years as the path of the wanderer once again approached Pern.

During this interval, the dragons multiplied and each successive generation became a little larger than the last, although optimum level would take many, many more generations to reach. And the humans spread out across the Northern Continent, creating holds to live in, and halls in which to train young people in skills and professions. Sometimes folks even forgot that they lived on a threatened planet.

However, in both Holds and Weyrs, there were masses of reports, journals, maps, and charts to remind the Lords and Weyrleaders of the problem; and much advice to assist their descendants when next the rogue planet approached Pern and how to prepare for the incursion.

This is what happened 257 years later.

Early Autumn at Fort's Gather

Dragons in squadrons wove, and interwove, sky trails, diving and climbing in wings, each precisely separated by the minimum safety distance so that occasionally the watchers thought they saw an uninterrupted line of dragons as the close order drill continued.

The skies above Fort Hold, the oldest of the human settlements on the Northern Continent, were brilliantly clear on this early autumn day: that special sort of clarity and depth of color that their ancestors in the New England sector of the North American continent would have instantly identified. The sun gleamed on healthy dragon hides and intensified the golden queen dragons who flew at the lowest level, sometimes seeming to touch the tops of the nearby mountains as they circled Fort. It was a sight to behold, and always brought a thrill of pride to those who watched the display: with one or two exceptions.

"Well, that's done for now," said Chalkin, Lord Holder of Bitra, the first to lower his eyes, though the fly-past was not yet over.

He rotated his neck and smoothed the skin where the decorative embroidered border of his best tunic had scratched the skin. Actually, he had had a few heart-stopping moments during some of the maneuvers, but he would never mention that aloud. The dragonriders were far too full of themselves as it was without pandering to their egos and an inflated sense of importance: constantly appearing at his Hold and handing him lists of what hadn't been done and *must* be done before Threadfall. Chalkin snorted. Just how many people were taken in with all this twaddle? The storms last year had been unusually hard, but then that wasn't in itself unexpectable, so why were hard storms supposed to be a prelude to a Pass? Winter meant storms.

And this preoccupation with the volcanoes going off. They did periodically anyway, sort of a natural phenomenon, if he remembered his science orientation correctly. So what if three or four were active right now? That did not necessarily have to do with the proximity of a spatial neighbor! And he was *not* going to require guards to freeze themselves keeping an easterly watch for the damned planet. Especially as every other Hold was also on the alert. So what if it orbited near Pern? That didn't necessarily mean it was close enough to be dangerous, no matter how the ancients had gone on about cyclical incursions.

The dragons were just one more of the settlers' weird experiments, altering an avian species to take the place of the aircraft they had once had. He'd seen the airsled that the Telgar Foundry treasured as an exhibit: a vehicle much more convenient to fly in than aboard a dragon, where one had to endure the black-cold of teleportation. He shuddered. He had no liking for *that* sort of ultimate cold, even if it avoided the fatigue of overland travel. Surely in all those records the College was mustering folks to copy, there were other materials that could be substituted for whatever the ancients had used to power the vehicles. Why hadn't some bright lad found the answer before the last of the airsleds deteriorated completely? Why didn't the brainy ones develop a new type of airworthy vessel? A vessel that didn't expect to be thanked for doing its duty!

He glanced down at the wide roadway where the gather tables and stalls were set up. His were empty: even his gamesters were watching the sight. He'd have a word with them later. They should have been able to keep some customers at the various games of chance, even with the dragonrider display. Surely everyone had seen that by now. Still, the races had gone well and, with every one of the wager-takers *his* operators, he'd've made a tidy profit from his percentage of the bets.

As he made his way back to his seat, he saw that wine chillers had been placed at every table. He rubbed his beringed fingers together in anticipation, the black Istan diamonds flashing as they caught sunlight. The wine was the only reason he had been willing to come to this gathering: and he'd half suspected Hegmon of some prevarication in the matter. An effervescent wine, like the champagne one heard about from old Earth, was to have its debut. And, of course, the food would be marvelous, too, even if the wine should not live up to its advance notice. Paulin, Fort Hold's Lord, had lured one of the best chefs on the continent to his kitchens and the evening meal was sure to be good: if it didn't turn sour in his stomach while he sat through the obligatory meeting afterward. Chalkin had bid for the man's services, but

Chrislee had spurned Bitra's offer, and that refusal had long rankled in Chalkin's mind.

The Bitran Holder mentally ran through possible excuses for leaving right after dinner: one plausible enough to be accepted by the others. This close to putative Threadfall, he had to be careful of alienating the wrong people. If he left *before* the dinner . . . but then he wouldn't have a chance to sample this champagne-style wine, and he was determined to. He'd taken the trouble to go to Hegmon's Benden vineyard, with the clear intention of buying cases of the vintage. But Hegmon had refused to see him. Oh, his eldest son had been apologetic—something about a critical time in the process requiring Hegmon's presence in the caverns—but the upshot was that Chalkin couldn't even get his name put down on the purchase list for the sparkling wine. Since Benden Weyr was likely to get the lion's share of it, Chalkin had to keep in good with the Benden Weyrleaders so that, at the Hatching which was due to occur in another few weeks, he'd be invited and could drink as much of *their* allotment of wines as he could. More than one way to skin a wherry!

He paused to twirl one of the bottles in its ice nest. Almost perfectly chilled. Riders *must* have brought the ice in from the High Reaches for Paulin. Whenever he needed some, he couldn't find a rider willing to do him, Bitra's Lord Holder, such a simple service. Humph. But of course, certain Bloodlines always got preferential treatment. Rank didn't mean as much as it should, that was certain!

He was surreptitiously inspecting the label of a bottle when there was a sudden, startled intake of fearful breaths from the watchers, instantly followed by a wild cheer. Looking up, he saw he just missed some sort of dangerous maneuver . . . Ah, yes, they'd done another midair rescue. He saw a bronze dragon veering from under a blue who was miming a wounded wing: both riders now safely aboard the bronze's neck. Quite likely that Telgar Weyrleader who was such a daredevil.

Cheers were now punctuated with applause and some banging of drums from the bandsmen on their podium down on the wide courtyard that spread out from the steps to the Hold down to the two right-angled annexes. Once again both the infirmary and the Teachers' College were being enlarged, if the scaffolding was a reliable indication. Chalkin snorted, for the buildings were being extended outward, wide open to any Thread that was purportedly supposed to start falling again. They really ought to be consistent! Of course, tunneling into the cliff would take more time than building outside. But too many folks preached one thing and practiced another.

Chalkin grunted to himself, wondering acidly if the architects had got Weyrleader approval for the design. Thread! He snorted again and wished that Paulin, chatting so cozily with the two Benden Holders as he and his wife escorted them back to the head table, would hurry up. He was dying to sample the bubbly white.

Rattling his fingers on the table, he awaited the return of his host and the opening of the tempting bottles in the cooler.

◆ ◆ ◆

K'vin, bronze Charanth's rider, put his lips close to the ear of the young blue rider sitting in front of him.

"Next time wait for my signal!" he said.

P'tero only grinned, giving him a backward glance, his bright blue eyes merry.

"Knew you'd catch me," he bellowed back. "Too many people watching to let me swing and give Weyr secrets away!" Then P'tero waved encouragingly at Ormonth, who was now flying anxiously at Charanth's wing tip. Though unseen from the ground, the safety-tethers still linked the blue rider to his dragon. P'tero unbuckled his end of the straps and they dangled free.

"Lucky you that *I* was looking up just then!" K'vin said so harshly that the brash lad flushed to his ear tips. "Look at the fright you've given Ormonth!" And he gestured toward the blue, his hide flushing in mottled spots from his recent scare.

P'tero yelled something else, which K'vin didn't catch, so he leaned forward, putting his right ear nearer the blue rider's mouth.

"I was in no danger," P'tero repeated. "I used brand-new straps and he watched me braid 'em."

"Hah!" As every rider knew, dragons had gaps in their ability to correlate cause and effect. So Ormonth would scarcely have connected the new straps with his rider's perfect safety.

"Oh, thanks," the rider added as K'vin snapped one of his own straps to P'tero's belt. Not that they would be doing more than landing, but K'vin wished to make a point of safety to P'tero.

While K'vin approved of courage, he did not appreciate recklessness, especially if it endangered a dragon this close to the beginning of Threadfall. Careful supervision had kept his Weyr from losing any dragon partners, and he intended to maintain that record.

Spilling off his blue before K'vin had passed the word was taking a totally unnecessary risk. Fortunately, K'vin had seen P'tero dive. His heart had lurched in his chest, even if he knew P'tero was equipped with the especially heavy and long harness as a fail-safe. Even if he and Charanth had not accurately judged the midair rescue, those long straps would have saved the blue rider from falling to his death. Today's maneuver had been precipitous instead of well-executed. And, if Charanth had not been as adept on the wing, P'tero might be nursing broken ankles or severe bruising as a result of his folly. No matter how broad, those safety straps really jerked a man about midair.

P'tero still showed no remorse. K'vin only hoped that the stunt produced the effect the love-struck P'tero wished. His mate would have been watching, heart in mouth, no doubt, and P'tero would reap the harvest of such fear sometime this evening. K'vin wished that more girls were available to Impress green dragons. Girls tended to be steadier, more dependable. But with parents keenly interested in applying for more land by setting up cotholds for married children—and no dragonriders, male or female, were allowed to own land—fewer and fewer girls were encouraged to stand on the Hatching Grounds.

The dragons who had taken part in the mass fly-by were now landing their riders in the wide road beyond the court. Then they leaped up again to find a spot in which to enjoy the last of the warm autumnal sun. Many made for the adjoining cliffs as space on Fort's heights filled up on either side of the solar panels. Dragons could be trusted not to tread on what remained of the priceless installations. Fort's were the oldest, of course, and two banks had been lost last winter to the unseasonably fierce storms. Fort, being the largest as well as the oldest northern installation, needed all its arrays in full working order to supply heat for its warren of corridors, power for air circulation units and what equipment still worked. Fortunately, a huge stockpile of panels had been made during the first big wave of constructing new Weyrs and Holds. There would be enough for generations.

Weyrleaders sought their tables on the upper level with Lord Holders and professionals, while riders joined whatever company they preferred at tables set up on the huge expanse of the outer apron. Not a sprout of vegetation anywhere on that plaza surface, K'vin noticed with approval. S'nan, Fort's Weyrleader, had always been fussy, and rightly so.

The musicians had struck up sprightly music, and couples were already dancing on the wooden floor set over the cobbles. Beyond the dance square were the stalls, tents, and tables where goods were being sold or exchanged. There'd been brisk business all day, especially for items needed during the winter months when there would be fewer big Gathers. The various Craftsmen would be pleased, and there'd be less for the dragons to haul back.

Charanth was now circling over the annexes, which had been started to increase living space for both Pern's main infirmary-research facility and teacher training. The dormitories were also going to house volunteers who were assiduously trying to save the records, damaged during last spring when water had leaked down the walls of the vast storage caverns under Fort. Riders had offered to spend as much time as possible from their training schedules to help in the project. Everyone who had a legible script was acceptable, and Lord Paulin had done a bang-up job in making the copyists comfortable. The other Holds had contributed material and workforces.

The exterior buildings of the College were designed to be Thread proof, with high peaked roofs of Telgar slate, and gutters that led into underground cisterns where errant Thread would be drowned. All the Craftsmen involved, including those destined to inhabit the facility, would have preferred to enlarge the cave system, but there had been two serious collapses of caverns, and the mining engineers had vetoed interior expansion for fear of undermining the whole cliffside. Even the mutant, blunt-winged, flightless photosensitive watchwhers had refused to go on further subterranean explorations which, their handlers insisted, meant dangers human eyes couldn't see. So build externally they did: stout walls more than two and a half meters thick at ground level, tapering to just under two meters beneath the roof. With the iron mines at Telgar going full-blast, the necessary structural beams to support such weight had posed no problem.

The new quarters were to be finished within the month. Even today there had been a workforce, though they had taken a break to watch the aerial display and would finish in time for the evening meal and entertainment.

Charanth landed gracefully, with Ormonth right beside him, so that P'tero might remove the tethering safety straps before they could be noticed. As he was doing so, M'leng, green Sith's rider, came up to him, scolding him for "putting my heart in my mouth like that!" And proceeded to berate P'tero far more viciously than his Weyrleader would.

K'vin grinned to himself, especially as he saw how penitent P'tero became under such a harangue. K'vin rolled up his riding straps and tied them to the harness ring.

"Enjoy the sun, my friend," he said, slapping Charanth on the wide shoulder.

I will. Meranath is already there, the bronze dragon said, his tone slightly smug as he executed a powerful upward leap, showering his rider with grit.

Charanth's attitude toward his mate, Meranath, amused, and pleased, his rider. No one had expected K'vin to accede to Telgar's Weyrleadership when it fell open after B'ner's death nine months before. Who would have expected that the sturdy rider, just into his sixth decade, had had any heart problems? But that is what the medics said killed him. So, when Meranath was ready to mate again, Telgar's senior Weyrwoman, Zulaya, had called for an open flight, leaving it up to the dragons to decide on the next Leader. She'd insisted that she had no personal preference. She had been sincerely attached to B'ner and was probably still grieving for him. There had certainly been no lack of "suitors."

K'vin had sent Charanth aloft in the mating flight because all the Telgar Weyr wingleaders were expected to take part, as well as bronze riders from the other Weyrs. He had no real wish to lead a Weyr into a Pass. He considered himself too young for such responsibilities. He had observed from B'ner that the normal duties of an Interval were bad enough, but to *know* that a high percentage of your fellow riders would be injured, or killed: that the lives of so many people rested on your expertise and endurance was too much to contemplate. Some nights, now, he was wracked by terrifying dreams, and Threadfall hadn't even started. On the occasions when he was in Zulaya's bed, she had been understanding and calmly reassuring.

"B'ner worried, too, if that's any consolation, Kev," she said, using his old nickname and soothing sweat-curled hair back as he trembled with reaction. "He had nightmares, too. Comes with the title. As a rule, the morning after a nightmare, B'ner'd go over Sean's notes. I figure he had to have memorized them. I've seen you do the same thing. You'll do well, Kev, when push comes to shove. I know it."

Zulaya could sound so *sure* of something, but then she was nearly a decade his senior and had had more experience as a Weyrleader. Sometimes her intuition was downright uncanny: she could accurately predict the size of clutches, the distribution of the colors, the sex of babies born in the Weyr, and occasionally even the type of weather in the future. But then, she was Fort Weyrbred, a linear descendant of one of the First Riders, Aliana Zuleita, and *knew* things. It was odd how the golden queens seemed to prefer women from outside the Weyrs—but sometimes a queen had a mind of her own and chose a Weyrbred woman, defying custom.

However, just like his predecessor, he constantly reviewed accounts of the individual Threadfalls, how they differed, how you could *tell* from the Leading Edge of Fall that this would be an odd one. Most often the accounts were dry statements of fact, but the prosaic language did not disguise the presence of great courage: especially as those first riders had to figure out how to cope with Thread, easy or hard.

The fact that he was a several times great-nephew of Sorka Connell, the First Weyrwoman—and Zulaya pointed this out more than once—constituted a secondary and subtle reassurance to the entire Weyr.

"Maybe that's why Meranath let Charanth catch her," Zulaya said, her face dead serious but her eyes dancing.

"Had you, I mean . . . did you think of me . . . I mean . . ." K'vin tried to summon appropriate words two weeks after that momentous flight. He had been overwhelmed by her response to him that night. But afterward she seemed very casual in her dealings with him, and she did not always invite him into her quarters, despite the fact that their dragons were inseparable.

"Who *thinks* at all during a mating flight? But I do believe I'm glad that Charanth was so clever. If there is anything in heredity, having a distant great-nephew of Fort Weyr's First Weyrwoman, *and* from a family that has put many acceptable candidates on the Hatching Grounds, as Telgar's Weyrleader gives us all a boost."

"I'm not my many-times-great-aunt, Zulaya . . ."

She chuckled. "Fortunately, or you wouldn't be Weyrleader, but Blood will tell!"

Zulaya had a disconcerting directness but gave him no real hint how she, the woman, not the Weyrwoman, personally felt toward him. She was kind, helpful, made constructive suggestions when they discussed training programs, but so . . . impersonal . . . that K'vin had to conclude that she hadn't really got over B'ner's death yet.

He himself was obscurely comforted that his great-great-aunt had managed to survive Fall and he would attempt to do the same. As, he was sure, would his two siblings and four cousins who were also dragonriders. Though no others were Weyrleaders . . . yet. Still, if his being of the Ruathan Bloodline, which had produced Sorka, M'hall, M'dani, Sorana, Mairian, offered reassurance to his Weyr, he'd reinforce that at every turn during the Pass.

Now, at probably the last large gather Pern would enjoy under Thread-free skies for the next fifty years, he watched his Weyrwoman leave the group of Telgar holders she had been talking to and stride toward him across the open courtyard.

Zulaya was tall for a woman, long-legged—all the better for bestriding a dragon's neck. He was a full head taller than she was, which she said she liked in him: B'ner had been just her height. It was her coloring that fascinated K'vin: the inky black curly hair that, once freed of the flying helmet, tumbled down below her waist. The hair framed a wide, high cheek-boned face, set off the beige of her smooth skin and large, lustrous eyes that were nearly black; a wide and sensual mouth above a strong chin gave her face strength and purpose which reinforced her authority with anyone. She strode, unlike some of the hold women who minced along, her steel-rimmed boot heels noisy on the flagstones, her arms swinging at her side. She'd had time to put a long, slitted skirt over her riding gear, and it opened as she walked, showing a well-formed leg in the leather pants and high boots. She'd turned the high-riding boot cuffs down over her calf, and the red fur made a nice accent to her costume, echoed in the fur trim of her cuffs and collar, which she had opened. As usual, she wore the sapphire pendant she had inherited as the eldest female of her Blood.

"So, did P'tero win M'leng's undying affection with that stunt?" she demanded, an edge to her voice. "They've gone off together . . ." and she looked in the direction of the two riders who were headed toward the temporary tents along the row of cots.

"You might have a word with both later. They're afraid of you," K'vin said, grinning.

"For that piece of stupidity I'll make them more afraid," she said briskly, hopping a step to match his stride. "You really should learn how to scowl menacingly." She glanced up at K'vin and then shook her head, sighing sadly. She had once teased him that he was far too handsome to ever look genuinely threatening, with the Hanrahan red hair, blue eyes, and freckles. "No, you just don't have the face for it. Be that as it may, Meranath's going to give out to Sith for allowing a blue to put himself in danger."

"Get 'em where it hurts," K'vin said, nodding, because Meranath was even more effective as a deterrent with the dragons than any human could be, even the dragon's own rider. "Damned fool stunt."

"However," and now Zulaya cleared her throat, "the Telgarians thought it was 'just marvelous!' " she added in a gushing tone. "Especially since they won't get much chance to see the dive in real action." Now she grimaced.

"Well, at least Telgarians believe," K'vin said.

"Who doesn't?" Zulaya demanded, looking up at him.

"Chalkin, for one."

"Him!" She had absolutely no use for the Bitran Lord Holder and never bothered to hide it.

"If there's one, there may be others, for all the lip service they give us."

"What? With First Fall only months away from us?" Zulaya demanded. "And why, pray tell, do we have dragons at all, if not to provide an aerial defense for the continent? Oh, we provide transportation services, but that's not nearly enough to justify our existence."

"Easy, lady," K'vin said. "You're preaching to the dedicated."

She made a disgusted sound deep in her throat and then they had reached the steps up to the Upper Court. She put her hand through his arm so that they would present the proper picture of united Weyrleadership. K'vin stifled a sigh that the accord was only for public display.

"*And* Chalkin's already into that new bubbling wine of Hegmon's," Zulaya said irritably.

"Why else do you think he came?" said K'vin as he deftly guided her away from the Bitran who was smacking his lips and regarding his wineglass with greedy speculation. "Though today's also a chance for his gamesters to profit."

"One thing's sure, I hear tell he's not on Hegmon's list," she said as they reached their table, which the Telgarians shared, by choice, with the High Reaches Weyr and hold leaders and those from Tillek. The senior captain of the Tillek fishing fleet and his new wife completed the complement at their table.

"That was quite a show you put on," said the jovial shipmaster, Kizan, "wasn't it, Cherry m'dear?"

"Oh, it was, indeed it was," the girl replied, clapping her hands together. While the gesture was close to an affectation, the young wife was clearly awed by the company she kept at this Gather, and everyone was trying to help her cope. Kizan had let it be known that she came from a small fishing hold and, while a capable shipmaster, she had little experience with a wider world. "I've often seen the dragons in the sky, but never so close up. They are so beautiful."

"Have you ridden one yet?" Zulaya asked kindly.

"Oh, heavens, no," Cherry said, modestly lowering her eyes.

"You may, and soon," her husband said. "We came overland here to Fort for the Gather, but I think we'd better see how good our credit is . . ."

"Very good, Captain," said G'don, the High Reaches Weyrleader, "as you've never applied to us half as much as you're entitled to." Mari, his Weyrwoman, nodded and smiled encouragingly at Cherry's almost horrified reaction.

"What?" Kizan teased his bride. "The woman who sailed through a Force Nine gale without complaint is nervous about flying on a dragon?"

Cherry tried to respond but she couldn't find words.

"Don't tease," Mari said. "Riding a dragon *is* considerably different to standing on your own deck, but I don't know many people who refuse a ride."

"Oh, I'm not refusing," Cherry said hastily, startled.

Just like a child fearful of being denied a promised treat, K'vin thought, and struggled to keep from grinning at her.

"All of you, leave her alone," said the Telgar Lady Holder, scowling at them. "I remember my first ride a-dragonback—"

"Back that far, huh," said her husband, Lord Tashvi, eyeing her blandly. "And yet you can't remember where you put that bale of extra blankets . . ."

"Don't start on that again!" Salda began, scowling, but it was apparent to the others at the table, even young Cherry, that the Telgar Holders often indulged in such sparring.

"Have you not opened your wine?" asked an eager voice, and they looked round at Vintner Hegmon, a stout, gray-haired man of medium height with a flushed face and a reddened nose which he jokingly called an occupational hazard.

"Do us the honor," Tashvi said, gesturing to the chilled bottles.

Hegmon complied and, in his experienced hands, the plug erupted from the bottle neck with speed and a "plop." The wine bubbled up but he deftly put a glass under the lip before a drop could be spilled.

"I think we've done it this time," he said, filling the glasses presented to him.

"I say, it does look exciting," Salda said, holding her glass up to watch the bubbles make their ascent.

Thea, the High Reaches Lady Holder, did likewise and then sniffed at her glass. "Oh, my word," she said, putting a hand to her nose just in time to catch a sneeze. "The bubbles tickle."

"Try the *wine*," Hegmon urged.

"Hmmmm," Tashvi said, and Kizan echoed the sentiment.

"Dry, too," the captain said. "Go on, Cherry," he urged his wife. "It's quite unlike Tillek brews. They tend to be foxy and harsh. This'll go down easily."

"Ohhh," and Cherry's response was one of sheer delight. "Oh, I like this!"

Hegmon grinned at her ingenuousness and accepted the approving nods from the others at the table.

"I quite like it, too," Zulaya said after letting a sip slide down her throat. "Rather nice."

"I say, Hegmon, wouldn't mind a refill," and Chalkin appeared at the table, extending his glass under the mouth of the bottle the vintner held.

Hegmon kept the bottle upright and regarded the Lord Holder coolly. "There's more at your own table, Chalkin."

"True, but I'd rather sample different bottles."

Hegmon stiffened and Salda intervened.

"Leave off, Chalkin. As if Hegmon would offer an inferior bottle to anyone," she said and waved him off.

Chalkin hesitated between a scowl and a smile, but then, keeping his expression bland, he bowed and backed away from the table with his empty glass. He did not, however, return to his own table but moved on to the next one where wine was being poured.

"I could—" Hegmon began.

"Just don't supply him, Hegmon."

"He's already insisting that I give him vine starts so he can grow his own," Hegmon said, furious at such importunity. "Not that he'd do that any better than any of those other projects he starts."

"Ignore him," Zulaya suggested with a flick of her fingers. "M'shall and Irene do. He's such a toady."

"Unfortunately," said Tashvi with a grimace, "he's managed to find like minds . . ."

"We'll settle him at the meeting," K'vin said.

"I hope so," Tashvi said, "though a man like that is not easily convinced against his will. And he does have a following."

"Not where it matters," Zulaya said.

"I hope so. Ah, and here's food to soak up all this lovely stuff before we're too muddled to keep our wits about us this evening."

Zulaya waved at the wine cooler. "I doubt there's more than two glasses apiece, scarcely enough to muddle us, though it's lovely stuff." And she sipped judiciously. "Hegmon is generous but not overly so. And here's our dinner . . ."

She sat back as a swarm of men and women in Fort colors began to distribute platters of steaming food among the tables. And bottles of red wine.

"You spoke too soon about muddling, Zuli," K'vin said, grinning as he served her roast slices from the platter before passing it around the table.

They had finished their meal and all the wine before Paulin rose from his table and signaled those in the Upper Court to follow him into the Hold for the meeting. Dancing was well under way in the square and the music made a cheerful processional.

K'vin hoped the musicians would still be playing when the meeting ended. Despite the height of her, Zulaya was so light on her feet she was a pleasure to partner, and because he was so tall, she preferred him as hers. And a full orchestra of professionals was far more entertaining than the half-trained, if enthusiastic players currently in the Weyr. Different music, too.

"Ah," said Zulaya appreciatively as they filed into Fort's Great Hall, "they've done a great job of freshening the murals."

"Hmmm," K'vin agreed, craning his neck around and impeding Chalkin's entrance into the Hall. "Sorry."

"Humph," was Chalkin's response, and he glared sourly at Zulaya as he passed, shrugging his garments away from touching them.

"Consider the source," K'vin said when he thought Zulaya might fire a tart comment after the Lord Holder.

"I want to be at Bitra when the first Fall hits his hold," she said.

"Isn't he lucky, then, not to be beholden to us, but to Benden?" K'vin said wryly.

"Indeed," said Zulaya, and allowed herself to be guided to Telgar Weyr's usual seat at the big conference table. "I wonder did anyone get any sleep in this hold the past week," she said, stroking the banner of Telgar's colors, which clothed their portion of the table. "Makes such a nice display," she murmured as she pulled out the chair which also sported Telgar's white field and black grain design.

The table itself was made up of many smaller units hooked together, forming a multifaceted circle: Telgar's Weyr and hold leaders were between High Reaches and Tillek since they were the northernmost settlements. Across from them were Ista Weyr and Hold, and Keroon Hold, with their brilliant sun-colors. Benden Weyr was seated with Bitra on one side and Nerat and Benden on the other. The Chief Engineer, the Senior Medic, and the Headmaster were also included in the meeting. Fort, traditionally the senior hold, with Ruatha and Southern Boll on either side, was at table center, and this time was the "Chair."

"Now, if any of us still have our heads after Hegmon's fine new wine, let's get this over with so we can get in some dancing," said Paulin, smiling around the table.

Chalkin banged the table in front of him with a very loud "Hear, hear!"

K'vin stifled a groan. The man was half drunk, if not all drunk, his face flushed red.

"I'm sure we're all aware of the imminence of Threadfall—"

Chalkin made a rude noise.

"Look, Lord Chalkin," Paulin said, scowling at the dissident, "if you managed to get too much of the champagne inside your skin, you can be excused."

"No, that's exactly what he wants," said M'shall, Benden's Weyrleader, quickly. "Then he can claim anything decided today was done behind his back."

"If he can't shut up, we can always hold his head under the tap until he sobers enough to remember common courtesy," put in Irene, Benden's weyrwoman. "He doesn't like getting his Gather clothes wet." Her expression suggested she'd had experience enough to know.

"Chalkin!" Paulin said, his voice steely.

"Oh, all right," the Bitran said in a surly tone, and he settled himself more squarely in his chair, leaning forward on his elbows at the table. "If you're going to be that way . . ."

"Only because you are," snapped Irene. Paulin gave her a stern look and she subsided, though she kept narrowed eyes on Chalkin for a while longer.

"Three independent calculations were made, and there's no doubt that the Red Planet is getting closer . . . spatially speaking."

"Is there any chance of a collision?" asked Jamson of High Reaches.

"Fragit, Jamson," Paulin said, "let's not bring that up."

"Why not?" Chalkin said, brightening.

"Because that . . . improbability . . . has already been discussed to the point of nausea," Paulin said. "There isn't a hint in any of the information collected by our forefathers to indicate there is any chance of a collision between the two planets. Or that they considered the . . . improbability . . . for any reason."

"Yes, but does it say anywhere that there *can't* be?" Chalkin was obviously delighted with this possibility.

"Absolutely not," Paulin said simultaneously with Clisser, who was not only the College Head but the senior of the trained astronomers. Paulin gestured for Clisser to continue.

"Captains Keroon and Tillek," and he paused in reverence, "both annotated the Aivas report, which included data from the *Yokohama*'s records. I have repeatedly reworked the relevant equations, and the rogue planet will Pass Pern on an elliptical orbit that *cannot* alter to a collision course with us. A matter of celestial mechanics and Rukbat's gravitational pull. I'd've brought the diagram of the orbits involved if I'd had forewarning." Clisser gave Chalkin a disgusted glare.

"Bad enough it brings in the Thread. Do you *want* to be blown to smithereens, Chalkin?" asked Kalvi, chief of the mechanical engineers. "And I checked the maths, too, so I concur with Clisser and everyone else who's done the equations. Why don't you, if you're so worried?"

Chalkin ignored the jibe since he had never been noted for scholarship in any field. He was also well pleased with the reaction to his remark. No matter what they said, there was no proof that they were really that safe.

"Now, calculations indicate early spring will bring the first Threadfall of this Pass. There are several falls that could be live, depending on the weather conditions, mainly the ambient temperature, at the time of Fall." Paulin reached under his table then and hauled up a board on which Threadfall areas had been meticulously delineated. S'nan cleared his throat, moving restlessly, as if he felt Paulin should not have usurped a Fort prerogative. "The first two will be in Fort Weyr's patrol area, the second two in High Reaches', and the third two in Benden's. These are due to occur in the first two weeks, about three days apart. The second Fall in Fort territory and the first one in High Reaches happen on the same day—different flows of the same Fall. Also, we know from the records that there will be live falls over the Southern Continent for about a week before they commence here in the North. S'nan," and Paulin turned to the Fort Weyrleader, "may we have your progress report?"

S'nan stood, holding up his ubiquitous clipboard. (Rumor had it that that item had been passed down from the Connell himself.) He peered down at it a moment. The oldest Leader of the premier Weyr on Pern resembled his several-times-great-grandfather, though his silvery hair was more sandy than red. Privately, K'vin didn't think Sean Connell had been such a martinet, even if he had promulgated the rules by which the Weyrs governed themselves. Most of these were common-sensible, despite S'nan managing to pursue them into the ridiculous.

"The First Fall," S'nan began, and there was a touch of pride in his voice, "will start over the sea east of Fort Hold and come ashore at the mouth of the river, passing diagonally across the peninsula and out into the sea in the west. The second two falls, which will occur three days later, will be over the southern tip of Southern Boll." He used his stylus and, at his most condescending, touched Paulin's chart. "This one may go south far enough to miss land entirely, and in any case will be over land for only a short while—and over the western tip of High Reaches, again proceeding out to sea, and so over land for only a short time. The third Fall will start on the south coast of the Tillek peninsula, east of the site of the hold, and proceed out to sea, again over land only for a short time."

"Thread giving us all a chance to get accustomed to fighting it?" asked B'nurrin of Igen.

"Your levity is ill-placed," S'nan said, but there were too many grins around the table for his reprimand to affect the irrepressible young Weyrleader. S'nan cleared his throat and launched once more into his discourse. "The next two falls will be the most dangerous for unseasoned wings," and he shot a stern glance at B'nurrin as he found the proper Thread path. "The first will start over the sea in the east and proceed over Benden Weyr and Bitra Hold, ending almost at Igen Weyr. This would normally be flown jointly by Benden and Igen Weyrs. The second will start at the northern end of the Nerat peninsula and proceed across it, over the east coast of Keroon and the east tip of Igen, and end just offshore from Igen. This also would normally be a joint Fall, flown by Benden over Nerat, Igen over the northern part of Keroon, and Ista over the southern part of Keroon . . ."

"We really do know what falls we fly, S'nan," M'shall said.

"Yes, yes, of course," and S'nan cleared his throat again. "However," and his glance went to the Lord Holders seated around the table, "it was decided at the last meeting of the Weyrleaders that, since any of these would be the first Fall in our experience, every Weyr would supply a double-wing at the initial engagement. Thus each Weyr would have firsthand experience."

"I still think we could all get *that* by hitting those first southern falls," B'nurrin began. "If the dragons miss, it's not going to fall on anyone's head or ruin any farmland."

"B'nurrin!" M'shall said sternly before the startled S'nan could open his mouth.

K'vin privately thought B'nurrin had a good idea and had backed him, but they were overruled by the older Weyrleaders. K'vin suspected that if he were to take some wings down south for that first Fall there, he'd be likely to find B'nurrin "practicing" there, too.

"I still think it's a good idea," the Istan said, shrugging.

Pretending such an interruption hadn't even occurred, S'nan went on. "As was customary in the First Pass, Lord Holders will supply adequate ground-crews and have them assembled as directed by the Weyrleaders. In this case, Weyrleader M'shall." He inclined slightly toward the Benden bronze rider. "Master Kalvi," and he bowed courteously to the head engineer, "has assured me that his foundry has turned out sufficient HNO_3 cylinders to equip the groundcrews but the HNO_3 must be made up on site. As in the First Pass, the labor and material are supplied by the engineer corps as part of their public duty. You all should have received your full allotment of tanks by Year's End." S'nan, as always, was precise in his language, scorning the new word "Turn," which the younger generation had begun to use instead of "year."

Kalvi rose to his feet. "I've scheduled every major hold with three days of training in the maintenance and repair of the flamethrowers and a practice session, which, I think," and Kalvi grinned, "you will find comprehensive as well as interesting." He shifted his stance and would have gone on but S'nan held up his hand and gestured Kalvi to sit.

With a bit of a snort and a grin, Kalvi complied.

Now the Fort Weyrleader turned his glance to Corey. "I believe you also plan a three-day seminar to instruct major and minor hold personnel in burn control and Thread . . . ah . . . first aid."

Corey did not rise but nodded.

"Lord Holders must assign suitable medics with every ground control unit, or have one member of each trained in first aid and supplied with kits containing numbweed, fellis juice, and other first-aid medications.

"Now," and he flipped over the top sheet, "I have done pre-Pass inspections of all Weyrs and find them well up to strength, with sufficient cadet riders to supply the wings with phosphine rock during the Pass. I have discussed all aspects of flight tactics and Weyr maintenance with the respective Weyrleaders . . ."

K'vin writhed a bit on his chair, remembering the exhaustive inspection carried out by S'nan and Sarai: they'd even inspected the recycling plant! Then he noticed that G'don, the oldest Weyrleader, was also squirming. So, the Fort pair had spared no one in their officious search for perfection. Well, they *were* heading into a Pass, and the Fort Weyrleaders were correct to want every aspect of dragon-riding at the highest possible standard and readiness. In the propagation of dragons, the pair had found no fault with Telgar Weyr: it had had the largest clutches of all the Weyrs in the last three years as the dragons themselves answered the tide of preparations for the coming struggle. K'vin was hoping that Charanth's first clutch would be larger than any that B'ner's Miginth had sired: maybe then Zulaya would warm to him. The two junior queens had done well in their latest clutches, producing more of the useful greens and blues. Telgar Weyr would soon be full! They might have to shift out some of the excess population to other Weyrs, but that could wait until the yearly review.

"And, in conclusion, let me state that we are as ready as we can be."

"Far more ready than the First Riders were," G'don remarked in his dry fashion.

"Indeed," said Irene of Benden.

K'vin contented himself with a smile. Unbidden, a little wiggle of fear shot up from his belly to chill him. He gave himself a shake. He came from a Blood that had produced First Riders and contributed many sons and daughters to the Weyrs.

And you ride me, Charanth said firmly. *I shall be formidable in the air. Thread will fly in the other direction when it sees my flame.* And that was not all draconic boast, for Charanth had racked up the Weyr record for the length he achieved in flaming practice. *Together we meet Thread, not just you on your own. I shall be with you and we shall overcome.*

Thanks, Charrie.

You're welcome, Kev.

"You've got that look in your eye, K'vin," Zulaya murmured for his ear alone. "What's Charanth's opinion of all this?"

"He's raring to go," K'vin whispered back, and grinned. Charanth was right to remind him that he did not fly alone. They were together, as they had been from the moment the bronze had broken his shell in half and stepped directly toward a fourteen-year-old K'vin of the Hanrahans waiting on the hot sands of the Hatching Ground. And K'vin had realized that that was the moment all his life had been aimed at: Impression. He'd seen his older brother Impress, and his second oldest sister, and three of the four cousins currently riders. From the moment he was Searched out, part of him had been sure-sure-sure, with all the fervor of an adolescent, that he would Impress favorably. The negative side of his personality had perversely suggested that he'd be left standing on the hot sands and he'd never live down such a humiliating experience.

"In conclusion," S'nan said, "let me assure this gathering that the Weyrs are ready." With that, S'nan sat down to an approving applause. "I hope that the holds are, too?" Not only did his voice end on an up note, but he raised his thick brows questioningly at the Fort Holder.

Paulin stood up again, shuffling until he found the right clipboard and cleared his throat. "I have readiness reports in from all but two major holds," and he glanced first at Franco, Lord Holder of Nerat, and then tilted his head toward Chalkin. "I know you received the forms to fill in . . ."

The tall, thin, bronze-skinned Neratian raised his hand. "I told you the problem we have with vegetation, Paulin, and we're still *trying* to keep it under control . . ." He grimaced. "Not easy with the excellent weather we've been having and the restriction against chemical deterrents. But I can assure you that we'll keep at it. Otherwise, we have emergency roofing for the seedling nurseries and sufficient stores of viable seeds to replant when that's feasible. We're also continuing our research into dwarfing plants for indoor propagation. All minor Holders are fully aware of the problems and are complying. Everyone's signed up for the groundcrew course."

Paulin made a notation, nodding. "Agriculture's still working on the problem of an inhibitor for your tropical weed types, Fran."

"I hope so. Stuff grows out of pure sand without any cultivation at all."

Then Paulin turned to Chalkin, who had been polishing his rings with every evidence of boredom. "I've had nothing at all from you, Lord Chalkin of Bitra," Paulin said.

"Oh, there's plenty of time . . ."

"A report was required by this date, Chalkin," Paulin said, pushing the issue.

Chalkin shrugged. "You all can play that game if you wish, but I do not believe that Thread is going to fall next spring, so why should I bother my people with unnecessary tasks—"

He wasn't able to finish his sentence for the acrimonious reactions from everyone at the table.

"Now see here, Chalkin . . ."

"Hey, wait a bleeding minute . . ."

"Just where do you get off . . ." Bastom was on his feet with indignation.

Chalkin pointed one thick, beringed finger at the Tillek Holder.

"The Holds are autonomous, are they not? Is that not guaranteed in the Charter?" Chalkin demanded, rounding on Paulin.

"In ordinary times, yes," Paulin answered, waving a hand to the others to be quiet. He had to raise his voice to be heard over the angry remarks and protests. "However, with—"

"This Thread of yours coming. So you say, but there's no proof," Chalkin said, grinning smugly.

"Proof? What more proof do you need?" Paulin demanded. "This planet is already feeling the perturbation of the rogue planet . . ."

Chalkin dismissed that with a shrug. "Winter brings bad storms, volcanoes do erupt . . ."

"You can't so easily dismiss the fact that the planet is becoming more visible."

"Pooh. That doesn't mean anything."

"So," and Paulin first had to quell angry murmurs to be heard, "you discount entirely the advice of our forebears? The massive evidence that they left for our guidance?"

"They left hysterical—"

"They were scarcely hysterical!" Tashvi bellowed. "And they coped with the emergency, and gave us specific guidelines to follow when the planet came back. And how to calculate a Pass."

"Hold it, hold it!" Paulin shouted, raising both arms to restore order. "I'm Chair, I'll remind you," and he glared at Tashvi until the Telgar Lord resumed his seat and the others had quieted down. "What kind of proof do you require, Lord Chalkin?" he asked in a very reasonable tone of voice.

"Thread falling . . ." someone muttered, and subsided before he could be identified.

"Well, Chalkin?" Paulin said.

"Some proof that Thread will fall. A report from this Aivas we've all heard about . . ."

"Landing is under tons of volcanic ash," Paulin said, and then recognized S'nan's urgent signal to speak.

"Nine expeditions have been mounted to investigate the installation at Landing and retrieve information from the Aivas," S'nan said in his usual measured tones. As he spoke he searched for and found a sheaf of plastic and held it up. "These are the reports."

"And?" Chalkin demanded, obviously enjoying the agitation he had aroused.

"We have not been able to locate the administration building in which the Aivas was located."

"Why not?" Chalkin insisted. "I remember seeing tapes of Landing prior to the first Threadfall . . ."

"Then you will appreciate the size of the task," S'nan said. "Especially since the blanket of volcanic ash covers the entire plateau and we have not been able to locate any landmark by which we could judge the position of the administration building. And since the housing was similar, it's difficult to establish where we are when we have dug one out of twenty feet of ash and debris. Therefore we have not been able to establish the location of the administration building."

"Try again," Chalkin said, turning his back to S'nan.

"So you have done nothing to prepare your Hold at all for the on-slaught?" Paulin asked calmly, reasonably.

Chalkin shrugged. "I don't perceive a need to waste time and effort."

"And money . . ." murmured the same heckler.

"Precisely. Marks are hard enough to come by to waste them on the off chance—"

"*Off chance?*" Tashvi erupted out of his chair. "You'll have a revolt on your hands."

"I doubt that," Chalkin said with a sly smile.

"Because you haven't bloody seen fit to warn your holders?" Tashvi demanded.

"Lord Telgar," Paulin said repressively, "I'm Chair." He turned back to Chalkin. "If the rest of us, however misguidedly, do believe in the forewarnings—backed by irrefutable astronomical evidence of an imminent Pass, how can you deny them?"

Chalkin's grin was patronizing. "A spaceborne organism? That drops on a large planet and eats everything it touches? Why wasn't Pern totally destroyed during previous visitations? Why is it every two hundred years? How come the Exploration Team that did a survey of the planet before it was released to our ancestors to colonize . . . how come they didn't see any evidence? Ah, no," Chalkin said, flicking the notion away from him with his beringed hands, "ridiculous!"

"My calculations were confirmed by—" Clisser said, feeling that he was being maligned.

"There was evidence of Threadfall," Tashvi said, bouncing once more to his feet. "I've read the report. There were hundreds of circles where vegetation was just starting to grow . . ."

"Inconclusive," Chalkin said with another flap of a hand. "Could have been caused by one of the many fungus growths."

"Well, then, when this inconclusive evidence comes dropping out of the skies onto your hold, don't bother us," Bastom said.

"Or come crying to my hold for help," added Bridgely, completely disgusted by Chalkin's attitude.

"You may be sure of that," Chalkin said, and with a mocking bow to Paulin, left the Hall with no further word.

"What are we going to do about him?" Bridgely asked, "because sure as night follows day, he will come running for aid to Franco and me."

"There is provision in the Charter," Paulin began.

Jamson of the High Reaches stared with wide and disbelieving eyes at Paulin.

"Only if he believes in the Charter . . ." Bastom said.

"Oh, Chalkin believes in the Charter all right," Paulin said sardonically. "The patent conferring the title of 'Lord Holder' on the original major northern stakeholders is what gives his line the right to hold. And he's already used the Charter to substantiate his autonomous position. I wonder if he also knows the penalty for failing to prepare his hold. That constitutes a major breach of the trust . . ."

"Who trusts Chalkin?" G'don asked.

". . . the trust that holders rest in the Lord of their hold in return for their labor."

"Ha!" said Bridgely. "I don't think much of his holders either. Useless lot on the whole. Most of 'em kicked out of other holds for poor management or plain laziness."

"Bitra's badly managed, too. Generally we have to return a full half of his tithings," M'shall said. "Half the grain is moldy, the timber unseasoned, and hides improperly cured and often rancid. It's a struggle every quarter to receive decent supplies from him."

"Really?" Paulin said, jotting notes down. "I hadn't realized he shorted you on tithes."

M'shall shrugged. "Why should you know? It's our problem. We keep at him. We'll have to keep at him over this, too, you know. Can't let him get away with a total disregard for the upcoming emergency. Not every holder in Bitra's useless, you know, Bridgely."

Bridgely shrugged. "Good apples in every basket as well as bad. But I'd really hate to have to cope with the problem come springtime and Thread falls. Benden's too near Bitra for my peace of mind."

"So what is the penalty for what Chalkin's doing? Or, rather, not doing?" Franco asked.

"Impeachment," Paulin said flatly.

"Impeachment!" Jamson was aghast. "I didn't know—"

"Article Fourteen, Jamson," Paulin said. "Dereliction of Duty by Lord Holder. Can you give me a printout on that, Clisser? Perhaps we all should have our memory refreshed on that point."

"Certainly," and the Head of the College made a note in his folder. "In your hands tomorrow."

"So your system's still working?" Tashvi asked.

"Copies of the most important official documents were made in quantity by my predecessor," Clisser replied with a relieved smile. "I've a list if you need any . . . handwritten but legible."

Paulin cleared his throat, calling them to order. "So, my Lord Holders, should we proceed against Chalkin?"

"You've heard him. What option do we have?" M'shall wanted to know, glancing about the table.

"Now, wait a minute," Jamson began, scowling. "I'd want to have incontrovertible proof of his inefficiency as a Lord Holder as well as his failure to respond to this emergency. I mean, impeachment's an extreme step."

"Yes, and Chalkin'll do everything he can to slide out of it," Bastom said cynically.

"Surely there's a trial procedure for such a contingency?" Jamson asked, looking anxiously about. "You certainly can't act without allowing him the chance to respond to any charges."

"In the matter of impeachment I believe that a unanimous agreement of all major holders and leaders is sufficient to deprive him of his position," Paulin said.

"Are you sure?" Jamson asked.

"If he isn't, I am," Bridgely said, bringing one fist down firmly on the table. His spouse, Lady Jane, nodded her head emphatically. "I haven't wanted to bring it up in a Council before—" Bridgely began.

"He's very difficult to confront at the best of times," Irene said, setting her lips in a thin line of frustrations long borne.

Bridgely nodded sharply in her direction and continued. "He's come as near to bending, or breaking for that matter, what few laws we do have on Pern. Shady dealings, punitive contracts, unusual harsh conditions for his holders . . ."

"We've had some refugees from Bitra with stories that would curl your hair," Jane, Benden's Lady Holder, said, wringing her hands in distress. "I've kept records . . ."

"Have you?" Paulin said. "I'd very much like to see them. Autonomy is a privilege and a responsibility, but not a license for authoritarianism or despotic rule. Certainly autonomy does not give anyone the right to deprive his constituents of basic needs. Such as protection from Threadfall."

"I don't know about going so far as to impeach him," Jamson said, his reluctance deepening. "I mean, such an extreme remedy could have a demoralizing effect on all the holds."

"Possibly . . ." Paulin said.

"Not being prepared for Thread will certainly demoralize Bitra!" Tashvi said.

Paulin held up his hand as he turned to M'shall. "Please give me specific instances in which Bitra Hold has failed to supply the Weyr. Jane, I'd like to look at the records you've kept."

"I've some, too," Irene added.

Paulin nodded and looked around the table. "Since his dereliction of primary duty in regard to preparation against Threadfall could jeopardize not only his own hold but those of his neighbors, I feel we must examine the problem as quickly as possible and indict him—" Jamson jammed an arm up in protest, but Paulin held up a placatory hand. "If, that is, we do find just cause to do so. Just now, he was acting as if he'd had too much of Hegmon's new wine."

"Ha!" was Irene's immediate response, a cynical response echoed by others around the table.

"We cannot allow personal feelings to color this matter," Paulin said firmly.

"Wait till you read my notes," was her wry answer.

"And mine," said Bridgely.

"But who could take his place?" Jamson asked, now querulous with anxiety.

"Not a task I'd like so soon to Thread," Bastom admitted.

Paulin grimaced. "But it may have to be done."

"Ah, if I may," and Clisser raised his hand. "The Charter requires us to find a suitable candidate from the incumbent's Bloodline—" he began.

"He *has* relatives?" Bridgely asked, mimicking surprise and consternation.

"I believe so," Franco said, "beyond his children. An uncle . . ."

"If they're of the same Blood as Chalkin, would that be an improvement?" Tashvi wanted to know.

"They do say a new broom sweeps clean," Irene remarked. "I heard that Chalkin did his uncle out of succession by giving him an isolated hold . . ."

"He got him out of the way fast enough, that's sure," Bridgely said. "Some mountain place, back of beyond."

"All of Bitra is back of beyond," Azury of Boll remarked, grinning.

"A replacement is not the most immediate concern," Paulin said, taking charge again, "if we can persuade Chalkin that all of us can't be wrong about Threadfall."

Zulaya this time snorted at that unlikelihood. "He'll admit he's wrong only when Thread is eating him . . . which might solve the problem in the most effective way. Bitra's in the path of the First Fall."

"Remiss as Chalkin appears to be," Jamson said, "Bitra Hold may be better off *with* than without him. You don't learn the management of a hold overnight, you know."

Paulin gave the High Reaches Lord a long look. "That is very true, but if he hasn't even told his people that Thread is coming . . ." and he opened up his hands to show dismay at such an omission. "That's a dereliction of duty right there. His prime duty and the primary reason for having a Leader during a crisis. As a group we also have a responsibility to be sure each of us is performing duties inherent to our rank and position."

Zulaya shrugged. "It'd serve him right to be caught out in the First Fall."

"Yes, well," and Paulin rattled papers. "I'll accept reports of malfeasance and irregularities in his conduct of Bitra Hold. We'll do this properly, gathering evidence and making a full report on the problem. Now, let's finish up today's agenda. Kalvi, you wish to broach the subject of new mines?"

The lean, hawk-nosed engineer sprang to his feet. "I sure do. We've got fifty years of Fall and we're going to need more ore: ore that's closer to the surface than the Telgar deposits."

"Thought they would last us a millennium," Bridgely of Benden said.

"Oh, there's certainly more ore down the main shafts, but it's not as accessible as these mountain deposits, which could be worked more efficiently." He unrolled an opaque plastic map of the Great Western Range where he had circled an area beyond Ruatha's borders. "Here! High-grade ore and almost waiting to leap into carts. We'll need that quality if we're to replace flamethrower equipment. And we'll have to." He said that with a degree of resignation. "I've the personnel trained and ready to move up there—which I'd like to do to get the mines going before Threadfall starts. All I need is your okay."

"You're asking to start a hold up there? Or just a mine?" asked Paulin.

Kalvi scratched the side of his nose and grinned. "Well, it'd be a long way to travel after the shift is over, especially if the dragons are all busy fighting Thread." He unrolled another diagram. "One reason I've backed this site is that there's a good cave system available for living quarters, as well as coal nearby for processing the ore. The finished ingots could be shipped downriver."

There were murmurs among the others as the project was discussed.

"Good thing Chalkin left," Bridgely remarked. "He's got those mines in Steng Valley he's been trying to reactivate."

"They're unsafe," Kalvi said scornfully. "I surveyed them myself and we'd have to spend too much time shoring up shafts and replacing equipment. The ore's second rate, too. There isn't time to restore the mine . . . much less argue with Chalkin over a contract. You know how he can be, haggling over minor details for weeks before he'll make a decision." He contorted his long face into a grimace. "If you," and he turned to the others at the table, "grant this permission, I'll have a chance to noise it about the Gather this evening and see who'd be interested in going along in support capacity and necessary Crafts."

"I'll second it," said Tashvi magnanimously, raising his hand.

"Good. Moved and seconded. Now, all in favor of the formation of a mining hold?" Hands shot up and were dutifully counted by Paulin.

"Chalkin's going to say this was rigged," Bastom remarked caustically, "and we drove him out of the meeting before the subject came up."

"So?" Paulin said. "No one asked him to leave, and he has a copy of the agenda same as everyone else." He brought his fist down on the table. "Motion carried. Tell your engineer he may start his project. High Reaches Weyr," and he turned to G'don, "Telgar," and he included K'vin now, "can you supply transport?"

Both Weyrleaders agreed. If a new hold was to be established, as many riders as possible from their Weyrs should become familiar with its landmarks.

"There won't be that much extra to protect against Threadfall," Kalvi said with a grin for the dragonriders. "It's all underground or within the cliff caverns. We'll use hydroponics for fresh food from the start."

"Any more new business?" Paulin asked.

Clisser raised his hand, was acknowledged and stood, glancing at the assembled: falling into his lecture mode, K'vin thought.

"Lord Chalkin's attitude may not be that unusual," he began, startling them into attention to his words. "At least, not in times to come. We, here and now, are not too distanced from the events of the First Pass. We have actual visual records from that time with which to check on the approach of the rogue planet. *We* know it is a rogue because we know from the excellent and exhaustive reports done by Captains Keroon and Tillek that the planet was unlikely to have emerged from our sun. Its orbit alone substantiates that theory since it is not on the same elliptical plane as the rest of Rukbat's satellites.

"I am assiduous in training at least six students in every class in the rudiments of astronomy and the use of the sextant, as well as being certain that they have the requisite mathematics to compute declension and ascension and figure accurately the hour circle of any star. We still have three usable telescopes with which to observe the skies, but we once had more." He paused. "We are, as I'm sure we all must honestly admit, losing more and more of the technology bequeathed us by our ancestors. Not through mishandling," and he raised a hand against objections, "but from the attritions of age and an inability, however much we may strive to compensate, to reach the same technical level our ancestors enjoyed."

Kalvi grimaced in reluctant agreement to that fact.

"Therefore, I suggest that we somehow, in some fashion, with what technology we have left at our disposal, leave as permanent and indestructible a record as possible for future generations. I know that some of us . . ." Clisser paused, glancing significantly to the door through which Chalkin had so recently passed. ". . . entertain the notion that our ancestors were mistaken in thinking that Threadfall will occur whenever the Red Planet passes Pern. But we can scarcely ignore the perturbations already obvious on the surface of our planet—the extreme weather, the volcanic eruptions, the other cosmic clues. Should it so happen in centuries to come that too many doubt—not wishing to destroy a flourishing economy and happy existence—that Thread will return, all that we have striven to achieve, all we have built with our bare hands," and dramatically he lifted his, "all we have around us today," and he gestured toward the music faintly heard outside the Hall, "would perish."

The denials were loud.

"Ah," and he held one hand over his head, "but it could happen. Lord Chalkin is proof of that. We've already lost so much of our technology. Valuable and skilled men and women we could ill-afford to lose because of their knowledge and skills have succumbed to disease or old age. We must have a fail-safe against Thread! Something that will last and remind our descendants to prepare, be ready, and to survive."

"Is there any chance we could find that administration building then?" Paulin asked S'nan.

"Too close to Threadfall now," M'shall answered. "And it's going into the hot season down there, which makes digging anything enervating. However, I most emphatically agree with Clisser. We need some sort of a safeguard. Something that would prove to doubters like Chalkin that Thread isn't just a myth our ancestors thought up."

"But we keep records . . ." said Laura of Ista Weyr.

"How much plasfilm do you have left?" Paulin asked pointedly. "I know Fort's stock is running low. And you all know what happened to our Repository."

"True. But we've paper . . ." and she looked over at the Telgar Holders, Tashvi and Salda.

"Look, how can we estimate how many forestry acres will survive Threadfall?" Tashvi asked, raising his hands in doubt. "I've the timberjacks working nonstop, cutting, and the mill's turning out as much lumber and pulp as it can."

"You know we'll do our best to protect the forests," K'vin said, though privately he wondered how good their best could be since even one Thread burrow could devastate a wide swath of timbered land in minutes.

"Of course you will," Salda said warmly, "and we will stockpile as much paper as we can beforehand. Old rags are always welcome." Then her expression sobered. "But I don't think any of us can know what will or will not survive. Tarvi Andiyar's survey when he took hold indicated that most of the slopes were denuded. Ten years before Threadfall ceased, he had seedlings in every corner of the hold, ready to plant out. We were just lucky that natural succession also occurred in the three decades after the end of First Pass."

"That is yet another item we must record for future generations," Clisser said.

"The ultimate how-to," said Mari of High Reaches.

"I beg pardon?"

"What to do when Threadfall has Passed is even more important than what to do while it's happening," she said as if that should be obvious.

"We've got to first survive fifty years—" Salda began.

"Let's get back to the subject," Paulin said, rising to his feet. "The chair concurs that we ought to have some permanent, indestructible, unambiguous, simple way to anticipate the rogue planet's return. Has anyone any ideas?"

"We can engrave metal plates and put them in every Weyr, hold, and Hall, where they're too obvious to be ignored," Kalvi said. "And inscribe the sextant settings that indicate the Pass."

"So long as there's a sextant, and someone to use it accurately," Lord Bastom said, "that's fine. But what happens when the last of them is broken?"

"They're not that complicated to make," Kalvi said.

"What if there's no one trained in its use?" Salda put in.

"My fleet captains use sextants daily," Bastom said. "The instruments're invaluable on the sea."

"Mathematics is a base course for all students," Clisser added, "not just fishermen."

"You have to know the method to get the answers you need," said Corey, the Head Medic, speaking for the first time. "And know when to use it." Her profession was struggling to maintain a high standard as more and more equipment became unusable, and unusual procedures became erudite.

"There has to be some way to pass on that vital information to future generations," Paulin said, looking first at Clisser and then scanning the faces at the table. "Let's have a hard think. Etching on metal's one way . . . and prominently placing tablets in every Weyr and hold so they can't be stored away and forgotten."

"A sort of Rosetta stone?" Clisser's tone was more statement than query.

"What's that?" Bridgely asked. Clisser had a habit, which annoyed some folk, of dropping odd references into conversations: references with which only he was familiar. It would lead to long lectures from him if anyone gave him the chance.

"On Earth, in the late eighteenth century, a stone with three ancient languages was discovered which gave the clue to translating those languages. We shall, of course, keep our language pure."

"We're back to etching again," Corey said, grinning.

"If it's the only way . . ." Clisser began and then frowned. "No, there has to be some fail-safe method. I'll investigate options."

"All right, then, Clisser, but don't put the project aside," Paulin said. "I'd rather we had a hundred sirens, bells, and whistles going off than no warning at all."

Clisser grinned slowly. "The bells and whistles are easy enough. It's the siren that will take time."

"All right, then," and Paulin looked around the table. Toe-tapping dance music was all too audible and the younger holders and Weyrfolk were plainly restless. "No more new business?" He didn't wait for an answer, and used the gavel to end the meeting. "That's all for now. Enjoy yourselves, folks."

The speed with which the Hall emptied suggested that that was what all intended to do.

Gather at Fort

"Cliss, what on earth possessed you?" Sheledon demanded, glowering. He was head of the Arts faculty at the College and constantly jealous of what free time he had in which to compose.

"Well," and Clisser looked away from Sheledon's direct and accusing glare, "we do have more records and are more familiar with the techniques of assessing them than anyone else. Information and training *are* what this College was established to provide."

"Our main function," said Danja, taking up the complaint—she wanted spare time in which to work with her string quartet, "is to teach youngsters who would rather ride dragons or acquire many klicks of Pernese real estate to use the wits they were born with. And to brainwash enough youngsters to go out and teach whatever they know to our ever-widely-spreading population."

Dance music swirled about them but Sheledon and Danja were so incensed that they seemed oblivious to the rhythms that were causing the other three at their table to keep time with foot or hand. Danja shot Lozell a peevish look and he stopped rattling fingers callused from harp strings.

"I don't think it'll be that hard to find some way to indicate a celestial return," he said in an attempt to appease the wrath of Sheledon and Danja.

"It isn't the 'hard' that bothers me," Danja said acidly, "but when will we have the *time*?" She stabbed her finger at the as yet unfinished extension to the teaching facility. "Particularly since there is a time limit," and she shot another dirty look at Clisser, "Winter Solstice."

"Oh." Lozell grimaced. "Good point."

"We're all working every hour we can spare from classes on what's *urgent* right now," Danja went on, gesturing dramatically and pacing up and down the length of their table. While Sheledon closed in on himself when threatened, Danja exploded into action. Now her nervous movements hit the chair on which she had placed her violin, and she reacted as quickly, to keep the valuable instrument from falling to the cobbles. She gave Lozell a second nasty look, as if he had been responsible.

Sheledon reached across and took violin and bow from her, putting them very carefully on the table, which had been cleared of all but wineglasses. Absently he mopped a wine spill near the precious violin, one of the few usable relics from Landing Days. He gave it a loving pat while Danja continued.

"Like today," she said, resuming her pacing, "we taught in the morning and managed to eat something before we spent an afternoon painting, so that there will be some finished rooms for the summer term. We had five minutes to change, and even then we missed the fly-past, which I, for one," and she paused to jab her thumb into her sternum, "wanted to see.

"We've played two sets," she went on earnestly, "and will undoubtedly still be playing when the sun rises, and tomorrow will be a repeat of today except no Gather, so we get a good night's rest to prepare us for more of the above, except maybe get a little work done on next term. Which starts in a week, and then we'll have no time at all since we now have to prepare the teachers who'll be graduated to carry the Word to the outer extremities of the continent." She gestured eastward in a histrionic fashion, then flounced down on the chair the violin had occupied. "So how are we going to find time to do yet more research, Clisser?"

"We always do find the time," Clisser said, his quiet rejoinder a subtle criticism of her rant.

"Use it as a history class project?" suggested Lozell brightly.

"There you have the answer," said Bethany, who had merely, as was her habit, watched the fireworks Danja was so good at sending up. "My juniors could use an independent project."

"So long as we have power to run the Library," Danja added sourly.

"We will, we will," Clisser said, with bright encouragement. "Kalvi had his engineers up on the heights during the fly-past, working on the sun panels. They'll hook them up to the main banks tomorrow. Other people worked today, you know."

"Well, that's a big consolation," Danja said acidly.

Clisser refilled her glass. "And we'll need some catchy tunes and good lyrics, too, I should think. Something to teach students from a very early age so that they learn all the signs of a Pass before they learn to ask questions about it."

" 'One and one is two, two and two are four?' " Danja sang the old multiplying song, then grinned wryly.

"The song remains an effective teaching aid," Clisser said, filling his glass. "Shel, would you put on your composer's hat and whip up some simple effective tunes?"

Sheledon nodded enthusiastically. "I've been saying for years that we ought to incorporate more basic stuff into a musical format. Jemmy's good at little popular airs."

Bethany's face lit up with a great smile. Jemmy was a favorite pupil of hers, and she was his staunchest champion. Even Danja looked mollified.

"So," Clisser went on, having solved one of his immediate problems, "what shall we do in the next set?"

"Just like that?" Danja demanded. " 'What'll we do in this set?' Clisser, will you get real!"

Clisser looked hurt. Bethany leaned over and patted his hand, smiling encouragingly.

"What did you mean by that, Danja?" Clisser asked.

"Don't you realize what a huge responsibility you just so casually . . ." and Danja lifted wide her arms, flinging her hands skyward in exasperation, "laid on us all?"

"Nothing we can't solve, dear," Bethany said in her gentle manner. "With a little thought and time."

"Back to time again. Do we *have* time?" Lozell was back in the discussion. "Especially if the winter's even half as bad as it was last year—and it's supposed to be, with that damned Red Planet leering down on us—how are we going to cope?"

"We will. We always do," Sheledon said with a sigh of resignation. "Paulin will help us out. And certainly the Weyrs do."

Danja glared at him. "We've changed tunes, haven't we? I thought you thought we didn't have time."

Sheledon shrugged diffidently. "I think Lozell's idea of making a survey a class project will solve that problem. And, if Jemmy can whistle up some lyrics, I can certainly churn out some tunes. Or maybe Jemmy can do both in his spare time." Sheledon's face softened into a wry grin. He had had a tussle with himself not to be jealous of Jemmy, whose brilliance was multifaceted. Though he wasn't officially "graduated" from the Hall, he already ran several smaller study groups and seemed able to do a bit of everything—on a high level. The Consummate Jack of all Trades, Clisser called him.

"And what if, by leaving it to the student body, who are, as most students, indifferent researchers, the best notion is *missed*?" Danja asked.

"That's why we're teachers, dear," Bethany said. "To be sure they don't miss an obvious solution. They can at least save us having to sort through pounds of material and present us with the most viable options. We can put Jemmy in charge. He reads the fastest and his eyes are younger."

Just then the instrumentalists on the stage wound up their last number and received an enthusiastic ovation from both the sweating dancers and on-lookers drinking at the tables. They filed off the stage.

"All right, what set do we do, Clisser?" Sheledon asked, tossing off the last of his wine as he got to his feet.

"Those seniors did a lot of fast dance music," Clisser said. "Let's give everyone a chance to catch their breaths and do some slow stuff . . . the old traditionals, I think. Start with 'Long and Winding Road.' Put everyone in a sentimental mood."

"Hmmm . . . then we can get some supper while the juniors do what they so erroneously call 'music,' " said Danja, who had considerable contempt for the contemporary loud and diatonic musical fad.

"Can't please everyone all the time," Clisser said, collecting his guitar. He drew back Bethany's chair for her and offered her an arm. Smiling in her gentle way at the courtesy, Bethany picked up the flute in its worn hard case, her recorders in their leather sleeves, and the little reed whistle that had won its maker a prize that year. It had a particularly sweet clear tone that young Jemmy had been trying to reproduce with other reeds. Then she limped forward, seemingly oblivious to her clubbed foot and awkward gait, her head high, her gaze directed ahead of her.

Jemmy joined them from his table, automatically taking Bethany's flute case from her. He was the drummer for their group, though he had been playing guitar with others. Unprepossessing in physical appearance, with pale hair and skin and oversized features, he was self-effacing, indifferent to his academic achievements. While not in the least athletic, he had won the long-distance races in the Summer Games for the last three years. He did not, however, relate well to his peer group. "They don't think the same way I do," was his diffident self-appraisal.

That was, of course, accurate, since he had tested off the scale of the standard aptitude tests given prospective scholars. His family, fishers at Tillek Hold, didn't understand him at all and at one point thought him retarded. At fourteen he had followed his siblings into training in the family occupation. He lasted three voyages. Though he proved himself an able navigator, he had such constant motion sickness—never acquiring "sea legs"—that he had been useless as a deckhand: a source of much embarrassment to his family. Captain Kizan had interested himself in the lad, recommended the boy be trained as a teacher and sent Jemmy to Fort Hold for evaluation. Clisser had joyfully accepted him—finding such an avid learner was a real boost to his morale. And, when Clisser had seen how Jemmy galloped through even the hardest lessons, he set up an independent study program for him. Although Jemmy had perfect pitch, he couldn't sing, and started playing instruments to make up for that lack in himself. There was nothing he couldn't play, given a few hours of basic training.

Although his family, and indeed the Lord Holder Bastom, too, had expected him to return to Tillek to teach, Clisser argued hard that anyone could teach the basics to hold children. He would supply a suitably trained candidate, he said, but Jemmy must be allowed to continue at the College Hall, benefiting the entire continent.

What no one at the Hall mentioned beyond their most private sessions was that Jemmy seemed intuitively to know how to fill in the gaps left by improper copying or damaged records. His notations, short and concise, were models of lucidity. The College could not afford to do without his skills and intelligence. He wasn't a good teacher, being frustrated by mental processes slower than his own, but he could, and did, produce manuals and guides that enhanced the basic texts the settlers had brought with them. Jemmy translated "Earth" into "Pern."

If his peer group did not enjoy his company, he enjoyed that of his mentors, and was fast outstripping all of them in knowledge and practical applications. It was also well known, if tacitly ignored, that he idolized Bethany. She was consistently kind and encouraging to everyone but refused to accept any partner. She had long since decided never to inflict her deformity on offspring, and refused any intimacy, even a childless one.

Clisser wondered, though, as he and Bethany made their sedate way to the stage, if Jemmy might not breach the wall of her virginity. He was certain that Bethany cared more for the Tillek lad than anyone else in the thirty years he had known her—student and teacher. She was a lovely gentle woman: she deserved to be loved, and to love in return. Since there were ways of preventing conception, her prime concern could be taken care of. Clisser thought the age difference was immaterial. And Jemmy desperately needed the balance that a fully rounded life experience would give him.

Clisser and Jemmy provided support for Bethany to ascend the unrailed steps to the stage, and then, with a swirl of the long skirts that covered the built-up shoe she wore, she settled herself in her chair. She placed her flute case and the recorders where she wanted them, and the little reed flute on the music stand. Not that this group of musicians required printed sheets to read from, but the other groups did.

Danja lifted her fiddle to her chin, bow poised, and looked at Jemmy, who hummed an A with his perfect pitch for her to tune her strings. Sheledon softly strummed his guitar to check its tuning, and Lozell ran an arpeggio on his standing harp. The continent's one remaining piano—his preferred instrument—was undergoing repairs to the hammers: they had not yet managed to reproduce quite the same sort of felt that had been originally used.

Clisser nodded at Jemmy, who did a roll on his hand drum to attract attention, and then, on Clisser's downbeat, they began their set.

◆ ◆ ◆

It was several days before Clisser had a chance to discuss the project with Jemmy.

"I've wondered why we didn't use the balladic medium to teach history," Jemmy replied.

"It isn't history we'll be setting to music."

"Oh yes, it is," Jemmy had contradicted him in the flat and tactless way he had. It had taken Clisser time to get used to it. "Well, it will be when the next generation gets it . . . and the next one after that."

"That's a point, of course."

Jemmy hummed something but broke off and sprang across to the table, where he grabbed a sheet of paper, turning it to the unused side. He slashed five lines across it, added a clef, and immediately began to set notes down. Clisser was fascinated.

"Oh," Jemmy said offhandedly as his fingers flew up and down the lines, "I've had this tune bugging me for months now. It's almost a relief to put it down on paper now that I've a use for it." He marked off another measure, the pen hovering above the paper only briefly, before he was off again. "It can be a showpiece anyhow. Start off with a soprano—boy, of course, setting the scene. Then the tenors come in . . . they'll be the dragonriders, of course, and the baritones . . . Lord Holders, with a few basses to be the professionals . . . each describing his duty to the Weyr . . . then a final chorus, a reprise of the first verse, all Pern confirming what they owe the dragons. Yes, that'll do nicely for one."

Clisser knew when he wasn't needed, and left the room, smiling to himself. Now, if Bethany was right and this term's students could perform the research satisfactorily, he could make good on his blithe promise to the Council. He did hope that the computers would last long enough for a comprehensive search. They had got so erratic lately that their performance was suspect at most times. Some material was definitely scrambled and lost among files. And no one knew how to solve the problem of replacement parts. Of course, the PCs were so old and decrepit, it was truly a wonder that they had lasted as long as they had. Was there any point these days in holding a course on computer electronics?

Which thought reminded him that he had interviews with two sets of parents who were insisting that their offspring be put in the computer course since that was the most prestigious of those offered. And the one involving the least work since there were so few computers left. Where would they practice the skills they learned? Clisser wondered. Furthermore, neither of the two students concerned had the aptitude to work with mechanical objects. They just *thought* it was what they wanted. There were always a few cases like that in an academic year. And one set of holder parents who did *not* like their daughter associating with "lesser breeds without the law" . . . as Sheledon put it.

As if there was room, or facilities, for more than one teachers' school. Or the private tutors some holders felt should be supplied them because of their positions. Ha! As it was, the peripatetic teachers were going all year long, trying to cover the basics with children in the far-flung settlements. Well, maybe one day they could site a second campus—was that the word?—on the eastern coast. Of course, with Threadfall coming, he'd have to revise all the schedules as well as instruct his travelers on how to avoid getting killed by the stuff. He had seen footage—when the projector still worked—of actual Threadfall. He shuddered. Accustomed as he had been all his life to the prospect of the menace, he still didn't *like* the inevitability. The reality was nearly *on them.*

The Weyrleaders could waffle on about how well-prepared hold and Weyr were, with dragon strength at max, and groundcrews and equipment organized, but did anyone really *know* what it would be like? He swore under his breath as he made his way to the rooms that still needed to be completed to receive occupants in five days. He'd work on the syllabus during his lunch break.

A sudden thought struck him so that he halted, foot poised briefly above the next step. What they really needed was a totally new approach to education on Pern!

What was the point of teaching students subjects now rendered useless here on Pern? Like computer programming and electronic maintenance? What good did it do the Pernese boys and girls to know old geographic and political subdivisions of Terra? Useless information. They'd never go there! Such matters did not impinge on their daily lives. What was *needed* was a complete revision of learning priorities, suitable to those who were firmly and irrevocably based on this planet. Why did anyone *now* need to know the underlying causes of the Nathi Space War? No one here was going to go into space—even the dragons were limited to distance that they could travel before they were in oxygen debt. Why not study the spatial maps of Pern and forget those of Earth and its colonies? Study the Charter and its provisions as applicable to the Pernese citizenry, rather than prehistoric governments and societies. Well, some of the more relevant facts could be covered in the course to show how the current governmental system, such as it was, had been developed. But there was so much trivia—no wonder his teachers couldn't get through the lessons. Small wonder the students got bored. So little of what they were presently required to learn had any relevance to the life they lived and the planet they inhabited. History should really begin with Landing on Pern . . . well, some nodding acquaintance with the emergence of Homo sapiens, but why deal with the aliens that Earth's exploratory branch had discovered when there was little chance of them arriving in the Rukbat system?

And further, Clisser decided, taken up with the notion, we should encourage specialized training—raising agriculture and veterinary care to the prestige of computer sciences. Breeding to Pernese conditions and coping with Pernese parasites was far more important than knowing what had once bothered animals back on Earth. Teach the miners and metalworkers where the spatial maps showed deposits of ores and what they were good for; teach not the history of art—especially since many of the slides of Masterpieces had now deteriorated to muddy blurs—but how to use Pernese pigments, materials, design, and tailoring; teach the Great Currents, oceanography, fish-conservation, seamanship, naval engineering, and meteorology to those who fished the waters . . . As to that, why not separate the various disciplines so that each student would learn what he needed to know, not a lot of basically useless facts, figures, and theories?

For instance, get Kalvi to take in . . . what was the old term—ah, apprentices—take in apprentices to learn fabrication and metalwork? And there'd have to be a discipline for mining, as well as metalworking. One for weaving, farming, fishing. And one for teaching, too. Of course, education in itself was designed to teach you how to solve the problems that cropped up in daily living, but for specialties, you could really slim down to the essential skills required by each. As it was, that sort of apprentice system was almost in place anyhow . . . with parents either instructing their kids in the family's profession or getting a knowledgeable neighbor to do it. Kalvi had both sons now in supervisory capacities in his Telgar Works. And there should be provisions to save other kids, like Jemmy, and see that they were able to develop a potential not in keeping with their native hold's main business. Administer a basic aptitude test to every child at six, and the more specific one at eleven or twelve, and be able to identify special abilities and place him or her where he or she could learn best from the people qualified to maximize the innate potential.

Even in medicine, a new curriculum should be established, based on what was now available on Pern, rather than what the First Settlers had had. Mind you, Corey was constantly regretting the lack of this or that medicine, or equipment and procedures that would save lives but was no longer available. Clisser snorted: too much time was spent bitching about "what had been" and "if only we still had" instead of making the best of what was available in the here and now. What was that old saying?

> Ours not to wonder what were fair in life
> But finding what may be, make it fair up to our means?

Well, he couldn't remember who had said it or to what it applied. But the meaning definitely applied! Pern had great riches which were being ignored in the regret of the "what had been." Even Corey had to admit that the indigenous pharmacopoeia was proving to be sufficient for most common ailments, and even better in some cases now that the last of the carefully hoarded Earth chemicals were depleted.

Basic concepts of math, history, responsibility, duty could indeed be translated into music, easier to transmit and memorize. Why, anyone who could strum an instrument could give initial instruction in holds; teach kids to read, write, and do some figuring; and then let them apply themselves to the nitty-gritty of their life's occupation. And music had always been important here!

He put his foot down on the step, pleased with this moment's revelation. A whole new way of looking at the education and training of the young, and entirely suitable to the planet and its needs. He must really sit down and think it all through . . . when he found the time.

His laugh mocked his grandiose ideas, and yet they'd had to revise and reform so many old concepts here on Pern: Why not the method in which education was administered? Was that the word he wanted: administered? Like a medicine? He sighed. He did wish that learning was not considered an unavoidable dose. Certainly someone like Jemmy proved that learning was enjoyable. But then, insatiable appetites like his for knowledge, for its own sake, were rare.

Clisser trotted up the last of that flight in considerably better humor. He'd find the time, by all that's still holy, he would.

CHAPTER
III

Late Fall at Telgar Weyr

Zulaya beamed at Paulin. "Yes, she rather outdid herself, didn't she?" She turned to regard her queen fondly as the golden dragon hovered proprietarily over the fifty-one eggs which would, by all the signs, hatch sometime this day.

All morning dragons had conveyed in guests and candidates.

"Aren't the Weyrs overproducing a trifle?" Paulin asked. Benden and Ista Weyrs had also had Hatchings in the past month. He had lost two very promising holder lads to the Weyrs: a felt loss, as riders would no longer be as free as they were during an Interval to journey easily between hold and Weyr, and to learn and practice other professions.

"Frequent clutches are one of the surefire signs that there will be a Pass," Zulaya said, obviously looking forward to the days when the dragons of Pern started the work for which they were engineered. "Have you heard that song the College sent out?"

"Hmmm, yes, I have," and Paulin grinned. "In fact, I can't get it out of my mind."

"Clisser says they have several more to play for us tonight."

"Just music?" Paulin asked, scowling. "It's a device we asked them for . . . something permanent so that no one can deny the imminence of a Pass."

Zulaya patted his hand encouragingly. "You can ask what progress he's made on that project."

K'vin, coming up behind them, casually laid a hand on his Weyrwoman's shoulder, acting as proprietary of her as her dragon was of her clutch. Amused, Paulin coughed into his hand and hurriedly excused himself.

"He's worried about that fail-safe," Zulaya said, almost amused by K'vin's show of jealousy but not about to remark on it.

"You're looking very beautiful in that new dress," he said, eyeing it.

"Do I? Why, thank you, Kev," she said, twisting her hips to make the skirt whirl. "Which reminds me . . ." and she held out a fold of the rich crimson-patterned brocade that she had had made for this Hatching. "Fredig suggested tapestries, hanging in every Weyr and hold, depicting the return of the Red Star—with the formulae in the borders. Make an interesting design, certainly."

"Colors fade and fabrics certainly deteriorate . . ."

"We've some that graced houses in Landing. That Earth-Moon scene . . ."

"Which was made, as I've been told, out of synthetic yarns which are more durable than what we have now—cotton, linen, and wool. And even they are looking worn and losing color."

"I'll have them washed . . ."

"You'll have them thread-worn . . . oops," and K'vin grinned at the pun.

". . . which is not what is wanted, but there's no reason, Kev, not to have a hundred different reminders."

"Something set in stone . . ." the Weyrleader said in a more sober tone.

"Even stones move . . ."

"Only prior to a Pass. Only *how* to perpetuate the critical information?"

"I think everyone's worrying too much. I mean, here we are," and Zulaya gestured broadly to include the Hatching Ground and the Weyr around them. "Why else have dragons? And Weyrs set apart to preserve them, if not for a very, very good reason. They're the planet's only sure defense."

A sound, subliminal, more than a real noise, alerted them. It issued from Meranath, who reared to her hindquarters, spreading her broad wings, her eyes glowing brightly green and beginning to whirl with excitement.

"Ah, it starts," Zulaya said, smiling in anticipation. "Oh, I love Hatchings!"

Hand in hand the two Weyrleaders raced to the entrance and called out the news, scarcely needed, for the Telgar dragons were already reacting to the queen's maternal croon with their deep masculine humming.

The Weyr Bowl became active with dragons a-wing in excitement, flipping here and there on seemingly unavoidable collision courses: with the Weyrlingmaster herding the candidates forward; with parents and friends of the lucky boys and girls rushing across the hot sands to take their places in the amphitheater: hustling to get the best seating for the Impression about to happen.

K'vin sent Zulaya back to keep Meranath company as he urged people inside, checking the nervous white-clad candidates who had been halted in a clump near the entrance until the spectators were all seated.

"You've long enough to wait on the hot sands as it is," T'dam, the Weyrlingmaster, told them. "Singe your feet, you could, out there . . ."

All this time the humming was rising in volume: Meranath joined by all the other dragons in a chorus of tones that Sheledon—and others—had tried to imitate without quite succeeding. Meranath's throat was swollen with her sound, which continued unabated and seemingly without her needing to draw breath. Soon, as the volume increased, her chest and belly would begin to vibrate, too, with the intensity of her humming. K'vin was aware of the usual response in himself, a jumble of emotions; a joy that threatened to burst his heart through his chest, pride, hope, fear, yearning—oddly enough, hunger was part of it—and a sadness that, on some occasions, could make him weep. Zulaya always wept at Hatchings—at least, until Impressions began. Then she was jubilant, picking up on her queen's acceptance of her clutch's partnering.

In Fort Hold's storage there were file boxes full of early psychological profiles about the effect of Hatching on riders, dragons, and the new weyrlings. The bonding that occurred was of such complexity and depth that no other union could be compared to it: almost overwhelming in the initial moment of recognition, and certainly the most intense emotion the young candidates had ever experienced. Some youngsters had no trouble at all adapting to the intense and intrusive link: some suffered feelings of inadequacy and doubt. Every Weyr had its own compendium of information about what to do in such-and-such a situation. And every weyrling was assiduously trained and supported through the early months of the relationship until the Weyrleaders and Weyrlingmaster deemed he/she was stable enough to take responsibility for her/himself and her/his dragon.

But then, a rider was the dragon, and the dragon the rider, in a partnership that was so unwavering, its cessation resulted in suicide for the dragon who lost his mate. The unfortunate rider was as apt to take his life as not. If he lived, he was only half a man, totally bereft by his loss. Female riders were less apt to suicide: they at least had the option of sublimating their loss by having children.

When the little fire-lizards, who had supplied the genetic material to bioengineer the larger dragons, had still been available, a former male rider found some solace in such companionship. Only three fire-lizard clutches had been found in Ista in the last five decades; though it was thought more might be found in the Southern Continent, that quest had so far been futile. The vets had decided that some sort of odd disease had infected the creatures on northern warm beaches, reducing their numbers and/or their clutches. Whatever the reason, no one had fire-lizard companions anymore.

As soon as most of the guests had crossed the hot sands, T'dam allowed the candidates to make a loose circle around the eggs. There was no golden egg in this clutch—a circumstance that had both relieved and worried the Weyrleaders. They had five junior queens, which was quite enough for Telgar's low-flight wing. In fact, there was no dearth of queens in any of the Weyrs, but there was safety in having enough breeders.

Five girls stood on the Hatching Ground. There should have been six, but the girl's family had refused to give her up on Search since they claimed a union had been arranged and they could not go back on that pledge. As K'vin thought that a good third or even half of this clutch might be greens, he hoped there'd be enough suitable candidates to Impress all the green hatchings. Green dragons were valuable to a Weyr for their speed and agility, even if they didn't have the stamina of the larger dragons. Still, they were perhaps the most problematic when it came to Threadfighting. Greens with male riders tended to be more volatile, apt to ignore their Weyrleaders' orders in the excitement of a Fall—in short, they tended to unnecessarily show off their bravery to the rest of the Weyr. Female riders, on the other hand, while more stable, tended to get pregnant frequently, unless they were very careful, since the greens were usually very sexually active. Even spontaneous abortions due to the extreme cold of *between* required sensible convalescence, so female green riders were all too often off the duty roster for periods of time. "Taking a short dragonride" was now a euphemism for ending an unwanted pregnancy. Still, K'vin had fallen on the side of preferring females when Search provided them.

The draconic humming—what Clisser called a prebirth lullaby—was reaching an almost unendurable level, climaxing when the first egg cracked open. The spectators were exhibiting the usual excitability, jumping about, weeping, singing along with the dragons. They'd calm down, too, once the Hatching had begun.

And it did. Three shells burst outward simultaneously, fragments raining down on nearby eggs and causing them to crack, as well. K'vin counted nine dragons, six of them wetly green, and revised his "third" of greens closer to "half."

The hatchlings were so dangerous at this stage, ravenous from their encapsulation, and some of the nearer candidates hastily avoided the bumbling progress of the newborn. Two greens seemed headed for Weyrbred Jule, but the blonde from Ista, already noted in the Weyr for her quick wits, stepped beside one and Impression was made for both. Three of the other greens made for lads who had demonstrated homosexual preferences in their holds. The remaining green, after lunging out of her shell, stood, weaving her head back and forth, crying piteously.

T'dam called out to the remaining girls to converge on her. The brunette girl from Ista made for her and instantly the little green covered the intervening distance, squeaking with relief.

K'vin swallowed against the emotional lump in his throat: that instant of recognition always brought back the moment he had experienced the shock of Impression with Charanth. And the glory of that incredibly loving mind linking with his: the knowledge that they were indissolubly one, heart, mind, and soul.

We are, are we not? Charanth said, his tone rough with the memory of that rapture. Despite the fact that Charanth, like the rest of the Weyr's dragons, was perched up along the ceiling, K'vin could "hear" the dragon's sigh.

Zulaya grinned up at K'vin, aware of what was taking place within him, tears flowing down her face as the high emotional level of the Hatching affected her.

Absently K'vin thought that the glowing bulk of Meranath behind Zulaya made a great background for her beautiful new gown . . . red against gold.

Then another dozen or so eggs split wide open and the raucous screeching of starving little dragonets reverberated back and forth on the Ground. There was a piercing quality to these screams like lost souls. As each hatchling met its rider, the scream broke off and a mellow croon began. That quickly segued into a piteous "hungry" appeal which was almost more devastating than the earliest screech the weyrlings made. K'vin's stomach invariably went into empathetic hunger cramps.

The noise of a Hatching, K'vin thought, was unique. Fortunately, because human eardrums were not designed to deal with such decibels and cacophony, it didn't last too long. He always felt slightly deafened—certainly ear sore—by the end of a Hatching.

He was suddenly aware of another sort of babble and fuss going on just outside the Hatching Ground. K'vin tried to see what was happening, but noting T'dam striding over to investigate, he turned his attention back to the pairing of the last few Hatchings, two browns and the last green. Two lads were homing on the green, desperate expressions on their faces. Abruptly the green turned from them and resolutely charged across the sands to the girl who had just entered. K'vin gave a double take. There were only five girls, weren't there? Not that he wasn't glad to see another. And she was the one the green wanted, for the hatchling pushed aside the boy who tried to divert her.

Then three men strode into the Ground, furious expressions on their faces, with T'dam trying to intercept their angry progress toward the lately impressed green pair.

"Debera!" yelled the first man, reaching out and snatching her away from the green dragonet.

That was his first mistake, K'vin thought, running across sands to avert catastrophe. Damn it all. Why did this marvelous moment have to be interrupted so abruptly? Hatchings should be sacrosanct.

Before K'vin could get there, the green reacted to the man's attempt to separate her from her chosen one. She reared, despite being not altogether sure of her balance on wobbly hindquarters. Extending her short forearms with claws unsheathed, she lunged at the man.

K'vin had one look at the shock on his face, the fear on the girl's, before the dragon had the man down and was trying to open her jaws wide enough to fit around his head.

T'dam, being nearer, plunged to the rescue. The girl, Debera, was also trying to detach her dragonet from her father, for that's what she was calling him.

"Father! Father! Leave him alone, Morath. He can't touch me now, I'm a dragonrider. Morath, do you hear me?"

Except that K'vin was very anxious that Morath might have already injured the man, he was close to laughing at this Debera's tone of authority. The girl had instinctively adopted the right attitude with her newly hatched charge. No wonder she'd been Searched . . . and at some hold evidently not too far away.

K'vin assisted Debera while T'dam pulled the fallen man out of the dragon's reach. Then his companions hauled him even farther away while Morath continued to squeal, and writhed to resume her attack.

He would hurt you. He would own you. You are mine and I am yours and no one comes between us, Morath was saying so ferociously that every rider heard her.

Zulaya joined the group and, bending to check the father's injuries, called for the medics who were dealing with the minor lacerations that generally occurred at this time. Fortunately, Morath had no fangs yet, and although there were raw weals on the man's face and his chest had been badly scratched by unsheathed claws—despite their newness—he had been somewhat protected by the leather jerkin he wore.

By now most of the newly hatched were out of the Grounds, being fed their first meal by their new life companions. The spectators, beginning to descend from the amphitheater's levels, managed to get a peek at the injured man. Undoubtedly they would recount the incident at every opportunity.

K'vin hoped the embellishments would stay within reason. Now he had to deal with the facts.

"So, perhaps you would tell us what this is all about?" he asked Debera who, confronted by the Weyrleader and Weyrwoman, was suddenly overcome with remorse and doubt.

"I was Searched," she said, urgently stroking Morath, who was trying to burrow her head into the girl's body. "I had the right to come. I *wanted* to come," and then she waved an indignant hand at her prostrate father, "and they didn't even show me the letter telling me to come. *He* wants me for a union because he had a deal with Boris for a mining site and with Ganmar for taking me on. I don't want Ganmar, and I don't know anything about mining. I was Searched and I have the right to decide." The indignant words rushed out, accompanied by expressions of distaste, resentment, and anger.

"Yes, I remember seeing your name on the Search list, Debera," Zulaya said, ranging herself beside the girl in a subtle position of support. The alignment was not lost on the older of the two men attending their fallen friend. "You are Boris?" she asked him. "So you must be Ganmar," she said, addressing the younger one. "Did you not realize that Debera had been Searched?"

Ganmar looked very uncomfortable and dropped his eyes, while the scowl on Boris's face deepened and he jutted his jaw out obstinately.

"Lavel told me she'd refused."

At that point Maranis, the Weyr's medic, arrived to have a look at the wounded man. When he had, he sent a helper for litter bearers. Then he began to deal with the injuries, pulling back the tattered jerkin, provoking a groan from the dazed man.

"Well, Boris," Zulaya said at her sternest. "As you seem to be aware, Debera does have the right . . ."

"That's what you Weyrfolk always say. But it's us who suffer from what you call 'right.' "

"Making more trouble, Boris?" asked Tashvi, arriving just then with Salda.

"You agreed, Tashvi," Boris said with little courtesy for his Lord Holder. "You said we could dig that new mine. You were glad to have me and my son here start. And Lavel was willing for Ganmar to have his daughter . . ."

"Ah, but the daughter seems not to have been so willing," Lady Salda remarked.

"She was willing, all right, wasn't you, Deb?" Boris said, staring with angry accusation at the girl, who returned his look by lifting her chin proudly. "Till they came from the Weyr on Search . . ."

"Search has the priority," Tashvi said. "You know that, Boris."

"We had it all arranged," the father said, speaking up now that his pain had been alleviated by the numbweed Maranis had slathered on his wounds. "We had it *arranged*!" And the look he gave his daughter was trenchant with angry, bitter reproach.

"*You* had it all arranged," Debera said, equally bitter, "between your-selves but not with me, even *before* the Search." A wistful moan from Morath interrupted her angry rebuttal. "She's hungry. I have to feed her. Come along now," she added in a far more loving tone. Without a backward glance, she led her green dragon out of the Hatching Ground.

"I'd say that the matter was certainly not well arranged, then," Tashvi said.

"But it *was*," Lavel said, jabbing one fist at the dragonriders, "until they came 'round, putting ideas in her head when she was a good, hardworking girl who always did as she was told. Then you riders tell her she's fit for drag-ons. Fit! I know what you riders get up to, and Debera's a good girl. She's not like you lot—"

"That's quite enough of such talk," Zulaya said, drawing herself up, insulted.

"Indeed it is," Tashvi said, scowling angrily. "The Weyrwoman will real-ize that you're not yourself, wounded as you are . . ."

"Wounds got nothing to do with my righteous anger, Lord Holder. I know what I know, and I know we had it all arranged and you should stick up for your holders, not these Weyrfolk and all their queer customs and do-ings, and I dunno what'll happen to my daughter." At that point he began to weep, more in frustrated anger than from the pain of the now well-anes-thetized injuries. "She was a *good* girl until they come. A good biddable girl!"

Tashvi gestured peremptorily to the two litter men to take the man out. Then he turned back to the Weyrleaders.

"I did approve the new mine, and Boris and Ganmar as owners, but I'd no idea that Lavel was in any way involved. He's a troublemaker from way back," Tashvi said, absently shifting his feet on the hot sands.

Zulaya gestured for them all to leave the Hatching Ground. Despite the extra lining she'd put in her boots this morning, she was uncomfortable standing there, and Tashvi was wearing light pull-ons.

"And it's not that he doesn't have other daughters," Salda said, taking her husband's arm to speed up his progress. "He's got upward of a dozen children and had two wives already. At the rate he's been making these arrangements of his, he'll have himself sufficient land among his relatives to start his own hold. Not that anyone in their right mind would want *him* as a Lord Holder."

They paused outside the Ground now. Adroitly, Zulaya and K'vin chose a position so that they could also keep a weather eye on the newly hatched who, with the help of their riders, were rapidly devouring the piles of cut meat prepared for their initial feeding.

Debera's situation was unusual. Most families were glad enough to have a child chosen on Search, because of the advantages of having a dragonrider in the family: the combination of the prestige accrued to the Bloodline as well as the availability of transport.

Listening to the vitriol in Lavel's criticism of Weyr life upset both Weyrleaders and Lord Holders. It was true that certain customs and habits had been developed in the Weyrs to suit dragon needs, but promiscuity was certainly not encouraged. In fact, there was a very strictly observed code of conduct within the Weyr. There might not be formal union contracts, but no rider reneged on his word to a woman nor failed to make provision for any children of the pairing. And few Weyrbred children, reaching puberty, left the Weyr for the grandparental holds even if they failed to Impress.

By now the festivities had started in the Main Cavern, with the instrumentalists playing a happy tune, one that reflected the triumph of a successful Hatching. Although the new riders were still feeding their dragons or settling them into the weyrling barracks, once the sated dragonets fell asleep, the new dragonmen and women would join their relatives.

Zulaya wondered if she should remind Lavel that the female riders were housed separately from the males. He obviously had no idea at all how much care a new dragonet required from its human. Most days the weyrlings fell into bed too exhausted to do anything *but* sleep. And had to be rousted out of their bunks by the Weyrlingmaster when they failed to respond to their hungry dragons' summonses.

The young lad, Ganmar, sulked, looking decidedly uncomfortable in his present situation. Zulaya doubted that his heart was the least bit broken by this turn of events. Of course, if he had to work with that father of his building a new hold, maybe a pretty girl to bed at night would have been a major compensation.

"What I should like to know," Salda was saying, "is why Debera arrived here so late, on her own and you evidently in hot pursuit. You realize, of course," and the stern expression in Salda's eyes was one Zulaya knew well, "that we—Lord Tashvi and I—would not be at all pleased to find that Debera has been denied her holder rights."

"Holder?" Lavel snorted and then moaned as the injudicious movement caused him pain. "She'll not be a holder now, will she? She'll be lost to us forever, she will."

"And any chance of bagging her legal land allotment," Salda said with mock remorse. Lavel growled and tried to turn away from the Lady Holder.

"You've claimed more than most as it is. I trust Gisa is in good health? Or have you got yet another child on her? You'll wear her out the same as you did Milla, you know. But I suppose there are women stupid enough to fall for your ever-increasing land masses. Sssh," and Salda turned from him in disgust. "Get him out of my sight. He offends me. And sullies the spirit of this occasion."

"He's not so wounded he can't travel," the medic said helpfully.

"Travel?" Boris exclaimed, pretending dismay as he had glanced in the direction of the Lower Cavern, where the roasts were being served.

"I could find him a place overnight," Maranis began hesitantly.

Just then four young Weyrfolk led up the visitors' horses, which they had recaptured.

"Ah, here are your mounts, Boris," Zulaya said. "Let us not keep you from a safe journey home. You should easily make it home before dark. Maranis, give Lavel enough fellis juice to see him to his hold. Lads, help him mount. Come, K'vin, we're overlong congratulating the happy parents."

She linked her right arm in K'vin's and her left with Lady Salda and hauled them along across the Bowl.

"A very good Hatching, I'd say," she began, without a backward look at the three dismissed holders. "Nineteen greens, fifteen blues, eleven browns, and seven bronzes. Good distribution, too. Good size to the bronzes as well. I do believe every clutch produces dragons just slightly larger than the last."

"Dragons haven't yet reached their design size," K'vin said, answering her lead. "I doubt we'll see that in our lifetime."

"Surely they're big enough already?" Salda asked, her eyes wide.

Zulaya laughed. "Larger by several hands than the first ones who fought Thread, which will make it all that much easier for us this time 'round."

"You know what to expect, too," Tashvi said, nodding approval.

Zulaya and K'vin exchanged brief glances. Hopefully what they could expect did not include unwelcome surprises.

"Indeed we have the advantage of our ancestors in that," K'vin said stoutly.

Zulaya gave his arm a little squeeze before she released him and strode to the first table, where the families of two new brown riders were sitting. K'vin continued in with Salda and saw her and Tashvi settled at the head table, where he and Zulaya would join them after they'd done their obligatory rounds of the tables. Then, making a private bet with himself, he started at the opposite end of the wide cavern.

By the fourth stop he had won his bet: news of the unusual Impression of the last green dragon was already circulating.

"Is it *true*," the holder mother of a bronze rider asked, "that that girl had to run away from her hold?" She, and the others at this table, were clearly appalled at such a circumstance.

"She got here in time, that's what's important," K'vin said, glossing over that query.

"What if she hadn't come?" asked one of the adolescents, her expression avid. "Would the dragon have—"

She stopped abruptly, as if she'd been kicked under the table, K'vin thought, suppressing a grin.

"Ah," he said, bridging the brief pause, "but I'm sure you saw that other lads crowded 'round, ready and willing. The dragonet would have chosen one of them."

That was not exactly true. Which was why every Weyr had more than sufficient Candidates on the Ground during a Hatching. Early on, the records mentioned five occasions when a dragonet had not found a compatible personality. Its subsequent death had upset the Weyr to the point where every effort was then made to eliminate a second occurrence, including accepting the dragonet's choice from among spectators.

There were also cases where an egg did not hatch. In the early days, when the technology had still been available, necropsies had been performed to establish cause. In most of the recorded instances, there had been obvious yolk problems or the creature had been malformed and would not have survived Hatching. Three times, however, the cause of death could not be established, as the fetus had been perfect, with no apparent deficiency or disability. The message was handed down to dispose of such unhatched eggs *between* immediately: a duty performed on such rare occasions by the Weyrleader and his bronze.

"I saw her ride up," the girl said, delighted to recount this fact. "And then the men who tried to stop her."

"You must have had the best seat in the house," K'vin said, grinning.

The girl shot a vindictive glance around the table. "Yes, I did, didn't I? I saw it all! Even when the dragonet tried to eat someone. Was that her father?"

"Suze, now, that's enough of that," said her own father, and the older boy beside her must have pinched her for she shot straight up on the bench and glared at him.

"Yes, it was her father," K'vin said.

"Didn't he know any better than to strike a dragon's rider?" asked Suze's father, shocked by such behavior.

"I think he has perceived his error," K'vin said dryly and caught Suze's startled reaction. "What has your son"—and Charanth, as he always did,

supplied the boy's name so quickly that the pause was almost unnoticeable—
"Thomas, decided on for a rider name?"

"Well, I don't think Thomas dared to hope," his mother said, but her expression revealed both her pride in his modesty and her delight in his
success.

"He never liked being a Thomas," Suze said, irrepressible. "He'll pick a
new name," and she gave a snide sideways glance at her parents.

"And here he is, if I don't miss my guess," K'vin said, gesturing toward
the lad making his way across the cavern floor. K'vin had lectured the candidates on their responsibilities to their dragonets, so he was familiar with
many of them. This Thomas, or whatever, bore a strong enough resemblance
to both sister and brother to make him easily identifiable. He hoped that a facial resemblance was all Thomas shared with his sister. She was a spiteful one.

"Well done, young man," K'vin said, holding out his hand. "And how
shall we style you now?"

"S'mon, Weyrleader," the new bronze rider said, still flushed with elation. He had a good firm handshake. "I considered T'om but I never liked
the nickname."

"You said you'd—" Suze got yet another kick under the table for she
yipped this time and tears started in her eyes.

"It's easier to say," S'mon said. "Tiabeth likes it." Now he showed the delightful confusion of pride and proprietariness so many brand-new weyrlings
exhibited while accustoming themselves to their new condition and duties.
As K'vin remembered so vividly, that took time. "And there was a T'mas in
the first group at Benden."

"He's long dead," his father said, not altogether pleased with his son's
choice. "Thomas is a family name," he admitted to K'vin. "I'm Thomas,
ninth of my line."

The boy looked at his father with that curious aloofness of independence
that came with being a newly paired dragonrider: sort of "You can't tell me what
to do anymore" and "This is my business, Dad, you wouldn't understand."

"Tiabeth and S'mon," K'vin said, lifting the glass he'd been carrying
from table to table and drinking a toast to the partners. The others made
haste to repeat it. "Eat, S'mon. You'll need every meal you get a chance to
eat," he added, and left the boy to follow that very good advice.

At each subsequent table he heard more speculation about the late arrival of Debera. There had been embellishments: one had her father bleeding
to death. Another variation suggested that Debera had been the reluctant
one and her family had insisted that she try to Impress, having been Searched.
Young Suze had had the best seat in the Hatching Ground after all, despite

having been so far from the center that she hadn't had a good view of Impression, but a perfect one for what was happening outside. So K'vin edited the facts to keep the incident from getting out of hand. Fortunately, the music the band was playing, and the lyrics, provided a happy distraction. Most of the music was new. Clisser's musicians had done their job very well indeed.

He avoided having his glass filled too often, and used slices of the roast wherry and beef to sop up what was required by the obligatory toasting of the new riders.

He had almost completed his circuit when he saw the Telgar holders and T'dam leading Debera in, all moving toward the head table. Salda and Tashvi rose and went to meet her halfway. She still had a dazed look on her face, and glanced, almost wildly, around the crowded cavern. Someone had given her a green gown which showed off a most womanly body, and the style of it as well as the color suited Debera. The deep clear green set off her fine complexion and a head of curling bronze-colored hair which was attractively dressed, not straggling unkempt around a sweaty distraught face. No doubt Tisha, the headwoman, had had a hand in the transformation. Zulaya had once said Tisha treated all the Weyrgirls like live dolls, dressing them up and fussing with their hair. Nor was Tisha herself childless, but her excess of maternal instinct was an asset in the Weyr.

Salda put an arm about Debera, her head inclined to the shorter girl as she chatted: evidently determined to make up for the lack of family members on what was generally a very happy occasion for holder or Crafter. Had Debera seen the last of her relatives? No matter, she was in the larger, extended family of the Weyr and could find more amiable and sympathetic replacements.

Zulaya was introducing Debera to Sarra, the sun-bleached blonde from Ista who was chatting away with such animation that Debera smiled—tentatively, K'vin thought, but with growing self-confidence.

"You got Morath to sleep all right?" he asked, joining the women.

"I thought she'd never stop eating," Debera said, a slightly anxious frown on her face. Her green eyes, K'vin saw, were also emphasized by the color of the gown. Tisha had done her proud.

"They're voracious," Zulaya said, with a kind laugh. "And so am I. Come, let's all be seated before there's nothing left for us."

Salda gave a good-natured snort, grinning down at Debera. "Not likely. We've been sending you the fatted calves for the past week in anticipation." She turned to the girl as she passed her over to K'vin. "One thing's sure, girl, you'll eat higher on the hog here in Telgar than you ever did at home. *And* not have to cook it."

Debera was so clearly startled by such jocularity that K'vin took her hand, guiding her to the steps up to the platform on which the head table was placed.

"I think you'll be very happy here, Debera," he said gently, "with Morath as your friend."

Immediately the girl's face softened with joy and her eyes watered. Her look of vulnerable wonder struck such a responsive chord in him that he stumbled in following her.

"Oh, and she is more than a *friend*," she said, more like a prayer than a statement of fact.

"Come, sit beside me," Zulaya said, pulling out the chair, and signaling K'vin to take the one beyond. They were not in their usual center table position, but quick eye contact with Salda and Tashvi had the holders pulling out those chairs as if such placement was normal. "Listen to that melody. How lovely . . ." she added, tilting her head as the music, not quite martial, but firm, was stopping conversation throughout the cavern.

"So are the words . . ." Salda said, eyes widening in surprise, as well as delight, at what she heard. When her husband started to say something, she hushed him.

K'vin was happy to listen, too.

Sheledon, who had insisted on using the Telgar Impression as the debut of some new music, was very pleased that conversation had trailed off and everyone was hearing what was being sung. Now was the time to spring the big one on them. As soon as the coda on what Jemmy called "Dragonlove" had finished, he held up the music to the Duty Ballad and then pointed it at his soprano spouse, Sydra, who would sing the boy soprano part. They hadn't found a lad with a suitable voice yet, but she could whiten her voice to approximate the tone. At Sheledon's signal, Bethany piped the haunting notes of the intro and Sydra rose to sing the opening verse.

All right, they didn't have enough trained voices to really sock the Ballad to this audience—in his mind, Sheledon "heard" what a *full* chorus would sound like—but the excellent acoustics in the cavern were a big help. And the music captivated. Sydra managed to sound very young and awed . . . Gollagee came in with his fine tenor as the dragonrider, Sheledon was right on cue with his baritone part, and then, with Bethany singing alto and the Weyr's own musicians adding their voices, they wound it all up.

There was just one split second's total silence—the sort that makes performers rejoice—and then everyone was standing, wildly cheering, clapping, stamping their approval. Even the dragons joined in from outside, caught up in their riders' enthusiasms. Sydra kept bowing and urging the rest of the musicians to stand and accept the accolades. Even Bethany stood, a few tears trickling down her cheek at such a unanimous reception.

They gave five encores of the Ballad—with people adding their voices to the chorus as they quickly picked up on the words. When Sheledon ruefully waved off a sixth repeat, there were calls for the "Dragonlove" song which was so appropriate for this evening.

All in all, Sheledon decided as he caught Sydra's smiling face, a very successful debut! Jemmy had outdone himself and Clisser would be delighted. Perhaps there was something to Clisser's notion of redesigning the educational system so less time would be wasted on unessentials and the Real Meaning of Life could be addressed sooner.

CHAPTER
IV

Telgar Weyr and the College

It was the Weyrwoman, Zulaya, who noticed Debera's increasing nervousness. "Go on back to Morath, m'dear. You're exhausted and you'll need your sleep."

"Thank you . . . ah . . ."

"We make no use of titles in the Weyr," Zulaya added. "Just go. I've given you permission, if that's what you were so politely waiting for."

Debera murmured her thanks and rose, wanting to slip out as inconspicuously as possible. She'd felt so awkward and unsocial, even when everyone, even the Lord and Lady Holder, had been so incredibly kind and easy. She thought they would expect her to give an explanation of her unusual behavior, but they'd supported her instantly. Really, it was as if her *real* life had started the moment she and Morath had locked eyes.

It had, she decided as she made her way along the side of the cavern wall, head down so she needn't make eye contact with anyone. She saw only smiles from folks as she passed them, smiles and courtesy. And certainly none of the lascivious behavior that her father had often said was prevalent in the Weyr.

Of course, he'd told her a lot of things. And not told her others. Like the fact that an official announcement of Search, with her name on it, had been delivered to the hold so that she'd know when to come, to be available for the Hatching. No, she'd had to find that, stuffed in the cupboard where bits and pieces that could be reused were kept. No one at Balan Hold, especially her father and stepmother, Gisa, would have thrown out a whole sheet of paper that had a clean side that could be recycled. How she hated that word! Cycle, recycle. Use, reuse. The concept dominated every aspect of Balan Hold. And they were not "poor" in material possessions: not the way some holders were. But "poor" Balan Hold had been in spirit ever since her mother died.

She'd been looking for something else entirely when she found the sheet. Not that she knew the day's date, but it was obvious that the announcement must have come sometime before, the paper being soiled and the creases well set. Maybe even weeks. She had been ready to accept Ganmar as an alternative to continued living in her father's house. She knew that she'd have to work as hard, if not harder, setting up a new hold, chiseling it out of rock above the mine, but it would have been hers—and Ganmar's—and something she could design to her own wishes. Not that she'd been inclined to believe any of the blithe and extravagant promises Ganmar or Boris had made her. All they wanted was a strong body with lots of hard work in it.

But she had seen many dragons in the sky the day before, most of them carrying passengers. Balan Hold was not that far from Telgar Weyr—not even by surface travel. So, the moment she'd read the message, she made her plans right then, without any wavering. She'd been Searched. She had the right to be there. No matter how life in the Weyr might be, it couldn't be worse than what she now endured. And if she could be a dragonrider . . .

She had tucked the paper into her hip pocket and slammed the drawer shut. She was alone in the kitchen, and sun streamed in, almost as if adding light to her resolve. She didn't even go back to the room she shared with her three half sisters. Grabbing her jacket, she made for the paddock where the riding horses were kept. There was no one about in the yard: all were at work. Assignments had been given out over breakfast, and everyone had to show their father completed chores or there'd be no lunch break until they were.

She didn't even dare collect a saddle or bridle from the barn, because her eldest brothers were restacking hay—they'd done a sloppy job of it the first time around. She just grabbed up a leather thong. Since she'd had the most to do with the hold horses, she'd have little trouble managing any of them with just a lip rein.

Bilwil would be the fastest. She had probably three hours before the midday meal, when her absence would be noticed. By then she'd be well up the track to the Weyr.

With one look over her shoulder to see if she was being observed, Debera walked quickly—as if she were on an errand—to the paddock. Bilwil was not far from the fence that she climbed—the gate would be too near the vegetable garden where two half sisters were weeding. They loved nothing better than to report her "idling ways" to either their mother or her father. Two brothers were in the barn, the next pair out with her father in the forestry, and her stepmother in the dairy hold making cheese. Debera had been grinding wheat for flour when the cotter pin snapped. That's what she'd been trying to find in the drawer, a nail or something to replace the cotter pin so she could continue her task. So Gisa wouldn't miss her for a while to sound an alarm. For until flour had been made there'd be no bread, and Gisa wouldn't want to turn that heavy stone, not pregnant as she was.

Bilwil nickered softly when she approached him and grabbed his fore-lock. No one had bothered to groom him last night and his coat was rough with perspiration from yesterday's timber hauling. Maybe she should take one of the others. But Bilwil had lowered his head to accept the twist of thong around his lower jaw. She could scarcely risk chasing a better-rested, less amenable mount about the paddock, so she inserted the rein, grabbed a handful of mane, and vaulted to his back. Would she be vaulting to the back of a dragon tomorrow? She lay as flat as she could across his neck, just in case someone looked out across the paddock, and kneed him forward, toward the forest.

Just before they reached the intertwined hedging that marked the far boundary, she took one more look back at the hold buildings, its windows chiseled out of the very rock, the uneven entrance to the main living quarters, the wider one into the animal holding. Not a soul in sight.

"C'mon, Bilwil, let's get out of here," she'd murmured, and kicked him sharply into a trot, heading him right at the fence, a point not far from one of the tracks through the forest.

It was a good thing Bilwil liked to jump anyhow, because she'd given him only enough room to gather himself up. But he was nimbly over and had planted his left front foot, swinging left on it in response to her pull on his mouth and to her right heel as he brought his other feet down. In moments they were among the trees and quickly reached the track. Bilwil tried once to pull to the left, to go back to the hold, but she kicked him sharply and he went right. They were far enough from the hold so that his hoofsteps wouldn't be audible—not unless someone had their ear to the ground, which was unlikely. Noses would be to the grindstones where hers no longer was. The thought made her grin, though she was not yet safe from discovery.

As soon as the track widened she set Bilwil to a canter, enjoying the one activity in which she took any pleasure.

She stopped several times, to rest her own backside as well as Bilwil's . . . and found late berries to eat. She really ought to have snatched up the last of the breakfast cheese or even an apple or two to tide her over on the way.

It wasn't until Debera reached the final leg of the journey up to the Telgar Weyr that she was aware of pursuit. Or at least spied three horsemen on the road. They could well be visitors, coming for the Hatching, but it was prudent to suspect the worst. Her father could be one, and possibly Boris and Ganmar the other two. She had to get to the safety of the Weyr before they caught up to her. How had they made such good time in pursuit of her? Had someone seen her, after all, and run to alert Lavel?

A long tunnel had been carved in the thinnest wall of the Telgar Crater as access for surface traffic. It was lit with glow baskets. Bilwil was tired from the last long steep climb on top of yesterday's work. She thought she heard male voices yelling at her and kicked Bilwil into a weary trot. No matter how she used her heels on his ribs, he wouldn't extend his stride. Then she heard the humming—as if it emanated from the walls around her. She knew what that meant. She gave a cry of despair.

After all this, she'd be too late and there wouldn't be a dragon left for her to Impress . . . even if she had been Searched. How could she possibly go back? She wouldn't. She knew her rights. She'd been Searched. She could stay at the Weyr until the next clutch. Anything was preferable to going back to what she'd just left. The union with Ganmar would not have been any real improvement, although she had been determined to establish a proper relationship with the young miner. He looked impressible. Her own mother had told her that there were ways of handling a man so he didn't even know he was being managed. But Milla had died before she could impart those ways to her daughter. And Gisa, who had probably given up all thought of a second union if she had been desperate enough to partner her father, was a natural victim who enjoyed being dominated.

More hoofsteps sounded in the tunnel and, desperate to reach her objective, Debera kicked Bilwil on. The gallant animal fell into a heavy canter that jarred every bone in her body, but they made it into the Bowl.

Debera could see that not only was the Hatching Ground full of people, but also new, staggering dragonets. But as she got close enough she saw there were still a few eggs. Her pursuers were catching up. She had no need to halt Bilwil at the entrance. He stopped moving forward the moment she stopped kicking him. She slid off and raced toward the Hatching Ground just as her father, Boris, and Ganmar caught up, yelling at her to stop, to come to her senses . . . She wrenched herself free of grasping hands . . . just in time to reach Morath. And finally came into her own.

Now, as she made her way back to the weyrling barracks, she was as tired as she had ever been in her life, and far happier! As she rattled the door in her nervousness to open it, T'dam poked his head out of the boys' barracks next door.

"Back, are you? Well, she hasn't moved so much as a muscle. And I don't think you will, either, will you?"

She shook her head, too tired to speak. She opened one side of a door wide enough to accommodate wing-trailing dragonets and slipped inside, turning to close it after her, but T'dam came in as well, reaching up to turn the glowbasket open. It was well he did because Debera would have knocked into the first of the dragonet beds.

These were basically simple wooden platforms, raised half a meter above the ground, ample for dragons until they were old enough to be transferred to a permanent weyr apartment. The rider's bed was a trundle affair to one side of the dragon's, with storage space underneath and a deep chest at the foot.

She skirted the bed, relieved she had not awakened the occupant, and got to Morath's, the next one in. And hers. There were several items of clothing on the chest.

"Tisha sent in some other things since you weren't able to bring any changes with you," T'dam said. "And a nightdress, I believe. Open the glow above the bed and then I'll shut this one."

When she had done so, he closed the larger one and the door behind him. As soon as he had, she examined Morath, curled tightly on her platform, wings over her eyes. Was that how dragonets slept? Wondering at the good fortune that had happened to her this day, Debera watched the sleeping dragonet as dearly as any mother observed a newborn, much wanted child. Morath's belly still bulged with uneven lumps from all the meat she had eaten. T'dam had laughed when Debera worried that the dragonet would make herself sick with such greed.

"They repeat the process six or seven times a day the first month," he'd warned her. "You'll end up thinking you've spent all your life chopping gobbets until she settles to the usual three meals a day. But don't worry. By the end of her first year she'll be eating only twice a week—and catch her own at that."

Debera smiled, remembering that conversation and thinking that T'dam had no idea what a relief it would be to have such an easy job, the doing of which would be a labor of love and so gratefully received. She held her hand over her beloved Morath, wanting to caress this so-beloved creature but not wishing to disturb her—especially when Debera was all but asleep herself. She lingered, though, despite weariness, just watching Morath's ribs rise and fall in sleeping rhythm. Then she could no longer resist fatigue.

She was the lone human in the weyrling barn . . . no, barracks. Well, the others had their families to celebrate with. Who'd've thought that Debera of Balan Hold would be sleeping with dragons this night? She certainly hadn't. She slipped out of the fine dress now, smoothing the soft fabric of the green gown one last time as she folded it. It had felt so good on her body and was such a becoming color: quite the loveliest thing she had ever worn. Gisa had got all her mother's dresses, which ought by custom to have come to her. Debera shrugged into the nightgown, aware of the subtle bouquet of the herbs in which it had been stored. She'd once had time to gather the fragrant flowers and leaves for sachets with her mother.

She pulled back the thick woolen blanket, fingering its softness, and not regretting in the slightest the overwashed and thin ones she had shared with her stepsisters. The pillow was thick under her cheek, too, as she put her head down, and soft and redolent of yet more fragrances. That was all she had time to think.

◆ ◆ ◆

Back at the College, Sheledon, Bethany, and Sydra arrived a-dragonback, full of the ardent reception they'd had at Telgar Weyr.

"I don't know why we didn't think of Teaching Ballads before now," Sydra said, slightly hoarse from all the singing she'd done the night before.

"Too bad we hadn't the selections ready for the other two Impressions," Sheledon said, for he invariably saw disadvantages everywhere. "Are there any more upcoming?"

"Well, there're Year's End celebrations . . ." Bethany said.

"We tend to stay here for them," Sheledon replied, not wanting to miss the feasts that Chrislee generally provided for those holidays. The senior teachers at the College invariably were included on the Fort guest list and never missed such opportunities, even if they had the option of returning to their native hearths for the three-day celebration.

"Maybe this once," Sydra began, looking at Sheledon, "we should go home and spread the word."

Bethany frowned. "The full chorus and accompaniment is what makes the songs so effective . . ."

Sheledon frowned. "We can certainly organize substantial groups for the main Holds. The dragonriders always come as guests anyway, so they'd all get a chance to hear . . ." Then he smiled down at his wife, settling an affectionate arm across her shoulders. "You sure did the boy soprano bit well. But I think we'd best get the juvenile voice for Year's End. You're hoarse today."

"Halllooo down there," and they all looked up to see Clisser, bending far out an upper window and waving at them. "Did the ballads work?" he yelled, hands to his mouth.

The musicians looked at each other, Sheledon counted the beat, and they roared back, "THEY LOVED US!"

Clisser made a broad okay gesture with both hands and then waved them to go to his office in the original section of the facility.

They reached it first, still elated with the success of their performance, an elation that began to disperse when they saw Clisser's expression.

"What's the matter?" Bethany asked, half rising from her chair.

"The computers went down and Jemmy thinks they're totally banjaxed now," Clisser said glumly, flopping into the chair at his desk, his body slack in despair.

"What happened? They were working perfectly," Sheledon said, scowling. "What was Jemmy—"

Clisser held up one hand. "Not Jemmy . . ."

"One of those students hacking around . . ." Sheledon's expression suggested dire punishments.

Clisser shook his head. "Lightning . . ."

"Lightning? But we had no storm warnings . . ."

"Fried all the solar panels, too, although, at least we can replace *those*. Corey lost her system, what was left of it, including the diagnostics she's been trying so desperately to transcribe."

Made speechless by such a catastrophe, Sheledon sat down heavily on the corner of the desk while Sydra leaned disconsolately against the wall.

"How much is gone?" Bethany asked, trying to absorb the disaster.

"All of it," and Clisser flicked his fingers before he clasped them together across his chest, chin down.

"But . . . but, surely, it's only a matter—" Sheledon began.

"The motherboards are charcoal and glue," Clisser said dully. "Jemmy's gone through every box of chips we had left, and there aren't enough to rebuild even a few meg, and that wouldn't operate the system. Even part of the system. It's gone," and he waved his hand helplessly again.

There was silence for long moments as those in the room coped with such a massive loss.

"How much did the students—" Bethany began, cutting her sentence off as Clisser waved, almost irritably, to silence her. "Surely they saved something."

"Something, but nowhere near what we *need*, what was waiting to be copied, a mere fraction of what we need to know . . ."

"Look, Clisser," Bethany said gently, "what have we really lost?"

He jerked his head up, glaring at her. "What have we really lost? Why, everything!"

Sheledon and Sydra were regarding Bethany as if she had run mad.

"The history we are already seeing as irrelevant to our lives *now*?" she asked softly. "Descriptions of archaic devices and procedures that have no relevance on Pern since we no longer operate an advanced technological society? Isn't that what you were doing anyway, Clisser? Changing the direction of teaching in line to what is *needed* in this time, on this planet, and disregarding

I don't know how many gigabytes of stored information that *is* irrelevant! Now that we don't have to worry about all that," and her hand airily dismissed the loss, "we can forge ahead and not have to concern ourselves with translating *useless* trivia for posterity. So I ask you, what have we really lost?"

Silence extended until Sheledon uttered a sharp laugh. "You know, she may be right. We've been knocking ourselves out copying down stuff that won't work here on Pern anyhow. Especially," and his voice hardened, "since no one back on Earth cares enough to find out what's happened to us."

Sydra regarded her husband with a blink. "Not that old Tubberman homing tube business again?"

Sheledon went defensive. "Well, we know from—"

"The records," Sydra said with a malicious grin, and Sheledon flushed, "that the message tube was sent *without* Admiral Benden's authority. Without the name of a colony leader on it, no one on Earth would have paid it any heed. If it even got to Earth in the first place."

"Someone could have come and had a look-see," Sheledon said.

"Oh, come now, Shel," Bethany said, as amused by his sudden switch, for he had always derided the Tubberman Tube Theory. "Pern isn't rich enough for anyone to bother about."

"So the precious records said, but I think that was to save face. They should have checked on us to see how we were faring . . . They got awfully proprietary about the Shavian colonies that were the basic reason for the Nathi Space War."

"That was over three hundred years ago, Shel," Bethany said in her patient teacher-tone.

"And it is totally irrelevant to *now*," Sydra added. "Look, the loss of the computers is undeniably a blow to us. But not something we cannot overcome . . ."

"But all that information!" cried Clisser, tears coming to his eyes.

"Clisser dear," and Bethany leaned across to him, patting his hand gently, "we still have the best computers ever invented," she tapped her forehead, "and they're crammed full of information: more than we really need to operate."

"But . . . but now we'll never find out how to preserve *vital* information— like early warning of the return of the Red Star."

"We'll think of something," she said in such a confident tone that it penetrated Clisser's distress. And briefly he looked a trifle brighter.

Then he slumped down in even deeper despair. "But we've failed the trust placed in us to keep the data available . . ."

"Nonsense!" Sheledon said vehemently, crashing one fist down on the desktop. "We've kept them going past their design optimum. I've read enough in the old manuals to appreciate that. Every year for the past fifty has been a miracle. And we haven't, as Bethany says, lost all. A gimmick from the past has failed, like so many of them have. And we're now going to have to bypass the easy access to data they provided and sweat through books! Books! Books that we have in quantity."

Clisser blinked. He shook his head as if mentally rejecting a thought.

"We have been planning to ignore much of the old data," Bethany said gently. "What was most important to us," and her hand indicated the Pern of the present, "has been copied . . . well, most of it," she amended when Clisser opened his mouth. "If we haven't needed it up to now, we never will."

"But we've lost the sum total of human—" Clisser began.

"Ha!" Sydra said. "*Ancient* history, man. We've survived on Pern and it is *Pern* that's important. As Bethany said, if we haven't needed it up till now, we never will. So calm down."

Clisser scrubbed at his skull with both hands. "But how will I tell Paulin?"

"Didn't the lightning affect Fort, too?" Sheledon asked, and answered himself: "I thought I saw a workforce on the solar heights."

Clisser threw both hands up in the air. "I told him we were checking the damage . . ."

"Which is total?" Sheledon asked.

"Total!" and Clisser dropped his head once again to his chest in resignation to the inevitable.

"It's not as if you caused the storm, or anything, Cliss," Bethany said.

He gave her a burning look.

"Was the system being run at the time?" Sheledon asked.

"Of course not," Clisser said emphatically, scowling at Sheledon. "You know the rule. All electronics are turned off in any storm."

"And they were?"

"Of course they were."

Bethany exchanged a look with Sheledon as if they did not credit that assurance. They both knew that Jemmy would work until he fell asleep over the keyboard.

"I tell you," and Clisser went on, "everything powered went down. It's just luck that the generators have all those surge protectors, but even those didn't save the computers. The surge came in on the data bus, not the power lines."

"The computers were dying anyway. They are now dead, really truly dead," Sheledon said firmly. "Rest in peace. I'll go tell Paulin if he's who you're worried about."

"I am not," and Clisser banged his fist on the table, "worried about Paulin. And it's my duty to tell him."

"Then also tell him that our new teaching techniques are in place and that we've lost nothing that future generations will need to know," Sydra said.

"But . . . but . . . how do we know what they might need to know?" Clisser asked, clearly still despairing with that rhetorical question. "We don't know the half of what we *should* know."

Bethany rose and took the two steps to the beverage counter.

"It's not working, either," Clisser said in a sharp disgusted tone, flicking one hand at it, insult on injury.

"I shall miss the convenience," she said.

"We all shall miss convenience," Clisser said and exhaled sharply, once again combing his hair back from his forehead with impatient fingers.

"So," said Sydra with a shrug of her shoulders, "we use the gas ring instead. It heats water just as hot, if not as quickly. Now, let's all go get a reviving cup, shall we?" She took Clisser by the hand, to tug him out of his chair. "You look as if you need reviving."

"You're all high on last night's success," he said accusingly, but he got to his feet.

"As well we are," said Sheledon. "The better to console you, old friend."

"Clisser," Bethany began in her soft, persuasive voice, "we have known from our reading of the Second Crossing that the artificial intelligence, the Aivas, turned itself off. We know why. Because it wisely knew that people were beginning to think it was infallible: that it contained all the answers to all of mankind's problems. Not just its history. Mankind had begun to consider it not only an oracle, but to depend on it far more than was wise. For us. So it went down.

"We have let ourselves be guided too long by what we could read and extract from the data left to us on computer. We have been too dependent. It is high time we stood squarely on our own two feet . . ." She paused, twisting her mouth wryly, to underscore her own uneven stance. ". . . and made our own decisions. Especially when what the computers tell us has less and less relevance to our current problems."

"You said it, Bethany," Sheledon said, nodding approval, his mouth in a wry twist.

Clisser smoothed back his hair again and smiled ruefully. "It would have been better if this could all have happened just a little," and he made a space between thumb and forefinger, "later. When we found what we need for the dragonriders."

"You mean, a fail-proof system to prove the Red Star's on a drop course?" Sheledon asked, and then shrugged. "The best minds on the continent are working on that problem."

"We'll find a solution," Bethany said, again with her oddly calm resolution. "Mankind generally does, you know."

"That's why we have dragons," Sydra said. "I could really murder for a cup of klah."

CHAPTER V

Weyrling Barracks and Bitra Hold

An insistent, increasingly urgent sense of hunger nagged Debera out of so deep a sleep she was totally disoriented. The bed was too soft, she was alone in it, and neither the sounds nor smells around her were familiar.

I really am most terribly hungry and I know that you were very tired but my stomach is empty, empty, empty . . .

"*Morath!*" Debera shot bolt upright and cracked her poll on the underside of the dragonet's head because Morath had been leaning over her bed. "*Ouch!* Oh, dearest, I didn't hurt you, did I?" Standing up in the bed, Debera wrapped apologetic arms about Morath, stroking her cheeks and ear knobs, reassuring her with murmurs of regret and promises to never hurt her again.

The little dragon refocused her eyes, whirling lightly but with only the faintest tinge of the red of pain and alarm, which dissipated quickly with such ardent reassurances.

Your head is much harder than it looks, she said, giving hers a little shake.

Debera rubbed underneath Morath's jaw, where the contact had been made.

"I'm so sorry, dearest," and then she heard a giggle behind her and swiveling around, half in anger, half in reflexive defense, she saw that she was not alone in the weyrling barracks. The blonde girl from Ista—Sarra, that was her name—was sitting on the edge of her bed, folding clothes into the chest. Her dragonet was still curled up in a tight mound from which a slight snore could be heard.

"Oops, no offense intended . . ." Sarra said, smiling with such good nature that Debera immediately relaxed. "You should have seen the looks on your faces. Morath's eyes nearly crossed when you cracked her."

Debera rubbed the top of her head, grimacing, as she descended from the bed.

"I was so deeply asleep . . . I couldn't think where I was at first . . ."

"Morath's been as good as she could be," Sarra said. "T'dam said to dress for dirty work. We're supposed to bathe and oil them after their first nap of the day."

That was when Debera remembered the pile of things she had not properly sorted the previous night.

Does dressing take long? Morath asked plaintively.

"No, it doesn't, love," and, turning her back in case Sarra might be embarrassed, Debera hauled off the nightdress and threw on the garments on the top of the pile—not new, certainly, but suitable for rough work.

The socks were new, knitted of a sturdy cotton, and she was especially grateful for them since the pair she had had on yesterday had already been worn several days. She stamped her feet into her own boots and stood.

"I'm ready, dear," she said to the little green, who stepped down off the raised platform and promptly fell on her nose.

Sarra jumped the intervening bed to help right Morath, struggling so hard to keep from laughing that she nearly choked. Once Debera saw that Morath had taken no hurt, she grinned back at the Istan.

"Are they always this . . . ?"

Sarra nodded. "So T'dam told us. You'll find a pail of meat just outside the door . . . We get a break this first morning," and she wrinkled her nose in a grimace, "but after today, it's up at the crack of dawn and carve up our darlings' breakfasts."

There was a long snorting snore from Sarra's green, and Sarra whirled, waiting to see if the dragonet was waking up. But the snore trembled into a tiny soprano "Ooooooh" and the snoring resumed its rhythm.

"Did she do that all night long?" Debera asked.

I am SO hungry . . .

Debera was all apologies, and so was Sarra, who sprinted ahead to fling open both leaves of the door. She made a flourishing bow for their exit. Morath immediately crowded against Debera, pushing her to the right, her young nose detecting the enticing smell in the two covered pails on the rack outside the barracks.

Debera lifted the pail down while Morath impatiently nudged off the cover and seemed to inhale the gobbets. Debera allowed her to fill her mouth and then started shielding the pail with her body.

"You will chew what you eat, Morath, you hear me? You could choke to death and then where would I be?"

Morath gave her such a look of pained astonishment and reproach that Debera couldn't remain stern.

"Chew," she said, popping a handful of pieces into Morath's open mouth. "Chew!" she repeated, and Morath obediently exercised her jaws before spreading them wide again for another batch. Debera had not tended the orphaned young animals of her hold without learning some of the tricks.

Whoever had decided on the quantity, Debera thought, knew the precise size of a dragonet's belly. Morath's demands had slowed considerably as Debera reached the bottom of the pail, and the dragonet sighed before she swallowed the last.

"I see she's had breakfast," said T'dam, appearing from behind so suddenly that Morath squawked in surprise and Debera struggled to get to her feet. T'dam's hand on her shoulder pushed her back down.

"We're not formal in the Weyr, Debera," he said kindly. "Now, lead her over to the lake there," and he gestured to the right, where Debera recognized the large mounds as sleeping dragonets. "Then, when she wakes up from this feed she'll be just where you can bathe and oil her." T'dam grinned. "Before you can feed her again, though . . ." and then he motioned to his left. "Are you squeamish?" he asked.

Debera took a good look in the direction he pointed and saw six skinned carcasses, swaying from butchering tripods. Weyrlings were busy with knives, carving flesh off the bones or at the table, chopping raw meat into dragonet morsels.

"Me?" Debera gave a cynical snort. "Not likely."

"Good," T'dam said approvingly. "Some of your peers are. Come now, Morath," he added in a totally altered tone, loving and kind and wheedling, "you'll need a little rest, and the sands by the lake are warm in the sun . . ."

Morath lifted her head, her eyes glistening bluey-green as she regarded the Weyrlingmaster.

He is a nice man, she said, and began to waddle toward the lake: her swaying belly bulged lumpily with her meal.

"When you've settled her, Debera, be sure to get your own breakfast in the kitchen. Good thing you're not squeamish," he said, turning away, but his chuckle drifted back to Debera's ears.

It's awfully far to the lake, isn't it, Debera? Morath said, puffing.

"Not really," Debera said. "Anyway, it's much too rocky underfoot right here to make a comfortable bed for your nap."

Morath looked down her long nose, her left fore knocking a stone out of her path. And sighed. She kept going, Debera encouraging her with every slow step, until they reached the sandier ground surrounding the lake. It had recently been raked, the marks visible between the paw and tail prints of the dragonets. Debera urged Morath farther onto the sand, to an empty spot between two browns who were tightly curled, with wings to shield their eyes from the autumn sun pouring down on them.

With a great sigh, Morath dropped her hindquarters to the sand with an I'm-not-going-a-step-farther attitude and sank slowly over to her right side. She curled her tail about her, curved her head around under her left wing and, with a sweet babyish croon rumbling in her throat, fell asleep.

Once again Debera could barely bring herself to leave the dragonet, lost in the wonder of having been acceptable to such a marvelously lovable creature.

She'd been lonely and lacking in love for so long—ever since her mother had died and her oldest full brother had left the family hold. Now she had Morath, all her very own, and those long years of isolation faded into a trivial moment.

She's perfectly safe here, Debera decided finally and forced herself to leave Morath and make her way across that quadrant of the Bowl to the kitchen caverns. Enticing smells of fresh bread and other viands made her quicken her steps. She hoped she'd have enough restraint not to bolt her food like her dragonet.

The kitchen cavern at Telgar Weyr was actually a series of caves, each with an entrance, varying in size, width, and height. As Debera paused at the entrance of the nearest and smallest one, she saw that hearths or ovens were ranged against the outside wall, each with a separate chimney protruding up the cliff face. Inside, the many long tables where last night's guests had been entertained were reduced to the number needed by the regular population of the Weyr. But the interior was busy as men and women went about the food preparation tasks.

"Breakfast's over there," a woman said, smiling at Debera and pointing. "Porridge's still hot and the klah's fresh made. Help yourself."

Debera looked to her left to the farthest hearth, which had tables and chairs set invitingly near it.

"There'll be fresh baked bread soon, too, and I'll bring some over," the woman added, and proceeded on her own business.

Debera had only just served herself a heaping of porridge—not a lump in it nor a fleck of burn—and a cup of klah when two boys, looking bewildered and not at all sure of how to proceed, wandered in.

"The bowls are there, the cups there," Debera said, pointing. "And use that hunk of towel to hold the pot while you spoon out the cereal. It's hot."

They sent her tentative smiles—they must just be old enough for Impression, she thought, feeling just a trifle older and wiser. They managed, but not without slopping gobs of porridge into the fire and jumping back from the hiss and smell, to get enough in the bowls and to pour klah into their cups.

"C'mon, sit here, I won't bite," she said, tapping her table. They were certainly not a bit sullen or grouchy, like her younger half brothers.

"You've a green, haven't you?" the first one said. He had a crop of black curls that had recently been trimmed very close to his skull.

" 'Course she has a green, stooopid," the other lad said, elbowing the ribs of the first. "I'm M'rak, and Caneth's my bronze," he added with a justi- fiable smirk of pride.

"My bronze is Tiabeth," the black-haired boy said, equally as proud of his dragon, but added modestly, "I'm S'mon. What's yours named?"

"Morath," and Debera found herself grinning broadly. Did all new rid- ers feel as besotted as this?

The boys settled into chairs and began to eat, almost as eagerly as drag- onets. Deliberately, Debera slowed the rhythm of her spoon. This porridge was really too good to gulp down: not a husk nor a piece of grit in it. Obvi- ously Telgar tithed of its best to the Weyr, even with such a staple as oats for porridge. She sighed, grateful for more than Impressing Morath yesterday.

The boys suddenly stopped, spoons half lifted to their mouths, and warned, Debera turned quickly. Bearing down on their table was the unmis- takable bulk of Tisha, the headwoman of the cavern. Her broad face was wreathed with a smile as generous as she was.

"How are you today? Settling in all right? Need anything from stores? Parents will pack your Gather best and you really need your weeding worst," she said, her rich contralto voice bubbling with good humor. "Breakfast all right? Bread's just out of the oven and you can have all you want." She had halted by Debera's chair, and her hands, shapely with long strong fingers, patted Debera's shoulders lightly, as if imparting a special message to her along with that pressure. "You lack something, come tell me, or mention it to T'dam. You weyrlings shouldn't worry about anything other than caring for your dragonets. That's hard work enough, I'm telling you, so don't be shy, now." She gave Debera a little extra pat before she removed her hands.

"I didn't think to bring with me the gown you lent me last night," De- bera said, wondering if that's what the subtle message was.

"Heavens above, child," Tisha said, big eyes even wider in her round face, "why, that dress was made for you, even if we didn't know you'd be coming." Her deep chuckle made her large breasts and belly bounce.

"But it's far too good a dress—" Debera began in protest.

Tisha patted Debera's shoulder again. "And fits you to perfection. I love making new clothes. My passion, really, and you'll see: I'm always working on something." Pat, pat. "But if I'd no one in mind when I cut and sewed it last year, I couldn't have worked better for you if I'd tried. The dress is yours. We all like to have something pretty to wear on Seventh Day. Do you sew?" she asked, eyeing Debera hopefully.

"No, I'm afraid not," Debera answered, lowering her eyes, for she remembered her mother with work in her hands in the evenings, embroidering or sewing fine seams in Gather clothes. Gisa barely managed to mend rips, and certainly neither of her daughters was learning how to mend or make garments.

"Well, I don't know what holder women are doing with their young these days. Why, I had a needle in my hand by the time I was three . . ." Tisha went on.

The boys' eyes were glazing over at the turn of the conversation.

"And you'll learn to sew harnesses, my fine young friends," she said, wagging a finger at them. "And boots and jackets, too, if you've a mind to design your own flying wear."

"Huh?" was M'rak's astonished reaction. "Sewing's fer women."

"Not in the Weyr it isn't," Tisha said firmly. "As you'll see soon enough. It's all part of being a dragonrider. You'll learn. Ah, now, here's the bread, butter, and a pot of jam."

Sure enough, another ample woman, grinning with the pleasure of what she was about to bestow on them, deposited the laden tray on the table.

"That should help, thank you, Allie," Tisha said as Debera added a murmur of appreciation and S'mon remembered his manners, too. M'rak made no such delay in grabbing up a piece of the steaming bread and cramming it into his mouth.

"Wow! Great!"

"Well, just be sure you don't lose it, preparing your dragonet's next meal," Tisha said, and moved off before the astonished bronze rider had absorbed her remark.

"What'd she mean by that?" he asked the others.

Debera grinned. "Hold bred?"

"Naw, m'family's weavers," M'rak said. "From Keroon Hold."

"We have to cut up what our dragonets eat, though, don't we?" S'mon said in a slightly anxious voice. "From the . . . the bodies they got hung up?"

"You mean cut it off the things that wore the meat?" M'rak turned a little pale and swallowed.

"That's what we mean," Debera said. "If you like, I'll do your carving and you can just cut up. Deal?"

"You bet," M'rak said fervently. And gulped again, no longer attacking the rest of the bread that hung limply from his fingers. He put the slice down. "I didn't know that was part of being a dragonrider, too."

Debera chuckled. "I think we're all going to find out that being a dragonrider is not just sitting on its neck and going wherever we want to."

A prophesy she was to learn was all too accurate. She didn't regret making the bargain with the two youngsters—it was a fair distribution of effort—but it did seem that she spent her next weeks either butchering or feeding or bathing her dragonet, with no time for anything else but sleeping. She had dealt with orphaned animals, true, but none the size nor with the appetite capacity of dragonets. Morath seemed to grow overnight, as if instantly transferring what she ate to visible increase—which meant more to scrub, oil, *and* feed.

"It's worth it. I keep telling myself," Sarra murmured one day as she wearily sprawled onto her bed.

"Does it help?" Grasella asked, groaning as she turned on her side.

"Does it matter?" put in Mesla, kicking her boots off.

"All that oil is softening my hands," Debera remarked in pleased surprise, noticing the phenomenon for the first time.

"And matting my hair something wicked," Jule said, regarding the end of the fuzzy plait she kept her hair in. "I wonder when I'll have time to wash it again."

"If you ask Tisha, she'll give you the most marvelous massage," Angie said, stretching on her bed and yawning. "My leg's all better."

She and her Plath had tripped each other up and she'd pulled all the muscles in her right leg so badly that at first they feared she'd broken a bone in the tumble. Plath had been beside herself with worry until Maranis had pronounced the damage only a bad wrenching. The other girls had helped Angie tend Plath.

"All part of being a dragonrider," T'dam had said, but he exhibited sympathy in making sure he was at hand to assist her, too. "Nothing you won't grin about later."

• • •

Although the room in which Lord Chalkin sat so that the newly certified Artist Iantine could paint his portrait of the Lord Holder was warmer than any other chamber in Bitra that Iantine had occupied, he sighed softly in weariness. His hand was cramped and he was very tired, though he was careful not to reveal anything to his odious subject.

He had to do a bang-up job of this portrait as fast as possible or he might not leave this miserable hold until the spring. Fortunately, the first snow was melting and, if he finished the painting, he'd leave before the paint was dry. And *with* the marks he'd been promised!

Why he had ever thought himself able to handle any problem that could occur on a commission, he did not know. Certainly he had been warned: more about not gambling with any Bitrans, to be sure, had he had any marks to wager. But the warnings had been too general. Why hadn't Ussie told him how many other people had been defrauded by the Bitran Lord Holder? The contract had *seemed* all right, *sounded* all right, and was as near to a total disaster as made no never mind. Inexperienced and arrogant, that's what he was. Too self-assured to listen to the wisdom of the years of experience Master Domaize had tried to get through his thick head. But Master Domaize had a reputation for letting you deal with your own mistakes—especially the ones unconnected with Art.

"Please, Lord Chalkin, would you hold still just a moment longer? The light is too good to waste," Iantine said, aware of the twitching muscles in Chalkin's fat cheeks. The man didn't have a tic or anything, but he could no more be still in his fancy chair than his children.

Impishly, Iantine wondered if he could paint a twitch—a muscle rictus—but it was hard enough to make Chalkin look good as it was. The man's muddy brown, close-set eyes seemed to cross toward the bridge of his rather fleshy, bulbous nose—which Iantine had deftly refined.

Master Domaize had often told his students that one had to be discreet in portraying people, but Iantine had argued the matter: that realism was necessary if the subject wanted a "true" portrait.

"True portraits are never realistic," his master had told him and the other students in the vast barn of a place where classes were held. "Save realism for landscapes and historical murals, not for portraits. No one wants to see themselves as others see them. The successful portraitist is one who paints with both tact and sympathy."

Iantine remembered railing about dishonesty and pandering to egos. Master Domaize had looked over the half spectacles he now had to wear if he wanted to see beyond his nose and smiled that gentle knowing smile of his.

"Those of us who have learned that the portraitist must also be the diplomat make a living. Those of us who wish to portray truth end up in a craft hall, painting decorative borders."

When the commission to do miniatures of Lord Chalkin's young children had been received at Hall Domaize, there had been no immediate takers.

"What's wrong with it?" Iantine demanded when the notice had stayed on the board for three weeks with no one's initials. He would shortly sit his final exams at Hall Domaize and had hopes to pass them creditably.

"Chalkin's what's wrong with it," Ussie said with a cynical snort.

"Oh, I know his reputation," Iantine replied, blithely flicking a paint-stained hand, "everyone does. But he sets out the conditions," and he tapped the document, "and they're all the ones we're supposed to ask for."

Ussie smothered a derogatory laugh in his hand and eyed him in the patronizing way that irritated Iantine so. He knew he was a better draughtsman and colorist than Ussie would ever be, and yet Ussie always acted so superior. Iantine *knew* his general skills were better, and improving, because, of course, in the studio, everyone had a chance to view everyone else's work. Ussie's anatomical sketches looked as if a mutant had posed as the life model . . . and his use of color was bizarre. Ussie did much better with landscapes and was a dab hand at designing heraldry shields and icons and such peripheral artwork.

"Yes, but you'll have to *live* in Bitra Hold while you're doing it, and coming into winter is not the time to live there."

"What? To do four miniatures? How long could it take?" Iantine had a sevenday in mind. Even for very small and active children that should be sufficient.

"All right, all right, so you've always managed to get kids to sit still for you. But these are Chalkin's and if they're anything like him, you'll have the devil's own time getting them to behave long enough to get an accurate likeness. Only, I sincerely doubt that an 'accurate' likeness is what is required. And I know you, Ian . . ." Ussie waggled a finger at him, grinning more broadly now. "You'll never be able to glamorize the little darlings enough to satisfy doting papa."

"But—"

"The last time a commission came in from Chalkin," Chomas said, joining in the conversation, "Macartor was there for nine months before his work was deemed 'satisfactory.'" Chomas jabbed his finger at the clause that began "on the completion of satisfactory work," and said, "He came back a ghost of himself and poorer than he'd started out."

"Macartor?" Iantine knew of the journeyman, a capable man with a fine eye for detail, now doing murals for the new Hall at Nerat Hold. He tried to think of a reason Macartor had not been able to deal well with Chalkin. "Great man for detail but not for portraiture," he said.

Ussie's eyebrows raised high in his long face and his gray eyes danced with mischief.

"So, take the commission and learn for yourself. I mean, some of us *need* some extra marks before Turn's End, but not so badly as we'd go to Bitra Hold to earn 'em. You know the reputation there for gambling? They'd sooner stop breathing than stop gambling."

"Oh, it can't be half as bad as they say it is," Iantine replied. "The sixteen marks, plus keep and travel expenses, is scale."

Ussie ticked the points off on fingers. "Travel? Well, you'd have to pay your own way there—"

"But he specifies travel . . ." Iantine protested, tapping that phrase impatiently.

"Hmmm, but *you* have to pay out for the travel there and account for every quarter mark you spent. Take you a few days to sort out right there. Chalkin's so mingy no decent cook stays with him, ditto for housekeeper, steward, and any other staff, so you may end up having to cook your own meals . . . if he doesn't charge you for the fuel to cook with. The hold's not got central heating, and you'd want a room fire this time of the year in that region. Oh, and bring your own bedfurs, he doesn't supply them to casual workers . . ."

"Casual? A portraitist from Hall Domaize is *not* classified as a casual worker," Iantine said indignantly.

"At Bitra, my friend, everyone's casual," Chomas put in. "Chalkin's never issued a fair service contract in his life. And read *every single word* on the page if you are foolish enough to take the commission. Which, if you had the sense of little green apples, you won't." Chomas gave a final decisive nod of his head and continued on his way to his own workstation, where he was doing fine marquetry work on a desk.

However, Iantine had a particular need for the marks the commission would bring him. With his professional diploma all but in his hand, he wanted to start repaying what he owed his parents. His father wanted to avail of Iantine's land allotment to extend his pasturage, but he didn't have the marks to pay the Council transfer fees: never a huge amount, but sufficient so that Iantine's large family would have to cut back on what few luxuries they had to save the sum. It was therefore a matter of self-esteem and pride for Iantine to earn the fee.

His parents had given him a good start, more than he deserved, considering how seldom he had been at the hold since his twelfth birthday. His mother had wished him to be a teacher, as she had been before her marriage. She had taught all the basics to him, his nine siblings, and the children in the other nearby Benden mountain sheep and farm holds. And because he had shown not only a keen interest in learning, but also discernible skill in sketching—filling every inch of a precious drawing book with studies of every aspect of life on the hillside hold—it had been decided to send him to the College. His help would be missed, but his father had reluctantly agreed that the lad showed more aptitude with pen and pencil than shepherd's crook. His next youngest brother, who had the temperament for the work, had been ecstatic to be promoted to Iantine's tasks.

Once at the College, his unusual talent and insights were instantly recognized and encouraged. Master Clisser had insisted that he do a portfolio of sketches: "animal, mineral, and floral." That had been easy to collect since

Iantine constantly sketched and had many vignettes of unsuspecting class-mates: some done at times he should have been doing other lessons. One in particular—a favorite with Master Clisser—was of Bethany, playing her gui-tar, bending over the instrument for intricate chording. Everyone had ad-mired it, even Bethany.

His portfolio was submitted to several private Craft Halls which taught a variety of skills, from fine leather tooling to wood, glass, and stone workings. None of those on the West Coast had a place for another student, but the woman who was master weaver in Southern Boll had said she would contact Master Domaize in Keroon, one of the foremost portraitists on Pern, for she felt the boy's talent was in that direction.

To Iantine's astonishment, a green dragon had arrived one morning at the College, available to convey him back for a formal interview with Do-maize himself. Iantine wasn't quite sure what excited him most: the ride on the dragon *between*, the prospect of meeting Master Domaize, or the thought of being able to continue with art as a possible profession. Afterward, Master Domaize, having set him the task of sketching himself, had accepted him as a student and sent off a message to his parents that very day, arranging terms.

Iantine's family had been astounded to receive such a message. Still more astonishing had been the information that Benden's Lord and Lady Holder were willing to pay more than half his fees.

Now he must earn as much as he could, as soon as he could, to show his family that their sacrifices had not been wasted. Undoubtedly Lord Chalkin would be difficult. Undoubtedly there would be problems. But the marks promised for the commission would pay the Land Transfer fee. So he'd ini-tialed the contract, a copy was made for Master Domaize's files, and it had been returned to Lord Chalkin.

Chalkin had demanded, and received, a verification of Iantine's skill from his Master and then returned the signed contract.

"Best reread it, Ian," Ussie said when Iantine waved the document about in triumph.

"Why?" Iantine glanced down the page and pointed to the bottom lines. "Here's my signature, and Domaize's, alongside Chalkin's. That is, if that's what this scrawl is supposed to be." He held it out to Ussie.

"Hmm, looks all right, though I haven't seen Chalkin's hand before. My, where did they find this typewriter? Half the letters don't strike evenly." Ussie passed the document back.

"I'll see if there're any other examples of Lord Chalkin's signature in the files," Iantine said, "though how—and why—would he deny the contract when he himself proposed it?"

"He's a Bitran, and you know how they are. Are you sure that's your signature?" Ussie grinned as Iantine peered with a suspicious glare at his own name. Then Ussie laughed.

"Sure, I'm sure it's mine. Look at the slant of the *t*. Just as I always make it. What are you driving at, Ussie?" Iantine felt the first twinges of irritation with Ussie's attitude.

"Well, Bitrans are known to forge things. Remember those bogus Land Transfer deeds five years ago? No, I don't suppose you'd have heard about them. You'd've still been a schoolboy." With an airy wave of his hand, Ussie left a puzzled and worried Iantine.

When he brought the matter up to his master, Domaize could produce a sample of Lord Chalkin's signature on a document much creased and worn. Domaize also put his glasses up to his eyes and peered at his own name on the current contract.

"No, this is mine, and I recognize your slanting *t* bar." He put the document in the "to-do" tray. "We'll copy it into our Workbook. If you have any trouble, though, at Bitra Hold, let me know instantly. It's much easier to sort things out when they start, you know. And don't," and here Master Domaize had waggled a stern finger at him, "allow them to entice you into any games of chance, no matter how clever you think *you* are. Bitrans make their living at gaming. You can't compete at their level."

Iantine had promised faithfully to eschew any gaming. He'd never had much interest in such things, being far more likely to sketch the players than join the game. But gambling was not a "thing" that the Master would have meant. Iantine was learning what did fall into that category: especially the nuances of the word "satisfaction." Such a simple word that can be so misconstrued. As he had.

He had done not *four* miniatures, but nearly twenty, using up all the materials he had brought with him, so that he had had to send for more from Hall Domaize since the wood used in miniatures had to be specially seasoned or it would warp, especially in a damp environment like Bitra Hold. He had done the first four on the canvas he had brought with him for the job, only to discover, along with a long list of other objections from Lord Chalkin and his wife, Lady Nadona, that canvas was not "satisfactory."

"If it isn't the best quality," and she ran one of her almost dragon-talon nails across one canvas, snagging a thread so badly the surface was unusable, "it doesn't last long. Skybroom wood is what you should be using."

"Skybroom wood is expensive . . ."

"You're being very well paid for these miniatures," she said. "The least we can expect is the best grade of materials."

"Skybroom wood was not stipulated in the contract . . ."

"Did it *have* to be?" she demanded haughtily. "I made sure that Domaize Hall has the very highest standards."

"Master Domaize provided me with the best canvas," and he pushed his remaining frames out of her reach. "He said that is what he always supplies. You should have stipulated skybroom wood in the contract if that's what you wanted."

"Of course it would be what I wanted, young man. The very best is none too good for *my* children."

"Is there any available in the Hold?" he asked. At least with skybroom, you could clean off "unsatisfactory" work without the risk of damaging the surface.

"Of course."

That was his first mistake. However, at that point he was still eager to do a proper job to the best of his abilities. And what skybroom was there turned out to be substantial lumber, being cured for furniture and not thin enough to be used for miniatures: "miniatures" which were now twice the ordinary size.

High on the list of "unsatisfactory" were the poses of the children, although these had been suggested by the Lady Holder herself.

"Chaldon doesn't look at all natural," Lady Nadona said. "Not at all. He looks so tense, hunching his shoulders like that. Whyever did you not tell him to sit up straight?" Iantine forbore to mention that he had done so frequently and within Lady Nadona's hearing. "And you've given him such an odious scowl."

Which had been Chaldon's "natural" expression.

"Standing?" he suggested, cringing at the thought of arguing any of them into standing for the "sittings." He'd had enough trouble getting them to sit still. They were, as Ussie had foreseen, not biddable, and had such short attention spans that he could never get them to strike the right pose or assume an even halfway cheerful expression.

"And why on earth did you paint on such a small canvas? I'll need to use a magnifying glass," Lady Nadona had said, holding Chaldon's likeness away from her as far as her arm would reach. Iantine had known enough about his patroness by then to suppress a remark about her farsightedness.

"This is the customary size for a miniature . . ."

"So you say," she replied repressively. "I want something I can see when I'm on the other side of the room."

As she was generally on the "other side of her room" whenever her children were in her vicinity, the need was understandable. They were the messiest preadolescents Iantine had ever encountered: plump, since they were indolent by nature; dressed in ill-fitting apparel, since the hold's seamstress was not particularly adept; and constantly eating: generally something that ran, smeared, or left crumbs on their chins and tunics. None of them bathed frequently enough and their hair was long, greasy, and roughly cut. Even the two girls showed no feminine interest in their appearance. One had hacked her hair off with a knife . . . except the long tress she wore down the back, strung with beads and little bells. The other had thick braids which were rarely redone unless whatever fastened the end of the plaits had got lost.

Iantine had struggled with the porcine Chaldon, and realizing that the child could not be depicted "naturally," tried to retain enough resemblance so that others would know which child had been depicted. But his portrait was "unsatisfactory." Only the youngest, a sturdy lad of three who said nothing beyond "No" and carried a stuffed toy with him from which he could not be parted, was deemed marginally "satisfactory." Actually, the dirty "bear" was the best part of Briskin's portrait.

Iantine had tried to romanticize Luccha's unusual hairstyle and was told that she'd look better with "proper hair," which he could certainly add in if he was any good at all. And why did she have such an awkward expression on her face when Luccha had the sweetest smile and such a lovely disposition? (Especially when she was busy trying to unite the hold's cats by tying their tails together, Iantine had said mentally. Bitra Hold did not have a single unscathed animal, and the spit boy said they'd lost seven dogs to "accidents" that year already.) Luccha's mouth was set aslant in her face, the thin lips usually compressed in a sour line. Lonada, the second daughter, had a pudding face, with small dark holes for eyes, and her father's nose: bad enough in a male but fatal for a female.

Iantine had also had to "buy" a lock from the hold steward to prevent his sleeping furs from walking out of the narrow little cubicle in which he was quartered. He knew his packs had been searched the first day; probably several times, by the variety of smeared fingerprints left on the paint pots. As he had brought nothing of real value with him—not having many possessions, he hadn't worried. Holds usually had one light-fingered person. And the hold steward usually knew who it was and retrieved what had gone astray from guests' rooms. But when Iantine found his paint pots left open to dry out, he protested. And "paid" for a lock. Not that he felt all that secure, for if there was one key to that lock, there could be duplicates. But his furs did remain on his bed. And glad he was to have them, for the thin blanket supplied was holey and ought to have been torn up for rug lengths long since.

That was the least of his problems at Bitra Hold. Having heard all that was wrong with the next set of miniatures he managed to produce, a third larger than the first, Iantine began to have a somewhat clearer grasp of just how the parents envisaged their offspring. On his fifth set he nearly won the accolade of "satisfactory." Nearly . . .

Then the children, one after another, succumbed to an infant disease that resulted in such a rash that they could not possibly "sit."

"Well, you'd better do something to earn your keep," Chalkin told his contract portraitist when Lady Nadona had announced the children were isolated.

"The contract says I will have room and board—"

Chalkin held up a thick forefinger, his smile not the least bit humorous. "*When* you are honoring that contract . . ."

"But the children are sick . . ."

Chalkin had shrugged. "That's neither here nor there. You are unable to honor the specific conditions of the contract. Therefore you are not entitled to be fed and housed at the hold's expense. Of course, I can always deduct your leisure time from the fee . . ." The smile deepened vindictively.

"Leisure . . ." Iantine had been so enraged, the protest burst from him before he could suppress it. No wonder, he thought, shaking with the control he had to enforce on himself, no one else at Hall Domaize would sign with Bitra.

"Well," Chalkin went on as if he were a reasonable man, "what else does one call it if you are not engaged in the labors which you are contracted for?"

Iantine had to wonder if Chalkin knew how necessary it was for him to earn the exact fee promised. Iantine had held no conversations with anyone in the hold: they were so sullen and uncommunicative a group at their best—which was usually at mealtimes—that he hoped he'd be spared them at their worst. He had steadfastly refused to "have a little game" with cooks or guards, which accounted for a good deal of the general animosity toward him. So how would anyone know anything about his personal life or his reasons for working here?

So, instead of already being on his way home with a satisfactory contract fulfilled and the marks of the transfer fee heavy in his pouch, Iantine spent his "leisure" time touching up the faces of Chalkin's ancestors in the main hall murals.

"Good practice for you, I'm sure," Chalkin had said, all too amiably, as he made his daily inspection of this project. "You'll be better equipped to do satisfactory portraits of this generation."

Pig faces, all of them, with the ancestral bulbous nose, Iantine noticed. Oddly enough, one or two of the ancestresses had been very pretty girls, far too young and attractive for the mean-mouthed men they had been contracted to. Too bad the male genes dominated.

Of course, Iantine had had to make up batches of the special paints required for mural work, having initially had no idea such would be required. He also found his supplies of the oil paints drastically reduced by the repeated unsatisfactory portraits. He had the choice of sending back to Hall Domaize for additional supplies—and paying transport charges plus having to wait for them to reach him—or finding the raw materials and manufacturing the colors himself. Which was the better option.

"How much?" he exclaimed in shock when the head cook told him how much he'd have to pay for the eggs and oil he needed to mix into his pigments.

"Yiss, an' that doan include cost of hiring the equipment," the cook added, sniffing. The man had a perpetually running nose, sometimes dripping down his upper lip. But not, Iantine devoutly hoped, into whatever he was in the process of preparing.

"I have to hire bowls and jars from you?" Iantine wondered how the cook could have become infected with Chalkin's greed.

"Well, if I aint using 'em, and you is, you should pay for the use, seems like." He sniffed so deeply Iantine wondered there could be any mucus left in his sinus cavities. "Shoulda brought yer stuff with ye if ye'd need it. Lord Holder sees you usin' things from his kitchen and one of us'll be paying for it. Won't be me!" And he sniffed again, shrugging one dirty white shoulder as emphasis.

"I came with adequate supplies and equipment for the work I was hired to do," Iantine said, curbing an intense desire to shove the man's face in the thin soup he was stirring.

"So?"

Iantine had walked, stiff-legged with fury, out of the kitchen. He tried to tell himself that he was learning, the very hardest way, how to deal with the client.

Finding the raw materials for his pigments had proved nearly as difficult since it was, after all, coming on to deep winter here in the Bitran hills. He discovered a hefty hunk of stone with a rounded end that would do as pestle and then a hollowed out rock that would act as a mortar. He had found a whole hillside of the sabsab bush, whose roots produced a yellow color; enough raw cobalt to get blue; and the pawberry leaves that boiled up one of the finest pure reds—with neither tint nor tinge of orange or purple. With the greatest of luck he also came across ochre mud. Rather than "rent" containers, he used chipped crockery he unearthed from the midden heap. He did have to pay the price of best oil for the substandard stuff that was all the cook would sell him. And that mark, he was sure, would never be passed on to Lord Chalkin as fee.

He managed to get enough saucers or mugs—they used a very cheap pottery in Bitra Hold—to hold the different colors he needed. He hadn't quite finished the repair work when Chaldon recovered sufficiently from the rash to be able to sit/stand—once more.

Chaldon had lost weight during the fever which accompanied the emergence of the rash. He was also lethargic, and as long as Iantine could think up funny stories to tell as he worked, he stayed reasonably still. Calling himself the worst kind of panderer, Iantine made the boy resemble the best looking of the ancestors he'd relimned. The boy was certainly pleased and ran off to find his mother, shouting that he did look like Great-granddaddy, just as she always said he did.

The same ploy did not quite work on Luccha's portrait when she had recovered. Her skin was sallower, she'd lost hair and too much weight to improve her undistinguished looks. While he had aimed for her great-grandmother thrice removed, she didn't have the right facial structure and even he had to admit the result was unsatisfactory.

"Her illness," he'd mumbled when Chalkin and Nadona recited the long catalog of dissimilarities between their daughter and the portrait.

He did better with Loñada and Briskin, who, several kilos lighter, had the look of his great-uncle—pinch-faced, lantern-jawed, and big-eared. Iantine had judiciously reduced the size of those even as he wondered what Artist had got away with such unflattering appendages on great-uncle.

He redid Luccha's after the other two: she'd put on some weight and her color was better. Not much, but better. And he set her eyes wider in her face, which improved her no end. Too bad it couldn't be done to the model. He vaguely remembered that the First Settlers had been able to remodel noses and bob ears and stuff like that.

So, grudgingly and after making him touch up each of the four not-so-miniature paintings to the point where he was ready to break something— their heads for preference—the Lord and Lady Holder considered the four paintings satisfactory. The final critiquing had lasted well into the night, which was dark and stormy: the winds audible even through the three-meter-thick cliff walls.

So, as he descended wearily but in great relief to the lower-floor cubicle, he became aware of the intense chill in this level. The temperature in the big Hall had been somewhat warmed by the roaring fires in the four hearths, but there was no heating down here. In fact, it was so cold that Iantine did no more than loosen his belt and remove his boots before crawling onto the hard surface that was supposed to be a mattress. It looked and felt like something recycled from the ships of the First Crossing. He curled up in the furs, more grateful than ever that he'd brought his own, and fell asleep.

Arctic temperatures swirling about his face roused him. His face was stiff with cold and, despite the warmth of his furs, when he tried to stretch his body, his muscles resisted. He had a crick in his neck and he wondered if he'd moved at all during the night. Certainly it was cold enough to have kept in the warm of the furs. But he had to relieve himself.

He crammed his feet into boot leather that was rigid with ice and, wrapping his furs tightly about himself, made his way down the corridor to the toilet. His breath was a plume of white, his cheeks and nose stung by the cold. He managed his business and returned to his room only long enough to throw on his thickest woolen jumper. With half a mind to throw his furs around him for added warmth, he ran up the several flights of stone steps, past walls that dripped with moisture. He paused at the first window on the upper level: solidly snowed closed. He went up the next short flight and opened the door into what should have been the relatively warmer kitchen area.

Had every fire in the place gone out overnight? Had the spit boys frozen on their bed shelf? As he turned his head in their direction, his glance caught at the window. Snow was piled up against the first hand's breadth of it. He moved closer and looked out at the courtyard but it was all one expanse of unbroken snow. Indeed, where the courtyard should have stepped down to the roadway, the snow was even, concealing any depression where the road should have been. No one moved outside. Nor were there any tracks in the expanse of snow-covered court to suggest that anyone had tried to come in from one of the outer holds.

"Just what I needed," Iantine said, totally depressed by what he saw. "I could be trapped here for weeks!"

Paying for room and board. If only the kids hadn't come down with measles . . . If only he hadn't already freshened up the murals . . . How would he survive? Would he have any left of his original fee—that had seemed so generous—by the time he could leave this miserable hold?

Later that morning, when half-frozen people had begun to cope with the effects of the blizzard, he struck another bargain with the Holder Lord and Lady: and very carefully did he word it. Two full-sized portraits, each a square meter on skybroom wood to be supplied by Lord Chalkin, one of Lady Nadona and one of Lord Chalkin, head and shoulder in Gather dress, with all materials and equipment to make additional pigments supplied by the hold; maintenance for himself and quarters on an upper floor with morning and evening fuel for a fire on the hearth.

He completed Lady Nadona's portrait without too much difficulty—she would sit still, loved nothing better than to have a valid excuse for doing nothing. Halfway through the sitting, though, she wanted to change her costume, believing the red did not flatter her complexion as well as the blue. It didn't, but he talked her out of changing and subtly altered her naturally florid complexion to a kinder blush and darkened the color of her pale eyes so that they seemed to dominate her face. By then he'd heard enough of the supposed resemblance between herself and Luccha so that he improved on it, giving her a more youthful appearance.

When she wanted to change the collar of her dress, he improvised one he remembered seeing in an Ancient's portrait—a lacy froth that hid much of the loose skin of her neck. Not that he had painted *that* in, but the lace softened the whole look of her.

He had not been as lucky with Chalkin. The man was psychologically unable to sit still—tapping his fingers, swinging one leg as he crossed and uncrossed them, twitching his shoulders or his face, making it basically impossible to obtain a set pose.

Iantine was nearly desperate now to finish and leave this dreadful place before another snowstorm. The young portraitist wondered if Chalkin's delays, and the short periods in which he would deign to sit, were yet another ploy to delay him—and rake back some of the original fee. Though Chalkin had even invited him to come into the gaming rooms—the warmest and most elegant rooms in the hold, Iantine had managed to excuse himself somehow or other.

"Do sit still, Lord Chalkin, I'm working on your eyes and I cannot if you keep moving them about in your face," Iantine said, rather more sharply than he had ever addressed the Lord Holder before.

"I beg your pardon," Chalkin said, jerking his shoulders about angrily.

"Lord Chalkin, unless you wish to be portrayed with your eyes crossed, *sit still for five minutes*! I beg of you."

Something of Iantine's frustration must have come across because Chalkin not only sat still, he glared at the portraitist. And for longer than five minutes.

Working as fast as he could, Iantine completed the delicate work on the eyes. He had subtly widened them in the man's face and cleared up the edemic pouches that sagged below them. He had made the jowly face less porcine and subtracted sufficient flesh from the bulbous nose to give it a more Roman look. He had also widened and lifted the shoulders to give a more athletic appearance and darkened the hair. Further, he had meticulously caught the fire of the many-jeweled rings. Actually, they dominated the painting, which he felt would find favor with Lord Chalkin, who seemed to have more rings than days of the year.

"There!" he said, putting down his brush and standing back from the painting, satisfied in himself that he had done the best job possible: that is, the best job that would prove "satisfactory" and allow him to leave this ghastly hold.

"It's about time," Chalkin said, slipping down from the chair and stamping over to view the result.

Iantine watched his face, seeing that flash of pleasure before Chalkin's usual glum expression settled back over his features. Chalkin peered more closely, seeming to count the brush strokes—although there were none, for Iantine was too competent a technician to have left any.

"Watch the paint. It's not yet dry," Iantine said quickly, raising his arm to ward off Chalkin's touch.

"Humph," Chalkin said, shrugging his shoulders to settle his heavy jerkin. He affected diffidence, but the way he kept looking at his own face told Iantine that the man was finally pleased.

"Well? Is it satisfactory?" Iantine asked, unable to bear the suspense any longer.

"Not bad, not bad, but . . ." and Chalkin once again put out a finger.

"You will not smear the paint, Lord Chalkin," Iantine said, fearing just that and another session to repair the damage.

"You're a rude fellow, painter."

"My title is Artist, Lord Chalkin, and do tell me if this portrait is satisfactory or not!"

Chalkin gave him a quick nervous glance, one facial muscle twitching. Even the Lord of Bitra Hold knew when he had pushed someone too hard.

"It's not bad . . ."

"Is it satisfactory, Lord Chalkin?" Iantine put all the pent-up frustration and anxiety into that question.

Chalkin shifted one shoulder, screwed up his face with indecision and then hastily composed his features in the more dignified pose of the portrait before him.

"Yes, I believe it is satisfactory."

"Then," and now Iantine took Lord Chalkin by the elbow and steered him toward the door, "let us to your office and complete the contract."

"Now, see here—"

"If it is satisfactory, I have honored that contract and you may now settle with me for the miniatures," Iantine said, guiding the man down the cold corridor and to his office. He tapped his foot impatiently as Chalkin took the keys from his inside pocket and opened the door.

The fire within was so fierce that Iantine felt sweat blossom on his forehead. At Chalkin's abrupt gesture, he turned around while the man fiddled with whatever it was he had in his strongbox. He heard, with infinite relief, the turn of the metal lock and then silence. A slamming of a lid.

"Here you are," said Chalkin coldly.

Iantine counted out the marks, sixteen of them, Farmermarks, but good enough since he would be using them in Benden, which didn't mind Farmermarks.

"The contracts?"

Chalkin glared but he unlocked the drawer and extracted them, almost flinging them across the desk at Iantine. Iantine signed his name and turned them back to Chalkin.

"Use mine," Iantine said when Chalkin made a show of finding a good pen in the clutter on his desk.

Chalkin scrawled his name.

"Date it," Iantine added, wishing to have no complaint at a later time.

"You want too much, painter."

"Artist, Lord Chalkin," Iantine said with a humorless smile and turned to leave. At the door he turned again, "And don't touch the painting for forty-eight hours. I will not come back if you smear it. It was satisfactory when we left the room. Keep it that way."

Iantine returned to collect his good brushes, but left what remained of the paints he had had to make. Last night, in a hopeful mood, he had packed everything else. Now, he took the stairs up two and three at a time, stored his brushes carefully, stuffed the signed and dated contracts into his pack, shrugged into his coat, rolled up his sleeping furs, looped both packs in one hand, and was halfway down the stairs again when he met Chalkin ascending.

"You cannot leave now," Chalkin protested, grabbing his arm. "You have to wait until my wife has seen and approved my portrait."

"Oh, no, I don't," Iantine said, wrenching free of the restraining hand.

He was out the main door before Chalkin could say another word, and ran down the roadway between the soiled snowbanks. If he was benighted on the road in the middle of a snowstorm, he would still be safer than staying one more hour at Bitra Hold.

Luckily for him, he found shelter during that next storm in a woodman's holding some klicks away from the main hold.

CHAPTER
VI

Telgar Weyr, Fort Hold

"Guess what I found?" P'tero cried, ushering his guest into the kitchen cavern. "Tisha, he's half frozen and starving of the hunger," the young green rider added, hauling the tall fur-wrapped figure toward the nearest hearth and pushing him into a chair. He deposited the packs he was carrying onto the table. "Klah, for the love of little dragons, please . . ."

Two women came running, one with klah and the other with a hastily filled bowl of soup. Tisha came striding across the cavern, demanding to know what the problem was, who had P'tero rescued and from where.

"No one should be out in weather like this," she said as she reached the table and grabbed up the victim's wrist to get a pulse. "All but froze, he is."

Tisha pulled aside the furs wrapped about his neck and then let him take the cup. He cradled the klah in reddened fingers, blowing before he took his first cautious sip. He was also shivering uncontrollably.

"I spotted an SOS on the snow—lucky for him that the sun made shadows or I'd never have seen it," P'tero was saying, thoroughly pleased with himself. "Found him below Bitra Hold . . ."

"Poor man," Tisha interjected.

"Oh, you're so right there," P'tero said with ironic fervor, "and he'll never return. Not that he's told me all . . ." and P'tero flopped to a chair when someone brought him a cup of klah. "Got out of Chalkin's clutches intact," P'tero grinned impishly, "and then survived three nights in a Bitran woodsman's hold . . . with only a half cup of old oats to sustain him . . ."

Through his explanation, Tisha ordered hot water bottles, warmed blankets, and, taking a good look at the man's fingers, numbweed and frost-bite salve.

"Don't think they're more than cold," she said, removing one of his hands from its fevered grip on the hot cup and spreading the fingers out, lightly pinching the tips. "No, no harm done."

"Thank you, thank you," the man said, returning his fingers to the warm cup. "I got so cold stamping out that emergency code . . ."

"And out of doors in such weather with no gloves," Tisha chided him.

"When I left Hall Domaize for Bitra Hold, it was only autumn," he said in a grating voice.

"Autumn?" Tisha echoed, widening her fine eyes in surprise. "How long were you at Bitra Hold, then?"

"Seven damned weeks," the man replied, spitting out the words in a disgusted tone of voice. "I thought a week at the most . . ."

Tisha laughed, her belly heaving under her broad apron. "What under the stars took you to Bitra in the first place? Artist, are you?" she added.

"How'd you know?" The man regarded her with surprise.

"Still have paint under your nails . . ."

Iantine inspected them and his cold-reddened face flushed a deeper red. "I didn't even stop to wash," he said.

"As well you didn't, considering the price Chalkin charges for such luxuries as soap," she said, chuckling again.

The woman returned with the things Tisha had ordered. While they ministered to the warming of him, he clung with one hand or the other to the klah. And then to the soup cup. His furs, which had kept him from freezing to death, were taken to dry at one fire; his boots were removed and his toes checked for frostbite, but he had been lucky there, too, so they were coated with salve for good measure and then wrapped in warm toweling, while warmed blankets were snugged about his body. Salve was applied to his hands and face and then he was allowed to finish the hot food.

"Now, your name, and whom shall we contact that you've been found?" Tisha asked when all this had been done.

"I'm Iantine," he said, and then he added in wry pride, "portraitist from Hall Domaize. I was contracted to do miniatures of Chalkin's children . . ."

"Your first mistake," Tisha said, chuckling.

Iantine flushed. "You're so right, but I needed the fee."

"Did you come away with any of it?" P'tero asked, his eyes gleaming with mischief.

"Oh, that I did," the journeyman replied so fiercely that everyone grinned. Then he sighed. "But I did have to part with an eighth at the woodsman's hold. He had little enough to share but was willing to do so."

"At a profit, I'm sure . . ."

Iantine considered that for a moment. "I was lucky to find any place to wait out the storm. And he did share . . ." He shrugged briefly, and a dejected look crossed his features as he sighed. "Anyway, it was he who suggested I make a sign in the snow to attract any dragonrider. I'm just lucky one saw me." He nodded thanks to P'tero.

"No problem," the blue dragonrider said airily. "Glad I came." He leaned toward Tisha across the table. "He'd've been frozen solid in another day."

"Were you long waiting?"

"Two days after the storm ended, but I spent the nights with ol' Fendler. If you're hungry enough, even tunnel snake tastes good," Iantine added. How long had it been since he'd eaten a decent meal?

"Ah, the poor laddie," Tisha said, and called out orders for a double portion of stew to be brought immediately, and bread and sweetening and some of the fruit that had been sent up from Ista.

By the time Iantine had finished the meal, he felt he had made up for the last four days. His feet and hands were tingling despite the numbweed and salve. When he stood to go relieve himself, he wobbled badly and clutched at the chair for support.

"Have a care, lad, filling the stomach was only half your problem," Tisha said, moving to support him with far more alacrity than her bulk would suggest. She gestured for P'tero to lend a hand.

"I need to—" Iantine began.

"Ach, it's on the way to the sleeping cavern," Tisha said, and drew one of his arms over her shoulder. She was as tall as he.

P'tero took up the packs again, and between them they got him to the toilet room. And then into a bed in an empty cubicle. Tisha checked his feet again, applied another coat of numbweed and tiptoed out. Iantine only made sure that his packs—and the precious fee—were in the room with him before he fell deeply asleep.

While he slept, messages went out—to Hall Domaize and to Benden Weyr and Hold, since Iantine nominally looked to Benden. Although Iantine had taken no lasting harm, M'shall recognized yet another instance of Chalkin taking unfair advantage. Irene had already sent in a substantial list of abuses and irregularities in Chalkin's dealings—generally with folk who had no recourse against his dictates. He held no court in which difficulties could be aired and had no impartial arbiters to make decisions.

The big traders, who could be counted on for impartial comment, bypassed Bitra and could cite many examples of unfair dealings since Chalkin had assumed holding fifteen years before. The few small traders who ventured in Bitra rarely returned to it.

Following that Gather and its decision to consider deposing Chalkin, M'shall had his sweep riders check in every minor hold to learn if Chalkin had duly informed his people of the imminence of Thread. None had, although Lord Chalkin had increased his tithe on every household. The manner in which he was conducting this extra tithe suggested that he was amassing supplies for his own good, not that of the hold. Those in a more isolated situation would certainly have a hard time obtaining even basic food supplies. That constituted a flagrant abuse of his position as Lord Holder.

When Paulin read M'shall's report, he asked if Chalkin's holders would speak out against him. M'shall had to report that his initial survey of the minor holders indicated a severe lack of civic duty. Chalkin had his folk so cowed, none would accuse him—especially this close to a Pass—for he still had the power to turn objectors out of their holds.

"They may change their minds once Thread has started," K'vin remarked to Zulaya.

"Too late, I'd say, for any decent preparations to be made."

K'vin shrugged. "He's really not our concern, for which I for one am thankful. At least we rescued Iantine."

Zulaya gave a wry chuckle. "That poor lad. Starting his professional career at Bitra? Not the best place."

"Maybe that's all he could aspire to," K'vin said.

"Not if he's from Hall Domaize," Zulaya said tartly. "Wonder how long it'll take his hands to recover?"

"Thinking of a new portrait?" K'vin asked, amused.

"Well, he's down an eighth of what he needs," she said.

K'vin gave her a wide-eyed look. "You wouldn't . . ."

"Of course I wouldn't," she said with an edge to her voice. "He needs something in his pocket of his own. I admire a lad who'd endure Bitra for any reason. And Iantine's was an honorable one in wanting to pay the transfer fee."

"Wear that red Hatching dress when you sit for him," K'vin said. Then rubbed his chin. "You know, I might have my portrait done, too."

Zulaya gave him a long look. "The boy may find it as hard to leave Telgar Weyr as it was Bitra."

"With a much fuller pouch and no maintenance subtracted . . ."

"And soap and hot water and decent food," Zulaya said. "According to Tisha, he'll need feeding up. He's skin and bones."

◆　◆　◆

When the singing woke Iantine, he was totally disoriented. No one had sung a note at Bitra Hold. And he was warm! The air was redolent of good eating odors, too. He sat up. Hands, feet, and face were stiff but the tingling was gone. And he was exceedingly hungry.

The curtain across the cubicle rustled and a boy's head popped through.

"You're awake, Artist Iantine?" the lad said.

"Indeed, I am," and Iantine looked around for his clothes. Someone had undressed him and he didn't see his own clothes.

"I'm to help you if you need it," the boy said, pushing halfway through the curtains. "Tisha laid out clean clothes." He wrinkled a snub nose. "Yours were pretty ripe, she said."

Iantine chuckled. "They probably were. I ran out of soap for washing three weeks ago."

"You was at Bitra. They charge for everything there." The boy threw up both arms in disgust. "I'm Leopol," he added. Then he lifted the soft slippers from the pile on the stool. "Tisha said you'd better wear these, not your boots. And you're to use the salve first . . ." He held up the lidded jar. "Dinner's ready." Leopol then licked his lips.

"And you must wait your meal until I'm ready, huh?"

Leopol nodded solemnly and then grinned. "I don't mind. I'll get more because I waited."

"Is food in short supply at this Weyr?" Iantine asked jokingly as he began to dress in the clean gear. Odd how important simple things, like freshly laundered clothing, assumed the level of luxury when you've had to do without.

Leopol helped him spread the salve on his feet. They were still tender to the touch. Even the act of applying the salve made them suddenly itchy. Fortunately, the numbweed, or whatever it was, reduced that sensation.

When he had relieved himself again and gingerly washed face and hands, he and Leopol made their way to the Lower Cavern, where the evening meal was in progress.

The lad led him to a side table near the hearth which had been set for two. Instantly, cooks descended with plates overflowing with food, wine for him and klah for Leopol.

"There now, Artist man," the cook said, nodding appreciation as Iantine attacked the roast meat, "eat first and then the Weyrleaders would like a few words with you, if you're not too tired."

Iantine murmured thanks and understanding and addressed himself single-mindedly to his food. He would have had additional servings of the main course but his stomach felt uneasy: too much good food after several days of semifasting, probably. Leopol brought him a large serving of the sweet course but he couldn't finish it all because the back of his throat felt raw and sore. He would have gone back to his bed then but he saw the Weyrleaders advancing on him. Leopol made a discreet exit, grinning reassurance at him. Iantine tried to stand in courtesy to his hosts but he wobbled on his numbed feet and dropped back into the chair.

"We don't stand much on ceremony here," Zulaya said, gesturing for him to stay seated as K'vin pulled out one chair for her.

He carried the wineskin from which he filled all the glasses. Iantine took a polite sip—it was a nice crisp wine—but even the one sip made his stomach feel more sour.

"Messages have been sent, and acknowledgments received, that you've been rescued," K'vin said, grinning over the last word. "Master Domaize was becoming worried so we saved him a messenger to Bitra."

"That's very good of you, Zulaya, K'vin," Iantine said, thankful that part of his training at Hall Domaize had included knowing the important names in every hold, Weyr, and Hall. "I certainly appreciated P'tero's rescue."

Zulaya grinned. "He'll be dining on that one for the rest of the year. But it proves the wisdom of sweep riding even during the Interval."

"You should know," Iantine blurted out, "that Lord Chalkin doesn't believe there will be a Pass."

"Of course not," K'vin replied easily. "It doesn't suit him to. Bridgely and M'shall would like a report from you, though, concerning your visit there."

"You mean, there's something that can be done about him?" Iantine was amazed. Lord Holders were autonomous within their borders. He hadn't known there'd be any recourse.

"He may *do* himself in," Zulaya said with a grim twist of her lips.

"That would be wonderful," Iantine said. "Only," and now honesty forced him to admit this, "he didn't really *do* anything to me . . ."

"Our Weyr Artist may not be trained," K'vin said, "but Waine informed me that it doesn't take seven weeks to do four miniatures . . ."

"I actually painted twenty-two to get four that they liked," Iantine said, clearing his throat grimly. "The hooker in the contract was the word 'satisfactory.' "

"Ah," Zulaya and K'vin said in chorus.

"I ran out of paint and canvas because I brought only what I *thought* I'd need . . ." He lifted his hands, then rubbed them because they were beginning to itch again. "Then the children all got measles, and so, rather than have anything deducted from the fee for room and board, I agreed to freshen up the hold murals . . . only I hadn't brought that sort of paint and had to manufacture the colors . . ."

"Did he charge you for the use of the equipment?" Zulaya asked, to Iantine's astonishment.

"How'd you know?" When she only laughed and waved at him to continue his telling, Iantine went on. "So I excavated what I needed in the midden."

"Good on you . . ." Zulaya clapped her hands, delighted by his resourcefulness.

"Fortunately, most of the raw materials for pigments are readily available. You only have to find and make the colors up. Which I'd have to do anyhow. Master Domaize was good about passing on techniques like that."

"Then I finally got them to accept the miniatures, which weren't exactly miniature size anymore, by the way, just before the first blizzard snowed me in." Iantine flushed. His narrative showed him to be such a ninny.

"So? How'd your contract go then?" Zulaya shot K'vin a knowing look.

"I was a bit wiser. Or so I thought," he said with a grimace, and then told them the clauses he'd insisted on.

"He had you on the drudges' level at Bitra?" Zulaya was appalled. "And you a diploma'd Artist? I would certainly protest about that! There are certain courtesies which most holds, Halls, and Weyrs accord a journeyman of a Craft, and certainly to an Artist!"

"So, when Lord Chalkin finally accepted his portrait, I made tracks away as fast as I could!"

K'vin clapped him on the shoulder, grinning at the fervor with which that statement came out.

"Not that my conditions improved that much," Iantine added quickly, and then grinned, "until P'tero rescued me." His throat kept clogging up and he had to clear it again. "I want to thank you very much for that. I hope I didn't keep him from proper duties."

"No, no," K'vin said. "Mind you, I'm not all that sure why he was over Bitra, but it's as well he was."

"How are your hands?" Zulaya said, looking down at him as he washed his itching fingers together.

"I shouldn't rub the skin, should I?"

Zulaya spoke over her shoulder. "Leopol, get the numbweed for Iantine, please."

The young journeyman hadn't noticed the boy's discreet presence, but he was just as glad he didn't have to walk all the way to his cubicle to get the salve.

"It's just the aftereffects of cold," he said, looking at his fingers, and noticing what Tisha had—pigment under the nails. He curled his fingers, ashamed to be at a Weyr table with dirty hands. And a deep shiver went down his spine.

"I was wondering, Iantine," Zulaya began, "if you'd feel up to doing another portrait or two. The Weyr pays the usual rates, and no extras charged against you."

Iantine protested. "I'd gladly do your portrait, Weyrwoman. It is of yourself you were speaking, isn't it?" That first shiver was followed by another, which he did his best to mask.

"You'll do it only if you are paid a proper fee, young man," Zulaya said sternly.

"But—"

"No buts," K'vin put in. "What with preparations for a Pass, neither Zulaya nor I have had the time to commission proper portraits. However, since you're here . . . and willing?"

"I'm willing, all right, but you don't know my work and I'm only just accredited—"

Zulaya caught his hands in hers, for he'd been wildly gesticulating in both eagerness and an attempt to disguise another spasm.

"Journeyman Iantine, if you managed to do four miniatures, two formal portraits, and refresh murals for Chalkin, you're more than *qualified*. Didn't you know that it took Macartor five months to finish Chalkin's wedding-day scene?"

"And he had to borrow marks from an engineer to pay off the last of his 'debt'?" K'vin added. "Here's Waine to greet you. But you're not to start work again until you're completely recovered from the cold."

"Oh, I'm recovered, I'm recovered," Iantine said, standing up as the Weyrleaders did, determined to control the next set of shiverings.

After they had introduced him to the little man, Waine, they left him, circulating to other tables as the Weyr relaxed. There was singing and guitar playing from one side of the room, cheerful noises, above a general level of easy conversation. That was something else Iantine only now realized had been totally absent at Bitra Hold: music, talk, people relaxing after a day's work.

"Heard you ran afoul a' Chalkin?" Waine said, grinning and ducking his head. Then he brought from behind his back a sheaf of large-sized paper sheets, neatly tied together, and a handful of pencils. "Thought you might need 'em, like," he said shyly. "Heard tell you used up all at Bitra."

"Thank you," Iantine replied, running his fingers appreciatively over the fine sheets and noticing that the pencils were of different weights of carbon. "How much do I owe you?"

Waine laughed, showing gaps in his teeth. "You been at Bitra too long. I've colors, too, but not many. Don't do more'n basics."

"Then let me make you a range of paints," Iantine said gratefully, gritting his teeth against yet another onslaught of ague. "You know where to find the raw stuff around here and I'll show you how I make the tints."

Waine grinned toothlessly again. "That's a right good trade." He held out a hand and nearly crushed Iantine's fingers with his enthusiasm. But he caught the paroxysm of almost uncontrollable shivering that Iantine could not hide.

"Hey, man, you're cold."

"I can't seem to stop shivering, for all that I'm on top of the fire," and Iantine had to surrender to the shaking.

"TISHA!"

Iantine was embarrassed by Waine's bellow for assistance but he didn't resist when he was bundled back into his quarters and the medic summoned while Tisha ordered more furs, hot water bottles, aromatics to be steeped in hot water to make breathing easier. He made no resistance to the medication that was immediately prescribed for him because, by then, his head had started to ache. So did his bones.

The last thing he remembered before he drifted off to an uneasy sleep was what Maranis, the medic, said to Tisha.

"Let's hope they all have it at Bitra for giving it to him."

◆ ◆ ◆

Much later Leopol told him that Tisha had stayed by his bedside three nights while he burned of the mountain fever he had caught, compounding his illness by exposure on the cold slopes. Maranis felt that the old woodsman might be a carrier for the disease: himself immune but able to transmit the fever.

Iantine was amazed to find his mother there, when he woke from the fever. Her eyes were red with crying and she burst into tears again when she realized he was no longer delirious. Leopol also told him that Tisha had insisted she be sent for when his fever lasted so long.

To Iantine's astonishment, she didn't seem as pleased to receive the transfer fee as he was to give it.

"Your life isn't worth the fee," she told him finally when he was afraid she was displeased with the missing eighth mark he'd had to give the woodsman. "And he nearly killed you for that eighth."

"He's a good lad you have for a son," Tisha said with an edge to her voice, "working that hard to earn money from Chalkin."

"Oh yes," his mother hastily agreed as she suddenly realized she ought to be more grateful. "Though whyever you sought to please that old skinflint is beyond me."

"The fee was right," Iantine said weakly.

"Don't take on so, now, Ian," Tisha said when his mother had to return to the sheephold. "She was far more worried about you than about the marks. Which shows her heart's in the right place. Worry makes people act odd, you know." She patted Iantine's shoulder. "She wanted to take you home and nurse you there, you know," she went on reassuringly. "But couldn't risk your lungs in the cold of *between*. I don't think she liked us taking care of you!" She grinned. "Mothers *never* trust others, you know."

Iantine managed a grin back at Tisha. "I guess that's it."

It was Leopol who restored Iantine's peace of mind.

"You got a real nice mother, you know," he said, sitting on the end of the bed. "Worried herself sick about leaving until P'tero promised to convey her again if you took any turn for the worse. She'd never ridden a dragon before."

Iantine chuckled. "No, I don't think she has. Must have frightened her."

"Not as much," and now Leopol cocked a slightly dirty finger at the journeyman, "as you being so sick she had to be sent for. But she was telling P'tero how happy your father would be to have those marks you earned. Real happy. And she near deafened P'tero, shouting about how she'd always known you'd be a success and to get the whole fee out of Chalkin was quite an achievement."

"She did?" Iantine perked up. His mother had been bragging about him?

"She did indeed," Leopol said, giving an emphatic nod to his head.

Leopol seemed to know a great deal about a lot of matters in the Weyr. He also never seemed to mind being sent on errands as Iantine made a slow convalescence.

Master Domaize paid him a visit, too. And it was Leopol who told the convalescent why the Master had made such a visit.

"That Lord Chalkin sent a complaint to Master Domaize that you had skivved out of the hold without any courtesy and he was seriously considering lodging a demand for the return of some of the fee since you were so obviously very new at your Art, and the fee had been for a seasoned painter, not a young upstart." Leopol grinned at Iantine's furious reaction. "Oh, don't worry. Your Master wasn't born yesterday. M'shall himself brought him to Bitra Hold and they said that there was not a thing wrong with any of the work you'd done for that Lord Chalkin." Leopol cocked his head to one side, regarding Iantine with a calculating look. "Seems like there's a lot of people wanting to sit their portraits with you. Didja know that?"

Iantine shook his head, trying to absorb the injustice of Chalkin's objection. He was speechless with fury. Leopol grinned.

"Don't worry, Iantine. Chalkin's the one should worry, treating you like that. Your Master and the Benden Weyrleader gave out to the Lord Holder about it, too. You're qualified and entitled to all the courtesies of which you got none at Bitra Hold. Good thing you didn't get sick until after Zulaya and K'vin had a chance to hear your side of the story. Not that *anyone* would believe Chalkin, no matter what he says. Did you know that even wherries won't roost in Bitra Hold?"

◆ ◆ ◆

Convalescence from the lung infection took time and Iantine fretted at his weakness.

"I keep falling asleep," he complained to Tisha one morning when she arrived with his potion. "How long do I have to keep taking this stuff?"

"Until Maranis hears clear lungs in you," she said in her no-nonsense tone. Then she handed him the sketch paper and pencils that Waine had given him his first night in the Weyr. "Get your hand back in. At least doing what you're best at can be done sitting still."

It was good to have paper and pencil again. It was good to look about the Lower Caverns and catch poses, especially when the poser didn't realize he was being sketched. And his eye had not lost its keenness, and if his fingers cramped now and then from weakness, strength gradually returned. He became unaware of the passage of time nor did he notice people coming up behind him to see what he was drawing.

Waine arrived with mortar, pestle, oil, eggs, and cobalt to make a good blue. The man had picked up bits of technique and procedures on his own, but picking things up here and there was no substitute for the concentrated drill that Iantine had had: drills that he once despised but now appreciated when he could see what resulted from the lack of them.

Winter had set in, but on the first day of full sun, Tisha insisted on wrapping him up in a cocoon of furs to sit out in the Bowl for the "good of fresh air." As it was bath time for the dragonets, Iantine was immediately fascinated by their antics and began to appreciate just how much hard work went into their nurture. It was also the first chance he'd ever had of seeing dragonets. He knew the grace and power of the adult dragon and their awesome appearance. Now he saw the weyrlings as mischievous—even naughty, as one ducked her rider into the lake—and endlessly inventive. None of this last Hatching were ready to fly yet, but some of the previous clutch were beginning to take on adult duties. He had firsthand observation of their not-so-graceful performances.

The next day he saw P'tero and blue Ormonth in the focus of some sort of large class. As he wandered over, he saw that not only the weyrlings from the last three Hatchings were attending, but also all youngsters above the age of twelve. Ormonth had one wing extended and was gazing at it in an abstract fashion, as if he'd never seen it before. The expression was too much for the artist in Iantine and he flipped open his pad and sketched the scene. P'tero noticed, but the class was extremely attentive. What T'dam was saying slowly reached through Iantine's absorption with line and pose.

"Now, records show us that the worst injuries occur on wing edges, especially if Thread falls in clumps and the partners are not sharp enough to avoid 'em. A dragon can fly with one-third of his exterior sail damaged . . ." and T'dam ran his hand along the edge of Ormonth's wing. "However," and T'dam looked up at Ormonth, "if you would be good enough to close your wing slightly, Ormonth," and the blue did so. "Thank you . . ." T'dam had to stand slightly on tiptoe to reach the area of the inner wing. "Injuries in here are far more serious, as Thread can, depending on the angle of its fall, sear through the wing and into his body. This," and he now ducked under the wing and tapped the side, "is where the lungs are and injury here can even be . . . fatal . . ."

There was a gasp around the semicircle of his students.

"That's why you have to be sharp every instant you're in flight. Go *between* the instant you even *suspect* you've been hit . . ."

"How do we *know*?" someone asked.

"Ha!" T'dam propped his fists on his thick leather belt and paused. "Dragons are very brave creatures for the most part, considering what we ask them to do. But," and he stroked Ormonth in apology, "they have exceedingly quick responses . . . especially to pain. You'll know!" He paused again. "Some of you were here when Missath broke her sail bone, weren't you?" and he pointed around the group until he saw several hands raised. "Remember how she squealed?"

"Went right through me like a bonesaw," a big lad said and shivered convulsively.

"She was squealing the instant she lost her balance and actually before she snapped the bone. She *knew* she would hurt even as she fell. Now, you don't have quite the same immediacy in Threadfall, since you'll be high on adrenaline, but you'll know. So, this brings up a point that we make constantly in all training procedures, *always*, ALWAYS, have a point to go to in your head. During Fall, it had better be the Weyr since everyone here," and now the sweep of his hand included those Iantine recognized as nonriders, "will be ready to help. *Don't* make the mistake of coming in too low. Going *between* will have stopped Thread burrowing farther into your dragon . . ." A muted chorus of disgust and fearfulness greeted that concept. ". . . so you can make as orderly a landing as injuries permit. What you don't need is a bad landing, which could compound the original Thread score. Start encouraging your dragon as soon as you know he's been hit. Of course, you may be hit, too, and I appreciate that, but you're riders and you can certainly control your own pain while seeing to your dragon's. *He's* the important one of you, remember. Without him you don't function as a rider.

"Now, the drill is," and once again he swept his glance around his students, "slather!" He picked up the wide brush from the pail at his feet and began to ply it on Ormonth's wing: water, to judge the way it dripped. The blue regarded the operation with lightly whirling eyes. "Slather, slather, slather," and T'dam emphasized each repetition with a long brush stroke. "You can't put too much numbweed on a dragon's injuries to suit him or her," and he grinned at the female green riders, "and the injury will be numb in exactly three seconds . . . at least the outer area. It does take time to penetrate through the epidermis to what passes for the germinative layer in a dragon's hide. So you may have to convince your dragon that he's not as badly hurt as he or she feels he or she is. Your injured dragon needs all the reassurance you can give him or her . . . No matter how bad you think the injury looks, don't think that at the dragon. Tell him or her what a great brave dragon they are and that the numbweed is working and the pain will go away.

"Now, if a bone has been penetrated . . ."

"Why, you've got P'tero to the life," said an awed voice softly in Iantine's ear, and he shot a glance at the tall lad standing behind him: M'leng, green Sith's rider, and P'tero's special friend. Iantine had seen the two riders, always together, in the kitchen cavern. "Oooh, is there any chance I could have that corner?" And he tapped the portion that contained P'tero and Ormonth.

M'leng was a handsome young man, with almond-shaped green eyes in an angular face. The light breeze in the Bowl ruffled tight dark brown curls on his head.

"Since I owe P'tero my life, let me make a larger sketch for you . . ."

"Oh, would you?" And a smile animated M'leng's rather solemn face. "Can we settle a price? I've marks enough to do better than Chalkin did you." He reached for his belt pouch.

Iantine tried to demur, pleading he owed P'tero.

" 'Ter was only doing his duty for once," M'leng said with a touch of asperity. "But I really would like a proper portrait of him. You know, what with Threadfall coming and all, I'd want to have something—" M'leng broke off, swallowed, and then reinforced his pleading.

"I've to do a commission for the Weyrleaders," Iantine said.

"Is that the only one?" M'leng seemed surprised. "I'd've thought everyone in the Weyr would be after you . . ."

Iantine grinned. "Tisha hasn't released me from her care yet."

"Oh, her," and M'leng dismissed the headwoman, with a wave of his hand. "She's so fussy at times. But there's nothing wrong with your hand or your eye . . . and that little pose of P'tero, leaning against Ormonth, why, it's him!"

Iantine felt his spirits rise at the compliment, because the sketch of the blue rider was good—better than the false ones he had done at Bitra Hold. He still cringed, remembering how he allowed himself to compromise his standards by contriving such obsequious portrayals. He hoped he would never be in such a position again. M'leng's comment was balm to his psyche.

"I can do better . . ."

"But I like the pose. Can't you just *do* it? I mean," and M'leng looked everywhere but at Iantine, "I'd rather P'tero didn't know . . . I mean . . ."

"Is it to be a surprise for him?"

"No, it's to be for *me*!" And M'leng jabbed his breastbone with his thumb, his manner defiant. "So I'll *have* it . . ."

At such intransigence, Iantine was at a loss, and hastily agreed before M'leng became more emotional. M'leng's eyes filled and he set his mouth in a stubborn line.

"I will, of course, but a sitting would help . . ."

"Oh, I can arrange that, so he still doesn't know. You're always sketching," and that came out almost as an accusation. Iantine, thanks to the lecture he had been overhearing, was considerably more aware of the dangers dragons, and their riders, would shortly face. If M'leng was comforted by having a portrait of his friend, that was the least he could do.

"This very night," M'leng continued, single-minded in his objective, "I'll see we sit close to where you usually do. I'll get him to wear his good tunic so you can paint him at his very best."

"But suppose—" Iantine began, wondering how he could keep P'tero from knowing he was being done.

"You do the portrait," M'leng said, patting Iantine's arm to still his objections. "I'll take care of P'tero," and he added under his breath, "as long as I have him."

That little afterthought made the breath stop in Iantine's throat. Was M'leng so sure that P'tero would die?

"I'll do my best, M'leng, you may be sure of that!"

"Oh, I am," M'leng said, tossing his head up so that the curls fell back from his face. He gave Iantine a wry smile. "I've been watching how you work, you see." He extended a hand soft with the oils riders used to tend their dragons. Iantine took it and was astonished at the strength in the green rider's grip. "Waine said a good miniature—which is what I want," and he patted his breast pocket to show the intended site of the painting, "by a journeyman is priced at four marks. Is that correct?"

Iantine nodded, unable to speak for the lump in his throat. Surely M'leng was dramatizing matters. Or was he? In the background, Iantine could hear T'dam advising his listeners on the types and severity of injuries and the immediate aid to be given to each variety.

What a bizarre, and cruel, lecture to give to the weyrlings! And yet, the thought stopped him, was it not kinder to be truthful now and ease the shock of what could possibly happen?

"This evening?" M'leng said firmly.

"This very evening, M'leng," Iantine said, nodding his head.

When the green rider had left him, it took the journeyman some long moments before he could return to his sketching.

Well, this was one thing he could do as a gift to the Weyr for all the kindnesses to him—he could leave behind a graphic gallery of everyone currently living in Telgar Weyr.

VII

Fort Hold

Classes were also being held that same day in Fort Hold. In the College assembly room, Corey, as Head Medic, was conducting a seminar for healers from all over Pern, who had been flown in for a three-day clinic. This included a first-aid session dealing with both human and dragon injuries. She was assisted by the Fort Weyr medic, N'ran, who had originally studied animal medicine before he inadvertently Impressed brown Galath. Galath was, on this occasion, outside, enjoying the sun, while a green dragon, who was small enough to fit in the Hall, was being used for demonstration purposes much as Ormonth was at Telgar Weyr.

"Now we have been able to duplicate the records of Doctors Tomlinson, Marchane, and Lao, which include some fading photos of actual injuries. Lunch is fortunately sufficiently in the future," she said with a quirky smile. Then her expression turned sober. "The verbal descriptions are worse, but it's necessary to impress on all those who have to deal with ground injuries how incredibly fast," she ticked off one finger, "how horrendous Thread is," another and then with a sigh, "and how quickly we must act to . . ." Her pause was longer now. ". . . to limit suffering."

Murmurs answered her, and she could see that some of the audience had paled. Others looked defiant.

"From what I, and my staff," and she indicated those in the front seats, "have determined, there is little option. The alternative of getting into cold *between* as the dragons can is not available to us . . . Yes?"

"Why not? If that's an alternative . . ."

"For them, not us," she said firmly. "Because all the records emphasize the speed with which Thread . . . consumes organic material. Too swiftly to call a dragon, even if any were available in your locale. A whole cow goes in less than two minutes."

"Why, that's not even time to . . ." a man began, and his voice trailed off.

"Precisely," Corey said. "If a limb is scored, there's the chance it could be amputated before the organism spread over the body . . ."

"Shards! You can't just—" another man began.

"If survival means loss of just a limb, it can be done."

"But only if you're right there . . ."

Corey recognized him as a practitioner in a large hold in Nerat.

"And many of us will be right there," Corey said firmly, "with the groundcrews, sharing their dangers . . . and hopefully saving as many as we can." She managed a wry smile. "Any body of water handy is useful since Thread drowns. Quickly, according to reports. Depending on the site of the injury, water can impede the ingestion long enough for an amputation to be performed. Even a trough is sufficient." She glanced down at her notes. "Thread needs oxygen as well as organic material. It drowns in three seconds."

"What if it's burrowed into flesh?"

"Three seconds. Flesh does not have the free oxygen necessary for Thread life. Ice, too, can retard progress, but that isn't always available, either.

"Let us assume that we have, somehow, halted the organism's progress but we have a bad scoring and/or an amputation. Numbweed, numbweed, numbweed! And bless this planet for inventing something it didn't know we'd need so badly. In the case of an amputation, of course, proceed with standard practices, including cautery. That at least would eliminate any final vestige of Thread. There will be significant trauma so fellis is recommended . . . if the patient is still conscious."

She glanced down at her notes. "Tomlinson and Marchane also indicate that the mortality rate, due to heart failure or stroke, is high in Thread injuries. Lao, who practiced until the end of the First Pass, notes that often patients, who had received slight scores, successfully treated, died from the pathological trauma of being scored. In preparing our groups for this problem, do stress that Threadscore can be successfully treated."

"If we can move fast enough," a man said facetiously.

"That's why it's important for a medic to accompany as many groundcrew teams as possible. And why first-aid procedures must be taught to every hold and hall within your practice. There are only so many of us, but we can teach many what to do and cut down on fatalities.

"And," Corey went on, "we must emphasize that all nonessential personnel are to *stay* safely indoors until groundcrews report the area safe.

"Now, we will go on to dragon injuries since these, too, will occur and those of us on the spot may need to assist the dragon and rider. They will have the one advantage we can't provide—the chance to go *between* and freeze the attacking organism. But the score will be just as painful.

"The larger proportion of draconic injuries are to the wing surfaces . . . if you please, Balzith," and she turned to the patient green dragon, who obediently extended her wing as the medic conducted that section of her lecture.

When they had adjourned for lunch, prior to discussing other problems—such as hygiene and sanitation within small and medium holds where the amenities were not as efficient as in the larger population centers—Corey was approached by Joanson of South Boll and Frenkal of Tillek Hold, both senior medics.

"Corey, what is your position on . . . mercy?" asked Joanson in a very thoughtful tone.

She regarded the tall man for a long moment. "What it has always been, Joanson. We have, as you realize, quite a few persons in this audience who have not received full medical training. I cannot ask them to do what I would find very, very difficult to do: administer mercy." She gave Joanson a long stare, then glanced at Frenkal, who seemed to enjoy the ethical spot she was in.

"We are sworn to preserve life. We are also sworn to maintain a decent quality of life for those under our care." She felt her lips twitch, remembering that there were occasions when those two aims were in conflict. "We must, each of us, reflect on how we will face such a desperate situation: whether to cut short a final agony is necessary, even ethical. I don't think there will be much time to consider morals, ethics, kind or cruel, at the time we are forced to take . . . action." She paused, took a deep breath. "I do remember seeing the tapes the Infirmary used to have, showing very graphically an animal being eaten alive by Thread . . ." She noticed Joanson's wince. "Yes, eaten alive because Thread caught the hind end of it. I think, if it was someone you knew, you'd opt for . . . the quickest possible end to *that*."

Since they were not the only two who approached her on that subject, she was almost glad when the lunch break ended and she could address the less vexatious matter of amputation. Everyone needed a refresher on that procedure, especially an emergency type of procedure when there might not be the time for all the preliminaries that made for a neat stump. She did have the new bonecutters—well, more axes than the traditional surgical tool—for distribution afterward. Kalvi had brought them with him.

"Best edge we've ever been able to make on a surgical tool, Corey," he told her with some pride. "Had them tested at the abattoir. Cut through flesh and bone like going through cheese. Gotta keep 'em honed, though. And I've made cases for the blades so no one slices off a finger by mistake."

Surgeons were not the only ones with a ghoulish sense of humor, Corey decided.

◆　◆　◆

Meanwhile, in the Great Hall of Fort Hold, with Lord Paulin seated in the front row, Kalvi himself was demonstrating to those who would form the Fort groundcrews how to use and service the HNO_3 cylinders, taking his audience from assembly of the parts and then a quick rundown of common problems likely to be encountered in the field. Every small holder within Fort's authority was present: many had brought their elder children. All had come on foot, their own or a horse's. Fort Weyr, like the other five, was beginning to restrict dragon rides. Lord Paulin understood and approved.

"We've had it far too easy, using the dragons the way our ancestors would have used the sleds and airborne vehicles," he was heard to say when one of his holders had complained that he had been denied his right to a dragonride. "We haven't been breeding horses just to run races, you know. And the dragonriders have been far too accommodating. Do us all good to walk or ride. You have, of course, extended your beast holds to shelter all your livestock?"

There had been moaning over that necessity, too, with complaints that the engineers should really have spent more time trying to replicate the marvelous rock-cutting equipment with which their ancestors had wrested living quarters out of cliffsides.

Kalvi had come in for considerable harangue over that, which he shrugged off.

"We have a list of priorities: that's not one. Nor could be. We still have two sleds in the North but no power to run 'em. Never did find out what they used," he said. "No way of duplicating such power packs, either, or I'm sure our ancestors would have. Otherwise why did they engineer the dragons? Anyway, renewable resources make more sense than erudite or exotic imports."

When the main lecture was concluded, everyone was told to reassemble after the noon meal for target practice. This was vastly more interesting than having to listen to Kalvi waffle on about how to adjust the wands of the HNO_3 throwers to give a long, narrow tongue of fire or a broader, shorter flame. Or how to clear the nozzle of clogged matter.

"You've got almost as much variation in flame as a dragon has . . ." Kalvi said as he slung the tanks to his back, his voice slightly muffled by his safety gear. "You, there, the hard hat has a purpose. Put it on your head! Lower the face screen!"

The offender immediately complied, Kalvi scowling at him.

"The effective range of this equipment is six meters on the narrowest setting, two on the broader. You wouldn't want it to get closer to you." He was fiddling with his wand. "Damn thing's stubborn . . ." He took out a screwdriver and made a slight adjustment. *"Always . . ."* he said loudly and firmly as he held the wand away from his body, "keep the nozzle of the wand pointed away from *you* and anyone in your immediate vicinity. We're flaming Thread, not folks. *Never . . .* never . . . engage the flow of the two gases without looking in what direction the wand is pointing. You can also burn, scorch, sear things without meaning to. *Can't you,* Laland?" he said, aiming his remark at one of his journeymen.

The man grinned and shifted his feet nervously, looking anywhere but at his Master.

"Now, signal the topside crews, will you, Paulin?" Kalvi said, setting himself firmly on both feet and aiming the wand up.

Paulin waved a red kerchief and suddenly a tangle of "something" catapulted off the cliff, startling everyone in the crowd behind Kalvi. Those with wands raised them defensively and others gasped as the tangle separated into long silver strands, some fine, some thick and falling at slightly different rates. As soon as they were within range, Kalvi activated his flamethrower.

There was a brief second when the fire seemed to pause on the ends of the launched strands before the flame raced along the material and consumed it so that only bits of smoking char reached the ground . . . and the rock that had been tied to the leading edge. There was a roar of approval and great applause.

"Not bad," Paulin said, grinning as he noted the new alertness in the crowd.

"Well, we tried for the effect we just delivered," Kalvi said, turning off both tanks. "Used a retardant on the rope, too. Had plenty of description of how Thread falls, and this is as near as we can get.

"Now," and he turned back to his students, "it's best to get Thread before it gets you or to the ground. We know there are two kinds: the ones that eat themselves dead—they're not a problem, even if they are in the majority and messy. Records tell us that the second kind find something in what they ingest that allows them to progress to the second step of their lifecycle: our ancestors could never do much with investigating this type. They only knew that it existed. We know it existed, too, because there are areas here in the

North which are still sterile two-hundred-odd years since the last fall. If this type gets the nourishment it needs, above and beyond organic materials, then it can propagate, or divide or whatever it is Thread does. This is what we needed groundcrews for. This is the type we don't want hanging around and burrowing out of sight. Our ancestors thought Thread had to have some trace minerals or elements in the dirt, but as they never figured out what, we're not likely to now." Kalvi heaved a sigh of regret. "So," and with a wide sweep of his arm, "we incinerate all the buggers the dragonriders miss."

He paused and looked up the cliffside where the catapult crews were waiting.

"OKAY UP THERE?" he yelled, hands bracketing his mouth. Immediately in response, red flags were waved at intervals along the cliff.

"All right, in groups of five, range yourself parallel to the red flags you now see. When we're all in place—and out of range of anyone's wand," and Kalvi gave a wry grin, "I'll give the signal and we'll see how you manage."

The results were somewhat erratic: some men seemed to get the hang of their equipment immediately, while others couldn't even get the right mix on the gases to produce flame.

"Well, it happens," Kalvi said in patient resignation. "Should make 'em climb the thread back up the cliff . . ." he added.

"Do 'em good."

"Take too much time. THROW DOWN THE NETS," Kalvi roared, and then grinned at Paulin. "Thought we'd have some trouble. We'll get our mock Threads back up and in use."

"How much did you bring?"

"Yards," was all Kalvi said with another grin.

By the time the short winter afternoon was closing into darkness, all the holders had had a chance to "sear" Thread, despite hiccups and misses. The mock Thread supply ran out before they lost interest in the practice.

"Now I don't want you to overdo it on your own," Paulin said to those nearest him as they walked back to the hold. The practice area had been some distance up the North Road from Fort Hold, where there were neither beasts nor cotholds that could be affected. "HNO_3 isn't all that hard to manufacture, but the equipment is. Don't wear it out before it's needed."

During their practice, the main Hall had been rearranged for the evening meal, and the trainees were as hungry as gatherers.

"Tomorrow we'll clean the gear," Kalvi announced while klah was being served, "and you'll strip down and reassemble the units so I'm sure you know what you're doing. The man who does it fastest and best will get Lord Paulin's reward."

A loud cheer resounded through the Hall.

"Morale's good," Paulin said to Kalvi, who nodded, well satisfied with the way this first instruction session had gone.

If all of those meetings planned for the head engineer at the other major holds went as smoothly, Kalvi thought he might even get a chance for a few days off to fish in Istan waters. In the frantic search during the run-up to the Second Pass for materials long left in storage, some reels of stout nylon fishing line had been found. The bar-coding on the carton had been damaged, so there was no way of knowing how long ago the line had been manufactured, but Kalvi was eager to put it to the test with some of the big 'uns that swam in the tropical waters. This sort of synthetic material was extremely durable and would certainly take the weight of packfish, which was sometimes substantial.

◆ ◆ ◆

A third group made up of teachers—novices and experienced—were gathered in the College's spacious refectory. Today this convocation had the happier task of learning and rehearsing the new ballads that were to be used in teaching the young. On the second day the Fort Weyrleader would instruct the peripatetic teachers on how best to shelter themselves if they should be caught out during Threadfall. Clisser had been inundated with complaints that the Weyrs were restricting rides that had been the accustomed mode of transport. Not all the teachers were familiar with nor competent enough to ride the sturdy horses that were bred for long-distance and mountain travel. He was going to have to reassign a lot of his older teachers, yet another headache.

But for this three-day period at least, the emphasis would be on the music and the new curriculum. Not that he hadn't had contentious reactions to *that*. He was beginning to think that Bethany had been right when she suggested that they, like the First Settlers, had relied too heavily on easy access to information. Oddly enough, some of the older teachers loudly approved the new curriculum.

"High time we brought things up to date, with relevance to the life we're leading here, not what folks had *there*," Layrence of Tillek said, "stuff we'll never have so what's the point of quizzing them on it?"

"But we have traditions we must uphold," Sallisha said, her brow creased in a frown. Which made Clisser realize once again that her reputation for being a "right wagon" was not without merit. "Traditions which they must understand to appreciate what we have . . ."

"Oh, Sallisha," and Bethany smiled in her soothing way, "we're incorporating all those traditions in the Ballads but *stressing* what they need to understand of the life they have here."

"But our glorious past—" Sallisha began.

"*Is* past," Sheledon said forcefully, scowling right back at her. "*All* past, *all* gone, and why dwell on contacts our ancestors severed for their own good reasons?"

"But . . . but . . . they should *know* . . ." Sallisha began again.

"If they wish to know more, they can read it," Sheledon said, "for advanced study. Right now, they have to cope with the problem of Threadfall . . ."

"And *that's* far more important than which planets outlasted the Nathi bombardments and who was World Leader in 2089," Shulse said. "Or how to plot a parabolic course around a primary."

Sallisha glared implacably at the maths teacher.

"Of course," Shulse went on, "I do approve of mentioning such history where it pertains to Emily Boll as governor, or Paul Benden as admiral of the fleet, because *they* are part and parcel of *Pernese* history."

"But you have to show students the overall picture . . ." Sallisha was persistence itself.

"And some students will be vitally interested, I'm sure," Shulse said, "but I agree with Clisser that we have to streamline the material to be studied to the point where it has relevance to *this* world and *our* civilization."

"Civilization?" Sallisha said at her most scornful.

"What? You don't call what we've made here 'civilized'?" Sheledon loved to tease the literal-minded Sallisha.

"Not in terms of what our ancestors had."

"And all that went with a high-tech society—like prepubescent addicts, city gangs, wild plagues, so much tech fraud that people were stuffing credits in their mattresses to protect their income, the—"

"Spare me," Sallisha said contemptuously, "and concentrate on the good that was done . . ."

Sheledon gave a chuckle. "D'you know how dangerous it was to be a teacher on old Earth?"

"Nonsense, our civilization," and she emphasized the word, "revered professors and instructors on every level."

"Only after they were allowed classroom discipline—" Sheledon began.

"And the use of stunners," Shulse added.

"That is not a problem on Pern," Sallisha said loftily.

"And we'll keep it that way," Clisser said firmly, "by adjusting what interests our classes and dispensing with irrelevancies."

Sallisha whirled on Clisser. "What *you* decide is relevant?"

Clisser pointed to the files along one wall of the library in which they were talking. "I sent out questionnaires to every teacher on the rolls, and to holders, major and minor, asking for input. I got it, and this curriculum," he lifted the thick volume, "is the result. You've all received copies. And the Teaching Ballads will be part of the package you receive during the conference."

Sallisha retired with poor grace, sulking as obviously as any intractable student would. He wondered if she saw the resemblance in attitude. Sallisha was, however, a very good teacher, able to impart knowledge at the level needed, and was therefore supervisor of southeastern Pern. But she had her little quirks—like everyone else in the world.

Making the children memorize the Teaching Ballads would improve their retention of words: a skill that Clisser realized he had lost with his dependence on technology. But then, one of the reasons the colonists had come to Pern with its limited resources was to revert to a society that was not so dependent on technology. He read accounts of persons who never left their home place, contacting others only by electronics, living as eremites. Not so much out of fear of the outside world, as out of indolence. No one could be indolent on Pern, Clisser told himself, and smiled. What a wasted life to remain in one place all one's days! Well, perhaps here on Pern events—like Threadfall—had forced them a little lower on the technological scale than the Settlers had anticipated, but they had adapted to Pern and were adapting it to their own use. And would meet the menace with a fully developed, renewable air defense force.

He hoped . . . Clisser sucked in his breath in a sort of reverse whistle. Everyone on the planet—with one notable exception—were girding their loins and securing their premises against that attack. Preparing was one thing, but enduring fifty years of an aerial attack was another. Briefly he reviewed the accounts published by the besieged colonists on Sirus III and Vega IV when the Nathi started bombarding the planets. Day after day, according to the history tapes, the worlds had been shelled with dirty missiles, rendering the surface uninhabitable. Whole generations had grown up on colonial planets, living in deep shelters . . . Clisser smiled to himself— not much different from the cave holds in which the Pernese now lived. And indeed those accommodations had benefited by the Sirian and Vegan experiences—using the magma core taps to provide heat, and solar panels for power. Humans had survived, under far worse conditions than pertained on this planet. At least on Pern you knew when and where Thread would fall and could mount effective defenses. And yet, the scale of Threadfall was awesome and failure had appalling consequences.

Failure usually did.

Therefore, Clisser hoped the music that had been composed as psychologically uplifting would have the desired effect: developing the morale and encouraging the effort. Briefly he wondered what would have happened on old Earth, during the National period, if there'd been a common extraterrestrial enemy to unite the diverse races.

Jemmy and Sheledon had certainly written some stirring music, martial as well as hopeful. Some of the less ambitious tunes had a tendency to stay with you so that you woke up in the morning whistling one or hearing it in your head: the mark of a good melody, to Clisser's way of thinking. And they had scored the music for various solo instruments or combinations of those readily available, so that even inexperienced players in the most isolated hold or hall would be able to accompany singers.

Jemmy's riddling song was a delight. Clisser hadn't quite got all the answers yet, but it would prove useful during the hours of Fall to distract folk from what was happening outside. Bethany's lament—the first song she had ever composed—was next on the program, and he settled back to listen to it.

But his mind, working overtime in anxiety over the success of his new program, refused to be caught up in the music. Among other things, *what* was he going to do about Bitra Hold? The last teacher he'd sent there had left, voiding his contract with Chalkin—not that Clisser blamed Issony when he'd heard the way the man had been humiliated and threatened by unruly Holder children—but children *had* to receive rudimentary education. You couldn't afford to let one whole province lapse into illiteracy.

To be sure, children learn at different rates: he knew that, and learning should be made as interesting as possible, to lay the foundations for further study, and for life itself for that matter. That was the purpose of education: to develop the skills required to solve problems. And to utilize the potential that existed in everyone—even a Bitran, he added sourly.

Maybe he should reappoint Sallisha to that area. Then he chuckled. Not much chance of that. She had enough seniority to refuse point-blank.

He made up his mind then, with the lovely phrases of Bethany's song soothing him, to bring the problem of Chalkin, Lord Holder of Bitra, up in the next Conclave. Something *had* to be done about the man.

◆ ◆ ◆

During the final evening meal in which all three groups joined up on the Fort court for a dinner featuring three whole roasted steers, Clisser heard Chalkin's name come up and homed in on the group discussing the man.

"That's not all," M'shall was saying, a deep frown on his usually amiable face. "He's put up guards at the borders, and anyone who wants to leave can take only their clothes with them. Nothing else, not even the animals which they may have raised themselves."

Clisser had not realized that the Benden Weyrleader had arrived, but his presence was certainly fortuitous.

"You're speaking of Chalkin?" he asked when the others acknowledged his presence and made room for him in their circle.

M'shall gave a scornful laugh. "Who else would turn folks out of their holds right now?"

"I've just heard from one of my traveling teachers, Issony, and he's quit and nothing would persuade him to go back to Bitra. But even they have to grow up literate."

"Ha!" M'shall's scoffing was echoed by the others.

"School hours keep Bitrans from other jobs which earn their holder more marks. What did he do to Issony?"

"He'll give you chapter and verse if you ask him. In fact, it would do him good. I understand one of your riders rescued him."

"We do a lot of rescue work in Bitra," M'shall said, not at all pleased by the necessity. "But only non-Bitrans," he added.

"Now, look," and Bridgely seemed about to explode, "I will *not* succor all his refugees. And I will *not* lift a hand to help him when his hold is over-run by Thread."

"Ah," and M'shall raised one finger in a sardonic gesture, "but you see, he doesn't *believe* Thread's coming."

"Wouldn't we feel silly if he was right after all," said Farley, one of the other minor Fort holders. "Oops, wrong thing to say," he added when coldly repressive stares rejected his witticism.

"Chalkin has always been contrary by nature," Clisser said. "But never such an outright fool."

"Well, he's exceeded even 'damned fool,'" Bridgely said. "Is your teacher, Issony, here now? Well, then, bring him up to Fort. We're about to do something definitive about Chalkin."

"Right now?" and Clisser couldn't help looking over at the roasting carcasses and sniffing at the succulent odors they were producing.

"I expect to eat, too," Bridgely said, relenting.

"I just finished eating at Benden," M'shall said, but his nose was twitching at the aromas. "Ah, well, we could have a slice to allow you to enjoy your meal."

"Timed it just right, didn't you?" Farley said, with a grin for their obvious interest in the roasting meats. "*Can* something be done about an irresponsible Lord Holder?"

"Read your copy of the Charter, Farley," Clisser said.

◆ ◆ ◆

"And how long have border guards . . ." Paulin paused, made indignant by such a measure. ". . . been in place?" He'd assembled those concerned in his office at the hold when they'd finished eating. Issony was on call if his testimony was required.

"As near as we can figure out, about seven days," M'shall said. "As you know, we've been canvassing all the holds, to see who, if any, of Chalkin's people has been told about the imminence of Thread."

"Surely they'd have heard that much at Gathers—" Paulin began.

"Ha!" Bridgely said. "Very few of his folk hear where or when Gathers are being held, much less attend them."

"That isn't right," Paulin said, shaking his head.

"Frankly, Paulin, I'd say his tithing of them is punitive. None of them ever seem to have a mark to spend even when they do bring work to sell at a Benden Gather. Not that they're encouraged to travel at all."

"Even to Gathers?" Paulin answered his own query. "No, he wouldn't encourage them, would he?"

"Not if he's afraid they'll compare conditions in another hold. Also he doesn't like Bitran marks to go past his borders."

"And gets every one those high rollers have when they attend those friendly little games he runs," M'shall said.

"I must confess I hadn't known how restrictive he is," Paulin said in a very thoughtful tone of voice.

"Well, how would you?" Bridgely replied, absolving him. "You're West Coast. We know because we see so few Bitrans at East Coast Gathers. Oh, his gamesters attend every one . . ."

"Hmm, yes, they're ubiquitous, you might say," Paulin murmured under his breath. "So, if he's had to close the borders, it would appear that some holders panicked when they learned Threadfall is indeed expected?"

"Indeed," Bridgely said with a grim expression, "and when a delegation got the nerve to approach him, he had them beaten out of the hold. I saw the lash marks so I know they aren't lying. They said they'd never seen him in such a temper. He announced that the dragonriders are trying to get extra tithing on false pretenses by spreading such rumors. He was also quite damning about the new mine being opened above Ruatha when good Bitrans could have worked the Steng Valley ones."

"The world is against Bitrans?" Paulin asked in a droll tone.

"You got it," M'shall said.

"Chalkin also refused to accept delivery of HNO_3 tanks . . ." Kalvi said.

"Wouldn't pay for them, you mean," M'shall said. "That's what Telgar riders told mine."

"Either way, there'll be no groundcrews. I think he's gone far enough to warrant impeachment," Paulin said with slow deliberation. "As a Lord Holder, it's his duty to inform, and prepare his folk, for Threadfall. That's why the Holder system was adopted: to give people a strong leader to supply direction during a Fall and to provide emergency assistance. By closing his borders, he's also abrogated one of the basic tenets vouchsafed in the Charter: freedom of movement. He's turned autonomy into despotism. I'll send all Lord Holders and Professional Heads particulars . . . Oh," and he glanced at Clisser in dismay, "we can't make quick copies anymore, can we?"

"One dragonrider could contact all the other Lord Holders," M'shall said. "Or one messenger on this coast and another on ours. That makes only two copies needed."

"I'll request a rider from S'nan," Paulin said, reaching for a pad.

"That'll please S'nan no end," M'shall said. "He's not been the least bit pleased with Chalkin's defiance. Simply isn't done, you know," and M'shall grinned as he mimicked S'nan's rather prim tones.

"We must take action against Chalkin now," Paulin said, "rather than leave it until the next formal Conclave at Turn's End. Time's running out." Then Paulin turned to Clisser. "Which reminds me. Clisser, any luck on finding some method of irrefutably determining the return of Thread?"

Clisser jerked himself into alertness. "We've several possibilities," he said, trying to sound more positive than he was. "What with the loss of computer access, it's taking longer to sift through ways and means."

"Well, keep at it . . ." and then Paulin touched Clisser's shoulder and smiled, "along with everything else you're doing. By the way, the teaching songs are very good indeed." Then he put a finger in his ear, drilling it briefly as he grinned more broadly. "The kids sing 'em all the time, not just in class."

"That's what we intended," Clisser said with droll satisfaction. "Shall I wait for your message?"

"No need for that, my friend, but thanks for offering. This I will take pleasure in penning." Fort's Lord Holder grinned. "And I'll remember to keep a copy for the Archives. By the way, wasn't there some ancient way of making copies . . . something that would transfer the writing to the next page under?"

Clisser bowed his head briefly in thought. "Carbon copying, I think you mean. We don't have it, but Lady Salda might have some ideas. We've got to figure a way to make multiple copies or spend hours copying." He gave a heavy sigh of regret.

"I'll leave it to you then, Clisser," said Paulin. "Thank you all. Now get out of here, the lot of you," and he grinned at the Benden leaders and Kalvi, "and enjoy the rest of the evening while I get on with this task. Not that I won't enjoy it in some respects," he said, picking up his pen and examining the tip.

At that polite dismissal, they all filed out of the office. Clisser thought that Issony looked disappointed at not being able to recite his catalog of complaints against Lord Chalkin. So Clisser made sure that Issony had as much of the good wine as he wanted.

VIII

Telgar Weyr

Iantine asked to be allowed out again on the next sunny day, so he was in the Bowl when the traveling traders arrived. The entire complement of the caverns flocked out to greet them. Iantine furiously sketched the big dusty carts with their multiple teams of the heavy-duty ox-types which had been bred for such work. They had been one of the last bio-engineering feats from Wind Blossom, whose grandmother had done such notable work creating the dragons of Pern.

Iantine had seen traders come and go on their routes since childhood and fondly remembered the stellar occasions when the Benden trading group had arrived at their rather remote sheephold. More specifically, he recalled the taste of the boiled sweets, flavored by the fruits that grew so abundantly in Nerat, which the traders passed out by the handful. Once, there'd been fresh citrus, a treat of unsurpassed delight to himself and his siblings.

For a remote holding, having travelers drop by was almost as good as a Gather. To Iantine's surprise, Weyrfolk were equally delighted. Despite the fact they could usually find a dragon to convey them wherever they wanted to go, the arrival of the traders was even better than tithe trains. (The tithe wagons were a different matter, since everyone had to pitch in to store the produce given to the support of the Weyr.) And traders brought the news of all the holds and halls along the way. There were as many clusters of folks just talking, Iantine noticed, as examining goods in the stalls the Liliencamp traders set up. Tables and chairs were brought out from the kitchen cavern: klah and the day's fresh bread and rolls were being served.

Leopol, always on hand for Iantine, brought over a mid-morning snack and hunkered down to give the journeyman the latest news.

"They've been setting up sheltered halts," he said between bits of his own sweet roll, "along the road to here. They won't stop doing their routes just because Thread's coming. But they gotta prepare for it. Half of what they got on those big wagons right now is materials for safe havens. 'Course, they can use what caves there are, but no more camping out in the open. That's going to cramp their style," and he grinned broadly. "But if ya gotta, ya gotta. See," and one honey-stained finger pointed to a group of men and women seated with the two Weyrleaders. They were all hunched over maps spread out on the table. "They're checking the sites over so's everyone here'll know where they might be if they're caught out in a Fall."

"Who trades through Bitra?" Iantine asked with considerable irony.

Leopol snorted. "No one in their right mind. 'Specially now. Didja hear that Chalkin's closed his borders to keep his own people in? Didja know that Chalkin doesn't believe Thread's coming?" The boy's eyes widened in horrified dismay at such irreverence. "And he never told his holders it is?"

"Actually, I got that distinct impression while I was there," Iantine said, "more from what wasn't said and done than what was. I mean, even Hall Domaize was stocking food and supplies against Threadfall. They'd talk enough about odds and wagers at Bitra, but not a word about Thread."

"Did they sucker you into any gaming?" Leopol's avid expression suggested he yearned for a positive answer.

Iantine shook his head and grinned at his eager listener. "In the first place, I'd been warned. Isn't everyone warned about Bitrans at Gathers? And then, I didn't have any spare marks to wager."

"Otherwise you'd have lost your commission fer fair," Leopol murmured, his eyes still round with his unvoiced speculations of the disaster Iantine had avoided.

"I'd say Chalkin's gambling in the wrong game if he thinks ignoring Thread will make it not happen," Iantine said. "Shelters are going to have to be huge," he added, gesturing toward the solid beasts who were being led to the lake to drink.

Either the great beasts were accustomed to dragonets, or they were so phlegmatic they didn't care. However, the dragonets had never seen *them* before in their short lives, so they reacted with alarm at the massive cart beasts, squealing with such fright that dragons, sleeping in the pale wintry sun on their weyr ledges, woke up to see what the fuss was about. Iantine grinned. He did a rapid sketch of that in a corner of the page. At the rate he was going, he'd use up even this generous supply of paper.

"Well, they've had to use a lot of sheet roofing, I know," Leopol said.

"The Weyr contributes, too, ya know, since the Liliencamps have to detour to get up to us."

Iantine had never given any thought to the support system required to serve a Weyr and its dragons. He had always assumed that dragons and riders took care of themselves from tithings, but he was acquiring a great respect for the organization and management of such a facility. In a direct contrast with what he had seen at Bitra, everyone in the Weyr worked cheerfully at any task set them and took great pride in being part of it. Everyone helped everyone else: everyone seemed happy.

To be sure, Iantine had recently realized that his early childhood had been relatively carefree and happy. His learning years at the College had also been good as well as productive: his apprenticeship to Hall Domaize had proceeded with only occasional ups and downs as he struggled to perfect new techniques and a full understanding of Art.

Bitra Hold had been an eye-opener. So, of course, was the Weyr, but in a far more positive manner. Grimly, Iantine realized that one had to know the bad to properly appreciate the good. He smiled wryly to himself while his right hand now rapidly completed the sketch of the Weyrleaders in earnest collaboration with the Liliencamp trail bosses.

That Bloodline had been the first of the peripatetic traders, bringing goods and delivering less urgent messages on their way from one isolated hold to another. A Liliencamp had been one of the more prominent First Settlers. Iantine thought he'd been portrayed in the great mural in Fort Hold, with the other Charterers: a smallish man with black hair, depicted with sharp eyes and a pad of some sort depending from his belt, and—Iantine had of course noted them—several writing implements stuffed in his chest pocket, and one behind his ear. It had seemed such a logical place to store a pencil that Iantine had taken to the habit himself.

He peered more closely at the trail bosses. Yes, one of them had what looked like a pencil perched behind one ear—and he also had an empty pouch at his belt: one that probably accommodated the pad on the table before him.

But even with such wayside precautions, would such traders be able to continue throughout the fifty dangerous years of a Pass? It was one thing to *plan*, and quite another, as Iantine had only just discovered, to put plans into operation. Still, considerable hardship would result in transporting items from Hall to hold to Weyr during Threadfall, especially since dragons would be wholly involved in protecting the land from Thread. They could not be asked to perform trivial duties. Dragons were not, after all, a transportation facility. They had been bioengineered as a defensive force: conveying people and goods was only an Interval occupation.

He wondered if the traders had any paper in their great wagons. Not that he had even a quarter mark left in his pouch. But maybe they'd take a sketch or two in trade.

As quick as he neatly could, he filled his last empty page with a montage: the train entering the Weyr Bowl, people rushing out to meet it, the goods being exhibited, deals being made, with the central portion the scene of the trail bosses discussing shelters with the Weyrleaders. He held the pad at arm's length and regarded it critically.

"That's marvelous," a voice said behind him, and he twisted about in surprise. "Why, you did it in a flash!"

The green rider, her dragon lounging beside her, smiled self-consciously, her green eyes shining with something akin to awe. Leopol had pointed this new rider out to him the other day and related the circumstances of her precipitous arrival at the Hatching.

"Debera?" he asked, remembering the name. She gasped, recoiling from him in her startlement. Her dragon came immediately alert, her eyes twirling faster with alarm. "Oh say, I didn't mean to—"

"Easy, Morath, he means me no harm," she said to the dragon and then smiled reassuringly up at him. "I was just surprised you'd know my name . . ."

"Leopol," and Iantine pointed his pencil to where the boy stood in earnest bargaining with a trader lad about the same age, "used to tell me everything that happened in the Weyr while I was recovering."

"Oh, yes," and the girl seemed to relax, and even managed a wider smile, "I know him. He's into everything. But kindhearted," she added hastily, glancing up at Iantine. "You've had some adventures, too, or so Leopol told me." Then she indicated his sketch. "You did that so well and so quickly. Why, you can almost hear them bargaining," she added, pointing to the trader with his mouth open.

Iantine regarded it critically. "Well, speed is not necessarily a good thing if you want to do good work." He deftly added a fold to the head trader's tunic, where he now saw there was a bulge over the belt. "Let's see if the subject likes it." He was amazed to hear the edge in his voice. She glanced warily up at him.

"If that's what you can do quickly," she said reassuringly, "I'd like to see what you do when you take your time."

He couldn't resist, and flipped over pages to where he had made a sketch of her oiling Morath.

"Oh, and I didn't see you doing this . . ." She reached out to touch it, but he was flipping to the page where he had sketched her and Morath listening to T'dam at the lecture. She'd had one arm draped over her dragon's neck, and he thought he had captured the subtle bond that prompted the embrace.

"Oh, that's marvelous," and Iantine was amazed to see tears in her eyes. In a spontaneous gesture, she clung to his arm, feasting her eyes on the drawing and preventing him from turning the page over. "Oh, how I'd—"

"You like it?"

"Oh, I do," and she snatched her hands away from his arm and clasped them behind her back, blushing deeply. "I do . . ." and bit her lip, swaying nervously.

"What's the matter?"

She gave an embarrassed laugh. "I haven't so much as the shaving of a mark."

He tore the sketch out of the pad and handed it to her.

"Oh, I couldn't . . . I couldn't," and she stepped back, although the look in her eyes told Iantine how much she wanted it.

"Why not?" He pressed the paper against her, pushing it at her when she continued to resist. "Please, Debera? I've had to get my hand back in after my fingers freezing, and it's only a sketch."

She glanced up at him, nervously and with some other fear lurking in the shadows of her lovely green eyes.

"You should have it, you know, to remind you of Morath at this age."

One hand crept from behind her back and reached for the sheet. "You're very good, Iantine," she murmured and held the sketch by fingertips as if afraid she'd soil it. "But I've nothing to pay . . ."

"Yes, you do," he said quickly with sudden inspiration and gestured toward the traders still in their group about the table. "You can be a satisfied customer and help me wheedle another pad out of the traders in return for this drawing of them."

"Oh, but . . ." She had shot a quick, frightened glance at the traders, and then, in as quick a change of mood, gave herself a shake, her free hand going to her dragon's head, as if seeking reassurance. The dragonet turned adoring eyes to her, and Debera's eyes briefly unfocused, the way Iantine had noticed in riders who paused to talk to their dragons. She let out a breath and faced him resolutely. "I would be glad to say a good word for you with Master Jol. He's by way of being a cousin of my mother's."

"Is he now?" Iantine said with fervor. "Then let us see if kinship is useful in trading."

"I can't, of course, promise anything," she said candidly as they moved toward the group. She found it hard to keep the sketch from fluttering. "Oh dear."

"Roll it up," he suggested. "Shall I do it for you?"

"No, thank you, I can manage." And she did, making a much tighter job of it than he would.

The conference was ending as they approached and the participants began to separate.

"Master Jol?" Debera said, her voice cracking a bit and not reaching very far. "Master Jol," she said, projecting a firmer tone. Iantine wondered if she was afraid the trader wouldn't recognize her at all.

"Is that Debera?" the trader said, peering at her as though he didn't believe his eyes. Then a broad smile of recollection covered his face and he strode rapidly across the distance between them, hands extended. Debera seemed to shy from such a warm welcome. "My dear, I'd heard that you'd Impressed a dragon."

Iantine put a reassuring hand at her waist and gave her an imperceptible forward push.

"Yes, this is Morath," and suddenly her manner became sure and proud. Dragon and rider exchanged one of those melting looks that Iantine found incredibly touching.

"Well, well, my greetings to you, young Morath," he said, bowing formally to the dragonet, whose eyes began to whirl faster.

Debera gave her a reassuring little pat. "Master Jol is my mother's cousin," she explained to Morath.

"Which makes me yours as well, my lass," Jol reminded her. "And very proud to have dragonrider kin. Ah, you're so like your mother. Did you know that?"

Iantine watched as Debera's expression turned sad.

"Ah, now, I didn't mean to grieve you, child," Jol said with instant dismay. "And how happy she would be to see you . . ." He paused and cleared his throat, and Iantine knew the trader was hastily amending what he had started to say. ". . . here, a dragonrider . . ."

"And out of my father's control," Debera finished with droll bitterness. "Had you heard that, too, Master Jol?"

"Oh indeed," Master Jol said, grinning even more broadly, his eyes twinkling with a slight hint of malice. "I was right pleased to hear that, indeed and I was. Now, what can I do for you? Some Gather clothes, good lined boots . . . you'll have come with little if I know your father."

Such plain speaking momentarily made Debera uneasy, but her dragonet crowded reassuringly against her.

"The Weyr has furnished me with everything I need, Master Jol," she replied with quiet dignity.

"Master? Am I not cousin to you, young woman?" Jol said with mock severity.

Now her smile returned. "Cousin, but I thank you, though I do have a favor to ask . . ."

"And what might that be?"

Debera flipped open her sketch and showed it to the trader. "Iantine here did this of me, and he has one of you . . ." On cue, Iantine offered his sketch pad, open to the montage. "Only Iantine's used up his pad and, like me, hasn't a sliver to spend."

Master Jol reached for the pad, his manner altering instantly to a trader's critical appraisal. But he had only cast an eye over the sketch when he paused, peering more closely at the artist.

"Iantine, you said?" And when both Debera and Iantine nodded, his smile quirked the line of his generous mouth. "I place the name now. You're the lad who managed to escape unscathed from Chalkin's clutches." Jol offered his free hand to Iantine. "Well done, lad. I'd had wind of your adventure." He winked, his expression approving. "But then we traders hear everything and learn to sift the fine thread of truth from the chaff of gossip."

Then he turned back to the sketch, examining it carefully, nodding his head as his eyes went from one panel to the next. He gave an amused sniff as he took a longer look at himself, pencil cocked behind his ear.

"You've got me to the life, pencil and all," and he touched the tool to be sure it was in place. "May I?" he asked courteously, indicating a desire to look at the other pages.

"Certainly," Iantine said, making a courteous bow. He could have kicked himself when he swayed a bit on his feet.

"Here now, lad, I know you're not long recovered from your ordeal," Jol said, quickly supporting him. "Let's just take a seat so I can have a good look at everything this pad seems to have on offer."

Ignoring Iantine's protests, Jol led him to the table he had just left and pushed him onto a stool. Debera and Morath followed, Debera looking very pleased with this consideration.

Jol went through the pad as thoroughly as Master Domaize would have done, making comments about those Weyrfolk he knew, smiling and nodding a good deal. He also knew when Iantine had left a pose unfinished.

"Now, what is it you require, Artist Iantine?"

"More paper, mainly," Iantine said in a tentative tone.

Jol nodded. "I believe I do have a pad of this quality paper, but smaller. I bring some in for Waine from time to time. I can, of course, get larger sheets . . ."

"It's not as if I'll be staying around the Weyr until your next round . . ."

Master Jol dismissed that consideration. "I've stores at Telgar Hold and can forward what you need in a day or two." He gave Iantine a thoughtful glance. "You'll not be leaving here all that soon, I'd say." He took the pencil from behind his ear with one hand and the pad from its pouch at his belt with the other. "Now, what exactly are your requirements, Artist Iantine?"

"Ah . . ."

"He wants to make sketches of every rider and dragon in the Weyr," said Leopol, who had eased himself unnoticed close enough to hear what was being said.

"So you've many commissions already, have you?" Master Jol said approvingly, pencil poised over the fresh leaf of his pad.

"Well, no, not exactly, you see—" Iantine stammered.

"You've three I know of," Leopol said. "P'tero for M'leng . . . and the Weyrleaders . . ."

Iantine almost bit Leopol's nose off. "The Weyrleaders're different. I will do them in oils, but the sketches are to thank those in the Weyr who've been so kind to me."

"Doing portraits of an entire Weyr is quite an undertaking," and Master Jol scribbled a line. "You'll need a good deal of paper and plenty of pencils. Or would you prefer ink? I stock a very good quality. Guaranteed not to fade or blot." He looked at Iantine expectantly.

"But I've only this sketch to trade with you," Iantine said.

"Lad, you've credit with Jol Liliencamp Traders," Jol said gently, touching his pencil to Iantine's shoulder and giving it a little push. "I'm not Chalkin, mind you. Not any way, shape, or form." And he gave a burst of such infectious laughter that Iantine grinned in spite of himself. "Now, give me your requirements straight. But to ease your mind, if you'd finish off this," and the pencil end tapped the montage, "in watercolor, I'm ready to give you two marks for it. Oh, and I'd like this one of T'dam giving his lecture," he added, flipping to that page. "That'll show some folks that dragonriders do something beyond glide about the skies. A mark and a half for that . . ."

"But . . . but . . ." Iantine floundered, trying to organize his thoughts as well as his needs. Debera was grinning from ear to ear and so was her dragon. "I've no watercolors with me—" he began, wishing to indicate his willingness to finish the montage.

"Ah, but I just happen to have some, which is why I suggested them," Jol said, beaming again. "Really, this meeting is most serendipitous," he added, and his smile included Debera. "And this," he touched the montage again in a very proprietary fashion, "colored up a bit and with glass to protect it, will look very good indeed in my wagon office. Indeed it will. Advertising, I believe the ancestors called it."

"Ah, Master Jol?" called someone from one of the trade wagons. "A moment of your time . . ."

"I'll be back, lad, just you stay there. You, too, Debera. I've not finished with the pair of you yet, no I haven't."

As Iantine and Debera exchanged stunned looks, he trotted off to see what was required of him, tucking the pencil behind his ear again and folding up his pad as he went.

"I don't believe him," Iantine said, shaking his head, feeling weak and breathless.

"Are you all right?" Debera asked, leaning across the table to him.

"Gob-smacked," Iantine said, remembering a favorite expression of his father. "Completely gob-smacked."

Debera grinned knowingly. "I think I am, too. I never expected—"

"Neither did I."

"Why? Don't you trust traders?" Leopol asked, sounding slightly defensive.

Iantine gave a shaky laugh. "One can trust traders. It's just I never expected such generosity . . ."

"How long were you in Bitra?" Debera asked tartly, giving him a long look.

"Long enough," Iantine said, grimacing, "to learn new meanings to the word 'satisfactory.' "

Debera gave him a little frown.

"Never mind," he said, shaking his head and patting her hand. "And thank you very much for introducing me to your cousin."

"Once he saw that sketch, you really didn't need me," she remarked, almost shyly.

"I believe you ordered these," said a baritone voice. Rider and Artist looked up in astonishment as a trader deposited an armful of items on the table: two pads, one larger than the other, a neat square box which held a full glass bottle of ink, a sheaf of pens, and a parcel of pencils. "Special delivery." With a grin, he pivoted and went back the way he had come.

"Master Jol does pride himself on his quick service," Leopol said with a wide grin.

"There now! You're all set," Debera said.

"I am indeed," and the words came out of Iantine like a prayer.

Fort Hold and Bitran Borders, Early Winter

*L*ord Paulin's message to the other Lord Holders and Weyrleaders received a mixed reception: not everyone was in favor of impeachment, despite the evidence presented. Paulin was both annoyed and frustrated, having hoped for a unanimous decision so that Chalkin could be removed before his hold was totally demoralized.

Jamson and Azury felt that the matter could wait until the Turn's End Council meeting: Jamson was known to be conservative, but Paulin was surprised by Azury's reservations. Those who lived in tropical zones rarely understood the problems of winter weather. To be sure, it would be more difficult to prepare Bitra Hold in full winter, which was Azury's stated concern, but some progress could be made to prepare the hold for the vernal onslaught of Threadfall. Preparations ought to have begun—as in every other hold—two years ago: larger crops sowed, harvests stored, and general maintenance done on buildings and arable lands, as well as the construction of emergency shelters on the main roads and for groundcrews. Not to mention training holders how to combat Thread burrows.

There was the added disadvantage that Chalkin's folk seemed generally dispirited anyhow—though that should not be used as an excuse for denying them news of the impending problem.

And who would succeed to the hold? A consideration that was certainly fraught with problems.

In his response, Bastom had made a good suggestion: the appointment of a deputy or regent right away until one of Chalkin's sons came of age; sons who would be specifically, and firmly, trained to hold properly. Not that the new holder *had* to be of the Bloodline, but following the precepts of inheritance outlined in the Charter would pacify the nervous Lords. To Paulin's way of thinking, competence should always be the prime decider in succession, and that was not always passed on in the genes of Bloodlines.

For that matter, Paulin's eldest nephew had shown a sure grasp of hold management. Sidny was a hard worker, a fair man, and a good judge of character and ability. Paulin was half tempted to recommend him up for Fort's leadership when he was gone. He had a few reservations about his son, Mattew, but Paulin knew that he tended to be more critical of his own Blood than others were.

He would definitely suggest Bastom's idea to the Council: good practice for younger sons and daughters to have actual hands-on experience in running a hold. Considering the state Bitra Hold was in, a team would be required. Such an expedient would certainly reduce the cry of "nepotism." And give youngsters a chance to display initiative and ability.

When the last of the replies came in, Paulin gave the young green rider a message for M'shall at Benden Weyr on the result of the polling. The Weyrleader was sure to be as disappointed as he was. He tried to convince himself that they could still get Bitra Hold right and tight in time for Threadfall. But the sooner it was done, the better. He hoped M'shall could get back to him about locating the Bitran uncle and whether he was competent to take hold. Otherwise a Search must be made of legitimate heirs to—

"Fragitall," Paulin muttered, pushing back from his desk and sighing deeply in frustration. One could no longer do a quick Search on the Bloodline program for a comprehensive genealogy. Surely that was one program Clisser had printed out and copied. "Well, we'll need a copy of whatever form that program's in," he told himself, sighing again. To cheer himself up he reviewed the progress report from the new mine.

They wanted permission to call the hold CROM, an acronym of the founders: Chester, Ricard, Otty, and Minerva. Paulin didn't see a problem with that but, as a matter of form—especially right now—the request should first be presented to the Council. During the Interval so many procedures had been relaxed, and the leniency was now coming back to plague them, as in the case of Chalkin becoming Lord Holder. At least Paulin was consoled by the knowledge that it was his father, the late Lord Emilin, who had voted Fort on that score. That evidence of bad judgment wasn't his own error, Paulin knew, even if it was now up to him to rectify the situation.

There was an abrupt rapping of knuckles on his door, and before he could respond it swung open: the Benden Weyrleader, M'shall, brushed past Mattew to enter.

"We've got to do something *now*, Paulin," the Weyrleader said, his expression grim as he hauled off his riding gauntlets and opened up his jacket.

"You got my message quickly enough . . . Bring klah, Matt," Paulin said, gesturing for his son to be quick. M'shall's face looked pinched with the cold of *between* . . . and more.

"I got it. And that's not the end of it. There's rough weather in Bitra and people freezing to death because they will not leave the border," M'shall announced.

"Will not? Or cannot?"

"More cannot than will not. Though Chalkin sent down orders that none of the 'ungrateful dissenters' could expect to reclaim their holdings— punishment for defying him—irrespective of the fact that he's putting their lives at risk by his notion of holding."

"How many are involved?" Paulin's sense of alarm increased.

M'shall ruffled thick graying hair that had been pressed down by his helmet. "L'sur says there must be well over a hundred at the main border crossing into Benden; women, children, and elderlies. There are as many or more at other border points, and no shelter at any, bar what the guards are using. The refugees have all been herded into makeshift pens. What's more atrocious, L'sur saw several bodies hung up by the feet that seemed to have been used as target practice. Benden Weyr cannot ignore such barbarity, Paulin."

"No, it can't, nor can Fort Hold!" Paulin was on his feet and pacing. "If that's what he calls hold management, he *has* to be removed."

"My thinking, too," M'shall said, running agitated hands through his hair again. "Another night like last and those people'll be dead of exposure and starvation. Bridgely concurs with me that something has to be done, now, today. And it's getting toward a cold night now there. I've come to you for Council authority since Bridgely says we'd better do this as properly as possible . . ." He paused, bitter. "Such a situation is not supposed to *happen*. Those people aren't defying *him*. They're just scared to death and desperate for security . . . which obviously they don't expect to find in Bitra." He hitched himself forward in the chair. "Thing is, Paulin, if we hand out supplies, what's to keep the border guards from just collecting them the moment we take off? So, I think I'll have to leave a couple of riders as protection . . . which'll give Chalkin a chance to cry 'Weyr interference.' "

Paulin felt nauseous. That sort of thing was straight out of the ancient bloody history the settlers had deliberately left behind: evolving a code of ethics and conduct that would make such events improbable! This planet was settled with the idea that there was room enough for everyone willing to work the land that was his or hers by Charter-given birthright.

"There's no interference if your riders stay on your side of the border. Besides which, Bitra Hold looks to Benden Weyr for protection—"

"Thread protection," M'shall corrected.

"In a manner of speaking," and Paulin's smile was grim, "this is partly Thread protection. They're looking for what they should have had from their Lord Holder, and who else should they turn to but the Weyr? No," and Paulin brought one fist down sharply on the desk. "You're within your rights . . . if you've riders willing to volunteer for such duty."

"L'sur's stayed on, or so his dragon told Craigath."

"But no firestone," and Paulin held up a stern finger, "much as some might like to show force."

"Oh, I've made myself clear on that point, I assure you," and M'shall gave a bitter twist to his lips. "And we haven't had any training at Benden recently so there's not a whisper of flame in any of the dragons. As for disciplining the guards, a short hop and a long drop *between* would be *my* preference, but . . ." He held up both hands to assure Paulin of self-restraint.

At that point Mattew returned with a tray containing steaming cups of klah, soup, and a basket of hot breads. He deposited it on the table and left.

M'shall didn't wait for Paulin's invitation but grabbed up the soup and blew on its surface, sipping as soon as he dared. "That hits the spot, and if you've a caldron of it, I'll take it back with me." He grinned, licking his lips. "It's certainly hot enough to survive a jump *between*."

"You may have it, caldron and all. L'sur has stayed on, you say? How about riders at other crossing points?" Paulin asked, stirring sweetener into his klah. M'shall nodded. "Good. Their presence ought to inhibit any further violence." But that presence was only a deterrent, not assistance. He would like to do more than send soup, but his position at this point, even as Council Chair, might be compromised. "At least the Weyr has a right to take action, and so does Bridgely," he added thoughtfully. He thumped his fist again. "But I will go personally to see both Jamson and Azury: especially since Chalkin has used such extreme measures. I'm hard-pressed to see the reason for them."

M'shall shrugged. "Fort holders have every reason to trust you, Paulin. Bitrans never have had any with Chalkin holding."

"What I'd like to do is haul the indecisive, like Jamson and Azury, and *show* them what's happening at Bitra. They probably think we've exaggerated the situation."

"Exaggerated?" M'shall was indignant, and it was as well the cup was empty of soup when he planted it hard on the table. "Sorry. What's wrong with them?"

"They wouldn't behave in such a manner. It's hard for them to believe another Lord Holder would."

"Well," and M'shall nearly growled, "he would and he has."

There was a more circumspect knock on the door, which Matt opened, showing in K'vin.

"I just heard about the border trouble, M'shall. Zulaya had Meranath bespeak Maruth, so Charanth and I thought to catch you here," the young Weyrleader said, his expression as grim as Benden's.

"So he's blocked the western borders as well?"

K'vin nodded. "Telgar has no grounds to object to his closing his borders, but he's deliberately killing people, turfing them out in this weather. I can't . . . and won't . . . permit people to be treated like that." He fixed an expectant stare on Paulin.

"M'shall and I have been discussing the intolerable situation. I've already polled the Lord Holders with a view to taking immediate action. The response was not unanimous, so even as Council Chair there is little I can do—officially, that is. But as M'shall pointed out, the Weyr has certain responsibilities to protect people. By stretching a point, you could say they're Thread-lost," and Paulin's smile was wry, "escaping a hold which is unprepared. So the Weyrs can move where the Council Chair may not."

"That's all I need to know!" K'vin slapped his riding gloves against his thigh to emphasize his approval.

"Of course," and Paulin held up one hand in restraint, "you must be careful not to give Chalkin due cause to cite an infringement against Hold autonomy . . ."

"Not if that includes deliberate mistreatment of people he's already misled," K'vin said, his voice rising in alarm.

"This is not the time to jeopardize the neutrality of the Weyrs, you know," Paulin said, looking from one to the other. "Thread hasn't started falling yet."

"C'mon, Paulin—" M'shall began in protest.

"I'm with you in spirit, but as Council Chair, I have to remind you—above and beyond my *private* opinion—that we don't have the *right* to interfere in the government of a hold."

"You may not, Paulin," K'vin said. "But M'shall and I do. There's truth in what you said about Weyrs protecting people from peril."

"From Threadfall . . ." Paulin reminded the younger Weyrleader.

"From peril," K'vin repeated firmly. "Freezing to death without shelter from inclement weather constitutes peril as surely as Threadfall does."

Paulin nodded approvingly. "I may even forget that you visited here this morning." He grinned. "M'shall, you don't happen to know where Chalkin's remaining uncle lives?"

"I already thought of that and he's not there," M'shall said. "Place was empty. Too empty. I know Vergerin was alive and well last autumn."

"How do you mean 'too empty'?" Paulin asked, jotting down the uncle's name.

"It had been cleaned out too thoroughly. Not," and M'shall held up one hand to forestall Paulin's query, "as if it had been set to rights after a man's death, but as if to prove no one had been there at all. But Vergerin had cleared vegetation back from his front court, as every smart holder should. Someone had thrown debris all around to disguise the clearance."

"Has Chalkin anticipated us?" Paulin asked in a rhetorical question. Then he looked from one dragonrider to the other. "Rescue those folks before either the weather or Chalkin's bullies kill them. And I'd like interviews from them, too, once they're not afraid to talk to outsiders." Just as M'shall had his hand on the doorknob, Paulin added, "And not so much as a trickle of flame, please. That could get magnified out of all proportion."

K'vin pretended wide-eyed shock at such a notion. M'shall glanced around.

"I didn't hear that, Paulin," the Benden Weyrleader said with stiff dignity.

"As if we would . . ." K'vin said to M'shall as they strode out of Fort Hold.

"I'd like to," M'shall said in a taut voice, "that's the problem. But then, I've known Chalkin longer than you."

Craigath and Charanth were already on the court, awaiting their riders.

"You'll take the western and northern crossings, K'vin?" M'shall asked as they separated to reach their bronzes. "Have you been checking on numbers for transport?"

"Yes, and had sweep riders checking in ever since Chalkin closed the borders. Zulaya will warn Tashvi and Salda that we're proceeding. We'll take all to the Weyr first. The entire Weyr is organized to help."

"You're a good man, K'vin," and M'shall grinned at his colleague. "So let's do it!" The Benden Weyrleader launched himself up his dragon's shoulder and swung neatly between the end ridges.

We go to help? Charanth asked K'vin.

Indeed we do. Tell Meranath to have Zulaya put our plan into operation. I'll meet my wing at the Falls road. And I think we'd better ask Iantine to come along.

When K'vin returned to Telgar, the first rescue wave was ready to take off at his signal. He paused long enough to haul Iantine behind him on Charanth.

"Get down as much in black and white as you can, Iantine. I want Chalkin nailed by the evidence."

Iantine was all too happy to comply with the request. It would be one way of paying back the arrogant Lord Holder for his snaking ways and meanness. But no sooner had Iantine dropped to the hard-packed snow of the border point than his attitude changed to horrified disgust. Using an economy of line, he sketched the "pen"—ropes looped around trees, and the shivering knots of people forced to stand, for there was not enough room to sit down—in the churned mud of an inadequate space. He drew the haggard faces, the chilled bodies bent inward from cold, or those clumped together to share what warmth they had. Some had been stripped of all but what covered private parts and were surrounded by their fellows in an attempt to keep them from freezing. Some were standing barefoot on the rough rags and boots of their neighbors, feet blue and dangerously white from frostbite. Children wandered weeping with hunger and fatigue or slumped in unconscious bundles in the mud at the feet of the adults. Three elderlies were stiff in death. Bloodied faces and bruised eyes were more common than the unmarked.

The guards, however, were warm with many layers of clothing, good fires with cooking spits turning to roast the meat of such animals as the refugees had brought with them. Others were tied or penned up for future use. Such belongings as the refugees had brought with them were now piled at the side of the guardhouse or in the barrows or carts lined up behind. Iantine faithfully recorded rings and bracelets, even earrings, inappropriately adorning the guards.

They had been alarmed at the arrival of the dragonriders, as many as could retreating into the shelter of the stone border facility. That had made it considerably easier to move the refugees. Of course many of them were in such a state of shock and fear that they were as frightened of the dragons and the riders as of the brutal guards.

Zulaya had brought Weyrfolk with her, and their presence reassured many. So did the blankets and the warm jackets. And the soup: the first sustenance many had had since they had left their holds.

What Iantine couldn't put down on paper were the sounds and the smells of that scene. And yet he did . . . in the open mouths of the terrified folk, their haunted eyes, the contortions of their abused bodies, their ragged coverings, the piles of human ordure because the guards had made no provision for that human requirement, and the abandoned belongings and carts.

Now that he had seen real privation, Iantine realized how lucky he had been in his brief encounter with the Lord Holder of Bitra.

Iantine returned with the last group, letting his hand rest only in *between*, sketching as they flew, his pad propped against P'tero's back.

"You haven't stopped a moment," P'tero shouted over his shoulder. "You'll freeze your hand up here, you know."

Iantine waved it to prove its flexibility and continued to sketch. He was adding details to the men who had been hung by their heels and used as target practice. The men had been cut down—one of the first things the rescuers had done. Iantine had only had time enough to do an outline, but the details—despite all the other sketches he made that day—were vivid in his mind's eye, and he had to get every one down on paper or he would feel he had betrayed them.

When the young blue rider deposited him in front of the lower cavern, Iantine, still filling in substance, managed to get himself to a table near enough to the fire to get the good of the warmth—and increase the fluidity of his drawing. His fingers gradually thawed and his pencil raced faster.

A touch on his shoulder startled him half out of his chair.

"It's Debera," and the green rider placed klah and a bowl of stew in front of him. "Everyone else has eaten. You'd better," she said severely, wrenching the pencil out of one hand and taking the pad from the other. "You look awful," she added, peering closely at his face.

He reached for his pad but she slapped at his hand, swinging it out of his reach.

"No, you eat first. You'll draw better for it. Oh, my word!" Her eye was caught by the scene, and her free hand went to her mouth, her eyes widening in shock. "Oh, they couldn't have."

"I sketched what I saw," he said, exhaling in a remorse that came from his guts and then inhaling the tantalizing odor emanating from the stew. He looked down at it, thick with vegetables and chunks of meat. They really could do miracles with wherry here. He picked up the spoon and began to eat, only then realizing how empty his stomach was. It almost hurt receiving food, and that nearly made him stop eating altogether. Chalkin's prisoners had been without food for three or four days.

"They're all fed now," Debera murmured.

Iantine gave her a startled glance and she patted his shoulder reassuringly, as she often patted her Morath.

"I felt the same way when I ate earlier on." She sat down across from him. "We'd been going flat out to feed them when Tisha made us all stop to get something to eat, too." She started turning the pages of his book, the look on her face becoming more and more distressed at each new scene of the tragedy. "How could he?"

Iantine reached over and gently pulled the sketch pad from her, setting it down, closed between them.

"He gave the orders—" Iantine began.

"And knew just what would happen when he did, I know. I've met some of his . . . 'guards.' Even my father wouldn't have one about the hold." She tapped the pad. "No one can ignore that sort of evidence."

Iantine gave a snort. "Not with dragonriders verifying what's in here!" He finished the last of the stew and stretched his legs out under the table, scrubbing at his face, still tingling with his long hours in the unremitting cold of the border crossing.

"Go to bed, why don't you, Iantine," Debera said, rising. She glanced around the cavern, which was occupied by only a few riders and folk finishing their evening meal. "They've all been sorted out and you'll be lucky if you have your room to yourself. But I'd better get some sleep, too. That Morath of mine! She wakes positively starved, no matter how much I give her."

Iantine smiled at the affection that softened Debera's voice. He got to his feet, swaying a bit. "You're right. I need sleep. Good night, Debera."

He watched her striding purposefully out of the cavern, at the proud tilt to her head and the set of her shoulders. She'd changed a great deal since she Impressed Morath. He grinned, picked up his pad, and slowly made his way to his quarters.

He wasn't sharing with any refugee, but Leopol sprawled on a bed pad along one wall and didn't even stir as Iantine prepared himself for bed.

◆　◆　◆

There were more refugees than originally estimated, and while the resources of the two Weyrs were stretched, the Lord Holders immediately sent additional supplies and offered shelter. Some of those rescued were in bad shape from the cold and could not be immediately transferred to the sanctuaries offered by Nerat, Benden, and Telgar Holds.

Zulaya had headed a rescue team of the other queens and the green riders. She came back, seething with rage.

"I knew he was a greedy fool and an idiot, but not a sadist. There were three pregnant women at the Forest Road border and they'd been raped because, of course, they couldn't sue the guards later on a paternity claim."

"Are the women all right?" K'vin asked, appalled by yet another instance of the brutality. "We arrived at the North Pass just in time to spare three lads from . . . very unkind attentions by the guards. Where does Chalkin find such men?"

"From holds that have tossed them out for antisocial behavior or criminal activities, of course," Zulaya replied, almost spitting in anger. "And that blizzard's closed in. We moved just in time. If we hadn't, I fear most of these people would be dead by morning. Absolutely nothing allowed them! Not even the comfort of a fire!"

"I know, I know," he said, as bitter about the sadistic behavior as she was. "We should have treated those guards to a taste of absolute cold. Like a long wait *between*. Only that would have been a clean death."

"We still can," Zulaya said in a grating tone. K'vin regarded her in astonishment. She glared at him, clenching her fists at her sides. "Oh, I know we can't, but that doesn't keep me from *wanting* to! Did you take Iantine with you? I thought of how useful on-the-spot sketches might be."

"In fact, he asked to come. He's got plenty to show Lord Paulin and the Council," K'vin said. He swallowed, remembering the stark drawings that had filled one pad. Iantine's quick hand had captured the reality, made even more compelling by the economy of line, depicting horrific scenes of deliberate cruelty.

The Weyrleaders introduced themselves to the first of the refugees and started off by interviewing the old couple.

"M'grandsir's grandsir came to Bitra with the then holder," the man said, his eyes nervously going from one Weyrleader to the other. He kept wiggling his bandaged fingers, though N'ran had assured him the pain and itch had been dulled by fellis and numbweed. "I'm Brookie, m'woman's Ferina. We farmed it since. Never no reason to complain, though the Holder keeps asking for more tithe and there's only so much comes out of any acre, no matter who tills it. But *he'd* the right."

"Not to take our sow, though," his mate said, her expression rebellious. "We needed that 'un to make more piggies to meet the tithe *he* set." Like her man, she laid a stress on the pronoun. "Took our daughter, too, to work in the hold when we wanted her land grant. Said we didn't work what we had good enough so we couldn't have more."

"Really?" Zulaya said, deceptively mild as she shot K'vin a meaningful glance. "Now that's interesting, Holder Ferina."

K'vin envied Zulaya's trick of remembering names.

You could've asked me, Charanth said helpfully.

You've been listening?

The people needed dragons' help. I listen. We all do.

When the pity of dragons has also been aroused, surely that's enough justification for what we've just done, thought K'vin, if the Council should turn up stiff. He must remember to tell Zulaya.

"But *he* says we got it wrong and we ain't had no teacher to ask," the man was saying. "An' thassa 'nother thing—we should have a teacher for our kids."

"At least so they can read the Charter and know what rights you all do have," Zulaya said firmly. "I've a copy we can show you right now, so you can refresh your memories."

The two exchanged alarmed glances.

"In fact," Zulaya went on smoothly, "I think we'll have someone read you your rights . . . since it would be difficult for you to turn pages with bandaged hands, Brookie. And you're not in much better shape, Ferina."

Ferina managed a nervous smile. "I'd like that real well, Weyrwoman. Real well. Our rights are printed out? In the Charter and all?"

"Your rights as holders are part of the Charter," Zulaya said, shooting K'vin another unhappy look. "In detailed paragraphs." She rose to her feet abruptly. "Why don't you sit over there, in the sun, Ferina, Brookie?" and she pointed to the eastern wall, where some of the Weyr's elderlies were seated, enjoying the warmth of the westering sun. "We'll make sure you hear it all, and you can ask any questions you want."

She helped the two to their feet and started them on their way across the Bowl as K'vin whistled for Leopol.

"Go get the Weyr's copy of the Charter, will you, lad?"

"You want me to read it to them, too?" the boy asked, eyes glinting partly in mischief and partly because he enjoyed second-guessing errands.

"Smart pants, are we?" K'vin said. "No, I think we need T'lan for this." He pointed toward the white-haired old brown rider who was serving klah to the refugees. "Just get the Charter now. I'll request T'lan's services."

Leopol moved off at his usual sprint, and K'vin went over to speak to the elderly brown rider. He had exactly the right manner to deal with nervous and frightened holders.

◆ ◆ ◆

Bridgely arrived in Benden Weyr, his face suffused with blood, torn between fury and laughter.

"The nerve of the man, the consummate nerve!" he exclaimed and threw down the message he carried.

It landed closer to Irene than M'shall so she picked it up.

"From Chalkin?" she exclaimed, looking up at Bridgely.

"Read it . . . and pour me some wine, would you, M'shall?" the Lord Holder said, slipping into a chair. "I mean, I know that man's got gall, but to presume . . . to have the effrontery—"

"Sssh," Irene said, her eyes widening as she read. "Oh, I don't believe it! Just listen, M'shall. 'This hold has the right to dragon messengers. The appropriate red striped banner has been totally ignored, though my guards have seen dragons near enough to see that an urgent message must be delivered.

Therefore I must add . . .' " She peered more closely at the written page. "His handwriting's abominable . . . Ah, 'dereliction' . . . really, where does he get off to cry 'dereliction' . . . 'of their prime duty to the other complaints I am forced to lay at their door. Not only have they been interfering with the management of this hold, but they fill the minds of my loyal holders with outrageous lies. I demand their immediate censure. They are not even reliable enough to perform those duties which fall within their limited abilities.' Limited abilities?" Irene turned pale with fury. "I'll unlimit him!"

"Especially when we've had an earful of how he treats his loyal holders . . ." M'shall said, his expression grimmer than ever. "Wait a minute. What's the date on his letter?"

"Five days ago," Bridgely answered, with a malicious grin. "He had to send it by rider. From what the fellow told me, Chalkin's also sent messengers to Nerat and Telgar as well. He wants me, you'll see in the last paragraph, Irene," and Bridgely pointed to that section of the missive, "to forward it by a reliable messenger to Lord Paulin, registering his complaint with the Council Chair. I suppose," and his grin was droll, "I'll get another one when he finds out about yesterday's airlift rescue."

"The man . . ." Irene paused, unable to find words. "When I think of how he's treated those poor people . . ."

"And when he's called to account, he'll probably whinge that his guards exceeded their instructions . . . and he's fired them all," said Bridgely with a cynical shrug.

"Oh," M'shall said brightly, "not all of them." He scratched the back of his head. "Ah . . . they wanted to know why they couldn't get to ride a dragon if the riffraff could."

"You didn't, M'shall?" Irene exclaimed, her eyes wide with delighted anticipation, "drop them off on the way, did you?"

"No," and M'shall shrugged with mock regret. "But I felt it might be wise to . . . ah, sequester? Yes, that's the word, sequester certain of them should they be required to stand before the Council and explain exactly what orders they received."

"Oh." Bridgely turned pensive.

"Oh, I was select, you might say," and M'shall's face was grim. "I found out which had had a hand in those killings and took testimony from bereaved witnesses. Not even guards, acting under a Lord Holder's orders, may execute without trial, you know."

"Oh, indeed, and you've acted circumspectly," Bridgely said, nodding with understanding. "Really, I don't think this can wait until Turn's End. And I shall so inform Jamson and Azury."

"I'd be happy to take you myself," M'shall said, "and speak for the Weyr.

In fact," and the Weyrleader reached for Chalkin's written message, "you could deliver this at the same time, Bridgely."

"You are all consideration, Weyrleader," Bridgely said, gesturing grandly and looking exceedingly pleased.

"My pleasure at any time, Lord Holder." M'shall swept his arm in an equally grand gesture.

"Whenever you can spare a moment from your duties, Weyrleader?"

"Why, I do believe I can spare an hour or two now, since I perceive that it is an appropriate time to visit the western half of the continent . . ."

"Oh, will you two stop your nonsense and *go*!" Irene said, laughter in her voice though she tried to look reproving. But their antics relieved the tension in the Weyr.

High Reaches, Boll, Ista Weyrs;
High Reaches Weyr,
Fort, and Telgar Holds

"Now, really, M'shall, Bridgely," said Jamson, fussing with his robes as he shifted uneasily in his chair. High Reaches was invariably a cold place, and today, in Jamson's private office, was no exception. The Benden Holder was glad he had riding furs on, and made no attempt to open his jacket nor unglove his left hand after the usual handshake with Jamson. He noted M'shall did the same. "I cannot believe that a Lord Holder would treat the very people he depends on in such a way. Not in midwinter."

"With my own eyes I saw it, Lord Jamson," M'shall said in an unequivocal tone. "And I thought it wise to ask several of the guards to stay in the Weyr so you may learn what their orders were."

"But here, Chalkin complains that you have not accorded him the courtesy of conveyance." Jamson frowned.

"If you had seen what I have, Lord Jamson, you might find it hard to oblige him," M'shall said, his face stark.

"Really, Jamson, don't be such a prick," Bridgely said, under no similar restraint of courtesy with his peer. "Nerat and Telgar are taking in refugees as well as Benden. You can speak to any you wish to determine the extent of Chalkin's perfidy . . ."

"I'll gladly convey you where you wish to go," M'shall offered.

"I've my own Weyr," Jamson said stiffly, "if I need transport. But it's not the weather to be traveling about in unnecessarily at all."

Which was true enough since the High Reaches Hold was cloaked in snow crusted as hard as ice on the ground.

"Agreed," Bridgely said, trying hard not to shiver and wondering at Jamson's parsimony with fires, or if the heating system in the hold was another victim to technological obsolescence. "So you will grant that only a dire need would bring me out, asking you to change your mind about taking immediate action against Chalkin. People would have frozen to death on Bitra's borders last night!" And he pointed vigorously eastward.

"He doesn't mention that in this," Jamson said, peering at the letter on the table.

"Doubtless he'll circulate a longer letter on that score," Bridgely said with deep irony. "But what I saw required me to give aid without any delay."

"As you know, Lord Jamson," M'shall put in, "Weyrs are also autonomous and may withhold services with sufficient justification. I feel perfectly justified in refusing him basic courtesies. Come, Bridgely. We're wasting Lord Jamson's valuable time. Good day to you."

Before the astonished High Reaches Holder could respond to such peremptory behavior, the two men had left the room.

"My word! And I always considered M'shall to be a sensible man. Thank goodness G'don is a solid, predictable Weyrleader . . . One simply does *not* impeach a Lord Holder overnight! Not this close to Threadfall." He buried his hands more deeply into the sleeves of his fur-lined jerkin.

Azury was so shocked he did not even comment on M'shall's "dereliction" of services. "I'd no idea, really," he said.

In direct contrast to High Reaches, Southern Boll's weather was hot enough for Bridgely to wish he'd worn a lighter shirt. Although they were well shaded from the morning sun on a porch decorated by a blooming plant with fragrant pink blossoms tangling in clusters, he had to open his collar and roll up his sleeves to be comfortable. Azury had ordered a fruit drink, and by the time it came, Bridgely's throat was dry enough to appreciate the cool tang.

"I know Chalkin's not exactly . . . reliable," and Azury then grinned wryly. "And I've lost sufficient marks in his little games of chance to wonder about his basic honesty. But . . ." He shook his head. "A holder simply doesn't keep his folk in the dark about something as critical to their survival as Thread. Does he really think it won't come? That we're all foolish or stupid?"

"*He* is both foolish and stupid," Bridgely said. "Why else did our ancestors bioengineer the dragons? And develop a totally unique society to nurture and succor the species if not for future need?" He glanced at M'shall, who merely raised his eyebrows. "It isn't as if we didn't have graphic proof of the existence of Thread, which was part of our education. Nor tons of records annotating the problem. It's not something *we* thought up to inconvenience Chalkin of Bitra."

"Preaching to the converted, Bridge," Azury said. "He's ten times the fool if he thinks to brace the rest of the planet on this score. But," and he leaned forward on his wickerwood chair, which creaked slightly, "holders can spin great lies . . ."

"And I can spot a whinge and a bitcher as fast as you can, Azury," Bridgely said, moving to the edge of his chair, which also reacted noisily to the weight shift. "Like this chair. You can interview any of those we've taken in . . . and the sooner the better so you can judge the condition they were in before we rescued them."

"I think I'd better have an eyes-on at that,". Azury said. He raised one hand quickly. "Not that I doubt you, but impeaching another Lord Holder . . . Nervous-making."

"That's as may be, but having a hold that is totally unprepared for the onslaught of Thread—one that's adjacent to me," and Bridgely jabbed a thumb in his chest, "is far more nervous-making."

"You've a point there," Azury admitted. He looked over his shoulder and beckoned one of the attendants, asking him to bring his riding gear. "You said that Jamson's reluctant? Doesn't impeachment require a unanimous verdict?"

"It does," Bridgely said and set his lips in an implacable line.

Azury grinned, thanking the attendant, who had quickly returned with his gear. "Then you also need me to add weight to a second delegation to High Reaches?"

"If you feel you can turn Jamson's opinion?"

Azury stamped into his boots. "That one's just perverse enough to hold out, but we'll see. Tashvi, Bastom, and Franco are involved, and I know Paulin is agitated . . . Who does that leave? Richud of Ista? Well, he will go along with a majority." He rose. "Now, let's leave before I swim in my own sweat . . ."

Azury interviewed each of the fourteen refugees still housed in Benden Weyr as unfit to be transferred elsewhere. He had a chat with three of the guards.

"Not that they were in a chatting mood," he said, his light blue eyes vivid with anger in his tanned face, "but they may soon have second thoughts on how much their loyalty is worth to Lord Chalkin. They do claim," and, as he grinned, his teeth were very white against his skin, "that they were outnumbered by the influx of so many ranting, raving maniacs and had to use force to restrain them until they could receive orders from the hold."

"That conflicts with what the ranting raving maniacs say, doesn't it?" M'shall replied.

"Oh, indeed," Azury said, grinning without humor. "And I do wonder that the guards came out of the ranting and raving mass unscathed while all of the maniacs seem to have a variety of injuries. Clearly the truth is being pulled in many directions. But it lies there, limpid as usual, to the eye that sees and the ear that hears."

"Well said." Bridgely nodded.

"So let's speak with Richud."

It was harder to find the Lord Holder of Ista because he had taken the afternoon off to fish—his favorite occupation.

The Harbormaster was unable to give any specific direction for a search.

"The dolphins went with him . . . circle your dragon, and see if he can spot them. Small sloop with a red sail but a lot of dolphins. Richud claims they understand him. He may be right," and the elderly man scratched his head, grinning with amusement at the notion.

"They do—according to the records," Azury said. "My fishers always watch out for them in the Currents."

"Wal, as you wish," the Harbormaster said, and went back to his tedious accounting of creel weights lifted ashore the previous seven days.

◆　◆　◆

Craigath flew his passengers in a high-altitude circle, spiraling outward from Ista Harbor. It was he who spotted the craft and, with mighty use of his pinions, dove for it.

Despite the broad safety band securing him to his position, Azury grabbed frantically at Bridgely, who was sitting in front of him, and Bridgely worried lest his own grip bruise the dragonrider.

M'shall merely turned his head to grin back at them. The words he spoke—for his mouth moved—were lost in the speed of their descent. Bridgely watched the sea coming nearer and nearer and arched himself slightly backward. He'd ridden often enough not to be alarmed by dragon antics, but never at such an angle or speed. He tightened his hold on his safety straps and argued himself out of closing his cowardly eyes. Just as it seemed as if Craigath would impale himself on the mast of the sloop—which wasn't all that small to Bridgely's mind—the bronze went into hover, startling the two crewmen who were watching Richud struggle with a pole bent almost double by his efforts to land the fish he'd hooked.

"Any time you're free, Lord Richud," shouted M'shall between his cupped hands.

Richud glanced once over his shoulder, then again, and lost control of pole and fish—the reel spinning wildly as pressure ended.

"Don't creep up on me like that! Lookit what you made me do! Fraggit. Can't I ever get an afternoon off? Oh well, what catastrophe's hit us now? Must be something bad to bring the three of you this far south."

He handed his pole to a crewman and came to the starboard side. There was still some distance between him and his visitors.

"I'd ask you aboard but the bronze would sink us," he said.

"No problem," M'shall said, and his eyes unfocused as he spoke to his dragon. *Can you get us a little closer, Craigath?*

Craigath, eyes gleaming bluely and whirling with some speed, set himself down in the water, wings neatly furled to his backbone while, with his left forearm, he took hold of the safety rail, pulling himself, and his passengers, closer to the hull of the ship. The sloop began to heel over at the strength of the dragon's hold.

The wind left the sail and the boom started to whip around when, just as abruptly, the sail caught wind again and the ship resumed her forward motion and speed.

M'shall laughed, thumping Craigath on the neck in appreciation of the completed maneuver.

"What'd he do? How'd he do that? What under the sun?" Richud was looking at the dragon, back at the ship, and then at M'shall in confusion.

"He's paddling to keep up so you won't lose headway," the Benden Weyrleader said.

This is fun. I like it, Craigath informed his rider.

"He's enjoying himself," M'shall said.

"He won't snap the rail, will he?" Richud asked, staring with some apprehension at the huge forepaw clutching the metal upright.

The dragon shook his head. *It is fragile so I don't hold it hard.*

M'shall paused a moment. "Good lad. He says he's well aware of its fragility."

"He didn't say that," Richud replied, shaking his head in denial. "Fragility?"

"His very word. Craigath's got quite a vocabulary. You know how Irene speaks . . . well, he has to keep up with Maruth, doesn't he?"

The dragon nodded.

"Well, I never. Never seen Ronelth or Jemath swim like this, either," Richud murmured. "So, what urgent matters bring you here?"

"Chalkin must be impeached as soon as possible. A hold is autonomous until it exceeds its rights," Bridgely said, and went on to give the Istan Lord Holder details of Chalkin's heinous behavior.

"I'd no idea he'd evict so many. Surely it's winter up there and they'd be in danger of freezing."

"They would be and have been," M'shall said.

"Their condition was appalling, Richud," Azury said. "I went to Benden myself to see. And the guards . . ." He dismissed them with a wide gesture. "You know the sort Chalkin hires . . ."

"Yes, toughnecks, layabouts, ruffians, and scoundrels like those Gather artists of his." Richud paused in thought. "Has that impeachment clause ever been used?"

"No, but it was put there as a safeguard. And there're a lot of people in Bitra who need their safety guarded . . . especially this close to Fall."

"Agreed. I'll go along with you. Only," and his tone turned entreating, "but not when I have an afternoon off to fish?"

Craigath let go of the rail and the two groups drifted apart. Suddenly the bronze shuddered from pate to tail.

I like that. Do it again.

Who are you talking to, Craigath? M'shall demanded, having had to clutch the neck ridge and lift his legs high above sudden waves sloshing Craigath's sides. His passengers had reacted as well to keep from a wetting.

Doll-fins rubbed me.

Playful, are they? Well, another time, my friend. We still have work to do. "Sorry about that. The dolphins were tickling Craigath."

"Dragons are ticklish?" Bridgely asked, startled.

"Their bellies, yes."

Dolphins flowed from under the dragon now, leaping up in the air and diving neatly back into the water as they sped off after the sloop.

"So, what do we do now? Beard Jamson again?" asked M'shall, stroking the bronze's neck affectionately. He was amused to see that Richud had retrieved his pole and was evidently baiting his hook.

"We'd probably have to drag Jamson down to Benden so he can see for himself, as you had to, Azury," Bridgely said, shivering as he thought of having to return to the frigid High Reaches.

Take the pictures, suggested Craigath, to his rider's astonishment. Dragons did not often offer unsolicited opinions, but then M'shall considered Craigath very intelligent.

"What pictures?" he asked.

"Pictures?" echoed Bridgely. "What pictures?"

Maruth says there are pictures. At Telgar.

"At Telgar?"

"Oh, that young painter," M'shall and Bridgely said in unison.

"What painter?" Azury wanted to know.

Bridgely explained.

"Very good idea, if Jamson will accept the proof as genuine," the Southern Boll Holder said skeptically.

Which was exactly what happened.

"How can you be sure these are accurate?" the High Reaches Lord Holder said when he had leafed through the vivid and detailed drawings on Iantine's pad. "I think the whole matter has been exaggerated out of proportion." He closed the pad halfway on the stark sketch of the hanging men.

"And you won't even accept my word, Jamson?" Azury said. "I've just been there and spoken to these people . . ." He riffled through the pages and came to one of a holder he'd interviewed. "That fellow, for instance. I spoke to him myself and I've no trouble accepting the truth of his story. He was four nights in an animal pen with no food and only the moisture he could get from snow, with his wife and elderly parents. Incidentally, they died of exposure despite all that Benden Weyr could do to try to revive them."

"I do not see why, Azury," Jamson said at his most pompous, "you do not content yourself with running your own hold. Leave Chalkin to run his. He has the right."

"But *not* the right to inflict atrocities on any of his people." Azury's reply was heated.

Jamson regarded him coldly. "A few lazy holders—"

"*A few?*" Bridgely exploded in frustration, which, even as he did so, he knew defeated his purpose. "A few hundred is more like it, Jamson. And for that many we should all stir ourselves!"

"Well, I for one shall not, Bridgely. And that's final." He folded his arms across his chest and sat there, glaring at his visitors.

"Jamson," Azury said in a very controlled, calm voice as he pushed Bridgely to one side and leaned across the desk toward Jamson, huddled in his furs. "I, too, was skeptical when Bridgely came to me, unwilling to believe his report, much less his solution to the problem. One does *not* lightly impugn the honor of a peer, and I could not understand why Bridgely was so agitated over a *few* insignificant holders. Then, too, Bitra is too far to affect anything in *my* hold. Though I quite took his point that Thread must not be allowed to burrow unchecked anywhere on the Northern Continent. So I conceived that it was my duty, my responsibility, to personally investigate the allegations.

"I have the witness of my own eyes and ears now. As well as the disparity between what the guards told me and the evidence of my own eyes. The Bitran situation is dire and must be rectified. We cannot, as intelligent, responsible leaders, allow such a situation to fester and spread. It affects the very roots of our society, the strength of the Charter, the fundamentals on which this whole society is based. We cannot ignore it as the internal problem of an autonomous holding. You as an honorable Lord Holder owe it to yourself to investigate the situation. Then you can come to a considered judgment. At least, set your own doubts to rest by going, as I did, to Benden and gather firsthand information."

"I have no doubts," Jamson said. "The Charter clearly states that a Lord Holder has autonomy within his borders. What he does is his business and that's that. I should certainly protest anyone poking his nose in my business. So I suggest you take your meddling noses and spurious charges out of here, right now!"

This time he rang a handbell, and when his oldest son opened the door in response, said, "They're leaving. See them out."

Bridgely took in a deep breath, but a sudden short blow to his midriff by Azury robbed him of wind to speak and he was helpless as the Southern Boll Holder dragged him out of the room.

"No matter what you say, he's not in a mood to listen," Azury told him, straightening Bridgely's jacket in a tacit apology.

"Lord Azury's right, I'm afraid," M'shall said.

"You came about Bitra?" the son asked, leaning against the heavy office door to be sure it was tightly closed. "I'm Gallian, his eldest and acting steward."

"You've heard?"

"Hmmm, the door was a bit ajar," Gallian said, not at all penitent about eavesdropping, "and during your last visit. Father's memory's slipping a bit so one of us tries to be nearby for important visits. He sometimes gets details muddled."

"Any chance you can unmuddle this visit to get his cooperation?"

"May I see the sketches?" He held one hand out.

"Certainly," Bridgely said and put the pad in his hand.

"Awful," Gallian said, shaking his head as he viewed the distressing scenes and peering briefly with intent gaze at one or two. "And these are accurate?" he asked Azury.

"Yes, inasmuch as I verified the condition of some of these people now at Benden Weyr," Azury said.

The bell jangled. Gallian thrust the pad at Azury.

"I'll do what I can. And not because I already consider Chalkin a thief and a cheat. I must go. See yourselves out, can you?"

"We can and will."

"What could the boy *do*?" M'shall wanted to know as they ran quickly down the steps to the front door and out into the icy air.

"One can never tell," Azury admitted. "Shards, but it's colder than *between* here. Get me back to my sun as fast as possible."

"Would a stop at Fort Hold be too much to expect from you?" Bridgely asked, grinning at the southerner's chattering teeth.

"No, and I expect it's a tactical necessity in this struggle with Chalkin."

M'shall nodded approvingly and, vaulting to Craigath's back, lent a hand to the other two to mount.

The ambient temperature at Fort Hold was not warm but a decided improvement over High Reaches. Warmer still was the greeting Paulin gave them, insisting on a hot mulled wine when he heard of their adventures.

"I don't expect Jamson will change his mind, especially now that he has been specifically asked to do so," Paulin said when his guests were settled near the good fire he had on his office hearth. "Jamson's always been perverse."

"Then the son is unlikely to be able to alter him?" Bridgely asked, depressed that they had obviously only polarized Jamson's opposition.

"Gallian's a good man," Paulin said, temporizing, "but the truth is Jamson's getting old, as well as odd, and Gallian has taken over a great deal of the management."

"Really?" Bridgely was surprised, for, despite his regret for Jamson's intransigence, the High Reaches Holder had a good reputation and his Hold showed his skill as a manager.

"Hmmm, yes. In confidence, now, my friends, but Gallian and his mother came to me a year or so ago when they noticed Jamson was having spates of memory loss. Even countermanded orders he had written out himself."

"But something like this—impeachment, I mean—Jamson would have to be present. Wouldn't he?"

Paulin rubbed his chin thoughtfully.

"And there is some urgency to our taking action," Bridgely added. "How could we wait until such time as Gallian thinks he can persuade his father that he said opposite to what he just told us?"

"We can wait a few weeks . . . now that we've removed the refugees from Chalkin's, ah . . . benevolent management," Paulin said, but there was a glint in his blue eyes when he turned them on Bridgely that was reassuring.

Bridgely opened his mouth and then closed it. It would be as well to keep his thoughts—and questions—to himself rather than queer Paulin's plans.

"Let me have a look at that pictorial evidence Iantine was clever enough to make," the Fort Holder asked, and Azury passed him the pad. He went carefully through the sketches. "Remarkable talent the boy has. So few lines to express so much: the cold, the squalor, the agony and the pathetic endurance of these poor folk. Issony mentioned that one of Chalkin's restrictions over his lessons was that the Charter wasn't to be included."

"He didn't!" exclaimed Azury, looking up from the pleasurable sipping of the well-spiced wine.

"That would explain why so few of his holders even knew it existed," M'shall said in a tense voice. "And didn't know they had rights, too."

"By the way, Clisser's new teaching program handles that very nicely, indeed," Paulin said, rising to refill cups from the beaker kept hot by the fire. "Children will learn their rights from the moment they learn to sing 'em."

"Really?" Bridgely looked intrigued.

"With this new Pass upon us, it's appropriate to redefine quite a few parameters, including the education we give our young folk," Paulin said. "Rote learning from an early age—and music is a great help in that—has much to commend it, now that we no longer have information at our fingertips."

◆ ◆ ◆

Iantine was painting Zulaya when his sketchbook was returned to him by K'vin.

"M'shall stopped by with this, and says to tell you it's been an enormous help," the Weyrleader said, but his attention was more on Zulaya, posing for her portrait.

She was seated on the edge of Meranath's stone couch, where the sleeping dragon lay, her head resting on her forepaws and turned toward her rider. K'vin was very pleased to see that his weyrmate was wearing the red brocade Gather dress, which was artistically draped so that the rich design was displayed. Zulaya had her hair up in an intricate style, held in place by the combs he had given her last Turn's End, the black diamonds in them sparkling when she moved her head. As she did just then, opening her mouth to speak.

"Stay still . . . please," Iantine said, stressing the last word as if he was tired of repeating the order. She snapped her mouth shut and returned to the pose.

K'vin stepped back, well behind Iantine as he worked, making delicate brush strokes on Zulaya's painted face. K'vin couldn't see any difference, but Iantine seemed to be satisfied and started working on highlights for her hair.

The young man certainly had caught the spirit of his weyrmate, slightly imperious, though the upcurve of her lips suggested humor. K'vin knew that

Zulaya found it amusing to be sitting for a portrait at all, and was twitting him about what he should wear to be immortalized. K'vin also knew about Iantine's project to do miniatures of all the riders. Ambitious, considering there were close to six hundred in the Weyr at the moment. On the one hand, K'vin was grateful there would be the gallery, while on the other hand, he dreaded those who would become casualties.

"Will it make it any easier *not* to have pictures?" Zulaya had asked the other night when she had required him to tell her why he was so preoccupied. "We have nothing to remind us of the first occupants of this Weyr. I think I would have liked that. Gives a continuity to life and living."

K'vin had supposed it did and decided that he had to have a more positive attitude.

"It's not as if we knew who will not be here next year this time," she added. "But it'd be nice to know that they *were* here."

"How much longer, Iantine?" Zulaya said plaintively. The fingers of the hand she had resting on her thigh twitched. "I can't feel my feet or my left hand anymore."

Iantine gave an exaggerated sigh and laid down the palette, scratching his head with the now free hand as he swished the fine brush in the jar on the table. "Sorry, Zulaya. You should by rights have had a break some time ago. But the light's perfect and I didn't want to stop."

"Oh, help me up, K'vin," Zulaya said, holding out a hand. "I don't usually get a chance to sit still so long . . ."

K'vin was glad to assist her, and she was stiff enough so that her first steps were awkward. Then she recovered her mobility and walked firmly to the easel.

"My word, you did do yards today, didn't you? Filled in that whole panel of the dress and . . . have you got my eyes crossed?"

Iantine laughed. "No, step a little to this side. Now back again. Do the eyes seem to follow you?"

Zulaya gave a little shake, widening her eyes. "They do. How do you contrive that? I must say, I'm not so sure I like me watching everything I do."

K'vin chuckled. "You won't, but your presence hanging in the Lower Cavern may spur the lazy to complete their tasks more quickly."

"I'm not sure I like that idea any more than having me leering at me up here." She turned to the table, mostly covered by Iantine's paraphernalia. "I had klah sent up not too long ago," and she cast an accusing eye on Iantine. "It should still be hot." She unscrewed the lid and steam obediently rose. "It is. Shall I pour for all of us?" Which she was doing even as she spoke.

"Maybe I should leave now?" Iantine said, looking from one to the other.

"No," she said quickly.

"I wanted to be sure your sketches were safely in your possession," K'vin said, taking a chair.

"And did they solve the problem?" Zulaya asked, spooning sweetener into the cups and passing him his. "Come, sit, Iantine. You must be more tired than I am. I've been sitting the whole time."

Iantine grinned as if, K'vin noted with a twinge of jealousy, totally at his ease with the Weyrwoman. Few were, except Tisha, who treated everyone like an errant child, or Leopol, who was impudent with everyone.

"So? What's the result?" She indicated with a wave of her hand that he should speak out in the portraitist's presence.

"M'shall's disgusted. They still don't have a unanimous decision about impeachment. Jamson's the holdout."

"He's not always dealing with a full deck," Zulaya said succinctly, "at least so Mari of High Reaches Weyr told me. And he's getting worse. Thea takes charge when she can, and that older lad of his—"

"Gallian's my age," K'vin exclaimed. "Can't they get around that?"

"Short of making Jamson abdicate, no. At least according to my understanding of the Charter. And it just got refreshed." She gave K'vin a droll smile. "As well I listened in to what T'lan was reading. I'd forgotten the half of it myself. Have you reread it recently?"

"I did," K'vin said, nodding and glad that he had. "Mind you, it isn't as ironclad as we used to think. Far more autonomy granted . . ."

"Where it can be abused by misdirection," Iantine said. "I borrowed the copy. It's going the rounds in the Weyr."

"No matter how Chalkin tries to interpret a Lord Holder's privilege, he can't deny that he's abrogated almost every right the holders are supposed to have . . . such as removal only after a jury of their peers had been convened. Which he certainly ignored in turfing them out . . . and *then* constraining them in unsuitable conditions. There certainly was no collusion or organized mutiny. They hadn't even presented him with a list of their grievances."

"Didn't know they could," Iantine said, his expression uncompromising. "Had to have the word 'mutiny' explained to them, and then denied that they'd do such a thing."

"And Jamson won't budge?" Zulaya asked.

K'vin shook his head.

"Won't he even come and speak to some of the refugees?"

"Doesn't feel it's his right to interfere in the autonomy of another Lord Holder," K'vin said.

Iantine growled in disgust. "I'll bet he really didn't believe my drawings were accurate."

K'vin nodded. "Even after Azury informed him that he thought you had glossed over *some* of the more gruesome injuries."

"Or some of the unseen ones, like those pregnant women," Zulaya added, her eyes flashing with outrage.

"How are they?" K'vin asked.

"One has delivered prematurely, but she and the babe will be all right. The others . . . well, Tisha's doing what she can . . . getting them to talk it all out before it festers too much in their minds."

"They can swear out warrants against the guards—" Iantine began.

"They have," Zulaya said in a harsh tone, her smile unpleasant. "And we have the guards. As soon as the women feel strong enough to testify, we're convening a court here. And M'shall wants to try the murderers he's holding at Benden."

"Two trials, then?"

"Yes, one for rape and one for murder. Not at all our usual winter occupation, is it?" Zulaya said in a droll tone.

"Is Telgar Hold joint with us?" K'vin asked, for the Weyr's Hold should be represented in such a process. He'd been surprised at how detailed the Charter was. His recollections of the Charter's contents were entirely too hazy. In this particular instance, they were also dealing with another holder's employees for a matter that had come up within that hold, not an incident in Telgar Weyr, or within the jurisdiction of Telgar Hold. "But the men are Bitran. Are *we* allowed to?"

"Indeed we're within our rights," Zulaya answered firmly. "Justice can be administered anywhere, provided the circumstances warrant. As the victims are currently in this Weyr and so are their attackers, we may legally hold trial here. However, we'll make sure to invite representatives of other holds and Weyrs to oversee that justice is done."

"How about making sure Jamson attends?" K'vin asked with some malice.

Zulaya gave him a broad smile. "That might alter the old fool's ideas about autonomy."

"And Chalkin?" Iantine asked, an intense expression of anticipation in his eyes.

K'vin chuckled. "We'll see about that. His attendance might just solve the problem."

"Or compound it," Zulaya said, shaking her head. "He's too clever to be caught out over what his men do. Or to come when he hears what it's about."

"No one's going to tell him, are they?" K'vin said.

"I wouldn't count on that, sir," Iantine said mournfully. "It's amazing what he does hear that he shouldn't."

"Then we keep what we've just discussed here," and Zulaya pointed her finger firmly down, "and not a whisper to anyone else. Right, Iantine?"

"Right!" Iantine nodded sharply.

XI

The Trials at Telgar and Benden Weyrs

As it happened, a blizzard covered most of the eastern mountain ranges and all of Bitra when the trial was convened. The winds were too fierce over Bitra for even a dragon to penetrate. Fortunately, the storm had not yet reached Benden, so representatives from every Weyr and hold were able to attend—with the exception of Lord Jamson of the High Reaches, who was very ill of a respiratory fever. The Lady Holder Thea came, annoyed that Jamson had a legitimate excuse for his absence and had sent Gallian in his place.

"It might have done that stubborn streak of his some good to hear just how Chalkin conducts his hold. Oh, he'd've spouted on about autonomy but he most certainly is against any harm coming to unborn children." Thea gave Zulaya a significant nod, reminding those around her that she had borne fourteen children to Lord Jamson in the course of her fertile years: sufficient to substantially increase the borders of the hold when the children were old enough to claim their land grants.

Held in the capacious Lower Cavern at Benden Weyr, the first of the two trials was a sobering, well-conducted affair. At one time there had been trained legists on Pern, but the need for such persons had waned. Most arguments were settled by negotiated compromise or, when all negotiation efforts failed, by hand-to-hand combat. Consequently, a spokesperson for the accused guards had to be found. One of the teachers from Fort Hold who specialized in legal contracts and land deeds reluctantly agreed to officiate.

Gardner had not been very enthusiastic about involving himself, however briefly, with rapists, but he recognized the necessity of representation and did his best. He had perfunctorily questioned the victims as to the identity of their alleged assailants and tried to shake their testimony. The three women were no longer the frightened, half-starved wretches who had been so abused. Their time in the Weyr had done wonders for their courage, self-esteem, and appearance. Gardner even insisted that they had been rehearsed in their testimony, but that did not mitigate the circumstances of the grievous bodily and mental harm inflicted on them.

"Sure I rehearsed," the oldest of the women said loudly. "In me mind, night and night, how I was flung down and . . . done by dirty men as wouldn't have dared step inside a decent woman's hold with such notions in their head. I ache still rehearsing," and she spat the word at him, "what they did, again and again and again." For emphasis she slammed one fist into the other hand. Gardner had ceased that line of questioning.

In the end he managed one small concession for the accused: the right to be returned to their Contract Hold, following the trial, rather than have to make their own way back to Bitra.

"Fat lot of good that'll do them," Zulaya muttered under her breath when he won that point. "Chalkin hates losers, and those guys have lost a lot more than their contract."

"I wonder what sort of tone Chalkin's next letter of protest will take," Irene said with a malicious chuckle.

Paulin had received a thick screed from the Bitran Holder when Chalkin discovered the "unmitigated interference of assorted renegade dragonriders in his affairs and the abduction of loyal holders from their premises."

"If he dares protest . . . Oh, why did it have to snow so hard?" Paulin lamented. "I'd love to have had him here when his guards said 'they was only following orders to keep the holders from leaving'! M'shall would have gathered him up in a ball and rendered him spitless!"

M'shall had assumed the role of prosecutor, claiming that right since his riders had been first on the scene. He was exceedingly precise in manner and in his questioning.

"Poring over the Charter and what books Clisser could send him on legal procedures," Irene told Zulaya with a broad grin. "It's done him a world of good. Taken his mind off . . . the spring, you know."

Zulaya had nodded approvingly. "He'd have been a good legist . . . or did they call them lawyers? No, barristers."

"Yes, barristers stood before the judge and handled the trial procedures," Irene replied.

"Gardner wasn't half bad, you know. He tried," Zulaya remarked. "I'll even forgive him asking for mercy for those miserable clods. After all, he had to appear to work *for* his clients," she added tolerantly. "I'm glad we had Iantine sit up close. I want to see his sketches of the trial. I wish he could work as fast with my portrait."

"Your portrait is scarcely the same thing as annotating a trial. And he's to come to Benden when he's finished with you two, you know."

Zulaya was pleased to hear the pride in Irene's voice when she mentioned Iantine. He was a Bendenian.

"You mean, when he's finished sketching our riders."

Irene gave a wistful smile, tinged with sadness. "You'll be glad he did. I wonder will he do the same thing for us at Benden?"

"Whatever he can fit in, I'm sure. That young man's got himself more work than he can handle."

"If he can get it all done before . . . oh, the jury's back."

The twelve men and women, picked at random by straw from those who had come to observe, had listened to all the evidence. Tashvi, Bridgely, and Franco had sat as judges. Now a silence descended over the room, so intense that a cough was quickly muffled.

The three rapists were accounted guilty as charged, and three more were sentenced as accessories, since they had helped pin the victims down. The penalty for the rape of a pregnant woman was castration, which was to be carried out immediately. The others were to receive forty lashes, well laid on by Telgar's large and strong stewards.

"They were lucky there isn't Fall," Zulaya remarked to Irene, Lady Thea, and K'vin. "Otherwise they could also have been tied out during the next Fall."

Despite herself, Thea gave a shudder. "Which is probably why there are so few cases of rape recorded in our hold's annals."

"Small wonder," K'vin said, crossing his legs again. Zulaya had noticed his defensive position and her lips twitched briefly. He turned away. His weyrmate had nearly cheered aloud when the verdict was delivered.

"You can't do that to me," one of the guards was roaring now as he belatedly realized the significance of the verdict. He had been the leader of the men stationed at the eastern border crossing. The other defendants were too stunned, their mouths moving in soundless protest, Morinst being loud enough to drown out any complaint they could voice. "You're none of you my Lord," he'd railed at three Lord Holder judges. "You've got no right to do this."

"And you had no right to rape a pregnant woman!"

"But Chalkin ain't even here." The man writhed in the grip of his guards.

"Chalkin's presence would have had no effect on the trial or the verdict," Tashvi said at his most repressive.

"But he should've been here!" Morinst protested.

"He was invited to attend," Tashvi said without regret.

"He's gotta know. You can't do nothin' without him knowing. I gotta contract with *him*."

"To rape, torture, and humiliate?" Bridgely asked in too soft a voice.

Morinst clamped his lips shut. He struggled more violently as the bailiffs aimed him toward the exit. And his punishment. Not that he could escape either the sentence or the Weyr. The other two were still too stunned to resist their removal to the infirmary where the verdict would be carried out. Those to be lashed were brought outside, though not all the audience followed to witness the corporal punishment.

When that, too, had been completed and the men removed to have their wounds treated, the observers filed back into the Lower Cavern. While this was scarcely an occasion for celebration, except that justice had been served, a substantial meal had been prepared. Wine was the first item sought and served.

"You were superb, M'shall," Irene said when her weyrmate joined her, a newly opened skin of Benden wine on his shoulder, "and do please give me a glass. Though I'm sure you need one more than I. Nice of Bridgely to supply it," she added to Zulaya.

"I think we all need it," the Telgar Weyrwoman said, glancing over to where the three plaintiffs were celebrating with considerable enthusiasm. Well, let them. "Now what do we do?"

"Well, we've the second trial to get through. I hope it goes as well," M'shall said.

"*No,* with *them,*" and his weyrmate pointed to the three women.

"Oh. That them. They say they just want to go back to their homes. Not going to let Chalkin take it because they're not there holding their places." He made a grimace. "Some of them don't really have much to go back to. Chalkin's bullies burned what was flammable and pulled down what they could. I'd say the storms kept more damage from being done. But," and he altered the grimace to a grin, "give 'em credit. They do own what they hold and now they know it. It may give them a tad more backbone next time they're chivvied, and more pride in what they do. They've also asked for groundcrew training."

"Nothing like losing something—however briefly—to value what you have," Thea said. "On the practical side, though, I think High Reaches can supply some basic items. Anyone organizing that?" She glanced about at others in the group. "D'you have numbers yet?"

"Actually we do," Zulaya said, including Irene in her nod. "Three hundred and forty-two—no, forty-three with that premature baby. It's very good of you to offer, Thea."

Thea snorted. "I've reread the Charter, too, and know my duty to my fellow creatures. You wouldn't also happen to know how many poor wretches hold in Bitra?"

M'shall had that answer. "Of course, you can't tell if Chalkin doctored the last census or not, but he's supposed to have 24,657 inhabitants."

"Really?" Zulaya was surprised.

"But then, Bitra's one of the smaller holds and doesn't have any indigenous industry—apart from some forestry. The mining's down to what's needed locally. There're a few looms working but no great competition for Keroon or Benden."

"And the gaming," Thea said with a disgusted sniff.

"That's Chalkin's main industry."

"Well, he's lost a lot on this gamble," Zulaya said.

"Has he?" K'vin wanted to know.

◆   ◆   ◆

The second trial was almost anticlimactic. Gardner again represented the seven defendants accused of "allegedly causing grievous bodily harm and death" to five innocent men and women.

While Gardner again stipulated that the men had only been following orders to "restrain by any means" anyone trying to cross the border out of Bitra Hold, their putative domicile, it was claimed that unnecessarily severe restraint had been used and caused the deaths of persons who should not have been denied "lawful" exit and a usurpation of their basic Chartered Right to freedom of movement.

The subsequent mutilation and/or torture of the seven, the prosecution said, was not inherent in the order to "restrain by any means." Chalkin had no right to take the lives of any holders without due cause and/or trial by jury.

The day's jury retired and, within half an hour, unanimously rendered a verdict of guilty. The men were sentenced to be transported to the Southern Islands by dragonback with a seven-day supply of food, which was the customary punishment for murderers.

"Are there many on the islands?" Thea asked. "I mean, there have been others sequestered there. Even families, I read, but that was years ago."

Zulaya shrugged. "Telgar's never had to take anyone there, so I wouldn't know."

"Benden hasn't," Irene said, "at least not as long as we've been Leaders."

"My father sent two," Paulin said. "And I do believe that both Ista and Nerat have sent killers there."

"Chalkin did, too," Gallian surprised them by saying. "About four years ago. I don't know where I heard about them. Some sort of real trouble down in his hold and he had Ista transport them since the men originated from that hold."

"Oh, I remember now," Irene said. "M'shall only mentioned he was glad he hadn't had to do the transport."

"Maybe we should send Chalkin's men there when they can travel," Zulaya said.

"No, let him see that we won't tolerate his methods of holding," Irene said, her tone implacable. "Maybe he'll come to his senses."

"That'll be the day!" Zulaya said facetiously.

When snow had melted sufficiently to allow any travel out of Bitra, Chalkin did send another blistering note of protest to Paulin, making it plain that he intended to demand compensation at the Turn's End Conclave for the "ritual disfigurement of men only doing their duty." This time, however, an elderly green rider collected the message when the urgent banner was seen flying from the panel heights of Bitra Hold. F'tol endured a long harangue from Chalkin that the letter had better be delivered, that dragonriders were parasites on the face of Pern, that there'd be some changes made or . . . F'tol was neither intimidated nor impressed. Stoically, he took the letter and responsibly delivered it.

Whether Chalkin knew, or cared, that the refugees had been returned to their holdings was not known. F'tol was reasonably sure that would have been included in the tirade since Chalkin seemed to have included every other shortcoming, mistake, and venial sin ever committed by a dragonrider.

Both Telgar and Benden Weyrs made daily checks on the returned, to reassure them as well as those concerned with their welfare. Of course, the conditions in Bitra, with dragon-high drifts blocking major roads and tracks, made it improbable that any of Chalkin's men would have been able to move, much less go the distance to the far-flung properties.

Benden Hold and Weyr became the latest winter victims as the blizzards which had hovered over Bitra made their way eastward, coating the eastern seaboard, even down into the northern section of Nerat, which hadn't seen any snow since the settlement of the Bendens in the early decades of the First Fall.

The dragons were the only living creatures who didn't mind the snow, since their tough hide was impervious to its cold as well as *between*. They much enjoyed the snow battles that the Weyrfolk indulged in, and then the warmth of sun intensified by the white landscape, so they lounged in reflected glory.

Despite the more northerly position, Telgar Weyr got only a hand's span of snow and made do with that. The young dragonets were fascinated by the stuff and by having to crack the ice of the lake to bathe. Bathing a dragon had become a hazard, but T'dam allowed the weyrlings to suds up a dragonet and allow it to rinse itself off in the frigid water. But daily washings resulted in some distress for the rider.

"I've chilblains again," Debera complained to Iantine, showing him her swollen fingers when he came out to watch her tend Morath.

The little green was a favorite subject of his because, he told Debera, "She has a tremendous range of expression on her face and gets in the most incredible positions."

Debera was far too besotted with her dragon to disagree with such an impartial opinion. If she herself figured in every sketch Iantine did, she did not wonder about it. But the other green riders did.

"You should get some of Tisha's cream. It stopped my fingers from itching," Iantine snapped his fingers, "like that!"

"Oh, I have some of that," she replied.

"Well, it doesn't do you any good in the jar, you know."

"Yes, I know," she said, ducking her head, her tone low and apologetic.

"Hey, I'm not scolding," he said gently, putting one finger under her chin and lifting her head. "What'd I do wrong?"

"Oh, nothing," she said and pushed his finger away, giving him a too-bright smile. "I get silly notions sometimes. Don't pay me any mind."

"Oh, I don't," he replied so blithely that she gave him a startled look. "Just go on with lathering up that beast of yours . . ." He turned to a new page and removed the pencil from behind his ear. "Go on . . ."

"Iantine's gone on you, Debera," Grasella said, eyeing her barrack mate shrewdly.

"Iantine? He's sketch mad. He'd do his big toe if he had nothing else to pose for him," Debera replied. "Besides, he'll leave soon for Benden . . ."

"Will you miss him?" Jule asked, a sly look on her face.

"Miss him?" Debera echoed, surprised at the question.

I will miss him, Morath said in such a mournful tone that the other dragonets turned toward her, their eyes whirling in minor distress.

"What did she say that's got them all upset?" Jule demanded.

"That she'd miss him. But, love, he's not Weyrbred," Debera told her dragon, stroking her cheek and then her headknob. "He can't stay here indefinitely."

"If anyone asked me, I'd say Iantine would like to," Sarra put in.

"No one's asked you," Angie replied tartly.

"Has he ever done anything . . . I mean, beyond sketching you, Deb?" Jule asked with an avid glint in her eyes.

"No, of course not. Why would he?" Debera said, annoyed and flustered. That was the trouble with having to sleep in with the others. They could be terribly nosy, even if they weren't as mean as her stepmother and sisters had been. She didn't pry into where they were when they were late in at night.

"I give up on her," Jule said, raising her hands skyward in exasperation. "The handsomest unattached man in the Weyr and she's blind."

"She's Morath-besotted," Sarra put in. "Not that any of us are much better."

"Most of us . . ." and Jule paused significantly, "know that while dragons may now be a significant factor in our lives, they are not *everything*, you know. Even ol' T'dam-damn-him has a weyrmate, you know."

"We don't have weyrs yet," Mesla said, speaking for the first time. She took everything literally. "Couldn't have anyone in here with you gawking."

Debera knew she was blushing: her cheeks felt hot.

"That hasn't held *you* back, I noticed," Sarra said to Jule, cocking her head knowingly.

Jule smiled mysteriously. "From the only Weyrbred resident in this barracks, let me assure you that our wishes can influence our dragons' choices."

"They won't rise for another eight or ten months," Angie said, though she had obviously taken heed of Jule's remark. "But, Jule, suppose your dragon fancies a dragon whose rider you can't stand?"

"You mean, O'ney?" and she grinned at Angie's discomfort.

The girl overcame her embarrassment and snapped back quickly enough. "He's impossible, even for a bronze rider. Have you ever *heard* him go on about how his wing is always tops in competitions! As if that was all that mattered!"

"To him it probably does," Grasella said, "but, Jule, I'm more worried about the blue riders. I mean, some of them are very nice guys and I wouldn't want to hurt their feelings, but they don't generally like girls."

"Oh," and Jule shrugged indolently, "that's easier still. You make an arrangement with another rider to be on hand when your green gets proddy. Then the blue rider gets his mate, if he's got one, or anyone else who's willing—and you'd better believe that anyone's willing when dragons are going to participate. So you bed the one you like, and the blue rider his choice, and you *all* enjoy!"

The girls absorbed this information with varying degrees of enthusiasm or distaste.

"Well, it's up to yourselves what you do, you know," Jule went on. "And we're not limited to this Weyr, either. Oh!" and she let out a gusty sigh. "I'll be so glad when we can fly out of here anytime we want."

"But I thought you were arranging matters with T'red?" Mesla said, her eyes wide with consternation.

"Well, so I am, but that doesn't mean I might not find someone I like better at another Weyr. Greens like it, you know."

"Ah, but can we go to other Weyrs?" Sarra said, waggling a finger at Jule. "In four, five months, we'll have Fall and *then* we'll really work hard, ferrying firestone sacks to the fighters." Her eyes gleamed brightly in anticipation and she hugged herself. "We'll be doing *something* a lot more exciting than having just one mate and plenty of kids."

Debera averted her face, not wanting to take part in such a ridiculous discussion.

Something bothers you, Morath said and slowly lowered her head to her rider's lap. *I love you. I think you're wonderful. Iantine does, too.*

That confidence startled Debera. *He does?*

He does! And Morath's tone was emphatic. *He likes your green eyes, the way you walk, and the funny crackle in your voice. How do you do that?*

Debera's hand went to her throat and she felt really silly now. *Can you talk to him, too? Or just listen to what he's thinking?*

He thinks very loud. Especially near you. I don't hear him too good far away. He thinks loud about you a lot.

"DEB'RA?" and Sarra's loud call severed that most interesting conversation.

"What? I was talking to Morath. What'd you say?"

"Never mind," and Sarra grinned broadly. "Have you got your Turn's End dresses finished yet?"

"I've one more fitting," Debera said, although that subject, too, caused her embarrassment. She had tried to argue with Tisha that the beautiful green dress was quite enough: she didn't need more. Tisha had ignored that and demanded that she choose two colors from the samples available: one for evening and another good one for daytime wear. Everyone in the Weyr, it seemed, had new clothes for Turn's End. And yet, something in Debera had delighted in knowing she'd have two completely new dresses that no one had ever worn before her. She had, she admitted very very quietly to herself, hoped that Iantine would notice her in them. Now, with Morath's information, she wondered if he'd notice at all that she was wearing new clothes.

"Speaking of weyrs . . ." Mesla said.

"That was half an hour ago, Mesla," Angie protested. "Well?"

"There aren't that many left, and the bigger dragons would have first choice, wouldn't they?" she said.

"Don't worry," Jule said, "some'll come free by the time we need them." Then she covered her mouth, aware of what she had just implied. "I didn't mean that. I really didn't. I mean, I wouldn't think of moving in . . ."

"Just shut up, Jule," Sarra said in a quiet but firm voice.

There was a long moment of silence, with no one daring to look at anyone.

"Say, who has the salve?" Grasella asked softly from the bunk beyond her, breaking the almost intolerable silence. "My fingers are itching again. No one told me I'd have to cope with chilblains dealing with dragons."

Angie found it in her furs and passed it on.

"After you," Debera said softly as she gave it to Grasella.

The easy laughing chatter was over for the night.

♦ ♦ ♦

"I haven't had much time," Jemmy told Clisser in his most uncooperative tone of voice when Clisser asked how he was coming on the last of the history ballads. "Had to look up all that law stuff. Why'd you have to take so much trouble with those fragging guards? They shoulda all been dropped on the islands, right away. None of this trial farce."

"The trials were not farces, Jemmy," Clisser said, so uncharacteristically reproving that Jemmy looked up in a state of amazement. "The trials were necessary. To prove that *we* would not act in an arbitrary fashion . . ."

"You mean, the way Chalkin would have," and Jemmy grinned, his uneven teeth looking more vulpine than ever in his long face.

"Exactly."

"You're wasting too much time on him," and Jemmy turned back to reading.

"What are you looking up?"

"I don't know. I'm looking because I *know* there's something we *can* use to check on the Red Planet's position . . . something so simple I'm disgusted I can't call it to mind. I know I've seen it somewhere . . ." Irritably, he pushed the volume away from him. "It'd help a great deal if the people who copied for us had had decent handwriting. I spend too much time trying to decipher it." Abruptly he reached across the cluttered worktop to the windowsill and plonked down in front of him a curious apparatus. "Here's your new computer." He grinned up at Clisser, who regarded the object—bright colored beads strung on ten narrow rods, divided into two unequal portions.

"What is it?" Clisser exclaimed, picking it up and finding that the beads moved stiffly up and down on the rods.

"An abacus, they called it. A counter. Ancient and still functional." Jemmy took the device from Clisser and demonstrated. "It'll take the place of a calculator. Most are down now. Oh, and I found the designs for this, too." He fumbled around his papers and withdrew an instrument consisting of a ruler with a central sliding piece, both marked with logarithmic scales. "You can do quite complicated mathematical calculations on this slide rule, as they called it. Almost as fast as you could type into a digital pad."

Clisser looked from one to the other. "So that's what a slide rule looks like. I saw one mentioned in a treatise on early calculators, but I never thought we'd have to resort to ancient devices. And mention of an abacus, too, actually. You *have* been busy reinventing alternatives."

"And I'll find that other device, too, if you'll leave me alone and don't dump more vitally important, urgent research on me."

"I'm hoping," Clisser said at his most diplomatic, "that you can give me something to show before the Winter Solstice and Turn's End."

Jemmy shot straight up in his chair, cocked his head and stared at Clisser so that Clisser leaned forward hopefully, holding his breath lest he disrupt Jemmy's concentration.

"Fraggit," and Jemmy collapsed again, beating his fists on the table. "It has to *do* with solstices."

"Well, if you've gone back to abaci and slide rules, why not a sundial clock?" Clisser asked facetiously.

Jemmy sat up again, even straighter. "Not a sundial," he said slowly, "but a cosmic clock . . . a star dial like . . . stone . . . stone *something* . . ."

"Stonehenge?"

"What was that?"

"A prehistoric structure back on Earth. Sallisha can tell you lots more about it if you'd care to ask her," Clisser said slyly, and was rewarded by Jemmy's rude dismissal of the suggestion. "It turned out to be rather an astonishing calendar, accurately predicting eclipses as well as verifying solstice at dawn."

Clisser stopped, looking wide-eyed at Jemmy, whose mouth had dropped open to form a soundless O as what he said astounded them both.

"Only that was a stone circle . . . on a plain . . ." Clisser stammered, gesturing dolmens and cross beams. Muttering under his breath, he strode across to the shelves, trying to find the text he wanted. "We must have copied it. We *had* to have copied it . . ."

"Not necessarily, since you've been interested only in relevant historical entries," Jemmy contradicted him. "I remember accessing it once. It's only that we'll have to adapt it to fit *our* needs, which is framing the Red Planet when the conjunction is right." He was scrabbling among the litter on his desk for a clean sheet of paper and a pencil. The first three he found were either stubs or broken. "That's another thing we've got to reinvent . . . fountain pens."

"Fountain pens?" Clisser echoed. "Never heard of fountain pens."

"I'll do them tomorrow. Leave me to work this out, but . . ." Jemmy paused long enough to grin diabolically up at Clisser's befuddlement. ". . . I think I'll have something by Turn's End. Maybe even a model . . . but only if you leave . . . *now*."

Clisser left, closing the door quietly behind him and pausing a moment.

"I do believe I've been kicked out of my own office," he said, pivoting to regard the door. His name, which had recently been repainted, was centered in the upper panel. "Hmm." He turned the sign hung there on a nail to DO NOT DISTURB and walked away whistling the chorus from the Duty Song.

He'd catch Sallisha before she climbed up the stairs to his office. That would please her. Well, it might.

He hurried down the steps and met up with her coming in the door.

"I'm not late," she said, at her most caustic, her arm tightening convulsively on the bulging notebook she carried.

He was in for it.

"I didn't say you were. Let's take the more comfortable option of the teachers' lounge."

"My conclusions are not something you'll wish to discuss in public," she said, recoiling. She might be one of his best teachers—though the rumor was that children learned their lessons to get out of her clutches—but her attitude toward him, and his proposed revitalization program, was totally hostile.

Clisser smiled as graciously as he could. "It's empty right now and will be for at least two hours."

She sniffed, but when he courteously gestured for her to precede him, she tramped in an implacable fashion. Like Morinst to his . . . Clisser shuddered and hurriedly followed her.

The lounge was empty, a good fire crackling on the hearth. The klah pitcher rested on the warmer, and for a change there were clean cups. He wondered if Bethany had done the housekeeping. The sweetener jar was even full. Yes, it would have been Bethany, trying to ease this interview.

As he closed the door he also turned the DO NOT DISTURB sign around and flipped the catch. Sallisha had seated herself in the least comfortable chair—the woman positively enjoyed being martyred. She still held the notebook, like a precious artifact, across her chest.

"You cannot exclude Greek history from study," she said, aggressively launching into an obviously prepared speech. "They've got to understand where our form of government came from to appreciate what they have. You have to include—"

"Sallisha, the precedents can be covered in the outline, but not the entire culture," he began.

"But the culture determined the form of government . . ." She stared at him, appalled by his lack of comprehension.

"*If* a student is curious enough to want to know more, we shall have it to give him. But there is no point in forcing hill farmers and plains drovers to learn something that has absolutely no relevance to their way of life."

"You demean them by saying that."

"No, I save them hours of dull study by replacing it with the history of Pern . . ."

"There is scarcely enough of that to dignify the word 'history.' "

"Yesterday is history today, but do you want to repeat it? 'History' is what happened in the life or development of a people . . . we," and he tapped his chest, "the Pernese. Also a systematic account of us," he tapped his chest again, "with an analysis and explanation. *From* . . . the beginning of the *Pern* colony . . . that is history, grand and sweeping, surviving against incredible odds and an implacable menace, derring-do, ingenuity, courage, and *of* this planet, not of a place that's only a name. It's better than our ancient history—if it's taught right."

"Are you impugning my—"

"Never, Sallisha, which is why I particularly need your complete cooperation for the new, enriched, relevant curriculum. On average, your students rank higher in their final examination papers than any other teacher's . . . and that includes the hill farmers and the plains drovers. But they never again *use* the information you imparted. Pern is difficult enough . . . with an external menace to contend with . . . Let them be proud of the accomplishments of their ancestors . . . their most recent ancestors. Not the confused and tortured mindlessness the Pern colonists left behind. Furthermore," he went on relentlessly as she opened her mouth to speak, "the trials at Telgar and Benden have proved that not enough time is spent teaching our people their rights under their Charter . . ."

"But I spend—"

"*You* certainly have never been remiss, but we must emphasize," and he slapped one fist into the other palm, "holder rights under their Lord: how to claim Charter acreage, how to prevent what happened in Bitra . . ."

"No other Lord Holder is as *wicked*," and her mouth twisted with disgust as she enunciated the last word, "as that awful man. Don't you think you can get me to teach there now that Issony's left!" She waggled her index finger at him and her expression was fierce.

"Not you, Sallisha, you're far too valuable to waste on Bitra," he said, soothing her. Bitra would need a more compassionate and flexible teacher than Sallisha. "But I'm amazed at just how many people were unaware of the

Charter Rights. And that's wrong. Not that I think the cowed folk up in Bitra would have dared cite the clauses to him . . . even if they had known about them. I mean, it was appalling to realize just how few people who attended the trial *knew* that ordinary holders had the *right* to freedom of movement, and lawful assembly, or to appeal for mediation for crippling tithes."

"Why haven't the Lord Holders impeached him?" she wanted to know, her fierceness diverted toward a new victim. "It's patently obvious he is unfit to manage a hold, much less one during a Fall. I cannot see why they have been waffling about over the matter."

"Sallisha, it takes a unanimous decision to impeach a Lord Holder," he said with a light admonishment.

She regarded him blankly for a moment. Then flushed. "Who's holding out?"

"Jamson."

She clicked her tongue irritably. "And that's another place you mustn't send me. The cold would exacerbate my joint problem."

"I'm aware of that, Sallisha, which is why I wondered if you'd consider Nerat South this year?"

"How much traveling?" she demanded, but not unappeased.

"Six major holds and five smaller units but all within reasonable distance. And, of course, your journeys would fall on Threadfree days. Excellent accommodations and a very good contract. Gardner made sure that everything complies with your wishes as regards conditions." He reached into his jerkin pocket and pulled out the document. "I thought you might like to see it today."

"Sweetening me up, are you?" she said with an almost coquettish smile, hand half outstretched to the sheets.

"You are my best teacher, Sallisha," he said and extended his hand until her fingers closed around the contract.

"This won't make me approve your butchery of pre-Pernese history, Clisser."

"It's not intended to, but we can't have you in danger on the plains of Keroon . . ."

"I did promise to come back . . ."

"They will understand . . ."

"There are some really fine minds there . . ."

"You will find them wherever you go, Sallisha, you have the knack." Then he hauled out the larger sheaf of papers, the new syllabus. "You may find this much easier to impart to your students."

She eyed it as she would a tunnel snake.

CHAPTER
XII

High Reaches and Fort Holds

"So," Paulin said to Thea and Gallian in the comfortably warm High Reaches solarium where the Lady Holder received her guest, "is there *any way we can get him to change his mind?*"

Thea shrugged. "Not by reasoned argument, that's for certain. He was indignant that 'a Lord Holder's right to deal with his own folk' had been set aside for the two trials. Not that he objected to the sentences . . ."

" 'That was only right and just, and they should have been sent to the islands as well for they'll only make trouble of a different sort now,' " Gallian added, mimicking his father's thin wheezing voice. "If he would only give me authorization to deal with *all* hold matters . . ." and he raised his hands in helplessness. "He's too sick . . ."

"Wait a minute. He *is* sick," Paulin interrupted, "and your weather here is only aggravating the respiratory problem, isn't it?"

Thea's eyes widened as she jumped to a conclusion.

"If he was sent to Ista, or Nerat to recuperate, why, he'd have to authorize Gallian—" she began.

"Precisely . . ."

"What happens when he recovers and finds out what I did, knowing, as he's made sure I do, his views on impeachment," Gallian asked his mother, "and finds out I've gone against him? I could very likely lose my chance of succession."

"That's not likely, dear. You know how he carries on about your 'stupid' younger brothers," Thea said reassuringly, laying a hand on her son's arm.

"You just know when to stand up to him. You've always had a flair for dealing with people. As for the nephews . . ." She threw up her hand in despair. Then her face clouded. "I really am worried about these constant chest infections. Frankly, I don't think he's going to last much longer." She sighed in regret. "He's been a good spouse . . ."

"Can you get your medic to recommend the warmer climate?" Paulin asked sympathetically.

"He's been doing so constantly," Thea said, setting her mouth in a firm line. "I'll make it so. Somehow! I couldn't live with myself if I didn't. For his sake as well as those poor wretches."

Gallian looked uncertain.

"Don't worry, lad," Paulin said. "You've already got full marks in my book for cooperation. And, as long as I'm Chair, you've my support. The Conclave doesn't necessarily have to abide by the deceased's wishes as to successor. But we've got to take action *now*. Even waiting until Turn's End is dangerous. We rescued those people, their rights were upheld in a duly assembled court, and Chalkin's in some state of mind over that." Paulin's laugh was mirthless. "We can't let him take his vengeance out on them or we've spent a lot of time and effort to no avail. With this thaw setting in, he'll be able to move about. And I think we all have a good idea that he'll retaliate in some fashion."

Thea shuddered, her comfortably plump body rippling under her thick gown. "I won't have *that* on my conscience, no matter what my Lord Jamson says." She rose. "Jamson spent such a poor night, I'll catch him now, before he can put up any more objections. One thing is certain, he doesn't *want* to die. He likes Richud more than Franco. I'll suggest Ista Hold. I wouldn't mind the winter there myself. In fact . . ." She straightened her shoulders. "I think I'm gomig dowd wif a gold, too," she said, sniffing. "He might just humor me, where he wouldn't do a thing for himself. If you'll excuse me."

Both men had stood when she did, and now Gallian strode to open the door for her as she sailed gracefully out, grinning mischievously as she left. Gallian returned to his guest, shaking his head.

"I've never gone against my father before," he said anxiously, his expression unhappy.

"Nor would I urge you to do so, lad. I appreciate your doubts, but can you *doubt* what Chalkin will do?"

"No, I can't," and Gallian sighed, turning back to the Fort Lord Holder with a resolute expression. "I suppose I should get accustomed to *making* decisions, not merely carrying them out."

Paulin clapped him on the shoulder encouragingly. "That's it exactly, Gallian. And I'll guarantee, not all the decisions you'll be called upon to make will be the right ones. Being a Lord Holder doesn't keep you from making mistakes: just make the right wrong ones." Paulin grinned as Gallian tried to absorb that notion. "If you are right most of the time, you're ahead of the game. And you're right in this one for the good reasons which your father declines to see."

Gallian nodded his head. Then asked more briskly, "Will you have some wine now, Paulin?"

"You've your mother's way with you," Paulin said, accepting the offer. "Which you will find is an advantage. . . . Not, mind you, that I in any way imply a lack in your father's manners."

"No, of course not," Gallian said, but he smiled briefly, then cleared his throat. "Ah, what happens to Chalkin when he's removed? I mean, it's not as if he could be dropped on the Southern Islands, is it?"

"Why not?" Paulin replied equably. "Not," he added hastily when he saw Gallian's consternation, "that he would be placed on the same one as the murderers. There is a whole chain . . . an archipelago of isles . . ."

"Aren't they volcanic?"

"Only Young Island, otherwise they're tropical and quite habitable. But one is certain then that the . . . ah, detainee cannot leave and cause ructions. Which Chalkin would certainly do if he was allowed to remain on the mainland. No, the most sensible and most humane solution is to put him where he can't do any more harm than he's already done."

"Then who's to take over managing Bitra?"

"His children are too young, certainly, but there's an uncle, not much older than Chalkin at that. I heard a rumor, though, that Vergerin and Chalkin had played a game, the stakes being an uncontested succession."

"My father mentioned that, too, early on when impeachment first came up. Said he ought to have insisted that Vergerin stand in spite of what the old Neratian Lord wanted. Chalkin's spouse is Franco's sister, you know."

"I'd forgot that. Amazing," Paulin added. "Franco's totally different, but then his mother was Brenton's first spouse."

They were discussing the ever-interesting problem of heredity when the door suddenly opened and Thea came in, almost bent double.

"Great stars, Mother!" Gallian rushed to assist her. "Why, what's the matter? You're so flushed . . ."

She slammed the door shut, waved aside her son's help, and collapsed in her chair with laughter.

"What's so funny?"

"Oh, your father, dear . . ." She wiped tears from her cheeks and some of the 'flush' came away, too. She looked at the handkerchief and rubbed her cheeks more vigorously, still laughing. "We did it. He's going to the warm. I left him writing to ask for Richud's hospitality. I said I'd have the message pennon flown, but your rider would take it, wouldn't he, Paulin? When he takes you back to Fort?"

"Indeed, he will . . . or rather I'll take it to Richud myself and ask him to connive with us to keep Jamson from knowing what's happening off the island," Paulin said, grinning with relief.

"But why are you laughing, Mother? And why the face paint?" Gallian demanded.

"Well," and she flitted her handkerchief, beaming at the two. "What he wouldn't do for himself, he'd do for his ailing mate," she said, again assuming a stuffed-nose voice. "So first I had your sister go in and fetch Canell, as if there were an emergency. I primed Canell to back me up and it was he who suggested the rouge. So when I came into your father's room, I arrived moaning over my aches and pains, which had developed so rapidly over-night. And sneezing constantly . . . Fortunately, I have a small sneeze so I can imitate it . . . Then Canell took over—really, the man was quite convinc-ing. He got alarmed over my rapid pulse and flushed face. He made much of worrying about the condition of my lungs and the strain on my heart. So, between us, why, Jamson agreed to take me south to Ista until I'm completely recovered. So there!" She beamed from one to the other, quite delighted.

"Mother! You are the living end."

"Of course," she said patronizingly. Then she surprised both men by sneezing. "Oh, good heavens!"

"Hmm," said Gallian with mock severity, "that's what happens when you tell stories. You *get* what you pretended you had."

"He's sent someone looking for you, too. So—"

There was a polite tap at the door. Gallian went immediately to answer it, opening only wide enough to be seen. "Yes, tell Lord Jamson that I'll be there directly," he said, and closed the door again.

"I'll wait with Lord Paulin until you can get the letter, Galli," she said, pouring herself some wine. "This is to fortify myself against my cold and any relapse I might have taken . . . Another small glass for yourself, Paulin? To toast my debut as an actress?"

"I wish you'd thought of that ploy earlier."

"So do I," she said with a little sigh. "But I hadn't such an overwhelming *need* to before. Those poor people. Who will take over from Chalkin once you get him out? And what will happen to him, for that matter?"

"That has to be decided."

"We were just discussing that, Mother," Gallian said. "There's Vergerin, the uncle on the father's side."

"But Vergerin gambled his succession rights away," Thea said sternly.

"You heard that, too?" Paulin said.

"Well, you know that Bloodline," Thea said. "Always gambling. On the most ridiculous things, too, and for the most bizarre wagers. But to gamble on the succession?" Her expression showed her disgust over that wager.

"Perhaps Vergerin learned a lesson," Gallian remarked—a trifle condescendingly, Paulin thought.

"Perhaps," Paulin said. "If we find him alive."

"Oh no!" Thea's hand went to her throat in dismay.

"If the Council votes to impeach—"

"Not if, Gallian, *when*," Paulin said, raising his hand in correction.

"*When* they do, how do they go about getting Chalkin out of Bitra Hold?" Gallian asked.

"I think that will require thought and planning," Paulin said. "But go now and see your father, Gallian. Mustn't keep him waiting. He might change his mind."

"Not when Mother's health is at stake," Gallian said, and, with a final grin, left the room.

"Promise me, Paulin, that Gallian's chance at succession won't suffer because of this?" Thea said, earnestly gripping his arm.

"I do promise, Thea," he said, patting her hand.

◆　◆　◆

Four days later, when Lord Jamson and Lady Thea had been safely conveyed to Ista Hold, the rest of the Lord and Lady Holders and the Weyrleaders convened an emergency meeting at Telgar Hold and formally impeached Lord Chalkin for dereliction of his duties and responsibilities to Benden Weyr, for the cruel and unusual punishment of innocent holders (Iantine's drawings were submitted as well as the proceedings of the recent trials), for refusing to allow the Charter to be taught so that all would know their rights as well as their responsibility (Issony gave testimony on that account), and for denying these rights to his holders without due reason.

Gallian soberly voted yea in his turn, having duly exhibited his authorization to act in all matters concerning High Reaches Hold.

"So, now what do we do?" Tashvi said, clasping his hands together with an air of relief at a difficult decision completed.

"Obviously, we inform Chalkin and remove him," Paulin said.

"No other trial?" Gallian asked, startled.

"He just had it," Paulin said. "Judge and jury of his peers."

"It would be against all precedent to employ dragonriders to effect his removal," S'nan said flatly.

Everyone turned to the Fort Weyrleader, showing varying degrees of surprise, disgust, anger, or incredulity at such a fatuous statement.

"Impeachment is also against all precedent, too, S'nan," M'shall said, "because this is the first time that clause has been invoked since it was written two-hundred-and-fifty-odd years ago. But it's now a matter of record. However, I disagree that the dragonriders should bow out. Fragit, S'nan, one of the main reasons for getting rid of him is that he has not helped to prepare his hold, which *we* are honor bound to protect. I'll drag him out of there myself if need be."

Irene beside him nodded vehemently in his support and then glared at S'nan. Sarai, S'nan's Weyrwoman, regarded Irene in horrified dismay.

"If you don't grab him first, he'll just flit out of that warren of a hold of his, and who knows what he might do then," Irene said. Then she blinked and cocked her head, puzzled. "You know, I don't know enough about the interior layout of Bitra Hold to know where to find him, much less grab him with all those bodyguards he has around him. Franco?"

"What?" The Nerat Lord Holder responded nervously. "I can't tell you what Bitra's like. I've never been in more than the reception rooms, even if Nadona is my sister."

"How curious," Bastom said.

"What will we do when we do get him out?" Franco asked. "Who's to hold? Those kids of his are too young."

"The uncle, Vergerin—" Paulin began.

"What about a regency till they're of age?" Azury suggested, cutting across the Fort Lord's beginning.

"Or a promising younger son from a well-conducted hold?" Richud of Ista asked, looking about brightly.

"We know the Bloodline's tainted with the gambling addiction," put in Bridgely.

"That trait can be remedied by strict discipline and a good education," Salda of Telgar said firmly. "As the seed is sown, so will it ripen."

"Vergerin . . ." Paulin said again, raising his voice to be heard above the various arguments.

"Him? He gambled his rights away," Sarai of Fort Weyr said at her most severe.

"Chalkin cheated . . ." M'shall said. "He did in every high-stake game I ever heard of."

Irene gave him a very thoughtful stare.

"So I *heard*!" M'shall repeated.

"VERGERIN," and Paulin roared the word, stunning everyone into silence, "must be considered first, since he is of the Bloodline. That's a stipulation of the Charter which I intend to follow to the letter. He is missing from the property where he has quietly resided since Chalkin took hold."

"Missing?"

"Chalkin do it?"

"Where? Why?"

"Vergerin would have had training from his brother in hold management," Paulin went on, "and I believe that the records state that Kinver was a capable and fair Lord Holder."

"He gambled, too," Irene said in an undertone.

"But he didn't cheat," M'shall said, giving his weyrmate a stern look.

"We all adhere, do we not," Paulin went on, "to the Charter Inheritance Clause which stipulates that a member of the Bloodline must be considered first. Now, if Vergerin is available . . ."

"And willing . . ." M'shall added.

"And *able*," G'don of the High Reaches Weyr amended in a firm voice.

"Able and willing," Paulin echoes, "we would then be following the Charter . . ."

"We've set one precedent today," Bastom said, "why not give Bitra a break and put in someone *trained* and competent. Especially since there's so much to be done to get that hold cleared for the spring action."

"Good point. How about a team? Give some young eager scions some practice in day-to-day management?" Tashvi suggested.

"All those with younger sons and daughters available for the job, raise your hands," said M'shall, not quite as facetiously as he sounded.

"No, you have to replace Chalkin with a member of the Bloodline," S'nan said loudly, pounding the table with both fists.

"Then it has to be Vergerin."

"If we can find him . . ."

"ORDER! ORDER!" and Paulin banged his gavel forcefully until silence prevailed. "There. Now, we can think again. First, we must remove Chalkin . . ."

"What good does that do if we've no one to put in authority in a hold that will be totally demoralized to find itself leaderless?" S'nan said, so incensed that he was speaking faster than anyone had ever heard him talk.

"Ah, but we could put in a new holder so quickly no one will have time to become demoralized," Tashvi suggested.

"I suspect that we will," Paulin said. "Vergerin is not in his known holding and indeed the place looks to have been deserted for some length of time."

S'nan was aghast. "Chalkin has removed him?"

"Probably to that cold storage he's said to have in his lower levels," M'shall said grimly.

"He couldn't have." One would think from S'nan's distressed expression that this latest evidence of Chalkin's complicity and dishonor was his final disillusionment. Sarai leaned over to pat his hand soothingly.

"We do not know that such suspicions are any more than that," Paulin said tactfully. "So, let us all be calm for a moment. Chalkin must be removed . . ."

"What do you do with him, then?" asked S'nan in a shaking voice.

"Exile him," Paulin said, glancing around the table and catching complete agreement with that decision. "That's the safest measure, and also the kindest. There are so many islands in that archipelago that he can have one all his own." Others chuckled at Paulin's droll tone.

"Yes, that would be fitting and proper," the Fort Weyrleader said, brightening somewhat from his gloom.

"We find Vergerin—" When others started to interrupt Paulin once more, he cracked the gavel hard once. "And to start preparing the hold for Thread and reassuring the holders right now, each of you will send a member of your family: one already competent in hold management. It's going to take a lot of work and time to get Bitra prepared. Too much responsibility for just one man or woman. If we find Vergerin and he's willing, he would in any case need assistants."

There was considerable murmuring at that, but the notion seemed to please all, even S'nan.

"We're back again to removing Chalkin," M'shall said. "And Bitra has more exits than a snake tunnel. If Chalkin suspects what we've just done, he'll make a break for it."

"Well, he can't! He's been impeached," S'nan said.

"He doesn't know that yet, S'nan," D'miel of Ista Weyr said, his tone tetchy.

"Considering how often he *knows* things he shouldn't," B'nurrin of Igen Weyr said, "we ought to *do* it now! He mightn't suspect me of anything devious," the young bronze rider said, grinning around the table. "I barely know the man. I'll volunteer."

"At the moment, I don't think any dragonriders are welcome at Bitra Hold," Bridgely said with a cynical lift of one eyebrow.

"You may be right," Irene said, "but only a dragonrider could get into Bitra easily right now. All the roads are snowbound. So it has to be one of us. I'll go."

"No, you won't," M'shall said firmly. "I don't want you anywhere near that lecher."

"Ah, but I could transport others in, you know, and drop them off quietly. He wouldn't be quite so upset at a queenrider coming." Irene gave a nasty chuckle. "He doesn't consider us dangerous, you know." She winked at Zulaya.

"If the snow's so bad at Bitra, where could he escape to anyhow?" Zulaya wanted to know.

"A good point, but he could also hide within the hold and impede progress when our deputies try to get things working again," Bastom said.

"Iantine was there for several weeks," Zulaya said. "Maybe he would know more about Bitra's levels and exits."

"Issony's been in and out for the past few years as teacher," M'shall said as he rose. "They're both still outside, aren't they? I'll just bring them in."

When the problem was explained to Iantine and Issony, they both hauled out writing implements, but it was Iantine who had paper.

"I did some explorations on my own," Iantine said, blocking out an irregular figure on the clean sheet.

"He didn't catch you?" Issony asked, his eyes on Iantine's fingers as the interior levels of Bitra were delineated in swift, sure strokes.

"I had a perfect excuse—I got lost. He lodged me down on the scullery level when I first got there," Iantine said.

Issony looked surprised. "Didn't anyone warn you about his contracts?"

"Yes, but not strongly enough. I learned."

"I could never do this!" Issony said in admiration. "And you've got the dimensions right, too."

"Master Domaize insisted that we learn the rudiments of architectural drafting," the young portraitist said.

"There's another level," Issony said, tapping the right-hand corner of the paper. "You were lucky not to visit it." He gave a snort. "Chalkin calls it his cold storage." The teacher glanced around the table. "A lot of small cubicles, some horizontal, some vertical, and none of them long enough or wide enough for the poor blighters shoved in 'em."

"You can't be serious?" S'nan's eyes protruded in dismay.

"Never more," Issony said. "One of the kitchen girls spilled a tub of sweetener and she was immured for a week. She died of the damp cold of the place." Then, as Iantine's pencil slowed, "There're steps down from his rooms here. They come out in the kitchen. He's always complaining that delicacies disappear from storage, but I know for a fact he's the one snitching." Issony grinned. "I was trying to get some food one night and he nearly caught me at it."

"There's an upper level over this section," Iantine said, his pencil poised. "But the door was padlocked."

"Supposedly due to subsidence," Issony said with a bit of a snort. "But there wasn't as much dust in the hall as usual in his back corridors. I think it could be an access to the panel heights."

"We'll have a dragon up there, too," Paulin said. He wasn't the only one to stand behind the artist to watch him work. "Quite a warren. Glad you looked about you when you were there, Iantine." He patted the young man's shoulder in approval. "So how many . . . ah, discreet exits are there?"

"I know of nine, besides the front one and the kitchen door," Issony said, pointing out the locations.

Paulin rubbed his hands together and, waving everyone to resume their seats at the table, stood for a long moment, looking at the floor plan.

"So, let us not waste time and agree on the . . . ah, strategy here and now. Irene, I appreciate your willingness to be bait, but let us use surprise instead. Issony, Iantine, when would the hold be at its most vulnerable?"

The two men exchanged glances. Issony shrugged. "Early morning, about four, five o'clock. Even the watchwher's getting tired. Most of the guards would be asleep." He glanced toward Iantine, who nodded.

"So, we will need dragonriders . . ."

"Let's stick to those of us in this room, if we can," M'shall said.

"It's totally improper to hound a man in his own hold," S'nan began, starting to rise from his seat.

G'don of High Reaches, seated just beyond him, pulled his arm to reseat him. "Give over, S'nan," he said wearily.

"You're excused from the force, S'nan," Paulin said, equally exasperated.

"But . . . but . . ."

Even his weyrmate shushed him.

"There're more than enough of us quite willing," Shanna of Igen said with a withering glance at the dismayed Fort Weyrleader.

"Good. Then we'll cover all the exits . . ."

"There's one window in the kitchen that they always forget to lock," Iantine said. "And I don't think they ever feed the watchwher enough. He's all bones. Something juicy might occupy him. And I think the window's beyond his chain's reach."

"Good points, Iantine," Paulin said. "Through the window, then, and we'll infiltrate immediately up to Chalkin's private quarters through the back stairs."

"The hidden door's the panel next to the spice cupboard. If you take me along, I can find it in a jiffy," Issony said, his eyes bright with anticipation.

"If you're willing . . ." Paulin said.

"I am, too," Iantine added.

"I rather thought you might be," Paulin said, and then rapidly issued the details of the plan.

With the exception of S'nan, all the Weyrleaders were involved, and even young Gallian was persuaded to come.

"I might as well be hanged for the sheep as the lamb," he said with a fatalistic shrug.

"You'll not suffer from this day's work, Gallian," Bastom assured him. "It's a unanimous decision and our presence there will make that plain to Chalkin. He has no allies among us," the Tillek Lord said, with a reproving glance at S'nan, who sat with face set in such a mournful expression that Bastom was nearly sorry for the punctilious Weyrleader.

"So we are agreed, Lords, Ladies, and Leaders?" Paulin said when he was sure everyone had grasped their roles in the deposition. "Then let us refresh ourselves and rest until it's time to depart."

XIII

Bitra Hold and Telgar Weyr

Except for the fact that the watchwher did not succumb to the choice bits of meat brought to lure it from its duty, and M'shall had to have Craigath speak sharply to it, entry was obtained easily. Whoever should have heard the watchwher's one bellow did not. Issony had no trouble entering by the unlocked window and opening the kitchen door to that contingent. Those who were assigned to watch the various other exits from the hold were by then in place. Iantine sped through the kitchen and up into the main reception rooms, where he opened the front entrance for the rest of the group. Meanwhile, Issony had found the hidden door in the kitchen. Although the stairway was lit by dying glows, there was enough illumination for Paulin and the "arresting" Lords, Ladies, and Leaders.

Paulin opened the access door at the top and entered Chalkin's private apartments first. Behind him came eight Lord and Lady Holders and M'shall, who insisted on representing the Weyrs. To their surprise, the room was brightly lit, glows shining from wall sconces so that the sleeping figures in the massive fur-covered bed were quite visible. All three of them. Chalkin's portly frame bulked the largest under the soft sleeping furs, though his head was covered by a fold of the fine white bedsheet.

One of the girls woke first. She opened her mouth to scream and did not when she saw Paulin's abrupt gesture for silence. Instead, she slithered across the mattress, sheet held up to her chin, to the edge of the bed and grabbed a discarded dress from the pile on the floor. Paulin indicated that she could clothe herself. As smoothly as she moved, or perhaps because she had the sheet up to her chin and let cold air in, the other girl was awakened. She did scream.

"As loud as a green in season," M'shall said later, chuckling at the memory. "At that, Chalkin didn't rouse."

His guards had been alerted, though, and charged into the room, to be flabbergasted by the sight of so many armed folk in Chalkin's most private apartment.

"Chalkin has been impeached for failure to prepare this hold for Thread-fall, for abuse of his privilege as Lord Holder, and for denying his holders their Charter-given rights," Paulin said in a loud voice, sword drawn.

"Unless you wish to join him in his exile, put up your weapons."

To a man they did, just as the reinforcements, led by Iantine, burst in from the hall.

That was what finally roused Chalkin from a drunken sleep.

Later Paulin remarked that he'd been disappointed at such an anti-climactic outcome of their dawn invasion.

"S'nan will be reassured," K'vin said. "I think he was certain we intended to humiliate Chalkin."

"We have," Tashvi said with a chuckle.

Chalkin showed every fiber of his cowardice, trying to bribe one Lord Holder after another, with hints of unusual treasure if they assisted him. If anyone had been in the least bit tempted, their resolve was strengthened when the broken, shivering wrecks were released from "cold storage."

"The place was full," Issony said, looking shattered by what he had seen on that level. "Border guards, most of them, but they didn't deserve that from Chalkin!"

Even the hardiest of them would bear the marks of their incarceration for the rest of their lives.

"Iantine? Did you bring . . . ah, you did. Do a quick sketch of them, will you," Issony said, pointing to the two so close to death: the two who had been castrated for rape. All that could be done for them was to ease their passing with fellis juice. "To show S'nan. In case he has lingering doubts as to the justice of what was done here today."

"Any sign of Vergerin?" Paulin asked when all the cells had been emptied.

"No," M'shall said grimly. "That shouldn't reassure you any." He jerked his thumb at some of the stretcher bearers who had previously been the "cold storage" guards. "They said there were four dead ones who were slipped into the lime pits day before yesterday. We may have moved too late for Vergerin."

Paulin cursed under his breath. "Did you ask if any had heard the name?"

M'shall grunted. "No one down there *had* a name."

Paulin winced. "We'd best send for the holder team."

"I have already dispatched riders to collect the deputies. They should be here . . ."

There was a commotion in the hall, with cheering and shouts of welcome.

"They can't have got here this soon," M'shall said, surprised. Both men went to investigate.

A tall man was shrugging out of thin and dirty furs and smiling at the riders clapping him on the back or whatever part of him they could touch.

"Guess who just walked in?" B'nurrin of Igen cried, seeing Paulin and M'shall.

"Vergerin?" Paulin asked.

"Optimist," M'shall muttered, and then, taking a second hard look at the face no longer hidden by a big furred hat, exclaimed, "It is!"

"It is?" Paulin hastened across the broad hall.

"Has the family eyebrows," M'shall said with a chuckle. "Where've you been hiding, Vergerin?"

"M'shall?" Vergerin peered around, a hopeful smile breaking across his weather-beaten face. He did bear a facial resemblance to Chalkin: as if Chalkin's features had been elongated and refined. "You don't know how glad I was to see all those dragons on the heights. I figured you had to come to your senses and get rid of him . . ." He jerked his thumb ceilingward. "You've no idea . . ."

"Where did you hide? When did you hide?" Paulin asked, clasping Vergerin's hand and shaking it enthusiastically.

Vergerin's grin turned wry. "I figured the safest place was under Chalkin's nose." He gestured in the general direction of the cotholds. "He houses his beasts better than his folk, so the smell of me is at least clean horse manure. I've been earning my keep at the beasthold."

"But your holding has been empty . . ."

"By my design, I assure you," Vergerin said, running a grubby hand through greasy hair and smiling apologetically. "I've a strong survival streak, my Lord Holders, and when I realized my nephew really was not going to do a single thing about the imminence of Thread, I knew I had better disappear before he thought of possible retaliation . . . and me as his only too obvious replacement."

He had unwound the layers that clothed him and stood with a quiet dignity in the midst of the warmly dressed riders and Lord Holders. It was that innate dignity that impressed Paulin. Nor was he alone in noticing it.

"Admittedly, my Blood claim to the hold was squandered foolishly, but then, I should have known that Chalkin was likely to cheat that night, if

ever, with such stakes. It took me quite some while to figure out *how* he managed it, for I'm not without knowing a few tricks myself, and most of those
that can be played on the unwary." He gave a self-deprecating little smile. "I
forgot just how hungry Chalkin was for a Lord Holder's power."

"But you kept your promises," Paulin said, nodding approval.

"The least I could do to restore self-esteem," and Vergerin executed a little bow to Paulin and the others. "Dare I hope that you wish to keep this
Bloodline in Bitra Hold?" He cocked one of his heavy dark eyebrows, his
glance candid and accepting.

Paulin did a quick check of the expressions on the other four Lord Holders who had arrived on the scene.

"You will certainly be considered by the Conclave when it meets at
Turn's End," Paulin said, nodding. The others murmured.

Loud protestations of innocence suddenly broke up the tableau as
Chalkin, bracketed by Bastom and Bridgely, was walked down the main
stairs. The tears of his wife and the frightened shrieks of his children added
to the tumult.

At the last landing Chalkin halted, wrenching his arms free from the two
Lords as he flung himself down the stairs at Vergerin.

"You! *You!* You betrayed me! You broke your word! You did it. You did
it all!"

Bastom and Bridgely, moving with creditable speed, managed to recapture Chalkin and restrained him from physically attacking Vergerin, who did
not so much as recoil from his nephew.

"You did it to me. You did it all," Chalkin said and shrieked louder than
his children when Vergerin, with an expressionless face, slowly pivoted away
from him.

Then Lady Nadona saw Vergerin and her cries turned raucous with
hatred.

"You've taken my husband and now you stand there to take my hold, my
children's inheritance . . . Oh, Franco, how can you let them do this to your
sister?" She fell against the Neratian's chest.

Franco's expression was far from repentant as he quickly unwound her
plump arms from his neck with the help of Zulaya and the Istan Laura.
Nadona was still in her nightdress with a robe half closed over the thin garment. Richud had the two boys by the arm, and his spouse had the two
weeping little girls, who certainly didn't understand what was happening but
were hysterical because their mother was. Irene took some pleasure in applying the slaps that cut Nadona's histrionics short.

Paulin took Vergerin by the arm and led him toward the nearest door,
which turned out to be Chalkin's office. Decanters and glasses were part of

the appointments, and Paulin hurriedly poured two glasses. Vergerin took his and drank it down, the draught restoring some color to his face. He exhaled deeply.

Paulin, impressed by the man's control in a difficult situation, clapped his shoulder and gripped it firmly.

"It can't have been easy," he said.

Vergerin murmured, then straightened himself. "What was hardest," and his smile was wry, "was knowing what a consummate idiot I had been. One can forgive almost anything except one's own stupidities."

Despite the thick stone walls, the screams and bellows continued, the sound altering slightly as Chalkin was hauled out of the hold and down the courtyard steps.

Lady Nadona was markedly absent. Despite her hysterics, she had decided quickly enough that she could not leave her darling children to the mercies of unfeeling men, and women, and would sacrifice herself to remain behind, while Chalkin went into exile. She was exceedingly well acquainted with her own rights as granted by the Charter, to the clause and relevant subparagraphs.

More shouting and confused orders! With an exasperated sigh, Paulin went to the shuttered window and threw it open on the most extraordinary scene: five men struggling to lift Chalkin to Craigath's back while the dragon, eyes whirling violently with red and orange, craned his neck about to see what was happening. Abruptly Chalkin's body relaxed and was shoved into position on Craigath's neck. M'shall leaped to his back and waited while two other Weyrmen roped first Chalkin to M'shall and then the collection of sacks and bags which would accompany the former Lord Holder into exile.

Craigath took off with a mighty bound and brought his wide wings down only once before he disappeared *between*.

"An island exile?" Vergerin asked, pouring himself another glass of wine.

"Yes, but not the same one we sent the guards to. Fortunately, there's a whole string of them."

"Young Island would be the safest one," Vergerin said dryly, sipping the wine. Then he made a face, looking down at the glass. "Wherever does he get his wines?"

Paulin smothered a laugh. "He's got no palate at all. Or did you like the idea of your nephew on an active volcanic island?"

"He's quick-witted enough to survive that. Does Nadona stay on?"

"Her children are young, but you would be perfectly within your rights to relegate her to a secluded apartment and take over the education and discipline of the children."

Vergerin gave a shudder of revulsion.

"Oh, there might be something worth saving in them, you know," Paulin said magnanimously.

"In Chalkin and Nadona's get? Unlikely." Then Vergerin walked to the cabinet where hold records should be kept and, on the point of opening the doors, turned back to Paulin. "Should I start right in? Or wait for the Conclave's decision?"

"Since we didn't know whether or not you had escaped Chalkin's grasp, we decided to let competent younger sons and daughters see what order they could contrive. However, since you would know a lot more about this hold than they could, would you take overall charge?"

Vergerin exhaled and a smile of intense relief lit his features. "Considering what I know of the state of this hold and the demoralization of its holders, I'll need every bit of assistance I can muster." He shook his head. "I don't say my late brother was the best holder in Pern, but he would never have countenanced the neglect, much less Chalkin's ridiculous notion that Thread couldn't return because it would reduce the gaming he could do."

There was a polite rap on the door, and when Paulin answered, Irene poked her head in.

"We managed to get the kitchen staff to prepare some food. I can't vouch for more than that the klah is hot and the bread fresh made."

Vergerin looked down at himself. "I couldn't possibly eat anything until I've washed."

Irene grinned. "I thought of that and had a room, and a bath, prepared for you. Even some clean clothing."

"Fresh bread and good hot klah will go down a treat," Paulin said, gesturing for Vergerin to precede him out of the room.

"No, my Lord Holder, after you," Vergerin said with a courtly gesture.

"Ah, but my soon to be Lord Holder, after you . . ."

"I didn't realize I smelled that bad," Vergerin said ruefully and led the way out.

He was looking about him now, Paulin noticed, as if assessing the condition of the place. He stopped so short that Paulin nearly bounced off him. Pointing to the inner wall where Chalkin's portrait by Iantine was ostentatiously illuminated, he pivoted, eyes wide, his expression incredulous.

"My nephew . . . never . . . looked . . . like that," he said, laughter rippling through his tone.

Paulin chuckled, too, having his first good look at the representation.

"I believe it took the artist some time to paint a . . . satisfactory portrait of your nephew."

"With so little to work on . . . but I can't have that hanging there," Vergerin exclaimed. "It's . . . it's . . ."

"Ludicrous?" Paulin suggested. Poor Iantine, to have had to prostitute his abilities to create *that*!

"That will do for starters."

Paulin leaned close to Vergerin, trying not to inhale because the warmth of the Hall was increasing the pong of manure emanating from Vergerin's clothing.

"I don't think you'll hurt the artist's feelings by removing it from such a prominent place."

"Would he consider repainting it to a closer likeness to the model?" Vergerin asked. "That would remind me of my youthful follies as well as how *not* to manage a hold."

"Iantine's here. Helped us get in, in fact. You can ask him yourself."

"*After* I've had that bath," Vergerin said, and continued on his way to the stairs and cleanliness.

◆ ◆ ◆

Younger sons and daughters were conveyed in from every major hold, dressed and prepared to work hard. If some were disappointed that Vergerin had been found, they hid it well, which did them no disservice. By the time a substantial breakfast had been served, Vergerin had spoken to each of the eight young men and women about what area of responsibility they should assume.

Irene put a wing of Benden riders at Vergerin's disposition to use in contacting the larger holdings in Bitra to announce Chalkin's impeachment and exile.

By then M'shall had returned. "I dumped him and his packages on Island Thirty-two. You'll need to know that for the records. It's rather a nice place. Too bad *he* gets it."

"Did you have any trouble with him?" Paulin asked.

M'shall looked amused as he unbuckled his flight gear. "With the wallop Bastom gave him? He was still unconscious when I left him. Near a stream." He made a face. "I should have dumped him in it. Serve him right for what he did to those he had in cold storage."

By mid-morning matters seemed to be in Vergerin's complete control and the Council members felt able to leave Bitra Hold.

Iantine begged a ride from K'vin for himself and Chalkin's portrait.

"When are you coming to Benden Hold?" Bridgely wanted to know, catching the young portraitist coming down the courtyard steps.

"Lord Bridgely, I am sorry not to be ready quite yet," Iantine said.

Bridgely jabbed his finger at the painting. "You're not letting *that* take precedent, are you?" And he scowled.

"No, never," Iantine said, recoiling slightly. Then he grinned. "Not that it will take me long to change the face on it. But it's last on my list. I've to finish K'vin's portrait and a few more of the Telgar riders and then I'll come. I can probably make it after Turn's End."

"Well, I'll give you until then, young man, but no longer," Bridgely said, sounding aggrieved. Then he smiled to allay Iantine's obvious anxiety. "Don't worry about it, lad. I just want to know where my lady and I fit into your appointment calendar."

With that he walked away.

K'vin was hiding his grin behind his gloved hand. "One can be too successful, you know," he said, then gestured for Iantine to mount Charanth while he held the painting, which he passed up to the artist when he was settled. "I'm glad you're going to fix this."

"Lord Holder Vergerin specifically requested me to. And I must say, I'm glad to do the sitter . . . justice."

"Justice?" K'vin laughed as he landed neatly between the bronze neck ridges. "I think that's possibly a dirty word to Chalkin now."

Iantine grunted as the dragon suddenly launched himself. Not only was Iantine going to be able to set right that inaccurate portrait—he felt he had demeaned himself and Hall Domaize by succumbing to Chalkin's coercion in spite of having no viable alternative—but he had given himself more time at Telgar Weyr. And Turn's End was nearing. Turn's End and the festivities that the midwinter holiday always incurred. Maybe then he could come to some agreement with Debera.

Dragonriders *could* and often did take mates from nonriders. It would have been easier if his profession was one that he could offer the Weyr in return for staying on in Telgar. But once Morath was able to fly, Debera could fly him wherever his commissions took him.

That is, if she felt anywhere near the same about him as he did about her. Never in his wildest dreams had he thought he'd be *in* a Weyr at all. He could almost have thanked Chalkin for being the catalyst on that score: almost. Until he remembered the stark horror of what Chalkin had done at the borders and in the cold storage cells. He shuddered.

"Thought you'd be used to this by now," K'vin said, leaning back to speak into Iantine's ear.

"It isn't this," Iantine said, shaking his head and grinning. He thoroughly enjoyed flying and, after the first experience with the utter cold and nothingness of *between*, had not been nervous about that transfer. He took a firmer grip on the strings about the painting. Charanth was now high enough above Bitra Hold to go *between*. Meranath, bearing Tashvi and Salda as well as Zulaya, zoomed up beside his right wing, the dragon's golden body gleaming in the bright morning sun as her riders waved at him.

As he waved back Iantine was surprised to think it *was* still morning. The invasion of Bitra Hold had begun in such early hours that the day was not that old. So much happened these days!

Blackness! Iantine couldn't feel the cord on the painting, his butt on Charanth's neck, and then they were out in the sun, hanging over Telgar's familiar cone.

Far below, above the prow of Telgar Hold, a sparkle announced Meranath's arrival. The big bronze now turned gracefully on one wing and headed down toward the Weyr.

For Iantine this happened all too swiftly, for he saw so much more from this vantage point than he did from the ground: the dragons sleeping in the sun on their weyr ledges, the younger riders practicing catch and throw with firestone sacks, even the weyrlings getting their morning scrub around the lake. Debera would be among them. He tried to see if he could identify her and Morath, but at that height details were lost. Two dragons, browns both, were eating their kill farther down the valley. Another rider burst into the air above the watchrider, who gestured broadly for him to land. Then Charanth had spiraled close enough to be identified, too, and welcomed back. Iantine could feel a rumble in the bronze's body. Did dragons speak out loud to each other? He had to tighten his hold on the painting or have the wind of their descent pull it free.

As they dropped, K'vin turned his head. "At the cavern?"

"Please," and Iantine nodded, struggling to keep a grip on the painting. Not that losing it would bother him, but then he'd have to waste another board.

He swung his leg over and slid down Charanth's shoulder as quickly as he could.

"My thanks, K'vin," he said, grinning up, having to shield his eyes from the sun.

"Not needed. You more than earned it with today's doings."

Charanth rumbled again, his gently whirling blue eyes focused on Iantine, who saluted him in gratitude. Then the bronze leaped up, flapped his wings twice and was landing on the ledge of the Weyrwoman's quarters.

"You're back, you're back, and safe," and Leopol came racing out of the Lower Cavern, leaping toward Iantine, who put out a restraining hand so the boy wouldn't carom off the edge of the painting.

"What have you done now?" Leopol demanded, taking care not to batter it.

"It's to be redone," Iantine said, knowing the uselessness of avoiding Leopol's interest.

"Oh, the Chalkin portrait?" Leopol reached for it and Iantine pivoted, putting his body between it and the lad's acquisitive hands.

"You're clever, aren't you?"

"Yup," and Leopol's grin bore not a single trace of remorse. "So? What happened when you deposed him?"

Iantine stopped in his tracks and stared at him. "Deposed whom?"

Leopol planted his fists on his belt, cocked his head and gave Iantine a long and disgusted look, finally shaking his head.

"One, you rode away on a Fort Weyr dragon. Two, you've been gone overnight so *something* was up. Especially when the Weyrleaders are gone, too. Three, we all know that Chalkin's for the chop, and four, you come back with a portrait and it isn't one you've done here." Leopol spread his hands. "It's obvious. The Lords and Leaders have got rid of Chalkin. Impeached, deposed, and exiled him. Right?" He grinned at the summation, cocking his head over the other shoulder. "Right?" he repeated.

Iantine sighed. "It's not my place to confirm or deny," he said tactfully, and started again for his quarters.

Leopol dodged in front, halting him again. "But I'm right about Chalkin, aren't I? He won't get ready for Threadfall, he's been far too hard on his people, and half the Lord Holders owe him huge sacks of marks in gambling debts."

Iantine stopped. "Gambling debts?" He brushed past Leopol, determined to get to the dubious safety of his room without giving anything away to such a gossip as Leopol.

"Ah, Iantine." Tisha caught sight of him and moved her bulk with surprising speed and agility through the tables to intercept him. "Did they catch Chalkin all right? Did he struggle? Did that spouse of his go with him? Which frankly would surprise me. Did they find Vergerin alive? Will he take hold or does he have to wait till the Conclave at Turn's End?"

Leopol bent double with laughter at Iantine's expression.

"Yes, no, no, yes, and I don't know," he said in reply to her rapid-fire questions.

"You see? I'm not the only one," Leopol said, hanging onto a chair with one hand to keep his balance while he brushed laugh tears from his eyes with the other, thoroughly delighted with himself and Iantine's reaction.

"I'd like to hear all, Iantine," Tisha said, and deposited the klah mugs and the plate of freshly baked cookies on the table nearest him. "Do. Sit. You've had a hard day already and it's not noon yet."

"I'll take it and put it very carefully in your room," Leopol said, grabbing hold of the wrapped painting and then snatching it out of Iantine's unconsciously relaxed grip. "And I won't look until you tell me I can."

"No, wait, Leo," Tisha said. "I want to see what Chalkin considered 'satisfactory.' "

"Do I have no privacy around here?" Iantine demanded, raising his hands in helplessness. "Is there no way to keep secrets?"

"Not in a well-run Weyr there isn't," said Tisha. "Eat. Drink. And, Leo, take the basket I made ready for K'vin up to his weyr. I didn't see Zulaya and Meranath so she may have stopped over at Telgar Hold."

His knees weakened, as did his resolve, and Iantine collapsed into the chair Tisha had invitingly pulled out for him.

"Shall I?" Leopol asked in his best wheedling tone, one hand on the cord knot.

"I'm not sure I could stop you," Iantine said, and caught the pad he had stuffed inside the wrapping as Leopol made short work of opening it.

Iantine put the pad to one side. He didn't really want to show the latest drawings he'd done. The two castrated rapists had died shortly after he finished the sketches. He intensely regretted how pleased he had been with their sentences. Had they had any idea of what additional torment Chalkin would inflict on them when they asked to be returned to their hold? No, or they wouldn't have gone. Then Iantine caught Tisha's sharp eye on his face and wondered if she had read his expression, which he had tried to keep blank. Fortunately, the much glamorized Chalkin stared out of the painting at them, and Tisha's first good look sent her into gales of laughter, with Leopol whooping nearly as loud.

The headwoman had an infectious laugh under any condition: a mere chuckle from her would have anyone in her vicinity grinning in response. Iantine was in sore need of a good laugh, and if his inner anxieties kept him from joining in wholeheartedly, at least he was made to grin.

Tisha's amusement alerted the rest of the Weyrfolk to Iantine's return, and the table was shortly surrounded by people having a good laugh over what Chalkin had considered to be a "satisfactory portrait" of himself. Iantine sated their curiosity by giving a brief report of what had happened. Everyone was much relieved that Chalkin was not only no longer Bitra's Lord, but also that he had been exiled far from the mainland.

"Too good for him, really," someone said.

"Ah, but he's lord of all he surveys, ain't he? Suit him!"

"No one was hurt?"

"Who's going to take hold there now, with so much to do so close to Fall?"

Iantine answered as circumspectly as he could, though he was amazed at how accurately the Weyrfolk had guessed what had happened. They also seemed to know a great deal about a hold that was not beholden to Telgar Weyr. He didn't think he'd talked much about his uncomfortable stay at Bitra, so they must have had their information from other sources. Weyrfolk did get to travel more than holders, so perhaps their level of information was more comprehensive.

Riders drifted in, early for the noontime meal and just as interested in what had happened at Bitra Hold. Some of the older ones remembered the wager that had cost Vergerin the holding, and knew other details about that Bloodline that certainly showed them well informed.

Iantine was grateful for the klah and cookies Tisha had brought and equally pleased to have Leopol bring him bread, cheese, and the sliced wherry meat that was being served for lunch. He did have a moment's anxiety when he saw K'vin, at the edge of the crowd, gesturing for his attention. Maybe he shouldn't have said a thing.

He told Leopol to take the notorious portrait to his quarters, bundled his pad under his arm—because he knew nothing would keep Leopol from looking at it—and then made his way to K'vin. Since he had obviously told all he was going to tell, he was allowed to pass, with good-natured mauling on his way.

"I'm sorry, Weyrleader, if I was speaking out of turn . . ."

K'vin regarded him with widened eyes. "Speaking out of turn? Ha, they probably had figured out everything on their own. What could you possibly tell them that they didn't know?"

"How many people Chalkin had in those appalling cells," Iantine said, blurting out the words before he realized what he was saying.

K'vin put a sympathetic arm around his shoulders. "I think I'll have a few bad dreams over that myself," and he gave a deep shudder. "Perhaps you'd best get some rest . . ."

"No, I'd rather not, if you've something else for me to do," Iantine said truthfully. He didn't even need to stop off at his quarters, as his tubes of oil and brushes were already in the Weyrleaders' quarters.

K'vin's solicitous expression brightened. "I've some time now, and you've the painting to finish of me . . . unless you'd rather redo Chalkin . . . but Bridgely made it very plain to me that he'd like you at Benden to do his commissions by Turn's End. You're much sought after, you know."

Iantine made a disparaging noise in his throat, embarrassed by his notoriety. K'vin, grinning at his reaction, slapped his back lightly in affection.

"So what's it to be?" the Weyrleader asked.

"You, of course. Did you . . ." He hesitated, not wanting to be thought pushy. "Did you like Zulaya's portrait?"

K'vin gave a low laugh and turned his face away. "You've done her proud, Iantine. Proud."

"She's easy. She's beautiful," Iantine said.

"Yes, isn't she?"

Something about the tone of his voice made Iantine wonder at such a response. They were Weyrleaders, together, weren't they? They always made such a stance of a good partnership. But Iantine was getting as good at hearing things that weren't expressed as he was at seeing all that could be seen. Not his place to comment, though, despite a growing admiration for K'vin as Weyrleader. Zulaya was a bit reserved, he knew from having spent so much time painting her, but she was much older than Iantine. And older than K'vin, too, for that matter.

"That gown was perfect for her," Iantine said to break an awkward silence.

"Yes, she had it made for the last Hatching," K'vin said, and the smile he turned toward Iantine was easy, relaxed.

Iantine wondered if all he'd seen that morning hadn't skewed his judgment. They were at the weyr stairs now and climbed up. At the top of the steep flight Iantine was glad he wasn't even out of breath.

"You're in good shape," K'vin said, with another friendly slap to his back to push him on into the high-ceilinged entrance to the weyr.

"I'd need to be, wouldn't I?" Iantine replied with a droll laugh. He paused briefly, his eyes seeking the weyrlings at the lake. Yes, Debera was there, oiling Morath. He'd have a chance to talk to her later: maybe even take dinner with her and show her Chalkin's portrait before he made the changes. Could he add to Chalkin's face what went on in that man's miserable soul? he wondered as he watched K'vin change into the Gather clothes he wore for his portrait. Was he good enough to attempt such a portrayal?

◆ ◆ ◆

Amid all the frantic preparations for Turn's End, Clisser braved S'nan's displeasure to request transport to the Telgar Engineering Hall to discuss the feasibility of the Stonehenge installation for Pern's purposes. All he told S'nan, however, was that he needed to discuss something vital with Kalvi; S'nan would not approve, believing that such bells, whistles, and signals should be unnecessary if the Weyrs were kept on their toes during Intervals.

Jemmy had meticulously drawn a replica of the prehistoric stone circle, plus another of a reconstruction of what it had originally looked like, and such description as might be valuable to Kalvi and his team.

Kalvi took one quick, almost derisive glance at the drawings, and then a second more respectful one.

"Eye Rock? Finger Rock? Solstice?" He gave Clisser a broad smile. "I do believe it will suffice, and rather neatly." Then he frowned. "Couldn't you have given me a little more time? Solstice is only two weeks off!"

"I—" Clisser began.

"Sorry, friend," Kalvi said with a self-deprecating smile, "you'd be busy with rehearsing and all that. Hmmm. Just leave it with me. I think we can contrive something . . ." He riffled through Jemmy's sketches. "Hmm, yes, the lad has real talent."

"Don't you dare seduce him away from the College," Clisser said, assembling as fierce a frown on his face as he gave to wayward students.

Kalvi grinned, pretending to recoil in terror, but his eyes were on the drawings. "We'll manage." He gave an exaggerated sigh. "It's what we're good at."

Clisser left, reassured that he would not fail the Conclave on this matter.

CHAPTER
XIV

Turn's End at Fort Hold and Telgar Weyr

Traditionally, the lord Holders and the Weyrleaders—and the invited heads of the various professions—met in Conclave the day before Turn's End—the Winter Solstice—to discuss what matters should be brought to those who would assemble for the festivities. Should a referendum figure on the agenda, its details would have been previously circulated. It would also be read out that evening in every main hold and Hall. If voting was required, votes were cast the morning of the first day of Turn's End, the results counted and returned to the second traditional sitting of the Conclave on the day after Turn's End, when the new year started.

The tradition was even more important in this 258th year after Landing with the Pass so imminent. Although Vergerin had been in charge but twenty days before the Conclave, it was obvious that he was taking a firm but just hold on Bitra. He was also working his assistants hard but fairly. None of them had any complaint to register when adroitly queried by their fathers or mothers. Vergerin's first official act had been to send riders to every single known holding and announce Chalkin's removal and that as many as could attend Turn's End at Bitra Hold would be made welcome. Vergerin paid for additional supplies out of his own funds. (No one had found Chalkin's treasury: nor had he taken it with him into exile. Nadona had denied any knowledge of its whereabouts and moaned that he had left her without a mark to her name.)

Altering a previously made decision, the Teachers' College planned now to supply a Turn's End concert to Bitra. They would bring copies of the Charter, which Vergerin had requested, to be given to each small holder. That would deplete to a few dozen the printed copies left in the College Library, but Clisser felt it to be in a very good cause. Since the Turn's End music featured Sheledon's ambitious "Landing Suite"—which made mention of the Charter—the audience would have a better understanding of what the music, and indeed the printed Charter, was all about. Bitran holders would no longer be kept in abysmal ignorance of their Charter-given rights.

Consequently, when the Conclave sat, the first business was to confirm Vergerin as Lord Holder of Bitra. He was not abjured to train his young relatives, Chalkin's sons, to succession, although he was in conscience bound to see them well taken care of, educated, and prepared to make their own living as adults. He was relieved of his promise to forgo having legitimate heirs and promptly installed at Bitra a nine-year-old son and a five-year-old daughter. No one knew who their mother had been. Vergerin made it plain that he was interested in acquiring a spouse suitable to hold as his Lady.

Clisser was called on to report on the matter of an indestructible and unambiguous method of confirming a Pass, and he said that Kalvi and he had agreed on the device and it would be installed on the eastern face of every Weyr. Kalvi, looking suitably smug, nodded wisely, so Paulin allowed himself to be reassured. He wanted no more problems like Chalkin to arise again! Ever! And now was the moment to prevent them.

The matter of a new hold being established and named Crom came up and there was considerable discussion.

"Look, they are entitled to use their Charter-granted acres, and that amounts to a fair whack of land," Bastom said, coming unexpectedly down on the side of the applicants. "Let 'em call it a hold . . ."

"Yes, but they want autonomy, and besides, they're too far from any other hold up there in the hills," Azury put in.

"It'll have to prove it's self-sufficient . . ." Tashvi said, looking reluctant to admit that much. Which was understandable since Telgar was also a mining hold.

"They have to follow the rules, same as everyone else," Paulin said in a neutral manner. "And supply basic needs to Contract workers."

"They're in good shape to do so," Azury remarked dryly, "what with the profit they can expect from supplying high-grade ore at the start of a Fall."

"Consider them on probation," was Bridgely's suggestion, and that motion was carried.

There were a few more minor details to be discussed, but they were carried as well. This year there was no referendum to be presented to the population.

"However, I want every one of you to give a *full* report of the trials and Chalkin's impeachment to the assembled," Paulin reminded the Lord Holders. "We want the truth circulated and believed: not a mess of rumors."

"Like the cannibalism!" Bridgely had been highly indignant over that one. "Sadistic Chalkin was, but let's squash that one *now*!"

"How under the sun did such a rumor ever get started?" Paulin asked, appalled. S'nan looked in a state of shock, staring incredulous at the Benden Lord Holder.

"The 'cold storage' I suspect," Bridgely said, disgusted.

"We didn't coin the term," Azury said with a shrug.

"Well, we don't want it circulated," M'shall said angrily. "Bad enough having to live with the facts without having to debunk the fantasies."

"We do want the swift justice meted out to the rapists and the murderers to be well publicized, though," Richud said.

"That, yes! Speculation, no," Paulin said. He rose, tapped the gavel on its block. "I declare this session of the Conclave dismissed. Enjoy Turn's End and we'll meet in three days' time."

He intended to enjoy every moment of it for the year he'd put in. He noticed a similar determination on other faces, especially young Gallian's. Apart from the Chalkin affair, Jamson had no need to fault his son's management of High Reaches. Though maybe that bit about "cannibalism" could be whispered in Jamson's presence. That would certainly alter his opinion about impeachment. Somehow Thea was still "ailing" and had persuaded her spouse to stay on in Ista for Turn's End. That gave more opportunity for the Chalkin affair to die a natural death.

◆ ◆ ◆

Turn's End was a holiday for everyone except those involved in the ambitious "Landing Suite" debut at all the Weyrs and the major holds. Clisser was run ragged with rehearsals and last-minute assignments, and understudies for those with winter colds. Then he had the extra burden of preparing for the precise calculations needed to set up the fail-safe mechanism to predict a Pass. Clisser, torn between the musical rehearsals and observing the installation of a permanent Threadfall warning device, opted for the latter. Of course, his role was supervisory, as the more precise location had to be conducted by teams of astronomers, engineers, and Weyrleaders on the eastern rim of all six facilities. He, Jemmy, and Kalvi were to set the apparatus at Benden, the first Weyr to "see" the phenomenon, then they would skedaddle on dragonback to each of the other five Weyrs to install the others.

It was imperative that the first installation, at Benden, had to be accurate in case there might be a distortion at any other. Though Clisser doubted it, not with Kalvi fussing and fussing over the components. Clisser'd been over and over the requisite steps to pinpoint the rise of the Red Star. Once that circular "eye" was set on the rim, they could install the pointer, the finger. But the eye had to be right on it! The teams had been in place for the past week, with predawn checks on the Red Planet's position at dawn. All that was necessary now was a clear morning, and that seemed to be possible across the continent, which had enjoyed some bright, clear, if wintry, skies. Fine weather was critically important at Benden, for the other Weyrs could take adjusted measurements from that reading if necessary.

Kalvi was still fiddling with the design of what he was calling the Eye Rock, which would bracket the Red Planet at dawn on Winter Solstice. His main problem was adjusting the pointer . . . the position at a distance from the eye itself at which the viewer would stand to see the planet. The pointer had to accommodate different physical heights. Old diagrams of Stonehenge and other prehistoric rings had surfaced. Actually, Bethany's students had found them after an intensive search of long unused documents. Fortunately, for Clisser's peace, Sallisha had gone to Nerat for the Turn's End celebration, ready to start her next year's teaching contract. He was spared any reminder from her of how important it was to keep such ancient knowledge viable. He had rehearsed arguments, in case he had a letter from her, about the fact that, in the crunch, someone *had* remembered.

He was quite excited—if freezing—to be on Benden Weyr's rim with the others, telescopes set up, aimed in the appropriate direction while Kalvi and Jemmy fiddled with their components. Kalvi had put up a cone for the pointer. The notion being that a person, resting their chin on the cone's tip, would see the Red Planet bracketed just as it cleared the horizon. They'd have to try it with folks of various statures to be sure the device worked, but technically, Clisser thought it would work. Kalvi was the shortest, he was tallest, M'shall was a half head shorter, and Jemmy between the Weyrleader and Kalvi. If all could see the Red Planet in the eye, the device would be proven.

Well, it would really be proven in another 250 years or so with the Third Pass.

But this moment was exciting. Clisser slapped his body with his arms, trying to warm himself. His feet, despite the extra lining, were frozen: he could barely feel his toes, and his breath was so visible he worried that it might cloud his chance to see the phenomenon.

"Here it comes," Kalvi said, though Clisser could see nothing in the crepuscular dawn light. Kalvi was looking at his instrument, not the sky.

A tip of red appeared just over the bottom of the Eye a breath or two later. A redness that seemed to pulsate. It wasn't a very large planet—from this distance, it wouldn't be, Clisser thought, though they had the measurements of it from the *Yokohama* observations. It was approximately the same size as Earth's old sister, Venus. And about as hospitable.

Somehow, Clisser thought—and told himself to breathe—as he watched, the wanderer managed to look baleful in its redness. Hadn't one of the other Sol satellites been called the "red planet"? Oh, yes, Mars. Suitable, too, since it had been named after a war god.

And equally a suitable color for a planet about to wreak havoc on them. How could such an avaricious organism develop on a planet that spent most of its orbit too far away from Rukbat's warmth to generate any life form? Of course, he was aware that very odd "life" forms had been found by the early space explorers. Who had blundered into the Nathi, to name another vicious species!

But the reports on this mycorrhizoid gave it no intelligence whatsoever. A menace without malice. Clisser sighed. Well, that was *some* consolation: it didn't really *mean* to eat everything in sight—people, animals, plants, trees— but that was all it could do.

Which was more than enough, Clisser thought grimly, remembering the visuals of recorded incidents. That's another thing he ought to have done—a graphic record—even a still picture would make vividly plain how devastating Thread could be. Iantine's sketches done at the Bitran borders had impressed the teacher immensely. Though it was a shame to waste Iantine's talents on a copy job. Anyone could copy: few could originate.

Meanwhile, the red edge crept up over the rim of Benden Weyr.

"THAT'S IT!" Kalvi cried. He made a final twitch to the iron circle on its pedestal. "I got it. Cement it in place now. Quickly. You there at the finger rock. Eyeball the phenomenon. All of you should see it bracketed by this circle."

The viewers had lined themselves up, and each took a turn even as Kalvi raced back to grab a look from this vantage point.

"Yup, that'll do it. You got that solidly in place? Good," and the energetic engineer turned to M'shall. "As you love your dragon, don't let anyone or anything touch that iron rim. I've used a fast-drying cement, but even a fraction out of alignment and we've lost it."

"No one'll be up here after we leave," M'shall promised, eyeing the metal circle nervously. Though he knew the ring was iron, it looked fragile sitting there, the Red Planet slowly rising above it. "But that's going to be replaced, isn't it? With stone?"

"It is, and don't worry about *us* messing up the alignment later. We won't," Kalvi said, blithely confident, rubbing his hands together, grinning with success. "Now, we've got some more dawns to meet."

"Yes, surely, but take time for breakfast."

"Ha! No time to pamper ourselves. But I was indeed grateful for the klah." Kalvi was gathering up his equipment, including five more iron circles, and gesturing to his crew to hurry up. "Not with five more stops to make this morning. The things I talk myself into." He looked around now in the semidark of false dawn. "Where's our ride?"

"That way," M'shall said, pointing to the brown dragons and riders, waiting well around on the rim.

"Oh, good. Thanks, M'shall." And, rings clanging dully where they rode on his shoulder, Kalvi gathered up his packs and half ran, his crew trailing behind. Clisser sighed and followed.

Well, he thought, he'd be well inured to the cold of *between*. They'd have an hour and a half between Benden and Igen but then only half an hour from Igen to Ista to Telgar, where they'd have a little over an hour, and time for something hot to eat before going on to Fort. High Reaches was actually the last Weyr to be done, which really didn't salve S'nan's pride all that much, but sunrise came forty-five minutes later in the northernmost Weyr due to the longitudinal difference. S'nan couldn't argue the point that Benden had to have its equipment installed first since it was the most easterly.

Clisser had heard the talk about S'nan's continued distress over Chalkin's impeachment. The Fort Weyrleader was not the oldest of the six: G'don was, but no one worried about his competence to lead the Weyr. S'nan had always been inflexible, literal, didactic, but that wouldn't necessarily signify poor leadership during the Pass. Clisser sighed. That was a Weyr problem, not his. Thank goodness. He had enough of them.

He'd catch some rest when they finished at Fort Weyr, so he'd be fresh for the final rehearsal at the Hall. If Sheledon had altered the score again during his absence, he'd take him to task. No one would know what to play with all the changes. Get this performance over with and then refine the work. It was, Clisser felt, quite possibly Sheledon's masterpiece.

"You're riding with me, Teacher," a voice said. "Don't want you walking off the rim!"

Clisser shook himself to attention. "Yes, yes, of course." He smiled up at the brown rider, who extended a hand.

Clisser reached up to grasp the proffered hand. "Oh, thank you," he said to the dragon, who had not only turned his head but helpfully lifted his forearm to make an easier step up.

Then he was astride the big dragon, settling himself, snapping on the safety strap.

"I'm ready."

Clisser did catch his breath, though, when the dragon seemed to just fall off the rim into the blackness of Benden's Bowl. He grabbed at the security of the safety strap and then almost cracked his chin on his chest as the dragon's wings caught the air and he soared upward.

They were facing east, and the malevolence of the Red Star was dimmed by the glow of Rukbat rising, altering the rogue planet's aspect to one of almost negligible visibility, almost anonymity, in the brightening sky.

Amazing! thought Clisser. *I must remember to jot that down.* But he knew he never would. And Pernese literature was thus saved another diarist, he amended. Clisser saw that the rider, too, had his eyes fastened on the magnificent spectacle. He must savor this ride. The dragon veered northward, pivoting slowly on his left wing tip. The dragons would soon have more important journeys to make. Clisser did observe the majestic snowcapped mountains of the Great Northern Range, tinted delicate shades of orange by the rising sun. What Iantine could make of such a scene! Then abruptly all he could see was the black nothingness of *between*.

◆ ◆ ◆

"What happens if you wear your fingers out?" Leopol asked Iantine.

The Artist hadn't even been aware of the lad's presence, but the comment—because Iantine was sketching the scene of the dragonets so fast that his elbow was actually aching—caused him to burst out laughing, even though he didn't pause for a moment.

"I don't know. I've never heard of it happening, though, if that's any consolation."

"Not to me, but for you," Leopol said, cocking his head in his characteristically impudent fashion.

"I'll miss you, you know," Iantine said, grinning down at the sharp expression on Leopol's face.

"I should hope so, when I've been your hands, feet, and mouth for months now," was the irrepressible answer. "You could take me with you. I'd be useful," and Leopol's expression was earnest, his gray eyes clouded. "I know how you like your paints mixed, your brushes cleaned, and even how to prepare wood or canvas for portraits." His pathetic stance could have persuaded almost anyone.

Iantine chuckled and ruffled the boy's thick black hair. "And what would your father do?"

"Him? He's winding himself up for Threadfall." A discreet question to Tisha had produced the information that a bronze rider, C'lim, was the boy's father; the mother had died shortly after Leopol's birth. But he, like every other child of the Weyr, had become everyone's child, loved and disciplined as the need arose. "He doesn't half pay attention to me anymore."

Which was fair, Iantine thought, since Leopol had become *his* shadow. "Tisha?"

"Her? She'll find someone else to mother."

"Well, I will ask but I doubt you'd be allowed. The other riders think you'll Impress a bronze when you're old enough."

Leopol tossed off that future with a shrug. What he could do *now* was more important than what might be three or four years in the future. "D'you *have* to go?"

"Yes, I *have* to go. I'm in grave danger of overstaying my welcome here."

"No, you're not," and Leopol looked significantly toward the lake, where the weyrlings were having their customary bath. "And you haven't drawn *all* the riders yet."

"Be that as it may, Leo, I'm due at Benden to do the holders, and that's a commission I've been owing since I started my training at Hall Domaize."

"When you do those, will you come straight back? You haven't done Chalkin's face like he really is, you know, and it isn't as if you were doing any-one else out of a place to sleep." Leopol's face was completely contorted now by his dismay. "Debera really wants you to stay, you know."

Iantine shot him an almost angry look. "Leopol?" he said warningly.

"Aw," and the boy screwed his boot toe into the dirt, "everyone knows you fancy her, and the girls say that she's gone on you. It's only Morath who's the problem. And she doesn't have to be. Soon as she can fly, she'll have a weyr and you'll have some privacy."

"Privacy?" Iantine knew that Leopol was precocious, but . . .

Leopol cocked his head and had the grace not to grin. "Weyrs're like that. Everyone knows everyone else's secrets."

Iantine hung amid irritation: relief in the information about Debera, and amusement that his carefully hidden interest was so transparent. He had never thought about loving someone so much that their absence could cause physical discomfort. He never thought he would spend sleepless hours re-viewing even the briefest of conversations; identify a certain voice in a crowded cavern; have to rub out sketches of imagined meetings and poses which his fingers did of their own accord. He kept close guard on his sketch pads because there were far too many of Debera—and the ever-present Morath. Morath liked him, too. He knew that because she'd told him she did.

That, actually, had been the first encouraging sign he'd had. He had tried, adroitly, to figure out how significant that might be, as far as Debera's awareness of him was concerned. He'd ask while he was sketching a rider, as if only politely inquiring about what was closest to his model's heart anyway. It appeared that a dragon could talk to anyone he or she wished. They did so for reasons of their own, which sometimes they did not discuss with their riders. Or they did. None of the other weyrlings, even the greens with whom Iantine was now quite familiar, spoke to him. It was Morath who counted. Not that the green dragon—who was the largest of that color from that clutch—ever explained herself. Nor did Iantine ask. He merely treasured the immense compliment of her conversation.

She did ask to see his sketch pad once. He noticed the phenomenon of the pad reflected in every one of the many facets of her eyes. They'd been bluey-green at the time, their normal shade, and whirling slowly.

"Do you see anything?"

Yes. Shapes. You put the shapes on the pad with the thing in your hand?

"I do." How much could a dragon see with that kind of optical equipment? Still, Iantine supposed it would be useful when Thread was falling from all directions. As the dragon eye protruded out from the head, it obtained overhead images, too. Good design. But then, dragons *had* been designed, though no one nowadays could have managed the genetic engineering. It was one thing to breed animals for specific traits, but to begin from the first cell to create a totally new creature? "Do you like this one of Debera oiling you?" He tapped his pencil on the one he'd done that morning.

It looks like Debera. It looks like me? and there was plaintive surprise in Morath's contralto voice. That was when Iantine realized that Morath sounded very much like her rider. But then, that was only logical since they were inseparable.

Inseparable! That's what bothered him most. He knew that his love for Debera would be constant. But any love left over from Morath for him could scarcely match his commitment. Did it have to? After all, he was totally committed to his work. Could he fault her for being equally single-minded? There was, however, a considerable difference between loving a dragon and loving to paint. Or was there?

Maybe it was as well, Iantine thought, tucking his pencil behind his ear and closing his pad, that he was going to Benden after Turn's End. Maybe if Debera—and Morath—were out of sight, they might also go out of mind and his attachment would ease off.

"You got your Turn's End clothes ready? Need ironing or anything?" Leopol asked, his expression wistful.

"You did 'em yesterday and I haven't worn 'em yet," he said, but he ruffled the boy's thick hair again and, looping his arm over the thin shoulders, steered him to the kitchen. "Let's eat."

"Ah, there's not much to eat," Leopol said in disgust. "Everyone's getting ready for tonight."

"They've been getting ready all week," Iantine said. "But there's bread and cold meats set out."

"Huh!"

Iantine noticed that Leopol had no trouble making himself several sandwiches of what was available and had two cups of soup and two apples. He noted that he had no trouble eating, either, though some of the smells emanating from the ovens—and all were in use—were more appetizing than lunch. He intended to enjoy himself this evening.

Then Leopol, eyes wide with excitement, leaped from the table. "Look, look, the musicians are here!"

Glancing outward, Iantine saw them dismounting from half a dozen dragons. They were laughing and shouting as instruments were carefully handed down from dragonbacks and carisaks were passed around. Tisha sailed out, her assistants with her, and shortly everyone was in the cavern and being served a lunch considerably more complicated than soup and sandwiches. Leopol was in the thick of it, too, the rascal, and the recipient of a huge wedge of iced cake. Iantine selected a good spot against the wall, sharpened his pencil with his knife, and opened his pad. This was a good scene to preserve. If he got them down on paper now, maybe he could listen to the music this evening without itchy fingers. As he worked he realized that Telgar had rated some of the best musicians, called back from wherever their contracts had taken them, for Turn's End celebrations. He'd finish in time for the concert and that would be that for the day!

It wasn't, of course. But then, he found it hard not to sketch exciting moments and scenes. Especially as he didn't want to leave this pad anywhere that it could be casually opened. And he could listen to the music just as well while drawing. Sketching also kept his hands where they should be and not itching to go around Debera's shoulder or hold her hand. Sketching did allow him some license, for he could always apologize that he didn't realize his leg was against hers, or that their shoulders were touching or he was bending his body close to hers. After all, he was so busy sketching, he wouldn't be noticing externals.

If Debera had found the contact unpleasant or annoying, she could have moved her leg away from his, or moved about on the bench. But she didn't seem to mind him overlapping her from time to time in the zeal to get this or that pose. Truth was, he was totally conscious of her proximity, the floral fragrance that she used that didn't quite hide the "new" smell of the lovely pale green dress she was wearing. Green was her color and she must know that: a gentle green, like new leaves, which made her complexion glow. Angie had told him the color of Debera's Turn's End gown, so he'd bought a shirt of a much deeper green so that they'd go together. He liked the way she'd made a coronet of her long hair, with pale green ribbons laced in and dangling down her back. Even her slippers were green. He wondered if there'd be dancing music, too, but there usually was at Turn's End. Although maybe not, what with the "Landing Suite" first. He bent to ask her to reserve dances for him but she shushed him.

"Listen, too, Ian," she said in a soft whisper, gesturing to his pad. "The words are as beautiful as the music."

Iantine glanced forward again, only now realizing that there were singers, too. Had he been that rapt in being next to Debera without Morath?

I'm here. I listen, too.

Morath's voice startled him, coming into his head so unexpectedly. He gulped. Would the dragon always be able to read his mind?

He asked the question again, more loudly, in his own head. There was no reply. Because there *was* no reply? Or because there was none needed to such an obvious question?

But Morath hadn't sounded upset that he was luxuriating in Debera's proximity. She had sounded pleased to be there and listening. Dragons liked music.

He glanced over his shoulder to the Bowl and could see along the eastern wall the many pairs of dragon eyes, like so many round blue-green lanterns up and down the wall of the Weyr where dragons made part of the audience.

He began then, obediently, to listen to the words, and found himself drawn into the drama unfolding, even tho' he'd known the story from childhood. The musicians called it the "Landing Suite," and this verse was about leaving the great colony ships for the last time. A poignant moment, and the tenor voice rose in a grateful farewell to them where they would orbit over Landing forever, their corridors empty, the bridge deserted, the bays echoing vaults. The tenor, with creditable breath control, let his final note die away as if lost in the vast distance between the ships and the planet.

A respectful pause followed, and then the ovation which his solo had indeed merited burst forth. Quickly Iantine sketched him, taking his bows, before he stepped back into the ensemble.

"Oh, good, Ian. He was just marvelous," Debera said, craning her head to watch what he was doing. She kept right on clapping, her eyes shining. "He'll be delighted you did him, too."

Iantine doubted that and managed a smile that did not echo the stab of jealousy he felt because Debera's interest had been distracted from him.

She likes you, Ian, said Morath as if from a great distance, though she was ranged with the other still flightless dragonets on the Bowl floor.

Ian? he echoed in surprise. Other riders had told him that while dragons would talk to people other than their own rider, they weren't so good at remembering human names. Morath *knows* my name?

Why shouldn't I? I hear it often enough. And Morath sounded sort of tetchy.

Morath may never know just how much that remark means to me, Iantine thought, taking in a deep breath that swelled his chest out. Now, if he could just get her by herself alone . . .

But she's never alone, now that she's my rider.

Iantine stifled a groan that he wanted neither dragon nor rider to hear and compressed his thoughts as far down in his head as he could. Would it all be worth it? he wondered. And tried to divorce himself from Debera for the rest of the concert.

He didn't pay as close attention to the second and third parts of the "Landing Suite," which brought events up to the present. A cynical section of his mind noticed that Chalkin's impeachment was not mentioned, but then it was a very recent incident which the composer and lyricist would not have known about. He wondered would it ever make history. Chalkin would love it. Which might well be why no one would include him. That'd be the final punishment—anonymity.

Dinner was announced at the conclusion of the suite, and the big cavern was efficiently reorganized for dining. In the scurry and fuss of setting up tables and chairs, he got separated from Debera. The panic it caused him made it extremely clear that he could not divorce his emotions from the girl. When they found each other again, her hand went out to him as quickly as his to her, and they remained clasped while they waited in line to collect their food.

Iantine and Debera finally found seats at one of the long trestle tables where everyone was discussing the music, the singers, the orchestration, how lucky they were to be in a Weyr that got preferential treatment. There was, of course, a tradition of music on Pern, brought by their ancestors and encouraged by not only the Teaching Hall but also Weyr and Hold. Everyone was taught how to read music from an early age and encouraged to learn to play at least one instrument, if not two or three. It was a poor hold indeed that could not produce a guitar or at least pipes and a drum to liven winter nights and special occasions.

The meal was very good—though Iantine had to concentrate on tasting it. Most of his senses were involved in sitting thigh to thigh with Debera. She was quite volatile, talking to everyone, with a great many things to say about the various performances and the melodic lines that she particularly liked.

Her cheeks were flushed and her eyes very bright. He'd never seen her so elated. But then, he knew he was feeling high with an almost breathless anticipation of the dancing. He'd have her in his arms then, even closer than they were now. He could barely wait.

He had to, for of course on First Day, ice cream, the special and traditional sweet, was available and no one would want to miss that. It was a fruit flavor this year, creamy, rich, tangy with lots of tiny fruit pieces, and he was torn between eating slowly—which meant the confection might turn sloppy since the Lower Cavern was warm indeed—or gulping it down firm and cold. He noticed that Debera ate quickly, so he did.

As soon as the diners finished, they dismantled the tables and pushed back the chairs so there'd be space for the dancing. The musicians, reassembling in smaller units so that the dance music would be continuous, were tuning up their instruments again.

When all was ready, K'vin led Zulaya, resplendent in the red brocade dress of her portrait, onto the floor for their traditional opening of the dance. Iantine caught himself wanting to sketch the distinguished-looking couple, but he'd hidden his pad in the pile of tables and had to content himself with storing the details in his mind. He'd never seen Zulaya flirt so with K'vin, and the Weyrleader was responding gallantly. He did notice some riders talking among themselves, their eyes on the two Leaders, but he couldn't hear what was said, and while the glances were speculative, it wasn't his business.

Next the wing leaders handed their partners out on the floor for three turns before the wing seconds joined them. Then Tisha, partnered by Maranis, the Weyr medic, whirled very gracefully in among the dancers. The first dance ended but now the floor was open to everyone. The next number was a brisk two-step.

"Will you dance with me, Debera?" Iantine asked with a formal bow.

Eyes gleaming, head held high and smiling as if her face would split apart, Debera responded with a deep dip. "Why, I was hoping you'd ask, Iantine!"

"I get the next one," Leopol cried, appearing unexpectedly beside them, looking up at Debera, his eyes exceedingly bright.

"Did you sneak some wine tonight?" Iantine asked, suspicious.

"Who'd give me any?" Leopol replied morosely.

"No one would give you anything you couldn't take another way, Leo," Debera said. "But I'll keep you a dance. Later on."

And she stepped toward the floor, Iantine whisking her away from the boy as fast as he could.

"Even for a Weyr lad, he's precocious," Debera said, and she held up her arms as she moved into his.

"He is at that," Iantine replied, but he didn't want to talk about Leopol at all as he swung her lithe body among the dancers and eased them away to the opposite side of the floor from Leopol.

"He'll follow, you know, until he gets his dance," she said, grinning up at him.

"We'll see about that," and he tightened his arms possessively around her strong slender body.

Will I dance when I'm older? Iantine clearly heard the green dragon ask.

Startled, he looked down at Debera and saw by the laughter in her eyes that the dragon had spoken to them both.

"Dragons don't dance," Debera said in her fond dragontone. Iantine had noticed that she had a special one for Morath.

"They sing," Iantine said, wondering how he was ever going to eliminate Morath from the conversation long enough to speak about *them.*

She'll listen to anything you say. Morath's voice, so much like Debera's, sounded in his head.

Iantine grimaced, wondering how under the sun he could manage any sort of a private conversation with his beloved.

I won't listen then. Morath sounded contrite.

"How long do you think you'll be at Benden, Ian?" Debera asked.

He wondered if Morath had spoken to her, too, but decided against asking, though he didn't want to discuss his departure at all. Certainly not with Debera, the reason he desperately wanted to stay at Telgar.

"Oh," he said as casually as he could, "I'd want to do my best for Lord Bridgely and his Lady. They've been my sponsors, you see, and I owe them a lot."

"Do you know them well?"

"What? Me? No, my family's mountain holders."

"So were mine."

"Were?"

Debera gave a wry laugh. "Don't let's talk about families."

"I'd far rather talk about us," he said and then mentally kicked himself for such a trite response.

Debera's face clouded.

"Now what did I say wrong?" He tightened his arms on her reassuringly. Her expression was so woeful.

She's been upset about something Tisha told the weyrlings yesterday. I know I said I wouldn't interfere but sometimes it's needed.

"You didn't," Debera said at the same time, so he wasn't sure who had said what, since the voices were so alike.

"But something is troubling you?"

She didn't answer immediately but her hands tightened where they gripped him.

"C'mon, now, Deb," and he tried to jolly her a bit. "I'll listen to anything you have to say."

She gave him an odd glance. "That's just it."

"What is?" ·

"You wanting to talk to me, dance with only me and—"

"Ooooh," and suddenly Iantine had a hunch. "Tisha gave all the riders that 'don't do anything you'll be sorry for at Turn's End' lecture?" She gave him a startled look. And he grinned back at her. "I've been read that one a time or two myself, you know."

"But you don't know," she said, "that it's different for dragonriders. For green riders with very immature dragons." Then she gave him a horrified look as if she hadn't meant to be so candid. "Oh!"

He pulled her closer to him, even when she resisted, and chuckled. All those casual questions he'd asked dragonriders explained all that she didn't say.

"Green dragons are . . . how do I put it, kindly? Eager, loving, willing, too friendly for their own good . . ."

She stared up at him, a blush suffusing her cheeks, her eyes angry and her body stiffening against the rhythm of the dance. They were about to pass an opening, one of the corridors that led back to the storage areas of the Weyr. He whirled them in that direction despite her resistance, speaking in a persuasively understanding tone.

"You're the rider of a young green and she's much too young for any sexual stimulation. But I don't think a kiss will do her any damage, and I've *got* to kiss you once before I have to go to Benden."

And he did so. The moment their lips touched, although she tried to resist, their mutual attraction made the contact electric. She could not have resisted responding—even to preserve Morath's innocence.

Finally, breathless, they separated, but not by more than enough centimeters to let air into their lungs. Her body hung almost limply against his, and only because he was leaning against the wall did Iantine have the strength to support them both.

That's very nice, you know.

"Morath!" Debera jerked her body upright, though her hands clenched tightly on his neck and shoulder. "Oh . . . dear, what have I done?"

"Not as much to her as you have to me," Iantine said in a shaky voice. "She doesn't sound upset or anything."

Debera pushed away to stare up at him—he thought she had never looked so lovely.

"You heard Morath?"

"Hmmm, yes."

"You mean, that wasn't the first time?" She was even more startled.

"Hmmm. She knows my name, too," he said, plunging in with a bit of information that he knew might really distress her, but now was the time to be candid.

Debera's eyes widened even more and her face had paled in the glowlight of the corridor. She leaned weakly against him.

"Oh, what do I do now?"

He stroked her hair, relieved that she hadn't just stormed off, leaving all his hopes in crumbs.

"I don't think we upset Morath with that little kiss," he said softly.

"*Little* kiss?" Her expression went blank. "I've never been kissed like that before in my life."

Iantine laughed. "Me neither. Even if you didn't want to kiss me back." He hugged her, knowing that the critical moment had passed. "I have to say this, Debera: I love you. I can't get you out of my mind. Your face . . . and . . ." he added tactfully because it was also true, ". . . Morath's decorate the margin of every sketch I draw. I'm going to miss you like . . . like you'd miss Morath."

She caught in her breath at even the mention of such a possibility.

"Iantine, what can I say to that? I'm a dragonrider. You know that Morath is always first with me," she said gently, touching his face.

He nodded. "That's as it should be," he said, although he heartily wished he could be her sole and only concern.

"I'm glad you do know that, but Ian . . . I don't know what I feel about you, except that I did like your kiss." Her eyes were tender and she glanced shyly away from him. "I'm even glad you did kiss me. I've sort of wanted to know . . ." she said with a ripple in her voice, but still shy.

"So I can kiss you again?"

She put her hand on his chest. "Not quite so fast, Iantine! Not quite so fast. For my sake as well as Morath's. Because . . ." and then she blurted out the next sentence, "I know I'm going to miss you . . . almost . . . as much as I'd miss Morath. I didn't know a rider could be so involved with another human. Not like this. And," she increased pressure on the hand that held them apart because he wanted so to kiss her for that, "I can't be honestly sure if it's not because Morath rather likes you, too, and is influencing me."

I am not, said Morath firmly, almost indignantly.

"She says . . ." Debera began as Iantine said, "I heard that."

They both laughed and the sensual tension between them eased. He made quick use of the opportunity to kiss her, lightly, to prove that he could and that he did understand about Morath. He had also actually asked as many questions about rider liaisons as discretion permitted. What he'd learned had been both reassuring and unsettling. There were more ramifications to human affairs than he had ever previously suspected. Dragonrider-human ones could get very complicated. And the green dragons being so highly strung and sexually oriented were the most complex.

"I guess I'm lucky she talks to me at all," Iantine said. "Look, love, I've said what I've wanted to say. I've heard what Morath has to say, and we can leave it there for now. I've got to go to Benden Hold, and Morath has to . . . mature." He gently tightened his arms around his beloved. "If I'm welcome to come back . . . to the Weyr, I will return. Am I welcome?"

"Yes, you are," Debera said as Morath also confirmed it.

"Well, then . . ." He kissed her lightly, managing to break it off before the emotion that could so easily start up again might fire. ". . . let us dance, and dance and dance. That should cause no problems, should it?"

Of course, the words were no sooner out of his mouth than he knew that having her so close to him all evening was going to be a trial of his self-control.

His lips tingled as he led her back, her fingers trustingly twined into his. The dance was only just ending as he put his arms around her, so they managed just one brief spin. Since he now felt far more secure, he did let Leopol partner Debera for one fast dance, lest he'd never hear the last of it from the boy. Other than that surrender, he and Debera danced together all night, cementing the bond that had begun: danced until the musicians called it a night.

He was going to hate to be parted from her, more now because they did have an understanding—of sorts—but there was no help for it. He had the duty to Benden Hold.

**New Year 258 After Landing;
College, Benden Hold, Telgar Weyr**

On the first official day of the new year, 258 AL, Clisser had a chance to review the four days of Turn's End. Frantic at times, certainly hectic despite the most careful plans and the wealth of experience, the main performances—the First Day "Landing Suite," and Second Day Teaching Songs and Ballads—had gone very well: far better than he had anticipated given the scanty rehearsals available for some of the performers. Fort's tenor, for instance, had been a bit ragged in his big solo: he really should have held that final note the full measure. Sheledon glowered from the woodwind section: he'd've sung the part himself but he hadn't the voice for it. But then, the only solos that Sheledon wouldn't find fault with would be Sydra's, and she never failed to give a splendid performance. Bethany's flute obbligatos had been remarkable, matching Sydra's voice to perfection.

Paulin had been on his feet time after time, applauding the soloists and, at the finale, surreptitiously brushing a tear from his eye. Even old S'nan looked pleased, also fatuous, but on the whole Clisser was relieved at the reception. He hoped the two performances had been popular elsewhere on the continent. A great deal of work had been put into rehearsals from folks who had little spare time as it was.

The Teaching Songs and Ballads had been just as well received, with people going about humming some of the tunes. Which was exactly what the composers had hoped for. Fortunately, honors were even between Jemmy and Sheledon for catchy tunes. He caught himself humming the Duty Song chorus. That had gone particularly well. He wouldn't have to deal with a laborious copying of the Charter once youngsters learned *those* words by heart. It certainly fit the bill. Copies of all the new songs were being made by the teachers themselves, who would then require their students to transcribe them, and that saved a lot of effort for his College.

Really, a printing press of some kind must be put high on the list of Kalvi's engineering staff. They'd managed quite a few small motor-driven, solar panel gadgets, why not a printing press? But that required paper, and the forests were going to be vulnerable for the next fifty years no matter how assiduous the Weyrs were in their protective umbrella.

One tangle of Thread could destroy acres of trees in the time it took to get a groundcrew to the affected area.

He sighed. If only the organics plastic machinery were still operating . . . but the one unit housed in the Fort storage had rusted in the same flooding that had ruined so much else.

" 'Ours not to wonder what were fair in life,' " he quoted to himself, "which is a saying I should get printed out to remind me that we've got what we've got and have to make do."

He couldn't help but feel somewhat depressed, though. There had been some high moments these last few days and it was hard to resume normal routine. Not every one in the teaching staff was back, though all should have checked in by late evening. He'd hear then how the performances went elsewhere. He'd have to wait to learn how the new curriculum was working. By springtime he'd know what fine tuning would be needed. He could count on Sallisha for that, he was sure. By springtime Thread would fall and the easy pace they had all enjoyed would be a memory.

Ah, that was what he had to do. He'd put it off long enough—write up the roster for groundcrews drafted from students over fifteen and teachers. He'd promised that to Lord Paulin and, what with everything else, never produced it. He pulled a fresh sheet of paper from the drawer, then stopped, put it back, and picked up a sheet from the reuse pile. A clean side was all he needed. Mustn't waste or he'd want soon enough.

◆ ◆ ◆

Lady Jane herself led Iantine to his quarters, asking all the gracious questions a hostess did: Where had he been for Turn's End? Had he enjoyed himself? Had he had the opportunity to hear the splendid new music from the College? What instrument did he play? What did he hear from his parents? He answered as well as he could, amazed at the difference between his reception here and the one he'd had at Bitra. Lady Jane was a fluttery sort of woman, not at all what he would have expected as the spouse of a man like Bridgely.

She must be extremely efficient under all that flutter, he thought, contrasting the grace, order, and appearance of the public rooms with those at Bitra, and seeing a vast difference between the two.

No low-level living for him here, either. Lady Jane led him onto the family's floor, urging the two drudges who were carrying the canvases and skybroom wood panels to mind their steps and not damage their burdens.

She opened the door, presenting him with the key, and he was bemused as he followed her into a large dayroom, at least ten times larger than the cubicle at Bitra, on the outside of the hold so that it had a wide, tall window, facing northeast. It was a gracious room, too, the stone walls washed a delicate greeny-white, the furnishings well-polished wood with a pleasing geometric pattern in greens and beige on the coverings.

"I do know that Artists prefer a north light, but this is the best we can do for you on that score . . ." Benden's Lady fluttered her hands here and there. They were graceful, small hands, with only the wide band of a spousal ring on the appropriate finger. Another contrast to the Bitran tendency to many gaudy jewels.

"It's far more than I expected, Lady Jane," he said as sincerely as he could.

"And I'm sure it's far more than you had at Bitra Hold," she said with a contemptuous sniff. "Or so I've been told. You may be sure that Benden Hold would never place an Artist of your rank and ability with the drudges. Bitrans may lay claim," and her tone expressed her doubt, "to having a proper Bloodline, but they have never shown much couth!" She noticed him testing the sturdiness of the easel. "That's from stores. It belonged to Lesnour. D'you know his work?"

"Lesnour? Indeed." Iantine dropped his hand from the smoothly waxed upright. Lesnour, who'd lived well past the hundred mark, had designed and executed Benden Hold's murals and was famed for his use of color. He'd also compiled a glossary of pigments available from indigenous materials, a volume Iantine had studied and which had certainly helped him at Bitra.

Lady Jane pushed open the wooden door into the sleeping room. Not large but still generous in size: he could see the large bed, its four posts carved with unusual leaves and flowers, probably taken from Earth's botany. She pointed at the back to the third room of the suite: a private toilet and bath. And the whole suite was warm. Benden had been constructed with all the same conveniences that Fort Hold boasted.

"This is much more than I need, Lady Jane," Iantine said, almost embarrassed as he dropped his carisak to the floor of the dayroom.

"Nonsense. We know at Benden what is due a man of your abilities. Space," and she gave a graceful sweep of her hand about the room, "is so necessary to compose the thoughts and to allow the mind to relax." She did another complicated arabesque with her hands and smiled up at him. He smiled back at her, trying to act gracious rather than amused at her extravagant manner. "Now, the evening meal will be served in the Great Hall at eight and you'll dine at the upper table," she said with a firm smile to forestall any protests. "Would you care to have someone put at your disposal to help with your materials?"

"No, thank you most kindly, Lady Jane, but I'm used to doing for myself." Maybe he could have borrowed Leopol for a few weeks? There was certainly enough space for the boy to be accommodated in with him.

So she left, after he once again expressed his profuse thanks for the courtesies.

He prowled about the rooms, washed his hands and face, learning that the water came very hot out of the spigot. The bath had been carved out of the rock, deep enough for him to immerse himself completely, and sufficiently long to lie flat out in the water. Even the Weyr hadn't such elegant conveniences.

He unpacked his clothing so the wrinkles would hang out of his good green shirt and began setting up his workplace. And then sat down in one of the upholstered chairs, plunked his feet down on the footstool, leaned back and sighed. He could get accustomed to this sort of living, so he could! Except for the one lack—Debera.

He wondered briefly if Lady Jane would flutter while she posed for him. And how would he pose her? Somehow he must put in the flutter of her but also her grace and charm. He wondered what instrument she played with those small hands. If only Debera weren't so far away.

◆ ◆ ◆

Iantine might not have been pleased to know that she was at that very moment the subject of discussion between the Weyrleaders at Telgar.

"No," Zulaya was saying, shaking her head, "she has more sense than to jeopardize Morath. And I think Iantine would not risk his standing with the Weyr in an indiscretion. I understand from Leopol that Iantine wants to come back. Tisha wasn't worried about *that* pair. They may have danced till the musicians quit, but they were visible all the time. Then, too, Debera's hold-bred. Jule's the one I might be worried about, especially since she and T'red have been weyrmates."

"They're not now?" K'vin asked sharply.

"Of course not," and Zulaya dismissed his anxiety on that and then grinned up at him. "T'red's biding his time. He knows he'd better."

K'vin sighed and checked off another matter discussed with Zulaya.

"Let's see—a tenth-month Hatching, so by this fourth month, the greens won't be flying yet."

"Oh, now, I'd say Morath might. If she keeps growing at the same rate, her wings'll be strong enough to test by late spring. But we don't need to include the latest Hatching in our calculations, K'vin," she said, and leaned toward him and the lists he was compiling. "They've got all the site-recognition training to do, the long-range flights to build wing muscle. If we don't need to force their training, let's not. We've got fifty years to use them . . ."

"Do we?" and K'vin tossed his pencil to the table, leaning back and sighing.

Zulaya reached a hand across to tap his arm reassuringly. "Don't fret so, Kev," she said. "That can't change events. I think that the group we're going to have trouble with is not the babies, but the elderlies. Those old riders're going to insist on being assigned to fighting wings, you know."

K'vin closed his eyes, shaking his head as if he could somehow lose that problem. "I know, I know," he said, all too aware that he couldn't avoid making a decision there. "They'll be more of a liability than the youngsters ever would—trying to show that they've lost nothing to their age."

"Well, the dragons won't have," she said, and then she, too, sighed. "But we can't baby them: that's not fair. And the dragons' reflexes are as fast as ever. They'll protect their riders . . ."

"But who'll protect the rest of the wing from slow reflexes? You know how close Z'ran and T'lel came to disaster yesterday morning?"

"They were showing off," Zulaya said. "Meranath chewed the two browns out as if they were weyrlings."

"We won't have time for that during a Fall . . ." K'vin rubbed the ache in the back of his neck. "I've called a safety-strap check for the entire Weyr."

"Kev," she said gently, "we had one last week. Don't you remember?"

"We can't have enough," he snapped back at her, and then shot her a look of apology.

"It's the waiting that's getting to you," Zulaya said with a rueful smile. "To all of us."

K'vin gave a snort. "So do we pray that Thread falls early?"

"I wouldn't wish that on us, but we could legitimately go south on an excursion . . ."

"Not," he objected emphatically, "another Aivas expedition."

"No, no!" She laughed at his vehemence. "But we could check on the Tubberman grubs: see how much farther they have penetrated. We should do so soon now anyhow, since we're supposed to check on their spread. A trip away, out of this cold, would lift spirits. After the excitement of Turn's

End, First Month is always a letdown. Who knows? We might even find some of those spare parts Kalvi's always whingeing about."

"Spare parts?" K'vin asked.

"Yes, ones lost in the Second Crossing storm."

"Now that's a real lost cause," K'vin said.

"Whether it is or not, it provides a training exercise in the sun, away from here and all of that," and she pointed at the disorder of lists and reports on the table.

"Where would we go?" K'vin sat upright in his chair, examining the possibility.

"Well, we should check the original site at Calusa . . ." She retrieved the relevant chart from the storage cabinet and brought it to the table. K'vin hastily cleared a space. "Then look along the Kahrainian coast where the Armada had a long stop for repairs."

"That's all been gone over so often . . ."

"And not much retrieved. Anyway, it's not so much what we find, but more that we went for a look," Zulaya said with a droll grin.

"The entire Weyr?"

"Well, the fighting wings, certainly. Leave the training ones here, give them responsibility . . . and see how they like it."

"J'dar had better be in charge," K'vin said, glancing to see if she agreed.

She shrugged. "J'dar or O'ney."

"No, J'dar."

Oddly enough, she gave him a pleased smile. He hadn't expected that, since she had specifically named O'ney, one of the oldest bronze riders. He tried to defer to her judgment whenever possible, but he'd noticed that O'ney tended to be unnecessarily officious.

"Now, this is as far as grubs had migrated on last winter's check," she said, running her finger along Rubicon River.

"How're the grubs supposed to get across that?" K'vin asked, tapping the contour lines for the steep cliffs that lined the river, gradually tapering down above the Sea of Azov.

"The Agric guys say they'll either go around or be carried across the river as larvae in the digestive tracts of wherries and some of those sport animals that were let loose. They have been breeding, you know."

Zulaya was teasing now, since she knew very well that Charanth had had to rescue him from a very large, hungry orange-and-black-striped feline. Charanth had been highly insulted because the creature had actually then attacked him, a bronze dragon! The incident was a leveling one for both rider and dragon.

"Oh, and don't I know it. I'll not be caught that way twice."

"It grew a mighty fine hide," she said, her eyes dancing with challenge.

"Catch your own, Zu. Now, let's see . . . should we check and see if any of the other Weyrs want to come? Make this a joint exercise?"

"Why?" she countered with a shrug. "The whole idea is to get our wings away for a bit for something besides Fall readiness. Meranath," and she turned to her queen, who was lounging indolently on her couch, her head turned in their direction and her eyes open, "would you be good enough to spread the word that the Weyr's going off on an exercise," and she grinned at K'vin, "tomorrow, first light? That should startle a few."

"Undoubtedly," and glancing at Zulaya for permission, K'vin made a second request of Meranath, "And ask J'dar and T'dam to step up here, please?"

The sun will be much warmer in the south, Meranath said, *and we will all like that, K'vin.*

"Glad you approve," he said, giving the gold queen a little bow. He was also considerably gratified that she was using his name more. Could that mean that Zulaya was thinking of him more often? He kept that question tight in his mind, where even Charanth wouldn't hear it. Did she really approve of his leadership? Zulaya never gave him any clues despite her courtesies to him in public: though he certainly appreciated that much. He didn't seem any closer to a real intimacy with her, and he wanted one badly. Would he ever figure out how to achieve that? Could that be why she had suggested this excursion?

"How long has it been since there was an update on the grubs?"

She shrugged. "That's not the point. We need a diversion and this makes a good one. Also, someone should do it for the Agric records. And we'll probably have to go down during Fall to see if the grubs really do what they're supposed to do."

"Do you want to put us out of business?" he asked.

Zulaya shook her head. "As long as Thread falls from Pernese skies, we won't be out of business. Psychologically, it's imperative that we keep as much of the stuff as possible *off* the surface of the planet. The grubs are just an extra added precaution, not the total answer."

The two Weyrleaders had forgotten to caution their dragons against mentioning the destination, and it was all over the Weyr by dinnertime. They were besieged by requests from Weyrfolk to be taken along. Even Tisha was not shy about requesting a lift.

"Some of the bronzes would need to carry two passengers," K'vin said, doing some quick calculations.

"The weyrlings would have to stay," Zulaya said, that necessity causing a brief hitch to the euphoria. But she shrugged. "We'll make an occasion for T'dam to take them down once they are flighted, but they're Weyrbound this time."

"That wouldn't be until after Thread has started," K'vin said, looking doubtful.

"Sure, we know when it falls, north or south, and a day off for the auxiliaries is no big thing. Plan it for a rainy day, here," Zulaya said, "and they won't mind having the sun down south."

So that issue was settled.

The entire Weyr assembled, loading passengers and supplies for an outing that was now scheduled for three days. K'vin allowed they would need that long to make a diligent survey of grub penetration. He brought with him maps and writing materials so he could make accurate records.

The morning had its moment of humor: getting Tisha aboard brown Branuth had been a struggle, involving not only Branuth's rider, T'lel (who laughed so hard he had hiccups), but four other riders, the strongest and tallest.

Branuth, an extremely quizzical expression on his long face, craned his head around to watch and got a bad cramp in his neck muscles doing so. T'lel and Z'ran had to massage him.

"Stop that and get up here, T'lel," Tisha was yelling, her thick legs stuck out at angles from her perch between the neck ridges. "I'll be split. And if I'm split, you'll suffer. I never should have said I'd come. I should know better than to leave my caverns for any reason whatsoever. This is *very* uncomfortable. Stop that guffawing, T'lel. Stop it right now. It isn't funny where I'm sitting. Get up here and let's go!"

Getting Tisha aboard Branuth had taken so much time that everyone else was in place and ready to go by the time T'lel did manage to get in front of Tisha.

"Not only am I being split, I'm also being bisected by these ridges. Did you sharpen them on purpose, T'lel? No wonder riders are so skinny. They'd have to be. Don't dragons grow ridges for large people? I should have had K'vin take me up. Charanth is a much bigger dragon . . . Why couldn't you have put me up on your bronze, K'vin?" Tisha shouted across the intervening space.

K'vin was trying to preserve his dignity as Weyrleader by not laughing at the sight of her, but he didn't dare look in her direction again. Instead he swiveled his torso so he could scan everyone, pleased to see all eyes on him— rider, passenger, and dragon. He peered upward to the rim, where more dragons awaited their departure, poised well clear of the newly positioned Eye and Finger rocks. Now he raised his arm.

Charrie, they are to assume their wing positions in the air.

They know. Charanth sounded petulant, for this was a frequent drill. K'vin slapped his neck affectionately with one hand while he gave his upheld right arm the pump.

All the dragons in the bowl lifted, swirling up dust and grit from the Bowl floor with such a battery of wings, and then those on the rim rose, sorting themselves out in the air to form their respective wings. Zulaya and the other queens positioned above the others.

And in formation in jig time, too. Let's go, Charrie.

With a great leap, Charanth was airborne. One sweep of his wings and he was level with the wings, another and he was in front of the queens. Heads turned upward and Charanth dutifully angled himself earthward so that all could see the Weyrleader.

Inform the Weyr that our destination is the Sea of Azov.

I have!

K'vin pumped his arm in the continuous gesture to signal *Go between!* The entire Weyr blinked out simultaneously.

Steady, he cautioned Charanth, pleased with that disciplined departure. *Now we go!*

Three seconds he counted and then the warm air above the brilliantly blue Sea of Azov was like the smack of a hot towel in his face. Charanth rumbled in pleasure.

K'vin was far more interested in discovering that the ranks of the dragons, wing by wing, had arrived still in formation. He grinned.

Please inform the wingleaders to take their riders to their separate destinations.

One by one the wings disappeared, with the exception of T'lel's, which had picked the sea area for their excursion site. The queens started to glide toward the shore, too, for they carried quite a few of the supplies that Tisha would need to set up her hearths for the evening meal.

Let's wait and let them all get safely to the surface, K'vin told Charanth, although part of him wanted to see how Tisha managed to dismount Branuth. He was therefore somewhat surprised, and at first a little concerned, when he saw a brown dragon detach itself from the main wing and glide in a landing, on the water, just short of the shore. Charanth had his head down and was observing the effort.

Branuth says she ordered it. She's swimming free of his back. Charanth sounded amused, too, and K'vin chuckled.

That was much more dignified.

Branuth says it was easier on him, too, but he doesn't think he should do the same back at Telgar.

Not with the water that cold this time of year.

We can now land? Branuth says the sun is warm.

I thought you wanted to hunt.

Later. NOW I want to get warm all over.

Charanth's preference was almost unanimous as the dragons spread out over both the pebbled beach and the shoreline, which was covered with a shrub that, when bruised by large dragon bodies, gave off a rich pungent odor, not at all unpleasant.

Tisha had some of the Weyrfolk off finding kindling and stones to make campfires, and to see what fruits might be ripe, and another group to fish where boulders had tumbled down into the sea like a breakwater.

"I'm going for a long swim," Zulaya called out to him as he and Charanth glided to a landing. She was already stripping off her jacket. "Meranath wants one, too." She touched down long enough to strip off the rest of her clothing, which she left in a neat pile on a boulder before making her way to the water.

"What about the grubs?"

"They'll wait," she yelled over her shoulder, wading out until the water was deep enough for swimming.

We don't have to go find grubs now, do we? asked Charanth plaintively, and the eyes he turned up to his rider whirled with a yellow anxiety.

"No, we don't," K'vin said. "Grubs were an excuse to leave the Weyr for a few days."

He shucked his clothes, and dragon and rider joined the others in the warm Azovian waters.

◆ ◆ ◆

It might not have pleased K'vin to learn that almost every rider procrastinated over the stated objective of the journey south: grubs were, in fact, probably the last thing on anyone's mind. Sunning, swimming in the pleasant waters, hunting for dragons, and food-gathering for humans took precedence—and space and time for absolute privacy.

P'tero and M'leng asked permission of V'last, their wingleader, to take their dragons hunting.

"Remember what K'vin told you about the sport creatures down here," V'last said, serving the same warning to the other riders wishing to hunt their dragons.

P'tero and M'leng nodded obediently but, as soon as they left the clearing where their wing had landed on the Malay River, they laughed at the very notion that any creature could be dangerous to *their* dragons.

"It's really hot here," M'leng said, glancing back at the river.

"We'll be hotter after we've hunted the dragons," P'tero said. "But once that's done we really don't have to do another thing until dinner."

"So let's not come back here until just before," M'leng said, laughing recklessly. "Or we'll end up having to hunt or fish or gather it."

"There're enough Weyrfolk with us to do all that. And enjoy," P'tero said, rather condescendingly. "Let's get out of here."

He made a running jump and neatly vaulted onto Ormonth's blue back. M'leng simultaneously boarded green Sith.

"What game shall we go after?" M'leng asked.

"Whatever we see first," P'tero replied, and pumped his arm to send them both aloft. M'leng preferred him to be leader.

They didn't have far to go to see grazing herds of runner beasts, smaller than the ones they were accustomed to seeing in the holds. But when they also saw other dragons in the sky, gliding in to hunt, P'tero signaled M'leng to fly on, in a southwesterly direction. They hadn't gone very far before both found it necessary to strip off their flying jackets, and then their shirts, which were winter weight anyhow. P'tero admired M'leng's compact body. The green rider was small-boned, which had always delighted P'tero, with a surprisingly strong and agile wiry frame. He was also winter-white, right to his collar. P'tero giggled. He looked so funny, as if he had two different skins.

Then the blue rider became fascinated with the tropical terrain around them, subtly different from the North's warmer holds. Nerat was rain forests and vast tracks of almost impenetrable jungle except along the western side, whereas Ista was sharp hills and deep valleys, also densely vegetated. But here, a vast grassland, similar in some respects to the plains of Keroon, spread out in all directions, dotted by upthrusts of bare yellow rock, occasional copses of angular trees with fronds spilling from the crests, and large, wide-branched trees like islands. The dragons' flight over some of these caused flocks of wherries and other avian forms to debouch in frantic escape.

Can I eat them? Ormonth inquired of his rider, speeding up in case he was allowed to give chase.

What? Those tough mouthfuls? P'tero asked scornfully. Then he cupped his hands and shouted at M'leng. "Ormonth's hungry enough to eat wherries!"

"Sith wanted to, as well. We'd better feed them," M'leng yelled back. "Over there!" and he pointed to one of the rock piles. One of the spreading trees had grown right up against the pile, shading the long incline to the top.

P'tero thought the formation looked like the prow of a ship, with midships plunging into the sea of ground. And the tree a muchly misplaced mast.

M'leng nodded vigorously in approval and pumped his arm, kicking Sith into a wide curve so that they came up to the prow to land. A fine breeze blew against them from the south, cooling the perspiration on their bare torsos.

As soon as they landed, the two young men stripped off their heavy flight pants and boots. They had to put their socks back on for the rock was far too hot for bare feet.

M'leng, who had good distance vision, covered his eyes with one hand, peering to the west, where a long dark line seemed to be moving.

"Oh, good, herd beasts." He hauled Sith's head around and then pushed it in the right direction. "See? You can eat those. Much better than wherries. Off you go now!" And he gave Sith a thump of dismissal.

"Follow Sith, Ormonth," and P'tero shoved the blue's head to the right. "Hunt with him, and you can't get into any trouble that way. We'll watch from here."

Ormonth shifted weight from one diagonal to the other, his eyes whirling with a trace of anxious yellow.

"What's the matter with you?" P'tero demanded, wanting both dragons to be away so he and M'leng could have some real privacy. And if the pair were busy enough hunting and eating, they'd pay no attention at all to what their riders were doing.

Smell something!

"M'leng, does Sith smell anything?" P'tero was annoyed but you didn't ignore your dragon.

"Different smells down here, that's all." M'leng shrugged, his eager expression indicating that he wanted the dragons away as much as P'tero did.

"I'll keep my eyes open," P'tero assured Ormonth, and slapped him peremptorily to be on his way.

The two launched upward at the same moment, and P'tero watched with some pride the blue's elegant flight attitude as he made height before he would glide down toward his prey.

M'leng slipped in under P'tero's arm. "Oooh, your hide is hot. We'd best be careful not to burn in this sun."

"We'll be all right if we move a lot."

"And we will, won't we?"

They enjoyed each other's company so much that neither were aware when the breeze altered to the west. It still cooled their bare bodies, drying the sweat they had generated. They weren't even aware of much until two things happened at the same instant: Ormonth's angry scream reverberated in P'tero's skull and he was rammed down hard against M'leng so that he cracked his chin on the rock as sharp things tore into his buttocks.

"ORMONTH!" he shrieked mentally and vocally.

M'leng was limp under him as he writhed in agony from whatever was attacking him.

Help me! he howled, struggling to turn and see what was trying to eat him.

A dark shadow and the air pressure above him seemed compressed: a most hideous roar sent a carrion stink and hot breath across his bare back. The talons were ripped from his flesh, causing him to shriek again. Something heavy and furry was being hauled across his tortured legs and away. He caught a glimpse of green hide and then blue. And then something large and tawny that seemed to come from nowhere. A blue tail curled protectingly around him. Above his head he heard Ormonth roaring, which turned to shrieks of pain and anger, but mostly anger. He was mentally assailed by vivid images and emotions of revenge that were totally alien to a dragon mind.

As waves of almost unendurable agony gripped him, he realized that Ormonth and Sith were rending whatever had attacked him into shreds; showering blood and gobbets of hot flesh all over him. Then he realized that he was lying on top of M'leng, who was suddenly being pulled away. To his horrified eyes, he saw a great brown paw, dirty big yellow claws unsheathing and curling into his weyrmate's shoulderblade, blood welling up. Despite the pain in his legs and back, he lurched across M'leng and beat at the paw, struggling to lift the claws out of his lover's body.

More noise, more draconic roars, and suddenly there was space above him, letting in fresh air, and the sight of other dragons. Two were attacking the tawny lean creatures that were swarming up the rock outthrust. The dragons hauled them backward by their tails or hindquarters while the creatures writhed and roared and spat defiance, turning to attack the dragons. One had curled itself around a brown's forearm, slashing out at a dragon face.

"M'leng, M'leng, answer me!" P'tero cried, turning his lover's face toward him, slapping his cheeks.

Booted feet stopped by M'leng's head.

"Oh help us, help us!" he pleaded, clutching at the boots. "Help me! I'm dying!" The pain in his legs was so awful . . .

"Who's got the fellis? Where's the numbweed?"

As P'tero felt himself slipping into oblivion, he wondered how under the sun Zulaya had got here and if he was dying.

CHAPTER XVI

Cathay, Telgar Weyr, Bitra Hold, Telgar

P'tero didn't die, although for some days he wished he had. The shame of being attacked, of endangering M'leng, of being responsible for injuring nine dragons—when K'vin had particularly warned everyone to be careful—was almost more than he could bear. M'leng might say that P'tero had saved his life—although he had to have his shoulder wound stitched—but P'tero knew that was incidental in the sequence of the attack. Both Sith and Ormonth had suffered from the fangs and claws of the attacking felines, for the creatures had not been easily quelled. Meranath nursed a bite on her left forearm and a slash on her cheek. P'tero hadn't yet been able to look Zulaya in the eye. V'last's Collith's worst injuries were to his forearm, gashed to the bone by the powerful hind legs of the female attacking him. The dragon-lion battle had been fierce while it lasted, for the lions had no fear of the dragons and the entire pride of some fourteen adult beasts had joined battle with the dragons.

Meranath had reacted instantly to Ormonth's shriek; in fact, so quickly that she had actually left Zulaya behind. The Weyrwoman had been astonished: dragons simply didn't do that. Though later, Leopol told P'tero, she had laughed about it—since she'd been swimming and would not have appreciated being hauled dripping wet to companion her dragon. She'd followed, quickly enough, with V'last, K'vin, and others who answered the mayday.

"She was some put out, too," Leopol went on, relishing the telling, "because the dragons made a mess of good lion fur . . . well, what they didn't eat."

P'tero gasped. "The dragons ate the lions?"

"Sure, why not?" Leopol shrugged, grinning. "The entire pride attacked the dragons. But they let the cubs go, you know, though some folks thought they ought to get rid of all they could find. V'last said Collith said they were quite tasty, if a bit tough to chew. Waste not, want not. But Zulaya really would have liked a lion fur for her bed."

P'tero shuddered. He never wanted to see anything to do with lions ever again.

"You shoulda seen yourself brought in, P'tero," Leopol added, gesturing to the temporary quarters that had been set up to tend the badly injured riders. "Charanth himself carried you back in his arms."

"He did?" P'tero's chagrin reached a new depth.

"And O'ney's bronze Queth brought M'leng in. Your wing helped Ormonth and Sith back. Actually, they came in sort of piggyback on Gorianth and Spelth. They were pretty shaken, you know."

P'tero had heard echoes of that journey from Ormonth, who, bless his heart, had never once criticized his rider: another source of infinite distress to P'tero. The blue had been intensely grateful to his weyrmates for their assistance as he couldn't leave his rider out of his sight. It had been all the other dragons could do—although Leopol did not relate this—to reassure Ormonth and Sith that neither of their riders would die.

The Weyr had set up a hasty camp to tend the injured, for some, like P'tero and Collith, couldn't risk being taken *between* until their wounds had scabbed over. K'vin had sent to Fort for Corey to stitch the worst wounds. Medic Maranis was more than competent for the dragons' wounds, but he needed reassurance on his treatment of the two injured riders. Messengers had gone back to Telgar Weyr to reassure those whose dragons had reported the accident and to bring back more equipment for an extended stay.

The two young riders had, in their innocence, chosen a site just above the cave home of a pride of lions. P'tero had never even heard of "lions." Evidently he could thank Tubberman for their existence, for they'd broken out of Calusa and bred quite handily in the wild. They were, Leopol told him with great relish, some of the sport beasts that Tubberman had been experimenting with.

This was not much consolation to P'tero while he lay on his stomach to let the deep fang and claw marks heal.

He worried endlessly that M'leng would no longer love him, with such a scarred and imperfect body. M'leng, however, seemed to dwell so on P'tero's heroism in protecting him with his own body that the blue rider decided not to mention the fact that it had not been entirely voluntary. M'leng had been unconscious from the moment of attack and had a great lump and a cut on the back of his head as well as the wound on his shoulder.

Zulaya had arrived to see P'tero trying to remove the claws from M'leng's body, so there was little the blue rider could say to contradict the Weyrwoman's version.

Tisha, coming to give him fellis early one morning, found him in tears, positive that he had lost M'leng with such a marred body.

"Nonsense, my lad," Tisha had said, soothing back his sweaty hair as she held the straw for his fellis juice to his lips. "He will only see what you endured for his sake, to save him. And those scars will heal quite nicely, thanks to Corey's neat stitching."

The reference to the skill of the Head Medic almost reduced him to tears again. He'd caused so much fuss.

"Indeed you have, but you've livened things up considerably, young man, and taught everyone some valuable lessons."

"I have?" P'tero would just as soon not have.

"For one, dragons think they're invulnerable . . . and they aren't. A very good lesson to take into Fall with them, I assure you. Cool some of the hotheads, so certain that it's just a matter of breathing fire in the right direction. For another, the Southern Continent has developed its own hazards . . ."

"Did the Weyr ever find out about the grubs?" P'tero asked, suddenly recalling the reason for the excursion.

Tisha burst out laughing, then stifled it, though P'tero's tent was a distance from any others. "There, lad, you've a good head as well as a brave heart. Yes, they completed the survey faster'n any other's ever been done."

P'tero learned later that the grubs had infested yet a few more kilometers westward and southward toward the Great Barrier Range in an uneven wave of expansion. Their progress into the sandy scrublands east of Landing had slowed to a few meters, and the agricultural experts were not particularly concerned: they were more eager to have the rich grass and forest lands preserved.

"So the trip hasn't been a waste?" P'tero said, relaxing as he felt the fellis spreading out.

Tisha gave him more maternal pats, settling the furs and making sure nothing was binding across his bottom and legs.

"By no means, lovey. Now you go back to sleep . . ."

As if he could prevent that, P'tero thought as the fellis took over and blotted out conscious thought as well as the pain.

◆ ◆ ◆

It was three weeks before P'tero's wounds had healed sufficiently for the trip back. The makeshift infirmary had more patients since there were other hazards besides large hungry and territorially minded felines in the Southern Continent: the heat, unwary exposure to too much sun, and a variety of other minor injuries. Leopol got a thorn in his foot which had festered, so he joined P'tero in the infirmary shelter until the poison drained.

Tisha and one of the Weyrfolk came down with a fever that had Maranis sending back to Fort for a medic more qualified than he in such matters. The woman recovered in a few days, but Tisha had a much harder time of it, sweating kilos off her big frame, to leave her so enervated Maranis was desperately worried about her. K'vin sent to Ista to beg a ship to transport her back North since he could not subject her to trying to climb aboard a dragon.

Her illness depressed everyone.

"You don't really know how important someone is," Zulaya said, having come down to reassure herself on the state of the convalescents, "until they're suddenly . . . not there!"

Her remark quite sunk P'tero's spirits. And Tisha was not there to jolly him out of his depression. M'leng was, and appeared in the shelter.

"How dare you be so self-centered?" the green rider said in a taut, outraged tone of voice.

"Huh?"

"Tisha's illness is *not* your fault. Leopol wasn't wearing shoes when he was told to and so his infected foot also isn't your fault. In fact, it isn't even your fault that we picked *that* rock out of all the ones we could have picked. It was *bad* luck, but nothing more, and I don't want Ormonth upsetting Sith anymore. D'you hear me?"

P'tero burst into tears. Just as he'd thought: M'leng didn't love him anymore.

Then M'leng's gentle arms went around him, and he was pulled into M'leng's chest and comforted with many caresses and kisses.

"Don't be such a stupid idiot, you stupid idiot. How could I *not* love you?"

Later P'tero wondered how he could ever have doubted M'leng.

When the convalescents did return to Telgar Weyr, they found Tisha once more in charge of the Lower Cavern. If her clothes were still loose on her frame, she was tanned from the sea voyage back from the mouth of the Rubicon and looked completely recovered.

Some of the green and blue riders in the wing had freshened up both P'tero's and M'leng's weyrs, with paint and new fabrics. The worn pillows had been replaced with plump ones.

"Because Tisha said you'd need to sit real *soft* for a while longer," and Z'gal giggled into his hand. "Lady Salda let us have feathers from the Turn's End birds."

Then Z'gal's lover, T'sen, brought an object from behind his back. P'tero stared at it, puzzled. It seemed to be a pad with very long thongs.

"Ah, what is it?"

Z'gal went into a laughing fit which annoyed T'sen, who scowled and kept pushing it at P'tero.

"To sit on, of course. It'll fit between neck ridges. We measured."

Belatedly but as effusively as he could, P'tero thanked T'sen for such a thoughtful gift. It wasn't so much his bottom that needed padding, but the muscles in the buttocks and down his legs that needed strengthening and massage to get them back in full working order. Of course, M'leng had been assiduous in the massage sessions, but P'tero was now concerned that he'd not be fit for fighting when Threadfall began. M'leng had been wounded in a much better site. He wouldn't miss a day's fighting.

There was wine, biscuits, and cheese for a small in-weyr party. M'leng capped the return celebrations by presenting P'tero with a flat wrapped parcel.

M'leng's eyes were shining in anticipation as P'tero untied the string, wondering what on earth this could be.

"Iantine's back, you know," M'leng said, breathlessly watching every movement of P'tero's hands.

The other riders were equally excited, and P'tero felt a spurt of petulance that they all knew what this was and were dying to see his reaction.

Naturally, the picture was picture side down when he finished unwrapping. P'tero was stunned silent when he turned it over, and his eyes nearly bugged out of his head at the scene depicted.

"But . . . but . . . Iantine wasn't even there!"

"He's so good, isn't he?" Z'gal said. "Did he get it all right? M'leng described it over and over . . ."

P'tero didn't quite know what to say, he was so bewildered. So much of it was what he would have given his right arm to have actually happened. The lion was clawing his backside, M'leng was sprawled under him, and there were more lions climbing up the rock, their vicious intent vivid in their posture, their open mouths showing fangs longer than a dragon's. P'tero was posed in an obvious act of defending his lover, his head turned, one arm upraised in a fist aimed at the attacking lion's head. But that wasn't the worst of the inaccuracies: both riders were fully clothed.

"P'tero?" M'leng's voice was quite anxious.

The blue rider swallowed. "I don't know what to say!"

Where am I? Ormonth wanted to know, evidently viewing it through his rider's eyes, as a dragon sometimes could.

"There!" and P'tero pointed to the dragons high up in the sky, wings straight up in a landing configuration, claws unsheathed, ready to grab the attacker, eyes a mad whirl of red and orange.

"Of course, I was unconscious," M'leng was saying, "but that's what Ormonth and Sith would have been doing. Wasn't it?" And he jabbed P'tero warningly.

"Exactly," P'tero said hurriedly. And it probably was, although he hadn't seen it, since he'd been looking in the other direction. "Everything happened so fast . . . it's almost eerie how Iantine has got it all down in one scene!" The amazement and respect in his voice was not the least bit feigned.

"Now," and M'leng pointed to the wall, "we've even got a hook for you to hang it on."

"Wouldn't you rather have it?" P'tero suggested hopefully.

"I've a copy of my own. Iantine did two, one for each of us," M'leng said, beaming proudly at his lover.

So P'tero had to hang the wretched reminder of the worst day of his life on his own wall, just where he couldn't miss it every morning of his life when he woke up.

"You'll never know how much this means to me," he said, and that, too, was quite truthful.

No one thought it the least bit odd that he got very, very drunk on wine that night.

◆ ◆ ◆

Ianath comes, Charanth told his rider.

"So Meranath tells me," Zulaya said before K'vin could speak. "He wants to know *all* about our trip south."

"I thought he'd given up on that notion to practice on the first Fall in the South," K'vin said. He tried to sound diffident.

Then Zulaya put a finger across her lips and pointed to the sleeping Meranath, a signal to K'vin to guard his thoughts to Charanth outside on the ledge. He nodded understanding.

"You don't fool me, Kev." She waggled her finger at him. "You and B'nurrin would give your eyeteeth to be in on the first real Fall—even if it does take place in the South where nothing could be hurt. Or, for that matter, saved."

"The grubs haven't spread across the entire Southern Continent, you know."

"That has nothing to do with *seeing* Thread for the first time in two hundred years."

He answered her droll smile with an abashed grin. "We don't need to have the dragons stoked up or anything," he said.

"Yes, but do you really want to have S'nan reproaching you for the rest of your career? That is, if you have one as a Weyrleader with this sort of antic in mind."

K'vin gave her a long look. "And don't tell me you like the fact that Sarai will be leading a queen's wing in the Fall before you will."

Zulaya rocked back in her chair just enough that K'vin realized he had made a palpable hit. She was honest enough to grin back.

"We don't even know that's what's on B'nurrin's mind," she said.

That's exactly what was on his mind, however, even after both Zulaya and K'vin enumerated the problems they'd had on that ill-favored excursion to the Southern Continent.

"In the first place," B'nurrin said, after repeating Zulaya's signal to shield their thoughts from their dragons, "we wouldn't be landing anywhere. And I don't mean for whole wings to go, Kev," he added quickly. "Not like it makes sense to fight the first actual Fall we do get—wherever *that* actually is . . ."

"And you're hoping S'nan doesn't go first," Zulaya said with a malicious grin.

"Too right on that," B'nurrin replied sourly. "He really gets up my nose, you know. I don't see any harm in having a look. I mean . . ." He paused, steeling himself a moment and staring straight into K'vin's eyes. "I'll be frank. I'm scared I'll be needing clean pants half a dozen times the first Fall I have to lead."

"I've wondered about that myself," K'vin admitted drolly. Out of the corner of his eye, he was surprised to notice a fleeting expression of approval on Zulaya's face. Surely B'ner had never mentioned that even as a remote possibility?

"So, I figure, if I get a good look at it *before* I have to act brave and unconcerned . . ."

"Anyone who isn't concerned about Thread's a damn fool," Zulaya put in.

"Agreed." B'nurrin nodded at her, grinning. "So, will you join me?"

"Because if two of us go, neither of us will be as much to blame?" K'vin asked, one eye on Zulaya's face.

B'nurrin scratched his jaw. "Yes, I guess that's the size of it."

"We're the first you've asked?"

B'nurrin gave a snort. "Well, I certainly wouldn't suggest it again to S'nan after the way he's clapped my ears back twice now. I figured you were more likely to than D'miel, though, you know, I think M'shall might come. If the weather's wrong at Fort and High Reaches, Benden's might be the first actual Fall we meet."

"M'shall might just be amenable at that," Zulaya said, "though he's the last one of the whole lot of you to doubt his abilities."

"That's true enough," B'nurrin said, then his enthusiasm got the better of him. "But look at it this way, even if old S'nan gets to fight this Pass's first Fall over Fort, we'll have been to one before him, so to speak." The Igen Weyrleader grinned with such boyish delight in the scheme that K'vin had to chuckle.

"How long is there between Southern's first and ours?" he asked. He was astonished to see that Zulaya was already unrolling Telgar Weyr's Thread chart onto the table.

"Roughly two weeks," she said.

"So we could go and see and not jeopardize the readiness of our own Weyrs," B'nurrin said.

"The first possible Fall over Fort is number seven. Number four is over the Landing site," Zulaya went on, tapping her finger on the various Thread corridors. "Five's no good, but six starts offshore of the mouth of Paradise River, not far from where we just were."

"What about the first three?" B'nurrin asked, craning his neck to see. "Oh, not really as good for safe coordinates, are they?" Then he looked up in a direct challenge at K'vin. "Will you join me?"

"I'd like to," K'vin said decisively, pointedly not looking in Zulaya's direction.

"I think I would, too," she said, surprising both men. When they regarded her in amazement, she added, "Well, queens' wings fly a lot lower into danger than the rest of the Weyr does. Makes it quicker for me to change *my* pants, but that doesn't mean I want to *have* to." Then, when they grinned with relief at her, she asked, "So, does Shanna want to come, too?"

Grinning even more broadly, B'nurrin said, "Only if you were going."

"At least one of you at Igen Weyr has some sense," Zulaya said. "Let's just sit on the idea for a few days. Just to be sure."

"Who will know, if we don't mention it?" B'nurrin asked, swiveling around to pointedly regard a sleeping Meranath.

◆   ◆   ◆

Paulin took Jamson with him to Bitra Hold. The older Lord Holder was still furious with his son for voting High Reaches Hold in the impeachment. But he had been unable to fault his son's management during his two-month convalescence. This had indeed restored Jamson to vigorous health, if not tolerance.

The change in Bitra was obvious from the moment Magrith dropped to the courtyard and Vergerin hurried down the steps to greet his guests. He had been alerted.

S'nan had insisted on being allowed to convey the two Lord Holders, for he had been as stunned as Jamson by the swiftness of the impeachment.

"My word!" the Fort Weyrleader said, staring about him. Magrith was staring, too, and Paulin had to suppress a grin since the dragon was looking in one direction, his rider in the other.

The courtyard was neat, and the recent snow swept from the paving, which showed fresh cement grouting. The road, in either direction, was no longer bordered by straggling bushes and weed trees. The row of cotholds sported fresh roof slates, repaired chimneys, and painted metal shutters, all obviously in good working order. Although some of the hold's upper windows were already shuttered tight, the facade was no longer festooned with dead vine branches. Sunlight glinted off solar panels that had been cleaned and repaired.

Piled under a newly built shed were HNO_3 tanks, racked for easy usage and the hoses and nozzles hung properly on pegs. Kalvi had told Paulin that he'd been asked to deliver the Bitran consignment within a week of Vergerin taking hold. And the following week he had sent his best teachers to instruct in their use and maintenance.

Vergerin wore a good tunic over his trousers but they were made of stout material and he had obviously been working before his guests arrived. He greeted Paulin affably and responded courteously to the introduction to Jamson, whose response was frosty.

"You've done a lot since you took over, Vergerin," Paulin said, giving the man the encouragement of his public support. "I wouldn't have believed it possible, frankly."

"Well," and Vergerin grinned in the most charming way, "I found Chalkin's hoard, so I've been able to hire in Craftsmen. Even the nearest holders aren't accustomed to me yet, and . . . shy?"

"Scared, more likely," Paulin said dryly.

"That, too, I'm sure, but I've done what I can to supply them with materials to make their own repairs. The hold was in an appalling state, you know."

Jamson grunted but his eyes widened as he saw the quiet order and cleanliness of the first reception room. S'nan made approving noises deep in his throat and even ran a finger across the wide table with its attractive arrangement of winter berries and leaves. A drudge, in livery so new the creases hadn't been lost, was hurrying across the hall with a heavy tray.

"My office is quite comfortable," Vergerin said, and gestured for them to enter.

Paulin noticed that the heavy wooden door gleamed with oil and the brass door plates were polished to a high gloss. The interior had been totally replaced, with worktops, tidy shelving, and bookcases. A scale map of Bitra Hold was nailed up on the interior wooden wall: beneath that was the Northern Continent and, oddly enough, the Steng Valley. Did Vergerin plan to reopen the mines there? A fire burned on the hearth, three upholstered chairs arranged cozily nearby, while a low table evidently awaited the tray. Polished metal vases on the deep window ledge held arrangements of bright orange berries and evergreen boughs: altogether a different room under Vergerin's management.

"There's klah, an excellent broth which I do recommend, and wine, mulled or room temperature," Vergerin said, gesturing for his three guests to take the comfortable chairs.

"You've a new cook as well, Vergerin?" Paulin asked, and pointed to the steaming pitcher when Vergerin grinned. "I'll sample the broth, then."

Jamson didn't mind if he did, too, but S'nan wanted the klah.

"You remember the back staircase, Paulin?" Vergerin said, taking the broth as well and pulling up a straight chair for himself.

"I do. Was that where the marks were hidden?"

"Yes, in one of the steps." Vergerin chuckled. "Chalkin must have forgotten that I knew about that hidey-hole, too. It's been a lifesaver, both to return unnecessary tithings and to buy in supplies. One thing Chalkin did do correctly was keep records. I knew exactly how much he had extorted from his people."

Jamson cleared his throat testily.

"Well, he did, Lord Jamson," Vergerin said without cavil. "They hadn't even enough in stores to get by on this winter, let alone have reserves for Fall. I'm still unloading what we couldn't possibly use from what Chalkin had amassed." He gave a mirthless laugh. "Chalkin would have weathered all fifty years of the Pass from what he had on hand—but none of his people would have lasted the first year, let alone have the materials to safeguard what they could plant out. Bitra being established after the First Fall, there were no hydroponics sheds, although the tanks are stored below."

Jamson gave another snort. "And the gaming? Have you curtailed that?"

"Both here and elsewhere," Vergerin said, flushing a little. "I haven't so much as touched dice or card since that game with Chalkin."

"What about his gamesmen?"

Vergerin's smile was grim. "They had the choice of signing new contracts with me—for I will not honor the old ones—or leaving. Not many left."

S'nan barked out a cackle of a laugh. "Not many would, considering the hazards of being holdless during a Pass. You have done well, Vergerin." He nodded an emphasis.

"You've had a second chance, Vergerin," Jamson said, waggling his finger. "See that you continue to profit by such good fortune." He had finished the broth and now stood. "We will go on a quick survey of the holds, if you please."

"Of course," and Vergerin rose hastily, pushing back his chair. "By horse—"

"No, no," Jamson dismissed that. "You've no need to accompany us. Better if you don't."

"Now, Jamson," Paulin began, for it was discourteous of the High Reaches Holder even to suggest Vergerin stay behind.

"Certainly, as you wish." Vergerin motioned them to pause at the map and indicated directions. "We've managed to complete all the necessary repairs on the holds adjacent or not far from the major link roads. Those high up have had to wait on supplies. I can't outstay my welcome at Benden Weyr, though M'shall has been far more obliging than I thought he'd be."

"It's to his advantage to oblige," S'nan said stiffly, at the merest hint of criticism of a Weyrleader.

Jamson had opened the door into the Hall and stopped so short, staring at the opposite wall, that Paulin nearly walked up his heels. Jamson muttered something under his breath and, pointing at the wall, turned to Vergerin.

"Why under the sun are you hanging his portrait *there*?" he demanded, almost outraged.

Paulin and S'nan peered in the direction indicated.

And Paulin had to laugh. "When did Iantine get a chance to . . . redo it?" he asked Vergerin, who was also broadly grinning.

"I got it yesterday." Vergerin walked across the Hall to stand beneath it. "I think the likeness is now excellent."

There was a moment of silence as they all viewed the portrait, now altered to an honest representation of the former Bitran Lord, including close-set eyes, bad complexion, scanty hair, and the mole on his chin.

S'nan sniffed. "Why would you want his face around at all, Vergerin?"

"One, to remind me to improve my management of Bitra, and two, because it's traditional to display the likenesses of previous Lord Holders." He gestured up the double-sided staircase, where hung the portraits of previous incumbents.

Jamson harrumphed several times. "And Chalkin? How's he doing?"

Paulin shrugged and looked to S'nan.

"He was supplied with all he needs," the Weyrleader said. "There is no need to exacerbate his expulsion by further contact."

"And his children?" Jamson asked, eyes glinting coldly.

Vergerin grinned, ducking his head. "I feel they have improved in health, well-being, and self-discipline."

"They stood in great need of the latter," Paulin said.

"They may surprise you, Lord Paulin," Vergerin said with a sly smile.

"I could bear it."

"As the branch is bent, so it will grow," Jamson intoned piously.

"Come this way," Vergerin said, putting a finger to his lips to indicate silence.

He led them down the corridor, toward what Paulin remembered as one of the gaming rooms. They could hear muted singing: Paulin instantly recognized the melody as one of the College's latest issues. As they got closer to the source he heard the words of the Duty Song. Jamson gave another one of his harrumphs and sniffed.

Carefully Vergerin opened the door on a mightily altered room. The students—and there were far more of them than Paulin had expected—were seated with their backs to the door. The teacher—and Paulin was surprised to recognize Issony back at Bitra—gave an additional nod to his head to acknowledge their presence as he continued to beat the tempo of the song.

Children's voices—even the ones who can't carry the tune—are always appealing: perhaps it is the innocence of the tone and the guilelessness in their rendition of the song's dynamics. Even Jamson smiled, but then the verse they were singing was about the Lord Holder's responsibilities.

"Which ones are Bitran Bloodline?" Paulin whispered to Vergerin.

He pointed, and only then could Paulin pick the children out in the front rows: the girls on the one side and the boys on the other. They were much better clothed than the others but no less attentive to their teacher, and singing lustily: the older girl had the most piercing voice. Somewhat like her mother's, Paulin thought.

Vergerin motioned for them to withdraw, grinning.

"Issony's been right that those youngsters needed competition. The holder kids need no incentives: they want to learn, and Chaldon is determined not to let mere holders get better grades than he. Oh, there's still whinings and pleadings and tantrums, but Issony has my permission to deal with them. And he does. Most effectively."

"Nadona?" Paulin asked.

Vergerin raised his eyebrows. "She's learning much the same lessons as her children, but she's not as quick a study, as Issony would say. She has her own quarters," and he inclined his head toward the upper levels. "She stays within."

"And leaves you to get along with the real work?" Paulin asked in a droll tone.

"Exactly."

"Hmm, yes, well, that's it here, I think," Paulin said, and then made much of fastening his riding jacket to indicate his willingness to depart on the inspection tour. "Do you agree, Jamson?"

Jamson harrumphed, but Paulin took the fact that he did not have questions as a good sign.

When they left the house, men and women were busy putting on the flamethrower tanks.

"I've scheduled a drill. Have to make up for lost time, you know," Vergerin said by way of explanation. Jamson and S'nan exchanged such fatuous glances that Paulin did his best not to laugh out loud. Vergerin caught his eye and winked. Then bade a polite farewell to his guests before he returned to the groundcrew.

"Well, he obviously learned a thing or two," Jamson said in a sanctimonious tone as they went down the steps to the waiting bronze dragon.

"Yes, it would seem he has," S'nan said and then frowned slightly. "Although I cannot like him turning loose Chalkin's gamesmen. They'll cause trouble at Gathers, mark my words."

"No more than they've always done," Paulin said, giving Jamson a discreet helping hand up Magrith's tall shoulder. "Probably less without Chalkin exhorting them to squeeze more out of innocent and guileless holders."

"No gambling should be allowed for any reason in a Weyr," S'nan said, as portentous as ever.

Paulin mounted silently, hoping that these two would see sufficient in a quick swoop to reassure S'nan about Vergerin's worth—and the wisdom of Chalkin's impeachment. The brief visit had satisfied him. Especially the sight of Chalkin's much improved portrait. He must send a message to Iantine at Telgar Weyr—Bridgely had said the artist returned there as soon as he was finished at Benden Hold—and inquire when he and his spouse could hope to have a sitting.

Paulin was well pleased he had taken the trouble to accompany Jamson. He hoped Lady Thea would be able to tell him that Gallian was off the hot seat.

◆ ◆ ◆

"You are *not* saving the entire world from Threadfall by yourself, P'tero," K'vin said, glaring up at the young blue rider. He was nearly beside himself with rage at P'tero's utter disregard of common sense. "You are *not* going to impress M'leng. If this is how you see your role in Threadfall, I think you'll be a long time on messenger duty."

"But, but—"

"Furthermore," and K'vin pointed a finger fiercely under the boy's nose, "Maranis tells me that your wounds are not well enough healed for you to be back on duty."

"But . . . but . . ." and P'tero, eyes wide with fright, recoiled from his Weyrleader's fury, clutching the neck ridge before he overbalanced. The pad that T'sen had given him now slipped, the ties torn loose sometime during the exercises. Blood spotted it.

"Get down here," K'vin roared, pointing to where he wanted P'tero: on the ground. "Right now."

P'tero obeyed, as promptly as he could, but he was stiff from sitting so long during the day's maneuvers and from the barely healed flesh of his buttock.

K'vin caught him by the shoulder and whirled him around.

"Not only new blood, but old stains," he said, his voice trenchant with scorn and fury. "You're off duty . . ."

"But . . . but . . . Thread's nearly here!" P'tero cried in anguish, almost in tears with frustration and the fear of being unable to show M'leng just how brave he really was. Not mock-brave, like the lion attack, but real brave in selflessness in the air.

"And Thread'll be here for fifty years, young man. That's plenty long enough for it to fear you and Ormonth in the air! Report to Maranis immediately. You're grounded!"

"But I have to be in the first Fall wings," P'tero cried, anguished.

"That wasn't the way to get there. Get to Maranis!"

K'vin didn't wait to see if P'tero obeyed. He stormed across the Bowl, the temptation to shake sense into the blue rider so intense he had to put distance between them.

Ormonth tried to keep him from flying today, Charanth informed his rider.

K'vin halted, glaring up now at his bronze dragon, who was settling himself on his weyr ledge to get what sun remained.

Then you're as bad as the pair of them! K'vin had the satisfaction of seeing Charanth quail at his fury.

From now on, you are to report to me—instantly—when any rider, or his dragon, is not one hundred percent fit for duty. Do you understand me?

Charanth's eyes whirled, the yellow of anxiety coloring the blue. His tone was remorseful.

I will not fail you again.

If they had been in real danger, I would have warned them off, Meranath said, entering the conversation.

I didn't ask you! K'vin was so irate he didn't really care if he offended Meranath, or her rider. But he was *not* going to lose riders from foolish and vainglorious actions. There *were* fifty years of Thread fighting ahead of them, and he was *not* going to lose partners. Or risk their injuries due to some cockamamie notion of what comprises courageous actions.

If you think that I would jeopardize a single rider . . .

K'vin took the stairs up to the queen's weyr three at a time, trying to work out his rage before he had to confront Zulaya and explain why he thought he could speak to her queen in such a peremptory fashion.

I should be informed of ANY unfit rider or dragon, at any time, anywhere, Meranath, and you should know that or, by the first egg, why are you senior queen?

"Because I am her rider!" Zulaya came storming out onto the weyr ledge, her eyes sparkling with indignation. "How dare you address my queen?"

"How dare she withhold information from *me*?"

Zulaya stared at him, surprised, for K'vin had never reprimanded either her or Meranath, though she had to admit privately that he could have legitimately done so on several occasions she would be embarrassed to admit.

"Did you know about P'tero's condition?" he demanded, and she backed into the weyr, away from him. He was rather magnificent furious, eyes blazing, face stern, the epitome of indignation.

"Tisha remarked that Maranis wasn't pleased with him assuming duty. The scar tissue is thin . . ."

"And you said nothing to me?"

"He's only a blue rider . . ."

"EVERY ONE OF MY RIDERS IS IMPORTANT TO ME!" K'vin roared, clenching his fists at his sides because they wanted to grab something to release the pent-up fury in him. "Threadfall is two days away. I need to have a Weyr in full readiness. I need to be sure of everyone I ask to face Thread in two days time. I don't need secrets or evasions or—"

"K'vin," Zulaya began, reaching a hand out to him, "Kev, it's all right. The Weyr is ready—perhaps tuned a little too tight, but that's all to the good . . ."

"All to the good?" K'vin batted her hand away. "When we have unfit riders taking positions they couldn't possibly manage in their condition?"

He began pacing now, and Zulaya watched him, smiling with relief and pride. He was going to be a splendid Weyrleader, much better than B'ner would have been.

He halted, just short of where she stood, his eyes, brilliant with his anger and frustration, fixed on her face.

"What on earth can you find to grin about right now?" he demanded, suspiciously, for there was a quality in her smile that he'd never seen before.

"That you're in full control," she said, leaving her smile in place.

"Oh, I am, am I?" Then, as she had always hoped he would, he took her in his arms and began kissing her with the full authority of his masculinity and his position as her Weyrleader, without a trace of hesitation or deference. Just what she'd always hoped she'd provoke him to.

◆ ◆ ◆

K'vin was still very much in complete control even very early the next morning, before dawn in fact, when Meranath told them that B'nurrin and Shanna were waiting for them.

"Waiting for what?" K'vin asked, pulling himself reluctantly away from Zulaya to reach for his pants.

It is time to go, Charanth added.

"Go where?" K'vin asked in a querulous tone of voice.

"Go where?" Zulaya asked sleepily.

South, they say, Meranath and Charanth echoed.

Suddenly K'vin remembered. Today was the day they would go see Thread. He said that very, very quietly in the back of his mind where Charanth might not hear it. Both dragons had been asleep when B'nurrin had made his visit. Which was just as well or the whole Weyr might have been privy to the notion of previewing Thread.

"B'nurrin wants us to join him," K'vin said, giving Zulaya a cautionary look.

She frowned for a moment, then her face cleared abruptly as she said "Oh." With a conspiratorial grin, she was out of the bed, trailing the sheet on her way to her riding gear.

When they passed each other once in the course of dressing, she pulled his head down to her mouth. "I could bring my flamethrower . . ."

"Might as well paint your destination on your forehead," he murmured back. "We're only going to *watch*."

"Yes, watch." Then she asked more loudly, "Where do we meet B'nurrin, Meranath?"

"We know that, too, remember?" K'vin said, grabbing Zulaya and giving her arm a little shake. Then he mouthed "Landing."

"Yes, how could I forget?"

If the dragon and rider on watch on the rim wondered why the two Weyrleaders were slipping away long before dawn, neither asked, and the rider gave a cheery swing of his arm as they passed over him.

Ianath says to count to three and then go, Charanth told his rider, still mystified.

Landing is where we're going, K'vin replied, glancing across the space between his dragon and Meranath. Zulaya showed him a thumb's-up signal to signify she had had the same message. Visualizing the arid sweep of desolate volcanic ash from Mount Garben down to Monaco Bay, K'vin nodded his head three times.

Go!

Abruptly, Charanth rumbled deep in his belly while his mind said in surprised shock *Oh!* K'vin felt him shift. Consequently he was perhaps not as surprised as he might have been to realize that the airspace around them, and Meranath and Zulaya, was well occupied. With that extra sense dragons had, the two had averted a collision. In fact, as K'vin swiveled about to check, the only two Weyrleaders he didn't see were S'nan and Sarai, although they might well have been among those who winked out of sight *between* so as not to be recognized. K'vin caught flashes of blue, brown, and even one or two green hides in the southern sun before they disappeared. Nor was this meeting composed now only of Weyrleaders and dragons: some thirty or so bronzes and browns were present.

The sight was too much for K'vin's sense of the ridiculous, and it was a good thing that he was clipped into his safety harness. He was seized of such a laughing fit that he reeled back and forth against Charanth's neck ridges. Had every rider on Pern been possessed of the compulsion to come here this morning? Of course, the particular site of Landing was well known to all riders. But for so many to decide independently to come here . . . probably every one certain he or she'd be the only ones daring enough.

Nor was K'vin the only one laughing hard. Right now he was more in danger of wetting his britches from mirth, not fright at seeing Thread for the first time. Which reminded him why he was here. Again that realization became universal. Laughter faded as every dragon and rider irresistibly turned northeastward.

It was there, too, the much-described silvery gray haze on the upper levels of the blue sky. Not a dragon wing moved, not a rider recoiled as the silver stuff began to drop onto the sea. *Thread!* And so aptly called.

Thread!

The word seemed to rumble from dragon to dragon, and K'vin had to grab hold of the neck ridge as Charanth started to lurch toward what he had known all his life as his adversary.

I have no firestone! How can I flame it! What is wrong? Why have you brought me here where there is Thread and I have no fire to char it!

It's all right, Charanth. We're here to watch. To see.

But it is Thread! I must chew to flame. Why may I not flame when there is THREAD!

Glancing wildly around him, K'vin realized that he was by no means the only rider having the same difficulty with a frustratedly zealous dragon, rapidly trying to close the gap to Threadfall.

I've seen enough, Charanth. Take us back to Telgar.

But THREAD? And the bronze dragon's tone was piteous, confused, and horrified.

We leave. Now!

Leave? But we have not met Thread.

Not here or now or in this place, Charanth.

It took K'vin every bit of willpower and moral strength, and Charanth's faith in him, to overcome his bronze's impassioned protest. Then, all of a sudden, Charanth stopped flying toward Thread.

Oh, all right! The tone was that of a petulant child forced by a senior authority to follow orders totally against the grain.

What?

The queens say we must go to the Red Butte.

Then let us go there. K'vin did not question the order, being far too glad that one was given that the dragon would obey.

The Butte was a training landmark in lower Keroon, a laccolithic dome so difficult to mistake that it figured in all weyrling training programs. And there the would-be observers managed to get their dragons to land. Even the queens' eyes were whirling at a stiff red-orange pace; some of the bronzes were so distraught with anger that their eyes pulsed wickedly, whirling at incredible speed in their anger. K'vin was almost relieved to swing down from Charanth's neck. But he and the other Weyrleaders all kept one hand on their dragons' legs, shoulders, muzzles: some contact was maintained. In a wide outer circle were the brown and bronze riders, who had also been "rescued": they remained mounted, soothing their dragons, allowing their leaders the center for discussion.

It was M'shall who spoke first. "Well, that was one good idea gone awry," he said in a droll tone. "Great minds, all of us."

"Except for forgetting one simple rule," Irene added, pulling off her flying cap. Her face was still pale from fright.

K'vin glanced at Zulaya, who was wiping sweat from her face, so he knew none of the queen riders had had an easy time to get their queens to insist on the disengagement.

"Dragons know what they're supposed to do when Thread falls," M'shall said, nodding. And then he started to laugh.

K'vin grinned and, when he heard G'don's bass chuckle, saw no reason any longer to hold his laughter in. B'nurrin was howling so, he had to clutch at K'vin to keep his balance. Even D'miel looked properly abashed, and Laura's giggle was infectious enough to increase the volume. Beyond the inner circle the rest of the riders caught the joke on themselves and joined in the laugh. It was a good release from the fright that they had all just had.

"Did anyone happen to notice a Fort rider disappearing in guilty retreat?" M'shall asked when the laughter died down. He'd been checking the identity of those on the rim of this informal assembly.

"They'd be the last to admit coming," Irene said.

"I doubt that, Renee," G'don said. "S'nan runs a strict Weyr, it's true, but I'll wager there're a few renegades among his wingleaders."

"I know there are," Mari said, blotting her eyes, which were still merry from laughter. "It's just such a hoot that we all," and she ringed them with a swirl of her hand, "thought to come have a peek."

"It's not going to inhibit any of the dragons, is it?" Laura asked, turning pale at the sudden thought, "turning them off like that?"

D'miel wasn't the only Weyrleader to dismiss that notion derisively. "Hardly! It's increased rider credibility a hundredfold. They now know without doubt that what we've been telling them since they were hatched is true!"

"Oh, yes, it would, wouldn't it?" she said, relieved.

"I myself would like to thank the queen riders for exerting their powerful influence on our bronzes," G'don said with a formal hand over his heart as he bowed to the five queen riders.

"The advantage of having three very senior queens," Zulaya said, "and two very strong-minded young women."

Laura blushed while Shanna stood even straighter.

"All right, then," M'shall said, having taken note that most of the male dragons' eyes were resuming normal color and speed. He took a step toward the center of the sandy circle and cupped his hands, turning as he spoke. "All right, then, every one of you. This is a meeting that never happened and isn't to be referred to in any Weyr for any reason. Do you understand me?" The response was loud and clear. He nodded and stepped back toward Craigath. "We'll meet . . ." he said now to the other leaders, "where Thread first—officially—falls North."

"We've sweep riders out all the time," G'don reminded them.

"And we're all very sure that S'nan does, too," B'nurrin put in, grinning. "So we'll know when and where to meet again."

"Wait a moment more, G'don," K'vin said. "Why don't we rotate the wings that meet that first Fall, wherever it is?" A little cheer from the outer circle gave instant approval to that suggestion. "That'll give even more riders a chance for at least a little experience before the individual Weyrs have to meet Thread on their own."

G'don paused at Chakath's side, looking around to check the reaction to that idea.

"In hourly intervals?" he asked.

"Make it two hours to allow wings to get properly into the routine," M'shall amended.

"It's not that we're green riders or anything," B'nurrin put in as protest.

"Two hours makes more sense than swapping around every hour . . ." D'miel said thoughtfully.

"I'd agree on two," G'don said. "We'll bring the matter up to S'nan. He deserves that much from us. I'll initiate the idea." He grinned again, since S'nan would listen to him as the oldest Weyrleader, where he would summarily dismiss a younger man. "I'll let you know when we'll meet to make the changes we've already agreed to."

Red dust swirled up in a cloud around the Butte as all the dragons leaped almost simultaneously from the ground.

XVII

Threadfall

Bitter cold weather and winds swept down from the icy poles of Pern on the day that S'nan set a meeting with the other five Weyrleaders to discuss the rotation of wings that G'don had suggested to him. Freezing weather was likely to do Fort Weyr out of its chance to be the first Weyr to meet Thread in this Fall.

That S'nan keenly felt deprived was obvious. Throughout the meeting he paced the floor, pausing to peer out the slanting corridor to the sleet falling heavily into Fort Bowl. He had only half his mind on the discussion. B'nurrin was all but laughing, only the kicks he received from K'vin under the table kept him from bursting out. Not that K'vin could blame the Igen Weyrleader, for the meeting was a charade: each of them giving soberly presented reasons for the two-hourly rotation while S'nan said little more than monosyllables. S'nan kept his expression blank. It was Sarai's petulant expression that was honest.

"She's been dying to get all of us under her wing," Zulaya whispered to K'vin when the Fort Weyrwoman's face was turned toward her anxiously pacing mate.

"Don't think she will, love," K'vin said, the endearment coming easily to his lips now. He sighed. "You know," and he moved his lips close to her ear. "I'm almost sorry for the old man."

Zulaya gave a little snort. "I'm not." Then she altered her expression to one of earnest attention as Sarai looked over at them for whispering.

Thread came down as black dust, sifted in with snow or sleet. Fort sweep riders brought buckets of it for S'nan to see and mournfully wave off. High Reaches were even more diligent in their efforts to locate live, dangerous Thread. Some riders even suffered frostbite, so earnestly did they watch for the reappearance of the old enemy, although one long piece of frozen Thread was brought for G'don to examine. The stench of it as it melted was enough for them to dispose of it completely.

By the time of Benden's First Fall—by the numbers, Ten—the weather pattern had shifted sufficiently on the East Coast to a warmer front so that a good deal of that projected Fall would be considered "live" and dangerous. The call went out to all the Weyrs of Pern.

◆ ◆ ◆

K'vin and Telgar Weyr's two full wings of dragonriders reassembled in the upper-right quadrant of air above Benden Weyr, not a rider out of alignment. Below him the Weyr was ablaze with lights in this dark predawn time, lighting the bellies of the dragons in their ranks. He wasn't sure if the Telgar contingent got there before the units of the other Weyrs, but they were certainly all present and accounted for at the designated hour and in the assigned positions. Everyone would have preferred a daylight defense, but Thread didn't need to see to fall. And according to Sean's reports of early morning or late evening Fall, the silvery stuff would be luminous enough for the practical purpose of flaming it out of the sky.

This First Fall of the Second Pass would start across the high mountains, still deep with winter snows, and would thus fall harmlessly. Much would probably fall as black dust in the still frigid temperatures of that area, though quite likely, on other occasions, Fall would merely be observed until it moved inexorably down to habitable lands. Today was the exception.

The final decision by the Weyrleaders had been unanimous, when M'shall had made S'nan put it to a vote—to ride the entire Fall over the ranges, harmless or not, "to see it for themselves." Everyone was too keyed up over the first three "dud" falls to wait any longer to go into action. Of course, some of the peaks jutted at altitudes where oxygen had thinned to an unsustainable level even for dragons. But it could be seen in actual descent and the general aspect of this Fall judged.

The wings would be rotated after two hours, giving as many as possible a chance at the "real thing." K'vin briefly thought of P'tero's vain attempt to be included in the fighting force Telgar would launch. Maybe he should have put the blue rider in, sore ass and all, to prove that there was a lot more to fighting Thread than having the guts to do it. But to include P'tero would have been to exclude a perfectly healthy and less erratic rider. K'vin had not selected M'leng of the green riders chosen for the First Fall. That would ease discord between that pair: that one had gone and the other had not. Basically, they were good weyrmates, having a reasonably stable relationship ever since P'tero, who was the younger, had Impressed Ormonth.

Movement and a shift in air pressure caught K'vin's attention and he looked down at Benden's rim.

Craigath warns us, Charanth told his rider. *Three, two, one . . .*
GO!

The command came from many minds and many throats in the dark above Benden Weyr. The blackness of *between* was more intense but scarcely less cold than the atmosphere above the peaks where the wings reentered real space. K'vin was glad of the wool fabric across his mouth and nose, though it did not altogether warm the thin air he inhaled. Below, the snowy mountains gave off a curious light of their own. Belior was setting in the west, and K'vin looked around to the east and saw the baleful orb of the Red Planet, vivid amidst the stars.

Spits of fire blossomed in the darkness all around as eager dragons belched. Too full a belly of firestone, K'vin thought with professional detachment, but he could hardly fault rider or dragon for overpriming.

For two centuries they had waited for this moment: centuries of training and lives lived so that dragons—and riders—would be here, right now, waiting to defend Pern.

Yet this was a first, too. For Pern had had no dragons the first time Thread had fallen, and the planet had been close to total disaster before the first eighteen dragons had emerged from *between* above Fort Hold to flame the parasite from the skies and give hope to the beleaguered defenders. K'vin had always been struck by the courage of the despairing Admiral Paul Benden—he should make P'tero read those entries in the admiral's diary, made just prior to that magnificent triumph. Even in his most recent reading of that journal, his throat closed over as he read the words:

And then that young rogue had the temerity to salute and say, "Admiral Benden, may I present the Dragonriders of Pern?"

More spurts of fiery breath and every dragon head turned northward.

It comes, Charanth said, rumbling deep in his chest, a vibration that K'vin felt through his legs. He was aware then that the only warm part of him was what was pressing against his dragon's neck. His nose had no feeling of the fabric across it. Maybe they should drop down a thousand feet or so . . . and he looked toward the central block of the massed wings, where M'shall and Craigath waited. It was the Benden Weyrleader's call, not his.

Then he saw it, or rather the mass of something lustrous against the black of night, like a banner spread from some distant source in the sky, a banner that rippled and spun. The pace of his heartbeat picked up. He felt an odd coldness in his guts, but it could be because it was very, very cold at this altitude.

Charanth's rumble increased and a little spit of flame spilled from his mouth.

Steady, lad!

I'm not moving! It is! And I can flame this time!

K'vin could not reproach Charanth for that snide reminder. And, oddly enough, he also felt no fear as he regarded the advance. There was this sense of inevitability, that he would be here, at this moment in time, to observe this phenomenon, to be part of this defense.

Closer and closer the waves of Thread came as the massed wings watched. The leading edge was now falling visibly on the mountainsides. In this cold air not even the steam of its dissolution was visible.

Thread was falling in a steady stream, freezing dead in the snow. A steady stream, no tangles, no bare spots.

Craigath says we regroup at the second meeting point.

Agreed.

Oddly enough, K'vin did not like even to regroup, though there was nothing Thread could have done to harm the snowy mountainsides and it was foolish to waste time and flame here. But it *felt* like retreat.

Charanth had broadcast the order and took them *between*.

The air was noticeably warmer at the altitude of the new position. He rubbed at his nose and cheeks to bring blood to the surface. Even his fingertips felt numb from the cold.

False dawn began in the east, the Red Star paling slightly in the graying skies. And Thread suddenly looked more ominous. More dragons spewed flame and he told Charanth to warn them to conserve their breath.

Suddenly the wait was chafing. They had waited so long, hadn't they? Two hundred years! When would they begin?

But Thread fell on snow, and K'vin was close enough to Leading Edge now to see the holes it made in the whiteness.

NOW! Craigath's command reached K'vin's mind in the same moment that Charanth roared, full flame erupting from his mouth as he beat his wings to power his forward surge. K'vin clutched at the flight strap, felt frantically for the rope that tethered the firestone sacks to the neck ridge in front of him, and clamped his knees as tight as he could to his bronze. His right arm rose and pointed forward, as if any rider could have missed Craigath's command or the roars that emerged from dragon throats across the sky.

They were flying in ranks, Telgar being the second and slightly behind the uppermost wings, which were from High Reaches. There was sufficient air between the two layers of dragons so that flame from one level would not interfere with another: and a corridor for maneuver as well. Every Weyr had drilled its wings for this strategy until it was instinctive to stay within the plane assigned them.

The moment when Charanth's breath sizzled up descending Thread was a transcendental experience for both partners. Charanth sustained his flame magnificently, crossing this cordon, and then they were out, beyond Thread's Fall and turning. K'vin spared a glance at the rest of his wings and saw them pivoting simultaneously, all those long, long hours and years of practice resulting in a perfect maneuver. His heart was like to burst in his chest with pride. Below and above him other wings were turning, all now flaming to catch the next band of falling Thread. And the next. And the next.

Meranath and the others are here, Charanth announced, dropping his head to peer far below.

They are? Turn. K'vin looked below and saw the unmistakable arrow of golden bodies in their low-level position, the flamethrowers that the queen riders used spouting here and there as they disintegrated stray strands escaping the higher ranks.

Does Meranath fly well?

Meranath flies very well, Charanth said proudly.

Tell the wings it is time to execute the first change-over, K'vin said. He swiveled his body around to watch that maneuver, holding his right arm up high, sweeping his eyes across Telgar's wings. He dropped his arm and counted nine or ten dragons still flaming. Then they, too, went off. He counted to five and suddenly full wings flew behind him. He raised his arm high in recognition of their arrival, which was all he had time for because the wall of Thread advanced to flaming distance and Charanth was ready with his fire. So far he could find no fault with the performance of Telgar's wings.

It seemed no time after that when he realized his sacks of firestone were empty. He had Charanth call for more. It surprised K'vin to notice that they had flown from night into day, for the sun slanted right into the eyes as they flew east again. There was good reason to use tinted glass in the goggles.

Z'gal and blue Tracath made the drop, swooping in neatly just above his head and depositing the new sacks across Charanth's neck. K'vin pulled the release knot of the empty sacks and saw Tracath swivel and dive beneath Charanth, Z'gal deftly catching the limp ones and disappearing instantly *between.*

Tell Tracath that was well done, K'vin said.

They were over the northernmost edge of Benden now, above pasturelands, forests, and small farming holds. The need for accuracy and complete destruction of Thread was more crucial now. The queens' wing was more visible, gold against the dark green or brown of fields not yet verdant with spring growth.

Sacks had to be replenished again. He called in the second change-over of wings, only then realizing that he was beginning to tire.

Are you all right, Charanth?

I flame well. My wings beat strongly. We are together. There is no problem.

The calm, strong tone of his bronze was like a tonic. Yes, they were together, doing what they had been bred and maintained to do.

Meranath says we are over Bitra Hold now. They were turning west again, back for another run. K'vin did notice that there seemed to be less Thread falling now, even gaps between the sheets of it. *This Fall is nearly over?*

K'vin wasn't sure if Charanth was pleased, surprised, or disappointed. He, for one, was enormously relieved. He had survived the ultimate test of the Weyrleader.

They did one more pass eastward and then there was no more Thread visible above. A cheer echoed from rider to rider, and all those within K'vin's range pumped both arms in jubilation.

We should land at Bitra Hold, in case we are needed for burrows that might have escaped us, K'vin told Charanth. *Tell the wings well done and all but J'dar's may return. He will wait with us for the all-clear. It is M'shall's pleasure to tell us that! Any casualties?*

That was the traditional Weyrleader's query, though reports would also be made to him during the Fall so that he could assess what replacements might be needed.

Today only some minor burns from char. Nothing bad enough that anyone cared to report to you.

K'vin wasn't that pleased that news had been withheld, but he could understand the reluctance of any rider in today's Fall to retire for a mere char burn. Now he noticed that he had quite a few black spots on his own riding leathers, but nothing had penetrated through to his flesh. Would that every Fall be so trouble-free! And the next one that Telgar flew would show up the foolhardy. He'd have to give the entire Weyr a hard bollicking to prevent the cocksure from disaster.

Today the queens' wing would join the wingleaders at Bitra Hold, though traditionally they stayed aloft to assist groundcrews.

Zulaya sought K'vin as soon as she was on the ground and embraced him, seeking his mouth to kiss him with enthusiasm.

"We did it. We did it."

"This time," K'vin said, hugging her tightly. He could almost have thanked P'tero for getting him so angry. It had done the world of good for his relations with Zulaya. The way she looked at him, the way she had to touch him . . . well, they were truly weyrmates now.

M'shall was moving among the riders, slapping one on the shoulder, thanking each Weyrleader for participating in this almost scatheless Fall, a wide smile plastered on his face.

"I'd say that this was a normal Fall," S'nan was saying portentously.

"How can we possibly tell?" G'don said.

"The records, man, the records," S'nan said, glaring. "It's exactly as Sean described Fall number 325, in his records of Fifty-eight A.L. Exactly."

"Oh, Fall number 325?" B'nurrin asked, his eyes dancing. "Myself, I felt it was more like number 499 in Sixty A.L."

"B'nurrin?" and M'shall's raised eyebrows suggested that the irrepressible young Igen Weyrleader should stop baiting S'nan.

"We got off much too easily," D'miel of Ista said, shaking his head. "I mean, we were all on a high. I for one was expecting far worse . . ."

"Isn't it nice to be disappointed?" K'vin said, but he agreed with D'miel. Everything had gone too well.

"Nonsense," G'don said. "We were all flying our best riders. We've been keyed up for weeks and nervous. And I don't mind admitting I was," he added, glancing around him, but he winked at K'vin and B'nurrin. Others nodded agreement. "So we were very cautious. It's when we're so accustomed to the menace that we're liable to be careless, to take unnecessary risks, to stop watching out of the backs of our heads."

A murmur of agreement and nods greeted that observation.

"We must never relax our guard during Fall," S'nan said, again sententious. "Never!"

"We'll have to be doubly cautious during the second Fall over south Benden and Keroon," Zulaya said softly to K'vin.

"Well, I for one was pleased with the way the wings performed. Not much got through," he repeated. "Between the upper flights and the queens' wing, only four incidents of burrow, and those were handled with great dispatch. Thanks to Vergerin . . ."

The Bitra Lord Holder was directing the distribution of Hegmon's sparkling wine to those crowding in his courtyard.

"Only think what might have happened if Chalkin was still here!" Irene said, raising her glass toward Vergerin.

"Who *wants* to think what might have happened?" Laura of Ista Weyr demanded, laughing with exaggerated relief.

"For one thing, we wouldn't have this champagne," Irene replied. "That's for damned sure!"

"How'd you get the sparkly out of Hegmon, Vergerin?" G'don wanted to know, cradling his glass lovingly.

"We're old friends, you might say," Vergerin replied with a droll grin.

"Did any wing report injuries?" M'shall asked, his expression turning sober.

"Nothing above char burns in mine," K'vin said. And that was what the other wingleaders reported one after another.

"Well, we're fragging lucky if that's all. Though I shudder to think how careless the average rider can get," M'shall said. "We'll have to keep them on their toes."

"And on their dragons," his weyrmate replied.

"Look at it this way," B'nurrin said, grinning from ear to ear, "we've only 6,649 more falls to attend, give or take a few, before it's all over for another two hundred years."

There was a moment of dumbfounded silence as that fact was absorbed, and then B'nurrin ducked away before the wrath of his peers could descend on him.

"But Fall has begun," K'vin said softly to Zulaya, standing proudly beside him, "and we have met the enemy again."

"What a time to be alive . . ."

"And riding a dragon!"

And thus began the Second Pass of Thread on Pern!

Moreta:
Dragonlady of Pern

This book is dedicated
to my daughter
Georgeanne Johnson
with great affection and respect
for her courage

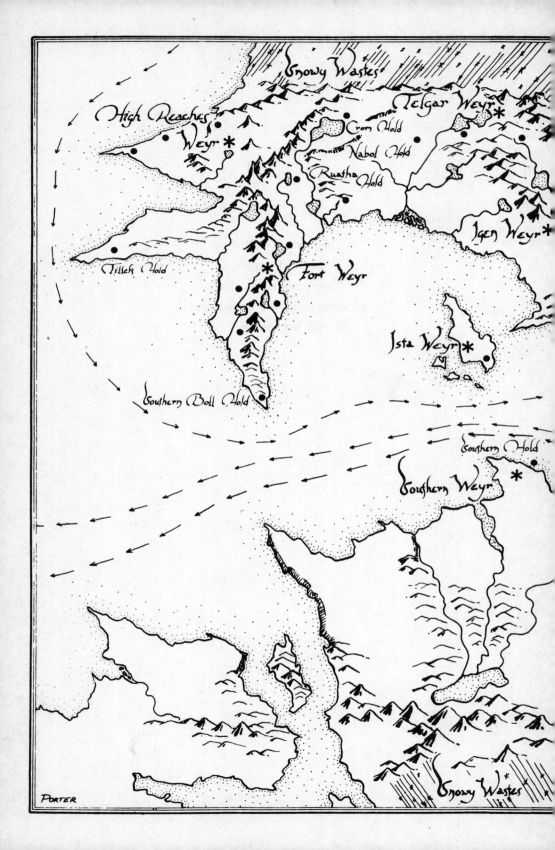

Benden Weyr

Bitra
Hold

Keroon Hold

Nerat Hold

N

W   E

S

Southern   Current

Cove Hold

Pern

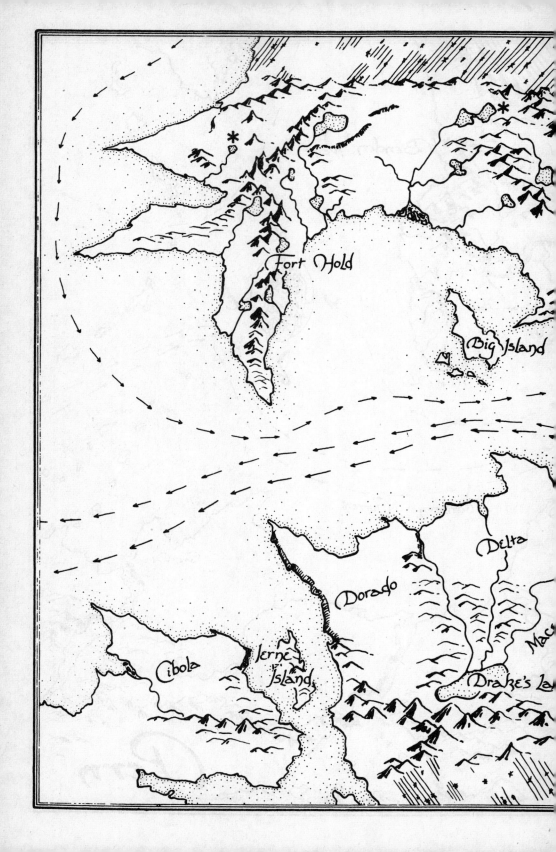

Rukbat, in the Sagittarian Sector, was a golden G-type star. It had five planets, two asteroid belts, and a stray planet that it had attracted and held in recent millennia. When men first settled on Rukbat's third world and called it Pern, they had taken little notice of the strange planet swinging around its adopted primary in a wildly erratic orbit. For two generations, the colonists gave the bright Red Star little thought—until the path of the wanderer brought it close to its stepsister at perihelion. When such aspects were harmonious and not distorted by conjunctions with other planets in the system, the indigenous life form of the wandering planet sought to bridge the space gap between its home and the more temperate and hospitable planet. At these times, silver Threads dropped through Pern's skies, destroying anything they touched. The initial losses the colonists suffered were staggering. As a result, during the subsequent struggle to survive and combat the menace, Pern's tenuous contact with the mother planet was broken.

To control the incursions of the dreadful Threads—for the Pernese had cannibalized their transport ships early on and abandoned such technological sophistication as was irrelevant to the pastoral planet—the more resourceful men embarked on a long-term plan. The first phase involved breeding a highly specialized variety of fire-lizard, a life form indigenous to their new world. Men and women with high empathy ratings and some innate telepathic ability were trained to use and preserve the unusual animals. The dragons—named for the mythical Terran beast they resembled—had two valuable characteristics: They could instantaneously travel from one place to another and, after chewing a phosphine-bearing rock, they could emit a flaming gas. Because the dragons could fly, they could intercept and char the Thread in midair before it reached the surface.

It took generations to develop to the fullest the potential of the dragons. The second phase of the proposed defense against the deadly incursions would take even longer. For Thread, a space-traveling mycorrhizoid spore, devoured with mindless voracity all organic matter and, once grounded, burrowed and proliferated with terrifying speed. So a symbiote of the same strain was developed to counter this parasite, and the resulting grub was introduced into the soil of the Southern Continent. It was planned that the dragons would be a visible protection, charring Thread while it was still skyborne and protecting the dwellings and the livestock of the colonists. The grub-symbiote would protect vegetation by devouring what Thread managed to evade the dragons' fire.

The originators of the two-stage defense did not allow for change or for hard geological fact. The Southern Continent, though seemingly more attractive than the harsher northern land, proved unstable, and the entire colony was eventually forced to seek refuge from the Threads on the continental shield rock of the north.

On the northern continent the original Fort, Fort Hold, constructed on the eastern face of the Great West Mountain Range, was soon outgrown by the colonists, and its capacious beasthold could not contain the growing numbers of dragons. Another settlement was started slightly to the north, where a great lake had formed near a cave-filled cliff. But Ruatha Hold, too, became overcrowded within a few generations.

Since the Red Star rose in the east, the people of Pern decided to establish a holding in the eastern mountains, provided a suitable cavesite could be found. Only solid rock and metal, both of which were in distressingly short supply on Pern, were impervious to the burning score of Thread.

The winged, tailed, fire-breathing dragons had by then been bred to a size that required more spacious accommodations than the cliffside holds could provide. The cave-pocked cones of extinct volcanoes, one high above the first Fort, the other in the Benden Mountains, proved to be adequate and required only a few improvements to be made habitable. However, such projects took the last of the fuel for the great stone-cutters, which had been programmed only for regular mining operations, not for wholesale cliff excavations. Subsequent holds and Weyrs had to be hand-hewn.

The dragons and their riders in their high places and the people in their cave holds went about their separate tasks, and each developed habits that became custom, which solidified into tradition as incontrovertible as law. And when a Fall of Thread was imminent—when the Red Star was visible at dawn through the Star Stones erected on the rim of each Weyr—the dragons and their riders mobilized to protect the people of Pern.

Then came an interval of two hundred Turns of the planet Pern around its primary—when the Red Star was at the far end of its erratic orbit, a frozen, lonely captive. No Thread fell on Pern. The inhabitants erased the signs of Thread depredation and grew crops, planted orchards and thought of reforestation for the slopes denuded by Thread. They even managed to forget that they had once been in great danger of extinction. Then, when the wandering planet returned, the Threads fell again, bringing another fifty years of attack from the skies. Once again the Pernese thanked their ancestors, now many generations removed, for providing the dragons whose fiery breath seared the falling Thread midair.

Dragonkind, too, had prospered during that Interval and had settled in four other locations, following the master plan of interim defense.

Recollections of Earth receded further from Pernese memories with each generation until knowledge of Mankind's origins degenerated into a myth. The significance of the southern hemisphere—and the Instructions formulated by the colonial defenders of dragon and grub—became garbled and lost in the more immediate struggle to survive.

By the Sixth Pass of the Red Star, a complicated sociopolitical-economic structure had been developed to deal with the recurrent evil. The six Weyrs, as the old volcanic habitations of the dragonfolk were called, pledged themselves to protect Pern, each Weyr having a geographical section of the Northern Continent literally under its wing. The rest of the population agreed to tithe support to the Weyrs since the dragonmen did not have arable land in their volcanic homes, could not afford to take time away from nurturing their dragons to learn other trades during peacetime, and could not take time away from protecting the planet during Passes.

Settlements, called holds, developed wherever natural caves were found—some, of course, more extensive or strategically placed than others. It took a strong man to exercise control over terrified people during Thread attacks; it took wise administration to conserve victuals when nothing could be safely grown, and it took extraordinary measures to control population and keep it productive and healthy until such time as the menace passed.

Men with special skills in metalworking, weaving, animal husbandry, farming, fishing, and mining formed crafthalls in each large Hold and looked to one Mastercrafthall where the precepts of their craft were taught and craft skills were preserved and guarded from one generation to another. One Lord Holder could not deny the products of the crafthall situated in his Hold to others, since the Crafts were deemed independent of a Hold affiliation. Each Craftmaster of a hall owed allegiance to the Master of his particular craft—an elected office based on proficiency in the craft and on administrative ability. The Mastercraftsman was responsible for the output of his halls and the distribution, fair and unprejudiced, of all craft products on a planetary rather than parochial basis.

Certain rights and privileges accrued to different leaders of Holds and Masters of Crafts and, naturally, to the dragonriders whom all Pern looked to for protection during the Threadfalls.

It was within the Weyrs that the greatest social revolution took place, for the needs of the dragons took priority over all other considerations. Of the dragons, the gold and green were female, the bronze, brown, and blue male. Of the female dragons, only the golden were fertile; the greens were rendered sterile by the chewing of firestone, which was as well since the sexual proclivities of the small greens would soon have resulted in overpopulation. They were the most agile, however, and invaluable as fighters of Thread, fearless and aggressive. But the price of fertility was inconvenience, and riders of queen dragons carried flamethrowers to char Thread. The blue males were sturdier than their smaller sisters, while the browns and bronzes had the staying power for long, arduous battles against Thread. In theory, the great golden fertile queens were mated with whichever dragon could catch them in their strenuous mating flights. Generally speaking, the bronzes did the honor. Consequently the rider of the bronze dragon who flew the senior queen of a Weyr became its Leader and had charge of the fighting Wings during a Pass. The rider of the senior queen dragon, however, held the most responsibility for the Weyr during and after a Pass when it was the Weyrwoman's job to nurture and preserve the dragons, to sustain and improve the Weyr and all its folk. A strong Weyrwoman was as essential to the survival of the Weyr as dragons were to the survival of Pern.

To her fell the task of supplying the Weyr, fostering its children, and Searching for likely candidates from hall and hold to pair with the newly hatched candidates. As life in the Weyrs was not only prestigious but easier for women and men alike, hold and hall were proud to have their children taken on Search and boasted of the illustrious members of the bloodline who had become dragonriders.

We begin our story toward the end of the Sixth Pass of the Red Star, some fourteen hundred Turns after men first came to Pern. . . .

CHAPTER

I

Fort Weyr, Present Pass, 3.10.43-1541, and Ruatha Hold

"Sh'gall is out on other Weyr business," Moreta told Nesso for the third time, beginning to loosen her sweat- and oil-stained tunic as a hint.

"His Weyr business should be accompanying you to Ruatha Gather." Nesso's voice had a whining note to it in the best of her humors. Now the Fort Weyr Headwoman was filled with aggrieved indignation at the fancied slight to her Weyrwoman, and her voice grated like a bone saw in Moreta's ear.

"He saw Lord Alessan yesterday. A Gather is not a time to discuss serious matters." Moreta rose, seeking to end an interview she hadn't wanted to give, one that could continue as long as Nesso could dredge up complaints, real or imaginary, against Sh'gall. Their antagonism was mutual, and Moreta often found herself in the position of placating or explaining the one to the other. She could not change Sh'gall and was loathe to displace Nesso for, despite her faults, the woman was an exceedingly efficient and hard-working Headwoman. "I must bathe, Nesso, or I'll be unpardonably late at Ruatha. I know you've arranged a good meal for those who remain. K'lon's comfortable now that the fever has broken. Berchar will look in on him. Just leave him alone."

Moreta fixed Nesso with an admonitory gaze, reinforcing her injunction. Nesso had an officious habit of "taking" Moreta's place whenever the Weyrwoman was absent unless specifically ordered not to. "Away with you now, Nesso. You've enough to do, and I'm longing to be clean." Moreta accompanied her words with a smile as she gave Nesso a gentle shove toward the exit from her sleeping room.

"Sh'gall should go with you. He should," the irrepressible woman muttered as Moreta held aside the vivid door-curtain. Only when Nesso neared the sleeping queen dragon did she cease her imprecations.

Heavy with egg, Orlith dozed on, oblivious to the woman's passing. The golden dragon had arranged herself on the stony couch so as not to mar the fine gleam of oil that Moreta had rubbed into her hide as part of the morning's preparation for the Gather at Ruatha. Moreta was heading for her own much-needed wash when she was asked to examine K'lon, so she'd been late for her chat with Leri to be sure the old Weyrwoman had what she required for the day. Leri would have no ministrations from Nesso's hands.

The interview with Nesso had proved unavoidable. The Headwoman had "heard" that Sh'gall and Moreta had "had words" that had caused the Weyrleader's abrupt departure, dressed in riding gear rather than in his Gather finery. Nesso had also to be reassured that K'lon was not wasting from a virulent fever that would spread rapidly through the Weyr, it being only three days to a Fall.

Moreta stripped off her clothes. She ought to have been at the Gather long since, getting through the obligatory courtesies before the racing started.

"Orlith?" Moreta called softly, concentrating the strength of her gentle summons in her head. As always, the sleepy response of her queen cheered her of Nesso's petulance. "Rouse yourself, my golden beauty. We'll be leaving soon for Ruatha's Gatherday."

It's still sunny at Ruatha? Orlith asked hopefully.

"It should be. T'ral did the morning sweep," Moreta said, opening her robe chest. The new gown lay in gold and soft, warm-brown folds, colors that would accent Moreta's eyes. "You know how accurate T'ral's weather sense is."

The dragon rumbled with satisfaction, and Moreta could hear her stretching and turning.

"Don't roll too much now," Moreta said politely.

I know. I mustn't lose my shine. Orlith spoke with patient acknowledgment. *I will keep clean until we reach Ruatha. And then I'll sun. When I get hot enough, I'll swim in Ruatha Lake.*

"Would that be wise so close to clutching, my dear? That lake's cold as *between*." Moreta shivered at her memory of those ice-fed waters.

Nothing is colder than between. Orlith spoke definitively.

Having laid out her Gather finery, Moreta strode into the bathing room. She grabbed a handful of sweet sand, then swung her legs over the lip of the raised pool, whose surface was faintly steaming. Standing waist deep, she sanded her body until her skin tingled. Submerging for a moment, she surfaced, tipping her head until her short hair fanned out in the water. Then she pushed back to the edge of the pool, reaching for more sand, which she scrubbed into her scalp and hair.

You take a long time to get clean though there's not much of you, Orlith remarked, somewhat impatient now that she was fully awake.

"There may not be much of me, but there was a great deal of *you* to be bathed and oiled."

You always say that.

"So do you."

The countercomplaints were lodged with total affection and understanding. Queen and rider had been partnered for nearly twenty Turns, though they had only recently become the leading pair at Fort Weyr when Leri's Holth had not risen to mate the previous winter.

Moreta gave her head a final drubbing, then flicked her fingers through her hair to make the short crop settle into natural waves. Wearing a leather cap during Threadfall made her scalp sweat so much that the long blond braids in which she had taken so much pride as a holder girl had been shorn. Once this Pass was completed, she could grow her hair!

Once the Pass was completed . . . In the act of pulling on a clean undertunic, Moreta paused in surprise. Why, this Pass would end in another eight Turns. No, seven if one counted this Turn a quarter gone. Moreta sternly corrected an optimistic attitude. The Turn was barely seventy days old. Eight Turns then. In eight Turns, she, Moreta, would no longer *have* to fly with Orlith against Thread. The Red Star would have passed too far to rain the devastating parasitic Thread over Pern's tired continent. Dragonriders would not have to fly because no Thread would blur the sky.

Did Thread just stop, Moreta wondered as she slipped on her soft brown shoes, like a sudden summer storm? Or did it dribble off like a winter rain?

They could use some rain. Snow would be even better. Or a good hard frost. Frost was always a Weyr ally.

She slipped into the dress now, smoothing it over her rather too broad shoulders, over breasts firm rather than large, a waist that was trim, and buttocks flat from long hours of riding astride. The gown hid muscled thighs that she sometimes resented, but they, too, were the legacy of twenty Turns riding a dragon and little enough inconvenience for being a queen's rider.

She did wish that Sh'gall had chosen to come with her. She wasn't acquainted with the new Ruathan Lord Holder, Alessan. She had a vague recollection that he was the leggy young man with light-green eyes that were an odd contrast to his dark complexion and shaggy black hair. He had always stood most correctly behind the old Lord Holder, his father. Lord Leef had been a stern if just holder from whom the Weyr could expect every traditional duty and the last tittle of tithe: just the sort of man the Weyr, and Pern, needed in command of such a prosperous Hold. But then, at Ruatha traditions had always been zealously maintained, and many of that bloodline had impressed queen as well as bronze.

None of the many sons that the old Lord Leef had bred had known which would be named his successor. Lord Leef had kept the whole tangle of them in hand, preventing discord. Despite Threadfall and the other dangers of a Pass, Lord Leef had contrived to build several new holds into the sides of Ruatha's steep valleys, to accommodate the worthiest of his sons and their families. Such expansion had been one of his many schemes to keep order in his Hold. Lord Leef had planned ahead for the end of the Pass as well as for an orderly succession. Moreta could not fault such provisions though Sh'gall, among other dragonriders, had become concerned over the creeping expansion of the hold populations. Six Weyrs, twenty-three hundred dragons, were hard-pressed to keep cultivated lands Threadfree in this Pass. There had been talk of founding another Weyr during the Interval. That would not be her problem, however.

Moreta set the gold and green jeweled band at her neck and slipped on her heavy bracelets. The light-eyed man *must* be Alessan. She had often seen him at the end of Fall with the flamethrower gangs. Always correct in his manner, nevertheless Alessan's presence was felt despite his reserve. For the life of her, Moreta couldn't remember as distinctly any of the other nine sons though they all seemed to have inherited the strong craggy features of their sire rather than those of their various mothers.

Today would be Alessan's first Gather since the Conclave of Lord Holders had confirmed his accession to Ruathan honors at the beginning of the Turn. Rest days, Threadfree days, and clear weather combined infrequently.

"Since there are the two Gathers, I shall attend Ista's," Sh'gall had told her that morning. "I told Alessan so yesterday, and it didn't displease him." Sh'gall gave a scornful snort. "He's got every rag and tag at the race meeting of his so you should enjoy yourself." Sh'gall did not approve of Moreta's uninhibited enjoyment of racing and, on those few occasions when they had attended a Gather since Orlith's mating flight with Kadith, he had put quite a damper on her pleasure in the sport. "I shall enjoy the sun and the seafood. Lord Fitatric always provides superb feasts. I can only hope you'll do as well at Ruatha."

"I've never found fault with Ruathan hospitality." Something in Sh'gall's tone required her to defend the Hold. Sh'gall had been awed by Lord Leef, but not by the new young Lord. Moreta did not always agree with Sh'gall's snap judgments so she would wait and form her own opinion of Alessan.

"Besides, I've promised to convey Lord Ratoshigan to Ista. He does not care to attend Ruatha. He does wish to see the curious new animal to be displayed at Ista."

"Oh?"

"Thought you might have heard?" Sh'gall's tone implied she should have known what he was talking about. "Seamen from Igen Sea Hold found the beast adrift in the Great Current, clinging to a floating tree. They'd never seen its like and took it to the Master Herdsman in Keroon."

Ah, Moreta thought, that was why she should have known. Why Sh'gall assumed she knew everything that transpired in her native hold she did not know. She was firmly and totally committed to Fort Weyr, and had been for ten Turns.

"It's some species of feline, I hear," Sh'gall added. "Probably something left behind on the Southern Continent. Quite a fierce beast. Wiser to leave that sort."

"With the way we're being overrun by tunnel snakes, a fierce, hungry feline might be useful. The canines aren't quick enough." Her comment annoyed Sh'gall, who gave her one of his dark, ambiguous glares and stalked out of the weyr. His unexpected reaction irritated Moreta. Not for the first time, she heartily wished that Sh'gall's Kadith had not flown Orlith a second time. Then she told herself firmly that old L'mal had considered Sh'gall one of the ablest wingleaders. Until the end of the Pass, Fort Weyr needed the ablest wingleader. Everyone had thought L'mal would last out the Pass, so his sudden illness and death had been a great loss. Moreta had always liked L'mal, and Leri spoke very highly of him as a weyrmate. Sh'gall was young, Moreta reminded herself; this was not an easy time to assume Weyrleadership, and Sh'gall suffered by comparison to the older, more experienced L'mal. Time would teach Sh'gall tolerance and understanding. Meanwhile Moreta must have those qualities in full measure to survive his learning period.

As Moreta lifted the fur cape about her shoulders, the bracelets slid up her arms. They had been the gift of old Lord Leef for her having ridden Thread down—perilously close for the safety of Orlith—to the Lord's cherished fruit trees, which were threatened by the parasite. Aided by Orlith's agile maneuvering, Moreta had seared the Thread to harmless char with her flamethrower. She had been very young then, just transferred to Fort Weyr from Ista and eager to prove to her new folk just how keen and clever Orlith was. She wouldn't take such a risk now, though it was not due to the memory of the rage in the eyes of L'mal, who had been Weyrleader then, when he had berated her for recklessness. Leef's gift had not appreciably lessened her disgrace or eased her conscience, but they looked well with her new gown.

Are we going to the Gather at all? Orlith asked wistfully.

"Yes, we are going to the Gather," Moreta replied, shaking her head clear of such reflections.

She'd have a good Gather, too, for Ruatha Hold would be gay and bright, dominated by the young Alessan's young friends. Sh'gall had said that they were still full of their success, that he'd had to remind Alessan that Thread brought no joy and he must attend his duties as Lord Holder before attending to his pleasures.

"Perhaps it's just as well Sh'gall decided to go to Ista . . . and take Lord Ratoshigan with him," Moreta told Orlith, convincing herself in the process.

He and Kadith are well occupied, Orlith said complacently as she followed her rider from their weyr.

Orlith paused on the ledge, glancing around the Weyr Bowl. Most of the sun-struck ledges usually occupied by dragons were empty.

Have they all gone? Orlith asked in surprise, craning her neck to see the shadowed west ledges.

"With two Gathers? Of course. I hope we're not too late for the racing."

Orlith blinked her great, many-faceted eyes. *You and your racing.*

"You enjoy it as much as I do and generally have a far better view on the fire-heights. Don't fret. It's fun to watch, but I ride only you."

Mollified by her rider's teasing assurance, Orlith crouched, setting her forearm so Moreta could climb to her place between the last two neck ridges above her shoulder. Moreta settled her skirts and pulled the cloak about her. Nothing would really keep her warm in the awesome total cold of *between* but the transition lasted only a few breaths, which anyone could endure.

Orlith sprang from the ledge. Though gravid, she was not a lazy dragon, to tumble off into the air before making first use of her wings. The old queen, Holth, trumpeted a farewell; the watchdragon spread his wings, masking the Star Stones on the summit. The watchrider extended his arm, completing the salute as Moreta waved acknowledgment.

Orlith caught the wind flowing down the oblong Bowl, the crater of an extinct volcano which was home to the Weyr. In a distant Turn, an earthslide had rampaged down the range, broken through the southwest part of the Weyr and into the lake. Stonecraftsmen had cleared the lake and shored up the edge in a massive wall but little could be done to clear the lost caverns and weyrs, or restore the symmetry of the Bowl.

"Surveying your Weyr, o Queen?" Moreta asked, indulging Orlith's leisurely glide.

At height, one sees many details in proper order. All is well.

Moreta's laugh was blown from her lips, and she had to hang on to the riding straps. Orlith constantly surprised her with gratuitous observations. Conversely, when Moreta needed guidance, Orlith might reply that she didn't understand any rider but Moreta. The queen could be counted on to comment on the Weyr in general, or on the morale of the fighting wings, or to supply information about the Weyrleader's dragon, Kadith. Orlith was not so forthcoming about Sh'gall. But, after twenty Turns of their symbiotic relationship, Moreta had learned to discover as much in the queen's impartiality or evasion as from her candid remarks. Being a queen's rider was never easy. Being the Weyrwoman, Leri had more than once told Moreta, doubled both honors and horrors. One took the good with the bad and used fellis sparingly.

Now Moreta visualized the fire-heights of Ruatha Hold, with its distinctive pattern of fire-gutters and beacons and the eastern watch rampart.

Take us to Ruatha, she said to Orlith and clenched her teeth against the cold of *between.*

> "Black, blacker, blackest; colder beyond frozen things,
> Where is *between* when there is naught
> To Life but fragile dragon wings."

Moreta often held the words of the old song as a talisman against the bitter breathless journey. Ruatha was not far from Fort Weyr by any means of travel, and Moreta had only reached "colder" when the warm sun shone on them and on Ruatha's fire-heights below. The host of dragons lounging on the rocky cliff summit, whole wings of them, voiced greetings at Orlith's appearance in the air. Orlith's thoughts echoed her pleasure in the accolade. Dragons met so rarely for pleasure, Moreta mused. Thread was the cause. Soon, in eight Turns . . .

As the queen glided down, Moreta recognized some of the dragons from other Weyrs by the scar patterns on their bodies and wings.

Bronzes from Telgar and High Reaches, Orlith reported, making her own identifications, *browns, blues, and greens. But Benden has been and gone. We should have come earlier.* The last held a plaintive note because Orlith had a partiality for the Benden bronze Tuzuth.

"Sorry, dear heart, but I had so much to do."

Orlith snorted. Moreta felt the jerk of chest muscles through the dragon's withers. She had begun to circle, dropping toward the fire-heights. Anticipating a landing, Moreta tightened her hold on the straps. Orlith overshot the heights, clearly headed down over the roadway crowded with the stalls of the Gather and a milling throng of folk gaily dressed for the occasion. Suddenly Moreta realized that Orlith meant to land in the empty dancing square ringed by lamp standards, trestle tables, and benches.

I do not forget that we are senior now, Orlith said primly, *and that the Hold's honors are due the Fort Weyrwoman.*

Orlith landed with neat precision in the dance square, her broad pinions vaned high to avoid excessive backwinds. The banners on the lamp standards flapped vigorously, but little dust rose from the square already swept to hard ground.

"Well done, dear heart," Moreta said, scratching her mount's back ridge affectionately.

She glanced over at the imposing precipice that housed Ruatha Hold, magnificently topped by ranks of sunbathing dragons. The Hold's unshuttered windows displayed banners and brightly woven rugs. Tables and chairs had been set out on the open forecourt so distinguished visitors could view the gather stalls and the dancing square without obstruction. Moreta glanced quickly in the other direction, toward the flats where the racing was held. She could see the picket lines off to the right. The brightly painted starting poles were not in position so she hadn't missed any racing.

The entire Gather had ceased its activity to watch Orlith's landing. Now there was a stir among the onlookers, who parted to allow a man to step from their midst.

See! The Lord Holder approaches, Orlith said.

Moreta swung her right leg over Orlith's neck, pulling her skirts about, preparatory to dismounting. Then she glanced at the man approaching them. She could just make out his features, which corresponded to her recollection of Lord Leef's light-eyed son. His broad shoulders were held at a confident angle and his rangy stride was assured, neither diffident nor hasty.

He came to an abrupt halt, bowing to Orlith, who lowered her head to acknowledge his greeting. Then he moved on quickly to assist Moreta to dismount, looking intently up at her.

His light-green eyes, unusual in one so dark-skinned, caught hers. His gaze was as formal and impersonal as his hands as he seized her by the waist and swung her down from Orlith's forearm. He bowed, and Moreta couldn't but notice that his shaggy hair had been neatly trimmed and attractively shaped.

"Weyrwoman, welcome to Ruatha Hold. I had begun to think that you and Orlith were not going to attend." His voice was unexpectedly tenor for a man so tall and lean, his words clearly spoken.

"I bring the Weyrleader's regrets."

"He gave them in advance yesterday. It would have been your regrets which I, and Ruatha, would have been sad to receive. Orlith is in splendid color," he added, his voice unexpectedly warming, "for a queen so near clutching."

The queen blinked her rainbow-hued eyes, echoing the surprise that Moreta felt in Alessan's adherence to formalities. Moreta hadn't expected so polished a delivery from so young a man but, after all, Leef had drilled his heir in the proprieties. Besides, she was always ready to discuss Orlith.

"She's in great health and she's always that unusual shade."

As her reply deviated from the tradition, Alessan hesitated.

"Now, some dragons are so light as to be more pale yellow than gold while others are dark enough to vie with the bronzes. Yet she is *not*"—Moreta eyed her queen candidly—"the classic shade."

Alessan chuckled. "Does shade make any difference?"

"Certainly not to me. I would scarcely mind if Orlith were green-gold. She is my queen, and I am her rider." She glanced at Alessan, wondering if he was mocking her. But his green eyes, with their tiny flecks of brown around the pupil, registered only polite query.

Alessan smiled. "And senior at Fort Weyr."

"As you are Lord of Ruatha." She felt slightly defensive for, despite the innocuous and formal phrases, she sensed an undercurrent in his speech. Had Sh'gall discussed his Weyrwoman with a Lord Holder?

Orlith?

The fire-height is warm in the full sun, the dragon replied evasively, swinging her head toward her rider. The many facets of her eyes were tinged with the blue of longing.

"Off you go, dear heart." Moreta gave Orlith's shoulder a loving thump and then, with Alessan at her side, she walked from the dancing square. As they reached the edge, Orlith leaped, her broad wings clearing the ground in the first downward sweep. The dragon had launched herself in a very shallow angle toward the sheer rock of Ruatha. As the queen flew a mere length above the stalls and gatherers, Moreta could hear the spate of startled cries. Beside her, Alessan stiffened.

Do you know what you're doing, my love? Moreta asked, reasonably but firm. *You're a bit egg-heavy for antics.*

I am demonstrating the abilities of their queen. It will do them good and me no harm. See?

Orlith had judged her angle finely, though from Moreta's perspective, she looked to be in danger of clipping her forearms on the cliff edge. But Orlith cleared the cliff easily and, dropping her shoulder, spun almost on wingtip. She set her hindquarters down directly over the Hold's main entrance, in the space vacated by other dragons. Then she flipped her wings to her back, sank down, and rested her triangular head on her forearms.

Exhibitionist! Moreta sent without rancor. "She's comfortable now, Lord Alessan."

"I had heard of Orlith's reputation for close flying," he replied, his eyes flicking to the jewelry Moreta wore.

So the young Lord knew of the old Lord's gift.

"An advantage in Threadfall."

"This is a Gather." With that slight emphasis on the pronoun, Alessan spoke as Lord Holder.

"And where is it more appropriate to display skill and craft and beauty?" Moreta gestured toward the gaily caparisoned stalls and the richly colored tunics and dresses of the crowd. She removed her hand from his arm, partly to show her annoyance with his criticism and partly to loosen her cloak. The chill of *between* had been replaced by the warmth of the afternoon sun. "Come now, Lord Alessan"—and she linked her arm through his again—"let us have no uncharitable words at your first Gather as Lord of Ruatha and my first outing since the winter solstice."

They had reached the roadway and the stalls where people were examining wares and bargaining. Moreta smiled up at Lord Alessan to prove her firm intention of enjoying herself. He looked down at her, blinking and creasing his dark brows slightly. His expression cleared to a smile, still reserved but considerably more genuine than his stiff formality.

"I fear I have none of my dam's virtues, Lady Moreta."

"And all of your sire's vices?"

"My good Lord Leef had no vices," Alessan said very properly, but his eyes had begun to gleam with an amusement that proved to Moreta that the man had at least a vestige of his sire's humor.

"The races haven't started yet?"

Alessan missed a stride and glanced sharply at her.

"No, not yet." His tone was wary. "We have been waiting for late arrivals."

"There seemed to be a good number at the pickets. How many races?" She gave him a quick glance. Didn't he approve of racing?

"Ten races are planned, but the entries have been lighter than I had anticipated. You enjoy racing, Lady Moreta?"

"I came from a runnerhold in Keroon, Lord Alessan, and I have never lost my interest in the breed."

"So you know where to place your wagers?"

"Lord Alessan," she said in a determinedly light tone, "I never wager. The sight of a good race well run is always a pleasure and excitement enough." His manner was still uncertain so she changed the subject. "I believe that we've missed the eastern visitors."

"The Benden Weyrwoman and Weyrleader have only just left us." Alessan's eyes sparkled at having acted the host to such prestigious guests.

"I had hoped to exchange news with them." Moreta's regret was sincere, but she was also relieved. The Benden Weyrleaders did not like Orlith's fascination with Tuzuth, the Benden bronze, any more than she herself did. Such cross-weyr interests were encouraged in young queens but not in seniors. "Did Benden's Lord Holder come, too?"

"Yes." Pleasure tinged Alessan's tone. "Lord Shadder and I had only the briefest but most congenial of talks. Most congenial. East and West don't often have much chance to meet. Have you met Lord Shadder?"

"When I was in Ista Weyr." Moreta smiled back at Alessan, for Shadder of Benden was undoubtedly the most popular Lord Holder on Pern. His warmth and concern always seemed intensely personal. She sighed. "I really wish I had been able to come sooner. Who else attends?"

The briefest of frowns crossed Alessan's face. "At the moment," he said briskly, "holders and Craftmasters from Ruatha, Fort, Crom, Nabol, Tillek and High Reaches. A long journey for some, but everyone seems well pleased that the warm weather had held for the Gather." He glanced about the crowded stalls, noting trades in the making. "Tillek's Lord Holder may arrive later with the High Reaches Weyrleader. Lord Tolocamp rode in an hour ago and is changing."

Moreta grinned in sympathy with Alessan. Lord Tolocamp was an energetic, forceful man who spoke his mind and gave his opinion on every topic as if he were the universal expert. As he did not have the least sense of humor, exchanges with him were apt to be awkward and boring. Moreta preferred to avoid his company whenever possible. But, as she was now senior Weyrwoman, she had fewer excuses to do so.

"How many of his ladies came with him?"

"Five." Alessan's voice was carefully neutral. "My mother, Lady Oma, always enjoys a visit with Lady Pendra."

Moreta had to choke back a laugh and turned her face slightly away. All Pern knew that Lady Pendra was angling to get Alessan to marry one of her numerous daughters, nieces, or cousins. Alessan's young wife, Suriana, had died the previous Turn in a fall. At the time, Lord Leef had not pressed his son to make another marriage, a fact that many had taken to mean that Alessan was not to succeed. As the Fort Hold girls were as plain as they were capable, Moreta didn't think much of Fort's chances, but Alessan would be obliged to marry soon if he wished his own bloodline to succeed.

"Would it please the Fort Weyrwoman for Lord Alessan to take a Fort Holder as wife?" His voice was cold and stiff.

"You can surely do better than that," Moreta replied crisply and then laughed. "I'm sorry. It is not really a subject for levity, but you don't know how you sound."

"And how do I sound?" Alessan's eyes glinted.

"Like a man sorely pressed in a direction he does not wish to travel. This is your first Gather. You should enjoy it, too."

"Will you help me?" Pure mischief played across his face now.

"How?"

"You're my Weyrwoman." His face assumed a proper respect. "Since Sh'gall has not accompanied you, I must be your partner."

"In conscience, I could not monopolize your time." Even as she spoke, Moreta realized that that was what she would rather like to do. There was a rebellion in him that attracted her.

"Most of it?" His voice was wistfully pleading, quite a variance with his sparkling eyes and grin. "I know what I have to do but . . ."

"There'll be girls here from *all* over—"

"Yes, a Search has been conducted for my benefit."

"What else did you expect, Lord Alessan, when you're now such a suitable match?"

"Suriana liked *me*, not my prospects," Alessan said in a flat bleak voice. "When that match was arranged, of course, I had none, so we could suit ourselves. And we did."

So that explained why he had been allowed to grieve and defer a second marriage. Moreta hadn't thought Lord Leef had so much compassion in him. "You were more fortunate than most," she said, oddly envious. Once she had Impressed a queen, personal choice had been denied her. Once she had Impressed Orlith, their love compensated for many things; love for another human paled in comparison.

"I was acutely aware of my good luck." In that quiet phrase, Alessan implied not only his loss but his realization that he must discharge the responsibilities of his new rank. Moreta wondered why Sh'gall had developed a curious antipathy to the man.

They were moving through the Gatherers, past the stalls. Moreta sniffed deeply of the aromas of spicy stew and sweet fruit pies, the odor of well-tanned leathers, the acrid smell from the glass-blowers' booth, the mingled smells of perfumes and garment herbs, the sweat of human and animal. And above all, the pleasant excitement that permeated the atmosphere.

"Within the bounds of Gather propriety, I accept your partnering. Provided that you like racing and dancing."

"In that order?"

"Since the one comes before the other, yes."

"I appreciate your courtesy, Weyrwoman!" His tone was mock-formal.

"Have the harpers arrived yet?"

"Yesterday . . ." Alessan grimaced.

"They *do* eat, don't they?"

"They *talk*. There are enough of them, however, to keep the dancing square filled until dawn, now that your queen has graced it. And our ever jovial Masterharper has promised to dignify our Gather with his presence."

Moreta frowned at yet another undercurrent in Alessan's speech. Didn't he like Tirone? The Masterharper was a big hearty man with a robust bass voice that he allowed to dominate every group he sang in. He favored the rousing ballads and stirring sagas that best displayed his own talents, but that was his one conceit, and Moreta had never considered it a flaw. But then, herself only lately the Weyrwoman, she had not seen as much of him in his capacity as Masterharper of Pern as had Alessan. She didn't think she would like to antagonize Tirone.

"He has a beautiful voice," she said noncommittally. "Is Master Capiam coming?"

"So I believe."

Shells, thought Moreta to herself at Alessan's terse reply. With the exception of Lord Shadder, Alessan apparently did not share any of her preferences among the leaders of Pern. She'd never heard of anyone who didn't like Masterhealer Capiam. Could Alessan fault the man for failing to mend his wife's broken back?

"Is that sort of exercise good for Orlith at this time, Moreta?" demanded Lord Tolocamp, bearing down on them suddenly. He must have been following their progress along the roadway to have intercepted them so neatly.

"She's not due to clutch for another ten days." Moreta stiffened, annoyed both by the question and the questioner.

"Orlith flew with great precision," Alessan said. "An ability well appreciated by Ruatha."

Lord Tolocamp checked, coughed, covering his mouth belatedly and plainly not understanding Alessan's reference.

"She's thoroughly shameless," Moreta said, "whenever there's a new audience for her tricks. She's never so much as bunged a claw."

"Yes, well, ah, Lady Pendra is just over here, Moreta," Tolocamp went on with his usual ponderous geniality. "Alessan, I would like you to become better acquainted with my daughters."

"At the moment, Lord Tolocamp, I am obliged to become better acquainted with the Weyrwoman, as Sh'gall is not here as her escort. Your daughters"—Alessan looked over at the young women, who were talking placidly with some of his subordinates—"seem well suited."

Tolocamp began to huff.

"A glass of wine, Moreta? This way." Alessan firmly propelled her away from Lord Tolocamp, who stood staring after them, somewhat surprised by their abrupt departure.

"I'll never hear the last of this from him, you know," Moreta said as she allowed herself to be hurried off.

"Then you can drown your sorrow in a Benden white wine I have chilling." He beckoned to a servitor, pantomiming the pouring of wine into a glass.

"Benden white? Why, that's my favorite!"

"And here I thought you were partial to Tillek's."

Moreta made a face. "I'm obliged to *assume* a partiality for Tillek wines."

"I find them sharp. Soil's acid in Tillek."

"True, but Tillek tithes its wines to Fort Weyr. And it's far easier to agree with Lord Diatis than argue with him."

Alessan laughed.

As the servitor returned with two finely engraved cups and a small wineskin, Moreta glimpsed Lord Tolocamp, Lady Pendra, and Lady Oma shepherding the daughters toward them. Just then a stentorian voice proclaimed the start of the runner races.

"We'll never elude Lady Pendra. Where can we go?" Moreta asked, but Alessan was staring toward the race course.

"I have a particular reason for wanting to watch that first race. If we hurry . . ." He pointed to the roadway that wound to the racing flats, but that path would not avoid the Fortian progression.

"Short of calling on Orlith's assistance, we'd never make it. And she's asleep." Then Moreta saw the scaffold surrounding the wall being built at the southern edge of the forecourt. "Why not up there?" She pointed.

"Perfect—and you've a head for heights!" Alessan took her hand and guided her deftly through the guests and away from the Fortians.

Those already standing by the unfinished courses of the wall made room for the Lord Holder and the Weyrwoman. Alessan put his goblet in her free hand and neatly jumped to the top course. Then he knelt, gesturing for her to hand up both wine cups.

For just a moment, Moreta hesitated. L'mal had often chided her about the dignity expected of Weyrwomen, especially outside the precincts of the Weyr, where holder, crafter, and harper could observe and criticise. Quite likely she had been stimulated by Orlith's outrageous exhibition. What affected dragon affected rider. It was a lovely warm Gather, just the respite she'd needed from her onerous responsibilities all Turn. There was racing and Benden wine, there'd be dancing later. Moreta, Weyrwoman of Fort Weyr, was going to enjoy herself.

You should, you know, Orlith commented sleepily.

"Hurry," Alessan said. "They're milling at the start."

Moreta turned to the nearest dragonrider at the wall.

"Give me a leg up, R'limeak, would you?"

"Moreta!"

"Oh, don't be scandalized. I want to see the race start." She arranged her skirts and bent her left knee. "A good lift, R'limeak. I'd rather not scrape my nose on the stones."

R'limeak's lift was not wholehearted. If Alessan's strong hands had not steadied her, she would have slipped.

"How shocked he looks!" Alessan laughed, his green eyes merry.

"It'll do him good. Blue riders can be so prim!" She took her wine from Alessan. "Ah, what a marvelous view!" Having observed that the race was not about to start, she turned slowly, to appreciate the sweep of the land from the foot of Ruatha's cliff hold, over the crude roofs of the decorated stalls, to the empty dancing square, the fields beyond, the walled orchards on each side, and then the slope that descended gradually to Ruatha's river, its source the Ice Lake high in the mountains above. True, the orchards were bare, the fields browned by what frost had fallen that Turn, but the sky was a vivid green-blue, not a cloud in sight, and the air was pleasantly warm. Favored with a long eye, Moreta saw that three laggard racers had yet to join the starters.

"Ruatha's looking so gay," she said. "Generally when I'm here, the shutters are all in place against Thread, not a soul or beast in sight. Today it's a different place entirely."

"We are often good company here," Alessan said. His eyes lay on the scene at the starting poles. "Ruatha is considered one of the best-placed Holds. Fort may be older but, I think, not so well laid out."

"The harpers tell us that Fort Hold was thrown together as a temporary accommodation after the Crossing."

"A mere fourteen hundred Turns *temporary*. Whereas we of Ruatha have always been planners. We even have special accommodations for visiting race enthusiasts."

Moreta grinned at him. She realized that they were both rambling on in excitement at the impending race.

"Look! They're finally lined up!"

The mild breeze cooperated by blowing the churned dust of the racing flats away from the straggling line of cavorting beasts. She saw the white flag drop, caught her breath at the incredible leap as the animals surged forward.

"This is the sprint?" she asked, trying to make out an early leader in the knot of nodding heads, bobbing bodies, and flashing legs. So close packed were the runners that neither riders' hat colors nor saddle pads could be identified.

"As is usual," Alessan replied absently, shielding his eyes with his hand to see better.

"Good field, too. Spreading out and . . . I'd swear the leader is wearing Ruathan colors!"

"I hope so!" Alessan cried in considerable excitement.

Cheers and exhortations rose from nearby and drifted up from the race course.

"Fort is challenging!" Moreta said as a second beast separated from the pack. "And fast!"

"It has only to hold!" Alessan's words were half threat, half entreaty.

"It will!" Moreta's calm assurance elicited a quick disbelieving glare from Alessan, who remained taut with suspense until the winners passed the post. "It did!"

"Are you sure?"

"Certainly. The poles are parallel to this vantage point. You've a winner! Did you breed it yourself?"

"Yes, yes, I did. And it did win!" He seemed to need her confirmation of his achievement.

"It certainly did. A very respectable two lengths the winner or I miss my mark. And I don't miss in racing. To your winner then!" She raised her goblet to his.

"My winner!" His voice was curiously fierce, and the light in his eyes became more defiant than triumphant.

"I'll come with you to the finish," she suggested, noticing that the sprinters were finally pulling up in the stubble.

"I can savor this moment just as fully in your company," he said unexpectedly. "And with no inhibitions," he added with a grin. "Dag's there. He's my herdsman, and this is as much his victory as it is mine. I won't detract from his moment. Then, too, it would be highly inappropriate for the Gathering Lord Holder to caper about like a fool over a mere sprint win."

Moreta found his admission of unlordly glee rather charming. "Surely this isn't your first winner?"

"Actually, it is." He was searching the enclosure and suddenly beckoned peremptorily at a servitor, signaling for more wine. "Breeding for special traits was the project Lord Leef assigned me eight Turns ago." Alessan went on in a more conversational tone though his voice still carried an edge. "A well-established Pernese tradition is breeding."

"Eight Turns ago?" Moreta gave Alessan a long look. "If you've been breeding since then, surely this can't be your *first* winner?"

"A race, yes. The quality Lord Leef wished me to perpetuate was stamina for long-distance carting, combined with more efficient use of fodder."

"More work out of fewer animals for less food?" Moreta didn't find that hard to believe of the old Lord, but she stared at Alessan with confused respect. "And out of that breeding, you got a sprint racer?"

"Not intentionally." Alessan gave her a rueful smile. "That winner is from a strain of rejects from the original project: tough, hardy, good doers even on poor feed, but small bodied and thin boned. They don't eat much, and everything they consume goes into short spurts of energy—fifty dragon-length sprint distances, to be truthful. Over the ninety-length mark, they're useless. Give 'em half an hour's rest and they can repeat that sort of winning performance. And they live long. It was Dag who saw the sprint potential in the scrubs."

"But, of course, you couldn't race the beasts during your father's lifetime." Moreta started to chuckle at Alessan's deception.

"Hardly." Alessan grinned.

"I imagine that your winnings today—an untried beast in its first race— will be substantial."

"I should hope so. Considering how long Dag and I have succored that wretched creature for just such an occasion as this."

"My sincerest congratulations, Lord Alessan!" Moreta raised her newly filled goblet. "For putting one over on Lord Leef and winning your first race at your first Gather. You're not only devious, you're a menace to racing men."

"Had I known you were such a race enthusiast, I'd've given you odds—"

"Spectator, not speculator. You'll race it next at Fort's Gather?"

"Considering its capability, I could race in the last sprint today and be sure of its winning, but that would not be courteous." The gleam in his eye suggested that if he weren't Lord Holder, he would not have felt any such restraint. "At that, most will assume it a lucky win. Only the one race in it, like as not." Alessan's voice imitated the pitch and inflection of the confirmed racer, querulous and skeptical. "So I shall get it to whatever Gathers we can reach. I like winning. It's a new experience."

His candor surprised her. "Are you sure your sire didn't know what you were about? Lord Leef always struck me as a man who had firm control of everything that occurred in his Hold—in the entire west."

Alessan gave her a long hard look, mulling her remark. "D'you know, I wouldn't be at all surprised if he *had* found out. We, Dag and I, took such extraordinary precautions. We thought we'd covered every possibility of discovery." Then Alessan shook his head, chuckling. "You wouldn't believe the lengths to which we went—but you could be right. The old Lord could have known."

"I expect he wouldn't have named you successor on your merits as a breeder alone. What else have you been up to?"

Alessan winked at her. "The Weyr commands my services, Lady, not my secrets."

"I've found *one* out. Shall I—" Moreta paused, suddenly aware that their laughing exchanges were being closely observed. Why shouldn't she laugh at a Gather? She gave R'limeak a stern glare, and the blue rider looked away.

Noting her change of expression, Alessan glanced about them and swore under his breath. "Not even on a half-built wall in full sight of a Gather!" he said acidly. He swore again as he saw Lord Tolocamp and the women moving purposefully toward the wall.

"Shards!" Moreta said. "I will not have the racing spoiled by chitchat and courtship. Look, we'll be able to see just as well from over there!" She pointed to a slight rise in the field below the roadway. Then she gathered her skirts and started to pick a careful path down the pile of stones waiting to be set into the wall. "And do collect that skin of white wine."

"Be careful, you'll break your neck!" Alessan urgently signaled the servitor to hand over the wineskin, then he was following her before anyone was aware of their intentions.

Rocks shifting under their feet, Moreta and Alessan reached the roadway without mishap, then hurried behind the stalls and down the open field to the rise. When Moreta felt burrs pulling at her full skirts, she bundled them higher.

"No propriety in you at all today." Alessan shook his head at her undignified lope, though he was placing his elegantly booted feet with a care for rough ground.

"This is a Gather. An informal occasion."

"You are not dressed informally." He caught her by the elbow as she tripped. "That gown was not designed for cross-country scrambles. Ah! Here we are"—he came to an abrupt halt, "an unimpeded view of the start and finish lines. Let me fill your goblet."

"Please." Moreta held it up.

"Why didn't I know that the Fort Weyrwoman liked racing enough to desert the forecourt and its pleasures?"

"I've been at all Ruatha's Gathers the past ten Turns—"

"Up *there*, though." He gestured back to the forecourt.

"Of course, as befits my rank. L'mal didn't like me to roam the picket lines."

"Which was where I generally was." Alessan grinned.

"Learning how to breed winners?"

"Of course not." Alessan feigned shocked innocence. "I was supposed to breed stamina, not speed. *My* Gather duties were to assist our race-course manager, Norman."

Moreta lifted her goblet again. "To the man who persevered and won the race!"

Alessan was quick-witted and grinned at her subtlety. Their eyes met in a candid gaze. Moreta felt a growing affinity for the new Lord Holder and not only because of their mutual interest in race runners. His mind was unpredictable, certainly not in the pattern of the usual Lord Holder, if she compared him to Tolocamp, Ratoshigan, or Diatis. He was good company, with a fine sense of humor; if he danced as well as he did everything else, she might just monopolize him this evening.

Two more dragons arrived midair as she glanced up, away from Alessan's light-green, compelling gaze. Then her eyes dropped slightly to admire Orlith, ensconced right above the main hold door, and she thought how well Orlith's golden hide complimented the window hangings on the top tier. Embarrassed, she looked away, aware that Alessan had been watching her.

"A habit, really," she said with a self-conscious shrug.

"Surely after twenty Turns as partners—"

"Are you already accustomed to being Lord of Ruatha Hold?"

"Not yet. I've only been—" Alessan broke off, his eyes on her face, noting her fond smile. "Even after twenty Turns?"

"Ah, look. The flag for the next race!" She diverted his attention. One could never explain the bond to someone who wasn't a dragonrider. Impression was a private miracle, a very private miracle.

CHAPTER

II

Ruatha Hold, Present Pass, 3.10.43

The second race was over a greater length, the winning poles having been moved down the field and farther apart to accommodate the larger number of middle-distance runners.

"Have you an entry in this race, too?" she asked Alessan as the runners charged away from the start.

"No. I got either spindly sprinters or massive carters from my crosses. But one of my holders has a strong contestant—blue with red hatching are the colors. Not that you can distinguish them."

The field had already begun to stretch out when suddenly an animal in the middle of the pack fell, tripping two others. Moreta could never watch a bad tangle without apprehension. She was holding her breath as she silently urged each animal to its feet. Two rose, one groggily shaking its head, the second running on down the field, riderless. The third made no effort to rise.

Moreta picked up her skirts and began to run toward the fallen runner.

"It shouldn't've fallen." *Orlith!*

"Close-packed field. Tripped." Alessan kept pace with her, caught up in her concern.

"Not that close, and it wasn't a trip fall." She saved her breath for running even when she had seen that the two riders were examining the fallen beast and that handlers were running up from the starting line. *Orlith, what's wrong? Why doesn't it get up?*

As she got closer, Moreta could see the sprawled beast's sides heaving. Its nose touched the ground yet it made no effort to rise. That was unusual enough. Runners preferred to stand.

Did it break a leg, Orlith?

"It can't get its breath," one rider was saying to the other. "It's got a bloody nose."

"Probably ruptured a vein falling. Just get it to its feet. Here, I'll help." The second rider begun to tug at the bridle.

Orlith, wake up! I need you.

"It should've got to its feet. Lord Alessan! Lady Moreta!" The first rider turned anxiously to them, and Moreta recognized the man as Helly, a capable herdsman and racer.

It cannot breathe, Orlith responded sleepily. She sounded a bit grumpy at being roused. *Its lungs are full of liquid.*

Moreta knelt at the animal's head, noticing the distressed flare of the nostrils, the bloody discharge. She felt for the pulse in its throat, weak and far too erratic for an animal that had only run a few dragon-lengths before falling.

Around her men were shouting that the runner should be assisted to its feet. Several positioned themselves to heave. Moreta waved them off imperiously.

"It can't breathe. No air is getting into its lungs."

"Cut into its windpipe. Who's got a sharp blade?"

"It's too late," Moreta said as she peeled back the upper lip, exposing the whitened gums.

The onlookers knew, as she did, that the animal was dying. From the finishing line the sound of cheering drifted back to those circling the faller. It gave one final sigh, almost apologetic, and the head rolled to the side.

"Ain't seen nothing like this before," the second rider said. "And I been riding since I could tighten a girth."

"You were riding it, Helly?" Alessan asked.

"Yes, doing a favor for Vander. His jock was sick. I've never ridden it before. Seemed quiet." Helly stopped, considered. "Too quiet, now I think about it. Rode in the first race, and this one was all ready for me . . . Broke well at the start as if it wanted to work!" Helly's tone was a mixture of despair, anger, and surprise.

"Could've been the heart," one of the onlookers suggested in a tone of broad experience. "That takes 'em sudden. No way of telling. Runner in good spirit one moment, dead the next. Takes people that way, too."

Not, Moreta thought, with a bloody nasal discharge.

"Here now," a loud voice cried. "What's the matter here? Why isn't this animal . . . Oh, Lord Alessan. Didn't know you were here!" The race manager had pushed his way into the circle. "It's dead? Excuse me, Lord Alessan, but we do have to clear the track for the next race."

Alessan took the shaken Helly by the arm. Moreta stepped to the man's other side, leading him through the pathway courteously made by the crowd.

"I don't understand it. No, I don't." Helly was obviously in shock.

Moreta realized that she still had the wine goblet and held it up to Alessan, who quickly unslung the wineskin and poured a full cup. Moreta gave it to Helly. The racer drank the contents in one gulp.

"Helly, what happened? Did it plait its legs or something?"

The stocky man, dressed in Ruathan colors, staggered as he realized who was assisting Helly. While trying to hold a pad of wet toweling to his forehead, he also attempted to bow to Alessan and Moreta. And staggered again.

"Helly, what happened? Oh, shards!" The last was said in a low voice as a cart bearing the dead animal off the track rumbled into view.

"Vander, are you all right?" Helly demanded. He handed Moreta her goblet and went to the stunned holder. Helly supported Vander in the wake of the cart.

Moreta, Alessan by her side, watched the activity of Gather races swirl and close behind the sad procession. Men, laden with tack or blankets or buckets of water, briskly moved toward the picket lines. The sound of urgent conversations and shouts was occasionally punctuated by the squeal of excited runners.

"I *cannot* remember a respiratory illness that would result in such a remarkably swift death," Moreta said.

"I'd've said the animal was only stunned by the fall and would have gotten to its feet," Alessan remarked. "How did you know what ailed it so fast?"

"My family has always raised runners," she explained quickly, for it was not common knowledge outside the Weyrs that she and Orlith worked together in healing.

"Your early training must have been remarkable. I thought I'd learned a thing or two about runners."

"If you bred that sprinter while looking for endurance stock, you have."

Just then two runners, long-distance racers by the look of them, were led past, and Moreta kept her eyes on them until they mixed into the crowd.

"Nothing wrong with them, is there?"

"Oh, no. They look racing fit. Not so much as a nervous sweat on them."

"Has it been crossing your mind that Vander's runner dropped dead of an illness?"

"It crossed my mind," Moreta agreed, "but it's highly unlikely. Helly said the runner *wanted* to race. A sick one wouldn't. Could have been the heart."

"Well, I'm not looking for trouble. Not today, at my first Gather." Alessan frowned and turned slowly on his right heel, casting his eyes down the rows of picketed runners. "It has to be a fluke. I know Vander. His hold's a good day's ride south. He's been saving that particular runner for this race." Alessan sighed. "We can have a look at the rest of his string. They'd be picketed over here if I recall the assignments." Alessan took Moreta's arm, guiding her to the right.

If the beast had been fit, Moreta thought, how could its lungs have filled so quickly? She considered asking Orlith but she sensed that the queen had returned to sleep. Runners did not have the same priority with the dragon as they did with the rider.

Alessan pulled Moreta to him suddenly as a rangy beast plunged past them, its eyes wild as it anticipated its race, the rider barely able to stay in the pad. Two handlers jogged along, at a distance respectful of the kicking range of an excited runner. Moreta watched its progress to the starting line.

"Well?" Alessan's tenor voice asked in her ear.

She was abruptly aware that she was still in his loose protective embrace. "No, that one seemed far from ill." She moved away from him.

"And here's Vander's picket." Alessan counted them. "As I recall he'd entered seven. Did you say you were from Keroon? This is a runner he bought from Keroon last Turn."

Moreta laughed as she let the runner sniff her hand. She stroked its head until it accepted her touch then she felt its warm ear for the breed tattoo.

"No, it didn't come from my family's hold."

Alessan grinned at her whimsy as he examined the other animals. "They're in good shape. Vander got here two days ago to rest them well before the races. I'll have a word with him later. Shall we get back to the races—Shells!" The shouts and movements of the crowd indicated that the next race had started. Alessan looked abashed. "Now you've missed *another* race."

"I watch the racing because, in my exalted position as Weyrwoman, that is much more dignified than scrambling around the pickets. Which is what I would rather do. Now that we're here, could I see your winner? I've a suspicion that only a sense of duty to your guest has kept you from checking it."

The relief and delight in Alessan's eyes confirmed her guess. He had just indicated the proper direction when a short man with the heavy chest, well-developed arms, and thin shanks of a rider trotted toward them, his face wearing the broadest of smiles.

"Lord Alessan? Have you been looking for Squealer?"

"I have indeed, Dag. Well done! Well done!" Alessan shook Dag by the hand and thumped him across the shoulders. "A fine race. Perfect!"

Dag gave Moreta a stiffly correct bow.

"You are to be congratulated on training a winner," Moreta said. Then she couldn't resist adding, "It's a few people could contrive against Lord Leef."

Dag's expression was one of shock, betrayal, and consternation. "Lady Moreta, I wouldn't . . . I didn't."

Alessan laughed and gave Dag a reassuring clout on the shoulder. "Lady Moreta's runnerhold bred. She approves."

"Where is this Squealer of yours, Dag? I very much want a closer look at such a success."

"This way, Lady. And now he's not all that much to look at close on, mind you," Dag began in the deprecating way of all devoted handlers. "Over to the right, if you would. I walked him cool, Lord Alessan, and washed him down with tepid water. Race didn't take a thing out of him. He could go again . . ." Dag caught himself short with a startled glance at the Lord Holder and the Weyrwoman.

"It's a full male then?" Moreta asked, rescuing Dag from indiscretion.

"That he is. On account of him looking so weedy, I always managed to convince the herdmaster that he was too young yet to be gelded, or too sickly, and shouldn't we wait awhile. Then I'd sneak him off to another field."

"Turn after Turn?" Moreta was impressed by such devotion.

"Squealer doesn't have any distinguishing marks to set him in a man's mind," Alessan said. "There he is."

Suddenly Moreta faced a scrawny, thin-legged, big-kneed, mid-brown runner, standing all by itself at the end of a half-empty picket line. In a pause during which she wracked her brain to find something creditable to say about the beast, all she could see was the length of empty pickets.

"He has a kind eye," she said, blurting it out. "Well placed in the head."

As if Squealer knew he was under discussion, he turned his head and regarded her.

"Intelligence, too. Heart. Calm."

Squealer ducked his head, seemingly agreeing with her points so that all three laughed.

"There really isn't much good you can say about Squealer," Alessan said, absolving her from further comment. He swatted the runner affectionately on the neck.

"Squealer won his first race, Lord Alessan. That's all that needs to be said of him. May he win many more. But not," Moreta added slyly, "all on the same day."

Dag groaned and turned away with embarrassed mortification.

"Lord Alessan, had you expected many more entries?" Moreta asked, gesturing toward the unused pickets.

"Dag, you were assisting Norman . . ."

"Well, we did expect a fair turnout, what with fine weather over the past sevendays and plenty of holds to shelter strings on the road. Come to think on it, I'd expected Lord Ratoshigan to sail his sprinter up—that one he's been winning with all season. That herdsman of his was boasting at their Gather—"

"I'm not sorry that we didn't get to pit Squealer against the best in the west, but perhaps Ratoshigan's absence ensured his win."

"It did no such thing," Dag protested vehemently and then realized that he was being teased. "He's cooled off now. I'll just take him back to the beasthold above."

"Starting line or finishing?" Alessan asked Moreta.

"Let's see if we can get in a finish."

They moved at a leisurely pace for people wishing to see an imminent finish, but their path took them between pickets and that pleased Moreta as well.

"I wonder why Ratoshigan didn't come."

"His absence is a boon." Moreta did not try to mask the acid edge to her voice.

"Perhaps, but I'd've liked to pit Squealer against that sprinter of his."

"For the joy of beating Ratoshigan? Well, I'd approve of that."

"Southern Boll is beholden to Fort Weyr, isn't it?"

"That doesn't mean I have to like him."

"Yet you'd drink that sour wine Lord Diatis makes."

Moreta had opened her mouth to reply when she was suddenly drenched with water. A colorful and original string of invective in Alessan's angry voice told her that he had not escaped the slops.

Who has distressed you? Orlith's response was immediate and, as Moreta stood there, eyes closed against the water draining from her hair, she needed the moral support of her queen.

"I'm only wet!" Moreta stolidly informed her queen.

The sun is warm. You will dry fast.

"Only wet?" Alessan roared. "You're soaked."

The erring handler, belatedly discovering that he had launched a full bucket of dirty water at the Weyrwoman and the Lord Holder—who didn't ought to be strolling along picket lines when everyone else was off watching the races—proffered Moreta a towel, but the rag had been used for many purposes and merely compounded the problem. Alessan was shouting for clean water and fresh clothes and the location of a vacant tent.

The commotion was sufficient to attract everyone not engrossed in the race just starting. Assistance was offered, and people began running here and there on Alessan's orders while Moreta stood, her beautiful new brown-and-gold gown plastered to her body. She tried to reassure the mortified handler that she took no offense, all the while knowing her long-awaited afternoon of racing was doomed. She might just as well summon Orlith and go back to the Weyr. She might get her death of cold going *between* in the soggy ruins of her Gather dress, but what choice had she now?

"I know this is not what you're accustomed to, Moreta," Alessan was saying, pulling at her sleeve to get her attention. "But it's clean and it's dry and will do to watch the rest of the races. I can't be sure if my mother's ladies or my sister can get your gown and cloak dry by evening, but I am certain that suitable gowns will be displayed in the Hold for your consideration when the races are over."

Alessan was holding out a clean brown shift in one hand, sandals and a pretty belt of colored cords in the other. He was gesturing toward the race manager's striped tent when the handler rushed up with clean, steaming water in his bucket and a bundle of clean towels draped over his shoulder.

"Come, Moreta, do let us set things to rights?" The softly spoken appeal and the very real distress evident in Alessan's eyes and manner would have swayed a character far more obdurate than Moreta's.

"And yourself, Alessan?" she asked courteously as she bundled her soaking skirts for the short walk to the tent. The right side of Alessan's Gather finery was soaked.

"You, I fear, took the brunt. I'll dry out in the sun. While we watch the races?" His sly question was part entreaty.

"I'll be quick."

She took the fresh clothing and let the handler place the bucket and clothes in the tent then she entered, dropping the flap.

Her undershift was wet as well, so she was pleased that the brown shift was woven of a sturdy fabric. Her hair was gritty from the slop water, which had been used to sponge down a runner's dusty legs. She buried her head quickly in the clean water, washed her face and arms thoroughly, making lavish use of the supply of cloths. She was dressed and outside the tent just as the cheers announced the finish of the fourth race.

"Now I believe that you were once a holder lass," Alessan said with a soft chuckle. He handed her a full goblet of wine. "The Benden did not get wet."

"Well, that's luck!"

The handler bobbed an approach, apologizing and bowing and generally so abasing himself that Moreta cut him short by remarking that worse things had come flying out of a picket line, and she was grateful it was no more than dirty water. Alessan escorted her toward the finish line.

"Last one was a sprint, only five entries," he mentioned as they walked.

"And Squealer wasn't entered?" She laughed as Alessan gave her a pained look, imitating Dag.

The next races were exciting enough to make up for those she had missed and to blot out the tragedy of the second. She and Alessan, looking far less the Lord of the Hold with his fine clothes puckered and soiled, found themselves vantages near the finish and sipped wine. They made private bets about winners when Moreta refused to allow Alessan to mark her with the wagermen. She enjoyed, too, being right in the midst of the racing crowd as she had so often been as a young girl in Keroon, in the company of her child-hood friend Talpan. She hadn't thought of him in Turns.

An enterprising baker passed among the finish-line crowds with a tray of hot spiced rolls. Moreta hadn't realized how hungry she was until the aroma wafted over to her.

"I'm host today," Alessan said, noticing her reaction. He took her arm and they pushed their way through to the baker.

The flaky pastry was stuffed with a savory mix, and Moreta quickly devoured three rolls.

"Don't they feed you in the Weyr on a Gather day?" Alessan asked.

"Oh, the stew pot's always simmering in the Cavern," she replied, licking her fingers appreciatively. "But stew wouldn't taste half as good as these spiced rolls do right now."

Alessan was eyeing her, a curious expression on his face.

"You're not at all what I expected in Weyrwoman Moreta," he said in a candid tone that captured her complete attention. Wearily she wondered what Sh'gall had said of her. Alessan went on, "I got to know Leri rather well. She usually stays on for a word with the ground crews . . ."

"I would if I could," Moreta said, countering his tacit criticism, "but I have to return to the Weyr immediately after Fall."

"Have to?" Alessan's right eye quirked high.

"Did you never wonder who takes care of dragon injuries?" She spoke more sharply than she intended because she had been able to forget that they would rise to Fall in two more days, and more dragons might be injured.

"I'd thought that the Weyr must have the best of the healers, of course." Alessan's reply was so formal that Moreta regretted the quick retort. She laid her hand on his arm, hoping to restore the ease of their relationship.

"I never realized it might be you." He smiled and covered her hand with his. "What about another spiced roll before someone else eats them all?"

"Lord Alessan . . ." Dag came rolling up to them. "Runel's going on about Squealer being a sport. I tol'im the breeding, but he won't take it from me."

Alessan's expression became pained, and he closed his eyes briefly.

"I was hoping to avoid Runel this Gather."

"You done pretty well with everyone else, Lord, but I can't do this for you."

Alessan inhaled the breath of one resigned.

"Who's Runel?" Moreta asked.

The two men regarded her with astonishment.

"You mean, you've escaped Runel?" Amusement chased resignation from Alessan's expression. "Well, you must meet him at least once."

Dag made a sound, half protest, half fear.

"And the race *is* due to start," Alessan reminded Dag. "Weyrwoman, that's the only thing, short of Fall, that will halt Runel's recitations."

By now, Moreta was intrigued.

"He's over there, with those cronies of his." Dag pointed.

Moreta noted first that the three men stood isolated by a clear space from any immediate neighbors. Two were holders by their badges, one from Fort and the other wearing Ruathan colors; the third was a wizened herdsman whose clothes reeked of his craft despite the fact that they looked well brushed. The tallest of the men, the Ruathan holder, drew himself up proudly as he noticed Alessan's approach. He spared Moreta only a passing glance.

"About that sprinter of mine, Runel," Alessan began briskly, addressing himself to the herdsman. "I bred the beast myself, four Turns ago, out of the sprint mare Dextra, Lord Leef's by Vander's brown stallion, Evest."

Runel's expression altered dramatically. He threw back his head and unfocused his eyes, wide-opened. "Alessan's sprinter, Squealer, won the first sprint race at the Ruathan Gather, third month, forty-third Turn of the sixth Pass, bred by Alessan out of Dextra, five times winner at sprint races in the west, Leef by Vander's Evest which was nine times winner over sprint distances. Dextra's sire, twice winner, by Dimnal out of Tran, nineteen times winner. Dimnal by Fairex out of Crick, Fairex . . ."

"There he goes," Dag said to Moreta in an undertone, shaking his head ruefully.

"He just keeps on?"

"And on and on. He'll recite the lineage of Squealer back to the Crossing," Alessan murmured, standing with hands clasped in front of him and seeming to give Runel the courtesy of his attention.

"He's only good with western racing, though," Dag added critically.

"He's eidetic? I've *heard* about them, but I've never heard one personally."

"Just give him a name of a racer and he's away. Trouble is he has to start at the beginning."

"Isn't he starting at the end with Squealer's win today?"

Runel's voice had settled into the sing-song of winners, sires, and dams.

"The latest race *is* his beginning, Lady Moreta."

"Does he go to all the Gathers?"

"Those he can get to." Dag shot Alessan a look.

I would be surprised if the Lord Holder knows half the races Runel attends, Moreta thought to herself.

"He's not much good otherwise, that's certain," Alessan said, unconcerned. "My father saw that the oldest sons were well apprenticed. Runel's memory serves a purpose—"

"Bore you to death, it would," Dag muttered unappreciatively, glancing over his shoulder at the race flats. "It's starting!" Reprieve was the overwhelming emotion. "Race!" he said in a loud voice directly at Runel.

Runel's companions began to tug at his arms. "Race, Runel! Race is starting!"

Runel came out of his recitation trance and looked about in surprise.

"Race is starting, Runel," the Fort holder said reassuringly as he began to guide the eidetic toward the finish line.

Alessan drew Moreta to one side, and Dag scurried behind the Lord Holder while the trio marched off. Moreta could not help but see that a path cleared before Runel more quickly than if Alessan and she had wished passage.

"You should hear him on the 'begats.' "

"As you have?"

"Indeed and I have, at every birthfeast." Alessan spoke with feeling and rolled his eyes upward.

"I'd've thought the man would be more valuable in the Harper Hall than in a hold."

"My father had the good sense to prevent that."

"Why? With that memory . . ."

"Because his granduncle was a harper here and remembered more than was prudent on too many occasions." Alessan grinned with malice. "I think my grandsire made sure to turn the trait to less . . . ah, shall we say . . . remunerative topics? I believe there have always been blood relations in the

Harper Hall, undoubtedly in the Records Rooms, scanning hides and committing them to memory before the ink fades completely."

They found a place at the line and observed the hotly contested finish of the sixth race. As they passed the wait for the next race, they overheard bits and snatches of conversations. References to the new Lord Holder and the quality of the Gather were in the main complimentary, though Moreta enjoyed Alessan's discomfiture at some of the candid remarks. The weather dominated most discussions.

"Too warm, too soon. We'll melt this summer."

"Can't say as I mind mild days instead of rain and blizzard, but it ain't natural. Upsets the rhythm of the Turn."

"M'herds won't settle with insects hanging on in the warm, pestering 'em. Terrible cases of sores. Beasts don't want to eat. Don't want to move. Muddle and moan together, they do."

"A bit of frost would do us the world of good. Freeze down those tunnel snakes. Breeding fierce they are this year with no cold to lay 'em."

"Can't decide to shear now for a short crop and give 'em relief from the heat or let 'em lose condition panting under long hair."

"We needs us some snow. We needs it to kill what grubs beneath the soil, what sucks life from our good seed, and what makes a field sour. We needs frost and snow in good measure."

"You ought to be relieved, Alessan, that all they complain about *is* the weather. After all, no holder expects the Lord Holder to be able to change the weather. The Weyrs do that, you know." She pulled her mouth down in a grimace that made him grin.

The final race had a surprise ending for two runners crossed the finish line, right in front of Moreta and Alessan, without so much as a nose between them. The argument over which animal won grew so heated that Alessan came forward to mediate, dragging Moreta with him. To settle what could have been a nasty situation, Alessan loudly proclaimed that he doubled the purse so that neither contender would be disappointed for the fine excitement they had provided the Gather.

That was just the right decision to end the race meeting on a high note. Owners, riders, handlers, and spectators dispersed from the flats in the best of all spirits.

"You're a sensibly generous man, Alessan."

"I thank you, Lady Moreta. Ah, just in time," he said, and Moreta turned as a handler lead up a big-boned, long-backed runnerbeast saddled with a thick pad in Ruathan colors. "My lady, your mount."

"*This* is what your father expected you to breed?"

"This is what I *did* breed for my father," Alessan replied with a broad grin. "Squealer's type was a bonus." He gave her a leg up and waited while she hooked her leg on the broad pommel before he swung up behind her.

"I think I prefer your Squealer," she said as the beast lurched forward at Alessan's urging.

"There speaks the racing enthusiast, not the prudent holder." He turned his head left as they moved off across the stubble field, and Moreta knew that Alessan had only deferred the puzzle of the empty picket lines for the duration of the races.

"It's not like Ratoshigan to miss a chance for Ruathan marks. They could sail right up the Ruathan River," Alessan said, giving her a tight smile for his inattention. "Soover—you know him from Southern Boll—ought to have come short of Fall, fire, or fog. I hadn't realized that the weather—for all your unwillingness to change it—was of such widespread concern."

"There's no lack of people at this Gather," Moreta said. The stalls were still doing a good business despite the numbers attracted by the racing.

People had already begun to take places at the tables about the dancing square. The aromas of roasting meats wafted enticingly on the wind, the pungency of spiced wherry dominating.

Alessan had ridden straight up across the field and now turned their mount up the roadway. Moreta glanced up to the fire-heights, covered in sun-baking dragons. There seemed to be more, and she noticed Orlith flanked by another queen. Tamianth of the High Reaches, judging by her size and color.

"Some creatures like the sun and the warm," Alessan said. "Does all the sunning help them endure the cold of *between*?"

Moreta shivered involuntarily, and Alessan's arms tightened about her. She rather enjoyed the unexpected intimacy.

"When we fly Thread, I'm grateful to the cold of *between*," she replied obliquely, her thoughts on the Fall in two days.

Then Alessan reined the beast up the ramp to the forecourt, its heavy feet clumping hollowly and alerting the guests there. Moreta waved cheerfully at Falga, the High Reaches Weyrwoman.

"Wasn't your new gown ready, Moreta?" Falga asked as she walked to meet them while Alessan halted their mount.

"A new gown?" Alessan's startled question fell on Moreta's ears only.

"You'll see it next Gather, Falga," Moreta replied blithely. "This is my race-watching dress."

"Oh, you and your races!" Falga smiled tolerantly and turned back to the holders with whom she'd been talking.

Suddenly Tolocamp appeared, his genial smile not completely masking his disapproval of Moreta's dusty appearance.

"I'll just slide off, thank you, Lord Tolocamp," she said, politely ignoring his offer of assistance.

"If you'll follow me, Lady Moreta," Lady Oma said, breaking through the press of people and taking charge.

Relieved to be able to retire gracefully from Tolocamp's critical gaze, Moreta followed Alessan's mother. In the instant her eyes met Lady Oma's, Moreta knew the woman disapproved of her as much as Tolocamp did but more for upsetting her own plans for her son's afternoon entertainment than for Moreta's hoyden behavior. As they proceeded through the Hall, splendidly decorated for the Gather, and up the stairs into the Hold's private corridors, Moreta felt the weight of Lady Oma's rebuke in her silence. In Lady Oma's own apartments, however, a variety of gowns, skirts, and tunics had been hastily assembled, and from the bathroom drifted the moist scent of perfumed water and the giggles of the girls who were preparing it.

"Your gown has been cleaned, Lady Moreta," Lady Oma said, closing the door behind Moreta. "But I doubt it will be dry before the dancing." She cast a measuring glance at Moreta, ignoring the dusty brown shift. "You're thinner than I'd thought. Perhaps the rust . . ." She indicated the garment, then canceled that suggestion with an impatient gesture of her hand. It was reminiscent of Alessan. "It is in no way comparable to your own gown. This green one is more suited to your rank."

Moreta went to the rust dress, fingering the texture of the plain but soft fabric. She held it up to her waist and shoulders. The fit would be good through the body, though the skirt was short above her ankles. She glanced at the fine material of the green dress. She'd sweat in it dancing the way she intended to dance for having lost part of her racing.

"The rust will do very well, and I'm grateful for the loan of it." She smiled around at the women in the room, trying to locate the donor but no one met her glance. "This will be fine. I won't be long," she added, smiling again as she entered the bathing room and pulled the curtain across. She hoped they would all take the hint and leave.

She lolled longer in the warm scented water than she intended, easing muscles made tense by the afternoon's excitements. Only when she finally emerged and was rubbing her hair dry did she hear a noise in the outer chamber and realize that someone was waiting for her.

"Lady Oma?" she called out, dreading the answer.

"No, it's only Oklina," an apologetic young voice replied. "Did you find the shift?"

"I'm in it."

"Do you need help with your hair?"

"It's short enough to dry quickly."

"Oh!"

Moreta smiled to herself for the chagrin in the young voice. "I'm distressingly self-sufficient, Lady Oklina," Moreta said, pulling the rust dress over her head, "except that I cannot do up the back of the gown." She pulled the curtain aside as Oklina rushed forward, nearly colliding with Moreta and almost collapsing with embarrassment at her awkwardness.

Oklina bore a marked resemblance to her brother but none to Lady Oma, if indeed the woman was the girl's mother. The dark complexion, which suited Alessan, did nothing for the girl yet she had a sensitivity in her face and a grace of movement that had its own appeal. And, Moreta noted enviously, thick long black plaits gleamed in the well-lit room.

"I'm awfully sorry it's only me, Lady Moreta, but it's time to serve the roasts and with so many guests . . ." Oklina deftly settled the bodice to Moreta's hips and began lacing the back.

"If I had been watching where I walked—"

"Oh, Marl wanted to sink into the ground with the slops, Lady Moreta. He rushed here to us with your gown and hovered in the washroom, fretting about the stains. You must have been furious to have a new gown ruined in the first wearing, before you had a chance to show it off or dance in it." Oklina's voice reflected her awe, which was quite understandable since she was obviously wearing a dress handed down from older sisters.

"I shall dance much more easily in this." Moreta twitched experimentally at the rust skirts.

"Alessan sent word that you *had* to be enticed with a gown pretty enough to make you stay for the dancing."

"Oh?"

"Oh!" Oklina's eyes widened at her indiscretion, and she blinked back sudden tears, her expression very solemn. "He hasn't been to a Gather or danced or sung or been himself since Suriana died. Not even when he became Lord Holder. Tell me, was he *pleased* when Squealer won?"

"Ecstatic!" Moreta smiled gently at the girl's obvious adoration of her brother. "Creditable win, too. Five lengths."

"And he actually smiled? And *enjoyed* himself?" At Moreta's reassurance, the girl clasped her hands under her chin, her dark eyes shining. "I did see the start"—her expressive face clouded briefly—"and *heard* the yells. I'll bet the loudest was from Alessan. Did you *see* Squealer afterward? And you met Dag. Dag is never far from that runner. He's been so devoted. He knows so much about racing because he rode for Lord Leef before he got so old. He can spot winners every time. He had faith in Alessan's breeding when everyone else thought he ought to give it up before Lord Leef—" Oklina broke off with a gasp. "I talk too much."

"I've been listening." Moreta was not unaccustomed to outpourings of repressed emotions. "I think Squealer is going to repay all the time and effort Alessan—and Dag—have put into him."

"Oh, do you really think so?" The prospect brought a fresh spasm of delight to Oklina. "Listen, the harpers have begun." At the sound of music, the girl wheeled to the window, its metal shutters open to the darkening sky.

"Well, then, let's go dance. It's time to enjoy ourselves."

For a moment, Oklina looked apprehensive, as if she wouldn't be allowed to enjoy herself. Younger members of Hold families were often saddled with the onerous duties of a Gather, but Moreta would make it a point to see that Oklina did dance. The girl smiled graciously and gestured for Moreta to precede her from the room.

The corridors and the Hall were empty, but drudges were opening the glowbaskets arranged on the forecourt as Moreta and Oklina hastened by. Moreta paused on the ramp, to look up to the fire-heights. Orlith slept, eyes closed, in the setting sun, likely to remain somnolent until the evening breeze chilled the air. Other dragons, their rainbow-colored eyes gleaming, watched the scene below.

"Oh!" Oklina's tone was a yip of delighted fear. "They are such awesome creatures." She paused, then blurted out, "Were you terribly scared?"

"When I Impressed? Very much so. The Search reached my father's hold the very day of Impression. I was scooped up and taken to Ista in a scurry, told to change, and then shoved onto the Hatching Ground before I knew exactly what was taking place. Orlith"—and Moreta could never suppress an exultant smile at the memory—"forgave me for being late!"

"*Ohhhh!*" Oklina expelled a long sigh of bliss.

Moreta smiled, recognizing the girl's yearning to be found on Search and to Impress a queen dragon. Once when faced with such envious yearnings, Moreta had felt unaccountable guilt over her good fortune at Impressing Orlith, her friend, her sure consolation, her life. That reaction had gradually been replaced by the knowledge of the great gap between wish, fulfillment, and acceptance. So Moreta could smile kindly at Oklina while her mind reached out to her sleeping dragon.

"If my brother hadn't been my father's successor, he might have been a dragonrider," Oklina confided to Moreta in a sudden whisper.

"Really?" Moreta was startled. She hadn't heard that Ruatha Hold had been approached for one of its sons, not since she joined the Weyr ten Turns before.

"Dag told me." And Oklina nodded her head vigorously to support her statement. "It was twelve Turns ago. Dag said Lord Leef was in a fury because Alessan was to be the heir, and though Lord Leef told the dragonriders they could have any other member of his Hold, Dag said that no one else was acceptable to the dragons—how do dragons know?"

"*Search* dragons know," Moreta said in a mysterious voice, a rote reply after so many repetitions. "Each Weyr has dragons who sense the potential in youngsters." Moreta deepened the mystery in her voice. "There are folk, weyrborn, who've known dragons and riders all their lives who don't Impress, and complete strangers—like myself—who do. The dragons always know."

"The dragons always know . . ." Oklina's whisper was half prayer, half imprecation. She stole a quick look up the fire-heights as if she feared the somnolent dragons might take offense if they heard.

"Come, Oklina," Moreta said briskly. "I'm dying to dance."

Ruatha Hold, Present Pass, 3.11.43

To Moreta, of all the Gathers she'd ever attended, the Ruathan Gather at that moment of dusk evoked best what Gathers should be—folk from weyr, hold, and craft assembled to eat, drink, dance, and enjoy one another's company. The glowbaskets on their standards cast patches of golden light on the crowded tables, on the dancers, on the clusters of people standing about talking, and on the circles of men near the wine barrels. The darting figures of children wove in and out of the light patches, and occasionally their laughter and shouts cut across the music and the stamping of the dancers. The smell of roasted meats and warm evening air, of dust and pungent glows, and wine reinforced all prospect of entertainment.

Nine harpers graced the platform and five more sat waiting their turns. Moreta couldn't pick out Tirone, but the Masterharper might be circulating among the tables. Alessan might not like the Masterharper, but Tirone would discharge his obligation to the new Lord Holder's first Gather.

Moreta and Oklina had reached the edge of the onlookers, who parted while respectfully murmuring greetings as the two moved closer to the dance square. Having guided Moreta to the head table, opposite the harpers' platform, Oklina would have left, but Moreta took the girl by the hand. When Alessan rose to his feet, gesturing for Moreta to sit beside him, she pulled Oklina down, too, ignoring the girl's protest.

"There's room enough, isn't there?" Moreta asked, giving Alessan a significant glare. "She was so good about waiting for me."

"Room enough, of course," Alessan replied graciously, motioning to the table's other occupants to adjust. As Moreta seated herself, Alessan peered at her, a frown beginning to pucker his brows. "Is that the best that could be supplied you?" He pinched at the sleeve with disapproval.

"This suits me very well. Much better for dancing than mine. Though I had many to choose from," she added hastily as the reason for his frown became clear to her. "I think I should make it a practice to bring two dresses to a Gather: one to see races in"—she grinned mischievously up at him—"and one to be seen in." She gave her chin an arrogant tilt and pretended hauteur.

Placated, Alessan smiled back at her and signaled for wine to be poured in her cup. "I've more of the Benden white for *you*." He raised his cup in a quick toast.

She had had not more than a sip when the harpers struck up a loud and lively dance tune.

"Will you honor me with a dance, Weyrwoman?" Alessan asked, jumping to his feet and extending his hand.

"Why else am I here?" She turned to Oklina with a smile. "Guard my place and my cup." Then she took Alessan's hand and allowed herself to be spun onto the square, finding the beat of the measure and stepping out into the pattern with a strong man's body against hers and firm hands guiding her.

She loved to dance and, though the Weyr had musicians and songs in the evening from time to time, dancing was generally reserved for Hatching festivities. Occasionally the blue and green riders indulged in wild acrobatics, usually when they were well into the wine after a bad Fall or the death of a dragon and rider, but Moreta dreaded those dances. Leri and L'mal had felt that such excesses purged the riders, but Moreta preferred to absent herself, taking flight on Orlith to be far from the maddening drum beat and the posturing dance.

But the Gather's music soon exorcised those memories and she was breathless by the time Alessan whirled her back to the table, both of them heartily applauding the harpers' music, the sweet, uncomplicated, merry, familiar tunes.

"I must dance now with Falga," Alessan said, seeing Moreta settled, "but save me another dance?"

"Did you enjoy dancing with Alessan?" Oklina asked in a shy wistful voice as she set the goblet of Benden wine before Moreta.

"Indeed I did. He's light on his feet and knows the dance well."

"Alessan taught me to dance. When there's music in the Hall, he always asks me at least once, but I don't expect he'll be able to tonight with so many other girls."

"Then I shall find you another partner." Moreta turned to search out an idle dragonrider.

"Oh, I mustn't." Oklina looked scared and her eyes flitted nervously to the crowded square where a new dance was forming. "I'm expected to help with the guests."

"You are, by making sure of my comfort and guarding my Benden wine." Moreta smiled warmly at the child. "But you *must* dance tonight!"

"Moreta!" A firm hand clasped her on the shoulder, and she looked up at B'lerion, bronze Nabeth's rider from the High Reaches Weyr. "There's good music begging your step. And me!"

The bronze rider did not wait for her consent, but took her hand and pulled her into his arms, laughing down at her. "I knew you couldn't resist me." And he winked over Moreta's shoulder at the astonished Oklina as he spun the Weyrwoman off to the square.

Moreta did not miss the wistful, yearning expression on Oklina's face, but then B'lerion had that effect on many women. He was handsome and tall with a fine strong body, sparkling dark eyes, a mobile expression, a ready laugh. He always had a quick remark and a fund of light gossip. Moreta and he had enjoyed a brief association when she'd first come to Fort Weyr and she was certain that he was the father of her third child. She regretted that she had had to foster, but she had always been the healer and that duty had priority. Though B'lerion was not the same caliber wingleader as Sh'gall, Moreta had hoped that Nabeth would have flown her queen during that crucial mating flight. But then, the strongest, cleverest dragon flew the queen: That was the only way to improve the breed. Twice Sh'gall's Kadith had been strongest and fastest. Or so Moreta kept telling herself.

B'lerion was in a good mood, not yet deep in his wine for his words weren't slurred and his step was firm. He'd heard of her dousing, teased her about monopolizing the young Lord Holder, told her that her love of racing would be her undoing, and asked why Sh'gall was not there to protect his interests.

"I never understood why you let Kadith fly your queen when she could have done much better with Nabeth and I'd be Fort Weyrleader. I'm much more fun to be with than Sh'gall. Or so you used to tell me."

By the intense gleam in his eyes and the sharp hold he took of her waist for the last figure of the dance, B'lerion was half in earnest, Moreta realized. Moreta reminded herself that B'lerion was always in earnest for the duration of any given encounter. A charming opportunist who didn't limit his activities to any one Weyr or Hold.

"What? You be Fort Weyrleader? You don't like that much responsibility."

"With you as Weyrwoman, I'd've improved beyond all knowing. And it's only eight more Turns and then we're all free to enjoy ourselves." He pulled her tighter still. "We did enjoy ourselves before, you know."

"When didn't you enjoy yourself, light wing?"

"True, and tonight is meant for enjoyment, isn't it."

She laughed and swung away from an embrace that had best be broken. B'lerion's attentions might be misconstrued by some. She owed Sh'gall her undiverted support at least until the Fall ended. As she made her way back to the table, B'lerion followed, smiling at Oklina in imperturbable good humor. Moreta wished he hadn't followed her, noting Oklina's breathless reaction as B'lerion smoothly set himself down beside the girl.

"May I have the next dance with you, Lady Oklina? Moreta will tell you I'm harmless. I'm also B'lerion, bronze Nabeth's rider from the High Reaches. May I have a sip of your wine?"

"Oh, that's Lady Moreta's wine," Oklina protested, trying to regain possession of the cup that B'lerion had seized.

"She'd never deny me a sip of wine, but I'll drink to you and your big dark eyes."

Schooling her own expression, Moreta watched Oklina's, saw her blushing confusion at B'lerion's compliments. She could see the pulse of excitement beating in the girl's slender neck, her quickened breathing. Oklina could not have been more than sixteen Turns. Hold-bred, she'd be married off very soon to some holder or craftmaster to the east or the south, far from Ruatha, strengthening Bloodlines. By the time the Pass ended, Oklina would have children and this Gather day would have been long forgotten. Or, perhaps, better remembered for B'lerion's attentions. She smiled when the harpers struck up a slow and stately dance and B'lerion lead the delighted girl onto the square.

As most people felt their talents adequate to that dance, the tables had emptied. Lady Oma remained at one end, listening gravely to a prosperously dressed holderwoman. When both smiled indulgently toward the dance square, Moreta caught sight of Alessan sedately guiding a young girl. The holderwoman's daughter, possible candidate for second wife? Lady Oma's faint smile was speculative. As Moreta made her own evaluation, the girl, pretty enough with dark curling hair, smiled simperingly up at Alessan. Such an innocent would never attract Alessan, now that as Lord Holder he could have his choice from any hold or hall on the continent. Then Moreta noticed S'peren, a Fort Weyr bronzerider, watching the dance. She'd thought S'peren had been to Ista.

"Is the Ista Gather over so soon?" she asked him, surprised.

"A bit disappointing, really, once they'd taken the animal away. No racing." S'peren gave her a tolerant smile. "Nowhere near as many people as Ruatha . . ." He nodded with satisfaction at the crowded dance square. "People weren't in such a festive mood, either. There's illness in Igen, Keroon, and Telgar."

"Runners?" The memory of the beast's unexpected fall flashed across her mind.

"Runners? No. People. A fever, I heard. Master Capiam was someplace about, I heard, though I didn't see him."

"Ista's Weyrleaders are well?" F'gal and Wimmia had been good friends during her Turns at Ista Weyr.

"And sent you their good wishes, as usual. Oh, by the way, I bear greetings for you from an animal healer named Talpan. Said he knew you from your father's hold."

Strange, Moreta thought, moving on after exchanging pleasantries with the High Reaches riders chatting with S'peren. Until that day she hadn't been reminded of Talpan in Turns, and now she even had greetings from him.

The dance ended and she tried to locate Alessan for another with him. He was such a good partner. Then she saw him in the square, partnering a girl whose long black hair made Moreta think at first he was dancing with Oklina. The girl turned slightly, and Moreta realized that he was doing his duty by yet another marriageable woman. She felt great sympathy for Alessan, remembering how bronzeriders had besieged her before Orlith rose to mate two Turns ago.

Moreta drained her goblet, then went in search of more wine or a partner. She very much wanted to dance again but paused by the nearest wine keg first. The barman quickly filled her cup and she thanked him. At the first sip, she realized her mistake. This wine had an acid aftertaste: Tillek, not the rich full mouth of the Benden. She nearly spat it out.

This dance was a short wild hop, as much fun to watch for the people losing balance as to dance. When the harpers finished with a swirl, they added the chords that announced an intermission. It was the time for harper songs. Moreta half expected Tirone to stride in, for he should be leading singer of a Ruathan Gather, but the young Masterharper of Ruatha Hold and an older journeyman moved to the fore in his stead.

When Moreta looked toward the head table, she saw Alessan flanked by a pair of pretty girls, one of them a redhead. Lady Oma was certainly wasting no time at this Gather. Disinclined to return to the head table, Moreta found an unoccupied stool.

She enjoyed the first song, a rousing ballad, and joined in the chorus with as much verve as those around her. Fine voices near helped her find the harmony for she didn't have a high enough voice to stay with the soprano line. Halfway through the second chorus, Moreta was conscious of Orlith's mind.

You do like the singing, too, don't you? she sent to the queen.

Singing is a pleasant occupation. It lightens the mind and all minds are together.

Moreta's voice faltered into a laugh, which she quickly suppressed for it wouldn't do, even if she were the Weyrwoman, to laugh through a serious song.

The harpers led the Gather in four traditional songs, each one sung with increasing zest as the dancers recovered their breaths. The young Ruathan harper, an excellent tenor, sang an unfamiliar song that he announced he'd found while going through old Records. The melody was haunting and the interval between the notes unexpected. A very old song, Moreta decided, but a good choice for the tenor's voice. Orlith liked it, too.

Our tastes generally coincide, Moreta said.

Not always.

What do you mean by that?

The harpers sing, Orlith replied, evading, and Moreta knew that she'd get no direct answer.

Then the harpers asked for favorites from the audience. Moreta would have liked to request one of the plains songs from her own Keroon, but it was a mournful tune unsuited to the mood of the evening. Talpan had often hummed it. Coincidence again!

After the serenading, Alessan went up on the platform, thanking the harpers and offering compliments for their music and their presence. He enjoined them to make as free of Ruatha's wine as necessary to keep them playing until the last dancer surrendered the square. Everyone applauded loudly, cheering and thumping the tables and kegs to signify their appreciation of a Lord Holder who would not stint on his first Gather. The cheering went on long past what was a courteous spate and followed Alessan back to his table.

The harpers began the next session with a circle dance that permitted Alessan to accompany both of the girls. B'lerion was on his feet with Oklina again. Lady Oma seemed not to notice, so concentrated was her attention on Alessan's partners.

Her throat dry from singing and cheering, Moreta was determined to find more of Alessan's Benden white. As she made her way to the head table, she was stopped by holders asking after Leri and Holth and expressing sincere regret that the Weyrwoman had not attended.

Pass the greetings on, Orlith. They'll like to know they were missed.

After a pause, Orlith replied that Holth was just as glad that she didn't have to sit through a long night on a cold cliff.

You're not feeling the chill, are you? Moreta asked anxiously.

The fire-heights hold the sun heat, and Nabeth and Tamianth keep me warm. You should eat. You're always telling me to eat. Now I you.

The smugness in Orlith's tone Moreta found amusing. And merited, for the rough Tillek wine was making her a trifle lightheaded. She was aware of a belly rumbling, and she'd best get to the food before the circle dance ended.

She detoured to acquire a full platter of spiced roast wherry, tubers, and other tempting morsels. As she was making her way to the head table and more of the Benden wine, the circle dance ended. Alessan had no sooner bowed to his two partners when Lady Oma was introducing him to yet another girl. Then Moreta caught sight of Lord Tolocamp bearing down on her and she moved off quickly at a tangent, as if she hadn't seen him. His expression was grim and she was not going to endure one of his lectures at a Gather. She wended her way through the crowds, briefly considered stopping at the harpers' table for they would have the best wine, but she decided she was no safer from Tolocamp in the harpers' company. Besides, they'd probably had enough of him since the Harper Hall was situated so close to Fort Hold. So, instead, she ducked behind the harpers' platform, standing a moment to accustom her eyes to the welcome darkness.

As it was, she nearly fell over the pack saddles stacked behind the dais. She upended one to make an informal seat and was quite delighted with her solitude and escaping Tolocamp. Come the end of Pass, that man was going to be high-flying irritant, and she didn't think that Sh'gall was going to be able to handle him as well as he handled Fall.

This is good, you are eating! Orlith said.

Moreta neatly folded a slice of the roast wherry and took a huge bite. The meat was as tender and succulent as its roasting odor had advertised.

It's beautiful! she told her queen.

She ate eagerly, licking her fingers, not wishing to miss a drop of the juices. Someone stumbled around the corner of the platform and Moreta, balancing her plate and cursing the interruption, slipped into the deeper shadow. Could Tolocamp have followed her? Or was this someone answering natural needs?

Alessan, Orlith told her, which surprised Moreta for Orlith wasn't all that good on remembering people names.

"Moreta?" Alessan sounded uncertain. "Ah, you are here," he added as she stepped forward. "I thought I saw you slip away to elude Tolocamp. I come laden with food and drink. Am I intruding on your privacy?"

"You're not if you happened to bring any more of that Benden wine. Mind you, the Tillek you're serving is not bad—"

"—But it doesn't at all compare with the Benden, and I hope you haven't mentioned the difference to anyone."

"What? And miss out on my share? And you brought more wherry! My compliments to your cook: The roast is superior and I'm starving. Here, sit on a pack saddle." She pushed one toward him and, after emptying her cup of the inferior wine, held it out to him. "More Benden, please?"

"I've a full skin here." Alessan poured carefully.

"But surely you must share it with your partners?"

"Don't you dare—" Alessan reached for her goblet in a mock attempt to retrieve the wine from her.

"That wasn't fair of me. You were doing your duty as Lord Holder, and very nicely, if I may say so."

"Well, I've done my duty as Lord Holder and will now resume the responsibilities of being your escort. I will now enjoy the Gather."

"Hosts rarely do."

"My mother, the good and worthy—"

"—and duty conscious—"

"Has paraded every eligible girl in the west, with all of whom I have dutifully danced. They're not much on talking. By the way, speaking of talking, is that bronze rider who's been monopolizing Oklina a kind and honorable man?"

"B'lerion is kind, and very good company. Is Oklina aware of dragonriders' propensities?"

"As every proper hold girl is." Alessan's tone was dry, acknowledging dragonrider whims and foibles.

"B'lerion is kind and I have known him many Turns," Moreta went on by way of reassurance. Oklina's adoration of her brother was not misplaced if he troubled himself to speak to a Weyrwoman about a bronze rider who was paying marked attention to his sister.

They ate in companionable silence, for Alessan was as hungry as Moreta. Suddenly the harpers struck up another tune, one of the spritelier dances, more of a patterned run, requiring the lighter partner to be lifted, twirled, and caught. She recognized the challenge gleaming in Alessan's eyes; only the young and fit usually attempted the toss dance's acrobatics. She laughed low in her throat. She was no timid adolescent, uncertain of herself, and no decorous hold woman, vitality and body drained by constant childbearing; she was the fighting-fit rider of a queen dragon and she could outdance any man— holder, crafter, rider. In addition, Orlith was encouraging her.

Deserting the remains of her food and her wine, she caught Alessan by the hand and pulled him after her toward the dancing square where already one pair had come to grief and lay sprawled, the subject of goodnatured teasing.

Weyrwoman and Lord Holder were the only pair to survive the rigors of that dance without incident. Cheers and clapping rewarded their agility. Gasping for breath and trying not to weave with the dizziness generated by the final spins, Moreta reeled to the sidelines. A goblet was put in her hand and she knew before sipping that it would be the Benden. She toasted Alessan as he stood beside her, chest heaving, face suffused with blood, but thoroughly delighted by their performance.

"By the Shell, with the right partner, you can really show your quality," Falga cried, as she walked up to them. "You're in rare form tonight, Moreta. Alessan, best Gather I've been to in Turns. You've outshone your sire who is, as of this moment, no longer lamented. He set a good spread but nothing to compare to this. S'ligar will be sorry he didn't come with me."

The other dragonriders with Falga lifted their cups to Alessan.

"See you at Crom," Falga said to Moreta in parting as the harpers began a gentle old melody.

"Can you move at all?" Alessan asked Moreta, bending to speak quietly in her ear.

"Of course!" Moreta cast a glance in the direction of Alessan's gaze and saw Lady Oma escorting a girl across the floor.

"I've had my shins kicked enough this evening!" Alessan clasped Moreta firmly, his right hand flat against her shoulder blade, the fingers of his left hand twining in hers as he guided her out in the center of the square.

As she surrendered to the swaying step and glide of the stately dance, Moreta had a brief glimpse of the smileless face of Lady Oma. She could feel Alessan's heart pounding, as hers still was, from the exertions of the previous dance but gradually the thudding eased, her face cooled, and her muscles stopped trembling. She realized that she had not danced to this melody since leaving Keroon—since the last Gather she had attended with Talpan, so many Turns ago.

"You're thinking of another man," Alessan whispered, his lips close to her ear.

"A boy I knew. In Keroon."

"And you remember him fondly?"

"We were to be apprenticed to the same Masterhealer." Could she detect a note of jealousy in Alessan's voice? "He continued in the craft. I was taken to Ista and Impressed Orlith."

"And now you heal dragons." For a moment, Alessan loosened his grip but only, it seemed, to take a fresh and firmer hold of her. "Dance, Moreta of Keroon. The moons are up. We can dance all night."

"The harpers may have other plans."

"Not as long as my supply of Benden white lasts . . ."

So Alessan remained by her side, making sure her goblet was full and insisting that she eat some of the small hot spiced rolls that were being served to the dwindling revellers. Nor did he relinquish her to other partners.

The wine got to the harpers before the new day. Even Alessan's incredible store of energy was flagging by the time Orlith landed again in the dancing square.

"It has been a memorable Gather, Lord Alessan," Moreta said formally.

"Your presence has made it so, Weyrwoman Moreta," he replied, assisting her to Orlith's forearm. "Shells! Don't slip, woman. Can you reach your own weyr without falling asleep?" His voice carried an edge of anxiety despite his flippant words.

"I can always reach my own weyr."

"Can she, Orlith?"

"Lord Alessan!" The audacity of the man consulting her dragon in her presence.

Orlith turned her head, her eyes sleepily golden. *He means well.*

"You mean well, Orlith says!" Moreta knew that fatigue was making her sound silly, so she made herself laugh. She didn't wish to end the marvelous evening on a sour note.

"Yes, my lady of the golden dragon, I mean well. Safe back!"

Alessan gave her a final wave and then moved slowly through the disarray of fallen benches and messy tables, toward the deserted roadway where most of the stalls had been dismantled and packed away.

"Let's get back to Fort Weyr," Moreta said softly, reluctantly. Her eyes were heavy, her body limp with a pleasant if thorough fatigue. It took an effort to think of the pattern of Fort Weyr's Star Stones. Then Orlith sprang off the dancing square, the standards whipping about with the force of her backwing stroke. They were aloft and Ruatha receding, the darkness punctuated by the last few surviving glows.

CHAPTER

IV

South Boll and Fort Weyr, Present Pass, 3.11.43

"Well?"

Capiam raised his head from the pillow he had made of his arms on the small wooden table in the dispensary. Fatigue and the tremendous strain disoriented him and at first he couldn't identify the figure standing imperiously in front of him.

"Well, Masterhealer? You said you would return immediately to bring me your conclusions. That was several hours ago. Now I find you sleeping."

The testy voice and overbearing manner belonged to Lord Ratoshigan. Behind him, just outside the door, was the tall figure of the Weyrleader who had conveyed Capiam and Lord Ratoshigan from Ista's Gather to Southern Boll.

"I sat down only for a moment, Lord Ratoshigan"—Capiam lifted his hand in a gesture of dismay—"to organize my notes."

"Well?" The third prompting was a bark of unequivocal displeasure. "What *is* your diagnosis of these . . ." Ratoshigan did not say "malingerers" but the implication would have been plain enough even if the anxious infirmarian had not repeatedly told Capiam that Lord Ratoshigan regarded any man as a malingerer who took his bread and protection but did not deliver a fair day's work in return.

"They are very ill, Lord Ratoshigan."

"They seemed well enough when I left for Ista! They're not wasted or scored." Ratoshigan rocked from heel to toe, a thin man with a long thin, bony face, pinched nostrils above a thin, pinch-lipped mouth and hard small eyes in dry sockets. Capiam thought the Lord Holder looked considerably more unwell than the men dying in the infirmary beds.

"Two have died of whatever it is that afflicts them," Capiam said slowly, reluctant to utter the terrifying conclusion that he had reached before exhaustion had overcome him.

"Dead? Two? And you don't *know* what ailed them?"

Out of the corner of his eye, Capiam noticed that Sh'gall had stepped back from the doorway at the mention of death. The Weyrleader was not a man who tolerated injury or illness, having managed to avoid both.

"No, I don't know precisely what ails them. The symptoms—a fever, headache, lack of appetite, the dry hacking cough—are unusually severe and do not respond to any of the commonly effective treatments."

"But you *must* know. You are the Masterhealer!"

"Rank does not confer total knowledge of my Craft." Capiam had been keeping his voice low, out of deference to the exhausted healers sleeping in the next room, but Ratoshigan exercised no such courtesy and his voice had been rising with his sense of indignation. Capiam rose and walked around the table, Ratoshigan giving way before him, backing out into the close night. "There is much we have forgotten through disuse." Capiam sighed, filled with a weary despair. He ought not to have allowed himself to sleep. There was so much to be done. "These deaths are but the beginning, Lord Ratoshigan. An epidemic is loose on Pern."

"Is that why you and Talpan had that animal killed?" Sh'gall spoke for the first time, angry surprise in his voice.

"Epidemic?" Ratoshigan waved Sh'gall to silence. "Epidemic! What *are* you saying, man? Just a few sick—"

"Not a few, Lord Ratoshigan." Capiam pulled his shoulders back and leaned against the cool stucco wall behind him. "Two days ago I was urgently called to Igen Sea Hold. *Forty* were dead, including three of the sailors who had rescued that animal from the sea. Far better that they had left it on its tree trunk!"

"Forty dead?" Ratoshigan was incredulous, and Sh'gall stepped farther back from the infirmary.

"More are falling ill at the Sea Hold and in the nearby mountain hold whose men had come down to see the incredible seagoing feline!"

"Then why was it brought to Ista Gather?" The Lord Holder was outraged now.

"To be seen," Capiam said bitterly. "Before the illnesses started, it was taken from the Sea Hold to Keroon for the Herdmaster to identify. I was doing what I could to assist the Sea Hold healers when a drum message summoned me to Keroon. Herdmaster Sufur had people and animals sickening

rapidly and curiously. The illness followed the same course as that at Igen Sea
Hold. Another drum message, and I was conveyed by brown dragon to Telgar. The sickness is there, too, brought back from Keroon by two holders
who were buying runnerstock. All the beasts were dead, and so were the
holders and twenty others. I cannot estimate how many hundreds of people
have been infected by the merest contact with those so contagious. Those of
us who live to tell the Harper will thank Talpan's quick wits"—Capiam
looked severely at Sh'gall—"that he linked the journey of the feline to the
spread of the disease."

"But that animal was the picture of health!" Sh'gall protested.

"It was." Capiam spoke with dry humor. "It seemed immune to the disease it brought to Igen, Keroon, Telgar, and Ista!"

Sh'gall defensively crossed his arms over his chest.

"How could a caged animal spread disease?" Ratoshigan demanded, his
thin nostrils flaring.

"It wasn't caged at Igen, nor on the ship when it was weak from thirst
and its voyage. At Keroon, Master Sufur kept it in a run when he was trying
to identify it. It had ample opportunity to infect people and plenty of time."
Capiam despaired as he thought of how much time and opportunity. The
healers would never be able to trace all the people who had seen the rarity,
touched its tawny coat, and returned to their holds, incubating the disease.

"But . . . but . . . I just received a shipload of valuable runners from
Keroon!"

Capiam sighed. "I know, Lord Ratoshigan. Master Quitrin informed me
that the dead men worked in the beasthold. He's also had an urgent message
of illness from the hold at which the men and the beasts halted overnight on
the way from the coast."

Ratoshigan and Sh'gall at last began to appreciate the gravity of the
situation.

"We're in the middle of a Pass!" Sh'gall said.

"This virus is as indifferent to us as Thread is," Capiam said.

"You have all those Records in your Crafthall. Search them! You have
only to search properly!"

Sh'gall had never had an unfruitful Search, had he? thought Capiam,
and suppressed his errant sense of humor. One day, though, he meant to
record the various and sundry ways in which men and women reacted to disaster. If he survived it!

"An exhaustive search was initiated as soon as I saw the reports on the
Igen Sea Hold death toll. Here is what you must do, Lord Ratoshigan."

"What I must do?" The Lord Holder drew himself up.

"Yes, Lord Ratoshigan, what you *must* do. You came to seek my diagnosis. I have diagnosed an epidemic. As Masterhealer of Pern, I have authority over Hold, Hall, and Weyr in these circumstances." He glanced at Sh'gall to be sure the Weyrleader was listening, too. "I hereby order you to announce by drum that a quarantine exists on this Hold and the one your beasthandlers used on the way from the coast. No one is to come or go from the Hold proper. There is to be no travel anywhere in your Hold, no congregating."

"But they must gather fruit and—"

"You will gather the sick, human and animal, and arrange for their care. Master Quitrin and I have discussed empiric treatments since homeopathic remedies have proved ineffectual. Inform your Warder and your ladies to prepare your Hall for the sick—"

"My Hall?" Ratoshigan was aghast at the idea.

"And you will clear the new beastholds of animals to relieve the crowding in your dormitories."

"I *knew* you'd bring that subject up!" Ratoshigan was nearly spitting with rage.

"To your sorrow, you will find that the healers' past objections have validity!" Capiam vented his pent-up anxieties and fears by shouting down Ratoshigan's objections. "You will isolate the sick and care for them, which is your duty as Lord Holder! Or come the end of the Pass, you'll find you hold nothing!"

The passion with which Capiam spoke reduced Lord Ratoshigan to silence. Then Capiam turned on Sh'gall.

"Weyrleader, convey me to Fort Hold. It is imperative that I return to my Hall as quickly as possible. You will wish to waste no time alerting your Weyr."

Sh'gall hesitated, but it was not to speak to his dragon.

"Weyrleader!"

Sh'gall swallowed. "Did you *touch* that animal?"

"No, I did not. Talpan warned me." Out of the corner of his eye, Capiam saw Ratoshigan recoil.

"You cannot leave here, Master Capiam," Ratoshigan cried, skittering fearfully to grab his hand. "I touched that animal. I might die, too."

"So you might. You went to Ista Gather to poke and prod a caged creature that has exacted an unexpected revenge for cruelty."

Sh'gall and Ratoshigan stared at the usually tactful Masterhealer.

"Come, Sh'gall, no time is to be wasted. You'll want to isolate those riders who attended Ista Gather, especially those who might have been close to the beast."

"But what shall I do, Master Capiam, what shall I do?"

"What I told you to do. You'll know in two or three days if you've caught the sickness. So I recommend that you order your Hold as quickly as possible."

Capiam gestured Sh'gall to lead the way to the courtyard where the bronze dragon was waiting. The great glowing eyes of Kadith guided the two men to his side in the predawn darkness.

"Dragons!" Sh'gall halted abruptly. "Do dragons get it?"

"Talpan said not. Believe me, Weyrleader, it was his primary concern."

"You're positive?"

"Talpan was. No whers, watchwhers, or wherries have been affected though individuals of all those species had contact with the feline at Igen Sea Hold or Keroon Beasthold. Runners are seriously affected but not herdbeasts or the indigenous whers and wherries. Since dragons are related . . ."

"Not to wherries!"

Capiam did not bother to disagree, though in his Craft the kinship was tacitly acknowledged.

"The dragon that took the feline from Igen to Keroon has not become ill, and he conveyed it over ten days ago."

Sh'gall looked dubious but he gestured for them to proceed to Kadith.

The bronze dragon had lowered his forequarters for his rider and the healer to mount. Riding dragonback was one of the most enjoyable perogatives of Capiam's Mastery, though he tried not to presume on that privilege. Gratefully he settled himself behind Sh'gall. He had no compunctions about drafting Sh'gall and Kadith to convey him to his Hall in this extreme emergency. The Weyrleader was strong and healthy and might survive any contagion Capiam carried.

Capiam's mind was too busy with all he must accomplish in the next few hours to enjoy the dragon's launching into air. Talpan had promised to initiate quarantine at Ista, to warn the east, and to isolate any who might have had contact with the beast. He would try to trace all runners leaving Keroon Beasthold in the past eighteen days. Capiam would alert the west and intensify the search of Records. The Fort drums would be hot tomorrow with all the messages he must send. The first priority would be Ruatha Hold. Dragonriders had attended Ista Gather and then flown in for a few more hours of dancing and wine at Ruatha. If only Capiam had not succumbed to fatigue. He had already lost valuable time in which the disease would be innocently spread.

Sh'gall's low warning gave Capiam time to take a good hold of the fighting straps. As they went *between*, he did wonder if the awful cold might kill off any trace of the disease.

They were abruptly above Fort Hold fire-heights and gliding in for a fast landing in the field before the Hall. Sh'gall was not going to stay in the company of the Masterhealer any longer than he had to. He waited until Capiam dismounted and then asked the healer to repeat his instructions.

"Tell Berchar and Moreta to treat the symptoms empirically. I'll inform you of any effective treatment immediately. The plague incubates in two to four days. There have been survivors. Try to establish where your riders and weyrfolk have been." The freedom to travel as they pleased had worked to the disadvantage of the Weyrs. "Don't congregate . . ."

"There's Fall!"

"The Weyrs do have their duty to the people . . . but try to limit contact with ground crews." Capiam gave Kadith's shoulder a grateful thump. Kadith turned his gleaming eyes toward the Masterhealer and then, walking forward a few paces, sprang into the air.

Capiam watched until the pair went *between* against the lightening eastern sky, the journey of a breath to the mountains beyond Fort Hold. Then he stumbled up the gentle slope toward the Hall and the bed he was going to welcome. But first he had to compose the drum messages that must go out to Ruatha.

The early-morning air held a bit of dampness that suggested fog was on its way. No glowbaskets were set in the forecourt of Fort Hold and only the one in the entryway of the Harper Hall. Capiam was surprised to see how much progress had been made on the annex of the Hall in the two days. Then the watchwher came snorting up to him, recognizing his smell and gurgling its greeting. Capiam slapped affectionately at Burr's ugly head, digging his fingers into its skull ridges and smiling at the happy alteration of its noise. Watchwhers had their uses, to be sure, but due to the freak of breeding that had perpetuated them, the creatures were so ugly that they revolted those who saw their debased resemblance to the graceful dragons. Yet the watchwher was as loyal and faithful as any dragon and could be trained to recognize those who were allowed to come and go with impunity. Legends said that watchwhers had been used in the earliest holds as the last-ditch defense against Thread. Though how, since watchwhers were nocturnal creatures that could not tolerate sunlight, Capiam didn't know.

Burr was quite young, only a few Turns old, and Capiam had cultivated an association with it since it had been hatched. He and Tirone had made it strictly understood that they would not tolerate apprentice abuse of the creature. When Thread fell on Fort, Capiam or Tirone, whichever of the two Masters was present, would take the watchwher into the main entrance of the Hall to remind the young men and women that the watchwher could provide an important function in that perilous period.

If Burr's ecstatic welcome nearly knocked him off his feet, at least the greeting was sincere, and Capiam was oddly touched by it. Burr bumbled along beside him, his chain rattling on the flagstone. He gave Burr a last drubbing across the scalp and then ran up the stairs to open the heavy door of the Hall.

One dim glow illuminated the inner hall. Capiam closed the door and moved quickly, so near his bed and much needed rest. He went to the left in the main hall, through the doorway that led to the Archives.

Discordant snores surprised him, and he peered into the vaulted library room. Two apprentices, one with head pillowed on the Records he had been examining, the other propped more comfortably against the wall, were vying unmusically. Annoyance warred with tolerance in Capiam's mind. Dawn was near and would bring Master Fortine to prod them to their labors and scold them for weakness. They'd be the better readers for his rebuke and the rest. Suddenly Capiam was too tired to answer the questions they would certainly tax him with if he did wake them.

Quietly then, he took a sheet of well-scraped hide and composed a terse message for the drummaster to broadcast to the Weyrs and the major Holds, to be relayed to lesser holds and halls. He put the message on Master Fortine's writing desk right on the page the Archivist was using. Fortine would see it as soon as he finished his breakfast, which was usually early, so the news of the epidemic would be spread before noon.

To the sound of the discordant snores, Capiam dragged his feet to his quarters. He'd get some sleep before the drums started. Quite possibly he was weary enough to sleep through them for a while. He walked up the steps into the healers' section of the Harper Hall. When the Pass was over, he must really start the construction of a Healer Crafthall.

He reached his room and opened the door. A mellow glow softly lit the chamber. A bowl of fresh fruit and a small wine jar had been placed on his bedside table, and his bed fur turned back invitingly. Desdra! He was once more grateful for her thoughtfulness. Tossing his pack to the corner, he sat on the bed, the effort of pulling off his boots almost beyond his remaining physical strength. He loosened his belt, then decided not to remove his tunic and pants—too much effort required. He rolled onto the mattress and in the same movement jerked the fur over his shoulder. The pillow was remarkably welcoming to his tired aching head.

He groaned. He had left the drum messages. Fortine would know that he had returned, but not at what hour. He had to have sleep! He had been across Pern and up and down it. If he wasn't extra careful of his own health, he'd be a victim of the plague before he found out what it was.

He staggered from his bed to his table. "Disturb me not!" he printed boldly and, hanging onto the door to keep himself erect for that one last task, he pinned the note where it could not be missed.

Then when he sank into the comfort of his bed, he could relax into sleep.

CHAPTER

V

Moreta was certain that she had only been asleep a few minutes when Orlith woke her.

Two hours you have slept but Kadith is in a frenzy.

"Why?" Moreta found it very difficult to lift her head from the pillow. It didn't ache, but her legs did. Whether from the dancing or from the wine, Moreta didn't know and probably would not have time to discover if Sh'gall was in one of his moods.

A sickness in the land, Orlith replied, sounding puzzled. *Sh'gall went first to see K'lon and woke him.*

"Woke K'lon?" Moreta was disgusted as she pulled on the first tunic she could reach. The clothing was slightly damp and her sleeping quarters were clammy. The weather must have changed.

There is a fine mist over the Weyr, Orlith obligingly reported.

Moreta shivered as she dressed. "Why on earth should he wake K'lon? The man's been ill and needs his rest."

He is convinced that K'lon has brought the illness here. Orlith sounded truly perplexed. *K'lon was in Igen.*

"K'lon is often in Igen. His friend is a green rider there."

Moreta splashed water into her face then rubbed the mint stick over her teeth, but it did little to improve the taste in her mouth. She ran her fingers through her short hair with one hand as she fumbled for a goru pear from the dish in her room. The tart fruit might neutralise the aftereffects of all that Benden wine.

"Moreta!" Sh'gall's summons resounded from the entrance to her weyr.

Moreta had time to give Orlith's muzzle a swift caress before Sh'gall burst into the chamber. The queen blinked her eyes shut, feigning sleep. Sh'gall charged ten paces into the weyr and stopped, holding his hand up as if fending off an approach.

"A sickness is all over Pern. Men are dying and nothing can be done. Runners are dying, too. No one must leave the Weyr."

Sh'gall's eyes were wide with a genuine fear, and Moreta stared at him in surprise for a moment.

"Thread falls tomorrow, Sh'gall. The dragonriders must leave the Weyr."

"Don't come close to me. I may have been infected, too."

Moreta hadn't moved. "Suppose you give me some details," she said, speaking calmly.

"That animal they showed off at Ista—it was infected with a deadly disease. It's spread from Igen to Keroon Beasthold to Telgar. It's even in Southern Boll! Men are *dead* of it in Lord Ratoshigan's Hold. And he's been quarantined by Master Capiam. So are we!"

"Runners, you said?" Moreta's breath caught in her throat and she turned fearfully toward her dragon. "Dragons?" She'd touched that runner and if she'd contaminated Orlith . . .

"No, no, not dragons! Capiam said Talpan agreed they weren't affected. They had the beast killed. It hadn't looked sick to me!"

"Tell me please how men could die in Southern Boll when that feline was still in Ista?"

"Because there's an epidemic! It started when the seamen hauled that beast out of the water and brought it home. Everyone wanted to see it, so they took it to Igen Hold, then Keroon Beasthold and Ista before this Talpan fellow realized it was a carrier. Yes, that's what Capiam said: The feline was a carrier."

"And they displayed it at Ista Gather?"

"No one knew! Not until this Talpan fellow came along and talked to Capiam. He'd been to all the infected holds."

"Who? Talpan?"

"No, Capiam! Talpan's an animal healer."

"Yes, I know." Moreta held on to her patience because Sh'gall was obviously so rattled as to be incoherent. "Nothing was mentioned of this at Ruatha Gather."

Sh'gall gave her a patient glare. "Of course, the truth wasn't known. Besides, who talks of unpleasant things at a Gather! But I just conveyed Capiam to his hall. I also had to convey Ratoshigan and Capiam to Southern Boll because Ratoshigan received an urgent drum message to return. *He* had deaths. He also had new runners in from Keroon; they probably brought that sickness to the west." Sh'gall glowered and then shuddered violently. "Capiam said that if I didn't touch the feline I might not get sick. I can't get sick. I'm the Weyrleader." He shuddered again.

Moreta looked at him apprehensively. His hair was damp, pressed in a wet ridge about his forehead by his riding helmet. His lips were slightly blue and his skin very pale. "You don't look well."

"I'm fine! I'm fine. I bathed in the Ice Lake. Capiam said that the disease is like Thread. Cold kills Thread and so does water."

Moreta took up her fur cloak, which lay where it had fallen from her shoulders a scant two hours before, and approached him with it.

"Don't come near me." He stepped backward, his hands extended to fend her off.

"Sh'gall, don't be idiotic!" She flung the cloak at him. "Put that about you so you won't get sick of a chill. A chill would make you more susceptible to whatever disease is about." She turned back to the table and poured wine, splashing it in her haste. "Drink this. Wine is also antiseptic. No, I won't come near you." She was relieved to see him settled, the cloak about his shoulders, and stepped back from the table so he could reach the wine. "An utterly foolish thing to do, plunge yourself into the Ice Lake before the sun is up and then travel *between*. Now sit down and tell me again what happened at Ista Gather. And where you went with Capiam and exactly what he said."

She listened with half her attention to Sh'gall's more orderly recounting while she mentally reviewed what precautions and measures she could take to ensure the health of the Weyr.

"No good comes from the Southern Continent!" Sh'gall commented gratuitously. "There's a very sound reason why no one is permitted there."

"Permission has never been denied. I always understood that everything we need was taken over in the Crossing. Now, what are the symptoms of the disease that's spreading?" Moreta recalled the bloody discharge from the dead runner's nose, the only external sign of its mortal distress.

Sh'gall stared uncomprehendingly for a long moment, then collected his thoughts. "Fever. Yes, there's fever." He glanced at her for approval.

"There are many kinds of fevers, Sh'gall."

"Berchar will know, then. Fever, Capiam said, and headache and a dry cough. Why should that be enough to kill people and animals?"

"What remedies did Capiam specify?"

"How could he specify when he doesn't know what the plague is? They'll find out. They've only to search hard enough. Oh, he said to treat the symptoms empirically."

"Did he mention an incubation period? We can't just stay quarantined in the Weyr forever, you know."

"I know. But Capiam said we mustn't congregate. He really tore into Ratoshigan for the overcrowding in his Hold." Sh'gall grinned unpleasantly. "We have been warning the Holders, but would they listen? They'll pay for it now."

"Sh'gall, Capiam must have told you how long it takes the disease to incubate."

The Weyrleader had finished the wine. He frowned and rubbed at his face. "I'm tired. I waited half the night for the Masterhealer at Ratoshigan's. He said it incubates in two to four days. He told me to find out where everyone has been and to order them not to congregate. The Weyr has its duties, too. I've got to get some sleep. Since you're up, you make sure everyone knows about this. Tell them all just what they may have caught yesterday." He gave her a hard, warning stare. "I don't want to find out when I wake up that you've jollied people along."

"An epidemic is a far different affair from reassuring a rider with a wing-damaged dragon."

"And find Berchar. I want to know exactly what K'lon was ill of. K'lon didn't know, and Berchar wasn't in his quarters!" Sh'gall didn't approve of that. Fully male and hold-bred, Sh'gall had never developed any compassion or understanding of the green and blue riders and their associations.

"I'll speak to Berchar." She had a fairly good idea she'd find him with S'gor, a green rider.

"And warn the Weyr?" He rose, groggy with fatigue and the wine he'd taken on an empty stomach. "And no one's to leave the Weyr and no one's to come in. You be sure that the watchrider passes on that order!" He waggled an admonitory finger at her.

"It's a bit late to cry Thread when the burrow's set, isn't it?" she replied bitterly. "The Gathers should have been canceled."

"No one knew how serious this was yesterday. You transmit my orders straightaway!"

Still clutching her fur around him, Sh'gall stumbled from the weyr. Moreta watched him go, her head throbbing. Why hadn't they canceled the Gathers? All those people at Ruatha! And dragonriders from every Weyr in and out of Ista *and* Ruatha. What was it S'peren had told her—sickness in Igen, Keroon, and Telgar? But he hadn't said anything about an epidemic. Or deaths. And that runner of Vander's? Had Alessan mentioned a new runner from Keroon in Vander's hold? Thinking of the long picket lines on Ruatha's race flat, Moreta groaned. And all those people! How infectious would that runner have been at the moment of his death, when anxious riders and helpful spectators had crowded around it? She shouldn't have interfered. It was not her business!

You are distressed, Orlith said, her eyes whirling in a soothing blue. *You should not be distressed by a runnerbeast.*

Moreta leaned against her dragon's head, stroking the near eye ridge, calming her anxiety with the soft feel of Orlith's skin.

"It's not just the runnerbeast, my love. A sickness is in the land. A very dangerous sickness. Where's Berchar?"

With S'gor. Asleep. It is very early. And foggy.

"And yesterday was so beautiful!" She remembered Alessan's strong arms about her in the toss dance, the challenge in his light-green eyes.

You enjoyed yourself! Orlith said with deep satisfaction.

"Yes, indeed I did." Moreta sighed ruefully.

Nothing will change yesterday, Orlith remarked philosophically. *So now you must deal with today.* As Moreta chuckled over dragon logic, the queen added, *Leri wishes to speak with you since you are awake.*

"Yes, and Leri might have heard about an epidemic like this. She might also know how I'm going to break the news to the Weyr the day before Fall."

Since Sh'gall had gone off with her cloak, Moreta slipped into her riding jacket. Orlith had been correct, as always, about the weather. As Moreta left her weyr and started up the steps to Leri's, the fog was swirling down from the ranges. Thread would Fall tomorrow, fog or not, so she devoutly hoped the weather would clear. If the wind failed to clear the mist, the possibility of collision would be trebled. Dragons could see through fog but their riders couldn't. Sometimes riders did not heed their dragons and found themselves in one-sided arguments with bare ridges.

Orlith, please tell the watchrider that no one, dragonrider or holder, is permitted into the Weyr today. And no one is to leave it, either. The order is to be passed to each watchrider.

Who would visit the Weyr in such fog? Orlith asked. *And the day after two Gathers.*

"Orlith?"

I have relayed the message. Balgeth is too sleepy to question why. Orlith sounded suspiciously meek.

◆   ◆   ◆

"Good day to you, Holth," Moreta said courteously as she entered the old Weyrwoman's quarters.

Holth turned her head briefly in acknowledgment before closing her eyelids and snuggling her head more firmly into her forelegs. The old queen was nearly bronze with age.

Beside her, on the edge of the stone platform that was the dragon's couch, Leri sat on a heap of pillows, her body swathed in thick woven rugs. Leri said she slept beside Holth as much for the warmth the dragon had stored up in her from so much sunning over so many Turns as to save herself the bother of moving. The last few Turns, Leri's joints rebelled against too much use. Repeatedly Moreta and Master Capiam had urged the woman to take up the standing invitation to remove to the south to Ista Weyr. Leri adamantly refused, declaring that she wasn't a tunnel snake to change her skin: She'd been born in Fort Weyr and intended to live out her Turn with those few old friends who remained, and in her own familiar quarters.

"Hear you enjoyed yourself past the first watch," Leri said. She raised her eyebrows questioningly. "Was that why Sh'gall was berating you?"

"He wasn't berating. He was bemoaning. An epidemic's loose on Pern."

Concern wiped the amusement from Leri's face. "What? We've never had an epidemic on Pern. Not that I ever heard about. Nor read either."

Her movement restricted by her joint ailment, Leri kept the Weyr's records to allow Moreta more time for her nursing. Leri often browsed through the older Records, for "the gossip," she said.

"Shards! I'd hoped you'd read something somewhere. Something encouraging! Sh'gall's in a rare taking and this time with due cause."

"Perhaps I haven't read far enough back for exciting things like epidemics." Leri tossed Moreta a pillow from her pile and pointed imperiously at the small wooden stool set aside for visitors. "We're a healthy lot, by and large. Tend to break a lot of bones, Threadscores, occasional fevers, but nothing on a continent-wide scale. What sort of disease is it?"

"Master Capiam has not yet identified it."

"Oh, I don't like the sound of that!" Leri rolled her eyes. "And, by the Egg, there were *two* Gathers yesterday, weren't there?"

"The danger was not fully appreciated. Master Capiam and Talpan—"

"The Talpan who was a friend of yours?"

"Yes, well, he's been an animal healer, you know, and *he* realized that the feline they had on display at Ista was the disease carrier."

"The feline from the Southern Continent?" Leri clacked her tongue. "And some bloody fool has been taking that creature here, there, and everywhere, showing it off, so the disease is also here, there, and everywhere! With riders, including our noble Weyrleader, all going to have a little peek!"

"Sh'gall's story was a little incoherent but he'd taken Lord Ratoshigan to Ista to see the feline; Capiam had arrived from seeing what ailed Igen Sea Hold, Keroon, and Telgar—"

"Great Faranth!"

Moreta nodded. "Ista, of course. Then Ratoshigan had an urgent drum message summoning him back because of illness, so Sh'gall conveyed him and Master Capiam."

"How did the sickness get there so fast? The beast only got as far as Ista!"

"Yes, but it was first at Keroon Beasthold to be identified by Master Sufur and no one realized that it was carrying sickness—"

"And because it's been an open winter, they've been shipping runners all over the continent!" Leri concluded, and the two women looked at each other gravely.

"Talpan told Capiam that dragons are not affected."

"We should be grateful for small mercies, I suppose," Leri said.

"And Fall's tomorrow. We'll have that over with before any of us fall sick. Incubation's two to four days."

"That's not a big mercy, is it? But you weren't at Ista." Leri frowned.

"No, Sh'gall was. However, a runner fell in the second race at Ruatha and it shouldn't have . . ."

Leri nodded, her comprehension complete. "And naturally you were close enough to go have a look. It died?"

"And shouldn't have. Its owner had just received some new stock from Keroon."

"Hooooo!" Leri rolled her eyes and sighed in resignation. "So, what medication does Capiam recommend? Surely he must have some idea if he's been flipping across the continent?"

"He recommends that we treat the symptoms empirically until he finds out just what it is and what the specific medicine is."

"And what is it we treat empirically?"

"Headache, fever, and a dry cough."

"They don't kill."

"Until now."

"I don't like this at all," Leri said, pulling her shawl across her shoulders and hunching into its warmth. "Though mind, we'd a harper here—though L'mal shooed him off for he was doleful—who used to say 'there's nothing new under the sun.' A slim hope in these circumstances, but I don't think we can ignore any avenues of exploration. You just bring me up more Records. Say the ones starting the last Pass. Fortunately I hadn't planned on going anywhere this morning."

As Leri only left her weyr to fly with the queens' wing, Moreta offered her a smile for her attempt to lighten the bad tidings.

"Sh'gall's left it to you to tell the Weyr?"

"Those who are awake. And Nesso . . ."

Leri snorted. "That's the right one to start with. Be sure she gets the facts right or we'll have hysteria as well as hangovers by noontime. And since you're up, would you fix my wine for me, please, Moreta?" Leri shifted uneasily. "The change in the weather does get to my joints." She saw Moreta's reluctance. "Look, if you fix it, then you'll know I haven't exceeded the proper amount of fellis juice." Eyes sparkling with challenge, she cocked her head at the younger Weyrwoman. Moreta did not like Leri to use much fellis juice and contended that if Leri went south where the warmer weather would ease her condition, she wouldn't need fellis juice at all.

But Moreta did not hesitate. The clammy cold made her feel stiff so it would certainly be making Leri miserable.

"Now, tell me, did you enjoy the Gather?" Leri asked as Moreta measured the fellis juice into her tall goblet.

"Yes, I did. And I got down on the race flats and watched most of the races from a very good vantage point with Lord Alessan."

"What? You monopolized Alessan when his mother and the mother of every eligible girl able to creep or crawl to that Gather . . ."

Moreta grinned. "He did his duty with the girls on the dance square. And we," she added, smiling more broadly than ever, "managed to stay upright in a toss dance!"

Leri grinned back at Moreta. "Alessan could be quite a temptation. I assume he's got over the death of that wild one he married. Sad, that! Now, his grandfather, Leef's sire . . . Ah, no, you'll have heard all that." Moreta had not, but Leri's comment meant she was unlikely to. "I always chat Alessan up while the ground crews are reporting. Always has a flask of Benden white with him."

"He does, does he?"

Leri laughed at Moreta's alert tone.

"Don't tell me he tried it on you, too, at his own Gather?" Leri chortled and then assumed a masculine pitch to her voice, " 'I just happen to have one skin of Benden white . . .' " And she laughed all the more as Moreta reacted to the mimicry. "He's got a full cave of 'em, I'd say. However, I'm glad Leef gave him the succession. He's got more guts than that elder brother of his—never could remember the man's name. Never mind. Alessan's worth three of him. Did you know that Alessan was Searched?"

"And that Lord Leef refused." Moreta frowned. Alessan would have made a superb bronze rider.

"Well, if the lad was to succeed, Leef was entitled to refuse. That was twelve Turns ago. Before you arrived from Ista. Alessan would have Impressed a bronze, I'm sure."

Moreta nodded, bringing Leri her fellis juice and wine.

"Your health!" she said ironically, raising the cup to Moreta before she took a careful sip. "Hmmm. Do get some rest today, Moreta," she said more briskly. "Two hours' sleep is not enough when there's Fall tomorrow and who knows how many dragonriders will do stupid things thanks to two Gathers, let alone Capiam's unidentified disease."

"I'll get some rest once I've organized a few matters."

"I sometimes wonder if we did right, L'mal and I, monopolizing your healing arts for the Weyr."

"Yes!" Moreta's quick reply was echoed by Holth and Orlith.

"Well, ask a silly question!" Leri was reassured, and she patted Holth's cheek.

"Quite. Now, what Records should I send you?"

"The oldest ones you can find that are still legible."

Moreta scooped up the pillow Leri had loaned her and threw it back to the old Weyrwoman, who caught it deftly.

"And eat something!" Leri shouted as Moreta turned and left the weyr.

Wisps of fog were infiltrating the valleys, oozing toward the western rim of the Bowl, and the watchrider was standing within the forearms of his dragon, finding what protection he could from the elements. Moreta shuddered. She didn't like the northern fogs even after ten Turns, but she hadn't liked the humidity of the southern latitude at Ista any better. And it was far too late to return to the comfortable climate of the highlands of Keroon. Was the disease in the highlands, too? And Talpan diagnosing it! How strange that he had been in her mind yesterday. Would the epidemic bring them together again?

She gave herself a little shake and began the descent to the floor of the Bowl. First she would see K'lon, then find Berchar, even if it meant invading the privacy of S'gor's weyr.

K'lon was asleep when she reached the infirmary and there was not so much as a bead of fever perspiration on his brow or upper lip. His fair skin was a healthy color, wind-darkened where the eyepieces left the cheek bare. Berchar had attended K'lon during the initial days of his fever so Moreta saw no point in rousing the blue rider again.

Folk were moving about the Bowl by then, swirling fog about them as they began the preparations for the next day's Threadfall. The shouts and laughter of the weyrlings filling firestone sacks was muted by the mist. Moreta thought to check with Weyrlingmaster F'neldril to find out how many of the weyrlings had drawn convey duty the day before. A rare animal in Ista might well have attracted some of them despite their strict orders to convey and return directly.

"Put some energy into the task, lads. Here's the Weyrwoman to see the sacks are properly filled for tomorrow's Fall."

Many Fort dragonriders insisted that F'neldril was the one rider all Fort dragons obeyed, a holdover from weyrling days under his tutelage. He did have an uncanny instinct, Moreta thought, if he could see her through the rolling fog. He appeared right beside her, a craggy-faced man with a deep Thread scar from forehead to ear, and the lobe missing, but she had always liked him and he was one of her first friends at Fort Weyr.

"You're well, Weyrwoman? And Orlith thrives? She's near clutching now, isn't she?"

"More weyrlings for you to tyrannize, F'neldril?"

"Me?" He pointed his long curved thumb at his chest in mock dismay. "Me? Tyrannize?"

But the old established exchange did not lift her spirits. "There's trouble, F'neldril . . ."

"Which one?" he demanded.

"No, not your weyrlings. There's a disease of epidemic proportion spreading over the southeast and coming west. I'll want to know how many of the weyrlings were on convey duty yesterday and where they took their passengers, and how long they stayed on the ground at Ista. The entire Weyr will be answering the same questions. If we are to prevent the epidemic's spreading here, we'll need to know."

"I'll find out exactly. Never fear on that count, Moreta!"

"I don't, but we must avoid panic even though the situation is very serious. And Leri would like to have some of the oldest Records, the still legible ones, brought to her weyr."

"What's the Masterhealer doing then with his time, and all those apprentices of his, that we have to do his job for him?"

"The more to look the quicker to find; the sooner the better," Moreta replied. F'neldril could be so parochial.

"Leri'll have her Records as soon as the lads have finished sacking firestone and had a bit of a wash. Wouldn't do to have stone-dust messing up our Records—You there, M'barak, that sack's not what I'd call full. Top it off."

Another of F'neldril's quirks was to finish one job before starting the next. But Moreta moved off, secure in the knowledge that Leri would not have a long wait for her Records.

She went on to the Lower Caverns and stood for a moment in the entrance, noting how few people occupied the tables, most of those few obviously nursing wineheads. How awkward and inconvenient it all was, Moreta thought with a rush of distressed exasperation, for an epidemic to break out the day after two Gathers, when half the riders would consider the news a bad joke and the rest wouldn't be sober enough to understand what was happening. And Fall tomorrow! How could she *tell* the Weyr if they weren't available to tell?

If you eat, you'll think of something, came the calm imperturbable voice of her dragon.

"An excellent notion." Moreta went to the small breakfast hearth and poured herself a cup of klah, added a huge spoonful of sweetener, took a fresh roll from the warming oven and looked around for a place to sit and think. Then she saw Peterpar, the Weyr herdsman, sharpening his hoof knife. His hair was rumpled and his face sleep creased. He was not really attending to the job at hand, which was honing an edge against the strop.

"Don't cut yourself," she said quietly, sitting down.

Peterpar winced at the sound of her voice but he kept on stropping.

"Were you at Ista or Ruatha?"

"Both, for my folly. Beer at Ista. That foully acid Tillek wine at Ruatha."

"Did you see the feline at Ista?" Moreta thought that it would be kinder to break the news gently to a man in Peterpar's fragile state.

"Aye." Peterpar frowned. "Master Talpan was there. He told me not to get too close though it was caged and all. He sent you his regards, by the way. Afterward"—Peterpar's frown deepened as if he didn't quite trust his memory of events—"they put the animal down."

"For a good reason." Moreta told him why.

Peterpar held the knife suspended, midstrop, shocked. By the time she had finished, he had recovered his equanimity.

"If it's to come, it'll come." He went on stropping.

"That last drove of runnerbeasts we received in tithe," she asked, "from which hold did it come?" She sipped at the klah, grateful for its warmth and stimulation.

"Part of Tillek's contribution." Peterpar's expression reflected the relief he felt. "Heard tell at Ista that there's been an illness among runners at Keroon. Same thing?" The tone in Peterpar's voice begged Moreta to deny it.

She nodded.

"Now, how can a feline that came from the Southern Continent give us, man and runnerbeast, a sickness?"

"Master Talpan decided that it did. Apparently neither man nor runnerbeast has any immunity from the infection that feline brought with it."

Peterpar cocked his head to one side, contorting his face. "Then that runnerbeast that dropped dead at Ruatha races had it?"

"Quite possibly."

"Tillek doesn't get breeding stock from Keroon. Just as well. But soon's I finish my klah, I'll check the herds." He returned his hoof knife to its case, rolled up his strop and shoved it into his tunic pocket. "Dragons don't get this, do they?"

"No, Master Talpan didn't believe they could." Moreta rose to her feet. "But riders can."

"Oh, we're a hardy lot, we weyrfolk," Peterpar said pridefully, shaking his head that she would doubt it. "We'll be careful now. You wait and see. Won't be many of *us* coming down sick. Don't you worry about that now, Moreta. Not with Fall tomorrow."

One was offered reassurance from unlikely sources, Moreta thought. Yet his advice reminded her that one of the reasons weyrfolk were so hardy was because they ate well and sensibly. Many illnesses could be prevented, or diminished, by proper diet. One of her most important duties as Weyrwoman was altering that diet from season to season. Moreta looked about the Cavern, to see if Nesso was up. She had better not be laggard with the tidings to Nesso who would relish disseminating information of such caliber.

"Nesso, I'd like you to add spearleek and white bulb to your stews for a while, please."

Nesso gave one of her little offended sniffs. "I've already planned to do so and there's citron in the morning rolls. If you'd had one, you'd know. A pinch of prevention's worth a pound of cure."

"You'd already planned to? You've heard of the sickness?"

Nesso sniffed again. "Being waked up at the crack of dawn—"

"Sh'gall told you?"

"No, he didn't tell me. He was banging around the night hearth muttering to himself half-demented, without a thought or a consideration for those of us sleeping nearby."

Moreta knew very well why Nesso imposed on herself the nighthearth duty on a Gather night. The prying woman loved to catch people sneaking in or out; that knowledge gave her a feeling of power.

"Who else in the Weyr knows?"

"Whoever you've been telling before you came to me." And she cast a dark look over her shoulder at Peterpar, who was trudging out of the Cavern.

"What did you actually hear Sh'gall saying?" Moreta knew Nesso's penchant for gossip and also her fallibility in repeating it correctly.

"That there's an epidemic on Pern and everyone will die." Nesso gave Moreta a look of pure indignation. "Which is downright foolish."

"Master Capiam has declared that there is."

"Well, we haven't got one here!" Nesso pointed her ladle at the floor. "K'lon's fine and healthy, sleeping like a babe for all he was woke up and questioned sharp. *Holders* die of epidemics." Nesso was contemptuous of anyone not connected intimately with Weyrs. "What else could be expected when so many people are crammed into living space that wouldn't suit a watchwher!" All of Nesso's indignation drained out of her as she looked up and saw Moreta's expression. "You're serious?" Her eyes widened. "I thought Sh'gall just had too much wine! Oh! And everyone here was either to Ista or Ruatha!" Nesso might love to gossip but she was not stupid, and she was quite able to see the enormity of the situation. She gave herself a little shake, picked up the ladle, wiped it off with her clout, and gave the porridge such a stirring that globs fell to the burning blackstone. "What're the signs?"

"Headache, fever, chills, a dry cough."

"That's exactly what put K'lon in his bed."

"You're sure?"

"Of course I'm sure. And for that matter, K'lon's fine. Weyrfolk are healthy folk!" Nesso's assertion was as prideful as Peterpar's and a matter of some consolation to Moreta. "And, saving your look-in on him yesterday afternoon, only Berchar tended him—but he was recovered by then. Mind you, I shouldn't go telling everyone suddenlike about the symptoms, as we'll have enough sore heads this morning and it's an epidemic of wine they had last night, that'll be all." She gave the porridge a final decisive poke and turned fully toward Moreta. "How long does it take this sickness to come on people?"

"Capiam says two to four days."

"Well, at least the riders can concentrate on Fall tomorrow with a clear mind."

"There's to be no congregating. No visitors into the Weyr and none to go out. I've told the watchrider so."

"Visitors aren't likely today in any case, with Gathers yesterday and the fog so thick you can't hardly see the other side of the Bowl. You'll find Berchar in S'gor's weyr, you know."

"I thought that likely. Sh'gall's not to be disturbed."

"Oh?" Nesso's eyebrows rose to meet her hairline. "Does he fancy he's already got this disease? And Thread Falling tomorrow? What do I tell the wingleaders if they ask for him?"

"Tell them to seek me. He's not ill in any case but he was conveying Master Capiam yesterday and he's exhausted."

Moreta left Nesso on that. By sleeping, Sh'gall would recover from the first flare of panic and be as eager as ever for the stimulation of a Fall. He was always at his best leading the Weyr's fighting wings.

Fog swirled around her as Moreta stepped out of the Lower Cavern.

Orlith, would you please bespeak Malth for me and ask for a lift to her weyr?

I'll come.

I know you would, my love, but you are egg-heavy, the fog is thick, and by making such a request, I give them due notice of my coming.

Malth comes. Something in Orlith's tone made Moreta wonder if Malth had been reluctant to obey the summons. Malth should have known that the Weyrwoman would not intrude unnecessarily.

Malth does, was Orlith's quick rejoinder, implying that the rider was at fault.

No sooner had the queen spoken than the fog roiled violently and the green dragon settled herself right beside Moreta so that the Weyrwoman need only to take one step.

Express my gratitude, Orlith, and compliment her on her flying.

I did.

Moreta swung her leg over Malth's neck ridge. She always felt a trifle strange when mounted on so much smaller a dragon than her great queen. It was ridiculous to think that she might be too heavy for the green, whose rider S'gor was a tall, heavily built man, but Moreta could never dispell that notion on the infrequent occasions when she rode the lesser dragons of the Weyr.

Malth waited a respectful moment to be sure that Moreta was settled and then sprang lightly upward. Diving blind into the fog disoriented Moreta despite her absolute faith in Malth.

You would not worry on me, Orlith said plaintively. *I'm not that egg-heavy yet.*

I know, love!

Malth hovered for a moment in the gray gloom, then Moreta felt the lightest of jars through the dragon's slender frame as she landed on her weyr ledge.

"Thank you, Malth!" Moreta projected her voice loudly to give further warning to the weyr occupants then dismounted and walked toward the yellow gleam spilling from the weyr into the corridor. She couldn't see her feet or the ledge. She looked behind her, at the dragon who appeared to be suspended in the fog, but Malth's eyes whirled slowly with encouragement.

"Don't come in here," S'gor called urgently, and his figure blocked the light.

"S'gor, I really cannot stand out here in the fog. I gave you plenty of warning." This was not the time for a rider to be coy.

"It's the illness, Moreta. Berchar's got it. He's terribly unwell and he said I mustn't let anyone in the weyr." S'gor stepped back as he spoke, whereupon Moreta walked purposefully down the aisle and into the weyr. S'gor backed to the sleeping alcove, which he now guarded with outstretched arms.

"I must speak with him, S'gor." Moreta continued toward the alcove.

"No, really, Moreta. It won't do you any good. He's out of his head. And don't touch me, either. I'm probably contaminated . . ." S'gor moved to one side rather than risk contact with his Weyrwoman. The incoherent mumbles of a feverish man grew audible during the slight pause in the conversation. "You see?" S'gor felt himself vindicated.

Moreta pushed back the curtain that separated the sleeping quarters from the weyr and stood on the threshold. Even in the dim light she could see the change sickness had made in Berchar. His features were now drawn by fever and his skin was pale and moist. Moreta saw Berchar's medicine case lay open on the table and walked over to it. "How long has he been ill?" She lifted the first bottle left on the table.

"He was feeling wretched yesterday—terrible headache, so we didn't go to either of the Gathers as we'd planned." S'gor fiddled nervously with the bottles on the table. "He was perfectly all right at breakfast. We were going to Ista, to see that animal. Then Berch says he has this splitting headache and he'd have to lie down. I didn't believe him at first—"

"He took sweatroot for headache?"

"No. He took willow salic, of course." S'gor held up the bottle of crystals. "Then sweatroot?"

"Yes, for all the good it did him. He was burning up by midday and then insisted on having this"—S'gor read the label—"this aconite. I thought that very odd indeed since I have been of assistance to him several times and he told me off rather abruptly for questioning a healer. This morning, though, he asked me to make him an infusion of featherfern, which I did, and told me to add ten drops of fellis juice. He said he ached all over."

Moreta nodded in what she hoped was a reassuring manner. Aconite for a headache and fever? She could understand featherfern and fellis juice.

"Was his fever high?"

"He knew what he was doing, if that's what you mean." S'gor sounded defensive.

"I'm sure he did, S'gor. He is a Masterhealer, and Fort Weyr's been fortunate to have him assigned to us. What else did he tell you to do?"

"To keep everyone from visiting." He stared resentfully at Moreta. She did not blink or look away, merely waited until he had himself in control again. "Essence of featherfern undiluted every two hours until the fever abates and fellis juice every four hours, but no sooner than four hours."

"Did he think he had contracted the fever from K'lon?"

"Berchar would never discuss his patients with me!"

"I wish he had this once."

S'gor looked frightened. "Has K'lon taken a turn for the worst?"

"No, he's sleeping quite naturally." Moreta wished that she could enjoy the same privilege. "I would like a few words with Berchar when his fever drops, S'gor. Do not fail to inform me. It's very important." She looked down at the sick man with conflicting doubts. If K'lon had the same disease that Master Capiam had diagnosed as an epidemic, why had he recovered when people in southeast Pern were dying? Could it be due to the circumstances of hold life? Were overcrowding in the holds and the unseasonably warm weather promoting the spread of the disease? She realized that her pause was alarming S'gor. "Follow Berchar's instructions. I'll see that you won't be troubled further. Have Malth inform Orlith when Berchar may talk to me. And do thank Malth for conveying me. I know that she was reluctant to disobey."

S'gor's eyes assumed the unfocused gaze that indicated he was conversing with his dragon. But he smiled as he looked down at Moreta.

"Malth says you're welcome and she'll take you down now."

Dropping back to the Bowl through the thick mist was an eerie sensation.

Malth would not dare drop her Weyrwoman, Orlith said stoutly.

I sincerely trust not but I cannot see my hand in front of my nose.

Then the green dragon daintily backwinged to land Moreta in the same spot by the Lower Caverns from which she had taken off. The fog rolled in a huge spiral as Malth spurted back to her weyr.

Not sweatroot, Moreta was thinking, to bring a fever out of a body. Featherfern to reduce it. Aconite to ease the heart? *That* bad a fever. And fellis juice for aches. Sh'gall had not reported aches in Capiam's symptoms. She wished she'd had a chance to talk to Berchar. Maybe she should see if K'lon was awake.

He sleeps, Orlith said. *You should sleep awhile.*

Moreta did feel weary now that the stimulus provided by Sh'gall's startling announcement had worn off. What had begun as a mist was now an impenetrable fog. She could get lost trying to find the infirmary.

You can always find me, Orlith assured her. *Turn slightly to your left and all you'll have to do is walk straight toward me. I'll have you back in the weyr safely.*

"I'll just have a few hours' sleep," Moreta said. She needed the rest that had been interrupted by Sh'gall's precipitous entry. She'd done what she could for now, and she'd check on her medicines before she went up the stairs to her weyr. She made the slight left turn.

Now just walk straight, Orlith advised her.

That was far easier for the dragon to say than for Moreta to do. In a few steps she couldn't even distinguish the bright yellow light from the Lower Caverns; then Orlith's mental touch steadied her and she walked on confidently, the mist swirling in behind her and pushing away before each time she raised a knee.

K'lon had recovered; her mind dwelled on that thought. Even if holders died, K'lon the dragonrider had survived. Sh'gall had been very tired, hadn't slept when he burst in on her, perhaps he had not got all his facts straight. No, S'peren had said something about illness. Fall was tomorrow and she'd had such a good day, with the exception of the runnerbeast's collapse.

Don't fret so, Orlith advised. *You have done all you can with so few people awake to tell. There is sure to be something in the Records. Leri will find it.*

"It's the fog, silly. It's depressing. I feel as if I'm moving nowhere forever."

You are near me now. You are almost at the steps.

And soon enough for Moreta to be wary. She kicked the bottom step with her right foot. Behind her the mist surged. She found the wall with one hand and then the frame to the storeroom. The tumblers of the lock were so old that Moreta often wondered why they bothered to use it. When the Pass was over, she'd speak to one of the mastersmiths. Now she didn't even need light for there was a click as the tumblers fell into place. She heaved at the massive door to start it swinging on its hinges. Even the fog could not mask the compound odors released by its opening. Moreta reached up and flipped open the glowbasket, her senses pleasantly assailed and reassured by the pungent spiciness of stored herbs. As she moved farther into the room, she could identify the subtler fragrances and smells. She didn't need to uncover the central light; she knew where the febrifuges were stored. To her eyes, the well-filled shelves and the bundles of featherfern drying on the rack looked more than adequate even if everyone in the Weyr were to come down with illness. She could very faintly hear the furtive slither of tunnel snakes. The pests had their own ways in and out of solid rock. She must get Nesso to put down more poison. Aconite was to the right: a square glass container full of the powdered root. Plenty of willow salic, and four large jars of fellis juice. Sh'gall had mentioned a cough. Moreta turned to those remedies: tussilago, comfrey, hyssop, thymus, ezob, borrago. More than enough. When the Ancients had made the Crossing, they had brought with them all the medicinal herbs and trees with which they had eased illness and discomfort. Surely some would answer the problem of the new disease.

She walked back to the door, closed the glow, resting her hand a moment on the door frame, smooth from generations of hands resting just as she did. Generations! Yes, generations that had survived all kinds of bizarre happenings and unusual illnesses, and would survive this one!

The fog had not abated, and she could see the staircase as only a darker shadow. Her foot kicked the first riser.

Be careful, Orlith said.

"I will." Moreta's right hand crept along the wall as she ascended. She seemed to be walking upward into nothing until her lead foot discovered the safety of the next step and the mist churned about her. But Orlith kept murmuring encouragement until Moreta laughed, saying she was only a few steps from her weyr and her bed. For all of that, she nearly missed her step at the landing for the light from her weyr was diminished to a feeble glow.

The weyr was noticeably warmer. The golden dragon's eyes gleamed as Moreta crossed to caress her, scratching Orlith's eye ridges. She leaned gratefully against Orlith's head, thinking that Orlith exuded an odor that was a combination of all the best herbs and spices.

You are tired. You must get some sleep now.

"Ordering me about again, huh?" But Moreta was on her way to her sleeping quarters. She pulled off tunic and trousers and, sliding into the furs, arranged them around her shoulders and was very quickly asleep.

CHAPTER VI

Ruatha Hold, Present Pass, 3.11.43

Alessan watched as the great dragon sprang into the air with Moreta lifting her arm in farewell. The dragon glowed in the dark-gray sky, and not from the feeble light of the dying lamp standards. Did her gravid state account for that luminescence? Then the phenomenon occurred for which Alessan waited: The golden glowing queen and her lovely Weyr-woman disappeared. A *whoosh* of air made the languid banners flutter.

Smiling, Alessan took a deep breath, well satisfied by the high moments of his first Gather as Lord of Ruatha Hold. As his sire had often repeated, good planning was the essence of success. True enough that good planning had resulted in his sprinter's win, but he had never counted on Moreta's company at the races—she had been such a spontaneous companion. Nor had he anticipated her dancing with him. He'd never had such an agile partner in the toss dance. Now, if his mother could find a girl in any way comparable to Moreta . . .

"Lord Alessan . . ."

He swung around, surprised out of his pleasant reverie by the hoarse whisper. Dag scuttled out of the shadows and stopped, bolt still, half a dozen paces from him.

"Lord Alessan . . ." The anxiety in Dag's voice and the formal address alerted Alessan.

"What's the matter, Dag? Squealer—"

"He's fine. But all Vander's animals are down with the cough, hacking out their lungs, feverish and breaking out in cold sweats. Some of those picketed next to Vander's lot are coughing, too, and sweating. Norman don't know what to make of it, it's so sudden. I know what I make of it, Lord Alessan, and so I'm going to take *our* animals, those that have been in the beasthold and ain't been near that lot in the pickets. I'm going to take 'em away before that cough spreads."

"Dag, I'm not—"

"Now, I ain't saying, Lord Alessan"—Dag raised his hand in a placatory gesture—"but what the cough could be the warm weather and a change of grass, but I'm not risking Squealer. Not after him winning."

Alessan suppressed a smile at Dag's vehemence.

"I'll just take our bloodstock up to the high nursery meadows—till *they* clear away." He jerked his thumb at the race flats. "I've packed some provisions and there're plenty of crevice snakes for eating. And I'll take that ruffian of a grandson of mine with me."

Second only to Squealer in Dag's affections was his daughter's youngest son, Fergal, a lively rascal who was more often in the black records than any other holding. Alessan had a sneaking admiration for the lad's ingenuity, but as Lord Holder he could no longer condone the antics that Fergal inspired. His most recent prank had so angered Lady Oma, involving as it did the smirching of guest linens, that he had been forbidden to attend the Gather, and the punishment was enforced by locking the boy in the Hold's cell.

"If I thought—"

Dag laid a finger along his snub nose. "Better safe than sorry."

"Get along then." Alessan longed for sleep and Dag was plainly in an obstinate frame of mind. "And take that . . . that . . ."

"Dirty piece of laundry?" Dag's grin was slyly infectious.

"Yes, that's an apt description."

"I'll wait for a message from you, Alessan, that all the visitors have gone and taken their cough with 'em." Dag's grin broadened and he turned smartly on one heel, setting off toward the beasthold at such a clip that his bandy figure rolled from side to side.

Alessan watched his departure thoughtfully for a moment, wondering if he gave Dag too much latitude. Perhaps the old handler was covering up some new prank Fergal had pulled. But a cough spreading through the pickets was not so easily dismissed. When he'd had some sleep, he'd have a word with Norman, see if they had discovered why Vander's runner had died. That incident bothered Alessan. But a cough hadn't killed the runner. Was it possible that Vander, keen to win at the Gather, had ignored the signs of illness to bring his middistance runner? Alessan would prefer not to think so, but he knew well how the desire to win could grip a man.

Alessan made his way back to the hold on the roadway, passing dark lumps of people rolled in sleeping furs. It had been a good Gather and the weather had held. A slight dampness in the dawn air heralded fog or mist. But the weather wouldn't be the only thing foggy that day.

The Hall, too, was crowded with sleepers, and he walked carefully so as not to disturb anyone. Even the wide corridor outside his apartment accommodated Gatherers on straw pallets. He considered himself fortunate that his mother had not insisted he share his quarters. But then, perhaps she had hoped that he would! He smiled as he closed the door behind him and began to strip off his finery. It was only then he remembered that Moreta had not retrieved her Gather gown. No matter. That gave him an excuse to talk to her at the next Fall. He stretched out on his bed, pulled the furs over him, and was asleep in moments.

In what seemed like no time he was being so vigorously shaken that, for one disoriented moment, he thought he was a boy again, being attacked by his brothers.

"Alessan!" Lady Oma's indignant exclamation brought him to complete awareness. "Holder Vander is extremely ill and Masterhealer Scand insists that it is not from overindulgence. Two of the men who accompanied Vander are also feverish. Your race-course manager informs me also that four animals are dead and more appear to be sickening."

"Whose animals?" Alessan wondered if Dag had known more than he'd admitted.

"How should I know, Alessan?" Lady Oma had no interest at all in the runnerbeasts that were Ruatha's principal industry. "Lord Tolocamp is discussing it with—"

"Lord Tolocamp presumes!" Alessan rolled out of the bed, reached for his trousers in a fluid movement, stuffed his feet into the legs and pulled them up as he rose. He dragged a tunic over his head, slammed his feet into boots, kicking aside his discarded Gather finery. He forgot about the sleepers in the hallway and nearly trod on an arm before he checked his haste. Most of those who had slept in the Hall were awake and there was a clear path to the door. Cursing Tolocamp under his breath, Alessan managed a smile for those who noticed his passing.

Tolocamp was in the forecourt, an arm across his chest, propping the elbow of the other arm as he rubbed his chin, deep in thought. Norman was with him, shifting anxiously from foot to foot, his face gaunt from a sleepless night. As Alessan strode out, Norman's face brightened, and he turned eagerly toward his own Lord Holder.

"Good day to you, Tolocamp," Alessan said with scant courtesy, controlling the anger he felt at the older man's interference, however well intentioned. "Yes, Norman?"

He tried to draw the manager to one side but Tolocamp was not so easily evaded.

"This could be a very serious matter, Alessan," Tolocamp said, his heavy features set in a frown of portentous concern.

"I'll decide that, thank you." Alessan spoke so curtly that Tolocamp regarded him with astonishment. Alessan took the opportunity to move aside with Norman.

"Four of Vander's runners are dead," Norman said in a low voice, "and the other is dying. Nineteen beasts near them have broken out in sweats and coughing something pathetic."

"Have you isolated them from the healthy?"

"I've had men working on that since first light, Lord Alessan."

"Lady Oma said that Vander's ill as are two of his men?"

"Yes, sir. I called Masterhealer Scand to attend them last night. At first I thought that Vander was upset from losing his runner, but his two men are fevered. Now Helly's complaining of a terrible headache. As Helly don't drink, it can't be from last night."

"Vander had a headache yesterday, didn't he?"

"I don't rightly remember, Lord Alessan." Norman released a heavy sigh, pulling his hand across his forehead.

"Yes, of course, you did have rather a lot to manage, and the races went off very well indeed." Alessan grinned, reminding Norman of the times when he had been his assistant.

"I'm glad you think so, but—" Norman's attention was held by something in the road and he pointed at a travel wagon, four runners led from its tailgate. "I'm worried about Kulan's leaving."

Even as the men watched, one of the led horses coughed violently.

"I told Kulan he hadn't ought to be traveling with that runner but he won't listen to me."

"How many decamped this morning?" Alessan felt the first stir of real apprehension. If a coughing illness spread through the Hold with the plowing only half completed . . .

"Some dozen left first light, mainly wagontravelers. Their stock wasn't pastured near the racers. It's just that I know Kulan's one is sick."

"I'll speak to him. You find out how many have started home. Tell some of the holders to report to me here as messengers. We'll retrieve our departed guests. No animals are to leave this Hold until we know what causes that cough."

"What about people?"

"Since the one usually takes the other, no, no people. And I'll want to have a word with Master Scand about Vander, too."

Kulan was not pleased to be halted. The animal only had a morning cough, he asserted, from the dust raised the night before and the change in grass. It'd be fine once it got moving. Kulan was anxious. He had three days' hard travel before he reached his hold. He'd left his next oldest son in charge and had doubts about the lad's capabilities. Alessan pointed out firmly that Kulan wouldn't want to bring an infected beast home to mingle with his healthy stock. Another day to find out what the ailment was would be well worth a delay.

Tolocamp followed, reaching Alessan and his holderman in time to catch the end of the argument. The older Lord's polite concern became an active anxiety but he held his peace until Kulan and his handlers had turned back to the Gather fields.

"Are such drastic measures necessary? I mean, these people must get back to their holds, as I must return to mine—"

"A slight delay, Tolocamp, until we see how the animals fare. Surely you and your good ladies would be glad of a longer visit?"

Tolocamp blinked, surprised by Alessan's smiling intransigence. "They may stay if they wish but I was about to request you to drum Fort Weyr for a conveyance."

"As you yourself said a few minutes ago, Tolocamp, this could be a serious matter. It is. Neither of us can afford to have a sickness run through our stock. Not at this time of the Turn. Of course, we may find that it only affects the racers, but I would fault myself severely if I didn't take preventive measures now, before the infection can spread from the Hold proper." Alessan watched Tolocamp's obvious reflections over the merits of a delay. "Kulan's one of mine, but I'd take it kindly if you would speak to those of your own Hold who gathered with us. I'm not spreading alarm but four racers dead and more coughing in the picket lines . . ."

"Well, now . . ."

"Thank you, Tolocamp. I knew I could count on your cooperation."

Alessan moved away swiftly before Tolocamp could muster an argument. He made for the kitchens where weary drudges were preparing large pitchers of klah and trays of fruits and sweetbreads. As he had hoped, he found Oklina supervising. From the fatigue apparent on her face, she hadn't had any sleep.

"Oklina, there's trouble," he told her quietly. "Sickness down at the flats. Tell Lady Oma that, until I'm sure what it is and how it can be cured, no one is to leave the Hold. Her powers of persuasion and hospitality are required."

Oklina's dark eyes had widened with alarm but she controlled her expression and peremptorily called one of the drudges to task for spilling klah.

"Where's our brother, Makfar?" Alessan asked. "Asleep above?"

"He's gone. They left about two hours ago."

Alessan rubbed his face. Makfar had had two runners in the racing. "When you've spoken to Mother, send a messenger after them. The way Makfar travels, they won't have gone far. Say, say . . ."

"That you have urgent need of Makfar's *advice*." Oklina grinned.

"Exactly." He gave her an affectionate pat on the shoulder. "And inform our other brothers that security is required for the Hold proper."

By the time Alessan returned to the forecourt, Norman had arrived with a number of Ruathan holders. Alessan told them to find short swords and ride in pairs along the main roads to turn back travelers on whatever pretext came to mind. The holders were ordered to use force where persuasion failed. His brothers, in varying stages of discontent, reported to him. He dispatched them to get arms and assist the messengers, if need be, but to be sure that no one else left the Hold. Just then Lord Tolocamp bustled out of the Hall. He looked full of arguments.

"Alessan, now I'm not sure that all this fuss is absolutely necessary—"

Echoing up from the south, the message drums of River Hold could be heard plainly. As Alessan counted the double-urgent salutation and heard the healer code as originator, he took a moment's pleasure in the astonishment on Tolocamp's face, but lost it as the meat of the message boomed out. Those who could not understand the code caught the fear generated by those who did. Drums were a fine method of communication but too bloody public, Alessan thought savagely.

Epidemic disease, the drums rolled, *spreading rapidly across continent from Igen, Keroon, Telgar, Ista. Highly infectious. Highly contagious. Two to four days' incubation. Headache. Fever. Cough. Prevent secondary infection. Fatalities high. Medicate symptoms. Isolate victims. Quarantine effective immediately. Runnerbeasts highly susceptible. Repeat Epidemic warning. No travel permitted. Congregating discouraged. Capiam.*

The final roll commanded the pass-on of the message.

"But there's been a Gather here!" Tolocamp exclaimed fatuously. "No one's sick but a handful of runners. And they haven't been at Igen or Keroon, or anywhere!" Tolocamp glared at Alessan as if the alarm was somehow at his instigation.

"Vander's sick and two of his handlers—"

"Too much to drink," Tolocamp asserted. "It can't be the same thing. Capiam just says the illness is spreading, not that it's here in Ruatha."

"When the Masterhealer of Pern calls a quarantine," Alessan said in a soft angry voice, "it is my duty, and yours, Lord Tolocamp, to respect his authority!" Alessan didn't realize that he sounded very much like his sire at that moment, but Tolocamp was silenced.

That was all the time they had to speak for those who had understood the drum message were now searching for the two Lords Holder.

"What's Capiam talking about?"

"We can't be quarantined! I've got to get back to my hold."

"I left stock near to birthing . . ."

"My wife stayed at the cot with our babies . . ."

Tolocamp rallied, standing stolidly by Alessan's side, confirming the dreadful message and Capiam's right to broadcast a quarantine restriction.

"Master Capiam is not an alarmist!" "We'll have further details once that message has passed." "This is just a precaution." "Yes, a runnerbeast did die yesterday." "Master Scand will tell us more." "No, no one may be permitted to leave. Might endanger your own hold and spread illness further." "A few days is not too much for health's sake."

Alessan answered almost by rote, letting the first panic roll over his head. He had already taken the first steps toward recalling people and to avert a mass exodus. He and Tolocamp did their best to quiet apprehension. Alessan rapidly calculated how much food he had in convenient storage. The Gatherers would soon exhaust their travel rations. Assuming some people might catch Vander's illness—if it was Capiam's epidemic, would it be better to house them in the Hall? Or clear one of the beastholds? The Hold's infirmary could accommodate no more than twenty and that with crowding. Four dead animals, another dying, and Norman said nineteen more were coughing? Twenty-four animals out of a hundred twenty-two in twenty-four hours? The emergency had nothing to do with what he had been trained to meet. Nothing to do with the immemorial evil that ravaged Pern. As impartially as Thread, this new and equally insidious menace would blight the inhabitants as Thread could devastate the land. "Fatalities high," the message had said. Were there no dragons to combat disease? Was this sort of disaster provided for in the Hold Records his father had always referred to?

"Here comes your healer, Alessan," said Tolocamp.

The two Lords Holder moved to intercept Master Scand before he reached the forecourt. The man's usually placid round face was nearly purple with his exertions, his mouth thinned by annoyance. He was sweating copiously and blotting his face and neck with a none-too-clean cloth. Alessan had always thought Scand merely an adequate healer, suitable to attend the Hold's large number of pregnancies and treat occasional accidents, but not up to a major emergency.

"Lord Alessan, Lord Tolocamp," Scand panted, his chest heaving, "I came as soon as I received your summons. Did I not hear drums? Did I not recognize the healer code? Is something the matter?"

"What ails Vander?"

The sharpness of Alessan's question put Scand on his guard. He cleared his throat and mopped his face, reluctant to commit himself. "Well, now, as to that I am perplexed for he has not responded to the draught of sweatroot which I prepared for him last night. A dose, I might add, that would have made a dragon perspire. It was ineffectual." Scand blotted his face again. "The man complains of terrible heart palpitations and of a headache that has nothing to do with wine because I was assured that he didn't indulge—he felt unwell yesterday even before the races."

"And the other two men? His handlers?"

"They, too, are legitimately ill." Scand's pompous speech had always irritated Alessan. Today he brandished his sweaty cloth in his affected pauses. "Legitimately ill, I fear, with severe headaches that render them unable to rise from their pallets, as well as the palpitations of which Holder Vander complains. Indeed, I am inclined to treat them for those two symptoms, rather than sweat them, although that is the specific treatment for unidentified sudden fevers. Now, may I inquire if that message from the Healer Hall in any way concerns me?" Scand cocked his head inquisitively.

"Master Capiam has called a quarantine."

"Quarantine? For three men?"

"Lord Alessan," said a tall lean man, wearing harper blue. He had grizzled hair and a nose that had suffered from many an unexpected adjustment to its direction. His glance was direct and his manner quietly capable. "I'm Tuero, journeyman harper. I can give Master Scand the full text so that you can get on." Tuero jerked his head to the people milling excitedly in the forecourt.

Just then Ruatha's drummer began to relay the news onward to the large northerly and western holds, the instruments' deep reverberations adding to the general atmosphere of apprehension. Lady Oma emerged from the Hall with Lady Pendra and her daughters. Lady Oma listened intently to the drum then gave Alessan one long steady look. She and the Fort Hold women converged on Harper Tuero and the healer, who was now dithering, his face cloth hanging from his limp hand.

For the first time in his life, Alessan had cause to be grateful for the unquestioning support of his bloodkin and even for the officiousness of Lord Tolocamp. A rider galloped back to request aid in bringing in one of the more aggressive holders with whom Alessan had already had trouble. Then

Makfar's family wagon thundered in, scattering folk in the roadway. Alessan put him in charge of improvising shelters from Gather stalls and travel wagons. It was one thing to doss down in a corridor for a night or grab a few hours' sleep in the Hall, but quite another matter to be so cramped for four nights. Tolocamp was not the only one who failed to see the irony of that as he countered Makfar's suggestions with some of his own. Alessan left the two to solve the housing problem so that he could accompany Norman to the race flats and survey the sick runners. People were already making small camps in the first of the fields.

Despite his errand, it was a relief to Alessan to get away from the turmoil about the forecourt.

"Never saw anything bring down so many so fast, Lord Alessan." Norman had almost to run to keep up with Alessan's long-legged stride. "And I can't think what to do for 'em. If there is anything. Healer's message didn't say much about animals, did it?" His voice was bleak. "A runner can't tell you if it ails."

"It goes off feed and water."

"Not wagon beasts. They go till they drop."

Both men looked across the fields where the Hold's sturdy cart and wagon runnerbeasts grazed—the ones Alessan had bred to his sire's specifications.

"Set up a buffer area. Keep racers and wagoners well separated."

"I will, Lord Alessan, but the racers have been drinking upriver of them!"

"It's a wide river, Norman. Hope for the best."

The first thing Alessan noticed at the flats was that the manager had utilized the entire spread of picket lines. The healthy beasts were on the outside, well away from the cleared circle surrounding the sick ones. The coughing of the infected beasts was audible on the still, slightly chill air. They coughed, necks extended, mouths gaping, in hard painful-sounding barks. Their legs were swollen, their hides dull and starring.

"Add featherfern and thymus to their water. If they'll drink, Norman. Use a syringe to get fluid into them before they dehydrate completely. We might offer nettleweed, too. Some runners are smart enough to know what's good for them. Nettles, at least, are in plentiful supply." Alessan gazed out over the meadows where the annual battle to reduce the perennial had not yet started. "Any coughs among the herdbeasts?" He swung in the other direction.

"Truth to tell, I've had little time to think about them." Norman had the dedicated racer's almost contemptuous disdain for the placid herd creatures. "Harper told me the drums only mentioned runners."

"Well, we'll have to slaughter herdbeasts to feed our unexpected guests. I don't have enough fresh meat left after the Gather."

"Lord Alessan, did Dag . . ." Norman began tentatively, with a half-gesture toward the cliff, to the great apertures where the Hold's animals were normally sheltered during Threadfall.

Alessan gave Norman a shrewd glance.

"So, you were in on that?"

"Sir, I was," Norman replied staunchly. "Dag and I got worried when the cough started to spread. Didn't want to interrupt your dancing, but as the bloodstock had no contact with these—Look at that!"

"Shards!"

They watched as the leader in a team of four hitched to a big wagon collapsed in the traces, pulling its harness mate to its knees.

"Right, Norman. Get some men up to take charge of that team. Use them as long as they last to haul carcasses. Burn the dead animals down there." Alessan pointed to a dip in the far fields, out of sight from the forecourt and downwind. "Keep track of the dead beasts. Reparation should be made."

"I've no recorder."

"I'll send down one of the fosterlings. I'll also want to know how many people stayed the night down here."

"Most of the handlers stayed, and some keen ones like old Runel and his two cronies. Some of the breeders were in and out, not caring much for the dancing after you were thoughtful enough to send a few kegs down here."

"I wish we knew more about this illness. 'Medicate the symptoms,' the drums said." Alessan looked back at the lines of coughing animals.

"Then we give 'em thymus and featherfern, and nettles. Maybe we'll get a message from the Masterherdsman. Could be on its way from the east right now." Norman looked confidently in that direction.

Help didn't usually come from the east, Alessan thought, but he clapped Norman reassuringly on the shoulder. "Just do the best you can!"

"You can count on me, Lord Alessan."

Norman's quietly issued assurance heartened Alessan as he took the shorter way across the stubble field to the hold. Was it only the day before that he and Moreta had paused on the rise to watch the racing? She had touched Vander's dying runner! Alessan's stride faltered. The Weyr would have received the drum message before Ruatha did. She would know by now the consequences of her act. She would also probably know better how to prevent falling ill herself.

As did everyone of Ruatha Hold, he knew the Fort Weyrwoman by sight, but Alessan had always been on the fringes of such Hold gatherings as she had attended since achieving her senior position in the Weyr. So he had thought her a distant, self-contained person, totally immersed in Weyr culture. The discovery that her fascination with racing was as keen as his own had been an unexpected delight. Lady Oma had rebuked him firmly at one point in the early evening for taking so much of Moreta's time. Alessan knew perfectly well that she meant that he was not making the most of the chance to meet eligible girls. He knew, too, that he must soon secure his bloodline and so he had tried to be properly receptive until he saw Moreta slip behind the harpers' dais. By then he had had enough of stammering insipidity and timorousness. He had acquitted his duty as Lord Holder but he was also going to enjoy himself at his first Gather. In Moreta's company. And he had. Alessan had been raised to anticipate both just reward and just punishment. Momentarily the thought that today's trials balanced yesterday's pleasures sprang to his mind but was quickly rejected as juvenile.

The situation at the racing flats observed, Alessan decided the next priority would be to send messages to those expecting the return of the Gatherers to those holds outside the message-drum system. Otherwise he would have anxious people coming to the Hold. Next he'd have to discover who else had brought in new stock from Keroon as Vander had done, whether the beasts were in holds or fields, and destroy them. He would also have to figure out how to deal with dissidents. The Hold's one small cell might secure a small boy like Fergal but not an aggressive holder.

Tolocamp, who had been directing those spreading a tent over the half-walled southern addition, intercepted Alessan.

"Lord Alessan," the older man said, stiffly formal, his face expressionless, jaw clenched, "while I realize that the quarantine affects me as well, I must return to Fort Hold. I will keep to myself in my apartment, making contact with no one. If this"—Tolocamp gestured toward the confusion in the roadway and Gather fields—"is occurring here, think of the turmoil caused by my absence from Fort Hold."

"My Lord Tolocamp, I have always been under the impression that your sons were superbly trained to take over any Hold duties and perform them flawlessly."

"So they are." Tolocamp stood even more stiffly erect. "So they are. I put Campen in charge when I left for your Gather. To give him experience in assuming leadership—"

"Good. This quarantine should afford him an unparalleled opportunity."

"My dear Alessan, this emergency is outside his experience, too."

Alessan gritted his teeth, wondering if he had underestimated Tolocamp's perception.

"Lord Tolocamp, you are more familiar than I with a double-urgent code sent by a Mastercraftsman. Would you permit anyone to disobey it?"

"No, no, of course not. But this is an unusual circumstance—"

"Quite. Your son has no Gather guests to deal with." Both men could see a group being shepherded back by two of Alessan's brothers and six men with drawn swords. "Campen has the Healer Hall as well as the Master-harper to instruct him in the emergency." Alessan moderated his harsh tone. He must not alienate Tolocamp. He'd need Tolocamp's support with some of the older men in his Hold who were not yet accustomed to taking orders from someone as young and untried in Holding. "As the drum message said, two to four days' incubation. You've been here a day already," he added persuasively, glancing up at the noon-high sun. "In another day, if you show no signs of discomfort yourself, you could discreetly return to Fort Hold. Meanwhile, you should set an example."

"Yes, well. Hold one, hold all." Tolocamp's expression mellowed. "It is true that it would be very poor discipline for me to break a quarantine." He became noticeably more amenable. "This outbreak is probably confined to the racing flats. I never have followed the sport." A disdainful wave of his hand dismissed one of the major pastimes of Pern.

Alessan did not take umbrage because a party of men now bore purposefully down on the two Lords Holder, their expressions determined and anxious.

"Lord Alessan . . ."

"Yes, Turvine," Alessan replied to the man, a crop holder in the southeastern corner of Ruatha. His companions were herdsmen.

"We've no drums near us and we're expected back. I'm not one to go against Healer's advice but there are other considerations. We can't bide here . . ."

Makfar had noticed the deputation and, although Alessan gave Turvine his complete attention, he was aware that his brother had signaled several armed holders to converge.

"You'll bide here! That's my order!" Alessan spoke forcefully and the men backed off, looking uncertainly for support from Tolocamp. The Fort Holder stiffened, ignoring their tacit plea. Alessan raised his voice, projecting it beyond the group to those watching and listening from the roadway and the forecourt. "The drums have decreed the quarantine! I am your Lord Holder. As surely as if Thread were Falling, you are under my orders. No one, no animal leaves here until that drum"—Alessan jabbed his arm at the tower—"tells us that the quarantine is lifted!"

In the silence that ensued, Alessan strode rapidly toward the hall door, Tolocamp in step beside him.

"You will have to get messages out to prevent people coming in," Tolocamp said in a low voice when they were inside the Hall.

"I know that. I just have to figure out how. Without exposing animals or people." Alessan swung to the left, into the Hold's office where the bloody Records he did not have time to peruse were stacked in accusing ranks. Although the office had been put to use as sleeping space during the Gather, it was vacant but sleeping furs were scattered about, their owners apparently having left them in haste. Alessan kicked several aside to reach his maps. He finally located the small-scale chart of the Holding on which the roads were marked in different colors for trail, track, or path, and the holds similarly differentiated.

Tolocamp exclaimed in surprise at the fine quality of the map. "I'd no idea you were so well equipped," he said with a want of tact.

"As the harpers are fond of telling us," Alessan said, with a slight smile to sweeten his words, "Fort Hold happened, but Ruatha was planned." He traced a forefinger up the northern trail, to the dividing tracks that went northwest, west, and northeast, reaching twenty holds, large and small, and three mineholds. The main western trail through the mountains wandered with occasional hazards into the plateau.

"Lord Alessan . . ."

He turned and saw Tuero at the door, the other harpers behind him in the corridor.

"I thought we might volunteer as messengers." Tuero grinned, which made his long, crooked nose slant even more dramatically to the left. "That's the subject of rather heated discussions outside. The harpers of Pern are at your disposal."

"I thank you, but you've been as exposed as anyone else here. It's the disease I wish to contain, not the people."

"Lord Alessan"—Tuero was smilingly insistent—"a message can be *relayed*." Tuero mimed putting something down quickly with one hand and taking it up in the other with a sharp pull. He walked quickly to the map. "Someone in this hold"—he stabbed at the first one of the northern track—"could take a message to the next one, and so on, relaying instructions as well as the drum call."

Alessan stared at the map, mentally reviewing the inhabitants of the holds and cots. Even the farthest settlement, the iron minehold, was no more than three days' hard riding. Dag would have taken the fastest runners, Squealer's ilk, with him, but there would be beasts to make the first leg of the relay, and no risk to other stock if the runner returned to Ruatha. If the runner returned . . .

"And as none of us has any reason to stay away from your bountiful hospitality, you can depend on us to return. Besides, this sort of thing is *our* duty."

"A very good point," Tolocamp murmured.

"I concur. So, may I leave it to you, Tuero, to organize the contents of the messages and instructions to be forwarded by this relay system of yours? Drum messages went here, here, here, and here." Alessan tapped the cardinal holds. "I doubt if they would have thought of communicating the bad news to the smaller places. Seven holds are capable of supplying runners for the relay, each covering outlying cotholds."

"How fortunate that we are seven!"

Alessan grinned. "Indeed, Tuero. Let the harpers spread the news that heralds are available. Our drummer is still in the drum tower, I take it—well, then, his supplies are in those cupboards: ink and hide and pen. Let me know when you're available. I've travel maps. I'll arrange mounts. You'll want to be quick about this business or risk sleeping out."

"That's no novelty for harpers, I assure you."

"And you might discover, if you can, who else brought in animals from Keroon over the past few weeks."

"Oh?" Both Tuero's eyebrows lifted expressing surprise.

"Vander picked up new runners from a ship out of Keroon—"

"The drum mentioned Keroon, didn't it? We'll find out. This winter's lack of ice is not the blessing it seemed, eh?"

"Not at all!"

"Ah, well, it's not ended yet!" With a quick courteous bow of his head, Tuero led his craftfellows off to the main hall.

"Alessan, there is so much to be done, too, at Fort—" Tolocamp pleaded.

"Tolocamp, Farelly is in the drum tower and at your disposal." Alessan waved him courteously toward the tower steps and then left the office. Lord Leef had once confided that the way to avoid arguments was to keep them from starting. Tactful withdrawal, he had called it.

Alessan paused briefly in the shadow of the Hall doors, observing the activity in the forecourt, along the roadway, and beyond. Tents had been raised, small fires had tripods, kettles hung above the flames, a new fire had been started in the roasting pit and the spit reset. From the east a party of mounted riders and a string of runners were slowly walking up the road, the leader flanked by Alessan's next oldest brother, Dangel, and two Ruathan cotholders, all three men with drawn swords. He'd asked Dangel where to put Baid, the reluctant cropholder. Above the din where he'd told Norman to burn the dead beasts, a thin gout of black smoke hovered.

Yes, anyone apprehended leaving the hold proper could serve on the burial detail.

A rider, running his mount hard, galloped up the stubble field, clattering over the roadway, dodging tent and fire. The rider jumped down, looking anxiously about him. When Alessan stepped out of the shadow, the rider dropped his reins and ran to him.

"Lord Alessan, Vander's dead!"

CHAPTER
VII

Healer Hall and Fort Weyr, Present Pass, 3.11.43

The booming reverberated through Capiam's head until he woke, clutching at his skull defensively. The drumming had even haunted his nightmares before he woke. He could hardly call the vivid scenes that had tortured him dreams, and his awakening was as much a protest against them as against the intrusive rhythms. He lay in his bed, spent with the effort of renewed consciousness. Another drum roll caused him to haul the pillows feebly over his head.

Would they never stop? He'd no idea that the drums were so infernally loud. Why had he never noticed them before? The Healers really deserved their own quiet precinct. He was forced to add his hands to his ears to obtain some relief from the throbbing. Then he remembered the messages that he had left to be relayed to all the major Halls and Holds. Had they taken so long to send them? It must be midday! Didn't the drum master realize how important a quarantine was? Or had some snide little apprentice mislaid the messages to allow time for his own sleep?

The ache in his skull was like nothing Capiam could remember. Intolerable. And his heartbeat had speeded up to the drum tempo. Highly unusual! Capiam lay in the bed, his head painfully resounding and his heart doing its own peculiar unsyncopated palpitation.

Mercifully the drums ceased presently, but neither his head nor his heart took any notice. Rolling to his side, Capiam attempted to sit up. He must have relief from this headache. Swinging his feet to the floor, he levered his body up. A groan of agony was forced from him as he managed to sit upright. The pain in his head intensified as he staggered to his cupboard.

Fellis juice. A few drops. That would do the trick. It never failed him. He measured the dose, blinking to clear his blurred vision, then splashed water into the cup and swallowed the mixture. He wove back to his bed, unable to remain perpendicular. He was panting from the slight effort and realized that not only had the frantic beat of his heart increased, but he was sweating profusely from a simple few steps across his own room.

He had had too much experience with sleepless nights and tight schedules to chalk up his condition to such things. He groaned again. He didn't have *time* to be sick. He ought not to have contracted the damnable disease. Healers didn't *get* sick. Besides, he'd been so careful to wash thoroughly in redwort solution after examining each patient.

Why didn't the fellis juice work? He couldn't think with the headache. But he had to think. There was so much to be done. His notes to organize, to analyze the course of the disease and the probability of dangerous secondary infections, like pneumonia and other respiratory infections. But how could he work when he couldn't hold his eyes open? Groaning again at the injustice of his situation, he pressed his hands to his temples and then to his hot, moist forehead. Shards! He was burning up with fever.

He was aware that someone else was in the room before he heard the slight sound of entry. "Don't come near me," he said urgently, holding up one hand abruptly and uttering another cry of pain when his injudicious movement increased the ache in his head.

"I won't."

"Desdra!" An exaggerated breath escaped his lips.

"I had an apprentice posted at your door to listen for sounds, but I wouldn't let anyone disturb you until you'd slept yourself out." Her calm unexcitable voice reassured him. "You've caught this fever of yours?"

"There's an ironic justice in that, you know." Capiam's sense of humor seldom left him.

"There would be if you weren't the most sought-after man on Pern."

"The quarantine isn't popular?"

"You might say so. Drum tower's been besieged. Fortine's been coping."

"My notes are in my pack. Give them to Fortine. He's much better at organizing than diagnosing. He'll have all I've discovered about this epidemic."

Desdra glided across the floor and took the Healer's note case from the pack. She flipped it open. "Which isn't much."

"No, but I'll soon understand it all much better."

"Nothing like personal experience. What do you need?"

"Nothing! No, not nothing. I'll want water, any fresh juice—"

"You cut off our supplies with that quarantine—"

"Then water will suffice. No one is to enter this room, and *you* are not to come farther than the door. Anything I ask for must be left on the table."

"I am quite prepared to stay in here with you."

He shook his head and regretted the motion. "No. I'd rather be by myself."

"Suffer in silence."

"Don't mock, woman. This disease is highly contagious. Has anyone else in Hall or Hold contracted it?"

"As of a half-hour ago, no."

"It's now?" Capiam was simply unable to see the timepiece.

"Late afternoon. Four."

"Anyone who was at either Gather and returns here—"

"Which is forbidden by your drum message—"

"Some wise-ass will think he knows better . . . Anyone who comes is to be isolated for four days. Two seem to be the usual incubation period, judging by the best reports—"

"And your good self—"

"Experience teaches. I don't know yet how long someone *stays* infectious so we must be doubly wary. I shall keep notes on my symptoms and progress. They will be here . . . in case . . ."

"My, we are being dramatic."

"You've always maintained that I'd die of something I couldn't cure."

"Don't talk like that, Capiam!" Desdra sounded more angry than fearful. "Master Fortine has apprentices and journeymen at the Records round the clock."

"I know. I heard their snores last night."

"So Master Fortine surmised when no one could tell him your time of return. Unfortunately Master Fortine must have only just retired himself for he didn't get back to his desk until noon. He will want to see you."

"He's not to come in here."

"He'll doubtless prefer not to."

Why wasn't the fellis juice taking effect? The palpitations of his heart were dramatic!

"Tell Fortine, will you, Desdra, that sweatroot has no effect and provides no relief. In fact, I think it is counterproductive. That's what they were using in Igen and Keroon for the first stage of the illness. Tell Fortine to try featherfern to reduce fever. Tell him to try other febrifuges."

"What? All on the same poor patient?"

"He will have patients enough for the different remedies." Capiam spoke from wretched certainty. "Go, Desdra. My head is a drum tower."

Desdra was cruel enough to chuckle softly. Or maybe she thought she was being sympathetic? One never knew what reaction to expect from Desdra. That was part of her charm, but she'd never make Master on the strength of it. She spoke her mind and sometimes a healer *had* to be diplomatic and soothing. She certainly didn't soothe Capiam. But he was relieved that she was in charge of him.

He lay supine, trying to rest his head as lightly as possible on a pillow that had apparently turned into stone. He willed the pain to subside, willed the fellis juice to dispense its numbing magic. His heart thudded. Erratic heartbeat had been mentioned by many of the patients. He'd had no idea that the symptom would be so severe. He hoped it would subside when the fellis juice took effect.

He lay for what seemed a very long time and, although the ache in his skull appreciably lessened, the palpitations did not. If he could just regain a normal heartbeat, he might be able to sleep. He was very conscious of his bone-deep weariness and that he had not benefited from that nightmare-filled sleep. He reviewed the appropriate herbs to relieve palpitations: whitethorn, adonis, glovecap, tansy, aconite, and decided on the latter, the old reliable root.

His rising from the bed was accompanied by much effort and suppressed moans—suppressed because Capiam did not want apprentice ears to witness masterly weakness. It was enough that the Masterhealer had basely succumbed; the grim details of his travail need not be advertised.

Two drops should suffice. It was a strong drug and must always be administered carefully. He remembered to secure a writing hide from his supply, gathered up ink and pen, and took all back to his bed, where he arranged his stool as his writing desk. Heart still pounding, Capiam composed his first entries, carefully noting the day and the exact time.

He was grateful to lie down again. He concentrated on his breathing, slowing it and willing his heart to slow. At some point in the exercise, sleep overcame him.

◆ ◆ ◆

Holth is upset. He is angry and so is Leri. Orlith's concerned but apologetic tone roused Moreta from a profound slumber.

"Why didn't he stay asleep and leave the ordering of the Weyr to me?"

He says Leri is too old to fly, and the plague kills the elderly first.

"Scorch him! This epidemic business has addled his wits!" She dressed quickly, grimacing as she stuffed her feet into clammy boots.

Leri says that she must speak with the ground crews, especially at a time like this, to find out who gets ill and to spread the word. She says she can do so without unnecessary physical contact.

"Of course she can." Leri had never been in the habit of dismounting to accept ground-crew reports. She was not tall and remaining on her queen gave her many advantages.

Moreta raced up the stairs through the thick fog. She could hear Holth's agitated rumblings by the time she reached the weyr entrance. Sh'gall's angry voice made her quicken so that she entered the weyr in a burst of speed.

"How dare you interfere with the queens' wing?" she demanded, allowing her momentum to carry her right up to him.

He spun around and, holding both hands up to keep her at a distance, backed off. Blinking with distress, Holth was swinging her head anxiously from side to side over Leri. A Weyrleader was an unlikely source of danger for her rider.

"How dare you upset Holth and Leri?" Moreta shouted.

"I'm not yet so decrepit I can't handle an hysterical bronze rider!" Leri retorted, her eyes snapping with anger.

"You queens stick together, don't you," Sh'gall shouted back, "against all logic and reason!"

Holth roared, and from the weyr below, Orlith trumpeted; then the fog resounded with dragon queries.

"Calm down, Sh'gall! We don't need the Weyr in an uproar!" Leri spoke in a tense but controlled voice, her eyes catching and holding Sh'gall's. She might have retired as senior Weyrwoman but just then she exuded the unmistakable authority of her many Turns in that position. When Sh'gall looked away, Leri glanced sternly at Moreta. The younger Weyrwoman spoke soothingly to Orlith and the furor outside the weyr subsided. Holth stopped her agitated head-swinging.

"Now!" Leri folded her hands over the cumbersome Record she was trying to keep in her short lap. "A fine time to be quarreling over small points. The Weyr needs undivided leadership now more than ever—we've a double threat to overcome. So let me tell you a few things, Sh'gall, that you seem to have overlooked in your very laudable concern for protecting the Weyr from this plague of Capiam's. As of yesterday's Gathers there can't be many of our dragonriders who haven't been exposed to it. In fact, you're the most likely carrier since you were actually in the infirmary at Southern Boll as well as at Ista, viewing that poor beast."

"I never went into the infirmary and I never touched the feline. I washed thoroughly in the Ice Lake before I returned to the Weyr."

"So that's why your wits are slow—too bad your tongue thawed first! Hold it, Weyrleader!" Leri's forceful tone and her stern face quelled the retort on the bronze rider's lips. "Now, while you slept, Moreta was busy. So was I." She hefted the heavy Record in her lap. "The watchriders all know to deny the Weyr, not that anyone's likely to be flying in this fog after two Gathers. The drum towers of Fort Hold have been booming all day. Peterpar's checked the herds for sign of illness, which isn't likely since the last drove came from Tillek. Nesso has been busy talking to those sober enough to absorb information. K'lon continues to improve. Moreta, exactly what do you think is wrong with Berchar?"

Moreta had never doubted that Leri kept an ear on everything that occurred outside her weyr, but the former Weyrwoman was too discreet to display her knowledge.

"Berchar?" Sh'gall exclaimed. "What's wrong with him?"

"Quite likely what ailed K'lon. At Berchar's instructions, S'gor isolated him and will himself remain weyrbound."

Sh'gall began to sputter with the questions he wanted to ask.

"If K'lon has recovered, Berchar should as well," Moreta continued reasonably.

"Two sick!" Sh'gall's hand went to his throat, then his forehead.

"If Capiam says two to four days before the onset of illness, you shouldn't be feeling ill yet," Leri said bluntly but not unkindly. "You'll lead in tomorrow's Fall. Holth and I will fly with the queens' wing and, as is my custom, I will receive ground-crew reports—that is, if any ground crew are about. It's unlikely that Nabol and Crom will panic. A disease would have to be desperate indeed to seek victims in those forsaken holds. As is my custom, I shall remain on Holth, thus keeping to a minimum any possible contagion. It is essential to the main duty of the Weyrs to keep in contact with every holder. Without ground crews to assist us, we'd have twice the work. Do you not agree, Weyrleader?"

Judging by the consternation on Sh'gall's face, he had not yet considered the possibility of inadequate ground-crew support.

"Not that it would matter if I did contract this plague of Capiam's. As well as being elderly"—Leri cast a malicious glance at Sh'gall—"I'm certainly the most expendable rider."

Holth and Orlith trumpeted in alarm. Even Kadith spoke as Moreta rushed to embrace Leri, her throat suddenly thick at the casual remark.

"You are not expendable! You are not! You're the most valiant of all the queen riders on Pern."

Leri gently disentangled herself from Moreta's fierce grasp then dismissed Sh'gall imperiously. "Go. All that can be done has been done."

"I'll get Kadith settled," he said, leaving as if pursued.

"And you settle yourself," Leri said to Moreta. "I'm worth no one's tears. Besides, it is true. I am expendable. I think Holth would like to rest and she can't until I do, you know."

"Leri! Don't say such things! What would I do without you?"

Leri gave her a long searching look, her eyes very bright. "Why, my girl, you'd do what you have to. You always will. But *I'd* miss *you*. Now, you'd best get down to the Cavern. Everyone will have heard the queens sounding off and Kadith's tizzy. They'll need to be reassured."

Moreta stepped back from Holth's couch and Leri, abashed by the intensity of her feeling.

"You're not worried because you touched that runner at Ruatha, are you?"

"Not particularly." Moreta shrugged diffidently. "But I did and it's done. My rash impulses always worried L'mal—"

"Not half as much as your ability to deal with injured dragons pleased him. Now go, before they have too much time to fret themselves. Oh, and would you take this piece of harness to T'ral to be mended?" She chucked a roll of leatherstrap to Moreta. "Would never do for me to tumble off, would it? Such an ignominious end! Go on now, girl. And check your own harness— routine is reassuring in times like these. I wish to continue my fascinating reading!" Leri made a comical grimace as she tugged the Record volume into a more comfortable position.

Moreta left Leri's weyr, her fingers finding the stretched length in the strap. She recoiled it. In a subdued mood, Moreta dutifully inspected her own harness, which she had oiled after the last Fall and hung neatly on its pegs.

I did not like to wake you but when Holth asked, I did.

"And you did exactly as you should."

Holth is a great queen. Orlith's eyes whirled brightly.

"And Leri is marvelous." Moreta went to her queen, who lowered her head to accept her rider's caresses. "This will be the last Fall you fly for a while!" she added, assessing the bulge in Orlith's belly.

I will fly tomorrow. I can fly in need as well.

"Don't you fret about my riding Malth that short hop!"

I don't. I do wish you to know that I can always fly you.

"There could be no need so great to take you from your eggs, my love." Moreta stroked the bulges appreciatively. "A good clutch, I think."

I know. A degree of smug satisfaction tinged her tone.

"I'd best get down to the Lower Cavern." Moreta pulled her shoulders back, bracing against the stresses. Then she reminded herself that weyrfolk were hardy, not only in body but in mind. Each Fall they faced the knowledge that some among them would suffer injury, possibly death. They endured the certainty with fortitude and courage. Why should an additional transient hazard dismay them? Why should something unseen appear more dangerous than the visible Thread that scored?

Sh'gall's apprehension was insidiously affecting her. There was even no surety that contact would result in illness. K'lon and Berchar? Well, that could be dismissed as misfortune—K'lon so often visited A'murry at Igen. At that, she was more likely to take ill than Sh'gall, after succoring that runnerbeast.

Moreta took Leri's strap then, with a backward look at Orlith, who was composing herself as comfortably as she could, she left the weyr. The fog appeared to be thinning. It eddied about her more freely, and she could make out the full flight of stairs although the Lower Caverns remained invisible until she was more than halfway across the Bowl.

When Moreta arrived, the Lower Cavern was already well populated. Most of the Weyr was about, in fact. Judging by the clutter of dishes and cups on the tables, a hearty meal had been consumed. Women and weyrlings moved among the diners with klah pitchers, but not many wineskins were in evidence. The other queen riders—Lidora, Haura, and Kamiana—were at the raised table to one side of the dining area, their weyrmates seated with them.

Moreta's presence was noted, and conversations subsided briefly. She located T'ral, who was busy at his leather-mending, then made her way across the cavern, nodding and smiling to riders and weyrfolk, feeling more at ease as she began to appreciate the receptive mood of the assembled.

"Leri's neck strap needs a mend, T'ral."

"We can't be losing her!" the brown rider said, taking the strap and putting it on top of other work.

"Did we mishear the drums, Moreta?" one of the younger brown riders asked in a voice suddenly too loud and brash.

"Depends on the strength of your morning headache," she said with a laugh, which drew a scatter of echoes.

"Klah or wine?" Haura asked Moreta as she stepped up on the dais.

"Wine," Moreta said firmly, a choice that was greeted appreciatively by those nearby.

"It's her legs that wobble," someone suggested.

"The dancing was good at Ruatha, wasn't it?" She took a sip of the wine and then looked out over the faces turned toward her. "Who doesn't know what the drums have been relaying?"

"Whoever slept through them heard the news from Nesso at the breakfast hearth," someone remarked from the center of the diners. Nesso brandished her ladle in that direction.

"Then you all know as much as I do. An epidemic's loose on Pern, caused by that unusual beast the seamen rescued in the Current between Igen and Ista island. Runnerbeasts are affected but Master Talpan says that watchwhers, wherries, and dragons don't contract the disease. Master Capiam hasn't a name for it yet but if the disease originated from the Southern Continent, the odds are it'll be mentioned in the Records—"

"Like everything else," a wit called out.

"Consequently it's only a matter of time before we know how to treat it. However"—Moreta altered her voice to a serious tone—"Master Capiam warns against any congregating—"

"He should have told us *that* yesterday—"

"Agreed. We may have Fall tomorrow but I want no heroes. Headache and fever are the symptoms."

"Then K'lon had the plague?"

"It's possible, but he's hale again."

A worried voice came from the eastern side of the cavern. "What about Berchar?"

"Caught it from K'lon, more than likely, but he and S'gor have isolated themselves, as you are probably aware."

"Sh'gall?"

An uneasy stir rippled around the Cavern.

"He was fine ten minutes ago," Moreta said dryly. "He'll fly Thread tomorrow. As we all will."

"Moreta?" T'nure, green Tapeth's rider, rose from his table to speak. "How long does this quarantine condition last?"

"Until Master Capiam rescinds it." She saw the rebellious look on T'nure's face. "Fort Weyr will obey!" Before she finished that injunction, the unmistakable trumpeting of the queens was heard. No lesser dragon would disobey the queens. Moreta thanked Orlith for the timely comment. "Now, in view of Berchar's indisposition, Declan, you and Maylone share responsibility for the injured. Nesso, you and your team must be prepared to assist. S'peren, can I rely on your help?"

"Anytime, Weyrwoman."

"Haura?" The queen rider nodded, none too keen. "Now, are there any other matters to be discussed?"

"Does Holth fly?" Haura asked quietly.

"She does!" Moreta spoke in a flat voice. She would not have that right challenged by anyone. "Leri, as is her custom, will speak to the ground crews, keeping her distance up on Holth."

"Moreta?" T'ral spoke up. "What about ground crews? I know Nabol and Crom will turn out tomorrow, but what happens next Fall—over Tillek and, after that, at Ruatha—if this plague spreads and we've no ground crews?"

"Time enough to worry about that in the next Fall," Moreta said quickly, with an unconcerned smile. Ruatha! With all the Gatherers there, crowded in! "The Holds will do their duty as the Weyrs discharge theirs."

An approving applause capped her restatement as she sat down, signaling that the discussion was at an end. Nesso stepped up on the dais with a plate of food.

"I think you should know," she said in a low voice, "that all the drum messages sign Fortine as sender now."

"Not Capiam?"

Nesso shook her head slowly from side to side. "Not since the first one this noon."

"Has anyone else noticed that?"

Nesso sniffed in offended dignity. "I know my duty, too, Weyrwoman."

◆ ◆ ◆

The headache didn't know when to quit, Capiam decided, trying for another position in which to ease his aching skull and his feverish body. His clock was slow: He had another hour before he could take a fourth draught of fellis juice. His heartbeat was more regular thanks to the aconite. Carefully the Healer rolled onto his right side. He forced himself to relax his neck muscles, let his head sink into the fiber-filled pillow. He was certain he could count every strand within the case from its pressure on the sensitized skin of his cranium.

To compound his misery, the drum tower began to transmit an urgent message. At this hour? Were they manning the drums on a twenty-four-hour basis? Could no one sleep? Capiam recognized that the message was being relayed to Telgar Weyr but that was as far as he could force himself to concentrate.

An hour before he could take more fellis juice? It was his duty to Pern not to be insensible as the disease followed its course with his resisting body. Sometimes duty was a very difficult task.

Capiam sighed again, willing his execrable headache to abate. He ought to have listened to that message to Telgar. How was he to know what was happening on Pern? How the disease was progressing? How could he think?

VIII

Fort Weyr, Present Pass, 3.12.43

The next morning when Orlith roused Moreta early, the fog had cleared from Fort Weyr's mountain slopes.

"And to the northwest? Toward Nabol and Crom?" Moreta asked as she donned riding gear.

Sweeprider's gone out. He'll know, Orlith replied.

"Sh'gall?"

Awake and dressing. Kadith says he's well and rested.

"What does Malth say about Berchar?"

The conversation paused while Orlith inquired. *Malth says the man feels worse today than he did yesterday.*

Moreta didn't like the sound of that. If Berchar had been taking sweat-root, the fever should have been sweated from his body.

Neither you nor the Weyrleader are ill, Orlith remarked by way of encouragement.

Emerging from her sleeping quarters, Moreta laughed and went to throw her arms around her queen's neck, scratching the eye ridges affectionately. She couldn't help but notice the protruberances marring the curve of Orlith's belly.

"Are you sure you should fly Fall today?"

Of course I can. Orlith craned her neck around to look at the bulges. *They will settle once I am airborne.*

"Holth and Leri?"

They still sleep.

"Staying awake until the small hours, poring over Records!"

Orlith blinked.

When Moreta had returned the mended strap to Leri after the Weyr meeting, she found the old Weyrwoman deep in her studies.

"Weyrfolk don't *get* sick," she had said with considerable disgust. "Bellyache from overeating or drinking raw wines, Threadscore, stupid collision, knife fights, abscesses, kidney and liver infections by the hundreds, but sick? I've looked through twenty Turns after the last Fall"—Leri paused to give a great yawn—"bloody boring. I'll read on, but only because duty requires. Dragonriders are a healthy lot!"

Moreta had been quite willing to take that reassurance with her to bed. Though Nesso might have found it curious that Fortine was sending drum messages, Moreta logically concluded that Capiam was sleeping off the exhaustion of his round of the afflicted Holds. Sh'gall said that the man had been traveling for days. Sh'gall's excessive alarm over the epidemic was likely compounded by his innate antipathy for injury or minor ailments. The Weyrleader had been overreacting. She felt more sanguine about her contact with the diseased runner: It had been so brief that she failed to see how she could be affected.

Consequently, after a good night's sleep, Moreta was able to face Fall in good heart as she stepped out in the brightness of a crisp wintry day. Moreta preferred an early start on a Fall day: that day especially for, with Berchar sick, she must check that the supplies for treating scored dragons had been set out properly.

Declan, Maylone, and six of the weyrfolk were already setting up supplies in the infirmary. Declan and Maylone were runnerhold bred like herself. Searched the previous Turn for Pelianth's clutch, they had not Impressed. Because Declan had proved himself useful to Berchar and Maylone was young enough to Impress again, the two had been allowed to stay on in the Weyr. Even if Declan made a dragonrider, his skill would give Moreta much needed assistance. A Weyr never had enough healers for men and dragons.

Declan, a thin-faced man of nearly twenty Turns, brought Moreta a mug of klah while she checked his efforts. Moreta had briefly considered sending a weyrling to the Healer Hall for a more experienced healer to replace Berchar, but because of the quarantine and the efficiency shown by Declan and Maylone, she decided the Weyr would be well enough tended. Most riders knew how to treat minor scores on themselves and their dragons.

She was serving herself from the porridge kettle when Sh'gall entered the cavern. He went straight to the dais and pulled all the chairs but one from the table. He sat down, beckoned to a sleepy weyrling, and, when the boy would have mounted the dais, Sh'gall warded him off with a peremptory command. While those in the cavern watched with amused surprise, the boy brought the cup of klah and the cereal bowl, placing them carefully at the far end of the table. Sh'gall waited till the boy had gone before he collected his breakfast.

Moreta felt impatience for such elaborate precautions. The Weyr had enough on its mind with Fall at midday. Out of deference to the Weyrleader's authority, she kept her expression bland. Nesso had added something flavorful to the cereal, and Moreta concentrated on identifying the addition.

Wingleaders and wingseconds began to arrive, to report the readiness of their wings to Sh'gall. They prudently observed his isolation.

The three queen riders arrived together and sought Moreta. She signaled a weyrling to serve the women and replenish her klah. Kamiana, a few Turns younger than Moreta, was her usual imperturbable self, her short dark hair spiky from the bath, her tanned face smooth. Lidora, who had flown enough Thread not to be unduly anxious, was clearly upset about something, but she had recently changed her weyrmate and her moods were often changeable. Haura, the youngest, was never at her best before Threadfall, but she always settled down once the queens' wing went into action.

"He's taking no risks, is he?" Kamiana said after noting Sh'gall's segregation.

"He did convey Capiam from Ista to Southern and Fort Hold."

"How's Berchar?"

"Still feverish." Moreta's gesture intimated that this was only to be expected.

"Hope there's no serious injuries." Kamiana aimed that remark at Haura, who was a capable if unenthusiastic nurse.

"Holth will fly lead," Moreta said, reproving Kamiana with a glance. "She's valiant in that position and we can all keep an eye on her. Haura and you fly as wing backs. Lidora and I will do the upper level. Nabol and Crom may not be cursed with fog—"

"Has a sweeprider gone out?"

"Sh'gall's less likely to fly blind than any other Weyrleader I've known," Moreta told Lidora dryly.

The weyrling returned with the porridge and klah, and served the Weyrwoman. Dragonriders began to arrive in groups, making their way to the breakfast hearth and then drifting to tables. The wingseconds moved about, checking their riders, giving instructions. All in a normal, perfectly routine fashion, despite Sh'gall, until the sweeprider came in.

"The High Reaches rider says it's all clear to the coast," A'dan announced in a cheerfully loud voice, peeling back his headgear as he strode to the hearth.

"The High Reaches rider says!" Sh'gall demanded. "You spoke to him?"

"Of course." A'dan turned round to the Weyrleader in surprise. "How else could I know? We met at—"

"Were you not told yesterday—" Sh'gall, appearing to enlarge with anger, rose. He glared at Moreta with piercingly accusative eyes. "Were you not told yesterday that contact with anyone was forbidden?"

"Riders aren't anyone—"

"Other riders! *Anyone!* We must keep this disease from reaching Fort Weyr and that means staying away from everyone. Today, during Fall, no rider of this Weyr is to approach any holder, any rider from High Reaches. Give any necessary orders adragonback, preferably on the wing. Touch no one and nothing belonging to anyone outside this Weyr. Have I made my orders perfectly clear this time?" He ended his outburst with another searing look at Moreta.

"What does Sh'gall think he can do to offenders?" Kamiana asked in an undertone meant for Moreta's ears alone.

Moreta gestured peremptorily for Kamiana's silence. Sh'gall had not finished speaking.

"Now," he went on in a stentorian but less forbidding tone that no one in the Lower Cavern could ignore. "We've Thread Falling today! Only dragons and their riders can keep Pern Threadfree. That is why we live apart, in Weyrs, why we must keep apart, preserving our health. Remember! Only dragonriders can keep Pern Threadfree. We must all be equal to that task!"

"He really is rousing us for Fall, isn't he?" Lidora said, leaning toward Moreta. "How long does he mean to keep us cooped up here?" Irritation colored her voice and sent a flush to her cheeks.

Moreta gave the dark woman a long measuring look, and Lidora caught at her lower lip.

"Aggravating to be sure, Lidora, but few Gather loves are ever caught for long." She had accurately guessed the source of Lidora's discontent and wondered who had caught the weyrwoman's fancy at Ruatha Gather. Moreta looked away, with apparent unconcern, but she thought again of Alessan and how much she'd enjoyed his company. She'd been showing off a bit, rushing to the runnerbeast's aid, trying to catch his attention.

The scuffling of bootheels and bench legs on stone roused her from her momentary lapse. She rose hastily. Custom dictated that she receive last-minute instructions concerning the queens' wing from Sh'gall. She stopped a few feet from the dais before he looked toward her, his expression warning her to keep her distance.

"Leri insists on flying?"

"There's no reason to stop her."

"You'll remind her, of course, to stay mounted."

"She always does."

Sh'gall shrugged, absolving himself of responsibility for Leri. "Tend your dragons, then. Threadfall is slated for midday." He turned to beckon the wingleaders forward.

"Is he complaining about Leri again?" Kamiana asked, perversely forgetting her own objections.

"Not really," Moreta replied then made her way out of the cavern, the queen riders following her.

Around the Bowl, on the ledges or on the ground, riders were harnessing dragons, arranging firestone sacks on dragon necks. Others daubed oil on recent scars and examined rough patches on hide or wing membranes. Wingleaders and wingseconds were busy overseeing the preparations. Weyrlings ducked around riders and dragons on errands. The atmosphere was busy but not frantic. The bustle had the right tone to it, Moreta decided as she made her way to the far side of the Bowl. The activity was routine, familiar, almost comforting when she considered the probability that, elsewhere on Pern, men and beasts might be dying of the plague.

That is not a good thought, Orlith said sternly.

"True. And not one to take into Fall. Forgive me."

There is no fault. The day is clear! We will meet Thread well.

Orlith's sturdy confidence imbued Moreta with optimism. The sun streamed in from the east, and the crisp air was invigorating after the clammy weather that had prevailed. A good deep frost now would be most beneficial, she thought as she climbed the stairs. Not too long a cold spell, just enough to freeze the pernicious insects and reduce the snake population.

"I'll do Holth's harness first."

Leri has help.

Moreta grinned at Orlith's impatience. That was a good spirit in a dragon. As she entered the weyr, Orlith was off her couch, her eyes sparkling, their whirl speeding up with anticipation. Orlith lowered her head. In a burst of affection and love for her partner and friend, Moreta flung her arms about the triangular muzzle, squeezing as tightly as she could, knowing that her strongest embrace would be as nothing to the husky beast. Orlith rumbled and Moreta could feel the loving vibration. Reluctantly she released Orlith. Briskly then, she turned to the harness hanging on its wall pegs.

As she arranged the straps, she ran the leather through knowing hands. The cold of *between* ate into equipment, and most riders changed harnesses three or four times a Turn. Finding all was well with the leather, Moreta then examined Orlith's wings despite the queen's growing impatience to be up on the Star Stone height, overseeing the final preparations. Next Moreta checked the gauge on the agenothree tank, made sure the nozzle head was clean, and strapped on the tank. Then queen and rider moved out to the ledge. On the one above, Holth and Leri were already waiting.

Moreta waved to Leri and received a jaunty salute. Settling her eyepieces, Moreta fastened her helmet, hitched back the cumbersome flamethrower, and mounted Orlith. With a mighty heave, Orlith launched herself toward the Rim.

"That's quite an effort, dear heart," Moreta said.

Once I am airborne, there is no effort.

To allay Moreta's anxiety, Orlith executed a very deft turn and landed with precision near Kadith. The dragon was a good-size beast, a deep rich shade of bronze with green undertones. He was not the largest bronze in Fort Weyr but, in his mating flights with Orlith, he had proved the most agile, daring, and energetic. Kadith looked up at Orlith and affectionately stroked his head on her neck. Orlith accepted the caress demurely, turning her head to touch muzzles.

Then Sh'gall signaled the blue, green, brown, and bronze riders to feed their dragons firestone. Considering it was an essential step in the destruction of Thread, Moreta could never take it as seriously as she ought. She kept her face composed and eyes straight ahead but she knew exactly the expression on the dragons' faces—pensive, eyes half closed as the dragon maneuvered firestone to the grinding surfaces of sturdy teeth, taking the greatest care to set the rock just *so* before applying pressure. The force that would pulverize firestone could also wreak considerable damage to a dragon's tongue. Dragons chewed firestone cautiously.

Once they'd stopped chewing firestone, the twelve wings of dragons— green, blue, brown, and bronze hides glistening with health in the sunlight, the many-faceted eyes taking on the reddish-yellow battle hue, wings restlessly flicking and tails slapping on the rock of the Rim—were a sight that never failed to inspire Moreta.

Orlith shifted her feet, sat back on her haunches. Moreta thumped her shoulder affectionately and told her to settle.

They are ready. Their bellies are full of firestone. Why are we not flying? Kadith?

Moreta was not one of those rare queen riders who could understand any dragon. Kadith turned his molten eyes on Orlith, and she steadied. Orlith was queen of the Weyr, as senior queen, the most powerful dragon in the Weyr, and since Fort was the first and biggest Weyr on the planet, she and her rider were the preeminent partners. But when Thread Fell, the Weyrleader was in command and Orlith had to obey Kadith and Sh'gall. So did Moreta.

Suddenly the farthest wing launched into the sky, high and straight. They would fly the high first westerly stack of the initial three wings. The second level wing moved out, then the third. Once all had achieved their assigned heights, the three wings went *between*. The north–south wings launched next for a cross-flight of the probable line of Fall. They went *between*. The diagonal wings, who would start in the northwest, went aloft and disappeared. Sh'gall lifted his arm yet again, and this time Kadith bugled, as impatient to be gone as Orlith. The Weyrleader would take his three wings east, to the line along Crom's plateau where the leading edge of Thread was due. The queens' wing took the final position, sweeping as close to the ground as they safely could. Their slower glide, their more powerful wings gave them more flight stability in erratic wind currents.

Now Kadith leaped from the Rim, Orlith following so quickly that Moreta was jerked back against the fighting straps. Then they were gliding into position. Leri on Holth had joined them, by what feat of acrobatics Moreta had not seen. Haura and Kamiana took their positions, and Lidora joined Moreta on the upper level.

Kadith says we go between.
You have the visual from him?
Very clear.
Take us between, Orlith!

"Black, blacker, blackest, coldest beyond living things,
Where is life when there is . . ."

The rugged mountains of Nabol were in the far distance, the sun warm on their backs in its cold-season arc. Below lay the bony plains of eastern Crom, glistening in patches and streaks that suggested there had been frost or a heavy dew.

Moreta's second glance was for Leri and Holth, who were perfectly fine. Haura and Kamiana were aligned behind them to form the V. Above were the fighting wings, the highest stack mere motes on a slow western glide. At the other assigned points of the defense, nine more wings were gliding toward the as-yet-unseen enemy. Now Moreta looked back over her shoulder. *Much wind?*

Not enough to matter. Orlith veered slightly to the right and left, testing.

Then Thread would make its entry on a slight slant, Moreta thought. There'd be more problems as they neared the mountains of Nabol where drafts would complicate Fall by sudden upward surges or drops. Thread fell at a faster rate during the cold season and, although the temperature was colder than it had been for recent Falls that Turn, the air wasn't frigid.

It comes!

Moreta looked back again. She saw that silvery smudging of a sky, a blurring that crept inexorably groundward. The Fall of Thread!

Leading edge! And Orlith began to pump her great wings, propelling them forward to meet the devastating rain.

Moreta caught her breath, as always exhilarated and apprehensive. She remembered to exhale as she settled against the fighting straps. Moments would pass before the high wings would close with Thread. It would be minutes before she and the other queens might be needed. She spared another glance for Holth.

She flies well! Orlith confirmed. *The sun is warm on their backs, too.*

Leading edge was visible and the sky ahead on either side was starred with quick bursts of flame. Moreta could see the stacks of dragons at their various altitudes covering the edge well. Then, from the pattern of dragon flame, she saw that the Fall was uneven. There were gaps where no dragon breathed Thread to char.

Kadith says the Fall is ragged. Widen the formations. Second stack is closing. Southern wings have contact. Orlith would keep up her commentary until the queens' wing was called to use its flamethrowers. Then her attention would be totally involved in keeping herself and her rider unscathed. *High level is dropping down now. No injuries.*

There rarely are, Moreta thought, not in the first few exciting moments of Fall, no matter how badly it drops. The riders are all fresh, their dragons eager. Once they assessed the Fall, thick or thin, racing or languid, then mistakes would occur. The second hour of a Fall was the most dangerous. Riders and dragons lost their initial keenness, they overshot Thread, or they misjudged. Falls don't always follow the pattern of the leading edge, particularly at the end of a Pass.

Kadith is checking. Kadith is flaming. Char! Excitement tinged Orlith's previously calm tone. *He's* between. *Back again. Flaming. All wings are now engaged. First flight returns for second sweep.*

The wind yanked at Moreta's body and she tugged briefly to settle the flamethrower strap on her shoulder. Now the wind carried with it tiny flecks of black charred Thread. On a stormy day, sometimes her eyepieces would be covered by a muddy film. They were under the first edge of Fall now.

Nothing passed the wings, Orlith said.

Sometimes great gouts of Thread would descend on the leading edge and riders would be hard put to acquit their duty. Some older riders preferred the first drop to be heavy, swearing that the heavier the leading edge, the lighter the die-off. So many Falls, so many leading edges, so many, many variations possible and so many comparisons. No two accounts, even by riders in the same wing, ever seemed to tally.

Old L'mal had told Moreta that the efficiency of the dragon was only hampered by his rider's ability to brag. However a rider flew, so long as no Thread reached the ground, the flight was well done!

The plains of Crom flowed beneath them. Moreta kept her eyes ranging ahead as did Orlith, in a synchrony of alertness long perfected. Moreta now caught the overvision from Orlith as the dragon saw hers. Moreta often experienced the desire to dive on Thread as the fighting dragons did, swooping down on the target, instead of having to wait passively for stray Thread to appear. Sometimes she envied the greens, who could chew firestone. That effectively sterilized them, which was all to the good or green dragons would overpopulate the planet. The danger was in the fight, but so was the excitement, and the golden queens could not indulge.

Thread!

"Haura!"

Werth sees. Werth follows!

Moreta watched as the younger queen veered, swung, and came up under the tangle of the deadly parasite. The flamethrower spat. The ash dispersed in the air as Werth accomplished the brief mission.

They are all alert now, Orlith told Moreta.

Tell them to broaden the interval since we're past leading edge. Kamiana is to stay with Leri and Holth. We'll go south. Haura, north!

Obligingly Orlith turned, gradually picked up air speed and altitude.

That was the hard part of Fall, coursing back and forth. The rich dark soil of the plateau held sufficient mineral nourishment to sustain Thread long enough to waste fields that had been brought to fertility over hundreds of Turns of careful husbandry.

They were nearing the initial rank of hills and the first of Crom's holds. The symmetry of the windows with their metal shutters tightly closed was visible against the protecting hillside. As Moreta and Orlith passed over the burning fire-heights, she wondered if all within the hold were healthy.

"Ask the watchwher, Orlith."

It knows nothing. Orlith's tone was a shade contemptuous. The queen did not enjoy interchanges with the simpleminded beasts.

"They have their uses," Moreta said. "We can check with all of them today. Sh'gall may not wish us to contact people but we can still learn something."

Orlith gained more altitude as the second fold of hills loomed. Rider and queen kept the silvery shower in sight, angling from one edge of their appointed line to the other. Over the next plateau they saw Lidora and Ilith swinging along their route.

Kadith says to converge on Crom Hold, Orlith told her after several long sweeps.

"Let's join them."

Moreta thought hard of Crom's fire-heights, chanted her talisman against *between,* and on "blackest" arrived in the air above Crom's principal Hold. It was situated near a river, the first cascade of which could be viewed from the Hold windows when unshuttered. The livestock that usually grazed the fields had been gathered in. Moreta remembered the gay and brave decorations on Ruatha's windows and asked Orlith to speak to Crom's watchwher.

It is only worried about Thread. Knows nothing of illness. Orlith sounded disgusted. *Kadith says the Fall is heavy now and we should be careful. There have been three minor scorings. All dragons are flaming well and the wings are in order. Cross over!*

Moreta glanced at the spectacular display as all the fighting wings overlapped one another above Crom Hold. Too bad the holders couldn't see it. Cross-over was a magnificent sight but the concentration of the wings in one aerial position left many openings for Thread.

Suddenly Orlith veered. Moreta saw the Thread patch. Saw the blue dragon heading for it.

"We're in a better position," she cried, knowing that Orlith would warn off the diving blue. She flicked open the nozzle of the flamethrower, leaning well left in her fighting straps as Orlith came up under the tangle. She pressed the button. The gout of fire found its mark but Moreta also had a blurred vision of blue wings and belly.

"Too close, you fool. Who was that?"

N'men, rider of Jelth, Orlith said. *One of the young blues. You didn't singe him.*

"A singe would teach him discipline." Moreta fumed, but was relieved that the young rider was unscathed. "Reckless stupidity to fly so low. Didn't he see us? I'll have his eyes for polishing."

More Thread! Orlith was off at another tangent. Lidora had also seen the Thread and she was nearer. Orlith desisted. *Kadith is diverting from cross-over. The others are coming.*

The queens' wing reformed, flying north, fanning out as gobbets of loose Thread Fell in a curious order caused by the dragon's distortions of the air currents. That was work indeed for the queens!

Moreta and Orlith were flying hard after this tangle, that patch, aware that Sh'gall had quickly redeployed sections of several wings to cover the upper levels. Cross-overs were hard to avoid, with the different stacks of dragons flying at varying speeds, especially when the prime requirement was that wings maintain the proper altitude and interval. Then Sh'gall sent sweep riders north to make sure there had been no burrowing.

The Fall continued as the wings reestablished their far-ranging patterns. Riders called for more firestone and set meetings with the weyrlings riding supply. Moreta checked her flamethrower and found half a tank. And Fall continued.

More casualties were reported by Orlith, none serious—wing tips and tails. Orlith and Moreta flew a watching level over the first of the snow-tipped mountains along the irregular border between Crom and Nabol. Thread would freeze and shrivel on those slopes but the queens ranged while Sh'gall and Kadith ordered the wings *between* to the far side and Nabol.

Haura said that she and Leri needed new fuel cylinders for their flamethrowers and were dropping down at the mine hold.

"Leri, please check with the watchwher!"

Holth says that the watchwhers are all stupid and know nothing of any use to us. I'll keep on asking.

Any landing was a strain for Holth, who was no longer agile. Moreta watched anxiously, but Leri had allowed for Holth's incapacity and directed the old queen to a wide ledge close to the mine hold. A green weyrling arrived from *between*, cylinders hanging on both sides of her neck. She landed daintily. Her rider detached one tank and dismounted. He ran toward Holth, up her forearm, clinging to the cylinder straps with one hand and the fighting leather with the other. The exchange of tanks was made as Moreta and Orlith glided over. Holth took several steps forward, leaning into the free air and got in her first downward sweep.

They pace themselves. All is well, Orlith said.

"Take us to Kadith!"

They went *between* and emerged above a rough valley just as a mass of Thread split across the nearest ridge.

Tapeth follows!

The green dragon, her wings flat against her dorsal ridge, fell toward the point of impact, her flaming breath searing the crest. Just when it looked as if the dragon would collide with the ridge, she unfolded her wings and swerved off.

Take us there! Moreta glanced down at the tank gauge. She'd need more to flood the ridge. No ground crew could get into the blind valley.

Then they were above the sooted stone. Obedient to her rider's mental directions, Orlith hovered so that Moreta could flame the far side of the ridge. Tendrils of Thread hissed and writhed into black ash. Methodically she pumped flame into the area, widening the arc to be sure that not a finger-length of the parasite escaped.

"We'll land a bit away, Orlith. I'll need another tank now."

It comes! Orlith landed easily.

"I want to check that ridge. I couldn't see if it was shelf, sheet, or shale."

Moreta released her fighting straps and slid down. Her feet, sore from the long ride and slightly numb despite the thick lining of her boots, were jarred by the impact of her jump. She slowly clambered on insensitive soles toward the blackened area, her finger ready on the flamethrower's ignition button. She began to sense the residual heat of the two flame attacks on the rock and moved forward more slowly as much to revive her cold feet as to be cautious. She never liked to rush in on a Thread site, not on foot. However, it had to be done and the sooner the better. Thread burrowed into any crevice or cranny.

The eastern side of the ridge was sheer rock, unmarred by a split or crack to harbor Thread. The western face was also a solid mass. Tapeth's flame must have caught the stuff on landing.

Her feet were beginning to warm up as she made her way back to Orlith. Just then a blue weyrling emerged. His claws were no more than a finger-length from the top of the protruding rock thrust. The next instant the blue backfanned his wings to land. Orlith rumbled and the blue shuddered at the queen's reprimand. The rider's expression altered abruptly from delight to apprehension.

"Don't be clever T'ragel! Be safe!" Moreta shouted at him. "You could have come out *in* the ridge, not on it! You've never been here before. Hasn't F'neldril drilled it in your skull to have air space landing as well as taking off?"

The young rider fumbled with the straps holding the tank to his blue dragon's side as Moreta stormed over to him, still seething with the fright he had given her. "Caution pleases me much more than agility."

She almost wrenched the tank from his hand.

"Get down. To make up for your error in judgment, stay until the ridge cools. Check for infestation. There's moss just below. You know how to use a flamethrower? Good. What's left in my tank should suffice. But have your dragon call if you see *anything* moving on that ridge. Anything!"

An hour or so's cold watch with fear as his companion would cool the young rider's ardor for fancy landings. No matter how often they were cautioned by the Weyrlingmaster and Weyrleader, weyrlings inexplicably disappeared and the older dragons grieved. The casualties were such a waste of the Weyr's resources.

She remounted Orlith, aware that the boy had taken a sentry's stance, but as close to the comfort of his blue dragon as possible. They looked shaken and forlorn.

Kadith calls!

"We must be nearing the end of Fall!" Moreta clipped back her fighting straps, remembering to tug them secure. Her harangue would lose its force if she came adrift on take-off.

B'lerion rides!

Moreta smiled as she told Orlith to get them airbound, to take them *between* to join the wings. She wondered, in the blackest of cold, just how B'lerion had fared with Oklina.

Then they were on the western side of the Nabol Range with Thread falling thick and fast. Moreta had no time to express gratitude for the presence of the fresh dragons and their riders. Moreta and Orlith had just dispatched a low snarl of Thread when Orlith announced abruptly, *The Fall is over!*

As the queen slowed her forward motion into a leisurely glide, Moreta leaned wearily into the fighting straps, the nozzle heavy in her tired hand. She felt the dull ache in her head from having to see too much at once, from having to concentrate on drift, and glide, and angle of the flame.

"Casualties?"

Thirty-three, mostly minor scorings. Two badly damaged wings. Four riders with cracked ribs and three with dislocated shoulders.

"Ribs and shoulders! That's bad flying!" Yet Moreta was relieved at the total. But two wings! She hated having to mend wings, but she'd had lots of practice.

B'lerion hails us. Bronze Nabeth flew well. Orlith was admiringly craning her neck as the High Reaches bronze matched their speed and level. B'lerion waved his arm in greeting.

"Ask him if he had a good Gather." Any diversion not to think of the Thread-laced wings to be mended.

He did. Orlith sounded amused. *Kadith says we should get back to the injured wings at the Weyr.*

"First ask B'lerion what he's heard of the epidemic."

Only that is exists. Then she added, *Kadith says Dilenth is very badly injured.*

Moreta waved farewell to B'lerion, wishing that Sh'gall or Kadith, or both, did not consider B'lerion and Nabeth rivals. Perhaps they were. Orlith liked B'lerion's bronze, and Moreta thought it would be far more pleasant spending the Interval with someone as merry as B'lerion.

"Take us back to the Weyr."

The utter still coldness of *between* acted as a bracer to Moreta. Then they were low over the Bowl, Orlith having judged her reentry as fine as that blue weyrling had earlier. The ground was studded with wounded dragons, each surrounded by a cluster of attendants. The piercing cry of wounded and distressed dragons filled the air and imbued Moreta with the most earnest desire to reduce their keening to a bearable level.

"Show me Dilenth," Moreta asked Orlith as the queen swung in over the Bowl.

His main wingsail is scored. I will soothe him! Pity deepened the queen's tone as she circled as close as was prudent above the thrashing blue. Riders and weyrfolk were trying to apply numbweed to the injured wing, but Dilenth was writhing with pain, making that impossible. As Orlith obligingly hovered, Moreta had a clear view of the crippled wing, its forestay tip flopping awkwardly in the dust.

It was a serious injury. From elbow to finger joint, the leading edge of Dilenth's wing had taken the brunt of the havoc wrought by Thread. The batten cartileges had wilted and were crumpled into the mass of the main wingsail; Moreta thought there was also some damage to the fingersail between the joint and batten ribs, where Thread had glanced off as Dilenth had tried to take belated evasive action. More damage marred the lub side of the wing than the leech. The spar sail appeared relatively whole. Nor could she discern if the finger rib was broken. She devoutly hoped it wasn't for without ichor to the head of the mainsail, the dragon might never regain full use and fold of his wing.

Dilenth's injury was one of the worst a dragon could sustain since both the leading and trailing edges of the mainsail were involved. Healed wing membrane might form cheloid tissue and the aileron would become less sensitive, imbalancing the dragon's glide. First Moreta would have to sort the puzzle pieces of the remaining tissue and support it, hoping that there was enough membrane left to structure repair. Dilenth was young, able to regenerate tissue, but he would be on the injured list for a long time.

Moreta saw Nesso bustling about in the group attending Dilenth. His rider, F'duril, was doing his best to comfort the dragon but Dilenth continually broke loose from his rider's grip, flailing his head about in anguish.

Orlith landed just in front of the blue dragon. As soon as her hind feet met the ground, Moreta released the fighting straps and slid to the ground. Weyrlings appeared to take the agenothree tank, her outer gear.

"Where's redwort to wash in?" she demanded loudly, more to mask the sound of the keening that beat between her ears. *Orlith, control him!*

The intensity of Dilenth's cries dwindled abruptly as the queen locked eyes with the blue. His head steadied and he submitted to his rider's ministration. The relieved F'duril alternately entreated Dilenth to be brave and thanked Orlith and Moreta.

"Half the noise is shock," Moreta said to F'duril as she scrubbed her hands in the basin of redwort. The solutions stung her cold fingers.

"The lacerations are major. The wingsail is nothing but rags and shreds," said Nesso at her elbow. "How will it ever mend?"

"We'll just see," Moreta replied, resenting Nesso for airing the doubts she herself entertained. "You can get me that bolt of fine wide cloth and the thinnest basket reeds you've got. Where're Declan and Maylone?"

"Declan's with L'rayl. Sorth took a mass of Thread on his withers. Maylone is somewhere or other with a dragon." Nesso was distracted by so many urgent requirements. "I've had to leave the injured riders with only their weyrmates and the women to tend them. Oh, why did Berchar have to be sick?"

"Can't be helped. Haura will be back shortly to help you with the riders." Moreta took a firm hold on her frustration and banished impatience as a useless luxury. "Just get me the cloth and the basket reeds. I'll want my table here, in front of the wing. Send me someone with steady hands, oil, and thin numbweed, then get back to the riders. And my needle case and that spool of treated thread."

As Nesso rushed off, shouting for helpers, Moreta continued her survey of the injured wing. The main wingbones were unscathed, which was a boon, but so much numbweed had been applied that she couldn't see if ichor was forming. Fragments of the leading sail dangled from elbow and finger joint. There might just be enough for reconstruction. Any shred would help. She flexed her fingers which were still stiff from the cold flying of Fall.

Dilenth's keening was muted but now another sound, a human one, penetrated her concentration.

"You know I had my feeling! You know we've both been uneasy. I *thought* we weren't flying true!" F'duril's litany of self-reproach reached Moreta. "I should have held us *between* a breath longer. You couldn't help yourself. It isn't your fault, Dilenth. It's mine! You'd no air space to dodge that Thread. And I let you back in too soon. It's all my fault."

Moreta rounded on the man to shock him out of his hysterics. "F'duril, get a grip on yourself. You're upsetting Dilenth far more than—" Moreta broke off, suddenly noting the Threadscores on F'duril's body. "Has no one tended you yet, F'duril?"

"I made him drink wine, Moreta." A rider in soot-smeared leathers appeared from Dilenth's left side. "I've got numbweed dressings for him."

"Then apply them!" Moreta looked around in exasperation. "Where *is* Nesso now? Can't she organize anything today?"

"How bad is Dilenth?" the rider asked while capably slitting away the remains of F'duril's riding jacket. Moreta now identified the slender young man as A'dan, F'duril's weyrmate. He spoke in a low worried voice.

"Bad enough!" She took a longer look at A'dan, who was coping deftly with the dressings he wrapped about F'duril. "You're his weyrmate? Have you a steady hand?"

A solicitous weyrmate was preferable to no help, and certainly more acceptable to Moreta than Nesso's moaning and pessimistic outlook. Beads of ichor were beginning to seep through the numbweed on Dilenth's wingbone.

"Where *are* my things, Nesso?"

Moreta had taken but one pace toward the cavern to collect her requirements when the stout Headwoman floundered into view, laden with reeds, a pot of thin numbweed liquid, the jug of oil, and Moreta's needle box. Behind her marched three weyrlings, one of them carrying a hide-wrapped bolt of cloth as tall as himself and a washing bowl while the other two wrestled the table close to the blue dragon's wing.

"Oh, a long time healing if it heals whole," Nesso moaned in a dismal undertone while shaking her head. She took one look at the expression on Moreta's face and scurried off.

Moreta took a long, settling breath then exhaled and reached for the oil. As she began coating her hands against contact with numbweed, she issued instructions to A'dan and the weyrlings.

"You, D'ltan." She pointed to the weyrling with the strongest-looking hands. "Cut me lengths of that cloth as long as Dilenth's leading edge. A'dan, wash your hands with this oil and dry them, then repeat the process twice, just patting your hands dry after the third. We'll have to oil our hands frequently or get benumbed by the weed as we work. You, M'barak." Moreta indicated the tall weyrling. "Thread me needles with this much thread"—she held her oily hands apart to the required length—"and keep doing 'em until I tell you to stop. You, B'greal"—she looked toward the third boy—"will hand me the reeds when I ask for them. All of you wash your hands in redwort first.

"We're going to support the wing underneath with cloth stitched to the wingbone and stretched from the dorsal to the finger joint," she told A'dan, watching his face to see if he understood. "Then we must—if you have to get sick, A'dan, do it now and get it over with. Dilenth and F'duril both will find it reassuring to have you helping me. F'duril knows you'll be the most loving and gentle nurse that Dilenth could have. A'dan!" She spoke urgently because she needed his help. "Don't think of it as a dragon wing. Think of it as a fine summer tunic that needs mending. Because that's all we'll be doing. Mending!"

Her hands oiled, she took the fine-pointed needle from the weyrling's hand, willing A'dan to fortitude. *Orlith?*

I can only speak to his green, T'grath, Orlith said a bit tartly. *Dilenth needs all my concentration and none of the other queens has returned to help.*

In the next second, however, A'dan shook himself, finished washing his hands, and turned resolutely to Moreta. His complexion was better and his eyes steady though he swallowed convulsively.

"Good! Let's begin. Remember! We're mending!"

Moreta jumped up on the sturdy table, beckoned him to follow, and then reached for the first length of cloth. As Moreta made her first neat tacks along the dorsal, Dilenth and A'dan twitched almost in unison. With Orlith's control and all the numbweed on the bone, Dilenth could not be experiencing any pain. A'dan had to be anticipating the dragon's reaction. So Moreta talked to him as she stitched, occasionally asking him to stretch or relax the fine cloth.

"Now I'll just fasten this to the underside. Pull to your left. The leading edge of the wing will be thick—no help for it—but if we can just save enough of the mainsail . . . There! Now, A'dan, take the numbweed paddle and smear the cloth. We'll lay on it what wingsail fragments remain. This is a very fragile summer tunic. Gently does it. M'barak, cut me another length. That tendon's been badly stretched but luckily it's still attached to the elbow." *Orlith, do stop him flicking his tail. Any movement makes this operation more difficult.*

Moreta was grateful when Dilenth's exertions abruptly ceased. Probably another queen had arrived to support Orlith. She thought she saw Sh'gall but he didn't stop. He wasn't attracted to this aspect of Threadfall.

"Retaining that tendon is a boon," she said, realizing that her verbal encouragement to A'dan had faltered. "I'll have those reeds now, B'greal. The longest one. You see, A'dan, we can brace the trailing edge this way, using gauze as support. And I think there're enough fragments of membrane. Yes. Ah, yes, he'll fly again, Dilenth will! Slowly now, very gently, let's lay the tatters on the gauze. M'barak, can I have the thinner salve? We'll just float the pieces . . . so . . ."

As she and A'dan patiently restored the main wingsail, she could see exactly how the clump of Thread had struck Dilenth. Had F'duril and the blue dragon emerged from *between* a breath earlier, F'duril would have been bowled off Dilenth by the searing mass. She must remember to point out to F'duril that good fortune had attended their reentry.

They retrieved more sail fragments than she'd initially dared believe. Moreta began to feel more confident as she stitched a reed to the tendon. In time the whole would mend although the new growth, overlapping the old, would be thicker and unsightly for seasons to come, until windblown sand had abraded the heavier tissue. Dilenth would learn to compensate for the alteration on the sail surface. Most dragons readily adapted to such inequalities once they were airborne again.

Dilenth will fly again, Orlith said placidly as Moreta stepped back from the repaired wing. *You've done as much as you can here.*

"Orlith says we've done a good job, A'dan," she told the greenrider with a weary smile. "You were marvelous assistants, M'barak, D'Itan, B'greal!" She nodded gratefully to the three weyrlings. "Now, we'll just get Dilenth over to the ground weyrs—and you can all collapse."

She jumped down from the table and would have sprawled had A'dan's hand not steadied her. His wry grin heartened her. She propped herself against the table edge for a moment. Nesso appeared, dispensing wine to Moreta first and then the others.

Dilenth, released from Orlith's rigid control, began to sag on his legs, tilting dangerously to his right. Orlith reasserted her domination while Moreta looked around for F'duril.

"He'll be no help to anyone," Nesso observed sourly as they all watched the blue rider sinking slowly to the ground in a faint.

"It was the strain and his wound," A'dan said as he rushed to his weyrmate.

Dilenth moaned and lowered his muzzle toward his rider.

"He's all right, Dilenth," A'dan said, gently turning F'duril over. "A little sandy—"

"And a lot drunk!" M'barak murmured as he signaled the other two lads to aid A'dan with F'duril.

"The worst is over now!" A'dan said with brisk cheer.

"He doesn't know what worst is," Nesso muttered gloomily at Moreta's side as the blue dragon lurched away, supported on one side by A'dan's T'grath and K'lon and blue Rogeth on the other.

It took Moreta a few moments to realize that K'lon and Rogeth should not be about. "K'lon? . . ."

"He volunteered." Nesso sounded peeved. "He *said* that he was fine and he couldn't stand being idle when he was so badly needed. And he the only one!"

"The only one?"

Nesso averted her face from the Weyrwoman. "It *was* a command the Weyr could not ignore. An emergency, after all. He and F'neldril decided that he must respond to the drum message."

"What drum message are you talking about, Nesso?" Abruptly Moreta understood Nesso's averted gaze, She'd been overstepping her authority as Headwoman again.

"Fort Hold required a dragonrider to convey Lord Tolocamp from Ruatha to Fort Hold. Urgently. There is illness at Ruatha and more at Fort Hold, which cannot be deprived of its Lord Holder during such a disaster." Nesso blurted out the explanation in spurts, peering anxiously up at Moreta to gauge her reaction. "Master Capiam is sick—he must be, for it is Fortine who replies to messages, not the Masterhealer." Nesso grimaced and began to wring her hands, bringing them by degrees to her mouth as if to mask her words. "And there are sick *riders* at Igen, Ista, and many at Telgar. There's Fall in two days in the south . . . I ask you, who will fly against Thread if three Weyrs have no riders to send?"

Moreta forced herself to breathe slowly and deeply, absorbing the sense of Nesso's babbling. The woman began to weep now, whether from the relief of confession or from remorse Moreta couldn't ascertain.

"When did this drum message come?"

"There were two. The first one, calling for a conveyance for Lord Tolocamp, just after the wings left for Fall!" Nesso mopped at her eyes, appealing mutely to Moreta for forgiveness. "Curmir said we had to respond!"

"So you did!" Nesso's blubbering irritated Moreta. "I see that you could not delay until we had returned from Fall. Surely Curmir responded that the Weyr was at Fall?"

"Well, they knew that. But F'neldril and K'lon were here—no, there"— Nesso had to find the exact spot near the Cavern—"so we all heard the drum message. K'lon said immediately that he could go. He said, and we had to agree with him, that since he had been ill of the fever, he was unlikely to contract it. He wouldn't let F'neldril or one of the weyrlings or the disabled take the risk." Nesso's eyes pleaded for reassurance. "We tried to ask Berchar about the danger of infection, but S'gor would not let anyone see him and could not answer for him. And we *had* to respond to Lord Tolocamp's request! It is only right that a Lord Holder be in his Hold during such a crisis. Curmir reasoned that, in such an unusual instance, we were constrained by duty to assist the Lord Holder even if it meant disobeying the Weyrleader!"

"Not to mention the Masterhealer and a general quarantine."

"But Master Capiam is *at* Fort Hold," Nesso protested as if that sanctioned all. "And what will be happening at Fort Hold in Lord Tolocamp's absence I cannot imagine!"

It was the happenings at Ruatha Hold that concerned Moreta more vitally, and the second drum message.

"What is this of sick riders? Did it come in on open code?"

"No, indeed! Curmir had to look it up in his Record. We did nothing about that. Not even forward it for it didn't have the pass-on cadence. F'neldril and K'lon said you should know. There are forty-five riders ill at

Telgar alone!" Nesso placed one hand on her chest in a dramatic gesture. "Nine are very ill! Twenty-two are ill at Igen and fourteen at Ista." Nesso seemed obscurely pleased by the numbers.

Eighty-one riders ill of this epidemic? Despair and fear welled through Moreta. *Riders* ill? Her mind reeled. It was Fall! All the dragonriders were needed. Fort Weyr was down thirty in strength from the last Fall, and thirty-three from this one. It would be a full Turn before Dilenth flew. Why this? Only eight Turns remained in this Pass and then the riders would be free of the devastation that Thread wrought on dragons, themselves, and Pern. Moreta shook her head in an effort to clear her thinking. She ought to have paid more heed to Sh'gall's agitated report of illness instead of discounting the truth because it was unpalatable. She knew that Master Capiam was not in the habit of issuing arbitrary orders. But riders were healthy, fit, less susceptible to minor ailments. Why should they, in their splendid isolation, pursuing their historic occupation, be vulnerable to an infection rampant in crowded holds, halls, and among beasts?

Yet, her rational self said, the damage was already spreading by the time Sh'gall brought her the news. Even she had already innocently compounded her involvement by showing off her sensitivity to impress Alessan. *How* could anyone at Ruatha Gather have realized the danger in approaching that dying runnerbeast? Why, when Talpan had correlated illness to the journeyings of that caged beast, she and Alessan had probably been watching the races.

You are not at fault, the tender, loving voice of Orlith said. *You did no harm to that runnerbeast. You had the right to enjoy the Gather.*

"Is there anything we should *do* about the other Weyrs, Moreta?" Nesso asked. She had stopped weeping but she still twisted and washed her hands in an indecisive way that annoyed Moreta almost as much.

"Has Sh'gall returned?"

"He was here and went off, looking for Leri. He was angry."

Orlith?

They are busy but unharmed.

"Nesso, did you tell him about the drum messages?"

Nesso cast a desperate look at Moreta and shook her head. "He wasn't on the ground long enough—really, Moreta."

"I see." And Moreta did. Nesso could never have brought herself to inform the Weyrleader of such fateful tidings had there been worlds of time. Moreta would have to present the matters to Sh'gall soon enough, a conversation that would cause more acrimony on a day when both had more problems than hours. "How is Sorth?"

"Well, now, he's going to be fine," Nesso said with considerably more enthusiasm for that topic. "He's just over here. I thought you might like to check over my work."

The westering sun glinted off the Tooth Crag above Fort Weyr and the glare hurt Moreta's tired eyes as she looked in the direction Nesso pointed. The repair of Dilenth's wing had taken far longer than she had realized.

There is still sun on your ledge, Orlith. You should enjoy it. Get the cold of between *and Fall out of your hide.*

You are as tired. When do you rest?

When I have finished what must be done, Moreta said, but her dragon's concern was comforting. Moreta scrubbed at her fingertips, which had become insensitive where numbweed had seeped through the oil. She rinsed her hands in redwort and dried them well in the cloth Nesso offered.

A blue dragon wailed plaintively from his ledge, and Moreta looked up, worried.

"His rider only has a broken shoulder," Nesso said with a sniff. "Torn harness."

Moreta remembered another blue rider. *Orlith, that blue weyrling—has he returned from the ridge?*

Yes, there was no Thread. He reported to the Weyrlingmaster. He wants to have a word with you about putting a very young rider at risk.

The lad would have been in more risk continuing his antics, and I'll have words with the Weyrlingmaster on another score. "Let's see Sorth," she said aloud to Nesso.

"He's an old dragon. I don't think he'll heal well." Nesso babbled out of a nervous desire to regain favor in Moreta's eyes, for she didn't know that much about dragon injuries and far too much about how she thought the Weyr should be managed.

Moreta had also come to the conclusion at some point in the last few moments that she would have ordered someone to convey Lord Tolocamp had she been in the Weyr when the message arrived, despite any protest Sh'gall might have raised about breaking quarantine. Fort Hold would need Tolocamp more than Ruatha needed an unwilling guest. She wondered fleetingly if any were sick at Ruatha. If so, how had Alessan permitted Tolocamp to break quarantine?

Sorth had taken a gout of tangled Thread right on the forward wing-finger, severing the bone just past the knuckle. L'rayl was full of praise for Declan's assistance, belatedly including Nesso in his recital while she glared at him. They had done a good job of splinting the bone, Moreta noted professionally, tying reeds into position on well-numbed flesh.

"Nasty enough," Moreta commented as Sorth gingerly lowered the injured wing for her scrutiny.

"A fraction closer to the knuckle and Sorth might have lost tip mobility," L'rayl said with laudable detachment. The man had a habit of clenching his teeth after he spoke, as if chopping off his words before they could offend anyone.

"A soak in the lake tomorrow will reduce the swelling once ichor has coated the wound," Moreta said, stroking the old brown's shoulder.

"Sorth says," L'rayl answered after a pause, "that floating would feel very good. The wing would be supported by the water and not ache so much." L'rayl was then caught between a grin and a grimace for his dragon's courage and, to cover his embarrassment, he turned and roughly scratched Sorth's greening muzzle.

"How many riders were injured?" she asked Nesso as they turned toward the infirmary. With eighty-one sick of the plague, they might have to send substitutes.

"More than there should be," Nesso replied, having recovered her critical tongue.

Nesso hovered while Moreta made her expected brief appearance in the infirmary. Most of the injured riders were groggy with fellis juice or asleep, so she didn't have to linger. She also seemed unable to extricate herself from Nesso's company.

"Moreta, what you need right now is a good serving of my fine stew."

Moreta was not hungry. She knew she ought to eat but she wanted to await the return of Sh'gall and Leri. In a brief flurry of malice, Moreta struck across the Bowl to the Lower Cavern in a long stride that forced Nesso to jog to keep up. Annoyed with herself, Moreta silently put up with Nesso's fussing to make sure that the cook served Moreta a huge plate. Nesso obsequiously cut bread and heaped slices on Moreta's plate before making a show of seating the Weyrwoman. Fortunately, before the last of Moreta's waning penitence was exhausted, one of the fosterlings came running up to say that Tellani needed Nesso "*right* now."

"Giving birth, no doubt. She started labor at the beginning of Fall." Nesso raised her eyes and hands ceilingward in resignation. "We'll probably never know who the father was for Tellani doesn't know."

"Babe or child, we'll have some trace to go by. Wish Tellani well for me."

Privately Moreta blessed Tellani for her timing; she would have respite from the Headwoman, and a birth after Fall was regarded as propitious. The Weyr needed a good dollop of luck. A boy, even of uncertain parentage, would please the dragonriders. She'd have a stern talk with Tellani about keeping track of her lovers—surely a simple enough task even for so loving a woman as Tellani. The Weyr had to be cautious about consanguinity. It might just be the wiser course to foster Tellani's children to other Weyrs.

It was easier to think of an imminent birth than tax her tired mind with imponderables such as sick riders in three Weyrs, a Masterhealer who was not signing outgoing messages, the disciplining of a rider and a harper who disobeyed their Weyrleader, a wing-torn dragon who would be weyrbound for months, and a sick healer who might be dying.

Malth says Berchar is very weak and S'gor is very worried, Orlith told her in a gentle, drowsy voice. *We have decided that the woman has carried a male,* Orlith continued. Moreta was astonished. Since Orlith very rarely used the plural pronoun, she must be referring to other dragons.

How kind you are, my golden love! Moreta shielded her face with her hands so that no one in the cavern would see the tears in her eyes for her dragon's unexpected kindly distraction, and her everlasting joy that, of all the girls standing on Ista's Hatching Ground that day Turns ago, Orlith had chosen the late arrival for her rider.

"Moreta?"

Startled, Moreta looked up to see Curmir, K'lon, and F'neldril standing politely before her table.

"It was I who *insisted* on conveying Lord Tolocamp," K'lon said firmly, chin up, eyes shining. "You could say that I hadn't actually *heard* the Weyrleader's order of quarantine since Rogeth and I were asleep in a lower weyr." Outrageously K'lon winked at Moreta. An older, weyr-bred rider, he had not been best pleased when Sh'gall's Kadith had flown Orlith, making the much younger bronze rider Weyrleader in L'mal's stead. K'lon's discontent with the change in leadership had been aggravated by Sh'gall's overt disapproval of K'lon's association with the Igen green rider A'murry.

Moreta tried to assume a neutral expression but knew from Curmir's expression that she failed.

"You did as custom dictates!" Moreta would allow that much latitude. "The Fort Holder must be conveyed by this Weyr. You brought his family back?"

"Indeed not, though I did offer. Rogeth would not have objected but Lady Pendra decided that she and her daughters could not break the quarantine."

Moreta caught Curmir's gaze again and knew that the harper was as aware as everyone else in the west as to why Lady Pendra would not break the quarantine. Moreta had great sympathy for Alessan's predicament. Not only was he still saddled with the Fort girls, but all the other hopefuls of the Gather were still at Ruatha.

"Lady Pendra said that she would wait out the four days."

"Four days, four Turns," F'neldril said with a snort, "and it wouldn't change their faces or improve their chances with Alessan."

"Did you see Master Capiam, K'lon?"

K'lon's expression changed, reflecting annoyance and remembered offense. "No, Moreta. Lord Tolocamp required me to set him down in the Hold forecourt, so I did. But immediately Lord Campen and Master Fortine and some other men whose names I can't recall bore him off to a meeting. I wasn't admitted to the Hall—to protect *me*, they said, from contagion, and they wouldn't listen when I explained that I'd had the plague and recovered."

Before she could speak, the watchrider's dragon bugled loudly. Sh'gall and his wing had returned at last. As Moreta rose hastily from the table, she could see the dust roiled up by the dragons' landing.

All are well, Orlith reassured her. *Kadith says the Fall ended well but he is furious that there were few ground crews.*

"No ground crews," she told the three men by way of warning.

Sh'gall came striding through the second dust cloud created as the dragons jumped to their weyrs. The riders of Sh'gall's wing followed a discreet distance behind their Weyrleader. Sh'gall made directly for Moreta, his manner so threatening that K'lon, Curmir, and F'neldril tactfully stepped to one side.

"Crom sent out no ground crews," Sh'gall shouted, slamming gloves, helmet, and goggles down on the table with a force that sent the gear skidding across the surface and onto the floor. "Nabol mustered *two* after Leri threatened them! There was no illness at Crom or Nabol. Lazy, ignorant, stupid mountaineers! They've used this plague of Capiam's as an excuse to avoid their obligations to me! If this Weyr can fly, they can bloody well do their part! And I'll have a word with Master Capiam about those drum messages of his, panicking the holders."

"There's been another drum message," Moreta began, unable to soften her news. "Ista, Igen, and Telgar have sick riders. The Weyrs may find it hard to discharge their obligation."

"This Weyr will always discharge its duty while I'm Leader!" Sh'gall glared at her as if she had disputed him. Then he whirled and faced those lingering at the dining tables of the cavern. "Have I made myself plain to you all? Fort Weyr will do its duty!"

His declaration was punctuated by the sound that every rider dreaded, the nerve-abrading shrill high shriek of dragons announcing the death of one of their kind.

Ch'mon, bronze rider of Igen, died of fever, and his dragon, Helith, promptly went *between*. He was the first of two from that Weyr. During the evening five more died at Telgar. Fort Weyr was in shock.

Sh'gall was livid as he hauled Curmir with him to send a double-urgent message to the Healer Hall, demanding to know the state of the continent, what was being done to curb the spread, and what remedies effected a cure.

He was even more upset when Fortine replied that the disease was now considered pandemic. The response repeated that there had been recoveries: Isolation was imperative. Suggested treatment was febrifuge rather than a diaporetic, judicious use of aconite for palpitations, willowsalic or fellis juice for headache, comfrey, tussilago, or preferred local cough remedy. Sh'gall made Curmir inquire double-urgent for a reply from Master Capiam. The Healer Hall acknowledged the inquiry but sent no explanation.

"Does anyone know," he demanded at the top of his voice as he rampaged back into the Lower Caverns, "if this is what K'lon had?" He glared at the stunned blue rider, his eyes brilliant with an intensity that was beyond mere fury. "What has Berchar been dosing himself with? Do you know?" Now he almost pounced on Moreta where she sat.

"S'gor tells me he has been using what Master Fortine suggests. K'lon *has* recovered."

"But Ch'mon has died!"

His statement became an accusation, and she was at fault.

"The illness is among us, Sh'gall," Moreta said, gathering strength from an inner source whose name was Orlith. "Nothing we can do or say *now* alters that. No one forced us to attend the Gathers, you know." Her wayward humor brought grim smiles to several of the faces about her. "And most of us enjoyed ourselves."

"And look what happened!" Sh'gall's body vibrated with his fury.

"We can't reverse the happening, Sh'gall. K'lon survived the plague as we have survived Thread today and every Fall the past forty-three Turns, as we have survived all the other natural disasters that have visited us since the Crossing." She smiled wearily. "We must be good at surviving to have lived so long on this planet."

The weyrfolk and the riders began to take heart at Moreta's words, but Sh'gall gave her another long stare of outraged disgust and stalked out of the Lower Caverns.

The confrontation had shaken Moreta. She was drained of all energy, even Orlith's, and it had become an effort to keep upright. She gripped the edge of her chair, trembling. It wasn't just Sh'gall's rage but the unpalatable, unavoidable knowledge that she was very likely the next victim of the plague in the Weyr. Her head was beginning to ache and it was not the kind that succeeded tension or the stress and concentration of repairing dragon injuries.

You are not well, Orlith said, confirming her self-diagnosis.

I have probably not been well since I went to that runner's rescue, Moreta replied. *L'mal always said that runners would be my downfall.*

You have not fallen down. You have fallen ill, Orlith corrected her, dryly humorous in turn. *Come now to the weyr and rest.*

"Curmir." Moreta beckoned the harper forward. "In view of Berchar's illness, I think we must demand another healer from the Hall. A Master-healer and at least another journeyman."

Curmir nodded slowly but gave her a long, searching look.

"S'peren is to contrive a support sling for Dilenth. We cannot expect T'grath to stand under his wing until it heals. Such sacrifices sour weyr-mates!" Moreta managed to rise, carefully planting her feet under her so as not to jar her aching skull. Never had a headache arrived with such speed and intensity. She was nearly blinded by it. "I think that's all for now. It's been a difficult day and I'm tired."

Curmir offered her assistance but she discouraged him with a hand gesture and walked slowly from the Lower Cavern.

Without Orlith's constant encouragement, Moreta would not have been able to cross the Bowl, which, in the sudden chill of the night air, seemed to have perversely grown wider. At the stairs, she had to brace herself several times against the inner wall.

"So, it's got to you," Leri said unexpectedly. The older Weyrwoman was sitting on the steps to her weyr, both hands resting on her walking stick.

"Don't come near me."

"You don't see me rising from my perch, do you? You're probably contagious. However, Orlith appealed to me. I can see why now. Get into your bed." Leri brandished her cane. "I've already measured out the medicine you should take, according to that drum roll of Fortine's. Willow salic, aconite, featherfern. Oh, and the wine has a dose of fellis juice from my own stock. The sacrifices I make for you. Shoo! I can't carry you, you know. You'll have to make it on your own. You will. You always do. And I've done more than enough for one day for this Weyr!"

Leri's chivvying gave Moreta the impetus to stagger up the last few steps and into the corridor of her weyr. At its end she could see Orlith's eyes gleaming with the pale yellow of concern. She paused for a moment, winded, her head pounding unbearably.

"I assume that no one in the Lower Caverns suspected you've been taken ill?"

"Curmir. Won't talk, though."

"Sensible of you in view of the Igen death. She'll make it, Orlith." Then Leri waved her cane angrily. "No, you will not help. You'd jam the corridor with your egg-heavy belly. Go on with you, Moreta. I'm *not* going to stand on these chilly steps all night. I need my rest. Tomorrow's going to be very busy for me."

"I hoped you'd volunteer."

"I'm not so lacking in sense that I'd let Nesso get out of hand. Go! Get yourself well," she added in a kinder tone, heaving herself to her feet.

Orlith did meet Moreta at the end of the corridor, extending her head so that Moreta could hang onto something to cross the chamber. Orlith crooned encouragement, love and devotion and comfort in almost palpable waves. Then Moreta was in her own quarters, her eyes fastening on the medicine set out on the table. She blessed Leri, knowing what an effort it had been for the old Weyrwoman to navigate the steps. Moreta took the fellis wine down in one swallow, grimacing against the bitterness not even the wine could disguise. How could Leri sip it all day? Without undressing, Moreta slid under the furs and carefully laid her head down on the pillow.

Healer Hall, Present Pass, 3.13.43;
Butte Meeting and Fort Weyr, 3.14.43;
Healer Hall, 3.15.43

Capiam could not remain asleep, though he tried to burrow back into the crazy fever-dreams as a more acceptable alternative to the miseries total awareness brought. Something impinged on his semiconsciousness and forced him awake. Something he had to do? Yes, something he had to do. He blinked bleary, crusted eyes until he could focus on the timepiece. Nine of the clock. "Oh, it's me. Time for my medicine."

A healer couldn't even be sick without responding to his professional habits. He hauled himself up on one elbow to reach for the skin on which he was recording his progress through the disease but a coughing spasm interrupted him. The cough seemed to throw tiny knives at his throat. Such spasms were exceedingly painful, and Capiam disliked them even more than the headache, the fever, and the boneache.

Cautiously, lest he provoke another coughing fit, he dragged the note case onto his bed and fumbled for the writing tool.

"Only the third day?" His illness seemed to have made each twenty-four hours an eternity of minor miseries. That day was mercifully three quarters done.

He could take little comfort in noticing that his fever had abated, that the headache was a dullness that could be endured. He placed the fingers of his right hand lightly on the arterial pulse in the left wrist. Still faster than normal, but slowing. He made an appropriate notation and added a description of the hardy, dry, unproductive cough. As if the note was the cue, he was wracked with another fit that tore at his throat and upper chest like a tunnel snake. He was forced to lie in a fetal position, knees up to his chin to relieve the muscle spasms that accompanied the cough. When it had passed, he lay back, sweating and exhausted. He roused enough to take his dose of willow salic.

He must prescribe a cough remedy for himself. What would be the most effective suppressant? He touched his painful throat. What must the lining of his throat resemble?

"This is most humiliating," he told himself, his voice hoarse. He vowed to be far more sympathetic to the afflicted in the future.

The drum tower began to throb and the message stunned him for condolences were being transmitted from Lord Tolocamp—what was *he* doing in Fort Hold when he should have remained at Ruatha?—to the Weyrleaders of Telgar and Igen for the deaths of . . . Capiam writhed on the bed, convulsed by coughing that left him weak and panting. He missed the names of the dead riders. Dead riders! Pern could ill afford to lose any of its dragonriders.

Why, oh why hadn't he been called in earlier? Surely nine people in the same Sea Hold falling sick was an unusual enough occurrence to have warranted even a courtesy report to the main Healer Hall? Would he have appreciated the significance?

"Capiam?" Desdra's query was low enough not to have aroused him had he been asleep.

"I'm awake, Desdra." His voice was a hoarse caw.

"You heard the drums?"

"Part of the message—"

"The wrong part from the sound of you."

"Don't come any closer! How many riders died?"

"The toll is now fifteen at Igen, two at Ista, and eight at Telgar."

Capiam could think of nothing to say.

"How many are ill, then?" His voice faltered.

"They report recoveries," Desdra said in a crisper voice. "Nineteen at Telgar, fourteen at Igen, five at Ista, two at Fort are all convalescing."

"And at Hall and Hold?" He dreaded her answer, clenching his fists to bear the staggering totals.

"Fortine has taken charge, Boranda and Tirone are assisting." The finality in her tone told Capiam he would not elicit any further information.

"Why are you in my room?" he demanded testily. "You know—"

"I know that you have reached the coughing stage and I have prepared a soothing syrup."

"How do you know what I would prescribe for my condition?"

"The fool who treats himself has only a fool for a patient."

Capiam wanted to laugh at her impudence, but the attempt turned into one of the hideously painful, long coughs and, by the time it had passed, tears rolled down his cheeks.

"A nice blend of comfrey, sweetener, and a touch of numbweed to deaden the throat tissues. It ought to inhibit the cough." She deposited the steaming mug on his table and was swiftly across the room by the door.

"You're a brave and compassionate woman, Desdra," he said, ignoring her sarcastic snort.

"I am also cautious. If at all possible, I would prefer to avoid the agonies which I have observed you enduring."

"Am I such a difficult patient?" Capiam asked plaintively, seeking more consolation than he could find in a mug of an odd-tasting syrup.

"What cannot be cured must be endured," Desdra replied.

"By which unkind words I assume that the Records have not given up either an account or a remedy."

"Master Tirone joined the search with all his apprentices, journeymen, and masters. They proceed backward by the decade for two hundred Turns and forward from the previous Pass."

Capiam's groan quickly degenerated into a spasm that again left him gasping for breath. Each of the two hundred bones in his body conspired to ache at once. He heard Desdra rummaging among his bottles and vials.

"I saw an aromatic salve in here. Rubbed on your chest it might relieve you, since you spilled most of that potion."

"I'll rub it on myself, woman!"

"Indeed you will. Here it is! Phew! That'll clear your sinuses."

"They don't need it." Capiam could smell the aromatic from his bed. Odd how the olfactory senses became acute in this disease. Exhausted by the last cough spasm, he lay still.

"Are you experiencing the severe lassitude as well as the dry cough?"

"Lassitude?" Capiam dared not laugh but the word was totally inadequate to describe the total inertia that gripped his usually vigorous body. "Extreme lassitude! Total inertia! Complete incapacity! I can't even drink from a mug without spilling half of it. I have never been so tired in my life—"

"Oh, then, you're proceeding well on the course of the disease."

"How consoling!" He had just enough energy for sarcasm.

"If"—and her emphasis teased him—"your notes are correct, you should be improving by tomorrow. That is, if we can keep you in your bed and prevent secondary infections."

"How comforting."

"It should be."

His head was beginning to buzz again from the willow salic. He was about to commend Desdra on the efficacy of her cough mixture when a totally unprovoked tickle bent him double to cough.

"I'll leave you to get on with it then," Desdra said cheerily.

He waved urgently for her to leave the room, then put both hands on his throat as if he could find some grip to ease the pain.

He hoped that Desdra was being careful. He didn't want her to catch the illness. Why hadn't those wretched seamen left that animal to drown? Look to what depths curiosity brought a man!

Butte Meeting, 3.14.43

Deep in the plains of Keroon and far from any hold, a granite butte had been forced to the surface during some primeval earthquake. The landmark had often been used as an objective in weyrling training flights. Just then it was the site of an unprecedented meeting of the Weyrleaders.

The great bronze dragons arrived almost simultaneously at the site, coming out of *between* full lengths clear of each other's wing tip, utilizing their uncanny perceptions of proximity. They settled to the ground in an immense circle at the southern face of the butte. The bronze riders dismounted, closing to a slightly smaller circle, each rider keeping a wary distance from those on either side until K'dren of Benden, who had an active sense of humor under any conditions, chuckled.

"None of us would be here if we were sickening," he said, nodding to S'peren who had come in Sh'gall's place.

"Too many of *us* have," L'bol of Igen replied. His eyes were red with weeping.

M'tani of Telgar scowled and clenched his fists.

"We have shared each loss," S'ligar of the High Reaches said with grave courtesy, inclining his head first to L'bol, M'tani, and F'gal of Ista. The other two bronze riders murmured their condolences. "We have gathered here to take emergency measures which discretion keeps from the drum and which our queens are unable to relay," S'ligar went on. As the oldest of the Weyrleaders, he took command of the meeting. He was also the biggest, topping the other bronze riders by a full head, and the breadth of him through chest and shoulders would have made two of most ordinary men. He was oddly gentle, never taking advantage of his size. "As our Weyrwomen have pointed out, we cannot admit the losses and numbers of the ill that the Weyrs have sustained. There is too much anxiety in the Holds as it is. They are suffering far more than we are."

"That's no consolation!" F'gal snapped. "I don't know how many times I warned Lord Fitatric that overcrowding hold and cot would have dire consequences."

"None of us had *this* in mind," K'dren said. "However, none of *us* had to run see the curious new beastie from the sea. Or attend two Gathers in one day—"

"Enough, K'dren," S'ligar said. "Cause and effect are now irrelevant. Our purpose here is to discuss how best to ensure that the dragonriders of Pern fulfill their purpose."

"That *purpose* is dying out, S'ligar," L'bol cried. "What's the purpose of flying Thread to protect empty holds? Why preserve *nothing* at the risk of our skins and our dragons? We can't even defend ourselves from this plague!" L'bol's dragon crooned and extended his head toward his distressed rider. The other bronzes rumbled comfortingly and moved restlessly on the warm sand. L'bol scrubbed at his face, leaving white runnels where tears had wet his cheeks.

"We will fly Thread because that is the one service we can provide the sick in the Holds. They must not fear the incursions of Thread from without!" S'ligar said in his deep gentle unhurried voice. "We have labored too long as a Craft to surrender Pern now to the ravages of Thread because of a menace we can't see. Nor do I believe that this disease, however fiercely it spreads, however ruthless it appears, can overcome *us* who have for hundreds of Turns defended ourselves from Thread. A disease can be cured by medicines, defeated. And one day we will fly Thread to *its* source and defeat it."

"K'lon, Rogeth's rider, has recovered from the plague," S'peren announced in the silence following S'ligar's statement. "K'lon says that Master Capiam is on the mend—"

"Two?" L'bol flung the number derisively back at S'peren. "I've fifteen dead, one hundred and forty sick at Igen. Some holds in the mideast no longer respond to their drum codes. And what of the holds which have no drums to make known their needs and the toll of their dead?"

"Capiam on the mend?" S'ligar said, seizing at that hope. "I have every faith in that man's ability to lick this. And more than those two must have recovered. Keroon Beasthold still drums, and they were the hardest hit by the plague. High Reaches and Fort Weyrs have sickness, it is true, but the holds of Tillek, High Reaches, Nabol, and Crom have none." S'ligar tried to catch L'bol's despairing gaze. "We have only seven Turns to go before this Pass is over. I have lived under the scourge of Thread all my life." Suddenly he straightened his shoulders, his face severe. "I haven't fought Thread as a dragonrider for nearly fifty Turns to quit now over some fever and aches!"

"Nor I," K'dren added quickly, taking a step toward the High Reacher. "I made a vow, you know"—he gave a short laugh—"to Kuzuth, that we would see this Pass through." K'dren's tone turned brisk. "There's Fall tomorrow at Keroon, and it has become the responsibility of all the Weyrs of Pern. Benden has twelve full wings to fly."

"Igen has eight!" Anger brought L'bol out of his despondency to glare fiercely at K'dren. Timenth, his dragon, bugled defiance, rearing back onto his haunches and spreading his wings. The other bronzes reacted in surprise, sounding off. Two extended their wings and gazed skyward in alarm. "Igen will rise to Fall!"

"Of course your Weyr will rise," S'ligar said reassuringly, raising his arm in an incomplete gesture of comfort. "But our queens know how many Igen riders are ill. Fall has become the problem of all the Weyrs, as K'dren said. And we all supply the muster from our healthy riders. Until this epidemic is over, the Weyrs must consolidate. Full wings are essential since, in many places, we shall be deprived of ground crews for close encounters with Thread."

S'ligar took a thick roll of hide from his pouch. With a deft flick of his wrist, the roll fell into five separate sections on the sand. Mindful to make no physical contact with the other Leaders, S'ligar slid a section to each of the other bronze riders.

"Here are the names of my wingleaders and seconds, since naming people seems to be a deficiency in our queens. I've listed my riders in order of their competence for assuming command of either wing or Weyr. B'lerion is my choice of a personal successor." Then a rare and brilliant smile crossed the High Reacher's face. "With Falga's complete accord."

K'dren roared with laughter. "Didn't she suggest him?"

S'ligar regarded K'dren with mild reproof. "It is the wise Leader who anticipates his Weyrwoman's mind."

"Enough!" M'tani called irritably. His dark eyes were angry under heavy black brows. He threw his lists down to join S'ligar's. "T'grel has always fancied himself a Leader. He reminded me that he hadn't been to either of the Gathers so I'll reward his virtue."

"You're fortunate," K'dren said with no humor in his voice. He added his lists to the others. "L'vin, W'ter, and H'grave attended both Gathers. I've recommended M'gent. He may be young but he's got a natural flair for leadership that one doesn't often see. He wasn't at the Gathers."

F'gal seemed unwilling to lose the sheets he unwound. "It's all on these," he said wearily, letting them flutter to the sand.

"Leri suggested me," S'peren said with a self-deprecating shrug, "though it's likely Sh'gall will make a change when he recovers. He was too fevered to be told of this meeting so Leri drew up the lists."

"Leri would know." K'dren nodded. He went down on his haunches to pick up the five slips of hide, aligning them at the top before rolling. "I shall be pleased if these can gather dust in my weyr." He stuffed the roll in his pouch. "It is, however, a comfort to have made plans, to have considered contingencies."

"Saves a lot of unnecessary worry," S'ligar agreed, bending to scoop up the scraps into his long-fingered hand. "I also recommend that we use entire wings as replacements, rather than send individuals as substitutes. Riders get used to their wingleaders and seconds."

The recommendation found favor with the others.

"Full wings or substitutes is not the real worry." L'bol glowered at the lists as he assembled them in his hand. "It's the lack of ground crews."

K'dren snorted. "No worry. Not when the queens have already decided among themselves to do that job. We've all been informed, no doubt, that every queen who can fly will attend every Fall."

M'tani's scowl was sour and neither L'bol nor F'gal appeared happy, but S'ligar shrugged diffidently. "They will arrange matters to suit themselves no matter what but queens keep promises."

"Who suggested using weyrlings for ground crews?" M'tani asked.

"We may have to resort to them," S'ligar said.

"Weyrlings don't have enough sense—" M'tani began.

"Depends on their Weyrlingmaster, doesn't it?" K'dren asked.

"The queens intend"—S'ligar put in before M'tani could take offense at K'dren's remark—"to keep the weyrlings under control. What other choice have we in the absence of ground crews?"

"Well, I've never known a weyrling yet who would disobey a queen," F'gal admitted.

"S'peren, with Moreta ill, does Kamiana lead?"

"No. Leri." S'peren looked apprehensive. "After all, she's done it before."

The Weyrleaders murmured in surprised protest.

"Well, if any of your Weyrwoman can talk her out of it, we'd be very relieved." S'peren did not hide his distress. "She's more than done her duty by the Weyrs and Pern. On the other hand, she *knows* how to lead. With both Sh'gall and Moreta sick, the Weyr at least trusts her."

"How is Moreta?" S'ligar asked.

"Leri says Orlith doesn't seem worried. She carries her eggs well and she is very near clutching. It's as well Moreta is sick or they'd be out and about Pern. You know how keen Moreta is on runners."

M'tani snorted with disgust. "This is not the time to lose an egg-heavy queen," he said. "This sickness hits so fast and kills so quickly, the dragons don't realize what's happening. And then *they're* gone *between*." He caught his breath, clenching his teeth and swallowing against tears. The other riders pretended not to see his evident distress.

"Once Orlith has clutched she won't go until they've hatched," S'ligar said gently to no one in particular. "S'peren, have you candidates safely at Fort Weyr?"

S'peren shook his head. "We'd that yet to do and thought there was worlds of time for Search."

"Pick carefully before you bring anyone new into your Weyr!" L'bol advised sourly.

"If the need arises, High Reaches has a few promising youngsters who are healthy. I'm sure an adequate number can be made up from the other Weyrs?" S'ligar waited for the murmur of assent to go round the circle. "You'll inform Leri?"

"Fort Weyr is grateful."

"Is that all?" L'bol demanded as he turned toward his dragon.

"Not quite. One more point while we are convened." S'ligar hitched up his belt. "I know that some of us have thought of exploring the Southern Continent once this Pass is over—"

"After this?" L'bol stared at S'ligar in total disbelief.

"My point. In spite of the Instructions left to us, we cannot risk further contagions. Southern must be left alone!" S'ligar made a cutting gesture with the flat of his huge hand. He looked to the Benden Weyrleader for comment.

"An eminently sensible prohibition," K'dren said.

M'tani flourished his hand curtly to show agreement and turned to S'peren.

"Of course, I cannot speak for Sh'gall but I cannot conceive why Fort would disagree."

"The continent will be interdicted by my Weyr, I assure you," F'gal said in a loud, strained voice.

"Then we shall leave it to the queens to communicate how many wings each Weyr supplies for Fall until this emergency is over. We've all the details we need to go on." S'ligar brandished his roll before he shoved it in his tunic. "Very well then, my friends. Good flying! May your Weyrs—" He caught himself, a flicker of uncertainty for his glib use of a courteous salutation not entirely appropriate.

"The Weyrs will prosper, S'ligar," K'dren said as he smiled confidently at the big man. "They always have!"

The bronze riders turned to their dragons, mounting with the ease and grace of long practice. Almost as one, the six dragons wheeled to the left and right of the red butte, to spring agilely into the air. Again, as if the unique maneuver had been many times rehearsed, on the third downstroke of six pairs of great wings, the dragons went *between*.

Fort Weyr, 3.14.43

At about the time the bronze dragonriders were meeting at the Butte, Capiam had discovered that if he timed a fit of coughing, he could miss some of the incoming, more painful messages. Even after the thrumming of the great drums in the tower had ceased, the cadences played ring-a-round in his head and inhibited the sleep he yearned for. Not that sleep brought any rest. He would feel more tired when he roused from such brief naps as the drums permitted. And the nightmares! He was forever being harried by that tawny, speckle-coated, tuft-eared monster that had carried its peculiar germs to a vulnerable continent. The irony was that the Ancients had probably created the agency that threatened to exterminate their descendants.

If only those seamen had let the animal die on its tree trunk in the Eastern Current. If only it had died on the ship, succumbing to thirst and exhaustion—as Capiam felt he was likely to do at any moment—before it had contaminated more than the seamen. If only the nearby holders hadn't been so bloody curious to relieve the winter's tedium. If! If! If? If wishes were dragons, all Pern would fly!

And *if* Capiam had any energy, he would apply it to finding a concoction that would relieve and, preferably, inhibit the disease. Surely the Ancients had had to cope with epidemics. There were, indeed, grand paragraphs in the oldest Records, boasting that the ailments that had plagued mankind before the Crossing had been totally eliminated on Pern—which statement, Capiam maintained, meant that there had been two Crossings, not one, as many people—including Tirone—believed. The Ancients had brought many animals with them in that first Crossing, the equine from which runners originated; the bovine for the herdbeasts; the ovine, smaller, herdbeasts; the canine; and a smaller variety of the dratted feline plague carrier. The creatures had been brought, in ova (or so the Record put it) from the Ancients' planet or origin which was not the planet Pern, or why had that one point been made so specifically and repeated so often? Pern, not simply the Southern Continent. And the second Crossing had been from south to north. Probably, Capiam contemplated bitterly, to escape feline plague carriers that secreted themselves in dark lairs to nourish their fell disease until unwary humans took them off tree trunks, days from land. Couldn't the Ancients have stopped bragging about their achievements long enough to state *how* they had eradicated plague and pandemic? Their success was meaningless without the process.

Capiam plucked feebly at the sleeping furs. They smelled. They needed to be aired. He smelled. He didn't dare leave his room. "What can't be cured must be endured." Desdra's taunt returned to him often.

He was a healer: He would heal himself first and thus prove to others that one could recover from this miserable disease. He need only apply his trained mind and considerable willpower to the problem. On cue, a coughing spell wracked him. When he had recovered sufficiently, he reached for the syrup Desdra left on the beside table. He wished she would look in on him.

Fortine had, conferring three times from the doorway, seeking authority on matters Capiam could not now recall. He hoped that his responses had been sensible. Tirone had appeared, very briefly, more to assure himself and to report to the world that Capiam was still part of it than to comfort or cheer the sick man.

Fort Hold proper had not been sullied by the plague, even though healers—master, journeyman, and apprentice—had journeyed to the stricken areas. Four of Fort's seaside holds and two coastal cropholds had succumbed.

The syrup eased Capiam's raw throat. He could even taste it. Thymus was the principal ingredient, and he approved of its use on his person. If the disease ran the same course in him as it had in the cases he had studied, the cough ought soon to pass. If, by virtue of the strict quarantine in which he lay, he did not contract a secondary infection—pulmonary, pneumonic, or bronchial seemed the readiest to pounce on the weakened patient—then he ought to improve rapidly.

K'lon, the blue rider from Fort Weyr, had recovered totally. Capiam hoped that the man had actually *had* the plague, not some deep cold, and his hope was substantiated by the facts that K'lon had a close friend in plague-stricken Igen, and that the Weyr healer, Berchar, and his green rider weyrmate were grievously ill at Fort Weyr. Capiam tried to censor his own painful thoughts of dragonriders dying as easily as holders. Dragonriders could *not* die. The Pass had eight Turns to go. There were hundreds of powders, roots, and barks and herbs to combat disease on Pern, but the numbers of dragons and their riders were limited.

Desdra really ought to be appearing soon with some of the restorative soup she took such pleasure in making him consume! It was her presence he wished for, not the soup, for he found the long hours of solitude without occupation tedious and fraught with unpleasant speculations. He knew he ought to be grateful to have a room to himself for the chances of further infection were thus reduced to the minimum, but he would have liked some company. Then he thought of the crowded holds and he had no doubt that some poor sod there would dearly love to exchange with him for solitude.

Capiam took no pleasure in the knowledge that his frequent haragues to the Lords Holder about indiscriminate breeding should prove so devastatingly accurate. But dragonriders ought not to be dying of this plague. They had private quarters, were hardy, inured to many of the ailments that afflicted those in poorer conditions, were supplied with the top of the tithe. Igen, Keroon, Ista: Those Weyrs had had direct contact with the feline. And Fort, High Reaches, and Benden riders had attended the Gathers. Almost every rider had had time and opportunity to catch the infection.

Capiam had had severe qualms about demanding a conveyance of Sh'gall from Southern Boll to Fort Hold. But, on the other hand, Sh'gall had conveyed Lord Ratoshigan to Ista Gather for the purpose of seeing the rare creature on display quite a few hours before Capiam and the young animal healer, Talpan, had their startling conference. It was only after Capiam had reached Southern Boll and seen Lord Ratoshigan's sick handlers that he had realized how quickly the disease incubated and how insidiously it spread. Expediency had required Capiam to use the quickest means to return to his Hall, and that had been adragonback with the Fort Weyrleader. Sh'gall had taken ill but he was young and healthy, Capiam told himself. So had Ratoshigan, but Capiam found a rather curious justice in that. Given the infinite variety of human personalities, it was impossible to like everyone. Capiam didn't like Ratoshigan but he shouldn't be glad the man was suffering along with his lowliest beasthandler.

Capiam vowed, yet again, that he would have far more tolerance for the ill when he recovered. *When! When!* Not *if. If* was defeatist. How had the many thousands of patients he tended over his Turns as a healer endured those hours of unrelieved thought and self-examination? Capiam sighed, tears forming at the corners of his eyes: a further manifestation of his terrible inertia. When—yes, *when*—would he have the strength to resume constructive thought and research?

There *had* to be an answer, a solution, a cure, a therapy, a restorative, a remedy! Something existed somewhere. If the Ancients had been able to cross unimaginable distances to breed animals from a frozen stew, to create dragons from the template of the legendary fire-lizards, they surely would have been able to overcome bacterium or virus that threatened themselves and those beasts. It could only be a matter of time, Capiam assured his weary self, before those references were discovered. Fortine had been searching the Records piled in the Library Caves. When he had had to dispatch journeymen and apprentice healers to reinforce their overworked craftsmen in the worst plague areas, Tirone had magnanimously placed his craftspeople at Fortine's disposal. But if one of those untutored readers passed over the relevant paragraphs in ignorance of the significance . . . Surely, though, something as critical as an epidemic would merit more than a single reference.

When would Desdra come with her soup to break the monotony of his anxious self-castigation? "Stop fretting," he told himself, his voice a hoarse croak that startled him. "You're peevish. You're also alive. What must be endured cannot be cured. No. What cannot be cured must be inured—endured."

Tears for his debilitation dripped down his cheekbones, falling in time to the latest urgent drum code. Capiam wanted to stop his ears against the news. It was sure to be bad. How could it possibly be anything else until they had some sort of specific treatment and some means of arresting the swift spread of this plague?

Keroon Runnerhold sent the message. They needed medicines. Healer Gorby reported dwindling stocks of borrago and aconite, and needed tussilago in quantity for pulmonary and bronchial cases, ilex for pneumonia.

A new fear enveloped Capiam. With such unprecedented demands on stillroom supplies, would there be enough of even the simple medicaments? Keroon Runnerhold, dealing as it did with many animal health problems, ought to be able to supply all its needs. Capiam despaired afresh as he thought of smaller holds. They would have on hand only a limited amount of general remedies. Most holds traded the plants and barks indigenous in their area for those they lacked. What lady holder, no matter how diligent and capable, would have laid in sufficient to deal with an epidemic?

To compound demand, the disease had struck during the cold season. Most medicinal plants were picked in flower, when their curative properties were strongest; roots and bulbs gathered in the fall. Spring and flowering, autumn and earthy harvest were too distant, the need was now!

Capiam writhed in his furs. Where was Desdra? How much longer did he have to endure before the wretched lethargy abated?

"Capiam?" Desdra's quiet voice broke into his self-pitying ruminations. "More soup?"

"Desdra? That message from Keroon Runnerhold—"

"As if we had only one febrifuge in our pharmacopia! Fortine has compiled a list of alternatives." Desdra was impatient with Gorby. "There's ash bark, box, ezob, and thymus as well as borrago and featherfern. Who's to say one of them might not prove to be specific for this? In fact, Semment of Great Reach Hold believes that thymus is more effective for the pulmonary infections he's been treating. Master Fortine holds out for featherfern, being one of the few indigenous plants. How are you feeling?"

"Like nothing! I cannot even raise my hands." He tried to demonstrate this inability.

"The lassitude is part of the illness. You wrote that symptom often enough. What can't be cured—"

Summoning strength from a sudden spurt of irrational anger, Capiam flung a pillow at her. It had neither the mass nor the impetus to reach its target, and she laughed as she collected the missile and lofted it easily back to his bed.

"I believe that you are somewhat improved in spirit. Now drink the soup." She set it down on the table.

"Are all healthy here?"

"All here, yes. Even the officious Tolocamp, immured in his quarters. He's more likely to catch pneumonia while standing at unshuttered windows to check up on the guards." Desdra chuckled maliciously. "He's got messengers stationed on the forecourt. He sails notes down to them to take to offenders. Not even a tunnel snake could slip past his notice!" A tiny smirk curved Desdra's lips. "Master Tirone had to talk long and hard to get him to set up that internment camp in the hollow. Tolocamp was certain that offering shelter would be an invitation to undesirables to lodge and feed at his expense. Tirone is furious with Tolocamp because he wants to send his harpers out with the assurance that they can return, but Tolocamp refuses to believe that harpers can avoid infection. Tolocamp sees the disease as a visible mist or fog that oozes out of meadows and streams and mountain crevices."

Desdra was trying to amuse him, Capiam thought, for she wasn't normally garrulous.

"I did order a quarantine."

Desdra snorted. "True! Tolocamp ought not to have left Ruatha. He overruled the brother when Alessan fell ill. And with every other breath, Tolocamp is said to moan for abandoning his dear wife, Lady Pendra, and those precious daughters of his to the mercies of the plague rampaging at Ruatha." Desdra's chuckle was dry. "He left them there on purpose. Or Lady Pendra insisted they all stay. They'll have insisted on nursing Alessan!"

"How *are* matters at Fort Weyr and Ruatha?"

"K'lon tells us that Moreta is doing as well as can be expected. Berchar probably has pneumonia, and nineteen riders—including Sh'gall—are weyred. Ruatha is badly hit. Fortine has dispatched volunteers. Now drink that soup before it cools. There's much to be done below. I can't stay to chat with you any longer."

Capiam found that his hand shook violently as he picked up the mug.

"Shouldn't've wasted all that energy tossing that pillow," she said.

He used both hands to bring the mug to his lips without spilling. "What *have* you put in it?" he demanded after a careful swallow.

"A little of this, a little of that. Trying a few restoratives out on you. If they work, I'll make kettlesful."

"It's vile!"

"It's also nutritional. Drink it!"

"I'll choke."

"Drink it or I'll let Nerilka, that laundry pole daughter of Tolocamp's, come nurse you in my stead. She offers hourly."

Capiam cursed Desdra but he drained the cup.

"Well, you do sound improved!" She chuckled as she closed the door quietly behind her.

❖ ❖ ❖

"I didn't say I liked it either," Leri told S'peren. "But old dragons can glide. That's why Holth and I can still fly Thread in the queens' wing." Leri gave Holth an affectionate clout on the shoulder, beaming up at her life-long friend. "It's the tip, the finger, and elbow joints that harden so the finer points of maneuverability go. Gliding's from the shoulder. Doesn't take much effort, either, with the sort of wind we're likely to get now. Why did it have to get so bloody cold on top of everything else? Rain'd be more bearable as well as more seasonable." Leri adjusted the furs across her shoulders. "I wouldn't trust the weyrlings to such dull work. They'd do something fancy, like the stunt young T'ragel tried on the ridge with Moreta.

"Now, you said L'bol is grieving badly?"

"Indeed he is. He's lost both sons." S'peren shook his head sadly before he took another sip of the wine Leri had served him "to wet your throat after the dust at Red Butte." S'peren took comfort in the familiar act of reporting to Leri. It was like the old times, only a few Turns past at that, when L'mal had been Weyrleader and S'peren had been much in this weyr. He almost expected to see L'mal's chunky figure swing into the chamber and hear the hearty voice greeting him. Now *there* was a Leader to encourage and comfort in this disastrous Turn. Still, S'peren thought with a blink, Leri was as brisk and quick as ever. "Could Igen put eight full wings up to Fall?"

"What?" Leri snapped out in surprise at the question, then snorted.

"Not likely. Torenth told Holth that half the Weyr is sick and the other half looks sick. Their damned curiosity and all that sun on their heads all the time. Slows 'em down. Nothing to do with their spare time but bake their brains. Of course, they all went to gawk at a raree! And we'll never hear the last of their moans for the unexpected tariff!" She made a business of scanning the lists S'peren had handed her. "Can't say as I can put a face or pair a dragon name with some of these. Must all be new. When L'mal was Leader, I kept up with all the new riders in every Weyr."

"S'ligar asked about Moreta."

"Worried about Orlith and her eggs?" Leri peered wisely over the lists at the bronze rider.

S'peren nodded. "S'ligar volunteered candidates in case—"

"Only what I'd expect." Leri's answer was tart but, seeing the expression on S'peren's face, she relented. "It was good of him to offer. Especially since Orlith is the only queen currently bearing eggs." Leri's round face produced a slightly malicious smile.

S'peren continued to nod for he hadn't realized that. It put another light on S'ligar's concern for Moreta and Orlith.

"Don't worry, S'peren. Moreta's doing well. Orlith's with her constantly and that queen's a marvel of comfort, as everyone in this Weyr should know by now."

"I thought it was just with injured dragons."

"And no comfort for her own weyrmate and rider? Of course Orlith helps Moreta. The other Weyrs could learn a thing or two from our senior queen dragon. Wouldn't surprise me if there were some pretty crucial changes made when Moreta's well. And when Orlith rises to mate again!" Leri winked broadly at S'peren. "That girl has got to show her true preference to her queen."

S'peren managed to hide his surprise at Leri's outspokenness. Of course, they were old friends and she probably felt able to be candid in his company. Then he took a quick sip of the wine. What could Leri possibly be suggesting? He liked Moreta very much. She and Orlith had done a fine job of healing a long Threadscore on his Clioth's flank last Turn. And Clioth had risen to fly in Orlith's last mating flight. He had been perversely relieved when Clioth had failed, despite his admiration and respect for Moreta, and despite a natural desire to prove his bronze dragon superior to the other bronzes of Fort. On the other hand, he had never questioned Sh'gall's ability as a flight leader. The man had an uncanny instinct for which dragon might be failing in strength or losing his flame, or which rider might not be as courageous as he ought in following Thread out of path, but S'peren did not covet the Leadership half as much as his Clioth yearned to mate with Orlith.

"K'lon?" Leri said, breaking into his thoughts. She and her dragon looked toward the weyr entrance.

Clioth confirmed the arrival of Rogeth to S'peren, telling his rider that he was moving over to permit the blue to land on Holth's ledge.

"About bloody time that young man came back to his own Weyr," Leri said, frowning. "There *has* to be another dragonrider able to do what K'lon's doing or he'll kill himself. Misplaced guilt. Or more likely the chance to get in and out of Igen to see that lover of his."

There was no question that the blue rider was exhausted as he entered the weyr. His shoulders sagged and his step had no spring. His face was travel-stained except for the lighter patches of skin around his eyes, protected from flight dirt by his goggles. His clothes were stiff with moisture frozen into the hide by constant journeys *between*.

"Five drops from the blue vial," Leri said quickly in an undertone, leaning toward S'peren. Then she straightened, speaking in a normal tone. "S'peren, fix a mug of klah laced with that fortified wine of mine for K'lon. And sit down there, young man, before you fall." Leri pointed imperiously to a chair. She had replaced her one stool with several comfortable seats positioned, as she phrased it, in noncontagious spacing in front of Holth's couch.

K'lon barely avoided falling into the appointed chair; his legs slid out in front of him as he slouched into the seat. Dangling helmet and goggles from one limp hand, he accepted the mug from S'peren.

"Take a long swallow now, K'lon," Leri said kindly. "It'll restore your blood to normal temperature after all that *betweening*. You're nearly as blue as Rogeth. There! That tastes good, doesn't it? A brew of my own to hearten the weary." Though her voice was kind, she watched K'lon intently. "Now, what news from the halls?"

K'lon's weary face brightened. "There is *good* news. Master Capiam really is recovering. I spoke to Desdra. He's weak but he's swearing out loud. She said they'd probably have to tether him to his bed to keep him there long enough to regain his strength. He's yelling for Records. Best of all"—K'lon seemed to shrug off his fatigue in his cheerful recital—"he insists that the disease itself doesn't cause the deaths. People are actually dying from other things, like pneumonia and bronchitis and other respiratory ailments. Avoid those and"—K'lon made a wide sweep of his hand, his helmet and goggles clacking together—"all's well." Then his expression altered dolefully. "Only that's just not possible in the Holds, you know. So many people crammed into inadequate space . . . and not enough facilities . . . especially now, when it's got so cold. The Lords Holder would put people into hide tents that are well enough for a Gather but not for the sick. I've been everywhere. Even holds that don't know what's been happening elsewhere and think it's only them that're in deep trouble. I've been so many places . . ." His face turned bleak and his body slumped deeper into the chair.

"A'murry?" Leri spoke the green rider's name gently.

K'lon's misery broke through the tight hold he must be keeping on his private anxiety. "He's got a chest infection—one of the weyrfolk nursing him had a bad cold." His condemnation was plain. "Fortine gave me a special mixture and a comfrey salve for his chest. I made A'murry take the first dose and it really did stop him midcough. And I rubbed the salve thick on his chest and back." Some instinct made K'lon look at the other two riders and he saw their unvoiced apprehension. "I've got to go to A'murry. Whenever I can. I can't *give* him what I've got over! And don't tell me it's enough that Rogeth and Granth stay in touch. I've very much aware that they do, but *I* have a need to be with A'murry, too, you know." K'lon's face contorted. He looked about to break into tears, a display he averted by drinking deeply of the wine-laced klah. "That's quite tasty, really," he said courteously to Leri. Then he finished the drink. "Now, what else can I tell you from my . . ."

He paused, blinked, swallowed, and then his head began to loll to one side. Leri, who had been waiting for that, signaled urgently to S'peren.

"Perfectly timed, I think," she said as S'peren caught K'lon before he slid from the chair. "Here." She tossed a pillow and pulled the fur from her shoulders. "Roll him into this, pillow his head, and he'll sleep a good twelve hours. Holth, be a pet and tell Rogeth to go curl up in his own weyr and get some rest. You"—she prodded the resisting flesh of her queen with her forefinger—"will keep your ears open for Granth."

"What if he's needed?" S'peren asked, arranging K'lon comfortably. "By the Halls or the Hold or A'murry?"

"A'murry is, of course, a priority," Leri replied thoughtfully. "I can't really condone his breaking of quarantine. I'll think of some discipline later, for K'lon *has* disobeyed a direct order. I have just decided that we can use other messengers in K'lon's place. Especially if most of what he does is convey supplies or healers. Weyrlings can do that! They'll feel brave and daring, and be scared enough to be careful. Packages can certainly be deposited without making contact and messages collected at a discreet distance from cots. Let them practice setting down by a pennant instead of a ridge. Good practice." Leri peered down critically at the sleeping K'lon. "However, you'd better circulate the news he brought us from the Hall—that the plague doesn't kill. We must be more wary than ever for our convalescents. No one with the slightest sign of a head cold or even a pimple is to attend the riders."

"It's hard enough to get weyrfolk to tend them," S'peren remarked.

"Hmm! Ask the laggards who will tend *them* in their hour of need?" Leri rolled up the rider lists and stowed them carefully on the shelf beside her. "So, old friend, you'll bring the good news from the Healer Hall to the Lower Caverns and *then* tell off the wings which are rising to Fall tomorrow!"

Healer Hall, 3.15.43

The light of the many glows that Capiam had ordered to illuminate the tight and fading script of the old ledgers shone harshly on the handsome countenance of Tirone, Masterharper of Pern, who had drawn a chair up to Capiam's wide writing desk. Tirone was scowling at the healer, a totally uncharacteristic expression on a man renowned for his geniality and expansive good humor. The epidemic—no, one had to state its true proportions, *pan*demic— had marked everyone, including those lucky enough not to have contracted it.

Many believed that Tirone bore a charmed life in the pursuit of his duties across the continent. The Harper had been detained on the border between Tillek and the High Reaches on a disputation over mines, which had prevented him from attending the Ruathan Gather. Once the drums had sounded the quarantine, Tirone made his way back to the Hall by runner relays, past holds where the plague had not penetrated and some where the news had not spread. He had a fine old row with Tolocamp to be permitted within the Hold proper, but Tirone's logic and the fact that he had not entered any infected areas had prevailed. Or had one of the guards told the Masterharper how it was that Lord Tolocamp had returned from Ruatha?

Tirone had also prevailed on Desdra to permit him to visit the Master Healer.

"If I don't get details from you, Capiam, I shall be forced to rely on hearsay and that is not a proper source for a Masterharper."

"Tirone, I am not about to die. While I laud your zealous desire for a true and accurate account, I have a more pressing duty!" Capiam raised the ledger. "I may have recovered but I have to find out how to cure or stop this wretched disease before it kills further thousands."

"I'm under strict orders not to tire you or Desdra will have my gizzard to grill," Tirone replied with a jocular smile. "But the facts are that I was woefully out of touch with the Hall at this most critical time. I can't even get a decent account from the drummaster though I quite appreciate that neither he nor his journeymen had the time to log the messages which came in and out of the tower at such a rate. Tolocamp won't talk to me though it's five days since Ruatha Gather . . . and he shows no signs of the illness. So I must have something to go on besides incoherent and confused versions. The perceptions of a trained observer such as yourself are invaluable to the chronicler. I am given to understand that you talked with Talpan at Ista?" Tirone poised his pen above the clean squared sheet of hide.

"Talpan . . . now there's the man you should talk to when this is over."

"That won't be possible. Shards! Weren't you told?" The Harper half-rose from his chair, hand outstretched in sympathy.

"I'm all right. No, I didn't know." Capiam closed his eyes for a moment to absorb that shock. "I suspect they thought it would depress me. It does. He was a fine man, with a quick, clever mind. Herdmaster potential." Capiam heard another swift intake of breath from Tirone and opened his eyes. "Master Herdsman Trume as well?" And when Tirone nodded confirmation, Capiam steeled himself. So that was why Tirone had been allowed to see him: to break the news. "I think you'd better tell me the rest of the bad news that neither Desdra nor Fortine voiced. It won't hurt half as much now. I'm numb."

"There have been terrible losses, you realize—"

"Any figures?"

"At Keroon, nine out of every ten who fell ill have died! At Igen Sea Hold, fifteen were weak but alive when the relief ship from Nerat reached them. We have no totals from surrounding holds in Igen, nor do we know the extent of the epidemic's spread in Igen, Keroon, or Ruatha. You can be very proud of your Craftsmen and women, Capiam. They did all that was humanly possible to succor the ill . . ."

"And they died, too?" Capiam asked when Tirone's voice trailed off.

"They brought honor to your hall."

Capiam's heart thumped slowly in his anguish. All dead? Mibbut, gentle Kylos, the earthy Loreana, earnest Rapal, the bone-setter Sneel, Galnish? All of them? Could it really be only *seven* days ago that he had first had word of the dreadful sickness? And those he had attended at Keroon and Igen already sick to their deaths with it? Though he was now positive that the plague itself didn't kill, the living had to face another sort of death, the death of hopes and friendships and what might have been in the futures of those whose lives were abruptly ended. And so near to the promise and freedom of an Interval! Capiam felt tears sliding down his cheeks but they eased the tight constriction in his chest. He let them flow, breathing slowly in and out until his emotions were in hand again. He couldn't think emotionally; he must think professionally. "Igen Sea Hold held nearly a thousand people; only fifty were ill when I attended them at Burdion's summons."

"Burdion is one of the survivors."

"I trust he kept notes for you." Capiam could not prevent his tone from being savage.

"I believe he did," Tirone went on, impervious to the invalid's bad temper. "The log of the *Windtoss* is also available."

"The captain was dead when I reached the Sea Hold."

"Did you *see* the animal?" Tirone leaned forward slightly, his eyes glinting with the avid curiosity he did not voice.

"Yes, I saw it!" That image was now seared in Capiam's memory. The feline had paced restlessly and vividly through his fever dreams and his restless nightmares. Capiam would never forget its snarling face, the white and black whiskers that sprang from its thick muzzle, the brown stains on its tusks, the nicks in its laid-back tufted ears, the dark-brown medallions of its markings that were so fancifully ringed with black and set off in the tawny, shining coat. He could remember its fierce defiance and had even then, when he'd first seen it, conceived the notion that the creature knew perfectly well that it would take revenge on the beings who had restricted it to a cage, who had stared at it in every hold and hall. "Yes, Tirone, I actually saw it. Like hundreds of other people attending Ista Gather. Only I've lived to tell the tale. Talpan and I spent twenty minutes observing it while he told me why he thought it had to die. In twenty minutes it probably infected many people even though Talpan was making the gawkers stand well back from the cage. In fact, I probably contracted my dose of the plague there. From the source. Instead of second-hand." That conclusion afforded Capiam some relief. Made more vulnerable by fatigue, he'd come down with the plague a bare twenty-four hours later. That was better than believing that he had been negligent of hygiene at Igen and Keroon. "Talpan deduced that the animal had to be the cause of the disease already affecting runners from Igen to Keroon. I'd been called to Keroon, too, you see, because so many of their folk were falling ill. I was tracing human contagion, Talpan was tracing runner. We both reached the same conclusion at Ista Gather. The creature was terrified of dragons, you know."

"Really?"

"So I was informed. But K'dall is among the dead at Telgar Weyr and so is his blue dragon."

Tirone murmured, all the while writing furiously. "How, then, did the disease get to Southern Boll if the creature was killed at Ista Gather?"

"You've forgotten the weather."

"Weather?"

"Yes, the weather was so mild Keroon Runnerhold started shipping early this winter, the tides and winds being favorable. So Lord Ratoshigan got his breeding stock early and an unexpected bounty. As did several other notable breeders, some of whom attended Ruatha Gather."

"Well, that is interesting. Such a devastating concatenation of so many small events."

"We should be grateful that Tillek breeds its own and supplies the High Reaches, Crom, and Nabol. That the Keroon-bred runners destined for Benden, Lemos, Bitra, and Nerat either died of the plague or were not herded overland."

"The Weyrleaders have issued an interdiction against any travel to the Southern Continent!" Tirone said. "The Ancients had excellent reason for abandoning that place. Too many threats to life."

"Get your facts straight, Tirone," Capiam said, irritated. "Most life *here* was created and nutured *there*!"

"Now, I have never seen that proved to—"

"Life and its maintenance are *my* province, Masterharper." Capiam held up the ancient ledger and waggled it at Tirone. "As the creation and development of life was once the province of our ancestors. The Ancients brought with them from the Southern Continent all the animals we have here with us today, including the dragons which they genetically engineered for their unique purpose."

Tirone's lower jaw jutted slightly, about to dispute.

"We have lost the skills that the Ancients possessed even though we can refine runners and the herdbeasts for specific qualities. And ..." Capiam paused, struck by an awful consideration. "And I'm suddenly aware that we are in a double peril right now." He thought of Talpan and all his bright promise lost, of Master Herdsman Trume, of the captain of the *Windtoss*, his own dead craftsmen, each with his or her special qualities lost to a swift, mortal illness. "We may have lost a lot more than a coherent account of the progress of a plague, Tirone. And that should worry you far more. It is knowledge as well as life that is being lost all over Pern. What you should be jotting down as fast as you can push your fist is the knowledge, the techniques that are dying in men's minds and cannot be recovered." Capiam waved the Record about, Tirone eyeing it with alarm. "As we can't recover from all the ledgers and Records of the Ancients exactly how they performed the miracles they did. And it's not the miracles so much as the working, the day-to-day routine which the Ancients didn't bother to record because it was *common knowledge*. A common knowledge that is no longer common. That's what we're missing. And we may have lost a lot more of that common knowledge over the past seven days! More than we can ever replace!"

Capiam lay back, exhausted by his outburst, the Records a heavy weight on his guts. That sense of loss, the pressure of that anxiety, had been growing inside him. That morning, when the lethargy had passed, he had been disquietingly aware of the many facts, practices, and intuitions he had never written down, had never thought to elaborate in his private notes. Ordinarily he would have passed them on to his journeymen as they grasped the complexities of their craft. Some matters he had been told by his masters, which they had gleaned from their tutors or from their working experiences, but the transfer of information and its interpretation had been verbal in all too many instances, passed on to those who would need to know.

Capiam became aware that Tirone was staring at him. He had not meant to harangue; that was generally Tirone's function.

"I could not agree with you more, Capiam," Tirone began tentatively, pausing to clear his throat. "But people of all ranks and Crafts tend to keep some secrets which—"

"Shells! Not the drum again!" Capiam buried his head in his hands, pressing his thumbs tightly into his earholes, trying to block the sound.

Tirone's expression brightened and he half-rose from the chair, gesturing for Capiam to unplug his ears. "It's good news. From Igen. Threadfall has been met and all is clear. Twelve wings flew!"

"Twelve?" Capiam pulled himself up, calculating Igen's crushing losses and the numbers of its sick riders. "Igen couldn't have put twelve wings in the air today."

" 'Dragonmen must fly, when Thread is in the sky!' " Tirone's resonant voice rang with pride and exultation.

Capiam stared at him, aware only of profound dismay. How had he failed to catch the significance of Tirone's mention of the Weyrleaders' joint interdiction of the Southern Continent? They'd had to consolidate Weyrs to meet Fall.

" "To fight Thread is in their blood! Despite their cruel losses, they rise, as always, to defend the continent . . .' "

Tirone was off in what Capiam had derisively termed his lyric trance. It was not the time to be composing sagas and ballads! Yet the ringing phrases plucked at a long forgotten memory.

"Do be quiet, Tirone. I must think! Or there won't be *any* dragonriders left to fight Thread. Get out!"

Blood! That's what Tirone had said. It's in their blood! Blood! Capiam hit his temples with the heels of his hands as if he could jolt the vagrant memory into recall. He could almost hear the creaky old voice of old Master Gallardy. Yes, he'd been preparing for his journeyman's examinations and old Gallardy had been droning on and on about unusual and obsolescent techniques. Something to do with blood. Gallardy had been talking about the curative properties of blood—blood what? Blood serum! That was it!

Blood serum as an extreme remedy for contagious or virulent disease.

"Capiam?" It was Desdra, her voice hesitant. "Are you all right? Tirone said—"

"I'm fine! I'm fine! What was that you kept telling me? What can't be cured must be endured. Well, there's another way. *Inuring* to cure. Immunizing. And it's in the blood! It's not a bark, a powder, a leaf, it's blood. And the deterrant is in my blood right now! Because I've survived the plague."

"Master Capiam!" Desdra stepped forward, hesitant, mindful of the precautions of the last five days.

"I do not think I am contagious any longer, my brave Desdra. I'm the cure! At least I believe I am." In his excitement, Capiam had crawled out of bed, flinging sleeping rugs away from him in an effort to reach the case that held his apprentice and journeyman's texts.

"Capiam! You'll fall!"

Capiam was tottering and he grasped at the chair Tirone had vacated to prevent the collapse. He couldn't summon the strength to reach to the shelves.

"Get me my notes. The oldest ones, there on the left-hand side of the top shelf." He sat down abruptly in the chair, shaking with weakness. "I must be right. I have to be right. 'The blood of a recovered patient prevents others from contracting the disease.'"

"Your blood, my fine feeble friend," Desdra said tartly, dusting off the records before she handed them to him, "is very thin and very weak, and you're going back to your bed."

"Yes, yes, in a minute." Capiam was riffling through the thin hide pages, trying in his haste not to crack the brittle fabric, forcing himself to recall exactly when Master Gallardy had delivered those lectures on "unusual techniques." Spring. It was spring. He turned to the last third of his notes. Spring, because he had allowed his mind to dwell more on normal springtime urges than ancient procedures. He felt Desdra tugging at his shoulder.

"You have me spend two hours fixing glowbaskets just to illuminate you in bed and now you read in the darkest corner of your room. Get back into bed! I haven't nursed you this far out of that plague to have you die on me from a chill caught prancing about in the dark like a broody dragon."

"And hand me my kit . . . please." He kept reading as he allowed himself to be escorted back to bed. Desdra tugged the furs so tightly in at the foot that he couldn't bend his knees to prop up the notes. With a tug and a kick, he undid her handiwork.

"Capiam!" Returning with his kit, she was furious at his renewed disarray. She grabbed his shoulder and laid her hand across his forehead. He pushed it away, trying not to show the irritation he felt at her interruptions.

"I'm all right. I'm all right."

"Tirone thought you'd had a relapse the way you're acting. It's not like you, you know, to cry 'blood, blood, it's in their blood.' Or in yours, for that matter."

He only half heard her for he had found the series of lectures that he had copied that spring, thirty Turns gone, when he was far more interested in urgent problems like Threadscore, infection, preventive doses, and nutrition.

"It is in my blood. That's what it says here," Capiam cried in triumph. " 'The clear serum which rises to the top of the vessel after the blood has clotted produces the essential globulins which will inhibit the disease. Injected intravenously, the blood serum gives protection for at least fourteen days, which is ordinarily sufficient time for an epidemic disease to run its course.' " Capiam read on avidly. He could separate the blood components by centrifugal force. Master Gallardy had said that the Ancients had special apparatus to achieve separation, but he could suggest a homely expedient. " 'The serum introduces the disease into the body in such a weakened state as to awaken the body's own defenses and thus prevent such a disease in its more virulent form.' "

Capiam lay back on his pillows, closing his eyes against a momentary weakness that was compounded of relief as well as triumph. He even recalled how he had rebelled against the tedious jotting down of a technique that might now save thousands of people. And the dragonriders!

Desdra regarded him with a curious expression on her face. "But that's homeopathic! Except for injecting directly into the vein."

"Quickly absorbed by the body, thus more effective. And we need an *effective* treatment. Desdra, how *many* dragonriders are sick?"

"We don't know, Capiam. They stopped reporting numbers. The drums did say that twelve wings flew Thread at Igen, but the last report I had, from K'lon actually, was that one hundred and seventy-five riders were ill, including one of the queen riders. L'bol lost two sons in the first deaths."

"A hundred and seventy-five ill? Any secondary infections?"

"They haven't said. But then we haven't asked. . . ."

"At Telgar? Fort Weyr?"

"We have been thinking more of the thousands dying than the dragonriders," Desdra admitted in a bleak voice, her hands locked so tightly the knuckles were white.

"Yes, well, we *depend* on those two-thousand-odd dragonriders. So nag me no more and get what I need to make the serum. And when K'lon comes, I'll want to see him immediately. Is there anyone else here in the Halls or the Hold who has recovered from this disease?"

"Not recovered."

"Never mind. K'lon will be here soon?"

"We expect him. He's been conveying medicines and healers."

"Good. Now, I'll need a lot of sterile, two-liter glass containers with screw tops, stout cord, fresh reeds span-length—I've got needlethorns—redwort and oh, boil me that syringe the cooks use to baste meats. I do have some glass ones Master Clargesh had blown for me, but I can't *think* where I stored them. Now, away with you. Oh, and Desdra, I'll want some double-destilled spirits and more of that restorative soup of yours."

"I can understand the need for spirits," she said at the door, her expression sardonic, "but more of the soup you dislike so?"

He flourished a pillow and she laughed as she closed the door behind her. Capiam turned the pages to the beginning of Master Gallardy's lecture.

In the event of an outbreak of a communicable disease, the use of a serum prepared from the blood of a recovered victim of the same disease has proved efficacious. Where the populace is healthy, an injection of the blood serum prevents the disease. Administered to a sufferer, the blood serum mitigates the virulence. Long before the Crossings, such plagues as varicella, diphtheria, influenza, rubella, epidemic roseola, morbilli, scarlatina, variola, typhoid, typhus, poliomyelitis, tuberculosis, hepatitis, cytomegalovirus herpes, and gonococcal were eliminated by vaccination . . .

Typhus and typhoid were familiar to Capiam, for there had been outbreaks of each as the result of ineffective hygiene. He and the other healers had feared they would result from the current overcrowding. Diphtheria and scarlatina had flared up occasionally over the past several hundred Turns, at least often enough so that the symptoms and the treatment were part of his training. The other diseases he didn't know except from the root words, which were very very old. He would have to look them up in the Harper Hall's etymological dictionary.

He read on farther in Master Gallardy's advice. A liter and a half of blood could be taken from each recovered victim of the disease and that, separated, would give fifty mils of serum for immunization. The injectable amount varied from one mil to ten, according to Gallardy, but he wasn't very specific as to which amount for which disease. Capiam thought ruefully of the impassioned words he had poured at Tirone concerning the loss of techniques. Was he himself at fault for not attending more closely to Master Gallardy's full lecture?

No great calculation was needed for Capiam to see the enormity of the task of producing the desirable immunity even for the vital few thousand dragonriders, the Lords Holder, and Mastercraftsmen, let alone the healers who must care for the ill and prepare and administer the vaccine.

The door swung before Desdra, who looked flustered for the first time that Capiam could remember. She carried a rush basket and closed the door with a deft hook of her foot.

"I have your requirements and I have found the glass syringes that Master Genjon blew for you. Three were broken, but I have boiled the remainder."

Desdra carefully deposited the wicker basket by his bed. She pulled his bedside table to its customary place and, on it, she put the jar of redwort in its strongest solution, a parcel of reeds, the leaf-bound needlethorns, a steaming steel tray that had covered the kettle in which he could see a small glass jar, a stopper, and the Genjon syringes. From her pocket, Desdra drew a length of stout, well-twisted cord. "There!"

"That is not a two-liter jar."

"No, but you are not strong enough to be reduced by two liters of blood. Half a liter is all you can lose. K'lon will be here soon enough."

Desdra briskly scrubbed his arm with the redwort then tied the cord about his upper arm while he clenched his fist to raise the artery. It was ropy and blue beneath flesh that seemed too white to him. With tongs, she took the glass container from the boiled water. She opened the packet of reeds, then the needlethorns, took one of each and fitted the needlethorn to one end of the reed. "I know the technique but I haven't done this often."

"You'll have to! My hand shakes!"

Desdra pressed her lips in a firm line, dipped her fingers in redwort, put the glass container on the floor by his bed, tilted the reed end into it, and picked up the needlethorn. The tip of a needlethorn is so fine that the tiny opening in the point is almost invisible. Desdra punctured his skin and, with only a little force, entered the engorged vein then flipped loose the tourniquet. Capiam closed his eyes against the slight dizziness he felt when his blood pressure lowered as the blood began to flow through the needlethorn and down the reed into the container. When the spell had passed, he opened his eyes and was objectively fascinated by his blood dripping into the glass. He pumped his fist and the drip increased to a thin flow. In a curious, detached way, he seemed to feel the fluid leaving his body, being gathered from his other limbs, even from his torso, that the draining was a totally corporeal affair, not just from the fluid in one artery. He really could feel his heart beating more strongly, accommodating the flow. But that was absurd. He was beginning to feel a trifle nauseated when Desdra's fingers pressed a redwort-stained swab over the needlethorn, then removed it with a deft tweak.

"That is quite enough, Master Capiam. Almost three quarters of a liter. You've gone white. Here. Press hard and hold. Drink the spirits."

She placed the drink in his left hand and he automatically held the compress with his right. The powerful spirit seemed to take up the space left by the release of his blood. But that was a highly fanciful notion for a healer who knew very well the route taken by anything ingested.

"Now what do we do?" she asked, holding up the closed glass jar of his blood.

"That top firmly screwed on?" And when she demonstrated that it was: "Then wrap the cord tightly around the neck and knot it firmly. Good. Hand it here."

"What do you think you're going to do now?" Her face was stern and her gaze stubborn. For a woman who had often preached detachment, she was suddenly very intense.

"Gallardy says that centrifugal force, that is, whirling the jar around, will separate the components of the blood and produce the useful serum."

"Very well." Desdra stood back from the bed, made sure she had sufficient clear space to accomplish the operation, and began to swing the jar around her head.

Capiam, observing her exertions, was glad she had volunteered. He doubted that he could have managed it. "We could rig something similar with the spit canines, couldn't we? Have to prod the beasts to maintain speed. One needs a constant speed. Or perhaps a smaller arrangement, with a handle so one could control the rotational velocity?"

"Why? Do we . . . need . . . to do this . . . often?"

"If my theory is correct, we'll need rather a lot of serum. You did leave word that K'lon is to be shown here as soon as he arrives?"

"I did. How . . . much . . . longer?"

Capiam could not have her desist too soon, yet Master Gallardy had said "in a very short time" or—and Capiam looked more closely at his own handwriting—had *he* erred in transcribing? A concerned healer with thirty Turns of Craft life behind him, he silently cursed the diffidence of the spring-struck young apprentice he had been. "That ought to suffice, Desdra. Thank you!"

Breathless, Desdra slowed the swing of the jar and caught it, placing it on the table. Capiam hunched forward on the bed while Desdra examined the various layers with astonishment.

"That"—Desdra pointed dubiously to the straw-colored fluid in the top level—"is your cure?"

"Not a cure, exactly. An immunization." Capiam enunciated the word carefully.

"One has to drink it?" Desdra's voice was neutral with distaste.

"No, though I daresay it wouldn't taste any worse than some of the concoctions you've insisted I swallow. No, this must be injected into the vein."

She gave him a long thoughtful look. "So that's why you needed the syringes." She gave her head a little shake. "We don't have enough of them. And I think you better see Master Fortine."

"Don't you trust me?" Capiam was hurt by her response.

"Completely. That's why I suggest you go to Master Fortine. With your serum. He has been too frequent a visitor at our cautious Lord Holder's internment camp. He's coming down with the plague."

CHAPTER

X

Fort Weyr and Ruatha Hold, Present Pass, 3.16.43

When Moreta woke, she felt Orlith's joyful presence in her mind.
You are better. The worst is over!

"I'm better?" Moreta was annoyed by the quaver in her voice, too much a remnant of the terrible lassitude that had enervated her the day before.

You are much better. Today you will get stronger every minute.

"How much of that is wishful thinking, my love?"

Even as Moreta spoke in her usual affectionate way, she realized that Orlith would know. During Moreta's illness, the queen had been as close in her mind as if the dragon had changed mental residence. Orlith had shared every moment of Moreta's discomfort, as if, by sharing, the dragon could diminish the effects of the plague on her rider. They, who had been partners in so much, had achieved a new peak of awareness, the one in the other. Orlith had dampened the pain of the fierce headache, she had eased the stress of fever and depressed the hard, racking cough. All she could do was comfort Moreta during the fourth day of physical and mental exhaustion. But by then the dragon queen had every right to rejoice.

Holth says there is other good news! Master Capiam has a serum which prevents the plague.

"Prevents it? Can he cure it?" Moreta had not been so detached in the course of her illness that she had not known that others in Fort had sickened—or that dragons and riders had died in other Weyrs. She was aware as well that two Fort Weyr wings had risen the day before to meet the Fall on Igen's behalf. That Berchar and Tellani's new babe had died. She knew as well that the epidemic had extended its insidious grip on the continent. It was time and enough for the healers to have found some specific means to control it.

The plague has a name. It is an ancient disease.

"What name do they give it then?"

I can't remember, Orlith said apologetically.

Moreta sighed. Naming was a dragon failing. Yet Orlith remembered quite a few, Moreta thought fondly.

Holth asks are you hungry yet?

"My greetings to our good Holth and our gracious Leri, and I think I am hungry," Moreta said with some surprise. For four days any thought of food had caused nausea. Thirst she had suffered, as well as the hard throat-searing cough, and a weakness so deep she feared at moments that she would never shake it. That was when Orlith had been closest to her mind. Had there been space enough, the queen would have forced her swollen body into Moreta's quarters to be physically near.

"How's Sh'gall?" Moreta inquired. She had been feverishly ill by morning when Kadith had mournfully roused Orlith and Holth with the news of his rider's collapse.

He is weak. He doesn't feel at all well.

Moreta grinned. Orlith's tone was tinged with scorn as if the queen felt her own rider had been more valiant.

"Do remember, Orlith, that Sh'gall has never been ill. This must come as a terrible shock to his self-esteem."

Orlith said nothing.

"What news from Ruatha Hold? You'd better tell me," Moreta added when she felt Orlith's resistance.

Leri comes. Relief marked Orlith's manner. *She knows.*

"Leri comes here?" Moreta tried to sit up, but gasped at the dizziness the sudden movement occasioned. She lay where she had flopped as she listened to the approach of shuffling steps and the tap of Leri's cane. "Leri, you shouldn't—"

"Why not?" Leri projected her voice from the larger weyr. "Good morning, Orlith. I'm one of the brave. I've lived my life so I'm not afraid of this 'viral influence,' as the Healers have styled it." Leri pushed back the bright door curtain, peering brightly at the younger woman. "Ah, there—you have color in your face today." A covered pot and the thong of a flask swung from her left hand. Two more containers had been stuck in her belt to allow her to use her right hand for her stick. As Leri entered the room, Moreta noticed that the old woman's gait seemed more fluid. She deposited her oddments on the chest that was now drawn to Moreta's bedside and then allowed herself to drop onto the space by Moreta's feet. "There now!" she said with great satisfaction, tucking her gnarled stick beside her. "Yes, you should do very well."

"Something smells good," Moreta said, inhaling the aroma from the pot.

"A special porridge I concocted. Made them bring me supplies and a brazier so I could nurse you myself. Nesso's finally down with it and out of my hair for a bit. Gorta's taken charge—rather well, I might add, in case you're interested." Leri looked slyly at Moreta as she spooned porridge in two bowls. "I'll join you since it's my breakfast time as well, and this stuff is as good for me as it is for you. By the way, I made Orlith eat this morning before she wasted away to nothing but the eggshells. She had four fat bucks and a wherry. She was very hungry! Now, don't look dismayed. You've scarcely been able to do for yourself, let alone her. She didn't feel neglected. She minds me very well, Orlith does, since she knows me so well. After all, Holth laid her! So she did as we told her and *she's* feeling better. She *had* to eat, Moreta. Her next stop is the Hatching Ground, and we had to wait till you recovered for that. Won't be long now."

Moreta did some swift adding. "She's early. She shouldn't clutch for another five or six days."

"There has been some stress. Don't fuss. Eat. The sooner you've got your strength back, the better all round."

"I'm much stronger today. Yesterday . . ." Moreta smiled ruefully. "*How* have you managed?"

"Very easily." Leri was serenely smug. "As I said, I had them bring me a brazier and supplies. I made your potions myself, I'll have you know! With Orlith listening to every breath you made and relaying the information to Holth, I'll wager you couldn't have been better cared for if Master Capiam had been at your bedside."

"Orlith says he's discovered a cure?"

"A vaccine, he calls it. But I'll not have him after your blood."

"Why should he be?" Moreta was startled and Orlith gave a bellow at Leri's protectiveness.

"He takes the blood of people who have recovered and makes a *serum* to prevent it in others. Says it's an ancient remedy. Can't say I like the notion at all!" Leri's short upright figure shuddered. "He practically attacked K'lon when he reported for conveying." Leri gave a chuckle and smiled with bland satisfaction. "K'lon was doing too much flitting *between* on Healer Hall errands. I've appointed weyrlings to the duty. Didn't like to but . . . they've followed orders well. Oh, there's been so much happening I hardly know where to begin!"

Beneath Leri's glib manner, Moreta could discern worry and fatigue, but the older Weyrwoman seemed to be thriving on the crisis.

"Have there been more . . . Weyr deaths?" Moreta asked, bracing herself for the answer.

"No!" Leri gave a defiant nod of her head and another pleased smile. "There shouldn't have been any! People weren't using the wits they were born with. You know how greens and blues panic? Well, they did just that when their riders got so sick and weak, *instead* of supporting them. In fact, there might be something to Jallora's theory that the one caused the other. . . ." Leri stared off for a moment in deep thought. "Jallora's the journeywoman healer sent with two apprentices from the Healer Hall. So we keep in touch with the sick riders. You were very ill, you know. Exhausted, I think, after the Gather—no sleep, all the excitement, then Fall and that repair on Dilenth. He's fine, but Orlith is so strong and her need of you so great that *you* hadn't a chance of dying! You and Orlith as a healing team were the inspiration"— Leri fixed Moreta with a mock stern gaze—"so we just told the other Weyr-women to have their queen dragons keep watch on the sick and not *let* the riders die. It isn't as if the Weyrs had the crowding that's causing so much concern in the Holds and Halls. It's ridiculous for dragonriders to die of this vicious viral influence."

"How many *are* ill, if the Weyrs must consolidate to fly Fall?"

Leri grimaced. "Steel yourself! Nearly two thirds of every Weyr except High Reaches is out of action. Between the plague and injuries, we can only just manage to send our two wings to cover Fall."

"But you said Master Capiam had a cure?"

"A preventive. And not enough of this vaccine yet." Leri spoke with an angry regret. "So the Weyrwomen decided that the High Reaches' riders must be vaccinated"—she stumbled over the unfamiliar term—"since we must all look to S'ligar and Falga. As more of the serum is prepared, other Weyrs will be vaccinated. Right now Capiam has the drums burning to find more people who have recovered from this viral influence. First dragonriders"—Leri ticked off each name on a finger—"then Healers, *then* Lord Holders and other Craftsmasters, except for Tirone, which, I think no matter how Tolocamp objects, is sensible."

"Tolocamp hasn't been ill?"

"Tolocamp won't leave his apartment."

"You know a great deal about what's happening for a woman who stays in her own weyr most of the time!"

Leri chuckled. "K'lon reports to *me*! Whenever, that is, Capiam hasn't his exclusive services. Fortunately blues have good appetites and, although

Capiam maintains that dragons, wherries, and watchwhers can't contract the plague, dragons had best eat from stock isolated in their own weyrs. So K'lon brings Rogeth home to eat. Daily."

"Dragons don't eat daily."

"Blue dragons who must flit *between* twice hourly do." Leri gave Moreta a stern glance. "I had a note from Capiam, could barely read his script, lauding K'lon's dedication—"

"A'murry?"

"Recovering. Very close thing but Holth was in constant touch with Granth once I realized how vital dragon support could be. L'bol lost both his sons and he grieves constantly. M'tani's impossible, but then he has fought Thread longer than most and sees this incident as a personal affront. If it weren't for K'dren and S'ligar, I think we'd have had trouble with F'gal: He's lost heart, too."

"Leri, there's something you're not telling me."

"Yes, dear girl." Leri patted Moreta's arm gently before she filled a glass from one of her flasks. "Take a sip of this," she said peremptorily, handing it to her.

Obediently Moreta did, and she was about to ask what on earth Leri had concocted, when she felt Orlith's presence in her mind, like a buffer.

"Your family's hold . . ." Leri's voice thickened and she avoided Moreta's gaze, staring instead at the bright central design of the door curtain. ". . . was very hard hit."

Leri's voice habitually broke but that time it was pronounced, and Moreta peered at the older woman's averted face. Tears were running unheeded down the round cheek nearest her.

"There'd been no drum message in two days. The harper at Keroon heights made the trip downriver . . ." Leri's fingers tightened on Moreta's arm. "There was no one alive."

"No one?" Moreta was stunned. Her father's hold had supported nearly three hundred people, and another ten families had cots nearby on the river bluffs.

"Drink that down!"

Numbly Moreta complied. "No one alive? Not even someone out with the bloodstock?"

Leri shook her head slowly. "Not even the bloodstock!" Her admission was almost a whisper. Moreta could barely grasp the staggering tragedy. Obscurely, it was the deaths of the bloodstock that she regretted the most. Twenty Turns ago she had acquiesced to her family's wish that she respond to Search. She regretted their deaths, certainly, for she had been fond of her mother, and several of her brothers and sisters, and one paternal uncle; she had enormous respect for her father. The runnerbeasts—all the bloodstock that had been so carefully bred for the eight generations her family had the runnerhold—that loss cut more deeply.

Orlith crooned gently, and her dragon's compassion was subtly reinforced by a second pressure. Moreta felt the terrible weight of her grief being eased by an anodyne of love and affection, of total understanding for the complexities of her sorrow, of a commitment to share and ease the multiple pressures of bereavement.

Tears streamed down Moreta's cheeks until she felt drained but curiously detached from her body and mind, floating in an unusual sensation of remoteness. Leri had put something very powerful in that wine of hers, she thought with an odd clarity. Then she noticed that Leri was watching her intently, her eyes incredibly sad and tired, every line of her many Turns etched in her round small face.

"No stock at all?" Moreta asked finally.

"Would young runners have been wintering on the plains? The harper couldn't check. Didn't know where and there hasn't been time to send a sweeprider."

"No, no. Of course there wouldn't be time. . . ." Moreta could quite see that impossibility with the present demands on available riders but she accepted the hopeful suggestion. "Yearlings and gravid runners would be in the winter pasture. Somebody of the Hold will have been tending them and survive."

The comforting presences in her mind wrapped her with love and reassurances. *We are here!*

Is Holth with you, Orlith? Moreta asked.

Of course, was the reply from two, now distinct to her, sources.

Oh! How kind! Moreta's mind drifted, oddly divorced from her body, until she became aware of Leri's anxious expression. "I'm all right. As Holth will tell you. Did you know she speaks to me?"

"Yes, she's got rather used to checking in on you," Leri said with a kind and serene smile.

"What did you put in that wine? I feel . . . disembodied."

"That *was* rather the effect I hoped to achieve. Fellis juice, numbweed, and one of the euphorics. Just to cushion the shock."

"Are there more?" From the wavering of Leri's smile, Moreta knew that there were. "You might as well give me the whole round tale now while I'm so remote. My family's hold . . . cannot have been unique." Leri shook her head. "Ruatha Hold?" That would follow the line of catastrophe, Moreta thought.

"They have been badly hit. . . ."

"Alessan?" She asked about him first because his would be the worst loss there, before he'd even had time to enjoy being a Lord Holder.

"No, he's recovering, but the decimation among the Gather guests—his brothers, almost all the racers—"

"Dag?"

"I don't have many names. Igen Weyr and Hold have been shockingly depleted. Lord Fitatric, his Lady, half their children . . ."

"By the Egg, isn't there *any* place spared?"

"Yes, in fact, Bitra, Lemos, Nerat, Benden, and Tillek have had relatively few cases, and those were isolated promptly to avoid contagion. Those Holds have been magnificent in sending people to the stricken."

"Why?" Moreta clenched her fists, hunching herself together in a sudden convulsion that was more mental than physical. "*Why?* When we're so near the end of the Pass? It's not fair so close to an Interval. Did you know"— Moreta's voice was hard and intense—"that my family started out after the end of the last Pass? My bloodline started then? And now—just before the next Interval—it's wiped out!"

"That isn't known for certain, if what you say of wintering stock applies. *Do* consider that possibility. That probability." The dragons reinforced Leri's optimism.

Moreta's outburst passed almost as swiftly as it had consumed her. She lay back, limp, her eyelids suddenly heavy, her body flaccid. Leri seemed to be retreating from her though she was conscious that the Weyrwoman still sat on the bed.

"That's right. You sleep now," Leri said in a gentle croon echoed by two dragon voices.

"I can't stay awake!" Moreta mumbled and, sighing, relaxed into a potion-induced sleep.

Ruatha Hold, Present Pass, 3.16.43

K'lon was intensely relieved when Journeyman Healer Follen, his lips pulled down in a sorrowful line, emerged from Lord Alessan's apartment. The death-stench of the cold corridor bothered K'lon, inured though he was to plague-ridden holds.

"I've vaccinated the sister and the harper and did that other poor fellow as well. Lord Alessan says that more patients may be found along this corridor, but they did manage to clear the upper levels. I don't know how the man had managed. I'd no idea it would be so bad or I'd've insisted that Master Capiam give us more serum."

"There isn't that much to distribute, you know."

"Don't I just!"

Follen gave K'lon a thin smile. The previous evening the bluerider had conveyed the journeyman to South Boll Hold when the drums had reported survivors of the plague. As Capiam's timely visit to South Boll and his recommendations to its healers had in fact prevented the plague from spreading as insidiously as it had in midcontinent, it was only just that all the survivors donate blood for serum. Lord Ratoshigan had been a donor though the ever-irascible Lord Holder had been under the distinct impression—adroitly fostered by bluerider and journeyman—that the blood-taking was part of the prescribed treatment.

"Donations can be taken here," Follen went on, combing his hair with his fingers. "I'll give them some of Desdra's brew first, but judging from Lord Alessan's tally, the Hold will be able"—Follen gave a dour snort—"to supply those left here. Do ask Lord Shadder if he can find a few more volunteers. I'm sure we can save many of those with secondary infections if we just have enough nurses. We've got to try. This Hold has been devastated."

K'lon acknowledged that with a slow nod of his head. The desolation and ruin of Ruatha Hall had appalled the relief party. K'lon and three Benden green dragons had conveyed Follen, an apprentice healer, and six volunteers from Benden Hold. The spectacle that greeted the party emerging from *between* over the Hold was the worst K'lon had seen. The monstrous burial mounds in the river field, the wide circle of charnel fires near the race flats, the abandoned tents built on Gather-stall frames had indicated the magnitude of Ruatha's attempt to survive. The sad tatters of the gaudy Gather flags, hanging from the upper tiers of the closely shuttered windows, had struck K'lon as grotesque, a mockery of the gaiety that was Gathering in the midst of the tragedy that had befallen the Hold. Bits and pieces of trash skittered across the forlorn dancing square and the roadway while a kettle swung noisily on its tripod over a long-dead fire, its ladle banging in time to gusts of the bitter-cold wind.

"Lady Pendra?" K'lon began.

A quick shake of Follen's head made it unnecessary for K'lon to continue. "No, nor any of the daughters he brought to Ruatha Gather. At that, Lord Tolocamp comes out better than Lord Alessan. *He's* got but the one sister left."

"Of all Leef's get?"

"Lord Alessan frets about her. And his runners. More of them survived than guests, I think. You speak to him," Follen suggested, clapping the blue rider on the shoulder before making off up the dark corridor to the next room.

K'lon squared his shoulders. In the last few days, he had learned how to keep his face from showing his emotions, how to sound not exactly cheerful, which would have been offensive, but certainly positive and encouraging. After all, with the vaccine, there was the hope of mitigating the plague and preventing the disease in those not yet infected. He knocked politely at the heavy door but entered without waiting for an acknowledgment.

Lord Alessan was kneeling by a toss-mattress, bathing the face of the occupant. There was another makeshift bed along the wall leading into the sleeping quarters. K'lon suppressed an inadvertent exclamation at the change in the young Lord Holder. Alessan might regain lost weight and his skin its healthy color, but his face would always bear the prematurely deep lines and the resigned expression that he turned toward the blue rider.

"You are many times welcome, K'lon, rider of Rogeth." Alessan inclined his head in gratitude and then folded the dampened cloth before placing it on the forehead of the man he was tending. "You may tell Master Tirone that, without the invaluable assistance and ingenuity of his harpers, we would be worse off at Ruatha than we are. Tuero here was magnificent. The journeyman healer—what was his name?" Alessan drew a shaky hand across his forehead as if to coax the identity back.

"Follen."

"Strange, I can remember so many names . . ." Alessan broke off and stared out the window. K'lon knew the Lord Holder could see the burial mounds and wondered if the distraught man meant the names of those who lay beneath the tumbled soil of the mass graves. "It takes you that way, lying in bed, waiting to . . ." Alessan gave himself a shake and, gripping the top of the table, pulled himself slowly to his feet. "You have brought relief. Follen says that Tuero here, Deefer"—he gestured wearily toward the other bed—"and my sister will recover. He even apologized that he hadn't more . . . vaccine? Is that what it's called? Yes, well—"

"Sit down, Lord Alessan—"

"Before I fall down?" Alessan gave a slight smile with his bloodless lips, but he eased himself into the chair, sighing heavily from a weariness that went beyond any physical fatigue.

"They've stirred up the fires, and soon there'll be some restorative soup. Desdra concocted it. She tended Master Capiam, and *he* says the soup worked miracles for him."

"We shall hope it does for us as well." As they both heard the sound of coughing, Alessan turned his head sharply toward the door of his bedroom, inhaling apprehensively.

"Your sister? Well, you'll see," K'lon said with conviction. "The vaccine will effect a great improvement in her condition."

"I sincerely hope so. She's all the family I have left."

Though Alessan spoke in a light, almost diffident voice, K'lon felt his throat close tightly with compassion.

"Oh, that serum will moderate the effects of the virus for her, I assure you. I've seen amazing recoveries after its administration. In fact, the serum Follen gave her is probably derived from the blood I donated." K'lon rattled on mendaciously. Others had taken consolation from that fact so he held it out as comfort to this sadly bereaved man.

Alessan regarded him with a slightly surprised expression and his lips twitched in wry humor. "Ruatha has always been proud of its dragonrider bloodties though they've never been so direct."

K'lon responded to Alessan's retort with a thin laugh. "You haven't lost your wits."

"They're about all I have left."

"Indeed, Lord Alessan, you have much more," K'lon said stoutly. "And you shall have all the help Weyr, Hold, and Hall can supply."

"As long as what you have already brought is effective." Once more Alessan's head turned toward the room where his sister lay. "It is more than we had hoped for."

"I shall have a look at your stores and see what is most needful," K'lon began, vowing to himself that one of his first tasks would be to remove the Gather banners. If their presence had affronted him as a hideous reminder of that unfortunate occurrence, how cruelly would they affect Lord Alessan.

The Lord Holder stood far more quickly than he ought to have for he had to steady himself against the chair. "I know exactly what we need. . . ." He walked shakily to the desk at the window, absently stacking dirty dishes as he looked. He found the sheet of hide he wanted with a minimum of search. "Medicines, first of all. We have no aconite, not a gram of febrifuge left, only an ineffective syrup for that wretched cough, no thymus, hyssop, ezob, no flour, no salt. Blackstone is almost depleted, and there have been no vegetables or meat for three days." He handed the sheet to K'lon, a wry smile on his lips. "See how timely your arrival is? Tuero sent the last drum message this morning before he collapsed. I doubt I should have had the strength to climb to the drum tower."

K'lon took the sheet with a hand that shook only slightly less than the hand that offered it. He bowed to hide his face, but when he looked up, he saw that Alessan was gazing out the window, his expression unreadable.

"Follen told me that scenes like this are repeated throughout the continent."

"Not like this," K'lon said, his voice cracking.

"Follen didn't go into detail—how badly are the Weyrs affected?"

"Well, we have had our casualties, it's true, but dragonriders have met every Fall."

Alessan gave him a long puzzled look, then he turned away again to gaze out the window. "Yes, I suppose they would, if they could. You're from Fort Weyr?"

As K'lon knew that Alessan was aware of his affiliation, he sensed that the man was trying to discover something else. Then he remembered what Nesso had said, about Moreta dancing in a scandalous monopoly of the young Lord.

"Lady Moreta is recovering and so is the Weyrleader. We have had only one death at Fort, an elderly brown rider and his dragon, Koth. The toll was fifteen at Igen, eight at Telgar, and two at Ista but, because of the vaccine, we are hopeful."

"Yes, there is hope."

Why Alessan should glance from the fields to the mountains, K'lon did not know, but the action seemed to hearten the man.

"Did you know that we had over a hundred and twenty of the best western racers here a few short days ago, and seven hundred Gatherers to enjoy the dancing, the wine, the feast, the plague . . ."

"Lord Alessan, do not distress yourself so needlessly! If you had *not* held the Gather festivities here, the *entire* Hold could have been destroyed. You were able to prevent the plague's spread. All Ruathan drumholds have reported in. There are a few deaths reported and some cases of the plague, but you did what had to be done, and did it well!"

Alessan turned abruptly from the window. "You must bear to Lord Tolocamp my most profound condolences for the loss of Lady Pendra and her daughters. They nursed the sick until they were themselves overcome. They were valiant." Alessan's message was no less sincere for the abruptness of its tone.

K'lon acknowledged the message with a sharp inclination of his head. He was not the only one who would forever fault Lord Tolocamp for running from Ruatha. There were those who held the opinion that Tolocamp had been eminently correct to put the welfare of his Hold above that of his Lady and his daughters. Lord Tolocamp had remained secure in his apartment at Fort Hold while Ruatha suffered and died. Tolocamp would be spared the disease since he had vehemently insisted on being vaccinated despite the priorities set by the Weyrwomen and Master Capiam.

"I will convey your condolences. All the supplies we brought," K'lon found himself explaining, "came from Benden or Nerat Holds."

Alessan's eyes sparkled briefly, and he looked at K'lon as if he were seeing the blue rider for the first time.

"Good of you to tell me that. My profound gratitude for the generosity of Lord Shadder and Lord Gram." The view from his window again drew Alessan's glance. His obsession was beginning to perturb K'lon.

"I must go," the blue rider said. "There is so much to be done."

"There is! Thank you for answering the drums . . . and for your reassurances, K'lon. My duty to Rogeth who brought you." Alessan held out his hand.

K'lon crossed the room to take it in both of his. He was almost afraid to return the pressure on the strengthless fingers but he smiled as warmly as he could, thinking that if Ruatha was proud of dragonrider bloodties, he was as proud to be part of it. Perhaps some of his blood *had* been in that serum batch. K'lon fervently hoped so.

He quit the apartment as fast as was polite, for he did not wish to give way to the emotions that possessed him. K'lon hurried down the dark corridor—they must put up glowbaskets—into the Main Hall, where two Benden volunteers were cleaning up. Their homey noises were a welcome relief from the preternatural stillness that had shrouded the Hall on their arrival. He told them about the need for glowbaskets and asked them to remove the Gather banners as soon as possible. He could hear Rogeth bellowing outside.

This place is most distressing, the blue dragon said piteously. *It is the most distressing place we have been. How much longer must we stay?*

K'lon gave the Bendenites warm thanks and then rushed out to the forecourt. Rogeth half ran, half flew up the ramp to meet K'lon, his eyes wheeling in distress.

This place distresses you, too. Can we not see Granth and A'murry now? The "now" was accompanied by an unhappy snort.

"We can leave now." K'lon swung up to Rogeth's back, his gaze inadvertently falling on the dreadful field with its ruined shelters, the race flats, and the burial mounds. *Were* they what drew Lord Alessan's eyes? Or the handful of runnerbeasts grazing in the far field? The rumble of the dead cart, a recalcitrant pair of herdbeasts between the shafts, startled K'lon.

"Get us out of here," he told Rogeth, sick to the soul of plague and death and desolation. "I *must* spend some time with A'murry. Then I'll be able to face this sort of thing."

K'lon was overwhelmed with longing for his gentle friend, for the respite of companionship. He should go right back to the Healer Hall. There was so much to be done. Instead he projected for Rogeth the sun-dappled heights of Igen Weyr, the bright sparkle of the Weyr lake. Rogeth leaped gladly from the ramp into the air and took him *between*.

Fort Weyr, Present Pass, 3.17.43

"Shards!" Jallora cried. "He's fainted!"

Kadith, in the outer chamber of the weyr, bellowed, and Moreta jumped up from the chair to reassure the startled dragon as the journeywoman healer examined her reluctant donor.

What has happened? Orlith asked in concern from her weyr.

"Sh'gall had a bad reaction," Moreta replied, knowing perfectly well that Leri would be instantly informed by Holth and know what had really happened. "Calm Kadith down!"

"It's generally the big strong ones who faint," Jallora was saying as Moreta resumed her place. "He's in no danger. Badly as we need the blood for serum, I wouldn't risk him."

"I didn't think for a moment that you would, Jallora," Moreta replied with a slight laugh.

The journeywoman had interrupted an interview between Moreta and Sh'gall in which he had been determined to find fault with every provision made in the Weyr since the onset of his illness. He utterly discounted the fact that Moreta had not made any of the decisions or that she herself had only just recovered.

"His sort don't generally make good patients, either," Jallora went on conversationally, though her attention was on the blood dripping into a glass container.

"Will his go to Ruatha?"

"Most of it, once the rest of your riders are vaccinated." When Moreta gestured warningly at Sh'gall, she added diplomatically, "I perfectly understand, I assure you. He's still out of it. There! That's all I'll take but he could donate more and never miss it." Deftly she pressed a small pad over the needlethorn, extracted it, and motioned for Moreta to continue the pressure as she dealt with the apparatus. "He'll regain consciousness in just a few minutes." Jallora began packing her tray, carefully covering the container. "F'duril told me that you did the reconstruction on Dilenth's wing. Fine work."

"The wing is healing well, isn't it?" Recognition of her achievement by another healer was gratifying to Moreta.

"Fortunately, so is F'duril and that nice young A'dan. I've never visited a Weyr before. And—you know something else? It never occurred to me that dragons suffered so from Thread. They're so impressive—"

"Unfortunately not invulnerable."

"We can thank our lucky stars they didn't catch this viral influence!"

Just then Sh'gall moaned. Jallora hurried to gather up the rest of her paraphernalia.

"There now! Back again, Weyrleader?" She took the glass of orange liquid from the table and, deftly propping Sh'gall's pillows behind him with her free hand, put the glass to his lips. "Drink this and you'll be just fine."

"I don't really think it was wise of you to take—" Sh'gall sounded petulant and took the glass from her with a bad grace.

"The riders of Fort need it, Weyrleader. They must all be vaccinated, you know, to ensure that no more have to endure what you've just been through."

The journeywoman took exactly the right tone with Sh'gall. Moreta could wish herself so fortunate as Sh'gall permitted Jallora to make a discreet departure.

"I don't think she should have!" Sh'gall repeated when he was certain Jallora was out of earshot.

"She got mine." Moreta pushed up her sleeve to exhibit the tiny bruise at the bend of her elbow. Sh'gall looked away. "We've a hundred and eighty-two riders out of action, sick or disabled."

"Why didn't Capiam attend us instead of that—woman?"

"Jallora is an experienced journeywoman healer. She was sitting her mastery exams when this plague occurred. Capiam is only just out of bed himself and he has the whole continent to worry about."

"I cannot believe that Leri did not know of my preference for P'nine as Leader." Sh'gall picked up his complaints as if Jallora had not interrupted the acrimonious interview.

"Leri made appropriate decisions based on her experience as a Weyrwoman. Kindly remember that she was one before you or I had Impressed."

"Then why does Kadith tell me that T'ral is taking *two* wings to Tillek today?" Sh'gall demanded angrily. "T'ral's a *wingsecond*."

"With the exception of the High Reaches, the Weyrs are still being led by wingseconds at this point. The sooner you can take over, the best pleased all the Weyrs will be."

That comment startled Sh'gall, but he didn't look pleased. "I've been ill. I've been very ill."

"I sympathize." Moreta tried not to sound facetious. "Believe me, you'll be feeling much better by evening."

"I don't know about that . . ." Sh'gall's voice faded.

"I do! I've been through it, too, don't forget."

Sh'gall gave her a look of pure loathing, but Moreta could not relent. Some of the burden of continuous Falls had to be removed from S'ligar's shoulders. Sh'gall was a damn good Leader and his abilities were desperately needed.

"Nerat's after Tillek," she went on. "You'll be in luck: *They* can supply ground crews."

"I didn't believe Kadith when he said that there hadn't been any ground crews. Don't holders realize—"

"The holders realize what this viral epidemic is like a lot more acutely than we do, Sh'gall. Talk to K'lon for a few minutes. He'll tell you a few hard unpleasant truths." She stood up. "I've a lot to do. Jallora said you must rest today. Tomorrow you can rise. Kadith may, of course, call me if you need anything today."

"I need nothing from you." Sh'gall turned away from her and jerked the sleeping furs around his ears.

Moreta was quite willing to leave him to surly convalescence. She sincerely hoped that he would want to lead his Weyr in three days more than he wanted to indulge his fancied grievances. Leading the consolidated Weyrs was a mighty temptation for a man with Sh'gall's love of power. She tried to consider him more charitably: He was shocked by the devastation caused by the pandemic and seeking refuge from the staggering losses by dwelling on the petty details he could cope with and understand. Like who rose to Fall from where, and how.

She walked down the steps to Leri's weyr at a fairly rapid pace, an exercise that did not leave her as breathless as it had the day before. She would harness Holth since she could not dissuade Leri from fighting in the queens' wing though the old woman was very tired. Then Moreta would distill and mix medicines from the Weyr's dangerously depleted stores. She knew K'lon had been raiding them but hadn't the heart to object.

"He fainted, did he?" Leri crowed in malicious jubilation. "And he wasn't satisfied with my decisions during his illness, was he?"

"Was Holth eavesdropping again?"

"She doesn't need to. I don't know another reason why you'd have anger spots on your cheeks. Ha!"

"I've as much trouble making you listen to reason." Moreta spoke more tartly than she meant and she could feel her cheeks flush again. "You *know* you're overreaching your strength—"

Leri flapped her hand. "I will *not* forgo the pleasure of flying the queens' wing. Not while I'm able. And I'm a lot abler today than I have been for Turns!" She sipped from her wineglass.

"Oh?" Moreta eyed the goblet significantly.

"I won't *have* any more fellis juice until you've brewed it, my dear Moreta," Leri reminded her with a saccharine smile.

"K'lon said he knew where he could get some dried fruit."

"Hmmm." Both women knew that many of K'lon's supplies probably came from a hold that didn't need such medicines any more. "Ah well." Leri lifted her glass in silent homage.

Moreta turned to the harness rack, tears stinging her eyes again. She must stop thinking of her family's empty hold. The memories of that place, shimmering in summer sunshine, children playing in the big meadow in front of the Hold, old aunties and uncles basking along the stone walls, see-sawed with the present empty lifeless dwelling. Snakes and wild wherries must have . . .

"Moreta?" Leri's voice was soft and kind. "Moreta, Holth says K'lon has arrived," she added in a brisker tone exactly as Orlith told her rider the same news.

"I sometimes think I have more than two ears and one head."

I don't have ears, Orlith remarked.

Then K'lon was striding into the weyr, exuding an enormous amount of energy and good spirits. Moreta was suddenly struck by the warm brown tan of his face. Then, as he pulled off his flying helmet, she noticed that his hair was bleached.

"Nerat has fellis juice to spare, Moreta," he announced cheerfully, swinging the bulging pack from his back. "And Lemos says they've aconite and willow salic."

"And how was A'murry when you stopped at Igen?" She gave him a warm smile to show that she didn't object to a short detour.

"He's much, much improved." K'lon radiated relief. "Of course he's still weak, but he sits in the sun all day, which is good for his chest, and he's beginning to get an appetite."

"Done a lot of sunning with A'murry, haven't you, K'lon?" Leri asked.

Moreta shot her a quick look for her voice was suspiciously coy.

"When I've had the time." K'lon stammered slightly, fussing nervously with the pack.

"You mean"—Moreta had at last reached Leri's conclusion—"you've *taken* time to be with A'murry!"

"When I think of how hard I've worked—" Rogeth bugled outside the weyr.

"No one is faulting you, K'lon," Leri said quickly. Holth crooned reassurance, her eyes whirling bluely. "But, my dear boy, you've been taking a dreadful risk timing it. You could meet yourself coming and going—"

"But I haven't. I've been very careful!" K'lon's tone was defiant and fearful.

"Just how many hours have you been putting into your days?" Leri spoke with great understanding and compassion, even a hint of amusement.

"I don't know. I never counted hours!" K'lon jerked his chin up, rebellious. "I had to, you know. To get everything done and still make time to be with A'murry. I had *promised* him that I'd be in Igen every afternoon no matter how busy I was. I had to keep that promise. And I felt *compelled* to render Master Capiam the assistance *he* had to have—"

"Believe us, K'lon," Moreta said when he turned to her in appeal, "we are profoundly grateful to you for your courage and dedication over the past week. But timing is a very tricky business."

"And something our Weyrlingmaster certainly never mentioned," K'lon replied with an edge to his voice.

"The information is restricted to bronze and queen dragons, K'lon. I presume you discovered it by chance."

"Yes, rather." K'lon's expression mirrored the surprise he must have had. "I was late. I knew A'murry would be worried. I thought of him, waiting for me, anxious, when I didn't appear on time, and the next thing I knew, I had!"

"Bit of a shock, isn't it?" Leri had a grin on her round wise face.

K'lon grinned back. "I wasn't all that certain how I'd managed it."

"So you practiced again the next afternoon?"

K'lon nodded, relaxing imperceptibly since the Weyrwomen had apparently accepted his feat with good humor. "I report to Master Capiam in the morning and he tells me the schedule. I'm at Igen in the afternoons and everywhere else on Pern in the mornings and evenings. I'm very careful." His smile was broad delight.

"You'll be more careful from now on," Leri said, her voice austere and her manner forbidding. "A'murry has improved—so you've informed us. But *you* cannot keep on being in debt to yourself for double time. Therefore, instead of flying Fall this afternoon, you will spend it—and only this afternoon— with your friend. From now on, you will keep to the normal number of hours in a day. Holth will supervise. And we will see that Master Capiam schedules you to drop in at Igen frequently."

"But—but . . ."

"Only one mistake, K'lon," Leri pointed her forefinger, oddly twisted now by the joint disease, shaking it at him in dire emphasis, "and you're too tired timing it to realize the risks you've been taking. Only one mistake, and you will deprive A'murry of yourself forever. Not just for an afternoon." Leri paused, judging the effect of her warning on K'lon, who lowered his eyes. Holth crooned on an admonitory note and Rogeth answered, startled, from outside. K'lon looked up at Leri, his eyes wide with astonishment. "Oh yes, we can, you know, when the matter is disciplinary. I think you'd prefer Holth to Sh'gall and Kadith in the matter of this infraction?"

K'lon cast a look of entreaty at Moreta, who shook her head in slow denial. K'lon looked bereft, quite different from the energetic assured man who had entered the weyr, but he had to be restricted.

"I'll be needed at Fall this afternoon," he said finally in a low uncertain voice. "How can I explain to A'murry? We can barely make up two wings as it is, and Ista can only supply one wing and ten replacements."

"You may tell A'murry that we have been considerably worried about the pace at which you've been working. That we felt it more advisable for you to *rest* this afternoon, because you've been working so hard that your judgment in Fall might be impaired, and we can't afford to lose you!"

"K'lon, *we* need you, too," Moreta added.

"In fact, the Healer Hall and the Weyr are deeply indebted to you," Leri said, her voice and manner kindly again. "Go on with you now, and send that scamp, M'barak, on any other duties Capiam scheduled for you. And you will never, K'lon—*never*—mention to anyone, especially A'murry, that dragons can slip between one time and another."

Holth's eyes gleamed with a red tinge as she extended her neck toward K'lon. He pulled himself up straight, awed by the dragon's fierce appearance.

"Yes, Leri."

"And?" Leri indicated Moreta.

"Yes, Moreta!"

"We shall never refer to this again. Give our regards to A'murry." Leri was all affability. "If it weren't so damn cold here right now, I'd suggest that you bring him and his Granth to Fort, but I suppose he *is* better off in the sun at Igen!"

The chastened rider left the weyr with a heavy tread. The two Weyr-women could hear Rogeth chirping.

"He's going to act the martyr for a while," Leri said with a sigh.

"Better that than a real one."

Then Leri began to chuckle. "I had the worst time keeping a proper face, Moreta. He was very clever about timing it, I must say. If he hadn't acquired that suspicious tan and bleached hair, we might never have guessed."

"He had too much energy! Positively obscene if you knew how dragged out I feel! Can Holth keep track of him?"

"As long as he thinks she is, it doesn't matter. You will check in on Rogeth now and again, won't you, my clever love?" Leri thumped her queen with affection. "Now, if you'll just harness her up, Moreta, we'll be off to Fall."

Moreta regarded her friend a long time until Leri gave an impatient shrug.

"Oh, go boil the fellis!" And she wriggled herself off the stone couch.

As Moreta harnessed the old queen, she wondered, in a very private way, if there was any restriction Orlith could put on Holth to prevent their martyrdom.

No.

Moreta blinked with surprise because she had put such a careful cap on her worry. And she didn't know which dragon had spoken, Orlith or Holth. Then she concentrated hard on the correct placement of the leather fighting straps. When Leri was ready, Moreta saw rider and queen to the ledge and watched them lumber off into the air with the two wings, Fort's contribution to Pern's protection against Fall. The bugling farewell from the Weyrbound dragons as the wings went *between* was a curious, prayerful compound of yearning, defiance, and encouragement. Moreta found that seeing so few dragons on the Rim reminded her that the Weyr was vulnerable, all the Weyrs—and Pern. It was hard enough to think of her family's hold, deserted, emptied by the pandemic in a matter of days. She knew but could not assimilate the fact that her personal loss was duplicated all over Igen, Ista, Telgar, and Keroon as well as at Ruatha. That wonderful Gather! To be so closely followed by such a disaster!

Resolutely Moreta turned from the chill blue skies and busied herself peeling and preparing the fellis fruit for juice. Her hands were not as shaky as they had been the day before and for that she was grateful, as the knife was sharp and the tough skins difficult. As the thick pulp was coming to the boil, she ran an inventory of the remaining stocks, amazed that what she had considered ample only six days before could have been reduced to a few bags of this or that. With all the riders vaccinated, the Weyr should not require massive amounts of febrifuges, stimulants, and chest remedies. Which was a good thing, for at that season of the year it would be impossible to restock.

"Where is K'lon?" she asked Orlith.

He is at Igen.

"How is Sh'gall?" Moreta asked out of a sense of duty.

He sleeps deeply and Kadith says that he ate well. He recovers.

Moreta was amused at the indifference in Orlith's voice—she didn't care, either, and that suited Moreta perfectly. When Orlith rose to mate again—

HOLTH COMES! Falga and Tamianth are severely wounded!

Moreta paused long enough to take the simmering fellis juice from the brazier before she hurried out. Holth emerged above the Star Stones and dove straight for her ledge. Moreta hurried up the stairs. With an agility that Moreta could not believe, Leri swung off her dragon, shedding the cumbersome agenothree tank so that it clanged hollowly on the stone, rolling to the wall.

"Tamianth has taken a terrible scoring, Moreta," Leri said, her face gray with shock and anxiety. "The healers can manage Falga's leg, but Tamianth's wing . . ." Tears runneled the flight dirt on Leri's face. "Here. Use my jacket! My helmet will fit and the goggles. Oh, go!"

"Orlith can't!" Moreta felt anguish, sensing Leri's distress through Holth.

"Orlith can't, but Holth will!" Leri was shoving her jacket sleeve on Moreta's outstretched arm. "You're more use to Falga and Tamianth than anyone else could be. You've got to go! Holth won't mind and neither will Orlith. This is an emergency!"

Both queen dragons were agitated, Orlith coming out to her ledge to croon and bellow, extending her neck up toward her rider, Leri, and Holth. Moreta pulled the jacket on. As Moreta was so much taller than Leri, it didn't quite come to her waist, and Leri's flying belt had to be cinched in to the last notch. Moreta crammed on the helmet and eyepieces and swung up on the fighting straps before she could reconsider.

Forgive me, Orlith! she cried, waving at her queen.

What is to forgive?

"Get going!" Leri bellowed.

Holth sprang, moving almost as heavily as egg-bloated Orlith. Moreta experienced confusion, linked for so many Turns to one dragon mind. How on earth was she going to understand Holth, when suddenly she did. Holth was there, with her, and Moreta could sense Orlith hovering protective. Jealously? No, she sensed nothing negative in her own dragon's mind other than a concern that Moreta could not deal with her friend Holth. Holth was by then airborne, and the first intimate connection Moreta had with the old queen was of her weariness and her compulsion to help Tamianth.

Slow and easy does it, Moreta said to Holth with all the encouragement and understanding she could muster.

The watchdragon saluted them, wishing Holth and Leri well. As the watchdragon was a green weyrling, mistaking Holth's rider could be forgiven but it stuck in Moreta's mind as Holth gallantly plowed upward in the blustery wind.

Moreta envisioned the distinctive ridge of the High Reaches Weyr, a jagged comb with seven unequal spires.

I know where we must go. Trust in me, the old dragon said.

I do, Holth, Moreta replied, aware that Holth's experience was far greater than Orlith's for all the younger queen's vigor. *Take us to the High Reaches.*

In place of her usual *between* litany, Moreta tried to analyze the difference between the two queen dragons. Holth's mind-voice was old and tired, but it was firm, rich, and deep, many layers denser than Orlith's. Perhaps, when Orlith had reached the fine age Holth enjoyed, she, too, would have the depth of Holth's responsiveness.

Then they were in the warmer air over the High reaches, and Holth was skimming the jagged spindles and swooping in a deep left-hand bank so that Moreta had an unobstructed view of the ground and the injured dragons there. Moreta blinked at the small clusters attending the wounded. Tamianth rated the most assistance. As Holth descended, Moreta could see that Tamianth had lost the trailing edge of all three wingsails. And she was badly scored down her left side.

How did that happen? Moreta was appalled.

Cross-over and too much to do. She wanted to help the wings, Holth said, and an echoing sadness welled in Moreta as Holth implanted the incident in her mind. Tamianth had risen at an angle so that Falga could bring the flamethrower into action but they had blundered into an updraft before they could correct. A great gout of Thread had fallen across her wing and into her shoulder. And across Falga's leg.

Holth could not turn on a wingtip as Orlith could, but the old queen gauged her descent to a finger and glided to a halt a wing-length from the injured Tamianth.

Can you help me ease her pain, Holth? Moreta asked as she slid in frantic haste from the dragon's back. Tamianth's howls had to be muted.

Orlith is with us, Holth said with great dignity, her eyes churning a brilliant sparkling yellow.

Falga lay to one side on a stretcher, her face turned toward her queen, but she was barely conscious. Two healers were swathing her leg in bandages soaked in numbweed.

Tamianth, Moreta said, hurrying to the dragon's injured side, hoping the dragon might hear her and would listen. *I am Moreta to heal you!*

Tamianth was thrashing her head and forearms from side to side, movement that hampered the efforts of the weyrfolk trying to apply numbweed to the wingbones. Moreta noticed in a quick glance that they had managed to salve the deep body score from which ichor flowed; the wing was causing Tamianth's agony.

"*Hold her!*" Moreta roared at the top of her voice and her mind.

The other injured dragons and the watchdragon bugled in response. Holth reared onto her hindquarters, trumpeting, her wings extended. From the weyrs emerged High Reaches dragons whose riders were too sick to fly Fall. And suddenly Tamianth was locked by the combined wills of the dragons around her.

"Come *on*!" Moreta exhorted the weyrfolk who were gawking in astonishment. "Get the numbweed on. Now!"

She grabbed a paddle and a pot from the ground and, as she worked rapidly, she assessed the extent of the injury. It was somewhat similar to Dilenth's. Though he had lost leading edge and sustained damage to bone and finger joints, Tamianth had lost more sail. She would be a long time out of the air.

"Is there anything we can do to help the dragon?" A bright-eyed little man with a broad jaw and a broad nose appeared at her elbow. Another man, not much bigger, frowning anxiously in what seemed a permanent grimace, stood just beyond him. Both wore Healer purple and the shoulder knots of journeymen. Moreta glanced quickly at Falga's stretcher. "She is unconscious and her wound dressed. That's all we can do for her right now. I will need oil, reeds, thin gauze, needle, treated thread—"

"I'm not of this Weyr," the bright-eyed man said and turned to the bigger one who nodded acknowledgment to Moreta and ran off to the low stone building that was High Reaches' main living quarters. "My name is Pressen, Weyrwoman."

"Keep applying numbweed, Pressen. All down the bones. I want them thickly coated, especially the joints. Just as you'd do any Threadscore on a human. And keep it thick on the body wound, too. I don't want her losing so much ichor."

An old woman stumbled up with a bucket of redwort, shouting at three children behind her to bring the oil and not dawdle. Two riders, each with bandaged scores, approached Moreta; their dragons, a blue and a brown—both scored—settled to the rocky ground, their eyes, spinning with distress, on Tamianth.

Moreta suddenly had more help than she could use effectively so she sent the riders to help the other healer find her requirements and the children to get a table for her to stand on. The old woman informed her that the Weyr's healers had died and the two new ones knew absolutely nothing about dragons but were willing. She used to help but her hands had "a trembling."

Moreta sent her off to find the gauze—that was her most urgent need. In the time it took Moreta to complete her preparations to repair the wing, Tamianth's crushing pain had been reduced to a throbbing ache, according to Holth–Orlith. Tamianth's wing was considerably larger than Dilenth's and the sail fragments fewer. The two riders were of great assistance in sorting the pieces onto the gauze. "I never would have thought of gauze," Pressen had murmured, fascinated at the reconstruction. He was able to assist her in the finer stitching, for his small hands were extremely deft. Nattal, the ancient High Reaches headwoman, forced Moreta to take time for a cup of soup, claiming that she knew the Fort Weyrwoman was only just recovered from the plague and it would give the High Reaches a bad name if Moreta collapsed on them, and then what would happen to Tamianth? It was soon obvious to Moreta that the soup contained a stimulating ingredient, for when she resumed her delicate repair it was with improved concentration and precision.

Nonetheless, Moreta was trembling with fatigue by the time she finished.

We must return, Holth said in an inarguable tone.

Moreta was more than willing, but oddly disturbed by some nonspecific anxiety. She looked toward Falga, who was either unconscious or sleeping under the furs of the stretcher. Troubled, Moreta looked over the rocky Bowl, at the other injured dragons.

"You look very pale, Moreta," Pressen said, lightly touching her arm with his red-stained hand. "I'm sure we can handle any other injuries. It was just that—the whole wing! Your work was an inspiration."

"Thank you. Just keep the bones saturated with numbweed. Once the joints have started to produce ichor, that will coat the wounds and the healing process will begin."

"I had never really considered that dragons get injured by Thread," Pressen said, his expression respectful as he flicked his eyes to the dragons on the ledges and the seven pinnacles.

Come! Mount! Holth's tone was more urgent, and there was nothing of Orlith in her voice.

"I must leave." Moreta swung up onto Holth's back, noting in the back of her mind that Holth was leaner than Orlith and no longer as tall in the shoulder. Or maybe it was the way Holth had of assuming a half-crouch.

As the old queen gathered herself, Moreta suppressed a concern that the dragon was too tired for a standing start. Her hindquarters—Moreta's head snapped back as Holth sprang powerfully upward, and she devoutly hoped that the queen had been unable to track her secret doubts. To cover her embarrassment, Moreta visualized the Star Stones of Fort Weyr, the largest of those monuments, and the mountain peak that soared behind the Stones.

Please take us to Fort, Holth!

Holth complied without clearing the High Reaches Weyr rim. During the searing moment of cold *between*, Moreta's hands stung in the gloves. She ought to have oiled them again. She was always acquiring little nicks and needle scratches during a repair. The green weyrling greeted them on their return, bugling on an unexpectedly joyful note.

Holth glided to her ledge, coming in a shade too fast, Moreta thought, bracing herself for the landing.

You are needed, Holth said as Moreta loosened the straps and slid down.

"I'll just remove your harness—"

I need you now! Orlith's voice was petulant. *I've been waiting for you!*

"Of course you have, love, and very goodnatured you were to let me go—"

Leri says you shouldn't waste any time, Holth added, the facets of her eyes beginning to whirl faster.

"Something's happened to Orlith?" Moreta skipped down the stone steps as fast as she could, her heart pounding. She raced around the corner into her weyr, knocking her shoulder as she bounced into the turn.

Orlith had her head angled to catch the first possible glimpse of her rider. As Moreta barreled into the weyr, Orlith bugled repeatedly.

As she threw her arms around her dragon's head, Moreta noticed Leri standing to one side, wrapped up in sleeping furs, looking excessively pleased.

"We managed just fine," she explained between Orlith's effusions, "but the sooner you get her to the Hatching Ground the better. I don't think she could have held out *much* longer, but you *were* needed badly at High Reaches, weren't you?"

Between apologies and encouragements to her dragon, Moreta agreed.

"No one even knew you were gone," Leri said, "but I doubt I could have sustained the deception getting Orlith to the Hatching Ground."

I really need to go, Orlith said plaintively.

CHAPTER XII

**Fort Hold, Fort and High Reaches Weyrs,
Present Pass, 3.18.43**

"J for one, am heartily glad to hear a piece of good news," Capiam said when the echoes of the drum message had faded.

They had all heard the sound of the drums but, closeted in the thick stone walls of Lord Tolocamp's apartment in Fort Hold, they had not been able to distinguish the cadences until the Harper Hall began to relay the tidings onward.

"Twenty-five eggs is not a generous clutch," Lord Tolocamp said in exaggeratedly mournful voice.

Capiam wondered if the Lord Holder's dose of vaccine had held some curious contaminant. The man's whole personality had altered. The charitable would say that he grieved for his wife and four daughters, but Capiam knew that Tolocamp had consoled himself rather quickly by taking a new wife, so his sorrow was suspect. Tolocamp had also made his losses the excuse for a variety of shortcomings, short temper, and dithering.

"Twenty-five with a queen egg is a superb clutch this late in a Pass," Capiam replied firmly.

Lord Tolocamp pulled at his lower lip, then he sighed heavily.

"Moreta really must not permit Kadith to fly Orlith again. Sh'gall was so ill."

"That is not *our* business," Tirone remarked, entering the discussion for the first time. "Not that the illness of the rider has any effect on the performance of the dragon. Anyway, Sh'gall is flying Fall at Nerat so he's evidently fully recovered."

"I wish they would inform us of the status of each Weyr," Lord Tolocamp said with another heavy sigh. "I worry so."

"The *Weyrs*"—Tirone spoke with a firm emphasis and a sideways look of irritation at the Lord Holder—"have been discharging their traditional duties to their Holds!"

"Did *I* bring the illness to the Weyrs? Or the Holds? If the dragonriders were not too quick to fly here and there—"

"And Lords Holder not so eager to fill every nook and cranny of their—"

"This is *not* the time for recriminations!" Tirone shot a warning glance at Capiam. "You know as well, if not better than most people, Tolocamp, that seamen introduced that abomination onto the continent!" The deep rumbling voice of the Masterharper was acid. "Let us resume the discussion interrupted by such good news." Tirone's expression told Capiam that he must control his antipathy for Tolocamp. "I have men seriously ill in that camp of yours." Tirone caught the Lord Holder's gaze, stabbing his finger toward the windows. "There is not enough vaccine to mitigate the disease, but they could at least have the benefit of decent quarters and practical nursing."

"Healers are among them," Tolocamp countered sullenly. "Or so you tell me!"

"Healers are not immune to the viral influence and they cannot work without medicines." Capiam leaned urgently across the table to Tolocamp, who drew back, another habit that irritated the healer. "You have a great storeroom of medicinal supplies—"

"Garnered and prepared by my lost Lady—"

Capiam ruthlessly suppressed his irritation. "Lord Tolocamp, we *need* those supplies—"

A mean look narrowed Tolocamp's eyes. "For Ruatha, eh?"

"Other holds besides Ruatha have needs!" Capiam spoke quickly to allay Tolocamp's suspicions.

"Supplies are the responsibility of the individual holder. Not mine. I cannot further deplete resources that might be needed by my own people."

"If the Weyrs, stricken as they are, can extend *their* responsibilities in the magnificent way they have, beyond the areas beholden to them, then how can you refuse?" Tirone's deep voice rang with feeling.

"Very easily." Tolocamp pushed his lips out. "By saying no. No one may pass the perimeter into the Hold from any outlying area. If they don't have the plague, they have other, equally infectious, diseases. I shall not risk more of my people. I shall make no further contributions from my stores."

"Then I withdraw my healers from your Hold," Capiam said. He rose quickly.

"But—but—you can't *do* that!"

"Indeed he can! *We* can," Tirone replied. He got to his feet and came round the table to stand by Capiam. "Craftsmen are under the jurisdiction of their Hall. You'd forgotten that, hadn't you?"

Capiam swung out of the room, so angry at Tolocamp's pettiness that bile rose sourly in his throat. Tirone was only a step behind him.

"I'll call them out! Then I'll join you in the camp."

"I didn't think it would come to this!" Capiam seized Tirone by the shoulder in an effort to express his appreciation at the Harper's swift reinforcement.

"Tolocamp has presumed once too often on the generosity of the Halls!" Tirone's usually smooth, persuasive voice had a hard edge. "I hope this example reminds others of our prerogatives."

"Call our Craftspeople out, but don't come to the camp with me, Tirone. You must stay in the hall with your people, and guide mine."

"My people"—Tirone gave a forced laugh—"with very few exceptions, are languishing in that blighted camp of his. You are the one who must bide at the halls."

"Master Capiam—"

The men whirled toward the woman's voice. The speaker emerged from the shadow of a doorway. She was one of the three remaining Fort daughters, a big-boned girl with large brown eyes well-spaced in an intelligent but plain face. Her thick black hair was pulled severely back from her face.

"I have the storeroom keys." She held them up.

"How did you? . . ." Tirone was uncharacteristically at a loss for words.

"Lord Tolocamp made plain his position when he received the request for medicines. I helped harvest and preserve them."

"Lady? . . ." Capiam could not recall her name.

"Nerilka." She supplied it quickly with the faint smile of a someone who does not expect to be remembered. "I have the right to offer you the products of my own labor." She gave Tirone an intense, challenging stare. Then she returned her direct gaze to Capiam. "There is just one condition."

"If it is within my giving." Capiam would give a lot for medicines.

"That I may leave this Hold in your company and work with the sick in that horrid camp. I've been vaccinated." A wry smile lifted one side of her mouth. "*Lord* Tolocamp was expansive that day. Be that as it may, I will not stay in a Hold to be abused by a girl younger than myself. Tolocamp permitted her and her family to enter this hallowed Hold from the fire-heights yet he leaves healers and harpers to die out there!"

And he left my mother and sisters to die at Ruatha. Her unspoken words were palpable in the brief silence.

"This way, quickly," she said, taking the initiative and pulling at Capiam's sleeve.

"I'll remove our Craftspeople from this Hold on my way out," Tirone said. He walked quickly toward the hall.

"Young woman, you do realize that once you leave the Hold without your father's knowledge, particularly in his present frame of mind—"

"Master Capiam, I doubt he'll notice I'm gone." She spoke with a light disregard for the matter, obviously more bitter about her sire's new wife. "These steps are very steep," she added and flicked open a handglow.

Steep, circular, and narrow, Capiam realized as his foot slipped on the first short step. He disliked blind stairways, of which Fort had more than its fair share. The Ancients had been fond of them in the construction of the first holds as auxiliary access between the levels of what were, essentially, natural caves. He was grateful for Nerilka's guidance and the soft glowlight but the descent seemed to take ages. Then the darkness lightened and they emerged on to a landing, with narrow high halls branching in three directions. Beside the circular stair they had just left was a second one that he hoped they would not need to use.

Nerilka led him to the right, then down a short broad flight and to the left. He was completely disoriented. Nerilka made a second left turn. Three drudges who had been lounging on long benches by a heavy wooden door got to their feet, their faces impassive.

"You are prompt, I see," Nerilka said, nodding approval to them. "Father appreciates promptness," she said to Capiam as she was separating the keys. Unlocking the door took three of the larger ones. Opening required the effort of one of the drudges and then Capiam could smell the mingled stillroom aromas, astringent, bitter, fragrant, and oddly musty.

Nerilka pulled open the glowbasket inside the door to illuminate sinks, braziers, tables, high stools, measuring apparatus and implements, gleaming basins and glass bottles. Capiam had been in the room often and when he had, he'd approached it from the other direction in the company of Lady Pendra. Now Nerilka was unlocking the storeroom and beckoning him to follow her. She smiled when she heard his surprised gasp.

Capiam had known that Ford Hold's storage rooms were ample, but he had not been beyond the dispensary. They were standing on a wide tier, balustraded from the vast, dark interior, with steps leading down to the main floor. He could hear the slither and rustle of tunnel snakes fleeing the sudden light. Capiam saw shelves, reaching, it seemed, to the high vaulted ceiling. Barrels and crates and drying racks, were ranged in rows and dusty ranks. He had the impression of staggering resources and doubly condemned Tolocamp's parsimony.

"Behold, Master Capiam, the produce of my labors since I was old enough to snip leaf and blossom or dig root and bulb." Nerilka's sarcastic voice was intended for his ears only. "I won't say I have filled every shelf, but my sisters who have predeceased me would not deny me their portions. Would that all of these hoarded supplies were usable, but even herbs and roots lose their potency in time. Waste, that's the bulk of what you see, fattening tunnel snakes. Carry-yokes are in the corner there, Sim. You and the others, take up the bales." She spoke in a pleasant authoritative tone, gesturing to the drudges. "Master Capiam, if you do not mind—that's the fellis juice." She pointed to a withy-covered demijohn. "I'll take this." She lifted the bulky container by its girth strap. In her other hand, she swung a pack over one shoulder. "I mixed fresh tussilago last night, Master Capiam. That's right, Sim. On your way now. We'll use the kitchen exit. Lord Tolocamp has been complaining again about the wear on the main hall carpets. It's as well to comply with his instructions even if it does mean extra lengths for the rest of us." She covered the glowbaskets.

She set down the demijohn to lock the storeroom, ignoring Capiam's expression, for it was apparent to him that she had gone to some pains to organize the unauthorized distribution. Her eyes met his once as she swept the chamber with one last long glance. The drudges were already halfway down the corridor with their burdens.

"I would like to take more, but four drudges added to the noon parade to the perimeter are not going to be noticed by the guard."

Only then did Capiam realize that Nerilka was dressed in the coarse fabric allotted the general worker, a plainly belted tunic over dark-gray trousers and felted winter boots.

"No one will care in the least if one of the drudges continues on to the camp." She shrugged. "Nor will anyone at the kitchen exit think it odd for the Masterhealer to leave with supplies. Indeed, they would wonder if you left empty-handed."

She had locked the outer door and now looked speculatively at the bunch of keys. "One never knows, does one?" she said to herself in the habit of one used to solitary tasks. She stuffed the keys in her belt pouch and then, noticing Capiam's look, gave him that little half smile. "My stepmother has another set. She thinks it is the only one. But *my* mother thought the still-room a very good occupation for me. This way, Master Capiam."

Capiam followed. The docility of the Fort daughters had been the source of ribaldry at the Halls whenever Lady Pendra had invited unmarried men of rank to the Hold. Nerilka, Capiam was chagrined to remember, was one of the oldest of the eleven daughters, though she had two full elder brothers,

Campen and Mostar, and four younger. Lady Pendra had been constantly pregnant, another source of indelicate comment among the apprentice healers. It had never occurred to Capiam—and certainly not to his shameless juniors—that the Fort Horde had any wits or opinions of their own. In Nerilka, rebellion was full blown.

"Lady Nerilka, if you leave now—"

"I *am* leaving," she said in a firm low voice as they entered the kitchen's back corridor.

"—and in this fashion, Lord Tolocamp—"

She halted and faced Capiam at the archway into the busy, noisy kitchen. "—will miss neither me nor my dower." She lifted the demijohn. She sighed with exasperation, glancing at the door through which the drudges had exited. "I can be of real use in the internment camp for I know about mixing medicines and decocting and infusing herbs. I shall be doing something constructive that is needed rather than sitting comfortably in a corner somewhere. I know your craftsmen are overworked. Every hand is needed.

"Besides,"—she gave him a sideways glance that was almost coquettish— "I can slip back in whenever it's necessary." She patted the keys in her pouch. "Don't look surprised. The drudges do it all the time. Why shouldn't I?"

Then she moved on and he followed her quickly, unable to think of any counterargument. The moment she passed the arch from the kitchen, her posture changed, her stride altered, and she was no longer the proud daughter of the Hold but a gawky woman, head down, shuffling, awkwardly overburdened and resentful.

Once out in the great roadway, Capiam looked, trying not to appear furtive, to his left, to the main forecourt and stairs. Tirone and the dozens of harpers and healers regularly in attendance at Fort Hold were moving down the ramp.

"He'll be watching them! Not us," Nerilka said. She chuckled. "Try to walk less proudly, Master Capiam. You are, for the moment, merely a drudge, burdened and reluctantly heading for the perimeter, terrified of coming down sick to die like everyone in the camp."

"Everyone in the camp is not dying."

"Of course not, but Lord Tolocamp thinks so. He has so informed us constantly. Ah, a belated attempt on his part to prevent the exodus! Don't pause!" she added, again in that authoritative voice.

Capiam would have halted in consternation but for her warning. He saw four guards hurrying after Tirone's group.

"You can walk as slowly as you want, that's in character, but don't stop," she advised.

She watched, too, and if her eyes sparkled and she grinned at the discomfiture of her father's guards, there was no one but Capiam to observe her unfilial delight. At that distance, Capiam couldn't tell whether the guards were halfhearted in their efforts or not. There was a brief mêlée from which Tirone and his companions continued unhurriedly down the roadway to the Harper Hall. Nerilka and Capiam continued toward the perimeter.

The internment camp had been established to the left of the massive Fort Hold cliff, in a small valley out of the direct view of the Hold. The guard lines had been set above it, in full view of Lord Tolocamp's windows. A rough timbered shack had been erected as a guard shelter from which temporary fencing had been built in both directions. Guards constantly patrolled the fence.

Nerilka's three drudges deposited their burdens at the guardhouse where others were leaving baskets of food. Then the men had begun to retrace their steps to the Hold, empty yokes balanced on their shoulders.

"If you go past the perimeter, Master Capiam, you will not be permitted back," Nerilka reminded him.

"If there is more than one way into the Hold, is there only one past the perimeter?" Capiam asked flippantly. "I'll see you later, Lady Nerilka."

As they approached the shack, guards were being assigned to carry certain of the baskets and bales into the prohibited area where a group of men and women waited patiently for the exchange to be made.

"Here now, Master Capiam." The guardleader came striding up, his expression alarmed. "You can't go in there without staying—"

"I don't want this medicine heaved about, Theng. Make sure they understand it's fragile."

"I can do that much for you," Theng replied, and he strode diffidently to add the demijohn to one side of the bales. "This is to be handled carefully and preferably by a healer. Master Capiam says it's medicine."

The internees moved forward to collect the supplies, and Theng backed up. Nerilka was right behind him and as he turned to come back to the guardhouse, she slipped past him and joined those picking up the baskets as if she were one of them.

Capiam waited for an outcry, for surely the other guards had noticed her. Nerilka was already trudging down the slope toward the tents of the internment camp when Theng took him by the arm to escort him back.

"Nah, then, Master Capiam, you know I can't allow you close contact with any of your craftsmen," Theng said as Capiam cast one more glance after Nerilka's retreating figure.

"I know, Leader Theng. The medicine was my concern. So little of its ingredients remain."

Theng made a conciliatory noise between his teeth and then his attention was taken by the spacing of his guards. Slowly Capiam turned in the direction of the halls.

As he walked, he realized that he could not walk out of his Hall as Nerilka could leave her Hold. Withdrawing his healers from the Hold was quite within his right as Masterhealer, but he must remain in his Hall, available to those who need him throughout Pern. However, he felt the better for his brief flirtation with the idea. And the camp had gained not only supplies but a valuable assistant. He must ask for volunteers to take the remainder of Nerilka's purloined supplies to Ruatha with all possible haste.

◆ ◆ ◆

"The ichor can be extracted from one queen and applied to the joints of another," Moreta told Leri. "And you shouldn't be coming all this way for a message someone else could have brought."

They were standing at the entrance to the Hatching Ground and talking in quiet tones, although it was doubtful that the sleeping Orlith would have paid them any attention had they bellowed. She was still exhausted from the laying of twenty-five eggs. Orlith had curled herself about the leathery eggs, the queen egg within the circle of her forearms, her head laid at an awkward angle. Her belly skin was beginning to shrink and her color was good, so Moreta had no more anxieties about her queen and time to worry about Falga's Tamianth.

"No one there is capable of doing that," Leri said with a fine scorn, "or so Holth was informed by Kilanath. Holth says she sounds very worried."

"She has reason to be if Tamianth is not producing any ichor on that damaged wing." Moreta paced up and down. "Is Falga conscious?"

"Delirious."

"Not the plague?"

"No, wound fever. Under control."

"Shards! Falga knows how to draw ichor. It would have to be Kilanath and Diona . . ." Moreta looked back at the slumbering Orlith.

"She'll be out a long while," Leri murmured, stepping inside the Hatching Ground and gripping Moreta's hands tightly in hers. "It doesn't take long to draw ichor and spread it—"

"That's abusing Orlith's trust in me!"

"She trusts me as well. Every moment you delay . . ."

"I know! I know!" Moreta thought wretchedly of Falga and Tamianth, of all that Weyr had done the last few days.

"If Orlith should rouse, Holth will know and, considering the emergency, Orlith will understand. The clutching's over!" Leri pressed urgently on Moreta's hands.

Unusual circumstances, of which there were far too many recently in Moreta's opinion, warranted unusual actions.

"Holth's willing. I asked her first, as soon as she told me about Tamianth."

Obviously Leri felt that no one at Fort realized that Moreta had been absent two days before to treat the injured High Reaches' queen. Moreta cast a distraught look toward her sleeping queen, returned Leri's clasp with an answering pressure, and walked hurriedly from the sheltering arch of the Hatching Ground, quickly leaving Leri behind.

"Don't stride so! I can't," Leri whispered after her.

Moreta adjusted her pace. Anyone really observant would have noticed the difference in height between the woman who had entered the Ground and the one who left, but it was the gray hour before dawn and no one was about. Thread would Fall later that day at Nerat and the dragonriders rested whenever possible with so difficult a schedule.

Moreta delayed long enough on her way to Holth to change into her own riding gear. Leri's had left a broad exposed band across her back and she couldn't risk kidney chill. Holth greeted her at the entrance to her weyr and Moreta stepped aside for the queen to reach the edge. Then she mounted, conscious once again of the difference between dragons. She wished fervently that she did not feel that she was somehow betraying Orlith.

"Take us to the High Reaches, please, Holth," she asked in a subdued voice.

The watchrider sleeps and the blue will not note our departure. Holth said impassively and, despite her dark reflections, Moreta smiled. So Leri and Holth had considered that detail.

Then Holth propelled herself from her ledge and was barely airborne before she went *between.* Moreta gasped at the audacity and hadn't time to think of her verse before the darkness around them was relieved by the glows surrounding the High Reaches Bowl.

Tamianth is below but it is easier for me to take off from a ledge, said Holth, neatly landing on one. *Tamianth will not object to my tenancy.* Then she added gently, *Orlith sleeps. And so does Leri.*

"The pair of you!" Moreta's exasperation was goodnatured.

Holth turned gleaming eyes toward her and huffed softly.

"Is that you? Moreta?" a quavering voice asked.

"It's Moreta."

"Oh, bless you, bless you. I'm so sorry to drag you here but I simply can't do it. I'm so afraid of hurting Kilanath. Hitting a nerve or something. They tried to explain to me how simple it all is but I can't believe them. Oh, do wake up, Kilanath. Moreta's come."

A pair of dragon eyes lit the darkness below the ledge. Moreta put her hand on the wall, her left foot seeking for the top step. Light spilled from the weyrling quarters now occupied by Tamianth but the stairs were still in confusing shadow.

"Oh, do hurry, please, Moreta!" Diona's plea was more wail.

"I would if I could see where I'm going." Moreta spoke sharply, irritated by Diona's ineffectuality.

"Oh, yes, of course. I didn't think. You don't know where anything is in this Weyr." Dutifully Diona opened a glowbasket but, before she held it up, she turned its illumination away from Moreta. "Yes, Pressen, she's here. Oh, do hurry, Moreta. Oh, yes, sorry." Then she remembered to hold the basket high enough to show Moreta the steps.

Moreta skipped down them as fast as she could before something else could distract Diona. Kilanath dipped her head close to Moreta and sniffed, as if testing the quality of the visitor.

"Now, don't fret, Kilanath," Diona crooned in a saccharine voice that Moreta thought ought to irritate a queen. "You know she came here just to help." Diona turned apologetically to Moreta. "She really will behave because she's terribly worried about Tamianth."

As Moreta entered the weyrling quarters, she could see why. Tamianth looked more green than gold except for the gray wing and gray-spread score on her side. The wing had been propped at the shoulder and put in a sling so that the queen could relax, but her hide twitched constantly from stress. Tamianth opened one lid of her eyes, which were gray with pain.

"Water! Water, please, water!" Falga's voice rose in feverish complaint.

"That's all she says." Diona was wringing her hands.

Pressen, the bright-eyed healer, ran to Falga's side and offered her water, but she pushed it away before falling back into her restless tossing.

Muttering an oath, Moreta strode to the queen, picked up a fold of hide on the neck, and cursed. The dragon was dehydrated, her skin parched.

"Water. Of course, it's *Tamianth* who needs the water! Has no one offered the queen water?" Moreta looked about for a water tank, for anything resembling a container.

"Oh, I never thought of that!" Diona snatched her hands to her mouth, her eyes wide with dismay. "Kilanath kept telling me about water but we all thought Falga . . ." She waved feebly at the fevered woman.

"Then, by the Egg of Faranth, get some!"

"Please, water. Water!" Falga moaned, restlessly trying to rise.

"Don't stand there, Diona. Are there weyrlings in the next building? Well, rout them out! Use a cauldron from the kitchen but get water for this poor beast. It's a wonder she's not dead! Of all the irresponsible, ineffectual, dithering idiots I have ever encountered—" Moreta saw the startled expression on Pressen's face as he rose from Falga's side. She pulled herself together, breathing deeply to dispel the impotent anger and dismay that boiled within her. "I *can't* keep coming here for oversights!"

"No, no, of course not!" Pressen's reply was conciliatory, anxious.

The poor beast was too weak to reach farther than her rider who had, even in her pain-wracked daze, tried to communicate! Fuming at Diona's ineptitude, Moreta snatched down the nearest glowbasket to examine Tamianth's wing. Two days without any lubrication and the wing fragments might not reconstruct. The glowlight glistened ominously on a stain on the floor, under Tamianth's injured side. With a muffled cry of despair, Moreta dropped to one knee, dipped her fingers in the moisture, sniffing it.

"Pressen! Bring me your kit—redwort and oil! This dragon's bleeding to death!"

"What?"

Pressen stumbled toward her and she held the basket high, at Tamianth's side. Grimly she recalled the instructions she had given Pressen, unused to dragon injuries: Keep the side wound covered with numbweed. Why hadn't she checked it? How could she have assumed, given the chaotic conditions at High Reaches, the inexperienced healers, and the tired riders, that the wound had been properly attended? Instead she had blithely flitted off, smugly pleased with her wing repair.

"The fault is mine, Pressen. I ought to have seen to the side as well. What has happened is that Threadscore ruptured veins along the side and shoulders. Numbweed covered the ooze. Ichor isn't reaching the wing. We'll need to repair the veins. The surgery is much the same sort you'd do on a human. Color is the main difference."

"Surgery is not my speciality, Lady, but," he added, seeing her desperate expression, "I have assisted and can do so now."

"I'll need surgical clamps, oil, redwort, threaded needle . . ."

Pressen was pouring oil and redwort into bowls. "I have all the instruments we'd need. Barly's effects were handed over to me when I arrived."

Dreading what she might find, Moreta examined the injured wing. Some ichor beaded the joints but far less than was required. Tamianth would have to be very lucky; stupidity had already worked against the poor beast. Possibly, with application of Kilanath's ichor at crucial points, the damage could still be reversed. Liberal and frequent dressings of numbweed had, at least, kept the fragments moist. Once Tamianth's veins had been mended and water brought the poor thirsty beast . . .

Moreta scrubbed her hands in the redwort, hissing at the sting in half-healed scratches. Then she oiled her hands thoroughly while Pressen made the same preparation.

"First we must clean the numbweed away from the wound. I'd say the stoppage is here . . . and here, and perhaps, even down here near the hearts." She lightly indicated the areas, then with oil-soaked pads, she and Pressen cleaned away the numbweed. Tamianth shuddered. "With all this numb-weed, she can't *feel* any pain. Here! See where the ichor is oozing . . ." Her father had always talked as he worked on injured runners. Much of what she had heard from her earliest years she had been able to apply to dragons. She oughtn't to think of her father at a time like this, but his habit would help her teach Pressen. Someone in the Weyr had to know. "Ah, here's the first one. Just below your left hand, Pressen, should be another. Yes, and a third, a major vein leading to the hearts, and the belly vein." Moreta reached for the fine needle and the treated thread Pressen had made ready.

"Yes, the colors are different!" Pressen saw the greenish flesh and the darker green ichor that was dragon blood, the curious shining fiber that was dragon muscle. He was absorbed. "Has she had any supply to the wing at all?" His nimble fingers were suturing the first severed vein.

"Not really enough."

"Thirsty! Thirsty. Water, please, water!" Falga raved.

"Can't that idiotic woman do anything? There's a lake full of water out there!"

There was suddenly a great amount of noise, the hollow sound of metal banging against another object, the sleepy complaints of young voices. The smell of desperately desired water roused the dragon from her stupor.

Hidden from sight behind the droop of the wing, Moreta could not see what was happening but she heard the bong of the kettle being dropped and the *plash* of buckets of water being poured. She heard the greedy slurping of Tamianth as the dragon sucked water down a parched throat.

"By the Egg, she'd drink barrels!" said the bemused voice of an older man. "She mustn't have too much at once, boys, so take your time with the refills. Anything else I can do—" The Weyrlingmaster ducked carefully under the wing and stared in surprise at Moreta. "I thought your queen had clutched, Moreta."

"She has, but this one would have died . . ."

When Moreta pointed to the ichor-stained puddle on the floor, the dis-approval in the Weyrlingmaster's face turned to shock.

"S'ligar's down with a touch of the plague, despite the vaccine," Cr'not said. "But"—he gestured impotently toward Pressen, at the sound of Diona's voice thanking the weyrlings—"I could hear Falga calling for water . . ."

"It's no one's fault, Cr'not. Everyone's tired, pushed beyond their strength or trying to take on unfamiliar tasks. *I* should have examined this wound two days ago!"

"Sometimes I think it's only the momentum of routine that keeps any of us going," Cr'not said, rubbing at his face and eyes.

"You could be right. There. That's the last! Thank you, Pressen. You've the makings of a good Weyr healer!"

"Once I get accustomed to such large patients!" Pressen smiled back at Moreta.

"And you're about to learn another invaluable technique for healing dragons," Moreta said, beckoning to Pressen to follow her. She took the largest syringe from Barly's kit, fitted a needlethorn to its opening, soaked a pad quickly in redwort and then ducked under Tamianth's wing. *Diona!*

"Oh, no," Diona moaned timorously, spreading her arms to protect her queen. "Tamianth's looking ever so much better. Her color's improved enormously."

"I should hope so, but, if we don't get some ichor on her joints, she may never fly again. Holth, tell Kilanath!"

Cr'not moved toward the weyrwoman, his expression ferocious, and Diona moaned again.

"It doesn't take long, and it won't hurt Kilanath."

The queen was a good deal more cooperative than her rider, dipping her wing as she knelt for Moreta's ministration.

"Pressen, see? Here, where the vein crosses the bone?" As Pressen nodded, Moreta rubbed on some redwort, turning the golden skin brown. The fine sharp needlethorn entered hide and vein so smoothly that the dragon never felt the prick. Moreta deftly drew ichor into the tube: It glistened green and healthy in the glowlight.

"Most interesting," Pressen said, his expression intent. Neither of them paid any attention to Diona's moaning or Cr'not's exclamation of disgust.

"Now we will apply this"—Moreta returned to Tamianth, Pressen right beside her—"to the joints and the cartilage. See how dry the cartilage is? Soaks the ichor right up. Well, ah, here, nearest the shoulder, see how the beads are forming? Tamianth's beginning to function again. We'll save that wing yet!" She grinned at the little man whose face beamed back at her. "And color's returning to Tamianth's eyes, too."

"Why, so there is! Is she winking at me?"

Moreta chuckled. The gray had certainly receded from Tamianth's huge eyes and the "winking" was just the sparkle returning to the facets as the dragon improved. "I believe so. She knows who's helped her."

"And Falga is sleeping." Pressen hurried to the cot, feeling the pulse along Falga's neck. He sighed with relief. "She's much quieter now."

Holth? Moreta asked, aware of other obligations.

They sleep! Holth was unperturbed.

"I must get back to Fort. Cr'not, will you keep checking on the wing for me? Pressen knows how to draw ichor and where to put it but not when. You would."

"I will!" Cr'not nodded solemnly. "Now, you ought not to leave your queen," he added, shaking his head worriedly.

"There is a point at which *ought* has little to do with actions, Cr'not. I was sent for! I came! Now I'm going!" She gave him a curt nod. Weyrling-masters were a breed of their own and felt they could criticize with impunity anyone in a Weyr. As she collected her riding gear, she gave Pressen a saucy wink and then strode out of the building.

She ran to the stairs and took the steps two at a time.

They sleep, Holth repeated, her eyes whirling serenely.

"And so shall we once we're back home," Moreta said, swinging up onto Holth's lean back. "Take us to Fort Weyr, please, Holth."

Obligingly, Holth sprang from the ledge and, once again, went *between* as soon as there was free air about her. As the chill of nothingness wrapped them, Moreta wondered if she should mention Holth's curious trick to Leri. Was it just that the queen was old and could not jump as forcefully? Did it not seem an impertinence on Moreta's part to criticize?

Then they were back in the dawn, skimming low above the lake in Fort Weyr. That was the explanation: Holth was practicing stealth. The watch-rider was unlikely to notice a dragon leaving so low in darkness.

Holth glided to her own ledge and accepted Moreta's effusive thanks before lurching wearily into her weyr. Moreta ran down the stairs and into the Hatching Ground. To the Weyrwoman's relief, Orlith hadn't so much as changed the angle of her head during her rider's absence. And Leri slept soundly on Moreta's cot.

CHAPTER XIII

Ruatha Hold and Fort Weyr, Present Pass, 3.19.43

Alessan had to stop. Sweat was beaded on his forehead, ran down his cheeks and chin. His hands were sweaty on the plowhandles and the team panting as hard as he from their labors in the rain-heavy field. Ignoring the sting of the blisters he had acquired in the last two days, he dried his hands finger by finger on the grimy rag attached to his belt. Then Ruatha Hold's Lord Holder rubbed the sweat from his face and neck, took a swallow from the flask of water, picked up the reins, slapped the rumps of his reluctant team, and managed to grab the handles of the unwieldy plow before the runners had pulled it out of the furrow.

Another day and he was sure they'd forget they'd ever been trained to race. Of course, he told himself that every day. One day it would have to be true. He had mastered feistier beasts to the saddle, and he must—if he wished to Hold—prove equally capable at retraining. With bitter humor, Alessan wondered if his predicament could be a retribution for his defiance of his father's wishes. Yet none of *that* breeding had survived. The heavier runners, the draft and plow animals, the sturdy long-distance beasts, had been especially susceptible to the lung infections that had swept the racers' camp after the first days of the plague. The light wiry runners of his breeding had survived to graze contentedly on the lush river pastures. Until he had had to harness them, and himself, to the plows.

The land had to be tilled, crops sown, the tithe offered, the Hold fed no matter how the Lord Holder managed to accomplish those responsibilities. He came to the edge of the field and wrestled the team into the wide arc, turning back on the furrows. They were uneven but the earth had been turned. He looked briefly out at the other fields of the Hold proper, to check on the other teams. He also had a view of the northern road and the mounted man approaching along it. He shaded his eyes, cursing as the off-sider took advantage of his momentary distraction. As he lined it up again with its teammate and the plow righted, he was certain that he saw a flash of harper blue. Tuero must be back from his swing of the northern holds. Who else would be brave enough to venture to Ruatha? Alessan had drummed for heavy plow-beasts and been told that no one had any to offer. Neither threats of witholding nor doubling the marks brought better results.

"It's the plague, Alessan," Tuero had said, for once unsmiling. "It was at its worst here in Ruatha. Until Master Capiam has sent the vaccine round to everyone, they won't come here. And even then they won't bring animals, I think, because so many died here."

Alessan had cursed futilely. "If they won't come, I'll have to go! I'll bring teams in myself! They can't deny their Lord Holder to his face!" While Alessan railed at his people, he understood their viewpoint—especially since he himself had not yet had the courage to send for Dag, Fergal, and the bloodstock. Follen had given him the most strict assurance that the plague was passed by coughing or sneezing—personal contact—and could not be in the soil of the race flats or the pickets where so many beasts had died, but Alessan would not risk the few priceless breeders that Dag had whisked away the morning after the accursed Gather.

After considerable discussion with Tuero, Deefer, and Oklina—his inner council—it had been decided that he couldn't leave the Hold proper, for there was no one else of sufficient rank to enforce his orders. He hadn't wanted Tuero to make the journey as the harper was only just out of bed. But Tuero had been a wily talker, which was why, Tuero had said at the con-clusion of the council, he was a harper and why he was the best emissary to send. A few days or so in the fresh spring air on an untaxing mission would complete his recovery. After all, while a harper was generally able to turn his hand to most tasks, Tuero couldn't plow. Alessan hadn't believed a word of Tuero's cheery bluff but he had no one else to send.

Despite the awkward height of its rider, Tuero's lean mount moved easily, with a quick high step, head held high and eager once it knew itself to be home. Tuero's feet were level with the wiry beast's knees, and the harper's gaunt frame towered above its ears. Certainly not the mount that Alessan would have assigned Tuero by choice, but they seemed to have gotten along. They were riding at a right angle to Alessan's field, but he could not remove his hands from the plow to hail Tuero. He'd reached the downslope of the field and the team was fractious with the pole hitting against their hocks.

The field was nearly done; he'd finish it! Once he had he could give all his attention to Tuero's news.

He would have wished to see Tuero returning with a sturdy team, but there did seem to be something in his pack. Two more furrows and the day's stint was done.

As he drove the weary team back to the beasthold, the sowers were still busy setting seed. They'd have some sort of a crop in spite of the bloody plague. That is, if the weather held, and some other disaster—like a Thread burrowing—did not overtake wretched Ruatha.

To Alessan's surprise, Tuero was waiting for him in the beasthold, sitting on an upturned pail, his saddlebags at his feet and a look of satisfaction on his long face. His mount was munching sweetgrass in its stall, all saddle marks rubbed from its back.

"I saw you at your labors, Lord Alessan," Tuero began, a sparkle of amusement in his eyes as he rose to take the bridles of the team. "Your furrows improve."

"They could stand to." Alessan began to unhook the harness.

"Your example inspires many. In fact, your industry and occupation are already legend in the Hold. Your participation does you no disservice."

"But brought me no team. Or is there more bad news?" Alessan paused before he removed the heavy collar from the off-sider.

"No more than you've probably figured out for yourself." Tuero nodded to the saddlebags and took the collar from the other runner. "I've some bits and stashes but I saw myself how bare the cupboards are of what is needed most. At least in the north."

"And?" Alessan liked all his bad news at once so he could absorb the different shocks according to their merits.

"Others have started working the land but in some of those holds"— Tuero gestured north with the twist of straw he made to rub the mount's sweat marks—"they had severe losses. Some Gatherers left before the quarantine and made it to their homes, bringing the virus with them. I've made a list of the deaths, a sad total it is, too, and no way I can ease the telling of it. They say misery loves company, and I suppose if you're of a dismal temperament, you get joy of it." Tuero quirked his eyebrows. "I've a list of needs and musts and worries. But I'd a thought on my way back which may sweeten all.

"I was right about people's being afraid to come here, to Ruatha Hold proper. I was right about their not wanting to send good stock to their deaths for all the marks you'd be willing to give. I had a time of it to get them to let Skinny there in their holds. They were afraid."

"Afraid?"

"Afraid it carries the plague."

"That runner *survived* it!"

"Precisely. It survived, you and I survived. I got over my bout faster because I had the serum. Wouldn't serum from recovered runners protect others the way it protects people?" He grinned at Alessan's reaction. "If that notion's valid, you got a field full of cures. And a good trade item."

Alessan stared at Tuero, condemning himself for not having thought of vaccinating runners. So many of his smallholders depended on their runner breeding that he could not, in conscience, have demanded his right to a portion of their labor in this emergency, recognizing their fear of bringing plague back to their holds.

"I'm disgusted I didn't think of it myself!" he said to the grinning harper. "Come on. Let's put these two away. I need a little chat with Healer Follen." He gave his beast an exultant swat on the rear to impel it into its stall. "How could I have been so dense?"

"You have had a few other problems on your mind, you know!"

"Man! You've revived me!" Alessan gave the lean harper a clout on the shoulder, grinning in the first respite from grim reality that he had enjoyed since Oklina had recovered. "And to think I hesitated about sending you."

"*You* may have, I didn't," Tuero said impudently, scooping up his saddlebags and following Alessan's quick lead to the Hold Hall.

They found Follen quickly enough, in the main Hall tending the sick. Alessan felt his nostrils pinch against the odors that the incense could not mask. He avoided the Hall whenever possible—the coughing, the rasping breaths, and the moans of the patients were a constant reminder of the sad hospitality he had offered. Follen's anxious expression cleared when Tuero raised the saddlebags. When the men had converged into the Hold office Follen now occupied, his hopefulness waned as he examined the bags and twists of herbs. Alessan had to repeat his question about vaccinating runners.

"The premise is sound enough, Lord Alessan, but I'm not conversant with animal medicines. The Masterherdsman . . . oh, yes, well, I forgot. But there must be someone at Keroon Beasthold who could give you a considered opinion."

Tuero sighed with disappointment. "It's too late now to drum across to Keroon. They wouldn't thank us for rousing them from their beds."

"There is someone else, much closer, who would know," Alessan said in a thoughtful voice. "And Follen, is there any human vaccine left? Enough for two people?"

"I can, of course, prepare some."

"Please do while Tuero and I drum up Fort Weyr. Moreta will know if we can vaccinate runners." Then he added to himself, I can bring Dag back and see what he managed to save.

❖ ❖ ❖

Moreta was startled when the request came in to the Weyr drummer. The quarantine no longer applied. Alessan had specifically mentioned that he had been vaccinated and was healthy. She had no reason to deny a meeting and more than a few to grant it, curiosity about why the Lord Holder of Ruatha would urgently require a meeting being the least of them. Orlith was not a broody queen and quite happy to have people admire her clutch, particularly the queen egg, though she kept it always within reach of a forearm. Once she indulged in her postclutch feeding, she had piled the other eggs in a protective circle about the unique one.

"As if anyone would rob your clutch," Moreta teased her affectionately. She had told Orlith all about her early-morning visit to High Reaches and received a serene absolution for her errand of mercy.

Leri was here. Holth was with you. Fair exchange in those conditions. I slept.

Moreta slept for a while after her return from the High Reaches, waking nervously almost as if she had expected another summons. She would have preferred to stay at Tamianth's side until she was certain that the ichor was flowing to the wing, but Pressen had learned of the dangers and was able to perform necessary countermeasures. Further, as Tamianth strengthened and Falga recovered from wound fever, another crisis was less likely to develop.

So Moreta ascribed her nagging sense of apprehension to the tensions of a long day and sent M'barak, Leri's favorite weyrling rider, to Ruatha Hold. K'lon told Leri and Moreta how appalled he had been by Ruatha. Moreta did not like to dwell on the scenes of a derelict Ruatha that her active imagination could conjure. What could she say in condolence to a man who had suffered so many losses?

Suddenly Alessan, dressed in rough leathers but a clean shirt showing at the neck, stood to one side of the entrance to the Hatching Ground. Beside his was a lanky man in a faded, patched tunic of harper blue. M'barak was grinning at their hesitation and waved them toward the portion of the tiers that Moreta had converted to a temporary living space. Orlith was awake and watched them enter, but displayed no agitation.

Moreta rose, one hand raised in unconscious protest against the change in Alessan. Too vividly she recalled the assured, handsome, buoyant young man who had greeted her at Ruatha's Gather eight days before. He had lost weight and his tunic was belted tightly to take up the slack. His hair no longer looked trimmed or brushed. She wondered why that detail should matter so much to her. The stains on his hands, witness of his efforts to plow and plant, were honorable ones, as was the redwort on hers. She grieved, too, for the lines of worry and tension in his face, the cynical slant to his mouth, and the wary expression in his light green eyes.

"This is Tuero, Moreta, who has been invaluable to me over the . . . since the Gather." After the slight pause, Alessan's voice deepened as if to ward off comment. "He has a theory against which I can raise no objections, but, as we cannot reach an authority at this hour in Keroon Beasthold, I thought you might give us an opinion."

"What is it?" Moreta asked, put off by his diffidence. The change in him went far deeper than appearance.

"Tuero"—Alessan gave the harper a slight bow of acknowledgment—"wondered if a vaccine could be made from the blood of runnerbeasts to protect them from the plague."

"Of course it can! You mean it hasn't been done?" Moreta was consumed by such a surge of fury and frustration that Orlith rose to all four legs from her semirecumbent position, her eyes whirling pinkly, and a worried question rumbled from her throat.

"No." In the one word, Alessan mirrored her own intense reaction.

"No one *thought* of doing it, or there hasn't been the time?" she demanded, sick at the thought of more loss, animal or human. The grim set of Alessan's mouth and the harper's sigh gave the answer. "I would have thought that—" She broke off the angry sentence, closing her eyes and clenching her fists. She recalled the heavy losses at Keroon Beasthold—the emptiness of her family's runnerhold.

"There have been other priorities," Alessan said. He spoke without bitterness but from a resignation to harsh fact.

"Yes, of course." She pulled her wits back from useless conjecture. "Have you any healers?"

"Several."

"Runnerblood would produce the same serum by the same method, centrifugal separation. More blood can be drawn from runners, of course, and the vaccine should be administered in proportion to body weight. The heavier—"

Alessan cocked his left eyebrow just enough for her to realize that there were no more of the heavier beasts at Ruatha.

"Would you have any spare needlethorns?" Alessan asked, breaking the silence.

"Yes." At that moment Moreta would have given Alessan anything he needed to alleviate his problems. "And whatever else is needed by Ruatha."

"We've been promised a supply train from Fort," Tuero said, "but until we can assure the wagoners that man and animal in Ruatha are plague-free, no one will venture near the Hold."

Moreta assimilated that information with a slow nod of her head, her eyes on Alessan. They might be discussing something completely foreign to him to judge by his detachment. How else could he have survived his losses?

"M'barak, please take Lord Alessan and Journeyman Tuero to the store-room. They may have anything they need from our supplies."

M'barak's eyes widened.

"I'll be right with you," Alessan told Tuero and M'barak, who left him. Alessan swung down the pack he carried. "I did not come," he said with a wry smile, "in expectation of bounty. I can, however, return your gown." He took out the carefully folded gold and brown dress and presented it to her with a courteous bow.

She managed to take it from him but her hands trembled. She thought of the racing, the dancing, her joy in a Gather as one should be, her delight in the perfection of that Gather evening as she and Oklina had made their way to the dancing square for an evening she would never forget. The pent-up frustrations, angers, suppressed griefs, the mandatory absences from Or-lith that she thought of as betrayals of Impression, the whole accumulation burst the barrier of self-control and she buried her face in the dress, weeping uncontrollably.

As Orlith crooned supportively, Moreta was taken into Alessan's em-brace. The touch of his arms, fierce in their hold, the mixed odors of human and animal sweat, of damp earth, combined to free her tears. Abruptly she felt the heave and swell of his body as his grief found expression at last. To-gether they comforted and were comforted by each other's release.

You needed this, Orlith said to Moreta but she knew that the dragon in-cluded Alessan in her compassion.

It was Moreta who recovered from the catharsis first. She continued to hold Alessan tightly, to ease his shuddering body, as she murmured reassur-ances and encouragements, repeating all the praise for his indomitable spirit and fortitude that had come to her through K'lon: trying to make her voice and hands convey her own respect, admiration, and empathy. She felt the shuddering subside and then, with one final deep sigh, Alessan was purged of the aggregation of sorrow, remorse, and frustration. She relaxed her grip and his arms became less fierce and clinging. Slowly they leaned apart so that they could look into each other's eyes. The lines of pain and worry had not diminished but the strain had eased about his mouth and brow.

Alessan raised his hand and with gentle fingers smoothed the tears from her cheeks. His hands tightened and he pulled her toward him again, bend-ing his head to one side so that she could evade him if she chose. Moreta tilted her head and accepted his kiss, thinking to put the seal of comfort to their shared sorrow with that age-old benison. Neither expected their emotions to flare to passion—Moreta because she had stopped thinking of relationships outside the Weyr, Alessan because he had thought himself spent from his losses at Ruatha.

Orlith crooned serenely, almost unheard by Moreta, who was caught up by the surge of emotion, the flow of sensuality so remarkably aroused by Alessan's touch, the hard strength of his thighs against hers, the sensation of being *vital* again. Not even her girlhood love for Talpan had waked such an uninhibited response, and she clung to Alessan, willing the moment to endure.

Slowly, reluctantly, Alessan raised his mouth from hers, looking down at her with incredulous intensity. Then he, too, became aware of the dragon's crooning and looked, startled, in the queen's direction.

"She doesn't object!" That amazed him further, and he was sensible of the risk he had taken.

"If she did, you'd know about it." Moreta laughed. His expression of dismay swiftly altering to delight was marvelous. Joy welled up from a long-untapped source in her body.

Orlith's croon changed to as near a trill as the dragon larynx could manage. With great reluctance, Moreta stepped back from Alessan, her smile expressing that regret.

"They'll hear it?" he asked, smiling back at her ruefully, his hands clinging as he released her.

"It may be chalked up to the joys of clutching."

"Your gown!" He grasped at the excuse of retrieving the crumpled folds where the dress had fallen unremarked to the stone at their feet. He was passing it to her when M'barak and Tuero entered the Hatching Ground, Tuero with a keen sparkle in his expressive eyes.

"With so much on your mind, Alessan," Moreta said, amazed at her self-possession, "it is very good of you to have remembered."

"If the simple courtesy of returning what had been misplaced is always rewarded with such generosity, leave more with me!" Alessan's eyes burned with amusement at his turn of phrase but it was Tuero's full pack that he indicated.

Moreta could not but laugh. M'barak was looking from her to Orlith, Tuero was aware that something had occurred but he couldn't identify it.

"I didn't take *all* we needed," the harper said as he looked from Weyrwoman to Lord Holder with a bemused smile. "That would have stripped your stores completely."

"I shall be able to get replacements more easily than you, I think. As I was telling Alessan"—Moreta felt the need to dissemble—"I think there are old Records about this sort of animal vaccination, though I cannot remember the details. I would try the serum on a worthless beast—"

"Just now there are *no* worthless beasts at Ruatha," Alessan said quickly, a slight edge to his voice. "I have no choice but to proceed and hope the animal vaccine is as efficacious as the human."

"Did you inquire of Master Capiam?" Moreta asked, wishing that Alessan had not distanced himself from her quite so soon though she could appreciate the necessity.

"*You* know runners, not Master Capiam. Why rouse them if the notion was not feasible?"

"I think it is feasible." Moreta put her hand urgently on Alessan's arm, yearning to recapture some trace of their encounter. "I think you should inform the Healer Hall immediately. And keep me informed."

Alessan smiled with polite acknowledgment and, under the pretense of a courteous pressure on her hand, his fingers caressed hers.

"You may be sure of that."

"I know Oklina lives." The words came in a rush from her lips as Alessan turned to leave. "Did Dag . . . and Squealer?"

"Why do you think I want so desperately to vaccinate the runners? Squealer may be the only full male I have left." Alessan left, pausing briefly at the entrance to bow toward Orlith.

With a startled expression, Tuero hastened after him, and M'barak hurried after his two passengers.

Orlith crooned again, her many-faceted eyes whirling with flashes of red amid the predominant blue. Feeling rather limp after the spate of emotions and resurgent desire, Moreta sank to the stone seat, clasping her trembling hands together. She wondered if there was any chance that Holth and Leri had missed that tumultuous interview.

CHAPTER
XIV

Healer Hall, Ruatha Hold, Fort Weyr,
Ista Hold, Present Pass, 3.20.43

"*L*ook at the situation as a challenge!" Capiam suggested to Master Tirone.

The harper slammed the door behind him, an uncharacteristic action that startled Desdra and sent Master Fortine into a spasm of nervous coughing.

"A challenge? Haven't we had enough of those in the past ten days?" Tirone demanded indignantly. "Half the continent sick, the other half *scared* sick, everyone suspicious of a cough or a sneeze, the dragonriders barely able to meet Thread. We've lost irreplaceable Masters and promising journeymen in every Craft. And you advise me to look on this news as a challenge?" Tirone jammed his fists against his belt and glared at the Masterhealer. He had fallen into the pose that Capiam irreverently called the "harper attitude." Capiam dared not glance at Desdra to whom he had confided the observation for it was not a moment for levity. Or perhaps that was all that was keeping his mind from buckling under the new "challenge."

"Did you not tell me yourself earlier this morning," Tirone continued, his bass voice resonant with vexation—"harper enunciator," Capiam's graceless mind decided, "that there had been no new cases of the plague reported anywhere on the continent?"

"I did. I'll be happier when the lapse is four days long. But that only means that this wave of the viral influence is passing. The 'flu'—as the Ancients nicknamed it—can recur. It's the *next* wave that worries me dreadfully."

"Next one?" Tirone stared blankly at Capiam, as if wishing he had misheard.

Capiam sighed. He was not at all happy with a discussion that he had hoped to put off until he had completed a plan of action. People were less apt to panic if they were presented with a course of action. He had nearly completed his computations for the amount of vaccine needed, the number of dragonriders (and he had to assume they wanted to avoid a repetition of the plague as much as he) needed to distribute the vaccine, and the halls and holds where it would be administered. The confrontation had been precipitated by apprentice gossiping: speculations about why healers were still asking for blood donations for more serum when the reported cases of the "flu" were dropping and why the internment camp had not been struck.

"Next one?" Tirone's voice was incredulous.

"Oh, dear me, yes," Master Fortine replied from his corner, thinking his colleague needed support. "So far we have found four distinct references to this sort of viral influence. It seems to mutate. The serum which suppresses one kind does not always have any effect on the next."

"The details would bore Master Tirone, I fear," Capiam said. No sense in fomenting total alarm. Capiam had seized on the hope that, if they could immunize everyone in the Northern continent, catching all the carriers of *this* type, they would be in less danger from further manifestations, the symptoms for which would now be easily recognized and speedily dealt with.

"I am less bored by details than you might imagine," Tirone said. He strode forward, pulled out the chair at Capiam's desk, and seated himself, folding his arms across his chest in an aggressive fashion. He stared pointedly at Capiam. "Acquaint me with the details."

Capiam scratched at the back of his neck, a habit he had recently acquired and that he deplored in himself.

"You know that we looked back into the Records to find mention of the viral influence . . ."

"Yes. Stupid name."

"Descriptive, however. We found four separate references to such 'flus' as periodic scourges before the Crossing. Even before the First Crossing."

"Let us not get into politics."

Capiam opened his eyes in mild reproof. "I'm not. But I always thought you were of the Two-Crossings school of thought and the language in the texts supports that theory. Suffice to say," Capiam hurried on as Tirone twitched his eyebrows in growing irritation, "our ancestors also carried with them certain bacteria and viruses which were ineradicable."

"Indeed they were, but they are necessary to the proper function of our bodies and the internal economy of the animals brought on both Crossings," Master Fortine said in earnest support of his colleague.

"Yes, as Fortine says, we cannot escape some infections. We *must* prevent a second viral infection. It can recur. Here. Now. As doubtless it does periodically on the Southern Continent. We know to our sorrow that it only takes one carrier. We can't let that happen again, Tirone. We have neither the medicines nor the personnel to cope with a second epidemic."

"I know that as well as you do," Tirone said, his voice rough with irritation. "So? Do those precious Records of yours say what the Ancients did?" He gestured at the thick Records on Capiam's desk with a contempt based on fear.

"Mass vaccination!"

It took Tirone a moment to realize that Capian had given him a candid answer.

"Mass vaccination? The whole continent!" Tirone made a lavish sweep of one arm, glaring at Capiam. "But I've *been* vaccinated." His hand went to his left arm.

"That immunity lasts only about fourteen days with the sort of serum we can produce. So you see, our time is limited . . . and might even be running out in Igen and Keroon unless we can vaccinate everyone and anyone who might harbor the virus. That's the challenge. My Hall provides the serum and the personnel to vaccinate; yours keeps Hall, Hold, and Weyr from panic!"

"Panic? Yes, you're right about that!" Tirone jerked his thumb in the direction of Fort Hold where Lord Tolocamp still refused to leave his apartment. "You would have more to fear from the panic than the plague just now."

"Yes!" Capiam put a great deal into that quiet affirmative. Desdra had moved perceptibly closer to him. He wasn't sure if her intention was supportive or defensive, but he appreciated her proximity. "And we have to proceed with speed and diligence. If there should be a carrier in Igen, Keroon, Telgar, or Ruatha . . ."

The vulnerable angry look in Tirone's eyes reminded him of his own reaction when he had had to admit the inescapable conclusions drawn from the four references Fortine, and then Desdra, had reluctantly shown him.

"To prevent a second epidemic, we must vaccinate now, within the next few days." Capiam turned briskly to the maps he had been preparing. "Portions of Lemos, Bitra, Crom, Nabol, upper Telgar, High Reaches, and Tillek have not had contact with anyone since the cold season started. We can vaccinate them later, when the snow melts but before the spring rains, when those people begin to circulate more freely. So we have to concern ourselves with this portion of the continent."

Capiam brought his arm down the southern half. "There are certain advantages to the social structure on Pern, Tirone, particularly during a Pass. We can keep track of where everyone is. We also know approximately how many people survived the first wave of the flu and who has been vaccinated. So it comes down to the problem of distributing the vaccine at the appointed day. As dragonriders are vulnerable to the disease, I feel we can ask their co-operation in getting vaccine to the distribution points I've marked out across the continent."

Tirone gave a cynical snort. "You won't get any cooperation from M'tani at Telgar. L'bol at Igen is useless—Wimmia's running the Weyr and it's a mercy Fall is a consolidated effort. F'gal might help . . ."

Capiam shook his head impatiently. "I can get all the help I need from Moreta, S'ligar, and K'dren. But we must do it now, to halt any further incidence of the flu. It can be halted, killed, if it does not have new victims to propagate it."

"Like Thread?"

"That is an analogy, I suppose," Capiam admitted wearily. He had spent so much time arguing lately, with Fortine, Desdra, the other Masters, and himself. The more he presented the case, the more clearly did he feel the necessity for the push. "It takes only one Thread to ruin a field, or a continent. Only one carrier is needed to spread the plague."

"Or one idiot master seaman trying to stake a premature claim on the Southern Continent—"

"What?"

Tirone took from his tunic a water-stained sheaf, its parchment pages roughly evened.

"I was on my way to see you about this, Master Capiam. Your healer at Igen Sea Hold, Master Burdion, entrusted this to my journeyman. I wanted it for an accurate account of this period."

"Yes, yes, you badgered me on my sickbed." Capiam made to take the book from Tirone, who reproved him with a look.

"There was no floating animal, no chance encounter, Capiam. They *landed* in Southern. Burdion was quite ill, you know, and during his convalescence he read the log of the good ship *Windtoss* for lack of anything more stimulating. He's been in a sea hold long enough to know sailing annotations. And he said that Master Varney was an honest man. He logs the squall, right enough, and that did send them legitimately off course. *But* they ought not to have landed. Exploration of the Southern Continent was not to be undertaken until this Pass was over. It was to be a combined effort of Hall, Hold, and Weyr. They were three days in that anchorage!" Tirone punctuated his remarks by stabbing his finger at the journal in such a way that Capiam couldn't see the page properly. Then Tirone relinquished it to his grasp, and Desdra sidled up to look.

"Oh, dear, oh, dear, how very presumptuous of Master Varney," Master Fortine said. "But that means this is not a case of zoonosis, Capiam, but a direct infection."

"Only if there were humans in the Southern Continent," Capiam said hopefully.

"The log entries do not suggest there are!" Tirone sank that possibility.

"Indeed the Records concerning the Second Crossing are clear on that point."

"Are we sure," Desdra asked, "that they *were* in southern waters?"

"Oh, yes," Tirone said. "A seabred journeyman harper confirmed that the positions correspond to the Southern Continent! He said there wouldn't *be* any place shallow enough to anchor anywhere *short* of the landmass of the continent. Three days they were there!"

"The log says"— Desdra was reading—"that they had to jury-rig repairs to the sloop after it was damaged by a storm."

"That's what it *says*," Tirone agreed sardonically. "Undoubtedly they did make repairs, but Burdion added a note"—Tirone produced a scrap that he flourished before he read it—" 'I found fruit pits of unusual size in the unemptied galley bucket and rotten husks of some specimens which were unknown to me though I have been many Turns in this Hold.' " Tirone leaned toward Capiam, his eyes brilliant. "So, my friends, the *Windtoss* made a premature landing. And look where it has landed us!" Tirone threw his arms wide in another of his grand gestures.

Capiam sank back wearily in his chair, staring at the maps, flicking his careful lists with his fingers.

"The log may shed light on certain aspects of this, my good friend, but also warns us against that projected return to the Southern Continent."

"I heartily agree!"

"And it reinforces my conclusion that we must vaccinate to prevent the spread of the plague. And vaccinate the runners as well. I really hadn't counted on that complication."

"Look on it as a challenge?" said Desdra dryly, her hands kneading at the tense muscles of Capiam's shoulders.

"Not one which I think our unofficial Masterherdsman is capable of answering, I fear," said Capiam.

"Would Moreta know? She was runnerhold bred, her family had a fine breeding hold in Keroon . . ." Even the brash Masterharper paused, knowing of the tragedy there. "She did attend that mid-distance runner at Ruatha Gather. That was the first case to be noted here in the west, remember."

"No, I don't remember, Tirone," Capiam said irritably. Did he have to cure the sick animals of this continent, too? "You're the memory of our times."

"Surely if we have a human vaccine, we can produce by the same methods an animal one," Desdra said, soothingly. "And there's Lord Alessan, who certainly has enough donors. I did hear, did I not, that some of his runner-beasts survived the plague?"

"Yes, yes, they did," Tirone said swiftly, glancing with an anxious frown at the despondent Masterhealer. "Come, my friend, you've solved so many of our recent problems. You cannot lose heart now." Tirone's bass voice oozed entreaty and persuasiveness.

"No, no, my dear Capiam, we *cannot* lose heart now," Master Fortine added from his corner.

Tirone rose, his manner suddenly brisk. "Look, Capiam, I'll drum for a convey. You can go to Fort Weyr, see what Moreta can tell you. Then on to that new man—what's his name, Bessel?—at Beastmasterhold. Meanwhile, since I take it that this vaccination program of yours is more urgent than ever, I'll sweeten hall and hold. I'll start with Tolocamp." Tirone jerked his thumb toward Fort Hold. "If he agrees, we'll have no trouble with the other Lords Holder, even that crevice snake Ratoshigan."

"Considering Tolocamp's mental state, however will you accomplish his cooperation?" Capiam asked, jarred from his depression by Tirone's obvious confidence.

"If you recall, my fellow Master, Lord Tolocamp has been deprived of our services for the past few days. As he has never encouraged any of his children or his holders to have ideas, he is going to need *ours*. He's had long enough to reconsider his intransigence," Tirone replied with a deceptively bland smile. "You take care of the vaccine; I'll organize the rest."

The Masterharper was careful to retrieve the log of the *Windtoss* from Capiam before he left with an energetic stride and a brisk slam of the door.

◆ ◆ ◆

The elation that Alessan had experienced after his visit to Fort Weyr was compounded of renewed hope and the unexpected sympathy of Moreta. He would have liked to savor that incident but the most urgent problem, producing a usable vaccine for runnerbeasts, especially those he devoutly hoped that Dag had saved, took precedence over any personal consideration.

M'barak returned Alessan and Tuero to Ruatha Hold, landing in the forecourt. The speed with which Oklina emerged from the Hold suggested she had been anxiously awaiting her brother's return. She paused on the top steps, her face turned up to him. As he slid down the blue dragon's side, Alessan let out a joyful whoop and her expression turned to relief as she rushed to meet him. Exuberantly Alessan swooped her up in his arms, achingly aware of the difference between his sister's slight body and Moreta's. He gave Oklina a gentle kiss on her cheek. There had been scant time for affection between brother and sister lately, and, during her illness, Alessan had come to know how much he valued Oklina. A kiss, he had good reason to know, was a kind gesture!

"Moreta said the serum idea is valid. We're going to try it! Now!" Alessan told her. "If it does work, then Ruatha is open again and my holders cannot deny me their labor. If it doesn't work, we're no worse off than we have been."

"It *has* to work!" Oklina cried fervently.

Alessan shouted for Follen. "We'll need his help, his implements, and that old brood mare. I know she caught the plague and I can't risk any of the team animals."

"Arith! Behave yourself. That's Lady Oklina!" M'barak called. The blue dragon had turned his head round toward brother and sister, and was now wiffling closer and closer to Oklina, his eyes whirling. By no means afraid of such attentions, Oklina didn't know what to do and clung to Alessan.

At his rider's reprimand, Arith made a tiny little noise, a disappointed snort, and turned his head away while M'barak apologized profusely.

"I really don't know what came over him. Arith is usually very well behaved. But it is late, he is tired, and we'd better get back to the Weyr." Arith snorted audibly and M'barak looked startled. "*I'd* best be back at the Weyr."

Thanking M'barak and Arith for their convey, Alessan guided Oklina out of the way, a bemused Tuero following.

"Blue dragons are not usually fascinated by the opposite sex," the harper remarked dryly to Alessan.

"Really?" Alessan's reply was polite for his mind was on the mechanics of turning runner blood into serum vaccine.

"There *is* a queen egg on the Fort Weyr Hatching Ground."

"And?" Alessan's courtesy turned crisp. He had a lot to do before he could see what Dag had salvaged of the Ruathan herds.

Tuero's grin broadened. "As I recall it, Ruatha has quite a few bloodties with dragonriders."

Alessan stared from Oklina to the dragon already airborne, and remembered K'lon's remark the day he had brought the vaccine to Ruatha Hold. "It couldn't be!"

At that point, Follen rushed out of the Hold, his expression hopeful, and Alessan devoted his full attention to putting vaccine theory to test.

Tuero brought the brood mare in from the field; she was quiet enough to be led by her forelock. Follen, Oklina, Deefer, and the trustworthy fosterlings bore the medical equipment to the beasthold. The momentum of exhilaration was briefly checked when they discovered that they didn't have large enough glass containers for the quantity of animal blood. Then Oklina remembered that Lady Oma had put away huge ornamental glass bottles long ago presented by Master Clargesh to Lords Holder as samples of apprentice industry and design. To spin such large bottles, Alessan, Tuero, and Deefer contrived a big centrifuge from a spare wagonwheel attached to spitcogs and a crank.

The runner mare stood quietly impassive since the bloodtaking caused no discomfort.

"Strange," Follen said as the first batch was completed and the straw-colored fluid drawn off. "It's the same color as human serum."

"It's only dragons who have green blood," Oklina said.

"We'll try the vaccine on the lame runner," Alessan said, wondering which blue rider was harassing his sister and why. All the time the wheel was turning, Alessan fidgeted. Since he'd no other option, he had been patient, but now that he could search out Dag, he was fretting to be gone. "If there's no ill effect on that creature, we can assume—we have to assume—that the serum works, since the same principle is efficacious for humans."

"It's too late to do more tonight anyhow," Follen said with a vast yawn when he had injected the serum in the lame beast.

"No one at the Harper Hall will think kindly of a message at this hour," Tuero agreed, knuckling his eyes.

"I think I'll just stay here tonight, in case there's a reaction." Alessan nodded toward the lame runner.

"And you'll be off first thing in the morning, won't you?"—Oklina leaned toward her brother, her dark soft eyes on his, her comment for him alone—"to find Dag and Squealer?"

He nodded and gave her shoulders an affectionate squeeze before he sent her off after the healer and the harper. Alessan watched the three until the glowbaskets they carried were out of sight in a dip of the roadway. Then he fixed himself a bed of straw in the stall next to the runner. Despite his good intention to remain alert enough to check on the beast, he slept soundly until first light. The injected runner was still lame but it exhibited no signs of a distress, no mark of sweat, and had eaten a good deal of the clean bedding with which it had been furnished.

Reassured, Alessan saddled the runner that Tuero had nicknamed Skinny—not a mount he would have chosen for anyone, but beggars couldn't be choosers at Ruatha those days. Alessan carefully packed the serums, needlethorns, and Follen's glass syringe into the saddlebag, cushioning them with clean straw, then mounted and urged Skinny onto the roadway.

The night before, he had had many doubts as they waited for the serum to be produced: doubts about many things, including Moreta's unexpected response to him. He thought of kindness and the kiss he had given his sister. Had Moreta only meant to be kind? Today, in the dawn of a bright fresh spring morning, he knew it had not been mere kindness in Moreta. He and the Weyrwoman had been of one mind in that brief instant. And the dragon queen had trilled in concord.

Skinny shied at some imaginary bogey in the greening bushes by the track. Alessan swayed to the motion, checking the animal's sideway plunge with a firm pressure of that leg, while he made sure that the flaps on the saddlebags were secure. Alessan liked an active mover but he couldn't risk the precious fluid or pause to school a fractious beast. He must concentrate on riding and not be diverted by visions of the impossible. Moreta was the Fort Weyrwoman. Although she might, just might, enjoy a discreet relationship with him, might even allow a pregnancy—and suddenly Alessan longed for a child as he had not with Suriana—Alessan was still Lord of a severely depleted bloodline. He had to have an acknowledged wife, and others to bear his children, as many as he could beget.

Old Runel was dead, he thought with a flash of regret. Old Runel and all the Ruathan begets as well as the bloodlines of runners back to the Crossing. He'd never thought he would rue the loss of that man.

Skinny trotted, its hocks well under it and with a fine forward extension. Too bad the creature was gelded. Ruatha had once had far better specimens to propagate. Alessan inhaled against the hope at the end of this track. He tried to keep from wondering which animals Dag had seen fit to take with him. If only Dag had included one breeding pair of the Lord Leef's heavy carters . . . The records of animals destroyed that Norman had started to keep had been lost when the race-flats temporary hospital had been abandoned. Alessan wished futilely that he had made time to look in on the beasthold that frantic morning before he had taken ill.

Alessan came to the fork in the track, each direction leading to nursery fields. Dag would have taken the less accessible one, he decided, but he paused long enough to see if there had been a message left at the division. Not a rag, a bone, or an unnatural formation of the pebbles. Nine days had passed since Dag left with Fergal. Fear burrowed from the trap in his mind to which Alessan had banished it.

He dug his heels into Skinny, and the beast responded instantly, skittering at a good rate up the track, high breathing as it caught the excitement generated in its rider. Runners were considered stupid, had few ways to communicate with riders, and yet occasionally one seemed to know exactly what was going on in the human it bore. Alessan laid a soothing hand on Skinny's arched neck and brought the animal to a more sensible pace.

Then they were at the rise that led to the pasture and, for a heartbreaking moment, Alessan could see nothing of man or beast in the rolling fields. But the barrier had been man-made, with prickly hedge and stone, high enough to contain docile beasts. He rose in his stirrups, numb with the fear that Dag had brought the plague with him and died with all the animals. Then he saw the thin column of smoke to his right, saw the flapping of a shirt drying on a branch. He heard a piercing whistle.

From the slope down to the stream, runners trooped obediently in answer to the summons. Alessan felt tears prick his eyes. He hauled Skinny smartly back down the road, turned, set his heels to the bony ribs, and Skinny charged the barrier, sailing nobly over it, clacking with surprise when they landed on the far side. Alessan hauled the delighted animal to a more sedate pace, remembering his mission. It was only then that he saw, among the beasts jogging up the slope, the wobbly-legged awkward infantile bodies, the waddling pace of the gravid. Alessan let out a whoop of jubilation and it reverberated from the hills. Had Dag taken *all* the pregnant mares with him? Alessan had bleakly had to assume that all the anticipated foals had died of the plague or been aborted, for all he found in the fields of the Hold proper had been gelded males and barren mares.

His whoop was answered from the rude shelter dug into the high side of the slope. The small figure standing at its entrance waved both arms. One small figure! Inadvertently Alessan checked Skinny and then urged it forward. One small black-haired figure, now with impudent arms cocked against ragged pants. Fergal!

"You took your time, Lord Alessan!" The boy's expression was as impertinent as his words were resentful and unforgiving.

"Dag?" Alessan's voice broke in consternation. He could not move from the saddle. Until that moment, he hadn't realized how much he had looked forward to seeing the old handler, how sorely he needed Dag's knowledgeable advice if Ruathan runners were ever to regain their former prestige.

Annoyingly, Fergal shrugged and then cocked his head up at Alessan.

"I thought you'd *forgotten* us!" He stepped to one side and gestured toward the shelter. "*He* broke his leg. I took care of all the runners, even the ones who birthed. Didn't I do a good job?"

Alessan would have swatted him for impudence had he been able to catch him but Fergal, grinning with positive malice at his little hoax, had slipped neatly out of range into the shelter of his charges.

"Alessan?" Dag's summons came from the shelter and Alessan put aside any thought of discipline to rush in to his old ally. "I saved all I could for you, Alessan. I saved all I could."

"You have also saved Ruatha!"

* * *

"I do apologize for intruding on the Hatching Ground, Moreta," Capiam said, peering cautiously around the entrance.

"Come in. Come in!" Moreta beckoned him eagerly to join her in her temporary accommodation in the first tier.

Capiam looked back over his shoulder a moment and then entered, keeping an anxious eye on Orlith among her eggs.

"She does seem quite serene, doesn't she?"

"Oh, she is!"

"M'barak, who conveyed Desdra and me here, said that she will even show off that splendid queen egg she clutched." With due respect for the hot volcanic sands, Capiam walked quickly to Moreta.

"Desdra's here? I've heard a great deal about her from M'barak and K'lon."

"She's chatting with Jallora so I could have a private word with you." Capiam cleared his throat in an uncharacteristic show of nervousness.

Moreta thought he was wary of Orlith and extended her hands to him. She supposed she must get used to the changes wrought in people by the plague. Capiam appeared only to have lost weight, for his eyes sparkled out of a craggy face that would become more attractive with age. His hair was thinning at the temples and she fancied that the gray had encroached farther into the black, but there was no diminution in the force of his personality, or in his grip as he clasped her hands.

"To what do I owe this unexpected pleasure?" she asked.

His eyes twinkled. "An unexpected . . . challenge is what I told Master Tirone."

Alerted by his geniality, Moreta searched his face. "What sort of a challenge?"

"I'll come to that in a moment, if I may. First, would you know if runner-beasts would respond favorably to a serum vaccine against the plague they also suffer?"

Moreta stared at him a moment, surprised to be asked the same question twice in a short space of time, and surprised that the question had to be asked at all. She was angry that no one had taken steps to safeguard the runnerbeasts, which were such valuable assets of the Northern Continent. She had tried to appreciate that saving human life had been the priority, but surely someone must have been rational enough in one of the runnerholds to apply the principal to the beasts. She had been complimented and touched that Alessan had sought her advice yesterday evening and, despite her varied irritations, slightly amused that she, Weyrwoman of Fort, was now being approached by the Masterhealer.

"I answered that same question for Alessan last night."

"Oh!" Capiam blinked with surprise. "Oh, and how did you answer Lord Alessan?"

"Affirmatively."

"He contacted Master Balfor?"

"It was too late to drum up the Keroon Beasthold. Is Balfor the new Masterherdsman?"

"He is acting in that capacity. Someone must."

"Alessan ought to have informed you, or at least the Harper Hall . . ." Moreta frowned. Tuero should have done it if Alessan was too busy. Perhaps Alessan had not had enough time to produce a serum? No. She had the impression that he wouldn't have wasted any time.

"It is not quite noon," Capiam said tactfully, willing to give the harried Lord Holder the benefit on any doubt. "In theory, serum vaccine ought to produce similar immunization in the runners. Alessan needs all the luck and help he can get."

Moreta nodded in solemn agreement. "So why does the Healer Hall concern itself suddenly with animal vaccines?"

"Because, unfortunately, I have good reason to believe that the plague is transmitted to man by animals and may break out again—'zoonotic' and 're-crudescent' are the terms the Ancients used to describe those qualities."

"Oh!" Moreta struggled to assimilate the information. The ramifications were staggering. "You mean, we could easily have a second epidemic? Shards! Capiam, the continent couldn't survive a second epidemic!" She threw up her arms in an excess of dismay that had to be vented. "The Weyrs are only barely able to get the requisite number of wings in the air with every Fall, what with riders recovering from secondary infections and new injuries. If the plague went through us again, I doubt there'd be a full wing available!" In her agitation, she began to pace then she noticed his patient watching. She halted and gave him a closer scrutiny. "If the animal vaccine works, then you could stop the zoonosis? You would vaccinate both man and animal against it? And your challenge is . . ."—she had to smile at the way he had led her to the conclusion—"to the dragonriders for their assistance in distributing the vaccines?"

"Preferably on the same day to all distribution points." Capiam carefully unfolded a copy of his plan. He peered at her from under his brows, watching her reactions as he handed her the document. "Mass vaccination is the only way to stop the plague. It would require a tremendous effort. My halls have already started to accumulate human vaccine. To be candid, my Hall had not quite evaluated the runner susceptibility. Between Tirone's reports and Desdra's exhaustive investigations, we can find no other way than zoonosis for the plague to have spread so rapidly and so far. We now know that the only way to prevent a recurrence of this viral influence is to stop it within the next few days or endure a second wave."

Moreta shuddered with dread. She studied his plan.

"Of course," he added, tipping the edge of the parchment, "the scheme depends first on the feasibility of the runner vaccine and the cooperation of the Weyrs to circulate both."

"Have you approached any of the other Weyrs yet?"

"I needed an answer to my question on runner vaccine and you are the nearest authority." He grinned at her.

"Surely Lord Tolocamp—"

"I'm leaving Lord Tolocamp to Master Tirone." There was considerable acrimony in the healer's voice. "And such a question as this to someone who can give me a rational answer. Not only have I an answer, I have a source."

"That is also an assumption—"

"Which I will confirm as soon as you can also assure me that the Weyrs can assist us in delivering the vaccines. One of my journeymen is a wizard at figuring out what he calls time-and-motion processes. If we could rely on a minimum of six riders from each Weyr to cover their traditional regions, in a scheduled roster of stops to the various halls, holds, and Weyrs, that would be sufficient."

Moreta was doing some calculations of her own. "Not unless the riders—" She caught herself and gulped in astonishment. In Capiam's broadening grin she had an unexpected answer.

"I've been doing rather a lot of reading in the Archives, Moreta." Capiam sounded more pleased than apologetic for the shock he had given her.

"How did that bit of information come to be in the Healer Archives?" she demanded, so infuriated that Orlith came fully alert, claws hooking protectively about the queen egg.

"Why shouldn't it be?" Capiam asked with deceptive mildness. "After all, my Craft bred the trait into the dragons. Can they really go from one time to another?" he asked wistfully.

"Yes," she finally replied, as austerely as she could. "But it's not encouraged at all!" She thought of K'lon, knew very well how often the blue rider had been at the Healer Hall, and wondered about such convenient Records. On the other hand, Capiam's Craft had been credited with many incredible feats and displays of skill, secrets forgotten by disuse. She chided herself for doubting the integrity of Master Capiam, especially at such a critical hour when any strategy that might restore the continent to balance might be condoned. "Capiam, traveling in time produces paradoxes that can be very dangerous."

"That's why I suggested the progressive delivery so there is no overlapping." The eagerness in his manner was disarming.

"There might be some trouble convincing M'tani of Telgar."

"Yes, I'd heard of his disaffection. I also know that F'gal of Ista is very ill of a kidney chill and L'bol of severe depressions—which is why I specify the minimum number of riders the effort would require. I don't know how the continent would have survived without all the assistance the dragonriders have given hall and hold up to this point."

"You have enough vaccine for people?"

"We will have. Master Tirone is adroitly broaching the subject to hall and hold."

"A wise precaution."

Capiam heaved a sigh. "So, what must be ascertained now is whether or not Lord Alessan has successfully produced the animal vaccine."

Go to Ruatha with them, Orlith said. After a flicker of a pause, she added, *Holth agrees.*

Illogically, Moreta resisted that gratuitous permission—and wondered why. She had a perfectly natural wish to see the results of Alessan's experiment, not necessarily Alessan. Was she resisting the attraction she felt for him? She was not normally bothered by indecision.

You have always liked runnerbeasts. They deserve your help now. Holth—Orlith was speaking, Moreta decided from the doubly deep tone. *You will have to see Ruatha sometime again.* That, undeniably, was spoken only by Orlith.

Moreta sighed deeply and sadly. Orlith had touched the core of her resistance, for Moreta did not want to see Ruatha in the ruins K'lon had described.

"I think, Capiam," she said slowly, steeling her mind, "that I should accompany you."

Arith is more than willing. He likes the girl, Orlith said. She unsheathed her claws from the queen egg. From the Bowl, Arith bugled agreement.

"Which girl?" Moreta was surprised at the remark.

Orlith shrugged and went about making a depression in which she rolled her egg. So, trying not to appear resigned, Moreta collected her flying gear.

"Arith says he will take us to Ruatha Hold."

"You can leave her?" Capiam looked toward the queen.

"My going is her idea. She's not a broody dragon, like some who must have their rider in constant attendance. Leri and Holth are nearby. I shan't be gone very long, you know." She gave Capiam a dour glance and then smiled at his startled expression.

When Moreta and Capiam reached the Bowl, Jallora was talking earnestly with a dark-haired woman who was standing a few lengths from M'barak and Arith. Desdra was older than Moreta had expected from K'lon's comments, older than Moreta herself, but then Jallora had said that the woman was taking her mastery at the Fort Healer Hall. Desdra had a reserved air about her, not quite haughty but certainly a woman who kept herself to herself—a trait that did not, however, keep her from being keenly aware of the activity in the Bowl. Two wings from Fort would fly later across Bitra and Lemos. Sh'gall had gone forward to Benden to see K'dren. The Benden Weyrleader was tactful, as M'tani of Telgar was not, and Moreta counted on K'dren to smooth matters over in the day's consolidation. She would be everlastingly grateful when the Weyrs could return to traditional territories.

"Desdra, Moreta is coming with us to Ruatha," Capiam was saying. "It would seem that Lord Alessan has anticipated the matter of runner vaccine."

Desdra inclined her head courteously to the Weyrwoman, her large gray eyes calmly taking Moreta's measure.

"Don't let Desdra make you uncomfortable, Moreta," Capiam said. "She takes no one at face value; claims detachment is required of a healer."

"Jallora had told me of the superb reconstruction work you do on Threadscored dragon wing," Desdra replied in a low unhurried voice, her eyes flicking a glance to Moreta's hands as she put on her gloves.

"When there is time again, please return and examine Dilenth. The Istan Weyr Healer, Ind, taught me the technique. I've had opportunity to perfect it."

"I'd forgot about Fall today, Moreta," Capiam was saying uncertainly, as he looked about and saw the unmistakable preparations.

"I must be back for the *end* of Fall, certainly," Moreta replied, now perversely compelled to go to Ruatha. "As it happens, the wings have taken fewer injuries since the plague. It might just be that flying against other Weyrs has improved performances."

"Really? How interesting." Capiam's surprise was genuine.

Then M'barak courteously gestured for Moreta to mount Arith first. She did so, settling herself at the back and assisting Desdra. Although Desdra made no comment and appeared perfectly composed, Moreta decided that the healer had not often ridden adragonback.

Capiam was clearly delighted, twisting about to grin past Desdra at Moreta then checking discreetly that Desdra was comfortable. "Four riders are not excessive weight for your Arith, M'barak?" he asked as the blue rider swung into his forward position.

"Not my Arith," the boy replied stoutly, "or I'd've mentioned it."

As if to prove his ability, Arith leaped from the ground so enthusiastically that his passengers were abruptly pressed backward. Moreta instinctively locked her legs and grabbed the ridge behind her to balance Desdra, who was pushed back by Capiam's weight. Arith made a quick adjustment as M'barak rapped his neck. Conscious of his Weyrwoman's presence, M'barak made a ceremony of taking leave of the watchrider, accepting and returning salutes as Arith winged to a respectable altitude. M'barak looked back at Moreta with a warning nod of his head before he gave Arith directions.

"Black, blacker, blackest—"

Moreta's litany broke as they appeared in the sky again above Ruatha. She caught her breath, closing her eyes against the sickening view of the violated field, the rutted racing flat, the great fire circles, and the appalling burial mounds. She knew that her grip on Desdra's waist had locked and she was aware, too, of warm hands that lay gently on hers in shared sympathy and dismay.

All too clearly, Moreta could recall her compliments to Alessan on Ruatha's Gather gaiety, a bitter memory now that she was faced with the grim reality of the Gather's aftermath. Arith glided across the racing flats, directly at the Hold. Moreta could see the starting poles forlornly tumbled about where the spectacular dead heat of the last race had been run. Moreta forced herself to look at the raw earth of the burial mounds and accept the fact of so many casualties from that carefree throng of visitors in their Gather finery. And to accept as well the cremation fires that had consumed dead animals, winners and losers both, of the ten races that had drawn them to Ruatha on that fatal occasion. For a callous moment she thought that Alessan could have found the time to clear the pathetic debris of travel wagons, trunks, and Gather stands from the roadway and the fields. She marked where campfires had blackened the stubble field from which she and the young Lord Holder had so blithely watched the racing. Where banners had brightly flown, the upper tiers of Ruatha Hold were shuttered, unneeded, reminders that Ruatha had withstood a siege more savage than any Threadfall.

Yet, even as her heart contracted at the disheveled look of the proud Hold, her eyes went to the fields and the runners grazing there—not the large, solid beasts that Alessan had bred on Lord Leef's instructions but the wiry, thin-boned runners of Squealer's ilk. The irony helped restore her composure. Her tears would not comfort Alessan now.

Arith was not going to land at the forecourt, for which mercy Moreta was extremely grateful. His line was taking them along the roadway to the beasthold where considerable activity was evident. Three runners were being disengaged from plows, saddles lay on the ground, and a small cart had been pulled from storage. People were rushing up the road, carrying baskets with careful haste. The basic vitality of Ruatha appeared resurgent.

"M'barak says that he has seen Alessan at the beasthold," Desdra said to Moreta, projecting her voice sufficiently to counter the glide breeze. Nothing in her expression indicated that she was aware of Moreta's painful first reaction to the plague-scarred Hold.

Those at the beasthold had become aware of the dragon's approach and, just as Arith landed neatly on the far side of the roadway, two men emerged. Both were tall and their faces in shadow but Moreta identified Alessan on the right. That he recognized her was apparent by his sudden start before he strode to meet his visitors as fast as a Lord's dignity would allow. And he walked like the Lord of Ruatha again, Moreta was relieved to see—confident and proud.

"Sorry to arrive at an awkward moment, Lord Alessan," Capiam called as he dismounted.

"Your arrival could never be awkward, your appearance is always welcome," Alessan replied, but his eyes held Moreta's for a long instant before he courteously handed Capiam to the ground. "Tuero and I"—he indicated the tall harper who had followed him—"were composing a message to you." Then Alessan abandoned his formal manner and grinned broadly up at Moreta. "Dag saved Squealer! We've foals, too. Three fine males!" He shouted the last sentence, giving vent to a joy he could no longer contain.

"Oh, how marvelous, Alessan!" Moreta swung her right leg over and behind her and dropped down Arith's side. Fortunately, for Arith was rather higher than she had thought, Alessan caught her about the waist and eased her to the ground. She turned in his arms, very much aware of his hold on her, his light-green eyes bright with elation and, she hoped, her unexpected visit. "And to think it's Squealer's breed that survived! And foals! Oh, how relieved you must be!"

"I'm only just back from the nursery meadows," he told her as he led her away from Arith, his hands moving along her arm, anxious to remain in contact with her and happy at a civil excuse to do so. "I didn't have enough vaccine with me. I never counted on foals. And Dag's got a broken leg so we have to send the cart. There'll be Fall here in six days! But Dag saved bloodstock for us. He saved enough and he's saved Ruatha!"

Moreta found herself grasping and shaking his hand repeatedly and wondering suddenly if anyone was noticing, but surely she could publicly congratulate him for such splendid good fortune. Then Capiam brought Desdra forward to introduce her, and Moreta saw that Desdra was measuring Alessan with the same penetrating gaze to which she had already been subjected. Moreta felt protective of Alessan and worried that the healer would divine her attraction to him.

"I deduce that you have produced a serum vaccine and used it."

"I have indeed, Capiam, for I couldn't risk the bloodstock in this infected area." Alessan's hand eloquently swept the Hold proper and its fields. "Journeyman Follen is in the process of making more." He nodded toward the beasthold. "The plague dealt us terrible losses both in men and animals." He motioned them all to follow him into the beasthold. "We prepared a serum as soon as I returned last evening, and I injected that beast." Alessan pointed to the lame one, its right front leg pointing despite the depth of the straw of its bed. "It seems none the worse for it. . . ."

"It won't be, I assure you," Capiam said warmly, adroitly steering them to an isolated area, away from others. "The theory is as sound for animals as it has proved for people. And"—he lowered his voice, peering first at Alessan and then at Tuero with a meaningful stare—"absolutely essential at this juncture." He shot Desdra a quick look at his inadvertent use of one of Tirone's favorite phrases. A twist of her lips showed that she had marked it. With a quick motion of his hands, Capiam circled the others closely around him, tucking his hands about Alessan's and Tuero's arms. He glanced about to be sure that everyone was busy, Follen with his group around the centrifuge and the holders about the animals being retacked. "Lord Alessan, the plague could break out again."

Moreta caught Alessan's free arm as he staggered back from Capiam. The Healer supported him on the other. Tuero's first reaction was to see how Alessan coped with the news. The harper's expression was unusually serious and compassionate.

"Animals as well as humans must be vaccinated this time round," Capiam continued. "All across the continent. I have worked out a plan of distribution, and Moreta will seek dragonrider assistance. What is needed is serum from recovered animals. You have them, sufficient at least to supply the needs of this Hold, Fort, Southern Boll, and that portion of Telgar which marches your boundaries. Lord Shadder, I know, will accommodate us in the east."

"But the herds in Keroon are vast . . ." Alessan was clearly stunned by the enormity of the project.

"No longer," Capiam said gently. "If this Dag of yours has saved bloodstock for you, you are richer than you think. May we have your help?"

Alessan looked at the Masterhealer, a curious expression playing in his light-green eyes and the oddest twist to his lips.

"Ruatha lost much—of its people, its herds, its honor, and its pride. Any help which Ruatha can now offer may perhaps remove the stain of our enduring"—Alessan indicated the burial mounds—"hospitality."

There was no bitterness in the young Lord Holder's voice but there was no doubt in anyone's mind that the aftermath of his first Gather had burned indelibly into his soul.

"What makes you think that *you* are responsible for that? Or any of this?" One flourish of Capiam's hand indicated the burial mounds, the next their meeting in the beasthold and the veterinary preparations being made to one side. "No blame adheres to you, Lord Alessan. Circumstance, unpredictable circumstance, drove the *Windtoss* from her course. Opportunism prompted its master to land in the Southern Continent, and greed kept him there for three days. What prompted the crew to transport that animal to the unprotected north will never be known for every witness to that reprehensible decision is now dead. But that circumstance was beyond your control. What *has* been in *your* control, my Lord Alessan, is the courage with which you have conducted yourself, your care of the sick, your effort to sow crops, and the preservation of Ruathan bloodstock. Most of all"—Capiam drew in a deep breath—"most of all, that you are, in the midst of the severe trials you have endured, willing to *help* others.

"When bad fortune occurs, the unresourceful, unimaginative man looks about him to attach the blame to someone else; the resolute accepts misfortune and endeavors to survive, mature, and improve because of it.

"A fishing ship is blown off course in an unseasonal squall and that minor event has influenced us all." Capiam's expression was rueful. He glanced at Desdra, who was staring at him in a baffled manner. "If you view justice as the foundation of your life, then it has been served—for captain, crew, and cargo are dead. *We* live. And *we* have work to do." Capiam gripped Alessan by the shoulder, emphasizing his words by shaking him. "Lord Alessan, take no blame to yourself for any of this. Take credit for your vision!"

Outside Arith suddenly bugled in welcome and was answered by a deeper note.

"A bronze? Here?" Moreta hastily made her way to the entrance of the beasthold. M'barak stood by Arith, who was gazing skyward. The blue was not agitated even if Moreta feared that Sh'gall might have followed. "M'barak! Who comes?" Why hadn't Orlith contacted her?

"Nabeth and B'lerion," M'barak said without concern, shielding his eyes from the sun.

"B'lerion!" Moreta was relieved but, when a slender figure rushed down the ramp from the Hold, she began to understand B'lerion's presence.

Arith rose on his hindquarters, emitting what Moreta could only interpret as a challenge.

"I don't know what's got into him, Moreta," M'barak cried, embarrassed. "He's gotten to be awfully protective of Lady Oklina."

"There is a queen egg on the Hatching Ground, M'barak," she said, and added when it was obvious her explanation eluded the weyrling. "Blue dragons are often very keen on Search. Arith would seem to be precocious, though." She frowned, observing Oklina awaiting B'lerion. "I don't think Fort Weyr has the right to deplete Ruathan resources . . ."

She swiveled around. Alessan was escorting Capiam, Desdra, and Tuero to the centrifuge. The big wheel was slowing and the next batch of serum could be examined. Turning her head, she saw that Nabeth had landed and B'lerion was sliding gracelessly from the bronze back. Oklina greeted him with restraint, pointing toward the beasthold. B'lerion caught her hand, and the girl fell in step with him willingly enough but did not reclaim her hand. As the pair turned down the roadway, Moreta could see B'lerion's left arm was in a sling. He could not fly Threadfall. Had he been glad to escape from his Weyr when the High Reaches wings rose? Did B'lerion feel—as she did when the wings rose without her—an irrational compulsion to be with them? Or did he feel the injury was little more than a valid excuse to visit Oklina?

Drawing back into the shadow, Moreta turned to join the group by the centrifuge, standing a little to one side—the better to watch Alessan—as the healers discussed the quantity of vaccine they would need, the minimum effective dose, and how they could discreetly discover how many runners were in-holded.

"Body weight is always the factor," Moreta said, slipping into the conversation.

"We must make the determination of dosage as easy for the uncertain and the inept as possible," Alessan said. "Some of the handlers in the back holds are going to be incompetent as well as skeptical. Where handlers are still alive, that is." He flushed as Capiam fixed him with a reproving eye.

"We have been relocating capable people and trying to ascertain where more might be needed. It is amazing what people can do when they have no other options available."

"Master Capiam, how crucial is it that the runners be vaccinated . . . at this juncture?" Desdra asked, her gray eyes intent on the Healer's face.

"With zoonosis the determining factor—and I thought we had agreed on that point—"

"We have, but we cannot also waste effort." Desdra indicated the ornamental glass, the layers of blood now at rest. "I am forced to admit to you now that we have barely enough needlethorn to vaccinate the *people*, much less the animals. It would be unwise to reuse needlethorns," Desdra went on softly. "The danger of contagion—"

"I know. I know." Capiam pulled his hand across his forehead and down his cheek, rubbing at his jaw. He gave a weak laugh, tossing his hand in the air in a futile gesture before he eased himself to a bale of straw. "And we can only be sure of eradicating the threat of plague if we vaccinate both."

"It is just needlethorn which you lack?" Moreta asked, catching Capiam's despondent gaze. The Masterhealer's eyes began to widen and his stricken expression changed to incredulity as he realized what her question implied.

"And will lack, unfortunately, until autumn," Desdra was saying, turning away from the disappointment she had just inflicted on her master. She did not see the exchange that passed between Moreta and Capiam. "I have appealed to every hall and hold on the drum network to send us their inventory. As it is, we may be forced to exclude some people—"

"How? Who? When?" Capiam's terse questions to Moreta were hoarse whispers but so intense was his voice that it caused a hush and Desdra whirled to face him.

Shrugging off discretion with a nervous laugh, Moreta answered him. "*How* is walking down the roadway. *Who* is us, for I can count on your silence and *that* is as essential as needlethorn, and *when* has to be now, before I have time to reconsider this aberration." She grinned in reckless glee. Knowing it was a dramatic gesture, but unable to resist, she pointed to the entrance just as B'lerion and Oklina entered. "Are you badly injured, B'lerion?" she said, hailing the bronze rider cheerfully and, in a lower voice to Capiam, "He can't be that bad or he wouldn't have risked *between*."

"No, my shoulder was only dislocated," the bronze rider replied diffidently, "but I can't stand seeing the wings form without me. Pressen needed someone to bring Ruatha what we can spare from our stores, so I volunteered." B'lerion did not look at Oklina, who was standing breathlessly beside him, but bowed with tacit sympathy to Alessan. "I have wanted to express—" He broke off, sensing Alessan's distress.

"There is something you can do to help, now that you're handy," Moreta said, and B'lerion gave her a startled look. She drew him to one side and explained the situation and made her audacious request.

"I concede," he said, darting quick glances at Capiam and Alessan, "that the matter is urgent, even overwhelmingly so"—he spread the fingers of his uninjured hand in appeal—"but it is quite one thing, Moreta, to add a few more hours to a day, and a completely different matter to flit across months. You know very well that it's damn dangerous!" He kept his reply low while trying to argue sense into her. Though B'lerion might often behave with apparent disregard for proprieties, he was far from careless and irresponsible.

"B'lerion, I know where we need to go, in both Ista and Nerat. I know when needlethorn is ripe to be harvested. The *ging* tree is always in bloom. I have seen the rainforest resemble a green face with a thousand dark-rimmed eyes—"

"Highly poetic, Moreta, but not exactly the guide I'd need."

"But it is a *when*. And to get the proper coordinates we've only to check the autumnal position of the Red Star. Alessan would have the charts. It's rising farther and farther west. One only has to calculate the autumnal degree." She could see that that argument did much to reassure B'lerion.

"I had not really expected to spend my free afternoon harvesting needlethorn . . . ." His protest was halfhearted as he came to a conclusion that Moreta hastily reinforced.

"We can spend as much time as we need there, B'lerion, and still harvest what is so desperately needed now. But we must go *now*. I have to be back at the Weyr for the end of Fall. Nabeth is equal to the feat."

"Of course he is. But *they'd* know"—he jerked his thumb at the waiting group—"that we had traveled forward in time, Moreta."

"Capiam and Desdra already know it's possible." She grinned at the expression on his face. "After all, the Healer Hall bred dragons."

"So they did." B'lerion recovered from his astonishment.

"We will also have to use the ability on the day the vaccine is distributed."

B'lerion blinked wildly, glancing about him, but his gaze fell more regularly on Oklina's figure and Moreta began to relax. "I could, actually, see the Weyrs condoning *that* application, Moreta."

"They do not need to know we have taken time today. Who knows you've been here?"

"Pressen and that lad out there."

"I'll send M'barak off on an errand. Surely we can expect silence from Oklina, so that gives us a working party of six. We must make the time, and take it, B'lerion. Weyr, hold, and hall cannot sustain a second epidemic."

"I have to concede that, Moreta." B'lerion looked out over the debris strewn in the roadway and fields. "The change here is staggering." He grasped her hands tightly, his grin giving her the assent she required. "I'll have Nabeth speak to Orlith. If she agrees, what difference would a few moments make among friends?"

"Tell Orlith it's for the runners. They deserve our help."

"You and your runners!"

When Moreta outlined her plan to Capiam, Desdra, and Alessan, she received startled demurrals from each one that they didn't have the time to join the expedition.

"Master Capiam, it *takes* no time from now, today, this hour, to do what I have in mind," she replied to their protests with vexed severity. "Alessan, you can surely arrange matters in your Hold for an hour's absence. It will take longer than that for the cart to collect Dag and the men to herd the mares and foals down. What will you do? Watch bottles spin? The risk I fear is a breach of discretion about the entire project. Capiam and Desdra already know about the dragons' ability, and they earnestly require the needlethorn. I know I can count on Ruathan honor to respect dragonrider privacy. B'lerion is fortuitously here, willing and able. Nabeth is well able to carry six of us and, in a day's hard harvesting, we will accomplish what is necessary to insure the plague does not spread across the continent again. No one else will be the wiser. And that is also essential!"

"Six?" Alessan asked into the thoughtful pause.

"It is your sister's company B'lerion seeks."

Desdra chuckled. Capiam grinned after he considered that development. Alessan reacted in surprise and then with dour amusement.

"You mentioned time paradox, Moreta," Capiam began.

"That would not apply to us in this venture, so long as none of us return to Ista on the day the *ging* trees flower."

"Highly unlikely," Capiam agreed with a humorous grimace.

"The ravines I have in mind can only be reached from a high cliff. I harvested there many Turns while I was still at Ista."

Alessan hesitated a moment longer, his eyes straying from Follen to the men waiting outside with saddled runners and the beast in the cart shafts.

"Another minor but extremely important detail, Alessan," Desdra said. "Your beasthold is well kept, but not exactly the proper environment if one is producing quantities of a serum which must be free of contamination." She indicated the droppings of the lame beast.

"A wise precaution," Alessan agreed, then smiled wryly as he added, "The removal should take not much more than an hour. What supplies should we bring with us?"

"Carry-nets," Moreta replied quickly. "The rainforests will provide everything else we're likely to need."

B'lerion came striding back, a grin wide on his face.

"Nabeth found it unusual to talk to two queens at once but you have permission to go and not be long about it. I sent M'barak off to High Reaches Hold for more of Master Clargesh's apprentice bottles. And there'll be more at every major hold in the west, I shouldn't wonder. Clargesh was so proud of them. That will keep *him* busy."

"Good, B'lerion, now find a jacket for Oklina to wear."

"She *is* rather special in an understated way, isn't she. Clever of Arith to notice. No wonder I've been attracted to her."

"Wait till the egg has hardened, my dear friend. Each one splits in its own way."

Capiam and Desdra were directing Follen and Tuero to reposition the vaccine manufactury. When Alessan returned from dispatching the men to collect Dag and the runnerherds, he suggested the vaccine apparatus be moved to the main Hall of the Hold since most of its patients could safely be moved to the upper storeys or their own cotholds. Moreta helped Alessan secure all the carry-nets hanging from the walls of the beasthold, lashing them into one large bundle. By the time B'lerion and Oklina returned from the Hold, the other four were impatient with the delay.

"Had to find the charts, my dear Moreta. I am not jumping without a more positive coordinate than 'a green face with a thousand dark-rimmed eyes.' We'll have to arrive at dawn to be perfectly certain, for the moons will both be visible then." He brandished his fist to signal success and readiness.

As they began to mount the stalwart Nabeth, Moreta turned to Alessan.

"Tuero's watching us. Has he any idea?"

Alessan moved his hands about her waist more than was strictly required to heave her toward B'lerion, who was already seated on Nabeth's neck.

"One can't keep a harper from having ideas, but he should be under the impression that we are going to see Master Balfor at the Beasthold about the animal vaccine. Moving everything up to the main Hall presently will occupy even his active mind."

Then all were aboard. B'lerion had insisted that Oklina ride before him, where he could secure her with his fighting straps. Moreta he positioned behind him to help direct Nabeth. Alessan rode behind Moreta, then Desdra and, finally, Capiam as the most experienced of the other passengers.

Orlith, I shan't be long but I must go, Moreta said.

So Nabeth has told me. Orlith sounded unconcerned.

"Moreta!" B'lerion's voice and a hard nudge of his right elbow interrupted her private communication. "I've got the moons and the Red Star visualized. Facing northwest, the Red Star is horizon, Belior half full ascending, and the quarter horn of Timor mid-heaven. You will please concentrate on how Ista looks with those *ging* trees in bloom. Think of them as *now* and in Ista, and the heat of autumn and the smell of those rotting rainforests."

Nabeth was excited but his launch had the smooth precision of the experienced dragon and did not even sway his passengers as he took off.

Moreta had become accustomed to two dragon presences in her mind; now a third one, a lighter one but by no means weaker, added itself. She conjured the image of Ista's southern palisades in their autumnal finery, the Red Star balefully glowering above the western sea, Belior half full and rising, and the quarter horn of the smaller Timor demurely above. She held that vision locked in her mind as she felt Nabeth take them *between*. She wanted to make use of her usual litany, but the blossom eyes of the *ging* tree and the heaven-held guides were sufficient comfort. Then, fearfulness mounting to an incredible pressure in heart and lungs, they were suddenly in the warm air, high over Ista's rocky coast, the creamy eyes of the *ging* tree blossoms seeking the early-morning sun just rising in the east. B'lerion let out a whoop and Oklina a tiny scream. This time it was Alessan who clung to Moreta for reassurance.

Nabeth immediately noticed the rocky ledge where Moreta had often landed Orlith to harvest needlethorn. It was high above the incoming tide that battered diligently at the rock palisade. Nabeth landed as competently as he had taken off, his wing strokes flattening the thick brush that clung to the very edge of the cliff.

"Needlethorn will be down that slope," Moreta called as they prepared to dismount.

B'lerion made an ostentatious descent from Nabeth, causing the dragon to turn his head with a startled exclamation.

"You could have broken your other arm, B'lerion," Moreta said, but she had to laugh because he'd succeeded. She explained to Oklina the proper and safer way of dismounting a tall dragon, and Nabeth obediently lifted his foreleg.

"Are we really in the future?" Capiam asked as Alessan handed out the cargo nets. He looked about him with an expression of awe.

"We'd better be," B'lerion said, glowering with mock ferocity at Moreta before taking another speculative glance at the three guides in the lightening sky.

"We are," she replied as calmly as she could, for she was becoming increasingly aware of a curious sense of disorientation within her—a sensation of weightlessness and a growing euphoria, neither of which she had ever experienced before. Action would dispel such contradictory agitations. She pointed down the slope. "We'll go this way and we'll know soon enough if we find needlethorn. I harvested here myself last year, with Ista's permission since they gather on more accessible slopes." And she led the way.

The ravine was ten or more dragon-lengths from the cliff edge, and Moreta was suddenly filled with apprehension. She hadn't cleared the bushes completely last autumn, but then the moons had been in a different conjunction and the Red Star was higher in the west. No one was more relieved than she to break onto the lip of the ravine and see needlebushes thick with brown spikes. Above them the rainforest closed over the sky. The ravine, winding away to the north and the south, had been caused by an ancient earthquake, and the shallow soil over solid rock could not support many of the lush rainforest plants though creepers draped its sides, keeping well clear of needlethorn bushes. Alessan commented on that.

"The needlethorn is omnivorous," she said. "The spines are poisonous through spring and summer. They'll suck the juice from anything that comes near them until the autumn when the thick stem of the plant has stored enough moisture and food, vegetable or animal. The vine grows during the winter and has to shed its old corona or leave too many unprotected gaps. I understand that the flesh is tasty."

Oklina shuddered, but Desdra went down on one knee by the specimen they were examining.

"During spring and summer the bush has an odor to attract snakes and insects. The hollow spines suck essential juices from the creatures the plant impales, and also rainwater. See, on that one there, the top is scarred. Some animal broke off the spines. That'll make it easier to harvest."

"You said the spines are poisonous." B'lerion was not too keen to start picking.

"In spring and summer, but right now the poison has dried up. See where new thorn buds are capping the scarred one? It's the new growth that forces the spines off. So all you do is—" With a sweep of her hand starting in the scar, she cleared a swath of needlethorns, holding the handful for all to see. "Very simple, but don't get too ambitious. Clear a small area first to give your hand room. You don't want to tick off the point and you want to avoid the fine hairs on the skin of the plant. They can cause an irritation and possibly an inflammation that would be rather difficult for us to explain."

"We can't transport them like that," Capiam said, looking at Moreta's handful.

"No. We have to wrap them in the fronds of the *ging* tree. Slice the edge, and sap from the frond provides its own glue. Very handy, and the fronds are thick and spongy enough to cushion and protect the needlethorn. It takes only a moment to strip a bush, so it might be more efficient if we paired off, one to pick and the other to pack."

"I'll pack for you, Moreta," Alessan suggested, and, taking his belt knife out of its sheath, went off to hack down the nearest *ging* frond.

"A grand idea," B'lerion said, his eyes dancing as he laid a possessive hand on Oklina's shoulder. "If you don't mind working with a one-handed man?"

"My dear journeywoman, pick or pack?" Capiam asked in high good humor as he bowed to Desdra. "Though we can switch off as the whim takes us."

"I daresay I've picked more often than you, good Master Capiam." She laughed as she led Capiam off down the ravine. "You'd best see how it's done."

"Take the tenderer fronds, Alessan," Moreta cautioned. "They've more sap and suppleness."

He had cut several, muttering about doing hatchet work with a table knife, when Moreta showed him how to break the frond off at the stem of the tree with a quick downward jerk. She laid the needlethorns on the petiole that was sufficiently concave to form a bed, and, deftly cutting away the excess leaf, she closed the needlethorns in a tough, tight little envelope, sealing the ends with the sap of the severed frond.

"No wonder you said we'd have everything in the rainforest. It's easy once you get the trick of it."

"That's all there is to it. Just a knack." She grinned up at him. "That package has roughly two hundred needlethorns. I tried to count as I picked but my concentration is abominable. Time distortion, I expect. Some of the bigger bushes will have thousands of spikes, each big enough for the largest runners on the continent."

Alessan caught her hand and she stopped her babbling, suddenly shy. They were alone, even though Desdra's amiable taunting of Capiam for his timorous dexterity and B'lerion's cheerful encouragement of Oklina were audible.

"You said that we could remain here as long as it took to complete the harvest," Alessan said quietly. He was kneeling beside her now. "And return with no more than an hour elapsed there. . . ." His eyes searched her averted face, and his hands captured hers before she could reach for more needlethorns. "Can we not make a *little* time for ourselves?"

Oklina's delighted laugh rang out, followed by B'lerion's startled curse.

"Damn things bite!"

Moreta grinned at the outrage in the bronze rider's voice and her eyes met Alessan's, saw his amused reaction. She lifted her hands to Alessan's face, her fingers tracing the lines that tension and anxiety had etched on a young man's countenance. Merely touching him in light intimacy evoked a response in her body, and she swayed quite willingly into his arms as they kissed. The resurgence of her own sensuality dispelled the last vestige of restraint and she slid one arm about his neck, the other clasping his strong hard body against hers as they knelt together by the needlethorn bush they had been stripping.

"What more can you expect of a one-handed man?" B'lerion demanded in a loud complaint.

Moreta and Alessan broke apart, but the bronze rider was still out of sight, if audible. Alessan grinned for their discomfiture, expressing regret at the parting.

"It will be far too hot to work midday, Alessan, and I have no doubts that we can find some privacy then."

"Clever of you to bring mixed pairs, wasn't it?"

"One is always more sorry for the things one didn't do than the things one has done." Moreta spoke with mock severity, and Alessan quickly silenced her the most effective way.

"Personally, I don't like it when it's too hot," Alessan was saying, releasing her lips to give her eyes and cheeks and ears and throat equal attention. An injudicious movement brought his arm in contact with the needlethorn bush and he spun away, dragging Moreta with him. "They really do bite, don't they?" He rubbed his arm where a fine row of bloody beads rose on the skin.

"Oh, dear, they do." She reached for the cut *ging* and squeezed some of the sap onto the punctures. "There, that'll seal them too. Really, Alessan"— and she gave him a quick kiss, fondling his ear—"we have to do what we came here for!" She tried to be stern, but he was still frowning from the indignation of having his ardor abruptly pricked.

"I'll settle a score for myself, too," he said, snatching handfuls of the needlethorns from the bush that had wounded him. "That'll teach you, my spiny friend! There! There! and There! You're stripped!"

Laughing at his outraged monologue, Moreta worked as fast as she could to pack the products of his vindictive harvest.

"You picked the first one. Now you pack for me!" Alessan said with a growl. But his hands impeded hers as she worked to close the last package. He kissed her at the base of her throat, then on her chin.

"Fastest packer on Pern," he said in a complimentary tone while his hands made investigations of their own.

"Now it's my turn to pick," Moreta said, nibbling at his ear and running her hands through his thick hair. "Someone must be able to give you a trim," she murmured solicitously. Alessan was beginning to look like his former shaggy self, and that annoyed her.

"I'll trim you if you don't get to work, Moreta."

"I work faster than you." She allowed herself to sound peevish as she snapped quick handfuls off the nearest bush, piling them for him to pack.

"Can't you two get along together?" B'lerion demanded, bursting suddenly from around a bend of the ravine.

"She'll learn!" "He'll learn!" they said in chorus, waving cheerfully. B'lerion looked at them for a long moment then stalked off.

"Work now, play later," Moreta said, continuing to strip the needlethorns down.

"It's as easy to combine work and play." Alessan drew a gentle finger from her ear to her shoulder.

They worked steadily, but each utilized every opportunity for a quick caress or a kiss exchanged as deft hands folded *ging* over a pile of needlethorns. They knelt by the bushes, knees or thighs touching. Moreta felt the light hairs of her arms rising toward his, she was becoming so sensitized to the delightful friction of his proximity. She had an idiotic desire to giggle and saw that Alessan, too, wore a rather foolish grin on his face most of the time. They were scarcely conscious of the others and almost forgot their existence until B'lerion and Oklina crashed to the top of the ravine.

"You have been busy," B'lerion said with grudging approval. "Haven't you noticed the heat?" He had stripped to the waist, and Oklina had tied her shirt up under her breasts, leaving her midriff bare. She carried four nets of packaged needlethorns. "I'm hungry, too, even if you aren't." He swung his shirt by the sleeves so that its burden was discernible. "Found some ripe fruit and chopped down one of those palms for the edible heart. You can't keep on at the pace you've been going"—he gestured to the filled nets—"without sustenance—and a bit of a rest in this humidity. Capiam! Desdra! Let's eat!"

Capiam and Desdra were arguing about the astringent properties of the *ging* sap when they sauntered up to join the others. Capiam, too, had stripped off his tunic, which was now draped over his shoulders. He was very thin, his ribs showing plainly.

"I know it's hot," Moreta began adroitly, "but none of us can return to Ruatha suffering from sunburn."

Capiam exhibited a leaf he was using as a fan. "Or heat prostration." He raised his eyebrows in satisfaction with the filled nets. "We left ours back a bit. I rather thought we should rest, as is the custom on this hot island, during the hottest part of the day."

Everyone agreed that that was a sensible idea.

"I found some melons and the red roots that Istans are so fond of," Desdra said, producing her contribution.

"There're clusters of softnuts on all the trees, Alessan. That is, if you can climb at all," Moreta said.

"I climb, you catch."

Alessan took off his shirt to keep it from being torn. Moreta used it as a receptacle for the softnuts. He was a dexterous climber and a swift picker. When finished, he sought his reward in a close embrace, his hands slipping up the back of her tunic, caressing her shoulders as she found, to her surprise, that his skin was as soft as Orlith's and the smell of him almost spicy in his maleness.

They recalled themselves to the task, not wishing to take too long for what was a simple enough operation. Moreta decided that her flush would be attributed to an incipient sunburn.

"Sun's rays at this latitude are too strong for winter-white skins," Desdra said, lounging on some *ging* fronds that she and Capiam cut just for that purpose. "And that heat's enough to drain anyone," she added, making use of Capiam's fan.

They relaxed during the meal. The red roots were succulent, the softnuts just ripe, and the melons so close to fermentation that the juice had a winey tang to it. The palm heart was crisply cool and crunchy, a nice texture to complement the others. Throughout the meal, B'lerion kept up a stream of quip and comment about his being one-handed in a venture that was destined to save the continent. Would he receive full marks for his participation or just half for the hand that had worked?

"Is he always like this?" Alessan asked quietly after B'lerion had told an extravagantly funny tale at the expense of Lord Diatis's reputation. "He's better than most harpers."

"He sings a good descant, but B'lerion's always seemed to be the epitome of a bronze rider."

"Why, then, is he not your Weyrmate?"

"Orlith chose Kadith."

"Do *you* not have any say in the matter?" Alessan was irritated for her sake. From remarks he had made during their morning's work, she knew that Alessan didn't like Sh'gall and wondered just how much their new relationship would strain Ruatha's dependence on Fort's Weyrleader. She was struggling to find an honest reply to a question she had evaded in her own heart, when Alessan contritely covered her hand, his expression pleading with her to forgive his rash remarks. "I'm sorry, Moreta. That is a Weyr matter."

"To answer you in part, B'lerion *is* always like that," she said. "Charming, amusing. But Sh'gall *leads* men well, and he has an instinct about Fall which his predecessor, old L'mal, considered uncanny."

"Well, well, B'lerion, I'd never heard that particular narrative." Capiam was still chuckling as he hoisted himself to his feet. "I suppose harpers must be discreet in circulating their tales." He extended his hand to Desdra. "Can you remember exactly where you saw those astringent plants, Desdra? I know we're here for needlethorn, but the Hall's supplies are dreadfully short."

"We'll look at the plants but, my dear Master Capiam, you are also going to rest through the heat of the day." Neither healer looked back as they disappeared up the ravine and around the first bend.

"Well, I suppose that one must allow an older man some rest," B'lerion said. "Come, Oklina, there's plenty of shade in our patch of needlethorn, and a smart breeze. We shall put our time to the use intended!"

Smiling affably, B'lerion made a running leap up the ravine, turning only to lend a long arm to Oklina. They disappeared from view, and the thick foliage settled to stillness in the thick noontime heat.

"If he expects me to believe that . . ." Alessan finished his sentence with a chuckle. Then, taking a deep breath, he pulled Moreta against him and kissed her deeply and sensually, his hand deftly stroking her to arousal. "Come on, Moreta, I'm not chancing another attack by those needlethorns." He led her from the ravine toward the cliff. "What I'd like to understand is why that blue dragon of M'barak's is sniffing around Oklina. I could understand Nabeth with B'lerion entranced by her, but Aritha . . . Would it have anything to do with that queen egg on the Hatching Ground as Tuero suggested?"

"It might, but Fort Weyr would not deplete your bloodline by Searching Oklina, Alessan."

"This will do. Let's just throw down some *ging* fronds," Alessan said, hauling on the nearest at hand. "I won't have you bruised, either. That would be almost as hard to explain as a sunburn or heat prostration." Moreta helped him arrange a bower, all her senses suddenly awake, wishing that Orlith, not Nabeth, were on the Istan ledge. "About Oklina, now, since I've been reliably informed"—Alessan paused to grin at her, his light eyes vividly sparkling with merriment—"that she already has dragonrider blood in her. . . ." Then he turned briefly serious. "If it could be understood that her children would return to Ruatha, I would not stand in Oklina's way if she had the chance to Impress a dragon." He dumped his last handful of frond on the ground with a decisive gesture and pulled Moreta into his arms. "I'm not my father, you know."

"I wouldn't *be* in a rainforest with your father."

"Why not? He was a lusty man. And I intend to prove that I'm a suitable heir to his reputation!"

She was laughing as he laid her down on the sun-dappled frond bed. And he proved himself as lusty—and tender—as any woman could wish a man. For a shining moment at the height of their passion, Moreta forgot everything but Alessan.

The heat of the day did overcome them briefly, and they slumbered in each other's arms until tiny insects sought the moisture of their bodies and made them uncomfortable enough to wake.

"I'm eaten alive!" Alessan cried, pinning one of the biting insects to his forearm.

"Take some of that broad-leafed vine, the one climbing the tree by your side," Moreta said. "Bruise its leaves. It'll neutralize the sting."

"How d'you know so much?"

"I did Impress at Ista. I know its hazards."

They spent considerably more time neutralizing one another's insect bites than was necessary. When Alessan, trying to kiss her, got too much of the astringent liquid on his lips and his mouth began to pucker, they laughed and were still laughing about that when they returned to the ravine, slightly cooler now that the westering sun no longer shone directly above it.

When the tropical dusk had made work impossible, the six of them gathered on the ledge where Nabeth lounged somnolently and began to stack filled nets.

"Nabeth says"—B'lerion thudded the bronze dragon affectionately on the cheek—"that the only moving things he saw were fire-lizards fishing! He's got a good sense of humor, my bronze lad. I hope we've got enough for your purpose, Master Capiam, because I'm telling you, this single hand of mine"—he held it out to display the tracery of thorn scratches—"has done enough today!"

Capiam and Desdra gazed speculatively at the nets and then at each other. Desdra covered her mouth and turned away. Capiam looked distressed.

"Did anyone remember to count?" he asked, beseeching each one in turn.

"I'll tell you another thing," B'lerion said firmly, "I'm not going to count 'em now."

"I wouldn't suggest it!"

"However, I would gladly return to this secluded spot to pluck whatever number you find you lack."

Moreta tapped him on the shoulder. "Not here, B'lerion. If, by any possible chance, we did not pick enough today, go to Nerat. Not here."

"Oh, yes. That would prevent a time paradox. And the moons would be in roughly the same alignment on Nerat tip."

"Well, if that's settled, I expect we'd best return," Capiam said wearily.

"On the contrary, my dear Master Capiam, that would be a sure clue to our day's employment." B'lerion clucked his tongue. "We leave Ruatha energetic and in great spirit and arrive, an hour later, exhausted, reddened, hungry. Oklina, which one is the dinner net? Oh, here we are. Just settle yourselves. Use Nabeth as a backrest. There's more than enough of him to go round."

Oklina handed him a net of tied vines, which he hoisted so that all could see balls of hard-baked mud.

"Did a bit of fishing during my rest," B'lerion said, his broad grin daring anyone to challenge the truth of his statement, "and Oklina found the tubers. So we baked them. On the rocks in the ravine this noon it was hot enough to fry a dragon egg—begging your pardon, Moreta. A good meal would go down now without a struggle, wouldn't it? And while there's light enough, Alessan, if you and Moreta could find a few more of those ripe melons, why, we'd have a feast fit for a—Hatching!" B'lerion caught himself so quickly that only Moreta knew that he had quickly substituted one festive occasion for another less painful one.

She had distracted Alessan by pulling him after her to find the melons. They knew exactly where to find more, since they'd raided the patch several times in the afternoon to slake their thirst.

Hunger was part of the fatigue they all felt, and Moreta was glad to take her share from Oklina and thank the girl for such foresight.

"It was B'lerion's idea, you know," Oklina said. "He actually tickled the fish to catch them."

"Did he teach you how?" Alessan asked.

"No," Oklina replied with admirable composure. "Dag did. The same principal works in our rivers as Ista's."

Moreta could not resist chuckling at Alessan's expression as he sank beside her.

"On mature reflection, I think she deserves to be in a Weyr," Alessan said in a severe undertone. Then he realized that he was leaning against a bronze dragon and jerked forward apprehensively.

"Nabeth won't mind. He's an old friend of mine, too."

With a mutter of mock discontent, Alessan cracked the mud to produce a long slender tuber, then Moreta broke one open to prize out the fish, and they shared bits of the contents, keeping the second course warm.

"What a clever fellow you are," Capiam said, his mouth half full. He and Desdra had arranged themselves in the curve of Nabeth's tail. Desdra nodded agreement, too busy licking her fingers to speak.

"I have a few talents," B'lerion said with a becoming show of modesty. "Eating is one of my few bad habits. Fruit is all very well in the heat of the day but something warms soothes the belly before sleep . . ."

"Sleep!" Capiam and Moreta protested simultaneously.

B'lerion held up a restraining hand. "Sleep"—he pointed his finger sternly at Moreta—"for you have to mend dragons after Fall in another four hours. You can't do that effectively after the day you just put in." He flipped his hand toward the carry-nets lying in the shadows. "You, Alessan, will have to vaccinate and escort those priceless brood mares and foals of yours down from the meadows. I do not see you permitting anyone else to head that expedition. Desdra and Capiam, you will be returning to the pressures of expanding this vaccination program of yours to include runnerbeasts. So we shall finish our meal and then we shall sleep." He allowed the sibilance of the word to emphasize his meaning. "When Belior has risen, Nabeth will rouse us, won't you, my fine fellow?" B'lerion thumped his dragon's neck. "And we'll all be the better for the time spent *here*."

"B'lerion," Moreta protested vigorously, "I really should get back to Orlith."

"Orlith's fine, my dear girl. Fine! You're only going to be gone an hour in real time. And frankly, dear friend, you look dead right now!" B'lerion leaned over to ruffle her hair in a proprietary gesture that made Alessan tense beside her. Moreta quickly checked him with a hand on his thigh. "And anyway," B'lerion continued affably, "you've no choice, Moreta." And his grin widened with keen amusement. "You can't leave here except on Nabeth and he follows *my* orders."

"You're a managing soul," Capiam said without rancor.

"He's sensible," Desdra said, making a minor correction. "I was dreading the thought of being plunged back into all that must be done. Not to mention explaining these." She examined her scratched hands.

"If you keep everyone as busy as you usually do, Desdra," Capiam replied at his dryest, "no one will have time to notice."

"So just make yourself comfortable beside Nabeth. He won't mind being pillow as well as windscreen, but there's enough cover on the ground to keep you from scratching yourselves and the landward breeze will keep the midges off."

B'lerion then had Nabeth stretch out his neck so that he and Oklina could settle themselves. Capiam and Desdra arranged themselves in the tail curve so Moreta lay down against Nabeth's ribs and gestured for Alessan to join her.

"He won't roll over or anything?" Alessan whispered to Moreta as he lay down.

"Not while B'lerion's lying on his neck!"

So Alessan fitted himself against Moreta, drawing her arms around his waist and clasping them in his. She could feel his breath slow as he began to relax, and she pillowed her forehead against his strong shoulder blade.

The tropical night was warm and fragrant. Moreta tried to compose herself for sleep. She could hear Capiam's baritone murmur and then silence. Alessan slept and she wanted to but was haunted by the sense of disorientation she had left that morning. Then the spicy smell of dragon, still tainted by a hint of firestone, began to soothe her and she realized that—for the first time in twenty Turns—she had passed a day without Orlith. She did miss her. Orlith would have liked Alessan's exuberant loving. All that had been missing from that experience had been the dragon's share of her rider's gratification. Comforted, Moreta slept.

◆ ◆ ◆

The moment Nabeth burst into the air above Ruatha, Moreta felt Orlith's distressed touch.

You are there! You are there! Where have you been?

Where could you have been? That deep-toned question was from an equally distraught Holth.

To Ista. As Nabeth told you.

We could not find you there! That came from both queens.

I am here. I have what we went for. All is well! I won't be long here now.

The time distortion that accounted for the strange feeling of separation and disorientation lingering even in her dreams at Ista had dissipated the moment Moreta felt Orlith's touch. She was not only rested but extraordinarily revived, to the point that the warm sphere of euphoria in her belly expanded to fill her entire body with strength. B'lerion had been sensible indeed to insist they take time for rest.

Seated behind Moreta, Alessan became suddenly tense, his hands tightening about her waist fiercely. She knew he was swearing though the wind of Nabeth's glide obscured the words. She looked down at sad Ruatha and knew that a dragonback perspective of the ruins could not fail to distress him. When she managed to twist to speak to him, his expression was full of urgent determination.

As soon as Nabeth came to a graceful landing across the roadway from the beasthold, he turned to Oklina. "Surely some of the convalescents must be strong enough to do maintenance, Oklina. Did you have a good look at the Hold proper? It's a shambles. Here, Moreta, I'll give you a hand." Alessan slid down Nabeth's side and extended his hands to her. It was, Moreta quickly realized, an excuse to hold her, and he kept one arm loosely about her shoulders as they backed far enough away from the dragon's bulk for Alessan to address the other riders. "I'll continue making the serum, Master Capiam, and wait for any further instructions. Oklina, have you seen what I mean? Then I'll help you down. My duty to you, Nabeth, and my eternal gratitude." Alessan bowed formally to the bronze dragon, who winked at him from eyes that whirled pleasantly green-blue.

"He says his duty was a pleasure," B'lerion replied, smiling as he handed Oklina down to his dragon's raised forearm. He waited until she was clear and then waved cheerily as Nabeth sprang aloft again.

They had made most of their farewells at Ista when Belior rose, round and greenly gold in the dark Istan sky. B'lerion would convey the two healers to their hall with the needlethorns. If more should be needed, B'lerion would harvest it discreetly at Nerat with Oklina and Desdra. Capiam had composed messages for the Masterherdsman and all the holds that bred or kept runners. Relays would go to drumless settlements.

The dust of Nabeth's departure was blowing away from them when Tuero came out of the beasthold, a look of surprise on his homely face.

"That didn't take you long," he said. "Alessan, we can't make up another batch unless M'barak finds more glass bottles. I don't know what's taking him so long."

The three travelers recoiled in a group, but before Tuero could comment on their reaction, Arith and M'barak hurtled across the fields to land almost exactly in the spot Nabeth had just occupied. Moreta clung to Alessan's hand for support.

"Who's he got with him?" Tuero demanded. As the blue dragon settled, it was obvious he bore three passengers as well as the carry-nets.

"Moreta!" M'barak called, gesturing to her urgently. "Hurry up. I need help with these silly bottles and I've people here who say they can handle runners. And we've got to hurry because I have to prepare for the Fall. F'neldril will skin me if I'm late!"

So Alessan, Tuero, Oklina, and Moreta rushed to unburden Arith of passengers and ornamental apprentice-blown glass bottles. Then Alessan gave Moreta a leg up to Arith's back and if his hands lingered on her ankle as she settled herself, no one remarked on the Lord Holder's behavior. As Moreta looked down at Alessan's upturned face, she wished she might give him more than a smile in farewell. Then he stepped back and one of the newcomers touched his arm. The woman was tall and thin, with dark hair as close-cropped as a weyrwoman's. She reminded Moreta of someone. Then they were airborne, and M'barak warned her that they'd go *between* as soon as Arith had air space.

Back at Fort Weyr, there was so much activity in the Bowl, readying the two wings, that no one noted their arrival though M'barak had craftily come in over the lake. Arith glided to deposit Moreta at the Hatching Ground cavern. After remembering to give the blue's ribs a grateful thump, Moreta ran toward Orlith across the sands, not totally surprised to see Leri's figure beside her.

You're here! You're here! Orlith was bugling in relief, her wings extended, sweeping sand over Leri's small figure.

"It's all right, Orlith. I'm here! Don't make so much commotion!" Moreta raced to her dragon, throwing her arms around Orlith's head and hugging her as tightly as she could, then scratching eye ridges and murmuring reassurances.

"By the first Egg," Leri was saying, leaning against Orlith's side, "am I glad to see you! What have you been doing? Holth couldn't find you either. Oh, do be quiet, Orlith! *Holth!*"

You have finally returned. There was more reproof in Holth's voice than Orlith would ever express.

"Couldn't you contact Nabeth?" Moreta asked Orlith, then Leri and Holth. Orlith's color was very poor and there was an ashen hue to Leri's complexion. She was full of remorse for having caused them a moment's anguish. "Why didn't you speak with Nabeth?"

I wanted you, Orlith said piteously.

"Could you spare me a word of explanation?" Leri asked in a caustic tone, her voice breaking effectively. Contrite, Moreta grasped Leri's shoulder. "The past hour has been dreadful. It took all my tact and patience to keep Orlith from blasting after you, wherever you were—which was where?"

"Didn't Nabeth explain? B'lerion said he had."

Leri waggled her hands irritably. "*He* only said that you had to go on an imperative journey that would take no more than an hour."

"And we were back at Ruatha within that hour." Moreta knew that had to be the truth and, indeed, now that she was back with Orlith, the past subjective twenty hours seemed the dream, not the reality. "Just an hour?"

"No, actually," Leri said firmly, "a little longer than an hour. You were talking with Capiam about something"—Leri underscored her ignorance of that interview by a significant pause—"before you, he, and that journeywoman of his went skiting off to Ruatha on M'barak. The next thing I hear is a request through Holth from Nabeth and B'lerion." She gave Moreta a stern look, an effect that was slightly spoiled by her changing from one foot to another during her reprimand.

"You look a bit uncomfortable on these hot sands, Leri. I think we'd better get off the Ground. I've rather a lot to tell you. No, Orlith, I won't leave your sight but what suits your eggs is hard on your rider." Moreta gave Leri a gentle shove toward her temporary living space and then fondled Orlith's muzzle.

Leri had already seated herself before Moreta had sufficiently reassured Orlith. The queen gently pushed her weyrmate off and began to reposition the queen egg.

"It all began," Moreta said to Leri as she settled herself, "when Master Capiam came to ask me the same question Alessan had"—Moreta caught herself before she could blurt out "two nights ago"—"about vaccinating the runners."

Leri gave a disgruntled snort. "I would have thought he had enough on his hands healing humans."

"He does, but the plague is an instance of zoonosis—animals infecting people *and* other animals."

Leri stared at Moreta, her jaw dropping in alarm. "Zoonosis? Even the term sounds repulsive!" She fiddled with the cushion behind her back. "So, now that I'm comfortable, give me all the details."

Moreta told Leri about Capiam's visit, his fears for the continent's health, how via zoonosis a second, more virulent, wave of the viral infection could spread, and why mass vaccination was so essential. Capiam had left his chart behind, and Moreta produced it for Leri to examine.

"Capiam has it all planned so that a minimum of dragonriders would be needed—" She broke off, seeing the shock on Leri's face as the method of distribution became apparent to the older Weyrwoman.

"The riders would have to time it!" Leri stared at her, the nostrils of her straight, finely arched nose flaring with indignation. "You did say that Master Capiam brought this—this incredible plan *with* him?" When Moreta nodded, Leri's voice crackled with fury. "*How*, may I ask, *how* did Master Capiam know that dragons can move in time? I'll flay K'lon to his bones!" Leri all but bounced off the stone tier. From above, Holth bugled a protest.

"It wasn't K'lon," Moreta said as she clasped Leri's wildly gesticulating hands in hers. "Calm Holth down. She'll have Sh'gall on us!"

"If you told Capiam, Moreta—" Leri freed one hand to raise it aggressively.

"Don't be silly. He knew!" Remembering her own outrage at Capiam's knowledge, Moreta could well appreciate Leri's reaction. "He knew because, as he had to remind me, his Craft bred the ability into dragons."

Leri opened her mouth to protest that statement, then took a deep breath and nodded her head in belated acceptance. "You still have some explaining to do, Moreta. Where have you been the past hour where neither Orlith nor Holth could reach you?"

Moreta was not so certain, suddenly, of Leri's reaction to the truth of her whereabouts, especially now that it was obvious that Nabeth's explanation had been somewhat less than candid. And she'd given B'lerion far too good a reason to prevaricate.

"We went to Ista. We went forward in time to Ista to harvest needle-thorn. There's not much point in producing vaccine if there's no way to administer it."

Meekly Moreta endured Leri's piercing stare, the expression of disbelief, anger, anxiety, and finally resignation that flashed through the woman's eyes.

"You just casually"—Leri flapped one hand in a careless motion—"jumped four or five months ahead?"

"Not *casually*—B'lerion checked the position of the Red Star and the two moons to be sure he was near the autumnal equinox. And we arrived back in Ruatha in an hour. Nabeth told you that much, didn't he?"

"That much!" Leri drummed her fingers on her short thighs, indicating a displeasure she evidently couldn't express in another way.

Moreta put out a tentative hand, a request for absolution, and Leri caught it, noticing for the first time the delicate tracery of needle scratches.

"Serves you right." With a snort of disgust she released the hand. Then, with a grudging smile, she added, "I'd have thought you'd've taken a lesson from K'lon's ineptitude. Sunburn. Scratches!"

"Nothing that redwort won't hide this afternoon." But Moreta tucked both hands under her thighs, the stone cool on the deeper slashes. "Nabeth didn't tell you he took us to Ista? I chose a spot that isn't easily reached through the rainforests. There're only two places on the northern continent where needlethorn grows, and I thought the ravine on Ista safer than Nerat. We were perfectly safe the entire time."

"*We?*" Leri eyed Moreta with renewed alarm.

"I could scarcely harvest the quantity of needlethorn required by myself." Then Moreta realized that, in her effort to reassure Leri, she had said altogether more than was strictly necessary.

"Who went?" Leri was quietly resigned to her indiscretions.

"B'lerion . . ."

"He would have to."

Moreta winced at Leri's dry sarcasm.

"Master Capiam and Desdra, the journeywoman. She knows about timing because she found the entries in the old Records."

"Could we ask Master Capiam to *burn* those old Records?" Leri asked hopefully.

"He's agreed to 'lose' them. Which is why *I* agreed to go."

"That makes four of you. So! Who else went? We've known each other far too long, my dear, for you to delude me!"

"Alessan and Oklina."

Leri sighed heavily, covering her eyes with one hand.

"Alessan has too much at stake and too much honor in him to prate about dragon capability. And judging by the way Arith has been snuffling around Oklina, she would make a candidate for Orlith's egg."

"You couldn't—you wouldn't take his sister from Alessan . . ." Leri was astounded.

"I wouldn't, but the queen might. Alessan said he'd be agreeable if any children she bears are allowed to go back to Ruatha."

"Well!" Leri's exclamation was complimentary. "You accomplished rather a lot in one hour, didn't you?"

"B'lerion insisted that we sleep six hours in Ista in *that* time, but we did have to leave an hour's leeway before appearing back at Ruatha!"

"So you skited back to Ruatha Hold bearing nets full of needlethorn and no explanations tendered?"

Moreta began to relax. Once Leri got over her shocks, she'd begin to see the humor of the whole adventure, that the sheer reckless momentum had worked to their advantage.

"B'lerion dropped off Alessan, Oklina, and me, and took off to the Healer Hall with Capiam and Desdra. The dust hadn't settled before M'barak arrived with more glass bottles and volunteers and . . . Besides, who will ask the Lord of Ruatha to explain an hour's absence or inquire of Master Capiam where he got needlethorn? He has it! That's all anyone needs to know!"

"A point to remember." Leri's humor had been restored enough for her to be witty.

"So," Moreta said, having achieved another minor miracle in soothing Leri, "tomorrow I have only to approach the other Weyrs to ask for aid in distributing the vaccine. I promised Capiam."

"My dear girl, you can skite out of here for an hour on a mysterious time-consuming errand, but what excuse could you possibly find to go Weyr-hopping?"

"The best. There's a queen egg in front of us. I can visit them on Search. Even Orlith would agree to the necessity for that! And if I remember correctly, the Weyrleaders promised at that historic Butte meeting of theirs that they would supply candidates for Orlith's clutch."

"Ah, but that was *then*," Leri pointed out sardonically. "This is now. You have surely been aware of M'tani's disaffection. He's unlikely to part with the dullest wit in his Cavern."

"I thought of that. Remember the lists the Weyrleaders gave S'peren? Or did you give them to Sh'gall?"

"Don't be ridiculous. They're safe in my weyr."

"We can figure out which of the bronze riders at Telgar are likely to time it. I can't imagine that Benden or High Reaches would renege on the offer of candidates—"

"Of course *they* wouldn't. T'grel would be the bronze rider you should see at Telgar. And you *could* apply to Dalova at Igen. She may tend to babble but she's basically rather a sensible person. You *have* thought this all out, haven't you?" Leri gave a little chuckle at Moreta's cunning. "My dear, you've the makings of a superior Weyrwoman. Just shuck that bronze rider and get someone you're happy with. And I do not mean that light-eyed Lord Holder, with his convenient stashes of Benden white. Though mind you, he's a handsome lad!"

Outside, the bronze voice of Kadith called the fighting wings to the Rim.

**Fort, Benden, Ista, Igen, Telgar, and
High Reaches Weyrs, Present Pass, 3.21.43**

"One day, M'barak, and not too distant at that," Moreta told the slim
young weyrling the next morning, "we'll all have nothing to do but
lounge in the sun."

"I don't mind conveying, Moreta. It's such good training for Arith."
Then M'barak averted his eyes and she could see the color staining his neck
and cheek. "F'neldril explained to me last night the responsibility of Search
dragons and why Arith's been so discourteous."

"It isn't discourtesy, M'barak."

"Well, it's not proper dragon behavior and it doesn't *look* right for him to
be doing such things to people like Lady Oklina."

"M'barak, she understands, too. And it is an instinct that we want very
much to encourage in Arith. He's a fine sensitive blue, and you've been of
great assistance to Weyr, hall, and hold! Now, today we must Search first at
Benden. The Weyrleaders promised us candidates—"

"Ones who've been vaccinated—" M'barak added hastily.

Moreta gripped him by the arm, amused by his conditioned qualifica-
tion. Then they mounted Arith and left Fort Weyr.

"You are always welcome at Benden," Levalla said when Moreta was ushered into the queen's weyr, "as long as you arrive without Orlith to plague
Tuzuth." The Benden Weyrwoman cast a sly glance at K'dren. "I trust she is
welded to the Hatching Ground."

"That's one of the reasons I'm here." Moreta was alone with K'dren and

Levalla since she had been able to recommend to M'barak that he remain in the Bowl with Arith. Both Weyrleaders looked tired and she wished that she did not have to tax their resources further, but there was no way one Weyr could manage to distribute the vaccine.

"Orlith's a reason for coming here?" K'dren grinned. "Ah, yes, of course. Candidates for your Hatching. Never fear that I will go back on that pledge. There are some promising fosterlings in our caverns. *All* have now been vaccinated—"

"That's the other reason I'm here." Moreta had to blurt out her real mission at the first opportunity he gave her.

K'dren and Levalla heard her out in weary silence, K'dren scratching at his sideburns, Levalla sliding a worry-wood piece through her fingers, its surface smooth from long use.

"What we don't need is another epidemic. I quite see that," Levalla said when Moreta had finished outlining the plan. "We didn't lose that many runnerherds here in the east but I'm sure Lord Shadder would be glad of the vaccine. Imagine Alessan being able to produce it with all he's been through!"

"I don't like asking riders to time it, Levalla."

"Nonsense, K'dren, we'll only ask those who do it. Only last Turn, Oribeth had to discipline V'mul, and he's only a brown rider. Bone lazy, the pair of them. You know how brown riders can be, Moreta. And you know perfectly well, K'dren, that M'gent makes time whenever it suits him."

"Then we'll put him in charge of the Benden riders assisting the Healer Hall," K'dren said with a snap of his fingers. "Just the sort of challenge to keep him out of mischief. He was annoyed, you know"—and he winked at Moreta—"that I recovered from the plague so quickly. He enjoyed Leading to Fall. He'll make Weyrleader soon enough, won't he, mate?" He cast such a ludicrously suspicious look at his beautiful Levalla that it was obvious he had no anxieties on that score.

Levalla laughed. "As if I had time for any dallying these days. You're looking exceedingly well, Moreta. Any injuries in your Weyr from yesterday's Fall?"

"A few Threadscores and another dislocated shoulder. I'd say that this consolidation puts each wing on its mettle."

"My thoughts, too," K'dren said, "but I shall be eternally grateful when we can resume our traditional regions. It isn't Sh'gall, I'll have you know— he's a bloody fine leader; it's that sour excrescence from Telgar—"

"K'dren . . ." Levalla spoke in firm remonstrance.

"Moreta's discreet, but that man . . ." K'dren balled his fists, setting his jaw as his eyes flashed with antipathy for the Telgar Leader. "He won't assist in either of your requests, you know, Moreta!"

"*He* might not." Moreta took out the lists. K'dren exclaimed in surprise at seeing them.

"So they will serve a purpose after all. Let me have a glance." He flipped the sheets till he came to the angular backhanded scrawl of M'tani's. "T'grel would be the man to contact at Telgar. Even if he weren't a responsible rider, he'd do it in reprisal for some of M'tani's tricks. And you must have riders from each Weyr, ones who know how to find the hole-in-the-hill cots that aren't well marked. Well, you *can* be sure of Benden support. I wondered why our healer was bloodletting again!" He rubbed his arm with a rueful smile.

"And Capiam's sure about this vaccination of his?" Levalla asked. Her fingers betrayed her anxiety by the speed with which she flipped her worry-wood.

"He likens it to Thread. If it can't get a grip, it can't last."

"About your Hatching, now. We do have a very keen young man from a Lemos highlands minehold whom we found on Search two Turns ago," Levalla said, reverting to Moreta's ostensible errand. "I don't know why he didn't take, but we'll have him back if he doesn't find a mate on your Ground. Dannell's his name, and he's eager to keep up with his mining craft if he can."

"Are you Searching more among the crafts than the holds these days?"

"With the end of Pass in sight, it's best to have men who can occupy their spare time profitably for the Weyr."

"We receive the tithe whether there's Pass or not," Moreta said with a frown.

K'dren looked up from his perusal of the names. "To be sure, but once a Pass is over, the Lords may not be quite so generous." K'dren's expression indicated that his Lords had better sustain the quality of their tithes. "I've underlined the riders who I suspect do time." His grin was raffish. "It's not something anyone admits to but T'grel must *have* to use it to cope with M'tani. Don't bother with L'bol at Igen. He's useless. Go directly to Dalova, Allaneth's rider. She lost a lot of bloodkin at Igen Sea Hold. She'd know who among her riders time it. And Igen has all those little cotholds stashed in the desert and on the riverbanks. Surely you've got a few good friends left at Ista. You were there ten Turns. Have you heard that F'gal's bad with kidney chill?"

"Yes, I'd planned to speak to Wimmia out of courtesy. Or D'say, Kritith's rider."

"You have a son by him, don't you?" Levalla said with a tolerant smile. "Such ties seem to help at the most unexpected times, don't they?"

"D'say is a steady man and the boy Impressed a brown from Torenth's last clutch," Moreta said with quiet pride. She rose. She would have liked to stay longer with the Benden Leaders but she had a long day ahead of her.

"We'll give Dannell time to pack up and send him on to you at Fort tomorrow, with M'gent. You can use the opportunity to go over any details with him. Shall I have a discreet word with my Lords?"

"Master Tirone is supposed to be sweetening them but your endorsement would be a boon."

As K'dren escorted Moreta to the stairs, Levalla waved an idolent farewell, still worrying the wood in her left hand.

The encouragement that Moreta received from the Benden Weyrleaders did much to sustain her during her next three visits. At Ista, F'gal and Wimmia were in her weyr, bronze Timenth on the ledge, the tacit signal for privacy. So Moreta directed M'barak to land Arith at D'say's weyr, where Kritith greeted Moreta with shining blue spinning eyes, rearing to his hindquarters and extending his wings. He peered out to the ledge, patently disappointed that Moreta had arrived on a blue instead of with her queen. Then D'say emerged from his sleeping quarters. To her chagrin she had obviously awakened him from a much-needed sleep. He was one of the few who had not succumbed to the first wave of illness, and he had ridden Fall continuously, nursed other sick riders, and tried to bolster F'gal's leadership during the latter's kidney ailment.

As she argued with D'say on the necessity of once again cooperating with the Healer Hall, she wished that he had had the plague; then he would not be so slow to comply. D'say resisted her presentation in such a glum silence that she was becoming depressed when their son M'ray suddenly charged up the steps.

"I beg your pardon, D'say, but my Quoarth told me that Moreta is here." The boy—in his height he was more manly than boyish—paused just long enough in the threshold to receive permission to enter. Then he rushed to Moreta, embracing her with a charming enthusiasm. He peered anxiously into her face with eyes the color of her own, set in a head with the same deep sockets and arching brows. Yet he was far more D'say's child in build and coloring. "I knew you were ill. It's very good to see you well."

"Orlith has clutched. I've had little to do except repair scored riders and dragons."

M'ray opened his arms, looking from sire to dam, hopeful of answers to his outspoken questions.

"Moreta needs help, which I don't think she'll get from F'gal in his state of health." D'say replied noncommittally. He refilled Moreta's cup with klah, tacitly giving her permission to tell their son.

She did, and the boy's eyes widened with apprehension and a growing eagerness that answered the challenge.

"Wimmia would agree, D'say—you know she would. We only have to present the urgency to her. She's not a passive person, like F'gal. He's—he's changed a lot recently." As M'ray blurted out his opinion, he eyed D'say to see if the bronze rider would try to refute him. D'say shrugged. "Anyway, *I'd* like to help and my wingleader, T'lonneg, is hold-bred. If there's anyone who'd know the rainforest holds, it's him. He caught the plague, too, and lost family. He should *know* about this, D'say, really he should. This isn't the sort of request you can deny, is it? No more than we can stop rising to Fall." M'ray faced his sire, shoulders back, jaw forward, a pose she remembered striking when she had acted on her own initiative in treating a runner in her family's hold. "I rose with Ista's wings at every Fall. Haven't got so much as char in my face."

"Keep it that way," D'say remarked in a flat voice that masked the pride he had for his lad. "T'lonneg says they fly well, M'ray and Quoarth."

"What we'd expect," Moreta said fondly, smiling all the more warmly at the lad. It was a pity that she hadn't been able to give him more time but she'd had to go on to Fort Weyr, and D'say had remained at Ista. "K'dren thought that six or seven riders would be needed from each Weyr."

D'say rose to stand beside his son; there wasn't a hair's difference in height between them. Moreta had never been motherly toward her children; as a queen rider, she'd had to foster them immediately. She could be proud of M'ray, though, of his eager enthusiasm. Though he was committed to the Weyr, it suddenly occurred to her that she had other children and her blood-line could be sustained in Keroon.

"We will recruit riders who are adequate to the task and will discharge this duty to the Hall," D'say assured her. "I'll speak to Wimmia as soon as she's free. She'll review the fosterlings for your queen's clutch, though I must remind you that we had heavy losses among the weyr and hold folk. Every-one wanted to see that peculiar beast when it passed through here on its way to the Gather."

"I grieved to know you had such heavy losses." Moreta looked up at the fine lad, grateful he had been spared. "When you've arranged the matter, send a messenger to Master Capiam. He has all the details worked out."

"I'll see you at the Hatching?" M'ray winked impudently at her.

"Of course!" Moreta laughed, and he embraced her again, a little more certain of where his arms should go and not quite so fierce with his strong arms.

Both riders walked her to the weyr entrance.

"You're off to Igen now?" D'say asked. "See Dalova. She'll agree." D'say's smile showed some of the charm that had once attracted her. The bronze rider had always been slow to make up his mind, but his loyalty never fal-tered after he had. "Don't try to talk to M'tani at Telgar. Ask for T'grel. He's sensible."

Then the bronze and brown rider locked fingers to give Moreta a lift to Arith's back, warning M'barak in a jocular fashion that he'd better be careful with that conveyance. M'barak replied solemnly that it was his sworn obligation.

Then they were above Igen Weyr, the brilliance of the sun glancing off the distant lake painful to eyes *between* blinded; but the heat, the dry intense desert heat, was welcome to chilled bodies as Arith bugled his request to the watchrider.

Dalova was at her weyr ledge to greet Moreta, her tanned face wreathed in delighted smiles for her visitor.

"You come in Search?" she cried, embracing Moreta and drawing her into the cool of her quarters. Dalova had a demonstrative and affectionate nature, though the strains of the recent past were apparent in her nervous gestures and grimaces, the way she constantly shifted her position by her queen, often tapping her fingers on Allaneth's forearm as she listened to Moreta's explanation of her double Search.

"There's no question of my refusing help, Moreta. Silga, Empie, and Namurra won't refuse either. Six, you say Capiam'll need? I'd wager any amount"—she laughed, a high nervous laugh—"that P'leen times it. You *do* get to know, you know. As I'm sure you do." She grimaced, causing the sunlines around her sad brown eyes to crease. "If only L'bol were not so terribly depressed. He feels that if he hadn't let our riders convey that dreadful beast about—" She broke off and threw her arms out as if she could scatter all the unpleasantness and misery. Absently she patted her dragon's face, and Allaneth regarded her fondly. "I can help you distribute the vaccines but I cannot, in conscience, give you any candidates. We have so few young people to present to hatchlings, much less a queen. Besides, Allaneth should rise soon; I'm counting on it." A flash of desperation crossed Dalova's mobile face.

"There's nothing like a good mating flight to buoy the spirits of the entire Weyr," Moreta said, thinking ahead to Orlith's next flight with increasing anticipation.

"Oh, my, not you, too?" Dalova asked with a shaky little laugh. Tears formed in her expressive brown eyes, and now her queen licked her hand.

Without hesitation, Moreta took Dalova in her arms and the woman wept, in the quiet forlorn way of someone who has cried often without relief.

"So many, Moreta, so many. So suddenly. The shock of it when Ch'mon and Helith went. Then . . ." She could not continue for sobbing. "And L'bol is sunk in apathy. P'leen has risen with the Igen wings. That's not out of order, but when we're no longer consolidated, if he cannot *lead* . . . So I'm counting on Allaneth's rising, and me! Once there's been a good mating flight, everyone's spirits will improve. And once the fear of this hideous plague is over, everyone will be restored."

Dalova raised her head from Moreta's shoulder, drying her eyes. "You know how firestone makes me sneeze, and I nearly burst myself to keep from doing it because a sneeze frightens people so! Ridiculous, but it is the truth." Dalova sniffled, found her kerchief, and blew her nose lustily. "I must say, I do feel better because *you* know what it's like. Now, let me have a look at our Weyr maps. Yes, I see what Master Capiam means and he's worked so much of the detail out, it'll be no trouble. I'll organize Igen. Have you been to Telgar yet? Well, ask for T'grel. Then you'll go to High Reaches? Is Falga improving? Will Tamianth really fly again? Oh, that is good news. Look, much as I'd love you to stay, you'd better go or I'll drip tears all over you again. I try *not* to for L'bol's sake because Timenth tattles on me and that depresses L'bol even more. You can't imagine what a relief it is to weep all over you. Look, I'll send Empie when we've decided, and I might not ask more than the queens or P'leen. I can trust them but L'bol never approves of timing it, for *any* reason, and now is not the moment to upset him on minor matters." Dalova had been ushering Moreta to the weyr entrance, holding tightly to her arm as they walked. She smiled warmly up at M'barak, stroked Arith's nose, and gave Moreta a leg up.

At Telgar the brown watchdragon bugled threateningly to Arith, ordering the blue to land on the Rim instead of proceeding down to the Bowl.

"My orders, Weyrwoman," C'ver said with no apology. "M'tani wants no strangers in the Weyr."

"Since when are dragonriders strangers to each other?" Moreta demanded, offended by the order and insolence with which it was delivered. Arith trilled with concern over their reception and he could sense Moreta's fury. "I've come in Search—"

"And left your queen alone?" C'ver was openly contemptuous.

"The eggs harden. I call M'tani to honor his promise to S'peren to send us candidates for Impression. I have vaccine with me if it is needed for the weyrfolk I seek."

"We have all of *that* we need for those who deserve it."

"If I were on Orlith, C'ver—"

"Even if you were on your queen, Moreta of Fort, you wouldn't be welcome here! Take your Search into your own Holds. If there're any holders left, of course!"

"If those are your sentiments, C'ver—"

"They are."

"Then have a care, C'ver, when this Pass is over. Have a care!"

C'ver laughed and his brown reared to his hind legs, trumpeting derisively. Arith trembled from muzzle to tail tip.

"Get out of here, M'barak." Moreta spoke through clenched teeth. Telgar could burn in fever and she'd never answer them. They could be down to the last sack of firestone and she'd not send them a sliver. The Weyr could be full of Thread and she—"Take us to the High Reaches."

A Rim landing indeed! The cold of *between* did not dampen Moreta's fury, but Arith stopped trembling only when the High Reaches watchdragon caroled a welcome.

"Ask Arith to request permission to land in the Bowl near Tamianth's quarters. Say we come in Search."

"I already did, Moreta," M'barak said, his eyes still shadowed by Telgar's rejection. "We are twice and twice times twice welcome at the High Reaches. Arith says Tamianth is warbling."

As Arith glided past the Seven Spindles and the waving watchrider, they could indeed hear Tamianth's intricate vocalization. B'lerion's Nabeth answered then charged out of his weyr to its ledge. S'ligar's Gianarth emerged as if catapulted, flapping his wings and uttering high crackling trills as Arith made his landing.

M'barak turned to grin at Moreta, his shattered confidence restored by the spontaneous greetings and goodwill. Then Moreta saw B'lerion standing in the wide aperture to the weyrling quarters that accommodated the wounded Tamianth. He waved his right arm vigorously and then trotted out to meet her.

"Just a quick word alone," he said, folding his good arm around her shoulders with careless ease. "I took Desdra and Oklina to the Nerat plantations late last night. We've all the needlethorn we could possibly require. I've not mentioned either of your Searches to Falga and S'ligar and there have been no awkward questions from any other source." He raised his voice, chatting casually. "Tamianth's wing is dripping ichor, and she's got a tub for diving; S'ligar's improving, the sun is shining, the Weyr is righted, and Pressan and I were just giving Falga a little walk. Pressen thinks very highly of you, my dear Moreta. Cr'not may *tell* me that Diona did it, but we know Diona, don't we? Pressen attended the dragon injuries from yesterday's Fall. Spends his free time badgering Falga about dragon cures, which keeps her from feeling useless. Ah, here we are, Falga, your waterbearer!"

The first thing Moreta noticed was the enormous water butt conveniently placed at Tamianth's left, full to its brim. Then she saw the neat stack of buckets.

B'lerion chuckled. "My idea. Everyone who wants to visit Falga goes by way of the lake and brings in a full bucket. Every hour a weyrling returns the empties to the lake. If you count the current buckets, you'll realize that Falga's been having entirely too much company. Or Tamianth's thirst has finally been slaked."

Falga was propped against cushions on a wide couch that had been made of several weyrling beds tied together. Moreta was delighted to see the good color in Falga's face and returned her embrace, almost embarrassed by the woman's profuse thanks for saving her queen's life. Then, out of deference to Falga's fervent request, Moreta checked the progress of Tamianth's wing with Pressen while Tamianth hummed softly, watching Moreta with softly glowing eyes.

Holth says Orlith sleeps. It was Tamianth who spoke.

Startled, Moreta glanced at Falga, who was equally surprised but smiled warmly at her.

"You've come on Search," Falga began. "Surely it's early, and even a shade unwise to assemble candidates." Falga indicated that Moreta should sit on one end of the couch, B'lerion on the other.

Moreta hesitated, glancing at Pressen, but he was busy in the far end of the large room.

"I've two reasons for coming."

"But there's only one queen egg." Then Falga slumped back against her pillows, resigned. "What else has gone wrong then?"

"No, I think you could say that something has come right," Moreta said in a positive manner, "but Master Capiam needs our cooperation." Quickly Moreta once more explained, irritated by the sincere way in which B'lerion expressed astonishment. "Parts of Nabol, Crom, and the High Reaches are totally isolated. Master Capiam feels that they could wait so your involvement won't be as large—"

"Moreta, after saving Tamianth you can have anything in this Weyr . . . except S'ligar and Gianarth. Fortunately"—Falga's delightful laugh pealed out—"he's feeling his age. B'lerion, I know you time it as a matter of everyday convenience. This is the sort of thing you're good at organizing. Besides, I doubt if there's a cot you don't know in any western hold."

"Falga!" B'lerion affected indignation and hurt, laying his right hand on his heart. "May I see this plan of Master Capiam's?"

The bronze rider was a very shrewd dissembler for he examined the plan as if that were his first viewing. Moreta wished that B'lerion were not so comprehensively charming.

"Moreta," Falga said, eyeing her thoughtfully, "if Tamianth says Holth says Orlith's asleep, High Reaches has not been your first stop."

"No, I kept the best for the last."

"Could that be why Tamianth tells me Holth now informs her that

Raylinth and his rider have arrived, in great agitation, at Fort?" When Moreta nodded grimly, she added, "M'tani would have none of it?"

"The watchrider made Arith land on the Rim."

B'lerion cursed with real fervor, all langor gone.

"If I'd been on Orlith, that squatty mildewed brown of C'ver's would—"

"Consider the source," Falga said earnestly. "A mere brown rider! Really, Moreta, save your wrath for something worth the energy to spit at. I don't know what has got into M'tani over the last Turn. Maybe he's battle-weary from fighting Thread for so many years. He's gone sour totally, and it's affecting his whole Weyr. That would be disastrous enough in ordinary times, but this plague has only shown up his deficiencies. Do we have to force a change there? We'll take up that matter later. Meanwhile, High Reaches will take up distribution on the eastern side of Telgar's region. Bessera can time it, and has, which accounts for that smug look so often on her face. B'lerion, which of the bronzes?"

"Sharth, Melath, Odioth," B'lerion closed a finger into his palm with each name. "Nabeth, as you suspected, Ponteth and Bidorth. That makes seven, and if my memory serves me, N'mool, Bidorth's rider, comes from Telgar Upper Plains. Of course, T'grel's not the only rider who's dissatisfied with M'tani's leadership. I told you, didn't I, Falga, that once those Telgar riders had had a taste of *real* leadership, there'd be trouble." He smiled winningly at Moreta. "I actually do defer to Sh'gall's abilities. He may be a dull stick in other matters—oh, no, you can't fool your old friend B'lerion—but he *is* a bloody fine Leader! Don't waggle your finger at me, Falga."

"Do stop your chatter, B'lerion. Holth has told Tamianth that Moreta had better get back to her Weyr. And we'll send you over a few weyrlings from our cavern. You can take your pick. If we discover any more likely lads and girls while we're delivering Master Capiam's brew, we'll bring them in."

"I'll just give Moreta a leg up," B'lerion called back over his shoulder as he hurried out with her.

"It's a good thing you've only the one arm, B'lerion," Falga called after them goodhumoredly.

"I was going back by way of Ruatha," Moreta said anxiously.

"I thought you might be. You don't have to. They're doing splendidly. Capiam's sent more people in to help. Desdra's overseeing. She says Tirone and his harpers are doing a magnificent job with the Lords Holder and Crafthallmasters."

"He must be. I haven't seen K'lon in days."

"Good fellow, K'lon; and I don't say that about just any blue rider."

Then they were beside Arith and, one-armed or not, B'lerion nearly lifted her over the blue dragon.

Orlith was awake on Moreta's return to Fort Weyr because Sh'gall had roused her while looking for Moreta. He was pacing up and down in front of the tier and whirled belligerently at her when she entered.

"M'tani sent a green weyrling," he cried, fuming, "hardly more than a babe, to give our watchrider the most insulting message I have ever received. He has repudiated any agreement made at the Butte, a meeting at which I was *not* present." Sh'gall shook his fist first at Moreta and then in the vague direction of the Butte. "And at which arbitrary decisions were made, which I cannot condone, though I've been forced to comply with them! M'tani has repudiated any arrangement, agreement, accord, understanding, undertaking. He is not to be bothered—bothered, he says—not to be bothered by problems of any other Weyr. If we are so poor that we have to beg and Search from other Weyrs, then we do not deserve to have a clutch at all." Sh'gall ended up swinging his arms about like a drum apprentice.

Moreta had never seen him so furious. She listened to what he had to say but offered no response, hoping he would vent his rage and leave. Having repeated himself at length on his displeasure with her shameless venture for the Weyr that had resulted in such an insufferable message from M'tani, he ranted on through his usual grievances, about his illness, about the puny size of the clutch. Finally Moreta could bear no more.

"There *is* a queen egg, Sh'gall. There have to be enough candidates to give the little queen some choice. I applied to Telgar Weyr as I did to Benden, Igen, Ista, and the High Reaches. No one else thought my appearance or my request importunate. Now leave the Ground. You've upset Orlith sufficiently for one day."

Orlith was visibly upset as Moreta ran across the hot sands to her, but not, Moreta knew very well, by Sh'gall. By Telgar Weyr. She paced in front of her eggs, her eyes wheeling from red to yellow and orange as she recited to her rider a list of the damages she would inflict on bronze Hogarth in such detail that Moreta was torn between laughter and horror. A mating dragon could be savage with the drive of that purpose, but a clutching dragon was usually passive.

Moreta scratched Orlith's eye ridges and head knob to soothe her, urging the dragon to have a care for her eggs and come lie down again and let the hot sands lull her.

She has some very good ideas, came the unmistakable voice of Holth. *Leri says that Raylinth's rider understands all that is necessary. She says that in the interests of tranquility, you are to stay in the Ground, eat and sleep well.*

Do you miss anything, Holth–Leri?

No. If Orlith does not finish Hogarth appropriately, I will do so.

*Leri says—*and the voice was now only Orlith's, her tone sullen—*that we* *must not stop Holth. Why not? If you had ridden me, you would not have been insulted.*

"Actually, I'd rather have C'ver's skin for a floor rug," Moreta said in a considered tone. "He's hairy enough."

The notion of flaying a rider was originally Leri's, but thinking about the process restored Moreta and indirectly placated Orlith. Perhaps she should go for Sh'gall's hide, too, except that she was fond of Kadith and wouldn't cause him anxiety.

Kamiana comes, Orlith said, her tone calmer, her eyes more green than yellow.

Moreta looked up and saw the Weyrwoman beckoning urgently for Moreta to join her on the tier.

"Leri told me to wait until you'd both had a chance to cool down!" Kamiana said, rolling her eyes and grinning sympathetically at Moreta. "Sh'gall will drone on when he's offended, won't he? You'd think the plague had been invented to annoy him alone. And that M'tani? We're all tired of Thread but we still do what is expected. He may find himself flying by his lonesome, and I know his Weyr's at half strength. Can *we* not replace him? Or must we wait until Telgar's Dalgeth rises to replace him as Leader? However, we're flying for Capiam tomorrow, Lidora, Haura, and myself. I wish you could persuade Leri not to, but she does know the hole-in-the-hill places better anyone else in the Weyr. She's talked S'peren into taking a few runs and K'lon, though he's only a blue." Kamiana frowned dubiously over that choice. "I think P'nine would have been wiser but he got scored."

"K'lon's already stumbled onto timing; besides, he's done a lot of conveying lately, you know."

"I didn't know"—Kamiana rolled her eyes expressively again—"just how much was going on around here, Moreta, and your queen on the Hatching Ground, pushing sand about to warm her eggs!"

3.22.43

In the main Hall of Ruatha Hold, which had so recently been a hospital, forty cartwheels had been rigged as centrifuges. A hundred or more ornamental bottles had also served their purpose and were now stacked against the stair wall where once the banquet table of Ruathan Lords had graced the raised end of the long Hall. The frenzied activity of the past three days had, in the late hours of this night, abated to weary preparations for the morning's final effort. It was no comfort to the fatigued that similar activity had wearied anxious men and women in Keroon Beasthall and Benden Hold.

In the corner nearest the kitchen entrance, a trestle table had been serving as dining table at appropriate hours and a worktable at all other times. The remnants of an evening meal were at the end nearest the wall, where maps and lists had been tacked to the hangings. On its long benches sat the eight people whom Alessan called his Loyal Crew, relaxing with a cup of wine from Alessan's skin of Benden white.

"I wasn't so taken with that Master Balfor, Lord Alessan," Dag was saying, his eyes on the wine in his cup.

"He's not confirmed in the honor," Alessan said. He was too weary to take part in an argument and well aware that Fergal was listening with avid ears to store bits and pieces of irrelevant information in his cunning young mind.

"I'd worry who else might have the rank, for Master Balfor certainly hasn't the experience."

"He has done all that Master Capiam asked," Tuero said with an eye on Desdra, who apparently was not listening.

"Ah, it's sad to realize how many good men and women have died." Dag lifted his cup in a silent toast. "And sadder to think of the fine bloodlines just wiped out. When I think of the races Squealer will walk away with and no competition to stretch him in a challenge."

Alessan poured a bit more wine in his cup, Fergal's eyes on the business. He'd been offered a portion but disdained it with an insolence that Alessan excused only because the lad had worked so diligently at any task assigned him. But then, the work had been to save runners, and the boy had obviously inherited his grandfather's total commitment to the breed.

"You say Runel died?" Dag continued, finding it hard to comprehend how few of his old cronies remained. "Did all his bloodline go?"

"The oldest son and his family are safe in the hold."

"Ah, well, he's the right one for it. I'll just have a look at that brown mare. She could foal tonight. Come along, Fergal." Dag swung his splinted leg off the bench and took up the crutches Tuero had contrived for him. For just a moment, Fergal looked rebellious.

"I'll come with you if I may," Rill said, rising and unobtrusively assisting Dag. "A birth is a happy moment!"

Fergal was on his feet in an instant, extremely possessive of Dag and unwilling to share the man's attention with anyone, not even with Nerilka, for whom he had taken a curious liking.

Tuero watched the curious trio until they had left the hall. "I know I've seen that woman before."

"I have, too," Desdra said, "or maybe her kinfolk. Faces have got blurred. Overdose!" She was leaning back against the wall behind her, hands limp in her lap, a few wisps of dark hair escaping from the tight braids. "When this is over tomorrow, I'm going to sleep and sleep and sleep. Anyone, anyone whosoever attempts to rouse me, shall be . . . shall be . . . I'm too tired to think of something suitably vile."

"The wine was excellent, Lord Alessan," Follen said, rising. He pulled at Deefer's sleeve. "We've just three more batches to decant tonight. There could be breakages, so we must have spares. It won't take long now."

Deefer yawned mightily then belatedly covered his mouth, apologetically glancing around. But a yawn was not in the same category as a sneeze or a cough.

"When you think that I thought," Tuero began with a long sigh as he regarded the interior of his empty cup, "that a Ruathan Gather would be less tedious than a Crom wedding, you may wonder what I was doing for wits that day."

Alessan looked up, his light-green eyes sparkling. "Does that mean, my friend, you have considered my offer of a post here at Ruatha?"

Tuero gave a little chuckle. "My good Lord Holder Alessan, there comes a time in a harper's life when he decides that the variety and change of temporary assignments begin to pall and he wishes a comfortable living where his capabilities are appreciated, where he can be sure of witty conversations over the dinner table—to save his fingers from the harping—where his energies are not abused—"

"I wouldn't post to Ruatha in that event," Desdra remarked caustically, but she smiled.

"You weren't asked," Alessan replied, mischief in his eyes.

"It's no joy to serve a cautious man." Tuero flung an arm about Alessan's shoulders. "There is one condition, however, which"—the harper held up a long forefinger, pausing before his stipulation—"must be met."

"By the first Egg," Alessan protested, "you've already got me to agree to a first-storey apartment on the inside, second tithe of our Crafthalls—"

"When you've got them staffed again—"

"Your choice of a runnerbeast, top marks as journeyman, and leave, if you wish, to take your mastery when the Pass is over. What more can you ask of an impoverished Lord Holder?"

"All I ask is what is fitting for a man of my accomplishments." Tuero humbly put one hand on his heart.

"So what is this final condition?"

"That you supply me with Benden white." He spoiled the gravity of his pronouncement by hiccuping and gestured urgently for Alessan to fill his cup. He sipped wine to stop the spasms. "Well?"

"Good Journeyman Harper Tuero, if I can procure Benden white, you may have your just share of it." He raised his cup solemnly and Tuero touched his to it. "Agreed?"

Tuero hiccuped. "Agreed!" He tried to swallow the next hiccup.

Desdra looked at Alessan then leaned forward and prodded the wineskin under his elbow. She made a noise of amused reproof.

"There's not much left in it," Alessan assured her.

"That's just as well. Tomorrow your heads must be as clear as can be," she said. "Come, Oklina, you're half asleep as it is."

Regarding her through the lovely euphoria produced by several cups of his superlative Benden white, Alessan wondered if Desdra was being solicitous of his sister or merely needed support up the stairs. The progress of the two women was steady but uncertain, and their indirect course not entirely due to the cartwheels, apparatus, and equipment that lay strewn about the spacious whitewashed Hall. That was another thing he must do, Alessan decided suddenly—repaint the Hall. The austere white was too much a reminder of too many painful scenes.

"I say, Alessan," Tuero said as he tugged at the Lord Holder's sleeve, "where do you get all that white Benden?"

Alessan grinned. "I have to have a few secrets." His head was wobbling and if he wasn't careful, it would fall sideways onto the table.

"Secrets? Even from your harper?" Tuero tried to sound indignant.

"If you find out, I'll tell you if you're right."

Tuero brightened. "That's fair enough. If a harper can't find out—and this harper is very good at finding things out—if a harper can't find out, he doesn't have the right to know. Is that right, Alessan?"

But Alessan's head reposed on the table; a snore issued from his half-open mouth. Tuero stared at him for a moment in mixed pity and rebuke, then pushed at the wineskin under his elbow and sighed in disgust. There wasn't more than a dribble in it.

Footsteps sounded behind Tuero. He turned.

"Has he finished it?" Rill asked.

"Yes, it's empty, and he's the only one who knows where the supply is!"

Rill smiled. "The foal is a male, a fine strong one. I thought Lord Alessan would like to know. Dag and Fergal are watching to be sure it stands and suckles." She looked down at the sleeping Lord Holder, an expression of ineffable tenderness lending her a look of quiet beauty.

Tuero blinked to be sure it was the wine that had enhanced the tall woman. She had good bones in her face, he decided after making an effort at concentration. With a bit of thought to her clothing, brighter colors, with hair longer than that unattractive crop, she'd be attractive. Unexpectedly her expression altered, and so did the illusion of beauty—once again she bore the resemblance that perplexed Tuero and Desdra.

"I know I know you," Tuero said.

"I'm not the sort of person a journeyman harper knows," she replied. "Get to your feet, Harper. I can't allow him to sleep in this uncomfortable position and he needs a proper rest."

"Not so sure I can stand."

"Try it." Her terse reply was issued with an authority that Tuero found himself obeying though he was shaky on his legs.

Rill was only half a head shorter than Alessan so she looped one limp arm over her shoulder, urging Tuero take the other. Between them they managed to get Alessan upright, though he remained only half-conscious of their efforts. Tuero had to cling with his free hand to the bannister but fortunately, Alessan's rooms were the first apartment past the head of the stairs. They got him through to the bedroom where Rill arranged his limp body comfortably before she covered him. Tuero was mildly jealous that Alessan could arouse such tenderness.

"I wish . . . I wish . . ." he began but lost the words to express that longing.

"The doss-bed is still in the next room, Harper."

"Will you cover me up, too?" Tuero asked wistfully.

Rill smiled and merely pointed to the pallet on the floor and shook out the blanket folded on it. With a sigh of weary gratitude, Tuero lay down on his side.

"You're good to a drunken sot of a harper," he murmured as he felt the blanket spread over him. "One day I'll rememmmm . . ."

◆ ◆ ◆

The morning began as any other in the Weyr. Though bothered by a lingering cough, Nesso had otherwise recovered from her illness. She brought Moreta breakfast and so many complaints about Gorta's management of the Lower Caverns during her illness that Moreta cut short the tirade by saying she had to check Leri's harness.

"I can't imagine why the queen riders would fly with Telgar after what M'tani did yesterday."

Moreta was grateful that the Fall would mask the queens' real activities and grateful, too, that Nesso had obviously not discerned that the rising to Fall was merely an excuse, that Telgar had nothing to do with the queens' flight that day.

"It's the last time," Moreta said, hastily draining her cup. "We had our duty to hold and hall!"

Orlith was carefully turning eggs on the hot sands, testing their shells with a gentle tongue. She was more solicitous of the queen egg and turned it nearly every hour; the lesser ones were rearranged only three or four times a day. Moreta would see Leri safely off on her mission and then take Orlith to the feeding ground. They would have to insist that drovers restock the Weyr, once the threat of plague was over. Just then there wasn't much choice among what beasts were left. She'd speak to Peterpar. Maybe wild wherries could be found nearby fattening on the spring growth in the lower range. Once the day was over, there'd be a lot of details she'd best attend and get affairs back to a normal pace. And then a real Search for candidates would be initiated.

Leri was dressed in her flying gear but grumpy.

"Maybe you'd better not fly your run if your joints are bothering you so much. Did you take enough fellis juice in your wine?"

"Hah! I knew there'd come a day when you'd beg me to take fellis juice!"

"I'm not begging you—"

"Well, you don't need to remind me either. Just didn't sleep well last night. Kept going over the details of what goes where and with whom. M'tani couldn't have picked a better time to be obnoxious." Leri was blackly sarcastic. "You're going to have to cope with Sh'gall today, you know, and all that injured dignity. Good thing we planned for you to stay in the Hatching Ground; otherwise he'd get suspicious."

"He's asleep."

"He should be! Gorta tells me he put away two wineskins on his own. Now, if you'll just pass that strap?—There!"

Holth nuzzled Moreta with unexpected affection as she bent her head to accept the neck strap, and Moreta gave her eye ridge a scrape.

"You'll take good care of Leri today, won't you, Holth?"

Of course!

"Of all the nerve. Talking behind a rider's back!" Leri pretended indignation, but she smiled warmly at Moreta before she tugged at the harness to be sure that the clips were secure. "There!" She thumped Holth on the neck. "We'd best be off. I'm taking the upper ranges. When I collect the animal vaccine from Ruatha, shall I leave in any messages?"

"You'll wish them well, of course. And see what Holth thinks of Oklina."

"Naturally!"

Moreta accompanied Leri to the ledge and, as Holth crouched low, helped her mount. Leri fastened her riding straps, settled her small frame against Holth's ridge, and waved a negligent farewell. Moreta stepped back against the wall while Holth leaped off, her wing strokes strong and sure. She flew toward the feeding ground and then, in an instant, was gone *between*.

Moreta worried at Holth's habit of flipping *between* so soon after takeoff, but the dragon was old. After they had treated everyone, Moreta was going to present the strongest possible arguments to Leri about continuing flight at all. The wise old Weyrwoman could be exceedingly useful down at Ista where the climate would be much kinder to both dragon and rider.

Other dragons were at the feeding ground, Moreta noticed, after reaching her decision about Leri's future. The sparse numbers of the Weyr herd stampeded to the lake and some ambled into the water. A pursuing green had a fine time splashing after a wherry, and sprays of water made rainbow dazzles in the midmorning sun. The green's triumphant bugle was somewhat muffled by the wet mass in her mouth. Instead of flying up to her ledge to savor her meal, the green veered low and deposited the wherry at the feet of the blue dragon on the far side of the lake. Tigrath had preyed for Dilenth, A'dan and F'duril standing by. Unless Moreta's eyes deceived her, the third man watching the exchange was Peterpar, the Weyr herdsman.

When she joined the trio, Peterpar was finalizing the details of a wherry hunt to be held that afternoon if the weather kept fair.

"They've nooks they squeeze into up in the ravines, Moreta," Peterpar explained. "If it stays sunny"—he twisted round to view the cloudless horizon—"and it looks to, they'll be out, browsing. A'dan here says he's willing."

"I was thinking of asking S'gor to join us," A'dan said. "Malth could use an excuse to spread her wings, and the chase would do S'gor a power of good!"

"He oughtn't to stay immured like that," F'duril agreed, glancing up toward S'gor's weyr in the western arc of the Bowl. "We'll do it," he added with a wink and a nod at Moreta. "A'dan here could get a snake to walk when he sets his mind to it." Grinning, he hooked arms with his friend.

"Nonetheless, Moreta, we'll hunt the hills out right quick," Peterpar said with a shake of his head. He frowned as he pushed together some stones with the toe of his boot. "How soon d'you expect the holders'll be willing to send up a drove?"

"Could we not just ask for permission to hunt until there's no more fear of spreading plague?" A'dan asked. Neither he nor F'duril had been infected since both had stayed close to F'duril's injured blue Dilenth during the worst of the contagion.

"That would spare holders the necessity of a drove when they're short-handed and behind on spring work," Moreta agreed, adding that detail to the others she was accumulating.

"Round up the strays for people in Keroon and Telgar," Peterpar said, nodding sagaciously. "I did hear that animals were let run when folk took sick with no one to care for them." Then he pointed skyward. "Where're the queen riders going? Is that S'peren with them?"

"On Search," Moreta said casually.

"Queens don't go on Search," Peterpar said presumptuously.

"They do when a Weyrwoman has been treated as uncivilly as Telgar treated me," Moreta declared with sufficient severity to quell Peterpar's curiosity. "Orlith does need to be fed. Do please get a few juicy bucks for her in your hunt."

Smiling, she left the men. Trust Peterpar to take an interest in everything. He hadn't mentioned Holth and Leri so perhaps Holth's shallow-angle approach to *between* had been justified. K'lon must have left earlier, but he was in and out of the Weyr so frequently on convey that his departure would not cause comment. It amused Moreta that she could turn M'tani's disaffection to advantage, so he was made useful instead of being merely obstreperous. Now if Sh'gall would just sleep all day. . . .

She felt inordinately good that morning, aware of the smell of the spring in the air, the warmth of the sun, the laughter of the children playing near the Cavern. Once the dragons had finished feeding, they would return to the lakeside, their favorite spot for games. The atmosphere in the Bowl was returning to a normal buzz of pleasant activity, no longer silent with anxiety. However, an air of anticipation, of suppressed excitement, hung over the infirmary when she visited looking for Jallora, who was vaccinating one of the riders scored the day before.

"Good morning, Moreta," Jallora said. "A well-timed arrival. Now I can give you the second vaccination which Capiam has ordered for the Weyrs. Dragonriders travel so much," she said with a mild apologetic smile. Nothing in her expression indicated that the procedure was anything but routine. She administered Moreta's dose with the deftness of long practice.

"Can I give you a hand?"

"I wouldn't object. I've got the Lower Cavern to do. I vaccinated the queen riders before they left on their errand."

Did Moreta imagine a twinkle in Jallora's eyes? At least she could keep busy helping the journeywoman, and so she passed the morning well occupied. When she saw Peterpar with A'dan and S'gor, she went to tell Orlith that there'd be more choice if she could contain her appetite until later in the afternoon.

Wild wherries are tough, Orlith remarked a trifle petulantly, *but generally tasty,* she added, sensing Moreta's concern and nuzzling her rider. *Kadith sleeps. Holth says that the errand proceeds well.*

Moreta was very grateful that Kadith still slept. Inevitably Sh'gall would discover that Fort Weyr riders had taken part in Capiam's vaccine distribution—preferably after he had recovered from the wine and when he had calmed down over M'tani's insult. Moreta could have been mistaken, but she had a fleeting thought that Sh'gall was obscurely pleased by M'tani's attitude toward her.

Suddenly Orlith reared up, her eyes flashing reddish orange with such alarm that Moreta whirled to the Hatching Ground entrance, alert to danger.

He will not let the bronzes go. Sutanith is worried. He is dangerous. Dalgeth, the senior queen, restrains all. Orlith sounded perplexed as well as defensive.

"Sutanith is speaking to *you?*" Moreta was amazed. Sutanith was Miridan's queen and she was a very junior weyrwoman at Telgar. Moreta didn't know her well at all for Fort did not often combine with Telgar Weyr even when traditional territories were observed.

The Leader has gone between *to the Fall, so Sutanith warns you of the trouble—that the bronzes cannot help.*

"M'tani found out that T'grel was going to distribute the vaccine?"

Sutanith has gone. Orlith relaxed her posture.

"And Dalgeth restrains? *How* did M'tani find out? I thought Leri and T'grel had worked out every detail. And Keroon *must* have the vaccine." Moreta began to pace, scrubbing at her short hair as if she could tease out a plan. "If Keroon doesn't get the vaccine, the whole plan could fail!" She dashed across the sands to the tier and found Capiam's notes. Keroon and Telgar had to be covered and there were many halls and holds. Who else among her riders knew Telgar and Keroon well enough to—

Oribeth comes. This time Orlith jumped in front of her eggs, spreading her wings, arching her neck in instinctive protection of her clutch from the proximity of a strange queen.

"Don't be silly, Orlith. Levalla's here to see me!"

Astonished that the Benden pair should appear in Fort Weyr, Moreta rushed out to meet Levalla. They had landed in the center of the Bowl, well away from both Hatching Ground and Cavern. As Moreta rushed out to meet her visitors, Levalla sighted the sun's position in relation to the Star Stones before sliding down her queen's shoulder to await Moreta.

"I timed that very well indeed. I didn't want you to worry unnecessarily."

"You timed it here? Orlith just relayed Sutanith's cryptic message. Do you *know* about it?" Moreta had to bellow over the noise made by the Weyr's dragons, which were bugling in bewilderment at Orlith's alarm and Oribeth's presence. Moreta sent powerful reassurances to her queen, who stopped bugling.

"Do calm everyone down. I didn't mean to put the Weyr in a panic. My apologies to Orlith and the watchrider and all that, but I had to see you instantly. I did rather well, you know, timing it across the continent on top of everything else." Levalla had stripped off one glove and now fingered the worry-wood. "And yes, we know all about it in the east. About midmorning, our time, M'gent thought something was amiss when Lord Shadder said no one from Telgar Weyr had collected any vaccine from him or Master Balfor—so we were slightly forewarned. Sutanith got her warning through to Oribeth, Wimmia, and Allaneth so I give Miridan full marks for courage. But then, K'dren says she's mating with T'grel, and *he's* determined against M'tani now. So we took a little time"—Levalla smiled eloquently at Moreta—"and we have assigned two brown riders who know Telgar Plains and the River holds. D'say has agreed to send one of his group on the runs along the Telgar coast to the delta. Dalova says she can expand her responsibility to include the mountains, skipping back pre-Fall because that's where it would choose to Fall today. But we don't have anyone who knows the Keroon Plains well enough." She paused then from her swift recital of emergency measures and gave Moreta a long stare. "You do. Could you fly it on that young blue?"

Holth comes. I come, said Orlith and Holth in different tones on the same breath.

"Oho, and here comes trouble without a shirt." Levalla looked up at the weyr steps and pulled Moreta to one side, to be shielded by Oribeth's bulk. "Does Sh'gall know, or was it Orlith's fussing that roused him?"

"He doesn't know." Moreta wasn't sure if she understood what was happening or half of what Levalla had so tersely explained. Then Holth arrived, no more that two wingspans above the Bowl.

"Shells, but she's flying near the mark!" Levalla instinctively drew back. "Sh'gall thinks you were only on Search yesterday, is that right?" When Moreta nodded, she went on. "All right then. I'll delay him. You do Keroon on anything that will fly you. Those runnerholds *must* get the vaccine. Master Balfor has it all ready, in order, and with handlers to help out at the appropriate holds. Find a dragon to ride. Oribeth and I have done all we have time for in one day!"

Then Levalla shoved the worry-wood back into her belt and strode off to meet Sh'gall, who was bellowing at such rude awakening and strange queens threatening the peace of his Weyr.

Holth had continued her glide to land right at the Hatching Ground entrance, glaring at Oribeth, who was beginning to react to the air of hostility. Moreta rushed to intercept Leri before Sh'gall saw her.

"What has been going on? Orlith called Holth in sheer panic about Sutanith and Oribeth—"

Moreta made wild gestures up at the steps, indicating Sh'gall. Holth crouched down on the ground so that Moreta didn't need to shout up at Leri, and the old queen hissed soothingly in Orlith's direction.

"M'tani had Dalgeth restraining T'grel and the other bronzes. No vaccine has been conveyed in Dalgeth or Keroon. Sutanith got a warning out to some of the queens but M'gent of Benden had already suspected something was wrong because no riders from Telgar had collected any vaccine. Levalla has made arrangements for Telgar Plains and River, D'say has taken charge of the coast to the delta, and Dalova is taking the mountains—"

"Which leaves the Keroon Plains and you! Get your riding things. The day's half done in the east. I'll tell Kamiana to take over the rest of my run. S'peren can do the western coast from the Delta. I had the oddest feeling that something was going to go wrong. I did all the hidey holes in the top range first. The others are easy to find. Go, girl! I'll stay with Orlith. In truth"— Leri had difficulty swinging her leg to dismount—"my bones are very weary today and I'll be quite content to sit sipping my fellis juice and wine by Orlith's side."

"Peterpar's gone to hunt wild wherries for her. Make her eat."

"I'll save a few fat ones for Holth when you two get back. She'll need to eat by then." Leri called cheerfully after Moreta as she ran to grab her riding gear. She started toward Orlith to give her a parting hug, but Leri cautioned her. "You've no time to waste and a lot to make. I'll give her all the affection she needs."

You must go to Keroon, Orlith said, still keeping one eye on the Benden queen in the center of Fort Weyr Bowl. *Holth will take you. I must guard my eggs.*

"Oribeth doesn't *want* your eggs," Moreta cried, scrambling up Holth's side.

I have told her that, Holth said.

Moreta quickly lengthened the riding straps to accommodate her longer body, secured them, then told Holth she was ready. Holth turned, charged a few lengths toward the lake, not quite in line with Oribeth, and then launched herself in the air. Moreta caught a glimpse of Levalla standing on the steps in earnest conversation with Sh'gall, who didn't even look up as Holth took to the air. With relief, Moreta realized that the bronze rider had not noticed the switch of riders.

"Please take me to Keroon Beasthold, Holth," Moreta said, visualizing the distinctive pattern of the fields that she knew as well from the ground as from the air. She didn't have time to think of her verse—she had to think of how much time she had to make. The Keroon region blazed in her mind, a map she had seen daily as a child in the big room of her family's hold. She knew it even better than she knew the northern holds, for she had trotted around it on runnerback as a child; she knew the north only from the back of a queen dragon.

The beasthold itself, set in its complex of paddocks, was a sturdy group of stone buildings and quadrangles of low, slate-roofed stables. It was there that the feline had been brought for identification and from those fields that runners had carried the disease. Few enough beasts occupied the fields, but more than she had expected. Perhaps in her family's hold the strays had been rounded up and all her father's careful breeding had not been wiped out. Holth glided in to land near the building where a group of men obviously awaited them, a line of nets arrayed on the ground.

Moreta recognized Balfor, an unsmiling man who generally confined his remarks to monosyllables. Or perhaps he had always diplomatically deferred to the affable and verbose Herdmaster Sufur. Balfor was certainly vocal now as he hurried to Moreta and Holth, beckoning his men to bring the first of the nets.

"We have them all in order for you, Weyrwoman," he said, "if you know the holds from east to west. We've taken pains to be sure there is enough vaccine for every beast and human registered with the drum census. Go speedily, for the afternoon is half gone."

Balfor exaggerated, too, for the sun was just past zenith.

"Then I shall make the most of it. Don't go wandering off. I'll be back directly."

Moreta angled Holth in takeoff so they both had a good look at the angle of the sun. Then she checked the first label: Keroon River Hold, situated where the river rushed through a gorge in its first wild charge from the higher plateaus. Holth jumped for the sky and went *between* as Moreta kept the gorge hard in her mind. She was met by the healer of Keroon River Hold and her delivery received with thanks. They had begun to worry since the vaccine had been promised for early morning. Moreta did not dally.

Next they went slightly northeast to the High Plateau Hold where the runners were cleverly penned in a canyon, awaiting the vaccine. The holder wanted reassurance about "this stuff" since they'd only had drum messages and no contact with anyone "below" since the quarantine was sent, and he wanted a fuller account of all that had been going on below. She answered him tersely but told him that once the vaccination had been administered, he could go below and hear the whole story. Her next stop was westward, along the great plateau fault at Curved Hill Hold where there had been a great in-gathering of runners—and that was the last of the first run she did.

She did four more holds, and each time she landed at the Beasthold for more vaccine, the sun had dipped by another hour's arc, though she and

Holth had been on the move hours longer than the sun told. And each jump Holth made seemed just that much shallower. Twice Moreta asked the dragon if she wanted to take time to rest. Each time Holth replied firmly that she was able to continue.

The angle of the sun dominated the coordinates Moreta envisioned for Holth in her valiant leaps: It had become a blazing beacon, turning slowly orange as it dipped farther down in the west. Moreta began to think of the sun as her enemy, fighting the time it took for Holth to recognize each new destination, to glide in to the hold or cot, hand over the bottles of vaccine and the packets of needlethorn, to explain, patiently over and over, exactly the dosage for animal and that for human, repeating instructions already sent by drum and messenger. Yet Moreta had to admit that, despite Master Tirone's best efforts, there was still panic in the more isolated holds that had not been touched by the plague and dreaded it more for its unexperienced terrors than its known qualities. Only the fact that she came adragonback allayed some suspicions. Dragons had always meant safety, even to the most secluded settlers. She had to use valuable time reassuring Holth and still make it back to the Beasthold for the next load of vaccine and the next run.

All during the last round, she kept the sun at a midafternoon position, feeling the strain of timing it in her bones, in Holth's heaviness. But when she asked Holth if they should stop, the dragon replied that she wished Keroon had a few mountains instead of all these dreadful plains.

Then they had delivered the last of the vaccine and the net across Holth's withers was empty at last. They were at a small western hold, stark amid the vast rolling plain, the runners held in an uneasy assembly around the great waterhole that supplied them. The holder was torn between administering the vaccine as long as he had light and offering hospitality to the dragon and rider.

"Go, you have much to do," she told the man. "This is our last stop."

Thanking her profusely, the man began to hand out the contents of the net to his handlers. He kept bowing to her and Holth, walking backward to his herd, all the while expressing his gratitude for their arrival.

She watched him go, numbly aware that Holth's body was shaking under her legs. She stroked the old queen's neck.

"Orlith is all right?" She had asked the question frequently, too.

I am too tired to think that far.

Moreta looked at the midafternoon sun over Keroon plain and wondered with a terrible lethargy exactly what time it was.

"One last jump, that's all we have to take, Holth."

Wearily the old queen gathered herself to spring. Moreta gratefully began her litany.

"Black, blacker, blackest—"
They went *between*.

• • •

"Shouldn't Moreta be back by now, Leri?" The blue rider had been prowling uneasily in the tiers, occasionally barking his shins.

Leri blinked, looking away from K'lon. His restlessness deepened her anxiety despite the soothing effect of the fellis-laced wine she had been sipping all afternoon. It had eased the pain in her joints caused by the morning's concentrated flying but did not allay her worry. She jerked her shoulders irritably, arching her back, and peered down at Orlith who lay drowsing beside her clutch of eggs.

"Take a hint from Orlith. She's relaxed enough. And I won't disrupt their concentration with an unnecessary question at what could be an awkward moment," she replied testily. "They'll be very tired. They'll have had to fight time and make every minute into twenty to get the vaccine distributed." Leri balled one hand into a fist and pounded her thigh. "I'm going to rend M'tani." She flexed her fingers as if to encircle M'tani's neck. "Holth'll rake that bronze of his into shreds."

K'lon regarded her with startled awe. "But I thought Sh'gall—"

Leri gave a snort of contempt. "L'mal would not have needed to 'discuss' the matter with K'dren and S'ligar. He'd have been at Telgar, demanding satisfaction."

"He would? What?"

"No Weyrleader can disregard a continental emergency. Capiam has not revoked his priority. Well, M'tani will wish he *had* cooperated. And"—Leri's smile was malicious—"Dalgeth will answer to the other queens."

"Really?"

"Hmm. Yes. Really!" Leri drummed her fingers on the stem of her wine cup. "As soon as Moreta comes back, you'll see."

K'lon peered out of the Hatching Ground. "The sun's nearly down now. It must be dark in Keroon . . ."

Afterward, K'lon realized that both the rider and the dragon knew in the same instant. But Orlith's reaction was vocal and spectacular. Her scream, tearing at his taut nerves, brought him round to witness the initial throes of her bereavement. Orlith had been lying at the rear of the Ground, her eggs scattered on the sand before her. Now she reared up on her hind legs, her awkwardly coiled tail all that prevented her from crashing backward as she arched her head back, howling her despair. The sounds she emitted were ghastly ululations in weird dissonances, like throat-cut shrieks. Then, in an incredible feat, Orlith launched herself from that fully extended posture, over her eggs, missing them by a mere handspan. She sprawled, muzzle buried in the sand as all color faded from her golden hide. Then she began to writhe, thrashing her head and tail, oblivious to the fact that she had caught her right wing under her, flailing the air with the left.

Holth is no more, Rogeth told K'lon.

"Holth dead? And Moreta?" K'lon could barely comprehend that statement and frantically tried to deny the corollary even as he watched its effect on the stricken queen.

Leri!

"Oh, no!"

K'lon whirled. Leri lay against the cushions, gasping, her mouth working, her eyes protruding. One hand was pressed to her chest, the other clawed at her throat. K'lon leaped toward her.

She cannot breathe.

"Are you choking?" K'lon asked, horror mounting as he scanned her contorted face. "Are you trying to die?" K'lon was so appalled at the thought of Leri expiring before his eyes that he grabbed at her shoulders and shook her violently. The action forced breath back into her lungs. With a thin wail more piteous than Orlith's shattering cries, Leri went limp in his arms, her body wracked with sobs.

Hold her. Rogeth's voice was curiously augmented.

"Why?" K'lon cried, suddenly aware that in his selfish panic, he had thwarted Leri. If Holth was dead, she had the right to die, too. His heart swelled with a crippling ache of compassion, anguish and remorse. "How?" he demanded, unable to comprehend what terrible circumstance could have robbed Orlith of Moreta and Leri of Holth.

They were too tired. They ought not to have continued so long. They went between . . . to nothing, the composite voice replied in the sad conclusion perceived by all the dragons in the Weyr.

"Oh, what have I done?" Tears streamed down K'lon's face as he rocked the frail body of the old Weyrwoman in his arms. "Oh, Leri, I'm so sorry. Forgive me. I'm so sorry. Rogeth! Help me! What have I done?"

What was necessary, the augmented Rogeth spoke in a tone ineffably sad. *Orlith needs her to stay.*

Now the air was filled with the lamentations of the Weyr's dragons as they joined Orlith's dreadful keen. Sound battered the Hatching Ground, echoing wildly in the great stony cavern. As K'lon rocked Leri, the dragons were respectfully gathering at the entrances to the Ground. They lowered their great heads, their eyes dulled to gray as they shared the grief of a dragon who was unable to follow her rider in death, held to the Ground by the clutch of hardening eggs.

People had edged past the guardian dragons now, pausing briefly in deference to Orlith. Then K'lon recognized S'peren and F'neldril, closely followed by the other queen riders and Jallora, Kamiana turned with a peremptory gesture to the weyrfolk to remain at the entrance. But Jallora hurried to the steps, sliding to the blue rider. The healer murmured tenderly to Leri, stroking her hair, before she took the weeping woman from K'lon's arms.

"She wanted to die," K'lon stammered, lifting his empty hands in mute apology to Kamiana. "She nearly did."

"We know." Kamiana's face was wretched.

"Pour some wine, Kamiana," Jallora said, rocking Leri as K'lon had. He was obscurely relieved that he had, at least, done that right. "Use plenty of fellis juice. From that brown vial. Pour a cup for K'lon, too."

"We could all use some," Lidora muttered as she helped Kamiana.

But when Jallora held the cup to Leri's lips, the Weyrwoman pressed them tightly closed over her sobs and turned her head away.

"Drink, Leri." Jallora's tone was deep with compassion.

"You must, Leri," Kamiana insisted, her voice breaking. "You're all Orlith has."

The rebuke in Leri's pained eyes was more than K'lon could stand and he buried his head in his hands, shaking with reaction. F'neldril laid a gentle arm across his shoulders to support him.

"Dear Leri, L'mal would expect it of you. I implore you. Drink the wine. It *will* help." S'peren's voice was hoarse.

"Oh, brave Leri, courageous Leri," Jallora murmured in approval and K'lon looked up as the old Weyrwoman accepted the wine.

Lidora pressed a cup into his hand. It must be half fellis juice, he thought as he recklessly downed the draught. Not that it would do any good. Not all the wine in Pern could assuage the pain and remorse in his heart. He willed the potion to numb his senses but he couldn't stop weeping. Even F'neldril's seamed face was tear-stained as he stroked S'peren's shoulder in comfort.

"Let's get her up to her weyr," Jallora said, motioning for S'peren and F'neldril to assist her.

"No!" Leri's response was vehement. Orlith screamed in echoing protest. *No,* said the voices and K'lon caught S'peren's arm.

"I'll stay." Leri pointed toward Orlith. "I'll stay here."

"Will *she*?" Jallora asked the other queen riders, meaning the dragon.

"Orlith will stay," Kamiana said in a barely audible voice while Leri slowly nodded affirmation. "She will stay until the eggs are ready to hatch."

"Then we'll both go," Leri added softly.

Her words would forever remain in his mind, K'lon knew, as indelible as the rest of the terrible scene. S'peren and F'neldril stood beside him, drooping in grief, their faces suddenly aged. Haura and Lidora clung to each other weeping, while Kamiana stood to one side, her figure taut. Beyond them, the arched entrances to the Hatching Ground framed the press of dragons, all gray in sorrow, and the silent cluster of weyrfolk bewildered by the grievous loss. Just then there was a stir and three riders slowly moved onto the Ground, Sh'gall escorted by S'ligar and K'dren. Sh'gall continued forward alone, his body bowed with grief. He fell to his knees, covering his face with his hands, unseen by the inconsolable Orlith who writhed in the soul-rending agony of separation from her beloved rider, Moreta.

Present Pass, 4.23.43

The occasion of a Hatching ought to be a joyous one, Master Capiam thought without a single buoyant fiber in his body as he watched the dragons glide to the knots of passengers awaiting conveyance to Fort Weyr.

He had not attended to what Tirone had been saying to him. Then the Masterharper's parting phrase penetrated his gloomy reflections.

"I will be singing my new ballad, composed in celebration of Moreta!"

"Celebration?" Capiam roared. Desdra caught his arm and prevented him from being trampled on by Rogeth. "Celebration indeed? Has Tirone gone mad?"

"Oh, Capiam!" Desdra's soft exclamation was unusually gentle for that caustic lady, newly made a Masterhealer. Capiam glanced quickly about to see why. Then he saw K'lon's grief-stricken face as the rider dismounted.

"Leri and Orlith went before dawn," K'lon said, his voice breaking. "No one could—would have stopped them. But we had to watch, to be with them. That's all we could do!" K'lon's tear-filled eyes begged for solace.

Desdra folded her arms around him, and Capiam stroked his back, offering the blue rider a kerchief that he needed himself in that instant. Desdra didn't weep but her face was flushed, her jaw muscles tight, and her nose very red.

"They only stayed because of the eggs, to be sure of the day. But we had to see them go." K'lon sobbed.

Wondering if he should administer a restorative, Capiam caught Desdra's eye, but she gave a little shake of her head.

"They were so brave. So gallant! It was dreadful, knowing they would go. Dreadful knowing that one day we would wake up and they would be gone! Just like Moreta and Holth!"

"They could have gone that day . . ." Capiam began, knowing that wasn't the thing to say, struggling to find something to ease K'lon's grief.

"Orlith could not have gone till the eggs were hard," Desdra said. "Leri stayed with her. They had a purpose and now it is accomplished. Today must also be a glad day, for dragons will hatch. Surely that is a good day for going. A day that had begun in unmeasured grief will end in great joy. A new beginning for twenty-five—no, fifty—lives, for the young people who Impress today begin a new life!"

Capiam stared in wonder at Desdra. He could never have expressed it so well. Desdra might not speak often but she chose the right words when she did talk.

"Yes, yes," K'lon was saying, dabbing at his eyes, "I must concentrate on that. I must think of the beginnings of this day. Not of the endings!" He straightened his shoulders resolutely and remounted the doleful Rogeth.

Dragons did not weep as humans did, but Capiam thought he might prefer tears to the gray tinge that came to their eyes and hides. Rogeth bore the color of mourning. They mounted and K'lon conveyed them to Fort Weyr. Old tears froze briefly on Capiam's cheeks, to be renewed as he saw the dragon-crowned Rim of Fort Weyr. He'd no time to count but surely even Telgar's disaffected Weyr must be represented to produce such an assembly. K'lon angled Rogeth to land as close to the Hatching Ground as possible, seemingly a dangerous task for dragons were leaping and landing all over the Bowl.

Everyone will have to make an effort today, Capiam thought and tears streamed down his face again. Desdra was stroking his hands and he knew she was aware of his intense feelings. He knew she wasn't untouched by the tragedies; but grief can be exhibited in many ways, and her quiet summary to K'lon had given Capiam some comfort, too.

They dismounted quickly from Rogeth, smiling up at K'lon, who had mastered his tears if not his mournful expression. Then the blue dragon leaped skyward again.

Capiam noticed that the usual tables and benches had been set outside the Lower Cavern for the Impression feasting. He hoped to get drunk enough at it not to hear Master Tirone's ballad. Capiam could smell the roast meats but they did not rouse his appetite as they usually did. It was a lovely day. It would have been a magnificent dawn, he thought, and rubbed his face harshly, to stop the ready tears. If the Masterhealer of Pern could not maintain his composure, what a poor example he would set. The day was a beginning not an ending!

As Desdra pulled him toward the Hatching Ground, he inadvertently looked to his right, to where Moreta had lived the last days of her life. He blew his nose fiercely and looked directly ahead of him, now pulling Desdra to a place as far from that tier as was possible within the confines of the Ground.

The eggs took his attention. They lay, neatly spaced, the queen egg separate on a neat mound of sand, lovingly piled to cushion and display it. He blew his nose again and stumbled on the first step of the tier.

There seemed to be a good deal of nose blowing, and kerchiefs of all colors were being flourished. There was no end to the sounds people made in clearing their nasal passages. Obscurely Capiam felt cheered that so many people were affected by the aura.

Could the dragons massed on the Rim have prevented Orlith and Leri going? Capiam chided himself for such wistful futile thoughts. No, the halves that were missing could never be replaced. Orlith yearned for Moreta, and Leri for Holth. As K'lon had done, Capiam must accept the inevitable.

Then he felt the vibration though his boot soles and looked down. It took him only a moment to realize that Hatching was imminent. The dragons had begun their hum. Not just the dragons taking their place at the top of the Ground, but those outside, until the solid rock of Fort Weyr was resonating. The note managed, in some inexplicable manner, to be melancholy as well as expectant. It was low, the crescendo to Hatching, but it produced an impetus. The audience rushed in.

Capiam looked around him again, to identify faces no longer obscured by kerchiefs. On the upper tier, to his left, he saw Lord Shadder and his lady, Levalla, K'dren and M'gent beyond, sitting next to Master Balfor, who had declined the honor of becoming Masterherdsman. Some said he felt keenly responsible that Moreta had died helping his Hold.

Desdra's hand tugged at his and he followed her gaze to see Alessan entering the Hatching Ground with Lady Nerilka. They were a striking pair, Alessan a half head taller than his consort, but, even at this distance, Capiam could see that Alessan was pale. He walked steadily, if slowly, his arm linked through Nerilka's. Tuero was on his right side, Dag and little Fergal a respectful pace, for once, behind their Lords Holder. Capiam had been surprised by Alessan's choice of wife, but Desdra said that Rill would support Alessan and he needed that.

Master Tirone arrived, with Lord Tolocamp and his ridiculous little wife. Capiam wasn't certain if the emergence of Lord Tolocamp from his self-imposed isolation was a tribute to the occasion or would be a trial, but he had made the effort today. As Nerilka had noted to Capiam, the man had never known he had a daughter missing. When told that Nerilka had become

Alessan's wife, Tolocamp had remarked about Ruatha swallowing up his women, and that if Nerilka preferred Ruathan hospitality to his, that was the end of her in his eyes.

Lord Ratoshigan arrived, alone as always, mincing across the hot sands to the fast-filling tiers. The dragon hum was swelling now, more confident, less mournful. Other Lords Holder and Mastercraftsmen scurried to the tiers. S'ligar supported Falga, who still walked lame though she rode every Fall; B'lerion walked by himself, quickly, and took a place without glancing about. Amid the journeymen, small holders, apprentices, folk from all the Weyrs, Capiam saw few wearing a Telgar badge—but many displaying Keroon.

The hum became excited as the dragons, gripped by a sense of occasion, sang their welcome. One of the eggs began to rock, and a hush of expectancy fell over the visitors while the dragon's song became ecstatic.

Sh'gall escorted the candidates in their white robes, the four girls leading. Sh'gall fussily motioned for the boys to walk on while he deferentially led the girls to the queen egg. Capiam rapidly counted the boys: thirty-two. Not as much choice as usual but then . . .

Capiam thought Oklina looked stunning. He remembered her as so shy and diffident in the bustling, lusty family that had once cramped Ruatha Hold as to be unremarkable. She had certainly bloomed. Then he noticed B'lerion watching her intently. He, too, had changed dramatically since Moreta died. *There,* the phrase had come out, hurtful though it was. Tears stung his eyes again. Desdra's hand renewed its clasp on his. Did she always know when sorrow overcame him?

People stirred and pointed as the first egg continued to rock and cracks became visible. The humming reached a new pitch of excitement, and Capiam felt his breath quickening. Another egg became agitated . . . and a third. One didn't know where to look first. The hum became more than vibration: It became a sound enveloping everyone in the Hatching Ground, almost visible about the eggs. They responded by frantic rolling and pitching.

The first one broke, and a moist dragon head appeared, crooning piteously as the dragonet shook itself free of the shell. It was a bronze! A sigh of relief rose from every throat. For a bronze to hatch first was a good sign! Pern needed every one it could discover. The little beast staggered directly toward a tallish boy with a shock of light-brown hair. That was also a good sign, that the dragonet knew whom he wanted. The boy didn't quite believe his good fortune and looked in appeal to his immediate neighbors. One of them pushed him toward the dragonet. The boy no longer resisted and ran, to kneel in the sand beside the little bronze and stroke his head.

Capiam had tears in eyes again, but they were joyful ones. The miracle of Impression had occurred and spread its anodyne, dispersing sorrow. While he was blotting his face, a second dragonet, a blue, found his rider. The hum of the mature dragons was joined by the crooning trill of hatchings and the excited exclamations from the newly chosen riders.

Suddenly a fresh flurry signaled activity about the queen egg, which rocked, Capiam thought, more imperatively than the others. In fact, three good wobbles and the egg cracked neatly in half, the fragments falling away from the little queen who seemed to spring from the shards. Another excellent omen! Two of the girls wavered in their stance but in Capiam's mind there was never any question of which girl the little queen chose.

Capiam turned to embrace Desdra in celebration. Clinging together, they watched Oklina lift shining eyes, her gaze instinctively finding B'lerion in the mass of faces confronting her.

"Her name is Hannath!"

Dragondex

IN ORDER OF FOUNDING

THE MAJOR HOLDS AS BOUND TO WEYRS

Fort Weyr

  symbol:
  color: brown

Weyrleader: Sh'gall; dragon bronze Kadith
Weyrwoman: Moreta; dragon queen Orlith
Wingleader: S'peren; dragon bronze Clioth

    Fort Hold (oldest hold), Lord Holder Tolocamp
    Ruatha Hold (next oldest), Lord Holder Alessan
    Southern Boll Hold, Lord Holder Ratoshigan

Benden Weyr

  symbol: **II**
  color: red

Weyrleader: K'dren; dragon bronze Kuzuth
Weyrwoman: Levalla; dragon queen Oribeth
Wingleader: M'gent; dragon bronze Ith

High Reaches Weyr

> symbol: 〰〰
> color: blue

Weyrleader: S'ligar; dragon bronze Gianarth
Weyrwoman: Falga; dragon queen Tamianth
Wingleader: B'lerion; dragon bronze Nabeth

> Tillek Hold, Lord Holder Diatis

Igen Weyr

> symbol: ◠◠◠
> color: yellow

Weyrleader: L'bol; dragon bronze Timenth
Weyrwoman: Dalova; dragon queen Perforth

Ista Weyr

> symbol: ∧
> color: orange

Weyrleader: F'gal; dragon bronze Sanalth
Weyrwoman: Wimmia; dragon queen Torenth
Wingleader: T'lonneg; dragon bronze Jalerth
Wingleader: D'say; dragon bronze Kritith

> Ista Hold, Lord Holder Fitatric
> Nerat Hold, Lord Holder Gram

Telgar Weyr

> symbol: ⋀⋀⋀⋀
> color: white

Weyrleader: M'tani; dragon bronze Hogarth
Weyrwoman: Miridan; dragon queen Sutanith
Wingleader: T'grel; dragon bronze Raylinth

PERNESE OATHS

By the Egg
By the First Egg
By the Egg of Faranth
Great Faranth
Scorch it
Shards
By the shards of my dragon's Egg
Shells
By the Shell
Through Fall, Fog, and Fire

agenothree: a common chemical on Pern, HNO_3. Agenothree fuels the flamethrowers used by ground crews to burn Thread, and traditionally carried by riders of the queens' wings.

Belior: Pern's larger moon

between: an area of nothingness and sensory deprivation between here and there

Dawn Sisters: a trio of stars visible from Pern; also called Day Sisters

Day Sisters: a trio of stars visible from Pern; also called Dawn Sisters

deadglow: a numbskull, stupid. Derived from "glow."

Dragon: the winged, fire-breathing creature that protects Pern from Thread. Dragons were originally developed by the early colonists of Pern, before they lost the ability to manipulate DNA. A dragon is hatched from an egg, and becomes empathically and telepathically bound to its rider for the duration of its life.

Green: Female (20–24 meters). The smallest and most numerous of the dragons. Light, highly maneuverable and agile, the greens are the sprinters of dragonkind. They breathe short bursts of flame. Greens are rendered sterile through a sex-linked disability triggered by chronic use of firestone.

Blue: Male (24–30 meters). The workhorse of the dragons. Medium-sized, the blues are as tough as the greens but not as maneuverable. They have more stamina under pressure and are capable of sustaining flame longer.

Brown: Male (30–40 meters). Larger than greens and blues, some well-grown browns are as big as smaller bronzes and could actually mate with the queens if they so dared. The browns are the real wheel-horses of the dragons, reasonably agile and strong enough to go a whole Fall without faltering. They are more intelligent than blues or greens, with greater powers of concentration. Browns and their riders sometimes act as Weyrlingmasters, training the young dragons and riders.

Bronze: Male (35–45 meters). The leaders of the dragons. All bronzes compete to mate with the gold queens; the rider whose dragon succeeds becomes Weyrleader. Bronzes are generally trained for leadership and assume Wingleader and Wingsecond positions along with browns. Bronzes and their riders often act as Weyrlingmasters, training the young dragons and riders.

Gold: Queen, full female (40–45 meters). The bearer of the young, the queen is traditionally mated by whichever bronze can catch her. Although browns can mate with queens—and sometimes do, in the case of junior queens—this is unusual and not encouraged. The queen is fertile and bears eggs which she oversees until they hatch. Clutch sizes range from ten to forty; generally, the larger clutches occur during a Pass. The senior queen, usually the dragon of the oldest queen rider, is the most prestigious dragon and is responsible for all the dragons in the Weyr and for the propagation of her species.

fellis: a flowering tree

fellis juice: a juice made from the fruit of the fellis tree; a soporific

firestone: a rock bearing phosphorous that, when eaten by a dragon, is digested to produce phosphine gas, which ignites on contact with air

glow: a light-source that can be carried in a hand-basket

harper: Harpers are the teachers and entertainers of Pern. They educate the young in hall, hold, Weyr, and cot; they guide the elders in the practice of their traditional duties. The Masterharper of Pern is responsible for the training of harpers, the appointment of trained harpers to Weyr, hold, hall, and cot, and the discipline of harpers. The Masterharper acts as judge, arbitrator, and mediator in disputes between Lords Holder and between Weyr and hold or hall, but any harper can be called in to mediate if necessary.

Headwoman: Selected by the Weyrwoman to run the Lower Caverns, the Headwoman supervises the general domestic machinery of the Weyr and the individual weyrs of the riders. Among her duties are the care of the young; the supervision of food collection, storage, and preparation; weyr maintenance; and nursing, under the aegis of the Weyr healer(s).

High Reaches: mountains on the northern continent of Pern (see map)

hold: A hold is where the "normal" folk of Pern live. Holds were initially caverns in rocky cliffs where Thread could gain no foothold; they began as places of refuge. They grew to become centers of government, and the

Lord Holder became the man to whom everyone looked for guidance, both during and after the Pass of the Red Star.

Impression: the joining of minds of a dragon and his or her rider-to-be. At the moment of hatching, the dragon, not the rider, chooses his partner and telepathically communicates this choice to the chosen rider.

Interval: the period of time between Passes; generally two hundred Turns

klah: a hot, stimulating drink made from tree bark and tasting faintly of cinnamon

Long Interval: a period of time, generally twice the length of an Interval, during which no Thread falls and Dragonmen decrease in number. The last Long Interval is thought to herald the end of Threads.

looks to: is Impressed by

month: four sevendays

numbweed: a medicinal cream that, when smeared on a wound, kills all sensation; used as an anesthetic

Oldtimer: a member of one of the five Weyrs that Lessa brought forward four hundred Turns in time. Used as a derogative term to refer to one who has moved to Southern Weyr.

Pass: a period of time during which the Red Star is close enough to drop Thread on Pern. A Pass generally lasts fifty Turns and occurs approximately every two hundred Turns. A Pass commences when the Red Star can be seen at dawn through the eye rock of the Star Stones.

Pern: third of the star Rukbat's five planets. It has two natural satellites.

Red Star: Pern's stepsister planet. The Red Star has an erratic orbit.

Rukbat: a yellow star in the Sagittarian Sector, Rukbat has five planets and two asteroid belts.

runnerbeast: also called "runner." An equine adapted to Pernese conditions from fetuses brought with the colonists. Quite a few distinct variations were bred: heavy-duty cart and plow animals; comfortable, placid riding beasts; lean racing types.

sevenday: the equivalent of a week on Pern

Star Stones: Stonehenge-type stones set on the rim of every Weyr. When the Red Star can be seen at Dawn through the eye rock, a Pass is imminent.

Thread: mycorrhizoid spores from the Red Star, which descend on Pern and burrow into it, devouring all organic material they encounter.

Timor: Pern's smaller moon

Tunnel-snakes: Tunnel-snakes are a minor danger and an annoyance on Pern. Of the myriad types of Tunnel-snakes, two are the most insidious: the type that lives in tunnels, and the type that makes tunnels by burrowing in the sand on beaches. The latter has a great appetite for fire-lizard eggs.

Turn: a Pernese year

watchdragon: the dragon whose rider has pulled watch duty on the Weyr roster. A watch is generally four hours long. Essentially Weyrs are military camps. Sentries are part of that ethos. During a Pass, they watch for any chance erratic Fall of Thread, for anyone entering or leaving the Weyr.

watchwher: the ungainly, malodorous product of an attempt to breed larger, more useful animals from the genetic material of the firelizard, an indigenous Pernese life form. Watchwhers are nocturnal, exceedingly vicious when aroused, and highly protective of those they recognize as friends. A watchwher is conditioned to know the people of its hold, hall, or cot, and to give warning of intruders of any sort; used as a watchdog, it is generally chained to the front entrance of the hold, hall, or cot. Watchwhers can communicate with dragons, but as they tend to be very trivial and rather stupid, dragons are not fond of touching their minds.

Weyr: a home of dragons and their riders

weyr: a dragon's den

Weyrleader: generally the rider of the bronze dragon who has mated with the senior queen dragon of the Weyr during her mating flight. The Weyrleader is in charge of the fighting wings of the Weyr, responsible for their conduct during Falls, and for the training and discipline of all riders. During an Interval, he is responsible for the continuance of all Thread-fighting tactics, for keeping alive the fighting abilities of dragons and riders. His rank symbol is a dragon.

weyrling: an inexperienced dragonrider under the tutelage of the Weyrlingmaster. His rank symbol is an inverted stripe.

Weyrlingmaster: usually an aging rider with good skills and the ability to discipline and inspire the young. Responsible for the training of young riders and their dragons.

Weyrsinger: the harper for the dragonriders, usually himself a dragonrider

Weyrwoman: The rider of a dragon queen and coleader, with the Weyrleader, of the Weyr. She is responsible for the conduct of the queens' wing during Fall, under the Weyrleader's orders; for the care of dragons, riders, and all Weyrfolk; and for the peace and tranquillity of the Weyr during a Pass and during Intervals. She appoints all subordinates, insures that all tithes are delivered or collected, and mediates all disputes except honor contests among riders. She is responsible for the training, fostering, and disposition of the Weyr's children and nonrider personnel, overseeing with the Weyrleader the training of weyrlings under the Weyrlingmaster. As any dragon will obey a queen, even against the wishes of his or her rider, the Weyrwomen are in fact the most powerful people on

Pern. Weyrwomen have autonomy in their own Weyr, but will act in concert with other Weyrwomen when necessary for the good of the Weyrs. Her rank symbol is a dragon.

Each Weyr has from two to five queens, the larger numbers occurring during a Pass. In the event of the death or voluntary retirement of a Weyrwoman, the position will be assumed by the oldest of the other queenriders in the Weyr. Although candidates for Impression generally come from nearby holds and halls, the Search for a queen candidate may extend throughout the continent.

weyrwoman: a female dragonrider. Her rank symbol is a gold star.

wherries: a type of fowl roughly resembling the domestic turkey of Earth, but about the size of an ostrich

Wingleader: the dragonrider in command of a Weyr's fighting wing, subordinate to the Weyrleader. His rank symbol is double bars.

Wingsecond: the dragonrider second in command to the Wingleader. His rank symbol is a single bar.

withies: water plants resembling the reeds of Earth

THE PEOPLE OF PERN

A'dan: rider, at Fort Weyr; dragon green T'grath
Alessan: Lord Holder of Ruatha Hold
A'murry: rider, at Igen Weyr; dragon green Granth
Baid: cropholder, at Ruatha Hold
Balfor: Master, at Keroon Beasthold
Barly: (deceased) Healer, at High Reaches Weyr
Berchar: Masterhealer, at Fort Weyr
Bessel: a man at Beastmasterhold
Bessera: weyrwoman, at High Reaches Weyr; dragon queen Odioth
B'greal: weyrling, at Fort Weyr
B'lerion: wingleader, at High Reaches Weyr; dragon bronze Nabeth
Boranda: Healer, at Healer Hold
Bregard: Healer, at Peyton Hold
Burdion: Healer, at Igen Sea Hold
Campen: heir to Tolocamp, Lord Holder of Fort Hold
Capiam: Masterhealer, at Fort Hold
Ch'mon: rider, at Igen Weyr; dragon bronze Helith
Clargesh: Mastercraftsman, glass, at Tillek Hold
Cr'not: Weyrlingmaster, at High Reaches Weyr; dragon bronze Caith
Curmir: Harper, at Fort Weyr
C'ver: rider, at Telgar Weyr; dragon brown Hogarth
Dag: runner handler, at Ruatha Hold
Dalova: Weyrwoman, at Igen Weyr; dragon queen Perforth
Dangel: brother to Alessan, Lord Holder of Ruatha Hold
Dannell: candidate for Impression from Lemos Minehall, at Benden Weyr

Declan: candidate, at Fort Weyr
Deefer: warden, at Ruatha Hold
Desdra: Journeywoman healer, at Fort Hold
Diatis: Lord Holder of Tillek Hold
Diona: weyrwoman, at High Reaches Weyr; dragon queen Kilanath
D'ltan: weyrling, at Fort Weyr
D'say: wingleader, at Ista Weyr; dragon bronze Kritith
Empie: weyrwoman, at Igen Weyr; dragon queen Dulchenth
Emun: Journeyman harper, at Ruatha Hold
Falga: Weyrwoman, at High Reaches Weyr; dragon queen Tamianth
Farelly: harper, at Ruatha Hold
F'duril: rider, at Fort Weyr; dragon blue Dilenth
Felldool: Healer, at Hold Brum
Fergal: grandson to Dag, runner handler at Ruatha Hold
F'gal: Weyrleader, at Ista Weyr; dragon bronze Sanalth
Fitatric: Lord Holder of Ista Hold
F'neldril: Weyrlingmaster, at Fort Weyr; dragon brown Mnanth
Follen: Journeyman healer, at Ruatha Hold
Fortine: Master of Archives, at Fort Hold
Gale: Healer, at Big Bay Hold
Gallardy: Healer, at Healer Hall
Galnish: Healer, at Hold Gar
Genjon: Master, glassblower at Tillek Hold
Gorby: Healer, at Keroon Runnerhold
Gorta: Apprentice to Headwoman, at Fort Weyr
Gram: Lord Holder of Nerat Hold
Haura: weyrwoman, at Fort Weyr; dragon queen Werth
Helly: race rider, at Ruatha Hold
H'grave: rider, at Benden Weyr; dragon green Hallath
Ind: Healer, at Ista Weyr
Jallora: Journeywoman healer, at Fort Weyr
J'tan: rider, at High Reaches Weyr; dragon bronze Sharth
Kamiana: weyrwoman, at Fort Weyr; dragon queen Pelianth
K'dall: rider, at Telgar Weyr; dragon blue Teelarth
K'dren: Weyrleader, at Benden Weyr; dragon bronze Kuzuth
Kilamon: Journeyman harper, at Ruatha Hold
K'lon: rider, at Fort Weyr; dragon blue Rogeth
Kulan: smallholder, at Ruatha Hold
Kylos: Healer, at Sea Cliff Seahold
L'bol: Weyrleader, at Igen Weyr; dragon bronze Timenth
Leef, Lord: father of Alessan, Lord Holder of Ruatha Hold

Leri: inactive Weyrwoman, at Fort Weyr; dragon queen Holth

Levalla: Weyrwoman, at Benden Weyr; dragon queen Oribeth

Lidora: weyrwoman, at Fort Weyr; dragon queen Ilith

L'mal: (deceased) previous Weyrleader, at Fort Weyr; dragon bronze Clinnith

Loreana: Healer, at Bay Head Seahold

L'rayl: rider, at Fort Weyr; dragon brown Sorth

L'vin: rider, at Benden Weyr; dragon bronze Jith

Makfar: brother to Alessan, Lord Holder of Ruatha Hold

Marl: handler of herdbeasts and runnerbeasts, at Ruatha Hold

Masdek: Journeyman harper, at Fort Hold

Maylone: candidate, at Fort Weyr

M'barak: weyrling, at Fort Weyr; dragon blue Arith

Mellor: Weyrwoman, at Telgar Weyr; dragon queen Dalgeth

Mendir: Healer, at Ground Hold

M'gent: wingleader, at Benden Weyr; dragon bronze Ith

Mibbut: Healer, at Keroon Beasthold

Miridan: weyrwoman, at Telgar Weyr; dragon queen Sutanith

Moreta: Weyrwoman, at Fort Weyr; dragon queen Orlith

Mostar: son of Tolocamp, Lord Holder of Fort Hold

M'ray: rider, at Ista Weyr; dragon brown Quoarth; son of Moreta by D'say

M'tani: Weyrleader, at Telgar Weyr; dragon bronze Hogarth

Namurra: weyrwoman, at Igen Weyr; dragon queen Jillith

Nattal: old Headwoman, at High Reaches Weyr

Nerilka (Rill): daughter of Tolocamp, Lord Holder of Fort Hold

Nesso: Headwoman, at Fort Weyr

N'men: rider, at Fort Weyr; dragon blue Jelth

N'mool: rider, at High Reaches Weyr; dragon bronze Bidorth

Norman: race manager, at Ruatha Hold

N'tar: rider, at High Reaches Weyr; dragon bronze Melath

Oklina: sister to Alessan, Lord Holder of Ruatha Hold

Oma, Lady: mother of Alessan, Lord Holder of Ruatha Hold

Pendra: Lady Holder of Fort Hold

Peterpar: herdsman, at Fort Weyr

P'leen: rider, at Igen Weyr; dragon bronze Aaith

P'nine: rider, at Fort Weyr; dragon bronze Ixth

Pollan: Healer, at Big Bay Hold

Pressen: Healer, at High Reaches Weyr

Quitrin: Healer, at Southern Boll Hold

Rapal: Healer, at Campbell's Field

Ratoshigan: Lord Holder of Southern Boll Hold

Rill: see Nerilka

R'len: rider, at High Reaches Weyr; dragon bronze Ponteth
R'limeak: rider, at Fort Weyr; dragon blue Gionth
Runel: old herdsman, at Ruatha Hold
Scand: Masterhealer, at Ruatha Hold
Semment: Healer, at Great Reach Hold
S'gor: rider, at Fort Weyr; dragon green Malth
Shadder: Lord Holder of Benden Hold
Sh'gall: Weyrleader, at Fort Weyr; dragon bronze Kadith
Silga: weyrwoman, at Igen Weyr; dragon queen Brixth
Sim: drudge, at Fort Hold
S'kedel: rider, at Fort Weyr; dragon brown Adath
S'ligar: Weyrleader, at High Reaches; dragon bronze Gianarth
Sneel: Healer, at Greenfields Hold
Soover: smallholder, at Southern Boll Hold
S'peren: wingleader, at Fort Weyr; dragon bronze Clioth
Sufur: Masterherdsman, at Keroon Beasthold
Suriana: deceased wife of Alessan, Lord Holder of Ruatha Hold
Talpan: Healer of Animals, at Keroon Beasthold
Tellani: woman at Fort Weyr
T'grel: wingleader, at Telgar Weyr; dragon bronze Raylinth
Theng: guardleader, at Fort Hold
Tirone: Masterharper, at Fort Hold
T'lonneg: wingleader, at Ista Weyr; dragon bronze Jalerth
T'nure: rider, at Fort Weyr; dragon green Tapeth
Tolocamp: Lord Holder of Fort Hold
Tonia: Healer, at Igen Seahold
T'ragel: weyrling, at Fort Weyr; dragon blue Keranth
T'ral: rider, at Fort Weyr; dragon brown Maneth
Trume: Masterherdsman, at High Reaches Hold
Tuero: Journeyman harper, at Ruatha Hold
Turvine: cropholder, at Ruatha Hold
Turving: smallholder, at Ruatha Hold
Vander: smallholder, at Ruatha Hold
Varney: Master of the *Windtoss*
V'mal: rider, at High Reaches Weyr; dragon brown Koth
V'mul: rider, at Benden Weyr; dragon brown Tellath
Wimmia: Weyrwoman, at Ista Weyr; dragon queen Torenth
W'ter: rider, at Benden Weyr; dragon bronze Taventh
W'ven: rider, at Fort Weyr; dragon green Balgeth

PASSES AND INTERVALS

Planetfall plus 8 years
First Fall

58	First Pass
258	Second Pass
508	Third Pass
758	Fourth Pass
	First Long Interval
1208	Fifth Pass
1458	Sixth Pass
1505	Moreta's Ride (The Plague)
1758	Seventh Pass
2008	Eighth Pass
	Second Long Interval
2405	Lessa's Impression
2408	Ninth Pass

ABOUT THE AUTHOR

ANNE MCCAFFREY was born in Cambridge, Massachusetts. She graduated cum laude from Radcliffe College, majoring in Slavonic Languages and Literatures. Before her success as a writer, she was involved in theater. She directed the American premiere of Carl Orff's *Ludus de Nato Infante Mirificus*, in which she also played a witch. Her first novel, *Restoree*, was written as a protest against the absurd and unrealistic portrayals of women in science fiction novels in the '50s and early '60s. Ms. McCaffrey is best known, however, for her handling of broader themes and the worlds of her imagination, particularly in her tales of the Talents and the sixteen novels about the Dragonriders of Pern. She is the winner of the Hugo Award, the Nebula Award, and the Margaret Edwards Lifetime Achievement Award.

Ms. McCaffrey lives in a house of her own design, Dragonhold-Underhill, in County Wicklow, Ireland. Visit the author online at www.annemccaffrey.org.